DESERTS AND AEOLIAN DESERTIFICATION IN CHINA

DESERTS AND AEOLIAN DESERTIFICATION IN CHINA

Wang Tao et al.

Responsible Editors: Han Peng, Wu Sanbao, Bu Xin, Guan Yan, Yang Shuaiying

ISBN 978-7-03-017338-6

Huge sand dunes and lakes (photoed by Geoge Stainmetz)

Badain Jaran Desert (photoed by Geoge Stainmetz)

Crescent dune

Taklimakan Desert (photoed by Ru Suichu)

Yardangs and sandy Land (photoed by GeogeStainmetz)

Wind-eroded post in hinterland of desert (photoed by Xia Xuncheng)

Yardangs and black gobi (photoed by Geoge Stainmetz)

Populus euphratica in desert (photoed by Gao Dongfeng)

Beautiful desert in autumn (photoed by Zhou Xingjia)

Natural *Sabina vulgaris* fixing dunes in Mu Us Sandy Land

Gobi in eastern Xinjiang

Crust fixing dunes in Gurbantünggüt Desert

☆ Sand ripples under wind forces (1) (photoed by Ling Yuquan)

☆ Sand ripples under wind forces (2) (photoed by Ling Yuquan)

☆ Microcosm of aeolian sand

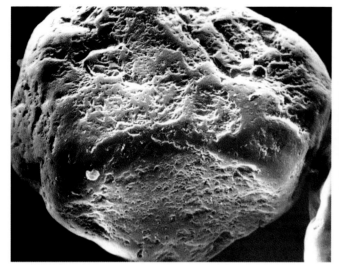

Impact traces:dish pit,mechanical
pitting and dehiscence furrow (×160)

Surface deposit under arid condition:difform SiO_2 (×200)

SiO_2 deposit on pocket surface of sand grains (×1200)

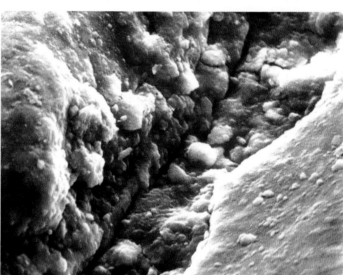

Impact fault and silicon deposit (×1700)

Features:edge
passivation, many impact
pits on surface (×180)

Tongwan City ruins of Xia Dynasty in Mu Us Sandy Land (photoed by Zhang Changjiang)

Dunhuang Mogao Grottoes hidden in desert (photoed by Geoge Stainmetz)

Shifting dunes crossing the Great Wall and encroaching farmlands (photoed by Geoge Stainmetz)

Shifting dunes burying the Great Wall in the Northern Shaanxi (photoed by Mo Bingchun)

Aedlian desertification processes due to shrub-coppice dunes

Steppe vegetation degrade toward hard shrub

Shifting sands accumulating under shrubs

Shrubs gradually die and
shifting sands emerge

Most shrubs die and
shifting dunes form

Aeolian desertification of farmland

Wind-eroded badlands

Grassland surface coarsening

Reactivation of fixed sand dunes

Sands covering loess

Shifting sands burying railway

Shifting sands burying house

Hazards of sand-storms

Shifting sands burying road

Irrational reclamation causing aeolian desertification

Over-grazing causing aeolian desertification

Over-cutting wood causing aeolian desertification (photoed by Hu Shunfu)

Mining under lacking protection boosting aeolian desertification (photoed by Zhang Tianceng)

Returning farmlands to woodlands or grasslands

Intercropping between wood belts

Restoring vegetation through building fences

Artificial sand-binding *C.korshinskii* belt

Vegetative sand barrier blockading sand dunes

Mechanical sand-control along desert road

Mechanical sand-protecting along desert railway

Baotou-Lanzhou Railway crossing over desert (photoed by Geoge Stainmetz)

Shelter-forest protecting oasis (photoed by Geoge Stainmetz)

Combined control measures in desertification areas

Xijingzi of Shangdu County in 1982

Late landscape of Xijingzi in Shangdu County

Huge sand dunes associated with lakes in the southeast of Badain Jaran Desert

The Map of Desert and Aeolian Desertified Land of North China

Legend:

Desert or Sandy land
- Shifting
- Semi-shifting
- Semi-fixed
- Fixed
- Gobi
- Salina

Aeolian Desertified Land
- Slight
- Moderate
- Severe
- Extremly severe
- Undefined International Boundary

0 250 500Km

1 Taklimakan Desert
2 Gurbantünggüt Desert
3 Kumtagh Desert
4 Qaidam Basin Desert
5 Badain Jaran Desert
6 Tengger Desert
7 Ulan Buh Desert
8 Hobq Desert
9 Mu Us Sandy Land
10 Onqin Daga Sandy Land
11 Horqin Sandy Land
12 Hulunbeir Sandy Land

Cities: Harbin, Changchun, Shenyang, Beijing, Tianjin, Jinan, Zhengzhou, Shijiazhuang, Taiyuan, Hohhot, Xi'an, Xining, Lanzhou, Yinchuan, Chengdu, Chongqing, ChangSha, Ürümqi

Summary

This book provides a comprehensive summary of the research on deserts and aeolian desertification and their rehabilitation practices in China over the past 50 years. This volume is composed of four parts. Part I presents the distribution and characteristics of deserts and aeolian desertification in China, as well as their physiographical conditions and socio-economic status. Part II discusses in detail the origin and evolution of deserts and aeolian desertification in China; reveals the physical, biological, and human impact processes of aeolian desertification; establishes the evaluation model and indicator system for monitoring aeolian desertification; and predicts the developmental trend of aeolian desertification. Part III gives a detailed description of the deserts, sandy lands and aeolian desertified lands in different zones in China. Part IV discusses the main problems confronting China's desert regions, puts forward strategies and optimization models for rehabilitating deserts and aeolian desertification in China, and summarizes the danger of blown sand movement to people's lives and infrastructure as well as engineering measures to prevent and control the wind erosion and desertification.

This book scientifically reveals the origins and mechanisms of deserts and aeolian desertification in China, effectively proves that deserts are the outcome of nature while aeolian desertification is a product of irrational human activities, clarifies the prolonged divergence of views on deserts and aeolian desertification, and solves some important theoretic questions concerning aeolian desertification control. Using this basis, as well as through summarizing China's practices and experiences in combating deserts and aeolian desertification over the past 50 years, this book puts forward strategies to combat aeolian desertification, basic principles and patterns for the rehabilitation of deserts and aeolian desertified lands, as well as patterns for development of deserts and the control of desertification in different climatic zones in China. Furthermore, fundamental technical systems to combat aeolian desertification are established.

This book represents a major scientific achievement in the research of deserts and aeolian desertification in China and provides an invaluable reference for the desert scientists and governmental policy-makers in China; this book can also be used as a reference for workers in other countries who are engaged in researching deserts, aeolian desertification, and their rehabilitation.

Preface One

Atmospheric protection, biodiversity conservation and combating desertification are environmental issues relating to human existence that need to be solved urgently in the new century. Aeolian desertification is one of the most significant desertification types. China is one of the countries suffering from the most serious aeolian desertification in the world. Deserts and aeolian desertified land in China covers an area of 1.669 million km^2, of which aeolian desertified land caused by human activity covers 385,700 km^2. Although the Government of China has been giving top priority to the control of aeolian desertification, it is still in a situation of "Local Rehabilitation and Overall Deterioration", and aeolian desertification is developing continuously and rapidly. Land aeolian desertification in China developed at a rate of 1,560 km^2/a during the 1960s–1970s, 2,100 km^2/a in the 1980s and 2,460 km^2/a during 1990—2000. With the accelerating development of aeolian desertification, sudden blown sand disasters—strong dust storms have been increasing in frequency. According to statistics, strong dust storms in northern China occurred 5 times per year in the 1950s, 8 times per year in the 1960s, 13 times per year in the 1970s, 14 times per year in the 1980s, and 23 times per year in the 1990s. The direct economic loss caused by aeolian desertification in China was estimated at 5.4 billion Chinese *yuan* per year, which seriously affects the sustainable development of the socio-economy. Aeolian desertification is a major eco-environmental problem facing the country today, and combating aeolian desertification is our long-term and arduous task.

Desert science is a discipline dealing with the research of desert and aeolian desertification processes and the prediction of their developmental trends and rehabilitation practices. Desert research in China was initiated in the 1950s, and from 1977 onwards its priority shifted to the study of aeolian desertification. This not only filled in the previous voids in aeolian desertification research, but also provided a scientific basis for China to work out a plan of action to combat aeolian desertification. The achievements we have made in aeolian desertification research have attracted the attention of international communities, especially developing countries. This book is a comprehensive summary of the research on deserts and aeolian desertification in China over the past 50 years; furthermore, it also deals with future research plans concerning deserts and aeolian desertification in China. I believe that the publication of this book will play an important role in promoting the development of desert and aeolian desertification science and advance the practice of aeolian desertification control in China.

Cheng Guodong

President, Lanzhou Branch, Chinese Academy of Sciences

Academician, Chinese Academy of Sciences

August, 2008

Preface Two

Since the economic reform and opening up of China to the outside world in the late 1970s, great progress has been made in constructing China's national economy and improving people's living standards. These achievements are unprecedented in modern Chinese history. However, owing to the large population and lower per capita share of land and natural resources, the rapid development of modernization constructions in industry, communication and building has consequently resulted in tremendous destruction to the eco-environment. In addition, rapid population growth and loss of arable land also pose a serious threat to the food security of the country. According to the predictions of both local and international scholars, environmental deterioration and food shortage would be two unsolvable problems for China in the future. In recent years, with the advances in agricultural science and technology great changes have taken place in the diet of the Chinese people (which includes an increase in meat and fruit consumption). Although the total grain output decreased, the country's grain reserve increased, and therefore grain prices remained stable. This is certainly a wonderful surprise, and both the Chinese Government and people are grateful for such an achievement.

Unfortunately, the prediction that China's eco-environment will deteriorate has proven true. After the lower reach of the Yellow River ceased to flow, the catastrophic flood of the Yangtze River and the serious water pollution of the Huaihe River in the late 1990s, frequent dust storms swept over the densely populated areas of eastern China in 2000. These dust storms not only caused serious economic loss but also badly damaged people's health. Though it most be said that those frequent dust storm events in 2000 were related to the atmospheric circulation of that year, it cannot be overlooked that it was also related to the rapid development of agriculture in arid regions of northwest China after beginning the policies of economic reform.

In the past, grain in China was transported from southern to northern regions, but by the late 1990s, the northern regions, especially the mixed farming-grazing regions, became the major grain-producing areas. For example, in 1978 the total grain output of Inner Mongolia was only 4.99 million tons and the per capita grain share was 274 kg. However, by 1997 its total grain output reached 14.21 million tons and the per capita grain share reached 661 kg despite a population increase. It is readily seen from these figures that such events are an inevitable outcome of extending cultivated land and reclaiming grasslands. During this same period, I made a trip to the northern front of the Yinshan Mountains, but I did not see the famous scene described in the "Song of Chile" of the Northern and southern Dynasties: "White clouds drift across the sky, the grassland stretches out of sight, and when a gentle breeze brushes against the grass, we see sheep and cattle here and there." What I saw during my trip was nothing but a vast expanse of bare reclaimed lands. Those lands have made great contributions to increasing the region's grain production, but on the other hand they also supplied a large amount of dust materials for dust storms. The same situation has been found in the Hexi Corridor region, which is the grain barn of Gansu Province; it is now producing a third of the grain and 70% of the commodities for the entire province by using 19% of the province's cultivated land. At the same time, excessive use of water resource in the midstream oases has led to a dramatic decrease in river runoff in downstream oases, such as Ejin Qi (the equivalent of a county) and Minqin. As a result, several lakes dried up, large areas of *Populus euphratica* forest died, desert vegetation rapidly degraded, some croplands were abandoned and black wind storms frequently occurred since the 1990s, thereby causing huge losses of both life and property. Certainly, the occurrence of natural disasters as a natural factor is unavoidable, but irrational human activities such as over-reclamation, overgrazing and over-cutting can be adjusted by mankind themselves. In response to the above problems, China has recently implemented strategies in the western regions of returning farmland to forests as well as ecological construction engineering projects.

It is impossible to effectively carry out government policies without the support of science and technology. We are glad to learn that dust storm events have been recently included in the country's weather forecast, and relevant governmental departments and scientific communities have put forward research plans and control strategies. The project "Research of the Aeolian Desertification Process and Its Control in Northern China" (GT2000048700) has been incorporated into the "National Key Basic Research Development Plan" (973 Program). This is no doubt a correct decision, and many of the leading participants of this project are the same researchers who contributed to this book. This book's aim is to sum up the research on deserts and aeolian desertification in China over the past several decades, and to reach a new level based on these achievements. This book fully and systematically presents the basic circumstances Surrounding deserts and aeolian desertification in China, gives detailed descriptions of their formation, evolution, extent and characteristics, and sums up the successful experiences of sand and aeolian desertification control created by researchers and people. In addition, it also puts forward reasonable measures and strategies to rehabilitate deserts and aeolian desertification by using theoretical evaluation.

It should be pointed out that since the founding of the People's Republic of China, the Chinese Government has attached great importance to the issue of aeolian desertification. In the late 1950s, comprehensive investigations of deserts and blown sand disasters were carried out and thus established special research institutes (such as the former Lanzhou Institute of Desert, Chinese Academy of Sciences) as well as local research organizations and sand control stations. Over the past several decades, we have trained a great number of qualified desert experts and had outstanding achievements in desert research such as shifting sand control along railways (in Shapotou of Zhongwei County). In addition, the highway construction in the Taklimakan Desert not only won a national prize and a UNEP award, but also attracted the attention of scholars from abroad. Furthermore, we have also made substantial progress in theoretical research. For example, the deserts in northwest China are temperate deserts located in the mid-latitude Asian interior and they are different from those deserts distributed in the vicinity of the Tropic of Cancer in North Africa and the Middle East. In the past, several foreign scholars tried to explain the origin of China's deserts by using theories such as "Continental Center" regions, with locations far removed from oceans, or this in combination with the rain shadow effects of the Himalayas and other mountains. But the authors of this book have put forward a new view and divided the evolution of arid zones in the middle regions of Asia into several stages since the Mesozoic Period, that is to say, the formation of modern deserts is directly related to the uplift of the Qinghai-Tibet Plateau (Qingzang Plateau). This resulted in the present monsoon pattern, and under the influence of Asia's winter monsoons, the deserts continuously spread. During the reworking processes of sand dunes, a large amount of dust materials was blown high in the air and transported to the surrounding grasslands to form thick-layer loess, which resulted in the formation of the Loess Plateau (Huangtu Plateau). Therefore, the uplift of the Qinghai-Tibet Plateau, desert expansion in northwest China and the formation of the Loess Plateau represent different links in the same causal chain of geologic processes. Thus the differentiation laws of the natural environment in northern China are correctly explained, which is a great advancement in scientific theory. This example alone can fully demonstrate the major progress we have made in desert research in China. However, compared with the arduous task we are now facing, namely implementing the strategy of developing the western regions, making full use of one third of the country's total area of arid zones, as well as simultaneously considering their use and protection, our knowledge and technical reserves are far from meeting the demand. Under global warming conditions, many problems, such as how to predict the future and what countermeasures should be adopted, need to be studied further. This is the reason why the state approved the implementation of the project "Research of the Aeolian Desertification Process and Its Control in Northern China".

This book is a summary of our previous work, and even though it looks as if it is an expansive sea of knowledge, the work we need to do in the years to come is even more arduous. The contributors of this book include both veteran scientists and young key members who continue to advance ideas and dare to blaze new trails; hence the research of deserts and aeolian desertification and their rehabilitation in China is bound to be pushed ahead to a new level. This book, with substantial content and a great wealth of data, deals with various aspects of deserts and aeolian desertification in China. I believe that this book will be of great assistance to researchers engaged in researching deserts and aeolian desertification as well as for others involved in this type of work.

Li Jijun

Professor, College of Resources and Environmental Sciences, Lanzhou University

Academician, Chinese Academy of Sciences

October, 2008

Foreword

Human society has entered a new era.

Reflecting upon the past, we have made considerable progress in science and technology; national economies developed rapidly, social wealth increased, people's living standards rose, and public welfare improved without precedence. It may be said without exaggeration that the 20th century was a century that mankind achieved the most brilliant accomplishments.

However, the development of mankind relies on the extortion of nature's resources, and society and civilization is created mostly at the expense of the natural environment. The 20th century was also a century when mankind's living environment was seriously destroyed through exploiting natural resources. As we fully enjoy modern civilization, the seriously destroyed fragile ecosystem warns us again and again. Human existence and sustainable development are now facing the serious threats of environmental issues, water crisis, climate warming, biodiversity loss and land desertification.

The international communities have been increasingly concerned about environmental issues since the 1970s. The United Nations Conference on the Human Environment was held in Stockholm, Sweden in 1972 and adopted the Declaration of the United Nations Conference On the Human Environment. In June of 1992, 102 heads of states and governments attended the United Nations Conference on Environment and Development held in Rio de Janeiro, Brazil and discussed a series of issues such as greenhouse gas emissions, global warming and other problems. The conference adopted the Rio Declaration on Environment and Development, Agenda 21, the United Nations Framework Convention on Climate Change, the Convention on Biological Diversity and the Statement on Forest Principles and also called on the governments of various nations to strengthen cooperation and formulate their own sustainable developmental strategies.

Land desertification, which occurs after the destruction of land surface vegetation, is a serious environmental and socio-economic problem threatening human existence and sustainable development. Combating desertification is included in Agenda 21 as an important topic. Shortly after the United Nations Conference on Environment and Development, the Convention to Combat Desertification in Those Countries Experiencing Serious Drought and/or Desertification, Particularly in Africa (also called the United Nations Convention to Combat Desertification for short) was adopted in Paris on June 17, 1994. The delegates of the Chinese Government also participated in the negotiations of the Convention to Combat Desertification, and China was one of the major signatories of the Convention.

China, one of the world's most populous developing country, lacks sufficient arable land and suffers from serious desertification. In light of the United Nations Convention to Combat Desertification and the actual situation, desertification in China mainly includes the following types: soil erosion, aeolian desertification and salinization. In the past 50 years, these disasters developed and spread rapidly and also increased in severity. Desertification in most parts of northern China is mainly manifested in land aeolian desertification. According to statistical data, the land area affected by water erosion, wind erosion, aeolian desertification and salinization occupies about one third of Chinese terrestrial area, of which desert, gravel desert (gobi), wind-eroded land and aeolian desertified land cover 1.67 million km^2, accounting for 17.4% of China's total land area.

Aeolian desertification is defined as land degradation in arid, semiarid and parts of semi-humid regions with the occurrence of blown sand activities (deflation, ground surface coarsening, and sand dune formation, etc.) on former non-desert areas as the main mark resulting from various factors including overusing land and upsetting the fragile ecological balance under the conditions of dry and windy climate and loose sand surface. Aeolian desertification in China mainly occurs in six provinces and regions in northwest China. Deserts and sandy lands in China can roughly be delimited with the 200 mm isohyet line as the dividing line. Arid and hyper-arid deserts dominated by mobile sand dunes occur in the zones where the precipitation is less than 200 mm, while sandy lands dominated by fixed and semi-fixed sand dunes, desertified land, desert grassland, steppe and forest grassland occur in the zones where the precipitation is more than 200 mm.

Natural environments in western China are complex and diversified, with an abundant amount of endemic species. For a long time this region has faced acute contradictions between environmental protection and resource development, ecological sensitivity and economical fragility. Hence, the protection and restoration of eco-environments and combating aeolian desertification are the key topics needing to be studied in the implementation of the national strategy of developing western regions.

The western regions affected by aeolian desertification in China are rich in light, heat, land and mineral resources. Especially the abundant energy resources are the key to the development of western regions. In the face of the current energy resource crisis, western regions of China will become one of the bases for future development. Promoting socio-economic development, raising people's living standard, and protecting and improving human living environments are the important and practical issues we are facing today.

At the end of the 1990s, the Chinese Government made a correct assessment of the situation from a broad and long-term view, and kept pace with times to work out the important strategy of "Implementing the Development of Western Regions and Quickening the Development of Mid-West Regions." This strategy has a profound significance to speed up the construction course of China's modernizations, to maintain the country's security and social stability and to fulfill the great cause of rejuvenating.

Aeolian sand activities, including soil and wind erosion, sand drift, sand deposition and sand dune movement are the common characteristics of sandy desert environments and aeolian desertified land. In localities where the climate is dry, vegetation is sparse and the surface is covered by sand, sand grains begin to move once the wind velocity reaches 4–5 m/s or more. However, there is a substantial difference between sandy deserts and aeolian desertified land. Sandy deserts are a natural product formed from long-term geological processes and man can do little or nothing to alter, these deserts which existed for at least 1–2 million years. With climatic changes, the already formed sandy deserts experienced positive developmental processes, during which blown sand activity was strong and sand dunes advanced, and they also experienced negative developmental processes, during which sand movement was weakened and sand dunes were fixed by vegetation. Aeolian desertification is a land degradation process resulting from the interaction between human activities and fragile eco-environments under modern climatic conditions. Irrational human economic activities changed the surface structure and vegetation cover, leading to the exposure of soil susceptible to wind erosion and sand movement; finally sand dunes will develop and thereby exhibit a desert-like landscape.

The earliest description of land desertification was mentioned in the ancient Babylon sphenogram about 4,000 years ago. Similarly, the environmental degradation caused by land reclamation in northern China during this same period was recorded in ancient Chinese works. However, the rapid spread of aeolian desertification over large areas occurred 2,000 years ago. Land aeolian desertification in the historical period is mainly attributable to human activities, such as land reclamation without considering the ecological conditions, overgrazing and cutting trees. In arid regions in northwest China, uncontrolled expansion of oases in the upper reaches of inland rivers, cutting off water supplies to downstream oases due to war or other causes, cropland abandonment, and population growth are the direct causes resulting in changes in land use, land cover and water shortage.

Prior to the Qin Dynasty (221 BC), China maintained a population of 11–13 million for a long time, by the second year of Yuanshi in the reign of Emperor Ping in Han Dynasty, the Chinese population increased to 59.6 million. It was the first period of a quick population increase in Chinese history. At that time, the cultivated land area was about 38.47 million hm^2, or about 6.4 times larger than that of the early Han Dynasty, and the farming limit extended as far away as Xinjiang, the Hexi Corridor, Yinchuan and the Hetao Plains, southern Inner Mongolia, and Xining. From the Eastern Han Dynasty (220 AD) onwards, the Chinese population decreased to about 10 million due to civil wars, then increased to 46 million in the Sui Dynasty and further increased to 52.9 million before An Lushan raised a rebellion in the Central Plains (755 AD). At that time cultivated land had increased to 73.33 million hm^2, and, almost all the plain lands had been reclaimed. In the Ming Dynasty (1368–1664), a large number of troops were stationed in the areas along both sides of the Great Wall and opened up a large area of grasslands to prevent nomadic invasion. In the sixth year (1720) in the reign of Qing Emperor Qianlong the head tax was rescinded and a tax policy to reduce the burden on farmers was carried out. As a result, China's population rapidly increased to 206 million from less than 100 million in the 29th year in the reign of the Qing Emperor Qianlong (1764), and further reached over 400 million in 1840. This was the second period of a rapid population increase in Chinese history. From 1858 onwards, the Government of the Qing Dynasty resettled a large number of people in border regions to open up grassland and thereby led to the extension of farming into Inner Mongolia, northeast China and northern Xinjiang. According to statistical data, in the 150-year period from the 10th year of the reign of the Qing Emperor Shunzhi (1654) to the 10th year of the reign of the Qing Emperor Jiaqing (1806), cultivated land area in China increased to 16.1 million hm^2. Therefore most forest regions and grasslands in northern China were disturbed or even destroyed. Under the influences of human activities over 2,000 years, the forest cover in China decreased to 21% in the early Qing Dynasty from the original 64%.

From 1949 onwards, China entered a third period of a rapid population increase. Over the past 50 years China's population has more than doubled, nearly reaching 1.3 billion, and this has therefore exerted tremendous pressure on the eco-environment. By 1995 the cultivated land area in western regions increased by nearly 10% compared with that in 1949, and in Xinjiang it increased by nearly 140% or more. By the middle of the 20th century China's forest cover had decreased to 8.6%, and in the same period grassland area also decreased. For example, in the 10-year period from 1987 to 1996 the grassland area decreased by 4%–9%. During the 1950s–1970s, northern China experienced three large-scale land reclamation periods; in total, over 6 million hm^2 of grassland were reclaimed. Grassland reclamation and rapid increases in animal population are the main causes responsible for grassland degradation and aeolian desertification; especially the grasslands in the eastern region have seriously worsened. According to statistical data, of the total area of aeolian desertified land in northern China, about 26.9% resulted from massive land reclamation, 32.7% resulted from uncontrolled removal of trees and vegetation, 30.1% resulted from overgrazing, 9.7% resulted from misuse of water resources and only 0.6% resulted from natural factors such as sand dune encroachment.

Over the past 50 years, considerable work has been done in aeolian desertification control in China; by the early 1990s about 260,000 hm^2 of aeolian desertified land had been rehabilitated. However, the general picture of the aeolian desertification situation is that of "local restoration and overall expansion". Furthermore, owing to feedback effects between aeolian desertification and the environment, the rate of aeolian desertification development has been continuously speeding up, i. e. increased from 1,560 km^2/a during the 1960s–1970s to 2,100 km^2/a in 1980s and to 2,460 km^2/a in 1990s. By the end of the 1990s aeolian desertified land area in northern China has reached 385,700 km^2.

With the accelerating development of aeolian desertification, the frequency of sudden blowing sand disasters—strong—dust storms greatly increased. According to statistics, the frequency of strong dust storms in northern China has increased from 5 times per year in the 1950s to 8 times per year in the 1960s, 13 times per year in the 1970s, 14 times per year in the 1980s, and 23 times per year in the 1990s. Dust storms directly damage northwest and northern China and can affect southern China or even the whole of East Asia.

Aeolian desertification poses a serious threat to the eco-environment and social economy. Firstly, it upsets the ecological balance, results in environmental deterioration and reduction of land productivity, affects the livelihood of people in aeolian desertification-prone regions and aggravates their degree of poverty. Secondly, it leads to the loss of large areas of productive lands. It is estimated that the land lost to aeolian desertification per year is roughly equivalent to the area of a medium-sized county in China. Finally, it poses a serious threat to rural communities, transport lines, water projects, mining and industrial infrastructures, national defense bases, as well as agricultural and industrial productions. It is estimated that aeolian desertification results in a direct and indirect economic loss of 54 billion Chinese *yuan* each year. Aeolian desertification is one of the major constraints to socio-economic sustainable development. Launching scientific research in light of the country's construction demand is a basic guiding principle of the Chinese Academy of Sciences. Based on the already achieved research results, further launching systematic and in-depth studies to understand the causes and development of aeolian desertification and dust storms as well as effective control ways in China is essential. In accordance with the national demand to implement "Strategy of Developing Western Regions" and "National Sand Control Engineering", the related departments of the country embarked on the "State Key Basic Research Development Plan" (973 Program) and "Research of the Aeolian Desertification Process and Its Control in Northern China" (GT2000048700). These studies will be contributive to solve some unsettled problems and achieve systematic and thorough research results.

Based on the famous geographer Zhu Kezhen's pioneer work, desert and aeolian desertification sciences in China were developed along with the development of the national economic construction. Through several generations of scientists' painstaking work over 50 years, considerable progress has been made. A strong research contingent has formed, and various organizations such as the key laboratory, experiment station and the International Center for Research and Education on Aeolian Desertification Control have been established. In summary, we have scored the following achievements in deserts and aeolian desertification researches: ① have clear understanding of the distribution of deserts and aeolian desertification and their extent and severity in China; ② the scientific theoretical frame and the methodology for deserts and aeolian desertification researches have been preliminarily established and some substantial results have been achieved; ③ we have preliminarily understood the developmental processes of deserts and aeolian desertification in China; ④ a national research contingent of deserts and aeolian desertification has begun to take shape; ⑤ several fixed site research and demonstration experimental stations have been established and aeolian desertification control work in different bioclimatic zones has been initiated; ⑥ we have conducted wide international cooperation and exchange work, some research results and experiences concerning aeolian desertification control have been accepted and adopted by international colleagues and friends.

However, our research work in deserts and aeolian desertification is still far from meeting the demand of improving eco-environments, combating desertification, and ensuring sustainable social and economic development.

The perfection of desert science requires a multidisciplinary intersection between earth science, mechanics, atmospheric science, biology, and socio-economics. It should be studied from the omnibearing and integrative angle of natural and social sciences. We are now taking measures to attract well-trained personnel in the above research fields so as to enhance our research level in deserts and aeolian desertification sciences, keep our leading position in the world in this respect, and make a greater contribution to the development of deserts and aeolian desertification sciences in the world.

This book is a comprehensive summary of the research work on deserts and aeolian desertification in China.

The contributors of this book include both veteran scholars who have been engaged in desert research for a long time and young experts who are willing to devote themselves to desert research and also have a strong command of scientific knowledge including physics, mathematics, geography, biology, socio-economics and hi-tech know-how. Multidisciplinary research in combination with innovative knowledge will contribute to the perfection of the theoretical system of desert and aeolian desertification science. The authors of this book are noted in various chapters, and this entire book was finally reviewed by Wang Tao. The publication of this book fills in a gap in this respect. It will not only play an important part in carrying on the past heritage and opening up the bright future but also have great significance for the research of deserts and aeolian desertification science. We hope this book will benefit readers who have an interest in deserts and aeolian desertification and their rehabilitation.

Dr. Wang Tao

Director, Cold and Arid Regions Environmental and Engineering

Research Institute, Chinese Academy of Sciences

September, 2008

Contents

Part II Evolution of Deserts and Aeolian Desertification in China

Part I
Overview of Deserts
and Aeolian Desertification in China

Chapter 1
Introduction

1.1 Progress in desert research in China

1.1.1 An overview of desert research history in China

Arid, semiarid and part of semi-humid regions in China are comprised of vast expanses of deserts, gobi and aeolian desertified land. The earliest description of deserts can be found in Chinese ancient writings such as *The Classic of Mountains and Rivers* (221 BC) and *The Book of Documents, Yugong*. In ancient times, Chinese people called deserts "shifting sand", "sand river", "sand sea", "big desert" or khoum and gobi words from the transliteration of minority languages. During the Western Han Dynasty (206 BC-25 AD) cultural exchange between Han People and other minorities including Hun (Xiongnu) in northern China gradually increased. During the Eastern Han Dynasty (25–220AD) Buddhism was introduced into China, and the Silk Road was later opened in the Tang Dynasty (618–907AD). Since the Yuan Dynasty (1271), more and more cavalry men, merchants, monks and envoys entered or traveled across the deserts. All these events increase our understanding of the deserts. What is worthy of special mention here is that many Chinese ancient writings described the deserts, such as *The Biography of Emperor Mu, Records of the Historian: the Account of Hun (Xiongnu)*, and the *Account of Ferghana* by Sima Qian, *History of the Late Han Dynasty: Western Region Account* by Ban Gu, *Natural Conditions and Social Customs in Western Regions* by Ban Yong, *A Record of the Buddhist Countries and Buddhist Record of the Western World in the Tang Dynasty* by Xuan Zang, and *Travel Notes of Western Regions* by Yelü Chucai, etc. In addition, some ancient geographical works also cursorily mentioned the deserts, but their emphases were mostly placed on the descriptions of the social economy and folk customs.

Modern desert investigations in China started from the expeditions of foreign explorers. Subsequently, several Chinese geographers also took part in these expeditions (Fig.1-1). One hundred years ago an upsurge in expeditions began. In the expedition teams, there were a few cultural thieves, whose disrespectful actions upset many Chinese people and overshadowed their geographic works. In addition, people in desert regions also had several successful experiences in the rehabilitation and development processes of deserts and sandy lands. For example, as early as the beginning of the 18th century, farmers in Shaanxi and Gansu used clay to cover shifting sand and to improve sandy land. In the 1940s, farmers in Jingbian of Shaanxi Province used methods of "diverting water to wash away dunes" and "diverting floods to irrigate dunefields" to open up farmlands. A few scholars even noted the damages of aeolian desertification. For example, in 1934 Cheng Boqun published his paper titled "The spread of desert in China" in *Science*. In this work, he described the aeolian desertification occurring at the southern edge of the Mu Us Sandy Land. However， before the 1950s, almost no scholars dealt with theoretical problems such as the origin of deserts and the causes of aeolian desertification, and no measures were taken to prevent their expansion. In other words, until the first half of the 20th century, the research on deserts and aeolian desertification in China was virtually nonexistent.

Fig. 1-1　Members of the Scientific Investigation Team of Northwest China (1928), Sven Hedin holding a stick

From the late 19th century to the early 20th century, a worldwide expedition of the "Silk Road—Western Region" occurred. The regions from the Central Asian deserts to the Mongolian grasslands became the explorer's favorite regions. Besides Russian scholars, many scholars from England, France, Hungary, America and Japan entered these regions.

Geographers Humboldt and Romancaiv first entered the desert regions in Xinjiang and investigated the Junggar region in 1829. From 1856 to 1857 the Russian geographer and biologist Semenov investigated the mineral deposits in the Tianshan Regions. He was awarded the title of "*Tianshanskii*" by the Russian Tsar for his publication titled "Travel to the Tianshan Mountains". In 1858 an expedition team headed by Russian captain Tonybek entered the Tianshan Mountains and the Junggar Basin. In the same year, Russian captain Walihanov, disguising himself as a merchant, arrived in the Kashi, Hotan and Aksu regions of southern Xinjiang. His travel notes were published in the "*Journal of Russian Geographical Society*".

Russian geographer Przewalski first arrived in China in 1870 and made investigations in Inner Mongolia, Qinghai and Gansu between 1870–1873. From 1875 to 1877 he made his second investigation in northwest China and entered Lop Nur along the Kaidu River and Korla. Based on his investigation, he corrected the location of the Altun Mountains in European maps. In his third investigation in Xinjiang, Qinghai and Tibet, he discovered a wild horse that was subsequently named Equus przewalskii after his name. During the investigation processes he collected a large number of animal and plant specimens which were exhibited in the Petersburg Museum. After his fourth investigation, he wrote the "Fourth Travel Notes of the Central Asian Regions" in which he mentioned his investigation route—from Qiaktu to the headwater of the Huanghe River (Yellow River) and from the border of northern Tibet (north Xizang) to the Tarim Basin via Lop Nur. On November 1, 1888, when he was ready for his fifth visit to China, Przewalski suddenly died. The Russian Tsar then sent an investigation team headed by Pevchov to investigate southern Xinjiang, the Kunlun Mountains and the Altun Mountains. As one of the members of the investigation team, the famous geologist Obluchev traveled over 15,000 km in Xinjiang, Gansu, Shaanxi and Shanxi and collected large amounts of geological data. His investigation laid the basis for the aeolian theory of the loess origin in China.

Famous Swedish explorer Sven Hedin investigated deserts and the Gobi in Xinjiang, Tibet and Inner Mongolia in 1894. On February 17, 1895 he entered the Taklimakan Desert via Markit and encountered a terrible sand storm; all of his camels and employers were swallowed up in the sand sea. Fortunately, he was saved by the Hotan River. Afterwards, he called the Taklimakan Desert "Sea of Death". After a short time of preparation, he again entered the desert along the Yurungkax River. Finally, he traveled through the Taklimakan Desert from south to north along the Hotan River and discovered the ancient towns of Dandanwulik and Karadun in the interior of the desert. In March of 1896 he entered Lop Nur and investigated the stream system of the lower Tarim River. Since then a considerable debate on whether Lop Nur is a wandering lake or not has been provoked. Funded by Swedish King Oscar and Nobel, Sven Hedin started his fifth Taklimakan Desert investigation in 1899. During that investigation he entered Lop Nur once again. He drew the shipping line of the Tarim River and 1,149 pieces of maps, and discovered a large number of ancient manuscripts and coins. After traveling about 10,500 km he determined the geographical location of Lop Nur and drew the 1 : 35,000 Map of the Tarim Basin. In 1928, with an invitation from the Chinese government, Sven Hedin led an expedition team consisting of 28 scholars from Sweden, Germany and China to investigate the ancient traffic artery south of the Taklimakan Desert. Chinese Scholars who participated in the expedition team included Professor Xu Bingxu (Xu Xusheng) of Beijing University, Chen Zongqi, Huang Wenbi, Ding Daoheng and Yuan Fuli. Sven Hedin passed away in 1952. Another person worthy of mention is Xie Bing—an official of the Ministry of Finance of China, who traveled 8,500 km in Xinjiang either by camel, horse or ass cart in 1916 and left his footprints in the surrounding areas of the Taklimakan Desert. In his work *Travel Notes of Xinjiang* he described the natural conditions and socioeconomic status in Xinjiang at that time. Many places he once arrived in have now changed into deserts, which provides vivid information for us to study the vicissitudes of the Taklimakan Desert and the oases around it.

1.1.2　Progress in desert research of China

Since the founding of the People's Republic of China, the Chinese government has attached great importance to the research of deserts and their rehabilitation. At the beginning of the 1950s an introduction experiment of *Pinus sylvestris* and the study of shelterbelt forest construction were initiated in Zhanggutai, Zhangwu County, Liaoning Province, and its aim was to prevent shifting sand encroachment on farmlands in the western part of the Northeast Plain. What is worthy of special mention is that in 1952 during the reconnaissance processes of the proposed Baotou-Lanzhou railway route, the Railway Survey and Design Institute, of the Ministry of Railway, in cooperation with the Institute of Geography under the Chinese Academy of Sciences, conducted research of aeolian landforms and observations of blown sand activities at the southern margin of the Tengger Desert. At the beginning of 1954 the first observation station of blown sand in China was established in the vicinity of Shapotou. Since then the shifting sand control in the shifting dune section of the Baotou-Lanzhou Railway at the southeastern margin of the Tengger Desert has been initiated. In response to the demands of national economic construction, the Chinese Academy of Sciences organized several comprehensive investigations teams including the Xinjiang, the Middle Yellow River and the Gansu-Qinghai-Ningxia-Inner Mongolia: Comprehensive Investigation Teams to make scientific investigations of natural resources and environments in northern China. The establishment of the Desert Control Team, Chinese Academy of Sciences, in 1959 marked the beginning of the systematic and comprehensive research of desert science in China.

The researches on deserts in China roughly went through the following stages and have made considerable progress.

1.1.2.1　Research work during the period of 1959–1960

In 1959, with the lead of scholars from the Desert Control Team of Chinese Academy of Sciences, 19 desert investigation teams, consisting of scientists from related institutes of the Chinese Academy of Sciences, national ministries, universities and local departments, were organized to conduct comprehensive investigations on the Taklimakan Desert, the Gurbantünggüt Desert, the Badain Jaran Desert, the Tengger Desert, the Ulan Buh Desert, the Mu Us Sandy Land, the Onqin Daga Sandy Land, the Hobq Desert, the Hedong Sandy Land in Ningxia, the desert in Qinghai and Gobi in western Gansu (Fig 1-2). The purpose was to make an in-depth investigation of the area, distribution and types of desert in China as well as their landforms, climate, hydrology, soil, vegetation, and socioeconomic conditions. Based on these investigations, preliminary rehabilitation plans and recommendations for certain desert regions were proposed. Based on the 1959 large-scale investigations, some supplemental surveys were conducted during the 1960–1961 period. The above scientific investigations mainly yielded the following results: (a). Basically found out the area, type distribution, and sand movement characteristics of deserts and gobi deserts in China; there after a classification system for deserts in China was established; (b). Preliminarily found out the existing resources and natural conditions in the interiors of various deserts; (c). The social and economic conditions of various deserts were better understood. On the whole, this work achieved a much better understanding about the deserts in China and therefore provided a basis for developing their rehabilitation plans.

During the scientific investigation period, the Desert Control Team, the Chinese Academy of Sciences, established six comprehensive experiment stations and scores of central stations in Inner Mongolia and five other provinces in northwestern China to conduct in-situ observations as well as experiments of sandy land use and dune stabilization. These stations preliminarily constituted a scientific experiment network in desert regions of northern China.

Fig. 1-2   Scientists from the Desert Control Team, Chinese Academy of Sciences, entered the desert in 1959

1.1.2.2   Research work during the period of 1961–1966

From 1961 onwards, desert research in China entered a stage of in-situ, semi-location or case studies. Research work in this stage included five aspects. Firstly, with the southern part of the Taklimakan Desert as the focus, the formation and development characteristics of the desert were studied, and emphases were placed on the Quaternary paleogeographic outline, underlying deposit composition and differentiation features. From this, the conclusion that "sands are of local origin" was put forward, and the distribution extents of fluvial deposits, lacustrine deposits and residual deposits in various deserts were determined. Based on the field investigations and aerial photograph analyses, the dune development processes from sands to dune chains and the relation between dune movement and height were elucidated. The work *Study of Aeolian Landforms in the Taklimakan Desert* by Zhu Zhenda et al. represents a comprehensive summary of the research results in this stage. Secondly, in combination with implementing sand control along the railway line, the in-situ research of shifting sand stabilization was carried out at the Shapotou Experiment Station during the 10-year period from 1956 to 1965. Based on the experiment results, some desert-adapted sand binding species, such as *Hedysarum scoparium*, *Caragana korshinskii*, *Calligonum arborescens*, and *Artemisia ordosica* etc were selected. The relations between plant growth and sand moisture content as well as compactness were elucidated, the variation laws of moisture content in sand were summarized, and the original design scheme to control sand encroachment on railway lines was modified. The collection of papers, "Research of Shifting Sand Control", represents the research results of this stage. This research result won the 1986 special prize of National Scientific and Technological Progress. Thirdly, human activities and desert vicissitudes in the historic period in the Mu Us Sandy Land and northern part of the Ulan Buh Desert were studied. Fourthly, the comprehensive utilization experiments of sandy land including planting fruit trees, melons and vegetables were conducted at Dengkou, Minqin and Yulin stations. These experiments proved the feasibility of agricultural use of sandy land. Lastly, during the period of 1965–1966, China's first Wind Tunnel Laboratory of Blown Sand Environments was constructed in Lanzhou, which provides the opportunity for indoor experiments and research on the physics of blown sand.

1.1.2.3 Research work after 1977

From 1977 onwards, desert research in China entered a new development stage. With rapid population growth and continuous progress in science and technology, both the extent and intensity of human exploitation of natural resources greatly increased, which is causing a series of eco-environmental degradation and socio-economic problems all over the world. The serious Sahelian drought of 1968–1973 resulted in great losses of life and property and forced the international community to focus great attention on developing methods to combat desertification. In view of this, the United Nations Conference on Desertification (UNCOD) was held in August-September 1977 in Nairobi, Kenya and worked out a "Plan of Action to Combat Desertification" (3337 Resolution). Desertification is one of the global eco-environmental issues related to the social economy. The Chinese government also sent delegates to the conference and from the exchange of views, the global community became fully aware that China was also facing serious aeolian desertification issues. Since then, desertification and its control have been listed as one of the important research subjects in China.

A new discipline generally forms in the processes of resolving social and economic problems, and its development depends upon a multidisciplinary approach. Over the past 50 years, in consideration of the demands of national economic construction, environmental protection and development, a series of field investigations, in-situ and semi-location experiments were conducted; the research methods were continuously improved; and the research of desert and aeolian desertification gradually formed into an independent discipline. Desert science, with aeolian sand activity-dominated regions (desert and aeolian desertified land) as the environmental complex, studies the formation and evolution laws of deserts, reveals their development processes in relation to human activities, predicts their future development trend, and seeks ways to reasonably develop and utilize them. In short, desert science is a disciplinary field studying the formation and evolution processes of desert and aeolian desertification, as well as predicting their developmental trends and finding ways to rehabilitate them. With a theoretical system of geography, agronomy, forestry, sociology and economics as a background, desert science has accepted the concepts, theories and research methods of modern science as well as gradually formed its own theories and research methods. Desert research is closely related to today's five worldwide social problems, namely population growth, food shortage, energy crisis, natural resource destruction and environmental pollution.

In China the formation and evolution of deserts have always been regarded as one of the main research contents. However, due to the limitation of available research conditions and methodological differences, scientists in geological and geographical scholars still hold different views as to the formation periods and origin of deserts in China. For example, based on historical literature and archaeological data, Professor Hou Renzhi suggested that the eastern sandy lands to the east of the Helan Mountains resulted from irrational human activities in the Han and Tang dynasties, especially in the Qing Dynasty. Through the studies of aeolian sand landforms and subsand soils, Zhu Zhenda and Wu Zheng thought the Taklimakan Desert was formed in the mid-Pleistocene. But from the field investigation results in the 1950s, Professor Zhou Tingru inferred that the Tarim Basin had been an arid desert since the beginning of the early Pleistocene; furthermore he thought that the sandy land in the Ordos Plateau was formed in the last glacial maximum. From the Yulin Formation, the Salawusu Formation and the "sand layer" intercalated in loess, Yang Zhongjian and Liu Tungsheng et al. inferred that "there may have been an ancient desert present "on the northern side of the Loess Plateau during the Quaternary. Soviet Union geologist Shinicun thought that the uplift of the Qinghai-Tibet Plateau led to the climatic aridification and the formation of deserts. However, from the aeolian quartz grains in boreholes of the North Pacific Ocean, French scholar Daiwa Rea inferred that deserts have existed in the Central Asian inland since the Cretaceous period, but there is no direct evidence supporting his view.

Through the large-scale scientific investigation in desert regions, Zhu Zhenda et al. suggested that deserts in China were formed over long periods of evolution processes under the conditions of dry climate and abundant sand sources, furthermore, they were affected by anthropogenic factors. It may be said that deserts are the outcome of arid climate. Globally, the formation of arid climatic zones (dryland) is mainly related to the latitude and atmospheric circulation. In the belts between latitudes 15°–35° north and south of the equator, which are controlled by the Subtropical High, the trade winds blow year round, and the descending high-pressure air gives rise to clear skies that are not conducive to precipitation. Therefore, it forms the earth's arid zones and most of the major deserts of the world occur in this zone, including the Sahara Desert in North Africa, the Arabian Desert in southwest Asia, and the Atacama Desert in South America. These tropical and subtropical deserts are also called hot deserts or trade wind deserts. Deserts in China mainly occur in the arid and semiarid regions of the temperate and warm temperate zones between 35°–50° N and 75°–125° E. Viewed from the latitude this zone is not an arid zone; however, due to their distant location from the oceans and the uplift influence of the Qinghai-Tibet Plateau, northwestern China and much of Inner Mongolia have extremely dry conditions. Under such a climatic condition, loose and bare sandy surface is exposed to strong wind, and sediments loosened by wind erosion are picked up and deposited elsewhere to finally form deserts.

A research group headed by Dong Guangrong used field investigations, indoor experiments and comparative research methods to conduct a detailed study on the formation and evolution processes of deserts in China in accordance with aeolian sand records and made considerable progress. A brief account is given below.

1) Desert deposits

Aeolian sands and gobi sediments are the major types of aeolian deposits. From the systematical researches of ancient aeolian sands in the strata after the Miocene, their characteristics of distribution, morphology, depositional structure, grain size, mineral composition and quartz grain microtexture were identified, and they were classified into buried ancient aeolian sand, residual ancient aeolian sand, sandy wind-deposited material and sandy paleosols in terms of their properties and lithologic characters. In the meantime, the characteristics of gobi pavement such as gravel mechanical weathering, salt weathering, gypsum wedge, wind erosion and deposition, and desert varnish were studied. According to their properties and underlying parent materials, they were classified into exposed gobi, buried gobi, gravel gobi and stony gobi. All these studies provide geological evidence for the formation and evolution of deserts.

2) Temporal and spatial distribution of desert evolution

According to lithologic characters and age determination data, ancient aeolian sand-bearing strata in northern China were compared and thereby used to preliminarily established the evolutional time series and spatial patterns of deserts in China. Before the Quaternary, the subtropic red desert transversed the country from northwest to southeast. During the Quaternary period the temperate yellow deserts existed in northwestern China; in the early Pleistocene they were scatteredly distributed with small area, but in the mid-Pleistocene their area rapidly increased and thus laid today's temperate desert pattern. During the latter part of the late Pleistocene, the deserts in eastern China rapidly mobilized, but its area was smaller than that of the mid-Pleistocene. During the Holocene the desert area decreased and in local places it was fixed or mobilized. Modern deserts represent a series of long-term evolutional processes of deserts. Like the continental aeolian red soil, loess deposits and deep-sea aeolian deposits, they provide the evidence for the researches of global changes and the regional responses.

3) Desert evolutional patterns and characteristics

From the Cretaceous period to the Eogene period, the differences between deserts in China was not evident. But in the period from the Miocene epoch to the Pliocene epoch, the red desert yielded some differences. With the Helan Mountains and Lanzhou as the approximate boundary, the eastern deserts were mainly comprised of ancient red aeolian sand, red soil and red soil interbeds; calcareous leaching was evident, sand dunes were mostly fixed and semi-fixed; and both positive and negative evolutional processes existed. The western deserts were dominated by ancient red aeolian sand and gypsum salt interbeds, paleosols developed poorly, and sand dunes were mostly mobile, showing a positive developmental process. Since the Quaternary, the regional difference of deserts was intensified. Roughly with the line extending from the Helan Mountains to Dulan of Qinghai as the boundary, the western desert existed west of that line and south of the Tianshan and north of the Kunlun Mountains, while the northern desert was located north of the Tianshan Mountains. The presence of the ancient aeolian sand-loess-paleosol interbeds showed that the eastern and northern deserts experienced alternating development processes of shifting sand spread, fixation, and soil formation. In the transverse direction the coexistence of desert and loess as well as a large area of dunes indicated that they are "steppe-type" desert. The western deserts, including the Taklimakan Desert, mostly experienced linear development processes of shifting sand spread. In the transverse direction, the desert, gobi, subsand soil and loess are interspersed with sparse rivers and lakes, and they are of "desert-type" desert (Fig.1-3). The deserts in the central region exhibit a development pattern between the former and the latter.

Fig. 1-3   Ancient sand dune and gobi remains in Xinjiang

4) Climate and environment

The Cenozoic stratigraphic deposits and other related data demonstrated that from the

Cretaceous period to the Eogene period, the red deserts in China were dry-hot tropical and subtropical deserts. During the Neogene period the bioclimatic zones in the western and eastern desert regions were respectively subtropic arid to hyperarid deserts and semiarid steppe savanna to steppe. During the Quaternary period, the limit of the deserts in northern China oscillated between the warm temperate zone and cold temperate zone. According to geological records such as stratigraphic sedimentary facies, vertebrates, sporo-pollens, soluble salts, $CaCO_3$, clay minerals, grain size, ancient moraine, and gypsum polygons, the climate and environment in various desert regions of China exhibited evident differences since the late Pleistocene. In the northern, but most especially the eastern desert regions, the warm-wet forest grassland and shrub grassland (meadow grassland) tended to change into steppe, desert steppe or even desert. The western desert region was always in an alternating dry-hot and dry-wet desert environment with little humidity variation. The central desert region exhibited a slightly large climatic fluctuation and roughly varied between dry-cold alternating hyperarid desert and semiarid steppe.

1.2   Aeolian desertification research and its progress in China

Land desertification is one of the largest environmental and socioeconomic problems facing the world today. The rapid spread of desertification resulted in environmental degradation, tremendous economic loss, and even caused local political unrest and social security problems; therefore it is attracting worldwide attention. French botanist A. Aubreville was the first scientist to use the term desertification (Aubreville, 1949). He pointed out that tree cutting, cultivation and soil erosion led to the land destruction of the tropical forest regions, and if nothing is done to stop this, productive land will turn into desert. This is what he termed desertification. The serious drought of the late 1960s and the early 1970s in West Africa accelerated the development of desertification and also attracted the attention of the international community. The United Nations Conference on Desertification held in Nairobi in 1977 stressed the implementation of the Plan of Action to Combat Desertification (3337 Resolution).

China is one of the countries suffering from the most serious desertification in the world. As early as the late 1950s, Professor Zhu Kezhen had pointed out that, owing to anthropogenic causes, some former non-desert land had turned into desert, and about 530,000 hm^2 of sandy grassland in Shaanxi and Ih Ju Meng, Inner Mongolia were "man-made deserts". He also stressed that water is a weapon to conquer the desert. In other words, we can use water to open up oasis in desert. In view of this, research workers of the Desert Control Team, China Academy of Sciences, conducted studies of aeolian sand movement, water balance, physiological and ecological characters of sand binders, and vegetation sand stabilization measures. In these studies, special attention was given to environmental degradation and desert spread caused by anthropogenic factors. Hou Renzhi et al. studied the environmental variations from analyzing the prosperity and decline of ancient cities in deserts. Zhu Zhenda analyzed the environmental changes and land degradation processes of the reclamation districts of historical periods. The historical vicissitudes of the deserts virtually reflect the historical processes of desertification (Zhu et al., 1981).

Desertification processes and its control, rational exploitation of agricultural resources in desert regions and sand disaster control were the key subjects of desertification research in China at that time. From 1979 onwards, in response to the national agricultural regionalization task, the projects "Aeolian desertification process and control regionalization in northern China", "Agricultural development strategies in mixed farming-grazing regions", and "Rational development and utilization of agricultural natural resources in the Shiyang River Basin" were carried out. All these projects have higher applicability and comprehensiveness. They require a multidisciplinary approach, and the implementation of the plan to combat desertification requires international cooperation.

1.2.1 Initial research into aeolian desertification in China

After the United Nations Conference on Desertification held in 1977, the priority in desert research of China was gradually shifted to the study of desertification processes and its control, and there was a gradual shift from studying regions of arid and hyperarid zones to semiarid and part of semi-humid regions that had relatively better eco-environmental conditions and higher productivity but were also facing desertification problems. In northern China, the main kind of desertification is aeolian desertification, which mainly results from wind erosion.

Aeolian desertification researches mainly include the following aspects: First, the occurrence and development processes of desertification and their types in arid, semiarid and part of semi-humid zones in northern China, especially in the regions with fragile eco-environments and frequent human activities. Second, the studies of desertification status, distribution, causes, damages and indicator system. Third, the establishment of the rehabilitation experiment and demonstration bases of different types of desertified land, for example, Linze at the margin of an oasis, Yanchi in the desert steppe zone, Fengning and Naiman in the semiarid mixed farming-grazing region, as well as Daxin and Yanjin in the semi-humid zone; Fourth, remote sensing monitoring, field investigation and mapping of aeolian desertification in northern China.

Through the systematic research we have achieved the following major results (Wang et al., 1999).

1.2.1.1 Aeolian desertification conception

According to the actual situation in China, aeolian desertification is defined as land degradation, and characterized by wind erosion in arid, semiarid and sub-humid regions mainly resulting from excessive human activities affecting natural resources. Such a conception contains the following implications:

(1) In time, it occurs in the human historical period, especially the most recent one hundred years.

(2) In space, it occurs in locations where the earth's surface is covered by loose sand materials and winds are frequent in arid, semiarid and part of semi-humid zones.

(3) Human irrational economic activities (over-cultivating, overgrazing, over-cutting and overusing water resources) are the main causes of aeolian desertification.

(4) On a landscape, aeolian desertification is a gradual process, and wind is the power that shapes the landscape of desertified land surfaces. Therefore, the blown sand activity and wind-eroded and morphological characteristics of wind-deposited surface can be used as the quantitative indicator of aeolian desertification development degree.

(5) Aeolian desertification intensity and its spatial extent are related to the drought degree, as well as human and animal pressure on land. These factors interact with each other, and under the action of wind force, desertification can spread spontaneously.

(6) Aeolian desertification leads to sand dune encroachment, biological reduction of land productivity and available land resource loss, but it can also be reversed or self-restored depending upon natural conditions (especially water conditions), landscape complexity and human activity intensity.

Here we need to clarify the following conceptions on deserts and aeolian desertification.

(1) Deserts in China mainly formed in different stages during the Quaternary period. They are the outcome of a dry climate and abundant surface sand sources, and they mainly occur in the arid zones, with large areas and complex aeolian shapes. Aeolian desertification has mainly occurred in the human historic period, especially over the past one hundred years. It is mainly distributed in semiarid regions or even parts of semi-humid regions. It has a limited area and mostly occurs in patches on farmlands and grasslands, with simple and small aeolian sand features.

(2) Deserts were formed under the influences of various natural factors, while the occurrence of desertification is mainly due to anthropogenic factors in addition to natural factors. Deserts varied with changes in the Quaternary climate; in the dry-cold stage it expanded and became mobile, but in the warm-wet stage it shrank and became fixed. Aeolian desertification develops or reverses in a short period under the same climatic conditions. In the past several decades, desertification developed rapidly due to the influences of human activities rather than climate changes.

(3) Modern climatic conditions and its variation amplitude are insufficient to cause larger expansion or shrinkage of deserts, and the positive or negative development of aeolian desertification is controlled by human economic activities.

In summary, the researches of desert and aeolian desertification are different in time, space, cause, developmental trend, restoration and utilization, but they are also interrelated.

1.2.1.2　Causes of aeolian desertification

With regard to the research on the causes of aeolian desertification in China, considerable progress has been made. To sum up, there are two types of causes, namely natural causes and human causes.

Aeolian desertification is a common problem in arid and semiarid regions of China. Wind erosion, sand dune encroachment and vegetation destruction are the natural causes of desertification. The mechanism of aeolian desertification in natural causes can be attributed to two points: one is the abnormal global climate changes, and the climate warming in the mid-latitude regions forms ecological conditions especially favourable to the occurrence of aeolian desertification; the other is adverse natural factors, such as dry climate, large precipitation variability, high sand content in soil, and strong and frequent wind. However, natural ecosystems have certain self-regulation abilities. When slightly damaged, they can self-restore to maintain their stability.

Aeolian desertification has mainly occurred in the human historical period, especially in the most recent one hundred years. Generally, the climate fluctuations over a timescale of less than one hundred years cannot cause great environmental changes, and the population pressure and rapidly increasing economic activities are the main causes resulting in eco-environmental deterioration and aeolian desertification development. At present, a widely accepted view is that under adverse environmental conditions, rapid population growth, over-reclamation, overgrazing and uncontrolled removal of vegetation results in rapid development of aeolian desertification.

Aeolian desertification in China mainly appears in three forms: aeolian desertification of grassland, fixed dune mobilization, and dune encroachment. According to field investigations and the analyses of aerial photographs and satellite images, over-reclamation-induced aeolian desertification accounts for 25.4% of China's total aeolian desertified land area, overgrazing-induced aeolian desertification is 28.3%, over-cutting-induced aeolian desertification is 31.8%, misusing water resources and industrial construction-induced aeolian desertification is 9%, and sand dune encroachment-induced aeolian desertification is 5.5%.

At present, scholars still have different views about the causes of aeolian desertification, some stress natural factors and others stress human factors. The former believe that deserts formed before the appearance of man on earth and were caused by the "aeolian desertification processes" of the geologic period; we call it the geologic historical view. The researchers of global changes mostly use the Quaternary methods. Others believe that aeolian desertification was man-made, and once human pressure was eliminated, the environment can be restored, and we call this the historical view. This view is favourable to the rehabilitation of aeolian desertification. These two different views directly affect the statistics of aeolian desertification area. In China, the combined area of desert, gobi and wind-eroded land is 1.283 million km^2, which is 3–4 times larger than the widely accepted aeolian desertified land area. As a result, the aeolian desertification area calculated by different scholars differs by 2–3 times. According to the definition of the United Nations Convention to Combat Desertification, desertification is land degradation in arid, semiarid and dry semi-humid areas resulting from various factors including climatic variation and human activities. It is reasonable to think that aeolian desertified lands are formed under the influences of human activities. The geologic historical view confuses the distinction between deserts and aeolian desertification and overlooks the possibility to reverse aeolian desertification by regulating irrational human activities and restoring ecological balance.

1.2.1.3 Aeolian desertification processes

Aeolian desertification has very complex processes. It occurs once the ecosystem is disturbed, ecological balance is upset, and vegetation and environment are severely degraded. In this respect we have made some progresses.

1) Vegetation degradation

Vegetation degradation is mainly manifested in the reduction of biodiversity, vegetation height, coverage, biomass production and perennial herb species; and increase of unpalatable annual species and shrub species. Communities tend to become simple and sparse, and surface bare spots increase or enlarge to form patches. Vegetation degradation may be gradual, continuous or abrupt. Its degradation rate depends on overgrazing degree and duration, sand damaging intensity and other factors. Vegetation degradation generally lags behind aeolian desertification. Vegetation has a self-restoration ability; once the foreign disturbance is eliminated, they can be gradually restored.

2) Soil degradation

Soil degradation is mainly manifested in wind erosion-induced coarsening, impoverishment and desiccation. Sandy soils have a coarse texture, with particles $\geqslant 0.05$ mm content exceeding 95%, while particle $\leqslant 0.001$ mm content is less than 1%; coupled with less than 1% of organic matter, their cohesiveness and water retention are poor. During the dry season plants can wilt or even die. Especially for the sandy farmlands, water and fertilizer deep seepage is a big problem.

3) Formation processes of aeolian landforms

For this aspect, emphasis was placed on exploring the occurrence and development laws of blown-sand activity on ground surfaces and the following problems were elucidated. (a) The development processes of sand surface features. When wind force acts on bare sand surfaces, particles move in creep, saltation and suspension to form wind-sand stream and further cause wind erosion and wind deposition geomorphological processes. (b) Fixed sand dune mobilization. During the wind erosion processes, as break points occur on the windward slopes of sand dunes, they can gradually form blowouts with the sand being blown downwind. With the windward slopes of blowouts becoming gentle, coppice dunes develop downwind in patches and with further accumulating sand, the surface exhibits a mobile sand dune landscape. (c) Sand dunes advance at the margin of sandy deserts. As winds blow over windward slopes, saturated wind-sand streams form. When it descends over the leeward slope, sand deposition takes place due to wind velocity reduction caused by vortex flow. The accretion of sand on the leeward slope leads to the gradual advance of sand dunes. Sandy desertification processes also include wind erosion, transportation and deposition processes of blown sand after vegetation is destroyed by human activities. Such processes deal with the development processes of sand surface features under the action of wind force, the mobilization processes of fixed sand dunes, and the migration processes of sand dunes at the margin of sandy deserts.

1.2.1.4 Aeolian desertification indicators

Aeolian desertification is a complex land degradation process. It is generally accepted that aeolian desertification indicators should be identified from natural, human and socio-economic conditions. However, owing to lack of consistency in the selection of the indicators, no universal aeolian desertification indicator system has so far been established in the world. According to the situation of aeolian desertification in northern China, namely its status and development trends, we established a classification system of aeolian desertification indicators, in which the changes in surface features are regarded as the main indicators, and the changes in soil, vegetation and ecosystem are also considered. Such indicators have widespread representativeness and are easily identified in the monitoring and evaluation of aeolian desertification in northern China. Vegetation cover, plant community structure, population composition, organic matter, thickness of soil layer and moisture content are directly related to the changes in the surface features and therefore can be used as additional indicators.

1.2.1.5 Monitoring and evaluation of aeolian desertification processes

According to the mapping of aerial photographs taken in the late 1950s and the mid-1970s and calculations, aeolian desertification in northern China, on average, was developing at an annual rate of 1,560 km^2. The main causes for this are attributed to two aspects; one is grassland reclamation as rain-fed farmlands and the other is fixed dune mobilization due to overgrazing and removal of vegetation for fuel. For example, in the Xin Barag Zuoqi in the Hulun Buir Grassland, aeolian desertified land increased from 9.2% in 1950 to 12% of its total area in 1984; in Naiman Qi in the Horqin Sandy Land, aeolian desertified land increased from 39.3% in the late 1950s to 65.6% of it's total area in the mid-1970s.

By the end of the 1980s, aeolian desertified land area in China reached 371,000 km^2, of which 10.2% was very severely aeolian desertified land, 18.3% was severely desertified land, 30.5% was moderately aeolian desertified land and 41% was slightly aeolian desertified land. Of this total area, 29% was in the eastern part of the semiarid zone and parts of the semi-humid zone, and in the mixed farming-grazing and dry-farming region, it mainly appeared as wind erosion and patches of shifting sand; 44% was in the middle-western part of semiarid zone and desert steppe zone, which was characterized by fixed dune mobilization and shifting sand encroachment; 27% occurred at the margin of oases in the arid zone and in the lower reaches of inland rivers, which was characterized by fixed dune mobilization.

The general development trend of aeolian desertification is that of local reversal due to rehabilitation but overall deterioration. From the mid-1970s to the late 1980s, desertified land area increased by 24,800 km^2, with an annual increase of 2,100 km^2. Aeolian desertification expansion mainly occurred in three regions. The first was the Bashang Region in Hebei, the Ulanqab Grassland and the Qahar Grassland in Inner Mongolia due to overgrazing and land reclamation. The second was the Horqin Sandy Land in Inner Mongolia, where over-cultivation, overgrazing and fuel gathering caused fixed dune mobilization. The third was energy source bases (e.g. Shenfu coal field etc) in the sandy grassland region.

At the beginning of the 1990s, aeolian desertification in northern China tended to accelerate and spread at an annual rate of 2,460 km^2 (CCICCD, 1996).

Continuous change is one of the most striking features of aeolian desertification processes. Therefore, it should be monitored continuously. In 2000 we monitored and calculated aeolian desertification in northern China by using American TM satellite data in combination with field investigations. The monitored region included 177 counties (Qis) and cities in 10 provinces (regions) in northern China, stretching from the Heilongjiang Provincial border in the northeast to the Bayan Har Mountains, Qinghai in the southwest, and including the Yellow River source area, with a total monitored area of 2.564 million km^2. The monitored results showed that by 2000 there were 385,700 km^2 of aeolian desertified land in northern China, accounting for 15% of the total monitored area. Of the total number, slightly aeolian desertified land was 139,300 km^2, consisting of 36.1%; moderately aeolian desertified land was 99,800 km^2, consisting of 25.9%; severely aeolian desertified land was 79,100 km^2, consisting of 20.5%; and very severely aeolian desertified land was 67,500 km^2, consisting of 17.5%. Compared with the monitored results of the late 1980s, slightly aeolian desertified land decreased, moderately aeolian desertified land kept constant, but severely aeolian desertified land increased. This is because the conditions of some slightly aeolian desertified lands have been improved.

1.2.1.6 Rehabilitation of aeolian desertified land

In China, the research and monitoring of aeolian desertification processes and the rehabilitation of aeolian desertified lands are conducted simultaneously. The former Lanzhou Institute of Desert Research established nine experiment stations in different types of aeolian desertification regions to explore their rehabilitation ways and also set up some demonstration plots to promote the regional rehabilitation of desertified lands. In addition, Xinjiang Institute of Ecology and Geography, Shenyang Institute of Applied Ecology, Changchun Institute of Geography, State Forestry Bureau and other forestry departments in northern China also set up experiment stations and sand control forest farms to combat desertification. As a result, about of 10% aeolian desertified land in northern China has been preliminarily improved.

According to natural and economic characteristics in the desertified regions of northern China and the problems relating to land use, we followed the ecological principles of proper development and polycyclic intercompensation to achieve ecological, social and economic benefits simultaneously. In the rehabilitation strategy, an overall plan was made to improve the ecosystem in the whole arid and semiarid zones, and we adhered to the policy of diversiform economy dominated by forestry, grass planting and a controlled population growth. Scientific research institutions, together with the production departments, conducted rehabilitation experiments and established demonstration plots to popularize successful rehabilitation measures. In the mixed farming-grazing regions where dwelling sites, farmland and grassland are scatteredly distributed, using the ecological household as a unit, measures were adopted to readjust land use structure, including fencing grassland, returning farmland to forest and grass, establishing forest networks and intensively managing lands with better conditions to combat aeolian desertification. In the grassland grazing region the number of grazing animal was determined according to the size of pasture; furthermore, efforts were made to establish artificial grassland, watering points and roads. In the arid zone, with the river basin as an ecological unit, an overall plan was made to rationally allocate water, establish a farmland protective forest network inside the oasis and tree-shrub sandbreak forest around the oasis, and erect mechanical sand fences to form an overall protective system.

Below are several successful examples in aeolian desertification control in experiment plots of the former Lanzhou Institute of Desert Research, Chinese Academy of Sciences.

Example 1　Naiman Qi (Yaoledianzi Village) Experiment Plot in Inner Mongolia.

The village's shifting sand area has decreased from 1,000 hm^2 to 330 hm^2, vegetation cover rate increased from 10% to 70%, grain output increased from 150,000 kg to 450,000 kg, and average income increased from 174 *yuan* to 1,290 *yuan*. The successful techniques have been adopted in other regions.

Example 2　Yanchi (Shabianzi Village) Experiment Plot in Ningxia

The village's 4,822 hm^2 of aeolian desertified land have been brought under control, 667 hm^2 of which has been transformed into forest land; vegetation cover increased from 30% to 50%, grain output increased from 139,000 kg to 219,000 kg, and average income increased from less than 500 *yuan* to 1,175 *yuan*. The successful techniques have been popularized in six villages of the county.

Example 3　Linze Experiment Plot in Gansu Province

Before adopting rehabilitation measures, shifting sand was encroaching on the oasis. In 1975, a protective forest belt was established on the surrounding aeolian desertified land to protect the 3,300 hm^2 of new oasis. As a result, the old and new oasis were protected, two new villages were established in the new oasis, and 125 households moved into the villages and per capita income reached 2,000 *yuan*. The successful techniques have been popularized on 27,000 hm^2 of land in the Hexi region.

Example 4　Yucheng Experiment Plot in Shandong Province.

After four years of rehabilitation, 80% of the 1,100 hm^2 aeolian desertified land have escaped damages from blown sand due to the construction of forest net and canal system, and the output was four times higher than the input. These successful techniques have been popularized in the Dezhou and Liaocheng regions.

As described above, scientists in China have made great progress in aeolian desertification control and also have provided a scientific basis for formulating the national plan of action to combat aeolian desertification. In view of the country's outstanding achievement in aeolian desertification control, UNEP and ESCAP entrusted the Lanzhou Institute of Desert Research, Chinese Academy of Sciences, to hold a number of training seminars and symposiums, and more than 300 persons from 46 countries participated in these events. In addition, the Institute was also entrusted by UNEP to jointly work out the local desertification control plan with Mali scientists.

1.2.2 Progress in aeolian desertification research over the past ten years

At the beginning of the 1990s, priority was given to basic research and applied research so as to enhance the overall research level of desert science. In the meantime, great efforts were made to promote the multidisciplinary researches and the application of research achievements in economic construction, environmental protection and aeolian desertification control.

1.2.2.1 Basic research

1) Blown sand physics and control engineering

Considerable progress has been made in the physical principles of aeolian desertification, including the dynamics of the two–phase flow of solid and gas, the bedform changes of aeolian sandbed, soil wind erosion, the theory of blown sand experimental similarity and sand control engineering (Liu, 1999; Han et al., 1999). Through the study of the movement trajectory of a single grain, a related mathematic model was established, and through a series of experiments, the physical model of the movement of two–phase flow and the theoretical parameters of blown sand experimental similarity were proposed. All these lay a theoretical basis for the design of blown sand control engineering. The research achievements described above were used to select the route and the design of the Tarim desert highway. In the study of the prevention of sand damage to the desert highway, a theory of transient behavior of sand flow was put forward. Furthermore, the sand control measures "fixation, blockage, transport and diversion" were successfully used in the sand control system of the 248 km long desert highway and yielded great profit. This achievement won the 1995 Prize of Ten Major Scientific Achievements of China and 1996 First-Class Prize of National Scientific and Technological Progress.

2) Desert evolution and climate change

In this respect systematic research has been made on the depositional types of deserts in China, including, researches on their climatic and environmental changes, their spatial distribution patterns and regional differentiation in different periods, especially the difference in climate, environment and composition of the quaternary red desert and yellow desert. In addition, the development processes, status and future trend of modern aeolian desertification and the control measures were also studied (Zhang et al., 1999). The study on desert evolution and climate change won the First-Class Prize of Natural Science from Chinese Academy of Sciences.

3) Study of micrometeorology concerning aeolian desertification

Over the past 10 years some advanced instruments have been used in the study of micrometeorological changes concerning aeolian desertification (Fig.1-4). Comparative studies at selected sites on farmland, grassland and sandy land showed that aeolian desertification had significant influences on micrometeorological conditions. Aeolian desertification alters the underlying surface, upsets the surface radiation balance, heat balance and water balance, and changes the near-surface turbulent flow and energy distribution. The wind profile over vegetated surfaces exhibits a logarithmic distribution in the day. In the daytime, the surface boundary layer is 2.7 m thick, while at night it is 5 m or more in thickness, with a drag coefficient of 3,200. The wind profile over mobile dunes exhibits a logarithmic distribution at night and bends to the Ln axis in the daytime. The thickness of the surface boundary layer is less than 0.7 m, with a drag coefficient of 1,900. Wind over mobile dunes has strong shear stress and therefore sand grains can be easily picked up. In the shifting aeolian desertification processes, vegetation destruction causes the surface albedo to increase sharply, while net radiation and latent heat exchange decreases. The albedo of non-desertified ground surface varies between 0.15–0.20, degraded land surface 0.25–0.30, and shifting sand surface 0.35–0.40. The transmission of heat flux of severely desertified land is greatly altered, the heat flux percentage in the stratum increases significantly but latent heat flux decreases. The phase lag time of dune surface temperature shortens, the daily range is large and absolute air humidity is low. The establishment of artificial vegetation reduces the surface albedo and vertical shear stress of wind velocity. Vegetation protects the ground surface and absorbs much of the airflow momentum; hence sand particle activity is reduced. This is not only favourable for surface

Fig. 1-4　Meteorological observations at fixed sites

stabilization but also can increase surface temperature. The micrometeorological indexes such as surface albedo, wind profile and latent heat exchange can also be used in the evaluation of aeolian desertification development degree.

1.2.2.2 Dynamical monitoring and evaluation of aeolian desertification in northern China

The remote sensing and GIS techniques have been widely used in the dynamical monitoring of aeolian desertification in northern China, including its distribution, damages and developmental trend, and this has also made it possible to give a quantitative and economic evaluation of aeolian desertification. For example, in the study of the "Remote sensing monitoring and evaluation of aeolian desertification in mixed farming-grazing regions in northern China", the $1 : 4,000,000$ evaluation map of aeolian desertification damage risk in China was compiled using TM data; the background database of aeolian desertification disasters in the Mu Us and the Horqin sandy lands was established; and the remote sensing monitoring evaluation, damage classification and indicator system of aeolian desertification were established. Researches showed that the identifiable aeolian desertification indicators include: ① Natural indicators—increased area of wind-eroded land, sandy land and dune; seasonal and annual variations of dust storm and precipitation; wind velocity and direction changes; soil layer thickness and organic matter content; groundwater table and quality; and surface albedo. ② Biological and agricultural indicators: vegetation cover, biomass, dominant plant species distribution and richness, land-use regime (farming, grazing, industry and mining, etc.), crop yield, livestock number, etc. ③ Social indicators: population change, public health index and mandatory or special policy, etc.

According to the characteristics of aeolian desertification and human activities as well as the monitored results in northern China, the following indicators can be acquired by remote sensing and computer methods can be directly used: ① Percent of area wind-eroded land or shifting sand land area; ② percent of mean annual expansion area of wind-eroded land or shifting sand land; ③ Vegetation cover (dominated by forest land and grassland); ④ Biological production.

From the comparison and analysis of the continuously monitored results in the Mu Us Sandy Land it has been found that during the 7-year period from 1987 to 1993 the area of aeolian desertified land decreased from 32,586 km^2 (67.5% of total area of the monitoring region) to 30,649 km^2 (63.5%), a decrease of 1,937 km^2, on an average, about 276.6 km^2 of aeolian desertified land were improved per year (Wang, 1998).

1.2.2.3 Aeolian desertification, vegetation succession and landscape ecological research

1) Aeolian desertification and vegetation succession

The succession of vegetation in sandy grassland is mostly related to the aeolian desertification degree. The vegetation succession stages and aeolian desertification degrees often mutually serve as the precondition. Vegetation succession in the aeolian desertified region may be gradual or sudden depending on the aeolian desertification degree and its own structural function. On different types of aeolian desertified land vegetation may experience sudden succession; while for the same type of aeolian desertified land the vegetation on the slightly aeolian desertified land exhibits a gradual succession and the vegetation on the severely aeolian desertified land exhibits a sudden succession (Wang, 1988). There is also large difference in the method and rate of vegetation degradation. On degraded grassland caused by overgrazing, the biodiversity, vegetation cover, grass height and yield significantly decreased; some perennial grass species first disappeared from the grassland, followed by palatable annual species and finally only non-palatable grass species remain. When the vegetation cover is reduced to a certain degree, small bare spots occur on the grassland, these small bare spots gradually enlarge to form patches, and this finally leads to aeolian desertification. On degraded grassland caused by sand encroachment and water changes, the degradation rate of vegetation was much higher than that of grazing-induced degraded grassland. The vegetation cover and species composition also decreased rapidly, but the vegetation height and yield did not necessarily decrease (Zhao et al., 1999). Under favourable environmental conditions, vegetation on degraded land may exhibit a positive succession, and species composition, vegetation height and herb percentage may increase largely.

2) Aeolian desertification and landscape ecological characteristics

Researches show that the aeolian desertification processes are closely associated with the landscape structural characteristics (Chang et al., 1999). Viewed from a landscape perspective, the initial small-scale aeolian desertification is related to erosion and deposition processes but does not affect the landscape characteristics. When aeolian desertification develops or a moderate scale, the stability of sand dunes change, which may alter the landscape characteristics but it does not affect the landscape properties. When the aeolian desertification develops on a large scale, the landscape properties will change. Among various landscape types, including the artificially fixed sandy land, fenced area and shifting dunes, the artificially fixed sandy land has the most complex landscape spatial pattern and high heterogeneity, followed by the fenced area, and the shifting dune has the simplest landscape pattern. Under the effects of aeolian desertification processes (overgrazing, overcutting and overcultivation) the landscape pattern of the sandy land tends to become simple and the heterogeneity decreases. In the reversal processes of aeolian desertification, the landscape pattern tends to become complex and the heterogeneity increases. In the artificially fixed sand plots, the patch types include fixed dune, semi-fixed dune, semi-shifting dune and shifting dune; and the patch pattern tends to become complex due to the influence of sand control measures. In the fenced area, the spatial structure of fixed dune patches and shifting dune patches is most complex due to seasonal grazing and fuel gathering. Semi-fixed dunes and semi-shifting dunes have a simple spatial structure and low patch diversity. Therefore, the landscape characteristic indexes can also be used to evaluate the degree of aeolian desertification development.

1.2.2.4 Aeolian desertification and plant stress physiology

In the past, the physiological research of desert plants mainly focused on the physiological characteristics of desert plants, such as plant bound water, free water, transpiration rate and coefficient, and water deficit. In recent years, the attention has been given to studying the relation between aeolian desertification processes and plant physiological changes, the adaptative mechanism of plants to aeolian desertification, and the research contents including plant morphological anatomy, photosynthetic rate, protective enzyme systems; osmotic regulators (Zhou et al., 1999a), plasma membrane permeability, membrane lipid peroxidation and plant stress-resistant succession etc. (Zhou et al., 1999b). Researches shows that under the conditions of drought and high temperature, the desert plants yield a bimodal photosynthetic rate and high transpiration rate, and under the conditions of environmental stress they have a low stomatal regulation and low water use efficiency. For plants with high moisture content, the situation is just the contrary. Under the conditions of drought and high temperature, cells of the stress-resistant plant species lose moisture slowly. Once their cells regain water, soluble sugar and proline accumulate rapidly; the activity of protective enzymes rapidly strengthens; and cells exhibit a good elasticity. However, the plants with low stress resistance are just the contrary. During the transformation processes from the shifting sand land to fixed sand land, the drought-escaping plant species are gradually replaced by physiologically drought-resistant species; blown sand-resistant species are gradually replaced by drought-resistant species, and their reproduction changes from single to multiple ways (Zhou et al., 1999c).

1.2.2.5 Effect of aeolian desertification on ecosystems

In recent years the material transformation and energy flow of the degraded ecosystem and the effect of aeolian desertification on ecosystems has become a subject of aeolian desertification research. Researches shows that the aeolian desertification of farmland is accompanied by a coarsening of surface, reduction in soil fertility and water-holding capacity, dramatic soil temperature change and low plant photosynthetic capacity, or even no harvest. For the grassland ecosystem, aeolian desertification leads to the strengthening of blown sand activity, microenvironmental deterioration, disappearance of wind-resistant plants and the reduction of species diversity. Due to the reduction of vegetation cover, both leaf area index and energy entering the grassland ecosystem also decrease; therefore the material transformation is hindered and productivity is reduced (Zhang et al., 1999). Furthermore, plant litter, soil microbes and organic matter also decrease. For artificial ecosystems established on shifting sand land, with increases in vegetation cover, the soil and water conditions deteriorate, which is unfavourable for the growth of pioneer plant species and the establishment of psammophytes (Lu, 1999).

1.2.2.6 High-efficiency use of water and soil resources and sustainable development in aeolian desertified regions

Over the past 10 years, in response to the development and environmental rehabilitation problems in aeolian desertified regions, a series of case studies were conducted regarding the available water resources and forestry construction in northwestern China, the carrying capacity of water resources in the Hexi region, the classification of blown sand soils and oasis warping soils, the resource system of water, soil, climate and grassland in some representative basins, the relations between resource use, human activity, economic growth and environmental problems, the effects of climate change on dryland agricultural ecosystems, oasis water balance and sustainable development, economic development and oasis eco-environment construction in the Hexi region. In the meantime, the plan for rational utilization of water and soil resources in several river basins was worked out; some demonstration bases were set up, including agricultural integrated development at marginal zone of oases, rain-harvesting farming and ecological agriculture in the Huang-Huai-Hai Plain region up (Xiao et al., 1999; He, 1999).

1.2.2.7 Aeolian desertification rehabilitation patterns and techniques

Aeolian desertification rehabilitation patterns and techniques are important parts of aeolian desertification research. In this respect considerable progress has been made. For example, the comprehensive rehabilitation model consists of "ecological nets", "polynary systems" and "small biospheres," and these have been widely used at the township, village and household levels in the mixed farming-grazing region of Naiman Qi. Such rehabilitation models require planning and establishing a large sandbreak forest net at the township level; readjusting planting structures, fencing grasslands, constructing basic farmland and developing agricultural, forestry and livestock production at the village level; engaging in agricultural production in interdune meadow zones that have better water conditions by establishing forest belts and grassland buffer zones, and to arrange grazing and control aeolian desertification at the household level. Practice has demonstrated that this three-level pattern is an effective aeolian desertification control system. The semi-humid blown sand region has better water and heat conditions, and in Yanjing and Yucheng, an aeolian desertification control and high-efficiency agricultural development model, including planting fruit trees, flowers, and commercial crops has been adopted and has yielded significant economic and ecological benefits. In the Bashang Region and the Yarlung Zangbo River and Its Two Tributaries region in Tibet, the biological sand stabilization and ecological agricultural pattern have been adopted. Other aeolian desertification control and farming techniques on sandy lands. include bottom-filmed rice cultivation technique; wheat, *Glycyrrhiza uralensis* and *Ephedra minuta* cultivation techniques on sandy land; water melon, corn and wheat cultivation techniques in high-cold regions; and water-saving farming and brackish water irrigation techniques in arid oases. All these techniques play a great role in aeolian desertification control of China.

1.3 Development trend in the researches of deserts and aeolian desertification in China

Over the past 50 years, in response to the requirements of the national economic construction and eco-environmental protection, scientists in China conducted a series of basic and applied researches dealing with desert formation, evolution and environmental changes; aeolian desertification processes and its control; shifting sand stabilization; ecological construction in arid zones; and resources, environment and sustainable development in desert regions. This not only filled in the gaps in desert science research but also formed an overall scientific system. For example, Lanzhou Institute of Desert Research, Chinese Academy of Sciences, completed about 200 research projects in the past 20 years, had 154 research achievements and won more than 50 prizes from the nation, ministries and provinces, of which one is the special prize of national scientific and technological progress; one is the first-class prize of national scientific and technological progress; 3 are second-class prizes of the country; 2 are special prizes, 14 are first-class prizes and 14 are second-class prizes from related provinces. In the past 20 years the institute published over 40 monographs including Introduction to Deserts of China, Aeolian Desertification Control in China, Aeolian Desertification and Its Control, Aeolian Sand Geomorphology, Aeolian Desertification in China, Sand Control Engineering, Experimental Blown Sand Physics and Sand Control Engineering, Desert Plant Flora, Shifting Sand Stabilization Principle and Techniques, Sand Damage Control on Farmland, Desert Ecosystems, Blown Sand Soils in China, Grasslands in Desert Regions of China, Climate in Deserts of China, Brackish Water Resources in Arid Zones and Its Use, Rational Development and Utilization of Water and Soil Resources in the Hexi Region and Study of the Application of Remote Sensing Techniques, etc. In addition, the institute published more than 70 kinds of desert and aeolian desertification thematic maps and over 2,200 research papers in domestic and foreign core periodicals as well as about 380 research papers that were presented at international symposiums.

Over the past 50 years much work has been done in the basic research fields of blown sand physics and desert environments. With an indoor wind tunnel, field wind tunnel and other related instruments and installations as tools, considerable progresses have been made in the quantitative researches of aeolian sand landform formation, sand movement, fluid mechanics of the two phase flow of solid and gas, soil wind erosion processes and sand control engineering design. In the aeolian desertification researches a new theoretical system and aeolian desertification control pattern have been put forward. It not only widens the research field of desert science but also provides a scientific basis for the country to work out strategies to combat aeolian desertification.

The research of dune fixation, afforestation and shifting sand control techniques is an important part of the basic and applied study of desert science. It deals with biological and mechanical dune fixation techniques, the construction techniques of the "the Three-North Shelter Forest Programme and shelterbelts inside oases, sand-binding species selection, sand land water balance, plant ecophysiology and succession. The establishment of the sand control system and artificial ecosystem "laying emphasis on fixation in combination with blockage and attaching equal importance to the fixation and blockage" along the Baotou-Lanzhou Railway is a creative achievement. Such sand control models have been adopted in other desert regions of China, such as the sand control system along the Lanzhou-Xinjiang Railway in Yumen and the sand control system along the oil-transporting highway in the Taklimakan Desert; until now it has created a direct economic benefit of several million *yuan*.

An enormous amount of work has also been done in the multidisciplinary researches such as hydrology and geology in arid zones, soils, climate, grassland, vegetation, farmland water conservation project, agriculture, forestry and horticulture. Furthermore, several experiment stations such as Shapotou Station, Naiman Station, Linze Station, and Yanjin Station were established in different representative regions. These field stations play a great role in transforming research results into practice, demonstrating and popularizing successful aeolian desertification control techniques, and have also made great contributions to local economic development and environmental protection.

The outstanding achievements of shifting sand stabilization techniques and aeolian desertification control patterns in China have attracted the attention of international communities. In 1987 the UNEP, Chinese Academy of Sciences and National Environment Protection Agency of China jointly established the International Center for Research and Training on Aeolian Desertification Control in the Lanzhou Institute of Desert Research. Entrusted by UNEP, ESCAP, UNESCO and MAB, the Center has organized 12 training seminars for combating aeolian desertification, and more than 300 persons from over 40 countries participated in these training seminars. The institute also sent experts several times to participate in the meeting of technical advisory groups on aeolian desertification assessment held by UNEP. The Center has also established relation ships with many international organizations such as UNEP, UNDP, FAO, ESCAP, WMO, Third World Academy of Sciences, and World Laboratory. In 1998, it was selected to be one of the "Global 500 Honour Roll" by UNEP for its outstanding achievements in the protection of the environment. In 1998, the institute was rewarded the Best Practice Award on Indigenous Technology for Combating Desertification and Mitigating the Effect of Drought by UNDP. In the past 20 years, the institute established relationships with more than 50 countries in cooperative research and academic exchange of desert and aeolian desertification sciences. Many experts, government heads and ambassadors of foreign countries, especially Third World countries, visit the institute and hope to study successful experiences of aeolian desertification control in China.

1.3.1 Development trend of desert research

Desert research as an independent research field is currently being established and is at the initial development stage. Its scientific system, rationale and research method need to be improved in future researches.

1.3.1.1 Research direction

With natural and anthropogenic factors, their interaction as variables, the earth system science as the frame, and sustainable development as the objective, future research will focus on the occurrence and development of blown sand activity, aeolian desertification processes, desert formation and evolution and its response and feedback to global changes. In the meantime, in response to national demands, the priority will be given to the study of the control principles of blown sand activity and the techniques to combat aeolian desertification. Efforts will be made to solve the scientific problems dealing with the desert and aeolian desertification researches and their rehabilitation so as to promote the development of the theory of desert science and related sciences.

1.3.1.2 Research content

1) Blown sand movement mechanism

Priority will be given to the researches of single grain movement, including the initiation of particle movement by wind, creep, reptation, saltation and suspension, their tracing (photographic) study, particle movement velocity and acceleration, lift-off angle, particle movement length and height and trajectory, energy transmission and transformation in the particle collision process, and the mathematic expression of sand particle movement (Fig. 1-5, 1-6).

2) Dynamics of blown sand boundary layer

Future research will focus on the characteristics of the wind velocity profile over a fixed sand bed, and its aerodynamic parameters and variation laws; wind-sand stream structure under different wind forces, its velocity field, velocity distribution, energy structure, aerodynamic parameters, and mathematic model; the coupling relation between wind velocity profile and sand stream structure, and the dynamic equation of two–phase flow of sand and gas.

3) Aeolian landforms

This research will focus on the exploration of the formation and evolution laws of different types of sand dunes through the studies of the characteristics of airflow field over sand dunes, sand movement characteristics, erosion and deposition balance, feedback effects of near-surface airflow fields, the formation of secondary airflow and its effect on the formation of aeolian landforms; the spatial assembly of aeolian landforms in relation to the airflow field; and sand dune movement in relation to their shapes and wind regimes.

Fig. 1-5　Wind tunnel simulating a blown sand environment

Fig.1-6　Field wind tunnel to observe wind erosion

4) Sand and dust entrainment and transport

The simulation experiments on the pneumatic activation processes over a static bed surface and the pneumatic creep processes over an activated bed surface will be conducted to study the sand and dust entrainment processes, to determine the transitional relation between the saltation layer and the suspension layer and to understand the aerodynamic characteristics of suspension movement; this will be done in combination with field observations to study the dust flow structure and aerodynamic distribution, and establish a dust transport model.

5) Blown sand control engineering

The researches in this aspect include studying the airflow field characteristics of different sand-blocking and sand-fixing engineering measures, wind-sand stream structure, erosion and deposition laws, and discovering the optimal sand control engineering system through simulation experiments and field observations.

6) Soil wind erosion

To build a bridge between wind erosion, blown sand physics and aeolian desertification, a quantitative study on soil erosion will be conducted to establish evaluation indexes of soil erodibility and erosivity, develop a physical evaluation model of soil wind erosion, reveal the changes in wind erosion intensity under the influences of natural and human factors, and predict the development trend of wind erosion and aeolian desertification under the influences of global changes.

7) Desert formation and evolution and global changes

The researches will concentrate on the formation and evolution processes of deserts at different temporal and spatial scales and their causes, and emphasis will be placed on the following: the late Tertiary to the early Quaternary as well as the last glacial maximum intervals; the relation between desert evolution in China and global changes; the temporal and spatial evolutional sequences of deserts in China over the past 5,000 years and the contribution percentages of natural and human factors; and the development trend of deserts in China in the future 30–50 years and the corresponding countermeasures.

1.3.2　Development trend of aeolian desertification research

Aeolian desertification is one of the main kinds of desertification. As an important global environmental and socio-economic issue, it is now threatening mankind's survival and development. China is one of the countries suffering from the most serious desertification in the entire world. Desert, gobi, wind-eroded land and aeolian desertified land in China cover an area of about 1.67 million km^2, 385,700 km^2 of which are modern aeolian desertified land caused by human activities. Aeolian desertified lands mainly appear in arid, semiarid and parts of semi-humid zones of northern China and roughly form a discontinuous curved belt extending from northeast China to northwest China via northern China, especially in the semiarid region to the east of the Helan Mountains where the distribution is concentrated. Aeolian desertification results from the interaction of irrational human activities with the fragile eco-environment and mainly appears as the reduction of land productivity and the occurrence of desert-like landscape. The development rate of aeolian desertification in China is continuously increasing. During the 1960s–1970s it developed at a rate of 1,560 km^2/a, in the 1980s at 2,100 km^2/a, and in the 1990s at 2,460 km^2/a. Along with the further development of aeolian desertification, the frequency of dust storm increases. According to statistical data, 5 strong dust storms occurred in northern China in the 1950s. Dust storms not only occur directly in northwestern and northern China but also affect southern China or even other areas in East Asia, and they have become a serious environment issue in the northeastern hemisphere.

Aeolian desertification destruction in China is mainly manifested in three aspects. First, it upsets ecological balance, worsens the environment, reduces land productivity, aggravates poverty or even creates ecological refugees. Second, large areas of productive land are lost and the land area lost to aeolian desertification each year is estimated to equal the area of a medium-size county of China. Third, it poses a serious threat to traffic, water conservancy, industrial installations, and agricultural production, and the direct economic loss caused by aeolian desertification is 54 billion *yuan* each year. China is now implementing a large development strategy for the western region, and it is essential to have systematic and in-depth research concerning the occurrence and development laws of aeolian desertification and its control.

1.3.2.1 Research direction

The research direction will closely combine with the scientific forefront and the national requirement and focus on the interaction processes of the soil-plant-atmosphere, the straying degree of these processes from natural conditions due to intensifying human disturbances and the application of different aeolian desertification control measures and patterns in different types of aeolian desertified regions.

With the man-land relation ship as the main focus, efforts will be made to systematize the researches of the background of aeolian desertification; its process as well as development trends under the influences of global changes and reveal the time line of its evolution; view eco-environment degradation processes in aeolian desertification processes beyond the region as a system to reveal the spatial differentiation of aeolian desertification and its influences on the environment and social economy; and quantitatively assess the influences of human activities on the evolution of aeolian desertification and its method, of control to provide a scientific basis for aeolian desertification control.

1.3.2.2 Research content

(1) Blown sand physics and desert environments. This is one of the basic research contents of aeolian desertification. With field stations, an indoor wind tunnel to simulate a blown sand environment and a field wind tunnel to observe wind erosion as supporting installations, in-depth

researches will be conducted on the natural and human factors of aeolian desertification, their feedback mechanism and contribution percentage, identification methods, material and energy flow between the interface of the adjacent ecosystems, coupling relation of various factors, dynamical model of aeolian desertification and future development trends.

(2) Restoration ecology of aeolian desertified land. The research will focus on the following points: (a) The ecological processes of the formation and evolution of the fragile arid eco-environments and the biological mechanism of aeolian desertification; (b) The structural function, energy flow, material flow and information flow of the ecosystem in arid zones at different levels and scales; (c) The temporal and spatial changes of landscape patterns and biodiversity in aeolian desertification processes and its reversal processes, as well as its stability and maintaining mechanisms; (d) The adaptative mechanism of desert plants to the harsh environment.

(3) Utilization of water and soil resources and their sustainable development in aeolian desertified regions. The research will focus on the following aspects. (a) Water balance in representative regions at different space-time scales, the ecological risk for the development of water and soil resources, the quantitative prediction of the changes in resources and environments under the background of global change. (b) In response to the major resource and environmental issues in the economic development processes in northwest ern China, emphasis will be placed on the study of the optimization arrangement of water and soil resources and the transformation model of resource advantages into economic advantages. (c) The application of advanced agricultural engineering techniques, especially the stereo high-efficiency and high-yield techniques and the regional sustainable development.

(4) Rehabilitation patterns of aeolian desertification. With field experiment stations in different zones as a base, the researches will focus on the reversal strategies and rehabilitation patterns or technical system of aeolian desertification to promote the regional rehabilitation of aeolian desertification through establishing demonstration and model plots.

(5) Establishment of aeolian desertification monitoring, evaluation, policy-making and management systems. In view of the increasing concern of the effects of aeolian desertification on human's living environment, economy and society, the "3S" techniques will be used to establish an information system of resources and the environment to achieve rapid information analysis and serve the regional sustainable development.

(6) Key scientific problems awaiting solution and research in the next five years. Many problems dealing with aeolian desertification and its control need to be solved through multidisciplinary crossovers and integration. In the next five years, enormous amount of work will be done, using the "National Key Basic Research Development Plan" (973 Program) and "Research of Aeolian Desertification Processes and Its Control in Northern China" (CT200048700) as the top priority, to solve some key scientific problems dealing with the aeolian desertification development processes and its control principles and techniques.

1.3.2.3　Key scientific problems awaiting solution

(1) Establishment and quantification of natural and human influence indicators affecting aeolian desertification. The occurrence of aeolian desertification is mainly attributable to climate change and human activity; however the relative contribution of these two factors, both separately and combined, on aeolian desertification are still an unsolved problem. How to reconstruct the spatial patterns of desert and aeolian desertification in certain periods, clarify the responses of aeolian desertification to natural and human factors, and establish the quantitative diagnostic indicators through example analysis are crucial problems that need to be solved.

(2) Mechanical model of multifield coupling near-surface blown sand flow. Under given surface and meteorological conditions, establishing the mechanical model of sand grain movement under the actions of the wind field and the electric field is a key subject in the research of blown sand physics. Through the researches of various mechanical mechanisms of sand grain movement (impacting saltation, turbulent motivation, material and energy exchange at gas-solid interface etc.) and the use of probability and mathematic statistical methods to establish near-surface sand flow model that can be simulated is also a problem awaiting solution.

(3) Establishment of the parameters of soil wind erosion factors and the wind erosion tolerance. The quantitative evaluation of soil wind erosion is achieved through the wind erosion model. The establishment of the parameters of wind erosion factors and the quantitative relation among various factors is a basis for the development of the multi-factored soil wind erosion model. The quantitative evaluation indicators must be determined in accordance with soil wind erosion degree, while the wind erosion degree is determined by the comparison of wind erosion intensity and soil-farming rates.

(4) Determination and numerical simulation of the emission rate of dust from source areas and the cause of dust storms. The simulation of dust emission rate, field observations and satellite remote sensing monitoring are the key ways to define the dust source area, understand the soil characteristics in the source area, the dust transport path, spatial distribution, and climatic effects. Dust storms are sudden and low-frequency events, and revealing their structural characteristics and formation mechanism is crucial for the early warning and forecast.

(5) Vegetation destruction and restoration mechanisms in the positive and negative aeolian desertification process. Understanding the external factors disturbing the vegetation, disturbing intensity, and adaptational countermeasures of vegetation in the positive and negative processes, defining the factors causing vegetation to deviate from a balanced state and begin destructive or restorative processes, and revealing the mechanism to maintain stability by the vegetation itself are the key to elucidate the biological processes of aeolian desertification and the vegetation restoration mechanism.

1.3.2.4　Priority in recent research

(1) Natural and human factors of aeolian desertification. The research will focus on the development processes and the mechanism of aeolian desertification in China in the historical period (over the past 2,000 years) and in the recent 50 years so as to determine the relative contribution of natural and human factors to aeolian desertification.

(2) Dynamical processes of dust storms and their control. The researches will concentrate on blown sand movement at different scales, electrification mechanism of sand, their environmental effects, soil wind erosion processes and physical mechanism of initiating dust storms so as to determine soil wind erosion tolerance and establish the dynamical model and quantitative evaluation indicator system of soil wind erosion; reveal the synoptic characteristics and formation mechanism of dust storms and further work out the monitoring, early warning and forecast methods.

(3) Biological processes of aeolian desertification and the mechanism of vegetation restoration. Researches will be conducted to understand the decreasing levels of C and N in the aeolian desertification processes and the ecological effects; reveal the stress-tolerant mechanism and adaptational countermeasures of psammophytes; understand the responses of individuals and the populations to environmental changes; elucidate their destruction and restoration processes; understand their succession and self-regulation mechanism; and understand water consumption of main species on sandy land in relation to their stability.

(4) Comprehensive control strategies and patterns of aeolian desertification. According to the status and the damages of aeolian desertification in northern China, there is a need to analyze the coordination degree of man-land relationships and predict the developmental trend of aeolian desertification, study the carrying capacity of water and land resources and rational landuse ways in desertified regions, select key rehabilitation regions and work out comprehensive control plans, evaluate existing rehabilitation patterns and technical measures, and sum up experiences, put forward suitable rehabilitation patterns and techniques for different regions, make some suggestions for the harmonious development of the society, economy and environment in several model regions to develop a policy-making basis for the country.

References

Aubreville A. 1949. Climate, forests et desertification de l'Afrique tropicale. Soc d'editions. Paris: geographiques et colonials, 352

CCICCD. 1996. China Country Paper to Combat Desertification. Beijing: China Forestry Publishing House, 18–31

Chang Xueli, Zhao Aifen. 1999. Application of landscape patterns in the study of desertification. Journal of Desert Research, 18(3): 210–214

Han Zhiwen, Liu Xianwan, Yao Zhengyi et al. 1999. Wind tunnel experiment and study of the sand control mechanisms of composite film sand bags and upright reed fences. Journal of Desert Research, 20(1): 40–44

He Xingdong. 1999. Comparative Study of Irrigation Ways of Sandy Land, Beijing: China Environment Science Press

Hou Renzhi. 1973. Approach to the evolution of Mu Us Desert from the ancient town ruins in Hongliu He, Cultural Relics, (1)

Hou Renzhi. 1981. Approach to the desertification in the Nanhu Oasis, Dunhuang. Journal of Desert Research, 1(1)

Liu Guifeng. 1999. Preliminary study of the seasonal changes of soil microorganism flora in Horqin Sandy Land, Journal of Desert Research, 19(Suppl.1): 107–109

Liu Lianyou. 1999. Preliminary study of regional wind erosion and deposition rates and intensities—an example from the Jing-Shaan-Mongol bordering region. Acta Geographica Sinica, 54(1): 59–68

Shen Jinqi, Gao Qianzhao. 1982. Study of desertification in Tarim Basin in historical period. Journal of Desert Research, 2(1)

Wang Beicheng. 1983. Historical evolution of the southern edge of Mu Us Sandy Land, Journal of Desert Research, 3(4)

Wang Tao, Chen Guangting, Qian Zhengan et al. 2001. Status and countermeasures of dust storms in northern China. Journal of Desert Research, 21(4): 322–327

Wang Tao, Zhao Halin, Xiao Honglang. 1999. Progress in the research of desertification of China, Journal of Desert Research, 19(4): 299–311

Wang Tao. 1998. Monitoring and evaluation of sandy desertification. Quaternary Research, (2)

Xiao Honglang, Li Fuxing, Gong Jiadong et al. 1999. Resource advantages and agricultural development of deserts and sandy lands in China, Journal of Desert Research, 19(3)

Zhang Tonghui, Zhao Halin, Zhao Xueyong et al. 1999. Preliminary approach to corn water consumption laws in Horqin Sandy Land, Journal of Desert Research, 19 (Suppl.1): 137–139

Zhang Weiming, Dong Guangrong, Li Sen et al. 1999. Desertification and control strategies in Rigze region, Journal of Desert Research, 19(1)

Zhao Halin, Zhang Tonghui, Chang Xueli et al. 1999. Study of the differentiation laws of plant diversity and niche on Horqin sandy pasture-land, Journal of Desert Research, 19(Suppl.1): 18–22

Zhou Ruilian, Sun Guojun, Wang Haiou. 1999a. Responses of osmotic regulator of psammophytes to high temperature and its effect on the stress resistance. Journal of Desert Research, 19(Suppl.1): 18–22

Zhou Ruilian, Wang Haiou. 1999b. Study of dehydration resistance of psammophytes under high temperature stress in relation to the membrane lipid peroxidation. Journal of Desert Research, 19 (Suppl. 1): 59–64

Zhou Ruilian, Zhao Halin, Wang Haiou. 1999c. Stress-resistant characteristics of process, Journal of Desert Research, 19(Suppl.1): 1–6

Zhu Zhenda, Liu Shu, Gao Qianzhao. 1983. Environmental changes and desertification processes in ancient Juyan Balck Town Region in historical period. Journal of Desert Research, 3(2)

Zhu Zhenda, Liu Shu. 1981. Desertification Processes and Its Control Regionalization in North China. Beijing: China Forestry Publishing House

Chapter 2
Outline on Natural and Socio-economical Features of Deserts and Aeolian Desertified Regions

2.1 Climate

Deserts are the outcomes of arid climate (Zhu et al., 1980). Continual drought is the basic characteristic of desert climates, as well as the fundamental basis for the evolution of deserts and aeolian desertified land. No or rare precipitation continued chronically is the essential reason for the arid climates.

China's arid regions are representative of temperate deserts in the Eurasian continent center (central Asia). These deserts are located at places farther north than others on Earth, and the central Asian deserts are not directly under control of the depressing air currents from sub-tropical high pressure belts. By temperature zoning, deserts in China are of the temperate and warm temperate belts; the wind regimes are the abnormal belt-featured, inner-continental belts influenced by the dried-up western belt. With distant locations from the oceans, and surrounded by mountains and plateaus that act as barriers to the moist air flows , deserts in China typically feature intense sunshine, rare precipitation, large temperature differences and high frequency of blown sand activities in the temperate continental climate.

2.1.1 Arid climate evolution in sandy regions

2.1.1.1 Atmospheric circulation systems in northern China

Two basic conditions must exist for precipitation to occur. The first is a certain amount of vapor in the air, which can be achieved by evaporation from the surface of the ocean, as well as snowy or icy polar areas. Therefore，precipitation is related by distance inversely from the shorelines, namely, the further the distance from the main vapor source, the lower the precipitation, if not accounting for disturbances from other factors. The second is aerosols, which may occur in two forms: organic and inorganic. The inorganic aerosols can be mineral particles, dust, fog and other chemical components, and the organic aerosols includes bacteria, spores, and pollens. As some researches pointed out，more precipitation over forests or thick vegetation can be found than over places lacking vegetation.

This is mainly due to the fact that vegetation cannot only increase vapor content of the air locally by transpiration, but can also release an abundant amount of organic aerosols. The schema of planetary atmosphere circulation is shown in Fig. 2-1.

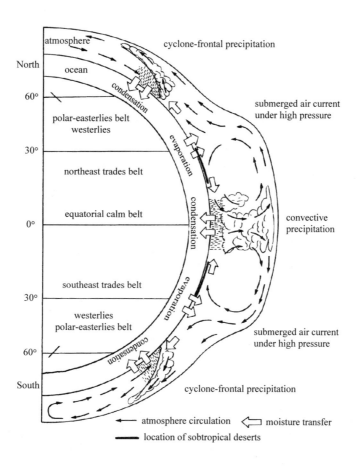

Fig. 2-1　Schema of planetary atmosphere circulation

As contemporary research on arid regions points out, the occurrence and adjacency of natural zones of desert, semi-desert, steppe and prairie results from the same origin but in unequal intensity—the mechanism of atmospheric depressing and divergence restricts atmospheric circulation and then precipitation. Horizontal and vertical movements of air mass in the atmosphere are the driving mechanism for cloud formation and precipitation. Convergence of airflow induces vapor and aerosols to condense and form raindrops; also, compressed airflow rises, and in the process, the temperature of the airflow decreases continuously while rising. When the temperature reaches the dew point, vapor begins to condense to form raindrops or ice crystals, and after absorbing each other to enlarge, precipitation occurs. In the areas over which airflows frequently converge, the climate is humid; contrarily, no precipitation occurs where airflows are divergent and in depression. Therefore, dry climate dominates places where divergent airflows are coming through or depressing vertically, and quite often the landscape is desert or semi-desert, and even the coastland is no exception. Thus, airflow mechanisms are the most important factor for precipitation.

As shown by facts, sandy and gobi deserts throughout the world are concentrated in zones between 15°–25° latitudes southward or northward from the equator since they are controlled by sub-tropical anticyclone belts of the planetary airflows depressing steadily (Fig. 2-1). Airflow depression is the determining factor for arid climates and deserts. However, it is not the whole story. Deserts, gobi deserts and even aeolian desertified lands can also be found elsewhere at higher latitudes outside the sub-tropical zones. The sandy areas in China are located in a warm-temperate zone, and connecting with those in Central Asia and the People's Republic of Mongolia, they form the largest temperate desert zone in the world.

The surface morphology of the earth is not uniform, and there are oceans, terrains and polar ice caps. Ocean currents with different temperatures affect the atmospheric airflows over them; the rolling mountain ranges, plateaus, hills, and plains also have different thermodynamic and kinetic effects. The surface covers of the earth has different physical properties that have a unique influence on the atmosphere above it, thus often changing the moving status of atmospheric currents and complicating the climate.

There are three circulation systems dominating the evolution of sandy areas in China: the East Asian monsoon, the north branch of the westerly in East Asia and the Qinghai-Tibet Plateau monsoon circulation.

1) The East Asian monsoon

The East Asian monsoon is induced by the high-pressure of the sub-tropics above the Pacific Ocean and the concomitant over the northern Siberia-Mongolia region. It not only controls the droughts-and-wetness and cold-warm dynamics of eastern China, but it is also an important factor behind sandy areas in China moving northward.

China is located in the eastern region of the Eurasia continent, and situated along the west coast of the Pacific Ocean. The northwest is the vast inland, while the southeast faces the Pacific Ocean. The location facing the ocean and backing on the inland is the very place where the Pacific Ocean sub-tropical high pressure system and the Siberia-Mongolia high pressure system contend. The position and intensity of these two high pressure systems change alternately with the seasons. The subsystem of high pressure circulation of the global sub-tropical high pressure system is caused by the Pacific Ocean. In its west, the warm-wet air current coming from the southwest or southeast brings abundant precipitation to mainland China. Especially, along China's southeast coast, the climate is humid subtropical with abundant vegetation, unlike other major subtropic areas of the world covered by vast sandy or gobi deserts (Fig. 2-2). As summer comes, the sub-tropical high pressure system of the Pacific Ocean gradually moves northward and stretches westward, and eventually arrives at and stays over about 30°N and the interim area between the land and the Ocean

(Fig. 2-2). Following the humid southern monsoon's track and derived from the movement of the Pacific Ocean's sub-tropical high pressure system, precipitation features a pattern with declining amounts and shorter precipitation periods from the south to the north. The humid air current also influences northern China at the end of summer. However, it is a 'power-losing arrow', characterized by a short rainy period that is concentrated but with sparse amounts. Almost from August on, the sub-tropical high pressure system starts to withdraw southward and shrinks eastwardly, and driven by the Siberia-Mongolia high pressure system, cold and dry air currents break out further down southward with the cold wave. Barely benifiting from small amounts of rainfall in the summer, sandy areas in China are first stricken by a cold dry front, and more often occupied by cold weather with strong and arid winds. Moistened only by the slight summer precipitation, sandy areas in China continue to suffer long-term droughts. This is the climate background that results in land becoming deserts and aeolian desertified land.

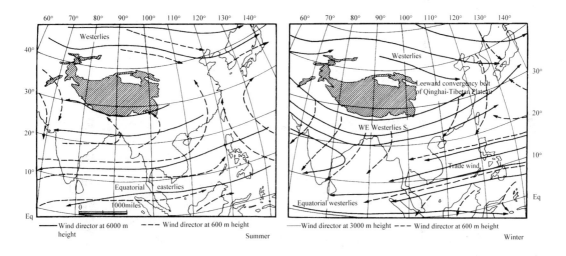

Fig. 2-2   Diagram for air flow conditions of the East Asian monsoon

2) The westerlies circulations

The westerlies over the middle latitude is part of global circulation which moves from the west to east, and the northern westerly winds separate into two branches when moving around the Qinghai-Tibet Plateau, which is an obstacle in front of it. The southern branch becoming wet as well as warm airflow from the southwest usually brings precipitation south of the Yangtze River. The north ern branch of the westerly airflow most importantly affects China's sandy areas, and it moves around north of the Qinghai-Tibet Plateau. Blocked by the Tianshan Mountains and the Altay Mountains, the northern branch of westerly airflow turns northeast and bypasses northern Xinjiang, then goes along the border between Mongolia and China, moves into China's sandy areas and then finally heads east. Thus, since the northern branch of the westerly moves around this area as an anti-cyclone, there is a constantly stable high ridge over the bordering scope along the 97°E longitude. This causes the airflow divergence to sink and depress, preventing precipitation from taking place. Therefore, there is a vast and barren area, covering stony mounds and black gobi, among Gansu, Xinjiang and the bordering areas. After crossing the Eurasian Continent, the northern branch of the westerly is almost dried up before reaching this area. Obstructed by the Kunlun-Qilian Mountain Chains at the northern edge of the Qinghai-Tibet Plateau, this branch is passively broken into two flows, the bigger one moving southeastward along the Hexi Corridor, while the smaller heads to the southwest, pouring into the eastern Tarim Basin through the basin's northeast inlet (Fig. 2-3). Both of them are too dry to cause precipitation. The existence of this kind of stabilizing situation causes eastern Xinjiang and western Gansu to be the driest places on the Eurasian continent. (Some scholars call it the "The extremely dry pole of the Eurasian continent"). Also it determines and controls the development of sand and duststorm centers in this area, as well as the evolution of deserts and aeolian desertification.

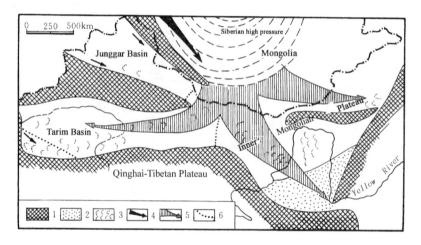

Fig. 2-3   Sketch map of the main directions of winds in the winter half-year for the sandy areas in China
1. plateau regions; 2. aeolian loess; 3. desert sands; 4. the northern branch across the plateaus; 5. main direction of wind flows;
6. the boundary of the main directions of wind flows

3) Monsoon of the Qinghai-Tibet Plateau

Besides the branches of the Westerly mentioned above, there is a regional air pressure system in this area due to the thermodynamic effect, and this drives thermal exchanges among the air currents over the Plateau and surrounding regions. Air circulations by thermal exchanges are also characteristic of monsoons. Land surface is warmer from May to October every year, especially in the summer. It brings about a "Tibetan warm high pressures system" over the plateau airspace of at least 300 hPa, which strengthens and stabilizes the northern branch of the westerly. Synchronously, the lower airspace is gradually controlled by a humid low-pressure system (From June to September). From October to April of the following year, the plateau becomes cold, introducing the control of the cold high pressure, hence the air pressure systems turns over. The cold high pressure in winter is stronger, and air overflows descend along the hill slope that is an important factor for the drier climate in winter of the western region of the sandy areas in China.

While changing along with the barometric systems of the inner plateau, the boundary layers of multiple barometric systems, which are called "plateau planetary boundary," move in a contrary direction to those over the plateau, both vertically over the plateau and horizontally in the surrounding profiles. Many researches show that, within a scope further away from it's margin surrounding this boundary layer, there is ring-shape belt of low precipitation (even thunderstorms and hail are infrequent), characterizing a small variability of daily-mean barometric pressure. Obviously, this stimulates droughts in western sandy areas in China. Therefore, the eastern boundary of this belt is an important zoning line for China's climate. Along this boundary from south to north (roughly in 106° E), is the east boundary of northern scope from the plateau with arid climate. Due to thermal sources for cold-warm functioning on the plateau, a series of barometric systems are changing. All of these manifestations prove that sandy areas and the western gobies in China are not an accidental occurrence.

2.1.1.2　Influence of geomorphologic structures and locations on climate

Regional systems of atmospheric circulation are the localized layout of geographic locations and geomorphologic environments. As mentioned above, as controlled by the depression of air flow from the subtropical high pressure system, deserts of the world are mainly located in a range from 30°S to the 30°N. Nevertheless, within this scope of latitude on the eastern side of the Asian continent, there is a humid climate and plenty of precipitation due to the East Asian monsoon. The deserts and aeolian desertified areas are driven northward to 35°N and further, which is partly caused by the Qinghai-Tibet Plateau upheaval in Asia.

Elevation of the Qinghai-Tibet Plateau is averages more than 4,000 meters, and the fastigium of this planet—the Himalayan Mountain Chain is higher than 8,000 meters, connected and integrated with the Pamier Plateau as a whole. It obstructs the northward advance of the southern monsoon that carries warm and humid air flows from the Indian Ocean. Air flows from the westerly winds are compelled to separate, and adding this up with the effects of the plateau itself as the source of cold-warm changes, these result in the obstruction of precipitation in the sandy areas and the northwest Qaidam Basin. Therefore, influence of the geomorphologic environment, especially the Qinghai-Tibet Plateau, on the arid climate of sandy areas in northwest China and the Qaidam Basin is yet another reason why sandy areas in China are located in the north.

Actually, the influence of the Tibetan Plateau is far greater. As pointed out by some researchers, with the upheaval of the plateau, the present Siberia-Mongolia High Pressure system is evolutionally formed from the Lhasa weak high pressure system, which is strengthened by the Ruoqiang high, and it gradually moves northward and joins with the Pacific sub-tropical high pressure system to form the East Asian monsoon circulation structure. This resulted in the above mentioned phenomenon, and the sandy areas in China moved northward. Therefore, the existence of the Tibetan Plateau not only formed the deserts and gobi in China, but also determined many features of the Chinese sandy area.

Sandy areas in China are basically surrounded by endless mountains and plateaus. Besides the lofty Qinghai-Tibet Plateau, from east to west are the Xiao Hinggan Ling Mountains, the Da Hinggan Ling Mountains, the Yanshan Mountains, the Taihang Mountains, the Luliang Mountains, the Qinling mountain chain, the Liupan Mountains, the Kunlun mountain chain, the Pamier Plateau, the Tianshan mountain chain, and the crossing and overlapping Altay Mountains' main branches and sub-branches. The stretched boundary between the north and the People's Republic of Mongolia is composed of open, flattened gobi steppes, and lowered hills and mounds, and the cold air flows of the northern monsoon certainly pass by this area. Further, northward in the north of the People's Republic of Mongolia and the bordering areas between Russia and Mongolia, there are the barriers of the Tangnu Mountains, the Khangai Mountains, and the east-west branches, sub-branches of the Yablonovy Mountains. Therefore, this kind of environment, including the sandy areas in China within the whole China-Mongolia Plateau blocked by higher mountains, mountain chains and plateaus (higher than 3,000 meters), and both plateaus and basins alike, obstruct the northward East Asian southern monsoon and lower the precipitation in this area. However, the northern East Asian monsoon can invade southward from the Peoples' Republic of Mongolia, bringing up dry and cold weather to replace the winter and summer monsoon. The above mentioned northern branch of the westerly and air flows from the Qinghai-Tibet Plateau is heavily obstructed by the mountain ranges and plateau, causing a local atmospheric depression, which consolidated the climatic background for the formation and existence of deserts and desertification. For example, even if located near the Pacific Ocean, the precipitation on the west side of Da Hinggan Ling, will still be less than that of the east. Moreover, in the Tarim Basin of the southern part of Xinjiang, due to the depression effect of air flows after crossing over surrounding plateaus of Qinghai-Tibet and the Tianshan Mountains, as well as resulting from the lowest content and source of air moisture in the deep inland, it lacks the most precipitation in all the sandy areas, and also has the driest climate and largest desert.

2.1.1.3   Radiation and land surface feedbacks

Researches on climate and aeolian desertification in recent decades brought up feedback theories on land surface radiation. As F. Kenneth Hare pointed out at the Conference on Desertification by the United Nations in 1977, atmospheric depression resulting in and strengthening an arid climate might result from the feedback of a barren land surface. This kind of feedback is due to the energy loss of effective radiation and the large amount of reflectivity of barren land surfaces. He pointed out, at the Africa Sahara Desert center, that although the mean radiation power of a day amounts to 275 W/m^2, the balance of radiation, however, is surprisingly low, only 80 W/m^2, and energy loss could be more than

70%. This astonishing result of energy loss was proven by satellite probing data: radiation balance of atmospheric temperature over the Saharan airspace is lower than that of surrounding areas, even for negative values. This means that the temperature of the atmosphere layer over it is lower than that of the surroundings at the same elevation. Differences in temperature layering structure of the atmosphere at the same height can cause a warming process of the depression to keep the balance of the temperature layering structure. This feedback effect of barren land surface also aggravates the atmospheric process for arid climates. He also pointed out this sort of radiation feedback is the result of the disappearance of large amounts of vegetation, as well as barren,dry land surfaces. Many simulated results calculated by computer experiments about the co-relationships between precipitation and reflectivity has proven the existence of this kind of feedback, and he therefore emphasized that vegetation protection is of important significance. What needs to be clarified is how large of an area of barren land surface is enough to induce this kind of feedback.

Statistical data shows that, the surface area of year round barren land surface in the sandy areas in China is quite large, with a total area of basically no-vegetated or totally barren land occupying 1,115.9 thousands km^2, accounting for 87.0% of the statistical area. At the same time there are many more steppes and farmlands having a period of roughly half a year of barren surfaces after the seasonal harvesting or natural withering, and this period can vary from six to nine months with very little snow cover. Obviously, these two land surfaces often have seasonal or yearly radiation feedback.

Studies on radiation balances for sandy areas in China clarified that radiation energy losses are dramatically huge in western sandy areas. Among them, there is an extreme radiation energy loss along the border of Gansu-Xinjiang, including eastern and southern Xinjiang. The loss is big enough to be compared with that of the Sahara Desert's center, also attaining up to 70%. In addition, all energy losses of the deserts are bigger than those of the nearby mountainous areas. The loss rate of the deserts is 66% to 68%, but the rate of the mountain areas reaches only 63% or much lower. The differences in feedback, as well as the larger feedback of China's desert areas can be explained by taking into account that sandy areas in China are located in the temperate-zone, as well as the strong reflectivity of the snow-ice surfaces on the high mountains and plateaus.

Content of air moisture or water vapor condensing and precipitation is correlated with land surface conditions. Although water vapor is carried by air flows from oceans which are far away from local desert areas, yet a portion of it comes from the vapor-transpiration of vegetation, soil and water bodies on the land, with vapor-transpiration from vegetation being an important component. Vegetation is also the main source for the organic nucleus of moisture condensation. Therefore, disappearance of vegetation decreases the water vapor transpiring from the land surface into the air, and also decreases the chance of precipitation from the condensation of moisture content. This results in an arid climate, which is yet another feedback from the land surface. In addition, vegetation disappearance enhances the blown sand activity and the aeolian desertification process. This is also another feedback as a result of vegetation vanishing from the land surface. In other words, the degradation and disappearance of vegetation cover on the land surface can trigger a series of feedbacks that aggravate the arid climate, which put the region into a malignant cycle of devastation from both the arid climate and aeolian desertification reinforcing each other.

The essential factors for arid climate are geographical location, atmospheric circulation and the geomorphological environment. They are also the origin for desert existence and aeolian desertification. These factors can't be changed. Although feedbacks of land surface seem to function extremely little, yet compared with the three factors mentioned above, feedback can be avoided and improved with effort. This is because the environmental destruction-development of aeolian desertification results from the pursuit of temporary economic benefits, and from ruthless de-vegetation activities.

2.1.2 Basic characteristics of the climate in sandy areas in China

With a vast territory of northern sandy areas, and regionally distinct variability, the notable features of climate in sandy areas in China in comparison with other deserts and arid regions in the world, are as follows:

2.1.2.1 Rare but intensive precipitation with great variability

The common point of desert regions in the world is drought, and while rare precipitation is the direct outcome of the arid climate, it is also the main reason for sparse vegetation. The general trend for precipitation amount in Chinese sandy areas: is a decrease moving westward as the distance from the coast increases. The annual precipitation of most regions (except for western Xinjiang) is below 400 mm (Fig. 2-4), which is lower than those areas of the same latitude in the Northern Hemisphere (according to the computed results, the mean annual precipitation of the land mass within 40°N–50°N is roughly 510mm). Secondly, precipitation decreases gradually from the surroundings to the center of the deserts, and deserts have an extreme arid center. In the west, sandy areas intersect with high mountain chains, plateaus and basins, like the northern and southern basins in Xinjiang, as well as the Qaidam Basin.

By delineating along the Wenduer Temple—Bailing Temple—Otog Qi—Dingbian, the eastern side is semi-arid, and under the monsoon's influence, precipitation is higher with an annual amount of 200–400 mm. The vast arid regions are on the western side, and the annual amount of precipitation is under 200 mm. Annual precipitation in the centers of the Taklimakan Desert and the Qaidam Basin is often below 30 mm.

According to measurements taken by the former Lanzhou Institute of Desert Research, the Chinese Academy of Sciences (CAS), during the period from July 1995 to June 1998, the three-year-mean precipitation in the center of the Taklimakan Desert was only 24.6 mm. Especially at Tuokexun, the center of the Turpan Basin, the consecutive 10-year-mean precipitation was only

3.9 mm, which is the minimum recorded in the entire country. In 1968, there were only two days when precipitation was recorded. One was in June, the other was in August, with an amount of 0.4 mm and 0.1 mm respectively. Both of these were non-effective precipitation, and for the entire year, the total precipitation merely 0.5mm. The annual multi-year mean precipitation of Ruoqiang County located in the southeast margin of the Tarim Basin, is 17.4 mm, and precipitation in Lenghu town located in northwest of the Qaidam Basin is 17.6 mm. The triangle district constituted by a delineation of Tuokexun, Ruoqiang, and Lenghu town is called "The Extremely Arid Spot of the Eurasia Continent", where precipitation gradually increases while moving outward.

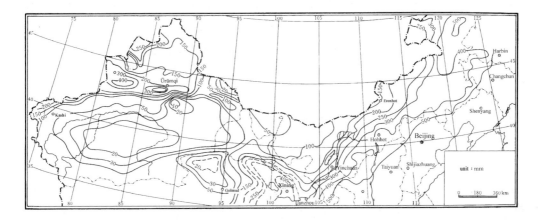

Fig. 2-4　Mean precipitation distribution map of desert regions in China

Precipitation in the sandy areas is not only rare, but also very uncertain; both the annual and yearly variances are very large. Usually, the lower the precipitation, the bigger the magnitude of variances. The annual mean precipitation rate for the eastern sandy areas is 25%–40%. But in the western part, it can go up to 40% or above, or even exceed 50%. For 12 years, no precipitation was recorded at Ruoqiang County. Seasonal amounts of precipitation is not extremely even. Except for the Gurbantünggüt Desert, precipitation in winter is commonly below 10mm for most parts of the sandy areas, which only amounts to below 10%. Contrarily, precipitation in summer are concentrated as high as 70% or above for the whole year, and in northwest Chadamu, it can even reach up to 80%. While precipitation in summer is usually concentrated within a few days, sometimes precipitation in one or two days can amount to that within half a year. In the southern Xinjiang region, precipitation within a day amounts to 70%–80% for the whole year, and sometimes even heavy rainstorms with possible flooding disasters occur Nevertheless, generally speaking, it is rare for precipitation of 10–15mm to occur all at one time. Due to intense evaporation, precipitation below 10–15mm will almost be exhausted at once, having almost no effect on the growth of crops and pastoral grasses.

The eastern region of the sandy areas is on the tail end of the East Asian monsoon. The relatively intense development of the Pacific Ocean Sub-tropical High and the Siberia–Mongolia High strongly affects wind blowing both in summer and winter. This kind of influence includes controlling the duration of either the humid-warm air mass or the cold-dry air mass. Thus the early or late arrival of summer precipitation impacts the length of the arid season. This continuous arid season, characterized by lack of precipitation, is usually longer than half a year in this region. The lack of precipitation and inconsistent variation is the basis of unexpected droughts or floods, fragile ecological-environments, and aeolian desertification.

The explanation needed here is: owing to lower temperature in winter in the deserts in China there are few snowfalls, which do not occur in the tropical deserts of the world. For example, in the Junggar Basin of northern Xinjiang, there are many snowfalls in winter that melt in the spring, and with good wetness of the sandy land, large quantity plants can complete their whole life cycle in 20–30 days, including germination, growing, blooming and fructifying. The vegetation coverage can be up to 20% or more and can have a tremendous effect on fixing sand dunes.

2.1.2.2 Large variations in temperature

Chinese deserts are located at a higher latitude compared to other areas, and no direct solar radiation reaches the land surface. Nevertheless, the percentage of relative sunshine is the highest when compared to areas of the same latitude because Chinese deserts have few clouds and drier air. It is generally more than 70%, and the annual sunshine is 2,800–3,400 hours. With about 3,400 hours of sunshine, western Inner Mongolia, eastern Xinjiang, the Qaidam Basin and the Hexi Corridor are the regions with the largest amount of sunshine in China; while, with 2,800 hours, eastern Inner Mongolia and the west of the Northeast Plain are regions that have the least. Especially in summer, the daytime is long, and the thermal energy acquired from sunlight and radiation is very rich. The total annual radiation from the sun in most parts of the sandy areas exceeds 4,700 MJ/m^2, which is 600–840 MJ/m^2 higher than that of northern and northeast China and 250–2,500 MJ/m^2 higher than that of the middle and lower reaches of the Yangtze River. The Qaidam Basin is the center for the highest total radiation in China with an amount that can reach 7,500 MJ/m^2.

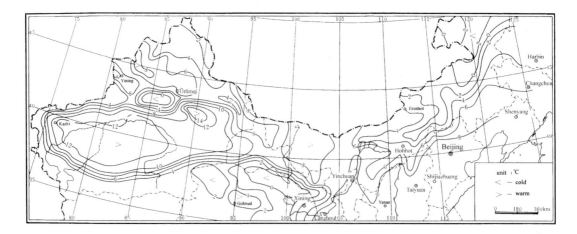

Fig. 2-5　Mean temperature distribution map of desert regions in China

Annual mean air temperature in sandy areas varies between 0–10°C (Fig. 2-5). The general trend is that it increases with an increase in latitude and elevation, and the isotherm is mostly cut up into pieces in anomalous shapes like blocked-circles or spatially-blocked belts because of high mountains and plateaus. Days with air temperature ⩾ 0°C varies from 180–240, and the accumulated temperature with daily-mean values ⩾ 0°C is between 2,200 to 4,500°C ranging from eastern Inner Mongolia through the Helan Mountains to plains on both sides of the Tianshan Mountains. Days with air temperature greater or equal to 0°C in the Turpan Basin can reach up to 275, while the accumulated temperture as mentioned above is 5,500°C. The same trend exists in distributions of both days with an average air temperature greater or equal to 10°C, as well as the relevant accumulative value. The active accumulated temperature is about 2,000–4,000°C in northern Xinjiang, the Hexi Corridor, the Alxa Plateau, and along the Great Wall. The most abundant areas are the Tarim Basin and the Turpan Basin with an active accumulated temperature ranging from 4,000–5,400°C.

There is an apparent seasonal difference in air temperature, with is cold winters and hot summers, and intense variations. The coldest monthly mean temperature from the western Northeast Plain to the Ordos Plateau and northern Xinjiang is between–10—–20°C. The lowest temperature even reached –51.5°C, which is the coldest recorded temperature in China. It occurred in Fuyun, located in the northeast margin of the Junggar Basin. However, in the summer, the hottest center is in the desert, deeply resided in the inland due to the extensive warming of the land surface. The Hexi Corridor, the Junggar Basin and the Tarim Basin have a mean air temperature for their hottest month of 24–26°C while the highest is 33°C in the Turpan Basin. Although the Turpan Basin is already near 43°N, the monthly average air temperature from June to August is over 30°C. The air temperature in Turpan changes drastically in a very short time, and both the spring and autumn in the desert are short, and it can be said that it has "only two distinct seasons". According to measurements taken at interior locations in the Taklimakan desert over the last several years, and based on the proper temperature for crops to determine the seasons, the spring is only 23 days and the autumn only 20 days. The maximum air temperature in Turpan once reached 48.9°C, and the sand surface temperature unexpectedly reached 82.3°C. Turpan, with its extreme dry and hot climate, is second to none in China and is called "the fire continent". Affected by the continental climate, annual variation of mean air temperature in sandy areas is generally 30–50°C. As an example, air temperature differences in the hinterland of the Taklimakan Desert is 36.3°C; in the Badain Jaran Desert it exceeds 40°C; in Turpan it amounts to 41.3°C, which is 22.4°C higher than that of the tropical desert of Aswan (yearly variation is 18.9°C). Therefore, the large annual variations of air temperature is notably different between deserts of China and and those of tropical and subtropical areas. At the same time, daily air temperature varies with abnormal intensity (Fig. 2-6); the daily temperature variance is similar to the changes of the four seasons in a year. Daily air temperature differences at each site is generally above 10–20°C, with a maximum of 35–40°C, which is greater than that in northern or northeast regions of China at the same latitude. The proverb "wear fur clothes in the morning, and change them with silk ones at noon; enjoy watermelon while embracing a stove" vividly depicts the violent changes of air temperature in the temperate-zone desert regions of China.

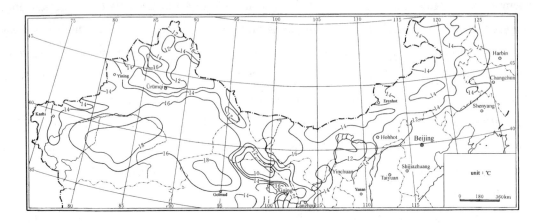

Fig. 2-6 Daily range of mean temperature distribution map of desert regions in China

2.1.2.3 Strong wind and frequent sandy weather

There is a lot of extreme and non-periodic weather in desert regions of China, as well as more weather processes such as cold waves, cold fronts, cyclones, and showers, than those in the tropics and sub-tropics. It is typical for "the breeze to stop once the summer moment comes" in other districts, but the wind blows all year-round in sandy areas. In the deep winter, because the arid regions in northwest China are near the center of the Siberia High, the most powerful anti-cyclone in the world, strong southward winds blow in a roar with extremely arid and cold weather. In the spring or autumn, both cold or warm air flows are vigorously exchanged with their counterpart. It is common for transient warm weather to be suddenly replaced by cold weather or vice versa, especially with many windstorms; in summer, the airspace of the deserts is controlled by the Low and air convections take place very often; many tornadoes, also the "Foehn," occur at the foot of the mountains. As for the annual variations in wind velocity, they are usually the biggest in the spring and the early summer of desert regions in China, which is related to the transition between the cold-frontier and the high airspace chamber, and many push against each other through cold and warm air flows.

Influenced by both the barometric distribution and atmospheric circulations, the regional distributions of wind velocity in the sandy areas in China are larger in the north, and smaller in the south; the strong areas emerge along the northwest borders, especially at neks, valleys of mountainous zone, where wind power is extremely strong. Taking the Anxi Area of Gansu as an example, since it is located right at the intersection of the northwest and northeast wind routes, there are an average of 80 days (with a maximum of 105 days) every year with wind blowing over No. 8 class (17.2–20.7 m/s), and it is consequently the called the "wind source of the world". The local people also have an expression, "there is only one wind which blows from spring until winter." At the Alataw Mountain Pass in the eastern end of the Junggar Basin, there are annually 164 days a year with wind blowing over No. 8 class, and the wind has a maximum speed over 55 m/s and annual mean of 7m/s. With these three records all exceeding that of Anxi, it is the most extreme place of China in this regard, and therefore called "No. 1 wind gorge".The Ebinur Lake, which is in the vicinity of the Alataw Mountain Pass, is called "wind lake" for short. There is also a folk song: "an evil wind resided in the Alataw Mountain Pass, No. 5 or No. 6 class is nothing, No. 7 or No. 8 class is breezing, and No. 10 class is commonly seen". In the northwest of the Turpan Basin, there is a famous wind gorge located near the "Three-springs", which is on the southeast of the Daban Town; strong wind blows with speeds higher than No. 6 class, and can continue for days. Annually, more than 100 days of the strong winds are No. 8 class, and 60m/s wind speed emerged as the record for the century. Smaller sands or gravels in the "Three Springs" were totally blown out; gravels of 2–3 cm in diameter were expelled as gravel-waves as high as 50–100 cm. The Turpan Basin, which is called "the wind warehouse", has strong winds 95% of the year, of which 100 days are class No. 8, and hurricanes of class No. 11 or No. 12 appear often. The "Qijiaojing" neck, between Bogeda Mountain. and Baliquen, has a segment of the "Lanzhou-Xinjiang Railway" from Liaodun, passing through the "Thirteen cabinets" to the "Fangqi Embankment". Because the long and narrow shaped terrain is parallel to the wind direction, this resulted in a "tunnel effect" that strengthens wind speed, and is thus called the famous "hundred *li* wind zone." "Sand particles were flying, stones were soaring, and even trains were stopped by the strong wind" is an accurate description of this area. On May 9th, 1993, rail tracks more than 100 meters in length from Liaodun to Shanshan were buried by sand drifts at 7 spots after strong wind, of class No. 12, 14 carriages and 34 freight trains were obstructed and over 10 thousands of passengers were stranded. On April 4th, 1999, the Lanzhou-Xinjiang Railway in the Turpan Basin was raided by a sandstorm. Windows of 24 carriage trains running on this section of the railroad were broken by flying stones blown up by the wind, and transportation on the Lanzhou-Xinjiang Railway was halted for 48 hours. Moreover, on April 10th, 1978, three freight coaches weighing 22 tons, while parked at the Hongliu station, were blown over from the roadbed and thrown down on the ground, resulting in the notorious freight accident from strong wind.

There is a big difference in seasonal distribution of winds between the east and the west. In the west, particularly in the region with wind gorges, there are more strong winds in the spring, although the magnitude does not vary significantly . However, in the eastern sandy areas, fairly strong winds appear in all seasons but the summer, and there is a significant range of magnitudes. It is fairly weak only in summer. Therefore, the spatial distribution of wind speed over sandy areas in China is summarized by the following:

(1) The wind is stronger in the west than in the east, and it is stronger in the north than in the south. Therefore, the south and southwest are often weak-wind zones, and the west margin of the

Tarim Basin located in southern Xinjiang is the weakest zone in all the sandy areas in China.

(2) Positions of both the high and low wind speeds are noticeably affected by terrains. High-speed zones can be found on steppes (the eastern sandy areas), deeply weathered downhills, and flat and vast gobi areas; lower wind speed is found on relatively lowland areas, which usually are in deserts or sandlands.

The fluid field of blown sand in the sandy areas as a whole is mostly eastward but deflected south southward year round. There are indications that the northwest wind system is the prevailing wind direction in sandy areas of China. However, the northeast wind regime along the border of Gansu-Xinjiang over the western sandy areas blows through the wide wind gorge between the eastern section of the Tianshan Mountains and the Beishan Mountains in the Hexi Corridor, then down southwestward for a thousand miles, eventually pushing deep into the hinterland of the desert of the Tarim Basin, and finally converging in a zone between the Hotan River and the Keriya River. The local wind system blows northwestward crossing over the Parmier Plateau so that a transition line is formed. Because the position of the Tarim Basin is close to the Qinghai-Tibet Plateau, it is directly influenced by the Plateau Monsoon. And also with the interweaving mountain chains and basins, local air circulations in this area are fully developed which inevitably result in multi-directionsal blown sand movements. Therefore,this is an in tersection for three wind systems featuring the northeast, the northwest, as well as the northward wind system in the Tarim Basin. Accompanying seasonal and yearly changes, the three wind regimes change respective of their forces and dependance on each other. The general rule of blown sand movements in the sandy areas is that it is multi-directional in the west and unidirectional in the east.

Blown sand activities are related closely to both the wind power and the condition of the land surface. In the west, a large amount of dry and loose sand materials are prone to be blown up, thus forming blown sand weather. However, in the east, although blown sand occurs every season except summer and the yearly mean forces are bigger than those in the west, yet blown sand events occur less frequently than those in the west due to the fairly vegetated surfaces.

The Annual blown sand events in the sandy areas in China generally occur between twenty to one hundred days (Fig. 2-7, Fig. 2-8). Among them, up to 35–60 days are sandstorms and more than 100 days have air dust. The amount and proportion of strong wind and blown sand weather, which includes sand blowups, sandstorms and dusty air, are closely related to geographical location, and local terrain (Geng, 1986). For example, the Taklimakan Basin has a northeastern opening, and through this mouth, air flowing from the north branch of the westerly that passes around the Qinghai-Tibet Plateau converges with that from the Mongolia High, and quite often blows over this basin. So, there is plenty of blown sand that causes floating dust to fill the air, but not strong enough to affect outside areas because dust and dirt settle down and deposit locally. The Hexi Corridor is an important passage for the northern branch of the westerly; blown sand weather occur all year-round, blown sand days amount to 60 (Fig. 2-9) in the windy seasons (March-June), and the biggest wind velocity is often higher than

20 m/s. With a vast gobi covering the western the Hexi Corridor and bordering Gansu and Xinjiang, ground air temperature rises rapidly under strong sunlight, triggering thermal convection that causes strong air flows Due to scarce vegetation in spring as will as loose soil in the oasis cropland, wind blows up sand and dust, and violent sandstorms occur. Therefore it is the most concentrated sandstorm region of China. Jinchang City located in the eastern the Hexi Corridor and south of the Badain Jaran Desert, as well as the Minqin Oasis located southwest of the Tengger Desert, suffer widespread-blown sand for more than 130 days a year. Generally, sandstorm duration is brief, but the toll is extremely heavy; soil erosion several centimeters deep can occur on cropland. Channels, ditches, railways and highways can also be buried by the piling up of sand deposited by sandstorms, and sandstorms can also cause other kinds of disasters including fires, blackouts, and cutting off water supplies. The northern zone of the Yinshan Mountains, located in the middle section of Inner Mongolia, also became a "windy corridor" (the north branch of the westerly), and exploitation of the southern steppe exhausted its primitive vegetation, which led to barren and loose land surfaces being prone to be the occorrence of sandstorms. In the last few years, sandstorms spreading to Beijing mainly originated from this region. They began east of the Yinshan Mountains, passed through the broad and flat Bashang Plateau in Hebei Province, and blew down to the Jing-Jin (Beijing-Tianjin) area.

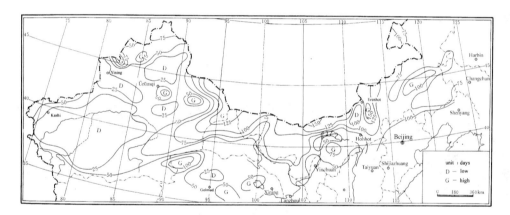

Fig. 2-7   Annual frequency of sand storm distribution map of desert regions in China

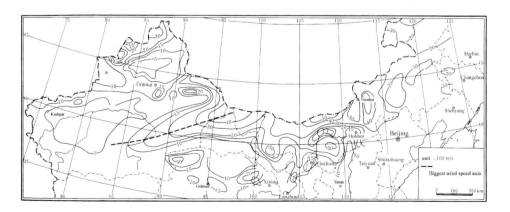

Fig. 2-8   Annual intensity of sand storm distribution map of desert regions in China

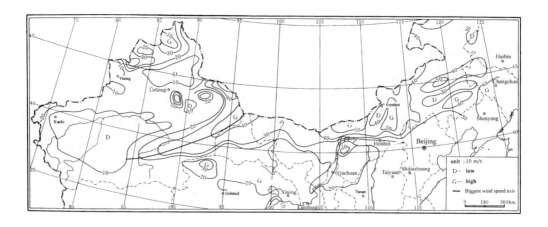

Fig. 2-9   Intensity of sand storm distribution map of desert regions in China in April

2.1.3   Climate zonation of sandy areas in China

Based on differences in the climatic environment as well as conditions and characteristics of heat, humidity and blown sand, (Figs. 2-10 and Fig. 2-11), Geng categorized the sandy areas in China into three climatic regions: the Western, the Eastern and the Qaidam region.

The ratio of thermal volume to precipitation of every location is presented here as $K=E/R$, where K is the aridity index, E (in mm) is the potential evaporation and R (in mm) is the precipitation, and is used to divide the sandy areas into six regions: I. Hyper-arid region ($K>32$); II. arid region ($K=4.0-32$); III. semi-arid region ($K=2.0-3.9$); IV. semi-humid steppe region ($K=1.0-1.9$); V. humid forest steppe region ($K<1.0$); VI. vertically distributed arid humid region ($K=1.0-74.0$).

Sandy areas in China are all in the temperate zone, so no sub-classification is made. However, based on accumulated temperature in degrees during the warm seasons, which is presented here as $\sum t_{10}$, it can be divided into four zones of thermal measurements in the temperate climate: B1, the warmer-temperate sub zone ($\sum t_{10}>3,500°C$); B2, the moderate-temperate sub zone ($\sum t_{10}=2,500-3,500°C$); B3, the cool-temperate sub zone ($\sum t_{10}=1,500-2,500°C$); BH the cold-temperate sub zone ($\sum t_{10}<1,500°C$), or high mountain zone with elevation above 3,000 meters. Considering circumstances of the blown-sand movements, based on the annual-mean advance rate V and the stable degree S, there are: ①straight fast [$V=1,200$ m/(s·a)]; ② swing moderate[$S>60\%$, $V=400-1,200$ m/(s·a)]; ③ hover around slow [$S>60\%;V>400$ m/(s·a)]and stable slow[$S>60\%$, $V<400$ m/(s·a)]; ④ windy but no blown sand (if comprehended as non-aeolian desertification or latent aeolian desertification areas).

According to the above criteria for sandy areas, regions, sub-zones and great belts, the sandy areas of China can be categorized into 62 climatic districts (Fig. 2-12).

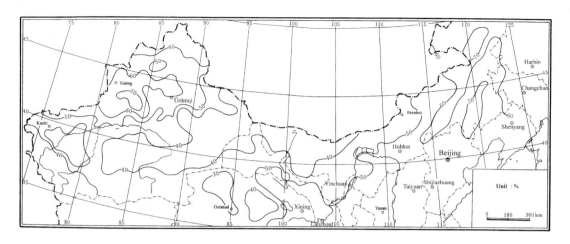

Fig. 2-10　Distribution map of relative humidity of desert regions in China

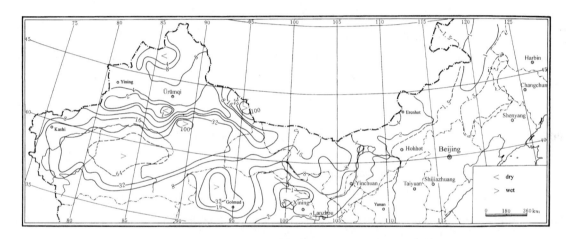

Fig. 2-11　Distribution map of aridity of desert regions in China

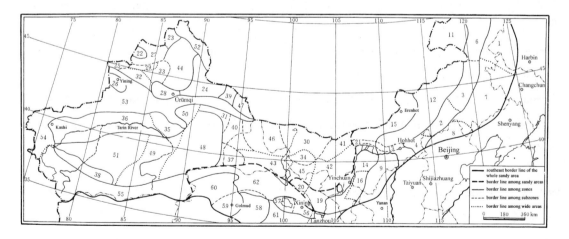

Fig. 2-12　Climatic districts map of desert regions in China

2.2 Geomorphology

2.2.1 Regionally controlled geomorphology units

Owing to the upheaval of the Qinghai-Tibet Plateau, three first-class terraces of geomorphology units in China emerged. The Qinghai-Tibet Plateau is the first unit with an average elevation of 4,000 meters, bordered in the north by the Kunlun Mountains and the Altun Mountains, and bordered in the east by the Hengduan Mountain Chain. The second unit has an average elevation of 1,000 meters, the Da Hinggan Ling Mountains, the Taihang Mountains are on the bordering line; from this line eastward, the third unit is constituted by low plains with mounds and downhills. Deserts in China are basically distributed on the second terrace. The Qinghai-Tibet Plateau is cold, and the physical cold-freeze weathering is intense; although desertification happened intensively in recent years, there is no desert with a large area, except those in the Qaidam Basin, in the Gonghe Basin, and surrounding the Qinghai Lake. Belonging to the third terrace, the Songnen Sandy Land and the Horqin Sandy Land are located on the Eastern Plain connecting westward to the Da Hinggan Ling Mountains.

2.2.1.1 Basic geomorphologic structure of two great plateaus and two great basins

There are two parts of the second great terrace divided into the south and the north. The north is basically occupied by two plateaus (the Inner Mongolian Plateau and the Ordos Plateau), and two basins (Junggar Basin, Tarim Basin) and the surrounding mountains. Both of the great plateaus and the great basins are the main portion of China's deserts (sandy lands), gobi and aeolian desertified lands (Zhao, 1990).

The eastern sandy areas China are basically plateau-type geomorphology, which belongs to the southeastern part of the famous central Asian Mongolian Plateau and its surroundings, which is commonly called the Inner Mongolian Plateau. The Inner Mongolian Plateau has a gently waved surface with an open view. Topographically it falls slightly down westward and northward. The Yinshan Mountains, the "backbone" of the Plateau, divides the whole plateau into two large parts. The northern one is regarded specifically as the Inner Mongolia Plateau, while the southern one is called the Ordos Plateau.

The Inner Mongolian Plateau, or the so-called "Northern Plateau," is a very broad area located to the west of the Da Hinggan Ling Mountains, and to the north of the Yinshan Mountains. With an extent of more than 2,000 km northeast to southwest, the surface of the Plateau is wide and smooth with an elevation of 600–1,500 m. Topographically, it is gently declining from the southeastern margin and mountains to the center of the plateau where it has an elevation of only 600–700 m. Dome-shaped mounds and lowered hills are inlaid and interlaced in the smaller basins, with layered high-plains basically characterizing the geomorphology in this area. Mountains located in the southeast, such as the Yinshan Mountains, the Da Hinggan Ling Mountains etc. are at an elevation of 1,500–3,000 m. They morphologically feature a one-facet shape of middle-range mountains that is lowered down and gentle in the side against the plateau and very steep and high on the other side. On the zones of the foothill of these mountains, there are fixed or semi-fixed dunes of large scope. They result from the fairly ample sand sources originating from the alluvial process by river systems.

The geomorphologic combinations of the Inner Mongolian Plateau can be divided into the Hulun Buir Plateau, the Xilin Gol Plateau, the Ulan Qab Plateau, the Alxa Plateau etc. from the east to the west.

The Hulun Buir Plateau is composed of the foothills of the western Da Hinggan Ling Mountains and the high plain. Its elevation is 400–600 m. Topographically, it declines slightly from southeast to northwest with the surface faintly incised. In the middle part of the plateau, the land surface undulates up-and-down, the underground materials are thick sedimentary layers of sand or sand-gravel, and the surface is covered with a thin layer of sandy-loess. Landforms are zonal-distributed, characterizing the interlaced distribution of sandy lands, sinks, wetlands and lakes.

The Xilin Gol Plateau is to the west of the Da Hinggan Ling Mountains. It is about 800–1,600 m high. The general trend in topography is a declination from south to north, and the plateau is surrounded by uprising mounds or down hills to the east, north, and south. The eastern and northern mountain bodies are stretched in an east-northeast direction, and the ramifications of the Yinshan Mountains are aligned east to west. Their tops are flat, smoothly domed with narrow ridges and a broad plateau-surface. There are many different-sized dry-valleys, channels and sinks; the terrain undulates up and down, similar to waves. Among them, the Ujimqin Basin in the northeast, the Abaga lava tableland in the west, and the Onqin Daga Sandy Land in the south together occupy quite a large area.

The Ulan Qab Plateau is located to the west of the Jining-Erenhot Railway, connecting the northern foothill of Yinshan Mountains. Mounds and basins are in the south of this plateau, while the middle is a wave-like highland covered with layers, and with down hill or weathered mounds appearing among the bordering area of Sino-Mongolia. With an elevation of 900–1,200 m, this plateau has declining northward terraces, with the lowest marsh sink at Naomugen in the northeast. The plateau is also cut with shallow marshes, channels and old-lake basins, and it features depressions and high plains inlaid upon each other.

To the west of the Helan Mountains is the Alxa Plateau, which is primarily piled up by mountains, mounds in stripped-weathering, and the depositary basins in complicated alignments. The southern margin of the Alxa Plateau is the Badain Jaran Desert and the Tengger Desert, and its eastern margin is the Ulan Buh Desert.

Surrounded by the Yellow River, the Ordos Plateau is connected to the Jinshan (Shanxi-Shaanxi) Loess Plateau in the south, with an elevation range of 1,200–1,600 meters and a square-table shaped high land. The land surface is wave-shaped and covered by aeolian sand, loess, strata of pebbles and sands of diluvium and alluvium, and the aeolian geomorphology is the most extensive. The geomorphology combination inside the Ordos Plateau is also obviously different. In the northern part is the Hobq Desert, in the south is the Mu Us Sandy Land, and in the east are mounds and knaps, the west has gullies, and the middle has gently waving roof-surface, lowland and sinks formed by wind erosion, with scarce rivers, but numerous lakes. Located farthest west is the Zhuozi (Table) Mountain, a block mountain with an elevation range of 1,500–2,000m, intensive arid denudation, and many crags and cliffs. Between the Yinshan Mountains and the Ordos Plateau, there are the Hetao Plains with an elevation of 1,000–1,100 m, a downthrow of the rift-valley basin. Bordering Xishanzui, they are divided into two parts called the Qiantao plain and Houtao plain. The Qiantao Plain has a triangular shape, which is narrower in the west and broader in the east, and the Daheihe River flows from the northeast gorge and along the eastern edge of the plateau. There is a huge foothill plain of the Yinshan Mountains, declining from northeast to southwest in topography. The Houtao Plain is similarly in a fan shape with a declination slightly to the north, and the current Wujia River is an ancient course of the Yellow River. Very deep and thick sediments and the passage of the Yellow River helped to irrigate the Hetao plain. For thousands of years, the Yellow River fed the Hetao Plain, resulting in a quite different landscape from the surrounding arid areas that have scarce vegetation and scattered sand dunes. The cropland in the Hetao plain is endless, with intersecting canals and ditches. Since ancient times, the Hetao Plain has been called "the Eden of the northern wastelands."

The west of the sandy areas in China is occupied by two tremendously huge inland basins, which are the Junggar Basin in northern Xinjiang and the Tarim Basin in southern Xinjiang, the two being separated by the Tianshan Mountains.

The Tarim Basin is the biggest inland basin in China, pertaining to a large scale built-up basin surrounded by mountains. Nipped by the Tianshan Mountains in the north and the Kunlun Mountains in the south, it stretches with a maximum width of 520 km from north to south, and a maximum length of 1,400 km from east to west. In tectonics, the Tarim Basin is a stable block or an ancient continental block, controlled by many surrounding and deep fracture zones. The base of it is pegmatite or old crystallized rocks, on the tilted facet is a set of sedimentary formations of the early Pleistocene and Paleozoic with a depth of 1,000 m. Above these sets, they are the sediments from the Mesozoic and the Cenozoic, and over them, sediments of the Quaternaries covering the biggest area. Based on geomagnetic probing, there are two large east-west fracture zones stretching through the middle of the block. The middle portion is upheaved, and in the west of the basin, there are a few convex peaks and weathered hills, such as the Mazhatage Mountains in the west of Hotan town and the Qokkatag Mountains in the south of Bachu. All these indicate that this old block has never been flattened.

The tectonics of the Tarim block are not consistent compared with the Tarim plain in geomorphology. The Tarim Block includes the surrounding low hills and mounds that include the Kuketage Mountains in the east and the Keping Mountains in the west. However, the Tarim Plain is only limited to the flat portion of the sediment covering in the Quaternary. Along both sides of the piedmont, influenced by tectonic movements, the plain fell down as a sink, with the Kuqa Depression in the north and the Shache Depression in the south. Under the Kuqa Depression, the tremendous thickness of continental sediments from the Mesozoic and the Cenozoic is as high as 10,000 m, which is valuable for fossil resources and fresh water reserves.

The exterior appearance of the Tarim Basin is like an irregular lozenge, surrounded by high mountains. In the east, the low elevation valley of the Shule River is the traditional passage to the Hexi Corridor, known also as the main route of the "Silk Road", However, because this corridor is higher than the Lop Depression, which is unable to develop outlet drainages, therefore the Tarim Basin is an entirely closed inland unit. Since the west is higher than the east, the Tarim Basin declines northward slightly, which causes the Tarim River in the north to flow eastward. This is the best indicator for the basin topography in general. At the lowest level of the basin, the old Lop Nur is 792 m in elevation.

The natural landscape of the Tarim Basin features a ring-shape: its margin is gravel gobi connecting to mountains, the center is endless desert, and the interim part is alluvial fans and plains where oases are distributed. Three morphologies are found within oases: (a) there are many delta–rivers in Kashi–Shache, with ample water resources, and oases are linked together with few deserted land surfaces; (b) clustered oases along rivers that run southward and located parallel to the northern hill foot of Tianshan Mountains, and running rivers ending on the alluvial Tarim Plains. (c) Oases in the southern Basin are all distributed in clusters with large surfaces in hungriness among them.

The vast territory southward from the Tarim River is the notorious Taklimakan Desert with an area of 330 thousand km², the biggest desert in China, and the second largest shifting desert in the world. The desert covered all the alluvial plains, the diluvial plains in front of the Kunlun Mountains and the ancient Tarim River flooding plains. Due to limited area, desert north of the Tarim River is distributed over the margin of apron as a discontinuous belt with flooding fans.

The Junggar Basin is located between the Altay Mountains and the Tianshan Mountains. On its west is the Junggar western mountains with a series of low mountains of 2,000–3,000 m. On its east is the Beita Mountains, an extended portion of the Altay Mountains. Topographically, the basin is tilted to the west, and the northern part is slightly higher than the southern. The Ulungur Lake (also known as the Buluntuo Sea or the Fu Sea) is situated in the north, and it's water level is 468 m; The Manass Lake is in the middle, with an old lake level of 257 m; the Ebinur Lake is in the southwest, with an old lake level of 189 m, and it is the lowest point of the Junggar Basin. The width of the basin from south to north is roughly 450 km, the length from the east to the west is about 700 km, and with an area of 180 thousand km², the desert roughly covers 30%. In the west, there are several gaps such as the valleys of the Ertix River, the Emin River, and the Alataw pass; through these gaps, the westerly air flow with relatively higher moisture brings precipitation to the basin and the surrounding mountainous zones.

Tectonically, the Junggar Basin is an old terrestrial mesa; this mesa had already emerged in the Craton Era, and its core might belong to the Cambrian System. Underneath the basin, the Paleozoic strata were overlaid by sedimentary formations of the Mesozoic and the Cenozoic in tremendous thickness. Mesozoic strata are continental sediments of mainly sandstone covering the Paleozoic base. The depth of the sediments increases southward, about 700 m in the north and 3,000–4,000 m in the south with coal and petroleum reserves. The Cenozoic strata thickness increases southward; in the north, it is only about 450 m thick, but in the sunken center of the south, it is as thick as 5,000 m. Among them the Quaternary sediments can be divided into three zones: Along the northern foothill of the Tianshan Mountains, the zone has a sink 500 m thick, in the middle it is only 100 m, and in the north it is relatively upraised with only few meters found covering the Tertiary. As mentioned above, spatial changes of the Quaternary sediments in this region reflect an obvious new tectonic movement. Within the three zones mentioned above, there were also characteristics of the attributed-class for tectonic movements, the most obvious being the upheaval of three young conformations in the southern sink, which starts east of Wusu and ends near Jimuser. In the north, the upheaval portions of the conformations in the lower class are represented as the valley of the Ertix River and the Ulungur Lake escarpment.

There are roughly three plains with geomorphological forms in the Junggar Basin. In the north, it is the foothill plain south of the Altay Mountains, starting in the north from the southern foothills zone of the southern Altay Mountains, ending at the desert margin in the south, including the declined plain in the north of the Ertix River, the alluvial plain between the Ertix River and the Ulungur River, and the alluvial plain in the Ulungur River. The main characteristics are thin strata of the Cenozoic, large areas of lowlands eroded by wind, and thin soil layers. In the south, it is the foothill plain in the north of the Tianshan Mountains, starting in the south from the northern foothills zone of the Tianshan Mountains, and ending at the northern margin of the desert. Soil thickness increases northward, the gravel gobi of the south is mainly used as pastures in the spring and the autumn while the northern fine-soil plains are the important irrigation districts for agriculture. Located in the middle of the basin, the Gurbantünggüt desert is the third largest desert in China, with fixed and semi-fixed dunes dominated features, and shifting sand dunes occupy about 3%. Precipitation is 100–150 mm in the desert area; snow is there in winter, and there is a higher percentage of vegetation than that of the desert in southern Xinjiang. It is about 20% with semi-fixed dunes and 40%–50% for the fixed. Pasturages in the trough of the dunes grow well, but in the past it was used as winter pastures and a water source for people and their livestock. At present, water is supplied by drilling wells sensibly divided in the region, and part of it is changed to ranches in summer. For balancing the seasonal carrying capacity of livestock, most areas are still winter pastures or harvesting field pasturages in summer. The desert can be divided into many slices having a local name of its own. From Mulei to Qitai there are Ailisen, Qiabila, Kala etc.; from Qitai to Fukang, it is called the Beishawo; sand dunes and in the south of Fuhai it is called Arcqumu; sand dunes near Burqin are called Tazikumu and Kumubaituo, etc.; sand dunes nearby Todog in the southeast of the Aibi Lake are called Shashanzi.

South of the Hexi Corridor is the grand Qilian-Altun Mountain Chain with an elevation of 4,000–5,000 m. Although the Hexi Corridor is flat and stretching up to 1,000 km from southeast to northwest, yet it is only 10–50 km wide, just like a corridor between two mountain ranges facing each other. Since it is west of the Yellow River, it is called the Hexi Corridor, which means "corridor west of the river" Two truncations appear on flat ground in the middle of the corridor by the Yanzhi Mountains and the Heishan Mountains, therefore, there exist three segments, namely the west, the middle, and the east. They are mainly formed by flooding deposits and alluvial plains at an elevation of 1,000–1,500 m. Water and soil resources are relatively abundant. From the foothill of the Altun Mountains to the north, the land surface tilts slightly, and diluvial gravel gobi, diluvial-alluvial sandy gobi, fixed dunes, shifting sand dunes, and plain oases successively appear. In the south foothill of the Mazong Mountains there is the extensive "black gobi", which is composed of base-rocks flattened by denudation, and there is often a black layer of varnishing over the surfaces.

Rivers in the Hexi Corridor are all inland rivers, mostly running out of the Qilian Mountains and the Altun Mountains. Their upper reaches are located in numerous mountains. After running out of the mountains, most of them disappear and merge as dry channels. Run off appears again at the fringe of the declined piedmont plain, as the irrigation source for oases agricultures; then water runoff gradually is reduced to disappear at last in the salty shoals or sand debris. In the past, there were some terminal lakes such as the Baitinghai Lake and the Qingtu Lake of the Shiyang River, but they are now dried up. Also, the Sogo Nur in the lower reach of the Heihe River was dried up in the 1990s.

2.2.1.2 Mountains surrounding the sandy areas

Among the mountains surrounding the sandy areas in China, the Tianshan Mountains, the Altay Mountains, the Yinshan Mountains and the Da Hinggan Ling Mountains are the most famous. Being sealed off and surrounded by mountains is an essential condition for the development and existence of deserts and the surrounding aeolian desertification. (Fig. 2-13).

The Tianshan Mountains is one of the highest mountains in the Eurasian continent. It extends roughly 2,500 km from east to west, and 100–400 km from south to north. The east segment starts at Yiwu County located on the border of Sino-Mongolia, continues through the border at the north bank of the Kezi River in Wuqia County, and finally reaches the Republic of Kyrgyzstan.

The Tianshan Mountains span through the middle of Xinjiang; located between the Junggar Basin and the Tarim Basin, they have an area of 244 thousand km^2. They are grouped by several nearly parallel mountainous ranges in an east-west direction. The width between the ranges is not the same, and the range from Wusu to Luntai is rather compact; with few branches it is called the mountain knot or mountain convergence. Eastward or westward from this area, mountain ranges all spread in a bundle; valleys and internal basins between mountains are broadly distributed. According to composition of ranges, the three mountain chains of the Tianshan Mountains are sorted as follows:

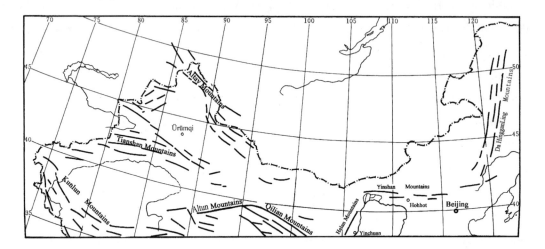

Fig. 2-13   Sketch map of the main mountains of desert regions in China

① The Northern Tianshan Mountains, including the Kaerkeli mountains betweens Hami and Balikun to Yiwu, the Bogda Mountains between the Turpan Basin and Ürümqi to Mulei, the Yilianhabierga Mountains between Ürümqi and Wusu, and the Potiankenu Mountains west of Wusu. The very western branch of the Northern Tianshan Mountains is the Alatan Mountain, located in the north of the Bertala Valley on the border of Sino-Kazakhstan. The crest of the Bogda Mountains is the Bogda summit with an elevation of 5,445 m.

② The Central Tianshan Mountains: The eastern edge is the Qoltag Mountains, the middle is the Turpan Basin, with the Narat Mountains. in the Yili valley as the western end.

③ The Southern Tianshan Mountains: The eastern starting point is the Kuruk Mountains south of the Hami Basin, to the Alai Mountains facing southward towards the Kezi River in Wuqia County. The western branch to Wenxu is customarily called the Tianshan southern branch that stretches with most of its boundary on the Sino-Kazakhstan border in Wenu County. In this area, the summit of the Tianshan Mountains is called the Tomür Peak with an elevation of 7,435.38 m. With high mountains and deep valleys near the summit, surrounded by a mountainous area more than 3,000 km^2, 60% of the area is above 4,000 m, and there are 15 mountains exceeding 6,000 m and 5 peaks above 6,800 m.

There are contemporary glaciers in the Tianshan Mountain ranges; the Tomür peak area is one area impacted by modern glaciers. There are more than 629 glaciers in this area, with coverage more than 3.800 km^2, and more than 509 glaciers and 2,700 km^2 coverage and a total volume of ice and snow up to 3,500 km^3, much greater than that of the Qilian Mountains and the Zhumulama area on the Himalayan Mountains. All of these giant glaciers stretch out from the Tomür summit with the center located in a radial status.

On the Tianshan Mountains, the Tianchi is a blocked lake on high mountains and formed with glacial-deposit materials, which were piled up on the course of the Sangong River taking the Bogda summit area as its source. The lake is at an elevation of 1,910 m shaped by the original course of the river, and extends along the canyon; it zigzags across and is very deep, with an area of 4.9 km^2; the deepest point is 105 m. With snowy peaks in the clouds, and the boundless verdure *Picea crassifolia*, it is the most attractive highlight.

There are many inner basins and valleys in the Tianshan Mountains interior, and they are all important bases for agro-pastoral industries. They include the Naomao Lake and the Tuerku Basin, the Santang Lake-Barkol Lake Basin, the Hami-Turpan Depressions, the Sayram Lake Basin, the Bole Valley, the Yanqi Basin, the Youledus Basin, the Baicheng Basin, the Zhaosu basin, the Tekes Basin, the Yili River valley, the Toxkan River valley, the Keping Basin, the Harjun Basin, and the Kezi River valley. Among them there are many outlets, and a considerable portion are mountain enclosed inland.

The Altay Mountains are located north of the Junggar Basin, stretching along the borders of China, Russia and Mongolia from the northwest to the southeast for more than 2,000 km. With it's southern piedmont of the middle segment located for more than 500 km in China, and the ranges generally more than 3,000 m high, it gradually descends from the northwest to the southeast. The summit is in the northwest and the elevation is 4,374 m. As for the Beita Mountain, it lowers to 3,200 m, and disappears in the gobi wasteland in the southeast. The Altay Mountains appeared as early as in the Craton movement, then after long-term erosion became a pre-plain. In the Himalayas movement, it was uplifted again with an un-even elevation on each side, so that several terraced topography emerged. From the ridgeline on the Xinjiang northeast border to the Valley of the Ertix River, there are apparently four terraces, and this kind of stratification is an important geomorphologic characteristic of the Altay Mountains. In the Mongolian language, Altay means "gold," which indicates the Altay Mountains are rich in gold reserves and many other minerals. By the Tang Dynasty it had already been called "the gold mountains".

The Yinshan Mountain range is located in the middle of the Inner Mongolian Plateau, and is also the boundary mountain between the Inner Mongolian Plateau and the Ordos Plateau. From east to west, the Yinshan Mountain range includes the Daqinshan Mountains, the Wula Mountains and the Langshan Mountains, with an elevation between 1,500–1,800 m, nearly 1,000 m higher than the southward Hetao Plain. However, it is not connected between these mountains; passes or breaches exist between them and these became the key-path for communication.

As the very western branch of the Yinshan Mountains, with an arc-extruded northwestward and embracing the southeastern Hetao Plain, the Langshan Mountains varies in its width from several thousand meters to 30 km. There are two branches of the east to the Langshan Mountains: the north one called the Serteng Mountains is the stretch of the Langshan Mountains, the other one in the south is the Wula Mountains, starting at Ulansuhai in the west and passing by Baotou, then ending eastward at the Hondlon River, with a ridge as narrow as 15 km with a crest of 2,300 m above sea level. One the east of the Kundulun River, it is called the Daqing Mountains, which stretches along the north side of the Hohhot Plain to nearby Jining with a wider body. The Daqingshan mountains is composed of many kind of rocks, and sandy shales often have a domed and lowered appearance, while the harder metamorphic rocks have erected stiff peaks or scarps. Nearby Jining, there is also basaltic mesa. The crest of the Daqingshan mountains 2,850 m high in the east of Jining, the Yinshan Mountains stretches continuously northeastward with an appearance of lowered hills and mounds to the Da Hinggan Ling Mountains. Gorges or passes among the weathered mountains became the "wind tuyere", allowing the arrival of the Mongolia High invasions and the Plateau blown sand northern regions of China.

The southern and northern slopes of the Yinshan Mountains are asymmetrical. The south facet facing the plain is very steep, but the north slope emerges gently into the Inner Mongolian Plateau, with no obvious mountainous features.

Abundant mineral reserves are found underneath the Yinshan Mountains. the Bayan Obo located on the north side of the Yinshan Mountains is also called in Mongolian as "the rich mountain". It is rich in minerals of ferrous and rare earths with certain importance in China and even over the world.

With the northern-northeast alignment, starting in the north from Muohe town located on the border of Sino-Russia, to the southern Chifeng, the Da Hinggan Ling Mountains are connected with the Yanshan Mountains lying west-eastly. It stretches more than 1,000 km in length up to 300 km in width in the north, but merely over 100 km in the south. Most of the mounts or peaks are 1,000–1,400 m high. The mountain body is composed of neutral-acid lavas formed in the Yanshan movement. With domed-tops and a vague ridgeline, and many passes or cuts between mounts as well as transverse valleys, the characteristics of the Quaternary sandy sediments on acustrine or fluvial at both flanks are very similar. The Da Hinggan Ling Mountains is usually regarded as the zoning line distinguishing the semi-arid from semi-humid areas.

The Helan Mountains is located to the west of the Yinchuan Plain, in a south-north alignment. With apparent asymmetrical slopes of both sides, that is the gentle and shallower cut-down gullies of the west but very deep valleys and steep slopes of the east facing the Yinchuan Plain. The ridge is in 2,000–3,000 m high and of meso-scale mountains weathered and stripped by arid climate. The summit of it is 3,556 m above sea level and located at the southeast of the Bayinhaote. Modern tectonic movement of this mountain is intensive, often accompanied by earthquakes. The middle segment and the northern part feature high-mount-steep-valley, steeper and narrower watersheds, and cliffs, but in the south it appears as a lower topography and is merged close to the Ningwei Plain by the Losses Plateau. It is similar to a running steed if viewed remotely. In Mongolian, "Helan" means a steed. The mountain is often considered as the zoning line between the eastern monsoon and the west arid regions. From a geographical standpoint, it is meaningful that both the Da Hinggan Ling Mountains and the Helan Mountains have similar north-south alignments.

The Kunlun Mountains start west from the Pamir Plateau and are located on the south of the Tarim Basin and the Qaidam Basin.The northern face is the margin of the Tibetan Plateau, and crests or peaks are above 7,200 m above sea level an extreme drop in the Tarim Basin.

2.2.2　Aeolian geomorphology in sandy areas

2.2.2.1　Factors for aeolian Geomorphologic features and distribution characteristics

1) Factors for aeolian geomorphologic features

Evolution of desert landform features in geomorphology results from the interactions among air flows and sandy surfaces, and is influenced by the topography underneath, the sand source supply and the moistures, and the vegetation conditions etc. (Zhu et al., 1994). These factors vary locally, so desert surfaces change a great deal in variety.

Sand dunes are the basic landforms of deserts. The general characteristics of sand dune regimes are related to the complexity of wind regimes in velocity for blown-sand flow that has different forms due to different wind circumstances. For example, in the southwest and the eastern parts of the Taklimakan Desert, due to the unimodal wind direction, barchan chains dominate; nevertheless, if areas with a prevailing wind are also affected by a secondary reversal wind, though the dune crest swings forth and back, the moving direction of the sand dune chains is generally that of the prevailing wind, such as the sand dunes in the southeast of the Mu Us Sandy Land. Pyramid or star sand dunes appear in areas where multi-directional wind blows with similar strength, which are those in the southern margin of the Taklimakan Desert between Qiemo and Minfeng. In areas such as the most of the Tengger Desert, with a prevailing wind and influenced by a secondary wind blow from a direction which is perpendicular to the prevailing wind, the grid-shaped sand dunes exists. Barchanized sand ridges arc located in places where two wind blows with intersected directions but the angles are not large, such as that in the southeast Taklimakan Desert. A prevailing wind influenced by several secondary wind blows from different directions benefits the development of domed sand dunes (dome-shaped irregularly and overlaid by intensified sand dune chains, generally distributing by individual with a length of 200–500 meters and an elevation of 30–50 m), as cases of the Ulan Buh Desert in its south, the central and the north of the Taklimakan Desert etc. Sand ridges were formed in an area with singular directions of wind blows.

General consistency can be found between the direction of sand dune alignment (which is represented by the aspect of the windward of the sand dune, or the heading azimuth angle of the sand ridges) and the resultant wind direction (above the threshold speed for sand saltation), but they do not always coincide; moreover certain degrees between them and the differences depend on the complexity of the winds. In the southwest or the east of the Taklimakan Desert with an unimodal wind regime, the angle is small and generally within 1°–5°, while its angle becomes up to 9°–15° in the west or the central north where wind regimes are more complex. According to this kind of relationship, recognitions of wind regimes where no metrological data is available, analyses of sand dune features reflected on aerial photos are practical.

With sand supply sufficient enough, sand mass quantities depend on the wind speed. Since natural wind blows are always turbulence which is largely unstable in velocity, the succeeding response is that sand drifting is always in a switching situation between saturated and un-saturated, and it is rarely stabilized and saturated. However, sand drifting is always prone to balance this unstable situation. When it is un-saturated, it will bring up more mass in quantity from the surface where wind erosion takes place. If it reaches the situation it take the mass overloaded, the extra or over-loaded portion will settle down on the ground and sedimentation takes place, and this is the cause and principle of the aeolian flow erosion-sedimentation action on the earth surface. In deserts, it is evidently true that developments or changes in morphology from simple to complex and vice versa everywhere. This results from the wind-sand geomorphology on its location and the local conditions in kinetics.

Although wind is the kinetic factor for sand dune evolution, various other natural factors may affect differently the forms in the process of sand surface change by wind. Giant sand dunes develop commonly on areas with plenty of sand sources, while small ones appear on site with sand mass lacking. Waving mountain ranges in an area are usually obstructive to wind-sand flows, giant sand dunes resulting from sediments in huge quantity appear on the upwind slopes; on the other hand fixed and semi-fixed nebkhas occur on foothill zones where air flows are influenced by the mountain relief. Owing to this mechanism, many cases of sand shifting occur in Ordos, eastern Inner Mongolia, and in the Horqin Sandy Land.

2) Spatial features in aeolian geomorphology of China

In districts of the Alxa, the Ordos, eastern Inner Mongolia and the Qaidam Basin eastward from the 96° E, transverse sand dunes exist generally with an alignment of NNE to SSW, or in an alignment of northwest to southeast, reflecting the northwest wind influences. On the opposite direction from the same longitude, the vast central and the eastern part of the Tarim Basin, transverse sand dunes generally exist with an alignment of northwest to southeast or NNW to SSE, reflecting the northeast winds influences. Nevertheless in the southwest of the basin, sand dunes align northeast to southwest, which results from the northwest winds. Also in the west of the Junggar Basin, wind from northwest functions on the alignment of northwest to southeast, the direction to which the sand ridges are parallel.

Shifting dunes exist mainly in the internal deserts located west of the Helan Mountains and the, Wushao Ling Mountains other than fixed and semi-fixed nebkhas in the Gurbantünggüt Desert with more precipitation and snow in winter, and those on both flanks of the intermittent channels in the inner deserts, as well as those in troughs of sand dunes with high phreatic tables, or in the margins of lakes and marshes, and in the lower margins of pediment-alluvial fans where artesian water emerges. However, in the east, benefiting from an annual precipitation of more than 200 mm, there is a higher degree of vegetation coverage, also mainly with fixed and semi-fixed sand dunes. Shifting sand flecks are distributed nearly to residential spots, farmland and ranges where vegetation is ruined.

Complicated sand dune types generally dominate the front belts of rolling mountain ranges, such as those at the Mazhatage and the north of Luostage in the west of the Taklimakan Desert, those along the regimental plain between the Qiemo and the Minfeng, and that of the Kumtag Desert on the northern slope of the Kerh-Chin Mountains, the southeastern Badain Jaran Desert which is located in the west of the Yaburai Mountains. Most ridges are developed in the fixed or semi-fixed deserts, such as the Gurbantünggüt Desert, the Onqin Daga Sandy Land and the Horqin Sandy Land. The low barchan sand dunes and barchan sand dune chains generally appear on margins of big deserts and in the gobi or pebble belts in front of the mountains.

2.2.2.2 Aeolian geomorphologic types

Characteristics of distinctive land surface morphology of deserts can be the result of analyzing the two categories in which the barren shifting sand dunes and the semi-fixed or fixed sand dunes with vegetation cover. This criteria is of practical importance in rehabilitating deserts. As to the bared shifting sand dunes, it generally means that the vegetation coverage is less than 15% or totally, therefore sand drifting is extremely intensified and morphologic changes are overwhelmingly controlled by wind forces. The semi-fixed sand dunes are those with a 15%–35% vegetation cover, and shifting sand appears in flecks with blown sand activities, though not extremely severe. The fixed sand dunes have good vegetation coverage of more than 35% of the dune surface and the blown sand is not remarkable. There is a complete difference in morphologies between sand shifting ones and the well vegetated ones under wind effects. For example, pyramid dunes appear in the shifting sand areas with multi-direction of winds and nearly equivalent wind forces of each.

Owing to the very long geological evolutional history of the mega deserts in western China, many kind of combinations in morphology existed by overlaid formations of the giant, the big and the middle-sized, also the small sand lands. Based on three different scales, we once produced a hierarchy for sand dunes in the Taklimakan Desert. (Chen, 1995): The biggest is that of the compound sand dunes forming the frame of the whole desert geomorphology; the middle sized scale is the simpler sand dunes which are situated on the mega ones as the completed sand dunes; the mini-scale is the ripples of the simple sand dunes. Although they are quite different in geomorphologic dimensions, the three classes are in a common or similar series of morphological appearance. Geomorphologic types with the same form can be treated as geometrical analogues with scaled sizes. Towards the dramatic mechanism in the development of the aeolian geomorphology in the three classes, disagreements exist among geomorphologists about desert research, even some think that there is no common place in developmental mechanism between the ripples and the sand dunes. Our viewpoint is that, they are all related to the turbulent nature of wind-sand flow, but only in different scales.

1) Compound morphologies of the shifting sand dunes

Compound morphology are giant sand dunes with secondary sand dunes overlaid on the first base, which are usually higher than 50 m and can even be higher than 500 m. We call those with a relative height greater than 100 m as compound sand dunes or sand mountains. This type cover about 60% of the shifting sand area in the whole country. Factors in their evolution include not only the plentiful sand sources, and relatively long development durations, but also the shearing effects of local relief to wind flows etc.

(1) Linear compound sand mountain. Situated east of the Taklimakan Desert, they feature mainly with a very long crest line perpendicular to its advancing direction, generally more than 10–20 km, more than 20 km as the longest with a width of 1–1.5 km. Their elevations generally are 100–200 m. The stretching line of the whole dune is considerably straight, and they are regularly aligned with no apparent Linguoid (curvature). If shown with a profile diagram, both flanks to the crest are very asymmetric, then the high, steep and obvious slipface and the upwind slope with much wider dimension generally take 80%–90% in width of the whole sand dune. Many sand dune chains of lowerclass overlaid on stratified, but their orientations are not the same with that of the compound dune itself, quite often with an angle lower than 30°. With very broad troughs separating the compound sand mountains, which are usually 1–3 km, while stretching a very long distance the compound dune is segmented with low sand dunes and their crest line is perpendicular to the main, therefore long belted and enclosed sunks generate, where the phreatic table is higher, somewhere with remains of ancient lakes left.

(2) Compounded barchans and compounded sand dune (sand mountains). They are primarily distributed in the Taklimakan Desert and the Badain Jaran Desert. Their alignment direction is perpendicular to the main direction of the prevailing wind or with an intersecting angle between 60°–80°. Giant barchan or sand dune chains are overlaid by layers of lower-class sand dune chains stretching aside in a general extent shorter than 2–3 km, and also with apparent chained barchanoid and Linguoid bodies, the height are usually be tween 50–100 m or so. In the Badain Jaran Desert, the higher ones are commonly 200–300 m high compared with those as low as 30–50 m. Moreover, this kind of sand dune is also featuring difference in the different local morphologies due to the variations occurring in their formation and evolution processes. Three kinds of types by primary

analysis recognized in the following: (a) It is apparently without very high slipfaces of the compound sand dune chains, the summit of the sand dune is the centre in geometry of the whole body, and both flanks of the slope are considerably symmetrical, and commonly with a height of 30–40 meters, stretching aside in 1–2 km or less. (b) Driven by winds, summit of the dune advances forth, toward the downwind slope so that asymmetry of both the flanks in morphology and obvious slip face appear, generally with a height scope of 50 meters around and stretching aside in 1–2 km. (c) The summit of the sand dune is right on the crest, the downwind slope is very apparent and high, with obvious asymmetry of both the flanks in morphology and generally with a height range in 50–100 m around and stretching aside in 2–3 km. Broad troughs exist between the compound sand dune chains, in which sand ridges or lengthways barchans are located (Fig. 2-14).

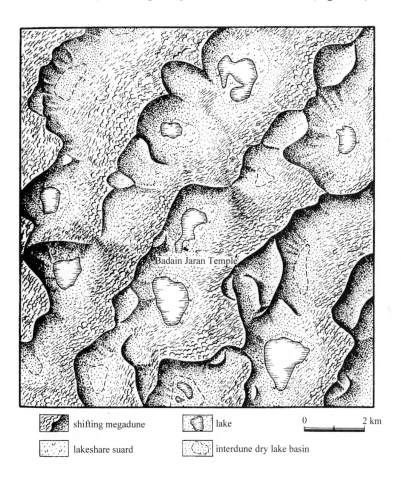

Fig. 2-14   Giant compound sand mountains located in the southeast Badain Jaran Desert

(3) Pyramid sand dunes (Sand Mountains). These are primarily distributed between Qiemo and Yutian in the south of the Taklimakan Desert, and those on northern slope of the Mazhatage in the northwest of this desert, and that in the margin of the Badain Jaran Desert, the Mingsha Mountains at Dunhuang in Gansu Province, and that in the south of the Kumtag Desert etc. They are called

"pyramid dunes" because they are morphologically very similar to the pyramids located on the riverside of the River in Africa. Furthermore, because general feature is a tetrahedron with four facets, it is also called tetrahedral sand dune. The characteristics specifically are: the titled facets are triangle-alike (with slopes generally in 25°–30°), the sharpened crest with narrow side lines, the dune is high, generally 50–100 m, even 100–200 m. Each facet usually represents a wind direction. There are generally three to four or five to six facets of the sand dunes located between Qiemo and Minfeng. This is because the pyramid sand dune is so high that it also becomes an obstacle for air flows, and changes the air flow direction, which may result in multi-facets on the neighboring pyramid sand dunes, nevertheless they are smaller than that formed by the prevailing wind. The pyramid sand dunes are individual and generally irregularly distributed with the exceptions of the irregularly ridges or hillocks one after another in long and narrow areas. Besides these, in some areas that sand dune chains overlaid densely, a few of the upraised and sharp tetrahedrons appear as a result of the crest line intersected of the sand dune chains, just looking like the summit of the pyramid but not a complete body as a pyramid sand dune. These can be seen in the northeast Tengger Desert as well as on both sides of the Hotan River in the Taklimakan Desert (Fig. 2-15).

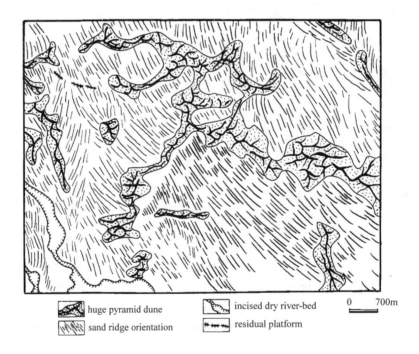

huge pyramid dune   sand ridge orientation   incised dry river-bed   residual platform   0   700m

Fig. 2-15　Diagram of pyramid sand dune in the east of Weituoke, Yutian of Xinjiang

(4) Compound lengthways sand ridges. They are primarily distributed in the southwest and central Taklimakan Deserts, within a scope of 82°–85°E. Their alignment direction is parallel to or having an intersecting angle smaller than 30° relative to the prevailing wind. The main characteristics are: There are many barchan chains stretching very long over the base of the ridge. Their length is generally between 10–20 km, with 45 km as the longest. Their heights are 50–80 m,

also longer ones are 30–80 m. The width is usually in 0.5–1 km, and the troughs, in which some low sand ridges or sand dune chains are located, generally have a width of 400–600 m (Fig. 2-16).

(5) Dome sand dunes. They are primarily located in the former southern course of the Tarim River, which is north of the Taklimakan Desert, northeast of the dried up river course of the Keliya River in the lower reach, and south of the Ulan Buh Desert, etc. Their main morphologic features are: Both flanks of the dunes are symmetric, many arc-shaped sand dunes of the lower-classes are overlaid, no apparent high and stiff slipface; the ratio of the length to width of the compound body is roughly 1, with a general height between 40–60 m. The horizontal plane is a dome-like circle or oval. They are individually irregular and randomly located, some connections between them exist but all with distinct dome features.

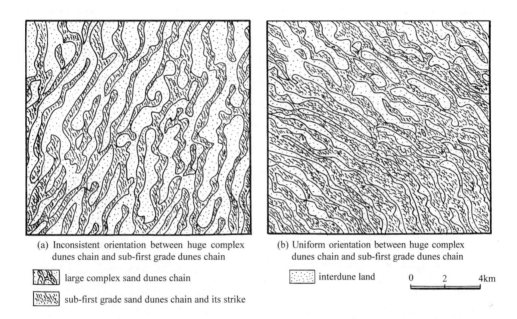

(a) Inconsistent orientation between huge complex dunes chain and sub-first grade dunes chain

(b) Uniform orientation between huge complex dunes chain and sub-first grade dunes chain

large complex sand dunes chain

sub-first grade sand dunes chain and its strike

interdune land

0   2   4km

Fig. 2-16   Diagram showing giant compound sand dune in the central part of the Taklimakan Desert
(a) Compound barchan; (b) Alignments of the sand dues both underneath and the lower-class overlaid

2) Simple morphologies of shifting sand dunes

Simple morphology indicates lower sand dunes with simple morphologies. These kinds of dunes are extensively located in the margins of the big deserts in the West, the sand lands in the East or on the surface of the mega-scale compound sand dunes (including the troughs of them) in China. There are four forms here:

(1) Barchans and barchan chains. This is the most essential morphology of the shifting sand dunes. They are extensively located west, north and east of the Taklimakan Desert, in the Kuruk Khoum Desert, the Tengger Desert, the Mu Us Sandy Land and the margin of the Badain Jaran Desert, in the flood plains surrounding the Qaidam Basin etc. Their apparent characteristics are the

crescent shape in a planar projection, and the Linguoids on both sides of the sand dune body stretched by wind formed by the transverse air vortices with a vertical axis. The intersecting angle (called the Linguoid broadness of barchan) of the Linguoid alignment varies locally. It depends on the strength of the local prevailing winds. The stronger the wind is, the smaller the intersecting angle is and also the Linguoid broadness will be. There are two inclining slopes in asymmetry as the morphology of the dune profile, the upwind one is the protrudent and gentle, with slopeness within 5°–20°, the slipface is crescented and steep with an inclining angle of 28°–34°. These kinds of dunes are not high, generally less than 1–5 m, primarily located in the margin of the deserts.

The barchan chains were formed with plenty of sand source, and connected by intensively located barchans. The heights are generally 1–5 m, and the morphology varies somehow based on the local wind regime. In areas with unimodal wind regime, sand dune chains keep themselves in morphology with crescent remains of the former individual sand dune. Nevertheless, in an area affected interactively by winds of two opposite directions, the sand dune chains are comparatively straight along, featuring in a complex profile of the crestal configurations with backward movements.

(2) Barchan sand ridges. They are primarily distributed in the southern Tuoclark Desert on the Kashi delta, the Katekhoum between Ruoqiang and Qiemo, northwest Minqin and the western the Qaidam Basin. They are also located densely, with comb-shaped compound features, in the troughs on the lee areas of the giant compound sand dune chains that are overlaid on the ancient alluvial plains north of the Taklimakan Desert. Generally they are 3–5 m high. They are formed by diagonally intersected winds of the prevailing and the secondary; the angle-intersected slant of wind directions is in certain degrees. When the intersected winds take effects on the barchan sand ridges, certain parts of the sand ridges often stretch downwind with the prevailing one. As long as the process continues, the barchans forms on the lee become vague or even disappear, so that the ridges have only one flank left to be longitudinal dunes.

(3) Grid sand dunes and grid sand dune chains. They are primarily distributed over the Tengger Desert, the Hobq Desert and the Hedong Desert in Ningxia, etc. Generally with heights of 5–20 m, they are formed with winds from two directions which are mutually perpendicular. Sand dune chain (the main transverse) is formed by the stronger wind; the smaller transverse (sub-ridge) is formed by the secondary and ephemeral wind with a direction perpendicular to the main. Grid-like or square shapes dominated by their intersection. In some areas grid sand dune chains mostly featuring a chain are results of stronger force of the main wind.

(4) Imbricate sand dune lineups. This kind of sand dune is extensively located in the northwest and west of the Taklimakan Desert. Its feature is: crowded lineups of sand dunes but not an individual, and without apparent troughs so that the foot of the leeward slope is just in front of the upwind slope of the next dune, multiple overlaid in an imbricate appearance. Morphologically from a profile of an individual, the sand dune crest is perpendicular to the main wind direction, and the

linguoid stretch and are connected with the upwind slope of the next dune forward, in this way downwind stretching ridge between sand dune chains is formed.

3) Vegetation fixed and semi-fixed sand dunes

(1) Sand ridges. This is one of the most basic forms of the fixed and semi-fixed sand dune. It is extensively located, with the most distributed in the Gurbantünggüt Desert. A considerable distribution is found in the Onqin Daga Sandy Land and the Horqin Sandy Land. The genesis and evolution here are much different from these in the circumstances of transforming from barchan ridges to sand ridges in the bared regions. They are in a nebkhas origin. Most nebkhas were reformed as a plait-shape sand dune along the resultant direction of the two wind directions intersected with small angle (less than 30°), then driven by the wind, these plait-shape sand dunes linked together to a sand dune ridge. While in stretching and development, nearby ridges were mutually connected and branches-alike sand ridges appeared. The sand ridges can come to a length range from hundreds to more than 10 thousands m, and a height of 10–25 m and the lower ones in 5–10 m high. Though mini asymmetry in the section diagram can be found, there is no significant difference from that of the upwind and the lee slopes of mobile sand dunes. Taking the sand ridges stretching from the south to north of the Gurbantünggüt Desert as an example, slopeness of the west side is generally 15°–24°, but in the east 19°–28°. There is a slightly curved surface on the ridge's top, some of them the crestal lines swing somehow.

(2) Parabolic dunes. They are mainly located in the Mu Us Sandy Land, in the Onqin Daga Sandy Land and the Horqin Sandy Land. It is most typically in the Gahaielesu Sandy Land of the Xi Ujimqin Qi in the northeast of Onqin Daga Sandy Land (Fig. 2-17). This landforms characteristics are just the reversed barchans in landform characteristics, that is both the linguoids are upwind, the upwind slope is gentle flat and concave, but the leeward slope is steep and protruded so that it is much like a parabola if projected on a plane.

Vegetation takes a very important role in the genesis of parabolic dunes. In the arid steppe zone, with good conditions of water content, plants generally grow well along the lower part (margins of both flanks), blanking wind forces by which the sand dune shifts, and keeping it settle down. Development of blowouts occurring on the upwind slope dedicates to the transforming of the sand dune as a whole into a morphology of a reversed barchan. Hollowing out results in enlargement of blowout on the upwind slope and stretching of the sand arms, which make the sand dune into a shape of hair-clip. Once the crest is eroded out, it will become parallel and fixed sand ridges eventually. This kind of sand ridges is no more than several meters.

(3) Beam nest form dunes. They are mainly located in the Gurbantünggüt Desert, the small deserts to the north of the Lang Mountains, the Mu Us Sandy Land, the Onqin Daga Sandy Land and the Horqin Sandy Land, generally with curvy uplifted sand ridge and concave sand nest, a morphology featured in densely fixed or semi-fixed barchans or barchan chains by vegetation with

herbage and bushes. In some areas such as in the Horqin Sandy Land, morphological confusion occurred after reclamation, and then former landscape was replaced by sand drifts.

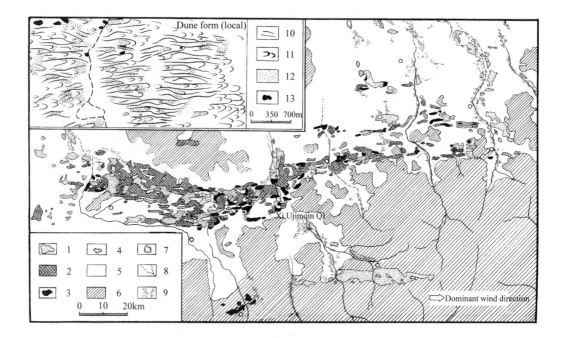

Fig. 2-17　The parabolic sand dunes in the Gahaielesu Sandy Land

1. Fixed dunes；2. Semi-fixed dunes；3. Shifting dunes；4. Giant blowouts；5. Waved highlands；6. Mountains and hills；
7. Lakes; 8. Rivers; 9. Marshes; 10. Linear dunes; 11. Parabolic sand dunes; 12. Shifting sand sheets; 13. Plashes from blowouts

(4) Alveolate sand dunes. They are mainly located in the southwest of the Gurbantünggüt Desert, the southeast of the Onqin Daga Sandy Land and the Hulun Buir Sandy Land. Morphological difference from the grid-like dunes is that they don't have stable sand ridges, and the sunks in a circular or oval shape and the surrounding edges (ridges) of the sunks alignment are directionless. The distribution is individual and scarce, or appearing in clustered collections, as that in the Hulun Buir Sandy Land. In the central and southern Gurbantünggüt Desert, hillock composed with very dense and much higher alveolate sand dunes and then compounded ridges with alveolate sand dunes are formed, secondary sand ridges on both sides of the main ridge spread at right angle to the main ones.

(5) Nebkhas. They are the most widespread and familiar of the fixed and semi-fixed dunes. They are located in places of the Chinese deserts and sandy lands that have good water conditions and plants well grown, and formed with lowdown and deposited sand by plants obstruction on the way, generally, they are named with the plant species such as the *Tamarisk* nebkhas, the *Nitraria Tangutorum* nebkhas. If viewed in a plane, they are circular or oval; not high, usually in 1–5 m, some individuals are up to 10 m. Nebkhas are the common morphological symbols of desertification on steppes, and appear after reclamations in the northern area of the Yinshan Mountains in Inner

Mongolia. Intensively distributed *Caragana* nebkhas appeared after the leeward steppe was reclaimed. After the appearance of nebkhas, sand mass enrichment begins and evolutionally a flat and waved sandland appears after the death of the shrubs.

4) Wind-erosion landforms

Wind erosion landforms develop in areas with earth sediments (clays, light clays) or loose rocks (such as the shales and interlaced shales with mudrocks). They are primarily located at mountain cuts or passes that have powerful wind, such as the famous Wuerhe wind castle located at the mountain cut in the western Junggar Basin. Wind erosion landforms at the Thirteen Cabins in eastern Xinjiang are also near a mountain pass. There are two categories.

(1) Yardangs. They generally develop in areas of earthy depositions. In Desert Geomorphology (Cooke et al., 1993), they are defined as "aeolian geomorphology stretching downwind, a smooth facet of the upwind, a lengthening and tipped leeward facet" (Fig. 2-18). Typical Yardangs are those with scarp upwind facet with concave pits on its lower part abraded by wind. There are many descriptions of the various Yardang morphologies in modern works. Its concepts and meanings have already been expanded; they are simply regarded as the combination of two morphologies: wind eroded earthy rocks and wind eroded lowlands. Their alignment direction is parallel with the prevailing wind direction, and the pedestal rock height is 2–10 m or so, such as those downstream of the Shule River. Yardangs have developed extensively, but are not very typical in the northern slope of the Yinshan Mountains and the aeolian desertified land surrounding the Onqin Daga Sandy Land. Therefore we call them wind-eroded badlands (Zhu et al., 1994). In the lop Nur Depression, the Yardangs surface is covered with salt and forms a square mount. Because of their white color, they are called "White Dragon Block" landforms.

Fig. 2-18   Typical Yardangs

(2) Wind castles. They generally develop in areas with underlying bedrocks (piedmont), and

Wuerhe in the north of Kelamayi in Xinjiang is the most famous. It was formed on strata with interlaid sandstone and sandy mudstone from the Cretaceous, and after being eroded by runoffs in the past, the erosion continued with wind to create the rolling and rugged land surface. Various kinds of peculiar landscape resulted from the different erosion patterns of these rocks, just like different building shapes in a castle. Therefore they are called "wind castles". South of the wind castles, a similar landscape called the Thirteen cabins can be found in eastern Xinjiang. They also appear frequently in the northwest Qaidam Basin.

5) Gobi

This is known as the gravel hunger (desert). Based on its origins, the two kinds of gobi desert are divided into wind eroded gobi and deposited gobi. Distributed over flood plains in the mountain front of arid areas, flat in appearances, deposited gobi are the remains of the selective erosion process by wind on the original flood sediments. Pebbles in the deposited gobi are different and perfectly rounded. The eroded gobi are distributed in areas of stripped peneplains and wave-like highlands with the strongest erosion process. Rolling in topographical features, the terrain uplifts and falldowns may simultaneously overlay the different strata with different heights, aspects and slopeness. Its pebbles are relatively smaller in volume than that of the deposited gobi, with sharpened tips and side edges. This kind of gobi is most focused in eastern Xinjiang, in the bordering areas of Gansu-Xinjiang, and in the boundary of Sino-Mongolia. In places where precipitation conditions are extremely rare, "black gobi" exists in a feature of numerous ventifacts or broken pebbles on the land surface，often apparent sharpened side edges and tip points, and black-shineness varnishes. Contemporary researches on the desert varnish are rare. Some regard it as the result of chronically oxidation rocks, manganese and other minerals under intense sunshine. Some deem it as the key function of bacteria's catalyzing. The desert patinas only exist in the land surface no deeper than 10–20 cm. For example, near the Gongpo Spring of the northwest Hexi Corridor, desert varnish was found on the upside of a stone buried about 20 cm deep, but the downside has already obviously diminished. Stones in a depth of 50 cm，there is no dark patinas all around.

2.2.2.3 Sand dune movements

1) Modes of sand dune movements

Located in the eastern and northwest Taklimakan Desert, the Qaidam Basin and the Alxa region, driven by a unitary regime of the northwest or northeast winds, sand dunes are in an advance-dominated mode, or advance with marginal retreat. Due to effects from the dual directions of the northwest and northeast winds, as well as seasonal variations, the advancing mode is characterized by a "zigzag" pattern with the sand dune moving north and northwest of the Qaidam Desert. In the eastern desert areas of China, since the two wind directions are opposite each other, sand dune movement is always in a mode of advancing back and forth. In winter, sand dunes advance southeastward under the northwest winds' control; in summer they move back a greant deal under the influence of the southeast winds, since the southeast winds are weaker than their counterpart, and therefore do not equal the effects of the northwest winds. Generally speaking, sand dunes in this region are slowly advancing southeastward.

2) Sand dune movement rate

Sand dunes near playas in the Gurbantünggüt Desert and the Tengger Desert, in the northwest of the Ulan Buh Desert, in the majority of the Mu Us Sandy Land, the Onqin Daga Sandy Land, the Horqin Sandy Land and the Hulun Buir Sandy Land, both water and vegetation conditions are good, so that the most sand dunes are fixed or semi-fixed and moving slowly. Rapid movement appears only in areas with drifting sand source as the result of vegetation exhausted. Also, in the vast interior of the Taklimakan Desert and the Badain Jaran Desert, though sand dunes are barren, high and dense, the moving intensity is small, and annual advancement distance is no more than 1 m. However, higher speeds appear in areas of smaller sand dunes, especially lower barchans on barren and flat surfaces with sand-pebble source, the annual advancement rate is up to 50 m. Based on the field measurements along the highway in the Tarim Desert, barchans with a height of 1–1.5 meters or rudimental barchans on the Tarim River plain area move toward southern-southwest 5–8 m a year. Sand dunes of the same kind and same heights but on a coarse-sand and flat surface in the hinterland of the desert, the annual-mean moving speed is up to 7–13 m, sand dunes with the maximum of 20 m a year was found at wind gorge (Fig. 2-19).

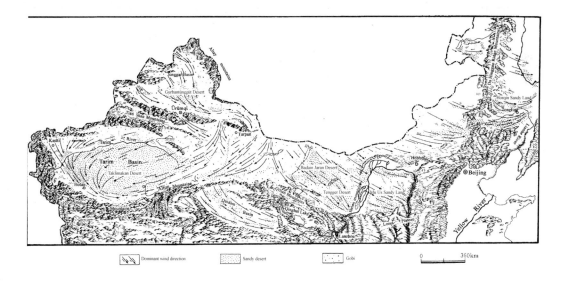

Fig. 2-19   Flux fields and moving directions of sand dunes in northern China

According to annual moving speed of various-sized sand dunes in every site of the sandy areas, we categorize them into four types.

The slow type: The annual-mean advancing speed is smaller than 1 m. The sand dunes include those located in the interior of the Taklimakan Desert, in the central part of the Badain Jaran Desert, and some areas of giant sand mounts in the Kumtag Desert.

The moderate type: The annual-mean advancing speed is between 1–5 m. The sand dunes include those located in the northwest and central part of the Taklimakan Desert, sand dune chains in the Badain Jaran Desert excluding the sand-mount area, and including most of those in the Tengger Desert, most of the Ulan Buh Desert and areas to its east, and those nearby some oases in the Hexi Corridor, etc.

The fast type: The annual-mean advancing speed is 6–10 m. They include sand dunes nearby some oases in the south of the Taklimakan Desert, those nearby the Minqin Oasis in the Hexi Corridor, some lower sand dunes located in the southeast of the Mu Us Sandy Land, sand dunes in the Tengger Desert, the Badain Jaran Desert, and those in the east of the Hobq Desert and the northwest of the Horqin Sandy Land, etc.

The very fast type: The annual-mean advancing speed of the sand dunes is above 20 m, such as the small barchans in the southeast and southwest margin of the Taklimakan Desert.

2.3　Hydrology

2.3.1　Runoff features in desert regions

Runoff in arid desert regions is formed directly and indirectly by precipitation, so the long-term average runoff depth of rivers is consistent with annual precipitation and decreases gradually from southeast to northwest China. Therefore, annual runoff near the ocean is higher than in the inland and is higher in mountains than in the plains. Especially, the runoff on windward slopes of mountains is far more than that of adjacent plains and basins. According to previous studies, about 20% of annual precipitation in mountainous areas around inland basins can be transformed into the stream-flow. The distribution of runoff has obvious regional and vertical variations. Even in the same region, the annual runoff is also affected by climatic and physical geographic factors. Based on runoff isoline of 10, 50, 200 and 800 mm in northern China (Fig. 2-20), the desert regions in China can be divided into four zones, including runoffless zone, dry zone, low-runoff zone and transition zone.

2.3.1.1　Runoffless zone

Runoffless zones are mainly distributed in the Taklimakan Desert, the Gurbantünggüt Desert, the Turpan Basin, the border of Gansu and Xinjiang, the Qaidam Basin, the Badain Jaran Desert, the Tengger Desert and the Hexi Corridor etc. In these regions, no runoff can be formed due to sparse precipitation and strong evaporation and infiltration.

2.3.1.2 Dry zone

In these regions, the annual runoff depth is less than 10 mm, and amounts of annual precipitation is about 50–200 mm. Dry zones occur in piedmont plains outside the runoffless region and occupy most parts is plain areas.

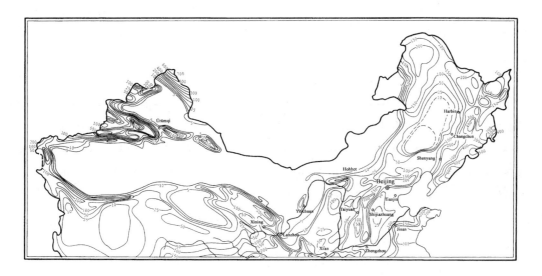

Fig. 2-20　The isoline of annual runoff depth in the desert regions, northern China

2.3.1.3 Low-runoff zone

The annual runoff depth in the low-runoff zone ranges from 10 mm to 50 mm; this corresponds to the semi-arid zone which has a precipitation of 200–400 mm. It is situated in the middle parts of the Song-Liao Plain, the upper reaches of the Liao River, the southern edge of the Inner Mongolian Plateau, most parts of the Loess Plateau, and the low mountains and hills in the northern and western Qinghai-Tibet Plateau. The coefficient of annual runoff in these regions is about 0.1, and in some areas is even less than 0.05.

2.3.1.4 Transition zone

Annual runoff depth of the transition zone ranges from 50 mm to 200 mm, which corresponds to semi-arid and semi-humid zones whose precipitation is about 400–600 mm. This zone includes part of the Songnen Plain, the Sanjiang Plain, the plain at the lower reach of the Liao River, the North China Plain, most parts of Shaanxi and Shanxi provinces, the middle part of the Qinghai-Tibet Plateau, and the mountainous areas of the Qilian Mountains, the Tianshan Mountains and western Xinjiang. The coefficient of annual runoff is generally 0.1 and can reach 0.2–0.3 in mountainous areas.

The seasonal distribution of annual runoff mainly depends on the features of the river's nourishment sources and its change laws. In northwest China, there are high mountains covered with snow and glaciers, so in these regions rivers are mainly fed by meltwater from glaciers, while in the eastern semi-arid regions, most rivers are fed by precipitation. Therefore, the seasonal distribution of runoff mainly depends on the seasonal distribution of precipitation.

In winter (from December to February), there is less rain and snow in most parts of the regions, therefore it is the low-flow period of the rivers. For most rivers, the runoff amount in winter only occupies 4%–6% of annual runoff, except for some rivers that are mainly fed by groundwater. In spring (from March to May), with the air temperature gradually rising from south to north, the river runoff begins to increase. The amount of spring runoff only occupies 6%–8% of annual total runoff. Where the rate of air temperature rising is far more than that of runoff, drought will occur frequently in early spring due to stronger evaporation and less soil moisture. However, in the Altay region of Xinjiang, due to more precipitation and early melt of accumulative snow in this season, the runoff could reach above 20% of annual total runoff. In summer (from June to August), with increasing precipitation and meltwater of glaciers and snow, most rivers enter the flood season. According to statistics, the runoff in most rivers in this season could occupy over 80% of annual runoff in semi-arid regions of northern China and 70%–85% in northwest China. Especially for rivers mainly fed by meltwater of glaciers at the southern edge of the Tarim Basin, the runoff in this season could occupy more than 90% of annual total. In autumn (from September to November), the runoff in most regions occupies about 15%–20% for the entire year.

Annual variations degree of natural annual runoff can be expressed by the coefficient of annual runoff variation (C_v) and the ratio of measured maximum to minimum values. Due to natural function of runoff in those rivers fed by meltwater of glaciers in Northwest China, the C_v values of these rivers have no obvious differences. For example, the C_v values of some rivers on the northern slope of the Tianshan Mountains in Xinjiang such as the Tekes River, the Kuytun River, the Jinggou River and the Manas River, the Kunmalik River, the Tailan River and the Muzat River on the southern slope are less than 0.15. To those rivers on the western part of the Qilian Mountains, which are mainly fed by meltwater of glaciers (such as the Qamalung River, the Hongshuiba River, the Dang River and the Haltang River), their C_v values are below 0.25. There are some rivers fed by glacier meltwater in Qinghai Province such as the Golmud River and Nomhon River, their C_v values are about 0.2, which is less than one third of that of rivers fed by precipitation on the Taihang Mountains and Yanshan Mountains.

The C_v values of some rivers in the middle Inner Mongolia and northern part of the east semi-arid zone are more than 1.0 generally and the maximum could exceed 1.2. The C_v values of some rivers in the Tarim Basin and the Qaidam Basin are over 0.8. The C_v values of some rivers in mountainous areas of Northwest China and the Yili River Basin in Xinjiang are 0.15–0.20.

2.3.2 Hydrology of rivers and lakes in desert regions

2.3.2.1 River hydrology in the inland region of northwest China

Rivers in the inland region of northwest China can be divided into 9 types according to their main recharge patterns and annual variation in runoff (Fig. 2-21).

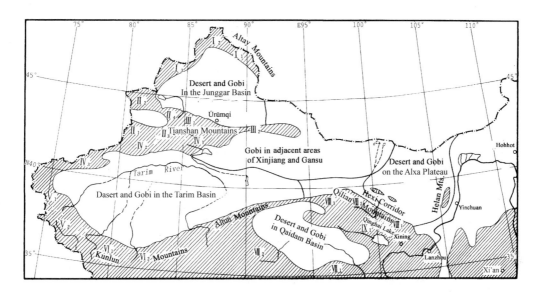

Fig. 2-21　Dynamic types of rivers in arid regions of Northwest China

(1) Altay type (I). This type of river is located in the mountainous areas of the Altay Mountains and Tacheng Region. The main rivers include the Ertix River, the Ulungur River, the Haba River and the Emin River, etc. They have a spring flood period caused by seasonal meltwater from accumulative snow. Flood period occurs between April through June every year.

(2) Yili type (II). This type of river occurs in the mountainous regions in the Yili River Basin in Xinjiang, including the Kukesu River, the Hashi River, the Künes River, the Piliqing River and other tributaries at the upper reaches.

(3) Type of North Slope of the Tianshan Mountains (III). This type of river mainly occurs on the northern slope of the Tianshan Mountains (except the Yili River Basin). There have more than 30 rivers, including the Manas River, the Gurt River, the Kuytun River, the Bortala River, the Kaiken River, the Sikeshu River, the Hutubi River, the Jing River, the Ürümqi River, the Shuimugou River, and the Mulei River, etc. Their annual runoff distribution is dominated by summer flooding, but the concentration degree is far smaller than those of the west Kulun type. There exists small spring flood peak resulting from some meltwater of seasonally accumulative snow and ice in rivers.

(4) Type of southern slope of the Tianshan Mountains (IV). This type of rivers occur on the southern slope of the Tianshan Mountains. There are many rivers, such as the Aksu River, the

Weigan River, the Kuche River, the Dina River, the Kaidu River, and the Tarim River. The runoff of these rivers is concentrated in summer. However, they have some differences between eastern and western parts.

(5) Pamier type (V). This type of river mainly occurs at the regions of the Pamier Plateau, and the main rivers include the Yarkant River, the Tizhinapu River, the Gaizhi River, the Kezhi River, etc. The hydrological dynamics show that there exists a 20-day spring flood in these rivers, which is favourable for farming.

(6) West Kunlun type (VI). This type of river mainly occurs on the northern slope of the Kunlun Mountains at the southern edge of the Tarim Basin. They have about 43 rivers, including the Yurungkax River, the Kalahashi River, the Keriya River, the Pishan River, the Qira River, the Qiemo River, the Niya River, the Ruoqiang River, and the Milan River, etc. In summer, the runoff of these rivers reaches their maximum, accounting for 70%–80% of annual total runoff or more.

(7) East-Kunlun type (VII). This type of rivers mainly occur at the southern edge of the Qaidam Basin, including the Golmud River, the Narengele River, the Urt Moron River and the Qagan Us River, etc. The runoff has a low concentration degree, and their annual distribution is uniform.

(8) Qilian Mountains type (VIII). This type of rivers occur on the north slope of the Qilian Mountains, and there are about 56 rivers in the Shiyang River, the Heihe River and the Sulehe River basins. The dynamic features of these rivers are that there have a dominant summer flow and a small spring floods.

(9) Qinghai Lake type (IX). This type of river mainly occurs within the inland basin of the Qinghai Lake. The rivers have some prominent features. For example, the daily change of runoff is large and their flood period is concentrated in the summer season.

The dynamic characteristics of various rivers are listed in Table 2-1.

2.3.2.2　River hydrology in semi-arid regions

The river systems in semi-arid regions include the Yellow River Basin, the Liao River Basin, the Heilong Jiang River Basin and some inland rivers and lakes in Inner Mongolia and the Ordos Plateau. Taking the rivers in Inner Mongolian Plateau as an example, their hydrological features are as follows.

The drainage area of inland rivers in the Inner Mongolian Plateau is $30\times10^4\,km^2$, which consists of many rivers such as the the Wulagai River, the Xilin Gol River, the Balaguer River, the Gaolihan River, the Tabu River, the Baying River, the Xar Moron River and the Aibugai River. Without high mountains in the semi-arid region, there is no windward-slope precipitation and glacier meltwater, and therefore the river density in this region is minimum. The rivers are usually short and their catchment basin is small. For most rivers, their length is less than 400 km and their catchment basin is less than 7,000 km^2. In general, these rivers become sinuous after entering the plains. Water can overflow the riverbanks during flood periods and finally concentrate in some inland lakes and

Table 2-1 The main characteristics of river types in the arid regions of China

Types	Typical river	Stations	Area (km²)	Flood period	Monthly runoff amount occupied proportion of the annual total (%)											
					1	2	3	4	5	6	7	8	9	10	11	12
Altay	Kuyirtesi River	Fuyun	1,965	Late spring	0.85	0.70	0.85	3.2	18.7	33.7	19.3	10.5	5.8	3.6	1.8	1.0
	Haba River	Kalatashi	6,111	Late spring	2.0	1.8	2.0	6.1	19.3	26.2	16.1	10.0	6.5	4.6	3.0	2.4
	Kalanggur River	Kalanggur	349	Early spring	1.2	1.1	3.0	12.7	36.6	16.8	9.3	6.5	4.9	3.4	2.5	2.0
Yili	Piliqing River	Piliqing	794	Spring-summer	1.6	3.5	4.0	16.1	21.5	15.7	10.0	7.1	5.6	5.1	4.2	3.6
	Kukesu River	Kukesu	5,379	Spring-summer	1.9	1.7	1.7	3.9	10.5	20.0	22.9	19.0	9.4	4.2	2.8	2.0
	Gongnas River	Zeketai	5,380	Spring-summer	4.6	4.7	6.3	9.9	12.6	11.9	10.8	9.5	8.4	8.2	7.3	5.8
	Hashi River	Wulasitai	5,081	Spring-summer	2.4	2.1	2.3	5.3	11.8	19.7	20.8	15.8	8.1	4.9	3.4	2.9
North slope of the Tianshan Mountains	Manas River	Kensiwate	4,637	Summer	1.6	1.3	1.4	2.1	4.8	16.0	28.3	25.9	9.8	4.1	2.6	2.1
	Guxiang River	Baiji	431	Summer and small spring	1.3	1.4	1.8	5.7	17.5	17.9	20.4	17.6	7.3	3.6	3.2	2.3
South slope of the Tianshan Mountains	Kaidu River	Dashankou	19,074	Summer and spring	3.5	3.3	3.6	8.4	10.5	14.1	16.4	15.0	9.6	6.8	5.0	3.8
	Muzhati River	Ahebulong	2,859	Summer	1.5	1.5	1.3	2.1	6.7	9.3	29.2	28.2	12.1	4.0	2.3	1.8
	Tailan River	Tailan	1,324	Summer	1.8	1.5	2.3	2.7	6.4	16.3	25.8	25.4	9.1	3.9	2.8	2.0
Pamir	Kezhi River	Yashi	5,196	Summer and small spring	1.9	1.9	2.1	5.4	10.8	25.1	21.7	13.0	9.7	3.8	2.6	2.0
	Tizhinapu River	Yuzhimenleke	5,389	Summer	1.2	1.3	1.8	1.9	4.9	19.5	31.2	24.7	8.4	2.3	1.5	1.3
Western Kunlun	Yurungkax River	Tongguziluoke	14,575	Summer	0.8	0.9	1.0	1.6	3.4	13.3	34.5	32.3	7.9	2.1	1.2	1.0
	Keriya	Maimaitilangan	7,358	Summer	2.3	2.4	2.6	3.4	5.6	15.0	27.3	24.3	7.8	3.9	3.0	2.4
Eastern Kunlun	Golmud River	Golmud	18,649	Summer and spring	15.8			23.6			35.3			25.3		
	Chahanwusu River	Chahanwusu	4,434	Spring and summer	6.6			40.3			34.8			18.3		
Qilian	Xiying River	Jiutiaoling	1,077	Summer and small spring	1.2	1.1	1.8	5.2	11.1	14.2	20.9	20.0	12.9	6.2	3.2	2.2
	Taolai River	Binggou	6,883	Summer	6.0	5.9	5.3	6.3	6.7	11.1	14.8	15.3	10.5	7.1	6.0	5.0
	Qamalung River	Changmabu	10,961	Summer	2.6	2.3	2.9	4.5	6.7	9.9	24.8	25.5	9.5	5.1	3.6	2.6
Inland of Qinghai Lake	Yikewulan River	Gangcha	1,442	Summer and small autumn	1.2			19.1			55.9			29.8		

Note: some rivers only have seasonal observation data; they are the winter, spring, summer and autumn discharges successively.

wetlands at the terminals, including the Tenge Nur, the Qagan Nur, the Dalai Nur and the Huangqi Lakes, etc. Some rivers disappear in steppes and deserts. Precipitation is a main recharge source, which occupies over 60% of total annual runoff usually. Recharge ratio of groundwater is small, accounting for less than 10% of annual runoff. Strictly speaking, most of the rivers in arid regions are a result of seasonal streams.

2.3.2.3　River hydrology in semi-humid regions

Climatic variations in semi-humid regions have obvious effects on river hydrology. Due to instability of both climatic and hydrological systems, the response of river hydrology to environmental change is very sensitive. Under the impact of a given background of physical geography, the rivers in semi-humid regions have the following features: ① Variation of annual runoff is large, and thus causes many flood and drought disasters in different seasons. ② Coefficient of runoff in plain areas is small while on windward slope of some mountains is large. ③ Runoff usually is concentrated in summer season, while runoff in spring is small. ④ There exists contradiction between water supply and demand. ⑤ sediment delivery is large and difference among areas is obvious, et al.

Due to flat and wide topography after river flowing into plains, flow speed decreases suddenly and a lot of sediment deposited in river course, this makes most of the river courses above the ground. Under such conditions, the river courses will occasionally change their route. So these abandoned river courses can supply abundant materials for aeolian desertification. The plain rivers in semi-humid regions have the following hydrological features: ① runoff-producing process is slow and runoff yield is small. ② Sediments are deposited along the river courses. ③ Surface water can recharge into groundwater directly, but groundwater can't enter into rivers courses. ④ River runoff is closely related with drought and flood disasters.

2.3.2.4　River hydrology in high-cold regions of Qinghai–Tibet Plateau

The Qinghai-Tibet Plateau is located at the middle latitude, with an area of $138\times10^4\,km^2$ and average elevation above 4,000 m, and surrounded by high mountains. The special cold-high environments were formed due to high and steep topography. The rivers in this region could be divided into external and interior drainage systems. The former belong to the Pacific Ocean and the Indian Ocean water systems. The latter belong to the river system of south Tibet and the Qiangtang Plateau of north Tibet. Most of the interior rivers have terminal lakes. According to the incomplete statistics, there exist 20 rivers with a total catchment basin over 10,000 km^2; among them the biggest one is the catchment basin of the Yalung Zangbo River.

The Qinghai-Tibet Plateau is called the "water tower of Asia". Besides the Yellow River and Yangtze River, many international rivers originate from it. The Yellow River, the Yangtze River and the Lancang River belong to the Pacific Ocean river system, while the Yalung Zangbo River, the Nu River, the Yiluowadi River and the Shiquan River etc. belong to the Indian Ocean river system.

The total catchment basin of interior water systems is about $61 \times 10^4 \, km^2$, among them the inland river systems in North Tibet (Xizang) occupy $58.56 \times 10^4 \, km^2$. The precipitation in this region is small and evaporation is strong, so surface water yield is small. Most of the rivers concentrated in the southeast Tibet are permanent streams, while most of the rivers in the northern and northwest Tibetan Plateau are intermittent. The biggest inland river catchment in the southern Tibetan Plateau is Yangzuoyong Cuo-Pulayon Cuo-Zhegu Cuo Basin (with a catchment basin of 9,980 km^2).

The rivers in the Tibetan Plateau are mainly fed by precipitation, glaciers and snow melt-water and groundwater. Some rivers such as the Jinsha River, the Lancang River and the Nu River in high mountains and valleys of East Tibet are flowing from northwest to southeast and across several climatic zones. River source regions are covered by large area of glacial deposits and weathering materials with the thick meadow and strong infiltration, so most of rainfall and meltwater could seep into the underground, therefore rivers replenished from groundwater can occupy over 50% of the total runoff. Rivers in the gorge region are mainly fed by rainfall and groundwater, but meltwater also occupies a certain proportion. The Yalung Zangbo River flows from west to east and suddenly turns to south at the Nanjiabawa Peak. So at its upper and middle reaches, groundwater is the main water sources, while at its lower reaches the replenishment is a mixture of rainfall and meltwater. In the rainstorm areas located in grand canyon, the replenishment is rainfall. As far as the whole river is concerned, the replenishment is a mixture of groundwater, rainfall and meltwater. Most rivers at the North and Northwest Tibet Plateau belong to groundwater-fed type due to special climatic and geomorphologic conditions. The replenishment ratio of groundwater in the Langqinzang Bu River occupies 50% of total runoff and in the Sungezang Bu River is more than 70%. The rivers in South and Southeast Tibet regions at the southern slope of Himalayas are mainly replenished by rainfall because of plentiful precipitation. For example, at the main tributaries of the Yarlung Zangbo River, such as the lower reaches of the Danlong Qu, the Danba Qu, the Chaou Qu and the Xi Baxia Qu, rainwater replenishment ratio is more than 80%.

2.3.2.5　Lake hydrology

The total area of inland lakes in northwest China, Inner Mongolian Plateau and the Ordos Plateau is $1.7 \times 10^4 \, km^2$, which occupies above 20% of total lake area in China. There are more than 400 lakes with an area more than 1 km^2. The lakes with area of over 1,000 km^2 include the Qinghai Lake, the Bosten Lake, the Qarhan salt Lake and the Hulun Lake. Bigger lakes are the Burulto Lake, the Ngoring Lake, the Ulan ul Lake, the Har Nur, the Gyaring Lake, the Ayakkum Lake, the Sayrim Lake, the Tuosu Lake, the Ulansu Hai, the Dali Nur, the Jiele Kol, the Dai Hai, the Huangqi Hai, the Hongjian Nur. etc (Table 2-2). There are many inland lakes formed in arid basins due to dry climate and less precipitation. Some lakes often become terminal of inland river system. Some lakes were developed as salt or saline lakes due to less surface runoff replenishment, strong evaporation and water concentration. The lakes developed in sandy desert regions are small and shallow, so lake

Table 2-2　Main characteristics of lakes in desert regions of China

Lake name	Region	location N	location E	Altitude (m)	Areas (Km²)	Depth(m) Max.	Depth(m) Average	Volume (10⁸m³)	Remarks
Qinghai Lake	Qinghai	36°40′	100°23′	3,196.0	4,635.0	28.7	18.4	854.0	Max. saline Lake
Lop Nur	Xinjiang	40°20′	90°15′	768.0	(3,006.0)				Dry
Hulun Nur	In. Mon.	48°57′	117°23′	545.5	2,315.0	8.0	5.7	131.9	
Nom Co	Tibet	30°40′	90°30′	4,718.0	1,920.0	6.5	2.8	64.3	
Silin Co	Tibet	31°50′	89°00′	4,530.0	1,640.0				highest. salt. Lake
Qarhan	Qinghai	36°20′	92°40′	2,677.0	1,600.0				Max. salt Lake
Bosten Lake	Xinjiang	41°59′	86°49′	1,048.0	1,019.0	15.7	9.7	98.8	
Zharinamu	Tibet	31°00′	85°30′	4,630.0	985.0				
Dangruoyon	Tibet	31°05′	86°36′	4,535.9	825.6	12.0	7.9	59.0	
Burulto Lake	Xinjiang	47°13′	87°18′	460.0	745.0	59.0	23.6	160.0	
Yangzuyon	Tibet	29°00′	90°40′	4,441.0	687.0	30.7	17.6	107.6	
Ngoring Lake	Qinghai	34°56′	97°43′	4,268.7	610.7				
Wulanwul	Qinghai	34°50′	90°30′	4,854.0	610.0		9.0	54.8	
Nuir Nur	In. Mon.	47°48′	117°42′		608.5	65.0	26.6	160.0	Boundary Lake
Har Nur	Qinghai	38°18′	97°35′	4,078.0	602.0				
Ayakkum	Xinjiang	37°35′	89°20′	3,809.0	587.0				
Anlaren Zu	Tibet	31°35′	83°00′	4,689.0	560.0				
Songhua Lake	Jilin	43°25′	127°00′	261.0	550.0	75.0	19.6	108.0	
Gyaring Lake	Qinghai	34°55′	97°15′	4,293.2	526.0	13.1	8.9	46.7	
Taluo Zu	Tibet	31°10′	84°10′	4,545.0	520.0				
Sayrim Lake	Xinjiang	44°36′	81°11′	2,671.0	464.0	85.6	50.0	232.0	
Mitijiangmu	Tibet, Qinghai	33°25′	90°20′	4,749.0	460.0			73.8	
Banggong	Tibet	33°44′	78°50′	4,241.0	412.5	41.3	17.9	202.7	Exclude Kashmir
Mabanyon	Tibet	30°40′	81°30′	4,587.0	412.0	81.8	49.2	75.0	
Tuosu Lake	Qinghai	35°10′	98°40′		318.5		23.5	11.10	
Juyan Lake	In. Mon	42°24′	101°15′	820.0	297.7			6.6	Dry
Ulansu Lake	In. Mon	40°55′	108°49′	1,019.0	250.0				
Dali Nur	In. Mon	43°15′	116°30′	1,226.0	238.0	13.0	6.7	5.80	
Jilikul	Xinjiang	46°50′	87°10′	462.0	172.6	12.8	8.7	2.75	
Aiximan	Xinjiang	41°50′	80°40′	131.0	149.6	3.5	1.8	5.30	
Huangqi	In. Mon	40°51′	112°17′	43.0	114.0	10.0	4.6		
Qagan Nur	In. Mon	43°25′	114°50′		108.9	5.0	1.3		

water is easy to evaporate and salt accumulates in it. These small lakes have seasonal changes in their recharge pattern: forming lakes in the rainy season and drying up in the drought season. These lakes contain abundant chemical substances, such as salt, alkali. Glauber's salt and so on. Some lakes become underground lakes due to encroachment of blown sand. Therefore, the deposits of inland lakes provide important evidence for environmental changes.

According to the previous statistics, there are 778 lakes each having an area of over 1 km^2 in the Tibetan Plateau, among them 47 lakes with an area of over 100 km^2 and 3 lakes over 1,000 km^2. The total area of lakes is 25,111 km^2, which occupies one third of China's lake area. According to the relationship between lakes and rivers, the lakes can be divided into exterior and interior lakes. Nearly 90% of lakes belong to the latter. These lakes have a total storage volume of 3,472×10^8 m^3, which occupy 47.5% of the total storage in China, among them 2,482×10^8 m^3 of water are stored in interior lakes and 630×10^8 m^3 in exterior lakes.

2.3.3 Flood and drought hazards

Oases occupy less than 5% of the total area of northwest desert regions in China, yet more than 90% of the population in this area live in oases. Although agricultural production conditions in oasis regions are stable, they also often suffer from flood and drought disasters, as well as soil secondary Salinization.

Water is a decisive factor for industrial and agricultural production in oases. There are some problems in water resource utilization, such as low efficiency and over-utilization. Therefore, cultivated lands are often abandoned due to water shortages in the lower reaches of rivers, and they ultimately suffer from desertification. In addition, precipitation in the arid regions is sparse and erratic. Therefore, oases face a water-deficiency issue on one hand, and also face flood disasters on the other hand. According to flood data statistics in Xinjiang, Qinghai, Gansu and Inner Mongolia, there were 291×10^4 hm^2 of farmland and 909×10^4 people in these regions that suffered from flood hazards during the 1950–1990 period. In addition, there were also about 1.1×10^4 km of highway, 1.5×10^4 culverts, 181 middle and small reservoirs, and 4,422 km of dikes that were destroyed by floods between 1950–1990. The total economic loss was about 35.2×10^8 *yuan* (RMB).

Low water use efficiency is a major problem in water resources management. According to data in 1990, the irrigation quota of farmland was very high in northwest China. The average irrigation quota in some regions such as Jiayuguan, Jiuquan, Jinchang, Turpan, and Kashi was as high as 1.5×10^4 m^3/hm^2, which is ten times the international level (Israel). In arid regions, drought and aeolian desertification are constant disasters, and secondary salinization of soil is also serious. According to previous data, during 1979–1986 in Xinjiang, there were 961×10^4 hm^2 of land that suffered from soil salinization, of which 107×10^4 hm^2 were farmlands, equal to 33.8% of the total cultivated land area in that period. In such a case, the food output decreased by 27×10^8 kg and the economic loss amounted to 38.6×10^8 *yuan* (RMB).

2.3.4 Groundwater basins

Abundant unconsolidated deposits in the Cenozoic tectonic basins are not only a material basis for desert formation, but also provide a place for the storage of interstitial water. Therefore, groundwater is plentiful in some basins of northwest China.

Glaciers and snow meltwater flowing into the basins from high mountains can replenish groundwater, while the thick layer of sand and gravel deposited in the piedmont belts around the basins can hold it. In the center of deserts, sand provides good conditions to store groundwater. However, due to sparse precipitation, strong evaporation and far distance from lateral replenishment sources, the groundwater is often mineralized.

2.3.4.1 Tarim Basin

The Tarim basin is situated in the warm temperate zone. The topography is inclined towards the northeast with an altitude from 980 to 1,200 m above sea level. There exist a gravel sloping plain, a fine earthy plain, a sandy desert plain and a salt desert plain from the mountain foot to the centre of the basin. The Lop Nur depression and the Taitema Lake are the regions where groundwater and salts accumulate. Fed by precipitation and meltwater from mountainous areas, about 149 rivers formed in the basin, and their total surface water resources equal about $373 \times 10^8 \, \text{m}^3$. The three biggest rivers are the Aksu River, the Yarkant River and the Hotan River, which originate from the Tianshan Mountains, the Kunlun Mountains and the Karakorum Mountains. respectively. They are incorporated into the Tarim River in the northern part of the basin and flow from west to east. There exist plentiful loose sediments in the basin. The thickness of the sand and gravel layer at the piedmont is about 50–300 m, the thickness of clay and sand layer at the clay plain is about 800–1,000 m, and the thickness of sandy layer at the sandy desert plain is 300–500 m. All of these sediments contain Quaternary phreatic water.

Groundwater resources mainly come from seepage of river runoff, infiltration of canal systems, reservoirs and farmlands, and inflow of temporary flood, precipitation and water overflow from river courses, which is not repeated with surface water resources. The Tarim Basin has groundwater resources of $292.7 \times 10^8 \, \text{m}^3$, of which $172.97 \times 10^8 \, \text{m}^3$ are in mountainous regions and $203.22 \times 10^8 \, \text{m}^3$ are in the piedmont. Except for the highly mineralized groundwater (degree of mineralization from 3 to 10 g/L) in the Taklimakan Desert and its marginal regions, the groundwater before entering the plains is fresh. It amounts to $121.6 \times 10^8 \, \text{m}^3$, of which 85% of the amount overlaps with surface water. So, these regions are favorable for groundwater development and utilization. At present, the development degree of groundwater is still not high; the pumped groundwater is less than 5% of the total volume. Groundwater has bright development prospects, but needs an overall development plan.

Groundwater resources along the banks of the Tarim River and in the Taklimakan Desert have been widely developed in recent years, mainly used as injection water for oilfields and greening-water to prevent blowing sand. Because of over-exploitation, water tables are declining and a groundwater drawdown cone is beginning to occur in local places. Due to sparse precipitation and strong evaporation in the centre of the desert, precipitation cannot feed the groundwater, so the replenishment of phreatic water only comes from the infiltration of water before entering the plains.

2.3.4.2　Junggar Basin

The Junggar Basin is located between the Tianshan Mountains and the Altay Mountains with an altitude of 290–800 m that inclines from east to west. The Ebinur Lake depression at its southwestern part is the lowest point of the basin, with an altitude of 189 m. The deposit in the Ebinur Lake region is 2,000–6,000 m thick, 800–3,000 m near Karamay and 2,000–4,000 m at the Karameili region. These deposits have an important effect on groundwater formation in the basin. In front of the Tianshan Mountains, the aquifer consists of pebbles, gravels and sands; the water table is more than 50 m deep. There is shallow groundwater and deep confined water in the middle and lower parts of the alluvial fans. There are 6 layers of confined water within the depth of 200 m in the western part of Shihezi. There is phreatic water in the central part of the basin; the water table is different in different areas, ranging from 1–4 m in most of the areas to 5–10 m in the northern part of the desert. The plains are the main regions for groundwater development and utilization. The plain at the north piedmont of the Tianshan Mountains has $80\times10^8\,m^3$ groundwater resources, of which about 80% of the amount overlaps with surface water resources according to infiltration calculations. At present, groundwater consumptions in most regions are still overflow of springs, evaporation of phreatic water and vegetation transpiration. With further development of surface water and groundwater, the agricultural and industrial water consumption in the plains is increasing rapidly. As a result, the water table is declining and the eco-environment is degrading. This is particularly obvious at the lower reaches of the Ürümqi River.

2.3.4.3　Qaidam Basin

The Qaidam Basin is a huge intermontane basin at the northern margin of the Qinghai-Tibet (Tibetan) Plateau. The basin includes the Qinghai Lake, the Har Nur and the Gonghe Basin, and has an area of $30\times10^4\,km^2$. The basin is surrounded by the Altun Mountains, the Qilian Mountains and the Kunlun Mountains, with an altitude of 2,675–3,000 m. Many small rivers originate from the surrounding mountains. The bigger rivers include the Narin Gol River, the Golmud River, the Nomhon River, the Qagon Us River, the Bayingole River, the Tataling River, and the Haltang River, etc. The total surface water resources in the basin is $44.4\times10^8\,m^3$. Besides the Qinghai Lake, there are many other salt lakes, such as the Dabsan Lake, the Tousu Lake, the East Taijiner Lake, the West Taijiner Lake, the Gaskule Lake, the North Huobusan Lake. and the Sugan Lake, etc. The total area of the lakes is 1,400 km^2. The basin is widely covered by Quaternary loose sediments. The surface runoff and bedrock interstitial water in mountain areas flow to the basin to be transformed into groundwater. Groundwater in the basin is present in four forms, including mountain interstitial water, phreatic water of alluvial and diluvial gravel layers, phreatic water of diluvial lacustrine layers and confined water of lacustrine plains. The groundwater resources are about 40.7×10^8 m^3 and its development degree is not high at present.

2.3.4.4 Hexi Corridor

The Hexi Corridor is partitioned into many tectonic basins by several NW-W and E-W-oriented basement uplifts. The larger basins are the Wuwei Basin, the Minqin-Chaoshui Basin, the Zhangye Basin, the Jiuquan Basin, the Jinta Basin, the Changma-Tashi Basin and the Anxi Basin etc. There are 56 rivers developed in the corridor, of which the three main rivers are the Shiyang River, the Heihe River and the Shule River. The Hexi Corridor has deep and loose Cenozoic sediments. On the southern side exists the continuously pluvial layer of the early and middle Pleistocene series, with thicknesses ranging from 50–300 m. The aquifer mainly consists of gravel and sand. The grain size gradually becomes finer as it transitions from the piedmont to the corridor and finally to the confined water zone at the plain, which is the most important aquifer in the Hexi Corridor. The groundwater is mainly recharged by infiltration from river courses, canals and farmlands at the alluvial fan zones rather than from the lateral runoff in mountainous areas. According to water balance calculations, the Hexi Corridor has groundwater resources of 44.7×10^8 m^3, of which infiltration from river courses, canal systems and farmlands accounts for 89% and only 5×10^8 m^3 is a natural supply of water resources that is not reused. At present, the exploitation degree of groundwater is generally over 20% and it reaches 70% in the Shiyang River basin. Overexploitation of groundwater has resulted in the decrease of spring flow in the Hexi Corridor. Especially at the lower reaches of the Shiyang River, the situation is even more serious.

2.3.4.5 Inner Mongolian Plateau

The Alxa Plateau includes the alluvial plain of the Ejin River as well as deserts. With an area of 3.8×10^4 km^2, the big alluvial fan of the Ejin River at the lower reaches of the Heihe River has more deep and loose Quaternary sediments and is favorable for storing groundwater. There exist Quaternary phreatic water and confined water in the plain and small areas of confined water in the delta at the lower reaches of the river. However, situated in the arid region, the annual precipitation in the plateau is only about 50 mm, which difficult to form surface runoff. Therefore, groundwater recharge from precipitation is very weak. According to calculations, the replenishment rate of precipitation infiltration in the basin is only 0.78×10^8 m^3, hence the groundwater in the plain region mainly comes from the seepage of the Heihe River water. With the decrease of inflow from the upper reaches, the terminal Juyan Lake dried up in the 1970s. The groundwater table in the whole river basin was declining and vegetation degraded rapidly. At present, the Chinese Government has taken some measures to divert water to the lower reaches. During the 2001–2003 period, $9 \times 10^8 \, \text{m}^3$ of water were diverted to lower reaches each year. There is no runoff formed in the Desert and the Tengger Desert. Storm infiltration and a little condensation water in deserts are favorable conditions for the replenishment of groundwater.

The eastern Inner Mongolian Plateau, with an annual precipitation of 200–350 mm, formed some short inland rivers such as the Wulagai River, the Bayin River, the Jilin River, the Xilin Gol River, the Tabu River, and the Olon Bulag River, and several inland lakes such as the Ulan Nur, the Dalai Nur, the Qagan Nur, the Huangqi Hai, the Dai Hai, and the Qagan Nur. The total annual runoff in the eastern Inner Mongolian Plateau is about $10 \times 10^8 \, \text{m}^3$. There exist bedrock crack water in lower hills, as well as phreatic and confined water in the valleys between hills. Natural groundwater resources are $27.7 \times 10^8 \, \text{m}^3$ and mainly distributed in basins and ancient river courses.

2.3.4.6   Ordos Plateau and Yinchuan-Hetao Plain

The Ordos Plateau, whose northern boundary is the Yinshan Mountains adjoining the Inner Mongolian Plateau, is bounded on the west by the Helan Mountains and the Alxa Plateau. The geological structure belongs to a platform syncline, which includes western Ningxia and the northern Hetao Plain. The Yellow River flows through the Heishan Gorge and forms a U-shaped valley in the front of the Mountains. The Hobq Desert and the Mu Us Sandy Land are distributed in its middle part. The annual precipitation is 150–400 mm. Besides the Kushui River, the Wuding River, and the Quye River, there exist many small lakes, most of which are saline lakes. The groundwater, replenished by river water and precipitation, is plentiful. The groundwater table in depressions between sand dunes is below 2–3 m.

The Yinchuan Plain and the Houtao Plain are the largest irrigation oases in the arid region. The long-term average annual runoff which could flow into the main course of the Yellow River in Ningxia is $325 \times 10^8 \, \text{m}^3$. In addition $8.9 \times 10^3 \, \text{m}^3$ groundwater comes from the southern mountains. The present irrigation area reaches $33.3 \times 10^4 \, \text{hm}^2$. It is favorable to recharge groundwater in the plains. The diverting water amount from the Yellow River is $80 \times 10^8 \, \text{m}^3$ each year and about $35 \times 10^8 \, \text{m}^3$ of water could return to the Yellow River. According to water balance analyses, the groundwater resources in the Yinchuan Plain is about $22.7 \times 10^8 \, \text{m}^3$.

The neotectonic movement in the Hetao Plain made the topography inclined northward slightly. The modern Yellow River flows through the southern parts that make the basin favorable for irrigation and unfavorable for drainage. The irrigation area is $50 \times 10^4 \, \text{hm}^2$ and annual channeling water from the Yellow River reaches $56 \times 10^8 \, \text{m}^3$. The return water into the Yellow River is small. Since 1960, land salinization has developed seriously and at least 50% of irrigation farmlands have suffered from it. The annual replenishment rate of groundwater is about $41.42 \times 10^8 \, \text{m}^3$ and extractable resource is $26.8 \times 10^8 \, \text{m}^3$.

The Horqin Sandy Land is distributed in the West Liaohe River Plain. The West Liaohe River has a length of 829 km and catchment basin of 14.7×10^4 km^2. Its total annual runoff with much sediments is 22×10^8 m^3. Due to vegetation degradation and serious water erosion, its upper reaches is the main sediment-producing region. The Horqin Sandy Land is covered by a thick layer of Quaternary sand deposits and the groundwater, recharged by the West Liaohe River water, is plentiful and fresh. The groundwater at the northern margin of the Horqin Sandy Land belongs to alluvial and diluvial phreatic water. The thickness of aquifers increases to 105m in the plain from 5m at the piedmont. The groundwater in the middle part of the Sandy Land belongs to the river alluvial and diluvial phreatic water, the grain sizes in the aquifers transit from middle and fine sands to silt with a thickness of 25–70 m. The groundwater at the southern part belongs to the phreatic water of sand dunes and the aquifers consist of fine sand and silt with a thickness of 50–150 m. At present, with the surface water depletion, the degree of groundwater exploitation is increasing. In some regions, water tables begin to drop. So it is necessary to strengthen water resource evaluation and management for rational development and utilization.

There are some scattered sandy lands and underlying Quaternary clastic sediments and loose deposits of different thickness in the Song-Nen Plain and the Huang-Huai-Hai Plain. With annual precipitation of 400–600 mm, groundwater resources in this region are plentiful. The plain at the lower reaches of the Nenjiang River has accumulated clastic sediments with a total thickness of over 6,000 m, of which the thickness of Quaternary deposits reaches over 150 m. It is one of the most prospective regions for groundwater development and utilization in northeast China.

Three large water systems i.e. the Haihe River, the Yellow River and the Huaihe River flow through the Huang-Huai-Hai Plain. The principal part of the plain comprises the alluvial fan of the lower Yellow River. However, with the continuous deposition and the heightening of artificial riverbanks, the lower courses of the Yellow River has become a "suspended river". In this case, groundwater seeps into the Haihe and the Huaihe River. The Plain could be divided into several hydrogeological units according to their hydrogeological conditions, including the alluvial fan and the flooding plain of the Yellow River, the northern Huaihe Plain and the coastal plain. Groundwater resources in the plain is about 462.5×10^8 m^3. Due to over-exploitation of groundwater, the water table is dropping to a large extent, especially in regions north of the Yellow River. Contradictions between supply and demand of water resources are very acute at present. Therefore, we need to intensify scientific management of water resources.

2.3.5   Hydrological regionalization in desert regions

Several hydrological regionalization schemes were put forward in China in the 1950s, 1980s and 1990s, respectively. But up to now, there is still no unified division scheme in desert regions due to lack of precise data. In general, the country can be divided into 10 first-class regions and 82 second-class regions. The first-class regions includes the hills and plains in northeast China, mountains and plains areas in the Huang-Huai-Hai Plain, grasslands in Inner Mongolia, the Loess Plateau in northwest China, the inland regions in northwest China and the Qinghai-Tibet Plateau regions. According to the division of water conservancy, the former four regions have been defined as the rainfed farming areas. In these regions, the principal problems are sparse precipitation and serious water erosion, so it is necessary to pay more attention to soil and water. conservation and drought-flood disasters. The latter two regions are located in the western part of China. In these regions, land area is large and population is small, with animal husbandry and serious drought disasters.

2.4　Soil

There are various types of soil in the desert and aeolian desertified regions of China, which provide a favorable condition for agriculture, forestry, animal husbandry and eco-environment. According to the *Classification of Soil System in China*, besides the Sandic Entisols, there exist other soil types in these regions such as artificial soil, arid soil, saline-sodic soil, gley soil, is-humus soil and the embryonic soil. These types of soil are distributed within Sandic Entisols, especially on the fringes of deserts. To avoid misunderstanding resulting from the change of soil classification system, Table 2-3 shows some references between system classification and genetic classification of soils in the desert and aeolian desertified regions of China.

Table 2-3　References between system classification and genetic classification of some major soils in desert and aeolian desertified regions of China

Soil genetic classification (1978–1992)	Soil system classification (2000)
Aeolian sandy soil	Freezing/dump/arid/semi-arid/wet sandic entisols
Oasis soil, anthropogenic alluvial soil, anthropogenic desert soil	Weak salt/ mellow/ water tillage/ speckle/general anthropogenic alluvial /arid tillage/ artificial soil
Chestnut soil	Calcic/ gley/semi-arid/ embryonic soil
Brown calcic soil	Calcic/ gley normal arid soil
Gray brown soil	Calcic/ gley normal arid soil
Gray desert soil	Calcic/ saline/ sliming /gley normal arid soil
Gray brown desert soil	Gypseous/ gley normal arid soil
Brown desert soil	Gypseous/ saline normal arid soil
Takyr soil	Gley normal arid soil
Saline soil	Arid/dump normal saline-sodic soil
Marshy soil	Organic/black / perch gley soil
Meadow soil	Gley/black/tint/speckle/dump embryonic soil

Remark: References just represent that most characteristics of them not all are the same.

2.4.1 Sandy Entisols

Sandy Entisols are those soils that possess sandy sediments characteristics. In previous soil classifications, these soils corresponded to aeolian sandy soils (Xiong et al., 1987; Chen et al., 1998, 1999; NSRI, 2000). Previously, shifting sands were not regarded as soil ingredient. But present researches have shown that there have vital movements (including microbe) and soil fertility in shifting sands, thus they belong to Sandy Entisols.

2.4.1.1 Distribution of Sandy Entisols

Sandy Entisols are distributed within three natural zones (the northwest arid regions, the eastern monsoon regions and the Tibetan Plateau). But they are mainly distributed over some inland basins and plateaus, ranging between 35°–50°N and 75°–125°E. They form an desert belt arc about 600 km long, starting from the Song-Nen Plain, crossing through northeast, northern and northwestern China, and finally ending in the Tarim Basin.

2.4.1.2 Soil forming features

1) Background of soil forming period

There is unified opinion on the formation time of desert, and the knowledge about the ages of Sandic Entisols is even more scarce. The previous studies indicated that the climate have undergone at least six stages with shifting sands and soil formation in the Holocene (1,000 a BP until the present), including 9,500–8,000 a BP, 7,500–5,000 a BP, 4,500–3,000 a BP, 2,500–2,000 a BP, 1,300–800 a BP and 100 a BP until the present (Dong et al., 1991, 1995). This conclusion has been conformed by some researches on paleosol and environment in northeast and northern China (Wang et al., 1992; Qiu et al., 1992).

Throughout human history, people's activities have exerted great influence on desert formation or its reversal (Zhou et al., 1983). That is to say, human activities played an important role in the formation of Sandic Entisols. First, due to over-cutting, over-grazing and over-cultivation, deserts appeared in originally non-desert regions. Second, some deserts have expanded during the historic time, such as the fringe of the Taklimakan Desert, Alxa and the Hexi Corridor.

2) Soil forming factors

(1) Climate. Desert is formed under arid climate, thus climate is the main factor for forming Sandy Entisols. In northwest China, winter is cold and dry but summer is hot and rainless, which provides the basic climate conditions for the formation of Sandy Entisols. Climate conditions of some typical Sandy Entisols are showed in Fig. 2-22.

(2) Pedogenic parent material. Sandy Entisols were formed above aeolian sands, so their parent

materials are aeolian sands. Their material sources include: river alluviums (dry delta or alluvial fan), lake sediments, diluvial deposits and bedrock weathering residues and so on.

(3) Vegetation. In the regions where Sandy Entisols are distributed vegetation is sparse. With the exception of some inland riverbanks, the majority of plants in these regions belong to grass and bush. In this case, the influence of organisms on the formation of Sandic Entisols is weak but cannot be overlooked.

(4) Topography. With the expectation of small patches of Sandic Entisols, most of them are distributed over large inland intermontane basins, such as the Tarim Basin and the Junggar Basin. In these basins, most of the ground materials are formed through wind erosion, sorting, transportation and re-accumulation of river alluviums or lake sediments. For example, the thickness of sandy sediments in the southern margin of the Gurbantünggüt Desert is about 200–400 m, while at the lower reaches of the West Liaohe River their thickness is about 100 m.

(5) Human activities. Man's economic activity is the provoking factor for the formation of Sandy Entisols. Some irrational economic activities such as over-cultivation, over-grazing and over-cutting can change the processes of Sandy Entisols' formation. On the other hand, rational economic activities can cause shifting sand to stabilize and even become an oasis.

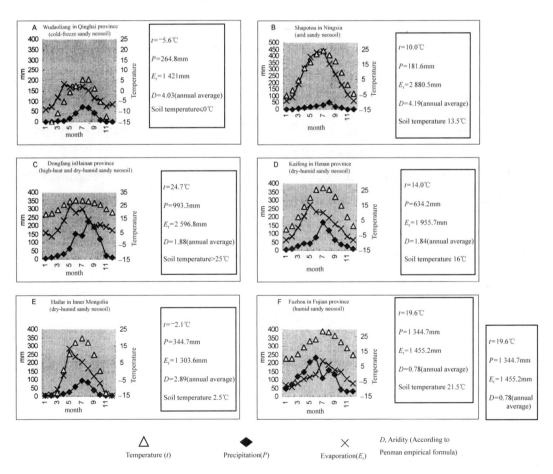

Fig. 2-22   Climate conditions of some major Sandy Entisols

3) Soil forming process

Sandy Entisols' Formation is closely related to the growth and succession of natural vegetation and results from the interaction between the geological cycle and the biological cycle. when sandy land is fixed, soil forms gradually. In general, aeolian sands can become Sandy Entisols through the following three stages. ① Soil forming stage in shifting sand. This is the early stage of soil formation. ② Soil forming stage in semi-fixed sandy land. ③ Soil forming stage in fixed sandy land.

4) Soil forming characteristics

These are the following characteristics during the evolution of aeolian sand into Sandy Entisols:

(1) Fine grains accumulation. Under the wind action, granulometric compositions of Sandy Entisols on shifting sand dunes are relatively uniform, mainly ranging from 0.25 to 0.05 mm (fine and extremely fine sand), while silty sand and clay particles are less. During the soil forming process, silty sand and clay particles will increase gradually. These fine grain materials have an important significance for soil formation. They can change soil's physical and chemical properties and improve soil fertility.

(2) Crust formation. In general, fall dusts in northwest China contain carbonate and silicon dioxide; these materials can make sand surface cemented. During precipitation, the water content of sand surface increases and its temperature decreases. Meanwhile, carbonic acid is produced when plant relics have been decomposed, thus causing $CaCO_3$ to transform into $Ca(HCO_3)_2$ and be in favor of $CaCO_3$ solution and infiltration easily. After precipitation, sand surface's temperature will rise and water will move up to sand surface. When calcium bicarbonate loses water, fall dusts on sand surface will be cemented and harden and finally surface crust will form.

(3) Accumulation of organic materials. During the soil forming process, organic materials are accumulated on the upper soil layer due to grass growth and litter decomposition. With soil forming, the organic materials increase gradually. According to statistics, organic materials contents in shifting, semi-fixed and fixed Sandy Entisols are about 1–2.3, 2–8 and 6–16.4 g/kg, respectively.

2.4.1.3 Classification and index of Sandy Entisols

According to the *Soil Classification System of China* (*modified scheme*), Sandy Entisols refer to soils which belong to Entisols and contain sandy sediments. In general, the structures of Sandy Entisols are simple and only have A–C profile. In addition, their textures are coarse.

According to water content and temperature, Sandy Entisols can be divided into cold-freeze, humid, arid, semi-arid and wet Sandy Entisols. Their definition is as follows:

Cold Sandy Entisols: Soil temperature of Sandy Entisols is low or even below 0 °C.

Humid Sandy Entisols: Water content of Sandy Entisols is high and there are oxidation-reduction features in at least a layer ($\geqslant$10 cm) within 50 cm.

Arid Sandy Entisols: Water content of soil is low.

Semi-arid Sandy Entisols: Water content of soil is moderate.

Wet Sandy Entisols: Other Sandy Entisols.

According to their specific properties, the above-mentioned groups can be divided into several subgroups (Table 2-4).

Table 2-4　Sandy Entisols taxonomic classification (High-level units)

Order	Suborder	Group	Subgroup
Entisols	Sandic Entisols	Cold Sandy Entisols	Permanent-freezing cold Sandy Entisols
			Semi-permanent freezing cold Sandy Entisols
			Acid cold Sandy Entisols
			Calcareous cold Sandy Entisols
			Common cold Sandy Entisols
		Humid Sandy Entisols	Calcareous humid Sandy Entisols
			Sodic humid Sandy Entisols
			Weak-saline humid Sandy Entisols
			Common humid Sandy Entisols
		Arid Sandy Entisols	Speckle Arid Sandy Entisols
			Calcareous arid Sandy Entisols
			Sodic arid Sandy Entisols
			Weak-saline arid Sandy Entisols
			Common arid Sandy Entisols
		Semi-arid Sandy Entisols	High-heat Semi-arid Sandy Entisols
			Speckle Semi-arid Sandy Entisols
			Calcareous semi-arid Sandy Entisols
			Leaf-litter Semi-arid Sandy Entisols
			Common semi-arid Sandy Entisols

2.4.1.4　Major Sandy Entisols

1) Cold Sandy Entisols

Cold Sandy Entisols are mainly distributed over the Tibetan Plateau, especially over those regions where the elevation is over 4,000 m and the annual mean temperature is below 0 °C (Fig. 2-22A). In these regions, the permafrost with thickness of 1–120 m is distributed continuously and its seasonal thawing depth is about 0.8–3.0 m. Zonal vegetations in these regions are mainly high-cold steppe and high-cold desert steppe. Cold Sandy Entisols mainly occur in high terraces of some lakes and their parent materials coming from aeolian sand. Sand occupies most parts, while silt and clay content is usually less than 100 g/kg. Cold Sandy Entisols can be further divided into several subgroups, including permanent-freezing, semi-permanent freezing, acid, calcareous and common cold Sandy Entisols.

Take the Calcareous cold Sandy Entisols as an example. Its physical and chemical proprieties can be seen in Table 2-5 (profile No. 94–qing–1). In this profile, $CaCO_3$ occupies 50–70 g/kg and reaches calcareous standard. Its soluble salt content is low, less than 0.5 g/kg. Gypsum content is also low, less than 1.5 g/kg. The differentiation of chemical constitution content in the whole soil profile is not obvious. In the lower part of the profile, there exist lamellar structures resulting from freezing-thawing processes. Organic content is about 2.0 g/kg and total N is about 0.1 g/kg. Land use patterns in the regions where cold Sandic Entisols exist should be limited, only allowing for light grazing during the warm season. Protection should be strengthened to prevent vegetation and soil damage.

Table 2-5 Physical and chemical properties of major sandy Entisols

Soil type	Profile No.	Location	Depth (cm)	(Organic C)	Total N	C/N	CEC[Cmol(+)/kg]	$CaCO_3$	$CaSO_4 \cdot 2H_2O$	PH 1:2.5 (H_2O)	Total salt (g/kg)	Sand	Silt	Clay	Silt/Clay
				g/kg				g/kg				Particle composition(g/kg)			
A. Calcareous	94–qing–1	Germud,	0–15	1.1	0.09	12.2	1.56	65	2	8.7	0.4	965	12	23	0.30
cold Sandy		Wudaoliang	15–50	1.1	0.11	10.0	1.79	63	1	8.8	0.4	967	11	22	
Entisols			5–150	1.1	0.10	11.0	1.97	68	0	9.0	0.3	958	21	21	0.43
B. Common	63–mao–11	Wuzao	0–7	14.8	3.94						1.2	830	60	10	1.0
humid Sandy			7–15	1.0	0.45						0.4	930	60	10	0.5
Entisols*			20–30	0.3	0.28						0.4	995	5		
			40–50	0.2	0.11						0.3				
			80–90	0.1	0.70						0.5				
C. Calcareous	Y–24	Zhongwei	0–1	3.5	0.38	9.2	4.06	58	0	8.7	0.4	694	267	39	1.97
arid Sandy			1–24	4.0	0.47	8.5	4.24	49	0	8.6	0.6	695	279	26	3.11
Entisols			24–39	3.3	0.35	9.4	3.37	22	5.1	8.3	3.6	916	65	19	1.21
			39–68	1.8	0.16	10.6	2.51	19	1.3	8.5	0.9	1,000	0	0	0
			68–106	0.7	0.07	10.0	2.21	18	0	9.1	0.4	1,000	0	0	0
			106–150	0.8	0.08	10.0	2.19	16	0	9.0	0.4	1,000	0	0	0
D. Common	Y–20	Hulun Buir	3–21	10.0	0.67	14.9	6.02	1		7.4	0.6	909	42	49	0.86
semi–arid			21–36	3.0	0.24	12.5	2.55	2		7.6	0.1	972	28	0	0
Sandy Entisols			36–67	1.3	0.10	13.0	1.45	3		8.4	0.1	1,000	0	0	0
			67–108	0.9	0.07	12.9	1.19	2		8.5	0.1	1,000	0	0	0
			108–150	0.4	0.05	8.0	1.14	4		8.6	0.1	1,000	0	0	0
E. common wet	87–F–1	Changle	0–7	2.0	0.16	12.5	2.12	1		6.7	0.1	975	3	22	0.36
Sandy Entisols			7–30	1.0	0.15	6.7	2.09	1		6.8	0.1	975	6	19	0.26
			30–50	0.9	0.14	6.4	2.15	2		7.2	0.2	977	2	21	0.33
			50–100	0.6	0.12	5.0	2.34	Tr		7.3	0.2	979	3	18	0.11

* Granulometric composition adopted unit systems of the former Soviet Union.

2) Humid Sandy Entisols

Humid Sandy Entisols are mainly distributed over interdune depressions or dune edges. In these places, there are high groundwater tables. In the majority of the years, when air temperature is over 5°C, soil layer in 50 cm will be wetted by capillary water. Humid Sandy Entisols can be divided into four subgroups, including calcareous, sodic, weak salt and common cold Sandy Entisols.

Profile 63–mao–11 in Table 2-5 shows the physical and chemical properties of typical cold Sandy Entisols. This profile indicates that there are obvious differentiations between A and C layer. Organic content in A layer reaches 25–30 g/kg, while in C layer this value decreases quickly below 2 g/kg and soluble salt content below 1.2 g/kg. In the whole profile, sands occupy 830–995 g/kg. However, there are more silt and clay in surface layer than in lower layer.

3) Arid Sandy Entisols

Arid Sandy Entisols are mainly distributed over the northwest Erdos Plateau, middle and eastern parts of the Hexi Corridor, and the Junggar and the Tarim basins. These regions belong to the semi-desert and desert climate zone, with annual precipitation of 50–200 mm and annual mean temperature of 3.5–10.0 °C. Mean temperature in January and July is –9–21 °C and 20–25 °C (Fig. 2-22B), respectively. Accumulative temperature of $\geqslant 10$ °C is about 2,000–3,000 °C and dryness is about 4–8.

According to grain size analysis of arid sandic entisols in Shapotou, sand content is more than 700 g/kg, while silt and clay content is less than 300 g/kg. Profile Y–24 (Table 2-5) shows that there is obvious differentiation between soil layer and crust developed on the earth surface. In the whole profile, $CaCO_3$ content is about 16–58 g/kg, organic content 1.9–8.9 g/kg, ratio of humic acid/ fulvic acid about 8.0 and gypsum content is very low. Chemical analysis shows that SiO_2 content is higher in the lower layer than in the upper layer, while content of Fe_2O_3, CaO, MgO, TiO_2, MnO_2, P_2O_5 is higher in the upper layer than that of the lower layer.

Arid Sandy Entisols can also be divided into five subgroups, including mottling, calcareous, sodic, weak salt and common arid Sandy Entisols.

4) Semi-arid Sandy Entisols

Semi-arid Sandy Entisols are widely distributed in China, including the Hulun Buir sands, river paleochannel of the Huang–Huai–Hai Plain and part of the shore sands in Hainan. Climate in these regions belongs to semi-arid/semi-wet temperate/warm temperate zone. Annual precipitation is about 250–600mm and annual mean temperature ranges from –2 to 14 °C. The mean temperature in January and July is –0.5–26.8 and 18.6–23.2 °C, respectively. Dryness ranges from 1 to 3.5.

This profile indicates that there are obvious differentiations from A to C layer. Organic content in A layer reaches 10 g/kg, and sometimes can even reach 167 g/kg. In general, the content of $CaCO_3$ is less than 10 g/kg, but in the warm temperate zone this value can reach 50 g/kg. Soluble salt content is usually less than 0.5 g/kg and ratio of humic acid/ fulvic acid is more than 1.0.

Semi-arid Sandy Entisols can be divided into five subgroups, including highly-heated, mottling, calcareous, forlia and common Semi-arid Sandy Entisols. As common Semi-arid Sandy Entisols an example, profile Y–20 (Table 2-5), shows its physical and chemical proprieties. Sand is the main ingredient of Semi-arid Sandy Entisols, and its content is more than 80%, and can even reach 100%. The contents of silt and clay in the upper layer can reach 20 g/kg, and the contents of total N, P and K and C/N also increase.

5) Wet Sandy Entisols

Wet Sandy Entisols are mainly distributed over shore sandy land and some sandy terraces of rivers in southern China, such as Changle in Fujian, Ganjiang and Haikou. In these regions, annual precipitation is over 1,000 mm and dryness is less than 1 (Fig. 2-22F). Soil temperature under 50cm ranges between 15 and 22 °C. Organic content in this type of soil is low, its value in the upper and lower layer is 3 g/kg, 1–2 g/kg respectively. In total profile, the content of $CaCO_3$ is also low, usually less than 2 g/kg. Soil pH is about 6.5–7.5 and the content of soluble salt is less than 0.2 g/kg. Wet Sandy Entisols can be divided into three subgroups, including calcareous, anthropogenic alluvial and common Wet Sandy Entisols. Taking common Wet Sandy Entisols as an example, expect for the surface layer, its sand content is more than 950 g/kg. Content of silt and clay in the upper layer is high, but in the lower layer this value is very low.

2.4.2　Other Sandy Entisols

2.4.2.1　Man-made irrigation-warping aridic soil

This type of soil is similar to oasis or irrigation-warping soil in soil genetic classification. The diagnostic horizon of the soil is irrigation–warping horizon and it was formed as a result of long-term cultivation, fertilizing irrigation. It is widely distributed in some irrigation farming regions, including the Hexi Corridor, the Yinchuan Plain, the Qaidam Basin, the Junggar Basin and the Tarim Basin, accounting for about 3%–5% of the total area of desert regions in China. In these regions, due to arid climate and rare precipitation, agriculture totally depends on irrigation water, which is sourced from rainfall as well as ice and snow meltwater from the mountain areas. There is obvious differentiation in the soil profile and the thickness of irrigation-warping horizon equal to or more than 50cm, sometimes even more than 1–2 m. Influenced by cultivation and artificial accumulation, irrigation-warping horizon can be partitioned into several sub-horizons, including cultivated irrigation-warping horizon (Aup1), plough irrigation-warping pan (Aup2), irrigation-warping cultivated illuvium (Bup), irrigation-warping marking horizon (Bur) and bottom soil parent material horizon (C) and so on. Nutrient accumulation in the soil is high. The content of organic matter, Total N and Total P (P_2O_5) are 10–20, 0.6–1.0, 2–3 g/kg, respectively and C/N value is 10–13. In addition, P enrichment in soil is very high. For example, the content of readily available P (P) is about 16–30 mg/kg and in mellow soil it can reach 35 mg/km and the maximum value is about 94mg/kg. Meanwhile, due to the increase of microbes and frequent activation of soil animals such as earthworms, soil fertility will be improved. Resulting from long-term irrigation and leaching, the soluble salt content is less than 0.5 g/kg; only in salinized soil can its content can reach 3.0 g/kg. The soil has good structure, with granular or blocky structure and moderate texture in cultivated horizon, and is favorable for farming. Therefore, soil-distributed regions of this kind are all grain and cotton production bases in the arid regions of China.

According to its development stage and properties, man-made irrigation-warping aridic soil can be divided into several subgroups, including weak salt, mature, water culture, marking and common irrigation-warping man-made aridic soil.

2.4.2.2　Common aridic soil

Common aridic soil represents the soil occurring in aridic moisture systems and has aridic epipedon or any one of diagnostic surface horizons and don't have cold soil temperature regime. In soil genetic classification, its counterpart includes sierozem, desert gray soil, gray-brown desert soil, brown desert soil, takyr and so on. The soil is widely distributed in the arid northwest China, including desert and semi-desert regions (their elevation less than 3,500 m) in temperate and warm temperate zones. According to aridity calculated from Penman's empirical equation, these regions can be divided into three subregions including weakly arid, arid and extremely arid subregion. Their descriptions are as follows:

(1) Weakly arid subregion. They are mainly distributed over semi-desert regions in the temperate zone, including middle and western parts of Inner Mongolia, Yinchuan, Lanzhou, Tacheng and Yili in Xinjiang. In these regions, the aridity ranges between 3.5 and 15.0 and vegetation belongs to desert steppe. In general, annual precipitation in these regions is less than 300 mm. Under the influence of biological agents, calcic horizon can be formed easily.

(2) Arid subregion. This subregion is mainly distributed over some piedmonts and conglomeratic gobi, including the middle and western Hexi Corridor, the western part of the Junggar Basin and the western part of the Tarim Basin. These regions are typical arid regions, with an aridity of 15–50 and an annual precipitation of 45–100 mm. Vegetation is sparse; shrub and undershrub belong to desert vegetation. In summer, carbonate and soluble salt are liable to be exposed on the ground surface and can be easily transported to the lower part of piedmont by storm rainfall. With generation of gypsum horizon, calcareous common aridic soil is formed in these regions.

(3) Extremely arid subregion. They are mainly distributed in gobi regions of eastern Xinjiang and the western Hexi Corridor and also exist in the Qaidam Basin. In these regions, aridity is more than 50 and annual precipitation is less than 50 mm. Vegetation is very sparse. Because any saline matters can't be leached out of soil profile, some soluble salts such as NaCl will be accumulated under 20–40 cm, thus a hard salt deposit is formed. We call this type of soil as salic common aridic soil.

As above-mentioned, there exist various common aridic soils in China. For example, there is calcareous common aridic soil in weakly arid subregion and cypsum common aridic soil in arid subregion. In addition, in each subregion, sliming common aridic soil often occur in old and stable surface and aquic common aridic soil often occur in newly and unstable ground surface.

2.4.2.3 Halogenic soil

In soil genetic classification system, halogenic soil is also called salt-affected soil or saline-sodic soil. In general, this soil profile contains salic horizon within 30 cm from the surface to subsurface or contains alkaline horizon within 75cm. It is widely distributed in arid, semi-arid and desert regions of China. It occurs in some low-flat basins, semi-enclosed depressions, river deltas and dry deltas. According to the features of soil forming factors and soil forming processes, halogenic soil in arid desert regions of China can be classified into two subgroups, including aridic common halogenic soil and aquic common halogenic soil.

2.4.2.4 Gleisoil

Gleisoil is also called marshy soil in soil genetic classification system. In its soil profile within 50 cm contain at least one layer that takes on gleization feature and thickness more than 10 cm. The distribution of gleisoil is closely related to low land, and it mainly occurs in some places such as a depression in the rim of alluvial fan, lake depression, river confluence and paleochannel. Gleisoil formation is mainly attributed to excessive soil moisture. According to its ecological form, the plants growing on gleisoil can be classified into aquatic plant, hydrophyte and mesophyte. According to the features of soil forming factors and soil forming processes, gleisoil in arid desert regions of China can be classified into three subgroups, including common gleisoil, umbric typical gleisoil and aquic common gleisoil.

2.4.2.5 Udorthent

Udorthent is a newly-named soil type, corresponding to chestnut soil in soil genetic classification system. It is widely distributed over arid desert regions of China and mainly occurs in some mountain hills and high plains. Its parent material is complex, including slope wash, eluvium, loess parent material and proluvial deposit, etc. Semi-arid climate is the major factor for soil formation. Annual precipitation in these regions is about 250–400 mm and vegetation is grassland. According to its major soil forming process intensity or features of secondary controlling factors, udorthent can be classified into calcic udorthent and aquic udorthent.

2.4.2.6 Aquic embryonic soil

Embryonic soil refers to the soil with low-developed profile. Aquic embryonic soil is one of subgroups of embryonic soil and it corresponds to meadow soil in soil genetic classification system. There is at least one oxidation-reduction layer in its profile within 50 cm. This type of soil is mainly distributed over some depressions and littoral land of river and lake. Parent materials of aquic embryonic soil are mainly fluviatile and lake facies deposits, and the minority are proluvial deposits or even aeolian deposits. Meadow is a major plant growing on it. These plants have large biomass and are favorable to humus accumulation. According to the major soil forming processes and their characteristics, aquic embryonic soil can be classified into three subgroups, including forlia, umbric and ochric aquic embryonic soil.

2.5　Vegetation

Deserts and desertification regions in China cover several climate zones, such as arid, semiarid, semi-humid, humid climate zones, and these regions also include various natural zones such as desert, steppe, and forest. Therefore, complex and diversified vegetation exist in these regions. Affected by sandy soil substrate, vegetation covers in different sandy land zones have some features in common with non-sandy lands.

2.5.1　Flora

2.5.1.1　Family and genus composition

According to preliminary statistics, there are about 800 common plant species in the middle and western desert regions of China. There are about 1,800 species if including the habitats such as piedmonts, residual mountains and salinized land. If including the species in deserts and mountain ranges, the total plant species reach 3,913 species. All these plants species belong to 129 families and 816 genera. If added to the plant species in sandy desert regions of northeast China, the Huang–Huai–Hai Plain and the Tibetan Plateau, the total plant species are more than 5,000.

According to the statistics, 79% of the total species are concentrated in 20 families, of which the former 5 families account for 40.7% of total species number. They are Compositae, Gramineae, Leguminosae, Cruciferae and Chenopodiaceae. According to regional distribution, there are parts of semi-humid and humid regions with typical wetlands and mountainous lands in eastern Inner Mongolia, which have significant effects on Cyperaceae and Rosaceae. However, the vertical zone in mountainous areas is narrow, causing the order of these two families to decline (the ninth and the tenth, respectively). Of the former 20 genera, Ranunculaceae, Labiatae, Scrophulariaceae, Liliaceae, Caryophyllaceae, Umbelliferae, Polygonaceae, Boraginaceae, Salicaceae, and Gentianaceae are the most common in sandy desert regions of China. Other genera in sandy desert regions are Papaveraceae, Zygophyllaceae and Tamaricaceae in the whole sandy desert regions, but Primulaceae, Orchidaceae and Saxifragaceae in Inner Mongolia. Judging from this, the composition of families in the sandy desert regions not only maintains basic characteristics of arid and semi-arid steppes, but also has the striking features of xerophytes.

First of all, there are more single and oligo-species in genus composition, which account for 74.5% of the total genera, but with the species included, only account for 27.2% of total species. Secondly, the species are concentrated in large genera. For example, although the genera of above

10–20 species only account for 10.3% of total genera, but account for 55.4% of total species. The genera include more species and important plants species in sandy desert regions are *Artemisia, Caragana, Tamarix, Stipa, Agropyron, Carex, Chenopodium, Corispermum, Salix, Populus, Calligonum, Zygophyllum, Ephedra, Bromus, Poa, Allium, Iris, Ulmus, Hedysarum, Oxytropis, Astragalus, Haloxylon, Salsola, Atraphaxis, Polygonum, Sympegma, Suaeda, Potentilla, Glycyrrhiza, Nitraria, Elaeagnus, Hippophaë, Reaumuria, Lespedeza, Limonium, Convolvulus, Lappula, Heteropappus, Saussurea, Taraxacum, Prunus, Sophora*, etc.

2.5.1.2 Geographical distribution

The geographical distribution of plants over sandy desert regions in China belongs to the Holarctic flora kingdom; it includes several flora regions and interacts with each other. This makes the geographical components of the flora have complex diversity and significant features. The core is the desert plant region of Asia, the second is the steppe plant region of Eurasia, and the third are the plant regions of East Asia and South Asia. The main flora components are as follows.

1) Composition of Central Asia

The center of sandy deserts in China belongs to the arid and hyper-arid desert zones of central Asia. The vegetation types include xerophytes, strong xerophytes and hyper-xerophytes. Most edificators in Chinese desert regions, especially in its middle and western parts, belong to central Asian components, such as *Stipa krylovii, S. bungeana, S. breviflora, S. glareosa, S. gobica, S . klemenzii, Agriotrib mongolicum, Caryopteris mongolica, Zygophyllum xanthoxylon, Z. mucronatum, Z. gobicum, Ephedra przewalskii, Calligonum mongolicum, Nitraria sphaerocarpa, N. tangutorum, Hedysarum laeve, H.Scoparium, Sympegma regelii, Anabasis brevifolia, Iljinia regelii, Salsola abrotanoides, S. pellucida, S. passerina, Agriophyllum squarrosum, Kalidium cuspidatum, K. gracile, Allium mongolicum, Caragana korshinskii, C. tibetica, C. intermedia, Oxytropis aciphylla, Convolvulus tragacanthoides, Ajania fruticulosa, A. achilloides, Scorzonera divaricata, Neoppalasia pectinata, Artemisia sphaerocephala, Brachanthemum gobicum, Psammochloa villosa, Asterothamnus centrali-asiaticus, Tugarinovia mongolica, Pugionium calcaratum*, and *Cornulaca alaschanica*.

2) Composition of the Tethys-sea region

The sandy desert region of China is one part of the arid and semi-arid Tethys-sea region. Some relic species include *Helianthemum songaricum, Gymnocarpos przewalskii, Frankenia pulverulenta*, etc. which exist locally in sandy regions. This indicates the relationship between the flora in sandy regions of China and the Mediterranean region. The species of the Tethys-sea flora hold an important position in the vegetation of the middle and western desert regions of China. They are edificators or dominant species in some deserts, desert steppes and sandy lands, including

Reaumuria, Nitraria, Haloxylon, Cynomoriaceae , Peganum harmala, Alhagi sparsifolia, Halostachys caspica, Kalidium caspicum, Kochia prostrata, K. Scoparia, Carex stenophylloides, Achnatherum splendens, Hordeum bogdanii, Glycyrrhiza uralensis, Halocnemum glomeratus, and *Suaeda corniculata*.

3) Composition of the Black Sea-Kazakhstan-Mongolia and Dawuli-Mongolia

These two components are mainly distributed over the Hulun Buir Sandy Land, the Horqin Sandy Land, the Onqin Daga Sandy Land, the Gahaielesu Sandy Land, the Mu Us Sandy Land and their surrounding areas, belonging to the components of Eurasian steppes. They include xerophytes and mid-xerophytes, dry mesophytes and halo-phytes. The main species include *Stipa baicalensis, S. grandis, Filifolium sibiricum, Caragana microphylla, Cleistogenes squarrosa, Agropyron desertorum, Serratula centhauroides, Hedysarum gmelinii, Iris tenuifolia, Artemisia commutate, A. mongolica, A. palustris, Potentilla acaulis, P. sericea, P. parvifolia, Convolvulus ammannii, Oxytropis glabra, O. myriophylla, O. grandiflora, O. filiformis, Astragalus adsurgens, A. galactites, A. melilotoides, Allium bidentatum, A. condensatum, Polygonum divaricatum, Silene jenisseensis, Delphinium grandiflorum, Papaver nudicaule, Orostachys fimbriatus, Haplophyllum dauricum, Limonium bicolor, Scutellaria baicalensis, Cymbaria dahurica, Echinops gmelinii, Leontopodium leontopodioides*, etc.

4) Compositions of East Asia

Sandy lands in China are mainly distributed over the eastern part of the country, mainly including semi-humid regions as well as semi-arid and humid regions. The plants in these regions are primary and secondary forests and shrubs. The forest plants (including trees, bushes and grasses under the forests) are main components of East Asian flora, with mesophytes as principal features. The species include *Pinus tabulaeformis, Larix pricipis-rupprechtii, Quercus liaotungensis, Q. mongolica, Juniperus rigida, Platycladus orientalis, Cratagus pinnatifida, Ulmus macrocarpa, Prunus sibirica, Schisandra chinensis, Spiraea trilobata, Viburnum mongolicum, Caragana rosea, Atraphaxis manshurica, Rhamnus parvifolia, Ziziphus jujuba, Vitex chinensis, Rosa xanthina, R. sibirica, Indigofera kirilowii, Periploca sepium, Artemisia gmelinii, A. giraldii, A. Oxycephala, Lespedeza daurica, Sophora flavescens, Euphorbia fischeriana*, etc.

5) Endemic compositions

Endemic plants species are distributed relatively less, but they have important effects on local vegetation. Most of these plants belong to dominant species; some endemic species are ancient relic species. The main endemic species include: *Artemisia intramongolica* in the Onqin Daga Sandy Land, the Bashan Plateau; *Artemisia ordosica* in the Ordos-Alxa sandy desert; *Potaninia mongolica* and *Tetraena mongolica* in the western Ordos Plateau; *Ammopiptanthus mongolicus, Prunus mongolica*, *Stilpnolepis centiflora*, *Brachanthemum gobicum* in Alxa deserts and Gobi; *Calligonum zaidamense* and *Reaumuria kaschgarica* in the Qaidam Basin; *Sophora moorcroftiana* in the Tibetan Plateau.

The above-mentioned species are the major components of vegetation in sandy deserts of China. Besides these species, there are many other desert plant species. However, there are fewer dominant species. Two endemic components are summarized as follows.

(1) The components of the northern temperate zone and the Eurasian temperate zone. These components include the Holarctic, palaearctic and East palaearctic flora. They are dominated by mesophytes and also include middle xerophytes, xerophytes and hygrophytes. Among them, the edificators, dominant, diagnostic and important economic plants species include *Pinus sylvestris*, *Sabina vulgaris*, *Salix*, *Betula platyphylla*, *Populus divaricata*, *Picea meyeri*, *Thymus mongolicus*, *Artemisia halodendron*, *A. frigida*, *A. sieversiana*, *Koeleria cristata*, *Festuca ovina*, *Calamagrostis*, *Elymus*, *Bromus inermis*, *Poa pratensis*, *Agropyron cristatum*, *Potentilla anserina*, *Eragrostis pilosa*, *Salicornia europaea*, *Trifolium lupinaster*, *Polygonum aviculare*, *Melissitus ruthenicus*, *Heteropappus altaicus*, *Saposhnikovia divaricata*, *Hypecoum erectum*, etc. The tropicopolitan species *Imperata cylindrical* is mainly distributed over tropic and subtropic zones as the companion species of evergreen broad-leaved forests, but it is the edificator of sandy grasslands of the secondary sandy lands in the Huang–Huai–Hai Plain.

(2) The world species. These species mainly grow in wetlands, swamps and farmlands. They are hygrophytes and hydrophytes and weeds. These species are few and they have little effects on vegetation covers. They include *Phragmites communis*, *Typha*, *Triglochin maritimum*, *Salsola collina*, *Setaria viridis*, *Chenopodium album*, *Amaranthus retroflexus*, *Convolvulus arvensis*, etc.

2.5.2　Vegetation types and their distribution

Owing to the vast area, complex topography and interaction of multiple factors, vegetations in desert regions of China have complex and diversified types and they could be divided into 9 types and 28 subtypes according to vegetation types (trees, bush and grass), land types (lower wetlands, sandy lands, mountainous lands and high-cold lands) and artificial influences (natural and artificial vegetation). Vegetations have obvious zonal and azonal distributional features. At first, they exhibit an obvious horizontally distributional pattern. The order from east to west is: deciduous and broad-leaf forest region in temperate zone at the Huang–Huai–Hai sandy lands; middle-temperate forest grassland in temperate steppe zone at the Song–Nen sandy lands; typical middle-temperature steep in temperate grassland zone at the Hulun Buir Sandy Land, the Horqin Sandy Land, the Gahelesu Sandy Land, the Onqin Daga Sandy Land and their surrounding areas; middle-temperature desert steppe at Ulanqab-Wulate Grasslands; warm temperate typical steppe zone at the Hobq Desert and the Mu Us Sandy Land to the south of the Yinshan Mountains; desert steppe zone of warm-temperate at western half of the Hobq Desert and the Hedong Sandy Land in Ningxia; temperate desert regions west of the line extending from the Helan Mountains to the Wushaoling Mountains and the Qilian Mountains; warm-temperate desert zone at the Kumtag Desert, the Taklimakan Desert and surrounding areas; high-cold vegetation in the deserts and sandy lands of Tibet. Secondly, the vegetation also exhibits vertically distributed features. The basic types of vegetation from bottom to top include: mountain steppe zone at the lower section above basic zone; the shady and sunny slopes at the mid mountain section above the mountain steppe zone; the xeromorphic grass-steppe and deciduous broad-leaf bushes on the sunny slopes of mountains; the forest vegetation on shady slopes of mountains; and the typical meadow at the high-mountainous regions. Because mountains are situated in different natural zones, so the vertical zonality of vegetation distribution is also influenced by the altitude and local climate.

Usually, the distribution of azonal vegetations has two factors. Firstly, hygrophytes, hydrophytes or desert riparian vegetation is distributed along the banks and beaches of inland rivers and lakes. Secondly, some azonal vegetation is distributed over sandy lands. The physical and chemical properties of soils in sandy lands are greatly different from those of zonal soils. Therefore, the azonal vegetation has particular features compared with zonal vegetation. ① The components and structures of plants are simple and easy to be influenced by seasonal precipitation and can easily be restored after taking artificial control measures. ② in arid and semi-arid regions vegetation in sandy lands tends to become mesophytes compared with surrounding zonal vegetation, and the life form of edificators is half to one order of magnitude higher than the surrounding vegetation. For instance, in the sandy lands of steppe zone, there can grow natural coniferous, broadleaf forests and shrubs, and semi-bushes, etc. If used as pasture land, its grass yield is higher than that of zonal steppe but the grass quality is poor. ③ The vegetations on the sandy lands from semi-humid to humid regions tend to become xerophytic compared with surrounding zonal vegetations. ④ the plants only occur in the interdune depressions where groundwater rises to the surface and no vegetation exists at all in other places in supper-arid gobi and sandy desert regions.

2.6 Social and economic situations

Sandy deserts in China occur in 217 counties or cities (Qis) of 11 provinces. They include 21 counties or cities in three provinces of Northeast China, 141 counties in 7 provinces (Shaanxi, Gansu, Ningxia, Qinghai, Inner Mongolia, Hebei and Shanxi) in central China, and 55 counties or cities in Xinjiang. They account for 9.68%, 64.98% and 25.34% of the total county or city numbers, respectively. Based on agricultural economic structure, the above-mentioned regions could be divided into four types, including grazing region, semi-farming region, semi-grazing region and farming region. Among them 42 counties depend on animal husbandry. These counties are located at the sandy lands of Song-Nen, Hulun Buir, Ujimqin, West Ordos, Horqin in northeast China, northern

Table 2-6　Agricultural economic types in sandy desert regions of China (with county as unit)

Type	Areas of sandy desert regions	Type	Areas of sandy desert regions	Type	Areas of sandy desert regions
Grazing district	*Ujimqin*: Dong Ujimqin Qi, Xi Ujimqin Qi, Abag Qi *Hulun Buir*: Ewenkiz Qi, Xin Barag Youqi, Chen Barag Qi, Hailar, Manzhouli *West Yikzhao*: Otog Qi, Otog Qianqi, Uxin Qi, Hangjin Qi *Alxa*: Alxa Youqi, Alxa Zuoqi, Ejin Qi. *Gansu Hexi*: Subei, Sunan, Aksay *Ningxia*:Yanchi *Qinghai Qaidam*: Golmud, Dulan, Ulan, Gonghe, Guinan, Haiyan, Tianjun, Delingha, Mangya, Da Qaidam, Lenghu *Total 31 counties, (Qis) or cities* *Northeast China*: Durbet, Fuyu, Tongyu, Taoan *Xinjiang*: Fuhai, Jeminay, Burqin, Habahe, Mori, Yiwu, Minfeng *Total 11 counties or cities* *Plus 31 Qis, counties or cities, total 42 counties or cities*	Farming district	*Hebei Bashang*: Guyuan, Zhangbei, Kangbao, Shangyi *North Shanxi*: Zuoyun, Youyu, Pinglu, Wusai, Hequ, Baode, Pianguan, Shenchi *Hexi Corridor*: Jiuquan, Yumen, Jinta, Dunhuang, Zhangye, Linze, Gaotai, Minle, Wuwei, Minqin, Gulang, Jingtai, Jinchang, Yongchang, Jiayuguan *Ningxia*: Wuzhong, Zhongning, Zhongwei, Lingwu, Taole, Pingluo, Shizuishan, Yongning, Helan, Yingchuan, Qingtongxia *Ulanqab*: Xinghe, Fengzhen, Liangcheng, Helinger, Chahar You Qi, Qingshuihe, Toktoh *Inner Mongolia Houtao*: Wuyuan, Linhe, Hangjin Hou Qi, Guyang, Baotou *Channeling Yellow River Irrigation District*: Dengkou, Wuda, Haibowan, Wuhai *Northeast China (9 counties)*: Liaoning: Zhangwu, Faku, Changtu, Kangping Jilin: Gongzhuling, Lishu, Fuyu, Shuangliao Heilongjiang: Zhaodong *Xinjiang (39 counties)*: Shawan, Hutubi, Jimsar, Fukang, Manas, Changji, Miquan, Tokxun, Shanshan, Turpan, Ruoqiang, Luntai, Korla, Aksu, Awat, Kulpin, Xinhe, Artux, Karghalik, Bachu, Yarkent, Mekit, Yopurga, Shule(include Kashi), Peyziwat, Shufu, Yengisar, Zep, Pishan, Hotan, Hotan City, Yutian, Qira, Muyu, Luopu, Ürümqi, Karamay, Kuytun *Total 48 counties or cities* *Plus 55 counties or cities in middle and eastern parts, total 103 counties or cities*	Semi-farming district	*Hebei Bashang*: Fengning, Weichang *Middle Ningxia*: Tongxin, Haiyuan *Gansu*:Shandan, Huan Xian *North Shuaanxi*: Dingbian, Jingbian, Hengshan, Shenmu, Fugu, Jia Xian, Mizhi, Wu Qi *Horqin*: Horqin Youyi Zhongqi, Naiman Qi, Horqin Zuoyi Zhong Qi, Horqin Zuoyi Huo Qi, Kailu, Jarut Qi, Huolinhe City, Coulomp Qi, Tongliao City, Tongliao, Arhorchin Horqin Qi *Ongin Daga*:Ongniud Qi, Bahrain Zuoqi, Bahrain Youqi, Linxi, Sonid Zuoqi, Sonid Youqi, Abagnar Qi, Zhenglan Qi, Duolun, Zhengxiangbai Qi, Xianghang Qi, Taibus Qi, Chifeng City, Hexigten Qi, Aoham Qi *Esat Yikzhao*: Dalad Qi, Dongsheng City, Zhunger Qi, Ejin Horo Qi *Ulanqab Houshan*: Wuchuan, Huade, Shangdu, Qiahar You Qi, Qiahar Zhong Qi, Siziwang Qi, Daerhan, Maoming Qi, Urad Hou Qi, Urad Middle Qi, Urad Qian Qi *Northeast China*: Tailai, Qiqihar City, Anda, Daan, Changling Qian'an, Qian Gorlo, Zhenlai *Xinjiang*: Huocheng, Jinghe, Qitai, Kumul, Bakol, Qiemo, Yuli, Wensu, Xayar *Total 72 counties or cities*

parts of northern Xinjiang, Alxa of Inner Mongolia, the Qaidam Basin and mountain regions of the Hexi Corridor. The production values of grazing in these regions account for 40%–50% of the total agricultural output value. There are 103 counties dependent on farming, and the animal husbandry production values account for about 10%–15% of total agricultural output value. These counties are distributed in the Ningxia Plain, the Hexi Corridor, Baotou, Houtao, Dengkou and Uhai, etc. These counties mainly develop irrigation agriculture with the water of the Yellow River, with precipitation in mountainous areas and glacier meltwater as water sources. Most flat lands and hills in these counties have been reclaimed as farmlands. Grasslands are distributed over mountain areas, low-wet meadows in lake basins and swamps. In addition, there are 72 counties dependent on both farming and grazing (semi-farming and semi-grazing). In these regions, the livestock production values account for about 20%–30% of total agricultural output values. They are mainly distributed over the rims of sandy lands in Horqin and Song-Nen, Onqin Daga, mountain areas of Ulanqab Meng, East/Ordos, 3 Qis of Ulate, Fengning and Bashang in Hebei Province, Tongxin, Haiyuan of Ningxia, Shandan and Huan counties of Gansu and a few counties in sandy desert regions in Xinjiang, etc. These counties have enough water, heat and grassland resources, but there exist serious contradictions between population, farming and animal husbandry. These counties are the main regions suffering from severe desertification and blown sand hazards (Table 2-7).

Table 2-7　Basic situations of 141 counties (Qis)
in the middle and eastern sandy desert regions of China

Type	Counties and cities	Population (Person)	Land area (km^2)	Population density (Person/km^2)	Per capita land area(ha)	Grassland area (ha)	Per capita grassland area (ha)	Total agricultural output value ($10^4 yuan$)	Livestock output value ($10^4 yuan$)	Percentage of livestock output value(%)	Per capita agricultural output value(yuan)
Arid region	54	8,204,515	971,793.05	8.44	11.845	44,380,259.1	5.41	290,321.63	55,359.49	19.07	353.86
Semi-arid region	87	18,212,394	732,367.95	24.87	4.02	54,168,927.1	2.97	522,555.3	138,367.76	26.48	286.92
Total	141	26,416,909	1,704,161	15.50	6.45	98,549,186.2	3.73	812,876.93	193,727.25	23.83	307.71

Note: Agricultural output value and livestock output value were calculated from 1985 values based on the constant price of 1980.

Some regions belong to semi-humid meadow grassland belts in the eastern and middle desert regions of China, such as the eastern part of the Hulun Buir Sandy Land, southeastern corner of the Song-Nen and the Ujimqin sandy lands. There are 18 counties in semi-humid regions, 90 counties in semi-arid regions, among them there are 98 counties located in the warm temperate arid regions and 11 counties located in high-cold arid regions. There are 3,195 towns or villages included in the region, among them 2 841 are villages and 354 are towns, state farms, and pastures. The total sum includes $1,125.05 \times 10^4$ families and 45,080,270 population. About 34,215,432 (75.89% of total population) people live by agriculture and stockbreeding. There are 12,136,252 labor forces (35.47% of rural population), so the labor force resources are sufficient. The land area of the region is 3,081,197.21 km^2, with a population density of 14.6 people per km^2. It seems that population density is low in the whole region; however it has large regional differences. For example, in the eastern part the population density is 24.87 per km^2, while in arid regions the population density is only about 8.7 people km^2. According to the standards recommended by UNEP (the population density are 20 and 7 people/km^2 for semi-arid and arid regions, respectively), it exceeds about 20% of land carrying capacity.

Table 2-8   Social and economic situation of sandy desert regions of China

Names of sandy desert regions	Town ships number	Number of farm, forestry and pasture field	Total household number	Total population (p)	Peasant population (p)	Rural men power (p)	Farmlands area (ha)	Agricultural output value (10^4 yuan)	Livestock Output value (10^4 yuan)	Percenta -ge of livestock output value (%)	Land area (ha)
3 provinces in NE China	484	698	2,011,541	9,540 966	7,786,441	1,997,397	29,254,533	207,882	36,158.4	17.39	9,646,600
13 districts in Inner Mongolia	1,198	260	4,500,000	14,330,970	10,082,628	4,084,464	43,778,667	454,588.92	122,135.71	26.87	93,938,845.5
Bashang in Hebei	154	26	440,819	1,826,278	1,684,133	687,432	872,624.5	56,015.58	13,939.85	24.85	3,182,971.9
North Shanxi	139	30	225,946	889,464	8,812,146	294,720	439,678.1	30,371.0	3,592.0	11.83	1,247,307.2
North Shaanxi	201	33	44,107	1,907,677	1,767,300	696,800	510,600	44,824.0	8,482.0	18.92	4,066,170.9
Middle and North Ningxia	194	72	583,380	2,916,901	2,269,753	778,212	455,135.7	74,799.8	11,806.2	15.78	4,050,667
Hexi Corridor plus Huan county in Gansu	307	70	840,000	4,043 499	3,247, 100	1,548,400	733,533.3	125,326.11	25,750.35	19.03	28,341,431.7
Qaidam Basin in Qinghai	61	25	94,200	502,120	179,831	76,627	99,200.0	16,911.52	8,021.14	47.43	35,588,686.7
7 provinces in middle and East China in sandy desert region	2,254	513	7,124,452	26,416,909	20,042 891	8,166,655	7,488,658.3	812,876.93	193,727.25	23.83	170,416,081
Xinjiang	457	182	2,114,546	9,128 400	6,386 100	2,152 200	1,732 040	247,599.0	35,672.1	14.41	128,057,040
Total	3,195	1,393	11,250,359	45,086,275	34,215,432	12,136,252	12,146,151.6	1,268,358.63	265,557.75	20.94	3,081,119,721

Note: Agricultural output value and livestock output value were calculated from 1985 statistical data. The agricultural output value and livestock output value for Northeast China were obtained from 4 counties in Liaoning, 10 counties in Baicheng district and Shuangliao County of Jilin and 16 counties, such as Daqing City and Duerbeit County in Heilongjiang.

In the agricultural economic constituents, land is a basic resource, just like labor force, climate and scientific and technical proficiency. The cultivated area in the region is 12,146,152 hm^2, per capita farmland and pasture land areas are 0.27 hm^2 and 2.975 hm^2 respectively. Among them there is 5.41 hm^2 of pasturelands in semi-arid areas and 2.97 hm^2 of pasturelands in arid areas of 7 provinces. This is 10–20 times the country's per capita pasturelands area of 0.28 hm^2 and about 3 times the per capita farmlands area of 0.09 hm^2. The whole sandy desert regions has 7,590×10^4

livestock and it is the main bases of animal husbandry in the northern parts of China. The livestock output value accounts for 20.94% of total agriculture output value, which exceeds the country's average level by 2.38%. The current situation of society and economy in sandy desert regions are listed in Table 2-6, 2-7, 2-8, respectively.

References

Chen Guangting. 1995. Characteristics of aeolian geomorphology and its unit division along Tarim Oil Road. International Science Symposium of the Taklimakan Desert. Arid Zone Research (suppl.)

Chen Longheng, Li Fuxing, Di Xinmin et al., 1998. Aeolian Soils in China. Beijing: Science Press. 1–188

Chen Longheng, Li Fuxing. 1999. Sandy neo-soils. In: Gong Zitong et al. Classification of Soil System in China: Theory, Methods and Practices. Beijing: Science Press. 716–742

Cooke R U, Warren A, Goudie A S. 1993. Desert Geomorphology. London: UCL Press

Dong Guangrong, Chen Huizhong, Wang Guiyong et al. 1995. Evolution of deserts and sandy lands and climatic change in northern China since 150 ka. Science in China (Series B), 25(12): 271–280

Dong Guangrong, Li Sen, Li Baosheng et al. 1991. A Preliminary Study on the Formation and Evolution of Deserts in China. Journal of Desert Research, 11(4): 23–32 (In Chinese)

Editorial Board of Hydraulic Division in China. 1989. Hydraulic Division in China. Beijing: Hydraulic and Electric Power Press

Geng Kuanhong. 1986. Climate in Desert Regions in China. Beijing: Science Press. 4–16, 155–161

Project Group of Soil Classification, Institute of soil science, CAS 2000. Classification of Soil System in China (Third Edition). Beijing: China Agriculture Science and Technology Press

Qiu Shanwen, Li Qusheng. 1992. Paleosol in western sandy lands of Northeast Plain and change of Holocene environment. Quaternary Sciences, (3): 230

Wang Peifang. 1992. A preliminary study on environmental change of the Hulun Buir Sandy Land during Holocene period. Journal of Desert Research, 12(4):19

Xiong Yi, Li Qingkui. 1987. Soils in China (Second Edition). Beijing: Science Press. 275–283

Zhang Chao, Ma Pinqi. 1989. Geographic Climatology. Beijing: China Meteorological Press

Zhang Qiang, Zhao Xue, Zhao Halin. 1998. Grasslands of Sandy Lands in China. Beijing: China Meteorological Press

Zhao Songqiao. 1990. Arid Zone in China. Beijing: Science Press

Zhou Tingru, Zhang Lansheng. 1983. Environment Change and Prediction in Holocene Period at Agro-pasture Cross-belt in China. Beijing: Geology Press. 69

Zhu Zhenda, Chen Guangting. 1994. Sandy Desertification in China. Beijing: Science Press

Zhu Zhenda, Wu Zheng, Liu Shu. 1980. Sandy Deserts in China. Beijing: Science Press

Chapter 3
Classification and Distribution of Deserts and Aeolian Desertified Lands in China

3.1 Classification and distribution of deserts in China

3.1.1 A history of the concept of deserts in China

The term "desert" was first used around 2,000 years ago in *Han History ·Biography of Su Jian*: "I traveled 10,000 *li*, crossing the sandy deserts, and I combated the Hun(Xiongnu) for my lord." Cao Zhi from the Wei Dynasty during the Three Kingdoms Period mentioned the desert in his *White Horse Poem* as follows: "He is a noble knight, who hails from You and Bing. He left his home in early youth, and now his name is known throughout the deserts." Ruan Ji, also from the Wei Dynasty during the Three Kingdoms Period, wrote in *A Teenager Learns to Remove Thorns:* "I waved my sword and faced the desert, and fed my horse in many fields." In these references, the word desert indicates land in the north of China covered by large naked regions of dry mobile sand or gravel, including the regions of sand dunes and gravel desert (gobi).

Before the Western Han Dynasty, references to the desert in northwest China were expressed as "mobile sand." In *The Classic of Mountains and Rivers* (a geographical and cultural account from the Warring States Period) it is written: "Walk west 400 *li*, and 200 *li* will be mobile sand." Another example is found in *Shang Book·Yu Gong*: "Part of the Ruoshui River is diverted to Heli, and the other part is diverted through mobile sand". From these early recordings, it is obvious that "mobile sand" is the earliest word representing the desert in China. In the Tang Dynasty, the term "mobile sand" is also often found in literature. In *Old Tang Book · Western World Biography*, it is written: "There are several hundred *li* of mobile sands in the northwest". This same period also witnessed the appearance of neologisms such as "shazi"(big desert) and "hanhai" (sand sea). Such an example appeared in *Collected Tang Poems,* a work by Cen Shen: "It has taken ten days to pass through the *shazi*, the morning wind blows endlessly! The horse walks on broken stones, and its four hooves are covered in blood"; "The *hanhai* was crisscrossed with miles of ice, and ominous clouds filled the gloomy sky. I saw you off at the east gate of Luntai, and the Tianshan Road was covered in snow".

After the Song and Yuan Dynasties, there appeared such neologisms as "gobi", "khoum" and "damo," as well as place names like the "Alxa Gobi desert", "Gashun Gobi", "Kuruk Khoum", and "Mongolian desert". Here, "gobi" (Mongolian) refers to flat sandy and gravelly land in which it is difficult to grow grass and trees"; "khoum" (Uigur) means the ground is covered with mobile sand dunes on a large scale; "Damo" refers to vast and bald, sandy or gravelly surfaces.

Since the 20th century, the word "desert" in China refers to a desert or a sandy desert. "Desert" refers to a region with low precipitation, high evaporation, low vegetation, including sandy, gravel, rock, mud and salt deserts. However, in Chinese "desert" is often translated into a word that literally means "sandy desert". In the new English-Chinese Dictionary (Shanghai Translation Press), a desert is expressed as ① desert, sterile lands; ② a desolate place. In *Ci Hai* (Shanghai Lexicographic Publishing House) "sandy desert" is a general term for the desert. To take another example, the Sahara Desert consists of large stretches of gulch (a vestige of a once well watered landscape, similar to the scabland formed by the erosion from flowing water), dry denudation mountain regions (rock desert), stone deserts (inhabitants call Hamada), gravel deserts (inhabitants call Reg), sandy deserts (which account for less than 10% of the whole area), and also includes oases., According to the standards of the Sahara, northwest China, the Qinghai-Tibet Plateau and Central Asia can all be classified as "deserts".

Through the above analysis, it is also easy to understand that the meaning of the word desert, including the words "shazi", "hanhai", "gobi desert" and "desert," still lack unanimous understanding. But one point is irrefutable, namely that sandy deserts refer to ground that is completely covered by sand dunes and lacks flowing water and vegetation due to the arid climate, for instance, the Taklimakan Desert, the Badain Jaran Desert and the Tengger Desert.

This shows that concepts of deserts in Chinese include both a broad and narrow meaning. In the broadest sense, deserts include gravel, rock, mud, salt and sandy deserts, and this definition is consistent with the English usage of the word "desert." The narrowly-defined desert refers to grounds that are covered by large dunes (or sands) and lacks both flowing water and vegetation.

Because of these two meanings, it can lead to some confusion about the classifications of deserts, and it is easy to create misunderstandings if the meaning of the word "desert" is not classified. For example, in some textbooks, the area of the Sahara Desert is 9,960,000 km^2; the area of Rub'al Khali Desert is 650,000 km^2. According to this data, the area of the Sahara is 15 times larger than that of Rub'al Khali Desert. However, it must be understood that the Sahara desert is usually classified under the broad meaning of desert, while the Rub'al Khali Desert is classified under the narrow meaning of the word desert. Using the narrow meaning of the word desert, the area of mobile sands in the Sahara is only 1,560,000 km^2; in actuality, the area of the Sahara Desert using the narrow meaning of the word "desert" is only 2.4 times larger than that of Rub'al Khali Desert.

3.1.2 Classifications of deserts

Classifications of deserts include:

(1) According to morphology and material composition, deserts can be classified into sandy

deserts, gravel deserts and wind-eroded land. This book classifies the following as deserts: sandy desert, gobi desert, wind-eroded lands, southern strand, lake banks, sandy bank land (sometimes referred to as sandy beach), as well as all the categories accumulated and transformed by wind-forces or with similar desert landscapes, The total area of Chinese deserts is 684,000 km^2; gobi desert (gravel desert) 570,000 km^2 (wind-eroded gobi 181,000/km^2, accumulated gobi 389,000 km^2); Yardang and other wind-eroded lands 29,000 km^2.

(2) Tropical, subtropical and temperate zone deserts are regionalized, according to their location along climate belts. There are a lot of differences between the reasons for formation, atmospheric circulation and water and heat conditions. Temperate zone deserts are distributed in the middle part of Eurasia in western basins as well as mountains plateaus in North America. They are on average located between 35°–45°N. Because these deserts are located in central mainland areas or are protected by alpine coast, they do not receive the humid air current from the ocean. Their climate is very arid, vegetation cover is low, and only a few sparse herbs and small bushes can grow. Desert areas of Asian temperate zones, including western Asian arid desert regions. Central Asian arid desert regions and arid desert regions of northwest China are very large and extend more than 5,000 kilometers continuously from east to west. In North America, deserts in the Temperate Zone are only distributed in the western part of the USA. In the Southern Hemisphere, Patagonia is a small arid desert located along the bank of the Atlantic Ocean in southern Argentina in South America.

Chinese deserts belong to the temperate zone deserts of Central Asia. The Asian and European Continents link together, in this area, and the area is vast. The centre is far removed from the ocean, separated by mountains. Most deserts are located in basins, where moist air currents cannot invade. This combined with heat from the Qinghai-Tibet Plateau controls the regional climatic conditions of the temperate zone deserts in China. The climate is cold in winter, with the lowest monthly temperature on average between −3–−10°C, In the center of the desert, temperatures reach 40°C in summer, and extreme temperatures can reach up to 90°C, corresponding to tropical and subtropical deserts. These temperate zone deserts are called "cold deserts."

(3) Sandy deserts can be divided into shifting sandy deserts (or sandy lands), semi-fixed sandy deserts (or sandy lands) and fixed sandy deserts (or sandy lands).

The total desert area in China is 684,000 km^2, of which shifting deserts encompass 446,000 km^2, semi-fixed deserts encompass 144,000 km^2, and fixed deserts encompass 94,000 km^2.

(4) The geographical educational circles of China, in order to emphasize the differences between natural conditions and landscapes in the western and eastern desert regions refer to the western deserts as sandy deserts and refer to the eastern deserts as "sandy land". The western sandy deserts are covered by large areas of sand dunes. They are in dry and windy regions, lack flowing water and have sparse vegetation, such as the Taklimakan Desert, Badain Jaran Desert and the Tengger Desert.

The eastern sandy lands are covered by fixed or semi-fixed sand dunes. They are in semi-arid or semi-humid windy regions with few rivers and sparse vegetation, such as the Mu Us Sandy Land, the Horqin Sandy Land and the Onqin Daga Sandy Land.

Usually an aridity index >4 is the boundary line between deserts and sandy lands. Aeolian sediments in semi-arid to humid regions in eastern China are called sandy lands and in western China are called sandy deserts. However, a discrepancy appears by taking an aridity index >4 as the boundary line as an aridity index above and below are both found in the Hobq Desert: its eastern region is in the half dry steppe, while the western region is in the dry desert steppe. Because the western range is larger than the eastern regions, the entire Hobq area is referred to as a desert.

The total area of deserts in China is 581,000 km^2; the total area of sandy land is 103,000 km^2.

Properties, characteristics, and climates are very different between deserts and sandy lands. The western sandy deserts located in the centre of Asia lacks rain throughout the year, has sparse vegetation, and is primarily composed of mobile dunes with various kinds of shapes. Eastern sandy lands, on the other hand, are influenced by the East cold and dry winter monsoon in the Northwest for a long time, while time is transient to influence by warm wet air current of southeast in summer and autumn, and is located in the end of southeast monsoon, transient in rainy season, and the precipitation is insufficient. Under modern climatic conditions, the natural appearance of sandy lands mainly on regular with the semi-stationary and lower sand dunes.

3.1.3 Distributions of deserts in China

Deserts or sandy lands in China are mainly distributed throughout 9 provinces and regions including Xinjiang Uygur Autonomous Region, Qinghai Province, Gansu Province, Ningxia Hui Autonomous Region, Inner Mongolian Autonomous Region, Shaanxi Province, Liaoning Province, Jilin Province and Heilongjiang Province (Fig. 3-1). They are distributed between 75°–125°E and 35°–50°N.

(1) 90% of the total desert area in China is distributed in the inland of China, far away from the ocean, and are more concentrated to the west of the Helan Mountains, Moreover, except for the Gurbantünggüt Desert in the Junggar Basin of Xinjiang, the majority of deserts have shifting dunes as the core, which totals to about 75% of all the deserts in this area. To the east of this line, the desert area is relatively small and scattered, and only accounts for about 10% of the total area of Chinese deserts. Except for the regions of the Mu Us Sandy Land in southern Erdos and the Horqin Sandy Land downstream of the Xiliao River that are part mobile sand, the majority of deserts are mainly composed of fixed and semi-fixed sand dunes (Table 3-1).

(2) From assessing climatic conditions, Chinese deserts are distributed in arid areas that lack rain, where the wind-force is strong and frequent, and the wind strength during the windy season usually reaches a force above 5–6 grades. The annual precipitation is less than 450 mm. The annual precipitation is lower than 150 mm in the areas to the west of the Helan Mountains, and it sometimes

is even below 100 mm. The annual precipitation is below 25 mm in the middle and eastern part of the Taklimakan Desert. The arid index is mainly over 1.5, and it is roughly 1.5–4.0 to the east of the Helan Mountains. The arid index reaches more than 4 in the west, and the aridity of the desert in southern Xinjiang is 20–60.

Table 3-1　The distribution of surface shapes in deserts in different natural zones of China

Natural zone	Representative deserts or sandy lands	Various dunes (%)	
		Mobile dunes	Fixed and semi-fixed dunes
Arid desert zone in Western China	Taklimakan desert	85	15
Steppe and semi-desert zone in Middle in China	Mu Us Sandy Land	64	36
Steppe zone in Eastern China	Horqin Sandy Land	10	90

Note: Quoting Zhu Zhenda. 1999a. Sandy Desert, Sandy Desertification, Desertification and Combating Countermeasures in China.

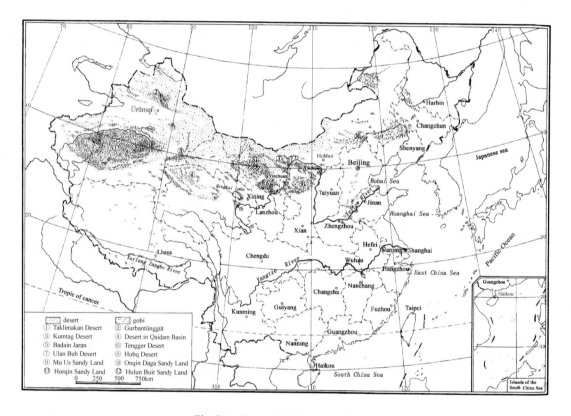

Fig. 3-1　Desert distribution in China

(3) The total desert area in Xinjiang is the largest in China, accounting for nearly 60% of the total area of China's deserts, followed in decreasing area by Gansu, Qinghai, Inner Mongolia, Ningxia, Jilin, Liaoning, Shaanxi and Heilongjiang (Table 3-2). The Taklimakan Desert in the Tarim Basin south of Xinjiang is the largest desert in China; including the fragmentary desert located around the edges, the total area reaches 327 thousand km^2, comprising 1/2 of the total area of Chinese deserts. It also has the largest shifting dune distribution of deserts in China, and the area of

mobile sand field is 277,000 km^2. The Gurbantünggüt Desert in the Junggar Basin north of Xinjiang, including the fragmentary desert around the edges, has a total area of 47,000 km^2 and is the third biggest desert as well as the largest regular semi-stationary desert in China. The Badain Jaran Desert in the Alxa Plateau in western Inner Mongolia is the second largest one in China; it has the tallest and largest dunes in China. The widest area of the Gobi desert is located at the border between Gansu and Xinjiang. The northwestern part of the Qaidam Basin, has the largest area of wind-eroded land, which encompasses an area of 22,400 km^2. Table 3-3 shows the area of every deserts in China.

Table 3-2　Total area of deserts in different provinces in China (Units: 10^4 km^2)

Province(Autonomous Region)	Xinjiang	Gansu	Qinghai	Inner Mongolia	Ningxia	Shaanxi	Jilin	Liaoning	Heilongjiang
Desert area	42.0	1.9	3.8	21.3	0.4	1.1	0.36	0.17	0.26

Note: ① figures do not include areas of gobi desert ; ② Quoting Zhu Zhenda (1999a) Sandy Desert, Sandy Desertification, Desertification and Combating Countermeasures in China.

Table 3-3　Area of major deserts in China

Desert or Sandy Lands	Location	Altitude (m)	Area (10^4 km^2)
Taklimakan desert	Tarim basin of Xinjiang	800–1,400	33.76
Badain Jaran Desert	The west of Alxa Plateau	1,300–1,800	4.92
Gurbantünggüt Desert	Junggar Basin of Xinjiang	300–600	4.88
Tengger Desert	The southeast of Alxa Plateau	1,400–1,600	4.27
Qaidam Desert	Qaidam Basin of Qinghai	2,600–3,400	3.49
Kumtag Desert	Areas to the north of Altun mountains	1,000–1,200	2.28
Hobq Desert	The north of Erdos Plateau	1,000–1,200	1.61
Ulan Buh Desert	The southeast of Alxa Plateau	1,000	0.99
Horqin Sandy Land	The downstream of Xiliao River	100–300	4.23
Mu Us Sandy Land	The middle-south of Erdos Plateau	1,300–1,600	3.21
Onqin Daga Sandy Land	The east of Inner Mongolia	1,000–1,400	2.14
Hulun Buir Sandy Land	The northeast of Inner Mongolia	600	0.72

Note: Quoting Chen Guangting (2001).

(4) The distribution of natural conditions varies in different deserts. For example, the Taklimakan Desert in the Tarim Basin is classified as a warm temperate arid desert, the desert in the Junggar Basin is a temperate arid desert, the desert in the Qaidam Basin on the Qinghai-Tibet Plateau is a cold arid desert, the western sandy land in the Erdos area is a temperate grassland desert, the eastern sandy land of the erdos area is semi-arid temperate steppe region, and some sandy land in the western part of the Northeastern Plain and eastern part of the Inner Mongolia is classified as a semi-arid temperate steppe region. Only the eastern Horqin Sandy Land is classified as a semi-humid temperate grassland region. As a result of the variance in natural conditions, natural features in China's deserts also are remarkably different.

(5) Except for the low altitude western Horqin Sandy Land in the Northeastern Plain located

only 100–300 m above sea level, other deserts are all distributed in basins located at higher altitudes above sea level and in between landlocked mountain. For instance, the Onqin Daga Sandy Land in the East Inner Mongolian Plateau is 1,000–1,400 m above sea level. Sandy lands on the Erdos Plateau are 1,200–1,500 above sea level; some deserts the Alxa Region are 1,200–1,800 above sea level; the desert in the Tarim Basin is 800–1,400 m above sea level; the desert in Qaidam Basin is 2,600 – 3,400 m above sea level; (see table 4-3). There are even sand dunes distributed in some river valleys on high mountains as well as on the Qinghai-Tibet Plateau located in southeastern regions of Qinghai and Xinjiang, all of which are around 4,000 m above sea level.

3.2   General characteristics of Chinese deserts

The characteristics of different natural environments in the world are determined by their geographical position. The characteristics of deserts are decided by their geographical position and environmental conditions.

Prof. Zhu and Prof. Zhao summarize the characteristics of deserts in China in the following several points (Zhu et al., 1980; Zhao, 1997).

3.2.1   Arid climate and low precipitation

Precipitation decreases progressively from east to west, and while the annual precipitation in most areas is less than 400 mm, but there are still some differences. The annual precipitation is about 250 – 400 mm, in western part of the Northeast Plain and eastern parts of Inner Mongolia Autonomous Region, 50 – 150 mm in Ningxia and the western Alxa region of Gansu, under 50 mm in the Badan Jarin Desert, and less than 10 mm in eastern Xinjiang and middle and eastern parts of the Taklimakan Desert.

In sandy areas in the western parts of the Northeastern Plain and eastern Inner Mongolia Autonomous Region, plants grow better, and fixed and semi-fixed sand dunes have a comparative advantage. With the exception of the Junggar Basin, which only 100–200 mm of precipitation, and the plant grows better, and the majority is fixed and semi-fixed sand dunes, the other most deserts are the mobile dunes. Not only is precipitation rare in desert areas, but the evaporation rate is also very high, generally between 1,400–3,000 mm per year, and often reaches 3,000–3,800 mm within the desert. The aridity increases gradually from east to west, the east is generally in the range of 1.5–4.0, but more than 4 to the west of the Helan Mountains; to eastern Xinjiang and the Tarim Basin, the aridity reaches between 20–60.

3.2.2 Abundant heat resources and high temperature difference

In desert areas, there is generally between 2,500 – 3,000 h of sunshine, 120–300 days free of frost, and with the exception of accumulative temperatures ≥10 °C in some sandy lands of Hulun Buir and eastern Inner Mongolia, the accumulative temperature is generally between 3,000 – 5,000°C.The temperature change is relatively large, with an average yearly difference in temperature generally ranging from 30–50°C and absolute temperature differences of more than 50–60°C. The daily temperature difference exhibits an extremely remarkable change, with 30°C as the largest temperature difference, though most daily temperature differences are between 10–20°C. Especially desert surface temperature changes are particularly violent, temperatures can reach up to 60–80°C at high noon in summer and autumn, and drop to below 10°C at night.

3.2.3 Frequent blown sand activities

Wind is relatively strong in desert areas, and wind velocity during the windy season usually reaches more than 5 grades, eroding loose sand on the surface. In the winter and spring windy season, the sandy surface is blown by wind into the air, and frequent sandstorms occur. Blown-sand days generally last about 20–100 days. Especially in mobile sand areas, vegetation is sparse, and sandstorms are more common. The blown sand days in the southern Taklimakan Desert accounts for 1/3 of the year, which is usually around 145 days; during 1995–1997, there were 182 sand-blown days every year on average in oil field No. 4 in the tower located in the desert hinterland. In 1959 there were 148 blown sand days in Minqin Basin, which is located at the edge of Tengger Desert. This accounts for 41% of the number of days of the year, and over 1/2 of the blown-sand days of that year occurred from March to June. The longest continuous blown sand activity lasted 17–48 hours, and they generally were above 10 hours.

3.2.4 Sparse and low vegetation, and few kinds of animals

Dense *P. euphratica* Oliver woods and narrow-leaved oleaster forest that grow along the bank of some river valley areas and rivers developed at desert edges getting deeply to the desert (i.e. the midstream and downstream of the Tarim River, the Hotan River, low reaches of the Keriya River, the Yarkant River and the Ejin River), and some aspen scattered, *P. armeniaca* var. ansu, elm, on fixed dunes in the Horqin Sandy Land and the eastern Onqin Daga Sandy Land growing, it is the most part herbaceous and bush (such as red willow and *Haloxylon*) However, in most desert areas, especially those with mobile dunes, the vegetation is sparse.

Plants are low and sparse in deserts, and have some arid landscape characteristics. In order to adapt to the arid climate, their leaf all shrink, or turn into bar-shaped and stinging type. For instance, *Haloxylon* and *C. mongolicum*, a lot of plants sink in order to reduce the air vent transpiration, and their cuticles thicken. Other plant nutrition organs turns into plump meat with one's own deposit moisture. To resist the strong summer sunshine, a lot of pieces of plants become white or ashen surface, like *N. tangutorum*. In order to absorb moisture in the sand layers, their roots try their best to spread deeply underground, and much areas by expanding and absorbing water of lateral root longer.

Arid climate, sparse vegetation, and lack of food, water and shelter, make it difficult for most animals to live normally. Animal groups of kind and quantity are poor, and animals concentrate in regions with sources of water, grass and trees, or close to growing vegetation located in piedmonts. Because some oases stretch into the desert hinterland, and the influence of the human activity, some grassland animals were forced to move to desert area for living, thus enriching animal species in desert areas (Zhang Linyuan et al., 1994).

3.2.5 Huge sandy sediments

Except for a small proportion of Chinese deserts distributed on landlocked plateaus, the majority of deserts are distributed in enormous inland basins. For example, the Taklimakan Desert lies in of the Tarim Basin, and of the Gurbantünggüt Desert lies in the middle part of the Junggar Basin. Sandy sediment thickness at the basins' edge can reach 200 – 400 m, sand layer thickness of the Taklimakan Desert in the Tarim Basin is generally 200 – 500 m, and the Quaternary Period loose sand thickness in the Xiliao River downstream alluvial plain of the Horqin Sandy Land located can reach 130 m. This kind of thick and loose sandy sediment becomes an important material source for the deserts and under the arid, windy climatic conditions, they are apt to be blown by the wind.

3.2.6 Shifting dunes moving along the dominant wind direction

The desert surface is covered with sand dunes. Though generally 10—25m high, the tallest and biggest sand dunes can reach 100–300 m, and the smallest ones are less than 5 m. Expect for fixed and semi-fixed sand dunes, sand dunes generally exhibit a remarkable phenomenon as they move along the dominant wind direction under strong wind conditions, However they move slowly, and their speed of movement. Under the same natural conditions and wind direction is directly correlated to its size. The higher the sand dune is, the more slowly it moves. For example, compound sand dunes with a height of 30–50 m in the Taklimakan Desert move at a rate of 1 m/a, the flat lands among the compound sand dunes, with 1.0–1.5 m high generally move 4–7 m/a, some can reach 12 m. Moisture is an important factor of the sand dune activity, in the area with better moisture and vegetation, most sand dunes are fixed by plants,and their advancement is not noticeable.

3.2.7　Little runoff, abundant underground water

In rare precipitation, vigorous evaporate and easy seepage regions, there is almost no river formed by local runoff, except several transit rivers (i.e. trunk stream and its tributaries of the Xiliao River in the Horqin Sandy Land, the Yellow River in the eastern Ulan Buh Desert). Input of rivers near Hotan, along with the alpine ice and snow supply, become the local main source of water, for instance, the Tarim River, the Qarqan River, the Yarkant River, and the Hotan River and the Keriya River stretching deeply into the desert, at the edge of the Taklimakan Desert, etc. Water systems, except for the trunk stream and its tributaries of the Xiliao River in the southern Horqin Sandy Land and the southeast of the Mu Us Sandy Land, etc. being exterior drainage, other deserts are all closed drainage.

Although the surface water in deserts is very scarce, except for some deserts, there distributed phreatic water and artesian water underground in most districts. This is because the majority of main deserts of China mentioned in just as former lies in the interior basin, this landforms, loose river alluviation or lake sediment of the basin can influx and store underground water. Among them some are very valuable in use, such as phreatic water of the pediment plain at the desert edge, phreatic water of a river valley inside a desert, pressure water and artesian water in alleviation and the lacustrine layer covered with sand dunes inside the desert.

3.2.8　Soil formation in the initial stage

The sections of soils in deserts possess thin layers, coarse texture, moisture and nutrients are scarce, and salt content (especially carbonate and gypsum) is abundant. Zonal soil in the areas to the east of the Wenduer Temple-Bailin Temple -Otog-Dingbian line is mainly chestnut soil, while soil in the areas to the west of the Helan Mountains is greyish brown desert soil and brown desert soil, and brown calcium soil and gray calcium soil between the two.

The Gobi desert can be divided into two kinds: accumulated Gobi desert mainly distributed in the pediment plains, piled up by water and repeated sorting of wind for the diluvian fan of the alluviation or the diluvian fan material, the ground materials mainly consist of gravel or sand gravel, the pediment plain in all mountains all belong to this kind in the Qilian Mountains, the Tianshan Mountains, the Kunlun Mountains; the other is denudation gobi type which refers to the denudation stony plain or broken stone remained cover the plain with incomplete mound and island mountain on earth's surface, the gobi desert of the Mazhong Mountains and eastern area of Xinjiang is the remarkable example.

The few above-mentioned characteristics determine the total characteristics of deserts in China, namely the obvious regional differences from the east to the west. Because the precipitation in the eastern area of Inner Mongolia is relatively higher than that in the west, plant grow well, and is covered mainly by fixed and semi-fixed sand dunes, while the mobile sand is only distributed in places where the vegetation is destroyed. In the Northwest arid area except that the Junggar Basin where winter precipitation is slightly more and fine for plants to grow, other most deserts are covered mainly by mobile dunes. Therefore, the mobile dunes reduce gradually from west to east, while the fixed, semi-fixed sand dunes increase gradually from west to east (Table 3-1) (Zhu, 1999a).

3.3　Types and characteristics of aeolian desertification in China

3.3.1　Aeolian desertification and aeolian desertified land

3.3.1.1　The concept of aeolian desertification and its development

In brief, aeolian desertification is the phenomenon where land is degraded to desert-like landscape in arid and semi-arid regions. It's the primary type of desertification.

In recent years, with the rapid occurrence of desertification all over the world, desertification has become a severe environmental issue which progressively blocks human advancement and economical and social development as well as worldwide attention. Today, there are also differences in how to understand and translate the word "desertification" globally. According to the consensus of United Nations Conference on Environment and Development (UNCED) held in Rio de Janeiro in 1992, the Convention to Combat Desertification in "Those Countries Experiencing Serious Drought and/or Desertification, Particularly in Africa" (abbreviated as "United Nations Convention to Combat Desertification") clarified the concept of "Desertification" in June, 1994.

(1) "Desertification" is land degradation in arid, semi-arid and dry semi-humid areas resulting from various factors, including climatic variations and human factors;

(2) "Desertification Control" is a series of activities on synthesized land exploitation in arid, semi-arid and dry semi-humid areas, it is supposed: to combat and/or decrease land degradation; to rehabilitate part of degraded land; to recultivate desertified land;

(3) "Drought" is a prolonged period of less-than-normal precipitation such that the lack of water causes a serious hydrologic imbalance, such as crop damage, and water supply shortages, in the affected area;

(4) "To reduce the impact of drought" is a series of efforts related to the forecast of drought; it aims to reduce drought's impact on social and natural systems by desertification control;

(5) "Land" means the terrestrial bio-productive system that comprises soil, vegetation, other biota and the ecological and hydrological processes that operate within the system;

(6) "Land degradation" means reduction and loss of the biological or economic productivity caused by land-use change, from a physical process, or a combination of two. These include

processes arising from human activities and habitation patterns, such as soil erosion, deterioration of the physical, chemical and biological or economic properties of the soil, and long-term loss of vegetation;

(7) "Arid, semi-arid and dry semi-humid areas" has the ratio of annual average precipitation to latent evaporation of 0.05–0.65, excluding polar and sub-polar regions.

As early as "Dust Bowl" swept the United States in the 1930s and similar environmental issues caused by large-scale land exploitation of the USSR on Central Asia that happened before the 1960s, people worldwide have paid attention to sandy desertification. French scientist, Aubreville put forward the word "Desertification" when he studied the ecological problems in the Sahara region in Africa. According to Aubreville's opinion, desertification is a process where tropical forest was changed into tropical steppe, even degraded to tropical desert-like landscape because of cutting and burning forests. During the 1960s–1970s, there was a long drought in the Sahara, which accelerated the degradation of the environment and resulted in the convulsion of the society. The word "Desertification" was adopted in a global conference on desertification, held in Nairobi, the capital city of Kenya, by the United Nations (UN).

Desertification or aeolian desertification is a kind of process of environmental degradation; land is the main body of degradation and desertified and aeolian desertified land are the result of environmental degradation.

3.3.1.2　The trend and harms of aeolian desertification in China

The history of aeolian desertification can be traced back to the origin of human culture and the speed of aeolian desertification is amazing. Aeolian desertification can lead to land degradation and even impede the development of social economy. Drought is a cause of aeolian desertification, but essentially, irrational human behavior is the main cause of aeolian desertification. Only a fraction of aeolian desertification land was caused by desert expansion. In China, only 5.5% of the total 38.57×10^4 km^2 of aeolian desertified land was caused by advancing sand dunes. Aeolian desertified lands don't include sandy desert, Gobi, salt desert and cold desert formed in the geological period. So, 128.3 km^2 of sandy desert, Gobi and cold desert are all excluded from aeolian desertification.

Aeolian desertification leads to the loss of land resources, debases the land productivity, reduces biodiversity and influences global climate. Aeolian desertification can severely influence the socio-economy in the following: ① By weakening the society's capacity to supply enough food for an increasing population; ② By arosing instability of economy and political turbulence and make local people leave their native place; ③ By increasing the pressure in non-desert areas, even resulting in conflicts in different areas; ④ To impeding the national, and even the global, sustainable development capability; ⑤ By directly threatening human health, even children's health and nutrition status.

Considering the extensive impact of aeolian desertification, the whole world has realized that aeolian desertification is not just a regional issue but rather a global economic, social and environmental issue.

Aeolian desertification is also a severe socio-economic and environmental issue in China. Though a great deal of works controlling aeolian desertification have been done, the rate of aeolian desertification control was less than that of aeolian desertification development. According to the report of State Environmental Protection Administration of China in 1997, there were 83.7×10^4 km^2 of all kinds of desertified land, accounting for 8.7% of the total territory. Of this, there was 38.57×10^4 km^2 of aeolian desertification land, accounting for 44.3% of desertified land. The report also showed that there is 141×10^4 km^2 of land susceptible to desertification, of which the area of land susceptible to aeolian desertification is 53.7×10^4 km^2. Desertified land and land susceptible to desertification amount to 224.7×10^4 km^2, and land of aeolian desertification and threatened by aeolian desertification amounts to 90.8×10^4 km^2. In addition to 219.1×10^4 km^2 of sandy desert, Gobi and blown land account for 22.82% of total area of continental territory.

The agro-pastoral ecotone in northern China is a typical region with rapid aeolian desertification over the last 50 years. Semi-arid steppe region lies at the end of Eastern Monsoon Region, and precipitation is rare and variable in this region. Furthermore, in spring, strong winds are frequent because of the retreat of cold high air pressure which controls the weather of the Mongolian Plateau in winter. So, there is a very famous belt with a fragile ecology. After more than 100 years cultivation, an interlacing belt of steppes and farmlands with a width of 140 km came into existence. The way of land use was completely changed in this area, and the vulnerability of the natural environment appeared. In addition, the temporary peasants ignored the appropriate management of land. Before the appearance of wind erosion breach and sand spackles, the land became barren, with low yields. Local peasants had to reclaim more new land for their living. It's a very typical example of over farming in dry farming in China. On the other hand, because of the expanding of farmland in the southern part of the steppe, the area of the rangeland contracted constantly. At the same time, population and livestock increased dramatically with the development of stockbreeding industry, which made the quantity of livestock per unit area of rangeland increased significantly and over grazing occurred. Livestock' grazing and trampling caused degradation of the rangelands. The imbalance between rangeland and livestock emerged. It's a process of land degradation before aeolian desertification. Once ground surface can't be covered by vegetation completely and breach by wind erosion appeared, aeolian desertification occurs.

Aeolian desertification in the southern Inner Mongolian Plateau occur very quickly, and 200×10^4 hm^2 of farmlands, and 300×10^4 peasants and herdsmen in 20 Qis or counties are influenced, what's more, it also influences the quality of air environment in Beijing. So it's of great importance to combat aeolian desertification.

The Inner Mongolian Plateau was historically a grazing region. In recent centuries, population and farmland increased constantly and grazing regions were turned into interlacing zones of steppes and farmlands. Excessive cultivation, over grazing and over cutting denuded a large area of vegetation on steppes. Based on the natural factors of aeolian desertification here which coincide with strong winds and drought in spring and winter, the surficial loose sandy materials and irrational human activities induce and aggravate land aeolian desertification.

Wind erosion made surficial organic matters being blown away constantly, which decrease soil fertility seriously. According to measurements, there was $32 \times 10^4 \, km^2$ of dry farmland where 1 cm of surficial earth has been blown away including 840.48 t of organic matters, 54,096 t of nitrogen and 830×10^4 t of clay. Dust eroded was transported by northwest wind to the North China Plain and resulted in environmental pollution in Beijing.

Sand-dust storms are a kind of natural catastrophic weather. When sand-dust storms occur, a great deal of surface sand-dust is blown up into high sky by gales, making the air dim and the horizontal visibility 1,000 m. Gales are the motivity of dust-sand storm's occurrence; bare earth surface and abundant sands are the surficial conditions and matter base for dust-sand storm's occurrence; local strong convection can raise sandy matters to upper air and is necessary thermodynamic condition. During a process of sand-dust storm, strong winds can erode surface soil severely, and a stronger wind-dust storm can blow away several centimeters of topsoil. So, sand-dust storm is not only a result of land aeolian desertification but also can accelerate the aeolian desertification process.

Northwest China, located in the interior of Eurasia, is far from ocean, so there is arid, less precipitation and sparse vegetation. What's more, there are abundant sand sources and strong winds in spring; days with average wind velocity exceeding threshold velocity is 200–300. When there is unstable air condition, sand-dust storm happens. Historical records show sand-dust storms happened 70 times during the past 2,154 years from 300 a BP to 1949 in northwest China, it happened once every 31 years averagely. 71 times from 1950 to 1990, and it almost happened every year after 1990s and its harm got more and more severe and the influenced range also got more and more extensive. Special severe sand-dust storm swept through Gansu, Xinjiang, Ningxia and Inner Mongolia in northwest China on May 5th, 1993, which resulted in 85 deaths, 31 disappearances, 264 people were injured, 12×10^4 heads of livestock were lost or died and more than $37 \times 10^4 \, hm^2$ of farmland was damaged; the direct economic loss was 0.75 billion *yuan* in all. Sand-dust storm happened frequently in 1998, with long durations, extensive incidences and serious damage, but it's rare in history. The strong sand-dust storm which happened in the midwest Inner Mongolia, mid-south of Ningxia and the Hexi Corridor of Gansu Province on April 15 caused the average TSP to reach $62.4 mg/m^3$, 230 times larger than the national environmental quality standard, the horizontal visibility less than 20 m in some areas. Blowing dust and floating dust appeared in Beijing, Jinan, and Nanjing, etc. The southernmost area where it's influence can reach Hangzhou. From April 17–19, northern, eastern and part of southern Xinjiang was attacked by strong sand-dust storm, the horizontal visibility is less than 10 m in some areas. On May 20, sand-dust storm happened again in

Alxa Meng of Inner Mongolia with wind force reaching 12th degree and horizontal visibility of less than 20 m. It lasted for 24 hours and made power, water and traffic cut off and shops close, 800 hm^2 of cotton seedling was damaged and 3,500 heads of livestock died or were lost and a large number of trees snapped or collapsed in the wind. The economic losses reached 24.993 million *yuan*. The strong sand-dust storm which occurred in eastern Xinjiang on April 22, 1999 also resulted in great damage, and the whole railway line from Lanzhou to Xinjiang was forced to shut down.

3.3.2 Types of aeolian desertification and aeolian desertified land

3.3.2.1 Regional differences of aeolian desertification in China

Northwestern China is located in the hinterland of the Asian continent and its climate is hypo-arid continental climate. The climate in eastern China is controlled by East Asian Monsoon; the aeolian desertification in eastern China is very different from that in northwestern China.

1) Arid regions in west China

First, for the driving factors of aeolian desertification, the fragile natural conditions and fluctuating climate play a very important role in western China. with natural conditions of hypo-arid, both natural and artificial vegetation depend greatly on water. Rivers supplied by precipitation and snow from mountains around desert are the basis for desert oasis's existence. So, water determines whether desert advances or recedes. The decrease of river water, whether it's caused by natural or human factors, can determine the development of aeolian desertification land in oases. Secondly, local people's destroying vegetation around oases accelerates the development of land aeolian desertification in oasis.

When there is water there are oases; otherwise there is desert. Because water resources are limited, the reasonable distribution of water between upper and lower reaches of inland rivers is very important. The opposed development of two oases at upper and down reach of the Shiyang River which lies in the eastern section of the Hexi Corridor in Gansu Province is the best example.

The Shiyang River is the convergence of 8 rivers all originating from the Qilian Mountains fosters Wuwei Oasis first, passes Hongyashan fault zone and irrigates the Minqin Oasis at last. Because the water resource is limited in the Shiyang River Valley, the phase of opposed development that one oasis flourish, the other must wane has been formed in history. The human civilization can be traced back to 4,000 years ago, where Shajingzi Cultures, the representative of Neolithic Cultures appeared. This oasis at that time can be regarded as "natural oasis" and the way of land use was grazing. Army and immigrants began to cultivate grassland in the reign of Emperor Hanwu. At the end of the Western Han Dynasty, the Wuwei Oasis formed. Because a large deal of water was used at the upper and middle reaches of the Shiyang River, the lower reach became a seasonal river and lakes also dwindled. Shortage of water resources resulted in the Minqin Oasis shrinking. When the Silk Road was opened in the Tang Dynasty, Guzang (present day Wuwei) in the Wuwei Oasis became the largest and most flourishing city in the Hexi region and the surrounding agriculture was also well developed. The overuse of water at the upper reach of Shiyang River made rivers dry up, lakes shrunk, oasis declined and aeolian desertification developed quickly in the Minqin Oasis. Years of war made these farmlands abandoned and suffer from intensive process of aeolian desertification. From the end of the Tang Dynasty to the beginning of the Yuan Dynasty, the Hexi region suffered from wars among several tribes and the Minqin Oasis was used for grazing by nomads. At the same time, the Wuwei Oasis also declined, so water for irrigation decreased. The water at the lower reach of the Shiyang River recovered. Lakes also recovered partly. When there was water, aeolian desertification was reversed. The policy that army cultivated farmland where they guarded was implemented during both the Ming and Qing dynasties. And the history of exploiting the Shiyang River Valley replayed, namely agriculture developed and the Wuwei Oasis expanded, at the same time, the Minqin Oasis receded southwardly. It was the same in the period of the Republic of China. According to statistics in 1944, 74.2% of plowland in the Hexi region can be irrigated, accounting for only 35.5% of the Hexi region. In the light of incomplete statistics, more than 6,000 manors and 1.72×10^4 hm^2 of farmland were buried by blown sand from 1950 to 1958.

After 1949, the Chinese Government organized local people to construct irrigation works in order to combat desert. Improved irrigation works enhanced the effective utilization of water. The Hongyashan Reservoir constructed in 1958 the artificial adjustment of surface water. Summarizing experiences to combat aeolian desertification in sandy region, people in the Shiyang River Valley took many measures to combat aeolian desertification, such as building shelterbelt systems. Benefiting from aeolian desertification control, both the upper and lower reach can well develop and the Silver Age of the Shiyang River Valley came. The area of plowland in Minqin reached 7×10^4 hm^2 at the beginning of the 1970s. During the 30 years (1950–1980), there was no severe sand dunes advance or manors buried by sands.

Conflicts became worse and worse along with the development of the economy people between the upper and lower reaches scrabbled for water. Many factors such as: climate warming, snow line rising, human's destroying forests and meadows for conservation of water supply, lack of efficient and appropriate management and wrong decisions, decreased the outflow of the Shiyang River by 3.6×10^9 m^3 (almost 20%)in the 1980s, compared with that in the 1950s. Water volume following in Minqin in the 1990s decreased to only 36.9% of that in the 1950s. To make up the lack of precipitation, local people began to pump out groundwater to irrigate farmlands. What's more, precipitation and replenishment of leakage in farmlands decreased synchronously, until to middle of the 1970s, $(1–2) \times 10^9$ m^3 of water was over exploited per year, which resulted in the decline of the water table significantly. Now, the water table in Minqin declined to 12–15 m under ground surface, which leaded to the downfall of sand-fixing plants and worsened the development of aeolian desertification. Since the 1960s, there was totally 2.52×10^4 hm^2 of abandoned farmland due to lack of water (Zhu et al., 1994).

Another example is the opposed development between the oasis at the upper reach and the sandy desertified land at the lower reach of the Tarim River. The length of the Tarim River is 2,200 km from the Yarkant River to the Taitema Lake and it is the longest continental river in China. The customarily Tarim River refers to the section from the point where the Aksu River, the Hotan River and the Yarkant River converge to the Taitema Lake, with a length of 1,280 km. The Tarim River ever has large runoff in history. Though there were no exact measuring figures, it can be deduced from some facts, such as foods were planned to be shipped to Shache from Xayar through the Tarim River in 1759 AD; Sven Hedin traveled from Markit the upper reach of the Yarkant River to Kalakunshun by large wooden ship from the winter in 1899 to the spring of the next year. The runoff from the Tarim River began to diminish at the beginning of the 20th century.

The reduction of runoff in the Tarim River is related to human factors. After the 1970s, the human start to overuse water at the middle of the Tarim River. 2.15×10^{10} m^3 of water was consumed in the section from the Tarim River Dam to Kala. On average, 6.83×10^6 m^3 of water is consumed per kilometer where the water rate is the largest in the Tarim River Basin. Local people breached the river bank to bring water to irrigate farmland extensively at will, which changed the river way and made water flow in nearby lakes, swamps, reservoirs, desert and holes. The evaporation and leakage are the main ways of water loss. The runoff was quite abundant in Tarim River in 1986, but the lower reaches of the Tarim River was much drier than past drought years due to water loss at the upper reaches. Because a large deal of water was consumed at the middle reaches, the volume of water flowing to lower reaches was greatly reduced. The annual average runoff in the Kala Station was 3.67×10^9 m^3 during 1982–1985, and it decreased to 3.40×10^9 m^3 in 1986, even dramatically to 1.2×10^9 m^3 in 1993.

In the 1950s, there was water perennially in the section of the Tarim River lower than the Daxihai Reservoir, and water passed Tingsu and Alagan and flowed in the Taitema Lake eventually. In the 1960s, there was water in Alagan only in flood period, and it was also only flood that can reach the Taitema Lake. The volume of water discharged from the Daxihai Reservoir was averagely 0.47×10^9 m^3 per year in the 1970s. People can plant crops by using flood, and there was also seeper in riverbed of Alagan section, where local people can fish. In the 1980s, 0.56×10^9 m^3 of water was discharged to the lower reach only in 1986, but stream interrupted before reaching Yingsu. At present, the river started drying up at the lower reaches in Yingsu, and blown sand was deposited in the riverbed lower than Alagan. Water interception of water can result in dramatic environmental degradation at the lower reaches. The first is the intensive development of aeolian desertification. ① Farmlands were discarded in irrigation area, and were degraded to aeolian desertified land eventually on the impact of strong wind. Xinjiang Production and Construction Corps of CPLA had five farms with 2.7×10^4 hm^2 of farmland in lower irrigation area in 1960s, but it decreased to 1.7×10^4 hm^2, thousands of people were obliged to migrate to make a living. 1.67×10^4 hm^2 of farmlands were reclaimed in Tieganlike Irrigation System, but 0.33×10^4 hm^2 were abandoned at last due to no water for irrigation, which is covered by shifting sands in different degrees now. ② A large area of *Populus euphratica* forest died. Due to interception of surface water, decline of water table and human cutting, in 1978, the area of *Populus euphratica* forest in the Tarim River Basin decreased by 56% compared with that in 1958 and the accumulated volume of lumber decreased by 37.6% during the same period. The area of *Populus euphratica* forest at the lower reach decreased by 56%, from 5.4×10^4 hm^2 to 1.64×10^4 hm^2, and the accumulated volume of lumber decreased by 77.1%. In recent years, because of water interception and decline of water table at the lower reach of the Tarim River, *Populus euphratica* forest lost its surviving conditions and faced the threat of becoming extinct. ③ Fixed sandy dunes reactivated and encroached farmlands.

The ecological environmental degradation is shown by: ① Lakes dried up; ② The degree of mineralization of lakes, rivers and ground water was all increased; ③ Biodiversity disappeared.

The third exemplification of aeolian desertification development in oases in West China was the Heihe River Valley. The Heihe River is namely past Ruoshui, is a comparatively big continental river in arid zone of Northwest China. It originates from the Qilian Mountains, passes Gansu Aisle and reaches eastern and western Juyanhai in Ejin Qi of Alxa Meng in Inner Mongolia. It covers 11 counties (or Qis) of 3 provinces with a length of 821 km. The Heihe River Valley is 1.3×10^5 km^2, with population of 1.25×10^6. The exploitative history of the upper reach of the Heihe River Valley can retrospect to 100 AD. For the lower reach, agricultural development results in the formation of ever famous "Black City Cultures". In recent 30 years, because population increased constantly, especially over exploiting and utilizing water and land resources at the upper and middle reaches, the ecological environment was seriously degraded at the lower reach. Because the Heihe River Valley is ruled by three provinces, it's difficult to manage and allocate water resource in the whole valley uniformly and appropriately. Presently, the area of natural forest reduced in the upriver Qilian Mountains area of Qinghai Province, so the capacity of headwater conservation also decreased and land desertification is obvious; for mid-river Zhangye City of Gansu Province, natural vegetation of agricultural oases decreased, aeolian desertification and salinization of land are very serious, and pastureland degraded. As for the downriver the Juyanhai Oasis of Ejin Qi of Inner Mongolia, ecological environment deteriorated severely, both eastern and western Juyanhai have dried up, areas of natural forest and grassland reduced sharply and the frequency of all kinds of catastrophic climates' occurrence increased.

Besides the above-mentioned aeolian desertification caused by lack of water, desert expansion also can result in aeolian desertification. A typical example is the southward advancement of the Taklimakan Desert in southern Xinjiang made oases in front of the Kunlun Mountains shrink, which is manifested most evidently in the Hotan region.

Influenced by atmospheric circumstance, at the southern edge of the Taklimakan Desert where the northeaster and northwester converge, sand dunes moves quickly. At the edge of desert, crescent dunes with a height less than 1 m can move 35–62 m per year. For comparatively higher sand dune, it can move 5–10 m per year, if it moves fast, it can cover 10–15 m in a year. These sand dunes can do great harm to oases. In the Hotan region, shifting sands border upon oases, in recent 50 years, area of sandy desertified land reached 1.67×10^4 hm^2, thereinto, sandy desertified farmland was 0.58×10^4 hm^2. Qira County seat was forced to relocate 3 times. currently, shifting sands are only 5 km from Qira County seat. Shifting sands can cause damages. Shifting sands can bury local people's houses, roadbeds, make road interdict. Aeolian desertified land caused by modern shifting sand encroachment amounts to 1.296×10^5 hm^2 (Table 3-4) at the edge of the Taklimakan Desert.

Table 3-4   Land area encroached by sand dunes at the edge of the modern Taklimakan Desert

Area	Modern sand dunes encroachment(km^2)	Percentage (%)
Southwestern edge (Yecheng-Hotan)	231	17.8
Middle southern edge (Qira-Qiemo)	279	21.5
Southeastern edge (Qiemo-Ruoqiang)	132	10.2
Southern edge of eastern part (downriver Tarim river)	302	23.3
Northern edge	170	13.1
Eastern part of Buguli and Tuokelake Desert	182	14.1
Total	1,296	100

In general, modern aeolian desertification in oasis of the arid zone in west China is mainly caused by improper allocation of water resource or conflicts of water resource using. Besides, it has the following characteristics:

First, Oasis establishment and aeolian desertification are coexistent. There exist both aeolian desertification in reverse and development. When an oasis at the upper reach expands, aeolian desertified lands at the lower reach may develop at the same time, and buffer zone between oases and deserts shrinks constantly. The general trend is that aeolian desertification develops from lower reach to upper reach, oases shrinks toward riverhead under the influence of human activities or water scarcity.

Second, ecological system of oases gets improved, but still threatened by salinization and aeolian desertification. Besides oases, ecological systems of mountain regions and deserts in plains have lost their balance or are getting worse.

Third, in recent 50 years, at the beginning, oases developed quickly at the upper reach of Tarim River, but limited by water resources, the rate of oases development decreased when it reached certain scale. On the contrary, the rate of aeolian desertification at the lower reach increased, the increased aeolian desertified land exceeded contemporary increased oases area. From another point of view, aeolian desertification lands are reversed partly but deteriorate holistically.

2) Semiarid regions in eastern China

Semiarid region in eastern China is a main region where aeolian desertification occurs and develops, especially in the latest 50 years, aeolian desertification developed intensively there.

85% of modern aeolian desertified land is concentratedly distributed in eastern China. The general characteristics of aeolian desertified lands in eastern China is that the pressure of human economic activities exceeded the environmental carrying capacity, which results in the appearance of desert-like landscape on former non-sandy-desertified land. The interlaced belt of pasture-lands and farmlands is the typical region of aeolian desertification in eastern China which stretches from the Horqin Steppe, along inside and outside the Great Wall to the Mu Us Sandy Land and southern part of Yanchi in Ningxia.

The fragility of ecology is determined by local natural conditions in the interlaced zone of pasture-lands and farmlands of northern China. Annual precipitation decrease from 500–550 mm in southeastern part of north China to 350–100 m, even 250–300 mm (Table 3-5) in northwest China gradually. Precipitation during the period when the daily average temperature $\geqslant 10°C$ is 350–400 mm in the eastern and southern part, 250–300 mm in central part and 200–250 mm in western part. The annual relative humidity is commonly 50%–60%, with annual sunshine time of 2,800–3,000 h and annual average percentage of sunshine arranging from 60% to 70%. Accumulative temperature of daily average temperature $\geqslant 10°C$ is 3,000–3,500°C in the east, 2,500–3,000°C in the west and 1,500–2,000°C in the central and northern part. Vegetation changes from *S.capillata* L.-*Leymus chinensis*. Steppe with sparse *Ulmus pumila* to *S. grandis* P. Smirn-*Stipa krylovi* steppe gradually from east to west. The topography of alluvial plains and undulant sandy plains with interlaced meadows and dunes in the east gradually changes into undulant sandy high plains in the west. As for soil, fertile chernozem and dark chestnut soil suitable for cultivation distribute in the east, light chestnut soil and brown soil which are shallow, weak in water holding and sandy distribute in the west. The above-mentioned transitional environmental characteristics show it can be used as good pastureland and farmland. But, the fragility of natural conditions is obvious: ① great variability of annual precipitation (Table 3-6), varying from 25% to 50% commonly, resulting in the instability of water conditions; ② Surficial matters are composed of loose sandy sediments, for example, the depth of loose sediments is 80–170 m in the Horqin steppe. Even in the Houshan area of the northern Ulanqab steppe, the depth is generally 5–25 m. Especially in the place where the earth's surface is mainly sand bed (Table. 3-7), under the impact of wind and human intensive utilization, it becomes fragile; ③ Frequent gales' blastation in arid Spring, the number of gale days ($\geqslant$8th class) is commonly 30–80 days (Table 3-8) (Zhu etc. 1994).

In the process of aeolian desertification, the change of earth surface substance's composition and micro-landscape includes: ① the process of earth surface's coarseness; ② the process of shrubs' aeolian desertification; ③ the process of badland's formation; ④ The process of sand dunes' reactivation.

Table 3-5　The annual average precipitation in aeolian desertified area of the interlaced zone of farmlands and pasture-lands

Place	Precipitation (mm)	Place	Precipitation (mm)	Place	Precipitation (mm)
Lubei	382.1	Wudan	361.3	Siziwang Qi	289.4
Gaoliban	377.1	Daban	376.0	Damao Qi	241.8
Ganqika	451.2	Duolun	391.0	Wuchuan	336.7
Hure	417.5	Taipusi Qi	410.8	Otog Qi	275.8
Eleshun	383.7	Huade	309.7	Xinjie	403.7
Naiman	364.0	Shangdu	337.2	Uxin Qi	370.2

Table 3-6　A comparison of the maximum and the minimum annual precipitation in aeolian desertified area of the interlaced zone of farmlands and pasture-lands

Place	The maximum annual precipitation (mm)	Year	The minimum annual precipitation (mm)	Year
Huade	445.4	1964	166.0	1965
Shangdu	583.4	1964	187.2	1965
Siziwang Qi	424.9	1969	181.8	1965
Damao Qi	356.5	1961	142.6	1966
Taipusi Qi	592.0	1964	240.0	1965
Duolun	474.0	1964	329.0	1965

Table 3-7　Composition (%) of grain size of surficial substances in sandy desertified area of the interlaced zone of farmlands and pasture-lands (0—20 cm depth)

Place	1–0.25 mm	0.25–0.05 mm	0.05–0.01 mm	<0.01 mm
Southwestern Taipusi Qi	30.18	54.99	10.93	3.90
Western Zhenglan Qi	28.50	68.92	2.14	0.44
Northwestern Hexigten Qi	42.55	56.02	0.71	0.42
Northeastern Ongniud Qi	35.04	60.53	3.38	1.05
Northeastern Alu Horqin Qi	17.97	70.87	8.12	3.04
Northwestern Kailu County	57.67	42.12	0.11	0.10
Southwestern Hure Qi	41.54	58.33	0.06	0.07
Southwestern Horqin Zuoyi Houqi	17.12	75.37	5.78	1.73
Northern Aohan Qi	17.99	81.65	0.27	0.09
Northern Zhangwu County	24.60	42.29	23.60	10.05
Northwestern Wuchuan County	11.38	44.62	24.00	20.00

The local environmental characteristics of transitiveness and fragileness show land use must be combined with mutual complementarity of agriculture and stockbreeding, considering local different conditions, then environment and land use can be promoted each other. Contrarily, if humans ignore the ecological balance and use land intensively and planlessly, it will result in aeolian desertification lands' spreading. According to the contrast of aerial pictures of different periods, it can be inferred that the process of aeolian desertification is very active, with a rapid expansion rate. This can be seen in Fig. 3-2.

Table 3-8   The monthly average number of gale (≥8th class) days in aeolian desertified area of the interlaced zone of farmlands and pasture-lands

Place	Jan.	Feb.	Mar.	Apr.	May	Jun.	Jul.	Aug.	Sep.	Oct.	Nov.	Dec.	Year
Aohan Qi	4.9	4.6	6.7	9.6	8.6	5.8	3.1	1.8	2.1	3.9	4.3	4.7	60.1
Linxi County	5.3	5.2	6.1	7.2	7.0	3.7	3.6	1.1	1.7	2.6	5.5	6.7	53.7
Daban	6.5	4.8	8.5	9.0	9.5	3.9	2.2	1.8	3.2	3.4	5.0	5.9	53.7
Baiyunhushuo	4.8	3.7	5.4	5.7	4.8	3.7	0.7	0.7	1.1	2.6	3.5	5.1	39.8
Ji'ergalang	1.3	2.6	4.4	7.9	7.3	1.9	1.3	0.3	1.0	2.0	1.5	1.0	32.2
Hure Qi	2.7	2.6	4.7	7.4	6.2	1.5	0.7	0.4	0.8	2.2	2.9	2.1	35.9
Lubei	2.4	2.8	4.4	6.0	2.5	1.7	0.9	1.0	1.0	2.3	1.8	2.6	32.2
Bayantela	1.3	2.3	5.5	8.6	8.3	2.8	1.7	0.7	1.5	3.1	2.1	1.1	38.7
Taipusi Qi	6.5	5.5	8.8	12.9	12.2	6.7	1.9	1.5	3.1	4.2	6.3	6.8	76.4

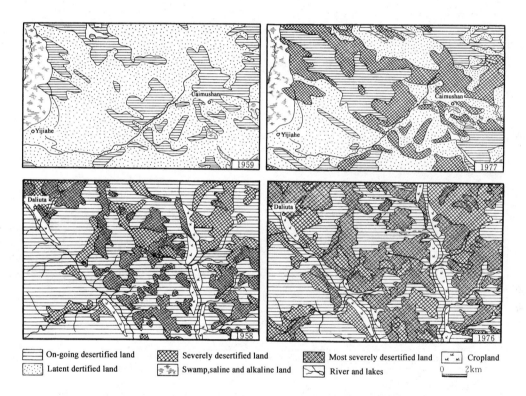

	On-going desertified land		Severely desertified land		Most severely desertified land		Cropland
	Latent dertified land		Swamp,saline and alkaline land		River and lakes		0 2km

Fig. 3-2   The status of development of aeolian desertification in the interlaced zone of farmlands and grasslands

From the above analysis, it can be concluded that the process of aeolian desertification has two types of characteristics:

① In sandy plains, aeolian desertification is characterized by blown sand activity. According to data from typical areas, the enlargement rate is 1%–1.8%.

② In fixed dunes and undulated sandy upland regions, aeolian desertification is characterized by an increase in shifting sand areas and aggravation of the aeolian desertification degree, with a rate of 0.5%–1% per year.

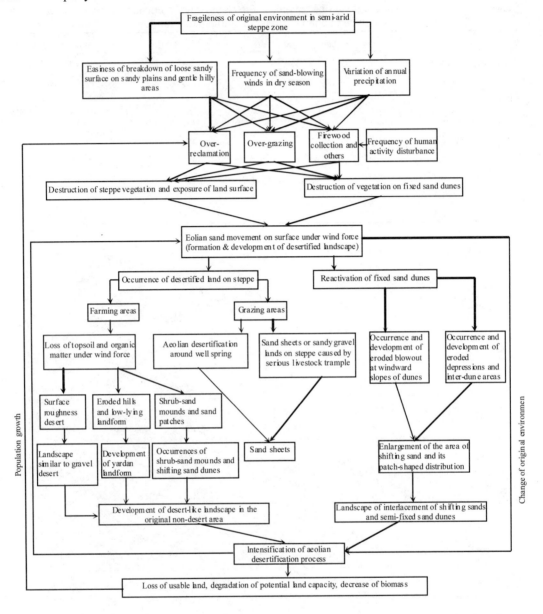

Fig. 3-3　Sketch map of the process of aeolian desertification in interlaced zone of farmlands and pasture-lands of semi-arid region

The spread of aeolian desertification in semi-arid regions is effectively the result of environmental degradation caused by economic development at the cost of the ecological environment. It also shows that environmental degradation caused by aeolian desertification is a dynamic process, which evolves from quantitative change to qualitative change. Namely, on original steppes, due to intensive land use, the area and configuration of land where speckles of aeolian desertification land scatter increases or gets complicated. Once the area occupies about 50% of the total area and the surfical configuration is primarily composed of dense shifting sand dunes, the whole environment will change in nature; the landscape of the steppe no longer exists; the earth's surface takes on a desert-like appearance with undulant sand dunes (Fig. 3-3). The environmental characteristics are different in different areas, which determines the different processes of aeolian desertification development.

3.3.2.2 The principles, index and system of aeolian desertification category

① At present, there are no uniform principles, indexes or system to categorize aeolian desertification in China. The most popular way is to classify aeolian desertified land into 4 basic types from the point of aeolian desertification development's phase (Table 3-9) (Zhu et al., 1981; Zhu, 1999).

Table 3-9   The symbols of aeolian desertified land development

Types	Percentage of aeolian desertification land	Features of shapes	Typical areas
Aeolian desertification-prone land	≤5	Patches of shifting sand sparsely scatter in farmland and around wells and residential area	Xilingol Steppe, Northern Ulanqab Steppe, etc.
Ongoing aeolian desertified land	6–25	Speckles of shifting sand or blown land, farmlands suffered wind erosion	Southern Ulanqab Steppe, Qahar Steppe, northern Horqin Steppe
Intensively developed aeolian desertified land	26–50	Sheets of shifting sand dunes and blown shrub sand dunes, interlaced with fixed and semi-fixed sand dunes	Hunshandake Sandy Land, Eastern Horqin Sandy Land, etc.
Severely aeolian desertified land	>51	Predominant shifting sand dunes distribute densely	Western Horqin Sandy Land between Laoha River and Balin Bridge, etc.

When judging the degree of aeolian desertification in certain areas from the view of ecology, we must consider changes of potential land productivity, biomass (including changes of plant structure and rate of vegetation cover) and energy transfer efficiency in biological systems (Table 3-10).

Table 3-10   Ecological indicators of aeolian desertification degree

Degree	Vegetation cover (%)	Land productivity (%)	Ratio of output to input (%)	Biomass [t/hm$^2 \cdot$ a]
Latent	Above 60	Above 80	>80	3–4.5
Ongoing	59–30	79–50	79–60	2.9–1.5
Intensively developing	29–10	49–20	59–30	1.4–1.0
Severe	9–0	19–0	29–0	0.9–0

If data of aeolian desertification monitoring in several periods are available, the annual increased rate of aeolian desertified land can be used to judge the degree of aeolian desertification. At the initial stage of aeolian desertification, the rate is less than 0.25%; 0.26%–1.0% at ongoing stage; 1.1%–2.0% at intensively developing stage; and the rate will be more than 2.1% when it is the most severe sandy desertified stage.

Four types of aeolian desertification shown in Table 3-9 represent different human activities pressures imposed on natural ecological system which caused environmental degradation, so this method of categorizing aeolian desertification not only puts forward the concept of dynamic aeolian desertification development, points out how danger the aeolian desertification degree is, arouses people's caution on aeolian desertification, but also supplies principles to rehabilitate aeolian desertified land. But, the terms of "ongoing aeolian desertified land" and "intensively developing aeolian desertified land" are not systemic concepts. Especially, "aeolian desertification-prone land" can give people an impression that aeolian desertification doesn't occur but with natural conditions to get sandy desertified. When reckoning the area of aeolian desertified land, this concept is disputed. Some people think some reports aggrandize the status of aeolian desertification in China, in which "aeolian desertification-prone land" is included into aeolian desertified land. In fact, indicators listed in Table 3-9 show "aeolian desertification-prone land" is not so called land with conditions of aeolian desertification but without occurrence of aeolian desertified lands but the degree of aeolian desertification is comparatively slight. So, it's fine to classify aeolian desertification into 4 types considering individual developmental stage, but some terms, such as "aeolian desertification-prone land", "ongoing aeolian desertified land" are not appropriate.

② To determine the stage of aeolian desertification according to configuration changes. When estimating the degree of aeolian desertification somewhere, we usually consider surficial "instant"

Table 3-11　Synthetical landscape symbols of all degrees of aeolian desertified land

Aeolian desertification degree	Synthetic landscape symbols
Slightly aeolian desertified land	1. Blowouts appears at windward slope, with shifting sand depositing at leeward slope; rate of vegetation cover is 30%–60%；Areas with speckles of shifting sand occupy 5%–25%
	2. Different scales of shrub sand mounds appear, shrubs grow luxuriantly and thickly
	3. A thin layer of sand deposits at the Earth's surface, even with gravels outcropped
	4. In Spring, farmland is eroded by wind, with less than 50% loss of humus and output is 50%–80% of original yields
	5. Blowouts appear where fine soil is thick, with certain vegetation cover
Moderately aeolian desertified land	1. The difference between blown slope and slip slope is obvious; vegetation cover is 10%–30%; area of shifting sand account for 25%–50%
	2. The whole sand mound can't be covered by shrub complete, with shifting sand's occurrence at windward slope
	3. Small patches of shifting sand appear at loess area, with much coarse sand and gravel at the surface, but still with sparse plant, vegetation cover is 10%–30%
	4. Productivity is decreased due to wind erosion, with more than 50% loss of humus and less than 50% of original output
	5. Blowouts are mostly bare, small-size steep ridges emerge at the ground surface
Severely aeolian desertified land	1. The whole sandy desertified area is shifting-sandy-land-like, with more than 50% of shifting sand, sparse vegetation, and vegetation cover is less than 10%
	2. Gravel desertified area takes on a Gobi-like look, vegetation cover is below 10%, farmlands with gravel desertification occurrence are deserted
	3. Humus layer is almost blown away completely, calcic horizon or soil parent material is outcropped and most farmlands are deserted
	4. Soil residues by wind erosion appears at Earth's surface

static characteristics reflecting the degree of aeolian desertification, but we don't know how it was or it will be. We determine the degree of aeolian desertification according to actual status, and concepts which can reflect actual status of aeolian desertification are used to name concrete aeolian desertification degree (Table 3-11).

③ Considering different aeolian desertification processes and different aeolian desertification land types, aeolian desertification can be classified into aeolian desertification in farmland, aeolian desertification in shrub, coarseness of soil by wind, badland desertification and reactivation of fixed sand dunes.

Considering different characteristics of aeolian desertification at different stages, especially great difference in aerial photos, satellite images, we constitute the below chart (Table 3-12).

Table 3-12　Aeolian desertification categories in northern China

Types Degree	A Reactivation of fixed sand dunes	B Aeolian desertification of shrubs	C Gravel aeolian desertification	D Badland aeolian desertification	E Aeolian desertification of farmland
Distributing area	Sandy lands in eastern China; margins of deserts or riverbanks deep in desert in western China	Deserts in western China or margins of sandy lands in eastern China; central Inner Mongolian Plateau	Peripheral area of Gobi; central and western part of Inner Mongolian Plateau	Lop Nur, peripheral area of Altun Mountain where Yardang landform distributes; southeastern part of Inner Mongolian Plateau (Bashang in Hebei Province)	Farm region in eastern steppe; northern part of Loess Plateau
1 Original status (aeolian desertification-prone land)	1a fixed sand dunes or oases, farmlands	1b Dry steppe or desert steppe, steppification desert	1c desert steppe or steppification desert	1d Dry steppe or desert steppe, steppe desert	1e Dry farmlands
2 Slightly aeolian desertified land	2a Blowouts appear at the windward slope; patchy shifting sand occupies 5%–25%; with more than 90% of original vegetation cover	2b Shrubs flourish; shifting sand deposits under shrubs	2c Gravels are getting concentrated at the ground surface	2d Shallow blown pits merge at the ground surface but without steep ridges	2e There is deposited sand in farmland in Spring, with obvious trace of wind erosion
3 Moderately aeolian desertified land	3a The difference between blown slope and slip slope is obvious; area of shifting sand account for 25%–50%	3b The whole sand mound can't be covered by shrub complete, with shifting sand's occurrence at windward slope	3c There are much coarse sand and gravels at the surface, but still with sparse plant, vegetation cover is more than 25%. The landscape is gravel steppe	3d Most blowouts are bare, obvious small-size steep ridges emerge at the Earth's surface	3e Small patches of shifting sand appear in loessial farmlands; productivity is decreased due to wind erosion, with more than 50% loss of humus

Types Degree	A Reactivation of fixed sand dunes	B Aeolian desertification of shrubs	C Gravel aeolian desertification	D Badland aeolian desertification	E Aeolian desertification of farmland
4 Severely aeolian desertified land	4a Sandy land is semi-shifting, area of shifting sand exceeds 50%, with less than 50% of original vegetation cover	4b A large patches of shrubs are dead; vegetation cover is below 25%, area of shifting sand exceeds 50%	4c Earth's surface is covered by gravels completely, with little sand in small holes among gravels, vegetation cover is 10%–25%	4d Soil residues by wind erosion appears at Earth's surface, with sparse vegetation at interdune area, farmlands with gravel desertification occurrence are deserted	4e Humus layer is almost blown away completely, calcic horizon or soil parent material is outcropped and most sandy desertified farmlands are deserted
5 Very severely aeolian desertified land	5a Shifting sand dunes or sandy land, with vegetation cover less than 10%	5b Undulated shifting sandy land, with vegetation cover less than 10%	5c Gobi; vegetation cover is less than 10%	5d Yardang landscape	5e Flat sandy land or gravel land; vegetation cover <10%

④ Classify aeolian desertification according to its development status. According to the rate of annual increased aeolian desertified land, it can be classified into reversed, stable and developing aeolian desertified land (Table 3-13).

Table 3-13   Classification of the status of aeolian desertification development

Status of aeolian desertification development	Rate of annual increased aeolian desertification land (%)
Being reversed aeolian desertified land	Negative
Stable aeolian desertified land	<0.25
Developing aeolian desertified land	>0.25
Thereinto: commonly developing	0.25–3
intensively developing	>3

3.4   Rules and characteristics of aeolian desertified land distribution in China

3.4.1   Spatial distributions

Chinese researchers began to do research work on aeolian desertification in the late 1970s, and summarized the spatial distribution characteristics of aeolian desertified land in China (Zhu et al., 1981, 1994, 1999b).

(1) Aeolian desertified lands are concentrated in semi-arid regions.

The semi-arid China ranges from the northern Hulun Buir Steppe to the eastern *Da Hinggan Ling* Mountains, and includes the western Horqin Sandy Land on the eastern Da Hinggan Ling Mountains, along the Jiliao Mountain, the Dama Mountains (Yanshan Mountains), the Great Wall, the Yellow River, to the Baiyu Mountain, including the northern part of Huan County in Gansu Province. It mainly includes semi-arid steppe and interlaced zones of farmlands and pasture-lands and 93 Qis (or counties) and cities in Inner Mongolian Autonomous Region, Liaoning Province, Jilin Province, Hebei Province, Shanxi Province, Shaanxi Province, Ningxia Autonomous Region and Gansu Province (Table 3-14).

The area of aeolian desertified land in semi-arid steppes 201,326 km^2, accounting for 52.2% of total aeolian desertification land in China, according to interpretive data of TM Images. There exist not only landscapes of aeolian desertification formed under the control of wind, but also badlands (rudiments of Yardang landscape) formed by the mutual erosion by wind and water. In the southern part of blown sand area, the ground surface is eroded by wind and water alternatively and seasonally, the fragmentized ground, with blown sand deposited takes on a special landscape of loess hill and mesa. This kind of landscape commonly appears in the transitional zone of sandy land and loess at the middle reaches of the Yellow River such as: northwestern Shanxi Province, northern Shaanxi Province, northeastern Gansu Province, northern side of the Ji-liao Mountains.

Table 3-14 Counties (Qis), cities influenced by aeolian desertification in semi-arid zones

Geographic units	Influenced cities or counties (Qis)
Hulun Buir steppe	Inner Mongolia: Manzhouli, Hailar, Xinba'erhuyou Qi, Xinba'erhu Zuoqi, Xinba'erhu Qi
Horqin steppe	Inner Mongolia: Horqin Zuoyi Zhongqi, Horqin Zuoyi Houqi, Horqin Youyi Zhongqi, Jarud Qi, Huolinhe city, Tongliao City, Kailu, Naiman Qi, Hure Qi, Aluhorqin Qi, Wengniute Qi, Balinyou Qi, Balinzuo Qi, Linxi, Hexigten Qi, Aohan Qi, Chifeng city Liaoning: Zhangwu, Kangping, Faku Jilin: Shuangliao
Xilin Gol steppe and Onqin Daga steppe	Inner Mongolia: Dong Ujimqin Qi, Xi Ujimqin Qi, Xilinhot City, Abaga Qi, Sonid Zuoqi, Sonid Youqi, Hexigten Qi
Qahar Steppe	Inner Mongolia: Zhenglan Qi, Duolun, Zhengxiangbai Qi, Xianghuang Qi, Taipusi Qi
Bashang area in Hebei Province	Hebei: Weichang, Fengning, Zhangbei, Guyuan, Kangbao, Shangyi
Ulanqab Steppe	Inner Mongolia: Huade, Shangdu, Qahar Youyi Houqi, Qahar Youyi Zhongqi, Siziwang Qi, Damao Qi, Guyang, Wuchuang
Qianshan area and Tumd Plain in Ulanqab Meng	Inner Mongolia: Qaharyouyiqian Qi, Fengzhen, Xinghe, Liangcheng, Helinge'er, Qingshuihe, Suburb of Baotou City, Tuoketuo
Northwestern Shanxi Province	Shanxi: Zuoyun, Youyu, Pinlu, Pianguan, Hequ, Baode, Suburb of Datong City, Huairen, Shanyin, Shuo County, Shenchi, Wuzhai, Kelan, Lan County, Xing County
Erdos Steppe and Mu Us Sandy Land	Inner Mongolia: Dalad Qi, Zhunge'er Qi, Dongsheng City, Yijinhuoluo Qi, Hanggin Qi, Otog Qi, Otog Qianqi, Uxin Qi Shaanxi: Shenmu, Fugu, Yumu, Hengshan, Jia County, Dingbian, Jingbian Ningxia: Yanchi
Sandy land on the eastern side of Yellow River in Ningxia Autonomous Region	Ningxia: Lingwu Gansu: Huan County

Source: Zhu Zhenda et al. (1994).

The reason why aeolian desertified land is extensively distributed in semi-arid zones is that there exist natural factors promoting the development of aeolian desertified land, such as the synchronous occurrence of the arid season and the windy season, thick loose sandy deposits and the erodibility of loose-like deposits in pasture area and interlaced zones of farmlands and pasture-lands. On the other hand, the population in this area is more than that of arid zones in China, with an average population density of 50–100 persons/km^2, so human activities are quite frequent in this areas, and over cultivation, over grazing and over cutting accelerate the process of land degradation in this fragile environments. In the Houshan area on the north of the Yinshan Mountains in Inner Mongolia as well as the Horqin Steppe and the Bashang pasture area in northern Hebei Province, 85% of farmland came into being by reclaiming undulated sandy pasture and fixed sand dunes (or fixed sandy land), and it takes on farmland view in summer and autumn. But in winter, there was full of blown sand, and soils were eroded by wind severely, organic matter was decreased by 23%, fine grains was decreased by 29%, so 3–5 years later, the soil will get barren. Land damaged by aeolian desertification increased from 37.1% in the middle 1970s to 41.2% in the middle 1980s; in pasture area, aeolian desertified land increased from 25.5% in the middle 1970s to 31.1% in the middle 1980s. In the southeastern part of Inner Mongolian Plateau, according to the northern boundary of dry farming, the Bashang area should be pastoral area, but in fact, the boundary of farmland is 140 km deep into pastoral area, which forms the extensive interlaced zone of farmlands and pasture-lands. Aeolian desertification is severest here, and it's also the region where aeolian desertification is intensively developing. At the end of the 1980s, there was 12.19×10^4 km^2 of aeolian desertified land, occupying 36.5% of total. From the mid 1970s to the mid 1980s, 17.5×10^4 hm^2 of land suffered from aeolian desertification due to wind erosion per year. So, the status of aeolian desertification here is the most serious in China, and it's imperative to take measures to combat aeolian desertification in this area. (Zhu et al., 1994).

The interlaced zone of farmlands and pasture-lands, lying in temperate semi-arid zones, is also the transitional zone of the East Asian Monsoon and continental climate zone. Local natural vegetation is shifting from steppe-forest vegetation to desert vegetation, as for the geographical location, it lies in the marginal area of the second terrain ladder of China where low plains is shifting to plateau or mountains. These transitional environmental factors are manifested in unstable land productivity, and they are the potential causes of aeolian desertification. Human activities and changes of land use are the driving force of land aeolian desertification.

① Precipitation is extremely variable, which can result in spring drought. Development of aeolian desertification is closely related to regional drought;

② Though drought influences aeolian desertification occurrence significantly, human factors are the primary factors determining aeolian desertification;

③ Both the causes and process of aeolian desertification are complex;

④ Because the semi-arid region lies in the transitional zone of sandy deserts and loess deposits, soils are loose and have an abundance of sand and dust; moreover, its southern part has been ‹reclaimed, when it blows, blown sand comes;

⑤ Fluctuations in climatic conditions and changes in human activities made the occurrence of aeolian desertification intricated;

⑥ Because there is certain amount of precipitation, aeolian desertified land can be reversed comparatively easily.

(2) Aeolian desertification lands in arid region are fleckily distributed around oases and in the marginal area of the Gurbantünggüt Desert where there are mainly fixed and semi-fixed sand dunes.

The arid region is composed of the Hetao Plain in Inner Mongolia, the Yinchuan Plain in Ningxia and northwestern arid zone on the west of the Wushaoling Mountain, including 95 counties (or Qis) in Xinjiang, Gansu, Inner Mongolia and Ningxia (Table 3-15). Aeolian desertification land in the Qaidam, the Qinghai Lake and the Gonghe basin is included. The area of aeolian desertified land amounts to 122,000 km^2, accounting for 31.4% of total in China.

The characteristics of aeolian desertification distribution are:

① 90% of sandy deserts, including the Taklimakan Desert, the Badain Jaran Desert, the Gurbantünggüt Desert, the Tengger Desert, the Kumtag Desert and the Ulan Buh Desert are concentrated in northwest China. There are oases supported by ground water in the proluvial fans at the edges of deserts or Gobi, or along rivers deep into sandy desert. Aeolian desertified land occurs or develops around oases or at the lower reaches of rivers where water is scarce. Aeolian desertified land is gathered in peripheral sandy desert oases.

Table 3-15　Aeolian desertified land in arid region in northwestern China

Geographic units	Related city and county (or Qi)
Junggar Basin	Xinjiang: Qitai, Mulei, Jimusa'er, Fukang, Miquan, Changji, Hutubi, Shawan, Suburb of Ürümqi city, Manasi, Kuitun, Jinghe, Suburb if Kelamayi city, Fuhai, Jimunai, Habahe, Bu'erjin
Tu-Ha Basin	Xinjiang: Hami, Turpan, Tuokexun, Shanshan, Balikun, Yiwu
Yili Basin	Xinjiang: Huocheng
Tarim Basin	Xinjiang: Korla, Yuli, Luntai, Kuqa, Xayar, Xinhe, Awat, Aksu, Wensu, Kalpin, Bachu, Jiashi, Yopurga, Shache, Zepu, Yecheng, Pishan, Moyu, Hotan, Lop, Qira, Yutian, Minfeng, Qimo, Ruoqiang, Artux, Shufu, Shule, Markit, Yingjisha
Hexi Corridor, front Qilian Mountains and marginal area of Tengger desert	Gansu: Dunhuang, A'kesai, Subei, An'xi, Yumen, Jiayuguang, Jiuquan, Jinta, Sunan, Gaotai, Linze, Zhangye, Jinchang, Shandan, Minle, Minqi, Gulang, Wuwei, Jingtai
Yinchuang Plain and Zhongwei Basin	Ningxia: Zhongwei, Zhongning, Wuzhong, Lingwu, Qingtongxia, Yongning, Suburb of Yinchuan City, Helan, Taole, Pingluo, Shizuishan
Alxa Plateau	Inner Mongolia: E'jina Qi, Alxayou Qi, Alxazuo Qi
Hetao plain and area along Yellow River	Inner Mongolia: Dengkou, Hanggin Houqi, Linhe, Wuyuan, Urad Qianqi, Wuhai City
Inner Mongolian Plateau (Houshan area)	Inner Mongolia: Urad Houqi, Urad Zhongqi

Source: Zhu Zhenda et al. (1994).

At the southwestern margin of the Taklimakan Desert, such as Pishan, Qira, Yutian, Minfeng, and its southeast marginal area, such as Qiemo, Washixia and Ruoqiang, and at the lower reach of the Tarim River, the Yarkant River, the Konqi River, the Shule River, the Heihe River and the Shiyang River, because human in arid region gather in oases, the population density is generally 200–400 person/km^2 in these areas. Frequent human activities reactivated fixed and semi-fixed sand dunes around oases, resulting in sand dune advancement and blown sand damage. For example, aeolian desertified land increased from 27% of total area in the late 1950s to 42% in the late 1990s around oases in Pishan.

Aeolian desertification caused by reactivation of sand dunes under the impact of human activities is not limited around oases; it also takes place in fixed and semi-fixed sandy desert areas. Aeolian desertification in the Gurbantünggüt Desert is a good example. In Manasi, Mosuowan and the southwestern margin of the Gurbantünggüt Desert, the width of the belt with sand dunes reactivation occurrence increased from 1–2 km to 5–10 km, and 0.33×10^4 hm^2 of farmlands were threatened by aeolian desertification in Mosuowan area. From west to east, this belt passes Changji, Miquan, Fukang, Jimusa'er, northern Qitai, and eventually reaches areas on the north of Mulei, with a length of more than 350 km. Besides, from southeast Alan Nur at the lowest reach of the Manasi River to Yanchi in the west of the Gurbantünggüt Desert, reactivation of fixed sand dunes is very severe. Shifting sand occupied 5% of the total area in the late 1950s, but it increased to 23% in the late 1980s. Due to petroleum exploitation in the north and northwest of the Gurbantünggüt Desert, reactivation of sand dunes made aeolian desertified land scatter fleckily at the spot of exploitation and along roadways.

What needs to be pointed out is that, as to the distribution of aeolian desertified land in arid regions, there is not only modern aeolian desertified land caused by human activities at the marginal area of oases, but also aeolian desertified land formed in history in continental river basin, such as relics of dry deltas in the Keriya River, the Niya River, the Andir River, the Yurungkax River, the Karakax River, the Damugou and the Konqi River (Zhou, 1989; Fan, 1993) (Table 4-6). There is some aeolian desertified land formed in history at the lower reaches of continental rivers in the Hexi Corridor, such as at the lower reach of the Heihe River, the Shiyang River and the Shule River. Shifting barchan dunes, chains and blown shrub sand mounds can be seen on aeolian desertified land formed in history, besides, relics of walls, castles, houses, channels, towers and temples can be found there. According to ^{14}C dating of structural materials, the age of Juyan site is 2,029±51 a BP–1,394±50 a BP; Kaladun is 2,135±75 a BP–2,133±94 a BP. Kaladun site at the lower reach of the Keriya River was 5–6 km long from south to north, characterized by lengthways aligned dead *Populus euphratica*, which shows there existed narrow oasis along the river. Thereafter, because the establishment of new oases at the upper and middle reaches made water flowing in downriver areas decrease, and even changed river's channel, so original plants around the oasis withered, even died. Under the force of northeast wind, sand dunes encroached on and buried houses, and the landscape of new barchan dunes, chains and blown shrub sand mounds came into being little by little, then original oasis turned into aeolian desertified land. The historical aeolian desertification almost took the same developmental pattern as Kaladun did in oases at the lower reach of rivers in the southern Taklimakan Desert. As far as the ancient city sites in the southern Taklimakan Desert are concerned, downriver oases flourished during the western and Eastern Han Dynasties and Jin Dynasty, middle oases thrived during the Sui and Tang Dynasties and modern oases were established since the Song and Yuan Dynasties. This shows that human activities decreased water resources in lower reaches, causing oases to shift from the lower reaches to the middle or upper reaches, which resulted in aeolian desertification expansion from the lower reaches to the middle and upper reaches. A survey of ancient cities at the southern margin of the Tarim Basin is shown in Table 3-16.

② Landscape of aeolian desertified land is characterized by an interlaced distribution of blown shrub sand mounds, barchan dunes and chains.

③ In the arid region of northern China, the annual average precipitation is less than 200 mm, the annual theoretic evaporation is 2,500–3,500 mm, and consequently the existence of oases completely depends on irrigation. Changes of water systems and reduction in irrigating water sources are the main causes of land aeolian desertification, and over cutting and over grazing at the edge of oases are the secondary causes.

④ The velocity of sand dunes movement in sand deserts is quite low, but the movement is notable as time passes.

Table 3-16 Survey of ancient cities at the southern margin of the Tarim Basin

Rivers	Ancient states	Ancient cities	Ages	Deserted causes	Status of sandy desertification
Lower Konqi River	Loulan (Han and Jin Dynasty)	Loulan	600 AD	River diversion	Blowland
Lower Tarim River		Haitou	500 AD	River diversion	Blowland
Middle Milan River		Yixun	500 AD	War	Blown shifting sand
Lower Qiemo River	Qiemo	Qiemo	unknown	River diversion	Shifting sand dunes and blowland
Lower Andi'er River	Duhuoluogu (Tang Dynasty)	Akekaoqikaranke	700 AD	River diversion	Shifting sand dunes and blowland
		Tiyingmu	1500 AD	River diversion	Shifting sand dunes and blowland
		Dawuzileke	1500 AD	River diversion	Shifting sand dunes and blowland
Lower Niya River	Jingjue (Han Dynasty)	Jingjue state	400–500 AD	River interruption	Blown shifting sand
		Nirang	800 AD	River interruption	Blown shifting sand
Lower Keriya River	Yumi (Han Dynasty)	Kaladun	400–500 AD	River diversion	Blown land and sand dunes
Lower Damagou River		Dandanwulike	800 AD	River diversion or interruption	Blown shifting sand
		Tete'ergelamu	1100 AD	River interruption	Blown semi-fixed sand dunes
		Laodamagou	1900 AD	River interruption	Blown semi-fixed sand dunes
Middle and lower Hotan River	Yutian (Han Dynasty)	Mazhatage	1000 AD	War	Blowland
Water systems in Pianshan county	Pishan (Han Dynasty)	Asaihujia	900 AD	River diversion	Shifting sand dunes and blowland
		Keziletake	300 AD	River diversion	Shifting sand dunes and blowland
		Ya'aqiwuyilike	1300 AD	River diversion	Shifting sand dunes and blowland
		Eqimailike	1500 AD	River interruption	Shifting sand dunes

⑤ Soil secondary salinization in the lower part of oasis. Soil secondary salinization is very severe in oases at the northern edge of the Tarim Basin and at the lower reach of the Heihe River, the Shule River and the Shiyang River in the Hexi Corridor. Take area in the middle reach of the Tarim River as an example, in the early 1980s, secondary salinized land accounted for 25% of farmland, but it increased to 31.1% in the early 1990s. In the oases at the marginal area of desert in Xinjiang, the area of current salinized land accounted for 31% of farmland, thereinto, severely salinized land accounted for

18%, moderately salinized land accounted for 33%, and slightly salinized land accounted for 49%. The analogous things took place in the Hetao Plain in Inner Mongolia and the Yinchuan Plain in Ningxia, blown sand and soil secondary salinization are the main damages impeding the development of agriculture in plain. Salinized land accounted for 73% of irrigation district in the Hetao Plain in 1980.

⑥ Establishments of transportation, industry and mining are susceptible to blown sand due to the fragile ecological balance.

(3) Aeolian desertified lands are mainly scattered in proluvial fans and along old riverbed banks in semi-humid regions.

Concentrated precipitation, dry and wind seasons are synchronous in northern China where climate is controlled by the East Asian Monsoon. Under these circumstances, land easily suffers from aeolian desertification. Aeolian desertified land is concentrated in floodplains and deltas; there are more than 80 counties suffering from aeolian desertification in ancient deltas at the lower reach of the Yellow River, and the others gathered in piedmont alluvial plains or floodplains of the Yongding River and the Chaobai River, the Luan River delta and lower valley, the Songhuajiang Plain and the Nenjiang Plain (Table 3-17). The area of aeolian desertified land is 24,660 km^2 in semi-arid region, accounting for 6.4% of the total aeolian desertified land in China. Because of the local semi-humid climate, aeolian desertified landscape is generally manifested in blown sand landforms in dry seasons such as in winter and spring, but it takes on a farmland view in summer and autumn, when characteristics of blown sand movement are not obvious. Therefore, the aeolian desertified landscape changes seasonally.

Table 3-17   Counties and cities suffering from aeolian desertification in semi-humid regions of northern China

Provinces	Counties (cities)
Heilongjiang Province	Suburb of Qiqihar city, Du'erbote mongolian autonomous county, Tailai, Gannan, Longjiang, Fuyu, Lindian, Nahe, Zhaoyuan, Suburb of Daqing city
Jilin Province	Baicheng city, Zhenlai, Da'an, Tongyu, Changling, Qianguo'erluosi mongolian autonomous county, Fuyu, Qian'an, Tao'an
Beijing City	Yanqing, Changping, Huairou, Shunyi, Fengtai District, Tongxian, Daxing, Fangshan
Tianjin City	Wuqing
Hebei Province	Qian'an, Luanxian, Luannan, Leting, Lulong, Changli, Zhuoxian, Gu'an, Yongqing, An'ci, Xinle, Zhengding, Shahe, Daming, Guantao, Weixian, Linxi, Qinghe
Henan Province	Neihuang, Qingfeng, Fanxian, Taiqian, Puyang, Junxian, Huaxian, Jixian, Xinxiang, Changyuan, Yanjin, Yuanyang, Fengqiu, Suburb of Zhengzhou City, Xinzheng, Zhongmou, Suburb of Kaifeng City, Kaifeng, Weidi, Tongxu, Qixian, Lankao, Minquan, Suixian, Ningling, Suburb of Shangqiu City, Shangqiu, Yucheng, Xiayi
Shandong Province	Dongming, Heze, Juancheng, Caoxian, Dingtao, Shanxian, Jinxiang, Yutai, Juye, Yuncheng, Jiaxiang, Yanggu, Xinxiang, Guancheng, Liaocheng, Dong'e, Chiping, Linqing, Gaotang, Xiajin, Wucheng, Yucheng, Pingyuan, Jiyang, Linyi, Shanghe, Leling, Qingyun, Huimin, Wudi, Zhanhua, Binxian, Lijin, Kenli
Jiangsu Province	Fengxian, Peixian
Shaanxi Province	Dali
An'hui Province	Dangshan

Note: Cited from "Aeolian desertification in China", Zhu Zhenda et al., 1994.

Characteristics of aeolian desertified land in semi-humid areas are obviously different from that in arid, semi-arid regions: ① seasonal characteristic of blown sand damage; ② obvious seasonal changes; ③ sporadic distribution of aeolian desertified land in semi-humid region; ④ Blown sand damage is mainly manifested in soil wind erosion in farmland; ⑤ Aeolian desertified land generally occurs in delta plains and at the lower reaches of rivers.

(4) Aeolian desertified lands under the wind force in humid regions is concentrated in sandy lands along riverbanks and in seashores.

There are good examples of aeolian desertification at the lower reach of the Yangtze River, such as Nanchang, *Xinjiang*, and at the lakefront of the Boyang Lake, such as Hukou, Xingzi, and Duchang. Besides, in xerothermic and arid river valley in the Jinshajiang River and the Minjiang River, sandy deposits in flood plains have been blown by wind for a long time, so aeolian desertified land came into being. Aeolian desertified land is also scattered in the Sanjiang Plain in northern China, the Nenjiang River basin and Yarlung Zangbo River basin. Its formation is related to river diversion and over cutting. Aeolian desertified land at the seashore develops based on seashore sand dunes, coastal pits and sand banks, such as the west coast of Taiwan, cities in Guangxi, such as Fangcheng and Jiangping, Changle, Pingtan in Fujian Province. Besides, Aeolian desertified land still scatters in western Guangdong Province, such as Wuchuan, Xuwen, and Dianbai, and in Hainandao, such as Wenchang in northeastern Hainandao. Inconsistent water and hot conditions and intensive human activities made climate much more drought in southwest Hainandao, and it became the only savanna in China. The process of aeolian desertification is similar to the evolvement of tropical forests in West Africa in that tropical forests evolved first into savannas, and eventually degraded to aeolian desertified land with desert-like landscapes.

Aeolian desertified land in humid regions of south China has the following characteristics: ① Seasonal changes are more obvious; ② The history of evolvement is short, but is developing at a rapid rate; ③ over cutting makes ground bare in winter, which aggravates the blown sand movement; ④ sand particles are coarse, with good sorting, and a high threshold velocity is required; ⑤ Sand sources are limited and landforms are simple.

(5) Aeolian desertified land fleckily scatters along riverbanks in high tundra zone.

Aeolian desertified land generally shows a patchy and scattered distribution pattern in high tundra zone, and it is mainly distributed in valleys of the Yalung Zangbo River, the Lhasa River and the Nianchu River. Shifting sand caused by over grazing and over cutting is interruptedly distributed. Aeolian desertified land developed around towns in Nimula, Naqu of northern Tibetan Plateau and Shiquanhe town in A'li area, which was mostly related to local construction of infrastructure and over cutting.

In summary, the distributions of aeolian desertified land are not limited to regions with a drought index value of 0.50–0.65 in China, but in all kinds of natural belts, which shows aeolian desertification is the product of interaction between intensive human activities and fragile ecological environments, and irrational human activities caused the environment degradation into a desert-like landscape. There was $38.57 \times 10^4 \, km^2$ of aeolian desertified land in northern China, thereinto, slightly aeolian desertified land was $13.95 \times 10^4 \, km^2$, accounting for 36.1% of total aeolian desertified land; moderately aeolian desertified land was $9.98 \times 10^4 \, km^2$, occupying 25.9%; severely aeolian desertified land was $7.91 \times 10^4 \, km^2$, occupying 20.5%; and very severely aeolian desertified land was $6.75 \times 10^4 \, km^2$, occupying 17.5%. Compared with the results of aeolian desertified land monitoring in the middle and late 1980s, in 2000, the percentage of slightly aeolian desertified land was reduced, that of moderate aeolian desertified land kept stable, but the percentage of severe aeolian desertification increased. This status is consistent with the principles of aeolian desertification development, and also conforms to principles of aeolian desertification control that area of light aeolian desertified land should be controlled first and rehabilitated.

3.4.2 Temporal trends of aeolian desertification

Aeolian desertification is a dynamic process, so the distributing scope and characteristics of surficial landforms are variable during different periods. Take aeolian desertification in northern China as an example, it has the following 3 points:

(1) During the historical period before 100 AD, aeolian desertified land was centered on historical ancient cities in arid zones, and it showed a specky distribution pattern.

This kind of aeolian desertified land was 53,616 km^2, accounting for 14.4% of total aeolian desertified land in China, such as Wucengtadi and Gudamagou in Qira, Ancient Pishan in Pishan, Jingjue at the lower reach of the Niya River, Kaladun at the lower reach of the Keriya River, Heicheng and Juyan at the lower reach of the Ruoshui River and Loulan at the lower reach of the Konqi River. The local landforms of aeolian desertified land is an interlaced distribution of blown shrub sand mounds along riverbanks and barchan sand dunes and chains in interdunes. Yardang landforms are extensively distributed in areas of thick clay deposits, such as Loulan. The reasons why these ancient cities (or ancient oases) were deserted are different. For example, establishment of oases at the upper and middle reaches could consume a large amount of water, and decreasing water resources made lower oases decay, even deserted, such as Kaladun, and Jingjue; or destruction of irrigation works during war resulted in impossible rehabilitation of lower oases, such as Heicheng. Besides, as for the oases lying in diluvial or alluvial fans, because of inappropriate irrigation, secondary salinization of soil occurred at the edge of fan, so farmland was deserted and oases withered, and former farmland was turned into desertified land, such as deltas of the Ogan River and the Dina River at the south foot of the Tianshan Mountain. The fact that sites of ancient cities in the Han Dynasty lied at the periphery of diluvial or alluvial fans, while sites of ancient cities in the Tang Dynasty were located at outer modern oases can prove the shrinkage of oases.

(2) During 1,100–1,900, aeolian desertified land was concentrated in semi-arid steppes, and it

was centered in historical farming regions, showing a patchy distribution pattern. Due to repeated process of aeolian desertification development and reversal, the landforms of aeolian desertified lands are characterized by interlaced distributions of shifting sands, fixed and semi-fixed sand dunes.

This kind of aeolian desertified land is 86,190 km^2, accounting for 23.23% of total aeolian desertified land in China, and its occurrence and development is closely related to reclamation of farmland. For example, the occurrence of aeolian desertification in the western Horqin Steppe in eastern Inner Mongolia has a close relationship with over reclamation along the Liaohe River. Qidan people who lived at the upper Xilamulun River reach were nomadic, and they learned to farm in the Tang Dynasty, and their life styles shifted from grazing to farming. After the foundation of the Liao Dynasty, traditional farming people were ordered to do farming at the economic center of the day, namely the upper Xiliao River, to develop agriculture. According to records from the "Liao History", more than 60 new counties had been established in west Horqin Steppe to meet the needs of exploitation of virgin land at that time, such as Qingzhou, Huaizhou, Fengzhou, Songshanzhou, Raozhou, and Yongzhou. Lands with abundant loose deposits, such as fine sands and clay, suffered from aeolian desertification due to over farming. Since the Nvzhen people governed the Xiliao River basin, political center was transferred southward. From the early 13th century to the middle 17th century, farming almost ceased in the Horqin Steppe. In addition to local semi-arid or semi-humid natural conditions, natural vegetation there can rehabilitate automatically, and large areas of shifting sand that formed in the Liao and Jin Dynasty had been recovered to fixed or semi-fixed sand dunes. After the middle 17th century, the Qing rulers encouraged Mongolians to reclaim grassland, so aeolian desertified land developed then. Aeolian desertification in the southeastern Horqin Steppe was initiated from about the mid 18th century to the 1980s. As for aeolian desertification in the northern Horqin Steppe, it began to occur approximately during the 1980s–2000s. In addition, aeolian desertification in the western Horqin Steppe got started from the late 1700s to 1940s.

Similar processes of aeolian desertification occurred in the Erdos Steppe. Large areas of shifting sand appeared during the Tang and Song Dynasties. In the Yuan Dynasty, this region was ruled by nomadic peoples, and because the Erdos area was used for grazing, farming almost ceased, and after the vegetation was rehabilitated, the landscape was primarily fixed and semi-fixed sand dunes. In the Qing Dynasty, the Qing Government encouraged Mongolians to reclaim grassland. Exploitation of grassland in interdune areas and sandy plains along rivers caused scattered shifting sand to connect, and the shifting sand belt came into existence at last, especially in Otog Qi, Uxin Qi, YijinHoro Qi and Hanggin Qi. Afterwards, the basic outline of aeolian desertification has formed in the Mu Us Sandy Land.

Characteristics of aeolian desertification in the Horqin and Erdos Steppe show reclamation of grassland is the main cause of aeolian desertification. This explains why aeolian desertified land is concentrated in farming areas, and the main channel for aeolian desertified land development is reactivation of fixed and semi-fixed sand dunes.

(3) Since the 20th century, over cultivation, overgrazing and irrational development of artificial oases at the upper reaches of continental rivers are the main causes of modern aeolian desertified land expansion.

During this period, the development of aeolian desertification was manifested in the following three points. First, further expansion of aeolian desertified land made separated patchy desertified lands jointed together in Erdos and Horqin Steppe, such as the joint of aeolian desertified land in fixed sand dunes and interdune flats in the Erdos Steppe. In the Horqin Steppe, it's manifested in the joint of shifting sand in eastern area, and the percentage of shifting sand increased from former 2% to 3.74% in the 1980s. Secondly, aeolian desertified land tends to develop toward the Ulanqab Steppe and the Bashang grassland, respectively on the north of Yinshan Mountain and Zhangjiakou, which has not yet suffered from large scale reclamation. For example, there were 80,000 people and $6.7 \times 10^4 \, hm^2$ of farmland in Shangdu County in the 1930s, but by the end of the 1970s, there were 35×10^4 people and $21 \times 10^4 \, hm^2$ there. Large scale exploitation of grassland aeolian desertified land to increase from 25% in the 1950s to 40% in the 1980s. Finally, over grazing promotes the development of aeolian desertified land in pasturelands. Degraded pastureland accounts for 42.3% of total pasture area.

As for the causes of aeolian desertification, it's not simply reclamation of grassland, but rather a combination of all kinds of human activities. For example, in the interlaced zone of farmlands and pasture-lands in northern China, 45% of aeolian desertified land was caused by over cultivation, over grazing resulted in 29% of desertified lands, over cutting accounted for 20%, desertified lands caused by construction of railways or roads and exploitation of minerals was 6%. So, it's obvious that human factor which can cause aeolian desertification is very complicated.

In general, characteristics of desertified land distribution at this stage are: the area of aeolian desertified land is increasing, not only in semi-arid steppe region but also in semi-humid zone and at the marginal area of oases in arid zone. Taking northern China as an example, the annual increasing area of aeolian desertified land was 1,560 km^2 from the 1950s to the middle 1970s, with a rate of 1.01%; from the middle 1970s to the middle 1980s, it was 2,100 km^2, with a rate of 1.47%; and it's 2,460 km^2 in the 1990s. What's more, the degree of aeolian desertification got aggravated, severe aeolian desertified land accounted for 0.93% in the middle 1970s, but it was 1.77% in the middle 1980s, during the same period, moderately aeolian desertified land increased from 14.87% to 21.8%, while slightly aeolian desertified land decreased from 84.2% to 76.4%. It shows the degree of aeolian desertification is getting worse and worse.

According to the above-mentioned temporal characteristics of aeolian desertified land distribution, it can be summarized into the following points:

(1) Before 1,000 AD, especially in the Han and Tang dynasties, desertified lands were concentrated at the lower reaches of continental rivers in sandy deserts in arid regions, which was caused by inappropriate utilization of water resources.

(2) From 1100 AD to 1900 AD, desertified lands were distributed in semi-arid regions, caused by large scale exploitation of grasslands. Because of different ways of land use (grazing or farming), there existed both development and reversal of aeolian desertified land during this period.

(3) Since the 20th century, great population pressure and frequent human activities has promoted the expansion of aeolian desertified land, especially in interlaced zones of farmlands and pasture-lands in semi-arid regions.

(4) New characteristics of aeolian desertification came forth in northern China at the turn of the 20th and 21st century. At the end of the 20th century, the Chinese Government put forward a strategic plan of "Western Development", which regarded rehabilitation of the ecological environment as the primary task, constituted "grain for green" policy, and carried out 10 great projects to combat desertification. As a result, a large area of aeolian desertified land was rehabilitated. On the other hand, in some areas of China, because of great population pressure, a weak economical basis and outdated modes of production, people pursue economic development simply to banish poverty and become rich, ignoring the capacity of environment, which results in the development of aeolian desertification. At the turn of the century, sand-dust storms attacked northwest and northeast China; what's more, northeastern China suffered much more damage from sand-dust storms in recent years. This fully proved the development of aeolian desertified land in northern China.

At the turn of the century, a new characteristic of aeolian desertification in northern China is the interlaced distribution of rehabilitated aeolian desertified land and intensively developing aeolian desertified land, new artificial oases and natural oases suffering from severe aeolian desertification. First, because of the implementation of the "grain for green" policy in the interlaced zones of farmlands and pasture-lands in semi-arid regions, local people all took this policy actively; in addition, local governments took other measures to combat aeolian desertification, such as afforestation. As a result, the rapid development of aeolian desertified land was controlled in farmlands of the interlaced zone of farmlands and pasture-lands in semi-arid regions since the 20th century, in most areas, aeolian desertified land even got reversed. Second, the increase of livestock amounts results in over grazing. Though local government carried out several policies, such as "prohibiting grazing on grassland", "enclosed grazing" etc, because of the shortage of money to establish artificial pastureland base and build enclosures etc, over grazing can't be prohibited completely. In addition to drought in successive years, aeolian desertification is rapidly developing in steppes of northern China. Third, since the 1950s, in continental river basins of arid regions, establishment of oases shifted from lower reaches to upper reaches, natural oases at lower reaches withered because of the shortage of water, then aeolian desertification was initiated. At present, on one hand, because of much attention from the Chinese Government, shortage of water was solved at the lower reach of the Tarim River and the Heihe River; on the other hand, because of irrational expansion of oases and reduction of water source at up reach, recently reclaimed farmland without water for irrigation was aeolian desertified at the marginal area of oases. Outward expansion of oases resulted in the shortage of water inside oases, and local people exploited ground water excessively, which destroyed the ecological balance. As a result, aeolian desertified land was overspread. Fourth, with the implementation of "*the Development of the Western Region*", construction of factories, roads, railways, etc. destruction of the stabilization of sand surface in sand desert, it's more and more urgent to combat aeolian desertification here.

In recent 20 years, since the policies of economic reform were carried out in China, China's economy has greatly improved especially in sandy areas. But there have been several contradictions related to the development of economy in sandy area, such as conflicts between extensive economic growth and limited ecological and environmental carrying capacity. In fact, it's very difficult to develop the economy and protect the environment at the same time. But, we have to insist on the sustainable development of ecology, economy and human society and continually adjust our activities in order to control aeolian desertification and promote the ecological environment in sandy areas.while maintaining the sustainable and stable development of the economy.

References

Chen Guangting. 2001. Origins of arguments on the area of desertified lands in China. Journal of Desert Research, 21(2): 209—212

Chen Yuqiong. 1986. Drought and its influence. Journal of Catastrophology, 56—62

China national committee to implement the UN Convention to Combat Desertification. United Nations to Combat Desertification in those countries experiencing serious drought and/or desertification, particularly in Africa

Dong Guangrong, Gao Shangyu, Jin Jun et al. 1993. Sandy Desertification and Control in Gonghe Basin in Qinghai Province. Beijing: Science Press, 164

Dong Guangrong. 1990. Discussion on the relationship between global climatic change and sandy desertification. Quaternary Sciences, (1): 36—43

Dong Yuxiang, Liu Yuzhang, Liu Yihua et al. 1995. Researches on Sandy Desertification. Xi'an: Xi'an Maps Press, 37

Fan Zili. 1993. Formation and evolvement of oases in Tarim basin. Acta Geographica Sinica, 48(5):421—426

Fang Xiuqi. 1987. The relationship between sandy desertification and precipitation variability in Erdos area in north Shaanxi Province. Journal od Beijing Normal University, (1): 90—95

State Environmental Protection Administration of China. 1999. Reports on Ecological Issues in China. Beijing: China Environmental Science Press, 24—25

Team of "Researches on Desertification (Land Degradation) Control in China" Project. 1998. Researches on Desertification (Land Degradation) Control in China. Beijing: China Environmental Science Press

Wu Zheng. 1991. Questions on sandy desertification in north China. Acta Geographica Sinica, 46(3): 266—274

Xia Guang, Wang Fengchun. 2000. Synthetic Decision-making on Environment and Its Development. Beijing: Science Press, 1—14

Zhang Linyuan, Wang Nai'ang. 1994. Sand Deserts and Oases in China. Lanzhou: Gansu Education Press,

15—17, 25—51

Zhao Songqiao. 1997. Selected Works of Zhao Songqiao. Beijing: Science Press, 161—162

Zhong Decai. 1998. Dynamical Evolvement of Sand Sea in China. Lanzhou: Gansu Culture Press, 1—2, 5—11

Zhou Xingjia. 1989. Sandy desertification in Tarim basin in historical period. Arid Zone Research, (1): 9—17

Zhu Zhenda, Chen Guangting. 1994. Sandy Desertification in China. Beijing: Science Press, 20—32

Zhu Zhenda, Liu Shu, Di Xingmin. 1989. Sandy Desertification and Control in China. Beijing: Science Press, 5

Zhu Zhenda, Liu Shu. 1981. Process of Sandy Desertification and Control in North China. Beijing: China Forestry Publishing House, 3—6

Zhu Zhenda, Wu Zheng, Liu Shu. 1981. Sand Deserts in China. Beijing: Science Press, 1—4

Zhu Zhenda. 1999a. Formation, distribution and characteristics of desert and rules of blown sand movement in China. Sand Desert, Sandy Desertification, Desertification and Control in China. Beijing: China Environmental Science Press, 108

Zhu Zhenda. 1999b. Spatial distribution of land desertification in China. Sand Desert, Sandy Desertification, Desertification and Control in China. Beijing: China Environmental Science Press, 351—356

Zhu Zhenda. 1999c. Measures to control sandy desertification in the interlaced zone of farmlands and pasture-lands in north China. Sand Desert, Sandy Desertification, Desertification and Control in China. Beijing: China Environmental Science Press, 159—173

Chapter 4
Natural Resources in Desert Regions

Abundant natural resources exist in desert regions of China, including land, light, heat, wind energy, coal, oil, kalium salt and common salt, etc. Due to the vulnerability of desert environments, the exploitation of natural resources often causes a series of eco-environment issues. Aeolian desertification is one of the most significant types of land degradation. The development of aeolian desertification not only can destroy the eco-system of desert regions but also can affect surrounding regions.

4.1 Climatic resources

4.1.1 Concept and characteristics

Climate is an important factor existing in the natural environment, and it is closely related to agriculture. The term "climatic resource" is a newly emerging terminology. H. E. Landsberg, a famous American climatologic scientist, first published a paper entitled "Climate is a kind of resource" in the 1940s, which promoted the observation, collection and management of climatic data. Actually, the term "climatic resource" was officially proposed at the "World Climate Conference" held in Geneva, Switzerland in February 1979. After that, a consistent conception gradually formed, that is "climate is an important renewable natural resource, as well as a valuable energy source which provides people with usable light, heat, water, wind and air directly or indirectly under certain technological conditions; it is also a basic condition for human existence and development.

As a kind of resource, climate has several peculiarities besides some common characteristics of other natural resources.

(1) Ubiquity: Climate resources exist in every place on the earth's surface but its abundance and structure are different in different places.

(2) Suitability: Climate factors can only become resources on a suitable scale. For example, there is a certain temperature and precipitation range suitable for agriculture. High temperatures beyond this range may cause scorching; low temperatures may result in frost damage; too little precipitation may cause drought and excessive precipitation may result in water logging.

(3) Exploitation and Usage risk: There exists risk in the process of exploitation and using of climate resources. Therefore, disaster control must be considered during the exploitation and utilization of climate.Through disaster prevention can decrease risk, thus allowing sufficient

resource utilization and development.

(4) Renewability: Climate is a kind of renewable resource and its value is only manifested in the process of usage. Rational usage of climate resources can allow for repeated use, which differs from oil, iron and other mineral resources.

(5) Variability: Climate resources have large variability, some of which belong to periodical variations and others which belong to non-periodical ones. For example, the diurnal change of temperature is important in the nutrient accumulation processes of crops. In the monsoon regions of China, there are evident seasonal temperature changes. High temperature, high humidity and strong radiation are especially suitable for the growth of crops in the summer. All of these are elements of periodical change. Non-periodical change mainly occurs during weather change and multiyear climate change processes, which includes temperature and precipitation. Considering this variability, a suitable time period should be considered during the exploitation of climatic resources

(6) Accumulative character: Climate resources must undergo an accumulation process due to its low density. During agricultural production, crops transform climate resources into consumable farm products over the whole growth period. Wind and solar energy usually are able to satisfy the demands of lowenergy consumption but cannot meet transportation and other industrial demands.

(7) Liability to human impact. Climate resources can easily change due to the effect of human activity, though such effects are usually unconscious. There are mainly two aspects: one is that enlarging farmlands, urbanization and deforestation cause the destruction of eco-systems which leads to local climate change and the exacerbation of drought and water logging disasters; the other is that large amounts of greenhouse gases are emitted into the atmosphere and thereby result in global warming.

4.1.2　Evaluation of climatic resources in desert regions

proper evaluation and research of natural resources and their rational exploitation in desert regions is very important for preventing eco-environment degradation while using desert, gobi and sandy lands.

(1) Radiation and sunshine.

The light energy dependent on solar radiation is the only energy source for the photosynthesis of green vegetation in nature. The calculation of solar radiation reaching the earth's surface (total solar radiation) is based on the relationship between sunshine or cloudage and total solar radiation. The empirical relation can be expressed as follows:

$$Q = Q_i f(a,b)\varphi(x) \tag{4-1}$$

where, Q is the total solar radiation; Q_i is the basic value used for the calculation of total solar radiation; $f(a,b)$ is the weakened function of the total solar radiation caused by atmospheric transparency, *a* and *b* are the empirical coefficients which are different in different regions; and $\varphi(x)$ is the weakened function of atmosphere coverage caused by climatic factor *x*. According to the difference in *x*, the above empirical formula can be divided into four kinds: (a) based on the sunshine percent: $Q/Q_i=a+bS_1$, where, S_1 is the sunshine percent; (b) based on the sunshine hours: $Q=m\sum t+n$, in which, $\sum t$ is the total sunshine hours, *m* and *n* are the coefficients that change with latitude and season; (c) based on the cloudage : $Q=Q_0[1-(1-k)n]$, where Q_0 is the monthly total solar radiation calculated from the clear days, *n* is the monthly average total cloudage; (d) based on mixed weather factors: $Q=Q_0[1-(1-k)r\ n]$, where *k* is the coefficient changing based on cloud forms, cloudage, solar altitude and reflectivity of the earth's surface, and *n* is the average cloudage. In desert regions of China, the formula: $Q=Qm(0.29+0.557S_1)$is usually adopted, where *Qm* is the total solar radiation under ideal (dry and clean) atmospheric conditions.

In desert regions of China, annual sunshine is between 2,600–3,400 hours, and sunshine percent varies between 60% and 80% (Fig. 4-1). The yearly total solar radiation in desert regions of China is about 5,000–6,500 $MJ \cdot M^{-2} \cdot a^{-1}$, which is next only to that of the Qinghai-Tibet Plateau but far exceeds other regions of China. On the whole, solar radiation tends to increase from east to west (Fig. 4-2). It also tends to increase from south to north in the eastern desert regions, while decreasing from south to north in the western desert regions. The highest values occur in the following two areas: the Taklimakan Desert, where the total solar radiation is 6,000–6,500 $MJ/(m^2 \cdot a)$; and Ejin Qi of Inner Mongolia, where the total solar radiation is 6,500–7,000 $MJ/(m^2 \cdot a)$. In the temporal distribution of solar radiation, the minimum value can reach 600–1,000 MJ/M^2 in winter and the maximum value can reach 1,800–2,400 MJ/M^2 in summer. The values in spring and autumn are higher than that of winter and lower than that of summer, and the value in spring is higher than that of autumn. The spatial and temporal distribution of photosynthetically active radiation is similar to above. High solar radiation provides ample light and heat energy for agricultural production in desert regions of China.

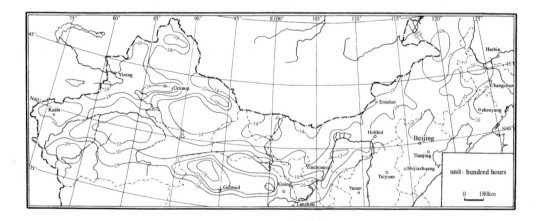

Fig. 4-1 Isoline map of sunshine time and percent in desert regions of China (Geng, 1986)

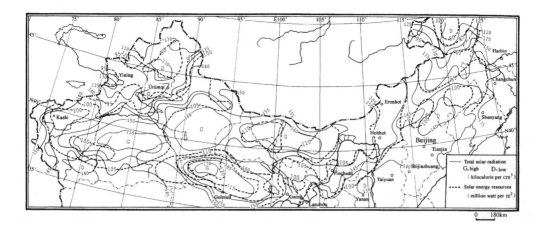

Fig. 4-2   Isoline map of total solar radiation and photosynthetically active radiation in desert regions

(Geng, 1986)

(2) Heat energy.

Heat energy, from solar radiation, is a necessary resource for human life and production. Because temperature is an important factor affecting the growth of crops, it is usually used to evaluate the heat energy in agricultural production and the study of climate resources. Heat energy resources are expressed by different temperature indexes that include annual average temperature, daily temperature difference, yearly temperature difference, accumulative temperature and extreme temperature. From the isoline map of annual average temperature, it can be seen that the temperature distribution of eastern desert regions is different from that of western desert regions. The temperature isoline in the eastern desert region stretches from northeast to southwest, while that in the western desert region exhibits a closed line in the basins, and the isoline between E100–110° is distributed along the longitude.

Mean annual temperature is 0–4°C in the eastern part, and 4–12°C in the western part. The highest mean annual temperature is above 12°C in the Tarim Basin. Below is a summary of accumulative temperatures and extreme temperatures, both of which have a major influence on agriculture in deserts.

There are many ways to express accumulative temperature, among which accumulative active temperature and accumulative effective temperature are extensively adopted. Active temperature is the mean daily temperature that is higher than the biological lower temperature limit, while accumulative active temperature is the sum of the active temperature during the period that a plant grows. Active temperature minus the biological lower temperature limit is effective temperature, whereas accumulative effective temperature is the sum of the effective temperature during the period that a plant grows. Let accumulative active temperature be A_a, and let accumulative effective temperature be A_e, then:

$$A_a = \sum_{i=i}^{n} t_i \qquad (t_i \geqslant B, \text{ when } t_i < B, \ t_i = 0) \tag{4-2}$$

$$A_e = \sum_{i=1}^{n} (t_i - B) \qquad (t_i > B, \text{ when } t_i \leqslant B, \ t_i - B = 0) \tag{4-3}$$

where, n is plant growing days; t_i is the mean daily temperature of the ith day; B is the biological lower temperature limit.

There are different accumulative active temperature indices depending on different biological lower temperature limits. For example, there exist $\geqslant 0°C$ accumulative active temperature, $\geqslant 5°C$ accumulative active temperature, $\geqslant 10°C$ accumulative active temperature, $\geqslant 15°C$ accumulative active temperature, $\geqslant 20°C$ accumulative active temperature, and they all have specific applications. Among the indices, $\geqslant 10°C$ accumulative active temperature is most extensively used. The first day when the mean daily temperature exceeds 0°C usually occurs between mid March and mid April in desert regions, though in the Tarim Basin, it occurs at the beginning of March. The last day is usually between mid October and mid November, and it occurs earlier in eastern regions than in western regions. The total number of days with a mean daily temperature exceeding 0°C is usually between 180–260 days. The first day with a mean daily temperature exceeding 10°C appears between mid April and mid May in most parts of the deserts, while in the western part, especially in the Hetian and Kashi areas, it is between the end of March and the beginning of April while in the Qilian Mountains, it occurs between mid June and mid July. The end day comes between mid September and mid October, and mid August in the Qilian Mountains. The total number of days with a mean daily temperature exceeding 10°C is the highest at the lowest in the Qilian Mountains at 40-80 days, while in the Hotian area of the Tarim Basin and in the Turpan Basin, it is the highest at about 200 days. The $\geqslant 0°C$ accumulative temperature is higher in western parts than in eastern parts, it is 2,500–3,000°C in the Hulun Buir and the Xilingol sandy rangeland while it is 4,000–5,000°C in the Tarim Basin and the Turpan Basin. The $\geqslant 10°C$ accumulative temperature is also higher in western parts than in eastern parts; it is 2,000–2,500°C in eastern parts, 3,500°C in the Tarim Basin, and 5,000°C in the Turpan Basin.

The annual extreme high temperature in the desert is usually 34–44°C. The lowest figure is between 26–28 °C in the Qilian Mountains, and the highest is above 42°C in the Tarim Basin, the Junggar Basin, the Turpan Basin and the Dunhuang area. The annual extreme low temperature is generally lower in eastern parts than in western parts. It is −34°C—−40°C in eastern parts, and −24°C—−34°C in western parts. There are several annual extreme low temperature centers, for example, it can reach −50°C in the Altay Mountains and −42°C in the Gurbantünggüt Desert and the eastern Tianshan Mountains.

(3) Wind energy resources.

Wind energy is a clean, renewable and on-the-spot natural resource. Its value is being re-recognized with conventional energy sources in short supply and extensive pollution of the environment. Wind energy comes from the movement of airflow. Compared with conventional fossil fuels, it is widespread, causes less pollution and is highly efficient. The utilization of wind energy is done by converting its kinetic energy to other forms of energy, so the evaluation of wind energy is the calculation of the kinetic energy of airflow. Wind energy can be measured by efficient power density (when wind speed is 3–20 m/s) and the hours of usable wind speed, or the product of them. Wind energy potential is calculated based on wind speed data. According to the dynamic theory (Tan et al., 1985), the kinetic energy of airflow W(J) is:

$$W = \frac{1}{2}mv^2 \tag{4-4}$$

Where m is the mass of airflow(kg); v is wind speed(m/s)。 Providing that airflow, in the speed of v, goes perpendicularly through a hypothetic section with an area of F, in time interval t(s), the bulk of airflow is:

$$S = vtF \tag{4-5}$$

Mass of airflow is:

$$m = \rho vtF \tag{4-6}$$

where, p is air density (kg/m^3).

　　Combining Equations (4-6) and (4-4), we get

$$W = \frac{1}{2}(\rho tF)v^3 \tag{4-7}$$

　　This is the equation measuring wind energy in t seconds that passes through the hypothetic section. Then the power of wind energy is:

$$W = \frac{1}{2}\rho Fv^3 \tag{4-8}$$

　　Equation (4-8) is the extensively used wind energy power equation, also called wind energy equation in wind engineering. It is obvious that wind energy is mainly related to wind speed. Let F be 1 in the wind energy equation, we'll get the wind energy density equation:

$$W = \frac{1}{2}\rho v^3 \ (W/m^2) \tag{4-9}$$

　　Because wind is of great variation and its mean value must be based on long-term observations, average wind energy density can be an integral:

$$\bar{W} = \frac{1}{T} \int_0^T \frac{1}{2} \rho v^3 dt \tag{4-10}$$

where, W is average wind energy density(W/m^2); v is wind speed; T is total hours (h); p is air density, which is a constant in general conditions, so (4-10) can be:

$$\bar{W} = \frac{\rho}{2T} \int_0^T v^3 dt \tag{4-11}$$

According to the above equation, air density and wind speed determine wind energy density. In the near ground layer, the order of magnitude of air density ρ is 10^0, while that of cubic wind speed v^3 is 10^2–10^3. So wind speed is the crucial factor that determines wind energy density. The following paragraphs will give a summary of wind-blown sand activities in Chinese desert areas.

From the maps of average wind speed and gale days, it can be seen that average wind speed is greater in eastern desert areas, and is about 4–5 m/s, while in western areas it is about 2–4 m/s because of the huge mountain ranges. Major gale areas are located near national borders, especially near the China-Mongolia and the China-Kazakhstan borders; the number of gale days is 75–150 d annually. The southwest Hulun Buir area, the northwest Onqin Daga Sandy Land, the north slope of the Yinshan Mountains Range, the Gansu-Xinjiang bordering area, and the eastern part of northern Xinjiang are major areas of wind-blown sand activities. In central parts of these areas, the intensity magnitude of wind is about 4,000 m/(s·a), and wind-blown sand days can be more than 125 days. Among these areas, the Gansu-Xinjiang bordering area is the strongest wind area, where gale axis extends 1,400 km southwest from national border area to the west of the Andir River. There are 3 famous gale passes – Alataw Pass, Daban City and Qijiaojing, where the magnitude of wind is above 5,000 m/(s·a). These gale passes are formed by local relief. Weak wind areas are mainly in the hinterland of deserts, especially in the Tarim Basin and the Junggar Basin, where wind-blown sand days are 20–25 days annually.

In the eastern desert, wind variability is large. It is strong in winter, spring and autumn, and weak in summer. In the western desert, only spring is windy season, and its annual variability is less than the eastern part. In the Qaidam Basin, wind is strong in spring and summer and weak in autumn and winter, and its variability is less than in the eastern part.

Wind energy resources in China's deserts are abundant. Potential wind energy in China's deserts is 20% more than Central Asian areas under similar wind conditions (Geng, 1986). Actually, the amount of wind energy resources depends, to a certain extent, on the use efficiency. As shown in Fig. 4-1, the distribution of wind energy resources in China's deserts is similar to that of wind sand strength. For comparing and evaluating the wind energy resources of different desert regions of China, the power of a wind wheel is adopted as the standard. At the boundary between China and Mongolia, the annual supplied wind energy can reach above 18,000–25,000 kW; several basins are wind energy deficient regions, of which the wind energy in Tarim Basin is the poorest, where the annual supplied wind energy is only around 1,500–7,350 kW. The wind energy resources in the eastern and western deserts is also different. The wind energy in the eastern desert is abundant; most of the area has over 11,000 kW of wind energy per year, and the maximum can reach 25,000 kW. The wind energy in the eastern desert has a decreasing trend from southeast to northwest. In the western desert, local differences exist in wind energy distribution; the annual supplied wind energy is from 1,500 kW to 42,000 kW, and the maximum value is 28 times as much as the minimum value. In the western desert, the wind energy in northern parts is more than that of southern parts except for in the mountains; in the two basins north and south of the Tianshan Mountains, the wind energy is more abundant in the surrounding areas than in the center. In the Qaidam Desert, the wind energy is abundant due to high relief; in most of the region annual wind energy could reach 11,000–30,000 kW or more. And the distribution of wind energy in the Qaidam Basin is contrary to that in the two basins north and south of the Tianshan Mountains.

The temporal change of wind energy is consistent with that of wind velocity, namely more in daytime and less in night, more in spring and less in winter and summer. The days with strong blowing sand activity are also the best days for wind energy use. A comparison of available wind energy in desert regions of China and Central Asia is shown in Table 4-1.

Table 4-1   Comparison of available wind energy in desert regions of China and Central Asia

Annual average wind velocity (m/s)	3	4	5	6
Chinese desert (kW)	12,014	26,548	40,259	53,823
Central Asian desert (kW)	9,776	20,510	33,115	44,962
Chinese desert in Center Asia desert (%)	123	129	122	120

From Geng Kuanghong (1986) "the climate of desert regions of China".

4.1.3   Climatic disaster and the exploitation and usage of climatic resource

4.1.3.1   Climatic disaster

As a kind of natural resource, the climate is favorable to human living and production if it is harmoniously combined with other factors. However, climate changes are out of man's control under present sci-tech level. So climatic disasters are inevitable. Especially in desert regions of China, climatic disasters are frequent and strong due to large temperature differences, frequent aeolian sand activity and special geomorphology. These disasters mainly include drought, shifting sand encroachment, dry-hot wind, frost and snow disasters.

(1) Drought. Drought is a basic characteristic of deserts. The drought caused by water shortage is the main natural disaster in Chinese deserts. The characteristics of drought are: large scale, large probability, long duration; most severe in spring; sometimes coexistence of drought and flood.

Droughts in Qinghai, Gansu, Ningxia, Inner Mongolia and Xinjiang are the most severe. According to statistical data, a drought that lasted four years from 1926 to 1929 in Qinghai resulted in the death of 1 million peoples; droughts in 1953 and 1966 caused a reduction of crop output by 91 million kg and 72.5 million kg respectively. According to literature records, 176 drought events occurred in Ningxia between 1470—1948. Six spring droughts, ten summer droughts and nine autumn droughts occurred in the most recent 30 years in Inner Mongolia. The analysis of historical materials shows that two drought years occur every three years, one strong drought event occurs every seven years, drought events which lasted one year occupied 54 % of the total drought events, those which lasted two years occupied 20%–30%, those which lasted three years occupied 10%–15%, and the longest drought events lasted seven years. According to the historical records of Gansu from 1470 to 1989, a slight drought event occurred every three years and a severe drought event occurred every ten years on a large scale while local and regional drought events occurred nearly every year. During that span of 520 years, there were eight extreme drought event. Drought greatly affects agricultural production. In recent years, the severest drought occurred in 1987; in that year the crop output was 9.7% less than that in 1986. In Gansu, 1,200,000 people died from starvation during a prolonged drought from 1928 to 1929; the average annual farmland area affected by drought was 730,000 –1,130,000 hm^2 in the most recent 40 years, which occupies 30% of the total farmland area, and the reduction of crop output was 0.25 billion to 0.37 billion kg per year on average.

(2) Strong winds and dust storms. Desert regions in China suffer from different degrees of sand disasters and they also constitute one of the sand storm centers of the world. The regions with frequent sand disasters mainly include the southwest Tarim Basin, the Turpan-Hami Basin, the Hexi Corridor, the Alxa Plateau of Inner Mongolia, the Ningxia Plain and northern Shanxi along the Great Wall, the Hetao plain and the Ordos Plateau. There are four centers and source regions for dust storms in China (Wang Tao, 2000): (a) the Hexi Corridor of Gansu and Alxa Meng of Inner Mongolia; (b) Boundary regions of the Taklimakan Desert of Xinjiang; (c) the north slope of the Yinshan Mountains and the Onqin Daga Sandy Land and its surrounding regions; (d) boundary regions between Inner Mongolia, Shaanxi and Ningxia along the Great Wall (Fig. 4-3). The sand and dust from the above source regions is often transported into eastern China by the west and northwest winds, which results in local dusty weather.

(3) Dry-hot wind. Dry-hot wind is a common disaster occurring in desert oasis regions of northwest China during the late spring to early summer. Local farmers often call it fire wind. The air temperature and humidity sharply change during this period of dry-hot wind, which damages crops in a short time (Xu Deyuan, 1989). As a major disaster in the late period of wheat growth, it often leads to evident reduction of crop output, especially in the Yellow River irrigation districts in Ningxia, the Hexi Corridor of Gansu and the east part of southern Xinjiang. According to data recorded between 1960 and 1980, dry-hot heat winds on average occur 0.9 times every year, while strong dry-hot winds occurs once every seven years in Ningxia and 2.4 times every year on average

in the Hexi Corridor of Gansu. Strong dry-hot winds can lead to the reduction of wheat yield by 20%.

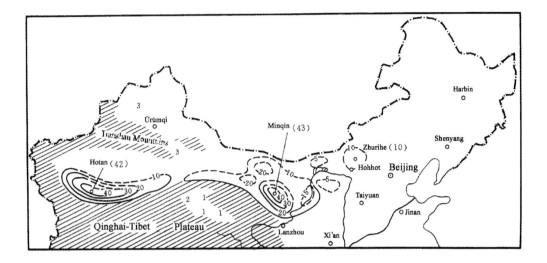

Fig. 4-3   The frequency of strong and extreme sand storms in China during 1952–1999
(From Wang Tao (2001), sand storm status and control strategy in China)

(4) Frost disaster. The Siberian-Mongolia high pressure system controls most areas of China's deserts. In these areas, frequent cold waves and unstable air temperature often lead to frost disasters. These areas mainly include: North Xinjiang, South Gansu, Hulun Buir Meng and Xing'an Meng of Inner Mongolia, the Liupan Mountains and the Helan Mountains of Ningxia and the   Qaidam Basin of Qinghai. Frost disasters can also result in large-scale reduction of crop output.

(5) Snow disaster. Snow disasters, also called "white disasters", often results in a mass of livestock to die from starvation due to the prolonged winter as well as grasslands covered by spring snow. It is the most severe natural disaster in the grasslands. In addition, snow disasters also affect transportation systems. The regions usually affected by strong snow disasters include Xilingol Meng, Ulanqab Meng and North Bayannur Meng of Inner Mongolia.

4.1.3.2   The exploitation and use of climate resource

In the deserts of China, water resources are sparse, and light, heat and wind energy are abundant. In the process of using these resources, regional resource predominance should be considered. According to the utilization status of resources, the consumption of water resource is high, but waste fulness and unbalanced water use among the upper, middle and down reaches has resulted in environmental deterioration. At the same time, consumption of heat, light and wind energy resources is low. Therefore, water resources should be used with high efficiency; light and heat energy consumption should be extended gradually based on experimental locations due to its high cost; and wind energy should be developed extensively due to the lower amount of pollution and cost.

4.2 Water resources

4.2.1 Water resources in inland desert regions of northwest China

Water resources are the most important factor affecting the environment and development of the social economy in arid regions. With the economic development in northwest China, the exploitation of water resources is rapidly increasing and the lack of availability of water resources has resulted in a supply shortage, especially for use in agriculture and industry. The conflict of using water resources between agriculture and industry, forestry and pasture, as well as between the upper, middle and lower reaches of a river is increasingly exacerbated. Therefore, the utilization of water resources needs to be comprehensively planned for the benefit of different industries. There is also a need to evaluate the quality and quantity of water resources in the desert regions of northwest China, analyse the present status of the exploitation and utilization of water resources and their development potential, and finally puts forward a reasonable approach for the exploitation and utilization of water resources in northwest China.

4.2.1.1 The quantity and quality of water resources

Water resources in northwest China include precipitation, glaciers, river runoff, lakes, reservoirs, underground water and soil water. There is a certain transformation relation among different kinds of water resources and they constitute a unified water body. Precipitation, glaciers, river runoff, lakes and reservoirs belong to surface water resources, of which a glacier is the solid water deposited in mountain regions. Water in lakes and reservoirs is the transformed form of precipitation, meltwater of glaciers, and runoff of rivers; glaciers and river runoff are fed by atmospheric precipitation in surrounding mountain areas of arid regions. Soil water and ground water belong to ground water resources. The relationship between surface water and ground water is very close in a river basin or in the upper and the lower reaches of a river; they are frequently transformed and strictly restricted each other. In addition, with the increase in global atmospheric temperature and human activities, the hydrologic cycle and its effect will be severely influenced. Therefore, there is a need to evaluate the quantity and quality of water resources.

1) Precipitation

According to the isoline of annual precipitation, average precipitation in arid inland regions of northwest China (including mountain regions) exceeds 400 billion m^3, equivalent to 148 mm of average depth of precipitation (Table 4-2). The area of Xinjiang accounts for 60%, and the precipitation occupies over one half. Although the area of plain in arid regions is large, about half of the precipitation falls in mountain regions around the basins. The water which reaches the ground surface is only a small fraction of water vapor transported in the region. According to the calculation by the Xinjiang Meteorological Bureau, water vapor transported in the region is about 1,154 billion m^3. But according to the estimation by the General Hydrological station, water falling down to ground surface is only 242.9 billion m^3, accounting for 20.8% of the water vapor in the air.

2) Alpine ice and snow resources

Glacier and permanent snow cover on mountain regions of northwest China are special forms of water resources in arid inland regions. Glacier resources, also known as "natural solid reservoirs" in desert oases, provide stable and efficient available water resources.

Table 4-2   The estimated volume of precipitation in arid regions of northwest China

Regions	area ($10^4\,km^2$)	Estimated precipitation resource ($10^8\,m^3$)	Average depth of precipitation (mm)
Xinjiang	164.7	2430	147
Southern part	119.8	280	106
Northern part	44.9	1150	255
Gansu Province	27.1	426	157
Hexi corridor	27.1	426	157
Blind drainage of Qinghai	36.5	414	113
Qaidam Basin	25.7	103	40
Blind drainage of Inner Mongolia Plateau	54.5	919	168
Alxa desert	24.9	224	90
Total	282.8	4,189	148

Glaciers and snow in arid desert regions of northwest China are mainly distributed on the Tianshan Mountains, the Kunlun Mountains, the Karakorun Mountains, the Pamier Plateau, the Qilian Mountains and the Altay Mountains. The total mountain area covered by ice and snow on mountain in these regions is about 2.58×10^4 km^2. The ice storage is over 2,330 billion m^3. The Tianshan Mountains is the most concentratedly distributed region of glaciers in northwest China, with 9,548.5 km^2 of glaciers, accounting for 1/3 of the total glacier area of northwest China. The biggest center of glaciers is in the Tomur Peak region, and many of them are big valley glaciers, which are the source areas and main replenishment source of the Aksu River, the Ogan River and the Tekes River at the upper reach of the Yili River. Tiemiersu glacier, Kalageyule glacier and Tugebieliqi glacier there have a length of more than 30 km, and the termini of their ice tongues extend the mid-mountain forest belt. Glaciers on the Kunlun Mountains are mainly concentrated in the headwaters of the Karakax River and theYurungkax River. On the Karokorum Mountains, glaciers are mostly distributed in the Qogir Peak area where glaciers are big and long. There 50 glaciers cover an area exceeding 50–70 km, which mainly occur in the Keshimier Mountains region. The Yinsugai glacier, the biggest one in China, is about 42 km long, and its terminus extends to the

Yarkant River valley at 4,200 m altitude. Glaciers in the Qilian Mountains are mainly concentrated in its middle and western section, with an area of 1,972.5 km^2 and ice storage of 95.4 billion m^3. The Altay Mountains is the northernmost region of glaciers in China, with smaller area of glacier (293.2 km^2), and the ice storage is estimated to be 16.5 billion m^3, which is the nourishment source of the Ertix River.

Statistics (Table 4-3) show that average meltwater supplied to rivers is about 20.0 billion m^3. The ratio of glacier runoff to river water is 19.9% in Xinjiang, 12.0% in the Hexi Corridor of Gansu Province, and 16.4% in Qinghai Province.

Table 4-3　Glacier resources in river sources regions of arid northwest China

Region	River system	Number of glaciers	Area of glaciers(km^2)	Melt water of glaciers ($\times 10^8$m^3)	Percentage in the river runoff (%)
Inland rivers in Hexi corridor	Shule River	975	849.38	4.692	28.0
	Heihe River	1,078	420.55	3.149	8.0
	Shiyang River	141	64.82	0.599	4.0
	Total	2,194	1,334.75	8.44	12.0
Inland stream system in Qinghai Province	Inland River in Qaidam Basin	1,581	1,865.00	11.15	25.1
	Hala Lake	106	89.27	0.354	34.4
	Qinghai Lake	22	13.29	0.105	0.6
	Hoh xil Region		869.45	4.82	43.0
	Total		2,023.29	15.49	16.4
Xinjiang	Inland Rivers in Central Asia	2373	2076.35	20.59	10.5
	Inland Rivers in Junggar Basin	3412	2254	22.57	17.8
	Inland Rivers in Tarim Basin	12157	20142	123.61	31.5
	Inland Rivers in Qiangtang region		30.75	5.11	24.2
	Ertix River	403	289	3.84	3.9
	Total		24792.1	175.72	19.9

3) River runoff

The rivers in arid regions of northwest China mostly belong to inland rivers, except the Yellow River and the Ertix River in northern Xinjiang. Meltwater of ice and snow is the main nourishment sources of the inland rivers.

Arid inland regions in northwest China has 678 inland rivers, including the Ertix River in northern Xinjiang. Among them, 570 rivers are in Xinjiang, 55 in the Hexi corridor, and 53 in the Qaidam Basin. Most of them have short flow distance and small discharge. The rivers with annual runoff less than 1×10^8 m^3 account for 70% or more, and their runoff accounts for less than 20% of the total runoff of inland rivers. There are 21 rivers with annual runoff exceeding 10×10^8 m^3, accounting for 3% of the total number of inland rivers, and their runoff amounts to 50% of the total runoff of inland rivers (Table 4-4).

Table 4-4 classifications of inland rivers in arid regions of northwest China

region	$\geqslant 10\times 10^8\,m^3$			$\geqslant 5\times 10^8\,m^3$			$\geqslant 1\times 10^8\,m^3$			Total		
	River number	Runoff $(10^8\,m^3)$	Percentage $(\%)$	River number	Runoff $(10^8\,m^3)$	Percentage $(\%)$	River number	Runoff $(10^8\,m^3)$	Percentage $(\%)$	River number	Runoff $(10^8\,m^3)$	Percentage $(\%)$
Northern Xinjiang	9	267.58	60.9	13	295.21	67.2	45	363.11	82.6	378	439.4	100
Southern Xinjiang	9	264.2	59.4	15	303.89	68.3	39	353.49	79.5	183	444.9	100
Qinghai Basin	2	22.2	32.1	3	25.7	37.1	21	51.1	73.8	91	94.54	100
Hexi Corridor	1	15.97	22.7	3	33.23	47.2	15	50.9	85.0	55	70.45	100
Inner Mongolia Plateau	0	0	0	0	0	0	1	1.16	11.5	41	10.25	100
Total	21	569.95	55.5	34	658.03	64.0	111	828.8		757	1,059.5	100

Recent statistics show that the total runoff resource is about $1060\times 10^8\,m^3$ (Table 4-5), based on the estimation of average river runoff discharged into arid inland region of northwest China. Among them, exterior river is about $132\times 10^8\,m^3$, accounting for 34%; inland rivers is about $928\times 10^8\,m^3$, accounting for 66% of the total runoff resources. Therefore, the runoff of inland rivers is the main form of water resources in arid region.

Table 4-5 Stream flow resources in arid regions of northwest China

Region	Region	Average runoff $(10^8\,m^3)$	Percentage in the total runoff (%)	Quantity of water	
				Entering the country's border $(10^8 m^3)$	Flowing out of the country's border $(10^8 m^3)$
Northern Xinjiang	Junggar Basin	127.53	9.1	2.31	
	Tacheng Basin	23.7	1.7		8.68
	Yili Valley	169.57	12.1	9.57	117.0
	Exterior river basin of Ertix	118.6	8.4	18.24	95.3
	Total	439.4	31.3		
Southern Xinjiang	Tarim Basin	392.89	28.0	60.74	
	Turpan Basin	9.79	0.7		
	Hami Basin	4.54	0.3		
	Tarim Basin	4.15	0.3		
	Inland region of Qiangtang	21.43	1.5		
	Pamier Plateau and Aksu River basin	9.27	0.7		
	Exterior region of Qipuqiabu River	2.93	0.2		
	Total	444.9	31.7		
Gansu	Hexi Corridor	70.45	5.0		
Qinghai	Qaidam Basin	44.4	3.2		
	Qinghai Lake Basin	19.3	1.4		
	Hala Lake Basin	3.23	0.2		
	Chaka-Shazhuyu Basin	2.31	0.2		
	Kekexili Basin	25.3	1.8		
	Total	94.54	23.0		
Inner Mongolia	Inland region of eastern plateau	10.01			
	Interior region of Alxa	0.24	0.6		
	Total	10.25			
	Total	1,059.54	100	90.83	220.98

Water quality of most rivers in arid regions of northwest China usually can meet common water requirements. Mineralized degree of water in river source region is about 0.1–0.3 g/L, and is mostly of Ca^{2+}-HCO_3^- type. While the runoff flowing out the mountain valley mouth becomes Mg^{2+}-Ca^{2+}-HCO_3^- type, with a salinity of 0.1–0.5 g/L. When the river flows in the plain, it is used for irrigation or infiltrates into the soil,and results in obvious deterioration of the water quality. Especially in the lower reaches of rivers in the plain region, irrigated water recharges underground water, the level of underground water rises, and increases the mineralized degree due to evaporation. For example, at the lower reaches of the Tarim River, the Heihe River, the Kezi River and the Wulun River, the mineralized degree is as high as 1.0–5.0g/L. At the headwaters of the Yellow River, its mineralized degree is 0.2–0.3g/L. When it flows into Ningxia and Inner Mongolia, the mineralized degree reaches 0.8g/L.

4) Lake (reservoir) water resources

There are many lakes in arid inland regions of northwest China, and lakes are a kind of water-storage form for surface water and ground water. Statistics show that there are thousands of lakes in arid inland regions of northwest China. About 4,000 lakes have an area exceeding 1 km^2 and their total area is more than 1.7×10^4 km^2.

According to the lake water quality, lakes can be divided into three types. ① There are about 80 fresh water lakes or brackish water lakes (mineralized degree less than 1–3 g/L), with a total area of 3,500 km^2 and water storage more than 300×10^8 m^3. ② The area of saline water lake or semi-saline water lake (mineralized degree 3–35 g/L) accounts for 80% of the total lake area, and mainly occurs at the terminus of inland rivers, the lowest site of basin center, or in interdune depressions in deserts. ③ The lakes with mineralized degree of more than 35 g/L belong to salt-water lake, and their area accounts for 25% and the highest mineralized degree is more than 300 g/L. lake water contains abundant salts and other mineral resources, though these lakes are difficult to utilize.

The Bosten Lake is the largest fresh water lake in the inland regions of China; it is located in the lowest depression of the Yanji Basin on the south slope of the Tianshan Mountains. It has an area of 1010 km^2, water volume of 77.4×10^8 m^3, and average depth of 7.66m. About 25×10^8 m^3 of water flows into the Bosten Lake and about 12.9×10^8 m^3 of water flows out every year. There are about 12×10^8 m^3 of water lost to evaporation every year. The Qinghai Lake is the biggest semi-saline water lake in China; its mineralized degree is about 15.5 g/L. Its area reaches 4568 km^2, with a water depth of 17.5m and water volume of 753×10^8 m^3. There are about 13×10^8 m^3 of surface runoff flowing into the Qinghai Lake every year, and the average evaporation of the lake is 492 mm. According to observations at Shatuoshi water level station between 1957–1978, water levels of the Qinghai Lake dropped by 2.14m and imported water volume decreased by 4.27×10^8 m^3 every year. This leads to the regional microclimate and environment degradation; desertification spreads, and ultimately affects the fish industry production.

5) Groundwater resources

(1) Groundwater is an important component of water resources in arid inland regions of northwest China. According to hydrogeological surveys in the piedmont plain region, natural nourishment volume of groundwater in the Junggar Basin, the Tarim Basin, the Qaidam Basin and the Hexi Corridor in arid regions of northwest China is about 316.35×10^8 m^3 (Table 4-6).

(2) Another storage zone of groundwater is in the intermontane valley and basin in arid inland regions of northwest China. Natural recharge volume to groundwater in the main intermontane valleys and basin is about 145.03×10^8 m^3 (Table 4-7). This groundwater is mostly distributed under the basins or valleys.

(3) Groundwater in lake basins and lowlands.

The collection centre of surface water and ground water mostly occurs below the piedmont plain or intermontane basins, alluvial-lacustrine plain in valleys, or lowlands in inland lake basins. Groundwater in the lowlands of lake basins in northwest China is about 33×10^8 m^3 (Table 4-8).

Table 4-6　Groundwater resources in the plain at the foot of mountain of arid region of northwest China (Unit: 10^8 m^3)

Basin	Field infiltration water	Underground runoff	precipitation infiltration	Natural recharge to ground water
Hexi Corridor	39.83	2.52	2.42	44.77
Qaidam Basin	23.30	5.65	1.02	29.98
Junggar Basin	53.27	3.77	5.84	62.88
Southern Xinjiang Basin	161.92	10.72	6.08	178.72
Total	278.32	22.66	15.36	316.35

Table 4-7　Groundwater resources in the main intermontane basins and valleys in arid inland regions of northwest China (Unit: 10^8 m^3)

Province	Basin (Valley)	Groundwater resources	Province	Basin (Valley)	Groundwater resources
Xinjiang	Yili Basin	8.17			
	Yili Valley	15.11			
	Dabancheng	2.93	Qinghai	Delingha Basin	3.56
	Jinghe-Bole Valley	16.23		Huahai Basin	5.67
	Barkol Basin	0.92		Mahai Basin	1.26
	Turpan Basin	5.67		Chaida Basin	0.64
	Hami Basin	3.07		Menyuan Valley	3.84
	Yanqi Basin	16.80	Gansu	Changmu Valley	2.56
	Bancheng Basin	24.12		Taoneng Valley	3.84
	Kechen Basin	1.32		Heihe Valley	1.82
	Haerjun Basin	2.31		Danghe Valley	0.47
	Mashi Basin	17.61			
	Kashikuergan Basin	5.55		Total	145.03

Table 4-8　Groundwater in some inland lowlands of northwest China (Unit: $10^8\,\text{m}^3$)

Lake basin (lowland)	Natural recharge volume	Lake basin (lowland)	Natural recharge volume
Minqin-Chaoshui	2.80	Jilantai	1.50
Jingta-Huahai	4.02	Qinghai lake	5.00
Anxi-Dunhuang	3.94	Lop Nur	8.65
Yabrai	1.79		
Juyanhai	5.39	Total	33.09

(4) Phreatic water in the desert.

Vast deserts are located in the center of large basins and the fringe of plateaus in arid inland regions of northwest China. Although annual precipitation in desert regions is usually less than 100 mm, it often falls in the form of sudden downpours, and sometimes once precipitation may reach 30 mm. The precipitation and snowmelt water can infiltrate into the ground and be stored in interdune depressions as phreatic water. Water in rivers, groundwater runoff in front of mountains and temporary runoff in mountainous area can also infiltrate into deserts and be stored as desert phreatic water.

In general, phreatic water in interdune depressions has a shallow water table, mostly ranging from 5 to 10 m or even lower. The mineralization degrees of desert phreatic water are variable depending on the replenishment type, storage location and season. Calculations based on the effective precipitation in desert regions has shown that groundwater replenished by natural precipitation can reach $50 \times 10^8\,\text{m}^3$. Artificial outcrop of groundwater in the Taklimakan Desert interior is shown as Fig. 4-4.

Fig. 4-4　Artificial outcrop of groundwater in the Taklimakan Desert interior

(5) Artesian water.

Terrain and geological conditions of Chinese northwestern interland region are advantageous to form artesian water, and some places formed artesian basins. There are widely shallow artesian aquifers in Quaternary unconsolidated formation under piedmont plain. Lots of materials also proved that there are deep-artesian water in Tertiary and mesozonic formation in many bigger basins and taphrogenic depressions (Table 4-9).

Table 4-9   Distribution of artesian water in arid regions of northwest China

Region	Location	Burial depth(m)	Age and features of aquifer	Quality and quantity of artesian water
Junggar Basin	Northern part	20–1,000	Tertiary sandstone and conglomerate	Salinity<2g/L, water storage is abundant
	Middle part	300–600	Tertiary sandstone and conglomerate	Salinity 5–102g/L, for livestock use
	North slope of Tianshan Mountains	5–60	Quaternary sandstone	Salinity <12g/L, water storage is abundant
		7,100–1,000	Tertiary sandstone and conglomerate	Salinity 10–302g/L or more
Tarim Basin	South slope of Tianshan Mountains	5–150	Quaternary sandrock	Salinity <12g/L, water storage is abundant
		400–600	Tertiary sandstone and conglomerate	Salinity 20–602g/L
		1,300–2,000	Tertiary sandstone and conglomerate	Salinity 10–302g/L
	Kashi and Hotan depression	10–200	Quaternary sandstone	Salinity <12g/L, water storage is abundant
		1,000–5,000	Tertiary sandstone and conglomerate	Salinity 80–1,502 g/L, belongs to brackish water
Qaidam Basin	Piedmont plain	20–100	Quaternary sandstone	Salinity <2g/L, water storage is abundant
		Less than 150	Quaternary sandstone	Salinity 3–10g/L, water storage is small
		150–200	Tertiary sandstone	Salinity 10–30g/L or more
Hexi Corridor	Jiuquan and Jinta Basin	10–50	Quaternary sandstone	Salinity< 1g/L, water storage is abundant
		1,000–2,000	Tertiary sandstone	Salinity 10–40g/L
	Shule River plain	100–120	Quaternary sandstone	Salinity< 1g/L, water storage is not too abundant
	Wuwei-Minqin Basin	20–50	Tertiary sandstone	Salinity <1g/L, water storage is relatively abundant
		300–500	Tertiary sandstone	Salinity 10–30g/L, water storage is moderate
Alxa	Juyan Lake Basin	30–50	Tertiary sandstone	Salinity < 2g/L, water storage is moderate
	Yingen Basin	10–300	Tertiary sandstone	Salinity <3g/L, water storage is not abundant
	Suhait Basin	Less than 100	Tertiary sandstone	Salinity <3g/L, water storage is not abundant
	Tengger Desert	10–30	Quaternary sandstone	Salinity <3g/L, water storage is not abundant
Inner Mongolia Plateau	From Erenhot to Chaoge Qi	40–150	Tertiary sandstone	Salinity 0.5–5g/L and there is obvious difference in quality and quantity

Note: modified from Zhang (1975).

4.2.1.2 Status and problems in the development and utilization of water resources

1) Status of water resource development and utilization

Since the Han Dynasty (about 2,000 years ago), agricultural production has been practiced in the arid inland regions of northwest China. This region, with a long irrigation history is a major area of artificial oasis construction in modern times. However, for a long time the utilization efficiency of water resources in these regions was very low. There are about 1.3 million hm^2 of irrigated farmland and grain yield was about 3,000 kg/hm^2.

From the 1950s to 1980s, the constructions of water resource project developed quickly. The effective irrigation area was more than 50 million hm^2 (Table 4-10).

Table 4-10   Irrigation area in the arid regions of northwest China (Unit: 10^4 hm^2)

Item		Inland river basin				Total
		Xinjiang	Gansu	Qinghai	Inner Mongolia	
Effective	Irrigated area	4,002.00	861.55	97.34	151.46	5,112.35
	Marshy field	89.50	2.98			92.48
Actual	Total area	4,156.85	861.55	97.34	113.00	5,228.74
	Marshy field	89.50	2.98			92.48
Grassland irrigation area		240.00	65.00	61.10	129.50	495.60
Actual irrigated area		3,003.70	544.68	87.30	83.42	3,719.10
Well-irrigation area		488.86	126.25	0.83	87.20	703.14
Water-raising irrigation area				0.15		0.15
Electric drainage and irrigation area		468.61	335.28	4.35		808.24
Irrigation district with an area of more than 100 hm^2 (Site/irrigation area)		436/3,900	76/ 600	25/65.69	2/ 50.01	539/4 615.61

Table 4-11   Water resources development in northwest China (Unit: 10^8 m^3)

Region	Agricultural irrigation water	Grassland irrigation water	Industrial water	City water consumption	Man and livestock water consumption	Surface water		Groundwater	
						Water storage	Use efficiency (%)	Exploited water	Use efficiency (%)
Xinjiang	387.98	9.50	7.94	0.43	2.05	335.6	53.1	63,38	17.0
Hexi Corridor	63.81	3.05	2.01	0.09	0.69	48.5	69.4	24.10	39.9
Qinghai	5.07	2.33		0.05	0.46	8.09	11.7	0.06	0.3
Inner Mongolia	5.35		0.23	0.06	0.57	1.84	6.30	4.37	20.8
Total	462.21	14.88	10.18	0.63	3.77	394.03	140.5	91.91	18
Percentage of total water consumption(%)	93.0	2.8	2.9	0.3	1.0	89.1		15.9	

According to previous statistics, in the mid 1980s, the total amount of water resources developed in northwest China was about 490×10^8 m^3, of which the water volume used for agriculture, animal husbandry, industry and human and livestock occupied 93%, 2.8%, 2.9% and 1.3%, respectively. At the beginning of the 1980s, the diverted surface water was about $400\times10^8\,\mathrm{m}^3$; accounting for 42% of total available surface runoff, in Xinjiang this value was more than 50%. In the Hexi Corridor, the diverted surface water reached $70\times10^8\,\mathrm{m}^3$ and the exploited groundwater was about $92\times10^8\,\mathrm{m}^3$, which amounted to 20% of the exploitable groundwater (Table 4-11). In recent years, owing to natural and man-made causes, both the surface water and groundwater volume have showed a decreasing trend, and the diverted water is also on the decline. However, the utilization efficiency is increasing gradually.

2) Main problems in the exploitation and utilization processes of water resources

The exploitation and use of water resources are of great importance to the economic development in Northwest China. Water storage has become an important factor affecting the economic development and eco-environmental stability of this region.

(1) The over-exploitation and use of water resources in the upper and middle reaches of inland river basins result in a decrease of water quantity, water quality deterioration, lake shrinkage, natural vegetation degradation and desertification spread in the lower reaches.

(2) In the irrigation districts of piedmont plains and newly reclaimed farmlands, large-scale irrigation causes the groundwater table to rise continuously, and thus results in the secondary salinization of soils.

(3) Over-exploitation of groundwater results in a dramatic lowering of water tables or even formed large cone of depression and finally leads to vegetation deterioration and land desertification.

(4) Lack of unified plans and distribution of water resources in the whole basin leads to water use conflicts between agriculture, forestry, grazing and industry in the upper, middle and lower reaches and results in eco-environmental degradation in the lower reaches.

4.2.1.3　Sustainable exploitation and rational use

Several aspects must be considered in the exploitation and utilization processes of water resources:

(1) Strengthening protection and rational use of water resources. In inland arid regions of China, the distribution of water resources can be divided into the runoff-forming zone around the mountains and the runoff-consuming zone in inland basins. The alluvial and proluvial fans and plains are the strong consumption zone of water resources due to human use. Strengthening water resource protection is to protect glaciers and water conservation forests in mountains; to prevent surface and ground water from pollution in plain regions; to keep balance of ground water extraction and recharge; and to protect the environment and resources in the lower reaches.

(2) Working out ecologic protection planning and halting desertification and other disasters. In China, the inland arid region consists of mountain ecosystems, plain-oasis ecosystems and desert

ecosystems. All of these three ecosystems are vulnerable and constitute a watershed ecosystem through the linkage of surface and ground runoff. According to the watershed function and characteristics, mountains regions are the water source regions covered by ice, snow and forests, therefore protecting ice, snow and forest resources is important to protecting water source regions and maintaining the water cycle. In the piedmont oasis regions, rational water use and pollution prevention is the key to protecting water sources.

(3) Rational exploitation and use of water resources with the basin as a unit. In inland regions of northwest China, water resource is formed, distributed and transformed with the basin as a unit, and the surface and ground runoff in upper, middle and lower reaches are interrelated and mutually controlled. Through the linkage of surface and ground water, a unified basin ecosystem comes into being. Great efforts should be made to maintain the water balance among the upper, middle and lower reaches and to meet water requirements in the areas surrounding oases.

(4) Preventing water pollution. The runoff-forming zone and water source regions should be protected to prevent water pollution. The factories releasing dangerous pollutants should not be established in these regions. The piedmont areas are the strongly transformed zones of surface runoff into ground water, and ground water quality must be protected.

(5) Strengthening the economic, social and environmental coordination of water resources. The distribution and management of water resources are the important problems affecting the sustainable development of society in the future. We should gradually accept the idea of water as a kind of special commodity. Working out rational water prices, increasing fund support, and encouraging irrigation construction work should be done to strengthen water management.

(6) Strengthening water resource management and conserving water resources. With the increase of water use degree, rational use of limited water resource becomes an important subject in future water management. Strengthening water resource management, coordinating the distribution of water resources and saving water resource are the basic measures to solve the discrepancy between water supply and demand.

4.2.2　Water resources in the eastern desert regions

4.2.2.1　Water resources evaluation

1) Precipitation

Precipitation is the main supply source of surface and ground water in eastern desert regions of China, and it determines the total amount of water resources and directly affects spatial and temporal distribution, river runoff, ground water, soil moisture and efficient use of water resources. In eastern desert regions of China, the precipitation is carried by monsoon weather systems under certain atmospheric circulation conditions.

Based on statistical data and calculations during the 1956—1979 period, the precipitation and yearly runoff depth of main river basins in northern China are shown in Table 4-12.

Table 4-12 Annual precipitation in the eastern desert regions of China

Basin name	Annual precipitation (mm)	Annual runoff depth (mm)	Annual total precipitation ($10^8 m^3$)	Percentage of total (%)
1. Upper and middle reaches of Yellow River	464.4	83.2	3,691	100
Huangshui River	502.1	152.8	165	7.6
Taohe River	603.3	208.0	154	8.0
Mainstream above Lanzhou	473.3	148.6	777	36.9
Lanzhou-Hekou	271.1	8.8	443	2.2
Hekou-Longmen	469.7	53.5	513	9.0
Fenhe River	529.5	67.4	209	4.0
Jinghe River	539.4	45.6	245	3.1
Luohe River	550.1	36.9	148	1.5
Weihe River	629.4	117.1	393	11.1
Longmen-Sanmenxia	573.3	72.8	95.3	1.8
Yiluo River	693.8	183.8	131	5.3
Qinhe River	642.2	136.0	86.9	2.8
Sanmenxia-Huayuankou	647.7	132.6	89.6	1.8
Interior region of Ordos	283.9	7.9	120	4.4
Lower reaches of Yellow River	673.9	130.3	151	0.5
2. Huaihe River basin	888.7	231.0	2,390	100
Upper and middle reaches	889.1	233.8	1,430	59.8
Lower reaches	1,045.3	258.1	308	12.9
Yihe, Mu he, Sihe River	836.0	215.1	653	27.3
3. Haihe-Luanhe River basin	559.3	90.5	1,781	100
Luanhe River	564.8	109.5	308	17.3
North branch of Haihe River	506.5	80.1	421	23.6
South branch of Haihe River	579.8	97.5	862	48.4
Tuhai-Maxia River	596.7	51.8	190	10.7
4. Liaohe River basin	551.0	141.1	1,901	100
Liaohe River	472.6	64.6	1,082	56.9
Yalujiang River	927.1	499.0	301	15.9
Tumenjiag River	568.7	223.1	130	6.8
Zhuhe River	638.8	207.4	388	20.4
5. Heilongjiang River basin	495.5	129.1	4,478	100
Nenjiang River	449.9	93.7	1,205	26.9
Second Songhuajiang River	665.6	209.6	524	11.8
Mainstream of Songhuajiang River	572.5	164.3	1,206	26.9
Ergun River	346.9	76.1	547	12.2
Mainstream of Heilongjiang River	513.2	161.3	614	13.7
Suifen River	551.5	131.9	380	8.5

The precipitation in the upper and middle reaches of the Yellow River and the Ordos Plateau is about $3,420\times10^8$ m^3, $5,377\times10^8$ m^3 in northeast China and $4,275\times10^8$ m^3 in the Huang-Huai-Hai Plain.

2) River runoff resources

In northwest China, the main rivers in desert regions can be divided into the Yellow River water system (including the Yellow River, the Haihe River, the Luanhe River and other small rivers that directly flow into ocean) and the Northeast Plain water system (including the Heilongjiang River and the Liaohe River)(Table 4-13).

Table 4-13   Statistics of stream-flow in desert regions of eastern China (10^8m^3)

Basin name	Catchment area (km^2)	Data-collecting period (a)	Annual runoff (10^8m^3)	Runoff of different P values				Percentage
				20%	50%	75%	100%	
Middle and upper reaches of Yellow River		24	619.6	728.0	606.0	539.0	463.0	100
Huangshui River	32,863	24	53.1	58.2	49.7	43.2	35.1	8.6
Taohe River	35,527	24	50.2	66.9	49.9	39.3	29.2	8.2
Above Lanzhou	164,161	24	244.0	293.0	237.0	200.0	159.0	39.4
Lanzhou-Tuoketuo	163,415	24	14.2	19.2	13.2	9.5	5.7	2.3
Togtoh-Longmen	111,595	24	59.7	72.2	58.5	47.8	36.4	9.7
Fenhe River	3,947	24	26.6	33.0	25.8	20.7	14.9	4.3
Jinghe River	45,421	24	20.7	26.5	19.9	15.5	10.6	3.3
Luohe River	28,095	24	9.9	12.3	9.6	7.8	5.6	1.7
Weihe River	62,440	24	73.1	93.6	70.2	54.8	37.3	11.8
Longmen-Sanmenxia	16,623	24	12.1	15.6	10.5	8.2	6.5	2.0
Yiluo River	18,881	24	34.7	45.8	29.8	22.2	16.7	3.0
Qinhe River	13,532	24	18.4	23.7	16.0	12.9	9.2	0.1
Ordos interior region	42,269	24	3.3	3.8	3.3	2.9	2.3	
Northwest region			1,653.0	2,096.0	1,591.0	1,243.0	856.0	100
Nenjiang River			251.0	348.0	230	158.0	82.8	15.2
Songhuajiang River	28,300		511.0	983.0	728	558.0	366.0	30.9
Ergun River	55,700		120.0	152.0	115	91.2	62.4	7.3
Wusuli River	(65 ,800)		90.9	130.0	80.9	51.8	24.5	5.5
Mainstream of Heilongjiang River	(883,000)		193.0	247.0	186	143.0	96.6	11.7
Liaohe River	21,900		148.0	189.0	142	110.0	74.0	8.9
Yalu River	(32,466)		162.0	202.0	157	126.0	89.0	9.8
Tumen River	(22,900)		51.0	68.9	47.4	33.7	19.4	3.1
Rivers along sea			126.0	169.0	118	85.7	51.7	7.6
Huang–Huai–Hai Plain		61	951.0	1,283.0	874	623.0	375.0	100
Lower reaches of Yellow River	31,609	61	41.4	57.8	35.9	23.9	14.1	4.3
Luanhe River	44,900	61	59.7	82.4	54.9	38.2	20.3	6.3
Haihe River	26,400	61	228.0	303.0	205	150.0	105.0	24.0
Huaihe River	26,900	64	622.0	840.0	578	411.0	236.0	65.4

The long-term average surface water resources in the Yellow River basin is $659 \times 10^8 \, \text{m}^3$ (Table 4-14), of which about $228.0 \times 10^8 \, \text{m}^3$ is in Qinghai Province and $340 \times 10^8 \, \text{m}^3$ at Lanzhou Station. In Ningxia, because a large amount of water isn't used for irrigation, so starting from Qingtong Gorge there is no surface runoff to feed the main stream. In such a case, there is only about $291.5 \times 10^8 \, \text{m}^3$ of runoff in this section. In the Hetao Plain, the Yellow River is the main water source for irrigation and about $44 \times 10^8 \, \text{m}^3$ of water resources is consumed in this region, about $247.6 \times 10^8 \, \text{m}^3$ of water flows through Hekou Hydrologic Station. From Hekou to Longmen, there are 21 tributaries (about $59.7 \times 10^8 \, \text{m}^3$) flowing into the main stream. From Longmen to Sanmen Gorge, there are 5 tributaries (about $142.4 \times 10^8 \, \text{m}^3$) flowing into it. From Sanmen Gorge to Huayuankou, there are 4 tributaries ($65.3 \times 10^8 \, \text{m}^3$) flowing into it. The runoff in the middle reaches of the Yellow River is about $267.4 \times 10^8 \, \text{m}^3$, if added the water recharged from lateral seepage along the mainstream, the annual runoff at the Huayuankou Station is $606 \times 10^8 \, \text{m}^3$. Below Huayuankou Station, the runoff reduces gradually. The runoff in this section is only about $29.2 \times 10^8 \, \text{m}^3$ and at Lijin Station the runoff is $30 \times 10^8 \, \text{m}^3$ less than that of Huanyuankou Station (Table 4-14).

Table 4-14 Surface water and runoff changes along mainstream of the Yellow River

Region	Catchment area (km^2)	Annual runoff ($10^8 \, \text{m}^3$)	Area		Runoff	
			$10^4 \, \text{km}^2$	Percentage (%)	$10^8 \, \text{m}^3$	Percentage (%)
Xunhua		223				
Lanzhou	222,551	347.3	222,551	29.6	347.3	
Lanzhou-Hekou			163,415	21.7	14.9	
Shizuishan		291.5				
Upper reaches of Yellow River	385,966			51.3	362.2	
Hekou-Longmen			111,595	14.8	59.7	
Longmen	497,561	411				
Longmen-Sanmenxia			190,860	25.4	142.4	
Sanmenxia	688,421	544				
Sanmenxia-Huayuankou			41,615	5.5	65.3	
Huayuankou		606				
Middle reaches of Yellow River	730,036		344,070	45.7	267.4	
Huayuankou-Lijin			21,839	2.9	15.0	
Lijin	751,869	621				
Below Lijin			574	0.08	14.2	
Lower reaches of Yellow River			22,407	3.0	29.2	
Yellow River basin	752,443	658.8	752,449	100	658.8	100

3) Groundwater resources

In the Yinchuan and Hetao plains in the upper and middle reaches of the Yellow River, large amounts of surface water is used for irrigation, and some large-scale oases have come into being there. In addition, there are several aquifer systems consisting of loose deposits and thus store abundant groundwater (Table 4-15). The synclinal structure in the Ordos Plateau provides a favorable condition for storing groundwater. The amount of groundwater is closely related with its replenishment and storage conditions. From the upper to the lower reaches of the Yellow River, the recharge modulus of groundwater increases gradually. For example, its values in Gansu, Ningxia, Inner Mongolia and Shanxi Province are 2.32×10^8, 5.15×10^8, 4.92×10^8 and 5.97×10^8 m^3/km^2, respectively. The values decrease in the order of pore water, karst water, crevice water, pore-crevice water and loess water (Table 4-16). According to statistics of groundwater resources in related provinces, there are 335×10^8 m^3 of groundwater in the Loess Plateau, of which fresh water (1g/L), weak saline water (1-3g/L) and saline water (>3g/L) occupy 86%, 1.0% and 4% of total water volume, respectively. The exploited water resource is 203×10^8 m^3, accounting for 60% of natural water resources and 79% are concentrated in plain areas.

Table 4-15   Groundwater resources in the plains (oasis) of the upper and middle reaches of the Yellow River ($\times10^8 m^3$)

Region	Basin area (km^2)	Ground-water	Percentage of precipitation recharged (%)	Exploited resources	Exploitable amount
Yinchuan Plain	7,000	11.8	25	11.0	4.9
Hetao Plain	21,000	17.9	50	10.9	10.7

Table 4-16   Different types of groundwater in the Ordos Plateau

Groundwater type	Pore water	Karst water	Crevice water	Pore-crevice water	Loess water	Total
Area (km^2)	16.97	4.55	10.82	10.00	20.00	62.34
Resources ($\times10^8 m^3$)	196.33	44.98	50.46	21.75	22.46	335.98
Percentage of total resources(%)	58.4	13.4	15.0	6.50	6.70	100.0
Modulus	11.57	9.89	4.66	2.18	1.12	5.39

The Huang-Huai-Hai Plain has exploitable groundwater resources of 481×10^8 m^3 and in northeast China the value is about $276\times10^8 m^3$.

According to the above-mentioned evaluation, the total water resources in the eastern desert regions of China are about $4,054\times10^8 m^3$.

4.2.2.2   Current situation and major problems in the development and utilization of water resources

1) Current situation

In the past 50 years, about 19,000 reservoirs were established in the Yellow River basin, the Huaihe River basin, the Haihe-Luanhe River basin, the Liaohe River basin and the Heilong River basin. The total storage capacity of these reservoirs reached $1,900\times10^8 m^3$ and the developed water energy was more than $400\times10^4 kW$. The effective irrigation area was $2,244.6\times10^4 hm^2$ and the actual irrigation area was about $1,975\times10^4 hm^2$. In addition, about $1,200\times10^4 hm^2$ of waterlogging land and $350\times10^4 hm^2$ of alkaline land were controlled. Under such conditions, the Huang-huai-hai and the Northeast Plain has become an important grain base in China.

In the Loess Plateau, about 10×10^4 hm^2 of land suffering from soil erosion was controlled, accounting for 23% of total erosion areas. In the Huang-Huai-Hai Plain and northwest China, great progress has been made in the development of water resources.

In the 1980s, the actual amount of water resource reached $1,850\times10^8$m^3, of which used river runoff was about $1,400\times10^8$ m^3 and the exploited groundwater reached 452×10^8 m^3. Except Songhua River, the utilization ratio of surface water resources exceeded over 50% and the exploitation ratio of groundwater more than 30%.

According to statistics, the total water consumption was about $1,627\times10^8$ m^3(Table 4-17), of which water consumed in industry, agriculture, and domestic water supply occupy 10%, 88% and 1.5% of total water consumption, respectively.

Table 4-17　Water development in eastern desert regions of China (Unit: 10^8 m^3)

Regions	Total development volume			Industrial water		Domestic water
	Total	Surface water	Groundwater	Total	Used by heat power plants	
Total water consumption of the country	4,438.91	3,817.91	619.00	457.32	157.48	67.69
Rivers in northeast China	353.72	268.86	84.86	63.86	14.74	9.47
Haihe River	383.88	181.44	202.44	48.69	11.78	10.72
Huanhe River and Shandong Peninsula	531.26	402.33	128.93	38.42	12.02	5.30
The Yellow River	358.37	273.96	84.41	27.93	5.56	8.03

Regions	Agricultural water					
	Total	Cropland irrigation	Grassland irrigation	Forest land irrigation	Man and animal drinking water in countryside	Water for sideline occupation
Total water consumption of the country	3,911.89	3,580.81	34.64	41.08	212.66	42.95
Rivers in northeast China	280.39	80.70	2.82	308	11.57	24.41
Haihe River	324.47	238.51	1.10	3.56	14.97	0.59
Huanhe River and Shandong Peninsula	487.54	304.25	0.01	0.16	27.20	6.73
The Yellow River	324.40	454.44	3.80	4.66	10.05	1.0

2) Major problems in the development of water resources

The northern part of China is a water-deficient region. Global warming, climate aridification and land desertification are accelerating; there exist many problems in the development of water resources. ① Acute contradictions between water supply and demand. ② Over-exploitation of groundwater. ③ Mismanagement of water resources and low water use efficiency. ④ Serious water pollution. ⑤ Severe environmental degradation.

4.2.2.3　Prospect of water resource development and utilization

In order to develop water resources in eastern desert regions of China rationally, the following measures should be taken. ① Controlling water and soil losses and promoting sustainable use of water resources. ② Utilizing water and land resources rationally. ③ Controlling water pollution. ④ Diverting water from regions with abundant water resources. ⑤ Strengthening water resource management.

4.3　Land resources

4.3.1　Types and distribution characteristics of land resources

In the arid and vast desert regions of China, the land resource types are diversified, and their origin and distribution have certain regularity. Their horizontal, vertical and zonal distribution are controlled by geologic and topographic conditions as well as human activities etc.

In the arid desert region of northern China, the topography is very complex，and much of the region is deserts, mountains, hills，basins and high plains, of which flat land accounts for about 35.5% of the total area, hills 8.86%, mountains 18%, deserts 37.27%, and water bodies 0.37% (Table 4-18).

Table 4-18　The landform types in desert regions of northern China

Region	Total	Flat land						Hill area			
		Subtotal		Bottom land (10⁴ hm²)	Flat(10⁴ hm²)	Mesa(10⁴ hm²)	Valley(10⁴ hm²)	Subtotal		Earth rock hill(10⁴ hm²)	Loess hill(10⁴ hm²)
		Area (10⁴ hm²)	Percentage (%)					Area (10⁴ hm²)	Percentage (%)		
Semiarid region of Inner Mongolia	5,348.88	2,791.14	52.18	179.93	1,950.59	509.92	150.70	1,019.93	10.09	1,019.06	0.87
Arid region of northwest China	18,862.05	5,803.62	30.77	304.35	4,970.50	444.66	84.11	1,125.23	5.97	1,125.27	
Total	24,210.93	8,594.26	35.50	484.28	6,921.09	954.58	234.81	2,145.16	8.86	2,144.29	0.87

Region	Mountain area					Desert		Water body	
	Subtotal		Mountains (10⁴ hm²)	Bare rock (10⁴ hm²)	Glacier (10⁴ hm²)	Subtotal		Subtotal	
	Area (10⁴hm²)	Percentage (%)				Area (10⁴hm²)	Percentage (%)	Area (10⁴ hm²)	Percentage (%)
Semiarid region of Inner Mongolia	574.60	10.74	574.60			928.5	17.36	34.71	0.65
Arid region of northwest China	3,784.32	20.06	1,993.81	1,617.09	173.42	8,095.08	42.92	53.80	0.29
Total	4,358.92	18.00	2,568.42	1,617.09	173.42	9,023.58	37.27	88.51	0.37

Data source: 1：1,000,000 Land resource map of China, 1991b. Some of the data in this table have been updated.

Soil types in the desert regions of China include Entisols, Anthrosols, Aridisols, Halosols, Gleysols, Isohumicosols, and Combisols. The vegetation types include grassland, desert grassland, and other desert vegetations. There are also desert riparian forests (such as *Populus euphratica, Salix sinopurpurea,* and so on) on the banks of the inland rivers, and in mountain areas, vegetation shows a vertical zonal distribution feature. Statistics of land use and land cover are shown in Table 4-19.

Table 4-19　Statistics of land use and land cover

Region	Total	Farmland		Woodland		Grassland		Bare land	
		Area (10^4 hm^2)	Percent(%)	Area (10^4 hm^2)	Percent(%)	Area (10^4 hm^2)	Percent(%)	Area (10^4 hm^2)	Percent(%)
Semiarid region of Inner Mongolia	5,248.88	610.80	11.42	260.97	4.88	3,915.21	73.20	2.76	0.05
Arid region of northwest China	18,862.05	552.38	3.28	473.02	2.51	8,347.17	44.25	1,854.90	9.83
Total	24,210.93	1,229.84	5.08	733.99	3.03	12,262.38	50.65	1,857.67	7.67

Region	Desert		Glacier		Water area		Others	
	Area (10^4hm^2)	Percent(%)	Area (10^4hm^2)	Percent(%)	Area (10^4hm^2)	Percent(%)	Area (10^4hm^2)	Percent(%)
Semiarid region of Inner Mongolia	152.63	2.85	—	—	34.71	0.65	371.80	6.95
Arid region of northwest China	7,089.92	37.59	99.17	0.53	53.80	0.29	325.02	1.72
Total	7,242.55	29.91	99.17	0.41	88.51	0.37	696.82	2.88

Data source: 1 ∶ 1,000,000 Land resource map of China, 1991b. Some of the data in this table have been updated.

4.3.2　Evaluation of quantity and quality of land resources

The land area suitable for agriculture is $1,510.1 \times 10^4$ hm^2, occupying 6.27% of the total land resources, and the land area suitable for agriculture, forest, and grazing is $1,435.38 \times 10^4$ hm^2, occupying 5.96%. The land area suitable for farming and forest is 1.45×10^4 hm^2, occupying 0.01%. The land area suitable for farming and grazing is 314.31×10^4 hm^2, occupying 1.3%. The land area suitable for forest and grazing is $2,475.84 \times 10^4$ hm^2, occupying 10.27%. The land area suitable for forest is 374.82×10^4 hm^2, occupying 1.51%. The land area suitable for grazing is $8,680.81 \times 10^4$ hm^2, occupying 36.02%. The land area that is difficult to use is $9,305.9 \times 10^4$ hm^2, occupying 38.62%. The most obvious feature of the land resources in the arid desert zone is that there is less land suitable for agriculture and much more land is difficult to use (Table 4-20).

1) Farmland

There are $1,229.76 \times 10^4$ hm^2 of farmland in the arid desert zone of China. In fact, about 104.24×10^4 hm^2 of land is unsuitable for agriculture, occupying 8.47%, which should be changed into woodland or grassland (Table 4-21).

Table 4-20　Statistics of land suitability types

Region	Total	Suitable for agriculture		Suitable for agriculture, forest, and grazing		Suitable for agriculture and forest		Suitable for agriculture and grazing	
		Area(10^4 hm^2)	Percent(%)	Area(10^4 hm^2)	Percent(%)	Area(10^4 hm^2)	Percent(%)	Area(10^4 hm^2)	Percent(%)
Semiarid region of Inner Mongolia	5,280.75	668.91	12.67	400.17	7.58			286.75	5.43
Arid region of northwest China	18,817.56	841.19	4.47	1,035.21	5.50	1.45	0.01	27.56	0.15
Total	42,916.07	1,510.10	6.27	1,435.38	5.96	1.45	0.01	314.31	1.31

Region	Suitable for forest and grazing		Suitable for forest		Suitable for grazing		Not suitable land	
	Area(10^4hm^2)	Percent(%)	Area(10^4hm^2)	Percent(%)	Area(10^4hm^2)	Percent(%)	Area(10^4hm^2)	Percent(%)
Semiarid region of Inner Mongolia	1,442.56	27.32	238.12	4.51	2,640.21	38.63	204.32	3.87
Arid region of northwest China	1,033.28	5.49	136.70	0.73	6,640.59	35.29	9,101.58	48.37
Total	2,475.84	10.27	374.72	1.55	8,680.80	36.02	9,305.90	38.62

Data source: 1：1,000,000 Land resource map of China, 1991b. Some of the data in this table has been updated.

Table 4-21　Statistics of farmland quality

Region	Total	First grade		Second grade		Third grade		Unsuitable for agriculture	
		Area (10^4 hm^2)	Percent (%)	Area (10^4 hm^2)	Percent (%)	Area (10^4 hm^2)	Percent (%)	Area (10^4 hm^2)	Percent (%)
Semiarid region of Inner Mongolia	610.80	121.51	19.89	270.30	44.26	131.00	21.45	87.92	14.39
Arid region of northwest China	619.04	293.42	47.40	195.61	31.60	113.68	18.36	16.32	2.64
Total	1,329.84	414.94	33.74	465.97	37.89	244.69	19.90	104.25	8.47

Data source: 1：1,000,000 Land resource map of China, 1991b.

2) Farmland in reserve

There are about 1,582.13 $\times10^4$ hm^2 of reserve farmland resources in the desert zone of China. The quality of these lands is presented in Table 4-22. According to Shi Zhujun, there are about 500×10^4 hm^2 of reserve farmland resources in the semiarid region of Inner Mongolia, 99.3% of which is of second or third grade. The main landform in this region is hills or hill-basins, and the annual precipitation is between 300–400 mm, so most of this area is suitable for grazing. There is about $1,050\times10^4$ hm^2 of reserve farmland resources in the arid region of northwest China, accounting for 31% of the total reserve land area of China, of which, Xinjiang has 950×10^4 hm^2, which is mainly second and third grade. 90% of them are aridisols or halosols. There are 530×10^4 hm^2 of reserve farmland resources in semiarid regions of Inner Mongolia, most of which are grasslands.

Statistics of limiting factors and intensity of reserve land resources are shown in Table 4-23.

Table 4-22　Statistics of the farmland resource in support

Region	Total	First grade		Second grade		Third grade	
		Area (10^4 hm^2)	Percent (%)	Area (10^4 hm^2)	Percent (%)	Area (10^4 hm^2)	Percent (%)
Semiarid region of Inner Mongolia	529.58	3.57	0.67	260.23	49.14	265.79	50.19
Arid region of northwest China	1,052.55	0.00	0.00	431.32	40.98	621.20	59.02
Total	1,582.13	3.57	0.23	691.57	43.71	886.99	56.06

Data source: 1 ：1,000,000 Land resource map of China, 1991b. Some of the data in this table has been updated.

Table 4-23　Statistics of limiting factors and intensity of reserve land resources

Region	Total	Without limitation	Total	Slope limitation		Erosion limitation		Bare rock limitation	
				Area (10^4 hm^2)	Percent (%)	Area (10^4 hm^2)	Percent (%)	Area (10^4 hm^2)	Percent (%)
Semiarid region of Inner Mongolia	529.58	3.57	526.02	11.70	2.22	0.00	0.00	0.00	0.00
Arid region of northwest China	1,052.55	0.00	1,053.21	0.00	0.00	0.00	0.00	0.00	0.00
Total	1,582.13	3.57	1,579.23	11.70	7.39	0.00	0.00	0.00	0.00

Region	Soil quantity limitation		Efficient soil layer limitation		Salt limitation	
	Area (10^4 hm^2)	Percent (%)	Area (10^4 hm^2)	Percent (%)	Area (10^4 hm^2)	Percent (%)
Semiarid region of Inner Mongolia	0.00	0.00	26.68	5.07	121.89	23.17
Arid region of northwest China	92.11	8.75	70.12	6.66	601.19	57.12
Total	92.11	5.82	96.81	6.12	223.08	45.70

Region	Water limitation		Hydrologic limitation		Temperature limitation	
	Area (10^4 hm^2)	Percent (%)	Area (10^4 hm^2)	Percent (%)	Area (10^4 hm^2)	Percent (%)
Semiarid region of Inner Mongolia	134.25	25.52	231.49	44.01	0.00	0.00
Arid region of northwest China	54.71	5.20	222.16	21.11	12.25	1.16
Total	188.96	11.94	453.65	28.67	12.25	0.77

Data source: 1 ：1,000,000 Land resource map of China, 1991b. Some of the data in this table has been updated.

3) Woodland

Woodland area is very small in the arid desert zone of China; generally the forest cover is less than 5%. The woodland mainly is distributed in the middle mountains area or on the banks of inland rivers, for example, the riparian forests of *Populus euphratica* or *Salix sinopurpurea* in the lower reaches of the Tarim River or the Heihe River. In addition, there are some artificial shelterbelts and sand-binding forests. Altogether, there are about $4,282.87 \times 10^4$ hm^2 of land suitable for forest (Table 4-24, Table 4-25).

Reserve woodland resource is shown in Table 4-26.

Table 4-24　Statistics of land resource suitable for forest

Region	Total	Farmland		Woodland		Grassland		Bare land	
		Area $(10^4 \, hm^2)$	Percent (%)	Area $(10^4 \, hm^2)$	Percent (%)	Area $(10^4 \, hm^2)$	Percent (%)	Area $(10^4 \, hm^2)$	Percent (%)
Semiarid region of Inner Mongolia	2,076.22	80.01	3.85	260.97	12.57	1,716.14	82.66	19.09	0.92
Arid region of northwest China	2,206.65	3.99	0.18	473.03	21.44	1,694.89	76.81	34.74	1.57
Total	4,282.87	83.99	1.96	734.00	17.14	3,411.03	79.64	53.83	1.26

Data source: 1 : 1,000,000 Land resource map of China, 1991b.

Table 4-25　Statistics of the woodland quality

Region	Total	First grade		Second grade		Third grade	
		Area $(10^4 \, hm^2)$	Percent (%)	Area $(10^4 \, hm^2)$	Percent (%)	Area $(10^4 \, hm^2)$	Percent (%)
Semiarid region of Inner Mongolia	260.97	97.00	37.17	102.08	39.11	61.90	23.72
Arid region of northwest China	473.02	84.25	17.81	150.38	31.79	238.39	50.40
Total	733.99	181.25	24.69	252.46	34.39	300.29	40.91

Data source: 1 : 1,000,000 Land resource map of China, 1991b.

Table 4-26　Reserve woodland resource

Region	Total	First grade		Second grade		Third grade	
		Area $(10^4 \, hm^2)$	Percent (%)	Area $(10^4 \, hm^2)$	Percent (%)	Area $(10^4 \, hm^2)$	Percent (%)
Semiarid region of Inner Mongolia	1,815.15	3.57	0.20	802.50	44.21	1,009.08	55.59
Arid region of northwest China	1,733.62	0.00	0.00	369.07	21.29	1,364.55	78.71
Total	3,548.77	3.57	0.10	1,540.63	33.01	2,373.63	66.89

Data source: 1 : 1,000,000 Land resource map of China, 1991b.

Table 4-27　Statistics of land resource suitable for grazing

Region	Total	Farmland		Woodland		Grassland		Bare land	
		Area $(10^4 \, hm^2)$	Percent (%)	Area $(10^4 \, hm^2)$	Percent (%)	Area $(10^4 \, hm^2)$	Percent (%)	Area $(10^4 \, hm^2)$	Percent (%)
Semiarid region of Inner Mongolia	4,172.03	203.59	4.88	60.51	1.45	3,901.93	93.67		
Arid region of northwest China	8,728.89	11.6	0.13	337.94	3.87	8,346.92	95.62	32.36	0.37
Total	12,900.92	215.25	1.67	398.45	3.09	12,254.86	94.99	32.36	0.25

Data source: 1 : 1,000,000 Land resource map of China, 1991b.

4) Pasture lands

In the arid desert regions of China, there is a large area of pastureland of many types, though the quality is rather poor, There is only about $12,894.85 \times 10^4\,\text{hm}^2$ of land suitable for grazing, while existing pasture land area is about $12,262.45 \times 10^4\,\text{hm}^2$ (Tables 4-27, 4-28). The pasture lands are mainly distributed in Hulun Buir, Xilin Gol, Ulan Qab, south or north of the Tianshan Mountains, and some sandy lands, such as the Horqin Sandy Land, the Onqin Daga Sandy Land, and the Mu Us Sandy Land.

Table 4-28　Statistics of the herd land quality

Region	Total	Fist grade		Second grade		Third grade		Unsuitable herd land	
		Area $(10^4\,\text{hm}^2)$	Percent (%)	Area $(10^4\,\text{hm}^2)$	Percent (%)	Area $(10^4\,\text{hm}^2)$	Percent (%)	Area $(10^4\,\text{hm}^2)$	Percent (%)
Semiarid region of Inner Mongolia	3,915.27	1,839.67	46.99	1,208.26	30.86	860.00	21.97	7.34	0.19
Arid region of northwest China	838,347.17	970.80	11.63	2,893.49	34.66	4,482.64	53.70	0.25	
Total	12,262.44	2,810.47	22.92	4,101.75	33.45	5,342.64	43.57	7.59	0.01

Data source: 1 : 1,000,000 Land resource map of China, 1991b.

In addition, there is about $646.08 \times 10^4\,\text{hm}^2$ of reserve pasture land (Table 4-29).

Table 4-29　Statistics of reserve pasture land resources

Region	Total	First grade		Second grade		Third grade	
		Area $(10^4\,\text{hm}^2)$	Percent (%)	Area $(10^4\,\text{hm}^2)$	Percent (%)	Area $(10^4\,\text{hm}^2)$	Percent (%)
Semiarid region of Inner Mongolia	264.10	153.68	58.19	14.10	5.34	96.32	36.47
Arid region of northwest China	381.97	3.98	1.04	95.63	25.03	282.36	73.92
Total	646.07	157.66	24.40	109.73	16.98	378.68	58.61

Data source: 1 : 1,000,000 Land resource map of China, 1991b. Some of the data in this table have been updated.

4.4　Vegetation in the deserts and aeolian desertified lands

In the vast deserts and desertified regions of China, there are abundant endemic plant species.

Special crop varieties form many important production bases, especially economic crop bases.

In desert regions most crop-producing bases are concentrated in irrigated oases in addition to rainfed croplands and alpine croplands. Generally, one crop can be grown each year.

Grasslands (including desert steppe) in China are mainly distributed in arid and semiarid regions, and they constitute important desert eco-system types. Of the seven major grassland provinces in China, six are located in arid and semiarid desert and desertification areas. According to the statistical data of 11 provinces of northern China, the total area of natural grassland is 224 million hm^2, accounting for 57.17% of the total grassland area of China. Of them 130 million hm^2 are distributed in desert and desertification areas, which occupy 34.1% of the total grassland area of China. The per capita grassland area is 2.98 hm^2 in desert regions, which is 3.5 times the average of 11 northern provinces and 3.6 times the average of the country. In the arid and semi-arid regions, the usable grasslands occupy 82.46 % of the total grassland area and produce on average 225 billion tons of grasses each year to support the livestock. The average per unit area yield of the grassland is 1,076.4 kg/hm^2, which theoretically can support 6,749.51 units sheep.

According to field surveys and statistics, there are 2,271 vascular plant species in Inner Mongolia, 1,839 in Ningxia, 2,054 in Gansu and 3,270 in Xinjiang. Most of these vascular plant species have been explored and used.

4.4.1 Pasture plants and forage crops

In the desert and desertification areas of China, there are 1,800 excellent pasture plant species, which occupies 70% of the total number of species in the country. These plant species include *Aneurolepidium chinense, Bromus, Festuca, Elymus, Hordeum, Medicago, Oxytropis, Hippophaë rhamnoides, Melilotus suaveolens, Medicago falcata* and so on.

4.4.2 Edible plants

In the desert regions of China, there are many types of wild edible plant species with abundant nutrients such as *Nostoc flagelliforme, Pteridumaquilinumvar latiusculum, Elaeagnus angustifolia, Crataegus pinnatifida*, and *Prunus armeniaca*.

4.4.3 Medicinal plants

Medicinal plants are the most important component of the economic plants. In the desert regions of China, there are about 284 medical herb species including *Glycyrrhiza uralensis, Ephedra sinica, Lycium chinense, Cynomorium songaricum, Cistanche deserticola* and so on. Some of them have been used as Chinese herbal medicine for a long period of time and most of them cannot be substituted by other cultivated species.

Cynomorium songaricum and *Cistanche deserticola* are shown as Fig. 4-5.

(1) Plant species used as antipyretic analgesics. *Arctium lappa, Ephedra sinica, Tamarix ramosissima, Bupleurum scorzonerifolium, Mentha arvensis, Anemarrhena asphodeloides, Artemisia capillaris, Scutellaria baicalensis, Rheum franzenbachii, Prinsepia uniflora, Gueldenstaedtia pauciflora, Corydalis bungeana, Potulaca oleracea, Pulsatilla chinensis, Menispermum dahuricum, Acorus calamus, Hyoscyamus niger, Datura stramonium.*

(2) Plant species used as cough suppressants. *Lepidium apetalum*, *Prunus armeniaca*, *Morus alba* and so on.

(3) Plant species used as hemostatics. *Leonurus heterophyllus*, *Eupatorium lindleyanum*, *Paeonia lactiflora*, *Carthamus tinctorius*, *Vaccaria segetalis*, *Siphonostegia chinensis*, *Limonium bicolor*, *Equisetum arvense*, *Euphorbia humifusa*, *Cirsium segetum*, *Hypericum ascyron*, *Rubia cordifolia*, *Sedum aizoon* and so on.

Fig. 4-5   Cynomorium songaricum (left) and Cistanche deserticola (right)

(4) Plant species used as sedatives. *Allium macrostemon*, *Celastrus arbiculatus*, *Polygala tenuifolia*, *Ziziphus jujuba* and so on.

(5) Plant species used as anti-rheumatic suppressant. *Artemisia argyi*, *Pedicularis resupinata*, *Gentiana macrophylla*, *Xanthium sibiricum*, *Periploca sepium*, *Incarvillea sinensis*, *Erodium stephanianum*, *Clematis hexapetala* and so on.

(6) Plant species used as diuretics. *Hemerocallis minor*, *Plantago asiatica*, *Polygonum orientale*, *Euphorbia kansui*, *Dianthus chinensis*, *Malva verticillata*, *Alisma orientale*, *Euphorbia helioscopia*, *E. soongarica*, *Prunus humilis*, *Humulus scandens*.

(7) Plant species used as digestants. *Polygonatum sibiricum*, *P. odoratum*, *Cuscuta chinensis*, *Orobanche coerulescens*, *Rehmannia glutinosa*. *Lilium pumilum* and so on.

(8) Plant species used as anthelmintics. *Lappula echinata*, *Ferula caspica*, *Delphinium grandiflorum*, *Stellera chamaejasme*, *Cnidium monnieri* and so on.

4.4.4　Other economic plants

(1) Wild oil yielding plant species. *Juglans mandshurica, Corylus heterophylla, Suaeda glauca* and so on.

(2) Wild amylum plant species. *Dioscorea quinqueloba* and so on.

(3) Wild fruit plant species. *Ribes tenue, Prunus tomentosa, P. davidiana, Fragaria elatior, Rubus, Viburnum* and so on.

(4) Wild fibrous plant species. *Apocynum lancifolium, Urtica cannabina, Miscanthus* and so on.

(5) Tannin and spice species. *Rumex crispus, Berberis, Galium verum, Bidens tripartita* and so on.

(6) Wild ornamental plant species. *Limonium aureum, Linaria vudicaule, Echinops gmelinii, E. pseudosetifer, Rosa bella, Syringa villosa, Primula maximowiczii, P. farinosa, Paeonia lactiflora, Lilium concolor, Polygonatum odoratum, Dianthus superbus, Cirsium esculentum, Ligularia sibirica, Spiranthes amoena, Scabiosa comosa* and so on.

4.5　Animal resources

Owing to dry climate, frequent strong winds, limited water supply, very low temperature in winter and sparse edible vegetation, most wild animal species living in the same latitude of other countries are absent in desert regions of China. Recent research shows that big animals, reptiles and amphibious animals are very few, but there are lots of small animals in desert areas (Zheng, 1979).

4.5.1　Big and middle size animals

There are some hoofed animal species in Chinese arid lands. The Main animal species in the eastern grassland areas is *Procapera gutturosa,* and there used to be over one thousand heads in a herd. But now it is very difficult to find large herds due to human hunting and habitat destruction. *Gazella subgutturosa* used to be a common species in western grasslands, but now they have disappeared. The main hoofed animal species in the desert and semidesert regions of China are *Camelus bactrianus, Equus przewalskii, E.hemions* and *Gazella subgutturosa,* of which *Gazella subgutturosa* is the most common, and usually lives in gravel or sandy deserts with a herd of 3 to 10 members. *E.hemions* often occur in the northern Junggar Basin and the western Qaidam Basin. In the desert areas of western China, there were lots of *Camelus bactrianus* and some *Equus przewalski.* In the Qinghai-Tibet Plateau, the most common species are Tibetan-antelope, wild Tibetan donkey, *Procapra picticauata, Pseudois nagaur* and *Ovis ammon.* The former two species mostly occur in basins or river valleys and the latter two species in mountain areas. In addition, there are Tibetan-antelopes and *Bos grunnieus* in the Qiang-Tang Plateau. In recent decades, owing to environment deterioration and human hunting, *E. hemion*, *Equus przewalski* and *Camelus bactrianus* have become endangered species. A national first-class protected animal—the wild camelis shown in Fig. 4-6.

The most common carnivorous animal species in semi-arid desert regions of China are *Mustela sibirica*, *M.eversmanni*, *Vulpes corsac*, *V.vulpus*, *Felis mamul*, *Vormela peregusna*, *Mustela altaica* and *Canis lapu*. In the desert regions of northwest China, the most common are *V.vulpus*, *Vulpes corsae*, *Vormela peregusna*, *Felis lupus* and *Canis lupu*.

Fig. 4-6   National first-class protected animal—the wild camel

4.5.2   Rodent animals

Rodent animals occur extensively in semi-arid steppe regions and arid desert regions or even cold and high mountain areas.

Rodent species in temperate grassland zones are *Microtus, Myospalax, Citellus, Marmota, Ochotona,* In eastern parts of the grassland, main species is *Microtus brandti,* and they extensively occur in the grassland of Inner Mongolia. In some regions, the number of *Microtus brandti* reaches 5,000-10,000 per hectare, and therefore the grassland is severely destroyed. *Myospalax* also has a big population and its number gradually decreases from northeast to southwest because water and vegetation conditions become worse. The *Meriones unguiculatus* and *Phodopus roborovskii* are often found in sandy land or saline land in the western parts of grasslands.

In northwestern arid areas including western Inner Mongolia, the Hexi corridor, Xinjiang and the Qaidam Basin, the species and number of rodent animals are much less compared with grassland areas. Extensively distributed species in the region are *Meriones meridianus. Meriones unguiculatus* mainly occurs in Xinjiang, Qinghai, western Gansu, eastern Ningxia and western Inner Mongolia. *Rhombomys opinus* is distributed in the Junggar Basin and the Hexi Corridor. (Wang Sibo, 1983)

There are eleven species of jerboas in deserts and steppe areas. The most extensively distributed species are *Allactaga sibirica* and *Dipus sagitta*. *Allactaga sibirica* exists in grassland and steppe areas, and it can even be found in the Qaidam Basin and mountain regions of northeastern Qinghai (altitude higher than 3,000 m) and in northern parts of the loess plateau, but it is seldom found in sand dune areas. The distribution region of *Dipus sagitta* is similar to *Allactaga sibirica,* but it fits for living in dune areas. Other rodent species are *Euchoreutes naso, Allactaga elater, Stylodipus telum* etc, and they mostly live in gravel and steppe areas and usually in a small population. *Alactagulus pumilio, Allactaga elater* and *Stylodipus telum* exist in bigger populations and can only be found in Gobi desert of northern Xinjiang. Generally speaking, ubiquitous species in these regions are *Lepus capensis, Hemiechinus auritus, Ellobius talpinus, Cricetulus migratorius, Phodopus roborovskii* etc.

In piedmont and low-mountain areas, besides the above-mentioned species, the dominant species are *Meriones erythrourus, Lagurus luteus, Citellus*. In the Qaidam basin, the common species are *Meriones meridianus, Euchoreutes naso, Allactaga sibirica, Dipus sagitta* and so on, but their populations are small. In desertified land of the Qinghai-Tibet plateau, there are many rabbits and rats. *Marmota himalayana, Pitymys leucurus, Cricetulus kamensis* and *Alticola stoliczkanus* are also commom in the region. *Cricetulus kamensis* can be found in rangeland of the western Qilian Mountains. *Pitymys leucuru* is easy to be seen in valley meadows of northern Tibet.

4.5.3　Bird resources

The number and populations of bird species in desert regions of China is rather small. Common dominant bird species in this region are *Alauda arvensis, Eremophila alpestris, Melanocorypha Mongolia, Oenanthe oenanthe, O.isabellina* and so on. In the Horqin and the Onqin Daga Sandy Lands, *O.isabellina* is dominant population. In eastern parts of the sandy land there are some *Emberiza aureola, E.spodocephala* and *Apus pacificus. Otis tarda* and *Syrrhaptes parodoxus* are often captured by humans. Along rivers or around water bodies in the grassland, *Fulica atr, Acrocephalus aurundinaceu, Anthus novaeseelandiae, Vanellus vanellus, Ardea cinerea, Tadorna tadorna, Anas clypeata, A.Formosa, Cygnus olor, Botaurus stellaris, Podiceps cristatus, Phalacrocorax carbo* and *Pelecanus philippensis* are often found in large populations. *Milvus korschun, Aquila chrysaetos, Accipiter gentiles, A.nisus* and *Buteo hemilasius* are common raptorial birds in grasslands.

In deserts and semi desert regions, the most common bird species are *Oenanthe oenanthe, Oenanthe deserti, O.hispanica, Galerida cristata, Calandrella cinerea, C. rugescens, Perdix dauuricae*, *Syrrhaptes parodoxus*, *Podoces biddulphi* etc, of which *Galerida cristata* is dominant. *Pterocles orientalis*, *Columba rupestris*, *C.livia* and *Streptopelia* occur in the piedmont belts or river valleys. *Perdix dauuricae* and *Syrrhaptes parodoxus* are economic animals.

Some dry river valleys are covered by shrubs or artificial *populus euphratica* forest, which provide good habitats for animals. *Streptopelia orientalis*, *S.decaocto*, *Columba livia*, *Lanius cristatus*, *Sturnus vulgaris*, *Motacilla alba*, *M.citreola*, *Hirundo rustica* etc are common in these places. *Galerida cristata* and *Podoces hendersoni* live in desert oases. Water birds are *Egretta alba*, *Ardea cinerea*, *Tadorna ferruginea*, *Sterna hirundo*, *Tringa* and *Gallinula chloropus*.

In cold rangelands and desert areas, common bird species are *Pseudopodoces humilis*, *Montifringilla ruficollis*, *M. taczanowskii*, *M.blanford* and *M.adamsi*. *Larus brunnicephalus*, *Anser indicus*, *Mergus merganse*, and *Ibidorhyncha struthersii* often occur in the areas around water areas like lakes. *Pyrrhocorax pyrrhocorax*, *P.graculus*, *Gypaetus barbatus* and *Columba leuconota* can be found in high-altitude mountains.

4.5.4   Reptile and amphibious animals

Common reptile species in grassland are *Eremias, Phrynocephalus, Elaphe dione* and *Agkistrodon halys*). *Elaphe dione* is a dominant species and has a big population. For amphibious animals, only *Bufo raddei* is a common species and has a big population. In steppe and desert areas, there are many species of lizards, especially in dune areas, *Eremias* and *Phrynocephalus* are dominant species. In deserts, *Eryx miliaris* and *Psammophis lineolatus* are common snake species. For amphibious animals, only *Bufo viridis* occurs in limited areas with better water condition such as oases of the northern Tarim Basin.

In cold rangelands and deserts, there are very few reptiles and amphibious animals. the reptile *Phrynocephalus theobaldi* can be found in sandy lands and valleys of the Yarlung Zangbo River and Ali region at an altitude of 4,800 m. Common snakes are *Agkistrodon strauchii* and *Thermophis baileyi*. The dominant amphibious species are *Nanorana pleskei*, *Altirana parkeri* and *Bufo tibetanus.*

4.6   Mineral resources

Deserts in China mostly lie in Mesozoic tectonic basins. Geological development history of the Tarim Basin can be traced back to the Tethys Sea. Therefore, abundant mineral resources are deposited in the basin such as coal, petroleum, natural gas, salt and so on. Due to active geological activities in mountain areas around the basin, many kinds of metallic mineral deposits formed. The main mineral resources such as coal, petroleum, natural gas and salt are presented as follows:

4.6.1 Coal

Coal resources in desert and desertified areas of northwestern China as well as Shanxi Province and Inner Mongolia, are abundant. The proven reserves in these regions account for 77% of the total reserves of China and rank first in the world.

4.6.1.1 Ordos Basin

There are several large-scale coal mines in the Ordos Basin and adjacent regions such as Datong, Shenfu, Jungar, Dongsheng, Wuhai, and Ningdong mines. The total proven reserves of the six coal mines are 265.9 billion tons, accounting for 38.8 % of 7 provinces' reserves.

(1) Datong coalfield. Datong coalfield lies to the southwest of Datong and extends across Zuoyun, Youyu, Shanyin, Huaiyin and Huairen counties. The coal beds spread 1,888 km^2, existing in the Carboniferous-Permian and Jurassic coal-bearing strata. The total thickness of coal seam is about 35 m, of which 6–7 layers (11–13 m) are in Jurassic, 9 layers (about 25 m) in Carboniferous–Permian strata. The proven reserve was 37.3 billion tons in 1985, of which 6.5 billion tons is in Jurassic strata, account for 17.4%, 30.8 billion tons in Carboniferous–Permian strata, accounting for 82.6%. The raw coals contain 10% of ash, less than 0.9% of sulfur. The calorific value is 33.5 MJ/kg.

(2) Shenfu Coalfield. Shenfu Coalfield, 130-150 km long from south to north and 50-70 km wide from east to west, is situated in Yulin, Shenmu and Fugu of northern Shaanxi Province, close to the Dongsheng Coalfield of Inner Mongolia. The coalfield covers an area of 9,000 km^2 and belongs to Jurassic coal-bearing strata with 27 coal layers; four of them (averaged 18 m thick) are extractable. This coal is a high quality with low contents of phosphorus, sulfur and ash. The raw coal contains 5.8%–9.7% of ash, 0.5% of sulfur and has a calorific value 32.2–33.1 MJ/kg. The proven reserves in 1985 were 65.6 billion tons. This coalfield was started to be developed at the end of the 20th century.

(3) Jungar Coalfield (Fig. 4-7). Jungar coalfield is located to the south of the Daqing Mountains in Inner Mongolia, eastern part of Jungar Qi, near Dongsheng coalfield, where geological structure belongs to northeast edge of the Ordos Basin. Coal exists in Carboniferous-Permian strata with a thickness of 30 m consisting of 10 layers. The maximum mineable thickness is 14.1–26 m. The ash content in raw coal is 20.5%–31.9%, sulfur less than 1%. Calorific value is 19.68–25.12 MJ/kg. The available reserve in 1985 was 25.9 billion tons.

(4) Dongsheng Coalfield. Dongsheng Coalfield, with an area of 11,000 km^2, lies in Ordos Plateau in Inner Mongolia connected with Shenfu coalfield and Jurassic coal deposits. Total thickness of coal layers is 17.2 m on average. Calorific value is 25.12 MJ/kg, ash content less than 10%, sulfur less than 0.5%. The proven reserves in 1985 were 95.3 billion tons.

(5) Ningdong Coalfield. Located in the middle part of Ningxia and to the north of the Yellow River, it belongs to Jurassic and Carboniferous—Permian coals strata. The calorific value is 27.63

MJ/kg, ash 8.4%, sulfur 0.58%.

Fig. 4-7　Coal covered by sand–Junggar coalfield

(6) Wuhai Coalfield. This coalfield is a part of Helanshan Coalfield and lies in Wuhai district in the central part of Inner Mongolia. It belongs to Carboniferous- Permian strata. The thickness of the coal bed is about 40 m. Calorific value of raw coal is 24.70–35.17 MJ/kg, ash content 11.1%–39.2%, sulfur 0.34% – 4.15%. The proven reserve in 1985 was 4.3 billion tons.

4.6.1.2　Eastern Inner Mongolia

There are plenty of coal resources in Inner Mongolia. It ranks second in China, just less than Shaanxi province. The proven reserves in eastern Mongolia are 43.4 billion tons mainly distributed to the west of Xing'anling. The Huolinhe River coal mine is a famous open pit in China which consists of two coalfields.

4.6.1.3　Xinjiang

Coal resources in Xinjiang have features of plentiful reserves, complete varieties, shallow burial depth, high quality and they are easy to develop but unevenly distributed. Up to 1992, total proven reserve was 94.9 billion tons, which ranks fourth in China.

The coal deposits in Xinjiang are mainly distributed in the Junggar Basin, the Tarim Basin, and the Turpan-Hami Basin, they were formed in Devonian, Carboniferous, Permian, Triassic and Jurassic Period, but most of them were formed in Jurassic and Triassic period.

The coals exist in many layers. In some areas it exists in 4 –10 layers. The thickness of the coal layer mostly is 3–20 m, in some areas reaches 180 m. Ash content usually is less than 10%, sulfur less than 1%, and calorific value 23–36 MJ/kg.

4.6.2 Oil and natural gas resources

In desert regions of north and northwest China, huge amount of oil and natural gas resources have been discovered, for example in the Taklimakan Desert (Fig. 4-8), the Gurbantünggüt desert, the Turpan–Hami Basin, and the Ordos Basin.

4.6.2.1 Tarim Basin

Much of the surface of the Tarim Basin is covered by the Taklimakan Desert. The geological reserves of oil and gas are 19.15 billion tons, including 11.06 billion tons of petroleum and 9,000 billion cubic meters of natural gas. Since 1989, some oilfields have been successively discovered, such as the oilfields of Lunnan, Jilake, Donghetang, and Sangta, especially No. 4 oilfield in the central Taklimakan Desert.

Fig. 4-8   Oil development in the central Taklimakan Desert

In Kuqa at the northern part of the Tarim Basin, five natural gas fields have been discovered with a proven geological reserve of 311 billion m^3. Another gas field discovered in April of 2004 has a proven reserve of 250.61 billion m^3.

Till the end of 2002, the proven reserve of natural gas reached to 1,000 billion m^3. The Chinese central government has started a west to east gas transmission project. The pipeline will be extended

4,200 km from Xinjiang to Shanghai.

4.6.2.2 Junggar Basin

The Gurbantünggüt Desert, the third largest desert in China, lies in the Junggar Basin. Since discovering the Karamay oilfield in the 1950s, other several oilfields have been discovered including Dushanzi, Qigu, Chepaizi, Huongshanzui, Baikouquan, Wusule, Fengpo, Xianzijie and Huoshaoshan oilfields. The predicted oil reserve is 9 billion tons and the proved reserve is 1.73 billion tons in addition to 140 billion m^3 of natural gas.

4.6.2.3 Turpan–Hami Basin

There are 1.7 billion tons of exploitable oil-gas reserves in the basin, of which the oil reserve is 1.6 billion tons and the natural gas reserve is 370 billion m^3.

4.6.2.4 Qaidam Basin

The oil and gas are mainly distributed in four regions of the basin. They are Mangai in the western part of the basin, Lenghu in the north, Sanhu in the south and Delingha in the east. 17 oilfields and 6 gas-fields have been discovered in these regions.

According to surveys, the estimated reserves in the basin are 1.7–2.0 billion tons of oil and 300 billion m^3 of natural gas.

4.6.2.5 Ordos Basin

Yan-Chang (Yan'an-Changqin) oilfield in Shaanxi province is one of the earliest developed oilfields. Changqin oilfield was developed in the 1960s and a natural gas field was discovered in the 1980s. The gas developed in the field is being transported to Xi'an, Taiyuan, Beijing and Tianjin for industrial and home uses. It is also supplied to Shanghai before completion of the West- East Gas Transmission Project.

4.6.3   Salt mines

Salt and saltwater lakes are extensively distributed in Qinghai, Tibet, Xinjiang, Inner Mongolia, Gansu, Ningxia, Shaanxi, and Shanxi. There are 2,848 lakes whose area is larger than one square kilometer in China, of which more than 1,000 are salt lakes, with an area of 45,870 km^2, accounting for 55% of China's total lake area.

Salt lakes refers to lakes with a soluble salt content of over 35g/L in water. There is large amount of soluble salts and useful elements in salt lake water; it provides very important raw materials for chemical and construction industries and agriculture.

4.6.3.1　Salt resources in Xinjiang

Xinjiang lies deep in the inland and is enclosed by mountains. It has an extremely dry climate, especially in the Tarim Basin and the Turpan-Hami Basin. Most lakes in the region have become salt lakes. About 2,000 salt lakes are unevenly distributed in Xinjiang.

These lakes contain 42 kinds of salt minerals including 8 kinds of carbonates, 18 sulphates, 3 borates, 6 chlorides and 7 nitrates. The sodium nitre and Magnesium nitre are local special minerals.

The lakes mostly are of sodium sulphate type, and a few of them are of carbonate and chloride types. The water in these lakes usually has a salinity of 70–200 g/L and maximum 494 g/L. The main salt ions in salt lake water are Na^+, K^+, Mg^{2+}, Ca^{2+}, Cl^-, SO_4^{2-}, HCO^- and CO_3^{2-}, accounting for 99%, they also contain B, Li, I, U and Th.

Wuzongbulak salt bed has a proved reserve of 400,000 tons of potassium nitrate.

Furthermore, these lakes teem with rock salt and Glauber salts, especially in Dabancheng, Aibihu, Balikunhu, Aidinhu and Qijiaojing salt lakes.

4.6.3.2　Salt Resources in Qaidam Basin

Qaidam means salt marsh in the Mongolian language. It covers 120,000 km^2, including 1 fresh lake, 7 semi-saltwater lakes, 27 salt lakes and 6 dried sebkhas. The basin can be divided into three zones: ①Mangya down faulted zone. Some sulphate lakes are distributed in this zone. They contain common salt, gypsum and glaube's salt. In the Dalangtan sebkha potassium content is very high, with a potassium chloride content of over 6 g/L in water. ② Severe downfaulted zone. Deposits include sulphates and chlorides, Li, K and Mg compounds. ③ Salt lake region in fault-block zone. This zone has a boron-potassium-salt mine and rock salt mine.

There are 45 kinds of salt minerals in the Qaidam Basin, including 7 carbonates, 20 sulphates, 12 borates and 6 chlorides. The soluble salt content in water is very high, on average 340.747 g/L, The highest value of 555.065 g/L occurs in the Niulangzhinu lake, and the lowest value appears in Gahai lake. Main ions in lake water are Na^+, Mg^{2+}, K^+, Ca^{2+}, Cl^-, so_4^{2-}, co_3^{2-} and HCO_3^-.

The proved reserves of potassium, magnesium, Glauber's salt, lithium and strontium rank first in China, while the reserves of boron and bromine rank second.

4.6.3.3　Salt Lakes in Inner Mongolia

There are more than 380 salt lakes in Inner Mongolia. Alkaline lakes are mostly located in Ordos region salt lakes in Alya, and glaube's salt in the Hulun Buir, the Xilin Gol and the Ulan Qab regions.

The minerals in these lakes include 8 kinds of carbonates, 7 sulphates and 3 chlorides.

The salinity of lake water is over 100 g/L or even reaches 4,279 g/L in the Hatongchahan Lake. The average pH value is 8.9, maximum 10.82 in Hatongchahan Lake, minimum 6.75 in Beidachi.

Main ions in lake water are Na^+, K^+, Ca^{2+}, Mg^{2+}, Cl^-, SO_4^{2-}, HCO_3^-, CO_3^{2-} and 27 other trace elements.

Edible salt development–Jilantai salt field is shown in Fig. 4-9.

Fig. 4-9　Edible salt development–Jilantai salt field

4.7　Tourism resources

Desert landforms, unique natural landscapes, historic sites and ancient irrigation projects etc. are important tourist resources in Chinese deserts. The Silk Road, passing through Gobi and desert in west China, has long been a famous and popular tourism destination. Currently, most tourist activities are limited to the periphery of deserts, but these activities will be extended to the interior of desert in the future.

Sheep-skin boats in the Yellow River are shown in Fig. 4-10.

4.7.1　Unique phenomena in desert

(1) Booming sand. Booming sand is a kind of sand that can emit a loud noise when someone walks on it. In China, booming sand mountains are mainly distributed in Dunhuang, Shapotou, Xiangshawan and Barkol.

(2) Sand therapy. Sand therapy, burying the human body with sand in the desert, is a unique treatment measure. It has special curative effects for some diseases.

Turpan in Xinjiang is an ideal place for sand therapy. The best time for sand therapy is between June through August, when the air temperature is about 40 °C.

(3) Wood fossil. Wood fossils are distributed extensively throughout the Junggar Basin In North

General Gobi, Qitai County, more than 10,000 wood fossils have been found. The longest one is 30 m and they may be more than 2 m in diameter.

Fig. 4-10   Sheep-skin boats in the Yellow River (Photographed by Li Chunsheng)

4.7.2   Natural scenic spots

4.7.2.1   Desert Lakes

(1) Crescent Spring in Dunhuang. The Crescent Spring, with a length of 218 m, a width of 54 m and a depth of 5 m, is a crescent-shaped lake in Dunhuang. It has been a famous scenic spot for 2,000 years.

(2) Bosten Lake. The Bosten Lake, located in the Yanqi Basin to the south of the Tianshan Mountains, is the largest fresh-water lake in China.

Its length is 55 km and width is 25 km, with a total area of 998 km^2.   Its average depth is 8–15 m, and the deepest part is 165 km. Several rivers, originating in the Tianshan Mountains, flow into the lake.

4.7.2.2   Yardang

A yardang is a typical aeolian landform. They exist in eastern Xinjiang, western Gansu and the western Qaidam Basin. Because yardangs are located in the hinterland of deserts and are difficult to access, they are poorly developed as a tourism resource.

In Xinjiang, many yardang landforms look like abandoned ancient castles despite being the natural result of wind erosion and water erosion. Local people call them "ghost cities". The Wuerhe, Qitai and Wubu ghost cities are among the most famous ghost cities.

4.7.3　Other scenic spots

4.7.3.1　Genghis Khan Mausoleum

The Genghis Khan Mausoleum, located in Ejin Horo Qi of Inner Mongolia, is a cenotaph of Genghis Khan. It has become a famous tourist attraction, but recently. desertification has started to quickly develop in the grasslands around this mausoleum. (Fig. 4-11)

Fig. 4-11　Genghis Khan Mausoleum

4.7.3.2　Karez

A karez is a horizontal underground channel that conveys water from aquifers in the piedmont alluvial fans to low-elevation farmlands. According to statistical data there are more than 2,000 strips of karez in Xinjiang, with the longest a length of 30 km. Water in a karez is fed entirely by gravity, thus eliminating the need for pumps. Karezs can be found in Hami, Shanshan, Turpan, Tuokexun, Qitai, Mulei, Yiwu and Balikun in Xinjiang.

4.7.3.3　Ancient city relics

Many once-flourishing cities and towns in desert regions of China have been abandoned. Several of these ancient cities have also been recorded in literature.

1) Loulan City

Loulan City relic is located in the eastern Taklimakan Desert, on the lower reaches of the Konqi River. It was once an important town on the Silk Road, and it was a center of trade, agriculture, communication, culture and military.

In 200 BC Loulan Kingdom had a population of 14,000, but after 300 AD it suddenly disappeared.

In 1901, Sven Hedin, a Swedish geographer, found the remains of Loulan City. Since then, many expeditions have been done here.

2) Black City

Black City relic is in Ejin Qi of Inner Mongolia, now lying in the desert area of lower reach of the Heihe River. It was built as a center of immigration for land reclamation during the Han and Tang dynasties. In its peak, the population exceeded 10 thousands. The total area of the city is about 160,000 m^2. The length of its wall is 440 m in west-east direction, and 370 m in north-south direction.

The Black City was abandoned due to land desertification, rivers changing course, and wars.

3) Gaochang City

Gaochang City relic is located 40 km southeast of Turpan City in Xinjiang. Once the capital of the Gaochang Kingdom, it flourished during the Han, Wei and Jin dynasties, but it was later abandoned in the early Ming Dynasty.

Gaochang City is divided into three sections, namely the outer city, the inner city and the palace. The outer city is a square city, the total length of its wall is more than 5 km, and its total area is more than 2,000,000 m^2. The height of its wall is 12 m. The length of the inner city wall is more than 3 km. Huge buildings are found in the inner city. The city was once a political, military, cultural and economic center in the Turpan area.

Drying up rivers and wars led to the abandonment of this ancient city.

References

1 ： 1,000,000 Land Resource Map of China. 1991a. 1 ： 1,000,000 Land Resource Map of China. Xi'an: Xi'an Maps Press

1 ： 1,000,000 Land Resource Map of China. 1991b. Land Resource Database of 1 ： 1,000,000 Land Resource Map of China. Beijing: China Renmin University Press

Cao Xinsun. 1990. Land degradation and control measurement in Wulanaodu Region. In: Integrated Control Research of Windblown Sand and Drought in the Eastern Inner Mongolia. Beijing: Science Press.

China Meteorological Bureau. 1994. Atlas of Chinese Climate Resource. Beijing: SinoMaps Press

Gao An, Chen Caifu, Gao Qianzhao. 1993. Reversed research of desertified lands in semi-humid regions. In: Supporting Technology Research on Integrated Control of Shallow Depression among Rivers. Beijing: Science Press, 30–38

Geng Kuanhong. 1986. Climate in Desert Regions in China. Beijing: Science Press, 4–16

Jing Guihe. 1990. System Dynamics and construction plan of wood-grass compound ecosystem in the middle-western sandy lands in Jilin province. In: Jing Guihe. Landscape Ecological Construction of Desertified Lands in the Middle-western Sandy Lands in Jilin Province. Shenyang: Northeast Normal University Press, 66–81

Li Fuxing, Chen Longheng. 1994. Strong sandstorm disaster and countermeasure. Natural Disaster Reduction in China, 4(2): 35–39

Liu Xinmin, Zhao Halin, Xu Bin. 1993. Mechanism of destruction and restoration of horqin steppe ecosystem. In: Liu Xinmi et al. Integrated Regulating Research of Ecological Environment in Horqin Sandy Land. Lanzhou: Gansu Science and Technology Publishing House, 12–26

Liu Xinmin. 1982. Research on controlling desertified lands in Northern Linze Oasis of Gansu province. Journal of Desert Research, 2: 9–15

Ma Shiwei, Ma Yuming, Yao Honglin et al. 1998. Desert Science. Hohhot: Inner Mongolia People's Publishing House. (In Chinese)

Ministry of Water Resources. 1989. Symposium of Water Resource Assessment. Beijing: Water Resources and Electric Power Press

"Natural Resources Series of China" Editorial Board. 1995. Natural Resources Series of China (Climate). Beijing: China Environmental Science Publishing House

"Natural Resources Series of China" Editorial Board. 1996a. Natural Resources Series of China (Qinghai). Beijing: China Environmental Science Publishing House

"Natural Resources Series of China" Editorial Board. 1996b. Natural Resources Series of China (Ningxia). Beijing: China Environmental Science Publishing House

"Natural Resources Series of China" Editorial Board. 1996c. Natural Resources Series of China (Inner Mongolia). Beijing: China Environmental Science Publishing House

"Natural Resources Series of China" Editorial Board. 1996d. Natural Resources Series of China (Gansu). Beijing: China Environmental Science Publishing House

"Physical Geography of China" Editorial Board of CAS. 1979. Physical Geography of China—Animal Geography. Beijing: Science Press.

Tan Guanri, Yan Jiyuan, Zhu Ruizhao. 1985. Applied Climate. Shanghai: Shanghai Science and Technology Publishing House

Wang Sibo, Yan Ganyuan. 1983. Xinjiang Rodent Fauna. Ürümqi: Xinjiang People's Publishing House

Wang Tao, Chen Guangting, Qian Zhengan et al. 2001. Dust storm status and countermeasures in northern China. Journal of Desert Research, 214: 322–327

Wang Xiangting. 1991. Gansu Vertebrate Fauna. Lanzhou: Gansu Science and Technology Publishing House

Xia Xuncheng, Liu Chongshun. 1991. Desertification in Xinjiang and Control of Sandstorm Disaster. Beijing: Science Press, 64–84

Xia Xuncheng, Yang Gensheng. 1996. Sand Storm Hazards and Control in Northwest China. Beijing: China Environment Science Press

Xu Deyuan. 1989. Agroclimatic Resource and Its Division in Xinjiang. Beijing: China Meteorological Press

Yu Huning, Li Weiguang. 1985. Analysis of Agroclimatic Resource and Its Use. Beijing: China Meteorological Press.

Zheng Zuoxin. 1976. Chinese Birds Distribution List. Beijing: Science Press

Zhu Zhenda, Chen Guangting. 1994. Sandy Desertification in China. Beijing: Science Press

Zhu Zhenda, Wu Zheng, Liu Shu. 1980. Sand Deserts in China. Beijing: Science Press

Part II
Evolution of Deserts
and Aeolian Desertification
in China

Chapter 5
Evolution of Deserts

5.1 Formation conditions for deserts

Almost all of the provinces in northern China have deserts and aeolian desertified land. The question is how did they came into existence? After the 1950s, research groups in the earth sciences have done much work regarding the formation period, cause and evolution dynamics of deserts in northern China. Especially in the last 20 years, some questions have been solved or nearly solved owing to the improvement of research techniques and the accumulation of data. But some other questions are still in debate. For example, the formation period of deserts in northern China is a difficult question. As a whole, we can regard aeolian deposits as deposit stratum, and the traditional methods to date the strata include ancient-biologic fossil, ^{14}C, thermoluminescence, element disintegration and so on. The difficulties in dating desert strata are as follows: firstly, a desert is a strong oxidation environment, where animal and plant species are scarce, so it is hard to find biological materials in it. Secondly, various dating methods are still in their initial stages, and their fluctuating values are higher than their true values. At present, the methods that researchers use most frequently are still the traditional stratigraphical correlation methods, in which there are many uncertain factors, such as lacking an accepted standard stratigraphical profile. All of the above make it hard to date desert deposits, and therefore there are still some debates as to the formation period of deserts in northern China.

It is without doubt that deserts are the result of dry climate. The main factors leading to the extremely dry climate in northern China include: (a) Far distance from oceans, moisture rich air can not reach in. (b) Topographical conditions cause airstreams to sink locally in basins, especially in western desert basins where airstreams are greatly blocked due to the uplift of the Tibetan Plateau. (c) The uplift of the Tibetan plateau disrupts the climatic pattern of East Asia, which causes the differentiation of westerly circulation to form anticyclonic westerly jets north of the Tibetan Plateau, the southwest monsoon and the southeast monsoon in southeast China. All of these result in a drier climate in northwest China. On the other hand, regarding the red oxidation deposits in vast regions in northern China after Mesozoic, it is generally accepted that the environment of northern China had turned dry since the Cretaceous period and that the aridification of climatic environment was a gradually changing process. However, there are still considerable debates as to the formation period of large-scale desert deposits, namely whether or not the appearance of ancient aeolian sand means the onset of a desert period, and whether or not the red desert appearance from the geological period is related to modern deserts.

After years of research, the debate on the nature of these deposits is nearly over. The first is that the current distribution of land and ocean is similar to that of the Cretaceous period, a hundred million years ago. The second is that the Tibetan Plateau started to intensively uplift at the beginning of the Tertiary, 40Ma BP years ago, and rose to 4,000 meters above the sea level and the western regions of China turned into the present landscapes at the beginning of the Quaternary, which is about 2.6Ma BP according to the latest result. Those who insist that China's deserts formed in the Cretaceous period emphasize that after the forming of Eurasia's land-ocean patterns, moist oceanic airstream could not reach the central Asian regions, including northwest China, and deserts began to appear. Furthermore, they divide Chinese desert deposition into three development stages: Cretaceous-early Tertiary desert (red desert), late Tertiary desert (red desert), and Quaternary desert (yellow desert). Those who emphasize that the Tibetan Plateau played a decisive role in the formation of dry climate in northwest China maintain that the drought at the beginning of the Cretaceous period was not strong enough to form vast deserts, and that the Tibetan Plateau's gradual uplift above the height of 4,000 meters hindered moist air corrects from the Indian Ocean to northern regions. This formed several branches of atmospheric circulations that affect Central Asia and East Asia, the climate was extremely dry, and extensive deserts came into existence.

5.1.1   Formation and evolution of dry climate in China

Extreme drought and strong wind are the basic factors for desert formation. Section 2.1 has described the formation and features of dry climate in China. In brief, the far distance of plateau basins from oceans is the background for dry climate in northwest China, and the thermodynamic and dynamic effects of the Tibetan Plateau and its circulation are the main factors for dry climate formation in Central Asia. Here we will provide an overview of the formation and evolution history of dry climate in China.

5.1.1.1   Formation and evolution of dry climate in hinterland of Asia

In 1962, Soviet scholar Cinisene. B. M. explored in his book, *Ancient Geography of Asia*, the evolution of dry climate in Central Asia as follows: "during the Neocene period, mountain-making movement was greatly strengthened in Central Asia, and mountains reached a considerable height by the Pliocene, which resisted airflows over land. The Himalayas prevented the penetration of more and more moist air from the Indian Ocean monsoon. In the meantime, the forming of the Kunlun Mountains, the Qilian Mountains and the Qinling Mountains stopped both the dry airflows from Central Asia and the cold anti-cyclonic airflows from Siberia. So with the gradual uplift of mountains, the closed regions in Central Asia turned into deserts, which were controlled by dry continental air mass." Both the ancient geographical and climatic data of arid northwest regions collected in the last decades, as well as the numerical simulating results from the uplift of the Tibetan Plateau and its effect on atmospheric circulation in China and Central Asia, prove that the uplift of the Tibetan Plateau is the main cause of the evolution of Asian temperate zone deserts. Concerning the evolution history of dry climate in Central Asia, local and international geographical research groups have done much work and achieved a lot of progress in many fields, especially in Quaternary climatic researches relating to the uplift of the Tibetan Plateau and the formation of aeolian loess deposits.

1) From the Cretaceous period to the early Tertiary

According to ancient geographical research, the dry climate in northwest China basically came into being during the time from the Cretaceous period (135–70 Ma BP) to the early Tertiary (70–25 Ma BP), when a large part of China was under the control of subtropical high pressure and northeast trade winds prevailed. One of the notable features of the ancient geographical lithofacies map of China was that there was a red NWW–SEE belt of evaporite rock. Gypsum deposits covered the zone from the Tarim basin to coastal regions in Zhejiang and Fujian provinces. The red rock strata of the early Cretaceous contains thin interlayers of gypsum, gingko species were rare, leaflet fern species were found, and pine and cypress were widespread. Northeast China and regions to the south of the Tanggula Mountains are respectively a humid temperate zone and a tropical zone. At the end of the Cretaceous period, the above mentioned arid zone expanded and the red layer covered an even larger region. In the early Tertiary, with further development of dry climate, xerophilous vegetation, especially Chinese ephedra, appeared and thousands of separate deposit basins of different sizes were distributed in dry and hot subtropics.The deposits contained oxidated red mudstone, sandstone and glauberite, which is an indicator mineral for high temperatures (Fig. 5-1). The thickness of gypsum layer could even reach more than 300 meters in the Tarim Basin. Besides gypsum deposits, halite was common in northern China's southern regions and in the middle and lower reaches of the Yangtze River. The early Tertiary sedimentary facies and the special distribution of animal and plant species clearly suggest that there were subtropical sparse grassland or semi-desert landscape in northwest China, even in the basin of the Yangtze River, and that ancient climate exhibited an obvious latitudinal zonal distribution at that time.

As a result of the Indian Plate's thrust into the Eurasian Plate, the Tibetan Plate shifted northwards, and thus caused the distortion of the arid zone of China.

2) The Tertiary

About 40 Ma BP the collision between the Indian Plate and the Asian Plate caused the disappearance of the Tethys Sea between India and China. At that time, Africa was closer to the European Plate, and the continental area in the subtropics of Asia, Europe and Africa notably expanded. From then on, the Indian Plate kept moving northwards at a speed of about 5cm per year, and the Tibetan region moved 2,000 km since the late Cretaceous period. By 20 Ma BP, the Indian Ocean basically came into being and the remaining sea in northwest China also disappeared in the

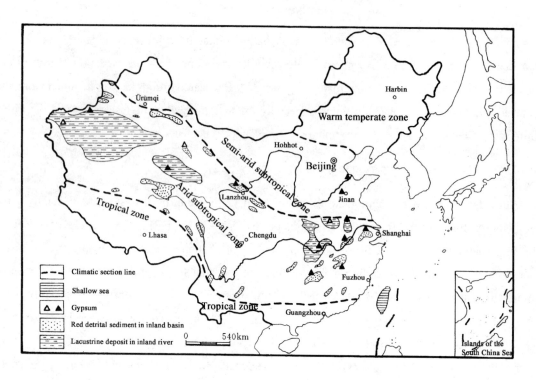

Fig. 5-1　Dry subtropics and their aberrations in China at the end of the early Tertiary

late Miocene. At the end of the Pliocene, the Tibetan region was an original plateau about 1,000 meters high, which basically changed the topographic structure of East Asia in the early Tertiary. At the same period with the Cenozoic land's expansion and the seawater's retreat, another feature of the earth's environmental change was the arrival of cold climate and the Quaternary Ice Age. Generally speaking, the air temperature of the early Tertiary was 10 ℃ higher than that of present, the temperature difference between high latitude and low latitude was smaller than present, and the climate was relatively uniform. At that time, except for parts of the warm temperate zone, most regions of the East Asian continent belonged to subtropical and tropical zones, and subtropical high pressure covered the central part of the continent. In China, there was sparse grassland or semi-desert landscape in the basin of the Yangtze River and south of Xinjiang. Sediment deposits generally contained evaporates such as rock salt and gypsum. However, after entering the Oligocene, the climate started to become remarkably cold in polar regions. For example, data from a deep ocean oxygen isotope covering the past 55 Ma indicates that there were abrupt changes occurring in stages under the background of the constant increase of $\delta^{18}O$. The first abrupt increase of $\delta^{18}O$ took place in the early Oligocene, 36 Ma BP, which was the same period as the first expansion of the Antarctic glacier. The second took place in the mid-Miocene, 15 Ma BP, which was the same period as the second expansion of the Antarctic glacier that covered the whole Antarctic continent. The third took place between the end of the Pliocene and the beginning of the Quaternary, 2.4 Ma BP, which indicated that land glaciers began to develop extensively and the Earth entered into an ice age. These three abrupt climatic changes had great effects on the global environment. According to estimates, the falling amplitude of global air temperature was over 12 °C in the past 40 Ma. The cold trend of the Earth's climate since the Mesozoic caused the climatic zones of middle and high latitude regions to separate and close off. This caused the height of the troposphere to decrease and the vertical gradient increase at the same time, which strengthened the influences of the difference between the land-ocean distribution and topographical height on the atmospheric circulation.

Research results show that land plays a leading role in the seasonal change of land-ocean temperature difference. The main reason why the early Tertiary did not create monsoons is that land did not expand into the latitude scope controlled by the peculiar sinking of subtropical high pressure, and especially that South Asia and North Africa were covered by ocean, which was not conducive to form low pressure terrestrial heat. In the late Tertiary, the land area obviously expanded and the land-oceanic distribution outline was almost the same as the present, which had two effects: one was that it made continental summer temperatures rise and the other was that it made winter temperatures acutely fall. Therefore, the continentality of the climate was strengthened, the land-oceanic thermodynamic difference was enlarged, and the seasonal features also became obvious. All of these represent the features of a monsoon climate. However, the altitude of the Tibetan Plateau was less than 1,000 meters in the late Tertiary, so if there was monsoon at that time, the result should be close to that without mountains, that is to say, the northern limit of the South Asian monsoon could only extend to central and southern India, about 15°N, the basin of the Yangtze River and mid-latitude regions were dry without rain, precipitation over the Tibetan Plateau was minimal, and the corresponding rain belt appeared on the boundary between the continent and ocean. Judging from the lithology of deposits, we knew that obvious seasonal changes took place over much of the East Asian continent and humidity difference appeared from west to east during the late Tertiary. For example, the Shandong Peninsula and the Liaodong Peninsula both had heterogeneous formations and alternating strata of coarse and fine grains. Clastic rocks in basins between the Changbai Mountains were also characteristic of seasonal deposits with horizontal and micro-laminations, and reflected the alternating cycle of dry and wet seasons. In inland regions such as Shanxi and Shaanxi provinces, the deposit was dominated by red soil-like deposits, and the climate was relatively drier than the eastern part of China.

Hipparion laterite and red weathering crust are extensively distributed in the inland region of northern China. They developed in environments with good drainage, high temperature and distinct seasonal variations which facilitated strong oxidation. In the Pliocene, the Hipparion group was basically distributed in latitudinal direction in Eurasia, so we can infer that the developing environment of Hipparion laterite belongs to the subtropical wet-dry type. Such climatic distribution patterns can help us infer that a subtropical high belt still existed in the East Asian continent during that period, and other regions were still controlled by planetary wind systems. For example, the carbonate content in Neocene sediments in the North Jiangsu Plain was between 2% and 7.8%, and 24% on the southern edge. In the Fang Mountains near Nanjing City, alternating layers consisting of sandstone and gravel were calcareously cemented, and judging by depositing fossils, it should belong to a much drier and hotter environment. The Tibetan region and the Tanggula region were in the savanna, and in the north, like the Kunlun Mountains, it was mainly covered by sparse grassland, and lacustrine strata contain rock salt and gypsum. In the Qaidam Basin, to the north of the Kunlun Mountains, Pliocene gypsum and other salts were well developed, that is the so called first salt-forming period. Paleo-aeolian soil or paleo-sand dunes from the late Miocene to the Pliocene have been found in recent years. A reasonable explanation for all these phenomena is that they are undoubtedly the results of dry climate controlled by a subtropical high.

3) The Quaternary

Under the background of the quasi–periodic fluctuations of global climate, the Asian monsoon seemed to strengthen in the early Quaternary. The most direct evidence was that the landscape of subtropical savannas had gradually disappeared and been replaced by evergreen broad-leaf and deciduous broad-leaf forests. For example, in the Pliocene, subtropical broad-leaf tree species were abundant in central China regions, and there were also many kinds of xeric species. In the early Pleistocene, the sparse-tree grassland controlled by the subtropical high gradually turned into a subtropical evergreen forest. In western China, plant fossils of the early Pleistocene were also evergreen species. For instance, pollens in the layers of the Tiebanhe formation in the Tarim Basin were mainly *Populus* and *Fagus*; phytolites of deciduous broad-leaf forests such as *Salix heterochroma*, *Chinese ash* and so on were found in ancient travertine at the northern slopes of the mid Kunlun Mountains. The layers from the early Pleistocene in the Qaidam Basin included much pollen of aquatic plants, which reflected the stop of salification and a stable water surface, high water temperatures and abundant nutrients.

In addition to including abundant tree species of warm temperate deciduous and broad-leaf forests, there were subtropical species in the Tertiary such as *Hemlock spruce*, *Cedar*, *Podocarpus*, *Hickory*, *Sweetgum* and others located in the layers of the Gonghe formation in the Gonghe Basin during the period from 2.26–0.69 Ma BP From the vegetation contrast, annual precipitation during the early Quaternary was obviously higher than today in the western regions of China, suggesting the Tibetan Plateau was located at an altitude with the highest precipitation. It could draw the southwest monsoon into the mainland without impeding the warm and wet airflow entering in the north of plateau. At the same time, air which flowed through the plateau was forced to rise to the highest level, which caused the most precipitation cloud in the plateau and its surrounding regions. In this case, palynofloras and ancient animals were different in the same magnetostrata in the eastern and western regions of China, which reflected the latitudinal zonality of the climate. Because the climate was warm and natural zones distributed from east to west were very different from today, the winter monsoon was weak and it influenced limited regions.

Palaeolakes developed widely and were the largest in eastern Asian, accompanied by an enhanced summer monsoon and disappearance of the subtropical dry zone. This period is called the "great lake-forming period". For example, the Pleistocene series lake or fluviolacustrine formations of southwest Yuanmao and Xigeda, northern Sanmen, Yushe and Nihewan, northeast Baitushan and Taikang formation were widespread from the south to the north in China. Freshwater lakes occupied almost the whole Qaidam Basin during the period of 2.32-1.6 Ma BP and the ancient Gonghe Lake also existed for a long period of time in the Gonghe Basin beginning from 2.26 Ma BP. According to the analyses of lacustrine strata and ancient lakeshore terraces, at early Quaternary there were many large lakes in the Lop Nur area of the Tarim Basin, Juyanhai area of the Alxa Plateau, Jiertai area of the Ulan Buh Desert and the Yinchuan Basin. The existence of so many freshwater lakes suggests that the climate was more humid than present. At the latter part of early Pleistocene, because of the deterioration of lake water quality and nutrition, many lakes shrank and gradually disappeared, which, in addition to construction factors, reflected the tendency for a dry climate. Because it was in the interior of the Eurasia and in the high latitude, northwest China started to experience a temperate continental climate. Its nature and origin were entirely different from the subtropical high dry climate in the Tertiary, and the hydro-thermal climate was "dry-cold" rather than "dry-hot". Afterwards, moisture carried by westerly circulations from the Atlantic gradually decreased, and the Siberian High Pressure was strengthened along, with the continuous uplift of the Tibetan Plateau and its periphery mountains. The above circumstances accelerated desertification in northwest China. As a result, the Taklimakan desert and other deserts markedly expanded.

5.1.1.2　Role of the near-surface winter monsoon in the formation and evolution of dry climate

Besides dry climate, the near-surface wind system was also an important controlling factor in the formation of deserts in China. Especially in winter, Eurasia was under the control of the strong Siberian High Pressure. Due to the open Gobi and grassland in the north, both the dry continental monsoon and cold current from the Arctic Ocean could enter this region. In the regions near 97°E, they were divided into the northwest wind and the northeast wind by the Tibetan Plateau. Northwest winds blew along the Qilian Mountains and Hexi Corridor to the southeast, controlling the central and eastern deserts. Northeast winds blew along the Altun Mountains to the Tarim Basin and were restricted by the basin terrain, and this usually resulted in anti-cyclonic circulation over the basin. In addition, a strong weathering effect, salinity accumulation and bare land under dry climate all strengthened the wind force to make it the most direct and important agent shaping the aeolian sand landscape. Under the movement of wind, loose and bare sandy land surfaces experienced strong wind erosion, and sands were blown up and carried away until the wind subsisted or was blocked by barriers. When wind-sand current could not carry sands further, sands accumulated to form dunes in the desert, and dust accumulated to form loess outside of the desert. As time progressed, dunes constantly grew and expanded and eventually vast deserts came into existence.

On the origin of the Asian Winter Monsoon, one popular view is that the initiation of loess deposition in China meant the establishment of the East Asian Monsoon Circulation. According to this background, the initial deposition of loess in the Loess Plateau occurred about 2.4 Ma BP, and therefore the establishment time of the modern East Asian Monsoon was also about 2.4 Ma BP. Some even suggest that the aeolian deposits of the Loess Plateau and the original development of the ancient East Asian Monsoon started at least about 6.5 Ma BP when the Tibetan Plateau reached its meaningful height. We can not fully support this view. As is well known, there are two main theories about the origin of loess. One is the traditional aeolian theory, which asserts that the loess above the Hipparion laterite was formed by wind. The other is the aqueous theory, or multi-cause theory, which asserts that the causes of loess are complex. As far as we are concerned, we prefer the typical aeolian theory, and believe that the temporal and spatial distribution changes of aeolian loess have some relation to the continuous strengthening of the winter monsoon. Therefore, we question the hypothesis that the initiation of loess deposition in China resulted from the establishment of the East Asian Monsoon Circulation because the deposition of loess cannot simply be the result of the winter monsoon.

Firstly, the latitudinal zonality of loess distribution is in consistent with the azonal monsoon distribution. Loess in the world is divided into two types, one is called "warm" loess, which is connected with deserts; another is called "cold" loess, which is related to continental ice sheets, both of them belong to the loess which is connected with planetary wind system and upper air current. It mainly occurs in the Northern Hemisphere, including the Rhine River basin, the Danube River basin, middle Asia, Yellow River basin of China, North America's Missouri River basin and Mississippi River basin etc. Its latitude range is 35°–62°N, which forms the world's discontinuous distributed zone of loess. Some places in the Southern Hemisphere, including New Zealand and Barana in South America, also have fragmentary distribution of loess, and it also occurs in mid-latitudes. It is evident that loess distribution is zonal; its basic cause is latitudinal climate zones controlled by planetary wind systems rather than the azonal monsoon circulation.

Secondly, the transport path of loess, to a considerable degree, depends on the high altitude westerly circulation and is different from the moving direction of the lower winter monsoon. According to the research of historical "dust rain" events in eastern China and several recent dust storm events, it was confirmed by Liu Dongsheng et al. that in the winter half-year, strong dry cold airflow and westerly airflow can carry the dust of Central Asia as far as several hundred to several thousand kilometers. Satellite observation indicates that loess and dust materials from dust source areas in northwest China can be carried by northwest winds and high altitude airflow across the mainland of China to the East China Sea, Korea and Japan, or even travel 9,600 km and be deposited in the northern Pacific Ocean and Hawaii, covering an area of 1 million–10 million km^2. It's obvious that the transport route of the upper dust is different from that of the lower winter monsoon.

Thirdly, loess dust rain events mostly occur in late spring to early summer, but not in winter when the winter monsoon prevails. According to meteorologic observation data, modern dust storms often occur between March and May.

Actually, the deposition of the loess plateau is polygenous in the early Pleistocene. The loess plateau is the center of loess distribution in China and mainly exists in a semi-circular ring closed off by the Qilian Mountains, the Qinling Mountains and the Taihang Mountains. Just as what many scholars think the deposits of the Loess Plateau in the early Holocene was not aeolian loess; there were other deposits such as lake deposits, sand or fluvial deposits. The bottom of the loess profile in the center of the Loess Plateau which is red or reddish and whose range is narrow is called Wucheng loess. It is quite different from the Lishi loess and Malan loess that is above the "Wucheng" loess in the structure. Due to obvious influence from surface water flow, this loess has not the feature of climate change in the Pleistocene, materiality cold and warm, dry and wet, so it belongs to pre-loess, loess-like, old loess, red soil or loess-like rock.

From the above we know that the typical loess deposit in eastern China is formed by several factors or dominated by wind transport. Teng Zhihong and Shen Xiping, through the comparative research of the representative loess profiles in western China, defined the lower limit and age of the typical wind loess; it began with the lower silt layer in the loess section and started to deposit at the end of the early Pleistocene, 1.20 Ma BP. Table 5-1 explains the universality of the quaternary aeolian deposition in China that began in the early Pleistocene. It is obvious that although the locations of the profiles are far away from each other, and the depth of the loess sediment is not the same, the initial deposition time is nearly identical, and 60% was deposited after 1.20 Ma BP. In the spatial distribution, the evidence about the intensification of the winter monsoon is that the southern edge of loess sediment at the end of the early Pleistocene changed from 34°N to 30°N. That is to say, 1.10 Ma B P is the turning point of the variation of loess susceptibility. As viewed from the variations of the B value (the ratio of paleosol susceptibility to loess susceptibility), we can find the fluctuation of B value is weaker in the early Holocene, but stronger from 1.10 Ma BP to 0.5 Ma BP. Such laws were also reflected in many loess sections. At the same time, deep oceanic $\delta^{18}O$ curve shows a low-level, low amplitude and high frequency fluctuations before 1.20 Ma BP. But starting from 0.9 Ma BP, it shows a high amplitude and low-frequency cold and warm fluctuations. The reason for the sudden change in the Pleistocene climatic frequency may be that the oceanic monsoon transformed into a continental monsoon, and the climatic contrasts between glacial and interglacial periods become large.

Not coming alone but in pairs, the netlike red soil developed on the terraces of Poyang Lake and the tributaries of the Yangtze River was formed around 1.2 Ma B.P. according to paleomagnetism and TL dating. Generally speaking, the dry and cold climate during the glacial period was favorable for the deposition of huge thick loess, and the netlike red soil was the product of desilication and richening iron and aluminum in the wet and hot interglacial period. Yang Huairen pointed out that the netlike red soil formed after the end of the early Pleistocene is different from the red earth formed before that time, and showed the changes of dry and wet seasons. Globally, the intensity and frequency of debris flow in eastern China is the highest in the world, which is caused by rainstorms or a direct result of monsoon rainstorms. As one of the monsoon geomorphological processes, the development degree of debris flow means frequent rainstorms, and this is an indicator of the intensity of the East Asian monsoon. The research by Cui Zhijiu et al. shows that the deposition pattern of monsoon debris flow only occurred in or after the mid-Pleistocenes, so we can infer that the modern winter monsoon basically formed in the mid-Quaternary. In addition, not only were the deposits of the Yangtze River in the mid-Pleistocene coarse, their sorting was poor. This is quite different from the early Pleistocene gravel layer and suggests the powerful influence of the monsoon climate. The modern valley of the Yangtze River was formed beginning from the mid-Pleistocene. It is the product of the monsoon climate as well as the rapid uplift of the Tibetan Plateau up to 3,000–3,500 m.

Table 5-1　The age of the typical loess deposits in China

Section name	Thickness (m)	B/M depth (m)	Age (Ma BP)	Dating method	Source of the material
Yutian, Xinjiang	120	73	1.2	K-Ar	Teng Zhihong et al., 1995
Dadunling, Xinning, Qinghai	250	147	1.2	paleomagnetism	Zeng Yongnian et al., 1992
Mengda mountain, Xunhua, Qinghai	105	101	0.76	paleomagneticm	Chen Fahu et al., 1993
Xiaoshigou, Wuwei Gansu	115	105	0.8	paleomagneticm	Wang Nai'ang et al., 1997
Jiuzhoutai, Lanzhou, Gansu	336	186	1.3	paleomagneticm	Burbank et al., 1985
Dunwa mountain, Lanzhou, Gansu	207	130	1.2	paleomagneticm	Zhang Yutian et al., 1991
Yandonggou, Lanzhou, Gansu	120	90	1.67	paleomagneticm	Zhu Junjie et al., 1994
Dongshanding, Linxia, Gansu	60	42	1.04	paleomagneticm	Wang Jianli, 1996
Caoxian, Jingyuan, Gansu	505	285	1.4	paleomagneticm	Yue Leping et al., 1991
Nuanquangou, Longxi, Gansu	95	48	1.15	paleomagneticm	Wang Junshu et al., 1992
Baicaoyuan, Huining, Gansu			0.66	paleomagneticm	Liu Junfeng, 1992
Bailongjiang, Wudu, Gansu	55	53	0.8	paleomagneticm	Fang et al., 1998
Huoxianggou, Xifeng, Gansu	87	55	1.2	paleomagneticm	Yue Leping, 1985
Changshougou, Baoji, Shaanxi		84	1.2	paleomagneticm	Yue Leping et al., 1996
Youhe, Weinan, Shaanxi	79	57.1	1.2	paleomagneticm	Yue Leping et al., 1996
Drill W7, Weinan, Shaanxi	128	84	1.2	paleomagneticm	Zhang Zonggu, 1989
Gongwangling, Lantian, Shaanxi		35	1.18	paleomagneticm	Liu Dongsheng et al., 1985
Duanjiapo, Lantian, Shaanxi	132	36.5	2.48	paleomagneticm	Yue Leping et al., 1989
Heimugou, Luochuan, Shaanxi	130	54.5	2	paleomagneticm	Liu Dongsheng et al., 1985
Yaozicun, Luochuan, Shaanxi			1.2	paleomagneticm	Wang Yongyan et al., 1982
Luojiayuan, Yulin, Shaanxi	80	56	1.1	paleomagneticm	Gao Shangyu et al., 1992
Liushugou, Wucheng, Shaanxi	118	105	0.9	paleomagneticm	Li Huamei et al., 1974
Wangning, Yushe, Shaanxi		7.5	1.15	paleomagneticm	Cao Jiaxin et al., 1995
Zhangbianyuan, Shanxian, Henan	75	57	1.2	paleomagneticm	Yue Leping, 1985

The nature of the difference between the modern East Asian monsoon and the paleo-monsoon is the annual temperature range. Especially the main feature of the East Asian monsoon climate is that the temperature in winter is lower than other places in the same latitude. There is no winter in areas south of 35° N in other parts of the world, but the East Asian continent is quite different; not only is the 0°C isotherm almost the same as the Qinling-Huaihe line in eastern China, but there are also 3 or 4 months' winter even in the Jianghuai basin of China. The northern limit of the subtropics is 5–7 degrees south than that in east America (38°–40°N) and about 10 degree south than that in Europe and the Mediterranean. If we use the theory that the temperature difference in the middle latitude zone is 0.6 °C per latitude, the middle latitude zone in East Asia would be 6° lower than that in the area with the same latitude all over the world after the modern East Asian monsoon circulation formed. In other words, after the formation of the modern continental monsoon, the climate in northern China changed from subtropics to warm temperate zone. The research showed that the Quaternary flora in China was formed based on the Tertiary flora. The composition of vegetation generally began to update in the Quaternary, and epibiotic species in Tertiary decreased gradually. There were many epibiotic species in north part of China in early Pleistocene, but in the mid Pleistocene ginkgo, metasequoia, silver fir, tulip tree, katsura tree diminished quickly in the north, and they only survived in the eastern, southern and middle parts. In the Wucheng loess deposits there are many fossils of vertebrates and many of which were left from the Tertiary, such as Hipparion and Prosiphneus sinensis. In the Lishi and Malan loess, it is difficult to find the species of the Tertiary and most of the fossils we found are recent species. Another example is the animal population of the Lantian princess ridge. At the end of the early Pleistocene (1.15–1.10 Ma BP), some animal species in the north and south had strong features of Oriental realm animals, such as pandas, hunting leopards, sword-teethed elephant, claw animals and tufted deer. Secondly, there are very few species of the Tertiary, such as sword-teethed tiger and the Lee cow, which are typical species of the early Pleistocene. When the Chenjiawo fauna appeared in the early mid-Pleistocene, it had already become a Palearctic realm and it had no southern features. Of the 14 animal fossil species, almost all of them appeared in the mid-Pleistocene and some of them even exist today. It is difficult to explain the reason why it is quite different between the two fauna that is only less than 25 km from each other and it reveals that the climate pattern of the Asian continent completely changed around 1.10 Ma BP, from a subtropical climate to a temperate zone monsoon climate. All of these prove that the modern winter monsoon circulation started to establish at the end of the Tertiary or the early Pleistocene rather than the end of the Tertiary or the beginning of the Quaternary, especially before the mid-Pleistocene.

5.1.2 Origin of sand materials in deserts

Dry and windy climate is a prerequisite to form a desert, but a desert can not be formed by dry climate alone. For example, annual precipitation in eastern Xinjiang, the western Alxa Plateau, the Tarim Basin, the Qaidam Basin and the mountainous areas of the Hexi Corridor is less than 100 mm, the climate is extremely arid, but these areas are not deserts; instead they are exposed bedrock areas or gravel-covered Gobi. Another example is the Arabian peninsula, which has 2.75 million km^2 of extreme aridity, but only 0.78 million km^2 or one third of this area is covered by sand. In the Sahara area, the sand surface occupies only 10% and most of the area is covered with rock and gravel.

Therefore, desert formation depends on abundant sand sources in addition to the dry climate. In other words, an abundant deposit source is the material basis for the formation of deserts.

Actually, desert sand has two origins, namely aeolian sand and non-aeolian sand. The latter is associated with the paleogeographic environment. It is carried by running water. Their sorting is poor but they have good roundness. In areas where precipitation is adequate and the water net is dense, sands mainly occur in both sides of the ancient or the modern river. For example, in the mountains around the Tarim Basin, precipitation is plentiful and glaciers are widely distributed. Because the climate in high mountains is extremely cold and the temperature between day and night changes sharply, rocks weather easily. In summer, the rainfall and the ice-snow melting water carry large amount of deposits to the basin and deposit there. Generally speaking, the deposits in the piedmont pluvial fan and alluvial fan can reach a thickness of hundreds of meters. The vast alluvial plain in the interior of the basin is formed by huge-thick sediments. The weathering substance and sediment are the main material source of aeolian sand in the Taklimakan Desert and adjacent deserts.

The situation of other deserts in China is just the same. In the Quaternary, the ancient rivers originating from the Tianshan Mountains carried weathering clastic deposits to the Junggar Basin to form a sand layer 2–400 m in thickness. It supplied a source for the Gurbantünggüt Desert. The huge thick Quaternary sediments formed by ancient rivers that originated from the Qilian Mountains offered a rich sand source for the Badain Jaran Desert and the Tengger Desert. In the Ulan Buh Desert, the alluvial deposits were formed by the ancient Yellow River. The diluvial deposits at the piedmont inclined plains of the Helan Mountains, the Langshan Mountains and the Bayinwula Mountains provide the sand source for the desert. The main sand source of the Hulun Buir Sandy Land comes from the Haila stratum (Q_3). The Quaternary loose sediments in the lower reaches of the Xiliao River are more than 130 m thick and it offers an important sand source for the formation of the Horqin Sandy Land. In other words, the reason why there are widespread deserts in China is that in inland basins in northwest China and the Inner Mongolian Plateau, the sand source is rich and it is easily transported by the wind under dry and windy climatic conditions to form deserts.

The dune sands mostly come from nearby underlying deposits. A small part is of long-range transportation origin and they are well sorted. Their mechanical composition is dominated by fine sand with diameters of 0.25–0.1 mm and medium sand with diameters of 0.5–0.25 mm. Since dune sands are mainly produced in local regions, their mineral composition is the same as the underlying deposits. For example, in the Taklimakan Desert, the heavy minerals in aeolian sand and fluvial alluvium are dominated by hornblende followed by mica, epidote and metal minerals; the predominant mineral composition of alluvial fan and dune sand near the Tarim River is mica (43.8%), followed by epidote, while the hornblende content is low (20.8%–30.3%); the eastern Lop Nur region is also dominated by hornblende (38.2%–60.9%). In the Wulanbuhe Desert the heavy mineral in dune sand and underlying deposits is hornblende-epidote with hornblende accounts for 34%–57%, and epidote 16%–39%.

Lower Cretaceous sandstone outcrop in the Ordos Plateau is shown in Fig.5-2.

According to the analyses of the Quaternary paleogeographic data of various deserts of China and comprehensive researches of the characteristics of the sand materials, there are 4 types of sediment sources in the deserts of China.

(1) Fluvial alluvial deposits. Including the Taklimakan Desert, the Gurbantünggüt Desert and most parts of the Hoba Desert; the north part of the Ulan Buh Desert; Xiariha-Tieguijian, the middle reaches of the Qaidam River; the Horqin Sandy Land in the Xiliao River basin.

(2) Fluviolacustrine deposits. Including the Badain Jaran Desert, the Tengger Desert, the Mu Us Sandy Land and a large part of the Onqin Daga Sandy Land; southwest of the Ulan Buh Desert; the Kulukokum west of the Lop Nur; the Manas-Dabasongnur lake basin in the Junggar Basin, and the desert in the Ebinur Lake area; parts of the deserts in the Hexi Corridor.

Fig. 5-2   Lower Cretaceous sandstone outcrop in the Ordos Plateau

(3) Diluvial and alluvial deposits. Mainly including Yaktokkumo between Ruoqiang and Qiemo, sand dunes between Qiemo and Yutian, north of the Kunlun Mountain; sandy dunes from the Gasikule Lake (Gezi Lake) in the west to the Wutomeireng in the east; southeast of the Badan Jarin Desert, the Yamaleike desert, the Haili desert; dune field in front of the Helan Mountains, the Langshan Mountains-Bayinwula Mountains.

(4) Bedrock weathering deposits. Sandy dunes in the dry denuded highland in the middle and west of Ordos in the north part of the Mu Us Sandy Land; to the north of the Mazatag of the Taklimakan Desert and the uplifted region of the north Minfeng; the Tazikumu and the Kumtag Desert in the low reaches of the Kuobubei-Akekum River and the Ertix River in the Junggar Basin; the middle part of the Kumtag Desert near the Shanshan of the Turpan Basin; the northwest part of the Tengger Desert and the west part of the Onqin Daga Sandy Land.

5.2 The formation and development of deserts

5.2.1 Occurrence of aeolian sand deposits and the formation of deserts

There has long been a considerable debate as to when the desert formed and the dispute mainly focuses on three aspects: ① Does the formation of arid climate imply the development of a desert? Scholars always believe that the Thar Desert in southern Asia is very young, and is the product of human irrational activity; it possibly developed in the post-glacial period (10 ka BP), or even in the Middle Ages. But much evidence shows that the Savanna appeared around 800 Ma BP in the Thar area, and at least two large arid periods had happened before the Holocene. In Fig.5-1, the main criterion of arid zones is evaporite rather than desert sediment. Deserts are a product of the arid climate, but there are other factors involved. We have not discovered the red desert under the yellow desert in the Taklimakan Desert until now. ② Does it imply the development of the desert following aeolian sand occurrance? Some scholars agree with this viewpoint. Dong Guangrong et al. (1991) thought paleo-aeolian sand and aeolian deposit are the direct or indirect evidence of the formation and development of deserts in geologic period, and thought there are late Tertiary aeolian deposits in Mazatag in the hinterland of the Taklimakan Desert, and affirmed Quaternary desert was developed from the late Tertiary red desert. But some scholars disagree. ③ Does the currently accepted inherent relation between red deserts and modern yellow deserts actually exist?

In conclusion, aeolian deposits identified by scholars include:

1) Cretaceous— early Tertiary ancient desert (red desert)

According to the distribution of the paleo-aeolian sand and the evaporite in the Cretaceous and the late Tertiary red layers and the study of the paleogeography, we concluded that in the Cretaceous—the early Tertiary red aeolian sand extensively existed in Northeast China, North China, central China and the central subtropical arid basins in southeast coastal regions, including the Junggar Basin between 25°–50°N, the Tarim Basin and the Kashi Bay, the Turpan-Hami Basin, the northern Tibetan Plateau basin, the Hexi Corridor intermontane basin, the Xi'ning-Minhe Basin, and Longxi Basin. For example, the distribution of aeolian sand and glauberite indicated that red desert had occurred in red basin in the Oligocene or even earlier. Deserts always occurred around salt lakes (earlier). They formed a red desert zone which diagonally extended through the middle subtropical zone of China. The formation of the desert zone was related to the subtropical high pressure belt at that time.

2) Late Tertiary ancient desert (red desert)

Dong Guangrong et al. found late Tertiary Paleo-aeolian sand in several regions especially late

Miocene to the Pliocene Paleo-aeolian sand and fossil dunes. They believe there are late Tertiary Paleo-aeolian sand in the Mazatag Mountains in the hinterland of the Taklimakan Desert, Anning in Lanzhou and Qingtongxia. According to the red aeolian sand and ancient aeolian loess, we suggest that in the late Tertiary there was a red desert zone in western and central China, but their distribution patterns, regional differences and the environmental features are different from the early Tertiary red desert zone.

At first, the scope of the late Tertiary red desert zone shrank largely. The southern limit retreated to the north of the Kunlun–Qinling Mountains and the eastern limit retreated to the Da Hingan-Taihang Mountains. In the southern and western limits, the large desert zone shrank or disappeared and was replaced by aeolian red soil and fluviolacustrine deposits. In large intermontane basins, for example, in the Junggar Basin, the Tarim Basin, the Qaidam Basin, the Longzhong Basin, the Ordos Basin, the Alxa Plateau and the Inner Mongolia plateau, there were several red deserts. All these deserts linked together, forming a red desert zone across northern China. Secondly, paleo-aeolian sand from the Miocene mainly existed in the forms of semi-fixed dunes and semi-fluid dunes.

3) Quaternary modern desert (yellow desert)

Although paleo-aeolian sand in some places occurred between 3–2 Ma BP or even 70–26 Ma BP, modern deserts in western China started to occur extensively at about 1–0.15 Ma BP. Quaternary paleo-aeolian sand has been discovered in northern China and early, medium-term paleo-aeolian sand has been discovered in some major deserts. In the Ordos Plateau, through extensive surveys of landforms and the Quaternary geology, we discovered large expanses of Quaternary paleo-aeolian sand. Generally speaking, the presence of large area of aeolian deposits is the most direct and credible evidence of desert existence. The dating of paleo-aeolian sand in early Pleistocene stratum indicates that the Mu Us Sandy Land in the Ordos Plateau had large areas of aeolian sand in the latter part of the early Pleistocene. For example in Yulin, we discovered the most representative paleo-aeolian sand section. The section included continuously developed "aeolian sand-loess-paleosol" sequence, recording the geological processes of desert development, which helped to reconstruct the development history of the desert. In the Horgin sandy land, early aeolian soil and medium-term aeolian sand have been found. There are vast tracts of early, medium-term Quaternary aeolian sand south of the Taklimakan Desert.

In the mid and late Quaternary, especially in the late Pleistocene, paleo-aeolian sand and loess extensively occurred in the curved desert zone and the surrounding regions of northern China. For example paleo-aeolian sand in the Taklimakan Desert, aeolian sand and subsand in the Gobi zone (Q_3) at the northern piedmont of the Kunlun Mountain, aeolian sand at the southern edge of the Qaidam Basin, thick aeolian sand on the Yellow River terrace in the southeast Tengger Desert, aeolian loess in the Gurbantünggüt Desert, and aeolian sand in the Mu Us Sandy Land, loess and fluviolacustrine deposits and aeolian sand in the Horqin Sandy Land, aeolian sand in the Hulun Buir Sandy Land, all of these are "yellow deserts", which were formed during the mid-Quaternary or the end of the early Pleistocene. At the beginning of the Miocene, with the uplift of the Tibetan Plateau, arid and cold climate formed and glacial and loess deposits provided abundant materials for deserts. The Xi'ning basin at the edge of the Tibetan Plateau started to generate shifting sand activity at the beginning of the mid-Pleistocene to the late Pleistocene. According to the study of lacustrine deposits, the kumkuli Desert, the highest desert of China, formed after 6,000 a BP. At the same time, paleo-aeolian sand occurred in coastal zones and on islands in southeast China, such as aeolian loess and subsand in Nanjing, late Pleistocene fossil dunes on the northern bank of the Poyang Lake, coastal dunes in the Shandong Peninsula, Putian in Fujian, the Xisha archipelago and the Zhoushan archipelago etc.

In other words, the development of Chinese deserts went through three periods: early Tertiary, late tertiary and Quaternary. Red desert and yellow desert were formed in various stages respectively, and at last they formed the modern desert zone in northern China. In other words, in the middle of the Pleistocene, the Tibetan Plateau had reached 3,000–3,500 m, the modern monsoon circulation had formed, and the temperate zone in Eurasia shifted to the south. At the same time, desert deposits developed in the middle of Asia and typical loess deposited universally. All of these are a unified physical and historical process, which result in the geographical distribution pattern of modern monsoons in Asia and arid regions of Asia.

5.2.2　Desert evolution

5.2.2.1　Responses of deserts to climate changes

Global climate has experienced a number of glacial and interglacial cold-warm and dry-wet changes during the Quaternary. In the wet climate period, plants thrived, sand dunes were fixed and the desert area decreased, while in the dry climate period, winds were very strong, sand dunes reactivated, and the desert area rapidly expanded. Such changes were quite obvious on the marginal belt of the East Asian monsoon. In recent years, scientists divided the environmental changes in northwest China into two regional patterns: the monsoon region and the westerly region. The changes in Xinjiang, the Hexi Corridor and Inner Mongolia follow the general characteristics of the westerly belt where the cold climate period was synchronous with the relatively wet period. The eastern region was primarily influenced by the East Asian monsoon. In the Ice Age, the weather was cold and dry, and the desert expanded and loess deposited. Under such a background, the desert evolution in China can be divided into two different types of zones.

1) Eastern steppe zone

Since aeolian sand and loess are located in the same layer in the transverse direction, and the sandy paleosol was formed with aeolian sand as mother material and the silty paleosol was formed with loess as mother material in the eastern desert region, we can conclude that not all the sand dunes were mobile dunes, even during the spread period of shifting sand. However, the semi-fixed and fixed dunes accounted for a high proportion, the vegetation was steppe type and the desert was steppe desert. Their characteristics are that loess and fluviolacustrine sediments and paleosol are interdispersed in aeolian sand and sand dunes. The sandy paleosol layers and the loess-paleosol layers are consecutive; furthermore their characters are very similar. Black sand strata (paleosol) buried in Holocene fixed sand dunes are shown in Fig. 5-3.

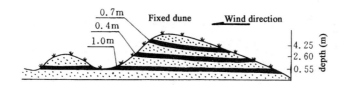

Fig. 5-3   Black sand strata (paleosol) buried in Holocene fixed sand dunes

They showed an alternate synchronous variation of warm-wet forest-steppe, cold-wet shrub-steppe (meadow steppe), cold-dry steppe, desert steppe, and desert. The total trend is forest-steppe, shrub-steppe transitioning to steppe, desert-steppe and desert. The natural environment was steppe, desert steppe and desert when shifting sand appeared and the desert expanded, or forest-steppe and shrub-steppe when shifting sand was fixed. For instance, the "aeolian sand, loess, paleosol" sequence recorded in the Yulin section reflects that the Ordos region has alternately experienced 11 cold-dry mobile dunes stages, 7 cold-dry fixed and semi-fixed dunes stages, 8 cold-dry aeolian deposition stages, 15 relatively warm-wet stages and 3 soil forming stages.

The evolution of the eastern desert was entirely consistent with the climatic fluctuations of the glacial-interglacial period and is directly controlled by the strength of monsoon circulation and the advance or retreat of the polar front. During the Ice Age, the global temperature decreased, the intensity of the southwest-monsoon and the southeast-monsoon weakened, the intensity of the Siberian cold anticyclone strengthened, the frequency and intensity of cold waves and anticyclones strengthened largely and the bioclimatic zones in arid areas of China moved southward. From northwest to southeast, the bioclimatic zones gradually changed from arid desert or desert steppe into semi-arid steppe. The land surface external agents were dominated by freezing weathering and wind action. Deserts expanded and loess deposition accelerated. During the interglacial period, because of global warming and the weakening and retreat of the Siberian cold anticyclone, the frequency and intensity of cold waves and anticyclones decreased sharply. At the same time, the rate and intensity of the southwest and southeast monsoons moving north and west strengthened remarkably. Bioclimatic zones moved northward on a large scale. The eastern desert region was influenced by moist oceanic airstreams, and precipitation mostly fell in the comparatively wet and warm forest grassland, bushy grassland and savanna climate zones. The land surface external agents are dominated by running water, growing grass and soil formation. The sand flow stopped, sand dunes were fixed, and the desert area reduced. So in a certain sense, the eastern desert is the monsoon marginal desert.

2) Western desert zone

Taking the Tarim Basin in the western desert as an example, according to the fact that the fluvio-lacustrine deposits occur in the same layer as aeolian sand, subsandy soil and loess in the transverse direction, and is co-existent with aeolian sand, subsand soil and loess in most regions, we can conclude that most regions are dominated by mobile dunes, and there are few areas with several fixed and semi-fixed sand dunes. Its notable characteristics are that the fluvio-lacustrine and lake-swamp sediments only exist in the low-lying land of deserts, but in the interior of desert, there are no paleosol layer, and calcium carbonate leaching and illuvium were found. In the longitudinal profile, based on the continuous sediment sequence of aeolian sand, we conclude that except for several fluvio-lacustrine areas that experienced development process similar to eastern desert regions, most areas experienced a linear development process where shifting sand continuously deposited and spread. It is indicated that western deserts in the Asian hinterland have always had dry and extreme dry climatic conditions, although the temperature changes are similar to the eastern desert zone. Its obvious characteristic is the alternating occurrence of warm-dry and cold-dry climates, not only in the glacial period but also in the interglacial period. This area is mostly influenced by the Siberian cold anticyclone and the Tibetan plateau anticyclonic westerly jet, the moisture carried by the westerly is quite limited due to foehn effect. So the desert is a "rain shadow" desert. It should be pointed out that in the Junggar basin, the sedimentary facies is similar to that in the Tarim Basin, but the calcification of aeolian sand and soil forming characters is roughly similar to the eastern desert zone due to the influence of moist airflow from the Atlantic and the Pacific oceans, but the paleosol color is light, soil thickness is thin and the leaching and illuvium of calcium carbonate are weak.

In other words, the different sediment environments of deserts in the Quaternary in northern China reflects that the regional differentiation of the yellow desert zone had already appeared. Under such a background, the response to climate fluctuations was different in different areas during the Holocene.

5.2.2.2 The vicissitudes of desert since 20 ka BP

As mentioned above, the expansion-diminution variations of desert in China follows the characteristics of glacial-interglacial climate changes. The northern deserts experienced about 19 obvious cold-dry and warm-wet climate cycles, of which the last glacial period (80–10 ka BP) in the late Pleistocene was the most important evolution period since the desert was formed. Especially during the last glacial maximum (21–10 ka BP), not ward various deserts expanded to the surrounding regions, but the aeolian activities expanded southward to the Datong Basin, Lanzhou, the southern bank of the middle and lower reaches of the Yangtze River, the Poyang Lake, northern Shandong Peninsula, Zhoushan Islands, and coastal zones of southern China. The discoveries of Paleo-Aeolian Sand offer evidence for this. From this we can conclude that the desert expanded southward to about 36°N, extended east to about 125°E, and its size was a little larger than today. Furthermore, there were large-areas of sand dunes present in Liaodong, Subei and Taiwan beaches of the continental shelf of the Huanghai Sea, Bohai Sea and the East China Sea.

The climate of the Northern Hemisphere was harsh during the last glacial period, which began in the late Pleistocene, and the atmospheric circulation was different from modern conditions because of the sudden drop in temperature. The simulated results of the paleoclimate since 21 ka BP using the Global Climate Model (GCM) indicate that during the LGM the high-latitude ice flow in western Eurasia rapidly expanded and forced the westerlies to shift southward. The high-latitude permafrost in eastern Eurasia thickened and expanded to the south, and so the winter monsoon strengthened. At the same time, the Asian summer monsoon weakened and the westerlies moved southward. This resulted in the precipitation and temperature differences in eastern and western China. From the LGM to late glacial period, arid regions in northern China were influenced by westerlies and the climate was cold and dry conditions. According to the computation, the annual average temperature in the Hexi Corridor region in the LGM and the Younger Dryas was 13°C lower than it is today (Table 5-2). The decline extent of the temperature is nearly the same as the result inferred from spore-pollen, sand wedge, and ice-core in northern China. Analysis from the stratigraphic grain size, sedimentary facies, and geochemical elements of the Late Pleistocene strata indicate that the bioclimatic zone in desert regions of northern China shifted 9–10 degree latitude southward, hence the eastern desert area was in a desert steppe to desert environment, while the western desert region had a classical desert environment.

Table 5-2　Descending value of average annual temperature during the last glacial period in northern China

Area	Estimation basis	Age	Temperature decreasing amplitude (°C)	Source
Beijing	Spore-pollen,Paleo-periglacial	LGM	8–13.6	AN Zhisheng, 1990
Datong Basin	Paleo-sand wedge	<26 ka BP	14–15	YANG Jingchun, 1983
Northwest Shanxi	Paleo-sand wedge	27–10 ka BP	9.6–15.5	SU Zhizhu, 1997
Weinan	Spore-pollen	27–18 ka BP	10–12	SUN Xiangjun, 1989
Weinan	Phytolith	23–14 ka BP	7–9	WU Naiqin, 1994
Ordos Plateau	Paleo-sand wedge	<25 ka BP	12–16	DONG Guangrong, 1985
Hexi Corridor	Mirabilite and Paleo-sand wedge	LGM and YD	9–13	WANG Nai'ang, 2000
Qaidam Basin	Isotope of mineral inclusions	21–15 ka BP	6–7	ZHANG Baozhen, 1995
West Kunlun Mountain	Guliya ice core	LGM and YD	12	YAO Tandong, 1999
Tibetan Plateau	Spore-pollen,Paleo-sand wedge etc.	LGM	6–9	SHI Yafeng, 1997

In the Holocene warm period, the area of the northern desert in China was largely reduced, especially the eastern desert. The eastern limit of the desert retreated from 125°E to 117°E in the last glacial maximum and the southern limit retreated to 38°N. The Mu Us Sandy Land, the Horqin Sandy Land and the Hulun Buir Sandy Land entirely disappeared; in the western desert areas, the Tengger Desert, the Badain Jaran Desert and the Gurbantünggüt Desert reduced significantly, and the Gonghe desert disappeared. Afterwards, under the effects of the climate changes of the late Holocene and human activities, the deserts and the sandy lands evolved into today's distribution pattern.

5.3　Sedimentary records of desert areas in China

5.3.1　The spatial and temporal characteristics of deposits in desert regions of China

The desert zones in China can be divided into four major subregions based on differences in geographical position, aridity and sedimentary composition (Fig. 5-4). The desert zone east of the line extending from the Langshan Mountains, lying at the west end of the Yinshan Mountains, to the China-Mongolia border passing through the Helan Mountains, the Wushaoling Mountains, Dulan, the Qinghai Lake and to the Zhaling Lake is called the eastern desert. West of the line, we can divide the desert into two parts with the Tianshan Mountains and Bogda Mountain as the borderline: to the south is the western desert, and to the north is the northwestern desert. East of the Ruoshui River, the west of the Yellow River, and extending from Linhe to Wuhai, Yinchuan and Zhongning, the Hexi Corridor and its northern region is the central desert, also known as the monsoon region desert or sandy land (Li Baosheng et al., 2001).

The desert sedimentary records refer to paleo-aeolian dunes and sand bed preserved in the strata or remaining on the surface. Apparently the paleo-sand is the most direct evidence to explore previous aeolian sand environments. It is important to note that its existence doesn't necessarily mean the existence of an ancient desert. We can see modern sand dunes or lands scattered on the Tibetan Plateau, along the eastern coastline in China, and near the banks of some rivers in the alluvial plain. They cannot be called deserts because of limited area and sand quantity. The investigated result reveals that paleo-aeolian sand widely exists in the Quaternary strata in the desert areas of China. Their color, cementation degree and grain size are close to those of modern aeolian sand, and they have a yellow-brown or grayish yellow color and poor cementation. The ancient shifting sand mainly consists of fine sand and extremely fine sand, and they also contain a certain amount of medium sand, but almost contain no silt or clay. The composition of ancient fixed or semi-fixed sand dunes is similar to ancient shifting sand, and they contain a certain amount of silt sand clay. The color and cementation degree of paleo-aeolian sand of the Tertiary is similar to laterite strata in northern China. They are red or brown-red, cemented or semi-cemented, and their grain size is similar to that of ancient shifting sand and fixed or semi-fixed sand dunes.

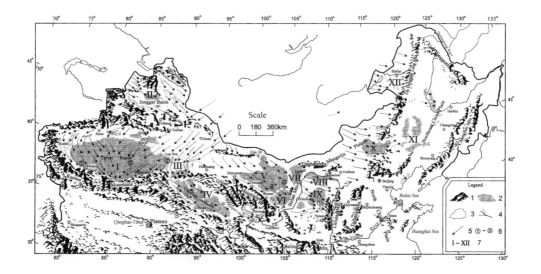

Fig. 5-4   Distribution of the deserts in China and the locations of related strata

1. mountains with bedrock. 2. desert or sand. 3. lake. 4. river. 5. the prevailing direction of the winter monsoon. 6. desert or sandy land in China: I. Taklimakan Desert; II. Gurbantünggüt Desert; III. Kumtag Desert; IV. Qaidam Desert; V. Badain Jaran Desert; VI. Tengger Desert; VII. Ulan Buh Desert; VIII. Hobq Desert; IX. Mu Us Desert or Mu Us Sandy Land; X. Onqin Daga Sandy Land; XI. Horqin Sandy Land; XII. Hulun Buir Sandy Land. 7. the locations of related stratigraphic sections: ① Milanggouwan in Salawusu River Basin; ② Lop Nur; ③ Chagelebulu at the eastern margin of the Badain Jaran Desert; ④ Badanhaizi at the southern margin of the Badain Jaran Desert; ⑤ Yuetegan in the Hotan Oasis; ⑥ No.1 well in the hinterland of the Taklimakan Desert; ⑦ Aqiang at the southern margin of the Tarim Basin; ⑧ Yulin in the north of Shaanxi Province

The paleo-aeolian sand of the Quaternary in various sub-regions of desert areas in China has no obvious difference in lithological character, but the stratigraphic assembledge is different, and sometimes differs greatly. Fig. 5-5 shows the result of the Quaternary paleo-aeolian sand, loess, other sedimentary facies, stratigraphic divisions and magnetic stratigraphic ages in different desert subzones and adjacent regions.

1) Eastern Desert Zone in China[1]

Paleo-aeolian sand and paleosol sedimentary sections mainly occur in the eastern desert zone. They are superimposed on each other. The Yulin section in the north of Shaanxi Province (Fig. 5-4) is a typical example. The aeolian sand and the river or lake sediments are often superimposed on each other. This situation is commonly found in the Wuding River and the Salawusu River basins of the Mu Us Sandy Land, Naiman Qi in the Horqin Sandy Land and the Northeast Plain (Dong Guangrong, 1994). Most of them were formed from the late Pleistocene to the Holocene. The fossils of vertebrates; mollusks and human cultural remains are more common than in other desert regions. As is well known, the fauna of Salawusu and Chengchuan, as well as the famous "Hetao man" and the cultural remains were found in this region.

---

1) Fig. 5-5: ⑬—⑳

2) Central desert zone in China[1]

The superimposed sections of paleo-aeolian sand and fluviolacustrine sediments are common in low-lying lands of the central desert zone (Gao et al., 1995); furthermore, we often see calcareous root pipes of plants and mollusk fossils in fluviolacustrine sediments (Li et al., 1998). The vertebrates' fossils are rare in this area, and only in the Gurinai Village in the western Badain Jaran Desert can we find eggs of ostrich in the paleo aeolian sand, tooth fossils of horses in the swamp facies, and calcareous root pipes of plants. Some ancient lakes existed during the late Pleistocene in some places in the central desert zone. According to a borehole survey by the Gansu Bureau of Geology, in Ejin Qi southeast of the Badain Jaran Desert, the stratum 70 m below the surface almost entirely consists of fine lacustrine deposits and fresh water mollusk fossils.

In the vast central desert zone, especially in the Alasa Plateau, megadunes with a relative height more than 150 m are widespread, and some of them may have been in existence from the late Pleistocene to the Holocene. Furthermore, the underlying stratum is cemented or half cemented by calcium carbonate. In the hinterland of the Badain Jaran Desert, near Yikeli Aobao, there are huge megadunes with a height around 500 m (Dieter, 1996). TL dating of underlying ancient mobile dune sand yielded an age of 139 ± 20 ka BP (Yan et al., 2001).

3) Western desert zone in China[2]

In the western desert zone, the thickest aeolian sand deposits occur in the hinterland of the Taklimakan Desert and the height of complex dune ridges varies from 100 m to 200 m. According to the strata sequence recorded at the No.1 well (east longitude 83°58′, north latitude 38°53′) in Tazhong and the research by Yanshun, most Pleistocene aeolian sand about 200–300 m thick exists in the inter-ridge depressions and covers the Pliocene stratum. There are several layers of alluvial silt and fine sand intercalated in it (Fig. 5-5: (6-1)). In this area complex megadunes and deflated hollows are alternatingly distributed, some new complex dune ridges are superimposed on old complex megadunes, and their mechanical composition is similar (Li et al., 1993a). The TL dating of the interface of new and old complex megadunes gave an age of $8,600\pm430$ a BP, its underlying sand layers have TL ages of $16,700\pm800$ a BP and $17,040\pm828$ a BP (Fig. 5-5: (6-1)). The TL age of the nearby older complex megadunes is $38,380\pm5,115$ a BP.

The lacustrine deposits in the Qaidam Basin are the thickest Quaternary lake sediments in desert regions of China. The Qarhan Saltlake is the lowest catchment center of the basin. According to the borehole records, the thickness of Quaternary sediment may reach 1,500 m (Liu et al., 1991). The thickness of lake deposits was about 100 m from 32 ka BP.

---

1) Fig. 5-5: ⑪–⑭

2) Fig. 5-5: ①–⑦

Another lacustrine deposit center in the western desert zone lies in the "Lop Nur Ancient Lake region" between the eastern edge of the Taklimakan Desert and northwest edge of the Kumtag Desert. According to Hong Li and Wang Wenxian, the lacustrine deposits have a thickness of at least 550 m, and each layer contains different amounts of Ostracode. The lower, middle, and upper Pleistocenes are named as the lower, middle and upper Qaidam Formation respectively, and their depths are 350–360 m, 150–200 m and 110–150 m respectively. The depth of Holocene sediment varies between 5–15 m. From the Pleistocene to Holocene rock core drilled in Lop Nur Ancient Lake, we can find several aeolian thin-layers of sub-sand.

Diluvial and alluvial conglomerates and gravel layers, lying in the oases from Hotan to Qiemo between the northern piedmont of the Kunlun Mountains and the southern Tarim Basin, is the deepest sediment in the western desert zone. The borehole records show that the thickness of Quaternary deposit could reach 2,000–3,000 m. On both sides of the Keriya River valley in the northern piedmont of the mid Kunlun Mountains, there are big boulders about 1–3 m in diameter mixed with the various gravel less than one meter. They are sub-rounded and sub-angular, with a thickness ranging from 100 to 200 m. There are also paleo-aeolian sand lens and two layers of basalt appearing on top of the gravel layer. The K-Ar age determined by Liu Jiaqi and others is 1.43 ± 0.03 Ma BP (lower basaltic layer) and 1.2 ± 0.03 Ma BP (upper basaltic layer) (Liu et al., 1990).

From the distribution of several sedimentary facies we can easily see that either paleo-dunes or lake sediments and alluvial-diluvial deposits mainly experienced a single-origin deposition process. In the western desert zone paleo-aeolian dunes have a large area, followed by lake sediments which mainly occur in the Qaidam Basin, while gravel deposits are only restricted to the marginal areas of deserts and at the foot of mountains. In the Taklimakan Desert, sand dunes mainly consist of fine and very fine sand. From the center of the desert to the south, dune accumulation facies gradually changed into aeolian subsand soil, mainly made up of very fine sand.

The assemblage of aeolian facies and other facies of the same origin but different lithological characters in the western desert zone, especially in the Tarim Basin, have the following characteristics:

(1) Paleo-aeolian sand and alluvial-diluvial deposits, lacustrine clay, and silt are superimposed on each other. They mainly occurred in the alluvial plains of the Tarim River and the Konqi River, the Lop Nur area and wind-eroded lowlands between huge complex dune chains in the Taklimakan Desert (Li, 1990).

(2) Paleo-aeolian sand, claylike silt, very fine sand, fine sand is superimposed on each other. They mainly occur in the center of the Taklimakan Desert (Fig. 5-5:ⓖ) and the Gobi-oasis areas from Yecheng-Yutian-Ruoqiang (Li, 1993a). In the alluvial and diluvial deposits, we can find shell fossils.

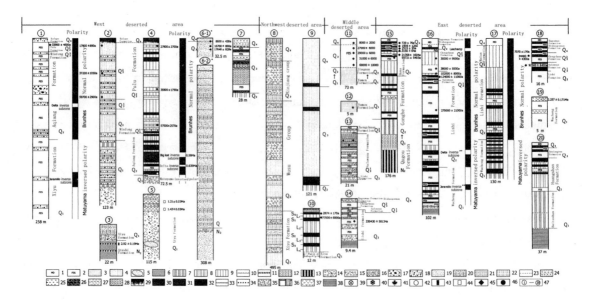

Fig. 5-5   Quaternary stratigraphical assemblage of the East, Central, West and Northwest desert regions of China

[① Shazidaban north of Ruoqiang in Xinjiang (Dong et al., 1995); ②gully at the north foot of the Altun Mountains north of Ruoqiang in Xinjiang; ③Mazatag residual mountain in the Tarim Basin (Dong, 1993); ④Aqiang village of Yutian County south of the Tarim Basin; ⑤grazing land in the upper Keriya River (Liu, 1990); ⑥-1. Tazhong in the Taklimakan Desert (83°58′E, 38°53′N); ⑥-2 No. 1 drill in the tower in the Taklimakan Desert (83°58′E,38°53′N)Yanshun; ⑦Yiliping of Qaidam Desert; ⑧ valley section from Kongnaisi to Yili in northern Xinjiang (Zhang Hongyi et al., 1985); ⑨composite section in northern Xinjiang (Zhang et al., 1985); ⑩Lujiaowan of Shawan County in north Xinjiang (the Comprehensive Investigation Team for Resource Development in Xinjiang CAS, 1994); ⑪Yikeli Aobao in Badain Jaran Desert (Yan et al., 2001); ⑫Dunes in the Badain Jaran Desert; ⑬Chagelebulu in the Badain Jaran Desert; ⑭Shapotou in the Tengger Desert (Yan et al., 1997); ⑮Fenghuang Mountain of Guinan in the Gonghe Desert in Qinghai province (Tao et al., 1994); ⑯Yunlin in the Mu Us Sandy Land; ⑰Jingbian in the Mu Us Sandy Land (Wang, 1989); ⑱,⑲Huiteng River in Onqin Daga Sandy Land (Dong et al., 1991); ⑳Sanjiazi of Hure Qi in the Horqin Sandy Land (Dong et al., 1992)]

1. modern dune; 2. Paleo-aeolian sand; 3. semi-cemented aeolian sand; 4. aeolian sub-sand; 5. aeolian sand lens; 6. red aeolian sand of Tertiary; 7. loss of lower Pleistocene loess; 8. mid-Pleistocene loess; 9. early-Pleistocene loess; 10. Holocene loess; 11. surface soil; 12. alluvial loess; 13. Tertiary laterite; 14. alluvial and diluvial gravel layer; 15. alluvial gravel layer; 16. diluvial sloping gravel layer; 17. diluvial gravel layer with grey-black desert varnish; 18. alluvial sloping gravel layer with grey-black desert varnish; 19. fluvial facies sand; 20. silty sand containing clay; 21. silty sand; 22. diluvial salt; 23. denudation surface; 24. interbed of silt and subclay; 25. subclay; 26. mud; 27. clay to subclay; 28. clay silt; 29. sod; 30. grey-black paleosol; 31. heilu soil; 32. brown paleosol; 33. peat layer; 34. gypsum layer; 35. calcareous concretion layer; 36. calcareous pan; 37. basalt; 38. early Tertiary bedrock; 39. vertebrate fossil; 40. mollusk fossil; 41. plant fossil; 42. cosmic dust; 43. sample of fission-track dating; 44. sample of K-Ar age; 45. sample of TL age; 46. sample of ^{14}C age; 47. histogram number

(3) Paleo-aeolian sand and alluvial-diluvial coarse sand are superimposed on each other. They mainly occur in the Gobi-oasis region from Yecheng-Yutian-Ruoqiang (Li, 1995).

(4) Aeolian subsand and alluvial-diluvial slope gravels are superimposed on each other. They occur in the subsand areas south of the Gobi-oasis region from Yecheng-Yutian-Ruoqiang. (Fig. 5-5: ① ②)

(5) Aeolian loess, fine loess and aeolian subsand are superimposed on each other. They occur on the northern slope of the Kunlun Mountains at an elevation of 2,600–2,800 m. (Fig. 5-5: ④)

(6) Mollusca fossil layers are intercalated in aeolian loess. They only occur in the source area of

the Keriya River on the northern slope of the Kunlun Mountains.

Paleosol is not very common in the western desert zone, and it can only be found in the loess layers on the northern slope of the Kunlun Mountains, reflecting the general feature of the region's arid environment: vast areas of sand dunes in the western desert zone and widespread gypsum evaporates.

4) Northwest desert zone[1]

Little is known about the Quaternary strata in the northwest desert zone. According to Hongli and Zhang Hongyi and Fig. 5-5: ⑧⑨, there occurred aeolian subsand deposition in the main stages of the Quaternary in this area.

Fig. 5-5: ⑩ shows the loess and paleosol sequence recorded at the edge of the Gurbantünggüt Desert by the Comprehensive Investigation Team for Resource Development in Xinjiang, CAS. It contained 5 layers of loess, L0, L1, L2, L3, L4, 4 layers of fossil soil, S0, S1, S2, S3. They are superimposed on each other. In addition, they also found L1–L4, S4 and L5 in the Xinyuan area at the northern piedmont of the Tianshan Mountains. The TL age of the upper layer of L5 is 390±30.3 ka BP. According to related research results, the temporal and spatial feature of deposition records in desert regions of China can be roughly summarized as follows:

(1) Aeolian sand activity might have started no later than the beginning of the Quaternary in desert regions of China. The following evidence supports this:

First, two layers of paleo-aeolian sand have been found under the basalt layer in the Onqin Daga Sandy Land, its K-Ar age of 2.257±0.171 Ma BP coincides with the lower limit of loess in China—about 2.48 Ma BP.

Second, paleo aeolian sand have been found in the overlying layer of the N/Q interface in borehole drilled in the center of the Taklimakan Desert (Fig. 5-5: ☺).

Third, paleo-aeolian sand was found in the cemented-half-cemented conglomerate on the Q1/N2 interface in the lower Xiyu formation of the western desert zone.

(2) Paleo-aeolian sand exists in all subzones in desert zones of China and they are superimposed with fluviolacustrine deposits. But the characteristics of paleo-climate reflected by river or lake deposits are different compared with the eastern desert zone. The river or lake deposits in the eastern desert reflect a warm and wet environment, while those in the western desert zone reflect a dry environment. Dry crack, evaporates such as gypsum and rock salt and desert varnish on the surface of gravels in the western desert zone also reflect a dry climate.

(3) As far as the development scale of paleo-aeolian sand is concerned, the paleo-aeolian sand in the shifting sand areas in the western desert zone and central desert zone seemed to have experienced a linear deposition process. This shows that the two big deserts have been in an active

---

1) (Fig. 5-5: ⑧–⑩)

state since the Pleistocene.

(4) The paleosol development in the western and central desert zones is poorer than the eastern desert zone (Dong, 1991). This may be caused by the different hydro-thermal condition in different zones affected by the location of land and sea.

(5) Owing to the existence of characteristics ②–④, vertebrate and primitive man fossils and historical cultural remains can be found in the Quaternary formation in the eastern desert zone, and especially in the Pleistocene-Holocene formation in the basin of the Salawusu River, but they were rarely found in older strata in other desert zones.

5.3.2 Examples of desert evolution records in desert regions of China since the early to mid-Pleistocene—research about stratigraphic sequences and ages of the Yulin and Aqiang Sections

The Yulin section and the Aqiang section are two representative sections with detailed and long sedimentary records (1,100 ka and 700 ka) in eastern and western desert zones respectively. The research of these sections will contribute a better understanding of the desert evolution and the environmental changes in desert regions of China. Here, we will discuss in detail the magnetic strata and geologic age recorded by these sections.

5.3.2.1 Sedimentary sequence and age of aeolian sand-loess-paleosol of the Yulin Section at the southeast edge of the Ordos Plateau since 1,100 ka BP

The Ordos Plateau (Fig. 5-6) is located in the transition belt of the arid desert steppe and semiarid steppe subzone in between the arid desert zone and sub-humid forest-steppe zone in northern China. Its elevation is about 1,300 m, with a maximum elevation of 1,700 m or higher. Its precipitation is 250–450 mm/a, and the aridity is 1.6–2.8. It has abundant aeolian sand materials. In the northern, southern and southwestern parts of the Plateau, there are the Hobq Desert, the Mu Us Sandy Land and the Hedong Sandy Land of Ningxia. In the southeastern part of the Plateau, there are mosaic distributions of shifting sand, fixed and semifixed dunes and loess. The area of sandy land is about 53,000 km^2. We call the desert and sandy lands in the Ordos Plateau the Ordos Desert for convenience.

In the 1920s to the 1930s, scholars from China and foreign countries investigated the geology in Ordos. They dealt with the topic of the desert in the Pleistocene. French scholars P. Teilhard de Chardin and E. EmileLicent investigated aeolian dune sediments in the Salawusu formation under the paleosol of the Yangshao Culture in the Salawusu River basin. P. Teilhard de Chardin and Yang Zhongjian named the 10-20m thick sediments the Yulin series, which resembles loess but contains abundant sand. Its age was believed to be from the late Pleistocene, and the sand came from the Hetao Desert. Unfortunately, these scientific conclusions were not recognized for a long period of time. From the late 1970s to the mid-1990s, new progress was made in the formation and evolution of the Ordos Desert (Dong, et al., 1995; Li, et al., 1993a; Shi Peijun, 1991), including the division of Quaternary deserts sedimentary age in Ordos and the relation between aeolian sand and loess. In recent years, Li Baosheng investigated the strata since 150 ka in the Salawusu River basin at the southeastern edge of Ordos (Li, 1993a; Li, et al., 2000). Other scholars studied the strata of the Yulin section and discussed the relationship of environmental change at the border of the desert and loess. They determined magnetic susceptibility and analyzed mechanical composition and organic content and tried to set up the contrast relationship with deep-sea deposits of the same time (Sun Jimin, et al., 1995). All these deepened our understanding on the formation and evolution of the Ordos Desert. Despite the accomplishments in research on desert environments in the past 20 years, the time of desert sediments of the early to mid of Quaternary still used whole units to divide strata (Dong, et al., 1995). Here, we select the Yulin section in the Ordos Plateau to research its sedimentary sequence and try to obtain some elementary views on the sedimentary age of the Ordos Desert in the most recent 1,100ka BP through the contrasts of lithologic character and lithofacies, age of sediment and loess-paleosol sequence in the Loess Plateau.

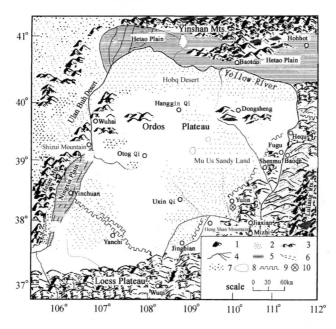

Fig. 5-6   The location of the Yulin Section and the Ordos Plateau

1. Bedrock mountains; 2. Desert; 3. Loess; 4. River; 5. Alluvial, diluvial and lacustrine plain; 6. Depression; 7. Gobi; 8. Lake; 9. The Great Wall; 10. The location of the Yulin Section

1) The characteristics of the Yulin section

The Yulin section is located at Caijiagou, Luojia Yuan at the southeastern edge of the Mu Us Sandy Land of the Ordos Plateau, 17 km south of Yulin City. The altitude of the plateau is about 1,200 m and the gullies are about 100 m deep. At the bottom of the gully is grayish green Jurassic sand shale. Above the stratum, there are nearly 100-m thick Quaternary deposits. There are 46 strata in the section, including 18 layers of aeolian sand, 8 layers of loess and 18 layers of paleosol superimposed on the cemented early Pleistocee gravel layer, 45G. (Fig. 5-7). The section is a typical section for the research of the formation and evolution process of the Ordos Desert.

The sedimentary characteristics and ages of the Yulin section are different and mainly manifested in the following several aspects.

(1) The color of sediments gradually become lighter from bottom to top. The color of aeolian sand and loess that occurs in the bottom and top of the mid-Pleistocene and the upper Pleistocene-Holocene layers are dark red brown (40FD, 42FD, 44D)-reddish, brown yellow and pale yellow. Cinnamon soil is red brown, dark red and reddish grey-black in color. Heilu soil has only one layer with a grey-black color.

(2) In the bottom of the aeolian sand, loess and cinnamon soil of the mid-Pleistocene, there are densely distributed calcareous nodules 30–40 cm in diameter that often developed into hard pans. Calcareous nodules in aeolian sand and loess in the top of the mid-Pleistocene significantly reduce. But in 19D, there are plentiful but scattered calcareous nodules. In the bottom of the cinnamon soil, calcareous nodules are present in stratified distribution with smaller diameter, generally between 1–5 cm. In the aeolian sand, loess and Heilu soil of the upper Pleistocene, there is no calcareous nodule but there are calcareous pseudohypha and film in the lower layer of Heilu soil. Small calcareous nodules with diameters of 1–2 cm can also be found in the bottom of cinnamon soil.

(3) Cinnamon soil and loess in the bottom and top of mid-Pleistocene are slightly cemented or semi-cemented. They have dense ferromanganese spots and needle holes. Cinnamon soil and loess of the upper Pleistocene are soft and have worm holes. Aeolian sand of the mid-Pleistocene has more ferromanganese spots. Its lower part is slightly cemented. Aeolian sand on the top of the mid-Pleistocene and the upper Pleistocene-Holocene is loose.

According to field investigations and grain size analytical data, Li Baosheng divided the aeolian sand strata in the Yulin section into modern mobile dune (1MD), ancient mobile dune (2D, 4D, 6D, 13D, 19D, 25D, 28D, 31D, 33D, 44D) and ancient fixed-semifixed dunes (9FD, 11FD, 15FD, 23FD, 35FD, 40FD, 42FD) in 1988. It is readily seen from Fig. 5-4 that aeolian dune strata, especially ancient mobile dunes, are the most prominent lithology and sedimentary phase in the section. The next are paleosol (3S, 8S, 10S, 12S, 14S, 16S, 18S, 20S, 22S, 24S, 27S, 30S, 32S, 34S, 36S, 38S, 41S, 43S) and loess (5L, 7L, 17L, 21L, 26L, 29L, 37L, 39L). Ancient mobile dune strata lack silt and clay. They can be divided into three mobile dune strata respectively based on medium sand ($\varphi1$–2), fine sand ($\varphi2$–3.32) and very fine sand ($\varphi3.32$–4.32). Coarse sand ($\varphi1$–2) is lacking. M_x and σ vary between $\varphi1.83$–3.75 and $\varphi0.32$–0.94 respectively. Ancient fixed-semifixed dunes consist of silty fine sand and silty very fine sand. The contents of coarse silt ($\varphi4.32$–6.64), fine silt ($\varphi6.64$–7.64) and clay ($>\varphi7.64$) are 51.07%–78%, 15.66%–37.37% and 3.34%–6.80% respectively. M_x and σ vary between $\varphi3.28$–4.22 and $\varphi0.54$–1.65 respectively.

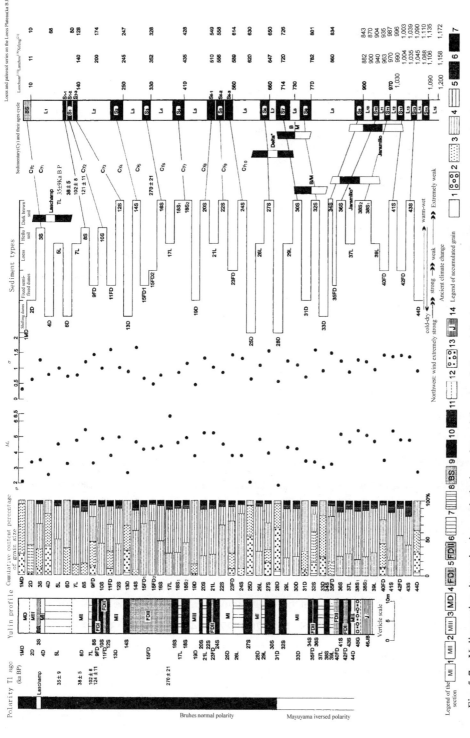

Fig. 5-7　Yulin section, its grain-size analytical results and the correlation to the loess-paleosol sedimentary sequences in the Loess Plateau

Legend of the section: 1. ancient mobile dune sand (medium sand); 2. ancient mobile dune sand (fine sand); 3. ancient mobile dune sand; 4. modern mobile dune sand;

5. ancient fixed-semifixed dune sand silty (fine sand); 6. ancient fixed-semifixed dune sand silty (very fine sand); 7.Malan loess; 8.Lishi loess; 9.Heilu soil; 10. silty brown drab soil; 11. sandy

brown drab soil; 12. denuded surface; 13.cemented gravel layer; 14. Jurassic sandy shale

Legend of accumulated grain size: 1. coarse sand; 2. medium sand; 3. fine sand; 4. vey fine sand; 5. coarse silt; 6. fine silt; 7. clay

Paleosol can be divided into sandy paleosol and silty paleosol according to lithologic character. The contents of sand, coarse silt, fine silt and clay in the former are 58.83%–81.87%, 10.67%–28.13%, 0.13%–6.27% and 2.20%–11.04% respectively. In the latter, their contents are 1.78%–46.60%, 44.20%–67.30%, 2.13%–8.37% and 4.10%–8.29% respectively. M_x and σ of the former are $\varphi3.2$–4.76 and $\varphi0.91$–1.75 respectively and those of the latter are $\varphi4.36$–5.37 and $\varphi0.80$–1.46 respectively. The grain size of the loess in the Yulin section is similar with that of sandy Malan loess in western Shanxi and northern Shaanxi. The contents of their sand, coarse silt, fine silt and clay are 14.88%–48.14%, 45.60%–76.13%, 2.83%–6.87% and 3.43%–6.80% and M_x and σ vary between $\varphi4.51$–5.34 and $\varphi0.80$–2.07, respectively.

Fig.5-7 shows the relative sorting degree of different sedimentary facies in the Yulin section. It can be seen that mobile dune sand is best sorted, and sandy paleosol sorting is poorest. The sorting for others is generally in between these two.

In the vertical direction of the section, paleosol and underlying aeolian sand and loess grain-size composition are roughly approximate. But M_x, φ and σ of the paleosol notably increase, suggesting that they developed from aeolian sand or loess parent material.

2) Geological age of the aeolian sand-loess-paleosol sedimentary sequence

As can be seen from the Yulin section, different strata have different sedimentary features, such as color, cementation degree, and calcareous nodules. From this we can make a comparison with the depositional features of loess in the Loess Plateau and obtain a frame for stratum division of the Holocene, upper Pleistocene, mid-Pleistocene and so on, as well as loess in the Malan Lishi periods.

As can be seen from Fig. 5-7, there are two layers in the Yulin section that can be used to make comparisons with contemporaneous strata in the Loess Plateau. One is compound paleosol of 8S–12S. It can be used to make comparisons with S1 that sometimes has three layers of paleosol. The TL age of 9FD in 8S–12S is 124±11 ka BP, approximate to the age of S_1 of 128 ka BP in the Xifeng section. Another is 15FD. Its TL age is 272 ±21 ka BP and corresponds to the age of L_3, which is 271 ka BP, in Xifeng section.

3S in the Yulin section and S_0 in the Loess Plateau belong to the same soil type. The latter is a product from 10 ka BP during the Holocene and the former has no determined age. But the ^{14}C age of the Heilu soil near Zhenbeitai is 5.28±1.4 ka BP (Dong Guangrong, et al., 1993a). The location of 4D-7L between 3S and 8S corresponds to L_1. The TL ages of 5L, 6D and 7L are 35±9 ka BP, 38±5 ka B.P. and 102±8 ka BP respectively and obviously belong to the same age of L_1.

The boundary of the top and the bottom of the Lishi loess is located between L_5/S_5 in the Loess Plateau. So S_5 is usually regarded as key stratum for the regional stratigraphic comparison. According to the contrast relation, the boundary between 21L/20S-24S of the mid-Pleistocene in the Yulin section ought to be in accord with the boundary between L_5/S_5. So we can divide the mid-Pleistocene boundary into a top and bottom. In fact, some characteristics of the top and bottom of the mid-Pleistocene are obviously different, for example, the size, density and arrangement of calcareous nodules. As mentioned above, calcareous nodules at the top of the mid Plerstocene are small, scattered and show a stratified distribution, while they are big, dense and often form hard pans in the lower part. Such difference is similar to that of the Lishi loess.

To answer the question of strata age，we collected 43 groups of paleomagnetism samples from 3S-44D in the Yulin section. Liu Chun from the Lab of Paleomagnetism, Institute of Geology, CAS completed the measuring work using alternating demagnetization with peak intensity of 250–350 Ost. The results are: the index of I (magnetic inclination) for the paleomagnetism samples 31E–44E is negative, and is positive for samples 3S-30S except 4D. The changes of the index of D (magnetic declination) are synchronous with the changes of I. From the result and tested age we can demarcate at 31D.

It can be seen from the results of magnetic strata that the sequence below 20S-24S and above the B/M interface in the Yulin section has better correlation with the sequence below S_5 and above B/M in the Loess Plateau. The corresponding correlation is: 25D and 26L to L_6, 27S to S_6, 28D and 29L to L_7 and 30S to S_7. And 31D corresponds to L_8 where the B/M interface in the Loess Plateau lies.

It should be pointed out that Gao Shangyu measured magnetic strata of the Yulin section in 1992. The B/M interface is also located in 31D. There occurred polarity drift event in the Matuyama polarity zone and its location was at 36S and 37L. No polarity drift occurred at 3S but rather at 27S in the Brunhes polarity zone.

If the polarity drift in the Matuyama polarity zone is regarded as a Jalamillo positive polarity subzone, the 36S and its underlying 37L can be compared with S_{10} and L_{11} of the Loess Plateau in Jalamillo positive polarity subzone. The reasons for this are that they are located in a positive polarity subzone and 32S, 33D, 34S, 35D, 36S and 37L below B/M interface of the Yulin section can be compared with S_8, L_9, S_9, L_{10}, S_{10} and L_{11} respectively. No intermittent deposition was found in these strata. The sequences in the Jalamillo are positive polarity subzone in the Loess Plateau, which not only include S_{10} and L_{11} but also include S_{10} and L_{11}. Samples 35D and 38S to L_{10} and S_{11} have no polarity drift. It is unclear whether the result is related to the sampling density.

The polarity drift of 27S in the Yulin section has age significance and can help to divide the stratum sequence of the section. According to the World Magnetic Strata Chronological Table by W. Brian Hariand, Allan V. Cox and others, the oldest polarity drift in Brunhes polarity zone is the Delta negative polarity subzone near the bottom of the positive polarity zone and its age is 635 ka BP. In the Loess Plateau, the age of S_6, 647 ka, 650 ka and 660 ka, are not only approximate to the Delta event, but also the Delta event was found in Lanzhou (Chen Fahu et al., 1993) and Xifeng.

To sum up, we can express the correlation of various layers of 3S-44D in the Yulin section and the loess-paleosol sedimentary sequences and their ages in the Loess Plateau in Fig. 5-7. From the figure, it can be seen that the 44D corresponding to L_{14} represents the oldest aeolian sediment in the Yulin section. For the age of L_{14}, it is respectively 1,110 ka BP and 1,088 ka BP in Xifeng and

Lanzhou calculated with magnetic susceptibility by Chen Fahu in 1993. But in Luochuan, the age of S_{14} under L_{14} is 1,090 ka. There is an obvious difference in age. We temporarily selected the age calculated by Kukla as the sedimentary age of 44D and viewed the sedimentary sequence of aeolian sand-loess-paleosol in the Yulin section as the product in the most recent 1,100 ka BP. And the ages of various layers in the section are the same as those of the corresponding loess-paleosol sequence in the Loess Plateau. Aeolian sand or loess and overlying paleosol are regarded as one sedimentary cycle from the viewpoint of sedimentology. The section is divided into 19.5 cycles and expressed by Cy_0–Cy_{18}. Cy_0 is a half cycle in which a sedimentary sequence has not been finished.

3) The significance of the Yulin section model

Lithologic and lithofacies characters of aeolian sand-loess-paleosol in the Yulin section, marker horizon i.e., compound paleosol, the events of magnetic strata and the TL age explain the relation between the timing of the sedimentary sequence and loess-paleosol in the Loess Plateau. So the defined ages of various layers in the section corresponding to various layers in the Loess Plateau are reliable. We consider that the Yulin section is an epitome of environmental changes in the Ordos Desert and it records a relatively perfect geologic historical process of the alternations of sand, loess and paleosol in the recent 1,100 ka BP.

It is well-known that loess in China records the most perfect geologic information of the paleoclimatic evolution in the Quaternary continental deposits. The vast desert in China is the main source area of basic materials of the Loess Plateau. But from a long-term viewpoint, much work remains to be done to confirm it. The causal relationship between the aeolian dune and sandy paleosol in the Ordos Desert represented by the Yulin section and loess-paleosol in the Loess Plateau reveals the changes of heteropic deposits since 1,100 ka BP.

Researches show that the sedimentary sequence of aeolian sand-loess-paleosol in the Yulin section is a result of regional responses to the changes of winter and summer monsoons under the background of global climate changes in glacial and interglacial periods. Accordingly, the 18.5 sedimentary cycles in the section can be viewed as climatic cycles. One cycle represents a whole process from dry-cold climate under which aeolian sand was formed to wet-warm climate under which paleosol developed. From the comparative study of the age, continental glaciers, loess and deep-sea cores, we can obtain a reference geologic historical record about the evolution of desert in China in the recent 1,100 ka BP.

4) Main conclusions

The Yulin section records a relatively perfect geologic historical process of the evolution of deserts, loess and paleosols in the recent 1,100 ka BP in the Ordos region, and it reveals the coupled relation of the sedimentary sequence of loess-paleosol in the Loess Plateau. Ancient mobile dunes, ancient fixed dunes, loess and paleosol dominated by sandy paleosol (and followed by silty paleosol) in the Yulin section are expressed by D, FD, L and S. Their contrast relation with loess-paleosol in the Loess Plateau is expressed by "→": $3S \rightarrow S_0$, $4D+5L+6D+7L \rightarrow L_1$, $8S \rightarrow S_{1-1}$, $9FD \rightarrow S_{1-1}/S_{1-2}$, $10S \rightarrow S_{1-2}$, $11D \rightarrow S_{1-2}/S_{1-3}$, $12S \rightarrow S_{1-3}$, $13D \rightarrow L_2$, $14S \rightarrow S_2$, $15FD \rightarrow L_3$, $16S \rightarrow S_3$, $17L \rightarrow L_4$, $18S \rightarrow S_4$, $19D \rightarrow L_5$, $20S \rightarrow S_{5-1}$, $21L \rightarrow S_{5-1}/S_{5-2}$, $22S \rightarrow S_{5-2}$, $23FD \rightarrow S_{5-2}/S_{5-3}$, $24S \rightarrow S_{5-3}$, $25D+26L \rightarrow L_6$, $27S \rightarrow S_6$, $28D+29L \rightarrow L_7$, $30S \rightarrow S_7$, $31D \rightarrow L_8$, $32S \rightarrow S_8$, $33D \rightarrow L_9$, $34S \rightarrow S_9$, $35D \rightarrow L_{10}$, $36S \rightarrow S_{10}$, $37L \rightarrow L_{11}$, $38S \rightarrow S_{11}$, $39L+40FD \rightarrow L_{12}$, $41S \rightarrow S_{12}$, $42FD \rightarrow L_{13}$, $43S \rightarrow S_{13}$, $44D \rightarrow L_{14}$.

5.3.2.2 Sand sedimentary sequence and age of the Aqiang section on the edge of hyperarid areas since 700 ka BP

Viewed from the distribution area and depositional scale of paleo-aeolian sand, the western desert zone is the largest among various desert subzones of China. Numerous desert sediment records have been found in the western desert zone. But the direct evidence relating ancient paleo aeolian sand to the formation and evolution processes of deserts is scarce. Fortunately, we discovered a satisfactory section with long-term stratigraphic records of desert evolution in a deep wadi several kilometers south of Aqiang in a border belt during the winter of 1990, and named it the Aqiang section. Located at the edge of a hyperarid region, the Aqiang sections sand sedimentary sequence and the age since 700 ka BP is discussed below.

1) The problem regarding loess regarding extremely arid areas

The thickness of loess strata is thin and its age is younger in arid areas, especially in the hyperarid regions of China. They usually do not have a perfect sedimentary sequence like the loess and paleosol in the Loess Plateau. They generally occur in the form of single stratum or aeolian earthy deposits. Therefore, whether there is thicker and older loess deposits in the arid region is still an open question. Hence, we will take aeolian sand deposits in the Aqiang stratigraphic section, located at the edge of an extremely arid area, as a typical example and try to answer these questions to put forward some preliminary views.

2) Aqiang section

The Aqiang section is located 4 km southwest of Aqiang, Yutian, Xinjiang and at the border of a sub-sand soil zone in the southern edge of the Taklimakan Desert and loess zone at the northern piedmont of the Kunlun Mountains. Its geographic coordinate is 81°56′E, 36°28′N and altitude is 2,420–2,492.5 m. Average annual precipitation, evaporation and air temperature is 170 mm, 2,590 mm and 12°C respectively. Aridity is higher than 16. It is located on the edge of a hyperarid area. The section is 72.5 m thick and has 29 layers of loess, 12 layers of sub-sand soil, 2 layers of gravel and one layer of sod. Loess and subsand soil is mainly an aeolian layer, with a thickness of 66.20 m. They cover the third terrace formed by alluvial and pluvial sands and gravels. The Aqiang section can be divided into 5 formations (Fig. 5-8).

(1) Holocene Kulafu Formation stratum number (1PE1–1PE5). The sod, dark brown yellow silt-silty very fine sand is loose and relatively compact, well-sorted and contains white pseudohypha, worm holes herb litters and root systems. It is often covered by grayish aeolian subsand soil which is 2.3 m in thickness.

(2) Upper Pleistocene upper Pulu formation (2A–27A). The interbed of subsand soil and loess is the main feature (2A–27A). The formation consists of grayish yellow silt-silty very fine sand. It is loose and well sorted and contains Ca-cemented subsand soil, loess and "salt horizon" due to the effect of running water. Furthermore, it is intercalated with several layers of brown yellow compacted loess.

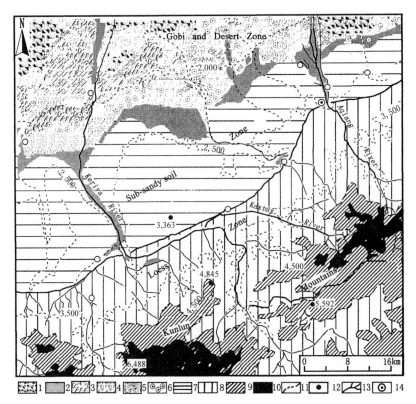

Fig. 5-8   The location of Aqiang section and main types of aeolian deposits

1. Gobi; 2. oasis forest land and irrigation farmland; 3. crescent dune and chain; 4. dune ridge and barchan ridge; 5. mobile dune; 6. fixed-semifixed dune; 7. sub-sandy soil; 8. loess; 9. bedrock mountainous region; 10. ice and snow; 11. contour line altitude (m); 12. elevation point (m); 13. river; 14. the location of the Aqiang section

(3) Upper Pleistocene lower Pulu formation (28G, 29FGL). The formation can be divided into two layers. The upper layer-28G is dark grey-pale yellow alluvial slope sand and gravels. The gravels vary between 0.02–0.05 m in diameter, are sub-angular and consist of granite, granodiorite and diabase. Their surfaces have grey black desert varnish and abraded aeolian pits. The lower layer-29FGL is loess and is dark brown-sandy beige silt and relatively tight. Its grain is fine. There are vertical joint, ferromagnesian spots and gypsum.

(4) Mid-Pleistocene Aqiang formation (30SL–43A). The formation consists of dark brown yellow silt and dark brown silt interbeds and has ferromanganese spots. The former is lumpish and compacted and has vertical joint. The latter is more compacted and darker in color and consists of finer grains and contains rock salt and gypsum. From the middle to the bottom of the formation there is light yellow sub-sand soil with crossbedding. Sometimes there are interlayers of alluvial sand and well-rounded fine gravels 0.10 m thickness.

(5) Lower Pleistocene Xiyu formation (44G). The formation is alluvial and pluvial gravels with sand soil, dark grayish yellow in color, slightly cemented and well rounded. The diameter of gravels is 0.05–0.20 m and the biggest diameter is 0.40 m. The gravels mainly consist of granite with small amount of basalt and diabase.

Fig. 5-10 shows the grain-size analytical results of the Aqiang section.

3) Geologic age of the Aqiang section

(1) The comparative analysis of stratigraphic age of the Aqiang section. Viewed from lithologic characters and sedimentary facies, the main characteristics of Kulafu formation and Pulu formation in Aqiang section are similar to those of the sod and the underlying subsand soil with loess in Pulu, west of the area. The formation ages of the latter two are 10ka BP and 70–10 ka BP i.e. Holocene and last glacial period. Zheng Benxing et al. (1990) and Wen Qizhong et al. (1995) researched loess in subsand soil in Pulu and adjacent areas. Ages of loess determined by them are 29,140±430 a BP, 18,200±1,600 a BP and 17,700±1,800 a BP. The ages of sand deposits underlaid by sod of the Pulu formation in the Aqiang section are 36,000± 1,800 a BP, 24,700±3,100 a BP and 25,400±1,260 a BP except 57,500±2,570 a BP (Fig. 5-10). The ages of the sods developed on the top of sand deposits in Pulu and the northern Piedmont of the Kunlun Mountains are 7,080±73 a BP, 6,610±70 a BP, 5,686±155 a BP, 5,338±132 a BP, 2,486±75 a BP (Wang, 1992) and 4,550±230 a BP (Li Baosheng et al., 1995).

The loess characteristics of the section in the Aqiang formation are similar to those of the loess in western Shanxi, northern Shaanxi, Qingyang and Xifeng in Gansu, such as ferromanganese spots and vertical joint of the former. The difference is that the former contains gypsum and rock salt and the latter contains secondary carbonate.

What is worth further discussion is the geologic age of sand and gravel layer-28G and the underlying dark brown-light drab loess layer-29FGL at the bottom of the Pulu formation. Their formation time should be in the initial stages of the Pulu formation after the Aqiang formation was formed. In loess areas in Shanxi and Shaanxi, the Malan Loess and the Lishi Loess usually take paleosol S_1 as the boundary, while the sediment between the Malan Loess or synchronous Chengchuan formation and Lishi loess take fluvial and lacustrine Salawusu formation as the boundary at the southern edge of the Mu Us Sandy Land. The upper and lower limits of it are 70,900±6,200 a BP and 50,200±19,100 a BP respectively (Li Baosheng et al., 1998a). So we can consider that the formation time of 28G and 29FGL is 15–70 ka BP corresponding to S_1 or the Salawusu formation.

The Xiyu formation in the section no doubt formed earlier than the Aqiang formation. Satellite images show that the Xiyu formation and the Kangsulake Conglomerate in the upper Keriya River and the alluvial and pluvial fans at the northern foot of the Kunlun Mountains seem to be contemporaneous. Their gravel composition and roundness are approximate. Liu Jiaqi and others determined the K-Ar ages of two basalt interlayers, lower Kangsulake and upper Kangsulake lavas, they are 1.43±0.03 Ma BP and 1.21±0.02 Ma BP. There are 8 m thick alluvial and pluvial conglomerates above the upper Kangsulake basalt. In other words, the age of the Kangsulake Conglomerate is early Pleistocene, and the Xiyu formation in the Aqiang section is of the same age.

(2) Magnetic stratigraphic age of the Aqiang section. A total of 107 groups of paleomagnetic samples on 321 pieces were collected. The sampling interval is generally 0.8 m and decreases to 0.4 m, or even 0.2 m, near the interface of formations. The paleomagnetic samples are treated with alternating demagnetization with 250–350 Ost Peak intensity. The determined results of the index of magnetic inclination and D (magnetic declination) of 1PE-42FGL in the Aqiang section are shown in Fig. 5-9. It can be seen from the figure that I has a positive bias for most paleomagnetic samples in the Aqiang section, except for samples $37FGL_2$, $39FGL_3$ and $40A_1$ which showed a negative bias. These exceptions are located at depths of 57.6–59.5 m and 63–64 m in the section. The changes of the index of D and I tended to be synchronous. This paleomagnetic data indicated aeolian sand deposition since 42FGL was in a positive polarity zone and there were two possible temporary negative polarity subzones near the bottom of the section. The I values of 8 groups of samples at the depth of 59.5–63 m between two subzones are positive or 31°–72°. The I values of 5 groups of samples at the depths of 64–68.2 m in the lower subzone are also positive or 54°–61°. From these results and the continuity of sand deposition, we consider that despite there are polarity drifts near the bottom of Aqiang section, it is farfetched to take them as Matuyama zone and it is feasible to take strata in and above 42FGL as a Brunhes positive polarity zone.

Liu Jiaqi, Zheng Benxing and Wen Qizhong believe the age of the Kangsulake Conglomerate to be early Pleistocene. Hence we can conclude that the conglomerate above Kangsulake Lava of 1.43 Ma BP or 1.21 Ma BP should be an upward extension of the Matuyama negative polarity zone. Furthermore, the age of loess above Kangsulake Conglomerate is 0.2 Ma BP and in Brunhes positive polarity zone. But the K-Ar age of the Heilongshan volcanic phase, the oldest volcanic phase of the mid-Pleistocene, is 0.67 Ma BP. This age is close to the lower limit of the Brunhes positive polarity zone or the upper limit of the Matuyama negative polarity zone which is 0.73 Ma BP. According to the deposition sequence, the surface of the Kangsulake Conglomerate can be viewed as interface of B/M. The interface of the Aqiang Formation and the Xiyu Formation in the Aqiang section also can be regarded approximatively as interface of B/M of magnetostraitigraphy. It looks as if two negative polarity subzones in Brunhes normal polarity zone of the Aqiang section correspond to Big lost negative polarity subzones and Delta negative polarity subzones. Their ages are 0.58 Ma BP and 0.635 Ma BP respectively (Fig. 5-9). It is obvious that the initial magnetostratigraphic age for the sand deposition in the Aqiang section should be at the beginning of the Brunhes and sand deposits in the Aqiang region gradually formed since Brunhes.

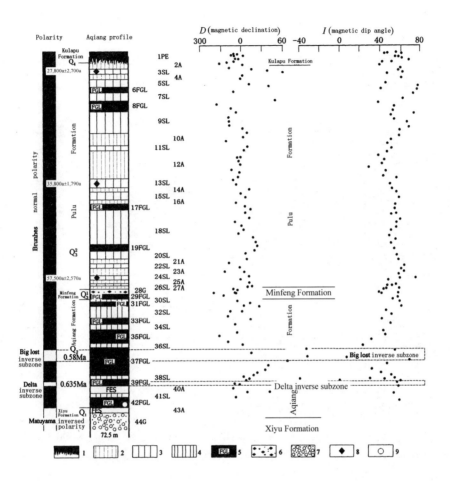

Fig. 5-9 Aqiang section and its magnetic stratigraphic result of sand deposits

1. modern loess; 2. sub-sand (soil silty very fine sand) 3. loess silt; 4. compact loess; 5. clay soil; 6. sand and gravel; 7. sand and pebble; 8. dating location; 9. cosmic dust

(3) The age comparison of loess-paleosol sequence in the Loess Plateau and sand sequence in the Aqiang section since Brunhes. Field investigations show that almost no paleosols exist in aeolian sand deposits in the extremely arid Aqiang or even all of southern Xinjiang. The comparative studies of the northern piedmont of the Kunlun Mountains and loess-paleosol sequence in the Loess Plateau and the paleoclimate show that the sand deposition environment was extremely arid when paleosol was developed in the Loess Plateau in Brunhes. The possible reason is that the Siberia-Mongolia anticyclone declined on a large scale between the Loess Plateau to Ordos during the interglacial period (Li Baosheng, et al., 1998) and the effect of the winter monsoon decreased but the effect of the summer monsoon strengthened. Because of the weak effect of the southeast and the southwest

summer monsoon, soil forming processes occurred in dunes and loess. In addition, the decline of the winter monsoon is reflected in changes of ancient aeolian sand in hyperarid areas, especially in oases. For example, aeolian sand deposition was the main characteristic of the Yutian-Hotan Oasis at the southern edge of the Taklimakan Desert during the cold period. In theory, although the area had no developmental conditions for S_0, S_1, S_2, S_3, S_4, S_5, S_6 and S_7 in the Loess Plateau, it should have isochronous deposits of paleosol. As described above, we confirmed the age of the Kulafu Formation in the Aqiang section is Holocene or corresponding to S_0 time. Here we will discuss the correlation of the Aqiang section and S_0, S_1, S_2, S_3, S_4, S_5, S_6 and S_7 from 4 aspects (Fig. 5-10).

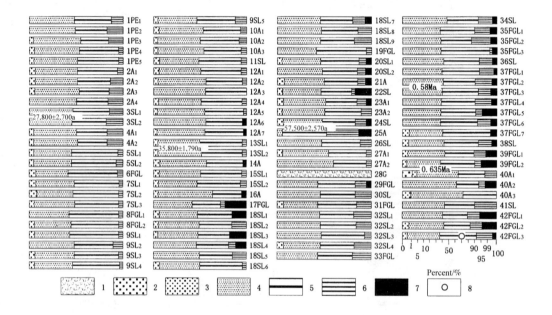

Fig. 5-10　The result of grain size of sand deposits in the Aqiang section

1. gravel; 2. medium sand ($\varphi1—2$); 3. fine sand ($\varphi2—3.32$); 4. very fine sand ($\varphi3.32—4.32$); 5. coarse silt ($\varphi4.32—6.64$); 6. fine silt ($\varphi6.64—7.64$); 7. clay ($>\varphi7.64$); 8. cosmic dust

① Under 28G and above 43G is almost entirely the strata of the Aqiang formation. The contents of silt and clay are relatively high in 29FGL, 31FGL, 33FGL, 35FGL, 37FGL, 39FGL and 42FGL. The sum of silt and clay content is higher than 61.40% and the rest is mainly very fine sand. The sum of silt and clay content in their interlayers is less than the content but very fine sand content is higher and forms the mode of grain size. In these layers there are rock salt and gypsum which developed in the dry and hot climatic condition (Zhang Pengxi, et al., 1991a). So 29FGL, 31FGL, 33FGL, 35FGL, 37FGL, 39FGL and 42FGL can be regarded as the marker layers of warm period and compared with S_1, ..., S_7.

② The age of 28G–29FGL was inferred to be 150–70 ka BP Salawusu period or S_1 period. If this view is correct, the 4th dark brown loess-37FGL under 28G–29FGL can be compared with S_5. The former is in the Big lost negative polarity subzone. The age is 0.58 Ma BP and very close to the lower limit of S_5 (age 0.56 Ma BP). The 5th dark brown loess-39FGL under 28G–29FGL and $40A_1$ is in the Delta negative polarity subzone. The age is 0.635 Ma BP. And the lower limit of S_6 is 0.66 Ma BP. The 6th dark brown loess-42FGL and the underlying aeolian sand-43A corresponds to S_7 and L_8 in the Loess Plateau.

③ S_5 in the Loess Plateau recorded the climatic optimum in the Holocene. The contemporaneous paleosol Paks in the Carpatii Basin in central Europe and F_6 of Atrai Slankmen loess section developed in a very warm and wet interglacial period. The content of aeolian sand in 37FGL in the Aqiang section is relatively low. The content of sand in 7 samples $37FGL_1$–$37FGL_7$ varies between 28.34%–37.76% and the average is 32.17%. The sum of silt and clay contents is higher than 62%. This shows that the formation of 37FGL, to a great degree, is related to the decline of the winter monsoon in Eurasia in the period of S_5 or F_6. So they should be contemporaneous.

④ The existing evidence indicates that there have been 6 collision events of huge celestial bodies since the Holocene (Xiao, et al., 1995). The latest collision occured in 0.7 Ma BP and its cosmic dust covered a vast area. The dust was discovered in deep-sea cores. It was also discovered in terrestrial strata, the top of L_8 to the bottom of S_7 above interface of B/M in the Luochuan Loess. Its age is 0.720–0.724 Ma BP (Li, et al., 1992). According to the determined results by Dai Fengnian using EPM-810Q electron microscope and electron microprobe, there are cosmic dusts in $42FGL_3$. They are spherical in shape and belong to a siliceous micrometeorite. Their surface texture and chemical composition are similar to some siliceous cosmic dust in Chinese deserts (Dai, et al., 1994). Obviously, this finding provides evidence to determine the boundary of B/M and sand deposition sequence in the Aqiang section during Brunhes. From this it follows that 1PE, 28G–29FGL, 31FGL, 33FGL, 35FGL, 37FGL, 39FGL and 42FGL in the Aqiang section can be compared with S_0, S_1, S_2, S_3, S_4, S_5, S_6 and S_7.

4) Main conclusions

The Aqiang section is the thickest section of aeolian sand deposits which has been discovered in the hyperarid area. It records the sand deposition and environmental evolution process in the western desert zone of China since Brunhes. The research results indicate that 1PE, 28G–29FGL, 31FGL, 33FGL, 35FGL, 37FGL, 39FGL and 42FGL in the Aqiang section can be compared with S_0, S_1, S_2, S_3, S_4, S_5, S_6 and S_7 in the Loess plateau. The sand strata in the section can be compared with loess in the Loess Plateau during Brunhes.

5.3.3 The high-resolution records of desert evolution in China since the late Pleistocene—the research of strata and their ages in the Salawusu River basin since 150 ka BP

The research of Quaternary strata in the Salawusu River basin was initiated in the late 19th century. During 1892–1894, the famous Russian geographer, Obruchev arrived at the Salawusu River basin in Jingbian of Shaanxi Province (Fig. 5-11). There, he observed the gravel stratum and fluvio-lacustrine deposits, i.e. "torrent facies", and inferred that its age is the same as the loess age on the southeastern slope.

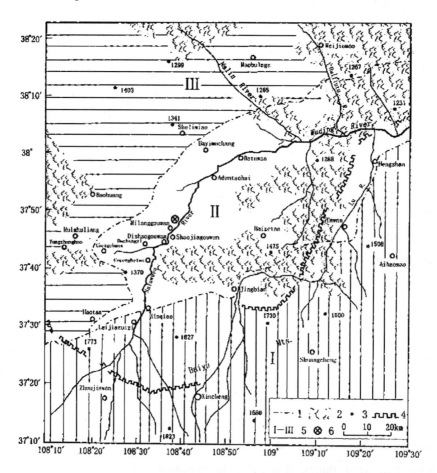

Fig. 5-11　Salawusu River basin and location of the Milanggouwan Section

1. Boundary of Geomorphologicgical Units; 2.Aeolian sand dunes of the Mu Us Sandy Land; 3. Elevation above sea level; 4. The Great Wall; 5.Position of the Milanggouwan Section; 6.Section position

In the 1920s, French paleontologist Teilhard de Chardin et al. did a lot of research in the Dagouwan village of the Salawusu River basin. According to their work on the Quaternary and paleontology in the areas including the Ordos Desert and the southern loess region from 1922 to 1923, they named a series of strata as the "Salawusu series" formed in late Pleistocene (renamed Salawusu Formation in

1956). Since the 1950s, much work has been done by Chinese scholars in the fields of stratigraphy, geochronology, paleontology, paleoanthropology, and the paleolithic and neolithic cultures (Jia, 1950; Pei and Li, 1964; Wang, 1964; Qi, 1975; Yuan, 1978; Dong et al. , 1982; Zhou et al. , 1982; Li et al. , 1988; Zheng, 1989). Based on previous study, Li Baosheng studied the Chengchuan Formation which is dominated by desert deposits on the Salawusu Formation (Li et al., 1993 b).

Since the 1970s, great progress has been made in studying the changes of continental glaciers and oceanic water bodies caused by "past global change" and their relation to changes of the paleomonsoon in China's Loess Plateau and environmental vicissitude (Kang et al., 1993). The results show that the global climate fluctuates with several cycles. There were a number of stadials and interstadials during the classical glacial and interglacial period, and there were also secondary climatic cycles in the latter two periods. These results gave us an important clue for further study of stratigraphical sequence at the southeastern edge of the Hetao Plain and the response of desert regions to global climatic fluctuation in the past 150 ka. In this section, we would like to take the Milanggouwan section as at model section of southeastern edge of the Hetao Plain to describe its characteristics and establish a chronology of desert formation and development over the past 150 ka BP.

5.3.3.1 Description of the Milanggouwan section

The milanggouwan section is located in the left bank of the middle reach of the Salawusu River with a thickness of 83 m, in which 29 layers are paleo-mobile dunes, three layers are paleo-fixed and semi-fixed dunes and one layer is modern mobile dunes. The color is mostly greyish yellow and brownish. The 9 layers of fluvio-lacustrine deposits are greyish green, rusty yellow and dark yellow; the 19 layers of lacustrine-swamp deposits are greenish yellow, caesious and dark gray etc.; the 5 layers of brown drab soil are light brown and ficelle; the 4 layers of Heilu soil are dark brown-greyish black; the 2 layers of loess are light greyish yellow; 3 layers of congeliturbated folds deformed after the lacustrine-swamp facies were deposited. Lithologic characteristics of various layers are shown in Fig. 5-12. The strata included the Lishi Formation of the mid Pleistocene, the Salawusu Formation and the Chengchuan Formation of the Upper Pleistocene, the Dagouwan Formation and Dishaowan Formation of the Holocene. From Fig. 5-12, it can be seen that sand dunes, especially palaeo-mobile dunes, are the most prominent characteristic of deposit facies in the Milanggouwan section, while fluvio-lacustrine deposits and palaeosols are the second most prominent. Compared with fluvio-lacustrine deposits and paleosols, grain-size of the aeolian sand is coarser, with better sorting. In the vertical direction, it exhibits an obvious coarse-fine alternation changes. There are calcareous nodules developing at the bottom of fluvio-lacustrine deposits and paleosols. Paleosols in the section have obvious soil genetic horizons, namely the upper part is claying horizon, the middle part is calcareous horizon, and the lower part is sand dunes or parent material layer composed of fluvio-lacustrine deposits.

Experimental results and examinations under a microscope indicate that brown drab soil and Heilu soil have a very obvious cemented speckled micro-structure. For convenient description, we abbreviate modern mobile dunes, paleo-mobile dunes, paleo-fixed and semi-fixed dunes, fluvial facies, lake-swamp facies, paleosols and loess to MD, D, Fd, FL, LS, S and L respectively, which is placed behind the serial number of corresponding layers in the section as shown in Fig. 5-12. Besides stratigraphic lithologic character, age and layers with fossils are also shown in Fig. 5-12. Mollusk fossils are chosen to date ages of the top of 2S, 14LS, 22LS, 26LS and 30LS; 3LS, 6LS and 8 LS have a silt age; ages of 12S, 24S, 36S and 28FL are obtained through dating organic matter from soils and plant remains. The ages mentioned above were determined by Hu at ^{14}C Laboratory of Cold and Arid Regions Environmental and Engineering Research Institute, Chinese Academy of Sciences. Samples of quartz grains were used to get ages of 21D, 23D, 25D, 29D, 64D and 60D. Ages of the former five layers were determined by Zheng Gongwang at Laboratory of Thermoluminescence of Department of City and Environment, Peking University; ages of 43D and 60D were determined by Pei Jingxian at Laboratory of Thermoluminescence, Institute of Geology, Chinese Academy of Sciences and Zhang Jingzhao at Xi'an Laboratory of Loess and Quaternary Geology, Chinese Academy of Sciences respectively. Fossils of wooly rhinoceros' tooth were used by Yuan Sicheng et al. at Laboratory of U-series of Department of Archeology in Peiking University to date age of 26LS. Because main boundaries of stratigraphic deposits of the Salawusu River basin are obvious and easy to compare, we compared the strata and their ages of Dishaogouwan, Dashibian and Batuwan near the Milanggouwan section with each other and obtained 3 ages related to the Milanggouwan section. In addition, ages of 4 layers of this section were dated recently, and the result is that the bottom of 2S has a ^{14}C age of 1,450±120 a BP; the bottom of 4LS yields a ^{14}C age of 1,480±85 a BP, the bottom of 62Fd dated by TL has an age of 148,000±12,500 a BP; the top of 65L has a TL age of 229±18 ka BP. The materials used for ^{14}C dating are organic matters in strata. ^{14}C dating was finished by Xu Qizhi and Cao Jixiu at ^{14}C Laboratory of Lanzhou University. The materials used for TL dating are aeolian quartz grains. TL dating was finished by Lu Liangcai at TL Laboratory of Institute of Geochemistry in Guangzhou at the Chinese Academy of Sciences. Fig. 5-12 shows that structures of aeolian dunes, fluvio-lacustrine deposits and paleosols (upper Pleistocene–Holocene) are obvious, and several layers are interbedded with each other. The time line of Lishi Formation/Salawusu Formation, Salawusu Formation/Chengchuan Formation and Chengchuan Formation/Dagouwan Formation is approximately 150 ka BP, 70 ka BP and 10 ka BP respectively.

It's obvious that the Milanggouwan section not only represents strata of this area but also implies when each main stratum came into being. It has general characteristics of regional and temporal strata. Detailed descriptions of this section are as follows.

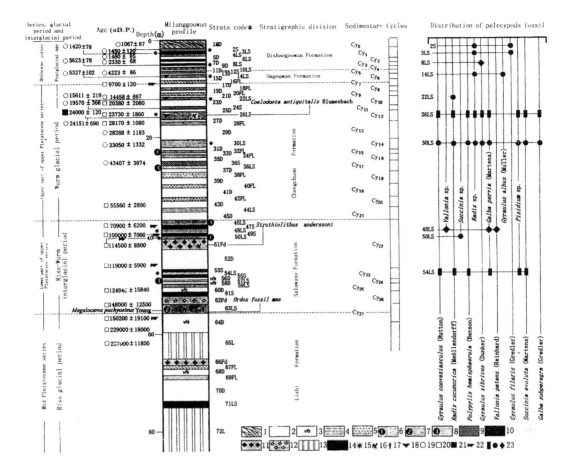

Fig. 5-12 Milanggouwan stratigraphical section and its magnetic susceptibility values

1. recent mobile dune; 2. paleo-mobile dune sand (fine sand); 3. paleo-mobile dune sand (very fine sand); 4. silty (very fine sand); 5. clay fine sand (fluvial facies); 6. silty fine sand; 7. clayey and silty fine sand; 8. clayey very fine sand; 9. black loam paleosol; 10. brownish-drab paleosol; 11. paleo-fixed to semi-fixed dunes (fine sand); 12. paleo-fixed to semi-fixed dune (very fine sand); 13. Lishi loess; 14. silt-clayey silt; 15. mollusk fossil; 16. vertebrate fossil; 17. Hetao Man fossil; 18. congeliturbated fold; 19. ^{14}C age; 20. TL age; 21. uranium age; 22. the ages obtained from the comparison with the related strata concerned in the Salawusu River basin; 23. the symbols represent that the number of the mollusk fossils is large, moderate and respectively

1) Dishaogouwan Formation of Upper Holocene

1MD, modern aeolian dunes in the Mu Us Sandy Land, greyish yellow, loose, well sorted and 2–5 m thick.

2S, dark grey black fine silty sand, with plenty of mollusk fossils. Heilu soil, soil genetic horizon is mainly lake-swamp deposits, its top and bottom have a ^{14}C age of $1,064\pm67$ a BP and $1,450\pm120$ a BP respectively, 0.5m thick.

3LS, greenish yellow or rusty yellow fine sand, with few mollusk fossils, lake-swamp deposits, with a ^{14}C age of $1,420\pm67$ a BP 0.15 m thick.

4LS, dark greyish yellow or rusty yellow very fine silty sand, lake-swamp deposits, its bottom yields a ^{14}C age of $1,480\pm85$ a BP.

5D, greyish yellow or rusty yellow aeolian fine sand, paleo-mobile dunes, 0.2 m thick.

6LS, greyish brown sand, horizontal stratification, containing roots of plants, swamp facies deposits, with ^{14}C age of 2,330±68 a BP.

7D, greyish yellow aeolian fine sand, uniformly sorted, with rare fluviation trace, dominated by paleo-shifting dunes, 0.2 m thick.

8LS, dark grey black sub-clayey silt, with few mollusk fossils, lake-swamp facies, with ^{14}C age of 3623±78 a BP, 0.05 m thick.

9D, greyish yellow fine sand. Paleo-shifting dunes, 0.55 m thick.

10LS, dark grey silt and very fine sand, containing plant roots, swamp facies, 0.4 m thick.

11D, greyish yellow, paleo-shifting dunes, 0.5 m thick.

12S, greyish yellow or light grey black silty fine sand, weakly developed Heilu soil with ^{14}C age of 4,223±86 a BP 0.05–0.1 m thick.

13D, greyish yellow fine sand, uniformly sorted, containing ferreous rusty spots caused by waterlogging, paleo-mobile dunes, 0.5 m thick.

2) Mid-lower Dagouwan Formation of the Holocene

14LS, dark grey green to versicolor, silty and very fine sand, containing plenty of mollusk fossils, this layer is congeliturbated fold layer, swamp facies, ^{14}C age: 5,327±102 a BP, 0.4 m thick.

15D, greyish yellow fine sand, paleo-mobile dunes, 1.0 m thick.

16FL, rusty yellow silty fine sand, with horizontal bedding, calcareous pan at the bottom, fluvial facies. ^{14}C age: 9,510±110 a BP, the corresponding layer of the Dishaogouwan section has a ^{14}C age of 9,700±120 a BP, 0.33 m thick.

3) Chengchuan Formation of Upper Pleistocene

17D, greyish yellow fine sand, paleo-mobile dune, 1.0 m thick.

18FL, greyish yellow silty very fine sand, with horizontal bedding, with calcareous pan at the bottom, fluvial facies, 0.4 m thick.

19D, greyish yellow fine sand, paleo-mobile dunes, 0.5 m thick.

20FL, greyish yellow silty fine sand, with obvious bedding, with calcareous pan at the bottom, fluvial facies, 0.4 m thick.

21D, greyish yellow fine sand, with obvious foreset bedding, paleo-mobile dunes, TL age:14458±867aBP, 0.25 m thick.

22LS, caesious, silty and very fine sand, with a few mollusk fossils. It's congeliturbated fold, lake-swamp facies, ^{14}C age: 15,611±219 a BP, 0. 4 m thick.

23D, greyish yellow fine sand, paleo-mobile dunes, a TL age: 20,380±2,080 a BP, 2.0 m thick.

24S, dark brown-greyish black, silty and very fine sand, paleosol is weakly developed to Heilu soil, soil parent material is lake-swamp deposits, the ^{14}C age: 19,570±366 a BP, 0.5 m thick.

25D, greyish yellow fine sand, paleo-mobile dunes, TL age: 23,730±1,860 a BP, 0.4 m thick.

26LS, dark gray, silty and very fine sand, containing numerous mollusk fossils, it's congeliturbated fold, lake-swamp facies, ^{14}C age at the bottom: 24,151±690 a BP, U-series age in the middle part: 24,000±120 a BP, 2.1 m thick.

27D, greyish yellow fine sand, paleo-shifting dunes, 0.6 m thick.

28FL, dark greyish yellow, silty and very fine sand, with calcareous pan at the bottom, fluvial facies, ^{14}C age: 28,170±1,080a BP 0.2 m thick.

29D, greyish yellow fine sand, paleo-mobile dunes, TL age: 28,268±1,183 a BP 3.0 m thick.

30LS$_{1-3.}$ 30LS$_3$, dark greyish yellow, silty and very fine sand, lake-swamp facies, 0.2 m thick, 30LS$_2$, rusty yellow to yellow, silty and very fine sand, containing many mollusk fossils, there are calcareous nodules at the top and bottom, lake-swamp facies.[14]C age: 33,050±1,322 a BP 0.5m thick, 30LS$_1$, dark gray, silty and very fine sand, with calcareous nodules at the bottom, 0. 8 m thick.

31D, greyish yellow fine sand, paleo-shifting dunes, 1.1 m thick.

32FL, alternatively occurred greyish yellow fine sand and dark grey or yellow fine clayey sand, with intercalated calcareous pan and calcareous nodules, fluvial facies, 0.35 m thick.

33D, greyish yellow fine sand, paleo-shifting dunes, 0.7 m thick.

34FL, light greyish yellow, silty and very fine sand, with calcareous pan at the bottom, fluvial facies, 0.3 m thick.

35D, light brownish red fine sand, paleo-shifting dunes, 0.8 m thick.

36S, dark gray, silty and very fine sand, Heilu soil, 1.1 m thick.

36LS, dark gray, clayey and very fine sand, containing calcareous pan, lake-swamp facies, ^{14}C age: 43,407±3,874 a BP, 0.3 m thick.

37D, greyish yellow fine sand, its top was influenced by running water, paleo-mobile dunes, 1.2 m thick.

38FL, greyish yellow, silty and fine sand, containing remains and roots of herbaceous and woody plants, calcareous pan and stratified calcareous nodules, fluvial facies, 1.0 m thick.

39D, greyish yellow fine sand, paleo-shifting dunes, 1.0 m thick.

40FL, greyish yellow, silty and fine sand, containing remains and roots of herbaceous and woody plants and calcareous nodules, fluvial facies, 0.15 m thick.

41D, brownish yellow fine sand, paleo-mobile dunes, 2.2 m thick.

42FL, dark gray, silty and fine sand, containing ferruginous rusty spots, inclined bedding caused by running water, remains and roots of herbaceous and woody plants and sparse calcareous nodules. Fluvial facies, 0.4 m thick.

43D, greyish yellow fine sand, with sparse ferruginous rusty spots at the bottom and horizontal bedding, paleo-shifting dunes, a TL age: 55,560±2,800 a BP, 1.8 m thick.

44LS, greyish yellow-dark greyish green, silty and very fine sand, containing calcareous nodules and calcareous pans, lacustrine facies, 0.8 m thick.

45D$_1$-D$_3$, D$_3$-D$_2$, greyish yellow fine sand, paleo-shifting dunes, 2.15 m thick. 45D$_1$, orange aeolian fine sand, probably semi-fixed dunes, 0.15 m thick.

4) Lower Salawusu Formation of upper Pleistocene

46LS, greenish yellow, silty and very fine sand, containing calcareous nodules, lacustrine facies, 0.6 m thick.

47S, light brown, clayey and fine to very fine sand, brown drab paleosols, with ferruginous and manganic spots, roots system of plants and calcareous nodules, with a thickness of 10–15 cm at the bottom, which became light pale green, silty and fine sand in transversed direction, lake facies. The corresponding layer of the Dishaogouwan section has a TL age of 70,900±6,200 a BP, 0.75 m thick.

48LS, light greenish yellow, silty and very fine sand, with 15 cm thick calcareous nodules at the bottom, lake facies, containing few mollusk fossils, 0.8 m thick.

49S, light brown, clayey and very fine sand, light brown paleosols, with wedge sands, containing root system of plants and rusty spots. There is an about 8 cm thick light gray calcareous nodules at the bottom, 0.5 m thick.

50LS, light gray, clayey and fine sand, lacustrine facies, containing mollusk fossils, 0.4 m thick.

51Fd, light greyish yellow, silty and fine sand, fixed dunes, vertical joints, containing calcareous nodules, ostrich egg fossils, rusty spots, calcareous nodules at the bottom, 2. 7 m thick.

52D, greyish yellow fine sand, paleo-shifting dunes, intercalated with greyish yellow, silty and fine sand of fluvial facies, containing sparse root system of plants, 4.0 m thick.

53S, brown drab clayey silts, brown drab paleosols, with 0.08 m thick calcareous nodules and pan at the bottom. The surface contacted 54LS was denuded slightly, where there are remains of calcareous nodules, 0.35 m thick.

54LS, grey green, silty and very fine sand, lake facies, containing numerous mollusks fossils, 0.25 m thick.

55S, light brown drab, clayey and very fine sand, light brown drab paleosols, with 5–10 cm thick nodules at the bottom, 0.4 m thick.

56D, grey yellow fine sand, paleo-shifting dunes, with orange sand at the top, due to waterlogging, 0.5 m thick.

57LS, light greyish yellow, clayey and very fine sand, fluvio-lacustrine facies, containing ferrugenous rusty spots, 0.3 m thick.

58D, light red, clayey and very fine sand, paleo-shifting dunes, 0.15 m thick.

59LS, greyish yellow, silty and very fine sand, lake facies, containing calcareous nodules, 1.1 m thick.

60D, greyish yellow very fine sand, paleo-shifting dunes, with sparse calcareous nodules and traces of fluviation, a TL age:124,940±15,840 a BP, 0.3 m thick.

61S, grey drab, sub-clayey and very fine sand, greyish brown drab paleosols, with scale-like structure, containing root system of plants and calcareous pan at both the top and bottom, 1.23 m thick.

62Fd, greyish yellow, dark greyish yellow to light brown clayey fine sand, paleo-fixed to semi-fixed dunes, compact, no bedding, and calcareous pan is intercalated in the middle part. The bottom has a TL age of 148,000±12,500 a BP, 2.25 m thick.

63LS, dark grey green, clayey and fine sand in the upper part, lake facies, containing rusty yellow plant remains and fossil of Hetao Man's bones, 1.1 m thick; greenish yellow, silty and fine sand at the bottom, lake facies, containing plant remains, deer fossils and grey green calcareous nodules, 0.9 m thick.

5) Lishi Formation of middle Pleistocene

64D, brownishred to light brownishred fine to very fine sand, greyish yellow fine sand 1.2 m below the top, paleo-shifting dunes, containing several layers of calcareous pans. The corresponding layer near the Dashibian Formation has a TL age of 150.2±19.1 ka BP, 2.8 m thick.

65L, greyish yellow, clayey and fine sand, Lishi loess, well sorted, lumpy, quite hard, vertical joint, containing rusty yellow strips or spots and calcareous nodules developed from root system of plants. There is a 5–10 cm thick calcareous pan at the top, and there are calcareous nodules layers at 3.9 m and 4.3 m beneath this layer. The nodules' diameter is 10–20 cm; this layer is 25 cm thick. TL age of the middle part: 237±11.8 ka BP, TL age of the top: 229±18 ka BP, 5.4 m thick.

66Fd, greyish yellow, silty and very fine sand, fixed dunes sand, compact and hard, vertical joint, without bedding, there is a 0.2 m thick calcareous pan and nodules layer, 1.1 m thick.

67FL, greyish yellow, silty and very fine sand, fluvio-lacustrine facies, nearly horizontal bedding, 0.3 m thick.

68D, greyish yellow very fine sand, paleo-shifting dunes sand, with obvious foreset bedding, 0.9 m thick.

69FL, dark grey green, silty and very fine sand fluviatile facies, ferruginous rusty spots, 0.4 m thick.

70D, greyish yellow fine sand in the upper part, brownish red fine sand at the bottom, there is a 3 cm thick calcareous pan in the middle, paleo shifting dunes sand, without bedding, 1.93 m thick.

71LS, light gray clayey silts, lake facies, horizontal bedding, with calcareous nodules, ferrugenous rusty spots and slope's angle of 75°, 0.6 m thick.

72L, greyish yellow light gray clayey silts, Lishi loess, with calcareous nodules, vertical joint and traces of fluviation, the angle of slope is 86°, there are calcareous nodules 0.28 m beneath the top surface, with scale-like clayey silt layer at the top, 6.88 m thick.

It's obvious that the three most prominent sedimentary characteristics of the Milanggouwan section are aeolian paleo-dunes, especially paleo-shifting dunes, fluvio-lacustrine facies and paleosols. The sedimentary cycle, which is composed of fluvio-lacustrine deposits or/and paleosols and underlying paleo-dunes sand, has 27 cycles since 150 ka (Fig. 5-12). Of these, 1MD and 63LS each is half of a cycle, if their underlying sand layer-age near the top of $150,200 \pm 19,100$ a BP is included, they constitute a cycle; Cy_0 is also 0.5 cycle. Its shifting dunes formed after Cy_1 when desert environment was recovered. From the ^{14}C age ($1,067 \pm 67$ a BP) of its underlying 2S, it can be inferred that Cy_0 is a climatic deterioration event in the recent 1,000 years. It indicates that the deposition frequency of aeolian shifting sand there was high with great fluctuations from then on. Without doubt, each perfect cycle indicates a process from sand dune mobilization to stabilization by overlying fluvio-lacustrine and swamp facies or paleosols.

5.3.3.2　Time stratigraphic table of desert formation and evolution events in the past 150 ka BP

Li Baosheng et al. surveyed Late Quaternary strata in the Salawusu River Basin several times since the 1970s. Until the 1990s, with the advancement of dating techniques and the accumulation of data, the time stratigraphic table of desert evolution events with high resolution in the past 150 ka BP was established.

Up to now, a total of 27 layers with defined ages in the Milanggouwan section have been identified. We chose two strata with closest age to calculate the deposition rate and obtained the ages of the Milanggouwan section in the past 150 ka BP. It's not difficult to see that the desert experienced alternating processes of dune mobilization-stabilization-remobilization-restabilization.

5.3.3.3　Conclusion

Through the above discussion, we updated our concept about the past division of strata in the Salawusu River Basin, especially the time stratigraphic table of desert formation and evolution processes in the past 150 ka BP.

The alternating frequency of desert expansion and shrinkage periods recorded in the Milanggouwan section in the past 150 ka is much more complicated than that of so-called classical glaicial-interglaicial period. It is generally accepted that aeolian sand deposition was more frequent in the glacial period than that in the interglacial period. The Salawusu Formation (Riss/Wurm Interglacial Period) recorded five deposition periods of aeolian sand, while the Chengchuan Formation (Wurm glacial Period) recorded 15 deposition periods. In addition, the time interval between desert expansion period (represented by aeolian dunes) and desert shrinkage period (represented by fluvio-lacustrine facies and paleosols) tended to become short. The Salawusu Formation (150–70 ka BP) experienced $Cy_{26.5}$–Cy_{20} cycles on average, a cycle of aeolian sand and fluvio-lacustrine facies or paleosols was 16 ka; the Chengchuan Formation (70–10 ka BP) experienced Cy_{20}–Cy_7 cycles or a cycle took 4 ka; the Dagouwan Formation and the Dishaogouwan Formation (from 10 ka BP to modern times) experienced Cy_7–Cy_0 cycles or a cycle took 1.45 ka.

Aeolian sand dunes, fluvio-lacustrine facies and paleosol records in the Milanggouwan section demonstrate that the desert environment and its positive and reverse processes have experienced tens of cycles in the past 150 ka or since the late Pleistocene.

5.3.4 Preliminary study on oasis deposits at the southern edge of the Tarim Basin since 13 ka BP—an example from the Yutian-Hotan Oasis

An oasis is a secondary system in the evolution processes of deserts in China. In theory, there is a mutual restraining relation between deserts and oases. However, little information is available to support this view. The authors try to give a review on the evolution processes of deserts in China based on the investigations of deposits in the Yutian-Hotan Oasis at the southern edge of the Tarim Basin as shown in Fig. 5-13.

Fig. 5-13　Paleo-aeolian sand deposits at the southern edge of the Tarim Basin

5.3.4.1　Physical geographic survey of Yutian-Hotan Oasis

The Yutian-Hotan Oasis is the general term for oases extending westward to Yutian, Qira, Luofu and Hotan, and then stretching westward to the oases in Moyu. The elevation varies between 1,350–1,450 m. It borders the Taklimakan Desert to the north and the slightly inclined plain of alluvial-pluvial fan—gravel Gobi at the northern foot of the middle Kunlun Mountains as shown in Fig. 5-14. The average annual precipitation, evaporation and temperature is 50 mm, 2,590 mm and 12°C respectively. The aridity here is above 16, and sand-dust weather occurs frequently. According to meteorological data recorded at the Yutian Meteorological Station from 1956 to 1994, the average annual number of dust storm days is 20.3; the number of days with floating dust is up to 155.4 days. The former is most frequent in late winter, early summer and the entire spring. In summer and autumn, the number of sandstorm events decreases obviously, but the days with floating dust increase. the water sources of the oasis are supplied by the melt-water of ice and snow and the stream systems such as the Keriya, the Yurungkax, the Kaxgar rivers, etc. and groundwater.

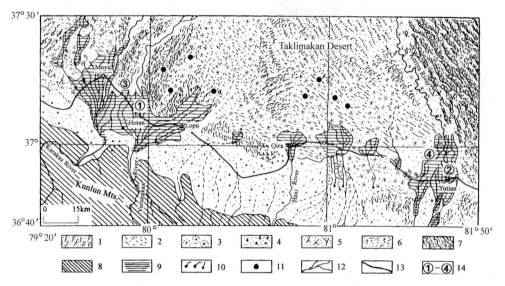

Fig. 5-14   Yutian-Hotan Oasis and the location of the section

1. barchan dune and barchan chain; 2. dune ridge; 3. coppice dune; 4. Gobi; 5. pyramid dune; 6. complex lengthways dune ridge; 7. complex transverse dune ridge; 8. mountain area; 9. oasis; 10. reservoir and channel; 11. ancient city ruins; 12. stream system; 13. road; 14. locations of the stratigraphic section mentioned in this item

5.3.4.2   Oasis deposits and their ages

The surface soil and cultivated soil in the Yutian-Hotan Oasis are brown desert soil, and the underlying strata consist of aeolian sand deposits and oasis surface soils. We called them "oasis soil". Oasis soils occur on the third terrace composed of alluvial-proluvial gravels or alluvial sand of the upper Pleistocene, with a thickness of about 5–6 m. They are light brown to brown in color, loose, porous, without bedding, with well developed vertical joint, containing abundant root systems and branches. We can also often find calcareous pseudohypha and large amounts of relics of human activities—fragmentized crockery, ashes and so on (Fig. 5-15: ①–③). The Vulun-kashi section (Fig. 5-15: ①), especially the Yutian section (Fig. 5-15: ②) is a typical model to describe the oasis soil profile. They have better development continuity and contain thin layers of lake deposit lens. But at the northern edge of the oasis, the soil contains snail fossils. The identification of 15 fossil samples showed that they are of Vallonia puchella.

Age determination of oasis soil in the Yutian section indicates that the oldest age of the oasis soil is about 12,410 ±158 a BP (Fig. 5-15: ②). Below this layer, there are nearly 2 m thick oasis soils. Its underlying stratum is the upper Pleistocene alluvial-proluvial gravel on the third terrace of the Keriya River. According to Cao Qiongying et al. (1992), the age of its top is about 13,525±510 a BP, that is the earliest age of the Yutian-Hotan oasis soil may be 13 ka BP. So we can consider that the Yutian–Hotan oasis soil was gradually deposited since 13 ka BP.

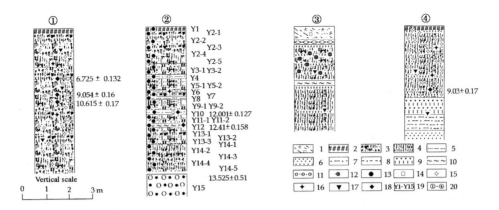

Fig. 5-15　Yutian-Hotan Oasis stratum cross section

1. modern mobile dune; 2. modern oasis soil; 3. ancient silty oasis soil; 4. ancient sandy oasis soil; 5. silty fine sand; 6. fluvial facies sand; 7. silt; 8. clayey silt; 9. interbed of fluvial facies sand and silt; 10. subclay; 11. sand and gravel; 12. snail fossil; 13. sample for particle-size analysis; 14. plant remnants or man-made ashes; 15. broken crockery; 16. animal fossil; 17. stone vessel; 18. location of ^{14}C sample; 19. samples chemical analysis; 20. ①②③④are the stratigraphic sections recorded in Yu Longkashi, Yutian, Hanaikelik and northern Yutian respectively

5.3.4.3　Material composition of the oasis strata

Soil protogenic material in the Yutian-Hotan oasis soil mainly comes from aeolian subsand and loess (Li et al., 1996) namely "aeolian sand accumulation" as described above. Thus, we call the oasis soil composed of the former sandy oasis soil and the latter silty oasis soil respectively. Analytical results of particle size of the Yutian section (Fig. 5-16) indicate that particle mode of oasis soil falls in the very fine sand and coarser silt fractions. The content of very fine sand is the maximum in sandy oasis soil, ranging from 49.93%–72.80%. The next is coarser silt, ranging from 20.23% to 40.66%. The contents of fine silt sand and clay are 1.03%–7.37% and 0.70%–8.73% respectively. The contents of fine sand and medium sand are lowest, ranging from 0.07%–6.30% and 0.03%–0.27%. The content of the coarse sand is negligible or non-existent. Accordingly, in silty oasis soil, the content of the coarse silt is highest, ranging from 39.07%–61.83%. The next is very fine sand, varying between 27.77%–47.69%. The contents of fine silt and clay are 0.13%–10.83% and 0.13%–10.77% respectively. The content of fine sand is only 0.19%–0.33%. The content of the medium sand is almost non-existent. The M_d variation ranges of sandy and silty oasis soil in the section are Φ4.22–Φ4.32 and Φ4.40–Φ5.20, on an average Φ4.29 and Φ4.79 respectively. However, the M_x variation ranges of sandy and silty oasis soil are Φ4.38–Φ4.96 and Φ4.86–Φ5.42, and the average values are Φ4.70 and Φ5.12. The sorting degree of these two types of oasis soil is moderate. The δ value of sandy oasis soil varies between 0.50–1.30, and the average value is 0.96. The δ value of silty oasis soil varies between 0.91–1.49, and the average value is 1.17. The particle composition of lake deposits in the section is similar to that of oasis soil. Its M_d, M_x and δ values are Φ4.35–5.36, Φ4.46–5.49 and 1.04–1.36 respectively, and the average values are Φ4.94, Φ5.11 and Φ1.19, respectively.

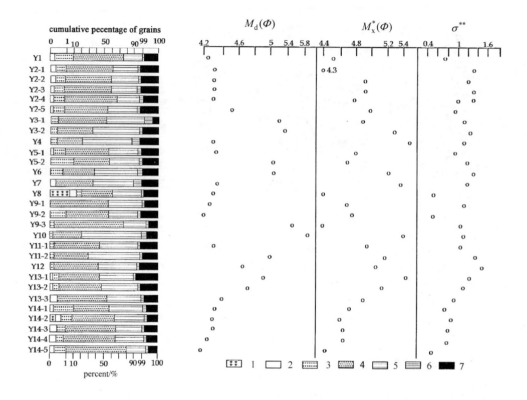

Fig. 5-16　Analytical result of particle size in Yutian section

1. coarse sand (Φ0–1); 2. medium sand (Φ1–2); 3. fine sand (Φ2–3.32); 4. very fine sand (Φ3.32–4.32); 5. coarse silt (Φ4.32–6.64); 6. fine silt (Φ6.64–7.64); 7. clay (Φ>7.64); M_x and M_d are: $M_x = (\Phi16 + \Phi50 + \Phi84)/3$; $M_d = (\Phi84 - \Phi16)/4 + (\Phi95 - \Phi5)/6.6$

Fig. 5-17 shows the distribution of some macroelements of oasis soil, modern oasis soil and modern shifting dune in the Yutian section. It can be seen that no matter if it is sandy oasis soil or silty sandy soil, their SiO_2 contents are roughly the same and the differences are not obvious in the content of K_2O, Na_2O, CaO, and MgO. However, the latter commonly has a higher content of Al_2O_3 and $Fe_2O_3 + FeO$. Their mean SiO_2 content is lower than those of fluvio-lacustrine deposits. Normally, the content of Al_2O_3 and $Fe_2O_3 + FeO$ in fluvio-lacustrine deposits is higher than that of underlying oasis soil, while CaO is lower, and the differences in K_2O, Na_2O and MgO content are not very obvious. If we compare the oxide content in modern oasis surface soil, oasis soil and modern sand dunes, we discover that their average values are approximate. But the soil oxide content in modern and ancient oasis soils is quite different from that of modern mobile dunes. The upper limit of SiO_2 content in modern oasis surface soil and oasis·soil is generally lower than 55%, while the minimum SiO_2 content in modern mobile dunes is higher than 63%. The average SiO_2 content of modern mobile dunes is higher than oasis soil by more than 13%. The average content of Al_2O_3, $Fe_2O_3 + FeO$, K_2O, Na_2O, CaO, MgO of modern oasis surface soil and oasis soil is higher than those of modern mobile dunes.

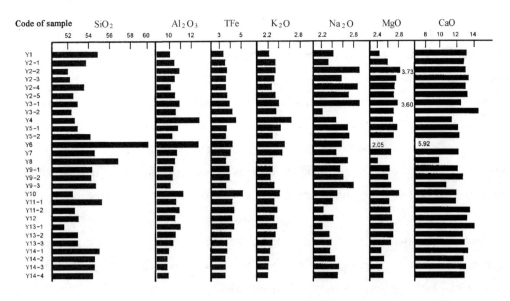

Fig. 5-17   Analytical results of some macroelements in the Yutian section

5.3.4.4   Deposition rate of oasis soil

According to stratigraphic deposition thickness and its age, we can calculate the deposition rate of oasis soil in the Yutian section by two stratigraphic intervals. The first stratigraphic intervals are 13–12 ka BP and the deposition rate is 2,400 mm/ka; the second stratigraphic intervals are 12 ka BP and the deposition rate is 266.64 mm/ka. In addition, according to the dating result of the Yulongkashi section, we worked out the deposition rate of strata from 12 ka BP to the present. Their ages are 10,615 a BP, 9,054 a BP and 6,725 a BP respectively; and their deposition rates are 263.78 mm/ka, 276.12 mm/ka and 252.79 mm/ka respectively. But the age at the depth of 2.45 m is 9,030 a BP and its deposition rate is 271.32 mm/ka. This shows that the deposition rate tended to slow down since the past 13 ka. But since 12 ka BP the deposition rate of oasis soil in the Yutian-Hotan oasis differed little at different depths and in different regions. From this we obtained the average value of 266.13 mm/ka of the five deposition rates.

5.3.4.5   Problems and discussion

Oasis soils are formed by sand materials (ϕ3.32–6.64), i.e. subsand and loess through soil-forming action. Like the modern oasis soils, their composition has experienced biochemical transformation and their formation environment is different from flowing sand in the Taklimakan Desert.

Oasis soils are true geological records in ancient oases, which are not only the natural barrier against flowing sand but also the storage place for atmospheric dust. They are relatively independent geological units in extremely dry deserts and the product of oasis environmental processes.

The dating result of oasis soils indicated that the Yutian-Hotan oasis had been there since 13 ka.

Oasis soil's continuous occurrence reflected that oases are the important sites for human activities at least since the beginning of the Holocene, and since then it has been one of human dwelling areas in the Taklimakan Desert.

In the Yutian section, deposition rate of the first stratum is much higher than that of the second one. Viewed from the time scale, either in the eastern or western regions of China, the deposition rate during the glacial period was obviously higher than that of the inter-glacial period. Viewed on a spatial scale, sand deposition rate was much lower in monsoon regions than that in extremely dry regions. It reflects that sand deposition rate in northern China was not only influenced by glacial and inter-glacial climates but also restricted by spatial distribution.

We can imagine that during the past 13 ka in the Yutian-Hotan oasis, sand deposition mainly occurred in cold period and gradually developed to sandy oasis soil; in the warm period, fluvial deposition took place and gradually turned into silt oasis soils. A number of dry-wet and cold-warm climate fluctuations led to the alternate depositions of sandy oasis, silty oasis soils and lacustrine facies in oases.

As described above, oasis soil contains much evidence of organism and human activities, which gives us confidence that the Yutian–Hotan oasis was always nourished by water resources during the past 13 ka. This is very important, and it is the lifeline for oases long term development. As for water resources, the situation is the same for modern and ancient oases; they mainly benefit from ice and snow meltwater and underground water for the mid and western Kunlun Mountains.

Many questions still remain in the Yutian–Hotan oasis, for example, the evolution sequence of cold or warm stages in oases age, and climate events. With the implementation of the development plan for western China, these scientific questions can be gradually solved.

5.3.5 The formation and evolution process and genetic information recorded in desert deposits in China

5.3.5.1 A general view of the existing desert in different periods of the Quaternary

From the deposition times of the Quaternary ancient aeolian sand and their spatial distribution laws, it can be seen that the time of desert emergence in China was at the beginning of the Pleistocene in the Quaternary, but its size was much smaller than it is today. Until now, we have seldom found aeolian sand layers that distinguish the boundary of the Tertiary and the Quaternary, which is in concordance with its overlaid and underlaid layers in deserts of China. But we can definitely conclude that there were aeolian sand activities between the late Tertiary and the early Quaternary in deserts of China. The direct evidence of this can be seen from the N/Q boundary line of the Taklimakan Desert in the western desert zone of China and ancient aeolian soil underlain in the basalt layer 2.257 Ma BP of Onqin Daga Sandy Land in the eastern desert zone in China (Fig. 5-5: ⑨) and (Fig. 5-5: ⑲). Meanwhile, the indirect evidence is the grain-size composition of aeolian Wucheng loess that transitions gradually from the late Pliocenethe Jingle laterite, which was found in the middle reaches of the Yellow River. Among which the very fine sand content of Wucheng loess near G/M polarities interface formed at about the 2.48 Ma BP is at least 14 percent. In line with to the saying that aeolian sand is the origin of loess, it is obviously caused by the southward invasion of sand drift.

If we take the B/M magnetic belt interface as the boundary of the middle and late Pleistocene, the primary outline of the modern desert may have formed in northern China after the early Pleistocene. This can be proved by the aeolian sand found in different subregions of the deserts in China.

In the western desert zone in China, we can see ancient aeolian sand lens before 1.43 Ma BP in the Xiyu conglomerate (Fig. 5-5: ⑤). Moreover, in the transverse direction, they changed into aeolian subsand and alluvial-proluvial, alluvial-slope gravel and loess with black desert varnish (Fig. 5-5: ②). The Xiyu conglomerate at the northern piedmont of the Altun Mountain is interrupted in the longitudinal direction by ancient aeolian soil, which appears as several layers of gray-black breccia, and its thickness is up to 100 m (Fig. 5-5: ①). We can often discover the superposition phenomenon of ancient aeolian sand and Xiyu conglomerate, especially at the western Kunlun Mountain piedmont, extending to Baicheng-Kuche-Korla and the Tarim River at the southern piedmont of the Tianshan.

Although there are less stratigraphic records of the early Pleistocene in the northwestern mountains and the central desert zones, there are thick ancient aeolian sand in the former area (Fig. 5-5: ⑧) and semi-cemented ancient aeolian sand can be seen in the latter area (Yan Mancun et al., 2001) (Fig. 5-5: ⑪,⑫). According to the investigations by Li Baosheng and Yan Mancun et al., ancient aeolian sand here transits partly with the Yumen Group.

The ancient aeolian soil in the early Pleistocene in the eastern desert zone is commonly found in the Ordos Plateau. Several layers of ancient aeolian sand can be found under the B/M layer of the Yulin section. But up to now, we have not found aeolian soil of this stage in the Horqin Sandy Land.

In addition, the loess deposits indicate that southward encroachment sand flow events might exist in desert zones of the early Pleistocene. In the Luochuan loess section situated at the inner part of the Loess Plateau, we have found two layers of sandy loess above and below the Jaramillo polar drifting layer at depths of 60 m and 80 m or so. That is to say, at least 1/3 of the material in these two loess layers came from sand flow.

Deserts in northern China were as large as they are today in the middle Pleistocene. This is inferred by the fact that aeolian sand can be found in different subregions of the deserts in China. So we think that there might be high sand mountains in the middle and western desert zones at that time, as mentioned in the first paragraph.

When the desert evolved to the late Pleistocene, the wind force action was so strong that the aeolian sand area was even larger than that today. As shown in Fig. 5-5, except for the widely distributed late Pleistocene aeolian sand in modern deserts, we can also easily find ancient aeolian dunes in the underlying bed of the non-sandy surface in the surrounding areas of today's deserts, most of which belong to the late Pleistocene.

The wind force action was so strong in the late Pleistocene that aeolian sand spread to the coastal areas in eastern China, including the Luanhe River basin in Hebei Province, Shandong Peninsula, Putian in Fujian Province, Shantou in Guangdong Province, northeastern Hainan Island, and Zhoushan Islands and so on.

In the Holocene, because of the effect of the postglacial deserts in the northwestern desert zone, eastern desert zone and southeastern part of the central desert zone were extensively fixed. Meanwhile, the desert area in the central and western desert zones decreased. The former appeared as biochemical stabilization and the development of paleosols, while the latter appeared as mechanical stabilization by the covering of fluvio-lacustrine deposits (Li et al., 2001).

The modern deserts in China began to develop slowly in the optimal warm and humid stage in the Holocene (8–3 ka BP) and later their development accelerated. Viewed from the 2S age of the Milanggou worm section, the acceleration of the development of deserts only occurred in the most recent 1,000 years. The reason for this is related to unreasonable human activities and climate factors.

5.3.5.2　The evolution process of the desert and its causes

In the discussion above, we have elucidated the basic conditions of Chinese deserts in the main periods of the Pleistocene and Holocene. And we have obtained a most profound image–since the Quaternary, the developmental trend of the Chinese deserts is consistent with the general characteristic of what is called the "glacial period". Obviously, at the time when nine tenths of the earth's surface was covered by ice, and the Chinese northern continent was controlled by the Mongolia high pressure system, the climate was very cold and dry, the physical weathering was violent, the aeolian sand flow was strong, and therefore the desert was widespread. However, there always existed a short climate fluctuation between two longer glacial periods, i.e. the "interglacial period". From Fig. 5-5, we can see that ancient aeolian sand and strata in various desert subzones presented traces of climate fluctuation in glacial and interglacial periods. In the eastern and northwest desert zones and southeast central desert zone, ancient aeolian sand and paleosol or river and lake deposits are superimposed on each other (Fig. 5-5: ⑧,⑨,⑬–⑱,⑳); in the central and western desert zones, ancient aeolian sand and the river and lake clay deposits, the alluvial and pluvial gravel layers are superimposed on each other (Fig. 5-5: ①,②,⑥,⑦); but the huge complex dunes which were seldom influenced by water or sand belts or megadunes exhibited a coarse-fine rhythm change as shown in the Luochuan section (Fig. 5-5: ④).

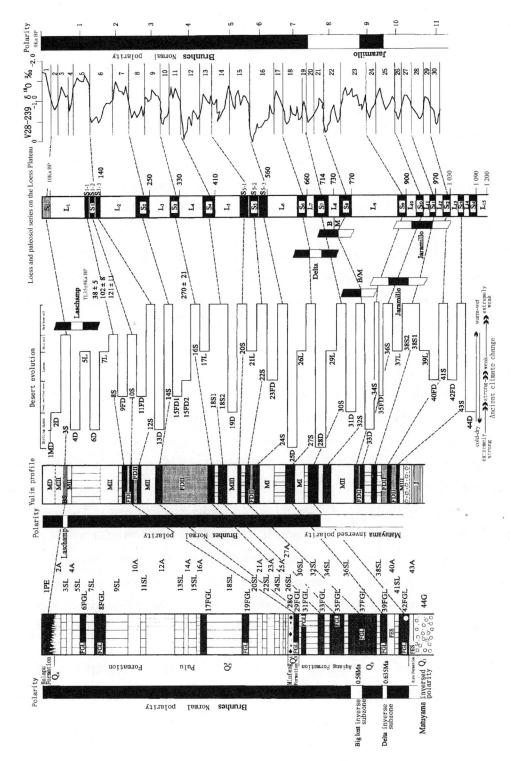

Fig. 5-18　Comparison of aeolian depositional sequences in the Yulin, Aqiang and Luochuan sections and the δ¹⁸O curves of V28-239 cores

It is obvious that it was the alternations of glacial and interglacial periods resulted in ancient dunes or aeolian sand—these representative elements of the ancient desert have undergone all of the changes described above.

How many stages have Chinese deserts undergone? And which climate type did these stages belong to? Is there a relationship between the various stages and the climatic fluctuations of the glacial period? We have partly answered these questions in the above discussion. Gao Shangyu also dealt with this question from analyzing the changes of the oxide ratio of SiO_2/Al_2O_3, FeO/Fe_2O_3, CaO/MgO, K_2O/Na_2O and $(CaO+K_2O+Na_2O) / Al_2O_3$ in the Yulin section and pointed out that these changes were caused by the dry-cold climate and the wet-warm climate. The research results of the loess-paleosol geochemistry in the Lujiaowan section at the southern edge of the Gurbantünggüt Desert demonstrate that the climate in the northwest desert zone was similar to that recorded in the Yulin section.

If we analyze the past climate changes recorded in the Aqiang section since 770 ka BP, we can see that there is a large difference in the climate between east, northwest and central desert zones. During the desert expansion stages the deposits were dominated by coarse particles, subsand and paleo-aeolian sand deposits and the climate was dry and cold. Regarding the shrinking stages of the desert, the sediments are fine particles, rock salt and thin layers of gypsum, indicating that the environment was dry and hot.

If we compare the stratigraphic sequence of the Yulin and the Aqiang sections to the loess-paleosol system of the Loess Plateau, and the $\delta^{18}O$ curves of V28–V239 cores of the Pacific Ocean, we can find that there is a coupling relation between them (Fig. 5-18). This reflects the corresponding region between paleo-aeolian sand, subsand loess plateau's loess and $^{18}O/^{16}O$ low valley—even number oxide isotopes. It can also reflect the relationship between $^{18}O/^{16}O$ peak-odd number oxide isotopes and paleosols developed on ancient sand dunes, as well as dust and paleosol of loess plateau. This implies that the fluctuation of the glacial and the interglacial periods led to the changes in the continent's ice amount. It also influenced the deposition processes of the desert's paleo-aeolian sand and paleosols, and the loess plateau's loess and paleosols. From this, it follows that the evolution of deserts in China was attributed to climatic fluctuations of the glacial and interglacial periods.

5.3.5.3 Regional environmental changes represented by polycyclic desert sedimentary sequences in the latest geologic period

The latest geologic period refers to the geologic period since 150 ka BP. This discussion focuses on the problem of environmental changes represented by 27 sedimentary cycles of the Milanggouwan section.

Aeolian sand activities in desert areas and loess regions of China mainly occur in winter and spring, and may persist until the late spring and early summer. Usually it is triggered by the

Siberian-Mongolian anticyclonic action. Its activity space is extensive, including 5 bioclimatic subzones in desert areas of China; the "dust haze" may pass over loess region and affect low-latitude regions (Yang et al., 1991).Strong dust storms may sweep over the Yangtze River basin or even reach Japan. Hence, it is not difficult to explain that the dune accumulation in the Milanggouwan section since 150 ka BP should be similar to the results of the modern winter aeolian process in Chinese desert areas, and the 27 layers of sand dune deposits represent 27 desert accumulation periods in desert areas of China since 150 ka BP.

The Chagelebulu stratigraphic section at the eastern edge of the Badain Jaran Desert (Fig.5-4: ②) has a lacustrine argillaceous layer at the depth of 13–17 m and contains a large number of mollusk fossils—*Galba pervia* (Martens), *Dolypylis hemisphaerula* (Benson), *Gyraulus convexiasculus* (Hutton), *Succinea erythrophana* (Ancey), which formed in the last interglacial period, which corresponds to the Salawusu period (Gao et al., 1996).

The Badanhaizi Lake is located in the megadune area at the southern part of the Badain Jaran Desert (Fig.5-4 ④). There are large number of mollusk fossils in lake deposits near the lake, such as *Gyraulus convexiasculus* (Hutton), *Gyraulus albus* (Muller), *Radix auricularia* C., *Radix aluminata* C., and *Lymnaea hagnnalis* (Linnaeus). The ^{14}C ages are between 68,402±95 a BP and 5,190±85 a BP.

The Yuetegan section in Hotan of the Taklimakan Desert (Fig.5-4 ⑤) has a light green subclay layer at a depth of 3.1–3.7 m and contains *Pianorbis sp.* fossils, whose age is 7–4 ka BP (Wen et al., 1995).

The large interdune depression of the terminal of the Andier River in the Taklimakan Desert (Fig. 5-4 ⑥) has a pluvial silt layer and contains a large number of the *Succinea pfeiferi* Fossmaeller fossils (Li et al., 1995), and its ^{14}C age is 5,474±96 a BP.

Obviously, because of the difference in precipitation distribution and the course changes of rivers and lakes in the vast central and western desert zones, there are sometimes grasslands, oases, rivers and lakes in desert areas, but this does not change the basic feature of the arid-hyperarid "mobile sand sea". Therefore, the natural vegetation is dominated by desert species such as *Artemisia*, Chenopodiaceae, Leguminosae, and *Ephedra*.

In conclusion, the eastern desert zone and other desert zones in China had some similarities and differences in deposition-climatic evolution patterns. In the cold period, they were mainly influenced by the Siberian-Mongolian anticyclone, and erosion-deposition processes were dominant under the action of the prevailing winter monsoon. Conversely, in the warm period, the eastern desert zone and the southeastern part of the central desert zone were affected by oceanic airflow and summer monsoons, hence soil-forming processes took place and large areas of shifting sand were stabilized. The situation in the central and western desert zone is not the same as the eastern desert zone in warm periods because it is located in the interior of Central Asia, and it is effected by landforms such as the Tibetan Plateau, western Pamirs, northern Tianshan, the Mongolian Plateau gobi, and the Helan Mountains, the Lvliang Mountains and the Taihang Mountains.

Especially due to the uplifting effect of the Tibetan Plateau and other mountains since 150 ka BP the summer monsoon became very weak in the central desert zone, therefore it had a high temperature and arid environment (Li Baosheng et al., 1998a) and paleosol development was weaker (Dong Guangrong et al., 1993a), water-heat conditions were poor compared to the eastern desert zone. This may be caused by the southward invasion of moist air mass from the Arctic Ocean.

5.4   Aeolian desertification in the historical period

Aeolian desertification in the historical period is complicated and mainly concerns the relationship between the land and man. Several scientists researched this question in the past from the view of historical geography and archaeology. It includes two aspects: one is the analysis of the environmental variations from the development and decline of ancient cities and the historical remains of human activity in desert regions; another is the analysis of the environmental and land degradation processes, from stationing troops to open up grassland in historical times, as well as using the changes of mature and immature soil as the criteria of land aeolian desertification. According to distribution and genetic features, aeolian desertification land can be divided into two types: one is aeolian desertification land occurring in adjacent land of oases in the lower reaches of inland rivers in arid desert regions, such as the aeolian desertification land around the Taklimakan Desert and in the Hexi Corridor and its adjacent area. Another is the aeolian desertification land in semi-arid and semi-humid areas, including the Mu Us Sandy Land in the Ordos Plateau and the West Liaohe River Sandy Land in the Horqin Grassland. These are the most areas of typical areas of desertification.

5.4.1   Adjacent area of the Taklimakan Desert

Researches confirmed that there was irrigation agriculture in the Neolithic Age along the banks of inland rivers in the biggest desert of China and its adjacent areas. For example in the second century BP Zhang Qian had seen many cities and farmlands in the desert when he was sent to Xiyu on a diplomatic mission. Afterwards, irrigation agriculture developed greatly in the Han, Tang and Qing Dynasties. But due to the influences of natural and human factors, many oases disappeared, and the ruins of ancient cities became the evidence of aeolian desertification (Fig.5-19).

According to archaeological data and historical records, the abandonment timeline of ancient cities and the timeline of aeolian desertification were not necessarily consistent. The ancient Loulan City was abandoned after 330 AD. The ancient Milan City was abandoned after 9th century AD. The abandonment of ancient cities and oases were closely related to the water diversion of the river and the shortage of irrigation water. This further caused the destruction of natural vegetation, the formation of sand dunes and the occurrence of aeolian desertification in oases.

According to investigations, there were ruins of a blockhouse and beacon tower in the low dunes along the Silk Road from Pishan to Yecheng. Judging from the sand-buried ancient city ruins along the southern Silk Road, the Taklimakan Desert has advanced more than 100 km southward over the past 1,000 years.

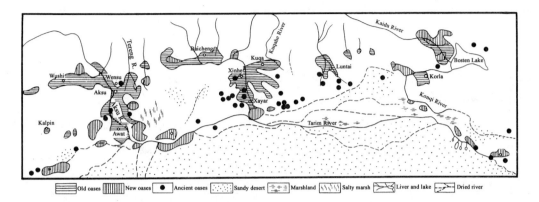

Fig. 5-19   The ancient cities and oases in the north region near the Tarim River, Taklimakan Desert

Ancient cultural remains of the Hexi Corridor and its adjacent area are shown in Fig. 5-20.

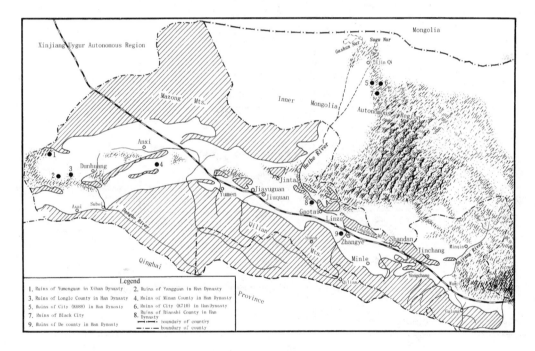

Fig. 5-20   Ancient cultural remains in the Hexi Corridor and its adjacent area

5.4.2   The Hexi Corridor and the Alxa area

The Hexi Corridor was an important and well-known passage for the Silk Road. Many ancient cities were established and large-scale land reclamation was initialized in the period under the reign of Emperor Wudi in the Han Dynasty in the Hexi Corridor region. Table 5-3 lists the abandonment timeline for several ancient cities in the Hexi Corridor and its adjacent area through the confirmation of archaeological data and ^{14}C dating. About 26.7% cities were abandoned during the Northern and Southern Dynasties, 26.7% at the end of the Tang and the Wudai Dynasties, and 46.7% during the Ming Dynasty and the Qing Dynasty. These three stages entirely correspond to the arid and cold climatic stages of the past 2,000 years. And in the past 300 years, the population density has exceeded the critical index of population pressure in the study region, the utilization factor of water resources has exceeded 40%, and human activities have become one of the important causes of land aeolian desertification in the Hexi Corridor region.

Natural landscape near the Shouchang ruins in Nanhu, Dunhuang is shown in Fig. 5-21.

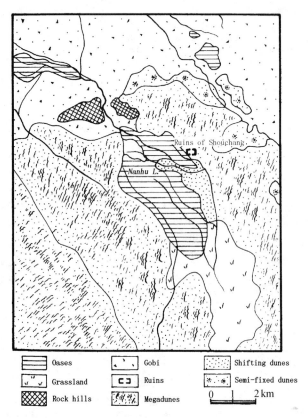

Fig. 5-21   Natural landscape near Shouchang ruins in Nanhu, Dunhuang

Table 5-3   Abandonment timeline for several ancient cities in the Hexi Corridor and its adjacent area

No.	Ancient city	Location	Continued time	^{14}C age (a BP)	Abandoned time
1	Gaogou Fort	Changcheng, Wuwei	Ming Dynasty		The early Qing Dynasty
2	Xuanwei Xian	Daba, Minqin	Han, Tang, Ming Dynasties		After Ming Dynasty
3	Wuwei Xianlian City	10 km northwest of Quanshan, Minqin	Han, Tang Dynasties		The middle of Tang Dynasty
4	Gucheng City	West Desert, Minqin	Han, Tang Dynasties		The middle of Tang Dynasty and the Wudai Dynasty
5	Sanjiao City	Hongshaliang, Minqin	Han Dynasty	2,520±80	Wei, Jin and Nanchao and Beichao Dynasties

No.	Ancient city	Location	Continued time	^{14}C age (a BP)	Abandoned time
6	Baiting Jun City	Xiqu, Minqn	Tang Dynasty		The middle of Tang Dynasty and the Wudai Dynasty
7	Dong'an Fort	Yanglu, Minqn	Western Xia, Yuan, Ming Dynasties		The early Qing Dynasty
8	Hongsha Fort	10 km northeast of Minqin City	Tang, Song, Ming Dynasties		The middle of Qing Dynasty
9	Qingsong Fort	Xuebai, Minqin	Ming, Qing Dynasties		The middle of Qing Dynasty
10	Shashan Fort	Xuebai, Minqin	Ming, Qing Dynasties		The middle of Qing Dynasty
11	Nanle Fort	Xuebai, Minqin	Ming, Qing Dynasties		The middle of Qing Dynasty
12	Hongya Fort	40 km southwest of Minqin City	Ming Dynasty		The end of Qing Dynasty
13	Shacheng City	Beidi, Shuiyuan, Yongchang	Han, Jin, Tang Dynasties		The middle of Tang Dynasty and the Wudai Dynasty
14	Dichi Xian	Northern Liju, Minle	Han, Jin Dynasties		Nanchao and Beichao Dynasties
15	North City of Heishuguo	Xicheng Post, Zhangye	Han, Tang Dynasties		The middle of Tang Dynasty and the Wudai Dynasty
16	South City of Heishuguo	Xicheng Post, Zhangye	Tang, Western Xia, Yuan Dynasties		Ming and Qing Dynasties
17	Luotuo City	Southeastern Minhai Desert	Tang Dynasty	1,428±56	The middle of Tang Dynasty and the Wudai Dynasty
18	Jiankang Jun	Southeastern Minhai Desert	Han, Jin Dynasties		Nanchao and Beichao Dynasties
19	Xusanwan City	Southern Minhai Desert	Han, Tang, Ming Dynasties		Qing Dynasty
20	Minghaizi City	Minhai Desert	Ming Dynasty	484±50	Ming and Qing Dynasty
21	Xindunzi City	Western Minhai Desert	Han, Wei, Jin Dynasties		South and North Dynasties
22	Caogoujing City	Western Minhai Desert	Han, Tang, Ming Dynasties		Qing Dynasty
23	Xianheqing Royal City	Western Minhai Desert	Han, Tang Dynasties		The middle of Tang Dynasty and the Wudai Dynasty
24	Suimi Xian	Gucheng, Linshui, Jiuquan	Han, Jin Dynasties		Nanchao and Beichao Dynasties
25	Huishui Xian	Jinta	Han, Northern Wei Dynasties		Nanchao and Beichao Dynasties
26	K710 City (Juyan)	Northern ancient Juyan oasis	Han Dynasty		Wei, Jin and Nanchao and Beichao Dynasties
27	A8 City (Pochengzi)	Northern ancient Juyan oasis	Han Dynasty		Wei, Jin and Nanchao and Beichao Dynasties
28	K688 City	Northern ancient Juyan oasis	Han Dynasty		Wei, Jin and Nanchao and Beichao Dynasties
29	F84 City	Northern ancient Juyan oasis	Han Dynasty		Wei, Jin and Nanchao and Beichao Dynasties
30	K749 City	Northern ancient Juyan oasis	Han Dynasty		Wei, Jin and Nanchao and Beichao Dynasties
31	K789 City	Southern ancient Juyan oasis	Han, Tang, Western Xia Dynasties		Ming and Qing Dynasties
32	Green City	Southern ancient Juyan oasis	Tang, Western Xia, Yuan Dynasties		Ming and Qing Dynasties
33	K799 City (Black)	Southern ancient Juyan oasis	Western Xia, Yuan Dynasties		14th century
34	Chitou Xian	Huahai, Yumen	Han, Northern Wei, Qing Dynasties		
35	Qiaowan City	Bulongji, Anxi	Qing Dynasty		The end of Qing Dynasty

No.	Ancient city	Location	Continued time	^{14}C age (a BP)	Abandoned time
36	Ming'an Xian	Qiaozi, Anxi	Han, Tang, Qing Dynasties		The end of Qing Dynasty
37	Suoyang City (Kuyu)	Qiaozi, Anxi	Tang, Yuan Ming Dynasties	1,230±58	The early of 18th century
38	Guangzhi Xian	Tashi, Anxi	Han Dynasty		Nanchao and Beichao Dynasties
39	Changle Xian	Nancha, Anxi	Wei, Tang, Song Dynasties		Ming and Qing Dynasty
40	Yiwu Xian	The lower reaches of Lucaogou River	Wei, Jin, Tang Dynasties		after 9 century
41	Ancient City in Tianshuijing	The lower reaches of Lucaogou River	Han, Tang Dynasties		The middle of Tang Dynasty and the Wudai Dynasty
42	Xuanquan Post	The lower reaches of Lucaogou River	Tang Dynasty		The middle of Tang Dynasty and the Wudai Dynasty
43	Xiaogu Xian	Guojiapu, Dunhuang	Han, Wei, Tang Dynasties		The middle of Tang Dynasty and the Wudai Dynasty
44	Shouchang Xian(Longle)	Nanhu, Dunhuang	Han, Tang Dynasties		10–11th century
45	Baiqi Fort	Xihu, Dunhuang	The end of Qing Dynasty		

Note: ^{14}C ages were determined in the Laboratory of Chronology, Lanzhou University and the Laboratory of Technological Archaeology and Cultural Relic Protection, Beijing University.

Archaeological data confirmed that the Suoyang City Ruin, located in the western alluvial and pluvial fanlike sector of the Changma River, was a Tang Dynasty ruin, and some researchers believe it was Guazhou City of the Tang Dynasty. The town's residential area and the remains of farmland are distributed on the middle-lower part of the alluvial sector plain. In front of this was a zone of groundwater extravasation, and the upper fanlike sector was a gravel fastigiated plain. According to the analysis of aerial phoyos and satellite images, it was found that there was a relatively large riverbed that flowed west of the alluvial and pluvial fanlike sector of the Changma River, which was the main irrigation riverhead and lifeline of the ancient oasis. The remains of an ancient channel system are clear. In the Ming and Qing dynasties, the river course that flowed west of the alluvial and pluvial fanlike sector of the Changma River was diverted by man. It caused discontinuation of the irrigation headwaters, and the city and the oasis were desolated. The land became aeolian desertified land, mainly characterized by areas of wind erosion and coppice dunes and mobile dunes were in the foreground of the fan-like. Similar circumstances existed in the Luotuo City area, located in western Gaotai, at the lower reaches of the Bailang River. The destruction from war and denudation in the Qilian Mountains after the Tang Dynasty decreased the headwater's ability for self-regulation. This rapidly increased the current and decreased the flux of river. The perennial river became a seasonal river, and the seasonal changes were large. The irrigation headwaters reduced sharply, and the oasis was abandoned finally. The Huqu Area of Minqin is an other example. After the Laxi River changed its course eastward, the Dongdahe River, the Xinhe River, the Xiaoxi River and the Daxi River flooded the terminal lake, and because of large amounts of sand volume, extended the alluvial plain into the central lake. Thereafter, the famous Baitinghai Lake of the Tang Dynasty became a lacustrine beach because of the lack of headwaters in the 19th century. The changes in the river system first affected the irrigation. Parts of farmlands and natural vegetation degraded because of the lack of water. At the same time, the dry sandy riverbed and farmlands in the sandy plain continually provided sand matter along with the action of a persistently strong dry wind. When shifting sand was formed, it reacted the river system and farmland. This unceasing and vicious circle was an important route of aeolian desertification in the area. The formation time of shifting sand south of the Western Desert in the Minqin Oasis was rather late. The Great Wall and forts located in the desert, such as Qingsong Fort, Nanle Fort, Shashan Fort, and others from the Ming Dynasty confirm this conclusion. The aeolian desertification land around Xicheng Post in the alluvial fanlike sector of the Heihe River has ancient city ruins and cemeteries from the Han Dynasty. Recorded in the Annals of Ganzhou Fu, the area was the Gongbi Post in the Tang Dynasty, the Xicheng Post in the Yuan Dynasty and the Xiaoshahe Post in the Ming Dynasty. Today, the abandoned riverbed can be distinguished and is roughly 7 m higher than the current riverbed of the Heihe River. This reflects the fact that abundant sand in the current of the Heihe River caused the riverbed to rise and forced the river to change its route east ward. The irrigation headwaters also changed along with these circumstances. The dry headwaters and abandoned farmlands in the sandy plains offered a sand source for the formation of dunes under wind action and ultimately brought about aeolian desertified land.

The aeolian desertified land of ancient Juyan, located in the northwest of the Badain Jaran Desert, included the famous Ancient Juyan City and Black City. The area is located at the ancient delta in the lower reaches of the Ruoshui River, (the Ejin River), whose upper reaches is called the Heihe River. During the Dynasty, Juyan Duwei was set up in the middle-lower part of the delta, and a series of military structures, for instance the Great Wall and beacons, were established for the safety of the Hexi Corridor. The military stationed and garrisoned around Juyan developed irrigation agriculture. There are relics of fortress walls and beacons, ancient farmlands, channels, abandoned cities and forts and abundant valuable Bamboo Slips from the Han Dynasty are located west of the ancient Ruoshui River (Ancient Juyanze Lake). All of these indicate the stationing of troops to open up grassland during the Han Dynasty was done on a considerable scale. After the Han Dynasty, economic activities reduced, military status weakened, and many farmlands were abandoned. Abandoned farmlands channels and dry riverbeds provided sand controlled by the wind action. As a result, the lower of dry delta and area around the ancient Juyanze Lake gradually became aeolian desertified land. Now, the east and west sides of Juyan City are dry riverbed, and larger and larger Chinese tamarisk dunes continue to crowd into the inner City. Black City, where Marco Polo, the famous Italy peregrinator had been, was built in the upper-middle part of the delta during the Western Xia Dynasty (1038–1227). Black City was built on a prodigious scale, with high and thick walls, and majestically stood out in the open plain. But now, quicksand nearly overflows the walls and fills up the riverbeds outside of the city. The Juyanhai Lake, the terminal lake of the Heihe River, included the ancient Juyanze Lake, Sogo Nur and Gaxun Nur, had been more than 2,000 km^2 during historical times when it was its largest. The agriculture scale was prodigious in the Han Dynasty, but three lakes still existed with a sizeable area. In the Yuan Dynasty and the middle of the Ming Dynasty, economic activities were centralized in the Hexi Corridor. Irrigation works built on a large scale in the middle reaches of the Heihe River caused surface water of the lower reaches of the Heihe River to decrease, and sand caused the riverbed of the east branch of the Heihe River to rise, so the ancient Juyanze Lake shrunk and became aeolian desertified land. The depravation of moisture conditions caused natural vegetation, such as *Populus diversifoha, Tamarix* to die. Then shifting sand and coppice dunes appeared. Since the 20th century, the water has mainly inflooded into the Sogo Nur and the Gaxun Nur. The Gaxun Nur's area was more than 262 km^2. Zhangye District, in middle reaches of the Heihe River, enlarged its irrigation area more than 60,000 hm^2 during 1949–1984 and increased water for agriculture irrigation 580 million m^3 with 40 m^3/hm^2 grass irrigation rate. This figure does not include the enlarged area in the lower reaches of the river. Surface evaporation capacity of the Juyan Lake is roughly 300–400 million m^3 according to calculations. Under the area of agriculture irrigation in the Heihe River, drainage area and grassland irrigation in delta of the lower reaches enlarged gradually, and waterpower of the Heihe River drainage are a consumed more than 400 million m^3. It is the main reason, for the decrease of water flowing into the lake (rough 700 million m^3) and drying of the lake. The shrinking and drying of lakes is a common natural phenomenon. But it was too fast in this area and can not be explained by climate changes. The main reason is the unscientific use of water, excess use of water resource in the upper reaches and victimization of the water in the lower reaches for maintenance eco-balance under the rapid increase of population and the rapid exploitation of land. In other words, the population and economic development of the drainage area had exceeded the critical index of ecological environment pressure. Especially in the most recent 300 years, after the middle of the Qing Dynasty, the sharply shrinking lakes and aeolian desertification had direct correlation with human activity, for example the destruction of forest of self-restraint in the upper-middle reaches, opening and cultivate of grass land and building of the water conservancy, and so on. The reclamation area in the ancient Juyan-Black City failed to revitalize after being abandoned is just another typical case of historical aeolian desertification.

The changes in area of major lakes in the Hexi Corridor and its adjacent regions are shown in Table 5-4.

Table 5-4　The changes in area of major lakes in the Hexi Corridor and its adjacent region (Unit: km^2)

Lake name	Qin and Han Dynasties	The early Qing Dynasty	The end of Qing Dynasty and Republic of China	1950s	1960s	1970s	Today
Zhuyeze				2,100–1,830	210	70–0	dry
Huahai Lake	445	49	10	>3	>3	3	dry
Juyan Lake	2,084	695	352	352	50	58	dry
Lop Nur	5,350		Markedly shrank	3,006	660	0	dry

5.4.3　The northern part of the Ulan Buh Desert

The northern part of the Ulan Buh Desert was formerly an alluvial plain of the Yellow River, and the desert is now located at the southeast of the Yellow River. According to historical literature records, the Western Han Dynasty sent Shuofang Jun to separate this area into 10 counties in 127 a BP (the 2nd year Yuanshuo of Han Wu Emperor) after defeating the Xiongnu. The westernmost three counties were located in the northern part of today's Ulan Buh Desert. The first county, Yuhun (established in 127 B.C.) was the key road through the Yinshan Mountain, where the famous Jilu Zhai was located, and then was Linrong (set in 124a BP) and Sanfeng (set in 120 B.C.) (Fig. 5-22). Migrants from inner China continuously entered this area, and along with the establishment of the three counties, large-scale land use began. After a century of management, this area became a rich and popular reclamation area, with more than sixty years of peace, prosperous people, and plentiful drove. Border Corn, as it was historically called, was produced in this area, and this is the evidence of affluent agricultural products of this area at that time. This area had been one of the centers for stationing troops to reclaim grasslands of northwestern China. There were no serious shifting sand problems for 300 years until the end of the the Western Han Dynasty. But after the Mang Xin Dynasty in 23 A.D., this agricultural nation were forced to emigrate out of this area because of the invasion of the Xiongnu. So the farmland was desolated, irrigated areas were abandoned and wind erosion strengthened. Surface clay pans of the ancient alluvial plain of the Yellow River, which was destroyed by plough, underwent serious wind-erosion without a crop cover.

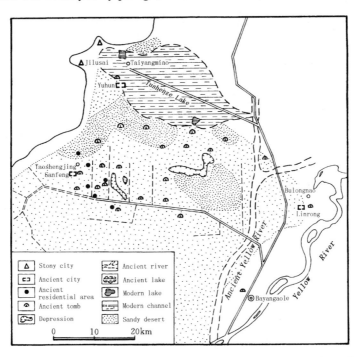

Fig. 5-22　Ancient area of stationing troops to open up grassland in the Ulan Buh Desert

Underground sand beds became shifting sand under wind action. The sight of the strong wind erosion in cemeteries of the Han Dynasty is shocking. Many arch tops were discovered in tombs of the Han Dynasty, and even stand out of the earth's surface like an island of sand sea because the surface soil in some tombs has suffered from wind erosion. The earth's surface of the ancient alluvial plain of the Yellow River had been wind-eroded about 1 m during recent 2,000 years when using the tombs' height during the Han Dynasty as a reference.

In 981 AD (the 6th year Taipingxingguo of the Northern Song Dynasty), when Wang Yande was sent on a diplomatic mission to Gaochang (today's Turpan) via this area, the situation was such "that they can not use a horse to travel, and had to use the camel over dunes three *chis* thick". He also recorded "that this area can not produce corns, but can produce a grass called *Dengxiang* which is edible as foodstuff". *Dengxiang*, with the formal name *Agriphyllum* squarrosum, has edible seeds and is a harbinger for mobile dunes. At that time, the use of *Agriphyllum squarrosum* as food indicated widespread distribution, prosperous growth and abundant production. *Agriphyllum squarrosum* was the primary species in shifting dunes according to the law of vegetation succession in sand. So we can conclude that the area was in the stage of initial aeolian desertification at the end of 10th century. In Spring of 1697 AD (the 36th year Kangxi of the Qing Dynasty), Gao Shiqi followed the Emperor on a punitive expedition to Gaerdan. They went directly northward to Dengkou along the west bank of the Yellow River in Ningxia. According to his records, cattail, Tamarix, *Caragana* and other vegetation fixed dunes on both sides of the Yellow River, and there was no shifting sand. When the road from Yinchuan, Dengkou, Sanshenggong to Baotou was built in 1925 shifting sand was far from the Yellow River. But after 1937 shifting sand reached the Yellow River in many places south of Dengkou, and the road was obstructed.

5.4.4　The Mu Us Sandy Land

The Mu Us Sandy Land, located in the northern edge of the Ordos Plateau, is a typical example of the southward invasion of deserts in the historical time. Its precipitation is 300–450 mm. Turf layers, which can reach several meters, are distributed around in interdunal depressions and Heilu soil is common in ridges. So there historically was a relatively wet period, and grassland was likely to exist at that time. Preserved between the dunes are large areas of *Rhamnus erythroxylon* coppice and *Salix* coppice, typical in appearance of a swamp woodland in the grassland. The ancient city ruins from the Han and Tang Dynasties to the Song and Ming Dynasties are spread along the Great Wall and covered with shifting sand, for example Ganfangcun in Gucheng Sands, Yulin; Tongwan City and Dashibian City on the riverside of the Hongliu River, as well as Baicheng Platform and Gucheng on the riverside of the Yingdiliang River. Copper cashes from the 1st–17th century interspersed among the dunes can prove this area was formerly not a desert environment with dunes.

From the data in historical records, the Mu Us Sandy Land was an abundant agriculture and stockbreeding area with fertile land, abundant production, rich grassland and numerous herds. In 413 AD, Helian Bobo of Xiongnu built Tongwan City as the capital of the Xia Dynasty, which is located on the north side of the Hongliu River in today's Jingbian County. At that time, the environment around Tongwan City was a delightful landscape "facing a big lake and with a clear river"; it was not a vast desert. Then, suffering from constant warfare, the city began recording shifting sand in the Tang Dynasty. In 822 AD, Xiazhou (Tongwan City) related the situation that sand dunes were as high as city walls during a blustery day. So the environment around the city underwent enormous change during the 400 years after its establishment. In the poems "See a Passenger out of Xiazhou from the Wall" and " on the Way to Xiazhou" were written by Li Yi, a poet during Xianzong Emperor's reign in the Tang Dynasty (806–821 AD) and Xu Tang, a poet during Xiantong's reign in the Tang Dynasty. They wrote several references to shifting sand. For example, "Horses herded on the sand dunes and wild geese fly alone"; "Vast desert is so wider; the Helian City is sparkling in the distance". The Song Dynasty destroyed and abandoned Xiazhou, recorded definitely that it was in that desert, and left a record about the extent of aeolian desertification. Today, only the 24 m high watchtower at the northwest corner of the ruined city stands out among the rolling quicksand. Its majestic appearance can be seen over 10 km of rolling dunes.

Ancient cities in the Mu Us Sandy Land are shown in Fig.5-23.

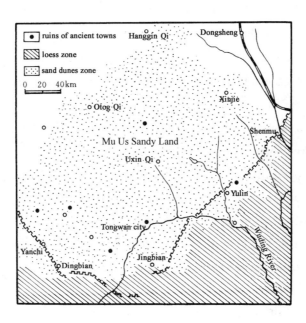

Fig. 5-23　Ancient cities in the Mu Us Sandy Land

In 1473 AD (the 9th year Chenghua of Xianzong Emperor in the Ming Dynasty), the Great Wall (divided into an inside and outside Border Wall) was built. It was the northern limit of the reclamation area. To resist the invasion of nomads who desired rich grassland, the flourishing areas were built inside the Great Wall. It was obvious that there were rich grasslands and flourishing areas suited for agriculture or pasturage, and it was not today's aeolian desertification landscape. After the middle of the Ming Dynasty, cities and forts were numerous between the inside and outside Border Wall. Grassland opened up by the garrison troops and peasants were prosperous. At that time there were grasslands covering more than several hundred *Lis* and herds were everywhere. But in the end of the Ming Dynasty, the agricultural economy could not be kept stable under government corruption and frequent wars among nations. The development of uncultivated farmland along the Great Wall offered appropriate conditions for aeolian desertification. At the same time, excessive economic activities and frequent wars seriously destroyed natural vegetation. For example, in the middle of the 15th century during the Ming Dynasty, one or two hundred kilometers of grass adjacent to the Great Wall were burned in the winter and spring to prevent of nomadic invasions. Thus it can be seen that there were neither stable agricultural activities nor the necessary time for vegetation recovery in the end of the Ming Dynasty. The earth's bure, sandy surface began to develop into aeolian desertified land. In the middle of the 16th century, in the Ming Dynasty, the phenomenon of piled-up sand on buildings in areas along the Great Wall began to appear in the northern part of Shaanxi. Yulin, an important northern city, had been almost encircled by desert.

The large development of aeolian desertification along the Great Wall was a result of migration and reclamation in the Qing Dynasty. In the middle of the 17th century, the Qing government repealed their policy of prohibiting reclamation to allow the opening up of grassland. Peasants in northern parts of Shaanxi were permitted to form a partnership to cultivate land outside of the Great Wall. So the recently recovered land encountered estrepement. At the same time, foreign forces invaded this area. They occupied and cultivated the land along the southern part of the Great Wall, such as Ningtiao Ridge. The destruction of grassland reached its culmination. The borderline between agriculture and stockbreeding moved to today's boundary line between shanxi Province and the Inner Mongolia Autonomous Region at that time. Seventy to eighty percent of the area in Jingbian was aeolian desertified land, Bala (fixed and semifixed dunes), alkali land and Liubo (Liuwan, interdunal depression with more *Salix* coppice); grassland occupied only twenty to thirty percent of the total area. At that time, cultivation of grassland was mainly distributed along the rivers, for example Chengchuan, Liushuwan and Xiaoqiaopan in the reaches of the Hongliu River; Hongshicheng and Hailiutu Temper in the reaches of the Hailiutu River; Jiumiaotan and Balasu in the reaches of the Yingdiliang River; Huanghaojie in the reaches of the Heihe River; and Hongdunjie in the reaches of the Getuan River. Those cultivated areas of bottomland in river valleys were the center for aeolian desertification, and aeolian desertification continued to extend outwards from these areas. Then the aeolian desertification along the Great Wall was accelerated. The landscape turned into an interlaced distributions of ploughland and shifting sand, fixed and semifixed dunes. Once the aeolian desertified land along the Great Wall came into existence, the continued influence of human actions made the ecological environment of fragile semi-arid grassland suffer and ultimately lose its ecological balance. Then aeolian desertification continually developed. Its processes were: a. The enlargement of area: Crescent dunes and chains moved at a speed of 5–8 m a year under the wind action. Then the area of aeolian desertification land enlarged. b. The increase of degree: Degree of aeolian desertification increased in the area which had already become aeolian desertified land. For example, semi-fixed dunes turned into mobile dunes and fixed dunes turned into semi-fixed dunes. These changes happened frequently around residential areas, farmlands, wells and springs. The Great Wall in northern Shaanxi and southeastern Ningxia was roughly 625 km long and 34 percent of it has been buried by shifting sand.

From the view of space-time, the process of aeolian desertification in the Mu Us Aeolian Land continued roughly a millennium from the Tang Dynasty. If the Great Wall of the Ming Dynasty is a time border, aeolian desertification north of the Great Wall took place between the 9th–15th century (from the Tang to the Song Dynasty), and the shifting sand nearly 60 km wide along and in the south of the Great Wall was developed in the most recent 300 years during the Ming Dynasty and the foundation of the P.R.C. The distribution of historical relics which has distributed as dynasties order from northwest to southeast confirm the direction and historical course of aeolian desertification in the Mu Us Sandy Land from another point of view.

Ruins of Tongwan City in the southern Mu Us Sandy Land is shown in Fig.5-24.

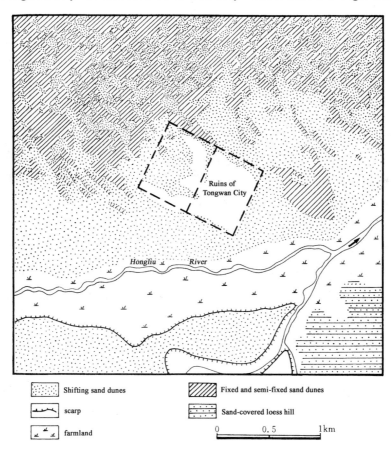

Fig. 5-24　Ruins of Tongwan City in the southern Mu Us Sandy Land

5.4.5 The Horqin Sandy Land

The Horqin Sandy Land, distributed east of the Da Hinggan Ling Mountains, is also a typical example in the historical course of aeolian desertification. With abundant precipitation, surface water and groundwater, the pasture is luxuriant and arbors, for example pine, elm, robur, maple and so on, grow in ridges and hills. According to historical data, in the 4–7th century, some tribes of Khitan lived between the Xar Moron River and the Laoha River with a lifestyle of "chasing the grass and managing the pasturage". At that time, besides the prosperous stockbreeding, people had begun to develop agriculture. It was an environment with fertile soil for planting and pasturage. At the beginning of the 10th century, the Yelü family of Khitan established the Liao Dynasty in the area of the Horqin Grassland and founded a capital in Shangjing Linhuang Fu near the eastern Wuerjimulun River and the Shalimo River. They set up several states and counties in the region beside the Huangshui River and the Xilamulun River. After capturing and plundering farmers from the states of Yan and Ji of the Northern Song Dynasty and Bohai Country in the east, they engaged in farming and developed agriculture. By the middle of the 10th century, the region had already developed into an agricultural region, in which there were several hundred thousand families and more than one thousand *Lis* of cultivated land. Discovered ironware and cultural ruins of the Liao Dynasty from the sandy land may reflect the scene of agricultural culture at that time. The great mass of cultural ruins were located between the Laoha River and the Jiaolai River. Under the circumstances of enlargement the agricultural and gathering scope, the vegetation was damaged and aeolian desertification developed. Su Che, a famous writer of the Northern Song Dynasty, wrote a poem when he was sent on a diplomatic mission to the Liao Kingdom:"the mountains are covered with sand, and groves are rare" Therefore, there was already a plentiful amount of aeolian desertification land in the West Liaohe River Plain at that time. By the 12th century in the Jin Dynasty, the circumstance became "no trees because of denudation". The residents, former migrants, had to look for a new place to live where there was grass and water, which reflected the serious aeolian desertification. Furthermore, there were records that the city state of Han Zhou had four seats and moved three times because of blown sand activity. After the 13th century, with the foundation of the Yuan Dynasty and the Ming Dynasty, the political center moved south, and with the scope of agricultural cultivation reduced, the natural vegetation gradually recovered. In the 17th century, the beginning of the Qing Dynasty, this area again became an excellent pasture with "flourishing woods and grass and millions of livestock". Therefore many paddocks and pastures were distributed in this region during the Qing Dynasty.

The latest aeolian desertification in the Horqin Sandy Land mainly happened after the 18th–19th century. Since the middle of 18th century, the Qing government promoted farming in this area and the grassland was gradually cultivated. After 2 or 3 years, the cultivated land was abandoned because of infertile soil and sand. Afterwards, new grassland was cultivated once again. The ploughed land largely destroyed the surface soil. Grassland without protection by vegetation formed mobile dunes because of sand flow during the arid and windy season. The dune, known as "Baishatuozi", first appeared as spots near residential areas, pasturages, farmlands and rivers. If gradually expanded, and the beautiful and rich grassland was degraded into aeolian desertified land. Even the famous Mulan Paddock of the Qing Dynasty, which was located west of the Horqin Grassland and north of Chengde, was cultivated in the beginning of 20th century. As a result, the natural vegetation coverage decreased to 5 percent, and aeolian desertification land has already taken over 48% of the northern region.

According to the above dissertation, it is obvious that the appearance and development of aeolian desertified land in the arid desert belt during the history time is on one hand, related to the changes of inland rivers and the stop of irrigation headwaters flow, and on the other hand, is related to political and military activities. In any case, the oases in the arid belt depended on rivers as an essential foundation. Aeolian desertification located at ancient cities or abandoned oases have traces of ancient riverbeds and springs, at their centers, and they didn't mutually link in the ancient hydrologic net. For example, some historical aeolian desertified lands on the edge of the Taklimakan Desert were Loulan in the lower reaches of the Konqi River, Jingjue in the lower reaches of the Niya River, Andier in the lower reaches of the Andier River, Kaladun in the lower reaches of the Keriya River and so on. Each area did not connect with each other. The aeolian desertification land in the north of the Tarim Basin (reclaimed area in the Han and the Tang Dynasty) has the lower reaches of the Dina River and the Weigan River respectively as the center. There were similar cases in the Hexi Corridor, such as Caogoujing City in the lower reaches of the Maying River, Xusanwan City in the lower reaches of the Bailang River, the Gaogou Fort in the lower reaches of the Hongshui River etc. These aeolian desertificatied lands developed after human and natural factors caused the river to change, irrigation riverhead flow to stop, and the area was finally abandoned. It was often difficult to reverse these circumstances, only leaving behind a landscape of an ancient city scattered in dunes. In the semi-arid and semi-humid belt, natural conditions were superior to arid and hyper arid belts, and when the weak ecological environment was destroyed, it was relatively easy for them to recover. At the same time, during the historical time, human activity was multifarious, and therefore the desertification process was more complicated. This was different from the linear development in the arid belt, and the forming aeolian desertified land in historical time took the emergence of sandstorm activity and large sand dunes in areas that were originally grassland. Most of the aeolian desertified land formed in the eastern and middle regions of Inner Mongolia is the result of excessive human activities during the historical time. With the basis of historical aeolian desertification processes, modern aeolian desertification can continuously develop. Besides the historical relics in the inner part of aeolian desertified land, broad quicksand, spotty quicksand, semi-fixed and fixed dunes and farmland, pasture and residential area distribution are all reflections in the earth's surface landscape of aeolion desertification. The Mu Us Sandy Land in the Ordos Plateau and the West Liaohe River Sandy Land in the Horqin Grassland are just two typical examples.

References

Cao Qunying, Xia Xuncheng. 1992. A preliminary study on landforms and quaternary geology at lower reaches of Keriya River, Xinjiang. Scientia Geographica Sinica, 12(1): 34–43

Chen Fahu, Zhang Weixin et al. 1993. Loess Stratigraphy and Quaternary Glacier Problems in Gansu and Qinghai, China. Beijing: Science Press, 9–46 (In Chinese)

Dai Fengnian, Wang Yuanping, Qu Jianjun et al. 1994. A preliminary study on cosmic dust in desert. Chinese Science Bulletin, 39(17): 1592–1594

Dieter Jakel, Jurgen Hofman. 1996. Glacial and periglacial features in the upper Keriya Valley (Kunlun Mountains). Reports on the "1986 Sino-German Kunlun shan Taklimakan Expedition". In: Dieter Jackl and Zhu Zhenda. ed. Die Erde, Zeitschrift der Gesellschaft fur Erdkunde Zu Berlin, Erg.-H.6

Dieter Jakel. 1996. The Badainjaran Desert: Its origin and development. GEO-WISSENSCHAFTEN, 14 Jahrgang, Juli/August: 272–274

Dong Guangrong, Jin Jiong, Li Baosheng et al. 1994. Some problems of desertification in Horqin Sandy Land—taking the southern regions as example. Journal of Desert Research, 14(1): 1–9

Dong Guangrong, Jin Jiong, Shen Jianyou et al. 1990. Desertification processes and its causes of Chinese terrestrial ecosystem since Late Pleistocene. Liu Dongsheng. Loess, Quaternary Geology and Global Change (Second Issue). Beijing: Science Press, 91–101

Dong Guangrong, Li Baosheng, Wen Xiangle. 1993a. Features and evolution of a eolian-sandland forms in China. In: Yang Jingchun ed. Features and Evolution of landforms in China. Beijing: Ocean Press. 149–172 (in Chinese)

Dong Guangrong, Wang Guiyong, Chen Huizhong et al. 1995. The formation and evolution of the deserts in China and their relation to the uplifting of Qinghai-Tibet Plateau. The China Society on Tibet Plateau. Symposium on Qingzang Plateau and Global change. Beijing: Meteorologic Press, 13–29

Dong Guangrong, Zhu Zhenda, Li Baosheng et al. 1992. On the origin and evolution of the modern Gobi,desert in North China. Quaternary Geology and Environment in China. Editor in Chief Liu Tungsheng, the Series of the 13th INQUA Congress. Beijing: Science Press, 34–40

Dong Guangrong, Gao Shangyu, 1993b. Land Desertification and the Ways to Prevention and Cure of It in Gonghe Basin. Qinghai Province. China. Beijing: Science Press. 226 (in Chinese)

Dong Guaugrong, Li Sen, Li Baosheng et al. 1991. A preliminary study on the formation and evolution of deserts in China. Journal of Desert Research, 11(4): 23–32 (in Chinese)

Fan Zili. 1993. A study on the formation and evolution of oases in Tarim Basin. Acta Geographica Sinica, 48(5): 421–437 (in Chinese)

Gao Cunhai, Zhang Qingsong. 1991. Loess sediment on northern slope of Kunlun Mountains and environment evolution during the latest Quaternary period. Xinjiang Institute of Geography, CAS. Arid Zone Geography Symposium. Beijing: Science Press

Gao Quanzhou, Dong Guangrong, Zou Xueyong et al. 1996. The Chagelebulu section; a strata recorded of the advances and retreats of the monsoons in East Asia since late Pleistocene. Journal of Desert Research. 16(2): 112—119 (in Chinese)

Gao Quanzhou, Dong Guangrong, Li Baosheng et al. 1995. Evolution of southern fringe of Badain Jaran desert since late Pleistocene. Journal of Desert Research. 15(4): 345—352 (in Chinese)

Gao Quanzhou, Tao Zhen, Dong Guangrong. 1998. The characteristics sediments geochemistry in Chagelebulu Section in the Badain Jaran Desert. Acta of Geographica Sinica, 53 (supp.): 44—51(in Chinese)

Gao Shangyu, Chen Weinan, Jin Heling et al. 1993. A preliminary on the desert evolution on the fringe of Chinese monsoon area in Holocene. Science in China (Series B), 23(2): 202—208 (in Chinese)

Gao Shangyu. 1992. Preliminary Studies on the Desert Evolution in the Northwestern Margin of the Monsoon, China. Lanzhou: Geography Department of Lanzhou University (in Chinese)

Jia Huilan, Li Baosheng. 1991. Chemical element distribution and Palaeoclimate in Late Pleistocene-Holocene Strata in East Gonghe Basin. Journal of Desert Research, 11(2): 27—32 (in Chinese)

Jin Heling, Li Baosheng. 1992. Discussion on the analytical results of calcium carbonate and soluble salt in pulu stratigraphic Profile in Xinjiang. Journal of Desert Research, 12(4): 27—33

Kang Jiancheng, Li Jijun. 1993. Loess profile in Linxia of Gansu: perfect records of environment evolution since 150,000. Geological Review, 39(2): 165—175

Li Baosheng, David Dian Zhang, Jin Heling et al. 2000. Paleo-monsoon activities of Mu Us Desert, China since 50 ka BP—a study of the stratigraphic sequences of the Milanggouwan section, Salawusu River area. Palaeogeography, Palaeoclimatology, Palaeoecology, 162: 1—16

Li Baosheng, Dong Guangrong, Ding Tonghu et al. 1990. Several problems about aeloian landforms in the eastern Taklimakan Desert. Chinese Science Bulletin, 35(23): 1815—1818

Li Baosheng, Dong Guangrong, Gao Shangyu et al. 1991. The changes in climatic environment of the Salawusu River area since the terminal stage of Mid-Pleistocene as indicated by detrital minerals in Quaternary sediments. *Acta Petrologica of Mineralogica* 10(1): 84–90 (in Chinese)

Li Baosheng, Dong Guangrong, Wu Zheng et al. 1993a. The establishment of the Upper Pleistocene Chengchuan Formation in Northern China. Geological Review, 39 (2): 91—100 (in Chinese)

Li Baosheng, Dong Guangrong, Zhu Yizhi et at. 1993b. The sedimental environment and its evolution of the dune desert and loess, Tarim Basin, since last glaciation. Science in China, Series B. 23(6): 644—651 (in Chinese)

Li Baosheng, Jin Heling, Lu Haiyan et al. 1998. Processes of the deposition and vicissitude of Mu Us Desert, China since 150 ka BP. Science in China (Series D), 41(3): 248–254

Li Baosheng, Li Sen, Wang Yue et al. 1988, Geological age of the sand and dust deposits of the Aqiang section in the extremely arid region of China. Acta Geologica Sinica, 72(1): 83—92 (in Chinese)

Li Baosheng, Wu Zheng, David et al. 2001. The environment and change in the monsoon sandy region of China during Late Pleistocene and Holocene. Acta Geologica Sinica, 75(1): 125—137 (in Chinese)

Li Baosheng, Yan Mancun, Barry B. Miller et al. 1998. Late Pleistocene and Holocene palaeoclimate records from the Badain Jaran Desert, China. Current Research, 15: 129—131

Li Baosheng, Yuan Baoyin, Zhou Xingjia et al. 1996. The Evolution of Yutian-Hotan Oasis since 13,500 a BP. Chinese Journal of Arid Land Research, 9 (2): 137—145, New York: Allerton Press Inc

Li Bingyuan, Zhang Qingsong, Wang Fubao. 1991.Evolution of lakes in Kalakunlun Mountains-Western Kunlun Mountains Areas. Quaternary Research, (1): 64—71

Li Chunlai, Ouyang Zhiyuan, Liu Dongsheng et al. 1992. Findings and its meaning of Microtektite and micro-glass-sphere in Loess. Science in China, 22(11): 1210—1219

Li Sen, Sun Wu, Li Xiaoze et al. 1995. Sedimentary characteristics and environmental evolution of Otindag Sandy Land in Holocene. Journal of Desert Research, 15(4): 323—331(in Chinese)

Liu Jiaqi, Maimaiti, Yi Ming. 1990. Quaternary volcanic distribution and K-Ar age in Western Kunlun Mountains. Science in China (Series B), 20(2): 180—187

Liu Zechun, Sun Shiying, Wang Yongjin et al. 1991. Quaternary stratum in the eastern regions of Qaidam Basin. Quaternary Research Association of China, Chinese Research Center of Quaternary Glacier and Environment, Quaternary Glacier and Environment of China. Beijing: Science Press

Roger Coque, Pierre Gentelle, Coque-Delhuille. 1991. Desertification along the piedmont of the Kunlun Chain (Hetian-Yutian Sector) and the southern border of the geomorphological observations (1). Geodynamique Externe Etude Integree du Milieu Naturel. Revue de Geomorphologie Dynamique. Tarif de L (Abonnement Pour 4 Numeros)

Shao Yajun, Li Baosheng. 1995. Spore pollen assemblage in the loess of upper reach of the Keriva River and its environment. Journal of Desert Research, 15(1): 37—41(In Chinese)

Shi Peijun. 1991. Theory and Practice of Research into Geography Environment Changes—Research into Geographical Environment Change during Late Quaternary Period in the Ordos Region of North China. Beijing: Science Press, 66—107 (In Chinese)

Shi Yafeng, Zhang Xiangsong. 1995. Climatic change's affection on surface water resources of arid Northwest areas and future trend. Science in China (Seri. B), 25(9): 968—977

Sun Jimin, Ding Zhongli, Liu Dongsheng et al. 1995. The environmental evolution of the desert-loess transitional zone over the last glacial-interglacial cycle. Quaternary Science (2): 117—122 (In Chinese)

Synthesis Science Investigation Team of Xinjiang, Chinese Academy of Sciences. 1994. Editorial board of Xinjiang Quaternary Geology and Environment. Xinjiang Quaternary Geology and Environment. Beijing: China Agriculture Press, 11—27

Tao Zhen, Dong Guangrong. 1994. Relation of land desertification and climatic changes since last-glacial period in Guinan Sandy Land. Journal of Desert Research, 14(2): 42—48

Wang Fubao. 1992. Dust accumulation in Kalakunlun Mountains-Kunlun Mountains Areas. Liu Dongsheng. Loess·Quaternary Geology·Global Change (Third Issue). Beijing: Science Press, 108—115

Wang Nai'ang. 1998. Adiscussion on the evolution of east asian monsoon. Marine Geology & Quaternary Geology, 18(3): 1—12

Wang Tao. 1990. Several problems on the formation and evolution of Badain Jaran Desert. Journal of Desert Research, 10(1): 29—40

Wen Qizhong, Qiao Yulou. 1995. Paleoclimate records in sediments on northern slope of Kunlun Mountains since Late Pleistocene. The China Society on Tibet Plateau. Symposium on Qinghai-Tibet Plateau and Global change. Beijing: China Meteorological Press, 96—104

Xiao Zhifeng, Ouyang Zhiyuan, Lin Wenzhu. 1995. Simulation on climatic effect of giant extraterrestrial body impacts against the Earth in the Cenozoic. Chinese Science Bulletin, 40(2): 151—153

Yan Mancun, Dong Guangrong, Li Baosheng. 1997. Terrace development of Yellow River and geomorphic evolution in Shapotou Area. Journal of Desert Research, 17(4): 369—376 (In Chinese)

Yan Mancun, Dong Guangrong, Li Baosheng. 1998. A preliminary study on the evolution of southeastern margin in Tengger Desert. Journal of Desert Research, 18(2): 111—116

Yan Mancun, Wang Guangqian, Li Baosheng et al. 2001. Formation and growth of high mogadunes, in Badain Jaran Desert. Acta Geographica Sinica, 56(1): 83—91 (In Chinese)

Yang Dongzhen, Ji Xiangming, Xu Xiaobin et al. 1991. An analysis of a sandstorm weather. Acta Meteorologica Sinica, 49(3): 334—342

Zeng Yongnian, Ma Haizhou, Li, Lingqin et al. 1997. Firstly discuss on problems of desertification in Xining Basin since 1.2 Ma BP. Journal of Desert Research, 17(3): 226—229

Zhang Pengxi, Zhang Baozhen. 1991. Preliminary study on paleoclimate and paleoenvironment of the Qaidam Region since three million years ago. Acta Geographica Sinica, 26(3): 327—335

Zhang Qingsong, Li Bingyuan, Zhu Liping. 1994. New recognitions of quaternary environment in the Northwest Tibetan Plateau. Acta Geographica Sinica, 49(4): 289—297

Zheng Benxing, Jiao Keqin, Li Shijie et al. 1990. New progress on aging Quaternary glacial epoach on Qinghai-Tibet Plateau: taking Western Kunlun Mountains as example. Chinese Science Bulletin, 35(7): 533—537

Zhou Xingjia. 1991. Evidence of Keriya River inflowed Tarim River. Xinjiang Science Investigation Team of Keriya River and Taklimakan Desert. *Science Investigation Report on Keriya River and Taklimakan Desert*. Beijing: China Science and Technology Press, 40—46

Chapter 6
Blown Sand Physics and Formation of Aeolian Landforms

6.1 Laws of blown sand movement

Wind is the driving force for near-surface sand movement. Blown sand movement processes can be divided into the initiation of sand particle movement, i.e. wind erosion processes, sand transport, and the deposition process. The main problems dealing with wind-blown sand movement include near-surface airstream characteristics, sand movement mode, the determination and calculation of wind erosion rate or sand transport rate etc.

6.1.1 Characteristics of near-surface air stream

6.1.1.1 Definition of near-surface layer

The lowermost zone of the atmosphere, where the motion of air is affected by ground friction force, is defined as the boundary layer. Since the closer to the ground surface, the higher the ground friction resistance, and the wind speed increases along with height above the ground surface. Within the boundary layer wind speed transits upwards from zero velocity to free airflow zone where it is no longer affected by ground friction force. The atmospheric boundary layer is generally about 1- 2 km thick (Fig. 6-1) (Thomas, 1977).

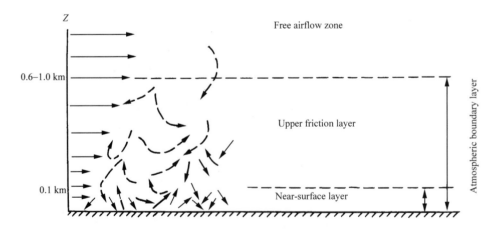

Fig. 6-1　A sketch of the atmospheric boundary layer

The structure of the airflow speed profile within the boundary layer is mainly determined by the airflow type, namely laminar flow and turbulent flow. In the case of laminar flow, the fluid in different layers basically does not mix and the momentum transfer is completed through molecular movement, the slow-moving molecules are carried to the rapid moving molecular layer, and as a result, a drag is produced in the rapid moving molecular layer. Such intermolecular momentum transfer causes the shear force between different airflow layers.

In the case of turbulent flow, the momentum exchange between different airflow layers is completed by gusts and turbulent vortex. The turbulent exchange is more effective than molecular movement so that it can deduce greater wind speed gradient and shear force (Fig. 6-2).

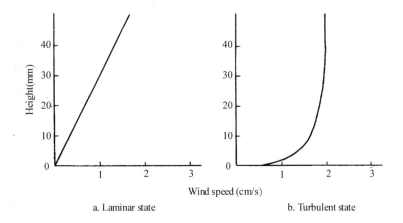

Fig. 6-2   Near-surface wind speed profile (Thomas, modified in 1997)

Laminar state can be distinguished from turbulent state by the Reynolds number:

$$R_e = \frac{\rho h v}{r} \tag{6-1}$$

Where, ρ is fluid density, h is fluid characteristic length, v is fluid speed, and r is the coefficient of viscosity.

Generally, when the Reynolds number is smaller than 2,000, the fluid is in a laminar state; when the Reynolds number is larger than 2,000, the turbulent flow is believed to have fully developed. Owing to low viscosity and large thickness, the airflow in the atmosphere is always in a turbulent state. Therefore, the priority of blown sand movement study is generally given to the wind profile under turbulent states.

6.1.1.2   Wind speed profile within boundary layer

Under the conditions of flat, unvegetated surface, no direct solar radiation and neutral stratification, wind speed mainly appears as semi-logarithmic form (Bagnold, 1941). This is generally thought to be the result of surface exerting a drag force on the near-surface airflow. Therefore, if the wind profile is given, the near-surface shear force can be calculated. In the study of blown sand movement, the term used to describe the velocity gradient is shear velocity (u_*),and it is mainly used to calculate wind erosion rate or sand transport rate. The relation between shear velocity and shear force is expressed as:

$$u_* = \sqrt{\frac{\tau_0}{\rho}} \tag{6-2}$$

Where, τ_0 is shear force. In the zone immediately above the ground surface the wind speed is zero. In the case of sand movement the depth of this zone is called aerodynamic roughness (z_0) (Fig. 6-3). The relation between aerodynamic roughness, shear velocity and wind speed can be expressed as:

$$\frac{u}{u_*} = \frac{1}{k}\ln\left(\frac{z-d}{z_0}\right) \tag{6-3}$$

Where k=0.4 is the Von Karman constant; d is displacement height above zero plane.

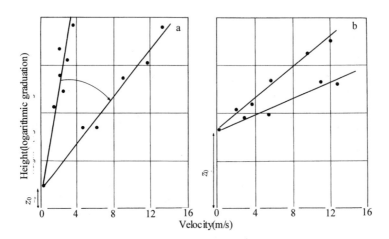

Fig. 6-3   Representation of dynamic roughness of blown sand movement

In previous literatures the roughness was generally regarded as a constant, but recent researches show that the roughness changes with wind speed even under neutral conditions.

6.1.1.3 Determination of shear velocity

Shear velocity can be determined by regression analysis of mean wind speed measured at several heights. Wilkinson (1984) thought that wind velocities at five different heights are required to calculate the meaningful shear velocity. If the roughness is given, the shear velocity over a flat ground surface can be calculated using the formula derived by Bagnold (1941).

$$u_* = \frac{k}{\ln z / z_0} u_z \qquad (6\text{-}4)$$

Where u_z is wind speed at the height of z. This formula has been widely used in the study of sand movement, but defining z_0 as a constant is problematic.

In the case of undulated ground surface, for example, the determination of shear velocity over the windward slope of sand dune, the wind speed profile is a zigzag line rather than a straight line (Fig. 6-4). Thus the determination of shear velocity has not been solved. In addition, the determination of shear velocity is also closely related to the temperature stratification; when near-surface heat convection is well developed, the buoyant force can also affect the wind speed profile. Therefore, in the determination of wind speed profile in field and in turn, the shear velocity, the Obukhov length or Richardson constant should be figured out together with the near-surface temperature gradient.

The obtained wind speed profile should be corrected. Literatures report that the instability of the determined wind speed can be expressed as a function of height. Generally, the correction coefficient can be overlooked at the height of 0.5 m and when the wind speed is greater than 10 m/s.

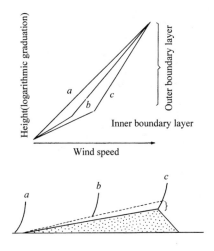

Fig. 6-4   Several types of wind speed profile over windward slope of sand dune (Frank and Kocurek, modified in 1996)

6.1.1.4   Determination of dynamic roughness

The dynamic roughness (z_0) in blown sand environments has obvious temporal and spatial variations and its accurate determination in the field is quite difficult. For sandy desert surfaces, the dynamic roughness height varies between 0.003–0.007 m and in the vegetated area it can reach 0.2 m or more. Bagnold (1941) obtained a dynamic roughness height of $d/30$, where d is the mean grain size of sands, however, this is only suitable for well-sorted uniform materials on flat ground surfaces. Based on the experimental results, Greeley and Iversen (1985) suggested that the dynamic roughness is related to the spatial arrangement form of sand grains and their values vary between $d/30$–$d/4$ (Fig. 6-5). Lancaster et al. obtained similar conclusions.

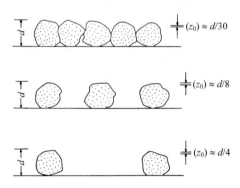

Fig. 6-5   Relation between dynamic roughness height and the arrangement of sand grains

Generally, the dynamic roughness height of a flat and uniform bed can be obtained from the wind speed profile but thus far there is no widely accepted method for the determination of dynamic roughness height over an undulated ground surface with complex composition. When wind moves from a flat surface to a rough surface, the thickness of the inner boundary layer will change and therefore the dynamic roughness will also change (Fig. 6-6).

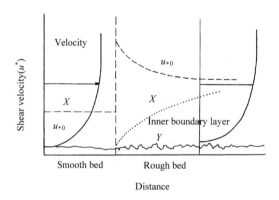

Fig. 6-6   Variations of inner boundary layer between smooth bed and rough bed

It can be seen from Fig. 6-6 that when wind moves from a smooth bed to a rough bed, near-surface airflow is retarded by the drag force, their dynamic roughness and shear velocity increase rapidly and then the shear velocity tends to become stable at a certain distance downwind. When the surface roughness increases, more sands of mean grain size are below the roughness height where the wind velocity is zero. Therefore, although the shear velocity increases, the wind erosion rate or sand transport rate does not increase.

In summary, although the dynamic roughness is an important parameter in the study of sand movement and there have been some new methods to determine regional roughness, such as radar and large meteorological observation towers, their accurate calculation is still difficult.

6.1.2　Sand movement modes and their structure

6.1.2.1　The initiation of sand movement by wind

1) Basic modes of the initiation of sand movement

When the force acting on the surface sand grains is larger than the resistance, sands begin to move. The basic types of force exerted on sand particles by airflow are shown in Fig. 6-7. Generally, particles maintain an equilibrium state under the action of three forces: lift force, drag force and shape resistance. Lift force is formed by the pressure difference between the upper and lower surface of particles due to the action of airflow; shape resistance is caused by the pressure difference around the particles; and drag force is caused by airflow shear force. Under the action of these forces, together with gravitational force and viscous force, particles begin to move and enter the airflow.

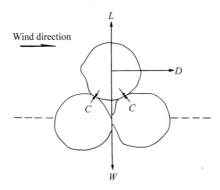

Fig. 6-7　Basic forms of forces acting on particles

L, lift force; D, drag force; W, gravitational force; C, internal friction force

Researches show that there is a functional relation between the initiation of particle movement, mean particle size and shear velocity of airflow. Bagnold et al. suggested the threshold shear velocity u_{*ct} as follows:

$$u_{*ct} = A\sqrt{gd\left(\frac{\sigma - \rho}{\rho}\right)} \tag{6-5}$$

Where, σ is particle density, g is acceleration of gravity, disparticle size and A is constant, which mainly depends on the Reynolds number and generally is 0.1.

Two modes of particle movement initiation, namely fluid initiation and impact initiation, have been studied in the 1940s (Fig. 6-8). It can be seen from Fig. 6-8 that large particles require a large threshold velocity, but particles <0.06 mm also require a higher threshold velocity due to the intermolecular and electronic attraction forces. In addition, it is also related to water molecules and the film effect of large particles. According to Greeley et al. (1985), particles in the size range of 0.04–0.4 mm are highly susceptible to erosion by wind. It is also seen from Fig. 6-8 that sediments on the downwind side of sand ripples or sand seas are generally well sorted and consist of fine-grained materials.

In the case of a flat and uniform bed, the shear velocity to initiate particle movement can be determined by formula 6-5. However, the actual beds are not uniform and variable, and many factors such as slope, water, vegetation and so on can affect the threshold shear velocity of sand particles.

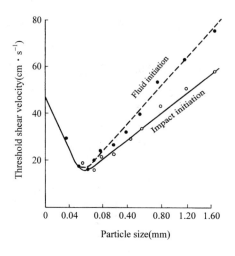

Fig. 6-8   Relation between threshold velocity and mean grain size

2) Influence of slope

Allen (1982) and Dyer (1986) analysed the influences of slope on the initiation of particle movement. From the comparison of wind tunnel experimental data of adjustable slope and theoretical values, Hardisty and Whitehouse found that they have a good consistency (Fig. 6-9). Iversen and Rasmussen (1999) put forward the relation of the threshold shear velocity for the initiation of particle movement on horizontal and inclined surfaces (Iversen et al., 1999).

$$\frac{v^2_{*t}}{v^2_{*t_0}} = \frac{\sin\theta}{\tan\alpha} + \cos\theta \tag{6-6}$$

Where v_{*t} is the threshold velocity when the slope is θ, α is the internal friction angle, and v_{*t_0} is the threshold velocity to initiate particle movement on a level surface.

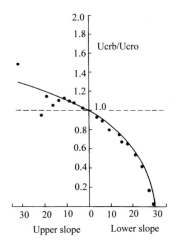

Fig. 6-9   Influences of slope on the initiation of particle movement

Solid line, obtained from Allen and Dyer's theoretical model. Circular points, obtained from Hardisty and Whitehouse's experimental results

3) Moisture

It has long been known that moisture has an important influence on the initiation of particle movement. Recent studies show that there is a function relation between the threshold shear velocity and moisture content; however, different scholars give quite different data (Fig. 6-10). Mckenna Neumann and Nickling believe that the function relation is caused by the sensitivity of different sizes of particles to the moisture content. But Belly and Kawamura found from experimental results that when the moisture content is below 8% the threshold shear velocity changes greatly. Sarre (1988) found that once sand is set in motion, even a moisture content over 14% has little influence on the transport of sand particles. In this aspect, further research is needed (Sarre, 1988).

6.1.2.2   Sand movement modes

Once entrained by wind, particles move in four ways: suspension, creep, saltation and reptation a transitional state between creep and saltation) (Fig. 6-11), but it is very difficult to define each of them clearly (Livingstone and Warren, 1996).

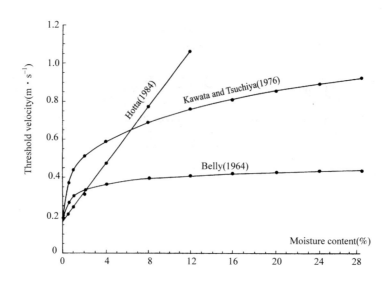

Fig. 6-10　Relation between threshold shear velocity and moisture content

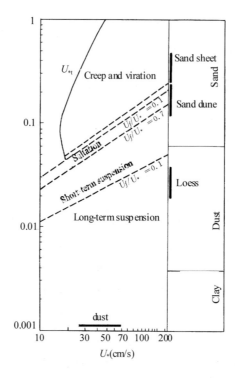

Fig. 6-11　Relation between particle size, shear velocity and movement ways

1) Suspension

Suspension refers to the turbulent particle flow in the air. Particles smaller than 0.06 mm can be carried in suspension for several days or more, such as dust and loess particles. A simple measure to distinguish suspension from the other transport ways is the ratio (U_*) of the settling velocity of a particle in air (U_f) to the shear velocity (U_*) (Fig. 6-11). The settling velocity of a particle is a function of the particle gravity and airflow resistance. If $U_f < U_*$, it may be thought that particles are moving as suspension. Under well developed turbulent conditions, some particles of a certain grain size can be transformed from a saltation state into a suspension state. The suspension distance of particles is related to their particle size; generally particles larger than 50 μm can be transported tens of kilometers and then deposit as wind speed reduces. Loess particles ranging in size from 20–30 μm can be transported about 300 km or more and particles smaller than 15 μm can be transported over even longer distances and remain in suspension for a long time.

2) Creep

Creep is generally caused by two processes. First, coarse particles are set in motion by the impact of saltating particles. Second, such particles are rolled into pits formed by saltating particles. For the creep process there is a function relation between shear velocity and particle size, and the creep velocity is slowest among the four movement ways. Researches show that when the shear velocity is 0.48 m/s, the particles with a diameter of 355–600 μm move at a velocity of about 0.005 m/s. At the initial stage they are creeping in the form of aggregates and then disintegrate due to differences in moving velocity. Finally some particles are deposited and microgeomorphologic features such as sand ripples are formed.

3) Saltation

Saltation is the most important way of sand movement. When sand particles are set in motion by pressure from a turbulent airflow they are initially rolled along the ground, but within a few meters, this gives place to bounding movement termed saltation. Saltating particles are taken up a short distance into the airflow and then return to the surface at an incident angle of 30°–50°; some particles may be moved in a reverse direction (Fig. 6-12). The bound velocity is about 50%–60% of the impact velocity. Researches also show that the saltating velocity appears as a Gaussian distribution and it may reach a large velocity when the ground surface has a certain slope.

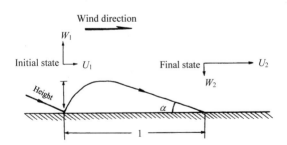

Fig. 6-12   Basic form of saltation (Livingstone and Warren, modified in 1996)

The saltation height of particles is closely related to particle size. Field observations and wind tunnel experiments show that there is a functional relation between mean particle size at different heights and their sorting. The experiments by Anderson and Bunas demonstrate that fine particles have a larger bounding velocity than coarse particles and such differences become more obvious with increasing wind velocity. The saltation length is 12–15 times the bounding height. However, there is still debate as to the relation between particle size and saltation length. For particles moving at high speed, their saltation length is directly related to the shear velocity and their falling is determined by the gravity and the drag of air.

In the saltation processes the movement of particles larger than 100 μm essentially cannot be affected by turbulent disturbance, their flying path cannot be affected by other saltating particles, and other forces such as Magnus force have little effect. Particles generally settle back to the surface at an angle of 10°–20°, and observational data show that it decreases with decreasing particle size and shear velocity. The impact velocity to the surface during falling process is lower than 4 m/s.

Saltation has a significant influence on near-surface wind speed profile. Experimental data show that when saltation takes place, wind speed profile has a turning point at a certain height; this height is larger than the roughness height under neutral conditions and is termed as "Bagnold kink". It changes with wind speed variations. Such variations can be viewed as a feedback mechanism between wind speed profile and saltation. Recent studies show that the wind speed profile in the saltating layer has a certain bend.

4) Reptation

Reptation is a kind of sand movement way discovered in recent years (Fig. 6-13). Anderson and Haff (1988) defined it as "particle movement caused by the dislodging of falling high-energy particles or low-angle saltation" (Anderson, et al., 1988). When one saltating particle impacts the ground surface, about 10 particles begin to reptate. Unlike creep, reptating particles are in an interchange state between vibration and saltation and their rate has an exponential distribution form. In addition, at any interval the particles are in a vibration state and there is a function relation between particle number, particle impact velocity and shear velocity.

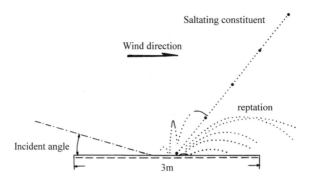

Fig. 6-13 Basic modes of vibration (Livingstone and Warren, modified in 1966)

6.1.2.3 Structure of sand flow

The height distribution of particles in the transport layer is called the vertical structure of sand flow. The research in this respect includes the flux of solid content and energy structure at different heights, as well as maximum distribution height and distribution form (Wu, 1987).

Field observations and wind tunnel experiments demonstrate that solid fraction decreases exponentially with height. From wind tunnel experiments (Butterfield, 1991), it is found that 79% of sand is transported at a height below 0.018 m. From the observations in 1940s, Bagnold found that saltating particles can reach a height of 2 m over gobi desert surface but only 9 cm over loose sand surface. Chepil found that 90% of wind-eroded material is transported within a height of 31 cm. Recent observations show that the maximum distribution height of saltating particles is 6–19 m and they are mostly transported within a height of 20 cm above the surface. Therefore, it may be said that wind-blown sand movement is a near-surface process.

The height distribution of particles in air flow has been studied in the 1950s, and Zingg (1953) suggested the distribution form as follows:

$$Q_z = \left(\frac{b}{z+a} \right)^{1/n} \tag{6-7}$$

When Q_z is the sand transport rate at the height of z, b is a function of particle size and shear velocity, n is an exponent and a is a reference height. Through statistical and theoretical analyses several scholars suggested that particle flux decreases with height, but recent studies, for example Butterfield's study(1999) showed that the height distribution of particles is discontinuous and its distribution is not a simple exponential function.

Former Soviet Union's scholar Znamenski put forward the characteristic index of sand flow structure in the 1950s–1960s, and through the analysis of particle distribution in 0–10 cm layer derived the index:

$$\lambda = \frac{Q_{2-10}}{Q_{0-1}} \tag{6-8}$$

Where Q_{2-10} is sand transport rate at the height of 2–10 cm, Q_{0-1} is sand transport rate at the height of 0–1 cm. They can be used to judge the relation between wind erosion, transport and deposition of particles. However, this concept is not widely accepted.

The vertical distribution of energy in the layer of sand flow is not an exponential relation (Fig. 6-14). When the shear velocity is 1.0 m/s and particle size is 250 μm, the maximum distribution height of energy is 0.8 m, and this height changes with the variation of ground surface. Researches show that there is a correlation between the energy and U_*^5 (McEvan et al., 1991).

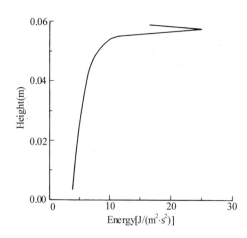

Fig. 6-14　The height distribution of energy in the layer of wind-sand flow

6.1.3　Determination and calculation of sand transport rate

At present, there are two equations obtained from the fitting of theoretical values and observed data that can be used in the calculation and determination of sand transport rate (wind erosion rate). In the past 100 years scholars have put forward tens of equations obtained from the fitting of theoretical, semi-theoretical and observed values; these can be found in more than 50 literatures, but about 10 equations are widely adopted at present. Table 6-1 presents several representative equations used for the calculation of sand transport rate.

Table 6-1　Several representative equations of sand transport

Bagnold (1941)	$q=C(d/D)^{1/2}V_*\rho/g$
Kawamura (1951)	$q=K(\rho/g)(V_*+V_{*t})(V_*-V_{*t})^2$
Hsu (1971)	$q=k_h\times10^{-5}[10V_*/(gd/10)^{1/2}]^{1/3}$, $k_h=-0.47+4.97d$
Lettau & Latteau (1978)	$q=C(d/D)^{1/2}(V_*-V_{*t})V_*^2\rho/g$
Borowka (1980), Wu Zheng (1987)	$q=A\times BV^C$

Note: A, B, C are regression coefficient; d is grain size; V_*, V_{*t} are friction velocity and threshold friction velocity m/s; V is wind velocity m/s, ρ is air density; g is gravity acceleration.

Bagnold (1937) studied and established the sand movement equation in the mid-1930s based on the theory of momentum transfer between airflow and particles (Table 6-1). According to the same assumption, Kawamura (1951) developed a sand transport equation. Through analysis of the impact processes of particles and bed and the momentum exchange between airflow and particles, Owen (1964) and Sorensen (1990) established a sand transport equation. Others, such as Anderson (1988), McEwan and Willetts (1994) also have done much work in this respect. However, the sand transport rates calculated by different equations differ greatly (Fig. 6-15).

At present, many scholars suggest determining the sand transport rate through field observations.

This is because environmental factors such as surface material composition, vegetation and moisture regime in different regions are quite different; therefore the theoretical values of sand transport rate are quite different from the determined values.

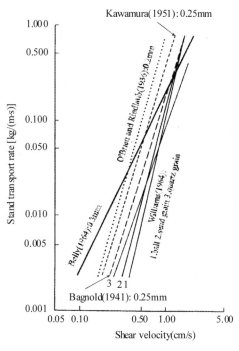

Fig. 6-15   Relation between sand transport rate and shear velocity

In field determination of sand transport rate, both environment conditions and measurement tool, for example the efficiency of a sand trap can significantly affect the accuracy of the determination. Since the 1930s, several types of sand traps have been developed. In recent years some newly developed sand traps have been adopted, for example, the sand traps developed by Nickling and Neuman (1988). However, there are still some problems in the field operation and the sand-collecting efficiency. Under natural conditions, wind direction is variable. Hence the determined data using uni-directional sand traps often cannot represent the actual sand transport rates. In addition, the wind fluctuation and turbulence are also major influential factors. From field observations Mckenna Neuman et al. found that there was a correlation between sand transport rate and mean wind speed at the height of 0.3 m (r^2=0.91). However, this conclusion still awaits further confirmation in other regions.

It is generally accepted that moisture in surface materials can affect the sand transport rate by increasing threshold shear velocity (Fig. 6-16), but their essential relation has not been solved. In addition to moisture content, vegetation, mechanical composition and grain shapes also affect the sand transport rate. Several scholars suggested that when the vegetation cover is larger than 14%, no sand flow occurs (Wiggs et al., 1995), but others found that when the vegetation cover is 45%, sand movement can not take place (Wasson, et al., 1986).

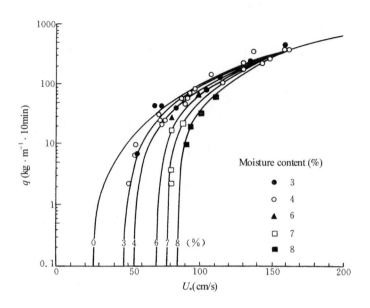

Fig. 6-16   Relation between sand transport rate and moisture content (Livingstone and Warren, 1996)

6.2   The role of sand movement in the formation of aeolian landforms

When winds blow over loose, dry and exposed sand surfaces, wind erosion and deposition may take place and thereby form different aeolian landforms. Generally, the wind-molding of sand surface includes two processes; one is wind erosion processes in which sands are blown away, and the other is wind deposition processes in which sands are deposited when wind ceases.

The complex relation among these processes can be explained by the equilibrium relation between kinetic energy of sand flow and the carried mass. The kinetic energy is manifested as the velocity of sand flow. Sand flow of a certain velocity maintains a dynamic equilibrium with the energy carried by sand material. When sand flow is accelerated, it is in an unsaturated state, which will cause wind erosion to re-establish equilibrium; when windspeed reduces, sandflow is in a supersaturation state, which will cause sand deposition. When the topography, vegetation or roughness changes, turbulence occurs in the near-surface air, which will cause wind erosion and deposition.

6.2.1   Wind erosion processes

In the recent researches on the sand movement and the formation of aeolian landforms, wind-deposited landforms hold an important place, while the study of wind-eroded landform is relatively rare. Generally, wind erosion can be divided into three processes (Fig. 6-17): deflation, namely winds blow sand particles away; abrasion, namely sand grains carried by wind impact the highly cemented ground surface and rock surface; and attrition, namely the collision between moving sand grains, which has a relatively small action in the formation of aeolian landforms as compared to the former two. Deflation and abrasion can create large wind erosion landforms such as Yardangs, ventifacts, wind scoured depressions and gobi desert etc. (Livingstone and Warren, 1996).

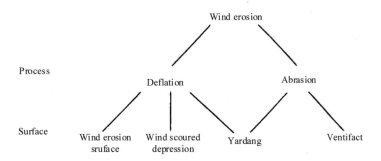

Fig. 6-17   Wind erosion processes and basic wind-eroded landform types

6.2.1.1   Main factors controlling wind erosion landforms

There are two factors controlling wind erosion landforms, namely erosivity and erodibility. Many scholars suggest that erosivity is a function of wind energy and time, while erodibility is the erodible degree of land surface or bodies and it is related to a number of factors. Researches show that particles of about 100 μm in diameter are most susceptible to wind erosion; high vegetation cover can increase roughness and reduce wind speed and therefore reduce ground surface erodibility. In addition, rough surface, undulated terrain, soil water content and soil crust can also affect the erodibility.

6.2.1.2   Wind erosion processes

1) Deflation

Deflation is the transport processes of loose particles by wind. Several scholars (Gillette, et al., 1982) divided the surface erodibility of desert and ranked them from strong to weak in the following order: loose soil→dune sand→deluvial and dry deposits→loose salty soil→playa beach→playa center→desert gravel.

Deflation processes generally cannot last long when most erodible particles have been blown away, as the microtopographic condition, mechanical composition and moisture regime will change, and the conditions will become unfavourable to deflation. The most significant landforms formed by deflation are wind-scoured depression, coarse sand land and gobi desert etc. Deflation is also the agent that shapes Yardangs.

2) Abrasion

It refers to the processes of wearing away of rocks or other particles by sand materials carried by wind. Abrasion on the surface of huge rocks may form niches; if the objects of abrasion are clasolites, ventifacts may be formed; when abrasion occurs in a vast region, Yardangs may be formed. However, there are still debates as to the relations between abrasion processes and the formation of ventifact and yardangs; for example, some scholars believe that abrasion does not play a leading role in the formation processes of yardangs.

6.2.2 Wind deposition

Under certain conditions, sand materials carried by wind are deposited to form aeolian landforms. The effects of blown sand activity on the wind-deposited landforms have been widely studied and it is an important subject in aeolian research at present. Wind deposition processes are closely related to wind erosion processes in the study of aeolian sand geomorphology. The most important landforms formed in the wind deposition processes are sand dunes.

Main factors affecting the formation of wind deposition landforms

Many factors affect the formation of wind deposition landforms, including wind environment, moisture, vegetation, grain-size composition and terrains etc. Many factors can cause sand deposition, such as the reduction of wind velocity, vegetation and topographic obstruction etc.

1) Wind environment

Wind environment includes the regional wind environment and the processes of wind acting on individual sand dunes. The regional wind environment controls the regional dune shapes and their development scale, while the action of airflow on individual dunes mainly refers to the mutual feedback of airflow and dune shapes.

Fryberger (1979), Wasson and Hyde (1983) systematically studied the effects of the regional wind environment on sand dune types. It is generally accepted that uni-directional wind mainly forms transverse dunes, bi-directional winds form linear dunes, and multidirectional winds form star dunes. Fryberger (1979) modified the sand transport equation derived by Lettau (1978) and put forward the wind environment index (Fryberger, 1979):

$$DP=V^2(V-V_t)t \tag{6-9}$$

Where DP is the drift potential, V is wind velocity larger than the sand entrainment threshold velocity V_t, and t is the duration of sand-moving wind.

According to equation (6-9) we can calculate the DP values of 16 directions or more, and then from the vector statistics of these DP values obtain the resultant drift potential (RDP). Some scholars use RDP/DP to judge the regional dune types (Fig. 6-18) and suggest that RDP/DP value and dune types have the following relation (Table 6-2) (Wasson et al., 1983).

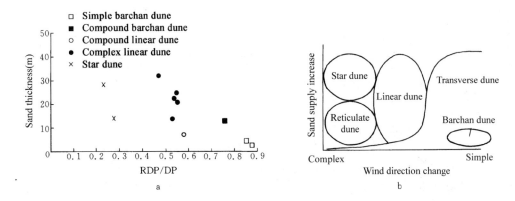

Fig. 6-18   Relation between resultant drift potential and dune forms

Table 6-2   Relation between RDP/DP and dune forms

Dune form	Barchan dune	Linear dune	Star dune
RDP/DP	>0.5, mean 0.68	0.45	<0.35, mean 0.19

2) Interaction between airflow and individual dunes

A large amount of information on the interaction between airflow and individual dunes is available and mostly covers all the dune types. The study methods include field observation, theoretical derivation and numerical simulation etc.

(1) Transverse dunes.

Field observation of transverse dunes was initiated in the 1930s, By the 1980s, they have been intensively studied, including wind velocity profile over dune surfaces, sand flux, and dune shape variations in relation to the maintenance of equilibrium. In the early 1980s the wind velocity profile over the windward slope of transverse dunes was assumed to be a straight line on the semi-logarithmic paper, but it has been proven to be a zigzag line through the field observations in the late 1990s. Wiggs et al. put forward the airflow pattern over the windward slope of transverse dunes (Wiggs et al., 1996) and the development process (Fig. 6-19). Stam (1997) analyzed the origin and the development processes of transverse dunes based on numerical model. Afterwards, Van Dijk (1999) simulated the sand flux and wind velocity profile over the transverse dune surface. Wipperman and Gross (1986), through wind tunnel experiments and numerical simulations, studied the transverse dunes(Fig.6-20).

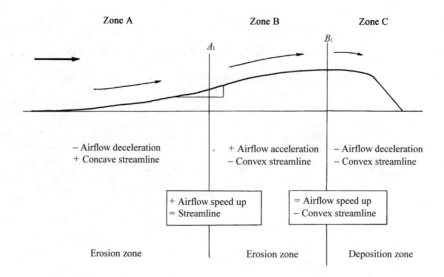

Fig. 6-19　Airflow patterns over the windward slope of transverse dunes

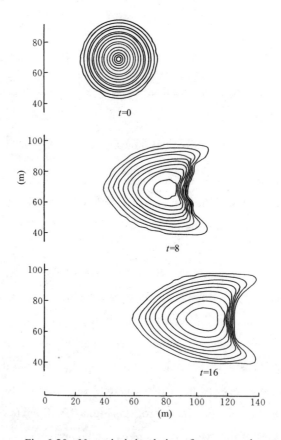

Fig. 6-20　Numerical simulation of transverse dunes

(2) Linear dunes.

As early as the mid-18th century, travelers had put forward a hypothesis for the origin of linear dunes. Some scholars thought that linear dunes resulted from the continuous erosion of interdune flat and they are unrelated to the deposition of sand materials. But this theory was refuted by Bagnold (1941). Afterwards, Hanna (1969) modified Bagnold's theory and put forward an improved theoretical system (Fig. 6-21). Through field observations of the dynamical variations of linear dunes, airflow pattern and structure over dune surface and analysis, Tsoar denied the dual helical flow theory. At present, many scholars believe that linear dunes are formed by bi-directional winds or wide uni-directional winds and Tsoar (1982) put forward an improved development pattern (Fig. 6-22). Some scholars suggested that linear dunes are evolved from simple barchan dunes and this has been demonstrated by the deposition structure of linear dunes.

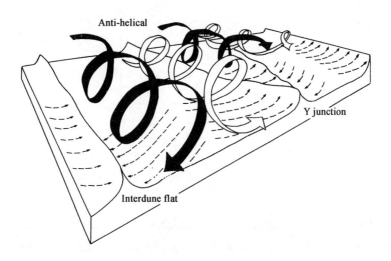

Fig. 6-21　Development pattern of dual helical flow of linear dunes

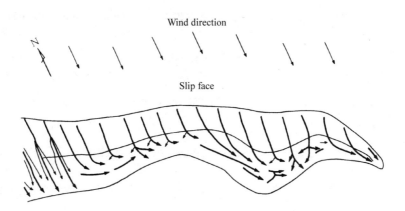

Fig. 6-22　Bi-directional wind theory of linear dune development

(3) Star dunes.

The formation of star dunes is associated with complex and variable winds. Owing to their large-scale and complex dynamical processes, star dunes are the least studied dune type. Some scholars believe that the formation of the main arms of star dunes is similar to that of transverse dunes (Fig. 6-23). As the dunes develop to a certain size, they maintain an equilibrium state due to the feedback effect between the dunes and airflow. Recent literature reports that star dunes are formed under three-set wind directional conditions and they can also be formed under two-set wind directional conditions.

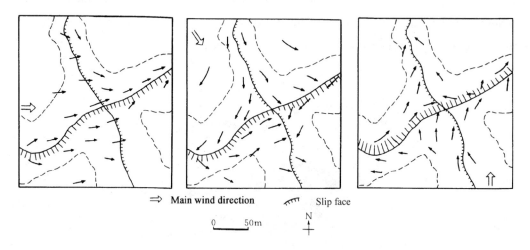

Fig. 6-23   Airflow pattern over star dune surfaces

In addition, the airflow patterns over reticulate dunes, parabolic dunes and other dune types including dunes in coastal regions also have their own features. Little information is available on these dunes and further research is needed.

6.3   Main dynamic types and characteristics of aeolian landforms

According to the formation mechanism, aeolian landforms can be divided into two major types, wind erosion landforms and wind deposition landforms and they can be further divided into several subtypes. In this section they are divided according to the morphological genetic principle.

6.3.1   Dynamic types and main characteristics of wind erosion landforms

Wind erosion landform types mainly include wind-scoured depressions, Yardangs, ventifacts and stone pavement etc.

6.3.1.1 Yardang

The shapes of Yardangs include deflation mushroom, deflation column and deflation residual hill etc. "Yardang" is a Turkish word first introduced by Sven Hedin in the early 20th century. Yardang landforms have been found in almost all arid zones. Their sizes vary from a few centimeters to several kilometers. At present, there are considerable debates about their formation mechanism. Halimov and Fezer (1989) systematically studied the yardang landforms in the Qaidam Basin in China and put forward eight types of Yardang (Table 6-3). The ratio between their length, width and height is $10 : 2 : 1$, while the ratio of their width to length in California is $1 : 4$. Researches by Goudie et al. (1999) in Egypt show that the ratio between their volume, length, width and length is $18.7 : 9.9 : 2.7 : 1$. This shows that there is a certain relation between morphological changes and the related parameters.

Table 6-3　Different types of Yardang in the Qaidam Basin

Type	Dipangle (°)	Height (m)	Width (m)	Length (m)	Spacing (m)
Flat-topped	0–10	10–15	100–2	100–2	Change
Zigzag	5–15	3–1	5–10	30–10	
Core	45	20	30		2
Pyramid		4–15	6–15	30	10–50
Long sand-ridge		>30	>50	100–5,000	200–350
Pig-back		10–30	15–6	100–35	
Whale-back		3	5	15	100
Low linear whale back		3–0.5	5–1	30–5	100–500

Reports on Yardang morphological parameters and their erosion rate in literatures are scarce. At present their erosion rate is mainly inferred from the Quaternary deposition rate, furthermore, their geomorphologic features are very difficult to describe compared to other landform types.

6.3.1.2 Wind-scoured depression

Wind-scoured depressions refer to saucer-like depressions formed in the arid zone consisting of loose surface materials. Satellite images show that such aeolian landforms are widespread in various regions of the world.

Wind-scoured depressions are generally formed on an erodible ground surface; in South Africa they mainly occur on the sand beds and in Australia they mainly occur on dry river beds or lake beds. In some cases, they co-existent along with Yardangs. Wind scoured depressions range in size from a few square meters to several hundred square kilometers and in depth from tens of centimeter to tens of meters. Another feature is that there are barchan dunes or small sand ridges at the downwind edges of Yardangs and they mainly consist of clay materials (Fig. 6-24). Such dunes and sand ridges may be a few thousand meter in length and 60 m in height.

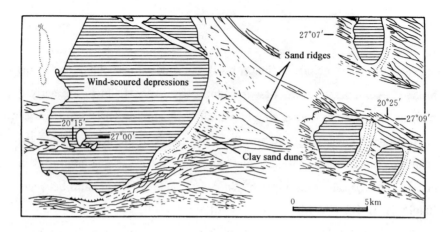

Fig. 6-24   Distribution relation between wind-scoured depressions, barchan and other dune types (Kalahari region)

6.3.1.3   Ventifacts

Ventifacts are formed by sand blast and dust abrasion of pebbles and they range in diameter from a few centimeter to several meters. A striking feature of ventifacts is their polished surface with pit sand scratches. Generally a ventifact has 2- 3 polished surfaces, in some cases it has more than 20 polished faces. Ventifacts generally form in the areas where wind can transport larger particles, for example in polar regions. Wind tunnel experiments by Miotke (1982) show that tens to several hundred years are required to form ventifacts, and their abrasion rate varies between 0.001–20 mm/a (Miotke, 1982).

6.3.1.4   Stone pavement

Stone pavement refers to stone mantle, or gobi desert in central Asia, which is covered on the surface by sandy and clay lands and formed through deflation. There is still debate as to the formation of stone pavement. Some scholars believe that they are formed by wind erosion but Cooke's study shows that deflation is only one of many factors, and their formation is also related to other factors such as freezing-thawing action, crystallization and running water action.

6.3.2   Main dynamic types and characteristics of wind deposition landforms

6.3.2.1   Wind deposition landform types

Wind deposition landform mainly refers to dunes; they are formed by the interaction of sand materials and wind. Sand dunes have a number of classification systems but they mainly can be divided into two systems: a. they are divided according to the relation between dune shape and wind environment or sand supply; b. they are divided according to genetic principle.

As early as the 1920s, sand dunes have been classified according to their shapes and wind environment or sand supply. Afterwards, some scholars divided them into three major types, longitudinal, oblique and transverse dunes according to the relation between dune strike and main wind direction (Fig. 6-25). Several scholars tried to divide the sand dunes into erosion type and deposition type but they were criticized (Lancaster, 1995).

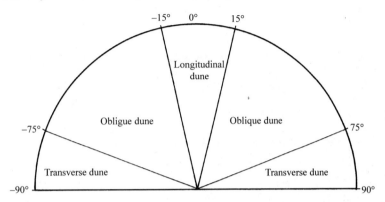

Fig. 6-25   Dune types divided according to the relation between dune strike and main wind direction

According to morphological and genetic classification, sand dunes are divided into five major types, e.g.barchan, linear, reversing, star and parabolic dunes in terms of their shape and number of slip faces. In addition, they are divided into simple compound and complex dunes. Compound dunes are those in which two or more of the same type coalesce or combine by overlapping each other. Complex dunes are those that result from the combination of two different types of shapes, for example, small barchan dunes are superimposed on large linear dunes or star dunes. According to the statistical data by Fryberger and Goundie (1981), about 46.6% of modern sand sea is covered by compound or complex dunes.

In addition, there are also other shapes in the sand sea, such as sand sheet, narrow and long dune without slip face known as zibar, phytogenetic dune or coppice dune (nebkha) and obstacle-anchored dunes such as echo dunes, climbing dunes and falling dunes etc. (Fig. 6-26).

6.3.2.2   Morphological characteristics of several typical dunes

1) Barchan dunes

(1) Simple barchan dunes. Simple barchan dunes mainly occur in deserts with uni-directional wind and meager sand supply and they occupy a very small area in the global sand sea. They exhibit a cresentic shape on the plane and their two wings extend downwind with a slip face. Their windward slopes range from 2°–15° and slip faces are 30°–35°. Most of simple barchan dunes have a height of 1–10 m, the ratio between their height and width is 1 : 10, and two wings are symmetric. In some cases, simple barchan dunes can be transformed into linear dunes (Lancaster, 1982 a, b).

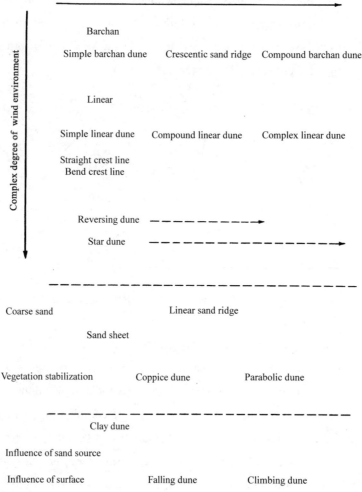

Fig. 6-26   Dune types divided in terms of morphology

(2) Crescentic sand ridges. Crescentic sand ridges occupy about 40% of the total area of the world sand sea; they are widely distributed in various sand sea and also known as transverse dunes. Their heights range from 3–10 m and spacings vary between 100–400m, the slope from the base of windward slope to the mid-upslope varies from 2°–3° to 10°–12°. Their crest line is bended. Some scholars called their projective part tongue or crescentic sand ridge. In some areas there is a good correlation between the height of crescentic sand ridges and their width (Fig. 6-27). Complex crescentic sand ridges are 20–80 m in height and a few hundred meters to tens of kilometers in length, with simple barchan dunes superimposed on their windward slopes (Table 6-4).

2) Linear dunes

Linear dunes occupy about 50% of the global sand sea area, but their areas are different in different regions, for example, in the Kalahari Sand Sea it occupies 85%–90% of its total area and in the Gran Desieto it accounts for 1%–2%. Simple linear dunes have two forms: the first one has flat and

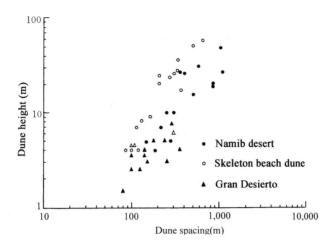

Fig. 6-27　Relation between height and width of simple barchan dunes

Table 6-4　Morphological parameters of compound barchan dunes in different regions

region	Spacing (m)	Width (m)	Height (m)
Gran Desierto	1,380	600	20–100
	500–2,300	300–1,500	
Algodones	1,070	880	50–80
	400–2,500	500–2,500	
Nafud	1,840	800	
	800–3,300	500–2,000	
Rub'al khali	1,430	670	
	850–2,200	300–1,100	
Thar Desert	1,440	1,300	
	700–2,500	750–2,000	
Taklimakan	3,000	2,200	
	2,000–2,500	1,100–3,400	
Aoukar	1,710	1,590	
	1,000–2,500	1,200–2,100	
NW Sahara	650	1,240	
	200–1,500	500–2,000	
Namib	694	680	18.6
	800–1,200	300–1,200	10–40

Source: Lancaster, 1995.

straight crest line and the surface is covered by vegetation, as can be seen in the Kalahari Desert; the second one has bend crest line and sharp crest, they mainly occur in the Arabian peninsula and are also known as "Seif "; compound linear dunes consist of 2–4 ridges with bend crest line; complex linear dunes have one main crest line, their tops show a star-like shape, with barchan dunes occurred on both sides. The simple morphological parameters of the three types of linear dunes are presented in Table 6-5.

(1) Simple linear dunes. Simple linear dunes are straight and partly covered by vegetation, as in the southwest Kalahari Desert. But in other regions their crest lines are bends. Such dunes are generally

Table 6-5　Several morphological parameters of linear dunes (Lancaster, 1995)

region	Spacing (m)	Width (m)	Height (m)
Simple type			
Simpson	648	290	11.4
	114–431		6.5–21.0
Great Sand Desert	1,134		9.09
	370–2,346		4.1–15.4
SW Kalahari	435	220	9.0
	431–1,148		2–20
Compound type			
Namib	1,724	650	34.5
	990–2,082		24–48
SW Sahara	1,930	940	
Complex type			
Namib	2,163	880	99.5
	1,500–2,700		44–167
Rub'al Khali	3,170	1,480	100–200
S Sahara	3,280	1,280	

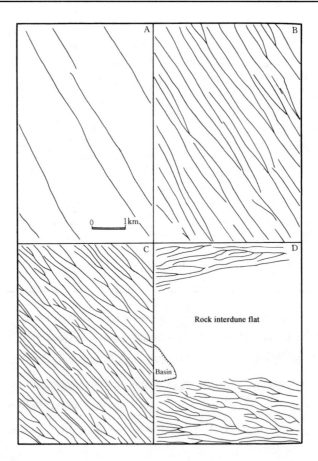

Fig. 6-28　Distribution patterns of simple linear dunes in SW Kalahari (Livingstone and Warren, 1996)

2–35 m in height, their spacing is 200–450 m, width 150–250 m, length 20–25 km and seldom exceeds 200 km. Bullard et al. (1995) analysed the shapes of four simple linear dunes in detail (Fig. 6-28). They have wide bases with a slope of 2°–4°and their side slopes are 5°–18°, and both sides are asymmetric. Some scholars found that there is a close correlation between the height and spacing of simple linear dunes.

The formation mechanism of linear dunes in western desert and eastern sandy land of China differs greatly. Linear dunes in the Onqin Daga Sandy Land and the Gaheelsu resulted from deflation and cutting through of the nose of parabolic dunes and vegetation play an important role in the formation of such dunes. Linear dunes in the Taklimakan Desert of west China are formed by downwind extension of one horn of a series of barchan dune arranged in longitudinal direction.

(2) Compound linear dunes. Compound linear dunes are common in the Namib Sand Sea. Generally, there are 3–5 main dunes running parallel with each other. Furthermore, their bend and sharp sand crests are 5–10 m high (Fig. 6-29). Such dunes are 500–800 m wide, 25–50 m high and 1,200–2,000 apart each other. Their crests consist of coarse sand, there are "Y" junctions and the interdune flats are often covered by sand.

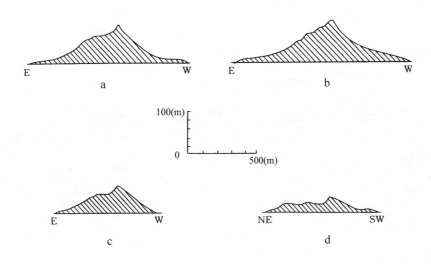

Fig. 6-29   Section forms of several types of linear dunes

a- c, complex type; d, compound type

(3) Complex linear dunes. Complex linear dunes are fairly common. Their height may reach 50–170 m, spacing 1,600–2,800m and mean spacing 2,000 m or so. There is a good correlation between their spacing and height (Fig. 6-30). Their crest lines generally are bend, leeward slope is 32° and there are 2–10 m high and 50–200 m wide secondary dunes superimposed on the main dunes.

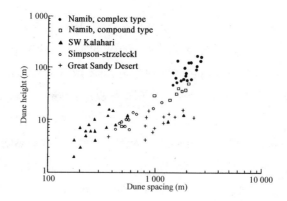

Fig. 6-30　Relation between height and spacing of complex linear dunes (Lancaster, 1995)

3) Star dunes

About 8.5% of the global sand sea is covered by star dunes. Star dunes are distinguished from other dune types by their pyramid shape and several slip faces. Their arms are not necessarily balanced. In many areas one of their arms has seasonal changes due to the changes in wind direction. There may be secondary barchan dunes or reversing dunes in the interdune flats. Their spacing ranges from 150–5,000 m, generally 1,000–2,400 m (Table 6-6). Star dunes are the largest dune type in the world, their mean height is 117 m, with maximum height of 500 m, and is different in different regions (Lancaster, 1982a, b).

Table 6-6　Morphological parameters of star dunes in the world (Lancaster, 1995)

region	Spacing (m)	Width (m)	Height (m)
Namib	1,330	1,000	145
	600–2,600	400–1,000	80–350
Niger	1,000	610	
	150–3,000	200–1,200	
Grand Erg oriental	2,070	950	117
	800–6,700	400–3,000	
SE Rub'al khali	2,060	840	
	970–2,860	500–1,300	50–150
Gran Desierto	2,982	2092	
	1,500–4,000	700–6,000	
Dunes in dusters	312	183	80
	160–488	90–363	10–150
Ala Shan	137	740	
	300–3,200	400–1,000	200–300

4) Parabolic dunes and coppice dunes

Parabolic dunes and coppice dunes are common in the coastal zones and semi desert regions but they also extensively occur in the Thar Desert. Parabolic dunes are distinguished from other dune types by their U-shaped paired arms. Their paired arms may reach 1–2 km long and 10–70 m high.

This kind of dune occurs where vegetation is locally destroyed and is formed by the downwind extension of blowouts. Their arms are fixed by vegetation and point toward upwind direction. With the retreat of their U-shaped nose and the extension of their paired wings, sand supply to the nose become less and less and finally the nose is cut through to form linear dunes. Coppice dunes generally have a height of less than 1 m but in some areas they may reach a height of 3.5 m or so. Owing to low sand flux they generally have a long development history.

6.3.2.3 Depositional features of several representative dunes

Depositional features of sand dunes include their depositional structure, particle-size composition, and color, shaped and mineral composition, but only the depositional structure and particle-size composition of sand dune are widely studied at present.

1) Depositional structure

Depositional structure of sand dunes is mainly formed by three dynamical mechanisms: a. sand ripple movement; b. saltation particle falling on slip face due to airflow separation; c. sand surface avalanche. Such processes mainly form three kinds of depositional structures: a. climbing bedding; b. particle falling bedding; c. particle cross bedding.

(1) Barchan dunes

Particle falling bedding and cross bedding are often found in the depositional structure of barchan dunes, they are formed on the avalanche slope as sand dunes move downwind. Climbing bedding is formed by wind pressure at dune crest, it is thin and roughly parallel to the windward slope of sand dunes (Fig. 6-31).

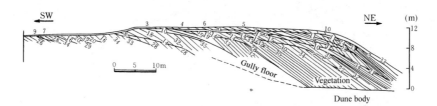

Fig. 6-31   Depositional structure of barchan dune

(number indicate the slope of depositional layers)

(2) Linear dunes

Bagnold (1941) put forward the depositional structural patterns of linear dunes (Fig. 6-32). McKee and Tibbitts (1964) studied the depositional structure of a simple linear dune 15 m in height and found that the cross beds at the upper part of the dune have a dip angle of 26°–34°, while the lower cross beds have a dip angle of 4°–14°. High-angle cross beds are mainly formed by sand avalanching in the bi-directional wind environment.

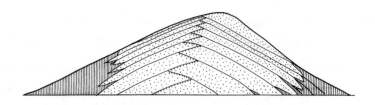

Fig. 6-32   Depositional structure of a linear dune (Bagnold, 1941)

Tsoar (1982) analyzed two sets of bedding of simple linear dunes (Fig. 6-33) and found that one set is formed by particle falling and particle-flow deposition, with a dip angle of 33°. The other set has a dip angle of 20°–25° and intersects the crest line at a certain angle. It is deposited on the slope formed by sand ripples as airflow changes. The avalanche of dune slopes and the deposition of sand ripples change with the prevailing wind direction.

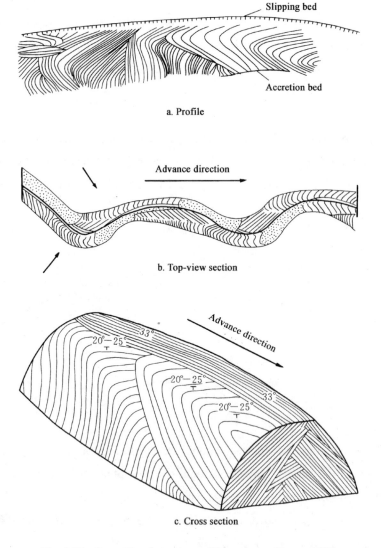

Fig. 6-33   Depositional structure of linear dunes (Tsoar, 1982)

The depositional structure of large complex linear dunes was also studied. Their slip face at dune crest is 27°–35° but the upper part of dune slope has a dip angle of 10°–20°. Bristow et al. put forward a general depositional structural pattern of linear dunes and thought that the development of depositional structure can be divided into five stages(Fig. 6-34): initial deposition of sand ripples→slip face formation, dune advance in resultant sand transport direction, similar to the formation of cross bedding in transverse dune→lateral movement of bend crest line and produce bi-directional dip angle→airflow separation on both sides of dune, secondary dunes start to develop→cross bedding formed by secondary dune becomes the main depositional structure of complex linear dune. However, such depositional structure obtained from linear dunes in the Namib Desert by using ground radar has not be demonstrated in other deserts (Tsoar, 1982).

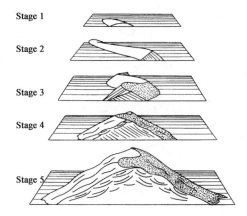

Fig. 6-34　Evolution stages of linear dune (Bristow et al., 2000)

(3) Star dunes

Depositional structure of star dunes is complicated (Fig. 6-35). Observations by Mckee (1966, 1982) show that the upper part of star dunes mainly consists of high-angle cross beds; they are formed by avalanching deposition under multidirection wind condition and have seasonal change. The base of star dunes consists of low-angle laminae.

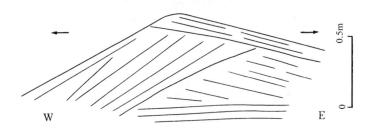

Fig. 6-35　Depositional structure of star dune

2) Grain-size features

Grain-size features mainly refer to grain-size composition of dune sand and their sorting. Most of dune sand consist of fine sand to very fine sand; mean grain size is 1.60–2.65 (160–330 μm). They are moderately sorted to very well sorted (0.26–0.55 μm). However, different dune types in different regions may have a certain difference in grain-size composition, as shown in Table 6-7.

Table 6-7   Mean grain size and standard deviation of dune sand in different sand seas

Region	Mean grain size (φ)	Standard deviation (φ)
Barchan dune		
Gran Desierto	2.43	0.41
Algodones dunes	2.46	0.42
White Sands	1.61	0.59
Skeleton Coast	2.02	0.51
Namib Sand Sea	2.20	0.55
Salton Sea	2.27	0.46
Tunisia	3.25	0.53
Kelso Dunes	1.80	0.49
Linear dune		
SW Kalahari	2.16	0.49
Simpson Desert	2.53	0.43
Namib Sand Sea	2.44	0.37
Saudi Arabia	2.67	0.32
Mauritania	2.20	0.60
Star dune		
Gran Desierto	2.43	0.41
Namib Sand Sea	2.29	0.29
Great Sand Sea	2.09	0.26
Kelso	2.26	0.30

(1) Barchan dunes. The variation of grain-size composition of barchan dunes are generally regular. Mean grain size decrease from the base of windward slope to dune crest, with finest particles occurred on the avalanche slope. The sorting of dune sand also shows a similar trend. Some scholars found that the sorting of dune crest is poorest and the skewness is dominated by negative skewness.

(2) Linear dunes. Grain-size composition of linear dunes has long been studied (Fig. 6-36) (Pye et al., 1990). Bagnold (1941) suggested that the sand materials at the crest line are finest and this has been demonstrated by the results from other deserts. But some scholars pointed out that the grain-size composition at crest line of simple linear dune is coarsest, for example, in the Simpson Desert.

(3) Star dunes. There is noticeable spatial change in grain-size composition of star dunes (Fig. 6-37) (Lancaster, 1989a). The sorting at dune crest is best. Star dunes in the Namib Desert consist of fine sand or very fine sand but in the Taklimakan Desert the grain-size composition of star dunes is coarsest as compared to other dune types. This shows that the dune sand composition is related to the underlying sand source.

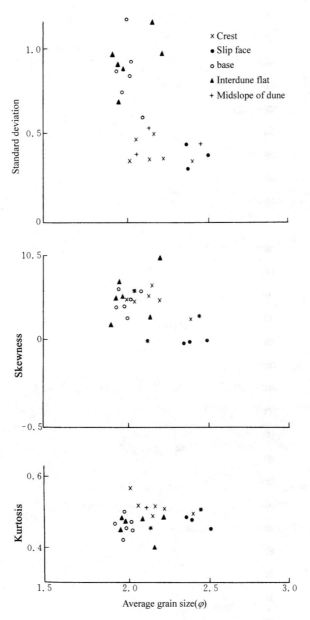

Fig. 6-36   Binary correlation between grain-size parameters of star dunes

(4) Comparison of grain-size composition of different types of dunes. Research results show that the grain-size composition of different types of dunes in different regions is different (Table 6-8), but there seems to be no definite relation between dune type and grain-size composition. In

the same desert, for example in the Namib Desert, the mean grain size from sand sheets→barchan dunes→linear dunes→star dunes tends to become fine (Lancaster, 1989b), but no such trend was found in other deserts.

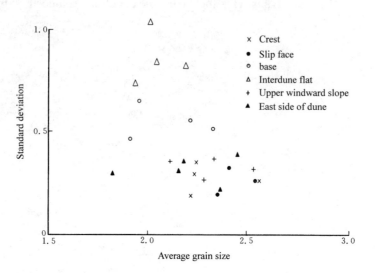

Fig. 6-37   Binary correlation between grain-size parameters of star dunes

References

Allen J R L. 1982. Sedimentary Structures. Amsterdam: Elsevier

Anderson R S, Haff P K. 1988. Simulation of eolian saltation. Science, 241: 820—823

Bagnold R A. 1941. The Physics of Blown Sand and Desert Dunes. Methuen. London Butteriield G R. 1991. Grain transport rates in steady and unsteady turbulent airflows. Acta Mechanica Supplement, 1: 97—122

Bristow C S, Bailey S D Lancaster N. 2000. The sedimentary structure of linear sand dunes. Nature, 406: 56—59

Bullard J E, Thomas D S G, Livingstone, Wiggs G F S. 1995. Analysis of linear sand dune morphological variability southwestern Kalahari Desert. Geomorphology, 11: 189—203

Dyer K. 1986. Coastal and Estuarine Sediment Dynamics. Chichester: Wiley

Frank A and Kocurek G. 1996. Airflow up the stoss slope of sand dunes: limitations of current understanding. Geomorphology, 17: 47—54

Fryberger S G. 1979. Dunes Forms and Wind Regimes, in McKee, 305—397

Fryberger S G, Goudie A S. 1981. Arid geomorphology. Progress in Physical Geography, 5: 420—428

Gillette D A, Adams J, Muhs D and Kihl R. 1982. Threshold friction velocities and rupture moduli for crusted desert soils for input of soil particles to the air, Journal of Geophysical Research, 87C, 9003—9005

Goudie A. 1969. Statistical laws and dune ridges in South Africa. Geographical Journal, 135: 404—406

Goundie A, Watson A. 1981. The shape of desert sand dune grains. Journal of Arid Environments, 4: 185—190

Greeley R, Iversen J D. 1985. Wind as a Geological Processes on Earth, Mars, Venus and Titan. Cambridge:

Cambridge University Press

Halimov M, Fezer F. 1989. Eight Yardang types in central Asia. Zeitschrift fur Geomorphology NF, 33: 205-217

Hanna S R. 1969. The formation of longitudinal sand dunes by large helical eddies in the atmosphere. Journal of Applied Meteorology, 8: 874-883

Iversen J D, Rasmussen k R. 1999. The effect of wind speed and bed slope on sand transport. Sedimentology, 46: 723-731

Lancaster N. 1982a. Dunes of the Gran Desierto sand sea, Sonora, Mexico. Earth Surface Processes and Landforms, 12: 277-288

Lancaster N. 1982b. Dunes on the Skeleton Coast, Namibia South West Africa): Geomorphology and grain-size relationships. Earth Surface Processes and Landforms, 7: 575-587

Lancaster N. 1989a. The dynamics of star dunes: an example from the Gran Desierto, Mexico. Sedimentology, 36: 273-289

Lancaster N. 1989b. The Namib Sand Sea: Dune forms, processes, and sediments, Balkema A A, Rotterdam

Lancaster N. 1995. Geomorphology of Desert Dunes. Routledge

Livingstone I, Warren A. 1996. Aeolian Geomorphology. Singapore: Addison Wesley Longman Limited

McEwan I K, Willetts B B. 1991. Numerical model of the saltation cloud. Acta Mechanica Supplement, 1: 53-66

McKee E D, Tibbitts G C. 1964. Primary structures of a seif dune and associated deposits in Libya. Journal of Sedimentary Petrology, 34: 5-17

Mckee E D. 1966. Structures of dunes at White Sands National Monument, New Mexico. Sedimentology, 7: 3-6

Mckee E D. 1982. Sedimentary structure in dunes of the Namib Desert, South West Africa. Special Paper of Geological Society of America, 188

Miotke F. 1982. Formation and rate of formation of ventifacts in Victoria Land, Antarctica. Polar Geography and Geology, 6: 97-113

Nickling W G, McKenna N C. 1997. Wind tunnel evaluation of a edge-shape aeolian sediment trap. Geomorphology, 18: 333-345

Pye K, Tsoar H. 1990. Aeolian Sand and Sand Deposits. London: Unwin Hyman

Sarre R D. 1988. Evaluation of aeolian sand transport equations using intertidal zone measurements, Saunton Sands, England. Sedimentology, 35: 671-679

Stam J M T. 1997. On the modeling of 2D aeolian dunes. Sedimentology. 44: 127-141

Thomas D S G. 1997. Arid Zone Geomorphology Second Edition. New York: John Wiley & Sons, Inc

Tsoar H. 1982. Internal structure and surface geometry of longitudinal seif dunes. Journal of Sedimentology Petrology, 52: 823-832

Van Dijk. 1999. Aeolian process across transverse dunes. II: Modeling the sediment transport and profile development. Earth Surface Processes and Landforms, 24: 319-333

Wasson R J, Hyde R. 1983. Factors determing desert dune type. Nature, 304: 337-339

Wasson R J. Nanninga P M. 1986. Estimating wind transport of sand on vegetated surfaces. Earth Surface Processes and Landforms, 11: 505-514

Wiggs G F S, Livingstone I, Warren A. 1996. The role of streamline curvature in sand dune dynamics: Evidence from field and wind tunnel measurements. Geomorphology, 17: 29-46

Wilkinson R H. 1984. A method for evaluating statistical errors associated with logarithmic velocity profiles.

Geo-Marine Letters, 3: 49—52

Wipperman F K, Gross G. 1986. The wind-induced shaping and migration of an isolated dune: A numerical experiment. Boundary-layer Meteorology, 36: 319—334

Wu Zheng. 1987. Aeolian Geomorphology. Beijing: Science Press

Chapter 7
The Causes and Processes of Aeolian Desertification

7.1 Natural factors leading to the formation of aeolian desertification

Aeolian desertification is land degradation in arid, semiarid and dry semi-humid areas resulting from various factors, including climatic variations and human activities.

The definition of the UN Convention to Combat Desertification has accurately explained the causes of aeolian desertification: climatic variations and human activities.

Environmental conditions such as drought, frequent wind and rich sand sources are the basis for the occurrence of aeolian desertification formation.

7.1.1 Analysis on the natural background of aeolian desertification

Of all the causes of aeolian desertification, the frequent winds above the sand entrainment threshold (5.5 m/s) in the dry season are the driving force of aeolian desertification. The surface materials, which mainly consist of loose sand, are the material basis for aeolian desertification. In addition, insufficient and unstable precipitation, fragile eco-environments, and exposed surfaces are the background of aeolian desertification occurrence.

7.1.1.1 The temporal and spatial consistency of frequent winds above the sand entrainment threshold and the dry season

Wind is the main agent shaping landforms in the aeolian desertified regions and plays an important role in aeolian desertification development. According to statistics, there are three windy areas in China: southeast coast, China-Mongolia border area and the Qinghai-Tibet Plateau. In Chinese aeolian desertified areas, the wind force is strong, with mean annual wind velocity ranging from 3.3 to 5.5 m/s. In spring, mean wind velocity generally ranges from 4.0 to 6.0 m/s. There are 200–310 days per year with wind above the sand entrainment threshold. The wind over force 8 on the Beaufort scale is 20 to 80 days in most regions per year. According to time distribution, spring is the windy season and its frequency occupies about 30% of the annual total number, especially the winds above force 8 mainly occurs in this season, occupying 40%–70% of annual total number. However, spring is also the season with less precipitation. Taking the Horqin Sandy Land and the

Ulanqab desertified grassland as an example, precipitation in spring occupies only 8%–13% of total annual precipitation. Therefore, a dry sandy surface easily experiences deflation, and results in the spread of aeolian desertification (Zhu et al., 1989).

Annual precipitation in Chinese desert regions is mostly below 400 mm, and reduces to lower than 50 mm from southeast to northwest. The annual variability of precipitation can reach 20%–50%.

In order to evaluate the comprehensive influence of climatic factors such as precipitation, wind velocity and temperature on wind erosion intensity, Dong Yuxiang et al. (1995) put forward a comprehensive index of wind erosion climatic factor C that includes these three variables. The calculation formula is:

$$C = \frac{1}{100} i \sum_{i=1}^{12} \overline{U^3} \left(\frac{ETP_i - P_i}{ETP_i} \right) d \tag{7-1}$$

Where: C is wind erosion climatic factor, a dimensionless index;

U is monthly mean wind velocity at a height of 2m (m/s);

P_i is monthly precipitation(mm);

ETP_i is monthly potential evaporation(mm);

d is days in a month(d).

Among them, ETP_i can be calculated by the formula below:

$$ETP_i = 0.19(20 + T_i)2(1 - \gamma_i) \tag{7-2}$$

Where: T_i is monthly mean temperature(°C);

Y is monthly relative humidity(%).

The calculated results (Fig.7-1, Fig. 7-2) show that the majority of arid, semiarid and dry semi-humid areas in China have infrequent precipitation and strong frequent wind. This results in strong climatic erosivity, and the mean climatic erosion factor is higher than 30; especially in spring (April), the value is higher than 50, and in most areas, it can reach above 100, an extremely severe degree ($C \geqslant 100$). The strong climatic erosivity provides dynamical conditions for sand movement in arid, semiarid and parts of semi-humid areas, and also provides strong power for aeolian desertification development (Dong, 1995).

7.1.1.2 Material basis for the occurrence and spread of aeolian desertification

Arid and semiarid zones in China are developed from mountains, plateaus and basins. The huge basins and plateaus once received large amounts of sandy sediment carried by mountain ice-snow meltwater and flood (storm runoff). This formed dry deltas, alluvial fans, alluvial plains, alluvial and lacustrine plains, alluvial-diluvian plains and lakeshore plains that consist of loose sandy materials. The loose sandy sediments can reach 200–400 m in thickness. With such loose sandy sediments as parent material, vast sandy areas were formed in the arid, semiarid and dry semi-humid zones in

China and soils are mainly sandy soils and sandy loam soils.

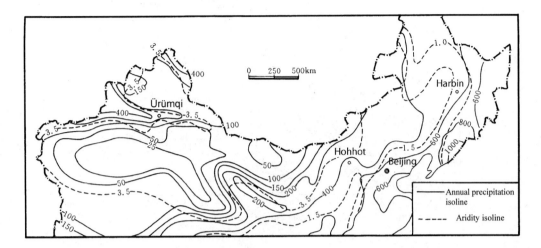

Fig. 7-1   Distribution of the index of wind erosion climatic factors in arid and semiarid regions of China
(Dong et al., 1995)

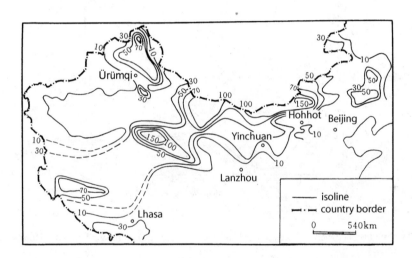

Fig. 7-2   Distribution index of wind erosion climatic factors in arid and semiarid regions of China in April
(Dong et al., 1995)

The sand content in sandy soils is more than 70% (Fig. 7-3), with coarse texture and low cohesion; they are prone to be eroded by wind (Fig. 7-4). Such unstable deflation-prone surfaces provide a material basis for the occurrence and development of aeolian desertification.

The analytical results of surface sediments in aeolian desertification-prone areas show that the surface materials mainly consist of sand grains. This is an important condition for aeolian desertification expansion after the surface vegetation is destroyed by intensive human economic activities.

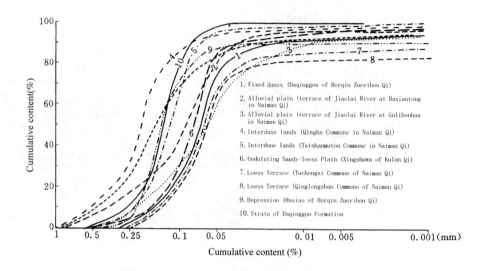

Fig. 7-3　Grain accumulation curves of different land types in the Horqin Sandy Land (Zhou et al., 1994)

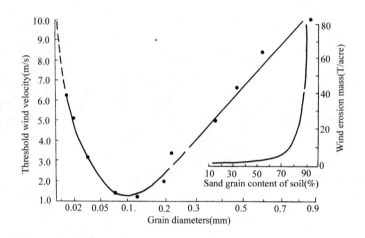

Fig. 7-4　Correlation between surface material composition and amount of wind erosion (Dong et al., 1995)

7.1.1.3　Sparse vegetation, exposed and semi-exposed sandy surface are favourable for wind erosion

Because of arid climate and impoverished soils, aeolian desertification-prone areas have sparse vegetation and low forest coverage. The forest coverage in most areas is lower than 5%. Vegetation is the vital factor to protect surfaces from wind erosion (Fig. 7-5). In Chinese arid and semiarid zones, large areas of land lack effective vegetation protection, and are in exposed and semi-exposed states. Especially in winter and spring, large areas of land are directly exposed to strong wind action, and surface materials are easily blown away.

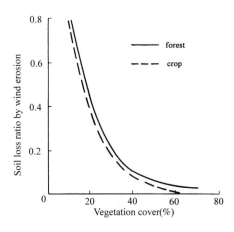

Fig. 7-5　Relation between vegetation cover and wind erosion of soil (Fryrear, 1985)

7.1.1.4　Insufficient precipitation resulted in fragile eco-environments and accelerated aeolian desertification processes

Among various potential natural factors affecting aeolian desertification, insufficient and erratic precipitation plays a vital role in the formation of the fragile eco-environment and accelerating aeolian desertification processes.

Annual climate change in typical aeolian desertified areas is shown in Fig. 7-6

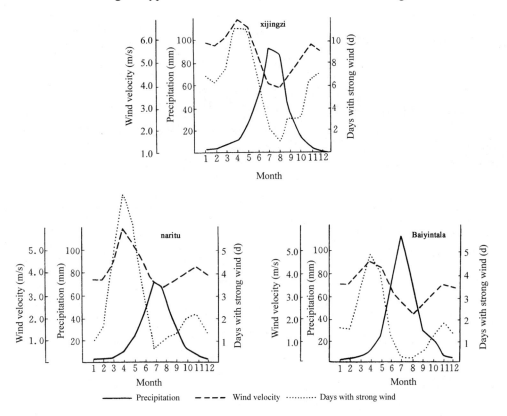

Fig. 7-6　Annual climate change in typical aeolian desertified areas (Dong et al., 1995)

According to the analysis of climatic data, besides some parts of semi-humid zone and arid zone, aeolian desertification mainly occurs in such areas with annual precipitation ranging from 200 to 500 mm and annual aridity of about 1.5. In such areas, the seasonal distribution of annual precipitation differs greatly: 70% of total annual precipitation falls in summer and 15% in winter and spring. As a result, combined with other agents (wind, temperature), the phenomena of "rain and heat occur simultaneously; drought and wind occur simultaneously." Rich rainfall in summer is favorable to plant growth, but the high variability of annual precipitation cannot guarantee the survival of plants. In the dry spring season, exposed surfaces are highly susceptible to wind erosion.

Interannual climate change in typical aeolian desertification areas is shown in Fig. 7-7.

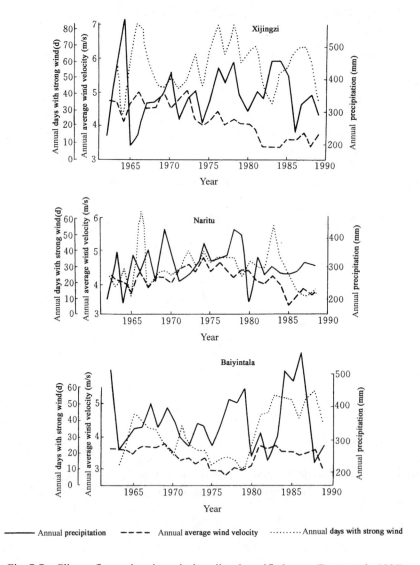

Fig. 7-7 Climate fluctuations in typical aeolian desertified areas (Dong et al., 1995)

The annual variability of precipitation in aeolian desertification-prone regions differs greatly. The precipitation in rainy years may be 2–3 times higher than that in low rainfall years. Taking the

Horqin Sandy Land as an example, the average variability of annual precipitation in different areas ranges from 58 to 87mm. The relative annual variability is 16%–22%, and the variation coefficient is 0.20–0.23. The same situation can be seen in the Ulanqab grassland. Taking Siziwang Qi as an example, during the period from 1959 to 1980, precipitation over 9 years was lower than the mean value, occupying 43%; precipitation over 8 years was higher than the mean value, occupying 38% and precipitations over 4 years was equal to the mean value, occupying 19%. Considering this data, inter-annual variations of precipitation is very high. Although its absolute value of variation range is not very high, ranging from 70 mm to 100 mm, the relative value is high, generally occupying 25%–30%. Hence, the frequency of drought is high, and fragile ecosystems may lose ecological balance and aeolian desertification may take place under disturbances from human economic activities. However, it should be pointed out that some areas of the semi-humid zone that has high variations in annual precipitation, total annual precipitation is much higher than that of the semiarid zone, so the decreased absolute value is still high. For instance, Daxing County in Beijing, located on the ancient sandy riverbed of the alluvial fan of the Yongding River, has an average annual precipitation of 580 mm and normally, the precipitation in low rainfall years can reach 400 mm annually. Although this may affect plant growth and corn yield, it still provides favorable water conditions for the recovery of natural vegetation, and can limit sand movement in the semi-humid zone to a certain degree.

In arid, semiarid and seasonal dry semi-humid areas, as long as the above conditions such as surface sand material and strong wind exist, aeolian desertification is likely to occur under continuous disturbance from human economic activities. In other words, the eco-environment in arid and semiarid areas is fragile. However, from the view of eco-environmental development, as aeolian desertification develops to a severe stage, some "climax landscape" environmental features occur. For example, an area that is full of shifting dunes, Gobi, badland, severe salinization that completely loses production capacity is another stable stage. Therefore, geoscientists and ecologists call the mixed farming-grazing zone in eastern sandy regions and oasis-desert transitional belts in the west as a fragile ecology zone that is prone to cause aeolian desertification and can be reversed. The most striking characteristics of the natural background in these areas are their fragile environments. When human factors exert positive influence, the aeolian desertified land can be reversed. When the pressure exerted by humans on the land exceeds its carrying capacity, the land will be desertified quickly.

Through a comprehensive analysis of the above potential aeolian desertification conditions, we give a quantitative evaluation to the possibility of aeolian desertification—internal risk of aeolian desertification in Chinese arid, semiarid and part of semi-humid regions. The evaluation result is shown in Fig. 7-8.

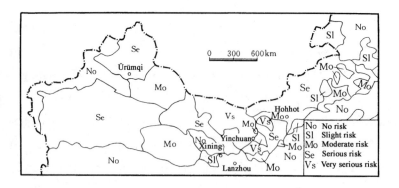

Fig. 7-8   Assessment map of latent aeolian desertification hazards in northern China (Dong et al., 1995)

7.1.2   The influence of climatic variations in recent years on aeolian desertification in arid and semiarid regions in northern China

The effect of climatic factors on aeolian desertification is mainly manifested in the influence of dry climate, such as annual precipitation over 1–2 years or more is lower than the multiyear mean value, or a long dry period that lasts up to 10 years. The changes in aridity can accelerate or delay the aeolian desertification process (Zhu et al., 1994).

7.1.2.1   Climatic variations and aeolian desertification in the historical period of China

Based on phenology-phenomenon recorded in ancient books, the famous Chinese geographer and climatologist Zhu Kezhen drew a temperature variation curve of the past 5,000 years in China. Zhang Chao et al., compared the curve with the variation curve of Norway's snowline height and found that the variation trend of the two curves is roughly consistent (Fig. 7-9). Besides precipitation, the rise and fall of the snowline has a close relation with climatic warming or cooling. Based on the temperature variation curve, we can divide the climate into four warm periods and four cold periods. The results studied show that under the influence of the East Asia monsoon, climatic variations in the historical period of China are directly related to the winter Mongolia high pressure and the influencing scale of southeast warm moist airflow. In the cool period, the winter Mongolia high pressure has a longer and larger influence, and its boundary noticeably shifts southward. Southeastern warm moist airflow stays in the south, and the whole climatic zone shifts southward. On the contrary, in the warm period, the scale of the winter Mongolia high pressure is small and its duration is short. Therefore, the moist airflow moves northward and the climatic zone shifts northward. The Mongolia high pressures are cold and dry. Therefore, as a rule, cold and dry, warm and wet are interrelated.

China's warm-humid periods over the past 3,000 years are: ① 3000–1000 BC (the Yangshao Cultural Time and the Shang Dynasty); ② 770 BC to the beginning of AD (the Qin and the Han

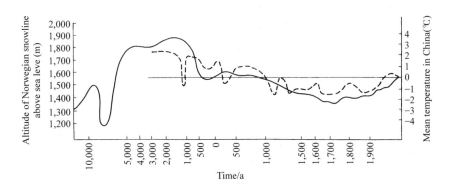

Fig. 7-9   Snowline height (bold line) since 10,000 years and temperature change (dash line) in China
since 5,000 years (Zhang Chao et al., 1989)

Dynasties); ③ 600 to 1000 (the Sui and the Tang Dynasties); ④ 1200–1300 (the beginning of the Yuan Dynasty). Cold and dry periods: ① 1000 to 850 BC (the beginning of the Zhou Dynasty); ② beginning of AD to 600 (the Eastern Han Dynasty, the Three Kingdoms, the Northern and southern Dynasties); ③ 1000 to 1200 (the Northern the Southern Song Dynasties); ④ Beginning of 1400 AD (the end of the Ming Dynasty and the beginning of the Qing Dynasty). During the fourth cold period over the past 500 years, the temperature still fluctuated obviously. A total of 4 relatively dry-cold periods and 3 relatively warm-humid periods can be derived from the temperature variation curve (Zhang et al., 1989). Since 1945, especially after 1963, China has entered another climatic fluctuation period with dry-cold characteristics. At the same time, the factors affecting the climate fluctuations become more and more complex and the influence of human activities on climate fluctuations is more and more significant. Experts have to consider more human factors when explaining the climatic variations. The factors include: ① The greenhouse effect resulting from increase of CO_2 emitted by industry; ② The destruction of the ozone layer by Freon; ③ The increase of surface albedo due to reduction of areas of green land and desertification.

By studying the relationship between several aeolian desertification periods and climatic variations in Chinese history, we can draw a conclusion that the positive aeolian desertification process occurs during dry-cold climatic periods, while its reverse process occurs in warm-humid climatic periods. The aeolian desertification period of the Mu Us and the Horqin generally coincides with the second and third dry periods respectively. During the Ming and Qing Dynasties, many ancient cities were abandoned land aeolian desertification developed rapidly in the Hexi region of Gansu. Especially at the end of the Ming Dynasty,a large number of strong dust storm records confirm this conclusion.

In the 1980s, from studying the relationship of nationality migrations, aeolian desertification and climate, some researchers drew a conclusion that during a dry-cold period, the northern grassland tended to degrade, land tended to be aeolian desertified, and the living environment tended to deteriorate. Therefore, nomads entered the Central Plains in search of development opportunities in the south, and this dry-cold climate accelerated the down fall of the Ming Dynasty. From a historical view, we can discover the time that the northern nationality enter the Central Plains and form "nationality great compromise" generally took place in the dry-cold period. From studying the dust storm records of the Beijing region in the historical period (since the Northern Wei Dynasty), we found that dust storm frequency reduced after the northern nomadic people began governing the Beijing region and changed the agricultural economy into a live stock raising economy. However, when the agricultural nationality moved northward, or the nomadic nationality paid more attention to farming and vigorously cultivated land nearby, aeolian desertification developed rapidly. This shows that the spread or reversal of aeolian desertification in the historical period was simultaneously affected by climate variations and human factors, and human factors were more and more prone to hold a dominant influence.

7.1.2.2　The influence of modern climatic fluctuations on aeolian desertification

Northern China is in a large dry-cold period that started at the end of the Ming Dynasty. As for the short term, the climate has entered a relatively dry-cold fluctuation beginning between the 1940s–1960s. However, temperature rises resulting from human factors leads to temperature variations far removed from the natural variation cycle, and makes the aridification trend obvious. In recent years, aridification continues unabated, or even strengthens. Most notably in the eastern semiarid zone and adjacent regions in northern China, the decrease of precipitation is very clear (Fig. 7-10), and the aridity index has increased remarkably (Fig. 7-11). Especially in the 20th century, the internal risk of aeolian desertification in arid and semiarid areas reached a medium degree, and most parts of eastern China have particularly reached a severe degree. This reflects that these areas are very prone to aeolian desertification and have a high internal risk of aeolian desertification. Since the 1950s, the precipitation has decreased by 6% throughout northern China, and the maximum reduction in northern China has reached 24%. Climate is the most active factor in arid, semiarid and semi-humid areas and climate variations inevitably cause changes in ecological factors such as vegetation and changes in the eco-environment, as well as leading to changes in the character and action of external surface agents to produce a very profound influence on aeolian desertification. The climatic aridification in northern China has led to a continual decrease in precipitation, rise in temperature, increase in evaporation, decrease in runoff and soil desiccation in the past 40 years. In such cases, it is inevitably causing the evolution of desert-like environments and leading to the occurrence and development of modern aeolian desertification.

As far as climate change is concerned, it is necessary to probe into the relationship between the El Niño Phenomena and aeolian desertification. Several intense El Niño events have occurred since the 1980s, and several corresponding La Niña events have caused abnormal weather in many areas of the world. Recent studies show that it has a great influence on short-term climatic fluctuations.

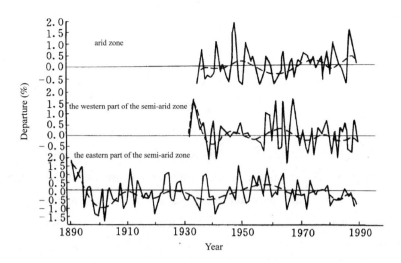

Fig. 7-10　Precipitation change in arid and semi-arid regions in China in the last 100 years (Xu, 1997)

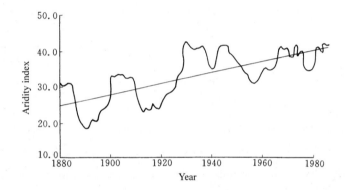

Fig. 7-11　Running curves for several years of annual DI (Drought Index) based on calculations
from 100 stations east of 100° E in China (Ye, 1992)

El Niño events refer to the abnormal warming phenomena of the Pacific Ocean surface temperature off the South American coast, adjacent to Ecuador and extending into Peruvian waters. There have been a total of 12 El Niño phenomena since the 1950s. Among them, the most obvious ones are those that occurred in 1957, 1958, 1965, 1972, 1973, 1976, 1982, 1983, 1997and 1998. From May 1997 to May 1998, one of the strongest El Niño events occurred and lasted for 13 months. It caused global climatic abnormality and great floods rarely seen in the history of China in the Changjiang River, the Nenjiang River and the Songhua River.

Later, scientists found that between two El Niño years, sometimes an anti El Niño phenomenon occurred where the ocean's surface temperature is lower than its lower layer and thereby leads to global climatic abnormality. This phenomenon is called La Niña. The years that La Niña events occurred are: 1954, 1962, 1964, 1967, 1970, 1971, 1973, 1974, 1975, 1978, 1981, 1984, 1985, 1988, and 1999.

It is still not clear about the primary mechanism of El Niño and La Niña at present. Chinese meteorologists have found that in El Niño years, tropical cyclones of the northwest Pacific and the South China Sea exhibit unusual activity. According to historical data, in El Niño years, the number of tropical cyclones that take place in the Northwest Pacific and the South China Sea is less than normal years, and the landing time is later. From 1949 to 1997, about 28 tropical cyclones were formed per year, and 7 landed. The minimal annual cyclonic number is 20 (1951), and the minimal landing number is 3 (1950, 1951, and 1988). All these events occurred in strong El Niño years. On the contrary, in La Niña years, the number of tropical cyclones that occur in the Northwest Pacific and the South China Sea is higher than that in normal years. The average number is 31 per year and the maximum number is 40. The average landed number is 9 per year and the maximum number is 12. Historically, the landing time of tropical cyclones in China is usually from June to July, and this was true for 47 of the past 50 years of the 19th century. There are only 3 years when it landed in August and these years are 1975, 1997 and 1998; all these years are El Niño years. In 1998, a tropical cyclone landed on Taiwan on August 4, which is the latest landing time since 1949.

The equator is the convergence zone of a tropical troposphere wind field and is also the area of concentrated rising tropical airflow. In this strong convergence zone, a tropical disturbance is frequently created and this disturbed airflow can be strengthened under suitable external conditions and develop into tropical cyclones. According to statistics, in the northwestern Pacific, about 80% of tropical cyclones occured in the equator, and only a few ones occur in other areas beyond the equator convergent zone. Therefore, the strength of the equator convergene zone directly affects the activities of tropical cyclones.

In the midsummer of normal years, the subtropical high-pressure zone is a little farther south, and the southern edge of the equator convergene zone generally lies between 10°–20°N with a width of 200–300 km. Nevertheless, in the midsummer of 1998; the northwestern Pacific had a prevailing easterly airflow, the equator's westerly airflow was very weak, and no obvious convergene zone existed. This anomalous inactive equator convergene zone is an important cause that resulted in fewer tropical cyclones.

The inactivity of tropical cyclones causes the subtropical high-pressure to remain in the Yangtze Basin, and brings no precipitation to the north. Therefore, the deserts in northern China are dominated by a dry air mass. The climate is dry-cold, and wind-sand activities are intense. In 1997, northern China experienced a severe drought in summer and fall. The year 1998 was a year with frequent strong wind 5 and dust storm 5. Strong winds occurred 6 times locally from March to May, and there were four very strong dust storms. Nevertheless, the La Niña phenomenon in 1999 also brought drought and strong dust storms to northern China. In previous history, during the El Niño years, northern China generally had plentiful precipitation, but the El Niño year of 1983 was a low rainfall year (Zhang Chao et al., 1989). The El Niño and La Niña phenomena can alter the synoptic situation over a large region, and directly influence the distribution of precipitation and the positive and negative development of aeolian desertification. However, because their influencing mechanism is unclear, their consequences remain to be further studied.

In summary, there are many factors leading to climatic variations. Besides the abnormal events caused by sea water temperature variation, the basic factors affecting China's desert climate include ground temperature, thermal properties of underlying surfaces such as ice and snow, and atmospheric circulation factors such as the locations of the Asian monsoon, the western Pacific subtropical high, the Qinghai-Tibet high, and the Eastern Asia high-pressure ridge; three oscillations, quasi-two-year oscillation, and extraterrestrial factors of the earth system such as solar activities. Until now, it is still unclear how some factors influence the climate of desert regions in China and much work remains to be done.

7.1.2.3 Effects of future climatic variations on aeolian desertification evolution in China

It is very difficult to forecast the future climatic variations, especially the forecast of the future development tendency of climatic variations, wet or dry. At the end of the 1990s, the National Science Committee invited 46 experts who were engaged in climatic forecast for many years to forecast the climatic variation tendency for the last 10 years of the 20th century to draw up the Blue Book of Climate. Most experts forecasted that the climate will become warm, and this conclusion has been confirmed. Nevertheless, as for precipitation, the number of experts who forecasted increasing precipitation is the same as those who forecasted decreasing precipitation. Confronted with the complicated situation of the last 10 years of the 20th century, it is impossible to judge who was correct.

Climatic variations are commonly caused by nature and humankind. Studies show that the main factors affecting the climate on a timescale over one hundred years are the internal interaction and feedback of the climatic system, solar activities, volcanic activities and human activities beyond the climatic system. All these factors interact with each other and will change in the future. Therefore, it is very difficult to forecast climate.

In the book of Evaluation of Environmental Evolution in Western China, edited by Qin Dahe in 2002, a prediction on the climatic variations in the future 10–50 years in 5 provinces in western China was made in the chapter "Climatic variations forecast".

For the prediction of natural change in the future 10–50 years in western China, a climate model was used. Special consideration was given to the factors that affect climatic variations including the physical factors of interannual variation, greenhouse gas increases and destruction of the ozone layer. The relationship between the periodical variations of solar activity over the past 2,600 years and climatic changes in western China was deduced. If human factors were not considered, the natural changes in the future 10–50 years would be warm-dry and cold-humid in dry desert areas (including the Qiangtang Plateau). The temperature from 2010 to 2050 will be 0.2–0.8°C lower than the present.

The variations in precipitation will turn from slightly dry to slightly humid in eastern parts of western China, and from slightly humid to slightly dry in arid desert areas (including the Qiangtang Plateau). But taking into account human factors (the CO_2 concentration will be doubled due to human activities) in 2030 will lead to a 2.0°C rise in temperature in western China, among which Qinghai will have the most obvious increase and will be 2.2°C warmer and Tibet in southwestern China will be 2.3°C warmer than the present. The precipitation will generally increase in desert areas, it will increase by 19% in northwest China, and it will increase the highest in Gansu at 23%. In Inner Mongolia, the increase is the least, at only 14%. Integrating natural variations and effects from human activity, we obtained the predicted values of the climatic variations in northwest China in the future 10–50 years: by 2050, the temperature in northwest China will increase 2.1°C, and the precipitation will also obviously increase. Therefore, the natural temperature decrease in the first 10 years will be generally offset by temperature increases due to human activities; thereafter, the influence of human activities will progressively strengthen, and temperatures will increase obviously.

When considering the influence of climate on aeolian desertification, the most important factor is the moisture condition of the atmosphere and soil that is affected by the combined action of temperature and precipitation variations. We try to give an evaluation of the aridity changes based on temperature and precipitation variations predicted by experts. The results showed that by 2030 the Turpan region in eastern Xinjiang will have the highest increase of precipitation, and the precipitation will increase by 47% compared to present levels. However, because the average annual precipitation is 16.6mm, the actual increase is only 7.8 mm, while local evaporation is 1,366.6 mm. According to the empirical relationship between temperature and evaporation, if temperature increases by 1–2 °C, the evaporation will increase by 273.32 mm, and aridity will increase by 46.3. Precipitation in Kashi will increase by 12.5 mm, and evaporation will increase by 241 mm. The aridity will increase by 20.8, exactly one-fold. The aridity in other areas also increases, indicating an increase in droughts. Among the factors causing aeolian desertification, the increase or decrease of precipitation is certainly an important factor, but the increase or decrease of evaporation is also important. Considering these two factors, one can assume that future climatic variations will lead to the spread of aeolian desertification.

7.2 Human activities and aeolian desertification

China is the world's most populous country and the arable land per capita is limited. The area of arid, semiarid and dry semi-humid land prone to aeolian desertification is about 300×10^4 km², occupying about 1/3 of China's total land area. China is also a country with many mountains and the area of mountains, plateaus, and hilly lands is 600×10^4 km², occupying about 2/3 of China's total land area. The area of plains, including arid and semiarid oasis plain (such as the Hetao Plain and the

Yinchuan Plain), is only $110 \times 10^4 km^2$. Human factors play an important role in the exploitation and usage of land resources. Over exploitation of land resources for feeding the population is one important cause of aeolian desertification. China is a developing country, and its development constantly needs plentiful resources. Calculated by per capita share, many natural resources in China, such as water, arable land, forest, grassland and important mineral resources, are far lower than the average level of most countries, and their spatial-temporal distribution is unbalanced. Taking water as an example, although northwestern China has a vast territory, some $2448.84hm^2$ of reserved arable lands were not reclaimed due to lack of water.

At present, China's ecological situation is very severe. The ecological problems characterized by land degradation, ecological unbalance, vegetation destruction and sharp decreases in biological diversity are a result of the tremendous pressure exerted by human economic activities on eco-environments that exceed the tolerance degree of the eco-environment. On the other hand, ecological destruction also intensifies the conflicts for resource supplies, severely restricts the development of many areas, and limits the living standard or even causes various disasters.

7.2.1 Rapid increase of population pressure

From the end of the 17th century to the end of the 18th century, also known as the "Kangxi-Qianlong Heyday Period", China's population began to increase rapidly. The population increased from less than 1×10^8, which had lasted for a long time, to more than 2×10^8. At the beginning of the 19th century, China's population increased to 3×10^8, and it surpassed the threshold of 4×10^8 in 1840. After the founding of PRC, with a stabilized society and rapid economic recovery, China's population entered into a period of rapid increase, and the total population increased from 4.5×10^8 in 1949 to 13×10^8 in 2000. It is estimated that the Chinese population will reach its peak in 2030, with a population of 16×10^8.

According to the existing situation in aeolian desertification-prone areas of China, intensive economic activities are usually related to the increase of population. The population growth exerts pressure on land resources. In order to meet the increasing demand for food and basic living materials, people are forced to reclaim land, destroy vegetation and increase grazing pressure on grasslands. Using the variation curve of population density, per capita arable land, and grassland possession per livestock in Jirem Meng, Horqin grassland as an example (Fig. 7-12), it is clear that with an increase of population, the pressure exerted on land by humans and livestock increased, thus accelerating the spread of aeolian desertification.

Since modern times, the population in northern China increased rapidly. The average annual growth rate was over 20% in the 100-year period from 1890 to 1990, and the population density increased from 2.06 people/km^2 to 17.09 people/km^2 during this time, an increase of over 7 times. Particularly during the period of 1949–1978, there was an accelerated population growth, and during this period, the annual average population growth rate reached 31.4% and population density also had a great increase. Taking Ningxia Hui Autonomous Region as an example, the population density rapidly increased from less than 10 people/km^2 at the beginning of the 1950s to 90 people/km^2 at present.

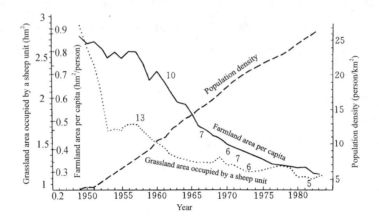

Fig. 7-12   Population density, per capita farmlands and grassland area occupied by livestock over previous years (Zou et al., 1994)

The rapid growth of human and livestock populations in arid and semiarid areas of China causes huge contradictions between humans, living demands and low productivity. For a long time, the per capita food share was lower than the basic standard of 350 kg, and in some years was even lower than the famine standard of 300 kg.

7.2.2   Unreasonable land development activities

Intensive land use is mainly manifested in three aspects: over-reclamation, overgrazing and excessive collection of firewood.

7.2.2.1   Over-reclamation

With the rapid increase in population, the per capita arable land area decreases rapidly. In order to meet human's increasing demand for food, large areas of lands unsuitable for agriculture have been reclaimed. Over-exploitation of lands for agricultural use results in the destruction of high-quality grasslands. The reclamation of large areas of land unsuitable for agriculture has destroyed the primary vegetation and soil structure, aggravated soil erosion by wind, and formed vast expanses of aeolian desertified land.

A new round of rapid aeolian desertification development in China began during the "Kangxi-Qianlong Heyday Period". Owing to rapid population growth, the Qing government repealed the policy which prohibited people from migrating north of the Great Wall Pass. At the beginning of the Qing Dynasty, northwest China, including the Horqin and the Xilin Gol grassland, was regarded as the "origin of the dragon". From the Rehe River to southern Liaoning province, a "wicker wall" was set up as a barrier to prevent farmers from moving north of the Pass. Once the policy was changed at the end of the Qing Dynasty, many farmers from Shandong, Hebei, Shanxi, and Shaanxi increasingly "adventured to Guandong" and "migrated to Xikou". In the beginning of the Republic of China, there were years of successive wars, and the migration of people from the south to northern grasslands reached a peak. The traditional grazing areas in Bashang, Hebei and Qahar Grassland, Inner Mongolia began to establish counties and changed from a live stock raising economy to farming. Many western missionaries and some business units also leased land and encouraged people to reclaim the grassland. By the 1930s, reclamation activities already extended as far as the Inner Mongolian Ulan Qab Grassland, southern Damao Qi (Bailing Temple) and Siziwang Qi. In the 1950s, the reclamation in Gongjitang of Siziwang Qi extended 140 km into the grassland. After that, the grassland experienced three large-scale reclamations at the end of the 1950s and the mid 1960s and 1970s. Moreover, the reclamation was conducted in an organized way and utilized some advanced farm implements (tractors).

Limited by natural conditions, mainly inadequate accumulative temperature, short growing periods and no irrigation (water), the newly reclaimed land has low productivity. Spring is the dry and windy season in northern China and conventional tillage techniques were explored by farmers, disturbing the dry and loose soils, and causing severe soil erosion. According to surveys in the southern Ulan Qab Grassland and the Qahar Grassland, the newly cultivated land can lose 2 mm of soil during one wind event and 5 mm in a windy season.

Wind erosion leads to continual loss of organic soil matter and severe reduction of soil fertility. Based on the data surveyed in 7 Qis (counties) of Houshan in Ulanqab Meng, Inner Mongolia, there are 32×10^4 hm^2 of dry farming lands where over 1cm topsoil is removed by wind annually, and annual loss of organic matter, nitrogen and soil clay fraction are 84×10^4 t, 5.4×10^4 t, and 830×10^4 t, respectively(Natural Department, National Environment Protection Bureau, 2000). Owing to severe wind erosion, the farmlands that have cultivated land for 50 years have turned into unproductive aeolian desertified land covered by gravels, sand patches, and coppice dunes (Chen, 1991). Furthermore, the eroded fine materials will form floating dust and can be transported to the North China Plain and pollute the environment.

The intense activities of human cultivation activities create favorable conditions for wind erosion, transport and deposition, and thereby greatly change the primary landscape of sandy grassland. Therefore, grassland reclamation is one of the main causes of aeolian desertification in grasslands.

7.2.2.2 Overgrazing

Overgrazing is also a main factor in the modern aeolian desertification process. Owing to uncontrolled reclamation, the grassland area was reduced, but the number of livestock has continually increased (Fig. 7-13). As a result, the per capita animal share of the grassland area has continually decreased. The grazing intensity on grasslands has rapidly increased, and grasslands have been severely over burdened for a long time (Table 7-1). This causes serious degradation of grassland; vegetation cover and height have obviously decreased, and deflation has exacerbated and resulted in the aeolian desertification of grassland.

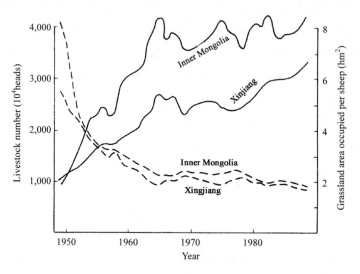

Fig. 7-13　Changes in livestock number (bold line) and grassland area occupied per animal(dotted line)(Dong et al., 1995)

Table 7-1　Livestock change in China in different years (10^4 sheep unit)

Years	Inner Mongolia	Gansu	Ningxia	Qinghai	Xinjiang
1950	2,447.30	1,746.46	292.43	1,851.46	2,309.41
1955	4,658.90	2,435.77	491.87	2,728.24	3,238.83
1959	5,189.20	2,222.78	472.36	1,817.00	3,307.12
1969	6,431.60	2,580.73	566.32	3,713.80	3,897.63
1979	6,800.60	2,975.53	597.19	4,379.18	4,350.47
1990	6,460.14	3,563.34	689.25	4,669.80	5,609.60
Reasonable number of animals sustainable	4,837.00	1,511.84	288.47	3,625.45	3,621.78
Overloading rate in 1990 (%)	33.56	135.70	138.93	28.81	54.89
Degraded grassland in total available grassland (%)	41.00	44.00	97.00	20.00	19.00

Source: Dong Yuxiang, 1995.

At the same time, the livestock number increased rapidly in Inner Mongolia, Gansu, Ningxia, Qinghai, and Xinjiang, i.e. increased from 7,671.96 $\times10^4$ sheep units in 1949 to 20,992.13 $\times10^4$ sheep units in 1990. The average annual increase rate is 29.3%.

Grassland reclamation resulted in the decline of grassland area. The continous increase of livestock number exceeded the ultimate bearing capacity of grassland, which has resulted in severe degradation of grasslands.

Overgrazing led to vegetation dwarfing and coverage reduction, as well as sporadic occurrences of bare land. Livestock trampled soil crusts and formed exposed sandy lands that become the breakthrough-point for wind erosion. The aeolian desertification process caused by overgrazing is most obvious around water wells. Generally, within a radius of 500m around a water well, the primary vegetation is destroyed and shifting sand and gravel appear on the surface. Within a radius of 500–1,000 m, inedible weeds, or even poisonous weeds, can grow around aeolian desertification. In undulating, vegetation-covered dunefields, besides water wells and overgrazing points, the aeolian desertified landscape resulting from overgrazing also includes small interdune lakes. This is because livestock trampling around the small lake produces shifting sand, and some fixed sand dunes turn into mobile dunes. Once shifting sand occurs, erosion action takes it as a basic point, leading to expansion of blowouts and forming the landscape of spot-distribution shifting sand between fixed dunes.

It should be pointed out that during the aeolian desertification processes on grassland, over-reclamation and overgrazing interact with each other and are closely interrelated.

7.2.2.3 Excessive collection of firewood

In the past 300 years, human beings have cleared about 1/5 forest on the earth's land surface. After the 1980s, about $15 \times 10^4 \text{km}^2$ of forests were cut down annually (Hu Zhaoliang, 2000).

During excessive human economic activities, fuel consumption destroys natural vegetation and causes a very serious aeolian desertification process characterized by fixed dune reactivation and sandy grassland wind erosion.

Vegetation destruction by collection of firewood usually directly leads to the occurrence of shifting sand. Especially in arid desert zones, destruction of vegetation on coppice dunes at the edge of oases is an important cause of aeolian desertification around oases.

Because of a vast territory with a sparse population, inconvenient transportation, and low levels of energy resource exploitation, biological energy sources are the main energy source in China's arid, semiarid and dry semi-humid areas. With the growth of population, the demand for fuel also increases; the energy-shortage conditions in villages is very severe. Due to energy shortages in villages, a great deal of straw and livestock dung is used as fuel and cannot be returned to farmlands; as a result soil organic matter is continuously reduced, the soil structure becomes worse, soil fertility declines, and land productivity decreases, which is one of the factors that intensifies over reclamation and overgrazing. Some typical examples are the aeolian desertification of oases around the Taklimakan Desert, and aeolian desertification development near many settlements along the Qinghai-Tibet Highway in the southern Qaidam Basin. Aeolian desertification caused by the collection of firewood is generally expanding outward with the settlements at the center. From 1954 to the end of 1984, in the Qaidam Basin, a total of 650–700 t of psammophytes such as *Sabina chinensis*, *Haloxylon ammondendron*, *Tamarix chinensis*, *aragana korshinskii*, *Nitraria tangutirum*, and sea-buckthorn were collected and the destroyed vegetation area totaled 1,330,000 hm^2. Currently along a highway at the center of Golmud, an area 240 km long, 25–35 km wide of psammophytes were almost entirely cut away. The area of natural *Populus diversifolia* in southern Xinjiang was reduced by 17.4×10^4 hm^2 from 1958 to 1980; the forest in northen Xinjiang retreated 20–30 km from the desert interior. Furthermore, the total afforestation area preserved was only 19.7×10^4 hm^2. In Ejin Qi of Inner Mongolia, the forest area destroyed annually can reach more than 1,000 hm^2 due to firewood collection. The destruction of vegetation causes the further exposure of sand surfaces unprotected by vegetation, and exacerbates wind erosion. Wind erosion causes reactivation of fixed sand dunes (Zhu, et al., 1989; Zhou, et al., 1994; Dong, et al., 1995).

According to statistics by Zhu Zhenda, the collection of firewood ranks as the first cause of aeolian desertification in northern China, followed by over-grazing and over-reclamation (Table 7-2).

Table 7-2　Different causes of aeolian desertification in northern China (Zhu et al., 1998)

Causes of aeolian desertification	Area (10^4 km^2)	Percentage accounting for the total area of desertification (%)
Over-cultivation on steppe	4.47	25.4
Overgrazing on steppe	4.99	28.3
Over-collection of firewood	5.60	31.8
Misuse of water resources	1.47	8.3
Technogenic factors	0.13	0.7
Encroachment of dunes under wind forces	0.94	5.5

The variations of sand dune mobility in different periods in the Onqin Daga area can illustrate the increasing intensity of human activities (over-reclamation, overgrazing and excessive collection of firewood) leading to fixed dune mobilization. In the past 30 years, mobile dunes and semifixed dunes notably expanded, but the area of well-covered fixed dunes and interdune depressions decreased. This reflects the aggravation of aeolian desertification in the Onqin Daga area. What is worth noting is the environmental variations in Haolaiku and its surrounding areas in the eastern Onqin Daga. The Haoluku region is primarily an interdune depression with large areas of grassland. In the 1950s, the vegetation cover was over 70%, with less shifting sand. Shifting sand slightly expanded during the 1960s, occupying 1.7% of its total land area and in the mid 1960s, occupying 3.8%. With the intensification of human activities, a national farm was founded and population increased; up until the mid 1980s, the shifting sand area occupied 19.8% but increased to 28.3% by the mid 1990s. Reactivation degree of dunes in different periods in the Onqin Daga Sandy Land is shown in Table 7-3.

Table 7-3　Reactivation degree of dunes in different periods in the Onqin Daga Sandy Land

Types	Percentage of distribution area in total sandy land area (%)	
	The end of the 1950s	The mid 1980s
Shifting dunes	2.0	4.5
Semi-fixed dunes	34.2	47.2
Fixed dunes	51.2	38.8
Interdune lowland	12.8	10.2

(Zhu et al., 1998)

7.2.3 Irrational use of water resources

Water is the main limiting factor in arid areas. The inappropriate use of water resources causes a decrease of water resources in downstream reaches of inland rivers, vegetation deterioration and destruction, and the occurrence and development of aeolian desertification in the downstream oasis along inland rivers in arid zones.

There would be no oasis in the desert region without water, and there would be no oasis agriculture without irrigation. The exploitation of oasis land must give overall consideration to upstream and downstream reaches, and the land utilization scale should be made in consideration of the water systems. From ancient times to the present, the rise and decline of oases in northwest China is mostly related to variations of water resources due to natural changes, excessive use of water in the upstream reach, and artificial changes of the channel. Historically, the destruction of ancient cities in the southern Taklimakan Desert is directly related to the cutting off of water supplies. The Wuwei Oasis and the Minqin Oasis are good examples as their development is limited by water resources due to lack of overall consideration of water distribution in upstream and downstream reaches. After the foundation of the PRC, the irrigation area has doubled and redoubled in flat areas in the Wuwei Oasis, together with industrial uses of water, it consumes a large part of the Shiyang River water. With the destruction of upstream water source conservation land-meadow, the water volume flowing out of the valley mouth greatly reduced, and the water flow that could reach the Minqin Oasis decreased rapidly. As a result, underground water was overexploited and therefore groundwater level fell greatly. In the 1990s, the groundwater level has declined to a depth endangering the survival of the whole oasis and has caused rapid development of aeolian desertification.

In the Heihe River Basin, the excessive use of water resources in the upstream reaches greatly reduced the water supply to Ejin Qi in Inner Mongolia. Consequently, ecological balance could not be maintained, lakes dried up, large areas of Populus diversifolia died, and aeolian desertification developed rapidly. After the founding of the PRC, excessive use of water in upstream oases of the Tarim River in southern Xinjiang resulted in the drying up of the Tarim River, the Lop Nur and the Taitema Lake. In downstream reaches of the Tarim River, the underground water level dropped from 3–5 m in the 1950s to 11–13 m in the 1980s. During the period of 1958–1978, the Populus area decreased from 5.4×10^4 hm^2 to 1.64×10^4 hm^2. In northern Xinjiang, the reclamation and irrigation in the upstream basin decreased the downstream discharge, and led to lakes shrinking or even drying up as well as rapid aeolian desertification around the lake.

7.2.4 Indirect influence of human activities on aeolian desertification

7.2.4.1 Changing heat balance, leading to climatic anomalies

There are 4 ways that human activities can influence the heat balance: ① increase of CO_2 in the atmosphere. CO_2 absorbs and reflects long wave radiation, and raises air temperature, which is also known as the greenhouse effect; ② increase of air-borne dust; ③ heat emitted through burning fuel; ④ irrigation, farming and construction changes the underlying surface layer characteristic, and influences heat circulation. Cities are densely populated areas leading to the heat island phenomenon. The temperature in the urban center is generally higher than that in the surrounding countryside.

The greenhouse effect has attracted worldwide concern at present. Before industrialization, the emission rate of CO_2 into the air was equal to its transformation rate. After industrialization, the CO_2 concentration in air increased, thus causing the greenhouse effect. In addition, methane, NO_2, fluorochloroparaffins, and ozone also have greenhouse effects. Rising air temperature speeds up evaporation, and cloud amount and albedo increase and causes self-regulation. However, the general tendency is temperature rises lead to thawing ice, rising sea levels, and atmospheric circulation changes. In some areas, the frequency of flood and drought disasters increases.

Many scientists believe that temperature rises not only has negative effects but also positive effects. The positive effect is the increase in effective accumulative temperature. In China, if temperature rises by 1–2°C, the crop growing period will be prolonged by one month. If the CO_2 concentration increases by 30%, the photosynthetic rate will theoretically increase by 10% and the yield of crops, fruits and pastures will increase. The negative effect is that evaporation will increase by 20%; the northern limit of suitable farming areas will shift from the 400 mm isohyetal line to the 450 mm isohyetal line and about 30×10^8 hm^2 of farmland will be lost; soil salinization will be aggravated; drought frequency will increase. In addition, summer continental temperature rises will speed up; the intensity and destructive power of typhoons will increase. Once the sea level rises, salt tides will intrude, salt-affected soil will increase and this will lead to the destruction of eco-environments in coastal region. About 40%–50% of permafrost will thaw; this will seriously affect the construction of the Qinghai-Tibet Railway and aeolian desertification will occur on the plateau's frozen soil region. In China's desert region, where the evaporation is greater than precipitation, the precipitation increase is limited but evaporation will double and redouble.

7.2.4.2 The feedback effect of vegetation destruction on climate

The studied results showed that vegetation destruction in China's arid, semiarid and parts of semi-humid areas resulting from human activities in modern times has caused changes in surface radiation and heat balance, which leads to climate change and has become one of several important factors currently affecting the climate.

Because of intensive economic activities, vegetation is destroyed and surface albedo increases (Table 7-4). In the lower atmosphere, convection action will weaken, and sinking air mass will enlarge or dismiss. This will lead to air compression, temperature rises and the reduction of relative humidity. Furthermore, it will continually inhibit convection precipitation, thus leading to decreases in precipitation, drought exacerbation and aeolian desertification expansion.

Table 7-4　Mean relative value of radiation equilibrium on a cloudless day with different underlying surface characteristics

Surface characteristics	Shifting dunes	Interdune lowland	Grassland	Fixed dunes	Poplar woods
Total radiation	100.0	100.0	100.0	100.0	100.0
Reflective radiation	38.7	18.1	23.9	18.6	18.4
Effective radiation	33.0	23.1	27.7	28.5	30.5
Radiation equilibrium	28.4	58.8	48.4	52.9	51.1

(Dong Yuxiang, 1995)

According to Shenal and Walli et al. (Charney, 1975), vegetation destruction and reduction of vegetation cover resulting from livestock trampling and overgrazing can influences the development of a condensation nucleus. Some substances secreted by plants can also impact the condensation nucleus. With the degradation of plants, the high-efficiency condensation nucleus is lessened, and the possibility of precipitation also reduces.

Analysis of comprehensive natural and human factors shows that in arid, semiarid and part semi-humid areas in China, fragile ecological environments are full of the basic factors for aeolian desertification. A quantitative study of the Mu Us Sandy Land shows that such factors as precipitation, wind velocity, land productivity and number of livestock have strong correlations with the aeolian desertification degree. Among these factors, the closest correlation is the number of livestock that represent land use intensity with the aeolian desertification degree (Table 7-5).

Table 7-5　Correlation of aeolian desertification and its influencing factors in the Mu Us Sandy Land

Factors	Coefficient of correlation	Level of significance
Precipitation	0.64	0.01
Variability of precipitation	0.66	0.01
Days of heavy wind	0.51	0.1
Mean wind velocity	0.70	0.1
Days of dust-storm	0.51	0.1
Gain of land	0.67	0.1
Number of livestock	0.76	0.01

Source: Chen Weinan, 1989.

Aeolian desertification results in the loss of large areas of arable land and land productivity continually decreases due to deflation of soil nutrients and fine-grained materials. The decrease in land carrying capacity and the continuous increase of human and livestock populations exert great pressure on land resources, leading to excessive use of land resources, and forming a vicious cycle of "excessive population pressure→over use of land resources→land aeolian desertification→land productivity reduction→population pressure increase" (Dong et al., 1995). This results in the increased expansion of aeolian desertified land area, and its degree of intensity increases.

Therefore, aeolian desertification is a process dealing with many issues such as natural, social, and economic factors, among which human factors are the most important. If there was no pressure from human activities, there would be no aeolian desertification under present climatic conditions. Only if the negative influence exerted by humans on the land was removed can the aeolian desertification land recover its productivity. This is the theoretical basis to combat aeolian desertification (Chen, 2001).

7.3　Aeolian desertification development processes

7.3.1　Pattern changes of landform features and landscape types

The changes in aeolian desertification landform features and landscape types is generally divided into 4 processes: sand dune mobilization, grassland shrub desertification, soil coarsening by wind erosion and land cutting by wind erosion (Zhu et al., 1994).

7.3.1.1　Sand dune (sandy land) mobilization process

The process of remobilization of sandy land (dunes) after the vegetation was destroyed in fixed deserts that were formed in the geological time is called sand dune (sandy land) activation (Fig. 7-14).

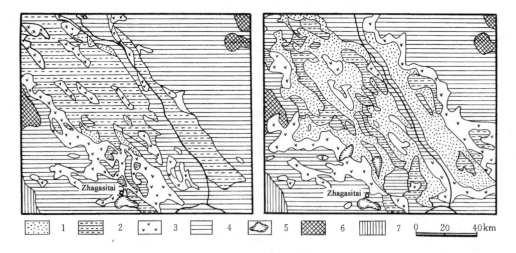

Fig. 7-14　Reactivation of fixed dunes in the Horqin Sandy Land

1. Most severely aeolian desertified land; 2. Severely aeolian desertified land; 3. On-going aeolian desertified land; 4. Latent aeolian desertified land; 5. Lake; 6. Rock mound; 7. Rock hill

Sandy lands in eastern China, no matter how long they were formed, were mostly fixed at the beginning of the Holocene 12,000 years ago. In the historical period, due to the disturbances from human activities, the sand dunes started to activate. This is the reason why eastern sandy lands are regarded as a part of the desert and also regarded as aeolian desertification regions. Sand dune (sandy land) activation is one type of aeolian desertification.

Due to farming reclamation, overgrazing and trampling by livestock, deforestation, and collecting fuel wood, the low vegetation cover cannot protect the land surface, and sand starts to move again. The initial landscape originally consisted of scattered sand, but they gradually connected together, and finally become large tracts of shifting sand. In the east of northern China, especially in the Horqin Sandy Land, the Onqin Daga Sandy Land, and the Hulun Buir Sandy Land, 3–6 layers of paleosols can be found in the dune section, indicating that several fixation and activation processes have occurred in parts of the sandy land due to climate variations. However, as for the modern aeolian desertification process, it was caused by human activities. Therefore, the activation process of dunes (sandy land) is mainly occurring on sandy farmland around arable land, settlements, drinking points, and along traffic routes.

Based on the initial topographic feature, another shape of dune forms through dune activation and the dune's shape change processes. The formation and development of parabolic dunes is the most typical representation. In the eastern sandy lands of northern China, such as Onqin Daga, Ujimqin, Hulun Buir, and Songnen Sandy Land, parabolic dunes are frequently found. Because the whole sandy land is semi fixed, the windward side of fixed dunes is eroded by wind and generates "breach", and then the "breach" gradually develops into blowout. The eroded sands enter the airflow and pass over the dune top to deposit on the leeward side. Without blowouts, the vegetation grows well and shifting sand is sparse. Therefore, the sandy land is still semi-fixed. With the development of blowouts, the convex nose of sand advances downwind, the dune develops a "U" shape and finally is completely eroded, and forms two rows of longitudinal ridges (Fig. 7-15). In the eastern sandy lands of northern China, many fixed dunes show a parabolic shape, indicating that the aeolian desertification development process of parabolic dune may possibly reverse at certain stages with changes in natural conditions and decrease of human pressure.

According to field observations, under the same wind conditions, aeolian desertification lands of different development degrees have quite different sand blown intensity due to the differences in their underlaying surface. From fixed sandy land to mobile sandy land, their roughness may differ by several orders of magnitude due to the difference of vegetation cover and therefore the threshold velocity has a large difference. The threshold velocity of free sand surfaces of mobile sandy land is about 5m/s at a height of 2 m; at the same height, the fixed grass-shrub sandy land with scattered blowouts and a thin layer of sand cover is 8 m/s; and the entirely fixed shrub sandy land cannot produce shifting sand under ordinary wind velocity (the maximum is 18.3 m/s). Under the same sand moving wind conditions, the intensity of sand transport can differ by two orders of magnitude (Table 7-6).

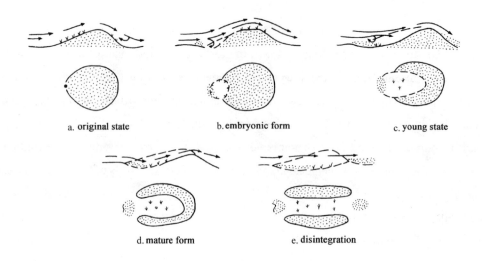

a. original state   b. embryonic form   c. young state

d. mature form   e. disintegration

Fig. 7-15　Formation and development of parabolic dunes

Table 7-6　Sand transport differences in different dune beds (Horqin Sandy Land)

Surface nature	Roughness of bed (cm)	Transport equation of sand	Correlation coefficient	T test (0.01)
Shifting dunes	1.00×9^{-3}	$Q=1.15 \times 9^{-4} V^{4.73}$	0.93	0.83
Semi-shifting dunes	2.850×9^{-1}	$Q=1.10 \times 9^{-5} V^{3.64}$	0.87	0.74
Semi-fixed dunes	1.600	$Q=1.78 \times 9^{-4} V^{3.56}$	0.88	0.71
Fixed dunes	2.330	$Q=1.70 \times 9^{-6} V^{4.57}$	0.83	0.77

Note：① V indicates wind velocity at a height of 2 m above ground. ② Zou Bengong et al., 1995.

The mobile sand beds not only have a greater intensity of sand transport than that of fixed sand beds, but also have more sand moving activities than fixed sand beds, namely, the duration of sand moving activities is much longer than that in the fixed sand beds. Therefore, from the view of wind action, the development rates of various dune activation stages are not the same.

7.3.1.2　Aeolian desertification process for grassland shrubs

The process generally occurs on the sandy or sand-gravel grassland at the outer edge of the sandy land—the region that aeolian desertification first takes place. It is the process of the formation, growth, and sand enrichment of coppice dunes which finally forms sandy deserts. This is the most basic desert formation process in former non-desert regions.

1) The formation of coppice dunes

The natural landscape in the mixed farming-grazing region of northern China is sparse-tree grassland, dry grassland and desert grassland. Once overgrazed, eco-environments degrade, soils become compacted and impoverished, grasses degrade and shrubs invade. In blown sand environments, shrubs trap sand grains carried by wind, the sand grains accumulate around shrubs to form small sand mounds, and these gradually develop into coppice dunes, developing a landscape similar to fixed dunes. when the shrubs die, the sand dunes change into undulated sandy land.

Coppice mound forms include shield, dome, strip and compound shapes.

The three formation conditions for coppice mounds are as follows:

(1) Suitable wind: this kind of wind is strong enough to cause sand flow but does not exceed the sandbreak capacity of shrubs. If the wind force exceeds the shrub's sand protection ability, coppice dunes will be blown away and no longer produce deposition features. No one has yet to predict the upper limit of wind force to produce coppice dunes. Nevertheless, the lower limit is approximately equal to the threshold velocity. In areas where the surface material is mainly composed of fine sand, it is about 5 m/s, 4 m/s for silt-fine sand, and over 7 m/s for coarse sand-gravel surfaces. In summary, the threshold wind velocity for sand movement is related to grain size (Wu, 1987).

(2) Necessary sand source: the primary condition for the occurrence of coppice dunes is the existence of sand-bearing flow, namely located in a blown sand environment. This condition requires a necessary sand source. Nevertheless, the areas that produce current coppice aeolian desertification generally lack sand material, namely, they are located at the edge of sandy land or the middle and front edge of piedmont alluvial and pluvial fans in semiarid areas.

(3) Vegetation: vegetation plays a very important role in the process of coppice dune formation. If the vegetation cover is large enough, wind erosion stops, and the formation process of coppice dunes will also stop. In other words, coppice dune formation processes require appropriate wind intensity, sand source, and vegetation, otherwise, coppice dunes cannot be formed.

2) Shrub and coppice mound types

In various vegetation zones in northern China, various shrubs or subshrubs can form coppice dunes. However, because of habitat requirements of the shrubs themselves, the shrub size differs greatly. The most common plant species in the semiarid areas is *Caragana sinica*, and the most widely distributed species is *C. microphylla*, which occurs over almost all of the semiarid grassland zone. In the west, the common plant species are *C. stenophylla* and *C. tibetica*. The widespread common *Caragana sinica* sand mound is about 1 m in height and 1.5–2 m in diameter. In areas with rich sand sources, their height can reach 1.5 m. In the typical desert sand-gravel grassland in arid zones, the common plant species is dwarf *Reaumuria soongarica* and *Oxytropis aciphylla* shrubs; their canopy diameter is less than 1 m, they have a height of 20–30 cm, and these sand mounds are entirely covered by *Reaumuria soongarica* and *Oxytropis aciphylla* et al. In sandy grasslands in arid zones, the common vegetation mounds are *Nitraria tangutorum* mounds and *Tamarix chinentsis* mounds; these are all large-size coppice dunes. The diameter of the former can reach 3 m, with a height exceeding 1 m, and the maximum height can reach 15 m. *Nitraria tangutorum* has a strong root system and flourishes, but its germination is late in spring and it has few branches. Its sand-binding ability is weak, so *Nitraria tangutorum* mounds exhibit semi-mobile movement in spring. Another characteristic of *N. tangutorum* mound distribution areas is that sand soil texture is fine, mainly consisting of silt, and because of its strong alkalinity, it is often in lake basin depressions. *Tamarix chinentsis* mounds are common on alluvial plains in arid zones. The dense *Tamarix chinentsis* mounds exhibit a fixed or semi-fixed aeolian desertified landscape, and their diameter can reach several meters or tens of meters, a large mound can reach a height of 10 m. In semi-fixed and semi-shifting deserts, the tall sand mounds can restrict sand flow and form circular or semi-circular shifting dunes around them.

In lake basins with good water conditions or depression, *Achnatherum splendens* shrub mounds are common. *Achnatherum splendens* can endure high soil salinity but need certain water conditions. In such damp areas, sand content in blown sand flow is less, so the size of *Achnatherum splendens* sand mounds is not very big, and their diameter is generally tens of centimeters. The highest height is about 50 cm.

Ceratoides latens shrub mounds are also common in arid desert grasslands. *Ceratoides latens* can endure sand burial, and the buried stem can produce new roots and branches. Therefore, the shrub is tall and luxuriant, and its sand-binding function is strong. In areas with an abundant sand supply, dense and big shrub mound groups can form, and develop into a fixed undulating sandy landscape. The biggest can have a diameter of 3 m, with a height of 0.7–0.8 m. The protein content in *Ceratoides latens* shoots and leaves is high and can substitute for fodder. In areas with frequent human activities, *Ceratoides latens* has died out. At present, *Ceratoides latens* is only present in enclosed pastures that are under intentional human protection, such as Red Flag Farm in Darhan Maomingan Qi, Inner Mongolia, but it is still on the verge of death resulting from ineffective protection.

3) Evolution of coppice dunes

According to field observations and wind tunnel experiments, the formation and evolutional processes of coppice dunes can be divided into 4 stages, namely sand strip, sand spit, sand mound and sand heap (Fig. 7-16).

(1) sand strip stage: The shrubs form a sand ridge strip where the ratio between length and width reaches ten times in the direction of the wind. The sand strip is mainly composed of fine-grained materials. The wider ones can also form paired sand strips. With the sedimentation of sand grains, the sand strip stage ends quickly. Because of the short process and lack of stable unidirectional wind, this stage is seldom seen in the field.

(2) sand spit stage: A sand spit is a shortened sand strip and its plane shape is an isosceles triangle with the shrub diameter as the bottom. The aspect ratio is 1 ∶ 5–1 ∶ 10 and the tails start to merge and sand ridges form a lasso. The sand spit is continually shortened and an forms embryonic sand mound. In areas with more unidirectional wind in the spring, young small sand mounds can be found in the field. In the arid grassland, the sand spit's height is generally less than 35 cm. The widest part is 50–60 cm and the length can reach 3–4 m.

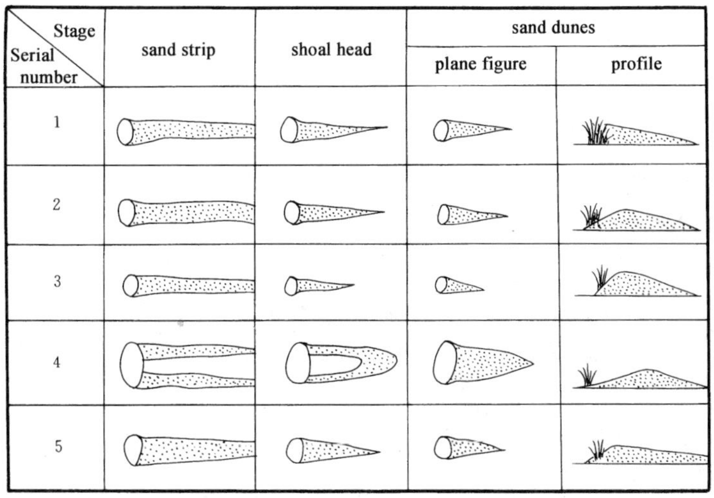

Stage Serial number	sand strip	shoal head	sand dunes	
			plane figure	profile
1				
2				
3				
4				
5				

Fig. 7-16　Process of coppice-dune formation in wind tunnel experiments (Zhu et al., 1994)

(3) sand mound stage: The extended part of the sand spit continually shortens and the height continually increases, and at last forms an egg-like feature with its big head pointing in the main wind direction. The section has a streamline shape, and the length width ratio is less than 2.

(4) sand heap stage: In the sand heap stage, the shape has little change compared to the sand mound, but vegetation entirely covers the dune due to large water storage in the heap; as a result, they grow higher and larger, and finally form mature coppice dunes. Nevertheless, the development of individual coppice dunes is not endless; their largest size is greatly related to habitat conditions such as sand source, water, wind and vegetation types, and shows a very strong zonality. As described above, in semiarid sandy grasslands, *Caragana sinica* heap can grow to 1.5 m in height and 3 m in diameter. However, in arid deserts and gravel grasslands, the heap's height is only 20–30 cm, and the diameter is less than 3 m. Once the heap reaches its highest height, it enters an equilibrium state. At this time, the shrub heap size no longer increases and reaches a well-developed sand heap stage. Namely, erosion occurs on the windward side forming a long gentle slope, and deposition takes place on the leeward side forming a short and steep slope, developing into a barchan-like dune. This is the last stage for the sand heap.

4) Changes in bedding and particle size

By observing the natural exposed profile of shrub sand heaps, the following bedding characteristic can be seen: a, inclined bedding, with the dune top as the center, sand layers dip toward windward and leeward side; b, the bedding dip angle changes gradually, from the bottom to the top of the heap, the dip angle increases gradually, and at the bottom, the dip angle is 7°-9°. At the upper part, the dip angle can reach 18°–22°; c, the bedding can be divided into several sediment groups according to its sediment rhythm and difference of dip angle, and each sediment group also can be divided into several laminae. The dip angle of all these are relatively uniform, indicating that during the coppice dune development process, they experienced environmental variations on a different scale, especially during the periodical changes of climate.

The soil particle size at different sites of coppice dunes is relatively uniform. The normal probability curve shows typical aeolian sand characteristics. The particle-size composition is dominated by saltation sand with diameters between 0.05–0.5 mm, but has a certain orderly change: a, the particle size of the windward slope is obviously larger than that of the leeward slope, and suspended particle content of the leeward slope is obviously increased, this is also reflected in the normal probability curve; b, the particle size at the middle part of the dune is generally much coarser. This is caused by the strong soil-forming action on the stable heap surface, which makes the soil particles fine.

In the southern part of the steppe, residual shrub sand mounds usually remain after the land is reclaimed as farmland. Because farmland provides a sand source, the heap grows quickly and has a large size. The height of farmland shrub heaps is usually 2–2.5 times higher than that of general grassland shrub heaps. Dense shrub heap groups usually can be found in the downwind grassland of the farmland.

7.3.1.3 Soil layer wind erosion and coarsening process

Wind erosion is the process of losing surface material under wind action, and it is the beginning of blown sand activity and aeolian desertification processes. The sub-process of aeolian desertification processes is directly or indirectly caused by wind erosion. The airflow's transportation that carries away sand grain from sandy surfaces is the cause of wind erosion. Coarsening by wind erosion is the process where the surface soil structure is destroyed by wind erosion, it loses fine-grained material loss, coarse material increases, soil fertility reduces, productivity declines, and finally leads to the degradation of the ecosystem and the alteration of the aeolian sand microtopography.

1) Soil erosion and coarsening process

The natural environment including wind force and soil water regime decides the soil grain size that can be carried by wind and may be lost under constant blowing wind. During a study of soil erosion in the Great Plains of the western United States of America, through numerous observations and experiments, W. Chepil called sand grain > 0.84 mm is a non-erosion factor. The results determined in Inner Mongolia by some experts show that the non-erosion factor are grains larger than 1.0 mm. In wind gaps, especially in some erosion valleys, this value is somewhat bigger and in the leeward side, the value is far smaller. Therefore, the non-erosion factor changes with wind force. Therefore, it was called the erosion difficulty factor by some experts in the study of wind erosion in Beijing Plain, and they determined that the lower limit of the erosion difficulty factor in the Beijing Plain is 0.8 mm (Chen et al., 1995). Besides wind force, the climatic factor affecting soil erosion is mainly precipitation. Precipitation influences soil grain movement by increasing water content in the soil. Wind tunnel experiments (He, 1988) showed that only when the water content in sand is below 1% can sand be moved by wind. When a certain amount of water exists in sand, grains are not only linked by water film, but also by electrostatic attraction. When wind force acts on the soil surface, surface soil dries up, sand grains detach from the surface and have rolling and saltation movement.

For a specific site, when soil has suffered erosion, the lost material is mainly the easily-eroded or erodible fraction. But for large regions, the lost material is mainly suspended materials ($d<0.05$ mm), because they can be carried or float out of the region with wind. Therefore, the eroded soil can be divided into 3 parts according to grain sizes. The first part is silt ($d<0.05$ mm) which can rise into the airflow. Because its sinking velocity is less than the upward-pulsed velocity component of common airflow, it can be moved in suspension by airflow, and may be deposited far away from the region to form loess sediment. The second part is erodible fine sands (diameter 0.05–0.08/0.10 mm). Although they move away from the primary surface, they only can roll and saltate, and travel downwards over short distances. They can move back and forth to a certain extent with seasonal wind directional changes and deposit in situ. The accumulated sand forms sand sheets, undulating sandy land, or even develops into sandy lands of varying features. The third part is coarse grain (non-erosion factor). Wind erosion leads to the blowing away of fine materials, leaving coarse grains on the surface.

On the southern side of deserts or sandy lands in China's arid and semiarid areas, there usually exists loess zones, for example at the southern side of the Mu Us Sandy Land is the northern Shaanxi Loess plateau; at the southern side of Hebei Bashang and Ulanqab Meng, Inner Mongolia is the Jinbei Loess Plateau; the Ji-Liao mountain region at the southern side of the Horqin Sandy Land is also loess tableland. The northern side of the loess zone is composed of sandy loess. The reason why we call it sandy loess is that its mean grain size is coarse and contains fine sand > 0.05 mm. The silt and clay particles (< 0.05 mm) in topsoil are continually lost, and form a very thin (2–3 cm) coarsening layer if not disturbed by other factors. The sand content can occupy above half of the total composition in the coarsening layer, and form shifting sand in local places. According to a study, sandy loess first undergoes the process of water erosion-transport-sediment deposits, and thereby increases fine sand content in local places. When fine sand content is less than 60%, through re-sorting by wind, it can form shifting sand (Chen, 1991). Through further water erosion and wind erosion sorting, as the sand grain content in surface layers reaches 75%–95%, the landscape of sand sheets and undulating sandy land develops. However, as described above, shifting sand only occurs in local places on the northern side of the loess zone near the desert, or the transitional zone between deserts and loess. Further southward, shifting sand decreases gradually and finally becomes sand patches. In northern Shaanxi Province, most loess covered by sand is mainly distributed along the Great Wall; south of the Horqin Sandy Land, the boundary of loess land cover sand is very obvious, and it is distributed on the loess tableland south of the Yangxumu River.

In the sandy loess arable land, the coarsening layer thickness is identical with the plow layer, and is usually 15-20 cm in depth. In addition, seasonal thin-layer shifting sand (or sand sheets) only occur in the windy season due to plowing disturbances, unless plowing has been abandoned (usually this aeolian desertified cropland is abandoned); otherwise, it cannot form large tracts of shifting sand. The consequence of wind erosion is the thinning, coarsening and fertility loss of soil (Table 7-7), and this is the typical coarsening process.

Table 7-7　Changes in particle composition of coarse cultivated farmland in sandy loess regions

Location	Depth (cm)	Particle composition/%						
		1–0.25mm	0.25–0.05mm	0.05–0.01mm	0.01–0.005mm	0.005–0.001mm	<0.001mm	>0.05mm
Yanchi	0–15	0.39	61.93	26.21	1.97	3.30	6.20	62.32
	15–35	0	28.29	53.64	3.24	4.91	9.92	26.25
Tongxin	0–15	0	46.34	37.85	4.26	5.99	5.56	46.34
	15–35	0	24.97	53.15	5.27	7.94	8.67	24.97
Haiyuan	0–10	0	28.39	53.92	7.61	4.19	6.29	26.89
	9–30	0	26.89	53.90	7.45	4.92	6.84	90.08
Otog Qi	0–14	27.39	62.69	6.90	1.40	0.27	1.33	90.08
	14–30	30.37	30.84	12.66	1.24	1.91	2.98	60.21

2) Formation of gravel mantle on piedmont diluvial plains or undulating eluvial plain

This kind of plain is mainly distributed at the edges of various deserts in northern China, especially in the middle and southeast parts of the Inner Mongolian Plateau. In these areas, the surface consists of gravels, sand, and fine soil mixtures; wind erosion results in fine particles being blown away, leaving behind coarse grains on the surface, and finally appearing as a land surface similar to gobi pavement.

The most widespread gravel mantle is in the Inner Mongolian Plateau. In this broad and flat plateau surface, there is a thin layer of residual slope sediments. It is a kind of mixture consisting of gravels, sand, and fine soil material. The gravels are distributed uniformly in the non-eroded layer, and through long-term deflation, silt is carried out of the region in the form of dust; most medium-fine sand (including coarse sand in strong wind areas) deposits on leeward slopes or depressions in the form of saltation, and gravel and roughness increase. When surface gravel increases to a certain amount, the surface reaches a relatively stable state, and the land surface develops a landscape similar to gobi, and the coarse surface can protect the subsoil from wind erosion (Fig. 7-17). In the grassland and barren land, the gravel layer is only a thin layer immediately below the surface, its thickness is less than 5 cm, and vegetation still can grow in the coarse sand between gravels. In Darhan Maomingan Qi and Siziwang Qi in the middle and northern parts of the Inner Mongolian Plateau, the dominant plant species are *Stipa gobicam*, *Stipa breviflora*, *Ajania achilloides*, *Artemisia frigida,* and *Cleistogenes sogonica*. The vegetation coverage is only 22%–33%, leaf layer height is only 7 cm, the genital branch height can reach 19 cm, the fresh grass yield is only 804 kg/hm^2, and every 2 hm^2 can raise one sheep. The plow-coarsening layer is generally 15–25 cm in thickness, gravel and coarse sand content increases with increasing cultivation time, and finally it is abandoned because of too many stones. After the land has been abandoned, the gravel mantle develops even more quickly, and then enters a relatively stable stage. In the abandoned farmland, the concentrated gravel layer can reach a thickness of 15–20 cm.

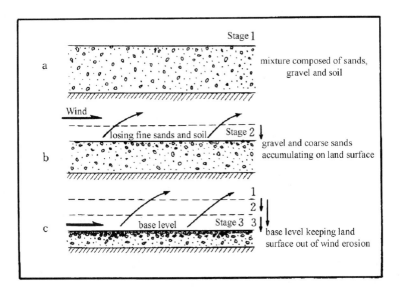

Fig. 7-17　Forming process of coarse gravel wind-eroded gobi land in the top layer

　　In the Houshan region of Ulanqab Meng, Inner Mongolia, fine materials in the farmland are continuously lost due to repeated plowing. The dust particles can be carried over long distances and fine sand is deposited in the leeward side of shrubs to form coppice dunes. The farmland is low and becomes a man-made depression. At the same time, the ridge of field has continuous deposits including sand fixation and accumulation by weeds as well as, gravels deposited by man. In some areas, the ridge of field is 1–1.5 m higher than the farmland. Many experts estimated the wind erosion rate from the height difference between the ridge of field and the farmland and concluded that the annual wind erosion depth is 4–5 cm and thereby yielded an error. From analyses of the coarsening layer and calculation of primary non-erosion factors, it has been found that the annual wind erosion depth in the intensive wind erosion farmland in the Houshan region of Ulanqab Meng is less than 3 cm, generally 1–2 cm. After cultivating for 30–50 years, most farmlands are entirely covered by gravels and therefore abandoned. According to the statistics from related departments, about $4.67 \times 10^4 \, \mathrm{hm}^2$ of farmland were abandoned annually in seriously aeolian desertified regions in the 7 Qis (counties).

　　With the development of gravel mantle, soils quickly become impoverished. From the analyses of soil samples in the farming regions of Bashang, Hebei Province and southern Ulanqab Meng, Inner Mongolia, it has been found that soil organic matter content in newly reclaimed land ranges from 4% to 2%. After long-term fillage and wind erosion over 5–10 years, this farmland becomes coarsening farmland and soil organic matter content decreased to 1% or less, and the lowest value is 0.75%. The decrease of crop yield is more obvious. In the farming regions of Bashang, Hebei

Province and southern Ulanqab Meng, Inner Mongolia, the yield of spring wheat or naked oats in dry farmland is 1,875–2,250 kg/hm^2 in the early years of reclamation. After 9–20 years, the yield decreased in half. In spite of many efforts in agriculture after the founding of the PRC, such as changing the farmers' habit of non-fertilizing cultivation, primarily using ammonium carbonate in potato fields, and gradually applying fertilizer in wheat fields, the yield fluctuated at a level of 525–750 kg/hm^2. In a poor harvest year, the yield was only 230–400 kg/hm^2, an amount only equal to seed amount.

7.3.1.4 Uniform wind dissection of land—the formation process of badlands

This process occurs regionally in gullies and lake depressions in Inner Mongolia. The stratum is relatively uniform and mainly consists of very fine sand, silt or even clay fractions. The land suffered unequal wind cutting and developed small, steep cliffs. This further leads to the generation of eddy current and makes it more uneven. There gradually appears wind eroded residual frusta and residual columns on the land. The general landform is similar to a yardang relief, and the surface is fractural, appearing as a badland landscape.

The residual frusta and residual columns in aeolian desertified regions in northern China are mainly scattered in the sandy lands around the grasslands, especially concentrated on the periphery of the Onqin Daga Sandy Land and south of the Ujimqin Sandy Land. However, their size is limited and rarely develops completely in to landforms such as whale-back yardang. Most of them are only the embryonic form of yardangs. Because of the indistinct definition and abuse of the word "yardang", we have not use the word "yardang" here; only use wind erosion badland to this kind of landform group of residual frusta and residual columns with small steep cliffs and blowout developing nearby.

Field observations show that the tops of residual frusta and residual columns usually have many layers of indistinct chernozem—chestnut paleosols. Vertical joints and large pores develop well in the paleosols, and sometimes root holes and root holes filled with preudomycelium—white sediment can be found. Much evidence shows that the deposition environment of these soil layers was similar to the modern environment: i.e., dry grassland and shrub grassland environments and is dominated by aeolian sediments. The multitude of perennial root grasses and water seepage, as well as the capillary action of underground water causes soil to become loess, which can be called loess rock. The vertical joints and development of large pores are important conditions for the occurrence of small cliffs, residual frusta and residual columns.

The badlands can be divided into 3 types according to their locations:

(1) Depression type: distributed in relatively wide intermontane depression, and consist of lacustrine/marshes facies and aeolian sediment, with more mud-calcium in the strata. The deposit is fine, showing gleying characteristics, and obvious horizontal lamination. The residual frusta are step-like, similar to the "Bailongdui" landform in Xinjiang, as can be seen in Baduandi Farm in Kangbao County, Hebei Province and fine seed farms in western Huade County, Inner Mongolia.

(2) Shallow ravine depression type: mostly occurs in the middle of gently undulating plains in interdune depressions. The fine sediment is dominated by aeolian sediment; after undergoing loess processes, the vertical joint develops well. Usually at the junction spot of two branch ravines, the airflow easily forms eddy currents, and causes the uniform cutting of the land surface to form badlands. The cliff of eroded table and frusta are developed from the vertical joints, and the cliff is nearly upright. In local places, it looks like whale back, and can only be seen as four upright cliffs. Wind-eroded grooves are present below the upright cliff. This kind of badland usually can be found Bayan UL Hot Town and Talinaobao, which is south of the Ujimqin Sandy Land. It can also be found in Dagai ia, Hbade province, and between Number Seven Haxat Village (Fig. 7-18).

(3) Piedmont type: occurs on the windward slope of hills, and mainly consists of slope deposits. The height of the eroded table is usually 1–1.5 m, and some relatively higher ones can reach 2 m. The lower layers below the steep cliff are mingled with gravel, and paleosols parallel to the slope are obvious. This kind of badland can be found near Gonglahutong in Huade County at Erdaohe. As a kind of wind erosion landform, wind plays a decisive role in the final formation process of badland landforms, with the abrasion from sand bearing wind being the most important. Nevertheless, at the beginning of the formation process of some other badlands, there are also other agents. In this case, other agents first generate a small steep bank in the ground, which leads to an eddy current that generates sand flow. The eddy current then cuts the ground uniformly, leading to badland development. In grassland regions of eastern China, most badland formation processes are related to running water cutting initially, especially in the wide shallow ravine-depression type. In the aeolian desertified farming areas where human economic activities are intensive, human activities have already become a special geological agent. Human activities such as excavating sand, digging soil, building roads, and cutting destroy ground surfaces directly, and provide a basis for the development of badlands. In the farming-grazing region south of the Onqin Daga, small patches of badlands can be seen nearby villages; most of them were caused by wind action after excavating soil for building houses.

Fig. 7-18   Wind-eroded badlands (Northern Shangdu County of Inner Mongolia)

Generally the badland can be classified into four types, namely single wind-force type, running water-wind force type, artificial-wind force type and mixed action type. In the modern time when human activities has affected all aspects of the natural evolution process, the human action in the process of aeolian desertification must be emphasized, especially after reclaiming of the steppe areas the farmland soil erosion completely enters a new stage controlled by man power.

The above is a classification of the physical processes of aeolian desertification itself. If classified from the results of aeolian desertification development—the "climax" landscape, it can be classified as: A, aeolian desertification—the climax landscape is dense mobile dunes; B, gravel mantle—the climax landscape is wind-eroded Gobi; C, badland-the climax landscape is wind-eroded badland similar to yardang. Here, we use the biogeographic term "climax", it means that as the natural conditions are not changed greatly, the aeolian desertification process can reach a relatively stable state, or the finally occurred geographical landscape. This usage may be not proper, but in the traditional geography or geographical environment landscape science, there is still no proper term to describe it. As for the aeolian desertification process, the entire loss of land productivity is the final result of the aeolian desertification process. The surface state of this stage is the final geographical landscape.

7.3.2 Biological processes of aeolian desertification

From an ecological standpoint, aeolian desertification includes two processes. One is the eco-environment degradation of soil and microclimate such as continuous worsening of soil moisture, nutrients, soil temperature, air temperature, humidity conditions etc, and this process finally leads to the formation of shifting sand environments. The second is the degradation processes of microorganisms as well as animal and plant communities, such as the reduction of species diversity, decrease of population, lowering of productivity etc, which finally leads to structural turbulence of ecological systems, and causes reduce in function, or even breakdown. These two processes interact with each other, and altogether make up the biological processes of aeolian desertification. Among them soil, plant and soil microorganisms provide mineral nutrients in the ecosystem, as well as being the primary producers and organic matter decomposers, and they play a key role in aeolian desertification and its reversal process. Biological processes of aeolian desertification introduced in this section refers to the degradation process of soil environments, soil microorganisms and plant communities.

7.3.2.1 Soil environment changes in the aeolian desertification process

Soil is the basis for the existence of all terrestrial organisms. Especially for plants, soil not only plays a role in fixing of plants, but also provides water and nutrients for plants. Therefore, for plants, the soil environment and the supply of water and nutrients are directly associated with their survival and reproduction. However, during the aeolian desertification process, soil and water conditions are worsening due to soil erosion and deposition.

1) Change of soil mechanical composition

Owing to wind erosion and sand deposition, soil mechanical composition is constantly changing (Zhao, 1993; Feng, 1993). Table 7-8 shows the changes of soil mechanical composition of sandy grasslands during the sandy desertification process. It can be seen that the sand content of sandy grasslands is relatively high, the sand content with particle size ⩾0.05 mm is usually 85%–95%; but soil particle size ⩽0.01 mm is very rare, with only 1%–2%. With the development of aeolian desertification, the content of grains ranging from 0.25 mm to 1.0 mm increases from 14.1% to 66.8%, a 3.73 times increase the content of grains <0.25 mm exhibits an obvious decreasing trend. Especially clay fractions <0.005 mm decreases from 6.61% to 0.15% with a decrease of 97.7%. This suggests that during the grassland aeolian desertification process with the continuous loss of large amount of fine-fractions, the clay content decreases and coarse sand content increases, and grassland soil obviously coarsens.

Table 7-8　Particle composition in soils of aeolian desertified lands with different levels of severity

	soil particle size distribution (%)					
	1–0.25mm	0.25–0.05mm	0.05–0.01mm	0.01–0.005mm	<0.005mm	Loss by HCl
Latent aeolian desertified land	14.10	74.01	5.58	0.59	0.61	1.75
Slight aeolian desertified land	22.77	69.06	5.72	0.12	little	1.43
Moderately aeolian desertified land	42.70	54.9	1.44	0.17	0.02	0.69
Severely aeolian desertified land	44.19	53.76	0.82	0.01	0.55	0.67
Most severely aeolian desertified land	66.81	33.71	0.42	0.01	0.15	0.50

Farmland erosion can not only lead to soil coarsening but also leads to sand deposition on the downwind side of farmlands and grasslands. Table 7-9 shows the changes of soil mechanical composition on farmlands during aeolian desertification process in sandy areas. The soil mechanical composition has obvious changes. Its changes are characterized by the decrease of clay content and increase of sand and is similar to sandy grassland. Furthermore, the effect of wind erosion is greater than sand deposition. This shows that the content of clay (<0.005 mm) in the wind-eroded land is obviously lower than sand-deposited land, the content of sand ranging from 0.05 mm to 1.0 mm is obviously higher than that in sand-deposited land, and the soil layer of farmlands in the desert area is thin. The underlying parent material is deep loose sandy sediment, and strong wind erosion often leads to destruction of this layer and exposure of the underlying sediments. Moreover, sand that has been blown up beats against the crops injures shoots and leaves, and the crops tend to die. However, the sand deposited on the ground surface usually only increases sand content in the plow layer, thickens plough pans, but does not destroy the plough layer. As for some clay soil, proper sand cover can increase soil aeration and increase crop yield. In the Horqin Sandy Land, farmers plow the clay farmland in autumn, which results in sand deposited on it in winter, which increases crop yield (Zhao, 1993).

Table 7-9　Particle composition in soils of aeolian desertified farmlands suffering from wind erosion

Site types	Wind-eroded lands			Shared border	Accumulating sand lands			Normal farmland
Serial number of quadrat	1	2	3	4	5	6	7	8
Intensity of desertification	Severe	Medium	Slight	Slight	Slight	Medium	Slight	None
0.05–1.00 mm	81.05	81.34	83.94	66.86	65.45	72.81	68.57	71.40
Mean		82.11		66.86		68.94		71.40
0.05–0.005 mm	13.53	12.89	8.58	24.13	23.54	16.47	18.42	19.90
Mean		11.67		24.13		19.47		19.90
<0.005 mm	4.01	4.16	5.69	6.50	8.55	9.74	9.92	9.92
Mean		4.62		9.92		9.40		9.92

2) Change of soil moisture content

The changes of soil mechanical composition inevitably alter the soil holding-capacity of water and nutrients, and change water and nutrient content in the soil. Table 7-10 shows the comparison of water content in aeolian desertified farmland and non-aeolian desertified farmland. It suggests that wind erosion and sand deposition cause an obvious decrease of water content in the plow layer (0–30 cm). For example, soil moisture content of wind-eroded farmland is 18.3% less than the non-desertified farmland and that in sand covered land is 10.7% less than the non-desertified farmland after rain. In the drought period, water content of wind-eroded farmland is 53.6% less than non-desertified farmland and that in sand covered land is 25.2% less than the non-desertified farmland. Furthermore,

Table 7-10　Soil moisture content in aeolian desertified farmlands and non-aeolian desertified farmlands (%)

Site types		Wind-eroded lands			Shared border	Accumulating sand lands			Normal farmland
Serial number of quadrat		1	2	3	4	5	6	7	8
Intensity of desertification		Severe	Medium	Slight	Slight	Slight	Medium	Slight	None
Wet period	0–5cm	23.1	22.3	23.6	22.6	21.9	21.4	21.5	22.1
	5–10 cm	22.4	22.5	25.7	25.8	25.1	23.5	23.2	24.2
	10–30 cm	23.3	23.8	26.6	33.0	34.6	32.3	29.9	40.7
	Average of layers	22.9	22.9	25.3	27.1	27.2	25.7	24.9	29.0
	Average of types		23.7		27.1		25.9		29.0
Dry period	0–5cm	2.98	3.47	3.94	6.11	5.47	3.16	3.73	5.57
	5–10 cm	4.67	6.69	8.77	11.64	8.59	5.81	8.34	10.34
	10–30 cm	8.30	6.15	11.64	24.34	22.81	16.42	17.05	24.69
	Average of layers	5.32	5.43	8.11	14.03	12.29	8.46	9.71	13.56
	Average of types		6.29		14.03		10.15		13.56

the more severe the wind erosion and sand deposition, the higher the decrease in soil moisture content. This suggests that with the occurrence and development of farmland aeolian desertification, the water conditions of farmland soil deteriorates obviously. Especially under arid conditions, the soil water condition is very poor in aeolian desertified farmlands and cannot satisfy the need of crop growth at all. Therefore, the crop yields decrease greatly or even produce no yield. Hence, the severely aeolian desertified farmland is not suitable for planting rain-fed crops (Zhao, 1993; Zhao, 1999).

During the aeolian desertification process, the trend of dune-grassland water regime change is obviously different from that in farmland soil. In dunefield lands, usually with the occurrence of aeolian desertification, there is a trend as vegetation decreases for soil water content to increase. Namely, with the occurrence and development of aeolian desertification, the soil water content in the sandy land tends to improve. Long-term field observations show that with soil water content in the 20–200 cm surface layer, is mobile dune > semi-mobile dune > semifixed dune >fixed dune. Among them, the soil water content in mobile dunes is 1.5%–2.0% higher than fixed dune. One of the reasons for this phenomenon is the low water-holding capacity of blown sand soil, which generally ranges from 3% to 4%. In the fixed sandy land, soil water content decreases greatly due to large amounts of transpiration by plants and evaporation from the land surface, and soil usually forms a dry sand layer below the root layer in arid years or seasons. However, in the mobile sandy land, transpiration by plants is very low, and plants are sparse plant or nonexistent. Furthermore, the land surface is usually covered by a dry sandy layer that can effectively decrease evaporation, and the soil water content is relatively high. However, this is only for the aeolian sandy soils, and it does not mean that aeolian desertification is favourable to improve the soil water regime. In fact, this is a characteristic of sandy soil formation and development at a specific stage when mobile blown sand soils evolve to sandy chestnut soil and sandy meadow soil etc. After a long-term grass-growing process, the water-holding capacity can obviously improve due to the increase of clay and organic matter content in the soil. The farmland soils listed in Table 9-8 come from reclaimed sandy meadow soil. Under normal conditions, the soil water content is about 20%, or 5–6 times as high as the aeolian sandy soil. During the aeolian desertification process, soil water environments for this kind of grassland tend to deteriorate rather than improve. Therefore, it is not acceptable to bring forward a viewpoint that the development of aeolian desertification is favorable for improving the soil water regime, or that we should conserve a section of mobile dunes for storing water.

3) Changes in soil nutrients

Large amounts of data shows that along with land aeolian desertification, soil nutrient conditions also changes obviously (Feng, 1993; Zhao, 1999a). Table 7-11 shows the nutrient variations in sandy grassland during the aeolian desertification process. It suggests that on a severely aeolian desertified land surface (0–30 cm), the contents of soil organic matter, N, P_2O_5 and K_2O are only

Table 7-11　Changes in soil nutrient content in during the aeolian desertification process in sandy grasslands

Aeolian desertification types	Depth (cm)	Organic content (%)	Contents of nutrient (%)		
			N	P_2O_5	K_2O
Latent aeolian desertified lands	0–31	1.40	0.047	0.074	2.88
	31–67	0.46	0.019	0.031	2.84
	37–103	0.18	0.005	0.035	3.04
Moderate aeolian desertified lands	0–28	0.41	0.019	0.018	2.64
	28–60	0.20	0.036	0.011	2.88
	60–90	0.10	0.019	0.01	3.18
Severe aeolian desertified lands	0–30	0.11	0.004	0.011	2.29
	30–50	0.08	0.007	0.012	1.93
	50–100	0.09	0.063	0.015	1.55

7.9%, 8.5%, 14.9% and 79.5% respectively, compared to potential aeolian desertified land. The situation in the lower layer is relatively better, which is 17.4%, 36.8%, 38.7% and 68% respectively. One reason for this is that a large amount of organic matter is blown away, leading to significant decreases of soil nutrients during the aeolian desertification process. Another reason is that soil water and nutrient retention ability is weakened, which leads to soil nutrient loss after soil coarsening. This suggests that the damage of aeolian desertification to sandy grassland soil fertility is very severe, and it not only influences surface soil, but also the sub-soil.

During the aeolian desertification process, like sandy grassland, the soil nutrient in farmland also shows a notable decreasing trend. However, the extent of decrease is generally less than that in sandy grasslands. Table 7-12 shows the changes of nutrients in the plough layer of farmland during the aeolian desertification process. Calculated from Table 7-12, the ratio of mean organic matter content of normal farmland, sand-covered land and wind eroded land is 1 ∶ 0.81 ∶ 0.44, and the ratio of total nitrogen is 1 ∶ 0.83 ∶ 0.50; the ratio of total phosphorous is 1 ∶ 0.86 ∶ 0.75; the ratio of total potassium is 1 ∶ 1.02 ∶ 1.09; the ratio of available nitrogen is 1 ∶ 0.48 ∶ 0.40; the ratio of available phosphorous is 1 ∶ 1.17 ∶ 0.96; the ratio of available potassium is 1 ∶ 0.88 ∶ 0.64. All of these ratios indicate that aeolian desertification has quite different influences on different soil nutrient elements. It has little influence on total potassium and available phosphorus, and the total potassium somewhat increases. It has the greatest influence on available nitrogen, and the decrease of available nitrogen content is the largest. In addition, the results in table 7-11 also indicate that the effect of wind erosion on soil nutrients is stronger than that on sand deposition. Correlation analyses show that the change of soil organic matter content is related closely with clay content, with a correlation coefficient of 0.94. The soil's available nutrient content is closely related with soil organic matter content, with a correlation coefficient of 0.94. This shows that when the clay is blown away, the soil organic matter is also greatly lost.

In the aeolian desertification process, along with soil coarsening, soil bulk density, pH value and soil temperatures also change (Zhao, 1993; Feng, 1993). However, according to observations, their extent of change is little and has a relatively weak influence on plants.

Table 7-12　Change of nutrients in farmland soil during the aeolian desertification process

Site types		Wind-eroded lands			Shared border	Accumulating sand lands			Normal farmland
Serial number of quadrat		1	2	3	4	5	6	7	8
Intensity of aeolian desertification		Severe	Medium	Slight	Slight	Slight	Medium	Slight	None
Organic matter (g/kg)		2.45	3.66	5.22	4.88	6.28	7.50	6.86	8.50
Mean (mg/100g)			3.78		4.80		6.88		8.50
Total nutrient content (g/kg)	N	0.15	0.24	0.29	0.29	0.36	0.42	0.36	0.46
	Mean		0.23		0.29		0.38		0.46
	P_2O_5	0.35	0.38	0.40	0.40	0.45	0.44	0.44	0.51
	Mean		0.38		0.40		0.44		0.51
	K_2O	29.5	28.0	28.0	26.3	26.3	26.3	28.0	26.3
	Mean		28.5		26.3		26.8		26.3
Available nutrient content (mg/kg)	N	23.6	25.5	31.4	41.0	42.1	22.7	31.6	66.5
	Mean		26.8		41.0		32.1		66.5
	P_2O_5	6.3	10.6	12.7	15.6	11.6	13.4	10.9	10.3
	Mean		9.9		15.6		12.0		10.3
	K_2O	65.0	73.0	83.0	83.0	90.0	116.0	100.0	116.0
	Mean		74.0		83.0		102.0		116.0

7.3.2.2　Change in soil microorganisms and soil animals during the aeolian desertification process

Soil microorganisms and soil animals are the organisms dwelling in soil, and they are most sensitive to soil's environmental changes. With land aeolian desertification, the population of soil microorganism and soil animal also changes obviously and finally forms communities adapted to an aeolian desertification environment. Therefore, the variations in soil microorganisms and soil animals is an important part of the biological process of aeolian desertification.

1) Change of soil microorganisms during the aeolian desertification process

Although the natural conditions of sandy land is atrocious, there still exists a certain number of microorganisms. They mainly include three major groups, namely bacteria, actinomycete and fungi, and bacteria is dominant (Lv, 1999; Gu, 2000). With the development of aeolian desertification, the number of actinomycete, fungi and spore decreases rapidly, but the number of bacteria changes relatively little (Table 7-13). Influenced by aeolian desertification, the bacteria number tends to decrease in the surface layer but increase in lower layers. It suggests that with aeolian desertification, soil aeration tends to improve and benefits the growth of aerobes. However, owing to the worsening of the surface soil environment, the densely distributed bacteria layer shifts downwards.

Table 7-13 Change of microorganism number in sand dunes during the aeolian desertification process

Types	depth (cm)	Total microorganism number (10^3 N/ g dry soil)	bacteria (10^3 N/ g dry soil)	actinomycete (10^3 N/ g dry soil)	fungi (10^3 N/ g dry soil)	spore (10^3 N/ g dry soil)
	0–25	4975	4444	528	2.0	215
Fixed dunes	25–50	1036	978	58	0.0	68
	total	6011	5422	586	2.0	283
	0–25	4464	3974	204	1.4	90
Semi-fixed dunes	25–50	1930	1604	47	0.8	57
	total	6394	5578	251	2.2	147
	0–25	3582	3538	44	0.7	15
Shifting dunes	25–50	1505	1470	37	0.1	3
	total	5087	5008	81	0.8	18

With the development of aeolian desertification, the microbial physiological groups also change. Table 7-14 shows that from fixed dunes to mobile dunes, the total number of nitrogen fixing microorganisms in 0–50 cm soil layer decreases by 37.6%, nitrifying bacteria decrease by 99.2%, and cellulose decomposing bacteria decrease by 73.3%. Although the number of silicate bacteria in mobile dunes is 33.4% higher than that in fixed dunes, it is 28.2% less than that in semifixed dunes. The decrease of all sorts of bacteria mainly occurs in the 0–25 cm layer and that in the lower layer (25–50 cm) changes relatively little. The decrease of these microorganisms in soil also indirectly reflects the deterioration of soil nutrients. It also suggests that the influence of aeolian desertification on soil microorganisms is more severe in the surface layer than in lower layers (Lv, 1999).

Table 7-14 Changes of microbial physiological groups during the aeolian desertification process

Types	Depth (cm)	nitrogen fixing microorganism			Nitrobacteria (N/g dry soil)	Cellulose decomposing bacteria (N/g dry soil)	Silicate bacteria (N/g dry soil)
Fixed dunes		Total (N/g dry soil)	Azotobacter (N/g dry soil)	Oligonucleotide (N/g dry soil)			
	0–25	666,755	58,688	465,347	1,442	4,005	89,823
	25–50	128,010	15,600	112,410	0	0	20,126
Semi-fixed dunes	total	794,765	74,288	577,757	1,442	4,005	109,949
	0–25	617,683	54,421	563,262	521	1,195	173,375
	25–50	140,706	5,051	135,655	31	0	30,852
Shifting dunes	total	758,389	59,472	698,917	552	1,195	204,227
	0–25	378,513	11,960	366,553	12	1,070	129,892
	25–50	117,366	5,751	111,615	0	0	16,771
	total	495,879	17,711	418,168	12	1,070	146,663

In the aeolian desertification process, with the decrease of microorganism number, the biomass of soil microorganisms also decreases (Table 7-15). Compared to fixed sandy land, the bacteria biomass in mobile sandy land decreases by 97.5% and the biomass of filiform microorganism decreases by 89.6%. Nevertheless, the mean individual number tends to increase, especially in mobile dunes. The mean individual mass is obviously higher than that in fixed dunes. Further study is needed to understand whether the number of microorganism larva in fixed sandy land is higher or the size of microbial individuals in shifting sandy land is much greater. However, there is no doubt that the soil environment in mobile dunes is worse than fixed dunes. In this atrocious soil environment, decreasing individual number and increasing individual volume and mass are favorable for survival and multiplying microorganism populations.

Table 7-15　Biomass of soil microorganism and individual weight in different types of aeolian desertified lands

Items	Fixed dunes			Semifixed dunes			Shifting dunes		
	Biomass (10^{-5}g/g dry soil)	Number (10^{-6}/g)	Individual weight (g/N)	Biomass	Number	Individual weight	Biomass	Number	Individual weight
Bacteria	5.51	172.37	0.00320	0.76	23.72	0.003,20	0.14	4.24	0.003,30
Filiform microorganism	2.02	0.44	0.45969	0.42	0.13	0.323,08	0.21	0.003	7.000
Total	7.53	172.81	0.00436	1.18	23.85	0.004,94	0.35	4.24	0.008,25

2) Changes in the soil animal community during the aeolian desertification process

With the occurrence and development of aeolian desertification, the growth of vegetation becomes poor, land surface is exposed, and aeolian sand activities are exacerbated. On the other hand, the deterioration of soil nutrients, temperature, and water regimes alters the living environment of soil animals, leading to changes in biological species and population density. Table 7-16 lists the major animal species in grasslands with different degrees of grazing and different degrees of aeolian desertification in the Horqin Sandy Land. It indicates that in the severely aeolian desertified and heavily grazed grassland, the soil animal number is the lowest, at only 83 per quadrat. In the slightly aeolian desertified and slightly grazed grassland, the number is the largest, 223 per quadrat; and the latter is 2.7 times higher than the former. Under livestock exclusion and moderately grazed conditions, the major animal number is roughly equal, 192 and 198 respectively. Compared to other grazing conditions, the decreased soil animal species in severely aeolian desertified areas are mainly Scarabaeoidea, Carabidaae, Elateridae, Homoptera, Formicidae, Hemiptera, Lepidoptera; and the increased animal species are large Formicidae, Curculionidae, and Coccinellidae. With population changes, the dominant populations also change greatly; the Scarabaeoidea + Formicidae + Hemiptera are dominant in the closed grassland; Scarabaeoidea + Formicidae + Carabidaae prevail in the slightly grazed grassland; Scarabaeoidea + Formicidae + Carabidaae in the moderately grazed grassland; Scarabaeoidea + Carabidaae in the severely grazed grassland. This suggests that in the grassland aeolian desertification process, soil animal number decreased but the dominance of Scarabaeoidea did not change and other dominant species were gradually replaced (Guan, 1999; Liu, 2000).

Aeolian desertification also leads to a decease in population and biomass of soil animals. Table

7-17 and 7-18 indicate that, except for the diptera animal, all of the soil animal density has decreased in severely aeolian desertified grassland owing to overgrazing, of which large animals decreased by 53%; ant family and nematode decreased between 76% to 81.4%. But the biomass change is different from the population density change: the biomass of Formicidae and Hemiptera animals decreased with increasing aeolian desertification degree, the biomass of Scarabaeoidea, Carabidaae, Diptera does not decrease but increases, and the biomass of big-middle size animals also increases. This suggests that with the development of aeolian desertification and deterioration of the soil environment, soil animal species decrease, density declines, but their size increases. It is an adaptation strategy of soil animals turing adverse conditions such as environmental deterioration and decreasing resource. This is important for population stabilization and reproduction.

Table 7-16　Change of soil animal community in sandy pastures with different aeolian desertification levels of severity (Unit:N)

Grazing aeolian intensity	Severe grazing	Moderate grazing	Slight grazing	Enclosure
Intensity of aeolian desertification	Severe	Slight	Micro	No aeolian desertification
Scarabaeoidea imago	9**	4	2	2
Scarabaeoidea larva	13**	38**	57**	36**
Carabidaae larva	10**	9*	22**	19**
Carabidaae imago	7*	19*	22*	7*
Cicindelidae larva	3*	2	0	0
Cicindelidae imago	0	0	5	0
Tenebrionidae imago	0	3	0	3
Tenebrionidae larva	1	4	0	8*
Coccinellidae imago	8*	1	5	2
Curculionidae imago	0	3	2	2
Curculionidae larva	5*	2	0	1
Buprestidae larva	0	0	1	0
Elateridae imago	0	1	1	2
Elateridae larva	5*	10*	6	14*
Staphylinidae	2	2	2	5
Homoptera	0	0	1	2
Tipulidae	2	0	0	0
Tabanidae	5	2	0	6*
Diptera	3	13*	8*	2
Formicidae imago	6	50**	31**	38**
Formicidae larva	0	13*	16*	2
Hemiptera	2	14*	21*	27**
Lepidoptera larva	1	2	12*	8*
Scutigeromorpha	0	0	0	1
Order Araneae	1	6	7*	2
Total	83	198	223	192

Note：①*Co-dominant species. ** Dominant species. Quadrat area：sampling quadrat of bigger soil animals, 0.25 m (length)×0.25 m (width) ×0.30 m (depth), sampling using 50 ml ring sampler for medium and small soil animals. ② After Guan Hongbin et al., 1999.

Table 7-17   Dominant population density of soil animals in grasslands with different aeolian desertification levels of severity (N/m^2)

Grazing intensity	Severe grazing	Moderate grazing	Slight grazing	Enclosure
Intensity of aeolian desertification	Severe	Slight	Little	No aeolian desertification
macrofauna	24	53.6	59.6	51.2
Scarabaeoidea	6.4	12.0	15.6	10.8
Carabidaae	4.4	7.6	11.6	6.8
Formicidae	2.0	16.8	12.4	10.8
Hemiptera	0.4	3.6	5.6	7.2
Diptera	2.8	4.4	2.4	2.4
nematode	79,388.5	174,318.5	204,993.6	330,853.5
acarus	356.7	764.5	1,273.9	356.7
Total	79,785.2	175,180.8	206,374.7	331,297.0

Table 7-18   Change of dominant population biomass and individual weight of soil animals in grasslands with different aeolian desertification levels of severity

Intensity of aeolian desertification	Severe		Slight		Little		No aeolian desertification	
groups	Biomass (g/m^2)	Individual weight (g/m^2)	Biomass	Individual weight	Biomass	Individual weight	Biomass	Individual weight
macrofauna	1.028	0.042,8	1.000	0.018,7	1.736	0.029,1	1.008	0.019,7
Scarabaeoidea	0.684	0.106,9	0.572	0.047,7	0.560	0.035,9	0.356	0.033,0
Carabidaae	0.200	0.045,5	0.156	0.020,5	0.208	0.017,9	0.112	0.016,5
Formicidae	0.004	0.002,0	0.012	0.000,7	0.024	0.001,9	0.036	0.003,3
Hemiptera	0.004	0.010,0	0.048	0.013,3	0.094	0.039,2	0.056	0.007,8
Diptera	0.308	0.110,0	0.060	0.013,6	0.024	0.010,0	0.044	0.018,3
Total	2.228	0.055,7	1.848	0.018,9	2.646	0.024,7	1.612	0.018,1

7.3.2.3   Vegetation changes during the aeolian desertification process

The most obvious visual characteristic of biological processes of aeolian desertification is rapid vegetation degradation and the invasion of psammophytes. Vegetation degradation in sandy areas differs from that in other areas. After developing to a certain stage, regardless of the causes, it becomes closely related to aeolian desertification. They mutually activate and accelerate each other's development, and this leads to further exacerbation of vegetation degradation and aeolian desertification. Therefore, once the blown sand environment has formed or vegetation cover decreases to a certain degree, land surfaces will be exposed, and the aeolian desertification process will aggravate itself.

1) The regressive succession of vegetation in the aeolian desertification process

In the aeolian desertification process, vegetation degradation is a kind of regressive succession. When vegetation in sandy land is disturbed and the disturbing intensity is stronger than the adjustment ability of vegetation, the vegetation's stability is offset and regressive succession takes place. Regressive succession can occur at any stages of succession, but the succession direction, speed and plasticity is greatly influenced by the surrounding environment, vegetation initial state and interference force. Therefore, the vegetation succession process varies greatly in different areas due to different driving factors (Liu Xinmin, 1996; Huang Zhaohua, 1992).

In blown sand regions of the Loess Plateau, the vegetation in semiarid areas is grassland vegetation with gramineous grasses as the dominant species. However, in arid areas, the grassland vegetation is desert steppe vegetation with dwarf grasses and shrubs as dominant species. The vegetation desertification process resulting from overgrazing has large differences. The grassland vegetation degradation process can be divided into 8 stages. In the initial stage of aeolian desertification, the vegetation gradually changes from densely bunched grasses to dwarf sparse grasses and then to dwarf subshrubs. In the middle stage of aeolian desertification, dwarf subshrubs give way to xeric shrubs and are further replaced by communities dominated by biennial herbs. In the severe stage of aeolian desertification, vegetation degrades into herbs dominated by rhizome-psammophytes and further degrades into root-sprout-psammophilic herbs + psammophilic subshrubs. In the later stage of aeolian desertification, the loess surface has been covered with a thick layer of shifting sand and vegetation consisting of psammophilic subshrubs. If the land is continually overgrazed, psammophilic subshrubs will entirely die away and finally will be dominated by annual pioneer herb communities. Regressive succession of vegetation in desert steppes can be roughly divided into 5 stages. In the initial stage of aeolian desertification, the vegetation gradually changes from moderate closed bunched grasses + dwarf subshrubs to dwarf subshrubs+hypo-weeds; in the middle stage of aeolian desertification, the vegetation changes to bulb geophyte herbs and further development produces creeping stem psammophyte communities. At the severe aeolian desertification stage, subshrub communities occur; at the very severe aeolian desertification stage, they give way to annual psammophilic pioneer plants (Zhang, et al., 1998).

2) Spatial evolution laws of sandy land vegetation during the aeolian desertification process

In aeolian desertified areas, owing to the influences of various natural factors such as shifting sand activities, aeolian sand landforms, and variations of groundwater level, vegetation exhibits an obvious spatial evolution. For example, in sand-damaged grassland, from unaffected areas to severely damaged areas, the vegetation shows a significant gradient change. This change varies greatly in the sand-covered and sandless zones. Several common spatial evolution laws of vegetation are introduced as follows.

(1) Vegetation evolution in the fixed sandy land and mobile sandy land. In desert regions, vegetation in the fixed sandy lands is generally normal vegetation or slightly degraded vegetation, and the number of plant species, plant density, vegetation cover, grass height and aboveground biomass are relatively higher (Table 7-19). Once aeolian desertification occurs, the number of plant species, plant density, vegetation cover, grass height and aboveground biomass obviously decrease. However, the different communities decrease to a different extent due to their different sensitivities

to aeolian desertification. The plant species and plant density of shrub and subshrub communities are very sensitive to aeolian desertification. When the fixed sandy land turned into semifixed land, the plant species of shrubs and subshrubs decreased by 40% and 70.1%, respectively. When the sandy land turned into semi-mobile sandy land, the decrease in vegetation cover is not obvious. On the contrary, the above ground biomass exceeds that in the fixed sandy land. Most notably, mean grass height in semi-mobile sandy land is 2.95 times that of the fixed sandy land. The reason is that some psammophilous shrubs and subshrubs that are able to tolerate sand burial invade semi-mobile sandy lands, which enhances the height and yield. As for herb communities, the slight aeolian desertification has little influence on vegetation, and moderate aeolian desertification can significantly reduce various indexes. The reason why there exists such difference between two communities is that the status, function and stability of the edificators or dominant species of various communities are different (Zhao, 1993).

Table 7-19　Vegetation change from fixed dunes to shifting dunes

	Fixed dunes		Semi-fixed dunes		Semi-shifting dunes		Shifting dunes	
	Number	(%)	Number	(%)	Number	(%)	Number	(%)
Shrub and subshrub communities								
Plant species	25	100.0	15	60.0	9	36.0	3	12.0
Density (plant/m^2)	164	100.0	49	29.9	6.9	4.2	18.5	22.3
Height (cm)	7.0	100.0	12.8	182.9	20.7	295.7	5.7	22.4
Cover (%)	70	100.0	55	78.6	53.3	76.1	9.5	23.3
Aboveground Biomass (g/m^2)	465	100.0	435	93.5	495	106.5	79	23.2
Herb communities								
Plant species	18		17	94.4	10	55.6	2	
Density (plant/m^2)	1848		824	44.6	239	12.9	22	1.2
Height (cm)	4.5		5.9	131.1	17.2	382.2	11.4	253.3
Cover (%)	72.7		52.3	71.9	32.3	44.4	7	9.6
Aboveground Biomass (g/m^2)	365.1		216.2	59.2	127.5	34.9	38.1	

Note: shrub and subshrub communities, C. microphylla+*Artemisia halodandron*+weed, herb communities, common lespedeza +*Setaria viridis*+ *Chloris virgata* Swartz.

(2) Vegetation evolution on leeward and windward slopes of sand dune. In China's semiarid areas, the prevailing wind in most sandy lands is the northwest wind. Under the action of wind, surface sand of windward slopes is constantly exposed and blown away, and deposited at the leeward slope, leading to dune migration from west to east. Because of continual wind erosion, coupling with poor soil water and temperature conditions, the vegetation on the windward slope is relatively short and sparse. However, on the leeward slope of dunes, continual deposition of sand also brings large amounts of plant seeds with it. Together with the better water and heat conditions on the leeward slope, it is easy for the vegetation to establish and grow there, which leads to plants spreading from interdune

depressions towards leeward slopes and gradually covering windward slopes of dunes. The plant species, grass cover, and grass height change obviously (Table 7-20) (Liu, 1996).

Table 7-20　Vegetation change from windward slope to leeward slope of dunes

	Leeward slope				Dune top			Windward slope			
	Slope foot	Lower	Middle-lower	Middle	Middle-upper	Upper	Top	Top	Upper	Middle-upper	Middle
Number of quadrat	1	2	3	4	5	6	7	8	9	1	11
Plant species	19	16	6	6	6	7	5	5	4	3	1
Cover (%)	94	40	38	36	46	13	40	15	3.2	0.4	0.1
Density (plant/m^2)	1,187	382	46	35	27	9	4	38	16	11	2
Height(cm)	26.8	14.0	23.7	36.6	30.5	19.2	19.1	14.4	7.5	4.8	3.0
Total frequency (%)	221	155	111	84	109	42	67	37	9	5	2
Biomass (g/m^2)	85.4	77.5	126.0	130.0	205.0	52.8	114	35.8	4.2	0.5	0.1

(3) Change of vegetation in interdune waterlogged depressions. In such semiarid areas as the Mu Us and Horqin Sandy Lands, many interdune depressions are permanently or seasonally waterlogged due to the shallow groundwater table. In waterlogged depressions, reeds or cattails grows vigorously and their height is usually 100–150 cm. The coverage can reach 80%–90%. This is one of the main pastures for farmers and herdsmen in the sandy area. However, because water conditions around the waterlogged depressions changes quickly, the vegetation exhibits an obvious transition from nygrophytes to mesophytes and xerophytes. Vegetation changes in waterlogged depressions in and around shifting and semi-shifting sandy lands is presented in Table 7-21. Obviously, plant species grown below the water surface are relatively fewer, but the indexes such as vegetation cover, density, and height are relatively higher. At the edge of waterlogged depressions, the plant species grown above the water surface increase quickly, but the indexes such as vegetation cover, density, and height decrease obviously. At a height of 7–8 m above water level, due to obvious decreases in soil water content, the vegetation exhibits a great difference compared to that in the marginal zone. The change of vegetation around waterlogged depressions is not only influenced by water regime but also influenced by soil aeolian desertification. Generally, the depressions are formed by wind erosion; around them are mobile and semi-mobile dunes. There exists obvious differences and gradient changes between depression vegetation and dune vegetation.

Table 7-21　Vegetation changes in interdune lowlands

Items	Middle of interdune lowland					Margin of interdune lowland		Lower part of dune			Middle-lower part of dune	
Number of quadrat	1	2	3	4	5	6	7	8	9	10	11	12
Plant species	8	4	4	4	2	4	1	1	1	1	2	1
Density (plant/m^2)	364	131	79	27	12	13	2	4	4	1	3	1
Height (cm)	18.2	16.3	11	20.3	35.7	22	45	29	30	48	4.4	6
Cover (%)	60	67	55	46	25	50	45	50	45	8	1.5	0.5
Total frequency (%)	107	92	81	68	30	65	54	74	87	12	3	2
Biomass (g/m^2)	313	241	239	100	620	34	650	392	44	0.1	0.4	

3) Main characteristics and laws of vegetation aeolian desertification

From the above succession process of vegetation aeolian desertification, it can be seen that the vegetation degradation process in sandy areas varies greatly from that of the non-sandy areas, and it has its own characteristics of development and evolution.

(1) With the development of aeolian desertification, species diversity within a community rapidly decreases.

In blown sand areas, species diversity within a community is the most sensitive to aeolian desertification. Once aeolian desertification occurs, the species composition within a community and species density of most plant species decreases rapidly. Taking the Mu Us Sandy Land as an example, the primary communities generally consist of about 30 species. At the initial stage of aeolian desertification, the primary plant species still can survive in the community and some other plant species may invade. However, in the mobile and semi-mobile sandy land stage, the number of species decreases to 1/4–1/10 of the primary communities (Table 7-22). In the Horqin Sandy Land, primary community species usually reach 30–50 species. With the increase in the aeolian desertification degree, the number of species decreases quickly. Firstly some rare species or unusual species such as *Delphinium grandiflorum*, *Dracocephalum moldavica* disappear, followed by *Corispermum dilutum*, *Chloris virgata* etc. In the severely aeolian desertification stage, the plant communities generally consist of 2–3 species such as *Artemisia halodendron* et al. (Chang et al., 2000; Zhao et al., 1999).

Table 7-22　Changes in community characteristics of vegetation in the Mu Us Sandy Land during the aeolian desertification process

Stage of development	Representative types	Communities' name	Communities' cover(%)	Species in quadrat (most in 25 m²)	Layers in community	Annual biomass, weight of grass (g/m²)
Initial stage of aeolian desertification	Chamaephyte+ dwarf subshrub dominating community	*A. frigida + Psammochloa villosa + Cleistogenes songorica* community	40	27	3	569
Middle stage of aeolian desertification		*Psammochloa villosa + A. frigida + A. scoparia+Setaria viridis* community	35	18	2	599
		Psammochloa villosa + A. scoparia + Salsola pestif er+ Setaria viridis community	45	9	2	484
Middle-late stage of aeolian desertification		*A. ordosica + C. tibetica + Pennisetum centrasiaticum* community	50	16	3	180.4
		A. ordosica + Pennisetum centrasiaticum + C. stenophyla community	35	6	2	300.2
Late stage of aeolian desertification	therophytes-herbaceous psammophyte dominating community	*Agriophyllum.* Community with little *Artemisia ordosica* Krasch	4	5	1	15

(2) With the development of aeolian desertification, community synusium structure and life forms tend to become simple.

In the semiarid sandy areas, grassland generally has 2–4 synusiums. Taking the Horqin Sandy Land as an example, the primary vegetation is sparse-tree steppe, and vegetation usually consists of 4 synusiums, i.e.tree layer, shrub layer, sub-shrub layer and grass layer. The situation is the same for the Mu Us Sandy Land. With human destruction, as well as the occurrence and development of aeolian desertification, the tree layer disappears first, and then the shrub layer gradually disappears from the community. Although the number of subshrub and grass layer species decreases during the moderate aeolian desertification stage, the synusium structure maintains a good condition. However, in the severe aeolian desertification stage, the subshrub layer also tends to disappear, only leaving behind the grass layer. If aeolian desertification continually develops, the grass layer can die away and the land surface is exposed entirely. The changes in life form is closely related to vegetation synusium change. With the occurrence of aeolian desertification, the species of all the life forms may be lost to different degrees. The first to disappear is phanerophytes, followed by hemicrytophytes, and finally therophytes (Zhang, 1998; Zhao, 1993; Xu, 1994).

Table 7-23　Life-form list of aeolian desertification development of vegetation on girder land

Development stages	Chamaephyte hemicrytophytes		Geophyte		Biennial		Therophytes	
	Range (%)	Mean (%)	Range (%)	Mean (%)	Range (%)	Mean (%)	Range (%)	Mean (%)
Initial stage of aeolian desertification, chamaephyte dominating		66.6		22.2		3.7		7.5
Middle stage of aeolian desertification, geophyte＋ herbaceous psammophyte dominating	33.3–44.3	38.8	11.2–22.3	16.7	11.1–5.7	8.4	27.7–44.5	36.1
Middle-late stage of aeolian desertification, subshrub-psammophyte dominating	50.0–84.7	67.4	16.7–25.0	20.8		3.1		9.4
Late stage of aeolian desertification, therophytes-herbaceous psammophyte dominating		40.0		20.0				40.0

(3) Vegetation cover and biomass decrease rapidly, with the development of aeolian desertification.

In all the regions, whether in sandy land or Gobi, the plant cover and above-ground biomass of primary vegetation are relatively high. This is because various plants have formed an optimal community compostition, density, coverage, and productivity in the long-term adaption process to the environment. Owing to the influence of aeolian desertification, the original environmental condition is destroyed, and the vegetation is accordingly affected. As the vegetation, density and biodiversity decreases, the vegetation cover and biomass also decrease rapidly (Huang, 1992; Han,

1994). As shown in Table 7-24, in the Horqin Sandy Land, the total coverage of primary vegetation usually can reach 70%–80%. In an area of good growth, the total coverage can reach 90%, and the ground biomass can reach 5,000–7,500 kg/hm^2. When the land is slightly aeolian desertified, the vegetation cover still can reach 50%, and the ground biomass can reach 5,000–6,500 kg/hm^2. In the moderately aeolian desertification stage, vegetation cover and ground biomass still can reach 45% and 4,500 kg/hm^2 respectively in the local places, but the overall total vegetation cover and ground biomass are only 20%–40% and 2,000–4,000 kg/hm^2 respectively. If aeolian desertification continues developing, the vegetation cover and ground biomass will decrease to below 10% and 500–1,000 kg/hm^2, or even become bare land.

Table 7-24　Change of vegetation cover and above ground biomass in different types of aeolian desertified lands

Items	Latent aeolian desertified land	On-going aeolian desertified d land	Severely aeolian desertified land	Severely aeolian desertified land	Most severely aeolian desertified land
Types of vegetation	sparse-tree steppe	shrubs+perennial herb	perennial herb +artemisia	artemisia +weeds	psammophyte
Number of synusiums	4	3	2	3	2
Total vegetation cover (%)	70–80	>50	30–40	20–30	<10
Total fresh grass yield (kg/hm^2)	5,000–7,500	5,000–6,500	4,200	2,100	500–1,000
Edible fresh grass (kg/hm^2)	3,750–5,250	3,750–4,500	3,000	1,500	375–750

7.3.3　Artificial development and reversal processes of aeolian desertification

7.3.3.1　Artificial process of aeolian desertification

Intensive economic activities are the driving factor of aeolian desertification. Based on field surveys, Zhu Zhenda classified the causes of the artificial process of 17.6×10^4 km^2 of aeolian desertification land surveyed at the end of 1970s. Among them, the aeolian desertified land mainly caused by human factors and less related to dune migration caused by wind action accounted for 5.5% of the total. According to the degree of influence of human economic activities on aeolian desertification, the impact can be arranged in the following descending order: collecting fuelwood, overgrazing, improper reclamation, improper use of water resources, and construction of cities, factories and mines (Table 7-2).

With the development of the social economy, the situation has changed. In 2000, when we surveyed aeolian desertification in the country once again, we found that the grassland became the most severely affected area by aeolian desertification, and overgrazing become the main cause of land desertification, followed by improper use of water resource. However, the situation has somewhat improved in the mixed farming-grazing region from the 1960s to the 1970s. The reason for this is as follows: firstly, natural vegetation has disappeared in this area and fuelwood was replaced by planting firewood; secondly, the policy of "return the cropland to woodland or grassland" and "control collection of firewood" has been carried out in severely aeolian desertified areas. Therefore, under certain conditions, governmental policy can also influence the ecological environment, including the development trend of aeolian desertification.

7.3.3.2 The regional characteristics of aeolian desertification

Under different land surface and climate conditions, when considering all the causes including improper reclamation, overgrazing, collecting fuelwood, improper use of water resource and construction of cities, factories and mines, only one or two play a leading role in the development of aeolian desertification, as shown in Table 7-25.

Table 7-25 Various human factors in aeolian desertification under different geographic conditions

Different types of aeolian desertification	Over-cultivation on sandy lands	Over-grazing on sandy steppe	Over-collection for firewood	Over-exploitation of underground water at marginal belts of alluvial fans	Over-using water resources in the upper and middle reaches of rivers	Constructing roads and mining on sandy lands
Aeolian desertification of fringes of oases and lower reaches of inland rivers in arid regions (e.g. Minqin Oasis)	√	√	√	√ √	√ √	√ √
Aeolian desertification on grasslands in semi-arid regions (e.g. Hulun Buir Steppe)	√ √	√ √	√ √		√	√ √
Aeolian desertification of riversides and plains in semi-humid regions (e.g. Songnen Plain)	√ √		√ √			

Note: √, factors with minor action; √ √, factors with major action.

(1) In the marginal zone of aeolian desertification, dunes move forward in the prevailing wind direction, resulting in the occurrence of a dune landscape in former non-dune areas. Taking the flat gravel surface between Yutian and Minfeng in the Taklimakan Desert as an example, its surface is covered by dune chains. About 1,000 years ago, its dune boundary was located about 5.4 km north of the current dune area, i.e., the 5.4 km wide mobile dune field between Yutian and Minfeng at the southern edge of the desert is the result of dune invasion over the past 1,000 years. The southward migration speed of the shifting sand is about 5 m per year.

(2) In some areas covered by fixed and semifixed dunes, aeolian desertification characteristics appear with the increase of mobile dune area and the decrease of fixed dune area, and indicate the aggravation of aeolian desertification.

(3) In the undulating sandy grassland, which was historically not seriously disturbed by human activities, aeolian desertification is on-going due to intensive use of land and over-reclamation in the

past 100 years. Aeolian desertification is manifested by the appearance of wind erosion in reclaimed farmlands, surface coarsening, and the occurrence of coppice dunes and sand sheets.

(4) In grazing grassland, aeolian desertification appears as the increase of circular desertified spots with wells, springs and grazing spots as the centers, and also appears as linear developments of aeolian desertification along the roads.

7.3.3.3　The reversal process of aeolian desertification

Controlling environmental degradation, improving and using aeolian desertified land, and restoring ecological balance are generally called the reversal process of aeolian desertification.

Unreasonable human economic activity is the important and decisive factor of aeolian desertification. When people understand that aeolian desertification must be controlled, they will adopt some effective measures to reverse the aeolian desertification process.

Aeolian desertification degree is different from place to place, and its reversal difficulty is also different. For example, the ongoing aeolian desertification in steppe and desert steppe zones may be naturally reversed once the human economic activity pressure decrease. Even on severely aeolian desertified land, if some measures that can promote ecological balance are adopted, it can have a significant effect. Taking the southern part of Chengchuan Township, Mu Us as an example, when the aeolian desertified land was enclosed from grazing for 20 years, the vegetation gradually recovered.

On the contrary, in aeolian desertified land in desert zones with harsh natural conditions, if no measure is adopted, the possibility of natural reversal diminishes. Especially after the activation of dense mobile dunes, the natural reversal possibility decreases even more. Even in desert grassland zones with excellent natural conditions, because of the encroachment of dunes, the natural grass growing process is very slow. Only by adopting some economic and technological measures can aeolian desertification be reversed.

All of the effective reversal measures are location-specific. The measures used in different zones are discussed as follows.

(1) Besides protecting existing natural vegetation and closing abandoned desertified farmlands in steppes and desert steppes, the following measures should be adopted: ① increasing woods/pasture proportion, establishing a farmland shelter belt, and developing a stable agriculture system of farming, forestry and animal husbandry; ② Establishing artificial vegetation in interdune depressions; ③ Decreasing the livestock pressure on grasslands and establishing artificial grasslands.

(2) The reversal measures for aeolian desertified land in arid desert zones. The measures mainly focus on reasonable use of water-soil resources and establishment of a protective system. ① From the viewpoint of maintaining and adjusting the ecological balance of the basin, the basic measures for combating aeolian desertification are: working out overall planning with inland river basins as an

ecological unit; reasonably allocating water in upper, middle and lower reaches; and adjusting the structure of farming, forestry and animal husbandry. ② Planting sand binding plants, using artificial ways to fix dunes, and promoting reversal of aeolian desertified land. ③ Establishing an oasis protection system.

As described above, the aeolian desertification reversal process is the process of restoring the destroyed environment, namely under unfavourable conditions to establish a reasonable ecosystem structure with biological population, to restore the environment and to ensure sustainable use of resources. Therefore, promoting recovery and reversal of aeolian desertification is related to the social economy. Analyzing the actual condition of China, the primary pressure resulting in destruction of the ecological balance is population pressure, which causes other excessive economic activities.

Humankind obtains their energy sources and materials from the natural environment. Therefore, the population number may be restricted by the capacity of the environmental system, abundance of energy and other materials. For recovering ecological balance, prompting aeolian desertification land reversal, and reducing population pressure, controlling population growth has a decisive significance.

Combating aeolian desertification and checking environmental degradation are social problems, and they cannot be solved with physical scientific techniques alone. Only by overall consideration of ecological and economic structure in the general plan of the national economic development and construction can the ecological environment be gradually improved over the course of resource use.

By analyzing the aeolian desertification process in the historical period, we can draw a conclusion that the governmental policy, to a great degree, influences the manner and direction of human economic activities in the environment. In the past 50 years, when we blindly put forward the slogans of "Taking food as the key link", "March towards barren mountains and barren land", and "taking food and oil from the desert", our activities were recompensated with the severe development of aeolian desertification. After the policy of economic reform was carried out, this situation was corrected. Following the guiding principle of "respecting the actual situations", the government adjusted many policies including the relationship between man and his natural environment. Since 1978, China has arranged "Ten great ecological constructions" in the country. Among them, five are in western China, including "three-norths protective forest system (Green Great Wall of China)"; "the protective forest system in middle and upper reaches of the Yangtze River"; "combating desertification"; "the protective forest system in middle and upper reaches of the Yellow River"; and "comprehensive recovery protective forest system in the Liaohe River basin". At the end of the 20th century, China put forward the strategic idea of "great development of western regions" and used ecological protection and establishment as the first strategic step. At the same time, the government successively implemented the projects of "return cropland to woodland (grassland)"as well as ecological construction and planting grass as "one of ten great projects in the western region". From 2000 onwards, this project was carried out in 13 provinces, including in the upper reaches of the Yangtze River in Yunnan and Sichuan, as well as in the upper and middle reaches of the Yellow River in Shaanxi and Gansu According to the national plan, some 34.3×10^4 hm^2 of cropland will be converted into forestland and grassland. At the same time, 43.2×10^4 hm^2 of barren mountains and barren land will be used to plant trees and grasses. In 2000, China quickly implemented the "project to encircle the capital for sand control". In the western region, ten projects for water and soil conservation will be constructed, including the water and soil conservation project in mixed farming-pasture regions; the oasis ecological restoration project in inland river regions; the sea-buckthorn ecological project in arsenical sandstone regions; the ravine realignment project in coarse sand areas in the Loess Plateau; the water-saving vegetation construction project in desertified grassland, the water and soil control project on sloping regions in the upper reaches of the Yangtze River; the land salvage project in limestone areas, the project to protect important water-source reservoirs; the monitoring net project of water and soil conservation; and the early warning and control demonstration project of debris in the upper reaches of the Yangtze River. The above projects do not include the ecological environment restoration projects in surrounding regions arranged by local departments and enterprises.

Once the natural balance is destroyed, it requires a long time for restoration. The recovery of the ecological environment cannot be realized after minimal effort. It needs several generations of constant effort. Reducing the negative influence of human activities on the deteriorated eco-environment areas is a serious scientific misson. If governmental departments in severely deteriorated ecological environment areas only consider economic activities in these limited areas, they cannot continue the important task of "allow nature recovery". Changing the backward system and mechanisms in western regions of China is a demand that cannot be ignored as nature continues to give warning signs.[1]

References

Chang Xueli, Zhao Halin, Yang Chi et al. 2000. Influence of plant species diversity on productivity of sandy grassland in Horqin Region. Chinese Journal of Applied Ecology, (113): 395–398

Charney J G. 1975. Drought in the Sahara: a biogeophysical feedback mechanism. Science, Vol.187

Chen Guangting, Zhang Jixian, Guan Youzhi el al. Blown sand and its control in Beijing. Memories of Institute of Desert, Chinese Academy of Sciences, Lanzhou, No 4. Beijing: Science Press, 1–69

Chen Guangting. 1991. The contemporary processes of desertification in southeast part of Inner Mongolian Plateau. Journal of Desert Research, (112): 11–19

Chen Guangting. 2001. Origins of arguments on the area of desertified lands in China. Journal of Desert Research, (212): 209–212

Dong Yuxiang, Liu Yuzhang, Liu Yihua. 1995. Research on some problem of desertification. Xi'an: Xi'an

---

1) Seeing *Science News*, 2001(15)

Maps Press. 44–105

Feng Zhongyun. 1993. Primary analysis of soil nutrient dynamics in the desertified area of the middle part of Naiman Qi, Inner Mongolia. In: Liu Xinmin, Zhao Halin, eds. Study on Comprehensive Control of Environment in Horqin Sandy Land. Lanzhou: Gansu Science and Technique Press, 80–87

Gu Fengxue, Wen Qikai, Pan Borong et al. Reasearch on soil enzyme activities of eolian soil under artificial plantation in Taklimakan Desert heartland. Journal of Desert Research, (203): 293–297

Guan Hongbin, Guo Li, Liu Yongjiang. 1999. The vertical distribution, seasonal dynamics and community variety of soil animal in the Horqin sandy land. Journal of Desert Research, 19 suppl (1): 110–114

He Daliang. 1998. The wind velocity of threshold sand affected by rainfall. Journal of Desert Research, (84): 18–26

Hu Zhaoliang, Chen Zongxing, Zhang Leyu. 2000. Introduction of Geographic Environment. Beijing: Science Press. 155

Huang Zhaohua. 1992. Desertification and ecological changes of the rangeland on the Ordos Plateau. Pratacultural Science, (91): 1–6

Liu Xinmin, Guan Hongbin, Liu Yongjiang et al. 2000. Diversity of soil and animal in the Horqin sandy grassland. Journal of Desert Research, 20 suppl (1): 110–114

Liu Xinmin, Zhao Halin, Zhao Aifen et al. 1996. Wind-sand Environment and Vegetation in the Horqin Sandy Land, China. Beijing: Science Press. 18–30, 56–70, 120–135, 150–160, 172–191

Lv Guifen. 1999. The preliminary study on seasonal dynamics of soil microbe in Horqin sandy land. Journal of Desert Research, 19 suppl (1): 107–109

Mainguet M. 1991. Sandy Desertification: Natural Background and Human Mismanagement: Berlin, Heidelberg. Springer-Verlag. 96

Wang Tao. 1989. Comparative study on desertification of typical area in Horqin sandy land. Journal of Desert Research, (91): 118–121

Wu Zheng. 1987. Aeolian geomorphology. Beijing: Science Press

Xu Bin, Zhao Halin, Liu Xinmin et al. 1994. An experimental study on the differential characteristics of plant communities under the different grazing gradation and the mechanism of desertification in the natural sandy rangeland. Journal of Lanzhou University (Natural Sciences), (304): 137–142

Xu Guochang. 1997. Climatic Changes of Arid and semi-arid regions in China. Beijing: China Meteorological Press

Ye Duzheng, Chen Panqin. 1992. Chinese Global Change Study: A Primary Perspective. Beijing: China Meteorological Press

Zhang Chao, Ma Pingqi. 1989. Geo-climatology. China Beijing: Meteorological Press, 277–279

Zhang Qiang, Wang Zhenxian. 1986. Relationship between vegetation succession and land desertification in the Yikezhao League. Memories of Institute of Desert, Chinese Academy of Sciences, Lanzhou, No. 3. Beijing: Science Press

Zhang Qiang, Zhao Xue, Zhao Halin. 1998. Sandy Grassland in China. Beijing: China Meteorological Press, 115–122, 198–210, 235–257

Zhang Tonghui, Zhao Halin, Ichiro Taniyama et al. 1998. Comparative study on features of different soil types of the Naiman Banner. Journal of Desert Research, 18 (suppl 1): 47–52

Zhao Halin, Zhang Tonghui, Chang Xueli. 1999b. The study on change laws of plant diversity and niche under grazing in Horqin sandy pasture, Inner Mogolia. Journal of Desert Research, 19 suppl (1): 35–39

Zhao Halin, Zhao Xueyong, Zhang Tonghui et al. 1999a. Relation between productivity formation of corn and soil environment in sandy farmland. Journal of Desert Research, 19 suppl (1): 88–91

Zhao Halin. 1993. Succession features of two main communities on Horqin sandy land. Journal of Desert Research, (133): 47–52

Zhao Songqiao. 1986. Physical Geography of China. Beijing: Science Press; New York: Wiley, 209

Zhu Zhenda, Chen Guangting. 1994. Sandy Desertification in China. Beijing: Science Press, 201–206

Zhu Zhenda, Liu Shu, Di Xingmin. 1989. Desertification in China and Its Controlling. Beijing: Science Press, 28

Zhu Zhenda, Liu Shu. 1988. Sandy Desertification Processes and Their Control in the North of China. Lanzhou:Inst of Desert, Chinese Academy of Sciences. 69

Zhu Zhenda, Zhao Xingliang, Ling Yuquan et al. 1998. Sandy Land Rehabilitation Engineering. Beijing: China Environmental Science Press, 56

Zhu Zhenda. 1986. Present condition and its development of desertification of north China. Journal of Desert Research, (53): 3–11

Zou Bengong, Chen Guangting, Wang Kangfu et al. 1994. Processes of land desertification and its control in the Horqin grassland. Memories of Institute of Desert, Chinese Academy of Sciences, Lanzhou, No. 4. Beijing: Science Press. 70–129

Zou Bengong, Chen Guangting, Wang Kangfu et al. 1995. Formation and evolution of desertification and its control in the Zhelimu League area, Horqin Grassland. In: Discourses of Arguments on the Ecological Building Stratagem of the Northeast China,(2): 62–63

Chapter 8
Formation and Damages of Dust Storms

Dust storms are disastrous synoptic events in which visibility is greatly reduced by sand and dust rises from the surface by strong wind action. The occurrence of dust storms is closely related to aeolian desertification. On one hand, dust storms are the consequences of aeolian desertification, and on the other hand they are also the manifestation of aeolian desertification. Each time a dust storm sweeps across the ground surface, serious erosion takes place, vegetation is seriously destroyed, large amounts of soil organic matter and nutrients are blown away, and this consequently speeds up the development of aeolian desertification.

The grades of dust storms can be divided according to wind speed and visibility. A dust storm is defined as that the visibility is less than 1000 and wind speed as fresh to strong breeze; strong dust storm refers to that the visibility is less than 200m and wind force as fresh gale to strong gale; strong dust storm is defined as that the visibility is less than 50m and wind force as more than whole gale, termed as "black haze".

When dust storms occur, fine particles can be emitted into atmosphere by turbulent air flow. If no precipitation occurs these dust can suspend in the atmosphere for a long time. According to radar remote sensing data, dust column can reach a height of 2,500 m or more.

Central Asia, North America, Central Africa and Australia are four regions that have the highest frequency of dust storms in the world. The worst-affected area by dust storms in northwest China is part of the region with the highest dust storm frequency in central Asia. In the past several decades, with rapid population growth and industrial development, the natural environment in northwest China was seriously destroyed and therefore the number of dust storm has greatly increased. Strong dust storms have powerful destructive effects; they destroy houses, cut off roads, damage agricultural production or even claim animal and human lives. Dust storms have become a serious environmental problem affecting the social and economic development in northern China, and therefore have attracted great attention from the Chinese government. Since 1993, scientists of the former Lanzhou Institute of Desert Research, Chinese Academy of Sciences have conducted systematic studies on the causes of dust storms, their temporal-spatial distribution and damages, and have published the monographs "Sand Storm Damage and Its Control in Northwest China" (Xia et al., 1996) and "Black Wind Storms" as well as over 20 research papers. In this chapter we will discuss the characteristics and damages of dust storms in China, the climatic and topographic conditions and human factors affecting the formation of dust storms, and its development trend.

In March 2001, scientists from the Cold and Arid Regions Environmental and Engineering

Research Institute and the Institute of Botany, Chinese Academy of sciences, completed a scientific investigation in the main dust source areas in northern China under the title, "Exploration of Sand Storms". The investigation results were summed up in the report of the "Status and countermeasures of sand storms in Northern China" and submitted to the central government.

8.1 "Dust rain" and dust storms in the historical period of China

Dust storms take place under the conditions of strong wind force, abundant dust sources and unstable air stratification. Dry and loose deposits on exposed surface can supply a lot of dust materials and the strong wind and unstable air stratification are the mechanisms that cause the occurrence of dust storms (Wang et al., 2001). In desert regions the solar radiation-induced strong heating of ground surfaces often forms a layer of superheated air over the near-surface, which leads to air expansion, causes vertical air convection, and therefore favours dust storm generation. Major dust storm centers are mostly distributed in the desert regions in the world.

According to statistical data, dust storms occur about 25 times each year in the Sahara Desert 30 times each year in the Arabian Peninsula, 80 times each year in Iran, 17 times each year in the Karakum Desert, 17 times each year in the Thar Desert, 5 times or more in the Simpson Desert, and 5 times each year in the mid-west prairie of North America. It is estimated that globally about 200–1,000 million tons of dust are emitted to the atmosphere per year and the annual dust-deposition rate over great distance is about 10–20 t/km^2. For example, Sahara dust can be transported over 7,000 km by wind to Bermuda and Latin America, dust from the desert of central Australia can be carried over 3,500 km to Singapore, and dust from northwest China has been identified as far as the Hawaiian Islands.

8.1.1 "Dust rain" events in the historical period of China

The determination of the physiochemical properties of deep sea core and ice-cap deposits revealed that dust storm events occurred on the earth as early as the early Cretaceous period (Cheng, 1994). In the geological period, dust storms exhibited some periodical changes, which may be related to changes in climate and land cover. According to aeolian theory, the Loess Plateau in north and northwest China resulted from the deposition of blowing dust. The "wind haze" and "dust rain" described in ancient Chinese literature are also related to dust storm events. Very fine dust particles, also known as floating dust, can be transported a long distance in suspension, but they settle rapidly when meeting wet air stream or even fall down in the form of "mud rain". According to Zhang De'er(1982), the "dust rain" weather in China has obvious seasonality; it mainly occurs between February and May, and its occurrence in April occupies about 26% of the year, and the material source of "dust rain" is long-range transported dust from the inland deserts in northwest China.

According to statistical data (Zhang, 1982), the frequency of "dust rain" events recorded from the 3rd century to 19th century in China are shown in Table 8-1.

Table 8-1   Number of "dust rain" events in historical period of China

Century	Number	Century	Number	Century	Number	Century	Number
before and in 3rd century	8	8th	10	12th	17	16th	24
5th	5	9th	6	13th	27	17th	40
6th	9	10th	4	14th	9	18th	22
7th	4	11th	10	15th	8	19th	34

From Table 8-1 it can be seen that the "dust rain" frequency increased from the 16th century to 19th century, "dust rain" occurred more than 20 times every 100 years or even reached up to 40 times. It occurred 120 times in the 400-year period or averaged once every 3 years. The years with higher "dust rain" frequency were 1060–1090, 1160–1270, 1320–1340, 1430–1560, 1610–1700, and 1820–1890. All these years were drought years. The "dust rain" affected regions starts from Xinjiang in the west and extends to the east coast, and starts from Inner Mongolia and stretches to the districts south of the Yangtze River, or even include Fujian, Guangxi and Guangdong Province.

8.1.2   Dust storm events in historical period of northwest China

In China the earliest recorded dust storm event can be found in Zhang Hua's work "Records of Anomalous Weather", in which a strong sand storm event occurred in 1600 BC was described. However, the earliest known sand storm event in recorded history occurred in the 3rd century BC. The sand storms occurred in northwest China from the third century BC to the twentieth century are presented in Table 8-2.

Table 8-2   Dust event records in northwest China

Time	Regions	Situation
205 BC	Gansu Province	A dust storm came from the west in April, with some houses destroyed and trees broken off
86 BC	Gansu Province	A dust storm occurred from the west in April, accompanied with "mud rain" in night
249	Gansu province	A dust storm occurred from the west in February, with some houses destroyed and trees broken off
300	Gansu Province	A dust storm lasted for about 6 days in November
351	Wuwei, Gansu Province	A dust storm occurred in February, with some houses destroyed, trees broken off, and many people and animals died
354	Western part of Gansu and Ningxia, eastern part of Xinjiang	A dust storm occurred, accompanied with thunders
488	Middle part of the Inner Mongolia	A floating dust lasted for about 6 days
503	Wuwei, Gansu Province	A floating dust occurred with "mud rain"
822	Uxin and Hanggin Qi of Inner Mongolia, and Jingbian County of Shaanxi province	A dust storm occurred

Time	Regions	Situation
1233	Gansu and Inner Mongolia	A floating dust lasted for about 7 days in December
1260	Inner Mongolia	A dust storm came from the north
1281	Ulanqab and Ih Ju of Inner Mongolia, northern part of Shanxi Province	A dust storm occurred in March, with thunders and some fire disasters
1306	Ulanqab and Ih Ju of Inner Mongolia, northern part of Shanxi Province	A dust storm with snowstorm occurred in February, with some houses destroyed, and people and more than 2,000 cattle and horses died
1410	Inner Mongolia	A dust storm occurred in February
1490	Jingyuan County of Gansu Province	A dust storm occurred in June
1503	Ningxia and Huanxian county of Gansu Province	A strong dust storm occurred in April with visibility of several meters
1511	Zhangye of Gansu province	A dust storm lasted for 2 days in November
1529	Ih Ju of Inner Mongolia	A dust storm occurred in February
1547	Ulanqab of Inner Mongolia, and northwestern part of Shanxi Province	Dust storms occurred in June and November
1550	Yulin county of Shaanxi province	A dust storm came from the northwest on March, 22, with some houses destroyed, and people and animals died
1567	Jinyuan county of Gansu Province	A floating dust event occurred
1608	Jiuquan of Gansu province	Several dust storms occurred continuously in February
1619	Yulin county of Shaanxi province	A dust storm occurred on February 12 with "mud rain"
1621	Ningxia and Ih Ju of the Inner Mongolia	A dust storm occurred in April
1657	Zhuanglang of Gansu	A strong dust storm occurred in February with a visibility of several meters
1704	Qingyang of Gansu	A blowing dust occurred in March
1708	Wuwei of Gansu	A dust storm occurred on March 15, with many birds dead
1709	Gulang of Gansu	A dust storm occurred in March
1710	Zhongwei of Ningxia	A dust storm occurred on March 7 and lasted for about 4 days, with some houses destroyed and trees broken off
1753	Shandan, Minle and Zhangye of Gansu	A dust storm occurred in July
1754	Qingyang of Gansu	A dust storm occurred in March
1757	Gulang of Gansu, Zhongwei of Ningxia	A dust storm occurred on June 6
1761	Hami of Xinjiang	A dust storm occurred in February and many people got ill
1814	Zhenyuan of Gansu	A dust storm occurred on December 25 with a visibility of several meters
1826	Zhangye and Jiuquan of Gansu	A dust storm lasted for about 3 days in May with trees broken off
1827	Kashi of Xinjiang	A dust storm occurred in February
1828	Hami of Xinjiang	A blowing dust event occurred in February
1830	Zhongwei of Ningxia and Lanzhou of Gansu	A dust storm occurred on March 28
1834	Hami of Xinjiang	A dust storm occurred with many houses destroyed
1853	Lingwu, Zhongwei counties of Ningxia	A dust storm occurred on March 14

Time	Regions	Situation
1857	Shache county of Xinjiang	A dust storm occurred in Yarkant on June 15
1876	Manas of Xinjiang	A dust storm occurred on October 15, with a visibility of about several meters
1877	Gulang of Gansu	A dust storm occurred in April, with a visibility of about several meters
1879	Northwestern part of Shanxi, and Ulanqab of Inner Mongolia	A dust storm occurred in April, with a visibility of about several meters
1886	Linze of Gansu	A dust storm occurred in April
1894	Zhangye and Linze of Gansu	A dust storm occurred in April, with a visibility of about several meters
1895	Markit of Xinjiang	Four dust storms occurred on April 23, 25, 28 and May 6, with a wind speed of 24 m/s
1896	Shandan of Gansu	A dust storm occurred in May, with "mud rain"
1912	Hami of Xinjiang	A dust storm occurred in May
1915	Yanchi of Ningxia	A dust storm occurred on May 26
1920	Shandan, Zhangye and Minle of Gansu	A dust storm occurred in December
1928	Shandan,Zhangye and Minle of Gansu	A dust storm occurred in December, with more than 140 hm^2 of farmland buried
1928	Gulang of Gansu	A dust storm occurred in April
1930	Linze of Gansu	A dust storm occurred in April, with a visibility of about several meters
1930	Lop Nur of Xinjiang	Two dust storms occurred on April 17 and 23
1934	Jiuquan of Gansu	Jiuquan suffered from dust disasters
1936	Toksun of Xinjiang	A strong dust storm occurred on May 6, and lasted for about 3 days, with more than 1,400 hm^2 of farmland destroyed, several wells and tens of canals buried, and 72 houses blown down
1938	Gulang of Gansu	A dust storm occurred in April
1939	Shaya of Xinjiang	A dust storm occurred on May 23, with 23 houses completely buried
1940	Xayar of Xinjiang	A dust storm on June 8 destroyed 138 houses
1949	Hami of Xinjiang	A dust storm occurred on March 18, with one adult and three children dead
1950	Turpan of Xinjiang	Several dust storms occurred from April 10 to May 1, with 270 hm^2 of farmland destroyed, 24 wells and 11 canals buried
1952	Hexi Corridor of Gansu	A dust storm occurred on April 9 with a visibility of several meters and a wind speed of 23 m/s in Zhangye
1952	Hexi Corridor of Gansu	A strong dust storm occurred in June with 23 people and 1,023 animals dead, 39 houses blown down, several hundreds of trees broken off
1955	Anxi of Gansu	Two dust storms occurred on March 18–23 and April 8-11, with a maximum wind speed of 27 m/s, about 80,000 hundred trees blown, and 10 houses blown down
1956	Daban of Xinjiang	A dust storm occurred on September 1 with a maximum wind speed of 32.6 m/s
1956	Dunhuang, Jinta and Shandan etc. of Gansu	Several blowing dust events destroyed 1,300 hm^2 of farmland
1958	Hami of Xinjiang	A dust storm occurred on April 4 with about 9,000,000 hm^2 of farmlands destroyed, 54 wells buried, 22,500 kg of forage lost, more than 40 big trees broken off and 3 roofs blown away
1960	Xiangride of Qinghai	A dust storm destroyed one third of the total farmland
1961	Dunhuang of Gansu, Yiwu of Xinjiang	On May 31, a dust storm with a maximum wind speed of 40 m/s overturned a train, 85 poles broken off, 23 25-ton oil tanks and more than 20,000 oil barrels blown away, and 90 t sheet irons blown off. And on June 1, another dust storm with 32.6 m/s of maximum wind speed swept cross Qijiaojin of Xinjiang and destroyed more than 9,000,000 hm^2 of farmland
1961	Xinhe of Xinjiang	On May 15, a dust storm with a maximum wind speed of 23 m/s destroyed 100 hm^2 of farmland, 30%–50% crops damaged, and nearly 1,000 big trees broken off, a - km water canal buried, more than 20 poles broken off

Time	Regions	Situation
1961	Yiwu of Xinjiang	On April 27–28, a dust storm with more than 30 m/s of maximum wind speed destroyed 8 hm^2 orchards. On June 1, a strong wind with a maximum wind speed more than 32 m/s destroyed 8 hm^2 of crop land, 30 animals died, and 28 houses were blown down, and about 30 trees broke off
1961	Turpan of Xinjiang	From May 31 to June 1, a dust storm with more than 30 m/s of maximum wind speed resulted in sand burial of Lanzhou-Xinjiang railroad in several sections, which overturned No.91 train. Several hundred poles broke off, more than 40 wells were buried, and about 20 people died and injured
1962	Toksun of Xinjiang	A blowing dust event occurred on March 18, 19, nearly 100 wheat-fields destroyed
1963	Turpan of Xinjiang	On April 14–15, a dust storm with a maximum wind speed more than 30 m/s destroyed 7,171 hm^2 of farmlands, 2 persons and 106 animals died, and 263 wells were buried, and about 1,066 big trees broke off
1965	Anxi of Gansu	On June 14, a dust storm with a maximum wind speed more than 22 m/s destroyed 216 hm^2 of farmlands
1966	Turpan and Toksun of Xinjiang	On March 15–16, a dust storm with a maximum wind speed more than 30 m/s destroyed 1,150 hm^2 of farmland, 64 animals died, and 81 wells and 69 water canals were buried, and 15 houses were blown down
1966	Lanzhou-Xinjiang railway in Xinjiang	On April3, a dust storm with snowstorm, with a maximum wind speed more than 30 m/s, resulted in sand burial of Lanzhou-Xinjiang railway in Shankou-Tudun section, which caused No. 1942 train running off the track
1970	Lanzhou-Xinjiang railway in Xinjiang	On March 18, a dust storm, with a maximum wind speed more than 26 m/s, resulted in sand burial of Lanzhou-Xinjiang railroad in Hongwei-Hongliu section, which caused No. 2402 train running off the track
1970	Turpan of Xinjiang	A dust storm occurred on April 10–12. There were reports on its disasters such as breaking off poles, burying wells, and killing some persons
1971	Ih Ju of Inner Mongolia	On May 23–26, a blowing dust event destroyed 6,660 hm^2 of farmland
1971	Minfeng of Xinjiang	A dust storm occurred on April 5, with a maximum wind speed more than 22 m/s
1971	Lanzhou-Xinjiang railway in Xinjiang	On April 6, a dust storm made Lanzhou-Xinjiang railway buried by sand in several sections, which caused a train running off the track
1972	Dunhuang and Jinta of Gansu	On April 12, a blowing event destroyed more than 300 hm^2 farmland
1974	Dunhuang of Gansu	On March 21, a blowing dust event destroyed more than 90 hm^2 farmland
1974	Ih Ju and Baotou of Inner Mongolia	On April 27–29, a strong dust storm occurred with a maximum wind speed 32m/s
1975	Hami of Xinjiang	On May 14, a blowing dust made Lanzhou-Xinjiang railway buried by sand in Hongwei-Hongliu section, which caused No. 2422 train turning upside down
1977	Minqing of Gansu	On May 19, a dust storm occurred
1978	Toksun,Turpan and Shanshan of Xinjiang	On April 12, a dust storm with a maximum wind speed more than 26 m/s destroyed 450 hm^2 of crop field, 19 wells were buried, 10 poles were blown down
1978	Toksun of Xinjiang	On May 5-6, a dust storm with a maximum wind speed more than 22 m/s destroyed 2,800 hm^2 of cotton field, 7 h m^2 of grape field, and 460 hm^2 of other crop field, 19 wells buried, 30 poles and 1318 big trees broken off, 2 wells and 35 water canals buried
1979	Middle part of Xinjiang	On April 10, a dust storm occurred in Hami with a maximum wind speed more than 32 m/s and a visibility of 6 m, which cut off telecommunication for 122 hours and interrupted railway traffic for 167 hours, blew down 21,000 farmer houses, caused 16,984,000 *yuan* of property loss, 3 pupils and 2 soldiers died On April 11, a dust storm occurred in Hami and Zhuomao lake areas with a maximum wind speed more than 30 m/s, which destroyed 540 hm^2 farmland, 10 persons and 7,800 animals died On April 10, 11, a dust storm occurred in Turpan with a maximum wind speed more than 32 m/s, which destroyed 30,000 hm^2 of farmland, 5,758 big trees were blown down, 108 wells and 402 water canals were buried, 16 houses were blown down, 26 houses were burned, 10 persons and 2,715 animals died, 40 persons injured and 1,043 sheep were missing On April 10, a dust storm occurred in Turpan, which caused serious fire disasters, 870 houses were destroyed, more than 800 t of grain lost, 4 people died and one person injured. The direct economic loss reached 1,439,000 *yuan*

Time	Regions	Situation
1979	Yuli of Xinjiang	On April 19–22, a dust storm with a maximum wind speed more than 20 m/s,, resulted in sand burial of Lanzhou-Xinjiang railway in several sections, which cut off the railroad traffic
1979	South Xinjiang	On April 19–22, a blowing dust event killed 15,000 animals
1979	Wulan of Qinghai	In March, a dust storm killed 20,000 animals
1980	Bayannur, Ih Ju,and Baotou of Inner Mongolia	On April 17–21, a dust storm with a maximum wind speed more than 30 m/s and a visibility less than 300 m destroyed 1,300 hm^2 of farmlands
1981	Lanzhou-Xinjiang railway in Xinjiang	From April 29 to May 21, a dust storm, with a maximum wind speed more than 32 m/s, cut off the traffic of Liaodun-Shanshan section of Lanzhou-Xinjiang railway on sandy land
1982	Yikezhao of Inner Mongolia	On May 1–8, a dust storm occurred in the middle and western part of Inner Mongolia, which destroyed 1,300 hm^2 of farmlands
1982	Lanzhou-Xinjiang railway in Xinjiang	On April 4-5, a dust storm made Lanzhou-Xinjiang railway buried by sand in several sections, which caused a train running off the track and the railroad traffic was interrupted for about 20 hours. The direct economic loss was 44,000 *yuan*
1983	Ningxia	On April 27, a dust storm, with a maximum wind speed more than 32 m/s and a visibility less than 20 m, destroyed 130,000 hm^2 of farmlands, 14 persons and 18,642 animals died, 3 persons and 1,000 sheep were missing
1983	Burqin of Xinjiang	On April 23–26, a dust storm destroyed 2,300 hm^2 of farmland
1983	Turpan,Toksun,Yopurga, Yengisar,Yanci of Xinjiang	On April 25–28, a dust storm destroyed 24,400 hm^2 of farmland 51,000 big trees broke off, 9.2 km of water canals were buried, 242 farmhouses were blown down, and 843 animals died
1983	Middle and western parts of Inner Mongolia, Yulin of Shaanxi	On April 27–29, a dust storm, with a maximum wind speed more than 38 m/s and a visibility less than 200 m, destroyed 130,000 hm^2 of farmlands, 14 persons and 18,642 animals died, 3 persons and 1,000 sheep were missing
1983	Delinha of Qinghai	On April 27, a dust storm, with a maximum wind speed more than 30 m/s, made 772 big trees broken off, 12 houses and 35 poles blown down
1983	Yiwu of Xinjiang	On May 19, a dust storm destroyed 20 hm^2 of farmlands, 4 houses were blown down, and 2 km water cannel were buried
1983	Jinta of Gansu	On May 18, a dust storm occurred with a maximum wind speed 35 m/s and a visibility of several meters
1983	Karamay of Xinjiang	On 27 November, a dust storm occurred with a maximum wind speed 40 m/s and a visibility of several meters
1984	Hanggin of Inner Mongolia	On April 4, a dust storm occurred with a maximum wind velocity of 25 m/s
1984	Toksun of Xinjiang	On April 18, 19 and 24, 25, two dust storms destroyed 3,300 hm^2 of farmlands, 84,667 trees broke off, 13 wells and 40 km water canals were buried, 29 farmer houses were blown down, 50 poles broke off, and several persons and 267 animals died
1984	Hami of Xinjiang	On April 25, a dust storm destroyed 700 hm^2 of farmlands, 13 km water canals were buried, 29 farm houses were blown down, railway traffic was interrupted for 26 hours, 719 animals died
1984	Turpan of Xinjiang	On April 28, a dust storm destroyed several hundred hectares of farmlands, 26 wells were buried, 155 houses were blown down. The direct economic loss was about 460,000 *yuan*
1984	Akto of Xinjiang	On November 4, a dust storm destroyed 102 hm^2 of farmlands. The direct economic loss was about 20,000 *yuan*
1985	Tokusn of Xinjiang	In May, five strong wind events destroyed 1,000 hm^2 of farmland, 15,000 little trees and 66 big trees broke off, 22 houses were blown down, 9 wells were buried and 22 km water canals were buried, 100 t of coal were blown away
1985	Lenghu of Qinghai	On April 1, a dust storm occurred with a maximum wind speed of 30m/s
1986	Anxi of Gansu	On April 14–16, a dust storm, with the maximum wind speed more than 30 m/s, lasted for about 7 hours and destroyed 5,800 hm^2 farm-land. Its direct economic loss was about more than 2,000,000 *yuan*
1986	Anxi and Dunhuang of Gansu	On May 18–20, a dust storm lasted for about 17 hours. It destroyed 14,800 hm^2 farmland, 25,000 big trees and 16,400 fruit trees were broken down, 29.4 km water channels were buried, 24.5 km electric wire were torn down, 1,800 t coal were blown away. The direct economic loss was about 12,000,000 *yuan*

Time	Regions	Situation
1986	Hotan of Xinjiang	On May 18–19, a dust storm caused an output reduction of 25,000 t of wheat and 7,000 t of cottons, 218 houses were blown down, 10 persons and 4,128 herds died, 736 poles broke off. Its direct economic loss was more than 50,000,000 *yuan*
1986	Hami of Xinjiang	On May 18–19, a dust storm destroyed 1,200 hm^2 of farm land, 30 km of water canal were buried, 359 farmer houses were blown down, 323 animals died. Its direct economic loss was more than 2,400,000 *yuan*
1986	Luopu of Xinjiang	On May 18-19, a dust storm destroyed 1,200 hm^2 of cotton-fields
1988	Yiwu of Xinjiang	On April 15–18, a blowing dust event destroyed 140 hm^2 of farmlands, 21 km water canal were buried
1989	Kashi of Xinjiang	On April 19–20, a strong wind caused a frost injury of 2,790 hm^2 croplands, 1,300 hm^2 of wheat field were buried by sand, and more than 30,000 trees broke off
1989	Burqin of Xinjiang	From April 30 to May 2, a strong wind destroyed 720 hm^2 of wheat field
1989	Hami of Xinjiang	On May 1–2, a blowing dust interrupted the railroad traffic for 6 hours, 22.26 t of salt blown away, the direct economic loss was about 850,000 *yuan*
1989	Zhangye of Gansu	On April 19, a dust storm occurred
1990	Turpan and Toksun of Xinjiang	On June 4–5, a strong wind occurred in Turpan and Tuksun. In Turpan it destroyed 2,900 hm^2 farmlands, 6 wells and 24 km water canal were buried, 76 poles and 2785 big trees broke off, more than 10,000 meters electric wire were torn down, 14 farm houses caught fire, one person and 18 animals died; In Tuksun, 135 hm^2 of farm lands were destroyed, 572 big trees were broken down, 4.8 water canals were buried by sand, 6 houses caught fire. The total economic loss was about 166,000 *yuan*
1990	Middle part of Inner Mongolia	On April 25, a dust storm occurred
1993	North China	On May 5, a strongest dust storm occurred in North China in the historic records. Its maximum wind speed reached nearly 40 m/s and its directly affected area was about 1,100,000 km^2. It destroyed about 400,000 hm^2 farmlands, more than 2,000 km water canals were buried, 4,412 houses were blown down, 349 persons and 120,000 animals died and injured. Its direct economic loss was 0.55 billion *yuan*
1998	North China and Yangzi Basin	On April 16–18, a dust storm swept across Northwest China. It caused "mud rain" in Beijing and had Nanjing TSP levels 8 times higher than the normal levels. The dust storm lasted for about 6 days and caused the direct economic loss of more than one billion *yuan*
2000	Inner Mongolia and Beijing	On March 3, a floating dust event occurred
	Beijing and its vicinities	On March 17-18, a floating dust and blowing dust events occurred
	Inner Mongolia and Beijing	On March 22-23, a blowing dust event occurred, but in Hexi Corridor of Gansu, it was a duststorm; and in Xian of Shanxi, the rain fell as mud rain
	North China	On March 27, a blowing dust occurred
	Beijing and its vicinities	On April 4, a floating dust event occurred
	Inner Mongolia, Shaanxi, and Hebei Provinces	On May 5-7, a blowing dust event, or a local duststorm occurred. It killed several persons
	Beijing and its vicinities	On April 4-9, a blowing dust swept across Beijing and its vicinities
	Beijing and its vicinities	On April 25, a floating dust event occurred

It can be seen from Table 8-3 that a total of 70 strong sand storm events occurred in northwest China from the 3rd century BC to the 20th century. However, 84.3% of the sand storm events recorded in historical period described the weather conditions without information on economic loss, and only 15.7% of which described the life and property losses.

As described above, we concluded that "dust rain" events in the 2,154-year period from the 3rd century BC to 1949 strong sand storms occurred in 354 (Gansu), 1306 (Inner Mongolia and Shanxi), 1619 (Shanxi and Shaanxi) and 1830 (Ningxia and Gansu) were very similar to the strong dust storms as we see in modern times.

Table 8-3   Number of strong sand storm occurred in northwest China in different periods

Century	Number	Century	Number	Century	Number
3rd century BC	1	6th	1	14th	1
2nd century BC	0	7th	0	15th	2
1st century BC	1	8th	0	16th	7
1st	0	9th	1	17th	4
2nd	0	10th	0	18th	10
3rd	1	11th	0	19th	17
4th	3	12th	0	20th	17
5th	1	13th	3	total	70

8.2   Characteristics and damages of dust storms in China

8.2.1   Characteristics of dust storms in China

Desert regions in northwest China are located in the Asian dust center. In winter and spring the Siberian- Mongolian high dominates the region, coupling with the influence of the 4,000 m the Qinghai– Tibetan Plateau, strong cold winds frequently blow over the desert and gobi surface or dry farmlands and pick up huge amount of dust materials to form dust storms. Dust storms in China mostly occur in spring and affect most parts of the country and cause tremendous economic loss.

8.2.1.1   Vast and diversified dust source areas

Arid and semiarid zones in China cover an area of 3.5 million km^2, accounting for one third of Chinese total land area, of which 2.6 million km^2 is arid desert, accounting for one fourth of Chinese total land area; semiarid zone covers an area of 9,000 km^2, accounting for one tenth of Chinese total land area. There are 1.669 million km^2 of desert, gobi, wind-eroded land and decertified land in arid and semiarid zones of China, and five provinces in northwest China and Inner Mongolia have 298,160 km^2 of dry farming land, 70% of which are rain-fed farmland. All these regions are the source areas of dust storms. Owing to rapid population growth, large-scale land development and misuse of water resources, the lower reaches of some inland rivers have dried up, the ground water table is falling and vegetation is degrading or even died. As a result, aeolian desertification around the oases and in the lower reaches of the inland rivers is accelerating, and the frequency, intensity, and duration of dust storms is increasing.

8.2.1.2　Vast effecting extent

Dust storms generally occur in the desert and aeolian desertified regions and affect about 212 counties (regions) in northwest China, northern China and northeast China. In some cases they have a much larger extent, including in eastern China, North Korea, South Korea and Japan, or even the west coast of America. For example, the strong sand storm occurred on 5 May 1993 affected 1.1 million km^2 of land in China, accounting for 11.5% of Chinese total land area, including 18 cities and 72 counties, with a population of 12 million people. According to statistical data, strong sand storm occurred once in less than two year from the 1950s to 1980s. After 1993, strong sand storm occurred every year, especially in 2000 increased to 3 times in northwest China and seriously affected Beijing region.

8.2.1.3　High frequency in spring

According to statistical data, strong dust storms mostly have occured in spring and about 51.6% of the dust storm events appeared between March and May. For example, since 1952 dust storms have occurred 37 times in Gansu Province, 7 of which were strong sand storms, and they occurred on 19 April 1952, 5–6 April 1971, 22 April 1977, 18 May 1983, 17–19 May 1986, 5 May 1993, and 12 April 2000 respectively.

8.2.2　Damages of dust storms in China

8.2.2.1　Damaging ways

Damaging ways of strong dust storms can be roughly divided into four forms, namely sand burial, wind erosion and sandblast, gale damage and air pollution.

1) Sand burial

During the passage of dust storms over an erodible surface, large amounts of dust materials can be carried great distance, when meeting obstacles they deposit rapidly. As a result, farmlands, villages, roads and canals are buried by sand. Such damages are fairly common in the oasis regions and newly reclaimed regions adjacent to sand sheets in northwest China.

2) Wind erosion and sandblast

Growing plants damaged by wind erosion and sandblast occur when they are being impacted by windblown particles. Dicot crops such as watermelon, vegetables, sugar beet, cotton and fennel etc, are less tolerant to sandblast. Especially at the seedling stage in spring, these crops can be seriously damaged.

Soil wind erosion not only results in serious losses of fertile fine particles and organic matter but also causes sand accumulation and exacerbates aeolian desertification. Therefore, the frequency of sand storm can be used as an indicator of the degree of aeolian desertification severity.

3) Gale damage

When dust storms pass over oases, near-surface sand flow ceases due to the effect of forest net but the gale may blow down trees, lift off roofs, pull down telephone lines, overturn cars, destroy various farm installations or even kill animal and human lives.

4) Air pollution

Dust can be lifted up in the troposphere and transported thousands of kilometers beyond the desert border. In some cases, it can form "mud rain". Suspended dust materials can seriously pollute the air and harm human health. For example, during the passage of the strong sand storm occurred on 5 May 1993, the dust concentration in air over Jinchuan city reached 1,016 mg $\cdot$ m^{-3} and indoor air dust content reached 867 mg $\cdot$ m^{-3}. Mine tailings in the area consist of 55.28% dust materials and contain some toxic metallic elements such as Cu, Ni, Mn and Co, they can seriously harm the health of animals and affect the growth of plants.

In addition, the advent of cold wave accompanied with sand storm may cause serious frost injury. For example, with the invasion of sand storm of 5 May 1993, the morning air temperature dropped to $-5 - -6$°C in Hexi region and caused serious freezing damage to fruit trees and dicot crops.

8.2.2.2　Main aspects of strong sand storm damages

Strong sand storms often cause serious damages to traffic transportation, buildings, industrial and agricultural production, lives and properties of people. Here we give some examples (Yang, 1993).

1) Damage to road transportation

During the period of strong sand storm, the visibility is very poor and in extreme case it may block the transportation. Sand accumulation on road bed may cause the train off the track; therefore mechanical removal of sand accumulated on the roadbed during a strong sand storm is essential. This not only affects the normal operation of the railway but also greatly increases its maintenance cost. For example, during the period of strong sand storm occurred on 5 May 1993, the traffic on the Wuda-Jilantai Railway was cut off for four days and the Lanzhou-Xinjiang Railway was interrupted for 31 hours.

Strong sand storms also can cause side slope deflation and sand accumulation on the surface of the highway. This can increase oil consumption, shorten cars life span and cut off the traffic. Similarly, they can also affect the air transport. For example, during the event of the strong sand storm of 5 May 1993, the Zhongchuan airport in Lanzhou closed.

2) Damage to industrial and agricultural production

Burial by sand is a common hazard for crops, forage grasses and fruit trees in the oases surrounded by sandy deserts and gobi, and it often causes serious economic loss. For example, the strong sand storm of 5 May 1993 destroyed 66,400 hm^2 of croplands in Jinchang. In Wuwei, Gulang, Jingtai and Zhongwei, about 10 cm of top soil were eroded, with maximum depth reached 50 cm, on an average, about 5 m^3 of soil were blown away per hm^2. In the meantime, some croplands were covered by sand, with maxi mum thickness reached 1.5m, sand accumulation per hectare cropland amounted to 9 m^3 averagely. In addition, 55,000 m of canals were buried by sand, 750 poles were blown down, 22,500 m of power line were torn down, 90,000 trees were broken off and 32,000 sheep and nearly 10,000 other livestocks were killed or were missing.

The strong sand storm of 5 May 1993 destroyed 35 kV and 6 kV power transmission lines and cut off water supply in Jinchang city, as a result, industrial production was partly stopped and caused a direct economic loss of 83 million *yuan*.

In addition, the strong sand storm destroyed 4,412 houses in the region, killed 85 people, injured 264 people, and 13 person were missing.

8.3 Meteorological and topographical conditions for the formation of dust storms

The formation of dust storms is closely related to meteorological and topographical conditions. The meteorological condition mainly refers to the atmospheric circulation condition, i.e. strong cold air invasion, cold-front heat low development and thermodynamic condition. Topographical condition can affect the path and intensity of dust storms.

8.3.1 Meteorological conditions

Strong wind is the dynamical condition for the generation of dust storms and the occurrence of strong wind requires suitable atmospheric circulations, i.e. aerodynamic processes and thermodynamic processes.

8.3.1.1 Astrosphere circulation conditions for the generation of dust storms in northern China

Owing to its vast territory, the influences of the weather system are different in different regions of China. The main wind systems affecting the wind regimes in China are the westerly circulation system, the East Asian monsoon and the monsoon over the Qinghai-Tibet Plateau. The synoptic systems affecting the dust storm weather in China include local thermal depression, prefrontal depression, the East Asian cyclone and anticyclone, and the Mongolian cyclone.

1) Local thermal depression

It is formed by intense solar heating of ground surface. Owing to the influences of terrain and thermal character, the heating of ground surface is uneven, and especially on the bare and flat gobi surfaces, intense solar heating can cause rapid expansion of air and result in unstable air stratification; this is favorable to the formation of local thermal depression and thereby causes dust storms. Such thermal depressions have marked daily change in intensity; in daytime its intensity gradually increases with increasing surface temperature and reaches the greatest intensity in the afternoon, and in the evening its intensity decreasing with the lowering surface temperature. Owing to limited height of non-adiabatic heating of the underlying surface, the thickness of the thermal depression is thin, generally less than 1.5 km.

2) Prefrontal thermal depression

The front is the narrow and inclined transition zone between cold and warm air masses. Owing to marked differences in humidity and temperature of the two air masses, air flow is extremely unstable near the front and the intense rising and falling movement of air flow in the frontal zone may cause dramatic weather changes, including the formation of the prefrontal thermal depressions. As the warm advection over the thermal depression continuously intensifies, the thermal low will be reinforced and vice versa. As thermal depression continuously intensifies, the thermal low will be reinforced and vice versa. Thermal depressions frequently occur in the desert and basin regions. If they reach a sufficient intensity they can cause gales or dust storms.

3) Cyclone and anticyclone

Cyclone and anticyclone are the areas in the air of low pressure and high pressure respectively. Owing to the differences in development stage, air mass character and geographical environment, they have quite different features but under a certain condition they may mutually transform.

A large-scale cold anticyclone (cold wave high) invades the country from Siberia and Mongolia, which may cause dramatic reduction in temperature and sharp increase in wind velocity, generally ranging from 10–20 m · s^{-1} or even exceeding 25 m · s^{-1}, this may cause dust storms. Mongolian cyclones generally develop in the middle and eastern parts of Mongolian between 40°–50°N and 100°–115°E and mainly occur in spring and autumn, followed by winter. The activities of Mongolian cyclones are often accompanied by gale, frost injury and dust storm weather.

8.3.1.2 Dynamical processes

According to the dynamical processes, dust storms can be classified into two types.

1) The type of strong cold air invasion.

The winter half year is the most active season of the cold air mass in the northern hemisphere, when cold air continuously moves southward and enters the country. From the high-level synoptic map it can be seen that there are a –30°C–40°C pressure trough and a 30–40 m/s strong northern belt behind the trough over Xinjiang and move southward. From the surface synoptic map it can be seen that there is a strong high of 1,050 hpa over the Siberia or central Asia and its leading edge has a cold front moving toward north Xinjiang and then entering western Inner Mongolia, the Hexi Corridor, Ningxia and Shaanxi, with a speed 70–80 km/h or even 100 km/h. As sweeping over the exposed ground surface with abundant dust materials, it may cause a duststorm weather.

2) The type of thermal depression development before cold front.

In spring and early summer, before the arrival of the cold front, the ground surface in Southern Xinjiang is intensely heated, causing the cyclonic convergence of warm air and the formation of a thermal depression in the basin. Such rising airflow can rise to a height of 3,000 m. Once the thermal depression has developed in the Tarim Basin, it causes gales and dust storm weather. The intensity of gales depends on the pressure gradient of the Mongolian high and the thermal depression in the Tarim Basin. In the center of the thermal depression the wind force is the largest. The duration of a dust storm depends on the duration of thermal depression.

In the sand storm-hit regions, air temperature changes greatly prior to the occurrence of a sand storm. On 5 May 1993, the mean temperature, extreme mean temperature and extreme maximum temperature in the Jinchang region of Gansu dramatically increased (Table 8-4). Prior to the occurrence of a sand storm on 31 December 2000, the mean temperature in the Minqin region was 40 °C higher than the historical value in the same month.

Table 8-4　Air temperature between January and May in Jinchang City in 1993

Monthly air temperature (°C)	Jan.	Feb.	Mar.	Apr.	May.
mean	−8.6	−0.6	5.2	11.2	15.8
extreme mean	−1.7	6.1	11.6	17.8	22.2
extreme maximum	7.8	15.9	18.5	28.1	29.6

8.3.2　Topographic conditions

8.3.2.1　Topographic structure and strong dust storm paths

Topographic structure has a significant influence on a strong dust storm path. Terrains such as mountain passes, canyons or flats create conditions for the invasion of cold air, and strong dust storms in China generally move along three routes, namely the western path, northwest path and northern path (Fig. 8-1).

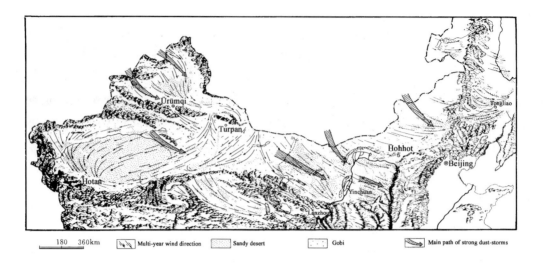

Fig. 8-1　Paths of dust storms in China

As can be seen from Fig. 8-1, the eastward migration of strong dust storms along the western and northwest paths are mostly affected by the Qinling and Yinshan mountain systems. As they move over underlying surfaces such as gobi and desert, their intensities increase due to increasing turbulent heat exchange. When the dust storms rapidly move southward along the north path from the Lake Baikal they directly sweep over the Inner Mongolian Plateau and form strong dust storms in the Ordos Plateau but do not affect the Da Hinggan Ling Mountains and the east region of the Taihang Mountains.

8.3.2.2　Influences of terrains on wind force

1) Influences of gullies on wind

When winds enter gullies from open flats, its speed may increase by 17% at the gully mouth due to streamline densification and the influence of mountain circumfluence.

Once inside the gully the wind speed gradually decreases due to increased friction resistance and at the outlet of the gully its speed reduces by 35% as compared to the wind speed over the open flat. After flowing out of the outlet, the wind speed will decrease due to the disappearance of the funneling effect and at a certain distance from the outlet the wind can gain its same normal velocity as over the open flat (Table 8-4, Fig. 8-2).

The facts described above represent a situation where the wind direction and the gully orientation are the same. If they are obliquely crossed, wind speed in the gully will decrease due to a weakened funneling effect. If a gully runs perpendicular to the wind direction, wind speed in the gully is low.

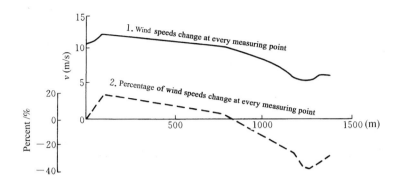

Fig. 8-2   Change of horizonal wind speed due to funneling effect

2) Influences of hills on wind speed

When wind encounters a steep hill (slope >70°), part of the airflow will climb up the slope and near-surface wind speed within a certain distance in the windward side of the hill will decrease and its deceleration range depends on the height of the hill. The higher the hill, the larger the deceleration range, generally that distance is four times as much as the height of the hill. The wind speed at the foot of the hill may be decreased by 67.4% compared to the normal wind speed over a flat (Table 8-5, Fig. 8-3).

Table 8-5   Changes of horizontal wind speed at 2 m height in gully due to funneling effect

Observation point	Distance to the flat outside the gully (m)	Wind speed (m/s)	Ratio of wind speed compared to the point outside the gully	Increase or decrease %	Note
1	0	10.8	100	0	
2	113	12.6	117	+17	
3	773	11.1	103	+3	
4	998	9.2	85	−15	Gully length 1,143 m
5	1,068	8.7	81	−19	
6	1,143	7.1	66	−34	Gully width 30 m
7	1,248	6.1	57	−43	
8	1,298	6.6	61	−39	
9	1,398	6.7	62	−38	

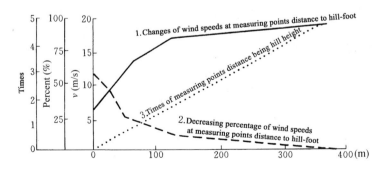

Fig. 8-3   Changes of wind speed in the windward side of a steep hill

In the leeward side of the hill, a vortex and wind-shadow zone will form and its range is related to the height of the hill. Generally, its influence is felt in an area of up to 12 times the height of the hill and wind speed at the foot of the hill may be decreased by 61.4% compared to the wind velocity over the flat (Dong, 2000) (Table 8-6, Fig. 8-4).

Table 8-6　Changes of horizontal wind speed at 2m height in the windward side of a steep hill

Observation point	Distance to the foot of the hill (m)	Wind velocity (m/s)	Ratio of wind velocity of each point to point 8	Wind speed reduction (%)	Times of hill height equivalent to distance	Remark
	Foot of the hill					Relative height of the hill is 75m
1	0	6.55	32.6	67.4	0	
2	34	10.45	52.1	47.9	0.45	
3	64	13.82	69.0	31.0	0.85	
4	94	15.07	75.2	24.8	1.25	
5	124	17.33	64.4	13.6	1.65	
6	179	18.02	90.0	10.0	2.49	
7	282	19.02	95.2	4.8	3.76	
8	382	20.06	100.0	0	5.09	

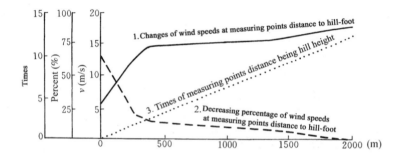

Fig. 8-4　Changes of wind speed in the leeward side of a steep hill

In the gentle hilly regions (slope 5°–7°), the deceleration range of wind in the windward side of the hill is related to the height of the hill and its slope. The higher the hill and the gentler the slope, the larger the deceleration range but the reduction in wind speed is small. If the hill has a lower height and steep slope, the wind speed may decrease by 22.6% (Table 8-7, Fig. 8-5).

Table 8-7　Changes in horizontal wind speed at 2m height in the leeward side of a steep hill

Point	Distance to the foot of the hill (m)	Wind velocity (m/s)	Ratio of wind velocity of each point to basic point	Wind speed reduction (%)	Times of hill height equivalent to distance	Remark
Basic point	no influence	17.8	100	0		
1	0	6.7	38.6	61.4	0	
2	150	11.2	63.0	37.0	0.91	
3	300	14.1	79.2	22.8	1.82	relative height of the hill is 165m
4	400	15.2	85.4	14.6	2.41	
5	700	15.6	87.6	12.4	4.24	
6	1,400	16.1	90.5	9.5	8.49	
7	1,700	17.2	96.0	3.4	10.39	

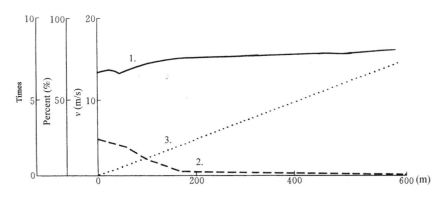

Fig. 8-5   Changes of wind speed in the windward side of a gentle hill

Wind speed in the leeward side of a gentle hill varies greatly due to the screen effect of the hill. According to observations, the influential range is 14 times as much as the height of a hill and the maximum reduction in wind speed occurs at a distance two times the height of a hill, generally reducing by 40% (Table 8-8, Fig. 8-6).

Table 8-8   Changes of horizontal wind speed at 2m height in the windward side of a gentle hill

Observation point	Distance (m)	Wind speed (m/s)	Ratio of wind speed of each point to point 6 (%)	Wind speed reduction (%)	Times of hill height equivalent to distance
1	0	12.7	77.4	22.6	0
2	51	13.2	80.5	19.5	0.63
3	105	14.6	89.1	10.9	1.24
4	178	15.4	94.9	5.1	2.14
5	378	15.8	96.2	3.8	4.67
6	578	16.4	100	0	7.14

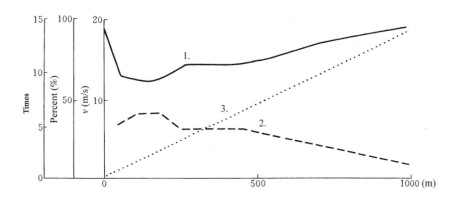

Fig. 8-6   Changes of wind speed in the leeward side of a gentle hill

For an isolated hill (width <200 m), the largest wind speed occurs at a distance two times the height of the hill in the leeward side; this is because the two branches of air flow from both sides meet there.

Owing to the difference in landforms, the frequencies of dust storms in southern and northern Xinjiang are different. On average, dust storms occurs 5 times per year in northern Xinjiang and

20–30 days per year in southern Xinjiang. The maximum wind speeds recorded at various stations from west to east in the Hexi Corridor are 21 m/s in Gaotai, 21 m/s in Linze, 23 m/s in Minle, 28 m/s in Yongchang, and 25 m/s in Gulang. Owing to the funneling effect, the wind speed gradually increases. Wind speed data are shown in Table 8-9–8-11.

Table 8-9　Changes of wind speed in the leeward side of a gentle hill

Observation point	Distance (m)	Wind speed (m/s)	Ratio of wind speed of each point to basic point(%)	Wind speed reduction (%)	Times of hill height equivalent to distance
basic point		20.1	100		
1	60	12.7	62.9	37.1	0.82
2	113	12.1	60.3	39.7	1.55
3	168	11.9	59.2	40.8	2.3
4	258	13.9	69.2	30.8	3.54
5	433	14.2	70.7	29.3	5.94
6	643	15.8	78.7	21.3	8.81
7	875	17.9	89.1	10.9	11.99
8	1,031	18.7	92.1	6.9	14.0

Table 8-10　Wind speed data in the west section of the Hexi Corridor

Region	Weather station	Mean wind speed (m/s)					Number of days with wind ⩽ grade 8
		Annual	Winter	Spring	Summer	Autumn	
Hexi Corridor	Dunhuang	2.2	2.1	2.7	2.2	1.8	15.4
	Anxi	3.7	3.4	4.4	3.5	3.3	68.5
	Yumen	4.2	4.7	4.7	3.6	3.9	42.0

Table 8-11　Wind speed data in the east section of the Hexi Corridor

region	Weather station	Mean wind speed (m/s)					Number of days with wind ⩽ grade 8
		Annual	Winter	Spring	Summer	Autumn	
Hexi Corridor	Gaotai	2.5	2.2	3.1	2.6	2.1	9.1
	Linze	2.5	2.8	3.4	3.2	2.5	21.7
	Minle	3.4	3.4	3.7	3.4	3.1	11.2
	Yongchang	3.2	3.0	3.7	3.0	3.0	18.3
	Gulong	3.5	3.7	3.3	3.7	3.5	4.5

8.4　Influence of anthropogenic factors on the formation of dust storms

Dust storm weather is the result of the interaction between synoptic processes and ground surface processes. The synoptic processes include aerodynamic processes and thermodynamic processes, and the ground surface processes include surface exposure and blown sand movement. The latter is closely related to climatic and anthropogenic factors. The climatic factors can be predicted and forecasted, while anthropogenic factors can be adjusted and controlled. In other words, vegetation destruction and desertification can be controlled. Similarly, dust storm hazards can be controlled or relieved through protecting and re-establishing vegetation, rationally using water resources and reducing surface exposure etc.

8.4.1 Effects of disturbed ground surface

Human activities often result in vegetation destruction, soil aggregate structural disintegration, soil loosening, and erodible material exposure to wind erosion. Observations showed that when the vegetation cover of sandy land reaches 15%–25%, its deflation rate decreases by 21%–31% compared to exposed sandy land; when the vegetation cover reaches 40%–50% its deflation rate is only 0.95% of shifting sand land. Covered by 2–5 cm of a gravel layer desert pavement, with a hardness of 2.42–7.49 kg $\cdot$ cm^{-2}, the gobi surface is less prone to wind erosion (Table 8-12). However, if disturbed by human activities, it is highly susceptible to erosion by wind. Human disturbed surfaces, especially the ploughed soil surface, generally has a hardness corresponding to a shifting sand surface. And its dust transport rate mainly depends on the silt and clay content (<0.063 mm) (Dong, 2000). Once disturbed by human activities, the sand transport rates of gobi, grassland and loess land increases greatly and becomes the new dust source areas.

Table 8-12   Changes of surface hardness under natural conditions
and after being disturbed by human activities

Site	Dunhuang, Jiuquan		Minqin, Yumen Mogutan		Dunhuang Mingsha mountain
Type	gobi		Fixed dune		Shifting sand
	Natural	Disturbed	Natural	Disturbed newly reclaimed land	
Surface hardness (kg $\cdot$ cm^{-2})	2.42—7.49	0.28	5.84	0.28	0.22

8.4.2 Contribution of disturbed dust sources to the atmospheric dust load

The global atmospheric dust sources include natural sources undisturbed by human activities and sources disturbed by human activities.

Ina Tegen and Inea Fung (1995) divided the global dust sources into "natural source" and "disturbed source", and used the GISS tracer model to calculate the contribution of disturbed dust sources to the global atmospheric dust load. Natural source (NS) includes natural deserts, bare sandy lands and sandy lands with sparse vegetation. Disturbed source includes destroyed forest land, overgrazed grassland, and abandoned cultivated land that have become dust source areas. According to the disturbed age, the disturbed sources can be divided into old source area (exceeding 20 years) and recent source area (less than 20 years). The former includes cultivated eroded soil (OA) and uncultivated eroded soil (OE), the latter includes Sahara boundary shift (RB), recently cultivated areas (RC) and recently deforested areas (RD).

Table 8-13　Silt and clay (<0.063 mm) contents in different types of ground surface

Site	20 km distance in eastern Dunhuang, Gansu	50 km distance in eastern Anxi, Gansu	Xilingol	East Meng of Xilingol	Ordos plateau	Zhangwu, Liaoning	Cibogou Of Shenmu, Shaanxi	Tijiapo of Yuling, Shaanxi	Tumengzhen Gansu	Mogutan of Yumeng, Gansu	Minqin sand control station, Gansu
Type	Alluvial-diluvial gobi	Diluvial gobi	Grassland	Primary grassland	Grassland	Grassland	Loess	Sandy loess	Newly reclaimed farmland	Wind-eroded hand	Shifting sand
Content	31.93	24.02	49.4	37.9	30.21	33.65	48.79	21.42	76.17	97.09	1.66

Table 8-13 shows the dust source type and area in various continents in the world. It can be seen that 10%–67% of dust source areas in various continents belong to natural sources or potential natural sources, 0.4%–4.7% of the dust source area fall into disturbed old sources and 0.01%–2.5% fall into disturbed new dust sources.

Table 8-14 shows the area of active source regions. It can be seen that about 10% of the global potential source area is an active area. In the case of old source, about 20%–25% of the potential source area is active, and the recent source areas are only about 20% of the old source area.

Table 8-14　Percentage of land area per continent that can potentially act as a dust source (Tegen and Fung, 1995)

Type	Global	Africa	Asia	Europe	North America	South America	Oceania
Total area ($10^{10}\,m^2$)	13,014	2,966	4,256	951	2,191	1,768	882
NS	34	54	26	10	18	38	67
OA	1.2	1.3	2	4.1	0.6	0.4	0.5
OE	2.0	4.7	1.9	0.4	1.2	0.9	1.4
RB	0.4	1.6	0	0	0	0.0	0
RC	0.5	0.3	0.2	0.007	0.7	2.2	0.003
RD	0.5	0.5	0.4	0.005	0.2	2	0.05
RL(RC+RD)	0.7	0.6	0.5	0.01	0.8	2.5	0.05

Total areas and percentages of global land area that are active dust sources in the model and dust properties from these sources (Tegen and Fung, 1995) are shown as Table 8-15.

From the restrictive conditions of δ and ρ we can see that: when $\delta>0$, it cannot meet the natural source type, when $\delta>0.7$, NS1–NS3 can meet neither natural type nor man-disturbed type (Condition 1); when $\rho>3$, it may overestimate the natural source but can meet the disturbed types except for RD and RL(condition 2).

As can be seen from above, natural source alone does not conform to the condition $\delta>0$ and $\rho>3$. Except RD and RL, other disturbed types coincide with the condition $\delta>0$ and $\rho>3$. For this reason, nine different experiments were designed to analyse the contribution of disturbed source to the atmospheric dust load (Table 8-16).

Table 8-15　Total areas and percentages of global land area that are active dust sources in the model and dust properties from these sources (Tegen and Fung, 1995)

Source type	Area (10^{10}m^2)	Land area (%)	δ	ρ
NS1, 100% of area each grid box acts as source	780	6	−0.28	1.9
NS2, 50% of area each grid box acts as source	390	3	−0.28	1.9
NS3, Asian deserts 100%, other deserts 50%	510	4	−0.2	2.9
OA, Eroded soil, cultivated	36	0.3	0.53	3.0
OE, Eroded soil, not cultivated	44	0.4	0.05	7.0
RL, land use change	9	0.07	0.17	1.6
RB, Sahara boundary shift	6	0.05	0.6	17.3

Table 8-16　Minimum percentage of anthropogenic dust per source type, depending on conditions 1($\delta>0$) and 2($\rho>3$) and emission factors for the case of 50% disturbance contribution to total atmospheric dust mass, 3,000 Mt. a^{-1} (Tegen and Fung,1995)

Experiment	Source types	Condition 1	Condition 2	Emission factor of natural source	Emission factor of human disturbance source
1	NS2, OA	>30%	>46%	0.6	19.3
2	NS2, OE	>88%	>30%	0.6	3.0
3	NS2,OA,OE	>66%	>30%	0.6	2.6
4	NS2, RD	>43%		0.6	179
5	NS2,RL	>64%		0.6	82
6	NS2,RL,RB	>8%	>73%	0.6	43
7	NS2,OA,OE,RL	>64%	>5%	0.6	2.5
8	NS2,OA,OE,RL,RB	>44%	>32%	0.6	2.4
9	NS3,OA,OE,RL,RB	>34%	>33%	0.83	2.4

It can be seen from Table 8-16 that when the condition $\delta>0$ is met, the minimum contribution of disturbed source to the atmospheric dust load is 8%–88%; when the condition $\rho>3$ is met, at least 5%–73% of the dust come from disturbed dust source.

According to the equation of the amount of uplifted dust derived by (Gillette. 1978):

$$q_a=c(u-u_{tr})u^2 \tag{8-1}$$

Where q_a is flux from the surface, u is near-surface wind velocity, U_{tr} is threshold velocity, C is constant, the C value of undisturbed surface determined by Gillette (1978) is 0.5–2 $\mu g \cdot s^2 \cdot m^{-5}$.

Table 8-16 lists the C values as the contribution of disturbed source to the atmospheric dust load is 50% in the Experiment 1–9. The dust entrainment coefficient of natural source (NS2) is 0.6 $\mu g \cdot s^2 \cdot m^{-5}$ and the dust entrainment coefficient of disturbed dust source is 4–300 times as large as the natural source. This is consistent with Gillette's wind tunnel experiment results.

As described above, the possible contributions of natural source and disturbed source to the atmospheric dust load are 50% respectively. It is estimated that natural source and disturbed source ech account for 1,500 Mt, respectively.

8.4.3　Man-made dust materials

Man-made dust materials include mine tailings, coal refuses, coal fly ash, cinder, and other industrial rubbish and solid wastes.

Such solid wastes have a loose structure and are prone to deflation. They are important man-made dust sources and can pollute soils, water bodies and the atmosphere.

According to 1990 statistical data, some 42.496 million tons of solid wastes were produced in northwest China Xinjiang, Gansu, Ningxia, Shaanxi and western Inner Mongolia per year (Table 8-17), of which 20.066 million tons or 47% were produced by Inner Mongolia, and 93% of mine tailings were produced by Inner Mongolia, Shaanxi and Gansu. In addition, some 69.747 million tons of accumulated solid wastes covered 8.54 million m^2 of land surface (Table 8-18).

Table 8-17　Annual output of solid wastes in northwest China (10^4 t/a)

Prefecture	Total output	Coal gauge	Cinder	Coal fly ash	Blast-furnace slag	Iron slag	Red mud	Non-ferrous metal slag	Mine tailings	Industrial rubbish	Industrial dust	Chemical industrial wastes
Inner Mongolia	2,006.57	131.94	178.9	66.41	117.6	21.63	0.17	3.31	567.8	39.0	22.93	856.93
Shaanxi	870.33	128	60.0	28.0		3.0			591.24	28.0	31.37	0.72
Gansu	736.14	136.28	61.84	35.99	1.08	0.49		44.92	360.02	47.43	18.95	20.57
Qinghai	120.8	8.63	8.26	14.37					80.08	4.19	5.2	0.06
Ningxia	290.55	202.1	11.29	22.31	0.5			0.35	36.37	2.65	14.98	
Xinjiang	225.16	86.49	31.35	6.07	1.95	0.06			3.09	85.37	8.61	2.18
Total	4,249.55	694.01	351.6	173.15	121.12	25.18	0.17	48.23	1,638.6	206.64	102.04	880.46

Table 8-18　Accumulated amounts of mine tailings and covered land area of several large enterprises

Region	Enterprise name	Accumulated tailing amount (10^4 t)	Covered land area (10^4 m^2)
Inner Mongolia	Boatou steel Co	2,847.00	300.00
Gansu	Jinchuan Non-ferrous Metal Co	2,785.14	300.00
Gansu	Jiuquan steel Co	770.00	
Shaanxi	Jinduichang Co		225.00
	Industrial Co	572.52	29.00

According to statistical data, 97% of metallurgical and chemical industrial solid wastes come from the Baotou Steel Co; 86% of coal refuses come from Ningxia, Gansu, Inner Mongolia and Shaanxi; 85% of cinder come from Xinjiang, Inner Mongolia, Shaanxi and Gansu; a large part of coal fly ash from power plants; and the Yongdeng Cement plant in Gansu produced 246,600 tons of dust material per year.

8.5　Status and development trend of dust storms in China

8.5.1　Status of dust storms in northern China

In 2000, more than 10 sand storms occurred in northern China and seriously affected communication and transportation. Before the end of March 2001, 9 dust storms occurred in Gansu and Inner Mongolia, especially the strong sand storm that occurred on 31 December 2000-1 January 2001 affected regions of Beijing and Nanjing. For this reason the National Environment Protection Administration entrusted the Cold and Arid Regions Environmental and Engineering Research Institute and the Institute of Botany, Chinese Academy of Sciences to send their experts to investigate the dust sources. Scientists from these two institutes, in cooperation with workers from CCTV, were organized into two teams to investigate the major dust source regions in the Hexi corridor, the Alxa plateau and the middle part of Inner Mongolia. In the investigation report some suggestions to control dust storms were put forward.

8.5.1.1 Features of dust storms occurring in China

According to the frequency, intensity and distribution of dust storms, dust composition, ecological status, water and land use ways and regional environment background, northern China is divided into four centers and source areas of dust storms: (a) the Hexi Corridor in Gansu and Alxa Meng in Inner Mongolia; (b) the Taklimakan Desert region in southern Xinjiang; (c) Northern slope of Yinshan to the Onqin Daga Sandy Land in Inner Mongolia; (d) Regions along the Great Wall in Inner Mongolia, Shaanxi and Ningxia (Wang et al., 2001). Dust materials in these source areas can be transported by westerly and northwesterly winds to northern China and lower reaches of the Yangtze River. Strong wind, abundant dust materials and unstable air stratification are three basic conditions responsible for the occurrence of dust storms. Dust storms in China mostly occur between March and May, especially in the afternoon of a day. Dust particles can be carried to a height of 1,000–2,500 m, or even 2,500–3,200 m.

The above dust source areas have been listed as the country's key dust storm monitoring and ecological protection regions.

8.5.1.2 Dust storm development trend

On the whole, dust storms in China had a decreasing trend with fluctuations during the 1950s, slightly increased during the 1960s-1970s, decreased in the 1980s, slightly increased in the 1990s (Fig. 8-7) and sharply increased in 2000; strong dust storms occurred nine times. This showed that a new active period of dust storms has come into existence.

Frequent occurrence of dust storms is one of the marks of eco-environmental deterioration. Desert, gobi and aeolian desertified land in China cover an area of 1.67 million km^2 and are expanding at a rate of 2,460 km^2/a. With the Helan Mountains as the dividing line, the regions to the west of the line are controlled by dry climate; land use is dominated by oasis irrigation agriculture. Misuse of water resources resulted in water shortage in the downstream farming region, farmland abandonment, vegetation destruction and serious wind erosion. The regions to the east of the line have relatively plentiful precipitation in summer and autumn due to the influence of monsoon wind,

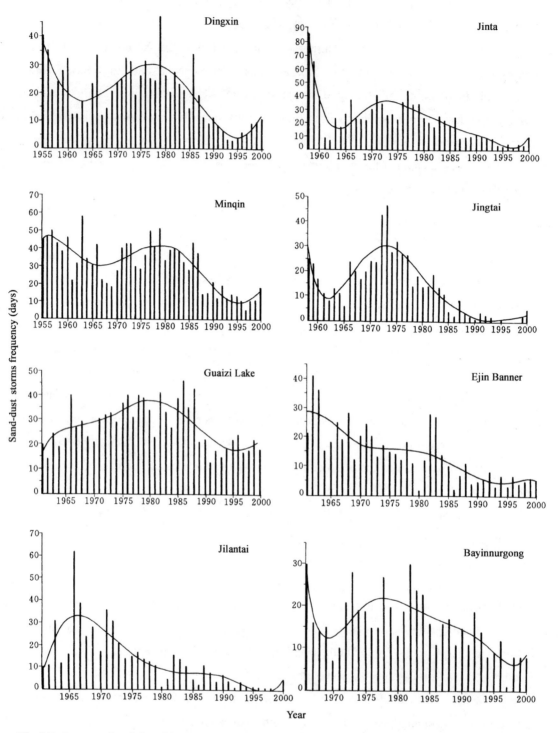

Fig. 8-7   Interannual variation of dust storm frequency in the Hexi corridor and the Alxa Meng region (Wang, 2001)

but the climate in winter and spring is dry, and coupled with overgrazing, aeolian desertification extensively occurs in the mixed farming and grazing zones.

Soil wind erosion rate increases exponentially with the reduction of vegetation cover. When the vegetation cover is larger than 60%, no wind erosion or slight wind erosion occurs; when the vegetation cover varies between 20% and 60%, moderate wind erosion occurs; when the vegetation cover is less than 20%, strong wind erosion occurs. The higher the soil moisture content, the higher the threshold wind velocity for dust entrainment, that is to say, the threshold wind velocity shows a linear increase with the increasing soil moisture content. Human disturbance may result in a ten-fold increase in soil wind erosion rate.

Viewed from the meteorological conditions, winter atmospheric circulation in East Asia suddenly changed after the late 1970s, and the high level East Asian trough shifted eastward and became weak. Hence wind speed in the dust source area in winter and spring reduced, and coupled with the El Nino effect in the mid 1980s, dust storm frequency was relatively low in the 1980s–1990s. Afterwards, the East Asian trough returned to normal or became strong, hence dust storm events sharply increased in 2000. In addition, the increase or decrease in dust storm frequency is also related to the precipitation changes in Inner Mongolia, south as in Xinjiang and the Hexi region.

Owing to a continuously deteriorated eco-environment and arid climate, coupling with the effects of global warming, it is predicted that in the near future dust storms in northern China will continue to stay in an active period.

8.5.1.3 Blowing dust weather in Beijing

In recent years, blowing dust weather, floating dust events or dust storms often occur in spring in the Beijing region. For example, on 6 April 2000 a strong dust storm occurred, with the maximum wind velocity reaching 14m/s and visibility reduced to 500 m.

According to statistical data, between 1971 and 1998 blowing dust events occurred 355 times, floating dust events 111 times and dust storms 25 times, accounting for 74%, 21% and 5% of their total number, respectively. From the 1950s to the mid-1990s, blowing dust weather in Beijing decreased with fluctuations, but significantly increased from 1998 onwards; in 2000 it occurred 12 times, which was roughly approximate to the level in the 1960s (12 times in 1965, 20 times in 1966 (Fig. 8-8).

According to the statistical data, the blowing dust weather can be divided into five types, namely blowing sand, floating dust, blowing dust-floating dust, gale-floating dust, and dust storm types; for the blowing dust floating dust type, the blowing sand occupies less than 50% and floating dust 30% or more; for the gale-floating dust type the blowing sand occupies 50% or more and floating dust 25%–40% and for the dust storm types the dust storm occupies 45% of blowing sand days (Chen et al., 1995).

According to the analytical results of geochemical composition and heavy minerals, sand materials in Beijing are of local origin, mainly coming from the ancient deposits in the Yongding,

Chaobai and Yuxi river beds, while dust materials are transported from the regions with high dust storm frequency, such as the regions to the north of the Yinshan Mountains the Onqin Daga Sandy Land, mixed farming and grazing region and degraded grasslands.

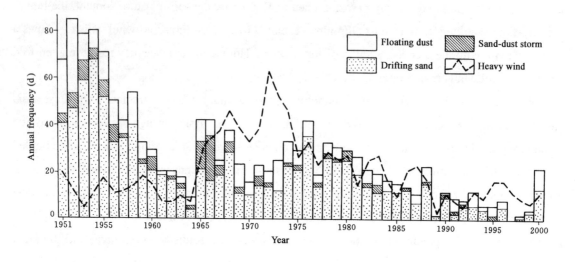

Fig. 8-8   Interannual variation of blowing dust weather in Beijing over the past 50 years

The earliest dust storm recorded in Beijing occurred in 440. During the period from the mid-15th century to the mid-17th century, the Beijing plain experienced a drought period with the most frequent and strongest dust storm events.

8.5.1.4   Analysis of the causes leading to early onset of dust storms in northwest China

During the 1949–1990 period, strong sand storms occurred 72 times in northwest China including Xinjiang, Qinghai, Gansu, Ningxia and Inner Mongolia, 64 of which occurred between March and May, and occupied 88.9% of its total number, while only 2 sand storms occurred in November, 1 occurred in August and 4 occurred in June. From 1952 to 2000, 7 strong sand storms occurred in Gansu, such as the strong sand storm that occurred on 9 April 1995 in Zhangye and Yongchang which had a wind velocity of over 25 m/s and a visibility of zero. From 2000 onwards, the starting time of sand storm event has shifted to an early date, such as the dust storm that occurred on 24-25 February 2000 in Yumen, Jinta, Minqin and Wushaoling in the Hexi corridor and two strong sand storms that occurred on 10 and 30 January 2001 in Zhangye, Linze and Gaotai in the Hexi region.

It is generally accepted that the increase in air temperature, gale and cold wave frequency caused by global warming, overgrazing, vegetation destruction, misuse of water resources and dune mobilization in dust source areas in northwest China has led to the early onset of dust storms in northwest China. According to satellite remote sensing investigations in 53 counties in Heilongjiang, Inner Mongolia, Gansu and Xinjiang during the 10 year period from 1986 to 1996, a total of 1.74

million hm^2 of grasslands were reclaimed, 884,000 hm^2 of cultivated land were left, accounting for 50.8% of total reclaimed area. A large area of this abandoned land developed into desertified land. From 1987 to 1996 the forest area in Bashang region of Hebei province decreased from 363,500 hm^2 to 222,400 km^2, shifting sand area increased from 68,000 hm^2 to 129,100 hm^2, from 1989 to 1996, shifting sand area in the Onqin Daga Sandy Land of Inner Mongolia increased by 93%, grassland area decreased from 602,500hm^2 to 430,100hm^2 due to overgrazing. During the 10-year period, degraded grassland area increased from 8,667 million hm^2 to 130 million hm^2, an increase of 43.33 million hm^2. Furthermore, it is still degrading at an annual rate of 4.333 million hm^2 (Earth science Department, Chinese Academy of Sciences, 2000).

During the period of strong sand storms that occurred on 21, 26, 27 March 2000, the maximum wind speed reached force 9, visibility was less than 400 m, dust concentration in air in Jinchang region reached 15.55, 12.67 and 2.74 $mg \cdot m^{-3}$, i.e. exceeded the state's second class air quality criterion by 51.8, 42.2 and 9.1 times.

From March to 25 April 2000, 8 strong dust storms occurred in northern China, occurred 3 times higher than the dust storm frequency of the 1990s, especially the sand storm on April 6 affected 5 provinces (regions) in the northwest China, northeast China, Jiangsu and Anhui provinces.

As described above, strong dust storms in China tended to increase in frequency and intensity but the number of dust storm days per year as a whole tended to decrease, which can be seen from the interannual variation curve of annual number of dust storm days from 1956 to 1996. This may be attributed to anomalous climatic changes and local improvement of ecological condition in dust source areas.

8.5.2   Development trend and control measures of dust storms in China

8.5.2.1   Factors affecting the formation of dust storms

The occurrence and development of dust storms are related to natural and anthropogenic factors. The main factors affecting the occurrence of dust storms in China are as follows.

(1) Overload of land resources. Owing to rapid population growth and relatively low agricultural productivity, agriculture in China has been under tremendous pressure. Population growth leads to a decrease in per capita cropland area. In order to increase grain output, large areas of grassland was reclaimed and thereby resulted in the deterioration of the eco-environment. Although great efforts have been made to improve farming techniques and enhance per unit area yield, excessive reclamation of grasslands seems to be unavoidable in a short period of time.

(2) Grassland degradation. Owing to overgrazing and unreasonable reclamation, grasslands in arid and semiarid regions of China are degrading and grass output has greatly decreased. It is estimated that in the past 10 years, grassland in China was degrading at a mean rate of 1.33 million

hm^2 per year, and the degraded grassland area has reached 87,000,000 hm^2. Due to large and long-term investments in grassland construction, coupled with road construction, uncontrolled fuel gathering, and digging medical herbs, the fragile eco-environment was further deteriorated.

(3) Serious water shortages. Owing to a dry climate and sparse precipitation, water resources in northwest China is limited. It is estimated that about 50 million rural people and 30 million heads of livestock cannot get sufficient drinking water. Unreasonable water allocation and misuse of water resources have caused serious conflicts between upstream and downstream water users in the Shiyang River Basin in the Hexi Corridor region, and as a result, some 4.5 million hm^2 of farmland in Minqin have been abandoned.

(4) Climate warming and aridification. The burning of fossil fuels and forest destruction have resulted in huge amounts of CO_2 emission. Since the 1960s, climate warming and aridification in northwest China have become increasingly clear and are mainly manifested in decreasing lake water levels, decreases in river runoff, retreating glacier and rising snow lines. It is predicted that in future decades, the temperature in the mid-latitude inland regions of the northern hemisphere will continuously rise due to the effect of global warming and aeolian desertification will be exacerbated.

8.5.2.2　Measures to control dust storms

Dust storms that occurred in the western part of America in the 1930s as well as the former Soviet Union in the 1960s became issues of global concern. From the 1930s onwards, the US government adopted a series of soil conservation measures such as inter-cropping, interplanting, stubble mulch farming and zero tillage, and they achieved great success in dust storm control; similarly, some water engineering and forest net construction measures were adopted in the former Soviet Union, and this also achieved great success. All these provide very useful experiences to learn from.

However, because dust storms are the outcome between the interaction of weather and ground surface processes, man can do little to entirely prevent them. To relieve the damages of dust storms we should adhere to the principle of "giving priority to prevention and attaching equal importance to protection and control", by protecting land cover and adopting various ecological protection measures.

(1) Define the northern limit of dry farming as quickly as possible to be able to implement the policy of "returning farmland to forest and grass".

(2) Work out the planning of "returning farmland to forest and grass" in different regions, select tree, shrub and grass species suitable to different climatic zones, and plant shrubs and subshrubs in dust source areas.

(3) Reasonable use of water resources. Irrational use of water resources in inland river basins in China has caused ecological problems in the lower reaches. Therefore, there is a need to control water use in the upper and middle reaches, adopt water-saving irrigation techniques and enhance

water use efficiency to protect downstream ecosystems.

In the 1950s, the Shiyang River supplied Minqin with 573 million m^3 of water per year, in the 1960s is supplied 445 million m^3, in the 1970s the value is 322 million m^3 and at present it is 70 million m^3. To maintain normal production, large amounts of groundwater were extracted, and by the 1970s, the groundwater table had lowered by 3–5 m. At present, the groundwater table is still lowering at an annual rate of 0.4 m. As a result, 90% of 13,300 hm^2 of *Elaeagnus augustifolia* forest planted in the 1960s has died and the mobilization of fixed sand dunes poses a serious threat to farmlands in Minqin.

The Heihe River is another large inland river in northwest China. In the 1950s, it provided downstream basin with 120.6 million m^3 water per year, in the 1960s, 103.5 million m^3 per year, and in 1985, only 79,000,000 m^3 water provided. As a result, the East and West Juyan lakes dried up, the eco-environment of Juyan oasis in Ejin Qi deteriorated, natural grassland area decreased, aeolian desertification exacerbated and dust storm frequency increased.

(4) Protect desert and establish natural reserves. Owing to repeated sorting, dune sands in desert regions are coarse with fine particles of only 2%–5%, and sand drift there can only affect the nearby area. Considering there is less than 100 mm precipitation and the current socioeconomic condition, there is no need to rehabilitate the desert at present. However, the sparse shrubs and coppice dunes in the isolation belt or the desert fringe area should be protected. The isolation belts around the desert are mostly covered by fixed dunes, and wind velocity at 2m above the surface is generally 50% lower than that of the exposed wind-eroded land; once the isolation belt is destroyed, the sand transport rate can reach 14 $m^3/a \cdot m$, which is 20 times higher than the 0.714 $m^3/a \cdot m$ of sand transport rate of the undisturbed isolation belt.

Establishing natural reserves have proved an effective measure to protect natural vegetation. For example, after six years of grazing exclusion in the Badaoqiao Natural Reserve in Ejin Qi the vegetation cover increased to 70%–90% from less than 20%, the leaf biomass of *Dopulusupules euphratica* trees reached 51,000 $kg \cdot hm^{-2}$, and the herb biomass under trees reached 15,000 $kg \cdot hm^{-2}$. After 20 years of grazing exclusion the vegetation cover in the outer protective area of oases increased from 15% to 50%.

(5) Establish protective forest system around oases. Farmland shelter forests should be established in combination with sand control engineering measures inside the oases. In the meantime, a 300-500 m wide grass belt should be established at the outer edge of the sand break forest. Grazing should be strictly prohibited and interdune depressions should be irrigated using flood water to promote vegetation restoration.

(6) Reform cultivation system. Efforts should be made to enhance cropland coverage in winter and spring, improve farm machinery, develop installation and greenhouse agriculture, return farmland unsuitable for cultivation to grassland and woodland, use solar energy and wind energy, stop cutting trees for fuel and halt blowing sand.

(7) Practise yard and confinement feeding of livestock, fence grasslands, establish artificial grassland and control animal population to restore eco-environment of grasslands.

(8) Strengthen the scientific study of the generation mechanism of dust storms, establish a monitoring network and early warning system to provide dust storm forecast services and reduce dust storm damages.

References

Chen Guangting, Zhang Jixian, Guan Youzhi et al. 1995. Blown Sand Control in Beijing Region. Articles Collection of Institute of Desert, Chinese Academy of Sciences Vol.4. Beijing: Science Press

Cheng Daoyuan. 1994. Atmospheric dust source and dust storms. World Desert Study, (1)

Dong Zhibao. 2000. Study of dust emission and control. Effects of sciences on society, (1)

Earth Science Department, Chinese Academy of Sciences. 2000. Causes of blowing dust weather and control strategies in northChina. Effects of Sciences on Society, (4)

Gilltte D. 1978. Wind tunnel simulation of the erosion of soil. Atmos Environ, 12: 1,735—1,743

Ina Tegen, Inea Fung. 1995. Contribution to the atmospheric mineral aerosol load from land surface modification. J Geophys Res, 100: 18,707—18,752

Wang Jiaying. 1963. Geological historic Materials of China. Beijing: Science Press

Wang Tao, Chen Guangting, Qian Zhengan et al. 2001. Dust storm status and countermeasures in northern China. Journal of Desert Research, (214): 322—327

Xia Xuncheng, Yang Gensheng. 1996. Sand Storm Hazards and Control in Northwest China. Beijing: China Environmental Science Press

Yang Gensheng. 1993. Formation process and control of "May 5" strong sand storm. Journal of Desert Research, (133)

Zhang De'er. 1982. Analysis of "dust rain" in historic period. Chinese Science Bulletin, (5)

Zhu Zhenda, Liu Shu, Di Xingmin. 1989. Desertification and Its Control in China. Beijing: Science Press

Chapter 9
Aeolian Desertification Monitoring and Assessment

9.1 Indicator systems for monitoring aeolian desertification by remote sensing

Aeolian desertification is a land degradation process characterized by aeolian sand movement, mainly resulting from human activities incompatible with the natural environment. During this process, physical and chemical properties of soil are altered by changes in landscape resulting from sand movement. Therefore, it is very important to establish a set of identifying indicators for monitoring aeolian desertification according to the degree of severity and development stage.

Since aeolian desertification is a complex land degradation process, it is usually considered that aeolian desertification indicators should be established according to natural conditions, human activities and socioeconomic regimes. But there is currently no globally accepted indicator system due to lack of consistency in indicator selection and its application. According to the aeolian desertification processes in northern China, we have established a universal aeolian desertification indicator and classification system, which places surface feature variations as the main factors and also considers the changes in soil, vegetation and the eco-system. The selected indicators have a common representativeness and it is easy to distinguish their differences while monitoring and evaluating aeolian desertification processes in northern China.

Aeolian desertification degree classification is important to evaluate aeolian desertification status and processes. Based on previous research results, it is divided into four grades, i.e. slight, moderate, severe and very severe degrees of aeolian desertification. The aeolian desertification degree can be developed or reversed, for example, moderately aeolian desertified land can develop into severely or very severely aeolian desertified land if the land is overused and wind erosion exacerbated; conversely, it can also be reversed to slightly aeolian desertified land or non-desertified land if some counter measures are adopted to control it.

For monitoring aeolian desertification processes, the most important issue is that the selected classification indicators should be representative and applicable. An indicator should be a statistic quantum or represent an envionment phenomena related to aeolian desertification processes, which represents an existing specific environmental condition (Wang Tao, 1998).

The indicators should have the following features: (a) contain clear information and are easy to obtain from observations; (b) sensitive to the changes in degree of aeolian desertification; (c) suitable to be used repeatedly; (d) able to be checked quantitatively.

From previous studies, such indicators are:

(1) Physical indicators: including dynamic data of wind eroded land, sandy land or sandy dune spread, dust storms, seasonal and annual changes of precipitation, wind direction, wind velocity, effective soil thickness, organic matter content, groundwater depth and quality and surface albedo etc.;

(2) Biological and agricultural indicators: including vegetation cover fraction, biological production, key plant species distribution, land-use regime (e.g. farming, grazing, fuel collection, industry, water resource use etc.), crop yield, livestock composition and number, and various economic input;

(3) Social indicators: including population, structure, variation processes and developmental trends, public health indexes, mandatory or stage-specific policies etc.

Aeolian desertification results from the interaction between natural conditions and human activities, of which human activities are the main contributors. Based on the causes of aeolian desertification, aeolian desertified land can be divided as: (a) aeolian desertified land caused by over-cultivation; (b) aeolian desertified land caused by overgrazing; (c) aeolian desertified land caused by over-collection of firewood; (d) aeolian desertified land caused by industry, city and communication constructions; e. aeolian desertified land caused by irrational utilization of water resources. The above-mentioned processes take place and develop under the action of external agents dominated by wind forces. They are manifested in two aspects: the first is wind erosion, which results in aeolian desertification of cultivated lands or grasslands or causes fixed or semi-fixed sand dunes to activate; the second is wind deposition occurring during the transportation process, which buries farmlands, pastoral lands, buildings and transportation lines.

Owing to some limitations and difficulties, not all the indicators can be used in monitoring aeolian desertification. Although a set of indicator systems of aeolian desertification had been established by FAO and UNEP in 1984, there is still a need to make a practical indicator system for regional desertification monitoring and assessment because of significant differences from place to place. According to human activity characteristics, existing monitoring results and the processes of aeolian desertification in northern China, we summed up the following directly usable indicators, which can be obtained and analyzed by remote sensing and GIS means: a) percentage of wind-eroded land area or shifting sand area in a region's total land area; b) percentage of annual expansion of wind-eroded land or shifting sand in a region's total land area; c) fraction of vegetation cover, mainly referring to grassland and forest land; d) biological production. A comprehensive classification of aeolian desertification degrees and their indicators are given in Table 9-1.

With the development of aeolian desertification, the land potential productivity and biological production are changed obviously. We can take these changes as supplementary indicators to evaluate the aeolian desertification degree (Table 9-2).

Table 9-1　Classification and indicators of aeolian desertification degrees

Degree	Blown-sand area (%)	Annual expansion area (%)	Vegetation cover fraction (%)	Annual reduction of biomass (%)
Slight (L)	< 5	< 1	> 60	< 1.5
Moderate (M)	5–25	1–2	60–30	1.5–3.5
Severe (S)	25–50	25	30–10	3.5–7.5
Very severe (VS)	> 50	> 5	10–0	> 7.5

Table 9-2　Supplementary indicators for aeolian desertification degrees

Degree	Soil deflation thickness (cm)	Accumulative thickness (cm)	Soil deflation rate [t/(hm²·a)]	Overload population (%)	Overload livestock (%)
Slight (L)	< 5	< 5	> 0.5	−50– −31	−50– −31
Moderate (M)	5–10	5–10	0.5–1.0	−31–0	−31–0
Severe (S)	10–20	10–20	1.0–3.0	0–31	0–31
Very severe (VS)	> 20	> 20	> 3.0	> 31	> 31

It is reasonable to divide the degrees of aeolian desertification based on ecology, but a great deal of information needs to be collected and detailed work must be done.

In fact, in the remote sensing monitoring practice, the percentage of eroded land or shifting sand areas and its changes in a certain period are taken as the main indicators, and others are considered supplementary indicators. This is because the change of eroded land or shifting sand area is a combined result of vegetation coverage biological production, soil properties and water content etc. It is easy derive by remote sensing during the aeolian desertification monitoring in northern China. This means that our indicator system mainly relies on the direct information of ground vegetation coverage species of plants and micro topographic features. The indicators we are able to practically use include: ① The area of shifting sands caused by wind erosion: i.e. the proportion of shifting sand, sand-mound and shifting sand dune areas in the region's total area, which is a main indicator for evaluating aeolian desertification degree. The larger the percentage, the degree of the aeolian desertification will be more severe. ② Vegetation coverage: it is a supplementary indicator. The lower the percentage, the degree of the aeolian desertification will be more severe.

Aeolian desertified land can be classified into four types as follows:

(1) Slightly aeolian desertified land. ① The blowouts appear on windward slopes of sand dunes and there are some accumulative shifting sands on leeward slopes; vegetation cover is 30%–50%, and patches of shifting sands occupy 25%. ② Shrubs grow well, sand mounds of different sizes appear around shrubs. ③There is a thin layer of shifting sands on the land surface. ④The ridges of cultivated field are eroded, and accumulated sands exist between the ridges. Humus layer of soil lose less than 50%. ⑤Crop yields only 50%–80% of that from the initial stages of cultivation. ⑥ Blowouts occur in shallow sandy areas, but some vegetation still exists; the blowouts

are gradually transformed without obvious steep benches.

(2) Moderately aeolian desertified land. ① An obvious differentiation between eroded slope and slip face appears, vegetation cover is 15%–30%, and the area of shifting sand occupies 25%–50%; ② Leaved shrubs cannot entirely cover sand mounds and there are shifting sands on the windward side of sand mounds; ③ Small patches of shifting sand occur in loessial farmland or on land surface covered by coarse sands or gravels, but sparse vegetation still exists with a coverage of 10%–30%; ④ There is obvious wind erosion in cultivated land, less than 50% of humus layer has been blown away, and crop yield is 50% of that from the initial stages of cultivation; ⑤ Blowouts are mostly exposed and ridges are easily found.

(3) Severely aeolian desertified land. ① Sandy land is in a semi-fixed state, the area of shifting sands exceeds 50%, and vegetation coverage is less than 15%; ② Gobi landscape occurs, vegetation cover is smaller than 10%; ③ Humus layer of soil is eroded and almost blown away, calcic horizon is exposed, and most desertified croplands are abandoned; ④ Deflation mounds and pillars appear on the land surface.

(4) Very severely aeolian desertified land. ① Land loses its productivity completely; ② A mobile sand dune landscape occurs in sandy lands; ③ Gobi landscape occurs in gravel lands; ④ Yardangs occur in wind-eroded lands.

9.2 Aeolian desertification monitoring methods based on 3S techniques

9.2.1 Technical principles

3S is an abbreviation for Global Positioning System (GPS), Remote Sensing (RS) and Geographical Information System (GIS).

9.2.1.1 Global Positioning System

Owing to lower population density, inconvenient communication and lack of ground objects in desertified areas, it is difficult to determine ground control points from satellite images. GPS is a very effective tool to determine an accurate position of ground points. It has the advantage of timesaving, precision and convenience.

The most important application of GPS is that we can know the exact position information of a point, the length of a forest belt and the areas of aeolian desertified land. Collected data can be computerized and displayed on various desertification maps with corresponding software.

The data of GPS provides us with position information including longitude, latitude, altitude, speed of a moving object and its direction. As a navigational tool, it can display the distance and time to a destination. It also can show the number of satellites and its technical information. Therefore, GPS is a very useful tool for monitoring desertification.

9.2.1.2　Remote sensing

Remote sensing is a new technique that uses a sensor to gather the information of ground objects from space or far distances. It is often used to obtain earth surface information like natural resources or environments. It has the following features: ① a large monitoring area; ② quick to obtain data; Landsat 4 scans the global surface every 16 days, climate satellite scans it every day; ③ almost no limitation from ground; ④ extensive usage and lower cost.

Remote sensing has a shortcoming that it is difficult to connect with Database Manage System (DBMS) and is not favorable for analysis. However, geodesy could provide digital information of land surface characteristics accurately. Especially GPS is a main data source of terrain in geographical information system and could be used for monitoring environmental changes.

9.2.1.3　Geographical Information System(GIS)

In GIS, geographical information is stored and processed in codes. The geographical position and object attributes are important content of this information.

GIS has three features: ① geographical information can be collected, managed, analyzed and outputted by the system dimensionally and dynamically; ②the data can be computerized and produce useful information; ③ complex information can be analyzed exactly, synthetically and rapidly.

The external appearance of GIS is a geographical information model constructed by computer software and geographical data. Users can select various contents from the model to make analyses and predictions according to their specific purpose. It can also be used to simulate natural processes to forecast results, and the best result can be selected for practice.

9.2.1.4　Integration of 3S

3S techniques provide a new tool for observation, description and analysis in scientific research and government management. The interaction of 3S constructs a frame with a brain and two eyes, of which RS and GPS provide regional information and dimensional position; GIS selects useful information from RS and GPS data, and then makes an analysis.

In the monitoring practice, 2S combinations are often used, such as the combination of GIS/RS, GIS/GPS or RS/GPS.

9.2.2　Aeolian desertification monitoring methods based on 3S techniques

Remote sensing is a widely used technique in monitoring aeolian desertification, of which air photos and satellite images are main information sources. They record the electromagnetic wave variations of ground objects. The satellite images are widely used because they have multi-wave bands and it is easy to discriminate between objects and landforms.

The purpose of aeolian desertification monitoring is to get the distribution maps of aeolian desertified lands in different periods based on the remote sensing data and field investigations. In previous research, some precise results of aeolian desertified land distribution have been made by relying on aerial photo information. Due to high cost, the complex procedure from inputting data in the database, and difficulty in updating data, aerial photos are only used in precise quantitative analysis of aeolian desertified lands in some example plots. For example, aerial photos were used to monitor the changes of aeolian desertified lands from the 1950s to the early 1970s. Afterwards, most of the data came from Landsat TM images from the 1980s and the 1990s. In processing, the data images from different periods of time were first corrected geometrically; secondly, a unified classification system was established and related information was selected; and finally the transformation process of aeolian desertified lands during a certain period was analyzed. Using the above-mentioned method, we obtained a practical method for aeolian desertification dynamic monitoring (Fig. 9-1).

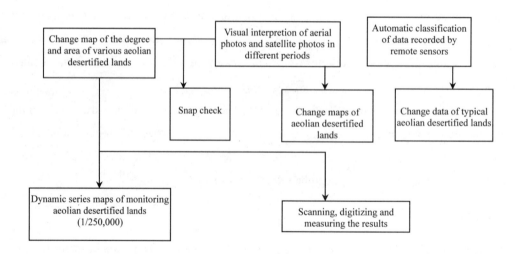

Fig. 9-1　Block diagram of technical route for aeolian desertification monitoring by remote sensing(Wu, 1997)

At present, TM image is a widely used information source as it has high resolution and high geometrical fidelity. The data is obtained by seven-wave band at the same time and covers a large area and long period compared to NOAA and SPOT imagery. TM image is used below as an example to explain some key issues in aeolian desertification monitoring.

9.2.2.1　Selection of acquired time for TM images

The selection of acquired time for TM images can greatly influence the monitoring results because it can enhance or reduce aeolian desertification degree determined by vegetation cover when interpretating images. Therefore, selecting an optimal time interval is a key issue for successful monitoring.

For the selection, winter and spring are not good seasons due to limited precipitation, sparse vegetation and monotonous reflective colors from ground objects. In summer, vegetation on sandy land is flourishing, and vegetation cover can be used to classify aeolian desertification degree, but dense crops are easily confused with forest. Therefore autumn is the best season to acquire optimal TM images for desertification monitoring.

9.2.2.2　The effects of image processing techniques on monitoring results

The purpose of image or information processing is to make them suitable to use. Processing techniques include radiance correction and enhancing the original image to make the image clearer. Automatic information identification and classification processing are also important steps. Regardless, the basic principle of the processing is to get the maximum information, i.e. intertype variance is large and key ground objects to be monitored should be discriminated clearly.

With the current monitoring and researches, standard false color composite of TM images is selected in TM band 4, 3, and 2 with three colors, i.e. red, green and blue, respectively. These wavebands are the best to reflect the vegetation-growing situation. TM band 4 can reflect vegetation features in different degrees of aeolian desertified lands; TM band 3 can reflect the brightness of sandy soils and whiteness of salinized soils; TM band 2 is sensitive to vegetation reflectance and can distinguish forest types and species of trees. The composite images of these bands can prominently display vegetation features, but the images of such wavebands have a comparatively weak reflection to sand dune information. Therefore it can be said that processing techniques of images and waveband selection have a great influence on monitoring results.

9.2.2.3　Visual interpretation of aeolian desertification monitoring

Visual interpretation is a basic method in TM image application, even in the process of digital image processing with computers. Although computer classification automatic is high speed, it is mostly used with simple and homogeneous situations of ground objects. Visual interpretation still is a main method in our research. The differentiation is that while traditional visual interpretation draw outline on paper with a pen, now the outlines are drawn on a computer screen through human and computer communication.

The interpretation experience and understanding about the local environment and related knowledge can affect the interpretation results or even get completely different results. Therefore, interpreters and analyzers must be familiar with interpretation content, image characteristics and interpretation marks of aeolian desertification of various types during the man-machine dialogue and visual interpretation processes. It is necessary to train interpreters and reduce the mistakes resulting from human factors.

The interpretation of images is an important part of aeolian desertified land monitoring by remote sensing. In the interpretation, we should first establish a monitoring classification system, based on the distribution, types and development degree of local aeolian desertified lands. Secondly, we determine some interpretation indicators and then match the indicators with image features. Colors and shapes are considered the main features of the images. Image colors reflect the difference of electromagnetic waves from ground targets, which are changed with the composition of objects and their surface structure or temperature; the shapes reflect landscape status and substance composition of land surface.

Some interpretation indicators are summarized and listed in Table 9-3 according to our study in the Mu Us Sandy Land.

Table 9-3   TM image features of landuse and aeolian desertification types

Land types	Image features	Other features
Cultivated land	Regular shapes, grid-like, red or light red color etc.	Road, canal and easy to judge linear objects
Grassland	Large patches, irregular shape, pink, red or grayish white colors	Flat surface
Forest	No fixed shape, red, red-brown, brown colors	Course surface
Orchard	Patches of regular shape, red-blown color	Clear boundary, uniform color
Residential area	Regular geometric graph, blue-gray, cinerous colors	Obscure boundary
Lake, reservoir	Irregular shape, blue-black color	Clear boundary
Sand dune	Crescent, patchy and wave shapes, grayish-yellow, light gray-white colors	Clear boundary, uniform color
Salinized land	Irregular patches, white, gray-white colors	Patchy shape, clear boundary
Shoaly land	Strip shape, white and even color, light red color if vegetation exists	Usually distributed along rivers
Bare rock	Rhombus shape, gray-green, blue-gray colors	Linear veins, clear boundary
Snow	Irregular wadding shape, even white color	Uniform colon
Slightly aeolian desertified land	Irregular block shape, light red color	Red patches occurring on light red color background
Moderately aeolian desertified land	Irregular block shape, light red color	Undulating land surface with sand dunes
Severely aeolian desertified land	Irregular patchy shape, blown-yellow color	Dunes and coppice
Very severely aeolian desertified land	Widespread, blown-yellow color	Clear landscape of sand dunes and sand ridges

9.3   Some results of aeolian desertification monitoring over the past 50 years

9.3.1   Monitoring and assessment of modern aeolian desertification

Modern aeolian desertification refers to the land desertification development processes that occurred in the past 100 years as a result of human activities. Considering there are limited observations and statistical data including those from meteorology, hydrology, soil, population, livestock, land use, input and output etc., the main focus is on monitoring aeolian desertification that occurred in the past 50 years.

Two large-scale investigations of aeolian desertified lands had been carried out in the mid-1970s and late 1980s by the former Lanzhou Institute of Desert Research, Chinese Academy of Sciences. The first investigation in the 1970s showed that there were 334,000 km^2 of aeolian desertified lands in 212 counties or Qis, located in the provinces of Heilongjiang, Jilin, Liaoning, Hebei, Shaanxi, Inner Mongolia, Shanxi, Ningxia, Gansu, Qinghai and Xinjiang, of which 176,000 km^2 have already been aeolian desertified and 158,000 km^2 are potential aeolian desertified lands. Compared with aerial photo data of the 1950s, aeolian desertified lands in northern China expanded at an annual rate of 1,560 km^2/a from the 1950s to 1970s. There are two causes for the expansion of aedian desertified land: one is dry-farming lands resulting in aeolian desertification due to over cultivation in steppes and desert steppe regions, and another is mobilization of fixed dunes due to overgrazing and over cutting of firewood in fixed sand dune areas. For example, in Xin Barag Zuoqi of Hulun Buir grassland, the area of aeolian desertified land increased from 9.2% in 1959 to 12% in 1984; in Naiman Qi of Horqin grassland, it increased from 39.3% in the late 1950s to 65.6% in the mid 1970s.

Funded by the government, a second investigation was carried out in the 1980's. Remote sensing was used as the main means for the investigation and monitoring. The monitoring results indicate that there were 371,000 km^2 of aeolian desertified land in China, accounting for 3.86% of its total land area, distributed in arid, semiarid and semi humid areas and covering 11 provinces. The agro-pastural zone along the Great Wall and in Inner Mongolia is the most rapidly developing region of aeolian desertification, where 36.5% of the total aeolian desertified land is distributed (121,900 km^2). It expanded about 24,800 km^2 from the 1970s to the late 1980s, with an average annual increase rate of 2,103.2 km^2 (development rate is 1.47%). Meanwhile about 2,250 km^2 of aeolian desertified land had been reversed. According to this development speed, there is an additional 32,100 km^2 of land that was aeolian desertified by the year of 2000, which is equal to 2,384 km^2 of useful land that is aeolian desertified in a year; the annual development rate is 1.20% (Zhu Zhenda, 1984).

The study showed that grassland reclamation, over-grazing, over cutting and excessive economic activities resulted directly from population growth. For instance, the population growth rate in agro-pastural zones was 3.08%, which is an average population density increase from 10–15 persons/km^2 in 1949 to 40–60 persons/ km^2, or even up to 80 persons / km^2 in 1980 in some regions. Increased population exacerbates landuse pressure and causes over-reclamation and overgrazing of grasslands. In Gurban Hua of Naiman Qi, 80% of fixed sandy land and grassland had been reclaimed into dry-farming land in the period from 1966–1977; in Chaolutu of Horqin Zuoyi Houqi, 110,000 hm^2 of grassland had been cultivated one to three times, and aeolian desertified land increased from

13.7% in the 1950s to 30.8% in the 1970s. The increased livestock resulted in overburdening the grassland, and the per livestock share of grassland was reduced from 3.07 hm^2 in the 1950s to 1-1.33 hm^2 in the 1970s, even as low as 0.33–0.67 hm^2 in some regions; in Horqin Zuoyi Houqi, one sheep occupied only 0.26 hm^2 of grassland, in Naiman Qi 0.2 hm^2. Another reason directly resulting in fixed dune mobilization and grassland erosion is over-collection of firewood and destruction of natural vegetation. Taking Elesun Village in the northern part of Hure Qi as an example, the annual firewood consumption of 1,340 families is equivalent to the destruction of 10,000 hm^2 of shrubs. Industry, communication and city construction as well as improper usage of water resources in arid and semiarid regions also results in the development of aeolian desertification.

The aeolian desertification development mentioned above is caused by wind action after destroying vegetation. Wind tunnel experiments showed that irrational cultivation, grazing and collection of firewood can greatly accelerate soil erosion, and these important factors resulted in aeolian desertification of grasslands.

In the 1990s, the speed of aeolian desertified land expansion further increased, and the annual development rate was 2,460 km^2 (Wang Jinfeng, 1995), mainly occurring in the following three regions.

(1) Agro-pastural zones of the semiarid region occupies 40.5% of total aeolian desertified land of northern China. For example in Bashang of Hebei province and Houshan of Inner Mongolia, the area of aeolian desertified lands increased from 3% in the 1950s to 13% in the 1970s and 25% in the late 1980s.

(2) Sandy grassland zones of the semiarid region occupies 36.5%. For example, the aeolian desertified land in the Horqin grassland increased from 20% in the 1950s to 53% in the 1970s and to 77.6% in the 1980s.

(3) Arid oasis edge and lower reaches of inland rivers occupy 23%, characterized by fixed dune mobilization or shifting sand encroachment. In the lower reach of the Heihe River, located in the Hexi corridor, the aeolian desertified lands increased from 5% of the region's total area in the 1950s, to 22% in the 1970s and to 36% in the 1980s.

If some control measures are taken, the aeolian desertified lands can be reversed. Remote sensing data showed that about 10% of aeolian desertified lands kept a stable state or exhibited a reversal trend.

9.3.2 Monitoring and evaluation of aeolian desertification in typical regions

With the application of remote sensing and GIS techniques, a larger scale investigation on the aeolian desertified land distribution, development and hazards have been made in northern China. The study of aeolian desertification has entered a new stage of quantitative analysis and evaluation (Zhu, 1991; Wu, 1991, 1997; Wang, 1992; Wang et al., 1994, 1998; Liu, 1996). During the study of the national key project "Aeolian desertification hazard monitoring and evaluation in agro-pastural zones in the northern China", an evaluation map of aeolian desertification hazards at a scale of 1 ∶ 4,000,000 was completed. A hazard database of Mu Us and Horqin Sandy Lands was established under the support of TM data and GIS. Based on the study of classification, indicator systems, evaluation models and remote sensing data processing, a tentative system of aeolian desertification hazard monitoring has been set up.

With the above system and TM data of 1987 and 1993, we monitored the aeolian desertification dynamic processes of the Mu Us Sandy Land. The aeolian desertified lands had been reduced from 32,586 km^2 to 30,497 km^2 in this period, with an average 276.6 km^2 of aeolian desertified land rehabilitated annually.

Xingrong district of Naiman Qi is another successful monitoring example. From the comparison of field survey and remote sensing monitoring results from 1974 and 1994, it can be seen that the land-use structure greatly changed before and after rehabilitation as shown in Table 9-4, and the economic benefit is obvious.

Table 9-4　Effects of aeolian desertification control in Xingrong district of Naiman Qi, Inner Mongolia (1974—1994)

Item		1974		1994		Effect	
		Area(hm^2)	Percent(%)	Area(hm^2)	Percent(%)		
Land use	aeolian desertified land	15,700	29.62	2,100	3.96	−13,600 ha	−86.62%
	Forest	777	1.47	15,840	30.10	+15,063 ha	+19 times
	Crop	4,960	9.36	6,900	13.02	+1,940	+39.11%
Total grain output		2,790t		13,110t		+10,320 t	+3.7 times
Grain yield per unit area (kg/hm^2)		562.5m		1,900m		+1,377.5m	+2.4 times
Grassland carrying capacity (sheep unit)		124,200		152,200		+2,800	+22.5%
Per capita income (Yuan/person)		80		1,120		+1.040	+13 times

9.4　Model of aeolian desertification assessment

9.4.1　Outline of the assessment model

9.4.1.1　Features of the aeolian desertification environment information system

In China, the aeolian desertification environment information system is a techique newly developed in the 1980s. This system provides a wealth of information on aeolian desertification development and has the following characteristics.

(1) It has the capability for data collection, dynamic management and output for geographical information.

(2) It can be used to conduct comprehensive spatial analysis and dynamic monitoring of aeolian desertification by a geographic model, and produce useful information for policy-making.

(3) Computerized aeolian desertification environment information is an important characteristic of the system. It can deal with various complex information with high speed and high accuracy, which is difficult to do when done by a human being alone.

9.4.1.2 Appearance and connotation of the aeolian desertification environment information system

The hardware and software of the computer are the appearance of the aeolian desertification environment information system; its application is a geographic information model consisting of computer programs and geographical data. When a user specializes in aeolian desertification or has certain knowledge of geography, the spatial data becomes a realistic world through an abstract model. It is much more flexible and contains more content than geographical maps. Users can observe all the contents or extract some phenomena or spatial data in the model according to their specific purpose. The most important characteristic is that natural phenomena and human thinking can be added in the data model to conduct analyses and predict information. These are meaningful applications of the aeolian desertification environment information system.

9.4.1.3 Tools of the aeolian desertification environment information system

The key software of the aeolian desertification environment information system is ARC/INFO developed by the American Environment System Institute. With the improvement of GIS software, the aeolian desertification environment information system supported by GIS shows many advantages such as saving cost and manpower to develop the software, shortened time period, and easy to use and popularize. More and more scientists who engage in geography or aeolian desertification studies have accepted this method.

9.4.1.4 Structure of the aeolian desertification environment information system

The aeolian desertification environment information system consists of three parts i.e., namely the computer hardware, software and geographical spatial data. Its core is the computer system. Spatial data reflects the geographical contents of the aeolian desertification environment information system.

(1) Computer hardware. Computer hardware usually includes a mainframe as well as input and output parts of data or graphics. GPS is also used in the aeolian desertification environment information system. The system scale, accuracy, speed, function and method are closely related to the hardware.

(2) Computer software. Necessary programs include the following three components:

① Computer system software: Operating system, programming languages, programming environment and so on.

② GIS software and other supporting software: ARC/INFO, ARCVIEW, Visual FoxPro, Photoshop, image processing systems and others.

③ Analytical software

Analytical software is compiled by users according to research content and specific tasks. It is the most important part for users and also a key part to extract aeolian desertification information from spatial data.

(3) Geographical spatial data. Geographical spatial data is the realistic contents of GIS and analytical object of system programs. It includes natural and social-economic information referring to surface position comprised of graphics, images, figures and other measurement data which are inputted into GIS with a digital scanner, a keyboard or the GPS method. It has three data types.

① Coordinate system of spatial data: It indicates the geographic position of any target or object on land surface, such as longitude and latitude.

② Topological relation of data: It includes the spatial relation between point, line and area, which is an important issue for data coding, input, storage management, searching and modeling analysis.

③ Attribute: It consists of qualitative and quantitative attributes. Qualitative attributes include name, type, and property, all of which describe the landscape, aeolian desertification types, land utilization etc. Quantitative attributes include the amount and degree, both of which can describe the area, length, hazard degree, population density, precipitation, days of strong wind, depth of groundwater etc. There is at least one attribute for any geographic object. Analysis, searching and expression of GIS are realized from the attributes.

9.4.2 Model of aeolian desertification assessment

The model of aeolian desertification assessment is the main part of the aeolian desertification environment information system and the core content of GIS.

9.4.2.1 Data source and selection principle for the model

The data source and selection principle should be thoroughly considered because aeolian desertification is a very complex process involving natural, economic and social factors. The main factors should be determined according to local characteristics. Data is mostly derived from geographic maps, remote sensing images, and the statistical data of natural and social economic information.

In the establishment of an aeolian desertification database the following aspects should be considered.

(1) Natural factors: Includes climate factors such as precipitation, wind, evaporation, sunlight, temperature etc. and ground factors like soil type, forest, vegetation, crop, land utilization. It even includes wind erosion, dust storm, organic matter content, depth and quality of groundwater etc.

(2) Economic factors: Includes gross output of industry, agriculture and stockbreeding.

(3) Social factors include population and its distribution structure, historical change and prediction.

9.4.2.2　Contents of the model

The contents of the model include attribute and background databases constructed with graphics and image information. Based on these databases, a series of studies can be conducted using the model, such as the study of aeolian desertification monitoring, hazard degree, and prediction as well as aeolian desertification simulation and modeling method.

9.4.2.3　Cluster and discriminant analytical model

1) Cluster analysis model

Cluster analysis is one of the statistical techniques. Its basic principle is to cluster similar samples according to their attributes and similarities and then determine their interrelationship. This can reduce the effect of subjective human factors.

Hierarchical map clustering is a commonly used method. Firstly aeolian desertification indicators were selected, such as land surface albedo, frequency of dust storms, wind speed, vegetation coverage, land utilization etc., then a hierarchical map was drawn and classification was made. With the work carried out in the Mu Us and Horqin Sandy Lands as an example, we introduce this method as follows.

Factor selection:

We selected 21 factors related to aeolian desertification. They are ① annual average temperature; ② number of sunlight days ⩾10°C; ③ accumulative temperature; ④ solar radiation; ⑤ frost-free period; ⑥ maximum depth of frozen soil; ⑦ annual average precipitation; ⑧ evaporation; ⑨ average wind speed; ⑩ number of strong wind days; ⑪ number of dust storm days; ⑫ days of hail; ⑬ population density; ⑭ number of big livestock; ⑮ number of small livestock; ⑯ artificial forest; ⑰ sandy badland; ⑱ cropland area; ⑲ grassland; ⑳ forest coverage; ㉑ agriculture production value.

Of these factors, ⑯-⑲ are expressed in percentage, and they are divided by the total area of the county. The data comes from 17 samples, which include Tongliao City, Horqin Zuoyi Zhongqi, Horqin Zuoyi Houqi, Kailu County, Hure Qi, Naiman Qi, Jarud, Otog Qi Qianqi, Ejin Horo Qi, Uxin Qi, Jungar Qi, Dongsheng city, Hanggin Qi, Fuxin County, Changtu County, Dalad Qi and Otog Qi.

Most active factors which have an accumulative contribution over 97% must be selected and some factors which have a large coefficient λ_i should be eliminated. The eliminated factors include ① annual average temperature; ② number of sunlight days ($\geqslant 10°C$); ③ accumulative temperature; ④ solar radiation; ⑤ frost-free period; ⑥ maximum depth of frozen soil; ⑦ average wind speed; ⑧ cropland area.

It can be seen from the result of principal components analysis: ① maximum frozen soil depth does not reflect its relationship to aeolian desertification, but the number of dust storm days conform to aeolian desertification status; ② average wind speed is not the best variable reflecting wind regime; ③ cropland area does not reflect a direct relationship to aeolian desertification owing to lack of inclusion of some aeolian desertified lands; ④ the number of hail days has a limited effect on aeolian desertification; ⑤ the factor of average temperature is much more important than accumulative temperature and solar radiation(Table 9-5).

Table 9-5　The contribution of major factors to aeolian desertification

Factors	Ratio (%)	Factors	Ratio (%)
Annual average temperature	31.09	Population density	5.12
Precipitation	16.00	Sandy land	4.62
Evaporation	6.65	Crop land	3.93
Number of strong wind days	7.84	Grassland	3.24
Number of dust storm days	7.49	Livestock	2.88
Forest coverage	6.22	Artificial forest	2.10

The remaining factors represent three aspects, i.e. nature, society and economy. Natural factors include annual average temperature, precipitation, evaporation, number of strong wind days, number of dust storm days and forest cover; social factors include population density; economic factors include percentage of sandy land, grassland, number of livestock, artificial forest etc.

2) System clustering methods

There are many kinds of system clustering methods. Commonly used methods are the nearest neighbor, the farthest neighbor, median clustering, centroid clustering, Ward's method, and between-group linkage method. System clustering methods belong to static clustering and can be further divided into stepwise clustering I stepwise clustering II, samples clustering, fuzzy clustering and crawling methods.

(1) Hierarchical clustering methods. Samples are first selected then classified and merged according to their similarity, resulting in several different classifications. The mathematic calculation basis is the matrix consisting of N samples with a proximity coefficient. What methods will be used depend on the proximity coefficient. The analyzed results of the above 17 samples are shown as follows:

① The result is not good with the nearest neighbor method.

② It can be divided into four types of pattern with the furthest neighbor method:

I. Severe (Kailu County, Naiman Qi, Hure Qi and Jungar Qi);

II. Very severe (Uxin Qi, Otog Qi, Dalad Qi, Otog Qianqi, Ejin Horo Qi, Hanggin Qi);

III. Slight (Tongliao city, Dongsheng city);

IV. Moderate (Horqin Zuoyi Zhongqi, Horqin Zuoyi Houqi, Fuxin County, Changtu County).

From hierarchical maps it can be seen that other system clustering methods, such as median clustering, centroid clustering, Ward's method, and between group linkage etc., also yield better results.

(2) The nearest neighbor method of stepwise clustering. The principle of stepwise clustering is to first divide samples into many initial types and then make adjustments to a stable state according to a certain regulation (specialized knowledge). There are many ways to produce initial types and conduct adjustment including merging and dividing the types, but they all use iterative equations to make calculations. The calculated results for the above 17 counties using this method are as follows:

① According to specified examples

I. Slight (Tongliao city, Fuxin county, Changtu County);

II. Severe (Horqin Zuoyi Zhongqi, Horqin Zuoyi Houqi, Kulen County, Naiman Qi, Ejin Horo Qi, Jungar Qi, Dongsheng City);

III. Moderate (Otog Qianqi, Hanggin Qi, Kailu County, Otog Qi);

IV. Very severe (Dalad Qi, Jarud Qi, Uxin Qi).

② According to maximum and minimum regulation

I. Slight (Tongliao City, Changtu County);

II. Very severe (Jarud Qi, Otog Qi, Hanggin Qi, Dalad Qi);

III. Moderate (Horqin Zuoyi Zhongqi, Horqin Zuoyi Houqi, Naiman Qi, Uxin Qi);

IV. Severe (Kailu County, Hure Qi, Ejin Horo Qi, Jungar Qi, Dongsheng City, Fuxin County, Otog Qi).

The results showed that method ② is better than method ①.

(3) Between-group linkage method of stepwise clustering. It uses the same principles as the nearest neighbor method, but the regulation, criteria and classification of initial types are different. With this method, the calculated results are:

Initial types classified according to serial number of samples

I. Moderate (Horqin Zuoyi Zhongqi, Horqin Zuoyi Houqi, Naiman Qi, Jungar Qi);

II. Very severe (Jarudqi, Otog Qianqi, Uxin Qi, Hanggin Qi);

III. Severe (Kailu County, Hure Qi, Ejin Horo Qi, Dongsheng City, Otog Qi, Dalad Qi);

IV. Moderate (Horqin Zuoyi Zhongqi, Horqin Zuoyi Houqi, Ejin Horo Qi, Uxin Qi).

Stepwise clustering methods are better than previous methods.

(4) Gray clustering. Gray clustering is a newly developed method based on the similarity and dissimilarity of factors and used to measure the correlation degree. Seven sample counties are analyzed with the following six factors.

① annual average wind speed; ② number of dust storm days; ③ sandy land (%); ④ vegetation coverage; ⑤ overload of population; ⑥ overload of livestock; Grayness is divided into 4 types, i.e. slight, moderate, severe and very severe.

The seven sample counties are Naiman Qi, Tongliao City, Hure Qi, Changtu County, Uxin Qi, Hanggin Qi and Kailu County.

Step 1, give a whitening cluster number d_{ij}. Where d_{ij} is action degree of factor j on sample i. It constructs a matrix D with 7 rows by 6 columns.

Step 2, determine whitening function F_{ij}. Where F_{ij} is whitening function of factor i to grayness type j. It is $6 \times 4 = 24$ totally (Table 9-6).

Table 9-6 Factor scales of aeolian desertification degree

Types	Very severe	Severe	Moderate	Slight
Average wind speed	$[20, \infty)$	$[15,20)$	$[10,15)$	$[5,10]$
Number of dust storm days	$[6, \infty)$	$[6, \infty)$	$[3,6)$	$[3,6]$
Sandy land	$[16, \infty)$	$[12,16)$	$[8,12)$	$[4,8]$
Vegetation coverage	$[12, \infty)$	$[9,12)$	$[6,9)$	$[3,6]$
overload of Population	$[50, \infty)$	$[0,50)$	$[-34,0)$	$(-\infty,34)$
overload of Livestock	$[50, \infty)$	$[0,50)$	$[-34,0)$	$(-\infty,34)$

Note: $-\infty$ fluctuates around threshold value, rather than negative infinity.

Step 3, calculate labeled clustering weight.

The clustering weight (η_{kj}) of a factor to grayness type j is expressed as

$$\eta_{kj} = \lambda_{ij} / \left(\sum_{i=1}^{N} \lambda_{ij} \right) \qquad (k=1, 2, \cdots, 6; \quad j=1, 2, 3, 4) \qquad (9\text{-}1)$$

λ_{ij} is determined by whitening function. Calculated results, can be seen in Table 9-7.

Table 9-7 Calculated results of each factor

Types	1 Very severe	2 Severe	3 Moderate	4 Slight
Average wind speed	0.4	0.3	0.2	0.1
Number of dust storm days	0.33	0.33	0.17	0.17
Sandy land	0.4	0.3	0.2	0.1
Vegetation cover	0.4	0.3	0.2	0.1
Overload of population	0.5	0.5	−0.34	0.34
Overload of livestock	0.5	0.5	−0.34	0.34

Step 4, calculate clustering coefficient.

σ_{ij} is the coefficient of sample county i to grayness type j and is given by

$$\sigma_{ij} = \sum_{k=1}^{N} f_{ji}(d_{ik})\eta_{ki} \tag{9-2}$$

The obtained results are shown in Table 9-8.

Table 9-8　Results of grayness weight fon each example

Item	Naiman Qi	Tongliao City	Hure Qi	Changtu County	Uxin Qi	Hanggin Qi	Kailu County
	1	2	3	4	5	6	7
1.Very severe	0.4	0.83	0.73	0.73	1.13	1.23	1.13
2.Severe	1.3	0.43	1.33	1.13	0.83	1.13	1.63
3.Severe	0.34	0.34	0.20	0.57	0.54	0.34	0.20
4.Slight	0.68	0.95	0.88	1.25	0.85	0.68	0.68

Step 5, construct clustering vector.

The clustering vector is obtained from grayness weight of various samples presented in the above table. It is expressed by

$$Q_i = (\sigma_{i_1}, \sigma_{i_2}, \sigma_{i_3}, \sigma_{i_4}) \tag{9-3}$$

Where i=1,2,3,4.

Step 6, clustering.

Select the largest vector from the Q_i to decide the grayness type, and the results are as follows(Table 9-9).

Table 9-9　Results of clustering

Samples	Naiman Qi	Tongliao City	Hure Qi	Changtu County	Uxin Qi	Hanggin Qi	Kailu County
	1	2	3	4	5	6	7
Results	Severe	Slight	Severe	Moderate	Very severe	Very severe	Severe

Discussion:

① Gray clustering method is simple, clear and involves less calculation.

② Clustering results are reasonable.

③ The accuracy depends on the structure of whitening coefficient matrix and whitening function, two parameters which are affected by human subjective factors.

(5) Other methods.

① Ordered sample classification.

Adjust sequence of samples, put similar samples together and classify in order.

I. Slight (Tongliao City, Fuxin County, Changtu City);

II. Moderate (Horqin Zuoyi Zhongqi, Horqin Zuoyi Houqi, Kailu County, Hure Qi, Naiman Qi,

Jarud Qi, Otog Qianqi, Ejin Horo Qi, Uxin Qi);

III. Severe (Jungar Qi, Dongsheng City, Otog Qi, Dalad Qi);

IV. Very severe (Hanggin Qi).

The results are reasonable.

② Fuzzy clustering.

17 simples are clustered by this method, the results are as follows.

When λ=0.99:

I. Tongliao City;

II. Horqin Zuoyi Zhongqi, Horqin Zuoyi Houqi, Kailu County, Hure Qi, Naiman Qi, Ejin Horo Qi, Jungar Qi, Fuxin County, Changtu County;

III. Jarud Qi;

IV. Otog Qianqi, Uxin Qi, Dalad Qi;

V. Dongsheng City, Otog Qi;

VI. Hanggin Qi.

When λ=0.988:

I. Tongliao City, Horqin Zuoyi Zhongqi, Horqin Zuoyi Houqi, Kailu County, Hure Qi, Ejin Horo Qi, Jungar Qi, Dongsheng City, Fuxin County, Changtu County;

II. Jarud Qi, Otog Qi;

III. Otog Qianqi, Uxin Qi, Dalad Qi;

IV. Hanggin Qi.

The classification is not accurate; the value of λ is too high.

9.4.3 Discriminant analysis model of aeolian desertification

The discriminant analysis is based on the cluster analysis mentioned above and produces a new variable from original aeolian desertification indicators according to Fisher's criteria. The new variable allows the difference between two groups reach the greatest limit as well as the difference within a group reach the lowest limit. Therefore we can easily find the differences among samples. Discriminant function can be expressed as:

$$R=\lambda_a A+\lambda_b B+\lambda_c C+\cdots+\lambda_k K \tag{9-4}$$

Where λ_a, λ_b, λ_c, $\cdots$, λ_k are coefficients; A, B, C, $\cdots$, K are variable indices.

The model can be used to discriminate and classify sample points and check the reasonableness of their classification. The contribution of each factor can also be calculated by the model.

There are many discriminant analysis methods, such as distance discriminant analysis method, Bayes method, Fisher method, stepwise discriminant analysis method etc. Here we use Fisher's discriminant method.

From previous results, Tongliao City, Fuxin County and Changtu County are selected as slightly aeolian desertified samples (group A), and Jarud Qi, Otog Qianqi and Ejin Horo Qi as group B. The other 11 samples are classified as follows(Table 9-10):

Table 9-10   Classified results

Original number	Region	Results	Original number	Region	Results
2	Horqin Zuoyi Zhongqi	A	11	Jungar Qi	B
3	Horqin Zuoyi Houqi	A	12	Dongsheng City	B
4	Kailu County	B	13	Hanggin Qi	B
5	Hure Qi	B	16	Dalad Qi	B
6	Naiman Qi	A	17	Otog Qi	B
10	Uxin Qi	B			

9.4.4   Prediction model of aeolian desertification

Aeolian desertification is a complex process and belongs to a typical gray system. So a gray system model is adopted to forecast the development trend of aeolian desertification. The key issue is to establish a gray dynamic model. For convenience, we use a GM (1, 1) gray forecast model. It is expressed as

$$X^{(1)}(t+1) = \left(X^{(0)}(1) - \frac{u}{a} \right) e^{-at} + \frac{u}{a} \quad \text{(Time function)} \tag{9-5}$$

or

$$X^{(0)}(t+1) = -a \left(X^{(0)}(1) - \frac{u}{a} \right) e^{-at} \tag{9-6}$$

9.4.5   Evaluation models of aeolian desertified land

Aeolian desertified land evaluation involves many aspects, such as the evaluation of aeolian desertified land status, hazard degree, land utilization, development, social economic effect and so on. Commonly used models include:

(1) Fuzzy evaluation model. This model is established based on the principle of fuzzy relation and belongs to a multi-objective model.

(2) System Dynamic model. This model is based on feedback control theory and studies social economic systems by simulation means. It can reveal the relations of mutual dependence and restriction of various factors and can also be used to analyze, compare and select the best implementation scheme for desertification control.

(3) Model of Analytic Hierarchy Process. The Analytic Hierarchy Process (AHP) was

developed in the 1970's by Prof. Thomas Saaty. It is a powerful and flexible decision making process to help people set priorities and make the best decision when both qualitative and quantitative aspects of a decision need to be considered. AHP is based on the assumption that when faced with a complex decision the human reaction is to cluster the decision factors according to their common characteristics. This involves building a hierarchy (ranking) of decision factors, making comparisons between each possible pair in each cluster (as a matrix), and then giving a weighting for each factor within a cluster. It consists of the following steps.

① Determine scope and concerned factors and find a mutual relation ship between the factors.

② Build a hierarchy (ranking) of factors and draw a map of hierarchy structure.

③ build matrices.

Discriminate the importance of each factor in the matrix. For example, the following matrix is analyzed(Table 9-11).

Table 9-11   Matrix of judgement

A_K	B_1	B_2	$\cdots$	B_N
B_1	B_{11}	B_{12}	$\cdots$	B_{1N}
B_2	B_{21}	B_{22}	$\cdots$	B_{2N}
$\vdots$				
B_N	B_{N1}	B_{N2}	$\cdots$	B_{NN}

Note: B_i is the judgment value of relative importance to B_j, B_{ij} is the judgement value of relative importance to A_K.

④ Ranking components in one hierarchy.

Calculate the importance order of various factors of a hierarchy relative to a factor of the previous hierarchy by a judgement matrix. Generally it is expressed by weight vector $W= (W_1, W_2, \cdots, W_n)$.

$$\sum_{i=1}^{n} W_i = 1$$

Where $W_i (i=1,2,\cdots, n)$ reflects the value of relative importance of various factors.

W is calculated with the Maximum Eigenvalue Method. Judgment-matrix B meet the relation of $BW=\lambda_{max}W$. Where λ_{max} is the maximum eigenvalue of matrix B, W is the eigenvector to λ_{max}. The W_i is the weight of various factors, which is what we want to obtain.

⑤ Total weight ranking of hierarchy.

The ranking of a hierarchy depends on the weight of all factors in the hierarchy. The analysis is a stepwise process from one hierarchy to another. For example, if the hierarchy B contains m factors $B_1, B_2, \cdots, B_m$, the weight ranking of the hierarchy is respectively $B_1, B_2, \cdots, B_m$. If the next hierarchy C contains n factors $C_1, C_2, \cdots, C_n$, the weight ranking to factor B_j is respectively $C_{1j}, C_{2j}, \cdots, C_{nj}$ ($C_{kj}=0$, if C_k has no relation to B_j).

The total weight ranking of hierarchy C can be obtained from Table 9-12.

⑥ Consistency test.

Matrix B is completely consistent if variables i, j, k meet the relation of $b_{ij}=b_{ik}/b_{jk}$, but usually because it is difficult to reach complete consistency, it can be checked by two indices:

Table 9-12　The total weight ranking of hierarchy

Hierarchy B Hierarchy C	B_1	B_2	...	B_m	Weight ranking of hierarchy C
	B	b	...	b	
C_1	C_{11}	C_{12}	...	C_{1m}	
C_2	C_{21}	C_{22}	...	C_{2m}	
$\vdots$					
C_n	C_{n1}	C_{n2}	...	C_{nm}	

I. index CI.

For components ranking:

$$CI = \frac{\lambda_{max} - n}{n-1}$$

Where λ_{max} is maximum eigenvalue of the matrix, n is rank of matrix.

For hierarchy ranking:

$$CI = \sum_i^m a_i(CI)_i$$

Where $(CI)_i$ is an index value of component ranking corresponding to a_i, usually CI<0.01.

II. Random consistency ratio CR,

For components ranking:

$$CR=CI/RI.$$

For hierarchy ranking:

$$CR = \sum_i^m a_i(CI)/\sum_{i=1}^m a_i(RI)_i$$

Where RI is a coefficient, they are as follows.

n	1	2	3	4	5	6	7	8	9	10
RI	0	0	0.58	0.90	1.12	1.24	1.32	1.41	1.45	1.49

We asked experts to make an evaluation of aeolian desertification and give a score to the following 14 factors:

Natural factors: wind erosion C_1, evaporation C_2, soil structure C_3, precipitation C_4, vegetation cover C_5, gathering firewood C_6, animal destroyed vegetation C_7.

Social factors: Population density C_8, total population C_9, number of scientists C_{10}.

Economic factors: Livestock number C_{11}, industry construction C_{12}, industrial products C_{13}, and agricultural output C_{14}.

The calculated results are as follows.

① A-B judgement matrix(Table 9-13).

Table 9-13　A-B judgement matrix

A	B_1	B_2	B_3
B_1	1	2	1/3
B_2	1/2	1	3
B_3	3	1/3	1

② C-B_1 judgement matrix(Table 9-14).

Table 9-14　C-B_1 judgement matrix

B_1	C_1	C_2	C_3	C_4	C_5	C_6	C_7
C_1	1	2	3	4	5	6	7
C_2	1/2	1	2	3	4	5	6
C_3	1/3	1/2	1	2	4	6	7
C_4	1/4	1/3	1/2	1	2	4	5
C_5	1/5	1/4	1/4	1/2	1	3	4
C_6	1/6	1/5	1/6	1/4	1/3	1	3
C_7	1/7	1/6	1/7	1/5	1/4	1/3	1

③ C-B_2 judgement matrix(Table 9-15).

Table 9-15　C-B_2 judgement matrix

B_2	C_8	C_9	C_{10}
C_8	1	2	3
C_9	1/2	1	2
C_{10}	1/3	1/2	1

④ C-B_3 judgement matrix(Table 9-16).

Table 9-16　C-B_3 judgement matrix

B_3	C_{11}	C_{12}	C_{13}	C_{14}
C_{11}	1	2	3	4
C_{12}	1/2	1	3	4
C_{13}	1/4	1/3	1	2
C_{14}	1/5	1/4	1/2	1

It can be seen from the results that:

① Natural and economic factors have a great influence on aeolian desertification. The influence of social factors is small; their scores are 0.540, 0.297, and 0.163, respectively.

② Weight scores of natural factors: wind erosion is 0.34, evaporation 0.2, soil structure 0.17, precipitation 0.10, vegetation cover 0.007, gathering firewood 0.04, and animal destroyed vegetation 0.02. The most important factors are wind erosion and evaporation.

③ Viewed from an economic aspect, the number of livestock and industrial construction are important factors; their scores are 0.49 and 0.30 respectively.

④ Viewed from a social aspect, the weight of population density is 0.53, total population 0.29 and number of scientists 0.16.

⑤ Using hierarchy analysis, according to their influence on aeolian desertification from large to small, the above mentioned 14 factors are ranked in the following order: population density, population, wind erosion, number of scientists, number of livestock, evaporation, soil structure, industrial construction, precipitation, vegetation cover, industrial output value, agriculture product, gathering firewood, animal destroyed vegetation. Their weight scores are shown in Table 9-17.

Table 9-17　Weight values of aeolian desertification factors

B	B_1	B_2	B_3	Total weight values for hierarchy C to hierarchy A
C	0.54	0.163	0.297	
C_1	0.34	0	0	0.102
C_2	0.23	0	0	0.069
C_3	0.17	0	0	0.053
C_4	0.10	0	0	0.032
C_5	0.07	0	0	0.021
C_6	0.04	0	0	0.012
C_7	0.02	0	0	0.008
C_8		0.53	0	0.291
C_9		0.29	0	0.160
C_{10}		0.16	0	0.088
C_{11}			0.49	0.080
C_{12}			0.30	0.050
C_{13}			0.12	0.021
C_{14}			0.07	0.013

References

Chen Shupeng, Lu Xuejun. 1999. An introduction on Geographic Information System. Beijing: China Science and Technology Press, 10–15

China National Committee to Implement the UN Convention to Combat Desertification. 1994. United Nations to Combat Desertification in those countries experiencing serious drought and/or desertification, particularly in Africa Beijing: China Science and Technology Press

Liu Jiyuan. 1996. Macroscopical Investigation of Remote Sensing and Dynamic Research on Resources Environment of China. Beijing: Science Press

Ma Lipeng, Li Xiaobing. 2000. "3S" technologies applying for desertification monitoring in Gansu province. Journal of Desert Research, 20(4): 278–282

Wang Tao, Wang Xizhang, Wu Wei. 1995. Disaster zoning of desertification in China. In: Wang Jingfeng. *Natural Disasters Zoning*: *Disaster Zoning, Assessing Influences and Countermeasures of Reducing Disasters.* Beijing: China Science and Technology Press

Wang Tao, Wu Wei, Wang Xizhang. 1998. Remote sensing monitoring and assessing sandy desertification: An example from the sandy desertification region of northern China. Quaternary Sciences, (2): 108–118

Wang Tao. 1992. A preliminary study on development trend of sandy desertification in Northern China. China Association for Science & Technology. *First Symposium of Young Scholars* (*cross-discipline*). Beijing: China Science and Technology Press

Wang Xizhang, Wang Tao, Xu Jiyan. 1994. A geographic system on monitoring and assessing desert disasters. In: He Jianbang et al. *Research Progress on Remote Sensing Monitoring and Assessment for Great Natural Disasters*. Beijing: China Science and Technology Press

Wu Lun, Liu Yu, Zhang Jing. 2001. An introduction on Geographic Information System: Theory Methods and Application. Beijing: Science Press, 7–299

Wu Wei, Wang Xizhang, Yao Fafen. 1997. Applying remote sensing data for desertification monitoring in the Mu Us Sandy Land. Journal of Desert Research, 17(4): 415–420

Wu Wei. 1991. Visual interpretation of TM images applying for investigation of resources. In: Wang Yimou. Symposium on Remote Sensing Application in Renewable resources. Beijing: Science Press

Wu Wei. 1997. Remote sensing monitoring methods of desertification dynamics and practice. Remote Sensing Techniques and Application, 12(4): 73–89 (in Chinese)

Zhu Zhenda, Chen Guangting. 1994. Sandy Desertification in China. Beijing: Science Press, 36–47

Part Ⅲ
Case Study of Deserts and
Aeolian Desertification in China

Chapter 10
Sandy Land and Aeolian Desertified Land in Steppe Zones

The strip zone extending southwestward from the northernmost Hulun Buir Sandy Land, along the Da Hinggan Ling Mountains to the Yinshan Mountains and both sides of the Great Wall, is the main steppe in China. With an aridity index of 4 and annual precipitation of 200 mm at its western borderline, the steppe includes a semi-humid area with an annual precipitation of 400–500 mm and a semi-arid area with an annual precipitation of 400–200 mm. As far as temperature is concerned, it covers both the warm temperate zone and the southern cold temperate zone. The plant biological zone is grassland, and it stretches from forest grassland in the east to steppe in the west.

Deserts in this area are generally called sandy land. Because of better natural conditions, sandy land differs greatly from deserts. It is covered by vegetation, and is mainly composed of fixed and semi-fixed sandy land. Most notably, the fixed and semi-fixed honeycomb dunes and parabolic dunes without distinctive differentiation between windward and leeward slopes account for more than 90%.

There are still different views about when these sandy lands were formed. Quaternary lacustrine and fluvial deposits extensively occurred in the sandy lands; for instance, the Daqinggou and the Gujiatun Formations in the Horqin Sandy Land and the Onqin Daga Sandy Land, and the Salawusu Strata in the Mu Us Sandy Land are the main sources of aeolian sand in the sandy land.

Aeolian desertification of grassland has recently been getting worse and worse in China. The nomads in northern China have lived there for a long time. Historically, stock-raising has been substituted by agriculture, and over-cultivation caused grassland desertification. In the middle of the 19th century, with continuous population growth, grassland cultivation reached its peak. From then on, aeolian desertification in grasslands kept developing. After more than a century of cultivation, a special economic zone in southern and eastern grasslands, namely the farming-grazing region was formed, and the livestock raising economy transitioned to agriculture. The conflict between fragile natural conditions and human economic activity turned potential aeolian desertification into severe aeolian desertification.

According to investigations in the 1980s, there were more than 120,000 km^2 of desertified land in semi-arid farming-grazing regions, accounting for more than 36% of the current sandy desertified area in China. Each year about 1750 km^2 land were lost to aeolian desertification, accounting for 80% of the country's newly aeolian desertified land. According to remote sensing data in 2000, there were 226,000 km^2 of aeolian desertified land in the eastern grassland occupying 58.6% of the total aeolian desertified land in China.

Because the grassland region is located in a semiarid zone in the middle latitude (including part of a semi-humid zone), as well as in the transitional zone of the East Asian monsoon zone and continental climatic zone, the characteristics of sandy desertified land in grassland regions are determined by its geographical environment.

(1) Lying at the end of the Southeastern Monsoon, the center, intensity and duration of dry continental air mass and humid maritime air mass in different years are quite different, which makes annual precipitation unstable, including the late onset of the first effective rainfall and rainy season, especially the occurrence of drought in spring. According to statistical data from 6 counties of Bashang in Hebei province, the precipitation's variability in winter is usually 100% and 46%–80% in spring. The probability of drought occurrence can reach 67% in spring and summer.

There is a close relationship between the development of aeolian desertification and regional drought. The instability of precipitation is the primary factor that causes ecological environment fragility. It also determines the fluctuation of aeolian desertified land's development. When precipitation is plentiful and evenly distributed, aeolian desertification is restrained, but it develops quickly in arid years.

(2) Though drought determines the expansion rate of aeolian desertification, human factors are the main cause of aeolian desertification development. In semi-arid regions, precipitation is 200–500mm. Grasses and drought-tolerant shrubs completely depend on precipitation. After cultivation, dry farming can maintain a certain output in normal years, and under the present climatic conditions, aeolian desertification doesn't occur. However, irrational utilization of soil resources causes rapid development of sandy desertification.

Human factors include uncontrolled reclamation of grassland, over grazing, excessive cutting for fuelwood and surface mining. All these factors can lead to the rapid development of aeolian desertification.

(3) The causes of aeolian desertification are diversified and complex. The geological conditions for the formation of sandy desertified land in semi-arid regions includes old sandy land evolved from Quaternary sediment basins, dry tableland denudated during the Quaternary, as well as hill and mesa composed of sandy loess. The affected lands mainly include grassland and rainfed farmland, dunefields and wind-eroded land.

(4) Because the semi-arid region is located in the transitional region between sandy land and loess, the soil is loose and sandy; coupling with repeated cultivation disturbances, blown sand is widespread. The occurrence of sand drift is an indicator of aeolian desertification. Sand drift phenomena includes blown dust, sand-dust storms, and floating dust. This powerful evidence demonstrates that the dust materials of dust storms not only comes from the center of the dust storm (desert, gobi), but also from aeolian desertified land in semi-arid region.

(5) The fluctuation of temperature and humidity and the impact of human factors make the

process of aeolian desertification much more complicated. Aeolian desertification has developed and reversed several times in many areas. The alteration of land use patterns in farming-grazing regions promoted the evolvement of aeolian desertification.

In the Horqin grassland, there widely exists 3 layers of paleosol, which means sandy land has been stabilized 3 times. There are also 3 layers of paleosol in the Onqin Daga Sandy Land. ^{14}C dating of these paleosols gave ages of 7,000 BP, 3,500 BP and 1,000 BP. The southern edge of the Onqin Daga Sandy Land as the center of stock-raising has been partly destroyed. This sandy land was stable before the 1950s–1960s and mainly composed of fixed and semi-fixed sand dunes. But by 2001, about one-half of them mobilized.

(6) If precipitation is plentiful, aeolian desertification can be easily reversed. This has been proven by the fact that large areas of desertified cropland in the middle of the Horqin grassland and the southern and middle parts of the Mu Us Sandy Land have been improved following the implementation of the "returning farmland to grassland" policy.

10.1 Hulun Buir Sandy Land

Both the Hulun Lake and the Buir Lake, located at the border of China and Mongolia, are very famous. The vegetation nearby is very lush, which is composed of steppe meadows. This area named after these two lakes is the most famous natural rangeland and the sandy land here are called the Hulun Buir Sandy Land.

10.1.1 General situation

The Hulun Buir Sandy Land is mainly distributed between Hailar city and the Hulun Lake in the Hulun Buir Plateau in eastern Inner Mongolia (Fig. 10-1). The climate is cold, and the average annual temperature is very low, below 0–2 °C. This area belongs to a semi-arid steppe climate with a ≥ 10 °C accumulative temperature of 1,800–2,000 °C, frost free period of about 100–110 days and an annual average precipitation of 350 mm. The annual average wind speed is 3.3 m/s, and it is 4–5 m/s in spring. The Hulun Buir Plateau is a steppe mostly composed of *Stipa* and *Leymus chinensis Tzvel.*, and the quality of grasses is very good. It's an important animal husbandry base for China.

The sandy land is located in an alluvial-lacustrine plain, mainly composed of fixed and semi-fixed dunes, accounting for 5,665 km^2 and 1,515 km^2 respectively. Vegetation cover is more than 30%, or even 50% locally. The height of dunes is mostly 5–15 m and there is a wide flat between dunes. The sandy land is formed by deep sand deposit. There exist 3 layers of interbeds of black sandy soil with plenty of organic matters and yellow fine sands in the section of fixed dunes, which means the sand dunes experienced several vegetation fixation processes. The modern aeolian desertification process is dominated by the mobilization of fixed dunes. The main causes of aeolian desertification are over grazing, over cutting and over cultivation since 1930.

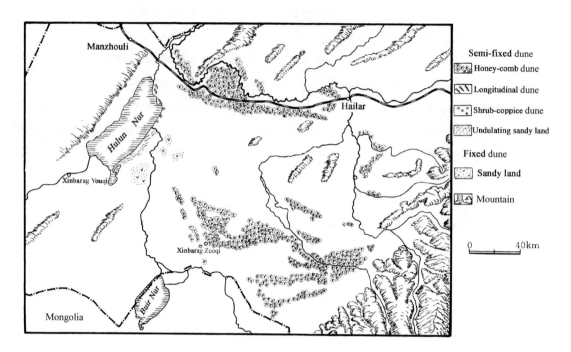

Fig. 10-1　Landscape of the Hulun Buir Sandy Land

10.1.2　Impacts of geological structure and paleoclimate on the Hulun Buir Sandy Land

As far as large-scale ecological structure is concerned, the Hulun Buir Plain belongs to the subsidence zone of *xi*-shaped structure-inland Cathasian subsidence zone. The Hulun Buir subsidence zone is the middle sunken district of *xi*-type and its structure is an oblique fold bunch, which is composed of Silurian and Devonian deposits, such as slate, quartzite and granite. At the northeast edge, it connects the new Huaxia Uplift Belt in the Da Hinggan Ling Mountains, and southwestwardly reaches Shiwudui in northeast Chenba'erhu Qi and gradually becomes parallel near the national boundaries. In this subsidence zone, thick Mesozoic sediment deposits form the famous Hulun Buir Plateau.

Lithosphere movement in the late Mesozoic formed the landforms in the Hulun Buir area. Mountains in western Inner Mongolia prevent humid maritime air mass from reaching the Hulun Buir area and the local climate is controlled by continental air mass, which determines the dry climate in the Hulun Buir area. Denudation and wind force play a dominant role in the landform formations in this area.

The function of modern rivers in the Hulun Buir area is very weak, but there are many scattered traces of water nets, as well as old eroded landforms and alluvial and lacustrine sediment. Many current depressions are the remnants of past rivers. If the river net has been restituted, it can be seen that many rivers once flowed into the Hulun Lake. The remnant bank of the Hulun Lake made of sand and gravel is 3–5 m higher than the current lake level. It suggests a period when the climate was humid and rivers and lakes began to evolve. This can be proven by the analysis of old strata (Fig.10-2). At the beginning of the Cretaceous, the climate was humid, and plants flourished. But at the end of the Cretaceous, the climate tended to be dry and hot. With the coming of the Eocene in the Tertiary, it returned to a humid climate once again. It can be speculated from the mudstone in the lake basin that there was a freshwater lake with humid and hot forest steppe at that time. That time was a blooming period for lake evolvement. During the Tertiary, the climate fluctuated several times, and it became significantly dry at the end of the Tertiary. Animal fossils of the Pliocene, such as giraffes, rhinoceroses, horses, rabbits, ermines and ostriches etc. were found in the red bed of the Tertiary. At that time, precipitation decreased dramatically, which made the Tertiary fluvio-lacustrine sediment exposed to the air and it suffered weathering. As denudation and wind force began to dominate, the formation of deserts began. In the early Pleistocene of the Quaternary, the climate became humid and hot, with rivers and lakes coexisting, and alluvial and lacustrine deposits evolved widely. In the middle Pleistocene, the climate was still humid and hot. In the late Pleistocene, the climate became dry and cold, and remnants formed in the periglacial climate period appear in many places. Fossils of animals and plants also prove the existence of a periglacial climate.

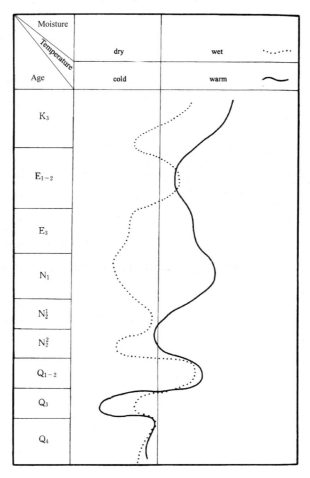

Fig. 10-2   The changes of the paleoclimate

With the coming of the Holocene, the cold climate began to ease up, and this area was occupied by grassland again. As the climate became dry, rivers and lakes retreated, which led to the formation of depressions and inland rivers. Under the action of wind force, exposed surface alluvial and lacustrine deposits evolved into the modern desert.

10.1.3 The development process of aeolian desertification in the Hulun Buir Grassland

(1) The material source of the Hulun Buir Sandy Land and the formation of modern aeolian sand landforms.

The material source of the Hulun Buir Sandy Land is closely related to paleogeographic sedimentary environments, especially the sedimentary environment in the Holocene. According to borehole data, the thickness of Tertiary strata is more than 200 m. Quaternary alluvial and lacustrine strata are also scattered very widely. The early Pleistocene strata is a series of gray, grayish clay and silt layers; the middle Pleistocene strata is a series of lacustrine sedimentary sand and gravel layers; the late Pleistocene sand layer also exists widely. Sand and gravel deposited in the Quaternary constitute the primary material base for the Hulun Buir Sandy Land.

The formation of the Hulun Buir Sandy Land has a very close relation with the monsoon circulation. Hulun Buir is far from the ocean, and with an annual average precipitation of 300–350 mm, it is a semi-arid steppe climate. Because of long winters, the ground surface is easily eroded by wind, which leads to the emergence of aeolian sand landforms. Gales are the primary cause of the formation of the Hulun Buir Sandy Land. Because Hulun Buir lies at the edge of the Siberian high, gales prevail in winter and spring. The wind speed in winter and spring is 4–6 m/s.

It's worth noticing that since the 1930s, due to unbalanced development of the grazing industry, there appeared spotted reactivated dunes along the Yimin River, the Huihe River and the Hailar River. Recently, with the growth of population, aeolian desertified land caused by human activities developed rapidly. Especially around towns, cultivation, cutting, over grazing and city construction led to aeolian desertification expansion. The main form of aeolian desertification is the mobilization of fixed dunes.

(2) Historical and modern processes of aeolian desertification in the Hulun Buir Grassland.

According to historical data, the earliest settlers of the Hulun Buir Grassland were the Tuobaxianbei people. In 1980, carved stones made in 443 AD were found in the Gaxian Cavity in the river valley of Ganhe River in the northern part of Daxin, which proved that the mountain historically called the Great Xianbei Mountains is actually the northern part of the current Da Hinggan Ling Mountains. The graves of Xianbei people were found repeatedly along the bank of the Hailar River. The black soil layer in these graves is comparatively thick, and the funerary objects are heads of cattle, horses and sheep. This means grass and trees flourished where the Xianbei people lived, and the stockbreeding industry was well developed. In 100 AD, the Xianbei people moved to the south because of the deteriorated environment.

It can be inferred that the second period of exploiting the Hulun Buir Grassland was in 1,000 AD. It was completed by the Qidan people originating from the Xiliao River Basin. According to the record of *Liao Shi*, during 939–940 AD, the Qidans moved to the Hulun Buir Grassland and resettled mostly along the banks of the Hailar River, Orxon Gol[1], Halhin Gol, Hui River and Herlen River. They reclaimed grassland and cultivated there, and engaged in agriculture. The residual canals that the Qidan people constructed are along the banks of rivers, and can be seen in the Hulun Buir grassland today.

According to archeologists' research, the cities of the Liao Dynasty were scattered in more than 10 sites along the banks of rivers. And the ancient Haotetaohai City in Chen Barag Qi was located on the northern bank of the Hailar River. Its perimeter was about 2,000 m and its height was 3–5 m.The reclamation of grassland, building moats and constructing castles in the Liao Dynasty destroyed the ecological environment, and led to aeolian desertification.

Exploitation in the Hulun Buir by the Liao lasted for two centuries. Reclamation and cultivation were continued by Mongolian maharajas in the Yuan Dynasty. Afterwards, the Hulun Buir was returned to pasture, and the environment gradually recovered.

Since 1949, the Hulun Buir grassland experienced two large-scale reclamation and aeolian desertification stages. The first one occurred in the 1950s–1960s, and about 25 state-owned farms were successively established in the Hulun Buir grasslandly. Until 1962, reclaimed grassland reached 198, 000 hm^2, which was mostly scattered along the Binzhou Railway, around Hailar City, along the banks of the Genhe River, the De'erbugan River and the Hawulu River. Because of impoverished soil and servere wind erosion, the output of crops decreased rapidly. By 1963, about 151, 000 hm^2 (accounting for 76%) of cropland were abandoned. But the lasting effect of aeolian desertification was irreparable. According to field surveys on 4,666 hm^2 of cropland in the Hadatu Farm, severely eroded land accounted for more than 50%. Blowouts, shifting sand pits and shifting dunes appeared in cultivated lands.

The second stage occurred during the 1960s–1970s. Under the impact of movements such as "All for food" and "In agriculture, learn from Dazhai", another reclamation occurred again in the Hulun Buir grassland. As a result, sandy desertified land in Hulun Buir Grassland added up to 470, 000 hm^2 in the 1970s and 1,160,000 hm^2 in 1982.

The Hulun Buir Sandy Land is a typical desert caused by human activity. But now, overgrazing is causing grassland degradation, and the threat of aeolian desertification still exists.

(3) Control and utilization methods in the Hulun Buir Sandy Land.

The sand hazards in the Hulun Buir Sandy Land can be generalized in the following 3 aspects. A. Pasture and farmland are covered by sand. During the advancement process of mobile dune, it can cover the pasture and farmland downwind. B. Top soil is blown away, which results in the loss

---

1) River

of soil nutrients. C. Wind and sandblast damage to seedlings of crops. The height of sand flow is near the ground surface, so the shifting sand is harmful to the growth of seedlings, finally leading to the reduction of crop yield.

The Hulun Buir Grassland is one of the most important natural pastures in China. The reasonable utilization method is to develop stock-raising rationally. To utilize the grassland resources rationally, the herd should be primarily composed of large livestock, and the number of small livestock should be reduced, which can reduce grassland trampling and protect natural vegetation; according to reasonable carrying capacity, rotational grazing must be implemented to protect pastures and promote the development of agriculture.

10.2   Songnen Sandy Land

10.2.1   General situation

The Songnen Sandy Land is located in the western part of Songnen Plain. It mainly lies in the flood plain, the first terrace and alluvial fan of the Nenjiang River and its tributaries, such as the Second Songhua River, the Taoer River, the Huolin River, etc. That is the origin of the sandy land's name. The sandy land covers western Jilin province and 22 counties or cities in southwestern Heilongjiang Province, with an area of 10,900 km^2. The structure of the Songnen Plain belongs to the Song-Liao Subsidence zone, and there is very deep and thick Holocene sediment. Middle Pleistocene and Holocene sediments are mostly composed of sand and loessial subsand. Holocene sediment is dominated by sand and covers the plain. It's the material basis of the sandy land. There are many lakes in the Songnen Plain. According to statistics, the number of lakes with an area more than 6.7 hm^2 is 7,378 and the total area is about 4,176 km^2. They are mostly fresh water lakes. Groundwater resources in the Songnen Sandy Land are very plentiful and buried shallowly, which provides water for controlling and utilizing the aeolian desertified land (Zhu Zhenda et al., 1994).

In the Songnen Plain, precipitation in spring only accounts for 10% of total annual precipitation. In addition, the temperature of the ground surface rises rapidly and evaporation is large, so the ground surface is very dry. Strong wind-induced deflation of unprotected ground surface by vegetation leads to the rapid development of aeolian deserification. The Songnen Plain was once covered by forest and grassland, but irrational land reclamation beginning in the Qing Dynasty resulted in grassland damage and the occurrence of aeolian desertification. Landscape of the Songnen Sandy Land is shown in Fig. 10-3.

Several large-scale land reclamations since 1949 greatly reduced grassland vegetation cover, thus exacerbating land aeolian desertification, especially rainfed farmlands.

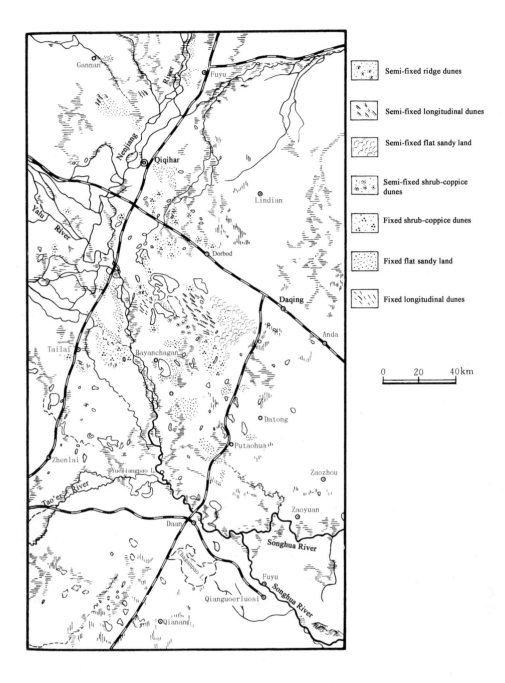

Legend:
- Semi-fixed ridge dunes
- Semi-fixed longitudinal dunes
- Semi-fixed flat sandy land
- Semi-fixed shrub-coppice dunes
- Fixed shrub-coppice dunes
- Fixed flat sandy land
- Fixed longitudinal dunes

Fig. 10-3　Landscape of the Songnen Sandy Land

10.2.2　Status of aeolian desertified land

The Songnen Sandy Land is one of the sandy lands with the best bioclimatic conditions in China and it was exploited as late as the end of the Qing Dynasty. Large scale land exploitation started since the 1950s, so the aeolian desertification degree is relatively light there. Latent aeolian desertified land, ongoing aeolian desertified land and intensively developed aeolian desertified land accounts for 56%, 36% and 8% respectively. But because the Songnen Sandy Land is the sandy area with the greatest population density and most intensive human activity in China, aeolian desertification has recently developed rapidly.

Because the Songnen Sandy Land was formed relatively late, the aeolian sand landform types are comparatively simple and mostly composed of wind-eroded flat sandy land. Wind-deposited landforms are mostly composed transverse complex and longitudinal complex ridge dunes. The flat wind-eroded sandy land appears on sandy terrace and high flood plains on alluvial fans. It's mainly characterized by the coarsening of surface materials without significant shape change. Blowouts and shifting sand appear in severely wind eroded sandy land. Transverse complex ridge dunes mainly appear on the upper windward slope and lakeshore and river terraces. Transverse complex ridge dunes at the leading edge of the river terraces are mostly distributed on the right bank of the Second Songhua River in Fuyu, the left bank of the Nenjiang River in the Dorbod sandy land and the right bank of the Tao'er River in the Sheli Sandy Land. Transverse complex ridge dunes in the front of the river terrace extend along the frontal edge of the terrace for more than 10,000 m. The relative height of transverse complex ridge dunes can reach more than 20 m. The windward slope is about 10°, and the leeward slope is less than 10°. Transverse complex ridge dunes on lakeshores mostly extend along lake-basin depressions. Their height is about 10 m. The upper slopes are almost symmetric, and its slope is generally 10°–20°and gradually decreases at the bottom of the leeward slope. The evolution of transverse complex ridge dunes is related to the prevailing wind direction. A series of longitudinal complex ridge dunes on the leeward side of transverse complex ridge dunes extend along the prevailing wind direction. Its relative height usually varies from several meters to more than 10 m, and its length varies from tens of meters to a few hundred meters. Its height and width gradually decrease along the prevailing wind direction (Li, 1996). Transverse complex ridge dunes and longitudinal complex ridge dunes join together and exhibit a comb-like shape on the plain (Fig.10-4).

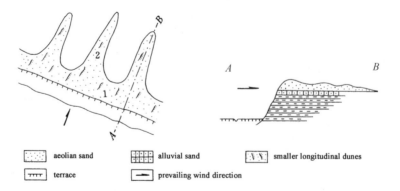

Fig. 10-4   The relationship of transverse complex and longitudinal complex ridge dunes

1. transverse complex ridge dune; 2. longitudinal complex ridge dune

Because of a short development period, the density of dunes in the Songnen Sandy Land and their undulating degree are small. Dunes around Sheli are relatively dense and dunes around Qiqihar are quite sparse (Table 10-1).

Table10-1　Density and undulating degree of dunes in various subzones of the Songnen Sandy Land

Sandy land	Density of sandy land (%)				Undulating degree of sandy land (m)			
	Sparse ⩽ 5	Middle (5,20]	Denser (20,25]	Densest >25	Flat ⩽ 2	Middle (2,10]	Higher (10,25]	Highest >25
Fuyu	21	12	39	28	17	64	17	2
Sheli	10	21	44	25	16	80	3	1
Dumeng	15	27	34	24	10	70	18	2
Tailai	15	26	43	16	6	60	29	5
Qiqihar	36	34	16	14	18	80	2	0
Total	18	24	35	23	13	71	14	2

10.2.3　Natural factors of aeolian desertification

(1) Loose sandy ground surface. The tectonics of the Songnen Plain belongs to the Song-Liao subsidence zone, and it has very thick Holocene sediment. Middle Pleistocene and Holocene sediments are mostly composed of sand and loessial subsand. Holocene sediment is dominated by sand, which largely covers the plain composed of loessial subsand.

(2) Spring drought, high temperature and frequent gale. Dry seasons and frequent continuous wind above the sand entrainment threshold are the potential natural factors of aeolian desertification. Precipitation in spring accounts for about 10% of annual precipitation in the Songnen Sandy Land. In spring, the humidity index is below 0.1 in most areas. It's the driest season in a year. Surrounded by mountains, the foehn effect is significant, and the temperature is obviously higher than other areas in the same latitude. High temperatures aggravate spring drought. Dry spring also has strong winds in the Songnen Sandy Land. Average annual wind velocity is 4.0 m/s and the average spring wind velocity is 5.1 m/s (Table 10-2). Gales acting on barren and loose sandy surface trigger aeolian desertification.

Table10-2　Wind velocity at representative stations in the Songnen Plain

Station	Type	1950s	1960s	1970s
Nenjiang	The number of gale days per year (d)	11.4	11.3	35.8
	Average annual wind velocity (m/s)	2.5	2.5	3.8
Keshan	The number of gale days per year (d)	18.4	16.0	28.7
	Average annual wind velocity (m/s)	3.1	3.0	3.2
Suihua	The number of gale days per year (d)	13.8	25.5	53.4
	Average annual wind velocity (m/s)	3.4	4.1	4.2
Harbin	The number of gale days per year (d)	25.0	38.7	38.5
	Average annual wind velocity (m/s)	3.8	3.9	4.6

(3) Great precipitation variability, frequent drought and flood disasters. Though average annual precipitation in the Songnen Sandy Land is 360–480 mm, precipitation varies greatly in a year, and

drought and flood disasters are very serious. During the 150 years from 1800 to 1950, droughts occurred once every 8 years, and floods occurred once every 5 years. When floods occur, they bring large amounts of sand to form sand badlands. In dry years, sand is blown away by wind force.

10.2.4　Human factors of aeolian desertification

In geological and human historical periods, there are no large-scale aeolian sand landforms in the Songnen Sandy Land. During the late Eocene, natural vegetation in Northeast China was broad leaved evergreen and conifer forests of warm temperate zones; during the middle Miocene it was broad leaved forest and forest grassland of warm temperate zones; and it was mostly forest grassland also in the Quaternary.

During 1901–1911, Russia built the Northeast Railway and cut off a large tract of forest. During the period of Japan's occupation, forests in Northeast China suffered severe damage. After 1949, this area experienced several large-scale land reclamations, which resulted in the dramatic decrease of forest and grassland area. Compared with the early 1960s, cropland area increased by 360 million hm^2 in the early the 1980s. In the early 1960s, forest coverage was 7.3%, and it decreased to 5.2% in the 1980s. More than 80% forest appears in the transitional zone between plain and mountains, but the forest coverage of plains was only 1%–2%. It's obvious that human factors played a key role in the aeolian desertification in the Songnen Sandy Land.

10.2.5　The damage from aeolian desertification

The Songnen Sandy Land is located in the northern end of a semi-humid blown sand zone, where the climate is dry and cold. Damage caused by shifting sand and aeolian desertification is very severe. Strong sand flow causes wind erosion in some places and deposits in other places. In Tongyu County of Jilin Province, 2,980 hm^2 land suffered from sand damage in the 1950s, and it increased to 14,400 hm^2 in the 1970s. During the 32 years from 1949 to 1980, about 21,850 hm^2 of cropland suffered from wind erosion and seedlings were destroyed, with a mean annual area of 6,733 hm^2. It reached 18,700 hm^2 in 1972. Because of wind erosion and sand burial, there was a total of 150,000 hm^2 of farmland without any output in Tongyu County in 1982. There were 20 hm^2 of wind-eroded cropland in the Maxiagentun of the Xinhua Village in the 1950s, and it increased to 60 hm^2, 137 hm^2 and 250 hm^2, in the 1960s, 1970s and 1980s respectively.

10.2.6　Combating aeolian desertification

Aeolian desertification in the Songnen Sandy Land has a short history of development, but it develops rapidly and poses a great threat. To prevent aeolian desertification from getting worse, the following strategies should be adopted.

(1) According to sustainable development principles, work out an integrated plan for land utilization and degraded land rehabilitation.

(2) According to the historical distribution of vegetation and the characteristics of modern climate, soil and hydrological conditions, return farmland to forest and grassland, control livestock numbers and prevent grassland from degradation and salinization.

(3) Observe the aeolian desertification process, study its characteristics and establish a standard system to evaluate the trends of aeolian desertification.

10.3　Horqin Sandy Land

Horqin was the name of a Mongolian tribe who once lived in this area. It is now used as the name of the desertified sandy land.

10.3.1　The distribution of the Horqin Sandy Land

The Horqin Sandy Land is located in the western part of northeast China and in the transitional zone between the Mongolia Plateau and the Northeast Plain (Fig. 10-5). It starts from the westernmost Qilaotu Mountain of the Yanshan mountain system and extends to the western part of the Songliao Plain. The Nuluerhu Mountain is its southern boundary and its northern limit is the Da

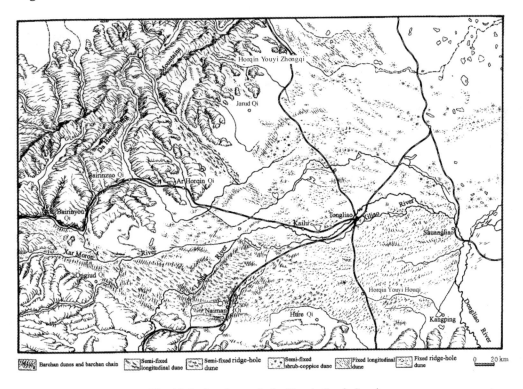

Fig. 10-5　Landscape in the Horqin Sandy Land

Hinggan Ling Mountain. It's approximately located between 113°30′E–123°30′E and 42°20′N–44°28′N, with a total area of 105,600 km². The actual area of aeolian desertified land was 50,168 km² in 2000, accounting for 47.5% of China's total aeolian desertified land area.

10.3.2　Natural conditions in the Horqin Sandy Land

10.3.2.1　Climate

The Horqin Sandy Land lies in a semi-arid continental monsoon climate region in the temperate zone. The climate has the following characteristics: the winter is cold and long, with little snowfall. It is arid and windy in spring. Summer is hot and short, and most rain falls in the summer. Temperature drops rapidly in autumn and frost comes early. Average annual temperature is 3–7 °C in most areas, and average temperature in the coldest month (January) is −12°C~−17°C, while in the hottest month (July) is 20–24°C. Annual accumulative temperature($\geqslant$10 °C) is 2,200–3,200 °C. The frostless season is 90–140 days. Average annual precipitation is 350–500mm, and 70% falls in the summer. Average annual evaporation is 1,500–2,500 mm. Aridity index is 1.0–1.8. Average annual wind velocity is 3.4–4.4 m/s, and average wind velocity in spring is 4.2–5.9 m/s. Sand moving wind ($\geqslant$5 m/s) occurs 210–310 days annually, or even 330 days. Sand duststorms occur about 10–15 days a year and mostly in spring.

10.3.2.2　Terrain

The characteristics of terrain in the regions undulating and open; the southern and northern parts are higher than the middle part, with an altitude of 120—800 m. There are great differences in geomorphologic structure. The southern, middle and northern parts belong to loess hill and tableland of the Chifeng Mountains, pluvial and alluvial plain in the Xiliao River Basin and piedmont inclined plains in front of the Da Hinggan Ling Mountains respectively. Because of intensive development of aeolian desertification, the ground surface exhibits a desert-like landscape with numerous fixed sand dunes.

10.3.2.3　Soil

The zonal soils are primarily chestnut soil, chernozem and chestnut cinnamon soil. Due to the impact of aeolian desertification, a large part of soil has been degraded to blown sand soil. At present, the area of chestnut soil accounts for 30% of total land area, while wind blown sand chestnut cinnamon soil and chernozem account for 30%–40% and 10% respectively. The underlying materials, except for stony mountain land and hills in the northern and southern parts of the Da Hinggan Ling Mountain, include thick Quaternary alluvial and lacustrine sand deposits.

10.3.2.4 Ground water

Despite lack of precipitation, there are ample surface and ground water resources in this region. The average annual total volume of water resource is 12.4 billion m^3, with an average annual runoff of 6 billion m^3 and reserved ground water volume of 6.4 billion m^3. In most areas, the ground water table is quite low, with a depth of only 1–3 m, so it's easy to exploit the ground water. But in some places, the ground water table is quite deep and it's difficult to be exploited.

10.3.2.5 Vegetation

The Horqin Sandy Land lies in the transitional zone between semi-arid and semi-humid climate zones and there is the special sparse-tree grassland in northern China. The Dominant grassland vegetation is primarily composed of mesophyte and xerophyte species, including *Ulmus macrocarpa, U. pumila, Acer truncatum, Crataegus pinnatifida, Prunus armeniaca, Lespedeza bicolor, Rhamnus dahurica, Ephedra sinica, Artemisia frigida, Leymus chinensis*, etc. There is no bare land. The biomass of fresh grass per hectare is commonly 4,000–5,000 kg.

In the past 100 years, primary vegetation was damaged severely, and aeolian desertification was becoming worse. The former sparse-tree grassland has turned into sandy land with interlaced fixed dunes and meadows and shifting sand. Its main species include *Caragana microphylla, Artemisia halodendron, A. scoparia, Salix gordejevii, Periploca sepium, Melissitus ruthenicus, Cleistogenes squarrosa, Setaria viridis, Lespedeza daurica, Pennisetum centrasiaticum* and *Agriophyllum squarrosum* etc. Because the habitat conditions were becoming worse, the number of plant species reduced and the structure became simplified. The vegetation cover was only 10%–40% and grass biomass was 300–3,000 kg/hm^2.

10.3.3　The process of aeolian desertification in the Horqin Sandy Land

Using different temporal scales, the causes of aeolian desertification are different. The process of aeolian desertification in the Horqin Sandy Land can be analyzed from three aspects. First, the cause of modern aeolian desertification process is analyzed according to information specifically recorded about regional development and environmental changes. Secondly, its historical process is analyzed according to historical materials and information obtained from archeological research. Finally, the geological process is analyzed according to the geological age of different strata and the age, species and quantity of organism remnants (including fossils and pollen etc.) preserved in the strata. Considering the data gathered with different temporal scales, we can analyze the process of aeolian desertification from the following.

In addition, the quantitative description of aeolian desertification can be expressed by degree and processes of aeolian desertification. To analyze it conveniently, we define the degree of aeolian desertification as:

$$DES_i = \frac{(M_i + k_1 * SM_i + k_2 * F)}{A_i} \tag{10-1}$$

Where, DES_i is the degree of desertification, A_i is the area of the study region, M_i is the area of mobile dunes, SM_i is the area of semi-fixed dunes, i is a certain period, k_1 and k_2 are weighting factors given by experts (Their values are 0.6 and 0.3 respectively). The value of DES_i is 0-1, namely, if there are no dunes of any kind, the value of M, SM_i and F_i are 0, so the degree of desertification is 0; if there is all mobile dunes, $A_i = M_i$, SM_i and F are 0, so the degree of desertification is 1. And the process of desertification DP can be expressed by the formula (10-2):

$$DP = \frac{DES_{i+1} - DES_i}{DES_{i+1} + DES_i} \tag{10-2}$$

Where the value of DP is 0-1. If DP is positive, it means aeolian desertification is developing; if DP is negative, it means aeolian desertification is reversed. If the value of DP is large, it represents an intensive process of aeolian desertification; otherwise, it represents a weak process.

10.3.3.1 Historical process of aeolian desertification in the Horqin Sandy Land

The Horqin Sandy Land was first inhabited as early as 8,000–9,000 years ago during the Xinglongwa Cultural Period in the early Neolithic age. According to archeological materials and historic records, it can be speculated that primordial agriculture appeared during the Xinglongwa Culture. The Xinglongwa Cultural stratum is comparatively thin, with a thickness less than 1 m, which means the scale of human activity wasn't great at that time. Furthermore primordial agriculture couldn't destroy vegetation and soil crusts severely, and it couldn't result in the frequent occurrence and intensive development of aeolian desertification, either.

The Hongshan Cultural Period was a branch of prosperous culture in the late Neolithic age in northern China that occurred around 5,300 a BP. According to Yuqin Song et al., it was the development of aeolian desertification that led to the rapid collapse of the Hongshan Cultural time in the Horqin Sandy Land and low human activity over a period of almost 1,000 years.

In the Bronze age, the Early Xiajiadian Cultural period existed in the Horqin Sandy Land with a span from the Xia Dynasty to the Shang Dynasty, when the population in the Horqin region was 2 times larger than that of the Hongshan Cultural Period and the intensity and efficiency of land exploitation must have been much larger than before.

From the Qin or the Han Dynasty to the end of the Tang Dynasty, the Xiliao River Basin has been governed by the Hun, Wuhuan, Xianbei and Qidan in turn. They were mostly engaged in stock-raising.

From the Xihan Dynasty to the Beiwei Dynasty, people in the Horqin Sandy Land were mostly the Xianbei people. During the 1,300 years from 400 BC to the Five Dynasties, the Xiliao River basin experienced a fluctuation of cold climate. But the cold climate didn't weaken Xianbei people's activity; on the contrary, their activity became more and more intensive, which proved that there were plenty of water and grass resources in the Xiliao River basin and the steppe in Horqin area was suitable for nomads to live.

After the foundation of the Liao Kingdom, large numbers of the Han people settled in Horqin, which resulted in the co-existence of stockbreeding and agriculture, but stockbreeding was dominant. As a result, the degree of land use in the Horqin Sandy Land during the Liao Dynasty exceeded that of any period since the Holocene.

After the mid-18th century, because the Qing Government implemented a policy which encouraged people to reclaim grassland, natural vegetation and soil crust were seriously destroyed in the Xiliao River basin and aeolian desertification slowly appeared in steppes. According to some counties or banners' records, agricultural reclamation in the southern and western Western Liaohe River basin was primarily conducted between 1750–1876, and in the northern Western Liaohe River basin, it was mainly conducted between 1877–1900. So there appeared dense mobile, semi-mobile and fixed dunes in the middle-southern part of the Horqin grassland. In the northern Horqin grassland, sporadic shifting and semi-mobile dunes were scattered between fixed dunes and undulating sandy plains.

From the 1950s to the 1970s, affected by the erroneous slogan of "all for grain", people abandoned stockbreeding to develop agriculture in the grazing areas of the Horqin region. Furthermore, due to the dramatic increase in population, the pressure exerted by mankind on the environment exceeded the capacity of the ecological system. So the ecological system in the Horqin region deteriorated and aeolian desertification extensively developed, until it finally reached the current degree of desertification.

Analyzing the process of formation and development of the Horqin Sandy Land have obtained the following conclusions:

(1) During the historical development process of the Horqin Sandy Land since the Holocene, local people were alternately engaged in stockbreeding or agriculture, resulting in a stable but progressive state of aeolian desertification over a long period. During this process, human factors were as a trigger for further aeolian desertification. According to analyses on the cause and historical process of aeolian desertification, we generalized the relationship between humans and land during the historical process of aeolian desertification in Fig. 10-6.

(2) The Horqin Sandy Land experienced four rapid agricultural development periods: the first one was the Hongshan Cultural Period that lasted about 1,000 years; the second one was the early Xiajiadian Cultural Period that lasted about 500 years; the third one was the Liao Dynasty and lasted about 200 years; the fourth one was in the late Qing Dynasty and lasted approximately several tens of years. These four periods lasted about 1,750 years. There were also four periods of decline: a

1,200-year interval between the Hongshan Cultural Period and the early Xiajiadian Cultural Period was the first; the second period was between the early Xiajiadian Cultural Period and the late Xiajiadian Cultural period; the third and the fourth periods were from the late Liao Dynasty to the early Qing Dynasty and the period of the Republic of China respectively, which altogether total about 2,450 years.

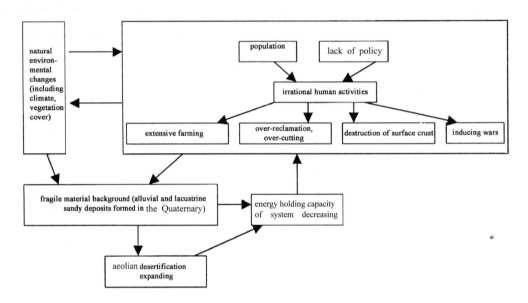

Fig. 10-6 Patterns of man-land relationship during the historical process of aeolian desertification

(3) According to the above analyses, the cycle of human disturbance in the Horqin Sandy Land has become shorter since the Holocene, but the intensity of disturbance has been getting stronger. The greater the intensity of human disturbance, the more difficult it is for the damaged ecosystem or environment to be restored. Considering the modern aeolian desertification process in the Horqin Sandy Land, due to the distinctly high intensity of human disturbances, the reversion of aeolian desertification has become more complex and it's more difficult to control.

(4) Because of the long-term impact of arid environments and the formation of deserts, there have been few plant species in northwest China, especially in the regions west of the Helan Mountains. This area has maintained a desert landscape since the Late Pleistocene. Due to the impact of the modern Southeast Monsoon, there is a relatively humid climate in the Horqin region in northeast China, and plant species are comparatively abundant there, so human activity has been quite frequent since the Neolithic Age. But this area has also experienceds four expansions and reversals of aeolian desertification.

(5) The formation and development of deserts are the result of the combined effect of natural factors and human factors. Since the Holocene, the resonance effect caused by both human factors and natural factors in different times and places accelerated the development and expansion of aeolian desertification in the Horqin Sandy Land.

(6) There appeared original extensive farming in the Horqin Sandy Land starting from the Xinglongwa Cultural Period since 8,000 a B.P., but the damage to vegetation and soil crust by agriculture was small, and the area affected by aeolian desertification was also limited. Farmland was cultivated every 2 years, and vegetation had a chance to recover. But agriculture in the Hongshan Cultural Period, the Early Xiajiadian Cultural Period, the late Liao Dynasty and the late Qing Dynasty was characterized by successive cultivation and furrowing with ploughs. Especially in the Liao Dynasty, many counties were set up in the Horqin Sandy Land where people cultivated farmland and reclaimed grassland. In the Qing Dynasty, farmers were encouraged to cultivate and reclaim sandy land, and the population expanded dramatically, which exerted pressure on the local environment and resources. So, modern aeolian desertification was accelerated and expanded in the Horqin Sandy Land.

(7) When climate was warm and humid, agriculture boomed and population rapidly increased in the Horqin Sandy Land. But agriculture ended with low human activity. According to historical experiences, the Horqin Sandy Land is suitable for both grazing and agriculture. But as far as the local ecological environment is concerned, it's not suitable for large-scale extensive farming; the best method of utilization is to develop stockbreeding. Simultaneous development of sustainable intensive agriculture and moderate stockbreeding is the best way to reverse aeolian desertification in the Horqin region.

10.3.3.2　Modern processes of aeolian desertification in the Horqin Sandy Land

Based on aerial photos and satellite images in typical areas in 1958, 1974, 1985, 1991, 1996 and 1998, the changing characteristics of fixed dune and sandy land are as follows:

The area of fixed dunes exhibited a fluctuating reduction tendency. It was 13,035.6 hm^2 in 1958, but it was only 7,321.4 hm^2 in 1998, accounting for 14.7% of the total area, with a decrease of 12.5%. In 1974, it decreased to a minimum of 5,661.3 hm^2. The area of fixed dunes tended to increase between 1974–1991 and reached 11,873.7 hm^2 in 1991, accounting for 23.8% of its total area. It has tended to decrease since 1991.

The changes of semi-fixed dunes were opposite to that of fixed dunes: their area increased from 5,082.6 km^2 in 1958 to 11,972.1 km^2 in 1998. From 1958 to 1974, the changes of semi-fixed dunes were consistent with that of fixed dunes. Its total area decreased from 10.2% to 3.3%.

The changes of mobile dunes area were consistent with that of fixed dunes. Their area decreased from 15,091.3 km2 (30.3% of total area) in 1958 to 11,866.9 km2 (23.8% of total area) in 1998. 1958–1974 was the first increase period, with an increase of 7.4%. Their area decreased from 18,811.6 km2 (37.7% of total area) to 14,720.7 km2 (29.5% of total area) during 1974–1991. It increased again from 29.5% to 32.4% between 1991 to 1996. Since 1996, it again decreased once more.

Between 1958–1998, the average aeolian desertification degree in the central sandy land of Naiman Qi was 0.70 (±0.06). It was a typical area with severe aeolian desertification. Average aeolian desertification degree was minimum (0.66) in 1958 and it was maximum (0.82) in 1974. After 1974, it decreased in fluctuations, with a second maximum of 0.72 in 1996 (Table 10-3 and Fig. 10-7).

Table 10-3   Changes of aeolian desertification degree in typical areas of the Horqin Sandy Land between 1958-1998

Years	Fixed dune and sandy land		Semi-fixed dune and sandy land		Shifting dune and sandy land		Total area		Degree of aeolian desertification
	Area (hm²)	Percent(%)	Area (hm²)	Percent(%)	Area (hm²)	Percent(%)	Area (hm²)	Percent(%)	Percent(%)
1958	13,035.6	26.2	5,082.6	10.2	15,091.3	30.3	49,840	100	0.66
1974	5,661.3	11.4	1,658.2	3.3	18,811.6	37.7	49,840	100	0.82
1985	9,940.4	19.9	6,696.5	13.4	16,067.0	32.2	49,840	100	0.71
1991	11,873.7	23.8	6,333.1	12.7	14,720.7	29.5	49,840	100	0.67
1996	8,673.4	17.4	8,273.1	16.6	16,139.4	32.4	49,840	100	0.72
1998	7,321.4	14.7	11,972.1	24.0	11,866.9	23.8	49,840	100	0.68

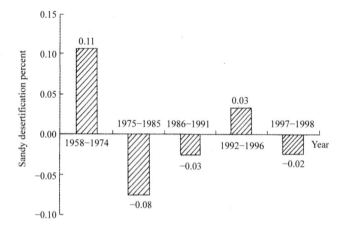

Fig. 10-7   Development and reversal of aeolian desertification in typical areas of the Horqin Sandy Land between 1958-1998

It can be seen from the calculated data of aeolian desertification degree in Table 10-3 that aeolian desertification in the Horqin Sandy Land experienced 4 stages during the 41 years from 1958 to 1998: the first stage was from 1958 to 1974 when the aeolian desertification was the most severe, with a DES value of 0.11; the second stage was from 1975 to 1991 when aeolian desertification was reversed with a DES value of −0.08; the third stage was from 1992 to 1996 when aeolian desertification developed slightly with a value of 0.03; the fourth stage was from 1997 to 1998 when aeolian desertification was reversed again, but compared with last reversal period, its speed reduced.

(1) Basic characteristics of vegetation, soil and soil water content in the Horqin Sandy Land.

In the past 100 years, with the increase in population and the development of aeolian desertification, the landscape of the Horqin Sandy Land degraded from sparse-tree grassland to sandy land with swamps, fixed dunes and meadows, while chestnut soils degraded to wind-blown sand soil. According to a survey in typical areas, plant species show a great difference in different aeolian desertification stages. As far as species richness is concerned (Table 10-4), there are 23 in the potential aeolian desertification stages, while there are 20, 9 and 3 species respectively in the slight, moderate and severe aeolian desertification stages.

Table 10-4　Composition of plant species in aeolian desertification stages in the Horqin Sandy Land

Species	Potential aeolian desertification stage	Slight aeolian desertification stage	Moderate aeolian desertification stage	Severe aeolian desertification stage
Caragana microphylla	√	√		
Atemisia frigida	√			
Atemisia halodendron	√	√	√	√
Mellissitus ruthenicus	√	√		
Cleistogenes squarrosa	√			
Lespedeza davurica	√	√		
Pennisetum centrasiaticum			√	
Phragmites australis		√	√	
Staria viridis	√	√	√	√
Eragrostis pilosa	√	√		
Digitaria sanguinalis	√	√		
Chenopodium acuminatum	√	√		
Euphobia humifusa	√	√	√	
Corispermum didutum	√	√	√	
Artemisia scoparia	√	√		
Salsola collina	√	√		
Ferula bungeana	√			
Ixeris chinensis	√	√	√	
Cynanchum thesioides	√			
Convolvulus arvensis	√	√		
Euphobia esula		√		
Chenopodium aristatum	√	√		
Aillum bidentatum	√			
Gueldenstaedtia stenophylla	√			
Erodium stephanianum	√	√		
Agriophyllum squarrosum			√	√
Leymus secalinus	√			
Echinops gmelini		√		
Bassia dasyphylla		√	√	

From the analysis of functional groups into which plants are divided according to whether it is C_3, C_4 or leguminous plants, it can be concluded that plant species in sandy land changed greatly in different stages of aeolian desertification. As far as functional diversity is concerned (Table 10-5), species richness for annual species is highest in various aeolian desertification stages. The value of importance for annual species is also higher than other life forms except during the potential aeolian desertification stage. Its primary characteristic for annual species was that its lowest importance was 34.6 in the potential aeolian desertification stage but had a highest species richness of 14. On the contrary, in the severe aeolian desertification stage, its species richness was the lowest with a value of 2, but with the largest value of importance of 62.01. This suggests that with the increasing intensity of the aeolian desertification process (from potential aeolian desertification to severe aeolian desertification), annual plants play different roles. In the potential aeolian desertification stage, the annual species are dominant. In the severe aeolian desertification stage, annuals are edifiers which then plays a decisive role in desertification. The value of importance and species richness of perennial plants are lowest in all three kinds of vegetation, with a highest value of 6 and 22.21 respectively in the potential aeolian desertification stage. In the severe aeolian desertification stage, they are both 0. The value of importance of shrubs changes very little in different aeolian desertification stages within a range of 27.36–43.19. This suggests that shrubs play a buffer role in the process of aeolian desertification.

Table 10-5　Species richness and importance value of vegetation composition in different stages of aeolian desertification in the Horqin Steppe

Item	Annual		Perennial		Shrub	
	IV	SR	IV	SR	IV	SR
Potential aeolian desertification stage	34.6	14	22.21	6	43.19	3
Slight aeolian desertification stage	56.69	14	9.97	4	33.35	2
Moderate aeolian desertification stage	61.59	6	10.62	2	27.36	1
Severe aeolian desertification stage	62.01	2	0	0	38.41	1

Note: IV, importance value; SR, species richness.

From the analysis of functional diversity divided according to C_3, C_4 and leguminous plants in different stages of aeolian desertification, it is found that in the composition of vegetation in the Horqin Sandy Land, nitrogen fixing plants exist only in potential and slight aeolian desertification stages, with low IV and SR values (Table 10-6), while C_3 and C_4 plants have comparatively high IV and SR value, and the IV of C_4 plants keeps increasing from the potential aeolian desertification stage to the severe aeolian desertification stage, from 35.63 to 61.59. In addition, as for SR of the functional group, C_4 plants have a relatively high value, ranging from 2 to 8, while C_3 plants have a value slightly below between 1-11. This suggests that C_4 plants are more adapted to wind-blown sand environments than C_3 and nitrogen fixing plants.

Table10-6　Species richness and importance value of functional diversity in different stages of aeolian desertification in the Horqin Steppe

Item	Legume		C_4 plant		C_3 plant	
	IV	SR	IV	SR	IV	SR
Potential aeolian desertification stage	26.44	4	35.63	8	37.93	11
Slight aeolian desertification stage	22.88	3	39.79	8	37.34	9
Moderate aeolian desertification stage	0	0	54.92	4	45.07	5
Severe aeolian desertification stage	0	0	61.59	2	38.41	1

Note : IV, importance value; SR, species richness.

(2) Soil characteristics.

Soil characteristics vary significantly in different types of dunefields in the Horqin Sandy Land. Viewed from leaching loss of soil treated by HCl (Table 10-7), the loss decreased from fixed dunes to semi-fixed dunes, i.e. from 1.18% (±0.51%) to 0.59% (±0.11%). This suggests that during the process of aeolian desertification (from fixed dunes to mobile dunes), the pH value of soil decreased. Viewed from soil mechanical composition (Table 10-8), the content of 1–0.25 mm particles increased from fixed dunes to shifting dunes, i.e. from 18.51% to 49.6%. On the contrary, the content of 0.005–0.001 mm and < 0.001 mm particles decreased from 1.64% to 0.17% and from 1.49% to 0.51%. This shows that in the aeolian desertification process, soil mechanical composition becomes coarse.

Table 10-7　Loss of soil treated with hydrochloric acid in different types of dunefields (%)

Item	Fixed dunes	Semi-fixed dunes	Semi-shifting dunes	shifting dunes	Flat sandy land	Wet land
1	1.1	0.9	1.13	0.65	1.76	1.39
2	1.91	0.55	1.54	0.65	1.21	1.23
3	0.48	1.68	1.23	0.65	1.26	0.68
4	1.31	0.55	0.76	0.58	1.08	0.45
5	1.11	1.15	0.84	0.4	0.91	0.34
Average	1.18	0.97	1.10	0.59	1.24	0.82
Variance	0.51	0.47	0.31	0.11	0.32	0.47

Table 10-8　Soil mechanical composition of different types of dunefields

Diameter (mm)	Fixed dune(%)	Semi-fixed dune(%)	Semi-shifting dune(%)	Shifting dune(%)	Flat sandy land(%)	Wet land(%)
1–0.25	18.51	23.68	18.84	49.6	16.92	30.8
0.25–0.05	68.74	67.03	75.74	48.05	67.66	65.87
0.05–0.01	7.33	5.99	3.07	0.14	11.15	1.21
0.01–0.005	1.19	1.15	0.04	0.88	0.53	0.27
0.005–0.001	1.64	0.21	0.07	0.17	0.99	0.14
<0.001	1.49	1.04	1.11	0.51	0.99	1.04

The analysis of soil moisture content of different types of dunes (Table 10-9) shows that, during the process of aeolian desertification, the contents of organic matter, both P_2O_5 and N, decreased. Aeolian desertification resulted in this loss of soil nutrients. But the changes in the content of available soil nutrient complicated. According to the variety of hydrolytical N, there is a comparatively high content of hydrolytical N in both fixed and mobile dunes, i.e. 24.6 mg/kg and 23.3 mg/kg respectively. This means that the aeolian desertification process has little impact on soil hydrolytical N. But hydrolytical P_2O_5 increases from 2.4 mg/kg in fixed dunes to 6.2 mg/kg in mobile dunes, which shows that aeolian desertification causes soil hydrolytical P_2O_5 content to increase.

Table 10-9   Soil moisture in different types of dunefields (mg/100g)

Items	Fixed dune	Semi-fixed dune	Semi-shifting dune	Shifting dune	Flat sandy land	Wet land
Organic materials(g/kg)	0.454	0.236	0.237	0.088	0.374	0.192
N(g/kg)	0.028	0.013	0.015	0.007	0.023	0.013
P_2O_5(g/kg)	0.023	0.02	0.02	0.01	0.026	0.014
Hydrolytical N(mg/kg)	2.46	0.97	1.94	2.33	2.6	0.82
Hydrolytical P_2O_5(mg/kg)	0.24	0.65	1.81	0.62	0.07	0.23

(3) Characteristics of soil moisture.

Soil moisture in different types of dunes in the Horqin Sandy Land are different. The comparative study of the characteristics of soil moisture in mobile dunes and fixed dunes showed that the former has a higher soil moisture content, with an average value of 3.44% (±0.81%) and 2.76% (±0.16%) in 0–200 cm layer respectively (Fig. 10-8). Soil moisture is highest at the bottom of mobile dunes, with an average value of 4.52% (±0.22%) at a depth of 200 cm; it is lower in the middle part, with an average value of 2.99% (±0.44%); it's lowest at the top, with an average value of 2.58% (±0.19%)(Fig.10-9).

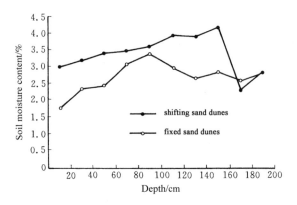

Fig.10-8   Characteristics of soil moisture in different kinds of dunes in the Horqin Sandy Land

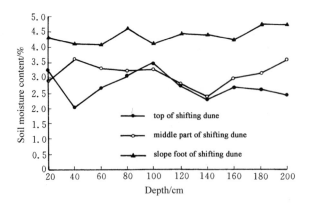

Fig. 10-9   Soil moisture in different parts of shifting dunes

10.4　Onqin Daga Sandy Land

The Onqin Daga is a Mongolian word that means a lonely two-year-old colt. There is a legend that a colt often haunts this beautiful sandy steppe, and brayed deeply towards the sky, as if he were searching for his owner. Afterward, Genghis Khan tamed this spirited horse which became one of his four steeds during war. Hence, this dune grassland was called the Onqin Daga by herdsmen.

10.4.1　General situation

The Onqin Daga Sandy Land was once called the small Tengger Sandy Land. It lies in the southeast part of the Inner Mongolian Plateau, and consists of the mid-southern part of Xilin Gol Meng and the northwest part of Zhaowuda Meng. The sandy land is approximately shaped like a rhombus, and its length from east to west and width from south to north are about 360 km and 30–100 km respectively. The sandy land covers 21, 400km^2, and is the eighth largest sandy land in China (Fig. 10-10) (Zhu, 1980).

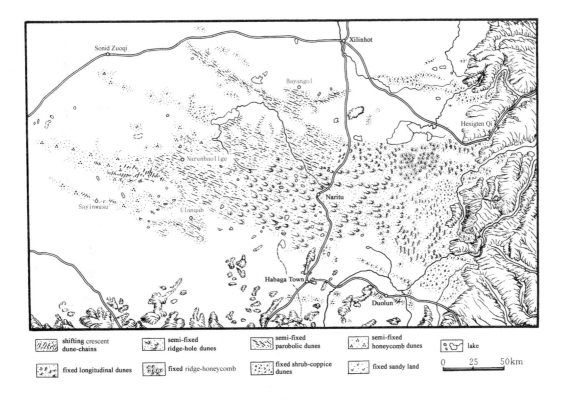

Fig. 10-10　Landforms of the Onqin Daga Sandy Land

(Zhu, 1980)

In addition, there is another sandy land called Gahaielesu which covers 1,660 km^2 in Xi Ujimqin

Qi and is located at the northern edge of the Onqin Daga Sandy Land and the northern side of the Huitengliang basalt mesa. Parabolic dunes are the most typical dunes in this sandy land (Fig. 2-18).

10.4.1.1　Geology and landforms

The geologic structure of the Onqin Daga Sandy Land belongs to the Paleozoic fold zone of Mongolian geosyncline. It rose and became land during the Hercynian orogeny, and after that it underwent a long erosion and planation process. Since the Yanshan Movement, it has suffered slow vibrational structure movements, and formed the strata after the Cretaceous period in the extensive basin. The sandy land itself is a rift-valley depressed zone and is mostly composed of lacustrine clay, sandy clay, and a sand-gravel layer of the Tertiary. The Quaternary system consists of river-lake facies, dune facies and loess sediments. Granite and metamorphite occur in several regions, and only local places are covered by basalt.

The landforms of the Onqin Daga Sandy Land descend slowly from the southeast to the northwest. The altitude of the southern hills is about 1,500–2,000 m, while the height of the northwestern high plain is 900–1,100 m. The whole undulating upland-plain ascends slowly from northwest to southeast. Thus the whole sandy land is still in the geosyncline. The undulation of the sandy land base is very small, and the edge consists of denuded hill, while dunes, lakes and rivers scatter in its interior. Fixed dunes in the sandy land occupy 67.5% of its total area, which are mostly sand ridges and ridge-honeycomb dunes; semi-fixed dunes occupy 19.6%, and shifting dunes 12.9%. The semi-fixed dunes are mostly distributed in the west of the sandy land. The middle is mostly covered by semi-fixed parabolic dunes, while the east is mainly occupied by fixed, semi-fixed ridge honey comb dunes and semi-fixed honeycomb dunes.

10.4.1.2　Climate and hydrology

The Onqin Daga Sandy Land is mostly in the semiarid dry steppe zone, with the northwest area transitions to an arid desert steppe, while its southeast transitions gradually to a semi-humid forest-steppe. It has a temperate continental climate. The water conditions between the east and the west are significantly different. The water quantity in the west is small and the water resources in the east are relatively abundant. The mean annual air temperature is about 0–3 °C. The difference between mean annual temperature and mean daily temperature is large. The sunshine hours per year is about 3,000–3,200 h. The accumulative temperature over 10 °C is 2,000–2,600 h, and the maximum in the west can reach 2,700 h. The frost-free days is about 100–110. The abundant heat and sunshine is favorable for crop and pasture growth. Affected by the southeast monsoon, the precipitation decreases from the southeast to northwest. The annual precipitation in the southeast is 350–400 mm, and that is only 100–200 mm in the northwest. The annual evaporation is 2,000–2,700 mm, and the aridity is 1.2–2. The wind in winter and spring is strong and frequent, especially in April and May, and wind can sometimes reach force 12. The annual mean wind velocity is 3.5–5 m/s, and the number of days with strong wind is 50–80 days. It is one of the areas with the strongest wind in China. The strong wind is the main cause of aeolian desertification development in the sandy land. At the same time, the abundant wind energy provides rich power sources for the production and livelihood of local residents.

The sandy land has many rivers. In the southeast is the Luanhe River and its upper reaches of the Shandian River and its branches, such as the Gongeryingol River, the Xilin River, the Gaogesitai River, and other seasonal streams. In the mid western areas are many seasonal rivers . Lakes in the sandy land are well developed, and they number over 110. There are many freshwater lakes in the eastern part, such as the Chagan Lake located at the southern part of Abaga Qi. With an area of 11,300 hm^2, it is rich in carp, crucian carp and other fishes; Dalai Nur is located at the western part of Hexigten Qi, its area is 22,600 hm^2 and the mean depth is about 7.3 m, and it has carp, crucian carp and other fishes. Most lakes in the west are alkaline, so the reserves of alkali mine is rather large. The Erlian Lake and the Chaganlimen Lake are the largest saline and alkaline lakes respectively. The underground water in the east is rich, and the burial depth is 1–3 m, with very good quality. The underground water is rare in the west, and the quality is poor. The depth of the dry sand layer is 3–10 cm on the shifting dunes and the moisture content of the wet sand layer is about 3%–4%, which provides water for pioneer plant's growth in the sandy land. The burial depth of underground water table in depressions is about 1–1.5 m.

10.4.1.3 Soils and vegetation

The zonal soil of the sandy land is mainly chestnut soil, followed by brown soil. The azonal soil is mostly aeolian soil. The formation and development of soils have significant differences. In general, the east is covered by meadow chestnut soil or dark chestnut soil, which is substituted gradually by light chestnut soil progressing westward. Near Erenhot, it becomes brown soil. The zonal soil is mostly aeolian soil and meadow soil. The fixed dunes in the east exhibits obvious soil genesis, and develops toward chestnut soil. According to developmental degree, it can be divided into chestnut-soil-type arenosol and loose-sandy primitive chestnut soil. The soils around lakes or low wetlands often show a circular distribution. The basic pattern of soil distribution from the center to outer margin is lake-marshy soil, meadow marshy soil, saline meadow soil, meadow soil and aeolian soil. The water and soil conditions in intervals are better, which is an important base for stockbreeding and forestry.

The Onqin Daga Sandy Land is mainly covered by steppe vegetation, and also by ultra zonal vegetation consisting of conifers and broad-leaved arbor, as well as elm sparse wood. The common psammophytes on shifting dunes are *Psammochloa villosa*, *Agriophyllum squarrosum*, *S. gordejecii*, little reed, *Pugionium cornutum* and other pioneer plants. The dominant species is *Salix microstachya*, and is often accompanied by reeds such as *Calamagrostis epigeios*, *Thermopsis schischkinii*, and so on. No plant grows on wind erosion blowouts on the windward slope of semi-fixed dunes, while *A. arenarum* and *Psammochloa villosa* are often intermingled. Moreover, some *S. gordejevii* often cluster on the eastern semi-fixed dunes. There are very rich species and populations on the fixed dunes, especially in the east where the constitution of psammophyte series is affected by fauna from the southern Da Hinggan Ling Mountains and the northern Yan shan Mountains. There are over 30 ligneous plant species. There are conifers such as *P. meyeri*, *P.tabulaeformis* and *Sabina vulgaris*, broad-leaved arbor such as *P. dividiana*, *Betula platyphylla* and *U. pumila* sparse wood, as well as mountains shrubs such as Malus Baccata, *P. humilis*, *P. tomentosa* and *S. mongolica*, etc. Large dunes often have evident sunny and shady slopes. There is sparse vegetation consisting of *Artemisia* ecological association on sunny slopes. On the contrary, there are *Artemisia* subshrub association—cluster herb and weedy association besides arbors and shrubs. *A. frigida*, *T.mongolica* and *P. acaulis* are the main species on the sand-covered section in the east of the sandy land. There is still elm sparse wood on the middle fixed dunes of the sandy land, but *A. mongolica,* and *A. frigida* association also can be found in many places. In addition, there are accompanying species such as *K.prostrata* (*L.*)*, Thymus serpyllum, E. sinica, Hedysarom fruticosum, Hedysarum laeve* and weeds tolerant to drought as well as multi-associations consisting of *agropyron desertorum*. There are *C. microphylla*, *C. pygmaea var. angustissima*, *A. mongolica* and *Psammochloa villosa* on the fixed and semi-fixed dunes in the west of the sandy land, mixed with *A. frigida, Caryopteris mongholia, E. gmelin, Asparagus gobicus, Cleistogenes, S. glareosa,* etc.

10.4.2　Sedimentary record

10.4.2.1　Strata

According to Li Xiaoze et al. (1998) and the different combinations of sedimentary facies, the sandy land can be divided into three major zones:

1) Gobi zone

It is mainly located in the western and northwestern parts of the sandy land, containing the Bagemalong rocky hill, Erlian Tala sandy high plain, Saihan Tala sandy and gravel high plain, and other landforms. It extends westward into the People's Republic of Mongolian. According to micro-topographic and eluvium characteristics, it can be classified as three specific types: A. Slope gobi: it is comprised of residual breccia material on the slope surface of hills, which was weathered directly from bedrock. B. Mesa gobi: residual sand-gravelly layer formed through wind erosion on the surface of flat Tertiary river and lacustrine strata, which developed on step sand-gravelly high plain. C. Lowland gobi: (In valleys, depressions and other negative landforms, sand-gravelly layer was deposited under the combined effects of wind and water force, where aqueous lamination and paleosol layers can be found.) The exposed strata in the gobi area can be divided into three epoches. There is the Lower Tertiary granitic crystalline rock on the western Sino-Mongolian border land, the old Tertiary river and lacustrine strata located at middle Erenhot, and the new Tertiary river and lacustrine strata in the east.

2) Sandy land zone

The Holocene sandy land surface is mainly covered by the Holocene aeolian sediments and river-lake deposits (Fig. 10-11).

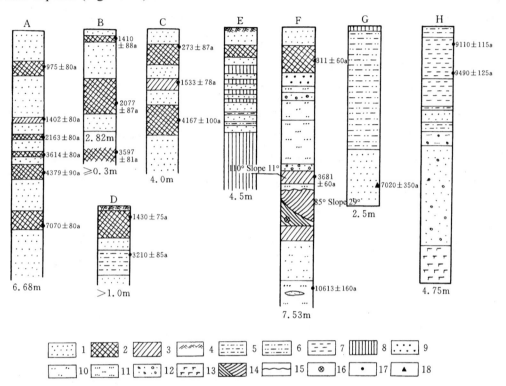

Fig. 10-11　Holocene stratigraphic column in the Onqin Daga Sandy Land (Li Sen et al., 1995)

1. Aeolian sands; 2. Sandy paleosol; 3. Weak sandy paleosol; 4.Surface soil; 5. Sandy clay; 6. Clayry silt; 7. Clay; 8. Sandy loess; 9. Coarse sands; 10. Middle sands; 11. Fine sands; 12. Gravels; 13. Basalt weathering layer; 14. Foreset laminae of aeolian sands; 15. Denudation plane; 16. Sampling site of animal fossils; 17. [14]C ages a BP; 18. U ages a BP

Section site: A. Hadan Huxu; B. Sanggin Dalai; C. Nari; D. Daerhanwula; E. west Sanyi; F. Bayan Huxu; G. Dalai Nur H. Anguli Nur

Aeolian sediment is widely distributed in the sandy land as well as its surrounding regions. There are 4–6 greyish yellow aeolian sand layers and 3–5 dark brown sandy paleosol layers which can be easily found in sections of dunes. The paleosols that developed on dunes usually cover the dune in the dome attitude. The paleosols developed on flat sandy land and interdune form interbed with aeolian sand layer, which constitutes the Holocene aeolian sand and paleosol sedimentary sequence.

At the east and south margin, the aeolian sediment phase changes into aeolian soil and loess, and forms interbeds with sandy paleosol, which develops into aeolian sand, sandy loess and paleosol sedimentary sequence.

River and lake deposits developed in river valleys or wide lowland, which are composed of river and lake sand-gravelly clay, aeolian sand and paleosol, etc. There are 3–4 dark brown sandy paleosol and yellow aeolian sand layers which can be found in the Holocene section at the river terraces. Paleosol often develops on alluvial flats, lacustrine beaches or aeolian sand layers, and its thickness can reach 30–60 cm. They are usually covered by aeolian sand or river and lake deposit. They form the superimposed deposit and river-lake, paleosol and aeolian sedimentary sequence.

The main characteristics of the Holocene sediments of the sandy land are as follows:

First, aeolian sandy sediment is the main sediment type, while river and lake sediments are secondary. They are interlaced or inserted in spatial distribution and form unique sedimentary facies and geomorphologic landscapes.

The two kinds of sediments, through phase change in the transverse direction, formed alternative arrangement patterns of aeolian sand, sand ridges, interdune flats, rivers and lakes. In the downwind direction of the sandy land, aeolian sand gradually changes into dust sediment.

Second, aeolian sediment, river and lake deposits and paleosol developed alternatively, and formed superimposed sedimentary sequences, which can be divided into six paleosol development periods. The sedimentary sequence of aeolian sand-paleosol and river-lake deposits—paleosol—aeolian sand possess the characteristics of alternative development, and superimposed deposit, which

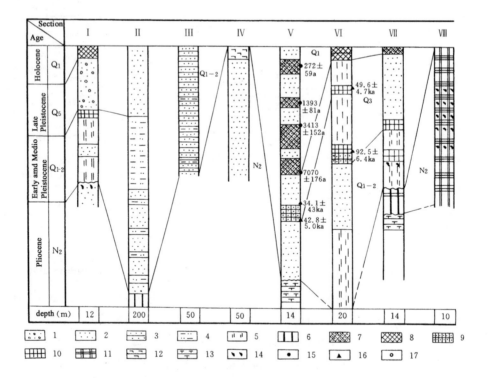

Fig. 10-12   Stratigraphic column in the Onqin Daga Sandy Land region

1. gravels; 2. aeolian sands; 3. alluvial sands; 4. alluvial sandy argillite; 5. sandy loess; 6. aeolian laterite; 7. black sandy paleosol; 8. black silty paleosol; 9. brown sandy paleosol; 10. brown sandy paleosol; 11. red silty paleosol; 12. basalt; 13. bedrock of former Tertiary; 14. calcareous nodule; 15. ^{14}C dating; 16. TL dating; 17. K-Ar dating

shows that the sandy land had complicated sedimentary modes. Two kinds of sedimentary sequence often have 3 or 4 sandy paleosol layers, and even can reach 6 layers. According to the ^{14}C dating paleosols as well as the strata section structure of this area, there are 6 paleosol development periods in this region during the Holocene. (The first period is about 9.8–9.0 ka BP, and the second, the third, the fourth, the fifth and the sixth are about 7.1–5.9 ka BP, 4.6–3.2 ka BP, 2.3–1.9 ka BP,1.6–0.9 ka BP, 0.33–0.27 ka BP respectively (Fig. 10-12).)

The Holocene ancient aeolian sand sediment does not have an obviously stratified structure (Fig.10-13). The scope of granuality is about 1–4ϕ, and probability cumulative curves mostly show a reversal S-distribution. The coordinate of the lower endpoint is (1.9ϕ, 50%), while that of the upper endpoint is (2.6ϕ, 65%), which has a triple segmentation and bimodal characteristics.

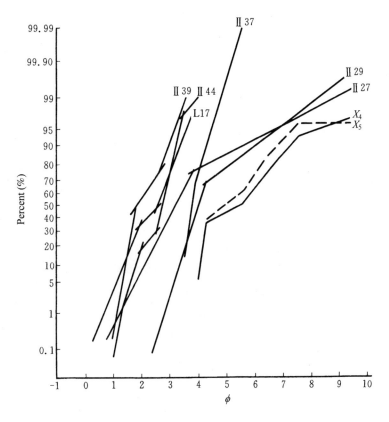

Fig. 10-13 Several granularity probability cumulative curves

The surface of quartz sand universally has pockmarks, dished pits and SiO_2 deposits. The particle-size composition of sandy paleosol is similar to that of ancient aeolian sand, except for higher silt content. River and lake facies sands were often a result of transportation and redeposition of ancient aeolian sand. The granularity probability cumulative curves of river and lake sandy sediments also show a reversal S-distribution.

The northern margin of the sandy land connects with the Abaga basalt mesa. According to borehole data and field observations, there is interbedded layer between aeolian sand and basalt at their joint. The three basalt layers in the section of basalt and aeolian sand located to the north of the Huiteng River correspond to grade I, II, III mesa of the five-grade Huitengxili basalt mesa. The grain-size analysis of white fine sands and brown-yellow fine sands between grade II and grade III basalt mesa show that granularity probability cumulative curves are similar to the common reversal S-distribution (Fig. 10-13). Pockmarks, dished pits and other aeolian phenomenon can be found on SEM photographs.

The whole sandy land basically consists of uniform sandy deposits. Its depth in the western desert zone is often less than 50 m, which is thinner than that of the central and eastern desert zone (over 200 m).

3) Loess zone

It mainly exists in mountains, hills and basins at the eastern and southern margin of the sandy land. The Quaternary sediments are characterized by the co-existence of ancient aeolian sand, sandy loess and loess. There are aeolian sands in the Huade–Kangbao–Baochang– Zhenglan–Duolun zones located at the margin of the sandy land.

Generally, the lower part is middle and late Pleistocene strata consisting of light red-yellow ancient aeolian sand or sandy loess, which has a yellow-red paleosol layer containing calcareous nodules. There are the late Pleistocene to the early Holocene strata in the middle part, and they are red-yellow sandy loess or aeolian sand intercalated with 1, 2 layers of dark brown or yellow-red paleosols. The upper part is the middle Holocene dark gray paleosol.

In addition, Neogene aeolian are widely spread in valleys and basins at the southern margin of the sandy land. There are the well-known Tonggur fauna fossil and Sanzhima fauna fossil in contemporaneous strata. The particle-size of aeolian laterite is dominated by silt and clay, of which the content of silt occupies over 90%. Quartz sands mostly are angular, subangular, and subrounded in shape. The mean granularity of aeolian laterite is about $5-6\phi$ which is similar to that of loess.

10.4.2.2 Granularity

In the aeolian sand-paleosol section, the scope of granularity is about $0-4.32\phi$, and they are mostly fine sands and very fine sands. Taking Hadan Huxu and Naritu sections as samples, fine sands are mainly $1.0-4.32\phi$. Their mean grain size (Mz) is about $2.19-2.35\phi$, and their standard deviation (δ_1) is 0.83–0.968. This reflects that this section is affected by combined effects of deflation and wind deposition, and is dune sediments with middle degree of sorting.

The granularity scope of river and lake deposit—paleosol—aeolian sediment of the sandy land are often broader, thus lithologic characteristics of different strata varies greatly. For example, in the Baiyinhushao section, Mz is 2.68ϕ, with a standard deviation (δ_1) of 1.2, and aeolian sand is mostly at $1.0-6.64\phi$. They belong to aeolian sediments that mainly consist of very fine sands with middle degree of sorting. The grain size of river and sandy paleosol is about $-1-0.64\phi$, Mz is about

1.10–3.36 ϕ, and δ_1 is about 0.729–2.604 ϕ. They belong to sandy sediments with great variety.

The grain size composition of different strata of the above sections exhibits obvious similarities and differences, which reflects the climatic changes of the region.

(1) The grain size composition of various soil layers is similar to that of underlying aeolian sand or fluvial sand, but with larger paleosol Mz and more silt content, which increased by 1.55% and 2.32% on the granularity scope of 4.32–6.64 ϕ compared to underlying aeolian sand or fluvial sand. Such thining trends are directly related to the soil-forming climatic conditions. This shows paleosol in this region developed from parent material consisting of aeolian sand or river sand of alluvial flats.

(2) Mz of aeolian sand in three sections varies among 2.130–2.594 ϕ, 2.410–2.954 ϕ and 2.39–2.96 ϕ respectively. This implies that the mean wind force had obvious changes during the deposition process of aeolian sand in this region. Obviously, coarse aeolian sands indicates strong wind, while the finer particles indicate weak wind (Li, 1988).

(3) Changes in grain size of fluvial deposits is larger, and Mz is 1.103–3.360 ϕ. This shows that hydrodynamic conditions had obvious changes during deposition, and its grain size composition indirectly reflects the dry-wet climatic changes in the deposition period.

(4) Mz and δ_1 of paleosol are often higher in various strata of the sandy land, however, those of aeolian sand are lower. This is particularly obvious in the Hadan Huxu section. Mz and δ_1 peaked in the fourth, eighth and twelfth paleosol layer, and had the minimum in the third, fifth and eleventh aeolian sand layer. This shows that more than three cold-warm and dry-wet as well as wind force climatic fluctuations had occurred in the Holocene in this region. Moreover, Mz peaking in the eighth, the ninth and tenth layers implies a persistent warm-wet climate.

10.4.2.3　Geochemistry elements

The sorting, migration and accumulation of trace elements are mostly related to the climatic environment in addition to the effects of their own physical and chemical properties. Usually, wet-type climatic elements (Fe, Mn, Cr, V, Co, Ni, etc.) tend to enrich under warm-wet conditions, and they disperse under dry-cold situations. Arid-type climatic elements (K, Na, Ca, Mg, Sr, Ba, etc.) have opposite behavior. Thus, the total accumulated quantity of the two kinds of trace elements and their ratio-ancient climatic index (C value) (Huang Ruchang, 1981) can denote climatic conditions during the period of deposit in semi-quantity. According to this, the C values of various layers in the Hadan Huxu Section and the Bayan Huxu Section were computed (see Table 10-10), and the statistics of mean C values in 4 types of strata consisting of sandy paleosol, fluvial fine sand, aeolian sand and fluvial middle-coarse sandy-gravel stone was calculated. The results show that the C value of sandy paleosol is largest up to 9.63, showing that wet-type climatic elements tended to accumulate during soil-formed periods when the climate was warm-wet. The average C value of aeolian sand is 8.92, showing that dry-type climatic elements tended to accumulate during aeolian sand development when the climate is dry-cold or arid. The average C value of fluvial fine sands and middle-coarse sandy-gravel stones are 9.19 and 7.46 respectively. According to analysis of average C values, the climatic conditions are similar in the fine sand deposition period and paleosol development period, while the climatic conditions of the middle-coarse sand deposition period is similar to that of the aeolian sand development period (Fig. 10-14).

Table 10-10　Ancient climatic index (C) of various horizons in the M section of Hadan Huxu and Bayan Huxu

Section	Horizon													
	1	2	3	4	5	6	7	8	9	10	11	12	13	14
Hadan Huxu	9.23	9.05	9.92	9.45	9.36	7.86	7.63	9.85	10.00	10.72	9.35	10.02	8.66	
Bayan Huxu	8.85	12.73	7.84	9.28	8.17	5.99	8.26	7.62	10.42	8.59	7.37	6.60	7.69	10.66

Note: Ancient climatic index (C) = $\sum$(Fe+Mn+Cr+V+Co+Ni)/$\sum$(K+Na+Ca+Mg+Sr+Ba) (Li Sen et al., 1995)

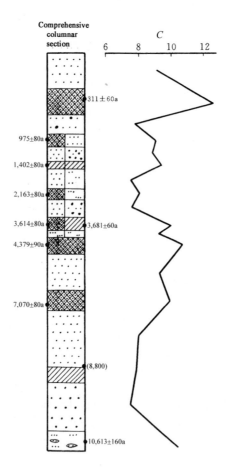

Fig. 10-14　Ancient climatic index curve obtained from C value(Li et al., 1995)

10.4.2.4　Spore pollen

1) The spore pollen assemblage characteristics of the Holocene Hadan Huxu Section

A total of 1580 grain sporopollens were identified from 14 samples in 13 layers of the section, of which herb and subshrub occupied 96.77%, and tree pollen and ferns spore occupied 1.65% and 1.58% respectively. They belong to 33 families or genus. From bottom to top, they can be divided into 5 sporopollen assemblage zones (Fig. 10-15).

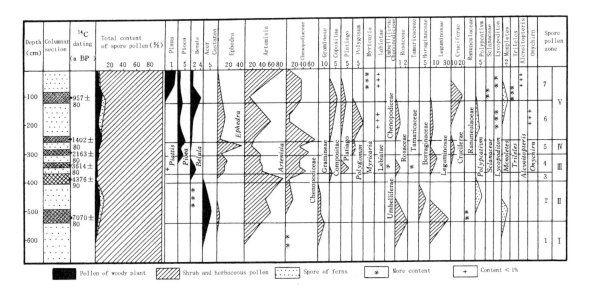

Fig. 10-15　Holocene sporopollen chart of the Hadan Huxu section (Li et al., 1995)

(1) *Chenopodiaceae*-dominated plant zone. This zone was characterized by small sporopollen amount and monotonic genus. Only one *Chenopodiaceae* pollen grain was identified, which means that the climate was dry and cold, lacking plants at the time.

(2) *Artemisia-leguminosae-gramineae* zone. This zone shows an increase in plant species and pollen amount. Pollen from herbs and subshrubs occupied 92.6% of the total. *Artemisia*, *Leguminosae* and *Gramineae* were dominant, and in the early period *Ranunculaceae* was dominant, while in the later period *Chenopodiaceae* was dominant. The woody plant pollens in the early period were warm-wet-loving acer and castanea, and in the later period was Quercus. They accounted for 2.3%–6.3% of the total. These show that the climate changed from warm-wet to warm-cool and dry in this stage.

(3) *Artemisia-chenopodiaceae-ephedra-betula* zone. The content of herb and subshrub pollen increased to 99.5% of the total. *Artemisia*, *Chenopodiaceae* and *Ephedra* were dominant, and there were *Plantago, Tamarix* and *Compositae* etc. Pollen from woody plants only accounted for about 1%, and no fern spores existed. This reflects that the temperature and humidity decreased compared to the previous stage, and represented a warm and moderate semi-humid climate.

(4) *Chenopodiaceae-ephedra- Artemisia-spruce* zone. The pollen content of *Chenopodiaceae* and *Ephedra* in herb and subshrub zone increased greatly, and accounted for 36.1% and 35% of the total respectively. However, the content of *Artemisia* decreased to 21.2%, and there were only a few

Chenopodiaceae and *Cruciferae* pollens. Woody plants only appeared in the early period. This reflects that the climate changed from cool - wet to dry-cold in this stage.

(5) *Artemisia-chenopodiaceae-ephedra-pinus* zone. The content and species of pollens are abundant in this zone. Herb and subshrub pollen occupied 86.6%–96.7% of the total. They were dominated by *Artemisia* and *Chenopodiaceae*, and there are a lot of *Ephedra*, *Compositae*, *Chenopodium*, *Cruciferae*, and herbs, etc. There were several *Pinus*, spruce and *Betula*. The bottom of this zone (the sixth section) is a *Artemisia-Chenopodiaceae-Betula* assemblage, and the upper layer is a *Artemisia-Chenopodiaceae-Pinus* assemblage. This suggests that the climate was dry-cold in the early period and warm-dry in the later period.

2) The spore pollen assemblage characteristics of the Holocene Bayan Huxu section

A total of 1,631 grain sporopollens of 14 samples in 14 layers of the section were identified, of which the woody plant pollen occupied 4.23%, while those of herb and subshrub occupied 95.77%, and fern spores was zero which belong to 16 families or genus. From bottom to top, they can be divided into 4 sporopollen assemblage zones (Fig. 10-16).

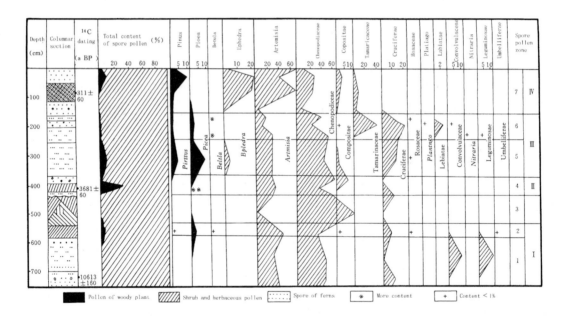

Fig. 10-16   Hollence sporopollen chart of the Bayan Huxu Section

(1) *Chenopodiaceae* and *Artemisia*-dominated plants zone. This zone was characterized by monotonic sporopollen genus and dominant xerophytic herbs and subshrubs. It can be divided into the upper, middle and bottom sections. The bottom was dominated by *Chenopodiaceae* and *Artemisia*, accompanied with a few *Cruciferae*, *Convolvulus* and *Leguminosae*, reflecting a dry-cold climate at that time. The middle section was *Artemisia-Chenopodiaceae- Cruciferae-spruce*

assemblage, the content of plant sporopollen increased, and spruce, *Pinus, Betula, Chrysanthemum*，rosebush，*Umbelliferae*, etc appeared. The content of Artemisia increased to 48.8%, while that of *Chenopodiaceae* decreased to 34.5%. These show that the climate was warm-wet. The upper section was dominated by *Chenopodiaceae*, and is similar to the *Hadenghushuo* section. This reflects that the climate was dry-cold at that time.

(2) *Chenopodiaceae-Artemisia-Betula* zone. This zone was dominated by herbs and subshrubs, of which *Chenopodiaceae* and *Artemisia* were dominant, and the content of *Cruciferae* and *Chrysanthemum* pollen was high. Only spruce belongs to woody plant. This reflects that the climate changed from dry-cold to warm-wet at that stage.

(3) *Artemisia-Chenopodiaceae- Cruciferae -Pinus* zone. The content of pollen were abundant and species were diverse in this zone. *Artemisia, Chenopodiaceae* and *Cruciferae* were the dominant herbs and subshrubs, with plenty of Tamarix, Ephedra, Plantago and woody plant pollens including *Pinus*, spruce and *Betula* species.

(4) *Artemisia-Chenopodiaceae-Ephedra-Pinus* zone. The content and species of pollens were sparse in this zone. The only woody plant pollen was *Pinus*. *Artemisia* and *Chenopodiaceae* were the dominant woody plants and subshrubs, and the drought tolerant *Ephedra* noticeably increased. This reflects that the climate tended to become dry and warm at this stage, belonging to a mild semi-arid climate.

10.4.2.5   Animal fossils

Fossils of skull and molars of the Coelodonta antiquitatis were found in the eleventh layer of aeolian sands layers of the Bayan Huxu section. According to *Xiejunyi* tutor's identification, the skull is composed of occipital, parietal bone, mandible and other shivers. Cheek tooth is M_2 and M_3 of left-upper gena. Mammoth-Coelodonta antiquitatis animals in zooecology include forest type, steppe type and river-marshy type. This represents the environment and climatic conditions of a cool temperature zone. According to Zhou Benxiong's research (1978), wooly rhinoceros once emigrated over a wide-range toward the south during the last glacial period. Based on the dating of upper and lower layers, the deposition times of the eleventh layer of the Baiyinhushao section is about 8.8–7.1 ka BP, and the fossils of wooly rhinoceros buried in the Bayinhushao section indicate it was a strong cold period of the early Holocene. The skulls and skin of wooly rhinoceros were preserved in aeolian sand. This proves that the climate was very cold at that time, and sand blown activities were frequent. The foreset laminated structure of aeolian sand layer indicates that the prevailing wind direction at that time was W–WNW.(West-West-North-West)

10.4.3   Formation age and evolution process

As to the time of the formation of the Onqin Daga Sandy Land, Yang Zhongjian (1930) proposed that it was formed in the Neolithicage; 101 hydro-geology and engineering geology team of Inner Mongolia thought that it was formed in the late Pleistocene. Gao Shanming (1985) thought this sandy land existed in the middle Pleistocene. According to aeolian sand evidence, Dong Guangrong et al. (1998) believed that this sandy land was present in the late Tertiary. The environment conditions, in major geological periods since the late Tertiary, are as follows.

1) Late Tertiary

Fossils of ancient vertebrate are abundant. Erlaintongur funa reflect a forest-steppe environment. There are some steppe-type animals such as Samotheriumv and Dorcadoryu, and some forest-type animals such as Sinohippus as well as some transition-type animals such as Palaetragus in the Huade Area. Rhinoceros with big lips were usually found in steppes or mixed forest-steppe belts.

In the Erdengtubaodeqi stratum, there are *Erinaceidae, Dipodidae, Muridae, Leporidae,* Ochotonidae, indicating the presence of desert-steppe. The Calcareous nodules in paleosols reflect a semi-arid climate at that time. Interlayered red clay and laterite paleosol layers reflect the periodical dry and wet climatic fluctuations. Generally speaking, during the Tertiary, there was a tropic or subtropic zone with obvious alteration of wet and dry season and local sandy land landscape in this region.

2) Early and middle Pleistocene

Sporopollens were dominated by *Artemisia* and *Chenopodiaceae*. Animals include *Eqidae, Bovidae, Gazella blacki*, etc. Aeolian sand, sandy loess and loess developed widely. The environment tended to become dry. The color of aeolian deposit is light red-yellow which shows that the oxidation was weaker than that of the late Tertiary, and temperatures were lower. The paleosol layer is yellow-red, containing calcareous nodules, which indicate a wet-warm semi-arid environment. The grain size of aeolian sediments gradually became finer from northwest to southeast, showing that the northwest wind was prevalent in this region at that time.

3) Early phase of the late Pleistocene

Sporopollens are mainly composed of *Artemisia* and *Chenopodiaceae*. Paleosol and river-lake facies strata developed widely. Paleosol is yellow-red, with sparse calcareous nodule. It is inferred that the environment was a semi-humid forest grassland environment.

4) Later phase of the late Pleistocene

Aeolian sediments spread widely, for example, the Malan Leoss is much thicker in the sandy loess zone. Sandy loess is gray-yellow. There is a large area of light brown-yellow ancient aeolian sand distributed in the desert region and sand-loess transition zone. There are ancient vertebrate fossils such as *Coelodonta antiquitatis, Camelus knoblochi, Equus prcewalskyi* and other desert-steppe species. *Artemisia, Chenopodiaceae* and *Gramineae* were dominant in sporopollen, which indicated a dry-cold desert-steppe environment. Wind and blown sand activity was strong, and sandy land was activated and expanded rapidly. A light brown paleosol layer appeared in the middle period. Sporopollens were mainly composed of *Artemisia* and *Compositae*, representing a warm-wet fluctuation in the dry-cold period.

5) Holocene

According to strata structure, sediment character and climatic records, the climate of the Onqin Daga Sandy Land in the Holocene can be divided into 8 alternating dry-cold and warm-wet cycles (Fig. 10-17). During the cold period, there were an extreme dry-cold and 7 dry-cold intervals, while there were 5 warm-wet and 3 warm-dry intervals in the warm period. Under extreme dry-cold and dry-cold conditions, desert and desert-steppe landscapes were formed. Dunes were reactivated, shifting sands spread, and aeolian desertification developed. Under warm-wet and warm-dry conditions, forest-steppe, steppe with sparse trees and dry-steppe landscape were formed, during which vegetation coverage increased, dunes were fixed, paleosol developed and aeolian desertification reversed. In 8 climatic cycles, the fluctuation period of the first and second cycles was about 2,500 a, and the landscape changed between desert-steppe and forest-steppe. The fluctuation period of the third, fourth and fifth cycles was about 1,000 a, and the landscape changed between steppe

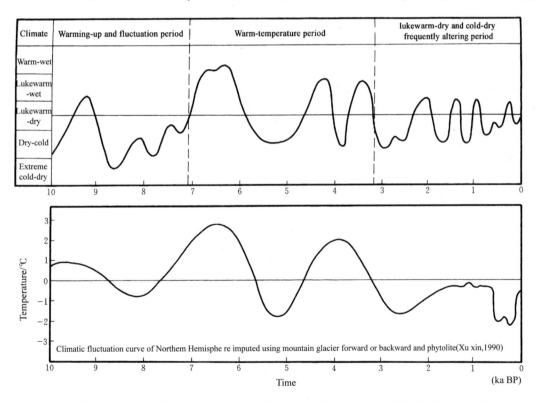

Fig. 10-17　Comparison of climate changes of the Onqin Daya Sandy Land and the Northern Hemisphere
in the Holocene (Li Sen et al., 1995)

with sparse wood and desert-steppe. The fluctuation period of the sixth, seventh and eighth cycles was about 500 a, and the landscape changed between desert-steppe and dry-steppe. This showed that the climatic change in this region had short fluctuating cycle and high frequency over 10,000 years.

The evolution process of the Onqin Daga Sandy Land in the Holocene can be divided into 3 stages: temperature rising period in 10–7.1 ka BP, warm period in 7.1–3.2 ka BP and cold-dry frequent fluctuating period until 3.2 ka BP.

After the last glacial period, this region entered rising temperature fluctuation period in the Holocene. In the initial stage, the climate was dry-cold, and during 9.8–8.8 ka BP the climate gradually became warm-wet. It is estimated that the mean annual temperature was 1–2°C higher than the present, and formed the sparse-tree grassland that mainly consisted of *Artemisia-Chenopodiaceae- Cruciferae-spruce*. The earliest weak sandy paleosol of the Holocene ^{14}C age of the bottom is 9,853±301 a BP was formed. After 8.8 ka BP，extreme cold events occurred in this region, and the climate was extreme dry-cold. The strong west wind prevailed, which led to the spread of shifting sands, vegetation damage and appearance of *Coelodonta antiquitatis* and other psychrophilic animals. Desert and desert-steppe landscape appeared. The extreme cold events lasted for about 1,700 a, and the bioclimatic zone moved at least 3 latitudes southwards.

The Holocene warm lasted for about 4,000 a in this region, and the climate changed between warm-wet and dry-cold. 7.1–5.9 ka BP was the warmest stage of the Holocene, when vast savanna steppe and sandy paleosol were formed. Warm broad-leaved forest appeared in the south part in the later period. During 5.9–4.6 ka BP, the second cold period of the Holocene, the climate was dry-cold, and the vegetation degraded to dry-steppe or desert-steppe. The climate during 4.6–4.1 ka BP was warm-wet,during which shifting sands shrank and fixed to form soil. The third cold period was 4.1–3.6 ka BP, which was drier and colder than the second cold period. The climate turned warm-wet during 3.6–3.2 ka BP, and formed steppe with sparse trees. Paleosol developed widely on dunes, interdunes and alluvial flats and this corresponded to the Xia-Shang Dynasty warm period in Chinese history. It was estimated that air temperature in the warm period was 2–3°C higher than it is now, and annual precipitation was 60–100 mm higher than present. And air temperature in the colder stage was 1–2°C higher than it is now, while annual precipitation was 20–70 mm less than today.

This region entered frequent fluctuating period of warm-dry and cold-dry climate since 3.2 ka BP. Under the climatic aridification circumstances, fluctuation cycles occurred. The 3.2–2.3 ka BP period was the fourth cold period. The climate was cool and wet during 2.3–1.9 ka BP which led to the formation of the landscape of grass-shrub in the southern part and steppe with sparse spruce and Pinus in the northern part. The climate became dry and cold during 1.9–1.6 ka BP when shifting dunes expanded and the desert-steppe landscape appeared. The climate had fluctuation periods of warm-dry and cold-dry during 1.9–1.6 ka BP. Temperature increased a little since 1 ka BP, the aridity was enhanced, and a warm-dry period appeared during 1.0–0.9 ka BP and a cold-dry period appeared between 0.9–0.33 ka BP; there was another warm-dry period during 0.33–0.27 ka BP and another cold-dry period after 0.27 ka BP.

10.4.4　Factors affecting the formation of the sandy land

10.4.4.1　Formation factors

The basic factors affecting the formation of the sandy land mainly include climatic changes, neotectonic movement and human activities.

1) Climatic change

First, the sandy land evolves with climatic changes. The climate in geologic times had different cycles and different degrees of cold-warm and dry-wet variations. Since the Cenozoic, the climate tended to become dry gradually, and up until the middle-late Miocene and the early Pliocene, the aridity reached its maximum. The Onqin Daga Sandy Land emerged just at this stage. The evolution processes of the sandy land are consistent with global climatic fluctuations in the glacial period. The development scope of the sandy land changed synchronously with variations in climatic fluctuation.

Second, the climate change controls the variation of wind force. Wind force is the energy source that shapes aeolian sand landforms. In the formation process of the sandy land, it was always affected by the Siberian-Mongolian high pressure. With the alternation of dry-cold climate in glacial stage and warm-wet climate in interglacial period, the continental high pressure caused by the difference between ocean and land was strengthened or weakened, and consequently the wind become stronger or weaker. Thus, the sandy land experienced fixed-shrinking and activated-expansion periods.

Third, the climate change has an important influence on the source of sandy material. The sand sources are the material basis for aeolian sand landforms. Under the action of a prevailing west wind, there is a trend of aeolian sand moving from west to east. This is why there are larger dunes, thicker ancient aeolian sand and complete sedimentary sequences in the east. The mineral composition shows that the main mineral ingredients of all aeolian facies, including coexistent alluvial-lake sediments, are similar, and approximate to those of granites around the sandy land. From this we conclude that the sand materials of the sandy land have three origins: A. Granite weathered materials around the sandy land; B. Tertiary alluvial-lake facies strata; C. Volcanic debris materials.

Fourth, the climate changes caused fixing-shrinking or activating-extending of dunes through changing vegetation cover and hydrological conditions.

2) Neotectonic movement

The development of the Onqin Daga Sandy Land trough mainly depends on effects of neotectonic movement. Reconstructing the geological history of this region, present landform patterns basically formed after the Yanshan Movement or during the late Cretaceous. The trough where the Onqin Daga Sandy Land is located in a secondary minus tectonic unit of the

Neocathaysian meridional tectonic system and the Yinshan latitudinal tectonic system. Neotectonic movement further developed the former depressed landforms and resulted in the Onqin Daga Sandy Land trough. Neotectonic movements were mainly vermicular movements and volcanic action.

Neotectonic movement had effects on the sources of sand. The sandy materials were transported from the outer edge of the basin to its center under certain conditions, but the basin land forms were controlled by neotectonic movement to a great extent. Volcanic debris might become part of ancient aeolian sands. On the other hand, structural landforms had effects on ancient wind. When the prevalent west wind blow across the sandy land, it was blocked by the Da Hinggan Ling Mountains in the east and weakened by the Bashang Plateau in the south, which promoted the mechanical differential process of aeolian deposition. The tectonic uplift led to river undercutting and a decreasing underground water table, and promoted climate aridification.

3) Human activities

Human activities have a long history in the study area. With the development of social productivity, the intensity of human activities is increasing. Human activities in recent decades have particularly tremendous effects on the formation of sandy land. From Table 10-11, we can find that fluctuations of temperature and precipitation were not much from the 1970s to the 1980s. Neotectonic movement and other natural conditions also have few changes. However, the degree of desertification development is increasing, and the spread of aeolian desertified land is also remarkable. It is obvious that this is related to irrational economic activities such as overgrazing, over-cultivation and other unsuitable activities. Therefore, the development of sandy land in the future not only depends on natural factors such as climatic change, but also human activities.

Table 10-11　The aeolian desertified land area and climatic changes in the 1970s and the 1980s in the Duolun county (km^2)

Items	Types	1970s	1980s	Variability (%)
Aeolian desertification	Sandy shrub-steppe	664.64	460.60	−30.70
	Coppice dunes	439.37	558.07	27.00
	Semi-shifting coppice dunes	49.44	81.63	65.11
	Shifting dunes	72.99	150.48	106.17
	Total	562.10	790.18	40.58
Gravel-like or Gobi-like Landscape	Sandy gravel gobi			
	Steppe with coarse-grained surface	36.45	330.52	806.80
	Gobi-steppe	44.76	52.86	18.10
	Wind-eroded gobi			
	Total	131.18	383.38	192.26
Farmland soil wind erosion	Sandy farmlands	757.45	198.60	−73.78
	Moderate wind-eroded farmlands	275.29	468.27	70.10
	Severe wind-eroded farmlands	99.30	336.70	239.07
	Total	374.59	804.97	114.80
Climate	Mean temperature (°C)	2.0	(1.6)	−20
	Mean precipitation (mm)	372.8	372.27	−0.14

10.4.4.2 Causes of the sandy land

Since the Quarternary, the subtropical northern boundary, which was located north of the sandy land in the late Tertiary, shifted southwards and retreated out of the sandy land, and the whole sandy land was controlled by the temperate East Asia monsoon. Landforms and environment of the sandy land experienced a series of evolutional processes, and formed aeolian sand or sandy loess/silty paleosol sediment in sequence. Aeolian sand or sandy loess are the results and signs of dune activation and desert expansion. This indicates that the northern limit of the summer monsoon did not reach this region, and it was mainly controlled by the winter monsoon and the environment was desert or desert-steppe. On the contrary, in the development period of paleosol, dunes fixed and deserts shrank, the northern limit of the summer monsoon moved northwards and across this region. Corresponding brown paleosol indicated a forest-steppe environment and black paleosol indicated a dry-steppe environment.

The climate and environment changes of the Onqin Daga Sandy Land in the Holocene are very similar to the temperature change curve of the Northern Hemisphere which was calculated based on the advance and retreat of mountain glaciers and plant fossils (Xu Xin et al., 1990), and consistent with 6 paleosol development periods of the Mu Us Sandy Land in the Holocene (Gao et al., 1993) and 8.5 cycles of the Gurbantünggüt desert. This shows that the main climatic events and evolution stages are consistent with neighboring regions except for individual cold and warm periods. That is, climatic change of this region was partially synchronous with the Northern Hemisphere, especially the northern arid area of China.

Aeolian desertification processes of the Onqin Daga Sandy Land is mainly manifested in the mobilization of fixed dunes.

For example, the Ujimqin grassland, the Abaga grassland and the Sunid grassland in the northern part of the sandy land are the main part of Inner Mongolian grassland which is one of five pasturelands of China. Especially the Ujimqin grassland was a very beautiful grassland with vigorous grasses, but it degraded severely in recent years. Desertified lands spread rapidly due to overgrazing, land reclamation and drought.

According to our investigation in Xi Ujimqin Qi, on average a sheep needed $0.54 \ hm^2$ grassland in this region in 1955. However, it needed $1.09 \ hm^2$ in the same place in 1982. According to the statistics in 1982, there are 16.2%, 26.5%, 20% of degraded grassland respectively in the southern, central and northern parts of Xi Ujimqin Qi. The total degraded grassland accounts for over 75%.

In recent years, China has implemented the policy of returning farmlands to forest or grassland, and the whole Onqin Daga Sandy Land and its surrounding regions are thought as the key dust control area, so aeolian desertification problems have garnered much attention. The policy was fully carried out in the mixed farming-grazing zone, and achieved substantial results, and some aeolian desertified lands began to reverse. However, the aeolian desertification problem in steppe areas still remains to be solved by feasible policies.

10.4.5 Modern wind erosion and aeolian desertification in reclaimed districts at the southern margin of the steppe

The southeast Inner Mogolian Plateau at the southern side of the Onqin Daga Sandy Land includes Xianghuang Qi, Zhengxiangbai Qi, Zhenglan Qi, Taibus Qi and Duolun County of Xilingol Meng, 4 counties of Bashang in Hebei province and the Bashang region of Chengde City as well as the Qahar Steppe.

The Ulanqab Steppe is the southward shifting passage of the Mongolian cold high pressure in winter and spring. The mean wind speed is high and strong winds are frequent. Therefore, according to climatic indexes, the margin of the southern Bashang region has almost no summer, while its winter is 7 months long with a shorter vegetation coverage period, and wind erosion is very severe. Landforms are denuded undulating plateaus (Fig. 10-18). Except silt sediments in dry riverbeds, lake depressions and bare rocks on the top of mounds, most areas are covered by a thin layer of sands, gravels, clay and aeolian soil. Due to long-term wind erosion, fine dust was blown away, leaving coarse gravels on the surface. Aeolian desertification processes in the whole region leads to the appearance of coarse-grained surfaces and wind-eroded badlands. Coppice dunes appear in shrub areas. The vegetation on fixed dunes is dominated by *Caragana microphylla* and *Achnatherum splendens*. Due to deflation over a long time, shrubs begin to die, and develop into undulating aeolian land. However, without enough sandy materials on denudated plateaus, coupled with strong wind, the modern aeolian desertification process in this region is mainly manifested as wind erosion.

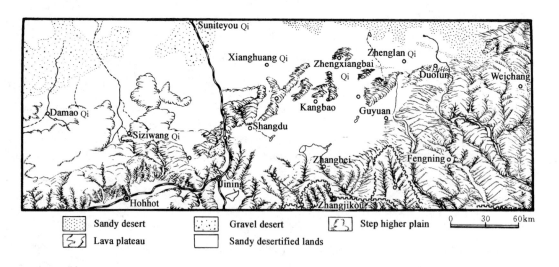

Fig. 10-18 Landforms of Bashang and its adjacent regions in Hebei Province

Since the end of the 19th century, the population in China increased rapidly. In the 20th century, the grasslands experienced three extensive reclamations, and the farmland area in the southern part consists of over 60% of the total reclamation. Under windy conditions, dryland cultivation accelerated the aeolian desertification processes (Zhu Zhenda et al., 1994). Because most grasslands were reclaimed as rainfed farmlands, wind erosion and desertification of farmlands became the most severe problem. Each year about 1 cm of zonal chestnut soil was removed by wind erosion, which exceeded the soil-formation rate. Farmland aeolian desertification results in the loss of soil organic matter, deterioration of physical and chemical properties and reduction of the land productivity as well as rapid decrease in crop yield (Table 10-12). The yield of wheat during the initial stage of reclamation was about 2, 250 kg/hm². But 30–50 years later, the yield reduced to about 750 kg/hm².

Table 10-12　Typical changes of chestnut soil from wind erosion and aeolian desertification processes

Soil name	Natural environment	Sampling depth (cm)	Mechanical composition <0.01mm (%)	>0.01 mm (%)	Texture	CaCO₃ (%)	Organic content (%)	Total N (%)	Total P (%)	Total K	Available P(10⁻⁶)	Available K(10⁻⁶)	pH	Exchange capacity (MΩ/100g)
Slightly wind-eroded dark chestnut soil	Low hills or high plains, shallow blowouts on surface; 1/4 of humus was blown away; sparse vegetation and some coppice dunes; few gravels on surface, sands sheet in farmlands, gravel content less than 20%	0–17	25.51	74.49	Light loam	4.20	1.39	0.103	0.069	2.60	3.3	136.9	8.28	10.33
		30–40	31.69	68.54	Medium loam	8.41	1.50	0.117	0.079	2.60			8.31	8.006
		50–60	35.70	64.30	Medium loam	12.92	0.54	0.036	0.067	2.34			8.43	7.148
Moderate wind-eroded chestnut soil	blowout, wind-eroded dish; 1/2–1/4 of humus was lost, coppice dunes area less than 30% and their height >50 cm, and some wind-eroded ridges and frusta, the content of gravels on surface about 20%–50%	0–9	17.34	82.66	Sandy loam	1.70	1.16	0.079	0.052	2.80	2.6	179.3	8.35	6.294
		40–50	15.32	84.68	Sandy loam	0.84	0.74	0.066	0.042	2.71			8.45	4.159
Slightly sandy desertification chestnut soil	developed higher plains, sands often less than 10 cm, some often less than 10 cm, some coppice dunes, thin shifting sands sheet, and local undulating sandy land	0–37	15.52	84.48	Sandy loam	0.29	1.13	0.070	0.052	2.66	1.5	138.6	8.32	5.467
		40–50	19.61	90.39	Sandy loam	0.42	1.29	0.085	0.045	2.57	2.0		8.30	34.91
Slightly wind-eroded chestnut soil	Undulating hills and higher plain, more sparse vegetation than that on dark chestnut soil; more thinner humus depth than wind-eroded dark chestnut soil, many stones in soil body, more shallow calcium accumulating layer, coarse-sand surface and small shifting sand sheet	0–13	18.97	81.03	Sandy loam		1.48	0.091	0.069	2.47	1.9	133.8	7.99	18.60
		60–70	18.01	81.99	Sandy loam		0.80	0.043	0.095	2.32		152.8	8.15	7.11
Moderate wind-eroded chestnut		0–15	28.29	71.71	Light loam	3.327	1.54	0.111	0.061	2.61			8.00	11.98
		25–35	29.28	70.72	Light loam	6.729	1.07	0.070	0.049	2.55			8.22	11.68

Slight aeolian desertification dominates the whole Qahar Steppe now, and occupies 76.43%, and severe aeolian desertification occupies 1.77%. However, it develops rapidly, with an annual increase rate of about 10%. Generally speaking, land desertification in this ragion is in a rapid development stage. Due to dune activation in the Onqin Daga Sandy Land, shifting dunes have reached the margin of the Bashang region. At the margin of the Bashang region in Xiaobaozi of Fengning County in Hebei province, 8% of land has become aeolian desertified land, the area of which exceeds that of the farmland area.

10.5　Mu Us Sandy Land

The Mu Us Sandy Land is located in the southern Ordos Plateau and the northern part of the Loess Plateau. The total area is about 32,100 km^2 occupying 4.7% of China's total desert area. The desert lies between 37°27.5′–39°22.5′N and 107°20′–111°30′E, and the altitude is 1,200–1,600 m. This region belongs to the steppe zone, and is also one of the typical regions suffering from severe aeolian desertification in China.

Viewed from atmospheric circulation, this region is located in the transition zone between the Mongolian—Siberian anticyclonic high pressure center and the southeast monsoon area. Seen from soils, this region is located in the transition belt between the chestnut soil subzone, the brown soil subzone and the Heilu soil subzone. And this region is also located in the transition belt between desert-steppe and forest-steppe. In hydrology, this region is located in the transition area between the interior and exterior areas, and also is the interlayered belt of wind erosion and water erosion. In geology and landforms, this region is located in transition area between the desert region and loess region. According to landscape ecology, this region possesses high heterogenity and provides complex and various habitats for shrubs. Also this region was the interlacing zone of steppe and farmlands where many people lived. It is a very special and sensitive ecological transition zone. Unique natural settings make the region fragile and susceptible to damage. In addition, long irrational human activities caused the rapid deterioration of the ecological environment in this region.

10.5.1　Ecological and geographic conditions

10.5.1.1　Geology and landforms

"Hard ridge", "Soft ridge", "shoal", "hill" and "valleys" are dominant landscape types of the Mu Us Sandy Land (Fig. 10-19). Geological conditions of various landform types are different. The northwestern part of the sandy land including ridges stretching from highlands in the middle-west Ordos is about 1,600 m above sea level; and the ridge stretching towards Uxin Qi in the southeast is about 1,500–1,300 m. The top surfaces of these ridges are relatively flat, however, many valleys are distributed between ridges due to dissection. Shoals are composed of parallel sloping lacustrine or alluvial aprons from the northwest to the southeast. Ridges consisted of the amaran thine Cretaceous sandstone and the Jurassic grayish-green sandstone are called "hard ridge". These sandstones have lower consolidation degree and are easy to be weathered. These produced abundant sandy materials that constitute the source of shifting sands in this region. Ridges consisting of the Quaternary sediments usually are distributed at the front of ridges consisting of bedrocks. Their heights are lower than those ridges that consist of bedrocks. Consisting of fine sands, silt and $CaCO_3$-cemented materials and calcareous nodules, they are also called "soft ridge".

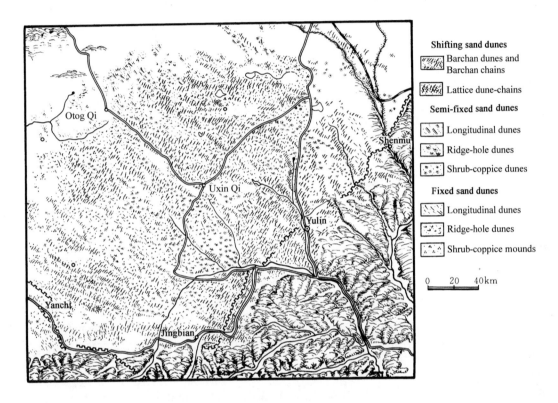

Fig. 10-19　Landscape of the Mu Us Sandy Land

Shoals occur in the whole sandy land, and their main deposits are fine sands and silt, but there are also deposits of oxbow lakes and swamps in local places. Sand is zonal substrate of the region, and it spreads widely on various ridges and hills as well as shoals and valleys, occupying over 75% of the total area. Thin undulating sand sheets, fixed dunes, and semi-fixed dunes are the most typical landforms in the Mu Us Sandy Land.

According to landscape ecology, Chen Zhongxin et al. (1994) divided the landscape of the Mu Us Sandy Land into 10 types; they are soft ridge, xili (a Mongolian word), ridges consisting of pink or Cretaceous and Jurassic grayish-green sandstones covered by a thin layer of soil, sand-covered ridges, wet shoal, alkaline shoal, shoals with Nitraria, sand-covered shoal, shoal covered by thick sands, shifting-semi- shifting dunes and fixed dunes. Fig. 10-20, is the TWINSPAN (two way indicator species analysis) dichotomy tree classes' diagram of the Mu Us Sandy Land.

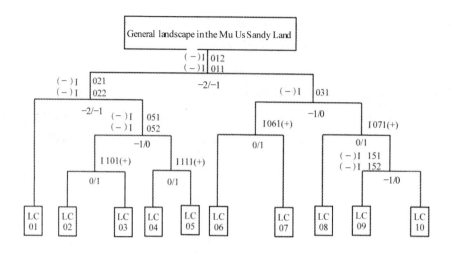

Fig. 10-20   TWINSPAN dichotomy tree classes' diagram of the Mu Us Sandy Land

LC01, alkaline shoal; LC02, wet shoal; LC03, sand-covered shoal; LC04, Shoal covered by thick sands; LC05, Shoal with
Nitraria; LC06, Soft ridge; LC07, Hard ridge; LC08, sand-covered ridge; LC09, fixed dunes; LC10, semi-shifting—shifting
dunes; I011, wet clay layer in section; I012, lowland; I021, water erosion; I022, alkaline crusts; I031, overlain sand <30 cm;
I051, thickness of soil layer>30 cm; I052, underground water table <1 m; I061, Cretaceous and Jurassic sandstone substrate;
I071, the thickness of overlying sand layer>3 m; I101, the thickness of overlying sand layer >30 cm; I111, undulating surface;
I151, thickness of soil layer>30 cm; I152, vegetation cover >50%

10.5.1.2   Climate

Average annual temperature is about 6.0–9.0°C in this region. Mean temperature in the coldest
month is about –9.5–12°C, and mean temperature in the warmest month of July is about 22–24°C.
Cumulative temperature (≥10°C) is about 2,500–3,500°C. Mean annual precipitation changes
between 420 mm in the east and 250 mm or even lower in the west. The total evaporation is
1,800–2,500 mm per year, and the frost free season is 130–160 days or so. According to heat
conditions, the Mu Us Sandy Land can be divided into a northern middle-temperate subzone and a
southern middle-temperate subzone. Most of this sandy land belongs to the former. The 3,000°C of
cumulative temperature ≥10°C and –10°C of average temperature in January are used as a dividing
line, the zone to the north of this line is a northern middle-temperate subzone, where accumulative
temperature ≥10°C is 2,600–2,800°C, and mean temperature in the coldest month is about –11°C to
–12°C, biologic temperature is 8.5°C to 9.9°C, and average annual temperature is about 5.1–7.5°C.
The warm index is 67–81, with a cold index of <–44, and Thornth waite heat coefficient is 59–65 in
this area. The southern middle-temperate subzone is only distributed in Yulin in the southeast edge
of the sandy land, where average annual temperature is about 8.5–9°C, mean temperature in the
coldest month is about –8.5°C to–10°C, and biologic temperature is 10°C, 11°C. The warm index is
81–87, cold index >–43, and Thornthwaite heat coefficient is 60–69. Fig. 10-21 illustrates the
eco-climatic characteristics.

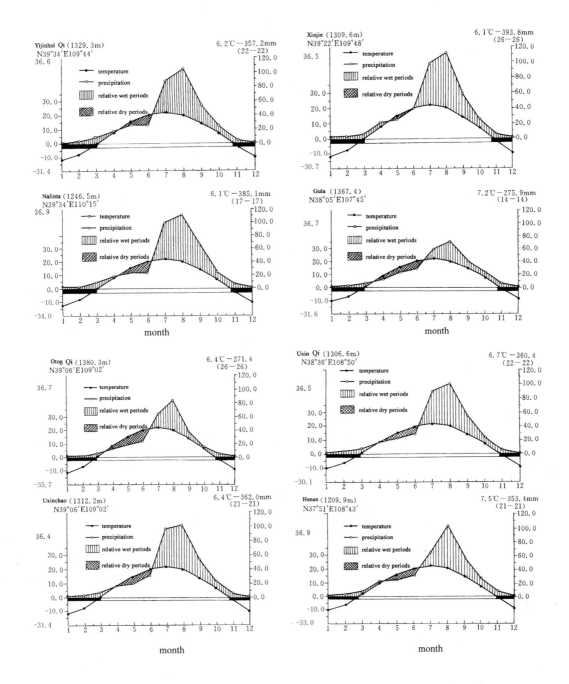

Fig. 10-21　Eco-climate chart of several weather stations in the Mu Us Sandy Land

10.5.1.3　Soil

Brown soil is a soil type formed under the driest steppe climatic conditions. It is mainly distributed in the western part of the Mu Us Sandy Land, which constitutes the brown soil belt matching with desert-steppe and steppe-desert. Brown soil is dominant in the region; there also exists salinized desert soil, salinized meadow soil, saline soil, blown-sand soil and mountain chestnut soil, etc.

Soil types change from brown soil to light chestnut soil, from the northwest to the southeast, namely, from semi-desert to dry steppe subzone. Most of the Mu Us Sandy Land was covered by this soil type. Further in the southeast, it transits to Heilu soil of warm temperate zone on the Loess Plateau. The distribution of soil exhibits obvious transitional features.

10.5.1.4 Hydrology

The surface runoff volume in the Mu Us Sandy Land reaches 1.4 billion m^3. Several rivers in the southeast part near northern Shaanxi Province join the Yellow River, such as the Wuding River, the Tuwei River, the Kuye River, etc. According to estimations, 400 million m^3 of water is available and representative inland rivers are the Bali River in Dingbian County and the Manggai River, the Qigaisu River, the Erlintu River as well as the Qianmiao River flowing into the Red Alkali Lake. The average annual runoff of inland rivers is about 105 million m^3. In addition, there are hundreds of small lakes in the desert, and most of them are alkaline lakes. Most freshwater lakes are formed by precipitation and infiltration water from underground water sources in depressions, and only a few evolved from abandoned riverbeds. The underground water resources are rich; however, they are irregularly distributed. Most of them are phreatic water in Quaternary loess deposits, and the storage volume of shallow underground water is 120.3 billion tons. The recharge of underground water mainly depends on precipitation, and the quantity of average annual recharge is about 1.4 billion tons per year. The water quality of most areas is good, and their salinities are lower than 1 g/L. Compared with other deserts or sandy lands in China, water resources in the Mu Us Sandy Land are relatively abundant.

10.5.1.5 Vegetation

Vegetation in the Mu Us Sandy Land can be divided into 3 subzones and 3 zones. According to the vegetation belt, it has transitional characteristics of desert-steppe and steppe-desert in the northwest margin of the sandy land, while most areas in the eastern and central sandy land belong to a typical steppe zone, and it shows a transitional character of typical steppe and forest-steppe in the southeast margin of the sandy land.

In addition, because most areas are covered by sandy materials, vegetation differences in this region are not obvious. Vegetation zones can be divided into steppe and shrubs on ridges, psammophytes in the sandy land (fixed, semi-fixed dunes) and shoal meadow, lalophilic, and swamp vegetation.

1) Steppes and shrubs on ridges

There are typical zonal steppe communities on the ridges without overlaying sands, such as *Stipa bungeana*, *S.breviflora*, *Lespedeza davurica*, *Thymus mongolicus*, *Aster altaicus* and other xerophytic species. There are several kinds of desert-steppe formations and ultra xerophytic subshrubs on the ridges in desert-steppe subzones located in the western sandy land. Xerophytic steppe components and desert components were reflected in the composition of communities. There are mainly *Stipa gobica, S.glareosa, Artemisia frigida, Allium polyrhizum, Kochia prostrata, Convolvulus ammannii, Caragana stenophylla, Oxytropis aciphylla, Ceratoides latens, Caragana tibetica, Ammopiptanthus mongolicus, Nitraria tangutorum, Clematis fruticosa,* etc. *Glycyrrhiza uralensis* communities appear in the zones between low ridges or loess areas of Dingbian County, Yanchi County and Otog Qi in the southwest sandy land.

2) Psammophytes

Psammophytes are the main vegetation in the Mu Us Sandy Land, and its distribution area is the largest, especially for the *Artemisia ordosica* community. Psammophyte communities include *A.sphaerocephala* and *Psammochloa villosa* communities on semi-fixed dunes and semi-shifting dunes, *Hedysarum leave* community on semi-fixed and undulating fixed dunes in the southern Mu Us Sandy Land, *Caragana Korshinskii* community on soft ridges covered by sands, *Sabina vulgaris* shrub community, *Periploca sepium* community and *Sophora alopecuroides* community in Ejin Horo Qi, Shenmu County and Uxin Qi of this region, and *Salix psammophila* and *Salix microstachya* shrub community distributed in interdunes or on the leeward side of semi-shifting dunes and the margins of shoals. In addition, *Rhamnus erythroxylon, R.parvifolia* and other shrub communities, distributed on ridges of Uxin Qi in the middle-southern part of the sandy land, are indicators of relic species of forest-steppe.

3) Shoal meadow and halophilous vegetation

Besides psammophytes, meadow vegetation distributed in shoals and river valleys is the widespread intrazonal vegetation. They are *Carex stenophylla* meadow, *Puccinellia distans* meadow, *Iris onsata* meadow, *Achnatherum splendens* meadow and others.

There is halophilous vegetation consisting of dominant *Suaeda glauca, Kalidium foliatum, Nitraria tangutorum* and others on saline soils of Dingbian County and Yanchi County in the southwestern part of the sandy land.

Although the plant community types are diverse in the Mu Us Sandy Land, shrubs are the zonal plant life form due to sand and moisture conditions. The Mu Us Sandy Land is the origin and center of shrub diversity of temperate steppes in China (Li, 1997, 2000).

According to statistics, there are 107 species of shrubs (see Table 10-13), and they can be grouped as 10 main types (Li, 2000):

(1) Evergreen shrubs with degraded leaves. There are mesic shrub *Sabina Vulgaris* of cypress and small shrub *Ephedra sinica, E.intermedia* and *E.equisetina* of Ephedraceae. Leaves of these evergreen shrubs are degraded and look like squama, spinous or membrane sheath. Young branches usually are green assimilation organs, and there are green branches over the whole year. *Sabina vulgaris* is edificatory of the Mu Us Sandy Land, and *Ephedra sinica* is also a main edificator in deserts of Central Asia.

Table 10-13   Life-form and ecotypes and the distributions of shrub species (subshrub and small half-shrub) in the Hobq Desert and the Mu Us Sandy Land

Number	Shrub name	Life-ecotype	Mu Us Desert	Hobq Desert
1	*Juniperus rigida*	Evergreen shrub or arbor	X	
2	*Sabina vulgaris*	Evergreen shrub	X	
3	*Ephedra equisetina*	Xerophytic upright subshrub	X	X
4	*E. przewalskii*	High xerophytic shrub		X
5	*E. intermedia*	Herbosa-like dwarf shrub	X	X
6	*E. sinica*	Herbosa-like dwarf shrub	X	X
7	*Salix cheilophilla*	Hygric-mesic shrub	X	X
8	*S. linearistipularis*	Mesic shrub or arbor	X	
9	*S. microstachya*	Mesic shrub in sandland	X	X
10	*S. psammophila*	Psammophyte-mesic shrub	X	X
11	*S. wilhelmsiana*	Xerophytic-mesic shrub	X	X
12	*S. flavida*	Mesic shrub in sandland	X	X
13	*Ulmus microcarpa*	Shrub or small arbor	X	
14	*Atraphaxis bracteata*	Psammophyte-xerophytic shrub	X	X
15	*A. bracteata* var. *angustifolia*	Psammophyte-xerophytic shrub	X	
16	*A. frutescens*	Xerophytic shrub	X	X
17	*A. manshurica*	Middle-xerophytic shrub	X	
18	*A. pungens*	Lithophyte-Xerophytic dwarf shrub		X
19	*Calligonum alaschanicum*	High-xerophytic subshrub		X
20	*C. mongolicum*	High-xerophytic subshrub		X
21	*Anabasis brevifolia*	High-xerophytic small subshrub		X
22	*Ceratoides arborescens*	Xerophytic subshrub	X	X
23	*C. latens*	High-xerophytic subshrub		X
24	*Sympegma regelii*	High-xerophytic subshrub		
25	*Kalidium cuspidatum*	Halobios subshrub	X	
26	*K. foliatum*	Halobios subshrub	X	X
27	*K. gricile*	Halobios subshrub	X	X
28	*Kochia prostrata*	Xerophytic small subshrub	X	X
29	*Salsola arbuscula*	Xerophytic subshrub	X	X
30	*S. passerina*	High-xerophytic subshrub	X	X
31	*S. laricifolia*	High-xerophytic subshrub	X	X
32	*Haloxylon ammodendron*	High-xerophytic Halobios shrub		X
33	*Helianthemum songaricum*	High-xerophytic dwarf shrub	X*	
34	*Clematis canescens*	Xerophytic upright shrub	X	X
35	*C. fruticosa*	Mesic-xerophytic dwarf shrub	X	
36	*C. sibirica*	Mesic -xerophytic subshrub	X	
37	*Berberis caroli*	Deciduous shrub	X	
38	*B. poiretii*	Xerophytic-mesic shrub	XX*	
39	*B. vernae*	Deciduous shrub	X	
40	*Ptilotricum canesscens*	Xerophytic small subshrub	X	X
41	*Pt. tenuifolium*	Xerophytic small subshrub	X	X
42	*Ribes diacantha*	Mesic-deciduous shrub	X	

Number	Shrub name	Life-ecotype	Mu Us Desert	Hobq Desert
43	*R. pulchellum*	Mesic-deciduous shrub	X	
44	*Cotoneaster acutifolius*	Xerophytic-mesic shrub	X	
45	*C. submultiflorus*	Upland mesic shrub		
46	*Malus transitoria*	Xerophytic-mesic shrub or arbor	X	
47	*Potaninia mongolica*	Xerophytic dwarf shrub		X
48	*Potentilla fruticosa*	Xerophytic-mesic shrub	X	
49	*P. parvifolia*	Xerophytic-mesic shrub	X X*	
50	*Prinsepia uniflora*	Warm-mesic shrub	X	
51	*Prunus mongolica*	Xerophytic shrub	X	X
52	*P. pedunculata*	Steppe mesic -xerophytic shrub	X	
53	*P. sibirica*	Steppe-mesic shrub	X	
54	*Rosa xanthina*	Steppe-forest mesic shrub	X	
55	*R. xanthina* f. *spotanea*	Steppe-forest mesic shrub	X	
56	*Spiraea aquilegifolia*	Steppe-forest mesic shrub	X	X
57	*S. trilobata*	Shrub	X	X
58	*S. mongolica*	Xerophytic-mesic shrub		
59	*Ammopiptanthus mongolicus*	Evergreen shrub	X	X
60	*Caragana brachypoda*	High xerophytic dwarf shrub	X*	X
61	*C. intermedia*	Psammophyte-xerophytic shrub	X	X
62	*C. kansuensis*	Mesic-xerophytic small dwarf shrub	X	
63	*C. korshinskii*	Desert xerophytic shrub	X	X
64	*C. leucophloea*	Desert xerophytic shrub	X	X
65	*C. microphylla*	Steppe xerophytic shrub	X	
66	*C. opulens*	Warm mesic-xerophytic shrub	X	
67	*B. pygmaea* var. *angustissima*	Desert xerophytic shrub		X
68	*C. stenophylla*	Xerophytic dwarf shrub	X	X
69	*C. roborovskyi*	High xerophytic dwarf shrub	X*	
70	*C. purdomii*		X	
71	*C. przewalskii*		X	
72	*Chesneya macrantha*	Desert xerophytic subshrub	X*	
73	*C. tibetica*	High xerophytic subshrub	X	X
74	*Hedysarum laeve*	Desert-psammophyte shrub	X	X
75	*H. scoparium*	Desert-psammophyte shrub	X	X
76	*Lespedeza daurica*	Herbosa-like mesic-xerophytic subshrub	X	X
77	*L. potaninii*	Xerophytic small subshrub	X	
78	*Oxytropis aciphylla*	Xerophytic subshrub	X	X
79	*Nitraria roborowskii*	Desert xerophytic-haloduric shrub	X X*	X
80	*N. sibirica*	Xerophytic-haloduric shrub	X	X
81	*N. tangutorum*	Xerophytic-haloduric shrub	X	X
82	*Tetraena mongolica*	Desert xerophytic dwarf shrub	X*	X
83	*Zygophyllum xanthoxylom*	Desert high xerophytic shrub	X*	X
84	*Haplophyllum tragacanthoides*	Steppe xerophytic subshrub	X X*	
85	*Securinega suffruticosa*	Upland xerophytic-mesic shrub	X	

Number	Shrub name	Life-ecotype	Mu Us Desert	Hobq Desert
86	*Evonymus bungeanus*	Upland mesic shrub or arbor	X	
87	*E. nanus*	Steppe mesic shrub	X	
88	*Xanthoceras sorbifolia*	Xerophytic-mesic shrub or arbor	X	X
89	*Rhamnus erythroxylon*	Steppe mesic-xerophytic shrub	X	X
90	*Rh. parvifolia*	Upland xerophytic-mesic shrub	X	
91	*Ziziphus jujuba* var. *spinosa*	Upland xerophytic-mesic shrub	X	
92	*Myricaria platphylla*	Xerophytic shrub	X	X
93	*M. alopecuroides*	Mesic-xerophytic shrub		X
94	*Rèaumuria songarica*	Desert-haloduric subshrub	X X*	X
95	*R. trigyna*	Desert-haloduric dwarf shrub	X*	X
96	*Tamarix austromongolica*	Haloduric xerophytic-mesic shrub	X	X
97	*T. chinensis*	Haloduric Steppe-forest mesic shrub	X	X
98	*T. ramosissima*	Haloduric xerophytic-mesic shrub	X	X
99	*Wikstroemia chamaedaphne*	Xerophytic-mesic shrub	X	
100	*Elaeagnus angustifolia*	Haloduric mesic-xerophytic shrub or arbor	X	X
101	*Hippophaë rhamnoides*	Mesic-xerophytic shrub	X	X
102	*Buddleja alternifolia*	Mesic-xerophytic shrub	X	
103	*Periploca sepium*	Xerophytic-mesic vine shrub	X	X
104	*Convolvulus tragacanthoides*	Xerophytic smallshrub	X*	X
105	*C. gortschakovii*	High-xerophytic subshrub	X*	
106	*Caryopteris mongholica*	Xerophytic subshrub	X	
107	*Dracocephalum fruticulosum*	Desert small subshrub	X	
108	*Thymus serpyllum* var.	Xerophytic small subshrub	X	
109	*Th. serpyllum* var. *mongolicus*	Xerophytic small subshrub	X	X
110	*Conicera microphylla*	Xerophytic dwarf shrub		
111	*Lycium barbarum*	Xerophytic shrub	X	X
112	*L. chinense* var. *potaninii*	Mesic shrub	X	X
113	*L. ruthenicum*	Xerophytic shrub	X	X
114	*L. truncatum*	Haloduric shrub	X	X
115	*Ajania achilloides*	Xerophytic small subshrub	X	X
116	*A. fruticulosa*	Xerophytic small subshrub	X	
117	*Asterothamnus centraliasiaticus*	Xerophytic subshrub	X	
118	*A. frigida*	Wide-xerophytic small subshrub	X	X
119	*A. ordosica*	Xerophytic-psammophyte subshrub	X	X
120	*A. sphaerocephala*	Ultra Xerophytic-psammophyte subshrub	X	X
121	*A. xerophytica*	Xerophytic subshrub		X
122	*A. restita*	Xerophytic subshrub	X*	
123	*Hippolytia trifida*	Xerophytic small subshrub	X	X
Σ	123		107	70

* Significance X, having.

(2) Xerophytic evergreen shrubs. There is only *Ammopiptanthus mongolicus* in this region, and it is the dominant species in sandy or gravelly desert.

(3) Mesic and Xerophytic-mesic shrubs. There are *Rosa xanthina* and *Spiraea trilobata* in this region. Some mesic shrub species can form sandy land communities and beach communities, such as *S. flavida*, *Salix cheilophilla* and *R. erythroxylon*, etc.

(4) Xerophytic shrubs with thorns. They have obvious xerophytic structure, morphological features, and hard thorns on their branches, including shoot thorn, stipule thorn, spine, thorn derived from stipe, etc. These plants are characterized by degraded leaves which minimize the transpiration area, and they have well developed protective tissues which is the result of natural evolution. The deciduous shrub formed through natural selection. This is one of the main life forms of desert vegetation and the shrub-steppe community. Many species of *Caragana* belong to this life form, such as *C. microphylla* and *C. intermedia* shrubs in the desert-steppe. *C. tibetica* is the edificator of the steppe-desert, with dwarf clump, narrow leaves, pin thorns degraded from stipes, an obvious xerophytic structure, and semi-cushion shrub with thorns.

(5) Xerophytic shrub without thorns. This kind of shrub possesses xerophytic characteristics, and their branches have no thorns, such as *Hedysarum scoparium*, *Lespedeza potaninii*, *Atraphaxis bracteata*, *A.frutescens*, etc.

(6) Xerophytic shrub with succulent leaves. They are typical desert xerophytic plants. Their leaves have different succulent characteristics and have water storage tissues. Such plant species in this region include *Zygophyllum xanthoxylon*, *Nitraria sibirica*, *N. roborowskii*, *N. tangutorum*, *Helianthemum soongarica* and *Tetraena mongolica*. They not only have strong drought resistance, but also salt tolerance. The three species of *N. tangutorums* are usually a desert community on salinized soil.

(7) Halophilic shrubs. They are the plant ecotype adapting to salinized soil. These plants can absorb water from salt soil, so the osmotic pressure of their cells is very high. However, they also have different adaptive means, and they can be divided into accumulative salt plants and secretive salt plants. *T. chinensis* is a typical representative of lalophilic shrubs in this region.

(8) Subshrubs with xerophytic leaves. It adapts widely to arid and semi-arid habitats, and is an important life form in steppe, desert, and sandy land vegetation, as well as in some lithophyte vegetation. These plants possess obvious xerophytic structures, lessening leaf area with cleft laminas, and most possessing floss or stoma sinking. Many species of *Artemisia* have this kind of xerophytic leaves. For example, *A. frigida* is the most common subshrub with xerophytic leaves which undergo 2–3 holoblastic cleavages, and small splits are thin strips with hoar dense floss. *Artemisia vestita* on stony sloping fields of low-relief terrain in the steppe zone can form a subshrub community, with cleft laminas.

(9) Xerophytic subshrub with thorns. Oxytropis aciphylla is the representative species, with obvious structure tolerance to droughts, and narrow and linear leaves. After they wither in autumn, their rhachises become hard pin thorns. They are the dominant species of sandy gravel deserts and the auxiliary species of desert-steppe. In addition, another species of such life form is *Haplophyllum tragacanthoides*.

(10) Subshrub with succulent leaves. These shrubs have salt tolerant ecological characteristics. For example, *Salsola passerina* and *Anabasis brevifolia* have high arid tolerance, and most of them are edificators or dominant species of the desert. *K. gracile* and *Kalidium cuspidatum* are typical subshrubs with halophilic roots and succulent leaves, and they appear in halophytic deserts or in salinized lowlands in steppe zones.

10.5.1.6 Origin of sandy materials and aeolian desertification

The origins of sandy materials are different in different morphologic regions. The aeolian sandy land in the Ordos Plateau is mainly the deflation production of the Cretaceous and the Jurassic bedrocks, and dunes are close to the crest and slope of bedrocks. Aeolian sands on the shoal are mainly derived from lacustrine sediments. The area covered by lacustrine sediments is larger than the exposed Cretaceous bedrock. Small sandy lands in lake depressions are formed from lacustrine sediments transported by wind. These alluvial deposits are formed through weatherings of bedrocks and carried by local runoff to lowlands.

The distribution extent of recent aeolian sediments—crescent dunes on the Ordos Plateau has a close relation with the impacts of mankind on vegetation on ancient aeolian sandy lands and fluvial sands. In areas where lands are over-grazed and over-cultivated, shifting dunes are widespread.

According to researches, the Mu Us Sandy Land formed in the Quaternary geological time, and its evolutional process was not a unidirectional development of shifting sand; instead it experienced a series of vicissitudes of shifting dune formation, expansion, fixing and shrinking. By the Holocene megathermal (8000 a BP), the whole sandy land or its majority had been fixed. During the human historical period, it entered an aeolian desertification development stage.

10.5.2 Socio-economic conditions

The Mu Us Sandy Land covers 151 towns of 14 counties (Qis or cities) in 3 provinces, and its population density reaches 34 persons/km^2. It is the most densely populated desert region in China. It covers an area of 40,000 km^2 and there are 4,358 km^2 of farmland occupying 10.2% of its total area. Most farmlands are rainfed, and they are mainly distributed on valley terraces, shoals and semi-fixed dunefields. And crops are mainly autumn ones. There are 1.01 million hm^2 of forest land sowed successfully by airplane in this region. However, ecological management needs to be strengthened to prevent vegetation degradation from human activity. Compared with other sandy lands or deserts in China, the economy in the Mu Us Sandy Land is relatively developed. Particularly, it is an important area for energy resources in China, and famous for coals and natural gases. Transportation is convenient, and there is a railway from Baotou to Shanbei. Highways extend in all directions. Rich and high quality underground water resources are good for farming and grazing.

10.5.3 Developmental process and combating aeolian desertification

Sand sources in the Ordos Plateau include the lower Cretaceous weathering product and the Quaternary lacustrine sand layers. There are many ancient aeolian sands layers embeded in lacustrine strata. This shows that there were strong blown sands activities and the Mu Us Sandy Land had formed in the Great Ice Age 1,000–700 ka BP. After the Holocene, the temperature was rising continuously, ice and snow melt, surface water was adequate, and plants grew well. Until the megathermal 8,000 a BP, most shifting dunes were fixed and formed wet meadow-grassland and shrub-grassland, black sandy soil developed, and fixed and semi-fixed dunes formed.

10.5.3.1 Aeolian desertification in the Tang Dynasty and the Song Dynasty

Thick sandy layer is in the southern part of the Ordos and steppe environment has been suitable for grazing ever since the ancient nomads lived there long time ago. In 407 AD, the leader of the Hun, Haolianbobo founded the Daxia regime. Since then the Hun had learned farming in addition to nomadism, and they reclaimed and cultivated grasslands. This affected the ecological environment of the Ordos Steppe.

After the foundation of the Daxia regime, the capital of Tongwan City was constructed north of the Suofang River and south of the Hei River. More than 100,000 people and soldiers participated in the construction that lasted for 5 years. Thus the ruin of the ancient city is still preserved in continuous dunesfield(Fig.10-22).

Fig. 10-22　Relics of ancient Tongwan City in the desert

Because the Ordos region was a frontier area in the Tang Dynasty, large numbers of troops were stationed in this area and opened up grasslands in order to strengthen frontier defence. However, opening up grasslands required cutting down trees and burning grasslands, which caused huge damage to the ecological environment of the steppe. Building castles also destroyed grassland vegetation and top soils. There is a very thick layer of silt below the surface of the Ordos Plateau. Once the surface soil layer was destroyed, silt would be blown away to form shifting dunes. The word "Sand Sea" recorded in the Song Dynasty was obviously associated with the land reclamation and wars of the Tang and the Song Dynasty.

At the beginning of the construction of Tongwan City, aeolian sand activity occurred, but it was not serious, and therefore did not attract people's attention(Fig.10-23). By the late period of the Tang Dynasty, land aeolian desertification had become quite severe.

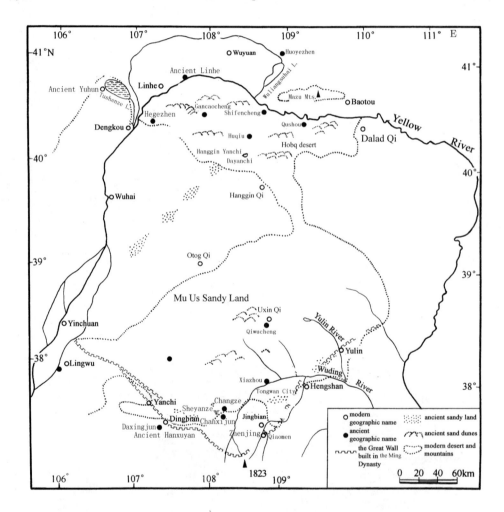

Fig. 10-23　Sketch map of aeolian desertification in the 6th century in the Ordos Region

Thus, many scholars thought that the Mu Us Sandy Land appeared in the Tang Dynasty. However, the sandy land mainly concentrated around Tongwan City had a limited extent at that time.

After that, due to wars and large-scale production activities, the ecological environment was destroyed seriously and the area of sandy land was greatly enlarged (Fig. 10-24).

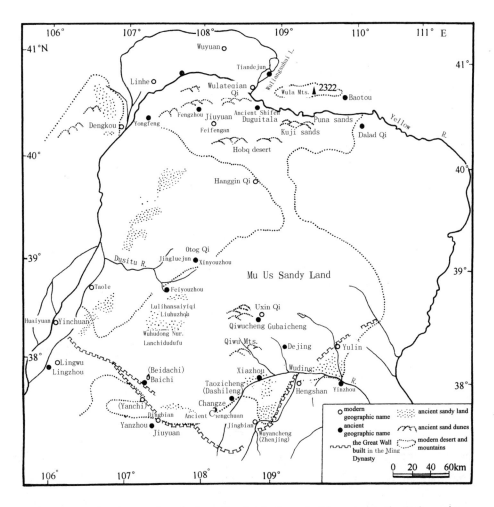

Fig. 10-24　Sketch map of sandy desertification in the early 9th century in the Ordos region

In the Song Dynasty, people called the sandy land between Shaanxi Province and Ningxia Hui Nation Autonomous Region a " Sand Sea ", and this shows that the Mu Us Sandy Land expanded at that time. Based on historical passages, the length of the Sand Sea was about 350 to 500 km, and there was no river or lake there.

10.5.3.2　Aeolian desertification in the Ming Dynasty and the Qing Dynasty

During the construction process of the Great Wall in the Ming Dynasty, the eco-environment along the Great Wall was seriously destroyed. It caused grassland degradation and aeolian desertification in the steppe zone. During 1465–1487, over 7,300 km of Great Wall were built from the Yalu River in the east to the Jiayuguan pass in the west.

Soil layer in the Ordos Steppe was very thin and there was a layer of loose, fine sand below the surface. Furthermore, the Great Wall was built on poor steppe with a thin soil layer. Soil excavation led to the exposure of loose sand susceptible to wind erosion. Large amounts of sand accumulated at the foot of the Great Wall, and finally the Great Wall was buried by sand (see Fig. 10-25).

Fig. 10-25　The Great Wall of the Ming Dynasty buried by sand

After building the Great Wall, local governments encouraged farmers to open up grasslands for cultivation. In addition, the army opened up grasslands nearby. According to records, there were about 600 hm^2 farmlands planted by farmers in the Yansui region. Troops also opened up large areas of grasslands, and most reclaimed land were formerly healthy grasslands along the Great Wall. After several years of planting, the underlying sand was exposed to wind erosion, farmlands were abandoned, and even parts of city walls were buried by shifting sands.

Owing to the influences of population growth and wars, more and more people moved to mountain regions, which caused even greater destruction. According to statistics, during the 100 years before 1949, about 140,000 hm^2 of farmlands, 6 cities and 412 villages in the Yulin region were buried by shifting sands and another 96,000 hm^2 of farmlands were surrounded by shifting sand. Yulin City, which originally earned its name from an elm forest, was forced to move three times.

10.5.3.3　Combating aeolian desertification over the past 50 years

More than 100 years before 1949, shifting dunes moved more than 40 km southward and buried 65,000 hm^2 of farmlands in Jingbian County. About 27,000 hm^2 of grassland suffered from aeolian desertification or salinization, 82 villages were encroached upon by shifting sands, and residents had to move to other places.

After 1949, the whole county implemented an ecological construction, laying emphasis on aeolian desertification control and shifting sand stabilization and consequently achieved significant improvements.

At present, the forest area of the county is 220,000 hm^2, which is 100 times larger than the area in 1949. Forest cover reached 45.2%, 88 times higher than that in 1949. During the construction processes of the Three-North Shelter Forest of China, Jingbian County established 250,000 hm^2 of forest belt altogether. As a result, about 120,000 hm^2 of mobile dunes have been turned into fixed or semi-fixed dunes. Through diverting water to wash sand about 10,000 hm^2 of dunefield have been transformed into farmland. In the areas with the most severe blown sand activity to the north and south of the Great Wall, a forest belt 2 km wide and 25 km long, with a total area of 15,000 hm^2, was established. In the border land between Shaanxi and Inner Mongolia, a forest belt 0.5 km wide and 67 km long was established. On both sides of the Yulin-Ling wu Highway, which crosses Yulin County, a 2 km wide and 84 km long sandbreak forest belt, with a total forest area of 170,000 hm^2, was established. In addition, the county built 67 protective forest patches and each forest patch covers an area exceeding 600 hm^2.

Planting trees is the most effective way to combat aeolian desertification. In the 1950s, the Mu Us Sandy Land spread at a rate of 4–6 m/a southward, but reduced to 1.4 m/a in the 1970s and further reduced to less than 1 m/a in the 1980s. It prevented large areas of farmlands and grasslands from being buried by shifting sands and restored 10,000 hm^2 of shoaly land in Ningtiaoliang, Zhangjiapan and Yangqiaopan, and over 300 hm^2 of sand-buried abandoned farmland were also recultivated.

Forests can reduce wind velocity, therefore it is often called a green barrier. Afforestation in Jingbian County reduced wind speed and dust-storm events. In the 1950s, mean wind velocity was about 3.6 m/s in Jingbian County, while it was 3.1 m/s in the 1960s, 3 m/s between the 1970s and 1980s, and it was much lower in the 1990s. Strong wind higher than 17 m/s was 43.8 days per year on average in the 1950s. Today, it has reduced to 6.4 days per year. The occurrence of dust-storms was 21.4 days per year in the 1950s, and reduced to 20.2 days per year in the 1960s, 15 days in the 1970s, 9 days in the 1980s and 7 days in the 1990s.

Forests can reduce evaporation by 10.7%–32.9%, and raise air humidity by 7% and raise soil moisture content by 8.9%. Therefore the crop yield per hm^2 increases by 25.3% on average.

In addition to huge ecological effects, forests also bring direct economic benefits. Forests can provide 2 million rafters and 1.75 million beans or posts for building houses every year, and this can increase the income in Jingbian County by 8.175 million *yuan*. Fruit trees can produce more than 3 million kilograms of fruit, including apple, pear and grape, etc. with 2.5 million *yuan* of economic income. Wickers exported to Europe and America can achieve an income of 1.5 million *yuan*. Tree seeds and firewood can be sold for 1 million *yuan* per year. There are over 30 hm^2 of nursery garden in Jingbian County which can produce 14 million saplings per year, and its production value can reach 430,000 *yuan*.

Jingbian County is only an epitome of the Mu Us Sandy Region. In fact, great progress has been made in aeolian desertification projects in Uxin Qi, Yijinhuoluo Qi and Otogqian Qi of the Inner Mongolian Autonomous Region and five counties of Yulin City in Shaanxi Province. On the whole, the process of aeolian desertification in the whole Mu Us Sandy Land is reversing and this sets up a model and strengthens our confidence for combating aeolian desertification in China.

References

Chen Zhongxin, Xie Haisheng. 1994. Preliminary study on the landscape ecotype in Mu Us Sandy Land and the biodiversity of its shrub comities. Acta Ecologica Sinica, 14(4)

Gao Shangyu, Chen Weinan, Jin Heling et al. 1993. Preliminary study on desert evolution at the northwest margin of monsoon area in China in Holocene. Science in China (Series B), 23(2)

Huang Ruchang. 1981. Ancient Climatic Change and Transfering, Accumulating and Evolution of Elements in Continental Deposit. Lanzhou Institute of Geology, Chinese Academy of Sciences, Corpus, No. 1. Beijing: Science Press

Li Baolin. 1996. The climatic factors of desertification and the development characteristic of Songnen Sandy Land. Journal of Desert Research, 16(3)

Li Baosheng, Dong Guangrong, Gao Shangyu et al. 1988, Analysis and discussion on the grain size of the quaternary stratigraphic profile in Yulin area of the northern Shaanxi. Acta Geographica Sinica, 43(2)

Li Sen, Sun Wu, Li Xiaoze et al. 1995. Characters of sediments in Holocene in Onqin Daga Sandy Land and environmental evolution. Journal of Desert Research, 15(4): 323—331

Li Xinrong. 1997. Land desertification and biodiversity protection in Mu Us Sandy Land. Journal of Desert Research, 17(1): 58—62

Li Xinrong. 2000. Discussion on the characteristics of shrubby diversity of Ordos Plateau. Resources Science,3

Liu Xinmin, Zhao Halin, Xu Bin. 1993. Mechanism of destruction and restoration of Horqin steppe ecosystem. In: Liu Xinmi et al. Integrated Regulating Research of Ecological Environment in Horqin Sandy Land. Lanzhou: Gansu Science and Technology Publishing House, 12—26

Ma Wenlin. 1995. Sandy desertification status and trend of Songnen Plain. Journal of Desert Research, 5(3)

Xu Xin, Shen Zhida. 1990. Environment in Holocene. Guiyang: Guizhou People's Publishing House, 58—60

Zhang Baizhong. 1991. Vicissitudes of Horqin Sandy Land from northern Wei to Jing Dynasties. Journal of Desert Research, 11(1): 36—43

Zhou Benxiong. 1978. Geographic distribution, paleoecology and relative ancient climatic problems of *Coelodonta antiquitatis* and mammoth. Vertebrate Paleontology and Paleoanthropology, 16(1)

Zhu Zhenda, Chen Guangting. 1994. Sandy Desertification in China. Beijing: Science Press

Zhu Zhenda, Wu Zheng, Liu Shu et al. 1980. Desert Generality in China (Revised). Beijing: Science Press

Chapter 11
Deserts and Aeolian Desertified Land in Desert Steppe

Desert steppe, as the name implies, is a rangeland with a natural landscape that transitioned from steppe to arid desert. The desert steppe zone covers a vast region starting from Erenhot in the northeast, which is the boundary between the grassland and the desert steppe, and stretches southwestwards across the staircase plateau of Inner Mongolia and the Yinshan Mountains. It extends into Yanchi of Ningxia and then to Lanzhou after crossing over the Yellow River from Baotou. At last, it stretches to the extremely arid desert regions in Gansu Province and Xinjiang.

The annual precipitation in the eastern desert steppe zone is about 200 mm, and is only 50 mm in the west. The Helan Mountains is a very important geographical boundary with north-south strike. The East Asian Monsoon reaches the area of the eastern Helan Mountains, and the precipitation in the area of the western mountains has decreased rapidly. Also, this mountain is the boundary between exterior and interior river systems. Geographically, the desert steppe is located in the second staircase plateau, which mainly includes the Alxa Plateau, the western high plain in Inner Mongolia and the western Ordos plateau.

The vegetation in desert steppes is mainly composed of sclerophyll shrubs, semi-shrubs and some species of Artemisia. There are also some dwarf grasses in the north (such as *Stipa gobica*). The zonal soil is gray desert soil due to limited precipitation for eluviation.

Deserts in the desert steppe zone include the Badain Jaran Desert, the Tengger Desert, the Ulan Buh Desert and the Hobq Desert. These deserts are mainly dominated by mobile dunes and some places are well fixed.

The characteristics of aeolian desertification in the desert steppe include:

(1) There are some oases nurtured by groundwater or surface water in proluvial fans or along the rivers stretching into sandy areas around the desert and Gobi aeolian. Desertification occurs mainly around the oasis. The cause of aeolian desertification, firstly, is that water resources are over-exploited in upstream regions due to expanded cultivated land, as a result the amount of water supplying the downstream area continually decreases; Secondly, improper expansion of oases, over-cultivation of land around oases, deforestation and collection of medicinal herbs lead to the destruction of the eco-environment of oases.

(2) Oases are sustained by irrigation. Therefore, vigorous evaporation may cause soil secondary salinization at the lower part of an oasis. Aeolian desertification seems to be symbiotic with salinization and the interspersed distribution of dunes and salinized soil is characteristic of the arid

zone. The most striking examples are in the northern Yinchuan Plain in the Ningxia Hui Autonomous Region and the Hetao Plain in Inner Mongolia, with a landscape of interspersed dunes and small salt lakes. Desert areas are also the main salt-producing areas of China.

(3) The Alxa Plateau and the Hexi Corridor are the main source areas of dust and frequently suffer from duststorms. The terrains are favourable to the generation of strong winds in winter. In addition, the eco-environmental destruction of oases also increase dust storm frequency and severely affects the traffic and industrial production there. The dust storms generated in these two regions can move south of the Yangtze River and influence the ecological safety of eastern China and adjacent countries; furthermore, the dust originating from northern China was recorded in the coast of California over the Pacific.

11.1   Ulan Buh Desert

Ulan Buh means "red bull" in Mongolian. Geomorphologically, it looks like a bull drinking at the bank of the Yellow River.

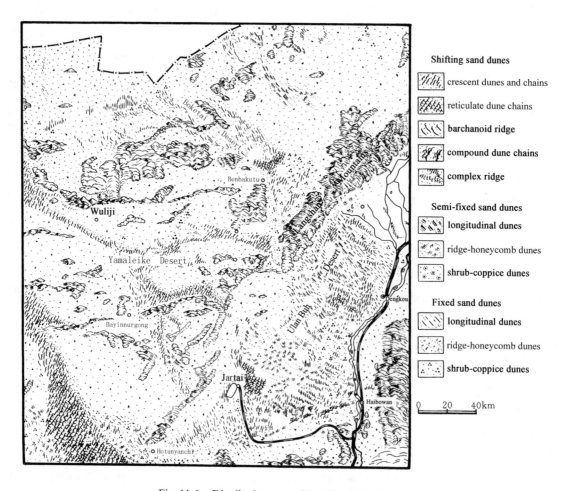

Fig. 11-1   Distribution map of the Ulan Buh Desert

The Ulan Buh Desert stretches northward to the foot of the Langshan Mountains, eastward to the Yellow River, northeast to the Hetao Plain, with the Wuda-Jilantai Railway to the south (Fig.11-1). It belongs to Alxa Meng and Bayannor Meng, with an area of 9,900 km² at the edge of the desert zone.

11.1.1   Eco-geographical conditions

11.1.1.1   Geology and geomorphology

The landscape is dominated by shifting dunes in the southeast of the desert, namely to the south of the line extending from DengKou-Aolong Bulug-Jilantai. There is an ancient lacustrine plain, with some preserved relics, to the west of the line. The Jilantai Salt Lake is one of famous salt lakes in China. The landscape is of fixed and semi-fixed *Nitraria tangutorum* coppice dunes and *Haloxylon ammodendron* sand ridges; furthermore there are still serious soil erosion and salinization problems. The area of the northern Dengkou-Shalajing line is an ancient alluvial plain formed by the Yellow River. The river bed once shifted from west to east and left behind many old river beds oriented southeast-northwest. These old river beds once were lowlands, wetlands and lakes, and are now scattered in the modern desert. The top soil is composed of clay or sub-clay, with medium and fine sand layers underneath. This set of strata, called the Houtao Formation, included the mid-Pleistocene series and the upper and lower Pleistocene series in the Quaternary System. The Inner Mongolia hydrogeological Investigation Team found that there was a delta under these lakes (formed by the ancient Yellow River) in the lower layer of medium and fine sand, and the upstream valley had developed into a mature river in the mid-Pleistocene. The Houtao Section of the Yellow River began to develop when the Lama Gulf was cut through by the Yellow River, and the clay and sub clay were sediments from the Yellow River. The lands distributed widely between dunes are good for agricultural development in this region.

The area of different dunes types is not very different. Shifting dunes, semi-fixed dunes and fixed dunes covers about 39%, 31% and 30% of the land, respectively. Shifting dunes mainly occur in the southern and middle section in the forms of crescent dune chains, reticulate crescent dunes and crescent megadunes, with a mean height of 10–30 m. Some dunes are 50–100 m high in the center, and lower than 10 m at the edge of the desert. The mound-like fixed and semi-fixed dunes mainly lie in the western part of the desert. The dunes are denser in the south than in the north. Sand covers the lake plain, the alluvial plain of the Yellow River， and the eroded bedrock. The sand mainly comes from the sediments of wind-eroded lacustrine and river deposits.

11.1.1.2   Climate

The desert is located at the eastern edge of the western desert in China and the climate is arid. According to meteorological data recorded at Dengkou (station), mean annual precipitation is 148.6 mm and mean annual evaporation is about 2,395.6 mm. The average annual wind velocity is 3.1 m/s, while the absolute maximum is 18 m/s, and gales (wind force ⩾8)occur 19 days per year. There are 27 days with a wind velocity higher than the sand entrainment threshold. The mean annual air temperature is 7.4 °C, and the mean temperature is −11.0 °C in January and 23.8 °C in July. The extreme temperature of soil surface is more than 70°C, and the lowest temperature is −20.3 °C. The accumulative temperature (⩾10°C) is more than 3,400 h. The growing period is 139 days. The large temperature difference between day and night in the desert is favorable for cash crops, such as melons, fruits and sugar beet.

Climate data recorded at Jilantai station shows that the mean annual precipitation is 116 mm while the mean annual evaporation is 3,006.0 mm. The mean annual relative humidity is 41% and the aridity is 5.8. The mean annual air temperature is 8.6 °C, with an average of −11.3 °C in January and 25.3 °C in July. The highest and lowest temperatures are 40.9 °C and −31.2 °C respectively. The accumulative temperature (⩾10 °C) is more than 3,577.9 °C. The frost-free period is 127 days. The amount of total solar radiation is 628 kJ $\cdot$ cm^2 and the amount of annual photosynthetic effective radiation is 324 kJ$\cdot$cm^2. The average annual wind velocity is 3.6 m$\cdot$s^{-1}. Dust storms occurs 18.9 days per year.

11.1.1.3 Vegetation and soil

Generally, the zonal vegetation in the Ulan Buh Desert is desert grassland, and the soil is grey desert soil. There are dense dunes in the northern and middle parts of the desert, where some bushes, such as *Agriophyllum squarrosum, Artemisia sphaerocephala, Hedysarun scoparium,* and *Calligonum mongolicum* are sparsely distributed. The vegetation at the northern and southern edge of the desert is composed of *Nitraria sibirica, Haloxylon ammodendron, Salix, Tamarix ramosissima, Zygophyllum, Ammopiptanthus mongolicus, Psammochloa villosa* etc, and the soil is gray brown desert soil. The semi-fixed and fixed dune fields in the west of the desert are natural grassland, with species such as *Haloxylon ammodendron, Reaumuria songarica* and *Nitraria tangutorum* etc.. In addition, there are solonchak or meadow soils. Soil salt content is high due to lack of water. There are plains of meadow soil type scattered along the Yellow River banks in the east of the desert. The sod well horizontal developed in soil profile with a surface occasionally covered by sand. The content of soil organic matter is about 1%–2%, and the salt content is 0.29% or so. The depth of the groundwater is about 1–3 m. There is good grassland dominated with *Achnatherum splendens* in this region.

11.1.2   Social and economic conditions

Administratively, the middle and southern parts of the desert belong to the Alxa Zuoqi of Inner Mongolia, and the northern part belongs to the Bayanor Meng. There are some farmlands and grazing lands distributed in this region, and some fixed residential areas with a population density of 1.2 person/km².

Some major characteristics of this region are listed below:

(1) There are fewer residents and less farmland in the southeastern part of the desert due to lack of earthy flats.

(2) There is a large area of fertile soil, gray brown desert soil, in the northern part of the desert, with sparse *Nitraria sibirica*. It is estimated that the area of such waste land in the desert is about $2.0 \times 10^5 \, hm^2$.

(3) This region is close to the Yellow River, and the plain gently dips from the river bank to the west. Hence, it can be irrigated by the Yellow River water. Dengkou, a desert area located largely in an irrigated district, has a developed economy and abundant products. There is sparse population in Alxa-Zuoqi, with harsh natural conditions. Hence, environmental construction issues such as exclusion of grazing must be considered, so as to alleviate environmental pressure and ensure a benign cycle of ecological restoration.

It is clear that although the Ulan Buh Desert lies at the edge of the desert zone, it has large areas of badlands near the Yellow River and can be irrigated by gravity flow. Large-scale windbreak forest belts have been established to prevent the Houtao Plain from being attacked by blown sand. However, effective measures should be taken to prevent re-activation of fixed sand and secondary salinization, especially in the section of the Yellow River, and to prevent shifting sand from entering the Yellow River.

11.1.3 Evolution of aeolian desertification

The Yellow River Plain northeast of the Ulan Buh Desert is a part of the Houtao Plain irrigated district in Inner Mongolia. This region has been irrigated as early as the Qin Dynasty. In 127 BC, the Shuofang District, including 10 counties, was established in the Western Han Dynasty. There were three counties west of the Shuofang District, or in the northern part of the today's Ulan Buh Desert. This region had been developed into one of the major military and cultivation centers in the last 300 years of the Western Han Dynasty. After 23 AD, farmers were forced to move out from this cultivated area because of attacks by the Huns, and the abandoned croplands were eroded intensively by wind. The underlying sand layer was exposed to wind erosion and formed shifting sand.

Until 981 AD, there were documents that recorded that 'horses can not travel through the sand and people use camels for transportation instead of horses'. Records also mentioned that 'crops cannot grow there' and one grass named 'Dengxiang' i.e. *Agriophyllum squarrosum*, a pioneer plant growing on dunes, was used as food. This indicated that *Agriophyllum squarrosum* grew well in the 10th century. Up until 1697, Gao Shiqi, an official, took an excursion with the emperor and noted that there were shrubs such as *Lepironia articutala*, *Salix*, *Tamarix ramosissima* and *Caragana microphylla* growing in the fixed dunefields along the western bank of the Yellow River in Dengkou. In the final stage of the Qing Dynasty, however, migrants from Shanxi and Hebei provinces started to reclaim this region, and dunes began to be re-activated. The shifting sand was far away from the Yellow River when a road from Yinchuan to Baotou was built by way of Dengkou in 1925, but shifting sand had moved to the bank of the river in some places by 1937, and the road was also cut off by sand.

In the 1960s, a garrison farm was established in the centre of the desert. Farmers paid attention to environmental protection and people also used flood water to irrigate deserts. However, water discharge from the upper reaches of the Yellow River is currently decreasing. The ecological environment in the western Ulan Buh Desert is improving now due to the development of animal husbandry, prohibiting land reclamation and planting shrubs such as *Haloxylon ammodendron* and *Ammopiptanthus mongolicus*, etc. However, the movement of re-activated shifting sand to the Yellow River in the southeast desert needs to be taken into account.

11. 2   Hobq Desert

The Hobq Desert is located in the middle section of the Yellow River, south of the Hetao Plain and at the northern edge of the Ordos Plateau (Fig. 11-2). It stretches in a narrow belt with a length of 400 km from west to east and covers an area of 1.61×10^4 km^2. The desert belongs to Dalad Qi and Hanggin Qi of Ih Ju Meng in Inner Mongolia. Most of the desert is covered with desert steppe except the eastern Dalad Qi, which is a typical steppe zone.

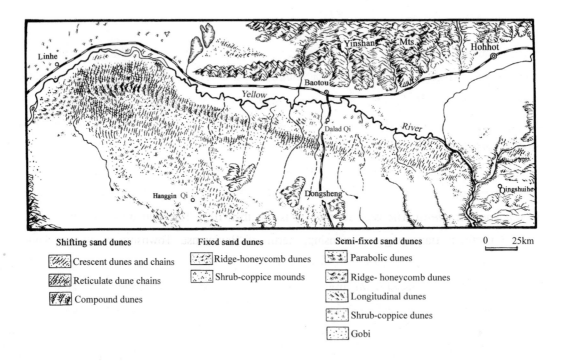

Fig. 11-2   Basic type of the Hobq Desert

11.2.1 Natural conditions

11.2.1.1 Geology and landform

The Hobq Desert is located on the Yellow River terrace, at the northern edge of the Ordos Plateau, and it is high in the north and low in the south, with an altitude of 1,000–1,400 m. Rivers originating from the Ordos Plateau the desert into several pieces. Its basal terrain terraces I, II and III of the Yellow River. The height of dunes and thickness of the sandy layer were different due to differences in underlying deposit thickness, constituent, cementation degree and water content. The crescent dunes and dune chains on washlands is about 3.0 m high and the dunes on the slope transitioning from terrace I to terrace II is in the range of 10–20 m, and some of them even rise to 25 m. There are compound dune groups in the transition zone from terrace II to terrace III with a height of 50–60 m, and slightly undulating dunes on terrace III. There are various types of dunes in the Hobq Desert. Reticulate dunes 10–15 m high are mainly in the middle and the western parts and there are crescent dunes and dune chains in washland. The slightly undulating dunes and coppice dunes are around the edge of shifting dunes with high moisture content and their height is not more than 3.0 m. The area of shifting sand accounts for 65.24% of the desert area, so shifting dune is the dominant landscape of the desert.

11.2.1.2 Vegetation and soil

The Hobq Desert can be divided into three parts including western, middle and northern sections in consideration of the natural conditions.

The western section lies in the west of Maobulakongdui of Hanggin Qi, which consists of two branches of dunes, namely the northern and the southern branch. The northern branch stretches from northwest to southwest along Zhaergelangtu, north of Saiwusu Township, south of Yongsheng Township, Duguimiao, south of Hangginzhuo Township and north of Tugelu Township. The dunes are shifting dunes with several plants on, such as *Agriophyllum squarrosum*, *Corispermum hyssopifolium* and *Psammochloa villosa*. The vegetation cover is less than 10%. The southern branch is distributed along the northern Baiyinengeer Township, north of Bayinwusu Township, south of Saiwusu Township, south of township and Baiyinbulage Township. The height of the dunes in the southern branch is lower than that of northern branch, and the water condition is better in the southern. The depth of groundwater is less than 10 m, while it is 3.5 m and 1.98 m in Saiwusu and Maobula. Shrubs are the dominant plant species. The climate conditions in the west are poor. This part is a steppe zone with brown soil. The vegetation includes species such as *Caragana stenophylla*, *Oxytropis aciphylla*, *Tetraena mongolica* and *Potaninia mongolica*; moreover, there are *Reaumuria songarica*, *Salsola passerina*, *Zygophyllum xanthoxylon*, *Ammopiptanthus mongolicus* and some endemic species, such as *Calligonum mongolicum*, *C.alxaicum*, *Haloxylon ammodendron*, *Artemisia sphaerocephala*,

A.xerophytica, Stilpnolepis centiflora, Myricaria platyphylla and *Prunus mongolica*, etc.

The middle section includes the region which is west of Husitaigou in Dalad Qi and east of Maobulakongdui in Hanggin Qi. This area is a semi-arid steppe with chestnut soil. The vegetation mainly consists of *A.ordosica, Atraphaxis bracteata* and some common plants on sandy land in the steppe zone.

The eastern section stretches from western Husitaigou eastward to the Yellow River. The natural conditions are better, and the soil is light chestnut. Sandy land appears on the Yellow River terrace I, terrace II and shoaly land. The bedrock is right under the shifting sand. In addition to the fluvial gravel layer, most of the area is composed of red clay from the Tertiary. There are three layers of black-sand soil covered on the older stratum with a height of 8–9 m, and most of them are present as chain-like and reticulate dunes. The data investigated in Wulanbulang showed that the thickness of the modern sand layer is about 2.0 m covered on the monadnock of black-sand soil. There are *A.ordosica* and residual *Rhamnus erythroxylon* growing in the interdune, while *Agriophyllum squarrosum, Corispermum puberulum* and *Pugionium cornutum* grow on dunes, and scattered *Salix matsudana* and *Populus* are also in this area.

The species diversity and zonal characteristics of the vegetation there are obvious, though the vegetation is sparse in the desert. Shrubs are dominant. Statistical data shows that there are more than 70 plant species in the desert. The species diversity of this area, together with the bushes in the Mu Us Sandy Land, forms the unique and rich biodiversity in the Ordos Plateau.

11.2.1.3 Climate

The precipitation in the western part of the desert is about 280 mm and less than 200 mm in most parts of the desert. The aridity is 3.89. The average annual wind velocity is 4.4–4.5 m/s, and the absolute maximum is 25 m/s. The prevailing wind direction is west-north –west and west, gales

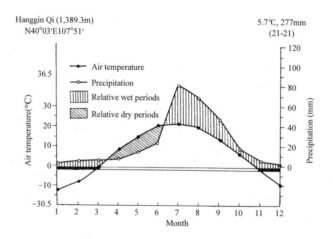

Fig. 11-3　Illustration of the eco-climatic conditions in Hanggin Qi

(wind force ≥8)occur 28.5 days per year, and dust storms occur 22.5 days per year. The precipitation in the middle of the desert is 310 mm. The average annual wind velocity is 3.2 m/s, and the absolute maximum is 24.0 m/s. The wind is dominated by the western winds, gales occur 25.2 days per year, and dust storm occurs 19.7 days per year. The precipitation in the eastern desert is 350–400 mm, or higher than that of the Ordos Plateau. The mean annual evaporation is 2,000–2,700 mm, and mean annual air temperature is 5–7 °C. Fig. 11-3 is the illustration of ecology-climate in Xini Town of Hanggin Qi, north of the desert.

11.2.2 Social and economic conditions

Farmland and pasture lands occupy a small proportion of the desert. Population in the desert is sparse. There are only a few grazing sites with low productivity. There are some small rivers in the desert, several of which originate from plateaus in the south and flow from south to north across the desert, but most of them are dry except in rainy seasons. So it is not favourable to develop and manage the desert. There is lower potential capacity to develop agriculture. The desertified land in Dalad Qi accounts for 75.81% of the total of 8,198.5 km^2. However, grazing is developing fast due to convenient communication. The Dalad electric power plant located in the county provides great energy supply to Beijing and other regions. It also promotes the ecological development of the Qi. The Xini village Hanggin Qi in the southern desert is in the centre of the Ordos Plateau. Its communication is inconvenient. The economy is underdeveloped and animal husbandry is the economic cornerstone of Hanggin Qi.

The desertified area accounts for 94.06%, or 18,789.03 km^2, of the whole Hanggin Qi. Balagong is an important town of the Hanggin Qi in the western desert against Dengkou County across the Yellow River. Convenient transportation plays an important role both in the economy and environmental protection in the Hanggin Qi.

11.2.3 Sand damage of the Hobq Desert

The northward expansion of the desert poses a serious threat to farmlands along the river. Its eastward invasion carries large amounts of sand to the Yellow River, and its southward extension buries grazing land. Especially, the desert northward and its migration severely affect the Yellow River mainly through the eight seasonal rivers. These seasonal rivers, originating from the central ridge of the Ordos Plateau, run across the desert from south to north and then flow into the Yellow River. The seasonal rivers or wadis include Kaersitaigou, Heilaigou, Xiliugou, Hantaichuan, Wubushitaigou, Husitaigou, Hashilachuan and Maobulagou. These seasonal rivers are long, and shave steep slope.They flood in summer and are dry in winter. They carry plenty of sand, for example, the sand content of the Xiliugou river is about 1,550 kg/m^3, maximum annual sand transport rate is 1.76×10^7 m^3 and mean annual sand transport rate is 3.855×10^6 m^3. Large amounts of sand are transported to riverside floodlands and covers large areas of farmlands, and at last deposit in the Yellow River. For example, one rainstorm that occurred in the south of Dalad Qi on August 20–23, 1961, led to flooding in all the eight wadis. The huge torrents flowed across the desert and poured into the Yellow River and made more than 2×10^4 households in 97 villages of four townships suffer great loss in northern of Dalad Qi, and all the water conservancy facilities on the flood route were destroyed. Especially, silt brought down by Xiliugou wadi blocked the Yellow River, caused the water to flow backwards and 3.75 km^2 of fertile farmland in four villages were covered with sand 1–2 m thick. Now, the Hantaichuan is a suspended river, 8.0 m higher than the site of Shulinzhao (equal to the bank height). (Yang et al., 1998).

11.3   Tengger Desert

Tengger means "sky" in Mongolian, and it has the meaning of "falling from the sky" or "flying from the sky"; it also can be thought as "the desert fell from the sky". The desert is located at 37°27′–40°00′N, 102°15′–105°41′E, west of the Helan Mountains, southeast of the Yellow River, northwest of the Yaburai Mountains, which is the boundary between the Tengger desert and the Badain Jaran Desert, and south of the Qilian Mounntains. Most parts of the desert belong to Alxa prefecture, Inner Mongolia. The southern part belongs to Baiyin City of Gansu Province, the western part to Wuwei District, while the southeast part is in Zhongwei County of the Ningxia Hui Autonomous Region.

The Tengger Desert covers 42,700 km^2, accounting for 6.2% of Chinese total desert area, and it is the 5th largest desert in China.

The Tengger Desert is mainly composed of shifting dunes, semi-fixed dunes and fixed dunes, and shifting dunes account 70%, while semi-fixed and fixed dunes account for about 26% of its total area. The semi-fixed and fixed dunes are dispersed among the shifting dunes and distributed in forms of belts and patches in the northeast or around the edge of the desert in the southwest. The types of dunes include crescent dune-chains, reticulate dunes, ridge-honeycomb dunes, sandy mounds, linear dunes, star dunes (megadune), compound dune chains and complex star dune chains (Fig. 11-4). Dunes become more complicated, the closer they get to the center of the desert.

Sand in this desert is from the lacustrine and fluvial sediments at the lower layer of the desert. Ancient lakes have been fragmented into more than 400 small seasonal lakes due to the arid climate, and some of them have evolved into salt lakes.Therefore this desert has the largest number of lakes among Chinese deserts.

Shifting sand dunes
- Crescent dunes and chains
- Reticulate dune chains
- Barchanoid ridge
- Compound dune chains
- Pyramidal dunes
- Compound megadune chains

Semi-fixed sand dunes
- Longitudinal dunes
- Ridge-honeycomb dunes
- Shrub-coppice dunes
- Undulating sandy land

Fixed sand dunes
- Longitudinal dunes
- Ridge-honeycomb dunes
- Shrub-coppice mounds

Others
- Gobi
- Oasis

0   20   40km

Fig. 11-4   Map of dune types in the Tengger Desert

11.3.1   Natural conditions and distribution patterns of the Desert

The basement of the desert is complex. It includes amaranth gritstone of Carboniferous- Permian, verrucano interbeddings of the Jurassic-Cretaceous, and flaxen gritstone and mudstone, identified from the exposed strata. The modern desert is covered by a plateau of peneplain which was made up of complex strata with many unakas of bedrock, and the southeast of the desert (Shapotou district) is covered by the multistage Yellow River terraces. The desert was formed by several lake basins according to the strata. The salt lakes scattered in the modern desert are the relics of ancient lake basins. The sand of the Tengger Desert is the finest in the three deserts of the Alxa Plateau (Zhu et al., 1980), and this also shows that the sand of desert is formed through repeated sorting processes. Someone stated that the Shiyang River once was a tributary of the Yellow River, which flows northeast into the Yellow River in Dengkou, Inner Mongolia, along the southern end of the Helan Mountain. If this was confirmed, it must be earlier than the development of the lakes of various sizes.

11.3.1.1 Climate condition

The climate of the desert is characterized by arid, windy and great diurnal temperature variations. The precipitation decreases gradually from southeast to northwest, for example the mean annual precipitation is 186.6 mm in Shapotou, 120 mm in Bayanhaote and 101.7 mm in Minqin. The mean annual evaporation is 2,200–3,000 mm, which is 16–25 times greater than precipitation. The mean precipitation in the period from May to September is about 154.8 mm, accounting for 83% of the annual total, and precipitation in summer is more than half of the annual (Table 11-1). The sychronization of high temperature and rainfall is favourable for plant growth. The precipitation has a ten-year periodicity in Shapotou. The precipitation was relatively adequate in the period from the middle of the 1950s to the 1970s with slight fluctuations, and it fluctuated greatly from the late 1970s until the present. The number of dry years was more than that of wet years (Li, 1993). The mean annual relative humidity is 40% and the aridity is 2.5, while it is 5.15 in Minqin.

Table 11-1　Seasonal precipitation in Shapotou (average between 1955–1990)

Season	Spring (March-May)	Summer (Jun-Aug)	Autumn (Sep–Nov)	Winter (Dec–Feb)
Percent of annual total (%)	14.6	58.8	23.6	3.1

The sunshine is extensive, and annual sunshine duration exceeds 3,000 h. The amount of heat is affluent and the annual accumulative temperature is more than 3,000 h, even more than 3,600 °C in the western part of the desert. In Shapotou, the mean annual air temperature is 9.7 °C and −6.7 °C in January. The absolute lowest temperature is −25.7 °C, and the mean temperature in July is 24.1 °C while the absolute highest temperature is 38.1 °C. The annual difference in temperature is 30.8 °C. In Bayanhaote, the mean annual temperature is 7.2 °C and the mean temperature in January and July are 12 °C and 24.2 °C respectively. However, the mean annual temperature is 7.8 °C, and the frost-free period is about 130–170 days in Minqin.

The annual average wind velocity is 2.9–3.9 m/s dominated by a northwest wind. The wind force is about 7–8, and the highest is more than 12. The annual threshold velocity for sand movement occurs 2,938 times (wind velocity ⩾5 m/s measured by electrical anemometer (once every 10 minutes at a height of 2 m above the ground)). The period from March to May is the windy season. On average, there are 1 or 2 dust storm events per year in Shapotou.

11.3.1.2 Soil and sandy material

The zonal soil in the desert is gray desert soil and brown desert soil with shifting sand in the center and gobi entisols in front of mountains. Also there are azonal soils distributed in the desert, such as meadow swamp soil, salinized meadow soil and salinized clay etc.

Table 11-2   Particle-size composition of aeolian sand in different directions in the Tengger Desert

Item Site	Northwest-southeast		South-north		
	Particle size	Content (%)	Site	Particle size	Content (%)
Xilinhu duge	0.5–0.25	1.82	Gaigen	0.5–0.25	0.1
	0.25–0.1	90.5		0.25–0.1	98.6
	<0.1	6.82		<0.1	1.3
Kergehu duge	0.5–0.25	1.18	Taohandonggen	0.5–0.25	0.1
	0.25–0.1	98.06		0.25–0.1	98.84
	<0.1	0.76		<0.1	1.1
Heigeta	0.5–0.25	0.1	Chetouhu	0.5–0.25	0.2
	0.25–0.1	98.60		0.25–0.1	94.74
	<0.1	1.3		<0.1	5.06
Masitu	0.5–0.25	0.82	Xierdaohu	0.5–0.25	0.12
	0.25–0.1	97.53		0.25–0.1	97.3
	<0.1	1.62		<0.1	2.58
Adigeyiker	0.5–0.25	10.0	Susaihu	0.5–0.25	0.96
	0.25–0.1	88.70		0.25–0.1	93.82
	<0.1	1.3		<0.1	5.12

Source: Zhu Zhenda, 1980.

The mineral and particle-size compositions of the aeolian sand are correlated with underlying deposits. The sand in the Tengger Desert is the finest among the three deserts in the Alxa Plateau, though it does not exceed the fine sand ranges of 0.1–0.25 mm (Table 11-2).

11.3.1.3   Vegetation

The vegetation is dominated by desert semi-desert dwarf brushs and semi-bushes, and it is identified as two types, psammophyte and hygrophyte in consideration of ecological differences.

1) Psammophyte

Psammophytes distributed in the fixed sandy land mainly include *Haloxylon ammodendron*, *Convolvulus lateens*, *Nitraria tangutorum*, *Caragana korshinskii*, *Ephedra sinica*, *Artemisia arenaria* and *A.ordosica*, and the secondary species are *Carex duriuscula*, *Crypsis schoenoides*, *Salsola ruthenica*, *Artemisia capillaries*, *Pennisetum centrasiaticum*, *Psammochloa villosa*, *Euphorbia humifusa* etc. The vegetation cover is about 15%–55%.

The vegetation on the semi-fixed dunes is mainly composed of *Calligonum mongolicum*, *A.ordosica Oxytropis aciphylla*, *Haloxylon ammodendron*, *Caragana intermedia*, *Artemisia sphaerocephala*, *Psammochloa mongolica*, *Agriophyllum squarrosum*, *Corispermum hyssopifolium*, *Stipa glareosa* and *Atraphaxis bracteata* etc. The vegetation cover is about 5%-16% on the semi-fixed dunes.

The shifting dunes are covered with *Artemisia sphaerocephala*, *Hedysarum scoparium* and *Agriophyllum squarrosum*, and also include *Stilpnolepis centiflora*, *Corispermum hyssopifolium* and *Psammochloa mongolica*. The vegetation cover is about 1%–2%.

2) Hygrophyte

Vegetation on salinized meadow soils is dominated by species of *Phragmites communis*, *Myricaria platyphylla*, *Iris onsata*, *Calamagrostis epigeios*, *Suaeda corniculata*, *Carex duriuscula*, *Polygonum sibiricum*, *Nitraria sibirica*, *Glaux maritima* and *Saussurea glomerata* etc. The vegetation coverage is about 30%–80%.

Vegetation on the salinized clay land and lowland covered with crescent dunes is mainly composed of *Nitraria sibirica*, *Inula salsoloides*, and *Messerschmidia sibirica*. In addition, *Thermopsis schischkinii*, *Reaumuria songarica*, *Agropyron cristatum*, *Pycnostelma lateriflorum* etc., develop together with the dominant species, with a vegetation coverage of 15%–40%.

3) Gravel land

Vegetation on gravel land includes the following species, *Pycnostelma lateriflorum*, *Nitraria sibirica*, *Oxytropis aciphylla*，*Ephedra sinica*, *Carex duriuscula*, *Convolvulus ammannii* and *Salsola pestifer* etc., with a vegetation cover of 10%–20%.

Shapotou Desert Research Station, Chinese Academy of Sciences, has achieved great success in desert research and control in China. According to investigations of the station, vegetation succession from shifting sandy land to fixed sand in Shapotou is in the following order: scattered *Artemisia sphaerocephala* or *Hedysarum scoparium*→*A. ordosica* community →*Caragana intermedia* community→*Convolvuluslatens* community→*Reaumuria songarica*, *Salsola passerina* community (relatively stable community).

4) Landscape

Landscape of the Tengger Desert has the following three characteristics:

(1) Natural landscape has a striking zonal change from Helan Mountains to the Tengger Desert. The piedmont belongs to semi-desert gobi steppe. There are salinized marshes in front of the proluvial fan with groundwater overflow. There are semi-fixed flat sandy lands and undulating sandy lands around the desert, and the natural vegetation mainly consists of *Reanmuria soongarica*, *Oxytropis aciphylla* and *Nitraria sibirica*, and *Artemisia arenaria* is located around shifting sand. Shifting dunes in the peripheral area is dominated by transversal sand ridges which are developed from crescent dune-chains, and the height increases from the edge to the desert centre. At the

junction of two crescent dunes, reticulate dunes develop.

(2) Dunes, lake basins, mountains, unakas and flats appear alternatively in the interior of the desert, of which dunes account for 71%, lake basins and grassland 7%, and mountains, unakas and flats 22%. The dunefield, fixed and semi-fixed dunes account for 7%, and mobile dunes 93%. Especially in the north-south ridge-hill zone in the southern desert, interdune flats are covered by sandy soil with vegetation, and shifting sand appears only on the top of dunes. Vegetation is mostly composed of *Ephedra sinica* and *A. ordosica*. Artemisia grows well in swales in the centre, as well as south and north of the desert, while *Calligonum mongolicum*, *Hedysarum scoparium*, *Psammochloa villosa* and *Artemisia sphaerocephala* etc., develop on the leeward slopes and interdune depressions. Mobile dunes are dominated by reticulate dunes and reticulate dune chains which are 10–20 m in height. And there are also some compound dune-chains. Megadunes of 50–100 m height mainly occur in the northeastern centre of the desert and dune-chains mainly at the edge (Zhu, 1980).

Main ridges of reticulate dunes are oriented in a north-north-east to south-south-west direction, while the secondary ridges are nearly perpendicular to the main ridge. The size of dunes changes in different regions. The relative height of the main ridge in Shapotou is about 7–20 m with a strike of 34°–47° N. The mean horizontal length of windward slopes and leeward slopes are 64 m and 25 m with a gradient of 28°–30°. The relative height of the secondary ridge is 3–5 m, and the eastern and western side are symmetrical. The end of the well-developed secondary ridge is high and often forms high dunes on adjacent dune-chains. The average horizontal distance between the secondary ridges is 30 m. Sandy soil and root coatings are exposed and these are relics of calcareous soil in the dune stabilization period. Reticulate dunes are formed by the wind from two or more directions under the exposed thick-layer sand source conditions. Wind direction is dominated by the northwest wind in the Tengger Desert, which determinates the direction of dune-chains. Investigation shows that the annual sand transport rate caused by dominant wind accounts for 60.5% of the total, while that caused by the secondary dominant wind, the northeast wind, accounts for 14.8%. The intersection angle of the two wind directions is 58.6°, which is the force that forms the secondary ridge of reticulate dunes. It causes the secondary ridge swift to the west and makes the end of the ridge shift generally southward. Reticulate dunes move forward in a wave manner. Erosion rates at the top and foot of the dunes are nearly equal, and both the variation coefficients of erosion and deposition are equal to 1, which shows the conformity of the dunechain movement and the relative stability of dune-chains' form.

There are some unakas that have not been covered by shifting sand in the Tengger Desert. Two mountain ridges, like islands standing in the sand sea with an approximate south-north direction, are distributed discontinuously in the south and west. In the west there are Alagushan, Qingshan, Toudaoshan, Erdaoshan, Sandaoshan and Sidaoshan, Dongqingshan and East-West Shuangheshan in the south. The Tonghu Mountains, oriented in a north-west to southeast direction, is located in the south of the desert. Scattered mountains and unakas such as the Tulantai Mountains and the Wugezi Mountains, etc. are distributed in the north. The height of these mountain ridges is about 50–200 m, and they differ slightly in height due to long periods of erosion. Plains in the interior of the desert mainly occur between the Chala Lake and the Tonghu Forestry centre in the heart of the desert, and also there are some small lakes distributed in the plains.

(3) There are 422 lakes of various sizes in the desert, except for areas in the north and southwest. Most of them are small water-logged or water-free grass lakes that are different from the lakes in the Badain Jaran Desert. The lakes can be divided into several types according to their distribution characteristics:

① Lake basins in the south are arranged in a regularly parallel pattern from south to north. The distance between the lakes is 3–5 km. Toudao Lake, Erdaoshan Lake and Sandaoshan Lake are distributed from east to west. Most of them are residual dried or shrunken lakes of the Tertiary lakes divided by scattered mountains. The length of the lake basins is mostly 20–30 km, with 1–3 km in width, and covers about 40-50 km^2. Topographically, the lake basins slope from south to north due to the influence of the isolated mountains.

② Most of the lake basins in the west and south of the desert are distributed irregularly. Larger lakes include the Dengmaying Lake, the Masha Lake and the Baijian Lake, with an area of 50–100 km^2. Most of the lakes originate from the swales of ancient diluvial plains, and others are the obstructed sections of the Shiyang River (such as the Baijian Lake). The area of small lake basins is not more than 1 km^2. Some of them belong to temporary water-collecting swales; also there are some small lakes with good water quality fed by spring water, such as the Gaolimahaizi Lake.

③ The areas of lake basins located in the interdune depressions of dune-chains from northeast to southwest in the mid-northeast part, are smaller. The lake basins are distributed regularly, and most of them are fed by spring water.

Landscapes of the lake basins is nearly similar, though there are differences in distribution. The basins are surrounded by fixed and semi-fixed dunes of *Nitraria sibirica*, *Achnatherum splendens* and *Psammochloa villosa*. Shifting dunes appear around fixed and semi-fixed dunes (Fig. 11-5). The depth of groundwater is about 1–3 m with a salinity of 1–2 g/L. Meadow soil mainly appears in lake basins except for the lowest places that have accumulated water. Salinized meadows appear in places with groundwater of higher salinity. The depth of underground water is 1 m. Now, some residential areas and fodder bases are distributed in the Tengger Desert. The larger ones are Toudaohu, Xiligaole, Yiker and Tengger etc.

Although the desert has large areas of shifting sand, it is separated by fixed sandy land, semi-fixed sandy land, lake basins, highlands and unakas, which facilitates its control. Some of the lakes can be used as the bases for deserts. Therefore, the Tengger is a desert with better development and utilization conditions in northwest China.

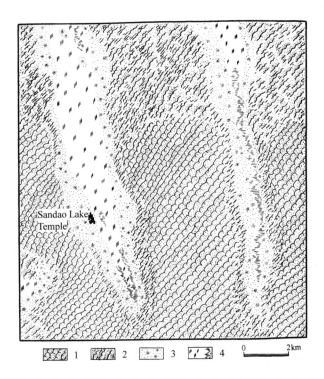

Fig. 11-5 Landscape of lake basins in the interior of the Tengger Desert—a case near Sandao Lake
Temple

1. Reticulate dune chains; 2. Crescent dune chains; 3. Coppice dunes; 4. Salinized swamp

11.3.2　Formation and changes of the Tengger Desert

Based on the analyses of the strata, sedimentary structure and particle size, surface texture of quartz, fauna, and composition of spore-pollen, we can conclude that the ancient climate of the desert was hot and dry; the alternation of wet and dry seasons was dramatic, and this area was bioclimatically a subtropical savanna, or a desert steppe in the late Tertiary. Also, we can conclude that the processes of erosion and deposition at that time were similar to those of modern time. To the east of the Helan Mountains and to the south of the Tonghu Mountains, the ancient aeolian sand was found in the Miocene stratum (Yan, 1992). At that time, the subtropical red desert gradually formed, which was dominated by the planetary wind system.

The Asian monsoon formed after the Qinghai-Tibet Plateau lifted over 4,000 m a.s.l. The variation of deserts in China are closely related to the circulation of the Asian monsoon. Using the Helan Mountains as a boundary, deserts in China can be divided into two big areas. This boundary can be pushed to the west of the the Tengger Desert if it is divided according to the position of the modern summer monsoon. The influence of the summer monsoon in the area east of this boundary was intensive and it was more humid during the interglacial period. To the west of this line, the variations were not obvious (Gao, 1993). This makes the Helan Mountains become an important climate boundary in China. The climate and bioclimatic zone of the Tengger Desert have obvious characteristics of a transition zone.

The modern desert (also called the Quaternary Desert) appeared at least 330,000 years ago. From then on, this area has gone through changes from desert expansion, shifting sand fixation or semi-fixation, and even formation of soil. The bioclimatic zone usually shifted between arid desert and semiarid steppe, which once developed dry wood's steppe during the wet period. The evolution of the deserts followed this pattern: the piedmont is characterized by the superposition of alluvial-proluvial gravels or alluvial-proluvial and sandy loess; the accumulated plain of aeolian sand is characterized by the mutual superposition of aeolian sand and caliche and calcareous root tubes, or ancient sandy soil. The transition zone between the above two was characterized by the mutual superposition of the alluvial-proluvial gravels and the lacustrine deposits, or aeolian sand (Yan, 1998).

Recent research shows that the deserts (or sandy lands) in eastern China, including the Tengger Desert, underwent large-scale development during last glacial period and established the basic structure of modern aeolian sand landforms. However, in the postglacial period, because the global circulation transferred from the ice age to that of the interglacial period, even to the Holocene megathermal period, the Tengger Desert underwent sod soil formation processes, which made the shifting sand fixed (Gao, 1993). The full development of the desert began at about 5,000 a BP.

According to recent investigation and analysis, the age of ancient soil formed from shifting sand via fixation is 8,000 to 5,000 a BP. Because of the strong wind erosion, the ancient soil has been blown away, or buried by shifting sand. Two soil profiles were found in Tuan Bu La Shui at the southeast and northeast edge of the Tengger Desert. The latter is about 2.5 km away from Xi 1 well. Among them, the ancient soil layer of the Xi 1 profile is about 80 cm thick and well developed in light black color. The ^{14}C age of the mid-upper part is 5,640±160 a BP. The ancient soil layer of the Tuan Bu La Shui profile is thick about 30 cm and well developed in black color, and the ^{14}C age is 8,090±130 a BP. at the bottom, and 7,870±70 a BP. at the top. Furthermore, gray white, calcareous root types were widely found in the flat land or interdunal lowland. These root tubes were formed in the ancient black soil. The ^{14}C age is 5,610±80 a BP (Gao et al., 1993). This is consistent with the Xi 1 ancient soil. This finding indicates that the ancient soil was once widespread in the Tengger Desert.

In addition, such ancient soil also developed in the Holocene loess section in Gulang County. Although the loessial evolvement sequences could not represent the desert evolution process, the section's position is right at the edge of the Tengger Desert and the evolution condition of ancient soil reflected by the sequence of loess is in accordance with the climatic variations of the desert. The section can be divided into two layers. From the bottom to the top, the first layer is about 1 m thick and better developed, which has a higher clay content, compact texture, abundant organic matter, and black colour. The ^{14}C age of the bottom is 9,020±100 a BP. and the top is 7,220±120 a BP., which is consistent with the 140 age of sandy ancient soil in the Tuan Bu La Shui section. The second layer is about 70 cm thick, and weakly developed with a light black color. The conclusion is that the second layer soil should be a same-period outcome of the sandy ancient soil of the Xi 1 section. When viewing the Gulang soil section using an average value measured by susceptometer (MS_2, Bartingon) at an interval of 5 cm with a magnetic susceptibility curve, there are obvious peak values in ancient soil, indicating a more humid climate and lush vegetation at that time (Gao, 1993).

The activities of ancient mankind, who lived on hunting, grazing and farming, were restricted strictly by natural environment. Expansion and shrinkage of the desert caused by climate change, e.g. from warm - wet to dry - cold, have important effects on human activities.

The 15 cm thick ash layer resulting from human activities were found in the black ancient sandy soil in the Tuan Bu La Shui section in the southeast of the Tengger Desert. The ^{14}C age is about 7,420±140 a BP. Some cultural relics were discovered near the interdunal lowland, such as a stone scraper, stone ax, etc. The human cultural relics of the same period were also discovered in many other desert places at the northwest edge of China's monsoon area. For example, the cultural relics discovered in the Mu Us sandy land were microlith, including some forged stone vessel, milled stone vessel, millstones, ceramics, agate beads, and burnt bone fragments from humans and animals. These facts revealed that the moderate climate and dense vegetation in the Tengger Desert during the Holocene megathermal were suitable for human settlement. The splendid neolithic culture was developed at that time.

The southeast side of the Tengger Desert is the Minqin basin, with rich lake sediments of the Late Pleistocene. This showed that a larger part of the Minqin basin was covered by lake water ten thousand years ago. In addition, Feng's analysis showed that the Zhuyeze Lake, mentioned in *Shang Shu Yu Gong,* was divided into the Baiting Sea and Qintu Lake. The accurate location is presently in the lake area of northern Minqin. Another viewpoint pointed out that the scene described in *Shang Shu Yu Gong* also included many small lakes in the Tengger Desert, in addition to the Zhuye swamp. Therefore, there should have been a large area of lakes 3,000 years ago or earlier. The Shajingzi culture belongs to the last phase of the Bronze Age and is the oldest culture discovered there. This time is equivalent to the Zhou Dynasty of Central China. According to the most current chronology of the Xia Dynasty and the Shang Dynasty, there are indications that the western Tengger Desert was characterized by large lakes and grassland about 3,000–2,800 years ago. The desert environment started to become dry and cold again 5,000 years ago and a great part of desert become active. However, the landscape in some parts (such as in the western edge of the desert) lasted for a long time. However, climate changes over the past 2,000 years and excessive manmade disturbance have caused desert reversal to be impossible.

11.3.3   Modern development and trends

A desert is the inevitable outcome of climate change, and it is a kind of extreme landscape. Unless there is a severe climatic change in the world, it is impossible for the desert to change greatly under modern climate conditions. This is the major difference between desert and desertified land.

Researches in desert development in China revealed that the reversing trend of the Tengger Desert was not very obvious (Zhong, 1998). In the past 50 years, there has been about 5.2% change in the Tengger Desert, of which 3.7% is due to desert reversal, and the reverse rate was 0.1% per year or about 40 km^2/a. The reversal resulted from conversion of shifting sand dunes to semi-fixed or fixed sand dunes, and conversion of semi-fixed and fixed sand dunes to farmland.

Most of the reversal occurred in Shapotou in the southeast and Minqin County in the west of the Tengger Desert. These two places are established as models of successful land management and development in China. At the same time, activated sand dunes led to 600 km^2 of land desertification in the Tengger Desert. The activation rate was 15 km^2/a due to reversal of semi-fixed and fixed dunes to shifting sand (Table 11-3).

Table 11-3 Modern development data of the Tengger Desert

	Sandy dune type	Area (km^2)		Sandy dune type	Area (km^2)
Activation type	Conversion of fixed sand dune to semi-fixed sand dune	191	Extension type	Conversion of original plain to fixed sand dune	16
	Conversion of fixed even sand flat to semi-fixed even sand flat	38		Conversion of original plain to semi-fixed sand dune	19
	Conversion of semi-fixed sand dune to shifting sand dune	373		Conversion of original plain to shifting sand dune	12
	Total	602		Total	47
Reversion type	Conversion of shifting sand dune to semi-fixed sand dune	675	No obvious change type	Fixed sand dune	1,379
	Conversion of shifting sand dune to fixed sand dune	71		Semi-fixed sand dune	8,234
	Conversion of shifting sand dune to flat farmland	105		Shifting sand dune	28,972
	Conversion of semi-fixed sand dune to fixed sand dune	536		Fixed sand flat	266
	Conversion of semi-fixed sand dune to flat cultivated dune	56		Semi-fixed even sandlot	1,200
	Conversion of fixed sand dune to flat farmland	129		Moving even sandlot	46
	Total	1,572		Total	40,097
Shrinkage type	Conversion of fixed sand dune to original plain	1		Final total	42,318
	Total	1			

(Zhong, 1998)

The area of the Tengger Desert increased by 46 km^2 during the past 50 years, at a rate of 1 km^2/a. This shows that the desert has been at a stable stage.

Except for the activated part, the reversal rate was 0.05% in the Tengger Desert. If this rate continues, the area of reversal will be increased twofold after 150 years. That is to say, the area of reversal would increase from 1,570 km^2 to 4,710 km^2 (Zhong, 1998). Air seeding, fencing and planting grasses can promote the reversal of shifting sand to fixed sand and semi-fixed sand in the southeast and southwest of the desert, with a mean annual precipitation of 200 mm.

11.4 Badain Jaran Desert

11.4.1 General situation

The Badain Jaran desert spreads in the center of the Alxa plateau, east to the Gurinai Lake which is on the eastern shore of Ruoshui, west to the Zongnai and Yaburai mountains, south to the Guaizi Lake, and north to the Baida Mountain. The Badain Jaran desert covers 4.92×10^4 km^2 and is the second largest moving desert in China (Fig. 11-6) (Zhu et al., 1980; Yan et al., 2001; Yang, 2000; Wang, 1990). The desert is famous in the world not only for its extremely huge dunes, but also the unique characteristics of interlaced distribution pattern of interdune lakes and dunes. Most of the dunes are huge, high and complex. The general height of the dunes is in the range of 200–300 m and the highest is more than 500 m. These kinds of sand dunes were called compound, complex crescent dunes with high ridges or mountain crescent dunes in some literature. Chinese scholars call it as "Sand Mountain" (Yan et al., 2001). There are a lot of permanent lakes in the interdunes depressions. The largest lake is 1.45 km^2 and the depth is about 16 m. The salinity varies over a wide scope in these lakes of various sizes. In some lakes, salinity is less than 5 g/L, and some are over 300 g/L. Most small lakes are already dried up. Wind eroded land has developed on some dried lake areas. Driven by wind, some sand patches moved directly from the lakeshore into the water and resulted in the lake bottom having aeolian sand deposits (Wang, 1990).

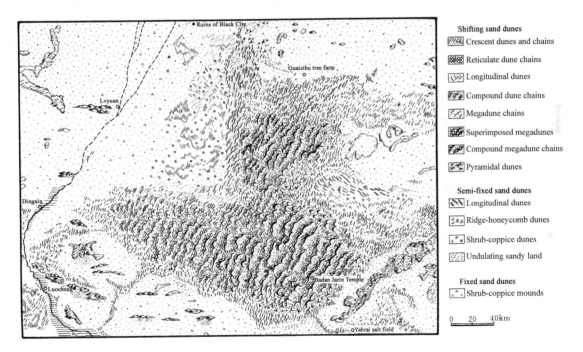

Fig. 11-6   Location and types of dunes in the Badain Jaran Desert [modified by Zhu et al. (1980)]

Controlled by the Mongolian Anticyclone, this desert is controlled by a typical continental climate: dry and cold winters, hot summers, and short springs and autumns. The annual precipitation is between 40 and 120 mm and 50% of it falls in July and August. Precipitation and relative humidity decrease gradually from east to west. The annual and diurnal difference of temperature is great; the sunshine is strong; the northwest and west winds prevail all the year round; the average annual wind velocity is 3.0 to 4.5 m $\cdot$ s^{-1}. The surface runoff is rare because of little precipitation. Therefore, Ruoshui River is the only river in the desert.

11.4.2 Dune types and characteristics

The Badain Jaran Desert is mainly composed of crescent dunes, crescent dune chains, compound crescent dune ridges and star dunes (Fig. 11-6). The crescent dunes and sand dunes are mainly distributed in the northwest, the compound crescent dune ridges are in the interior and the south, and the star dunes are also in the southern desert. In general, the desert has the following characteristics:

(1) The compound, complex crescent dune ridges (sand mountain) are mostly distributed in the middle of the desert, accounting for about 61% of the total area. Their average height is 200–300 m and the highest height is more than 500 m. They can be divided into three types according to their shape characteristics. The first type is a compound sand ridge with superimposed sand dunes on the windward slope. Its direction is 30°–40° from north to east, reflecting the influence of the local prevailing wind (northwest wind). Generally speaking, sand ridges are 5–10 km long and 1–3 km wide. Its figure is high in the middle part and low at both ends. There is a twist at the 1/3 or 1/4 of the upper part of the windward slope, which makes the windward slope have two slopes: the upper part is about 24°–27° and the lower part is about 12°–15°. The leeward slope is tall and steep. The shape of the secondary superimposed dunes on the windward slope is different. It is a dune chain, or a horizontal sand ridge, or a reticulate dune. This is not only due to the local prevailing wind, but also to the airflow altered by the sand ridges. The wind direction is variable, and reflects the influence of the northwest, west, and southwest winds. The second type is also a huge sand ridge, but there is no obvious superimposed sand dune chain on the windward slope. The third type is the star dune, mainly occurring in the south and east near the mountains, especially on the windward side of the mountain range. It is different from the former in that the dune chains are linked to each other, but the latter is pyramidal and usually isolated. The above-mentioned sand mountains are very high and big, because the modern sand dune superimpose on the old ones, or it is overlaid on the ancient calco-cemented dunes, or the sand dune covers the underlying denudes bedrock hills. In the surrounding areas of the high and big sand mountains are dune chains, which account for 25% of the desert area. The dune chains are also very high, generally 25–50 m high; some can reach about 100 m. The interdune area is small and there is no waterlogged low land. The low sand dune chains only occur in piedmont plains at the edge of the desert (Zhu et al., 1980).

(2) Although the Badain Jaran Desert has large areas of shifting sand, which accounts for 83% of the total, there are some plants growing on these dunes or on the sand mountains. These sparse plants occupies about 1/3 of the total area of the sand mountains. Plants mainly grow on the windward slope and the lower part of the leeward slope. Sometimes they are found on the upper part of the slope. The plant species composition is different in the western and eastern parts of the desert. *Calligonum rubicundum, Artemisia sieversiana, Hedysarum scoparium, Zygophyllum xanthoxylon, Ephedra sinica, Atraphaxis frutescens* are dominant species in the west, while *Artemisia sieversiana* and *Psammochloa villosa* are the dominant species in the east, and *Calligonum rubicundum* is no longer dominant. *Zygophyllum xanthoxylon, Ephedra sinica, and Atraphaxis frutescens* gradually decline from west to east. Such characteristics, namely plants growing on the big sand mountains, show that the Badain Jaran Desert is not bare shifting sand land as stated by some scholars in the past (Wang, 1990).

(3) In the interdune lowlands between sand mountains there are many small inland lakes (Haizi) (Fig. 11-7). The number amounts to 144. These lakes are mainly distributed in the southeast of the desert, and are much less in the north and west. Most of the lakes are salty, and the water is undrinkable and can not be used to irrigate due to high salinity caused by high evaporation. However, spring water exists at the edge of the lake basin and in the center of some small lakes. This kind of water also originates from sand dunes, and is replenished by precipitation and condensed water. Therefore, the water quality is better and the salt content is less than 1 g/L. These lakes can provide drinking water.

Fig. 11-7　Sand mountains and lake basin in the southeastern Badain Jaran Desert
(Near the Badan Jarin temple)

The lake areas are generally less than 1 km^2, the largest area is 1.51 km^2 and the maximum depth is 6.2 m (Yihezagede Lake, 40 km west of the Badan temple). Their natural landscape shows a concentric ring-like differentiation. Haizi (a smaller lake), generally occurs in the center, with very high salinity, and Tamayike Haizi, east of the Badan temple, has a salinity amounting to 8.64 g • L^{-1}. Swamp meadow around Haizi has a ground water level of less than 1 m, and it surrounds Haizi. The plants are low and dense, and the dominant species are *Triqlochin maritimum, Glaux maritima,* and *Aeluropus litoralis* etc. Around the swamp meadow is a halophytic meadow, where the underground water depth is about 1 m. The dominant species are *Phragmites australis* and *Achnatherum splendens* etc. Outside of the halophytic meadow is sand drift dominated by *Nitraria sibirica Artemisia halodendron*. The underground water depth is more than 3 m. The outermost edge of the lake basin is fixed and semi-fixed sand dunes, which connect with shifting sand. These lake basins are mainly used for grazing now. There are two permanent residential sites (Badan temple and Yindeertu) in the lake basin. It is not a land without human activity as was reported before.

In addition to lakes distributed between high mountains and in the middle of the Badain Jaran desert, there are also some large lake basins distributed in the western and northern edges. For example, the Guizi Lake in the northern part is more than 100 km long from west to east and 6 km wide; the lake basin of the Gulunai Lake in the western part is about 180 km long and 10 km wide. Their formation is related to the ancient water system. These two lakes are relics of the ancient water system, which was broadened and cut deep by wind erosion. The thin layer of modern lake sediment at some sections shows that they developed from blocked riverbed rather than primary lakes.

The common characteristics of these two lake basins are as follows: a. the water exists only in the center with a high salinity (4.5 g • L^{-1}) and a poor water quality; the soil is generally salinized; b. there are terraces at the edges of the lake basins, for example, there are two terraces at the southern edge of the Guaizi lake. The first one is 30–40 m thick and the second is 20 m; the terrace of the Gulunai Lake is also about 20 m high; c. there is an obvious circlular landscape from the center to the edge. Water exists at the lowest part of the lake growing *Phragmites australis*; the edge of the lake is occupied by *Achnatherum splendens* and *Haloxylon ammodendron* (such as Guaizi lake), or drift sand dominated by *Nitraria sibirica*, and *Haloxylon ammodendron* (such as Gulunai lake); and the outer edge is dunes. Gobi desert is only distributed at the southern edge of the Guaizi Lake, where there are no sand dunes (Zhu et al., 1980)

Haloxylon ammodendron are extensively distributed at the edge of the Badain Jaran Desert, with an area of more than 3.0×10^5 hm^2, mostly in the Gulunai lake, Kunaitou temple, and the Guaizi Lake and so on. These three lakes have better water resources because they lie in lake basins, or in the aggraded flood plain, or in the zone with a high groundwater table in the dry delta. Therefore, *Haloxylon ammodendron* grows well and becomes the dominant natural vegetation at the edge of the Badain Jaran Desert.

From the above description, it is clear that the Badain Jaran Desert is dry and mountainous. On the other hand, there are some lake basins between sand mountains. Especially, the grasslands around some lakes in the southern central and southeast desert can be used as a water source and rangeland. This is an advantage to manage the desert in the future. At the same time, the above characteristics also indicate that the Badain Jaran Desert is not comprised of 100% shifting dunes, and there are also some lakes,which is not like the many maps that show no lakes area distributed in the area north of 40° N (actually, most lakes are concentrated south of 40° N). Furthermore, the western boundary of the desert is also not like some maps which presents that the western boundary is between 40°N and 41°N and ends at the border of the Ruoshui River. The area west of Gulunai Lake is actually a gravel gobi rather than sand dunes shown in some maps.

11.4.3 Landforms

11.4.3.1 Sand source

Sand sources are the material base for the development of the desert and sand dunes. Sand sources are related to the adjacent landform and underlying strata. According to field investigations, aerial photography interpretation data, aerial image analysis and borehole data, from the Black City to Jianguoying in the west and northwest, the Badain Jaran Desert has received huge thick (more than 300 m) fluvial and lacustrine deposits. Paleomagnetic dating shows that this sediment was formed in Brunhes period. From the Black City to Gurinai there are terraces formed by alternately distributed fluviolacustrine deposits and aeolian sand. The fluvial and lacustrine sediments consist of fine sand, silt and clay. There are two types of aeolian sand: one is calco-cemented dune sand with a clear crossbed, 0.4–1.0 m thick, and occurs under the fluvial and lacustrine facies; another is loose ancient dune sand, which is 0.5–1.8 m thick.

The large terraces are replaced by wind-carved Yardang landforms south of the Guaizi Lake, eastern Gurinai, that are on the edge of modern shifting sand. The wind-carved Yardang is 1–5 km wide and the widest section is more than 10 km. The side near the lake is wilted *Populus euphratica* land with a width of 1–3 km, and some parts are covered by crescent dunes or dune chains. The side close to the shifting dunes is Yardangs, consist of wind-carved ridges, hillocks, terraces, dunes and mounds and so on. Yardangs are distributed in patches; with an average height of 2–15 m. Yardangs are also found in shifting dune fields south of the Guaizi Lake, and 10–15 km east to the Gurinai Lake.

A layer of caliche or fluvial and lacustrine facies has developed on the top of Yardangs. All Yardangs are almost at the same level and represent the highest position of lake invasion in this region. Yardangs are made up of alternative fluviolacustrine and aeolian sand facies. The former is stable and mainly consists of silt, fine sand and clay. The soil colour is gray and rust-yellow, and the calcareous root tubes are extensively distributed in this region. The latter is unstable and can be divided into two types: one is tongue-shaped calco-cemented dune sand, which is 0.2–1.5 m thick and has clear aeolian cross-bedding, inclined eastwards and southeastwards at 15°–33°; another is loose ancient dune sand, which is 0.5–2.5 m thick, and there are some calcified patches or calcified aggregates distributed in the crossbeds. TL dating shows that the loose sand near the top of the terrace is 139±10 ka BP, and indicates that the Yardang layer was formed before the last interglacial period (Yan et al., 2001; Yang, 2000).

Analyses of the particle size of Yardang fluviolacustrine sediments in Yikeli sand mountain, the Guaizi Lake, and Gurinai in the southeast of the desert indicate that coarse sand, medium sand, fine sand, very fine sand and clay account for 0.33%–15.04%, 6.36%–50.77%, 21.6%–52.0%, 16.47%–38.67%, and 0.33%–3.9% respectively (Table 11-4). In Yardang fluviolacustrine facies, the contents of coarse, medium, fine, very fine sands and clay are approximate to those of sand dunes. The difference is that the silt content is higher in fluviolacustrine facies, which indicates that the fluviolacustrine deposits are the material basis for the development of dunes and deserts. At the same time it indicates that the formation process of wind-carved Yardangs is also a sand transportation process for desert and sand dunes (Yan et al., 2001; D. Jakel, 1996; J. Hofmann, 1996).

Table 11-4   Grain-size characteristics of sand mountain and fluviolacustrine sediments in the Badain Jaran Desert

Item	Horizon	Coarse sand (0.32–1.00)	Medum sand (1.00–2.00)	Fine sand (2.00–3.00)	Very fine sand (3.00–4.00)	Silt (<4.00)
Yikeli heap	Sand mountain crest	3.37	14.40	52.00	29.90	0.33
Yikeli	Upper sand mountain	1.47	21.46	49.87	23.77	3.90
Yikeli	Middle sand mountain	15.04	30.07	21.60	27.10	3.20
Yikeli	Lower sand mountain	0.33	6.36	53.54	38.67	1.10
Yikeli	Sand mountain foot	2.55	50.77	28.23	16.47	2.83
Guaizi lake	Yardang lake facies	0.20	22.47	37.07	30.10	10.17
Guaizi lake	Yardang lake facies	0.14	16.27	48.17	30.67	4.66
Gurinai	Yardang lake facies	0.33	24.19	37.03	31.50	6.93
Gurinai	Yardang lake facies	6.47	38.80	28.50	23.73	2.50
Gurinai	Yardang lake facies	2.60	18.20	33.10	43.57	2.53

(Yan et al., 2001)

The surface microtexture of quartz sand shows that the surface structures are pockmarked mainly by wind transportation, as well as silica dissolution and deposition due to dramatic changes in temperature in the southeastern Badain Jaran desert. Pockmarked structures, crescent pits, and dished pits were formed by sand collision driven by wind. Because of dramatic changes in daily temperature in arid regions, water is condensed in the interparticle pores when sand surface temperature is lower than that of subaerial air. The condensed water contains soluble salt and the pH value increases accordingly, which makes the SiO_2 dissolve on the sand surface; the evaporation causes the dissolved SiO_2 to deposit on the particle surface when the temperature increases in daytime. With the mechanical action and weathering process, some parallel thin slices develop at the edge of the particle cleavage plane. Afterwards, these slices overlap on the silica layer and make the schistosity blurry. But the outline of the slices can still be distinguished with an upshot edge. The upshot slices appeared with high frequency on the quartz sand surface in the study region, and show that strong wind and significant changes in daily temperature are the regional climate characteristics (Yang, 2000).

There are color differences between new and old sand dunes. However, the heavy mineral composition in sediments has few differences. Sediments consist of hypo-stable, stable, unstable, and the much fewer ultra-stable mineral. This indicates that the new and old sand dunes have a similar developmental environment. The heavy mineral component of lake facies is very similar to that of the new and old dunes, which overlaps on lake facies. This indicates that there is a very close relation between the local lake sediments and aeolian sand. The lake sediment in the interdune lowland is one of the main sand sources of dunes.

11.4.3.2 Wind

The morphological characteristics and development scope of sand dunes in this region are determined by wind. Data from the weather station at the edge of the Badain Jaran Desert indicate that this region belongs to a low wind energy environment (Fig. 11-8). The wind data from the weather station in Dingxin and the northern desert indicate that the prevailing wind direction travels west in Dingxin at the western edge and northwest in Guaizi Lake at the northern edge of the desert. The average sand transportation rate is 140 VU and 129 VU per year in the two regions respectively; the direction variation ratio is 0.57 and 0.40 respectively. They belong to a low energy wind regime. The sand transportation direction is south-east-east in Dingxin all year round, east in February, south-east in April to August, and east or south-east-east in September to the following January. The sand transportation rate is higher between December and the following May, and is the highest between March and May in a year. In the Guaizi Lake, the sand transportation direction is south-east over the whole year. The sand transportation rate is higher between December and the following June, and it is highest between March through June. Results discussed above are consistent with that reflected from the leeward slope of sand dunes (Yan et al., 2001).

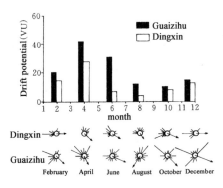

Fig. 11-8   Variations of sand transportation rate in the Dingxin and Guaizi Lake

(Yan et al., 2001)

11.4.3.3 Landforms

There are mountains distributed in the eastern and southern Badain Jaran Desert. Shifting sand can be transported to the mountains by wind, and the transported sand can make another "sand mountain". For example, Yaburai Mountains is 1,600–2,000 m a.s.l, and stretches from the northeast to the southwest. The relative height is 100–500 m; it has a border with the Yaburai Basin in the southeast and it is lower in the northwestern part with a relative height less than 100 m; to the northwest, it gradually merges into the Badain Jaran Desert.

Impacted by the prevailing northwest wind, the aeolian sand from the Badain Jaran Desert usually flows across the bajada and deposits on the northern slope of the mountain and forms a lower "sand mountain". It looks like a sand cover on the barren undulating mountain. From a distance, it looks like the sand mountain stems from the center of the desert. However, approaching closer to the mountain, it becomes clear that the "sand mountain" is actually an eroded bedrock mountain. Space shuttle radar echo data shows that thin sand layers (approximately 2 m) cover the bedrock directly in many places on the mountain. If the underlying bedrock undulates with slight differences in elevation, then it is reasonable to think that this difference formed the sand mountain as described above (Wang, 1990).

Some high sand mountains were formed because of mobile sand overlapping on hummocks at the eastern and western edges of the desert. For example, granite gneiss appears occasionally on sand ridges with an elevation of 1,485 m to the south of Nanshuang Haizi; also, there is light red sandstone distributed in grasslands 1,400 m a. s. l. The highest elevation of this sand mountain is about 1,550 m. However, the relative height of large dunes is no more than 150 m if the bare bedrock is assumed as the initial position. There is a large area of granite gneiss in Baoritaole Gainuoerxi, which almost constitutes one corner of the pyramid sand mountain. There is a sand ridge of about 20 m thick extending westward. Its eastern part is a star sand dune. According to altitude, the top of the bare bedrock is 1,385 m, and most of the sand mountain on the bedrock is 1,470 m. Thus, the relative height of this sand mountain is only 85 m.

In some places the bedrock covered by thick aeolian sand has already become a part of the Badain Jaran Desert. The original landscape can not be identified from the whole body. This may be an auspice or epitome that the northwestern slope of the Yaburai Mountains could be covered with shifting sand completely. If more and more movable sand moves upon the northwestern slope of the Yaburai Mountains, many sand mountains dominated by underlying bedrock will be developed. Connecting them with the sand mountains at the southeast edge of the Badain Jaran Desert, an integral desert landscape will come into being and it will be difficult to distinguish the causes of sand mountains in different regions.

11.4.4　Developmental history of the Badain Jaran Desert

Researchers have different views on the ages of the Badain Jaran Desert. Some scholars think that the deposition of the Badain Jaran Desert started from the Late Pleistocene to the beginning of the Holocene, and its fast development occurred from the middle of Holocene to modern times; others think it began in the early Pleistocene; even some believe that it began from the Pliocene to the Pleistocene. This shows that there are quite different views on the ages of the Badain Jaran Desert.

Tectonically, the Badain Jaran Desert is in the sunken basin of the Alxa mesa. It is separated from Alxa by the rift of the western Zongnai Mountain. Analysis of strata and structure shows that this region was integrated into the Alxa Plateau uplift in the Paleozoic. Hercynian orogeny caused the Alasan uplift. The fracture also occurred during the Alxa uplift. The Yanshan movement resulted in the deposition of the Jurassic and Cretaceous strata due to the uplifting process around mountains and sinking in lake basins when this area was geologically re-activiated. During the Tertiary, this region generally deposited huge Tertiary red continental lake basin sediments; the prevailing climate was warm and humid at that time. Most of the Tertiary was dominated by steppe landscape at least. Large scale lift of the Qinghai-Tibet Plateau made continental climate stronger at the late Tertiary (about $2.5 \times 10^7 - 2.0 \times 10^6$ years ago) in this area.

During the Quaternary the continental glaciers widely developed in China. Although it is not confirmed that there were ancient glaciers in the Quaternary in the Alxa Plateau, some higher mountains, such as the Qilian Mountains, the Mongolian Altay—Gobi Altay and so on, have confirmation that they experienced 2–3 glacial periods. The growth and decline of the adjacent mountain glaciers in glacial periods certainly affected the environment in this region. The intermontane basin or plain generally has 2–3 terraces (consisting of the Tertiary and Quaternary system), showing the influence of the Quaternary climatic variations (possibly glacier and interglacial) (Wang, 1990).

Many researches point out that the alternating variations from cold-dry to warm-humid climates are a low in Quaternary climate. This is because most of the ocean's evaporative water was gathered to polar regions in solid form due to the decrease of global air temperatures, and the areas of glaciers, snow cover and permafrost extended in high-latitude region and a part of middle and low-latitude mountain plateaus; the sea level dropped, shorelines receded on the land, and the continentality was intensified. On the contrary, all the processes mentioned above went through a reverse track in the interglacial period. China is located in the East Asia monsoon zone. So, the alternation of the dry-cold and warm-humid periods caused by glaciation and interglaciation exerts more obvious impacts. In the world wide arid desert regions, the dry period (or interpluvial, interdiluvial, interlacustrine) occurred in the global ice age and the wet period (or rainy period, pluvial age, lake period) occurred in the interglacial period. Based on the study of the ancient climate in the eastern and western deserts, Chinese scholars concluded that in an ice age, the arid desert region was in a dry period and the desert expanded; under opposite circumstances, the desert shrunk and was fixed in the interglacial periods.

It has been confirmed that there were at least three ice ages in the Qilian Mountains in the Quaternary. Taking the ice age of the Lenglongling Mountains as an example, there were the Xiehe ice age in the mid-Pleistocene (Q_2), the early Donggou ice age and the Sanchakou ice age in the late Pleistocene (Q_3), and there were also two interglacial periods between these three ice ages. The ice ages and interglacial periods are reflected by the climate changes in eastern and western China. Growth and decline of the glaciers in the Qilian Mountains and the nearby mountains corresponding to the alternation of glaciation and interglaciation had important effects on the variation of natural environments in the Alxa Plateau, where the Badain Jaran Desert is located. Therefore, it had an important effect on the origin and development of the Badain Jaran Desert.

The Alxa Plateau began to uplift due to neotectonic movement and fractures were produced in the basin and evolved into fracture terraces. Lower Pleistocene alluvial and lacustrine sand were deposited in the terraces. The alluvial and diluvial layers developed in the lower middle Pleistocene. In the Badain Jaran Desert, some places, such as Angcike, Badain Jaran Temple, Bayinnuoer, and Engeliwusu, have late Pleistocene exposed lacustrine deposits. Its lower part is thick caesious, orange, yellowish and green medium-fine silt or semi-cemented sandstone, with a stable structure and lithofacies; its upper part is caesious, greyish-white medium and fine sandstone and marlite (including the stick of bulrush, and concentric or grape-shaped epigenetic concretion). Also, it is the bare region of the lower Pleistocene series alluvial-lacustrine layer in the areas of northwest Gulunai Lake, east of the Ejin River and west of the river valley. The lacustrine layer of the middle Pleistocene mostly is distributed at the western edge of the Badain Jaran Desert, which formed bed-like or hillock-like topography, with a height of 5–20 m. That is composed of greyish-white, brownish-yellow, reddish-brown, and yellowish-green clay soil, sub-clay soil, sub-sandy soil, sandy clay soil, and a sand layer. Its edge has thin and coarse deposits containing gravel; the center has a small amount of sand, whose total thickness is 20–100 m. The alluvial deposits from the upper Pleistocene to the Holocene is distributed in alluvial flats of the Ejin River valley. Its upper layer consists of interbedding of gray, greyish-white, tan, and grayish yellow sub-sandy soil, sub-clay soil, and fine sand. The thickness of each layer varies from 0 to 5 m. Its lower layer consists of interbed sand gravel, medum fine sand, sub-clay soil, and clay soil. The above sediments in various periods are the main sand sources of the Badain Jaran Desert (Wang, 1990).

The above-mentioned facts indicate that the lower Pleistocene alluvial-lacustrine deposits cover a greater part of the Badain Jaran Desert. However, the fluviolacustrine sediments of the middle and upper Pleistocene exist only in the western of the Badain Jaran Desert.

Field investigation proved that there are exposures of loose and fine sandstone in lake-basin (Haizi) lowlands between the Badain Jaran Desert and the high Sand Mountain. For example, sandstones were discovered at the edge of Hazi in Baoritaolegai, Badain Jaran temple, Bagajilin, Yideertu, and Kuhejilin; some are semi-cemented. The distance from the flat sandstone in the southern Badain Jaran Desert to the lake surface is 10–15 m, and it is covered by deposited sand. The sandstone to the east of Hazi in Kuhejilin is about 20 m higher than the lake surface, with an oblique angle of 24 degrees, on which is covered with a sand mountain. In addition, this kind of stratum is also exposed to Bayinnuoer, Angcike and Engeliwusu and so on in the desert interior, which resulted from the lower Pleistocene alluvial-lacustrine deposits. Supposing the study of stratum era is correct, the formation age of the lower part of the high sand mountain should be the mid-Pleistocene (Wang, 1990). There was once an ice age during that period, called the Xiehe ice age in the Qilian Mountains. According to the above-mentioned relations between ice ages and desert development, the Xiehe ice age is the period in which the Badain Jaran Desert had developed on a large scale. Therefore, the formation of the Badain Jaran Desert began in the middle Pleistocene, and then continued to develop gradually until present.

11.5 Aeolian desertification in the Hexi Corridor

The Hexi corridor is located between the Qilian Mountains and the Tengger Desert. Its southern part is moistened by glacier water from the Qilian Mountains, and the northern part is invaded by aeolian sand. The diligent people in Hexi have taken full advantage of the river water for irrigation, which helped the agriculture to develop and the economy to flourish in the arid Hexi Corridor. It is also part of the Silk Road.

Aeolian desertification in arid regions is a process where oases change into deserts due to aeolian sand activity. The main reason for aeolian desertification is irrational exploitation of water and soil resources; the second is firewood cutting around oases. At present, it is very important to pay great attention to aeolian desertification resulted from industrial development, mining, and road construction.

Human civilization in Hexi can be traced back 4,000 years ago, and the area was exploited in the Qin Dynasty and the Han Dynasty. It once was the most developed region in China. However, conflicts always exist between the scale of land exploitation and the carrying capacity of water resources. Furthermore, this conflict becomes intensified with the continuous population increases.

11.5.1 Main characteristics of aeolian desertification

11.5.1.1 Classification of desertification

There are many common characteristics in the occurrence and developing processes of aeolian desertification and natural deserts. Hexi is located in a desert zone, and most of its aera is desert except for the forest and grassland in the southern mid-high mountain area. Land types are diversified and dominated by gobi and desert, which account for 46.64% of the total area. Aeolian desertification caused by human activities has many similarities with the natural desert. They are an undivided unit, or interlaced at many plots. Therefore, the basic principles of the classification of desertification types are consistent with natural desert types.

The main cause leading to desertification is irrational exploitation of resources by mankind. So, desertification can be generalized into two types: one is desert landscape caused by water erosion, due to cutting and overgrazing in middle-high zones of the Qilian-Altun mountains system; the other is dominated by the degradation of oasis into aeolian desert on plains.

11.5.1.2 Distribution of aeolian desertification

According to the above reasons, desertified lands in the Hexi Corridor can be classified into four types: desert dune, wind-eroded land, salinized land, and water eroded land. The spatial distribution of desertified lands in various regions is presented in Table 11-5. The total area of various desertified lands is 5,030,000 hm^2 in Hexi, accounting for 18.25% of the total. About half of the desertified land is distributed in the Jiuquan district, with an area of 2.46×10^6 hm^2. According to the percentage of local land area, Wuwei has the highest value (51.83%). Desertified land formed in the past 2,000 years takes up the biggest proportion (50.14%), and is mainly distributed in the lower reach of the Shiyang River, the Shule River and the Danghe River. Water eroded land ranks second place, with a proportion of 31.62%, and is mainly distributed in the southern mountains and piedmont of the Qilian Mountains. The irrigating oases in the Hexi corridor depend on water conservation in the Qilian Mountains. The expansion of water eroded land will accelerate the desertification process in the Hexi Corridor. The third type is alkaline soil, with a proportion of 16.27%, including primary saline soil and secondary salinized soil. In addition, over-exploiting causes the underground water levels in the lower reaches of Shiyang River to decrease. Wind eroded land accounts for the smallest proportion of 1.79% and is mainly distributed around sandy desertified lands.

According to the proportion of aeolian desertified land in different districts and cities of the Hexi Corridor (Tables 11-6, 11-7, 11-8), Wuwei has the highest proportion (51.38%); the second is Jingtai County (21.08%); the rest is not more than 20%. This maybe reflects two facts: one is that they are located at the edge of the desert and influenced by the natural environment; the other is that their exploitation histories are long. Especially, resource exploitation is more intensive in Wuwei. This can be confirmed by the fact that desertified land is declining with the decrease of exploitation from east to west.

According to the distribution pattern of different desertified lands, Jiuquan has the largest proportion of desertified land, accounting for 48.91% (Table 11-7). Except for water-eroded land, Jiuquan has the largest area of the other three types of desertified land. The salinized land in Jiuquan is 74.48%. One reason for this is that natural climate in western China is drier; another reason is that aeolian desertification is closely related to distribution of cropland and unreasonable utilization of water and soil resources. The wind eroded land in Zhangye and Jiuquan accounts for a large proportion. This reveals that the land use in the mountainous forest and grassland in the southern part of these two regions is irrational.

Table 11-5 Desertified land in the Hexi Corridor

County	Desert dune (km²)	Wind eroded land (km²)	Salinized land (km²)	Water eroded land (km²)	Total (km²)	Land area (km²)	Percent (%)
Jingtai	33.32		45.10	1,069.68	1,148.10	5,445.92	21.08
Wuwei	1,656.90	11.24	7.49	1,049.86	2,725.49	6,083.67	44.80
Minqin	7,923.74	21.06	1,226.96		9,171.76	16,622.28	55.18
Gulang	1,348.36	20.40		1,604.22	2,972.98	4901.43	60.66
Tianzhu				532.92	532.92	2,372.55	22.46
Subtotal	10,929.00	52.70	1,234.45	3,187.00	15,403.15	29,979.93	51.38
Jinchang	41.69	44.54	405.38	575.72	1,067.33	7,513.31	14.21
Zhangye	41.82	74.21	61.98	150.00	328.01	3,722.68	8.81
Linze	237.02	53.73	94.27	10.93	395.95	2,724.30	14.53
Gaotai	683.46	79.75	261.72	55.30	1,080.23	4,383.60	24.64
Shandan		82.09	26.58	1,403.69	1,512.36	5,094.82	29.68
Minle	5.12	34.03	37.86	282.70	359.71	2,844.99	12.64
Sunan	249.23	34.90	243.63	3,841.26	4,369.02	22,052.82	19.81
Subtotal	1,216.65	358.71	726.04	5,743.88	8,045.28	40,833.21	19.70
Jiuquan	130.10	37.65	280.15	38.37	486.27	3,399.72	14.30
Jintai	2,185.62	64.87	256.66		2,507.15	18,943.25	13.24
Yumen	470.82	26.93	574.79	219.17	1,291.71	13,327.41	9.69
Anxi	275.90	58.03	1,488.72	463.80	2,286.45	24,359.12	9.39
Dunhuang	8,210.62	74.43	2,521.68	8.95	10,815.68	31,396.80	34.45
Subei	164.47	270.73	180.23	3,225.05	3,840.48	66,040.71	5.82
Akesai	1,536.05	1.22	465.35	1,371.74	3,374.36	33,103.41	10.19
Subtotal	12,973.58	533.86	5,767.58	5,327.08	24,602.10	190,570.42	12.91
Jiayuguan	27.41	0.46	4.44		32.31	1,310.65	2.47
Total	25,221.65	990.27	8,182.99	15,903.36	50,298.27	275,653.44	18.25
Hexi	25,188.33	990.27	8,137.89	14,833.68	49,150.17	270,207.52	18.19

Table 11-6 Proportion of desertified land to the total land in various counties(%)

District	Desert dune	Wind eroded land	Salinized land	Water-eroded land	Total
Wuwei	36.45	0.18	4.12	10.63	51.38
Zhangye	2.98	0.88	1.78	14.07	19.70
Jiuquan	6.81	0.28	3.03	2.80	12.91
Jinchan	0.55	0.59	5.40	7.66	14.21
Jiayuguan	2.09	0.04	0.34		2.47
Jingtai	0.61		0.83	19.64	21.08
Total	9.15	0.36	2.97	5.77	18.25

Table 11-7 Distribution of different desertified land in various districts (%)

District	Desert dune	Wind eroded land	Salinized land	Water-eroded land	Total
Wuwei	43.33	5.32	15.09	20.04	30.62
Zhangye	4.82	36.22	8.87	36.12	16.00
Jiuquan	51.44	53.91	70.48	33.50	48.91
Jinchang	0.17	4.50	4.95	3.62	2.12
Jiayuguan	0.11	0.05	0.05	0	0.06
Jingtai	0.13		0.55	6.73	2.28

Table 11-8 Constitution of desertified land in various districts (%)

District	Desert dune	Wind eroded land	Salinized land	Water-eroded land
Wuwei	70.95	0.34	8.01	20.69
Zhangye	15.12	4.46	9.02	71.39
Jiuquan	52.73	2.17	23.44	21.65
Jinchang	3.91	4.17	37.98	53.94
Jiayuguan	84.83	1.42	13.74	
Jingtai	2.90		3.93	93.17
Total	50.14	1.97	16.27	31.62

The distribution of desertified lands in the Hexi Corridor has its unique characters: ①aeolian desertified lands are mainly distributed in Wuwei, Jiuquan and Jiayuguan; ②water erosion mainly occur in Zhangye, Jinchang and Jingtai; ③water-eroded land is the second largest desertified land type in Hexi, while the wind-eroded land has the smallest proportion in various districts in Hexi.

Considering the characteristics of aeolian desertified land in different districts in the Hexi corridor, it is recommended to first pay attention to the control of desertification, especially in the western and eastern parts of Hexi, and secondly to control soil erosion in the mountains. Although the mountain area has no characteristics of an arid area, it plays a vital role in water source conservation of the drainage basin.

11.5.1.3 Aeolian desertification characteristics

Aeolian desertified land accounts for a large proportion in Hexi and it influences a large scope (Fig. 11-9). As for the time sequence of succession, desertified land is the main type in Hexi. Desertified land generally appears around the desert due to the influence of natural conditions. Shifting sand

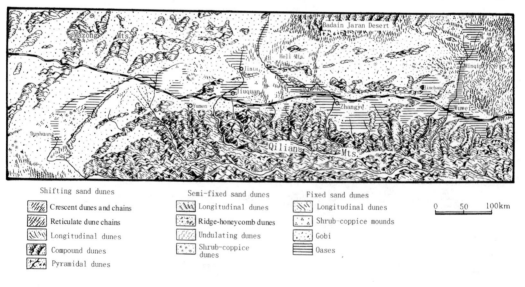

Fig. 11-9 Map of desertified land distribution in the Hexi Corridor

landscape often appears in areas where human activity is strong, and transferring the surface water resulted in the drop of the underground water table, abandonment of large areas of cropland and overuse of vegetation. Aeolian desertified land often occurs in regions such as the lower reaches of drainage basins, the fringe of oases, the downwind side of abandoned cropland and places where ground water was overused.

According to the mobility of sand, aeolian desertified land can be divided into three classes: fixed dune, semi-fixed dune and shifting dune, and they can be converted from each other. Any one of these lands could become the sand source of the others due to the influence of natural processes or human activities. Generally speaking, the mobility of dunes is intensified from an oasis to the surrounding sand. Fixed dunes mainly appear at the margin of oases, with higher plant cover such as, *Slaix microostachya* Turcz. var. *bordensis* (Nakai) C. F. Feng, *Nitraria sibirica* (Pall). The vegetation cover is 40%. Fixed dunes are a natural protection system of the oasis. It is also the result of long-term ecological protection. Semi-fixed dunes have the same vegetation composition as fixed dunes, but the vegetation cover is reduced to about 20% due to collection of fuelwood at the periphery of the oasis. The ground water in lower reaches of the Shiyang River is over exploited, leading to re-activation of larger areas of dunes. Desertification in oases is caused by abandonment of cultivated land and destruction of vegetation. Shifting dunes mainly appear at the fringe of deserts and on abandoned fields in oases. Coverage is about 5%. Dunes at the fringes are distributed continuously in the form of crescent barchan chains 3–5 m high, while dunes in abandoned fields are in a scattered pattern, and abandoned cropland remains are found in the interdune lowland. Generally, the height and density of dunes increase along with the age of abandonment. For example, the cultivated land of the Western Han Dynasty in Minqin is a desert now.

Desertified land caused by wind erosion or badlands has the smallest proportion in Hexi. This land mainly occurs in the middle and lower reaches of alluvial and lacustrine plains. The thicker silt is produced by long-term fluviolacustrine activity and experienced different cementation in the late aridification process. These places once were natural and artificial oases, but became desertified land due to transfer of water resources, drying-up of rivers or overuse of water in the upstream basin. Consequently, the original hydrophyte and mesophyte vegetations have gradually evolved into desert vegetation, with a vegetation cover of about 10%, and the productivity dramatically decreased. The landscape is evolving toward a more arid one. The ground is eroded by wind into blowouts, troughs and depressions. Local people call them 'Upper Gobi'. Moreover, Yandangs a wind eroded landform, develop in some well-cemented places. This landscape typically develops in the area north of Tianshuijing, Anxi County.

11.5.2 Resource exploitation and oasis aeolian desertification

In 1949, Hexi had a population of 1,700,000 and cultivated land of 450,000 hm², of which irrigated lands was about 350,000 hm^2, but the actual irrigated area was only about 130,000 hm^2. In 1993, the population increased to 4,290,000, and the cultivated land increased to 680,000 hm^2, of which the irrigated land was about 668,200 hm^2; however the guaranteed irrigated land was only 130,000 hm^2 (in 1990). Two large-sized reservoirs, 17 median-sized reservoirs and more than 120 small-scale reservoirs have been built on 32 rivers out of 56 rivers in Hexi. At the same time, more than 12,000 km canals were built. About 23,000 motor-pumped wells irrigated 13,000 hm^2 of cropland. The use status of water resources in Hexi is that water use has already been overloaded in the Shiyang River basin; the Heihe is in a critical state (this is only considering the upper and middle reaches; if considering ecological needs in lower reaches, water use has already exceeded its carrying capacity). There is a surplus of 2.0×10^7 m^3 water for the Shulehe River basin.

However, water resource use is intensified dramatically and has inevitably caused many adverse influences. In addition, the lack of knowledge about using natural resources with administration region as a unit by taking into account resource structure have caused regional aeolian desertification.

11.5.2.1 Eco-environment of the Shiyang River Basin

The Shiyang River is located in the eastern of Hexi Corridor and has a relatively high precipitation for arid areas. But there are many problems from the past until the present, and it is worthy of being analyzed as an integral eco-environmental system.

The Shiyang River basin is situated at the northern piedmont of the Qilian Mountains. It covers an area of about 41,600 km^2, bordering Wushaoling and the Yellow River in the east, Dahuang Mountains and Heihe basin in the west. The total area of mountain, gobi, desert and abandoned land occupies about 68%, while grassland, forest and farmland account for 32%. The whole basin includes the following counties: Jinchan, Wuwei, Minqin, Gulang and parts of Tianzhu, and besides these there are some mountain area across Sunan in Zhangye district and Menyuan of Qinghai province.

Wushaoling is located in the intersection zone of the eastern monsoon, the Qinghai-Tibet plateau and the northwest arid region. Therefore, the Shiyang River, lying at the foot of Wushaoling, not only has natural characteristics of the arid area in the northwest, but also has the characteristics of the other two zones: dry and little rainfall, intensive evaporation, with large areas of temperate semi-desert, arid desert and desert-oasis landscape. The relief inclines sharply from southwest to northeast. In its south, the Ganshikadaban in the Qiliang Mountains in the upper reach of the Dongda River is 5,254 m high, and it is surrounded by the Badain Jaran Desert and the Tengger Desert in the north, and the lowest place in Minqin is 1,230 m. The total slope is 1.64%. Annual precipitation increases by 28.6 mm and temperature decreases by 0.33 °C as the altitude increases by 100 m. These results show obvious vertical zonal features in climate, soil, moisture, vegetation and animals.

1) Mountainous cushion vegetation in the cold and frost zone

Mountainous cushion vegetation appears in the cold and frost zone of the alpine belt, where the altitude is over 3,800 m, annual precipitation is more than 600 mm, aridity is less than 0.49, annual average temperature is below 1 °C, and annual average accumulative temperature ($\geqslant$ 0 °C) is not over 12,001 °C. The vegetation is short, and coverage is about 5%–20%. The Qilian peak, with an altitude over 4,000 m, makes Lenglongling a rain center with an annual average precipitation of 800–1,000 mm by blocking the moist air carried by the southeast monsoon and the westerly. Most of the water is stored in the form of snow and ice. There are many unique characteristics in this place: the height of the snow line is 4,400 m, the average height of the glacier bottom is about 4,259 m, the glacier area reaches 64.82 km^2, water storage is 2,143,400,000 m^3, and the average annual meltwater is 55,690,000 m^3.

2) Cold alpine meadow, shrub meadow and forest meadow

Cold alpine meadow, shrub meadow and forest meadow is located in the mid-alpine area with an altitude between 2,600–3,800 m, where the annual precipitation is 380–560 mm and the aridity is 0.49–1.5; the average annual temperature is –1–2.6°C, and the vegetation growing period is 120–170 days. The 3,800–3,500 m zone is covered by alpine meadow, and the sub-alpine scrub meadow zone is at an altitude between 3,500–3,400 m; the forestry scrub meadow zone is at an altitude between 3,400–2,600 m. This place is the 'green reservoir' in the arid desert and a 'life' line for Hexi.

3) Mountain desert and grassland eco-region of the cold temperate zone

Mountain desert and grassland eco-region of the cold temperate zone mainly includes the intermontane basins, rocky low-mountains, denuded hillbelts and sloping land in front of the mountains. The 2,300–2,600 m zone belongs to alpine grassland, and desert grassland appears at an altitude between 2,000–2,300 m. The natural characteristics of this region are as follows: annual precipitation is 350–400 mm and the aridity is 0.8–3.3; the annual average temperature is –1.0–5.8 °C, and the growing period is 150–250 days a year. This region is one of the poor ecological areas in the Shiyang River basin.

Eco-economically, the above three eco-regions are runoff-generating regions. There are eight rivers originating from this area and total discharge at the mountain valley mouth is 1,628,000,000 m^3, of which 34.9% is from the mountainous eco-region in the cold and frost zone and 1.6% from the mountain eco-region in cold temperate zone. Thus, it is concluded that the 'solid reservoir of alpine ice-snow' and 'green reservoir of forest-steppe' play an important role in arid desert areas.

4) Stony desert and semi-desert eco-region in front of mountains

Stony deserts and semi-desert eco-regions in front of mountains mainly appears in the low mountainous area with an altitude of 1,600-2,000 m, hills in front of mountains, and stony tilted plains on the alluvial and proluvial fans. The annual average temperature is 5.5–7.2 °C, the annual precipitation is 150–320 mm, and the growing period is 200–230 days. When a river flows through this region, more than 70% of the water infiltrates into the thick stony layer and forms an underground reservoir. This creates a so-called 'cool-cold' irrigated agricultural zone.

5) Central warm temperate oasis eco-agricultural zone

The central warm temperate oasis eco-agricultural zone mainly lies on the alluvial and proluvial fine soil plain at 1,600 m a.s.l. It is also the springs-overflow zone and the mid-downstream zone of the river. The annual mean temperature is 7.6–8.0 °C, annual mean precipitation is 110–170 mm, and annual accumulative temperature ($\geqslant$10 °C) is 2,980–3,150 °C. The zonal soil is desert soil, but the oasis irrigated soil, formed due to long-term utilization and irrigation, becomes dominant. Vegetation includes steppe desert, meadow and halophilic meadow vegetation, swamp vegetation, and weeds in cropland, as well as the commercial forests of arbor and shrub, and shelter forest, such as *Populus pseudo-simonii Kitag*, *Salix*, *Elaeagnus angusti folia* L., *Haloxylon ammodendron* and so on. The growing period is about 8 months, the duration of sunshine is long, and the temperature is high, with potential productivity possibly reaching 30,000 kg $\cdot$ hm^{-2}, equal to that in Jiangxi and Zhejiang. In addition, there is plenty of water from springs and rivers. It has become one of the richest areas in dry desert regions.

6) Small semi-shrub desert, desert and salt desert region of northern warm temperate zone

This area lies in the vast area in the north margin of oases, where annual precipitation is 80–160 mm, and potential evaporation is 2,640–3,040 mm. The mean annual temperature is 7.8–10.0 °C, the sunshine duration is over 3,000 h, and solar radiation is stronger. The aridity is 4.5–8, and dust storms can occur more than 130 days. The soil types include sandy and stony grey-brown desert soil, saline-alkali soil and aeolian sand soil etc. Vegetation species are very limited, consisting of xeric, ultra-xeric and halobiotic shrubs, small semi-shrubs and perennial psammophilous herbs. Vegetation coverage is 5%–40%, and the grass yield is 1,500 kg in an area of 3.33–5.67 hm^2, just enough to feed one sheep.

11.5.2.2   Aeolian desertification restoration in the Shiyang River Basin

Since the founding of the People's Republic of China, the government organized people in the sandy region to construct irrigation systems, control shifting sand and develop the agro-pastoral production. At first, the local government launched a campaign to build irrigation canals and facilities, and to substitute half-natural water systems. In June, 1958, Hongyashan Reservoir, with a desiged capacity of 127,000,000 m^3, was put into operation and it became an artificial water irrigation source. The lining of main and branch channels made the surface water utilization efficiency of canal systems increase to about 0.5 from 0.2–0.3 before the foundation of the People's Republic of China. The improvement of surface water utilization efficiency resulted in the irrigating land increasing to 36,700 hm^2. From the end of the 1960s to the beginning of the 1970s, the area of farmland increased to 70,000 hm^2 (25,200 hm^2 was later abandoned for lack of water). Until the end of 1985, about 39,500 hm^2 of cropland were built into a high standard strip-field. As early as 1949, the government had organized a sand control campaign on a large scale. In 1951, clay was used to cover sand, and then planted sand binders *Artemisia sphaerocephala* and *Agriophyllum squarrosum* on the dunes. Afforestation was mainly carried out in oases. The Desert Control Team, Chinese Academy of Sciences summarized the experience and disseminated it in the whole region. In 1959, the Minqin Desert Control Experimental Station was established. They set up sand barriers on mobile dunes as wind-blocked walls and planted grasses to fix the sand around the oasis, built shelter belts along sand belts, paved clay barriers around farmlands and planted *Haloxylon ammodendron* to protect the land. After years of work, protective systems were established with trees, bushes and grasses (Fig. 11-10). Therefore, in the past 30 years between the 1950s to the 1980s, there was no dune encroachment or villages buried by sand that occurred in this area (Zhu et al., 1994).

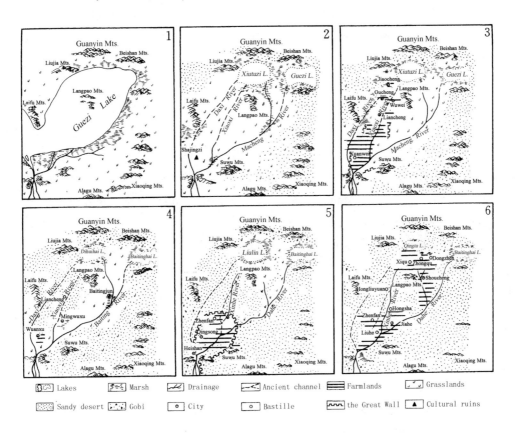

Fig. 11-10   Minqin oasis and its protective system in the early 1970s

However, with the development of the entire Shiyang River basin, the balance of its environment was destroyed and sand disasters started to occur in this region again. At first, water shortage became a threat to this region. The runoff in the Shiyang River basin in the Minqin Oasis decreased from 580,800,000 m^3/a in the 1950s to 217,000,000 m^3/a in the 1990s. In order to meet the need for irrigation, farmers had to dig wells to pump ground water for irrigation. Until the middle of the 1970s, the over-extraction reached about 1.0×10^8–2.0×10^8 m³, leading to a drop in the water table. This further led to the death of vegetation in larger areas, and at last, the cropland was abandoned due to lack of water and land aeolian desertification expanded again.

11.5.2.3　Oasis evolution and ecological crisis in Minqin

(1) Decrease of water resources in the Minqin Oasis is related to the upset of the ecological balance in the whole Shiyang River basin. Since the vegetation in the Qilian Mountains was destroyed, the general function of headwaters gradually declined. The forest area in the Qilian Mountains of the Shiyang River basin was 227,000 hm² in the early 1950s. This forest, together with the grassland, constituted a basis for water resource conservation. However, from the 1960s onwards, the forest in this area suffered four times from serious destruction. About 30,100 hm² of forest land were destroyed and 66,700 hm² of grassland were reclaimed into farmland. After the 1980s, hundreds of gold seekers rushed into this region and vegetation at hundreds of mining sites were destroyed. Even after the 'Soil and Water Conservation Law' and "Regulations for Soil and Water Conservation' were issued, the destruction was still not stopped. The total runoff of the 8 rivers in the 1980s decreased by about 306,000,000 m³, compared to that in the 1950s. Owing to vegetation degradation, global warming, aridification and its feedback mechanism, air temperature in the Qilian Mountains increased by 0.2–0.4 °C from the 1960s to the 1980s. As a consequence, the snow cover decreased, glaciers retreated, and water storage was reduced. Monitoring shows that glaciers on the Lenglongling are retreating at an annual rate of 12.5–22.5 m, and the snow covered area decreased by 30% in the upper reach of the Jingta River.

The use of water resources in the Shiyang River never has had long-term planning and unified management. There was also no pre-assessment on the effects of engineering on the eco-environment. Water consumption and diversion in the upper reaches become larger and larger, and huge amounts of water resources are consumed in the cool irrigation districts in front of the mountain. Oases are enlarged and the ecological balance of the whole basin is upset. According to statistics, building reservoirs and canals resulted in the irrigated area to extend from 61,300 hm² in the 1950s to 101,000 hm² in the late 1980s. Correspondingly, with an increase of 4640 hm² of irrigation land in the intermontane basin, the irrigation area expanded by 44,000 hm² and annual net water consumption reached 286,000,000 m³.

Wuwei basin is a gravity irrigation region with the Shiyang River water and spring water overflowing from the ground water in front of the mountain. The spring water output was about 800,000,000 m³ in the 1950s. From the 1960s onward, canals in the upper reach were lined to prevent leakage and spring water replenishment decreased, as did the wells and the nearby spring water. Many wells and springs dried up due to lack of replenishment. By the end of the 1970s, the total spring water flux decreased to 203,000,000 m³ and the area irrigated with spring water output reduced from 33,300 hm^2 to 6,000 hm^2.

The Hongyashan Reservoir play an important role in flood adjustment in Minqin Oasis. But this plain reservoir is in the desert. Its surface area is over 7.5 km^2 and directly exposed to wind, dry air and high evaporation. Hence, the annual evaporation is about 135,000,000 m^3, about 15.0% of the reservoir capacity. This is a direct loss in water circulation.

The runoff flowing into the Minqin Oasis continuously decreases due to excessive water exploitation in the upper reaches; it was 546,000,000 m^3 in the 1950s, 448,500,000 m^3 in the 1960s, 322,600,000 m^3 in the 1970s, and 221,700,000 m^3 in the 1980s. The averaged rate of decrease was 2%. That is to say, about 108,100,000 m^3 of water was lost every 10 years. Therefore, farmers have had to dig wells and pump ground water on a large-scale from the 1970s onward. As early as the middle of the 1970s, the ground water had been over-exploited. On average, about 100,000,000–300,000,000 m^3 of ground water were over-exploited per year. The accumulated over-exploitation was 3,628,000,000 m^3 in 15 years. Therefore, the water table declined by 4–17 m in 15 years. And three cones of ground water depression with a total area of 986 km^2 were created in the oasis. Water table at the center of one of the cones reduces by 0.6–1.0 m per year. The surrounding water was mineralized due to land salinization, vegetation degradation and desertification expansion (Zhu et al., 1994).

For accurate description, the Hydrological Department summarized the ecological changes in the Shiyang River basin into 'four advances' and 'five decreases'. They are: desert advances to oasis, farming area advances to pasture area, pasture area advances to forest region and glacier and snow line advances to mountain tops; forest and grassland decrease, precipitation decrease, river runoff decrease, water table and reserve decrease, and living resources decrease. The ecosystems are facing a series of threats, and most it likely will be destroyed.

Nowadays, the development and utilization of natural resources in the Shiyang River basin have far exceeded those at any time in history. Especially, the over-exploitation of water resources has extended from the surface water to ground water and from the mid-lower reaches to the source area. Hence, its impact on the environment balance and aeolian desertification is also different from that in the historical period.

Owing to water table decline, both the natural and artificial vegetation died in Minqin. 70% of the 72,400 hm^2 of natural psammophyte vegetation in the oasis have been degraded. And 8,527 hm^2 of vegetation was seriously degraded or even wilted with dead branches. As a result, vegetation cover decreased from 44.8% in the 1950s to less than 15% in recent years. The vegetation has been gradually evolving from hygrophytic meadow to xerophilous or even super-xerophilous vegetation. For example, *Phragmites communis* which was 2 m high in the Qingtuhu Lake, has disappeared and been replaced by sparse reeds 10 cm high. *Iris onsata and Calamagrostis epigejos* were almost extinct and replaced by halophytic vegetation, such as *Kalidium foliatum* and *Karelinia caspia* etc. The primary hygrophilous vegetation which grew around the lake or in the lowlands were replaced by *Nitraria sibirica Pall* communities. The decrease of water flow in canals made the 2 m-high *Salix microostachya Turcz. var. bordensis(Nakai)* along the canals degrade to a 1 m height. *Haloxylon ammodedron* on semi-fixed dunes degraded and was replaced by *Calligonum mongolicum* and *Artemisia ordosica*. Decrease of vegetation cover has led to decrease in biomass. For instance, the biomass of *Phragmites communis* in Sanquwan was 400,000 kg in the 1950s, but at present, is only 200,000 kg.

After the foundation of the People's Republic of China, afforested land of *Elaeagnus angusti folia L* and *Haloxylon ammodedron* once increased to 77,000 hm². Nowadays, 67% of the land has degraded. According to the statistics of the local forestry department, about 2,973 hm² of *Elaeagnus angusti* folia died, 5,800 hm² *Elaeagnus angusti* folia's top branches died, accounting for 41.2% of the total. Even worse, about 6,667 hm² of *Haloxylon ammodedron* died and 33,400 hm² degraded. There were 45,300 hm² of shrubs that degraded on the fixed or semi-fixed dunes, which once was fenced in the 1950s. 17% of the degraded woodland had a coverage less than 10%, hence the land was desertified (Zhu et al., 1994).

(2) Due to water shortages, the actual aridity in the Minqin oasis has increased from 1.14 in the 1950s to 2.21. Owing to the shrinkage of the ecological scope of animals' activity, Mongolian gazelles and mallards, once existing in large flocks, have disappeared from this place due to illegal hunting. Rabbits and rats move into oases from degraded woodland; foxes, wolves, eagles, peckers and snakes markedly decrease in number. Rabbits and rats browse trees and damage crops, which exacerbate the ecological crisis.

(3) Due to lack of water, cropland area in Minqin never exceeds 40,000 hm². On the contrary, about 25,200 hm² were abandoned since the 1960s, of which 6,133 hm² are located around the lakes or villages at the edges of deserts. The abandoned land has been desertified. For instance, 40 hm² of cropland irrigated for planting millet in the Production Team I of Xiqu Township have been abandoned due to lack of irrigation water. Four years after the land has been abandoned, the mean deflation depth of the abondoned cropland reached 10 cm and the deepest blowout was 40–50 cm. At the same time, 30% of the abandoned land was covered by sand. The thickness of sand layer increased downwind (southeast), and a crescent dune, 35 m long, 18 m wide and 0.5–1.3 m high, developed in the middle of the sand-deposited area. The height of small dunes was about 0.5 m. If effective measures are not taken to protect this abandoned land, it will inevitably be turned into shifting dunes.

After natural water systems were replaced by man-made water systems, the original water channels were abandoned and dried up. The shifting crescent dunes develop when the barren and loose alluvial sand is exposed to strong wind. The shifting sand can encroach on grassland, bury cropland and damage woodland. At last, the riverbed exhibits a strip desert landscape.

(4) Minqin Oasis is located between the Tengger Desert and the Badain Jaran Desert. The area of interlaced dune and cropland is about 560 km², of which shifting dunes occupy 18 km². After the founding of the PRC, a protective system for the oasis was established, and the shifting dunes inside and on the edge of the oasis were fixed to a certain degrees. Aeolian desertification reversed, and the

aeolian sand disasters were alleviated. Now, the fixed and semi-fixed dunes have started to re-activate and shifting crescent dunes develop with the destruction of the protective system. This poses a serious threat to the croplands and villages.

There were about 6,133 hm^2 of cropland desertified and 5,200 hm^2 of land buried by sand. About 32 villages in the lake area and 867 hm^2 of cropland were covered by sand, accounting for 8.7% of its total.

(5) High mobile dunes around the oasis are increasing at a rate of 8 m per year. And, in some places the height of sand dunes is 20 m.

(6) Historically, the Minqin Basin is an accumulated area of water and salts in the lower reaches of the Shiyang River. In recent years, water amounts reduced and ground water was excessively exploited, and an aridification trend developed in the entire region. Salt accumulation is tending to take place in shallow stratum and cultivated horizons. Following the formation of the cone of ground water depression, high-salinity water recharges the oasis. The salinity of groundwater is increasing at a rate of 0.3–1.48 g $\cdot$ L^{-1} per year. In particular, the terminal lake in the basin has a salinity of 4–6 g $\cdot$ L^{-1} and 76,100 people and 124,600 livestock lack drinking water. In the 1980s, the salinized land increased to 8,067 hm^2.

(7) Owing to the reduction in the underground water table, the well-drilling depth is getting deeper and deeper. Farmers in Minqin have to change their pumps five times. The cost of well construction, management and pumping greatly increased. The cost of grain production in 1988 was 3.6 times more than that in 1980. The county once had plenty of grain to feed the people, but by the end of the 1980s, it had to buy 1,500,000 kg $\cdot$ a^{-1} of grain and received relief funds of 180,000 *yuan* per year. At present, this place has become an impoverished region of common concern.

It is noticeable that environment degradation caused by this exploitation of groundwater has influenced not only Minqin County, the Wuwei Oasis, but also the entire Hexi region.

References

Bao Y. et al. 1984. Land desertification and control regionalization. Journal of Desert Research, 4(2)

Beijing University et al. 1983. Natural Condition and Utilization of Mu Su Sandy Land. Beijing :Science Press

Chen G T. 1992. Sand control effect along the highway in Tengger Desert. Journal of Desert Research, 12(3): 18–26

Denton G H, Karlen W. 1979. Holocene Climatic Variations: Their Pattern and Possible Cause. Quaternary Research, 3

Desertification Investigation Team of Ih Ju Meng, Lanzhou Institute of Desert, CAS. 1986. Land desertification and control in Ih Ju Meng of Inner Mongolia. In: Memories of Lanzhou Institute of Desert, CAS. No.3. Science Press, Beijing

Dong G R, Gao S Y, Li B S. 1983. Variations of Mu Us Sandy land since late Pleistocene viewed from strata in Salawnsu River basin. Journal of Desert Research, 3(2): 9–14

Dong G R. et al. 1986. Paleo-periglacial phenomena and relation between aeolian sand and loess since late Pleistocene in Ordos Plateau. In: Memories of Lanzhou Institute of Desert, CAS. No.3. Beijing: Science Press

Feng Shengwu. 1963. Water system evolvement of Minqin Oasis. Acta Gegraphica Sinica, 3:241-249

Gao S Y, Chen W N, Liu L Y et al. 1993. Tengger Desert of Holocene mega thermal period. In: Annuals of Shapotou Desert Scientific Research Station, Chinese Academy of Sciences (1991-1992). Lanzhou: Gansu Science and Technology Press, 212—214

Hofmann J. 1996. The lakes in the SE part of Badan Jarin Shamo, their limnology and geochemistry. Geowissenschaften, (7, 8): 275—278

Inner Mongolia Investigation Team, CAS. Inner Vegetation in Mongolia. Beijing: Science Press. 371—391, 427—466

Jakel D. 1996. The Badan Jarin Desert: its origin and development. Geowissenschaften, (7, 8): 272—274

Lanzhou Institute of Desert, CAS. 1979. Desert Map of the People's Republic of China. Sinomaps Press

Li B. 1990. Study on Natural Resource and Environment in Ordos Plateau of Inner Mongolia. Beijing: Science Press. 80—90

Li J G. 1993. Analyses on air temperature and precipitation in Shapotou. In: Annuals of Shapotou Desert Scientific Research Station, Chinese Academy of Sciences (1991-1992). Lanzhou Gansu Science and Technology Press. 112—114

Li J J. et al. 1979. Discussion on age, range and form of the Tibetan Plateau's uplift. Science in China, (2): 608—616

Li X R. 1997. The characteristics of the flora of the shrub resource in Mu Us Sandy land and the countermeasures for their protection. Journal of Natural Resources, 12(2): 146—152

Liu D S. et al. 1965. Quaternary Climate and Quarternary Geology in China. Beijing: Science Press

Liu Y X. 1995. Discuss on occurrence and formation of flora in desert area. Acta Phytotaxonomic Sinica, 33(2): 131—143

Shapotou Desert Scientific Research Station, Lanzhou Institute of Desert, CAS. 1980. Study on shifting sand control in Shapotou Region in Tengger Desert. Yinchuan: Ningxia People's Publishing House. 5—8

Sun J M, Ding Z L, Liu D S. et al. 1995. Environmental evolution at marginal belt of desert and loess since last interglacial age. Quaternary Sciences, 2: 117—121

Wang H S. et al. 1992. Flora Geography. Beijing: Science Press

Wang T. 1990. Several problems on formation and evolution of Badan Jarin Desert. Journal of Desert Research, 10(1): 29—40

Yan M C, Dong G R, Li B S et al. 1998. A preliminary study on the desert evolution of southeastern margin in Tengger Desert.18(2): 111—117

Yan M C, Dong G R, Tao Z et al. 1992. Neogene palaeo-aeolian sands and environment at southeastern margin in Tengger Desert. Journal of Desert Research, 12(3): 10—15

Yan M C, Wand G Q, Li B S et al. 2001. Study on formation and development of high sand hills in Badain Jaran Desert. Acta Geographica Sinica, 53(suppl): 45—51

Yang G S, Lu R. 1998. Sandy desertification and integrated control techniques in Ih Ju Meng of Inner Mongolia. Beijing: China Environmental Science Press. 19—21

Yang X P. 2000. Landscape development and precipitation change in the past 30ka in Badain Jaran Desert. Chinese Science Bulletin. 45(4): 428—434

Zhang X S. 1994. Ecological background and fundamental, optimizing pattern of grassland construction in Mu

Us Sandy land. Acta Phytoecologica Sinica, 18(1): 1—16

Zhong D C. 1998. Desert Dynamic Evolution in China. Lanzhou: Gansu Cultural Press

Zhu B H. 1963. Chinese climate. Beijing: Science Press

Zhu L Y, Bao Y. 1993. Evaluation on Site Quality of Arbor and Shrub in Mu Us Sandy Land. Beijing: China
  Forestry Publishing House

Zhu Z D, Chen G T. 1994. Sandy desertification in China. Beijing: Science Press

Zhu Z D, Wu Z, Liu S. 1980. Introduction of Deserts in China (Revised edition). Beijing: Science Press. 68—76,
  71—73

Chapter 12
Deserts and Aeolian Desertified Lands in the Arid Regions

The Xinjiang Uygur Autonomous Region of China lies in the hinterland of Eurasia. (It is calculated that the geometrical center of Eurasia is near Ürümqi.) It is located very far from the Pacific Ocean in the east, the Atlantic Ocean in the west and the Arctic Ocean in the north. It is difficult to get the warm and humid airflow from oceans due to the obstruction of the Qinghai-Tibet Plateau in the south whose height is over 4,000 m, together with the subsidence of airflows due to the two basins in the northern and southern Tianshan Mountains. All of these factors make it arid and hot, and difficult to form precipitation. Therefore, it is the most arid location in Eurasia. But along with the uplift of the Pamir Plateau, the Tianshan Mountains and the Kunlun Mountains, the mountainous region has obvious vertical bioclimatic zones. Consequently, Xinjiang is not covered entirely by desert, and because of precipitation moistening in the alps and streams formed by melted ice and snow, oases appear in front of mountains. On the other hand, the peculiar locality and topography of northern Xinjiang favoring moisture passing through from the Atlantic and Arctic oceans, has formed the unique Gurbantünggüt Desert,which is composed of fixed and semi-fixed sand dunes and isolated from the desert system in China.

The characteristics of aeolian desertification in the extremely arid region are as follows:

(1) Aeolian desertification only develops on the periphery of natural oases, which is usually called oasis aeolian desertification. The oases existence relies on water, and the water resource quantity determines the development of aeolian desertification. When there is a shortage of water, aeolian desertification will develop, and when there is plenty of water, the desert will change to oasis. Unplanned development of oases in an inland upriver leads to aeolian desertification intensification in the downriver.

(2) The physiognomy characteristics of aeolian desertified land are the alternating distribution of the wind-blown shrub-coppice dunes, crescent dunes and dune chains. The representative examples are in Pishan, Moyu, Qira, Luopu, Yutian, Minfeng etc., located on the southern edge of the Taklimakan Desert. As time lapses, they further develop into numerous crescent dune chains with shrub-coppice dunes among them. The landscape is dominated by crescent dune chains near the ancient castle in the Taklimakan Desert.

(3) The movement of shifting sand dunes is slow, but if it moves in one direction, it will move a considerable distance. The Taklimakan desert is moving southward due to the prevailing northeast and

northwest wind. It had moved over 10 km southward in the last 1,000 years and 2–3 km in the past 100 years.

(4) In the past 10 years the precipitation in Xinjiang increased. Together with climate warming and the thawing of ice and snow, some lakes' water tables rose. But in the downstream there is still no water and some lakes dried up due to overuse of water in the upstream. According to estimates of climatologists, with greenhouse gases increasing, precipitation will increase in arid regions. But the absolute increment is very little because the precipitation is low. With continuous global warming, especially the persistence of warm winter, aridization will continuously intensify. Additionally, since the anthropogenic influence is increasing, aeolian desertification will be a severe problem.

12.1 Gurbantünggüt Desert

The Gurbantünggüt Desert is the biggest fixed and semi-fixed desert in China. The climate is mainly controlled by the westerly, and the effect of the Pacific summer monsoon is weak. The dune modality, desert type and sand structure, surface biology state and the generic community are typical for present desert environment. The evolutional process of desert environments is evident in the stratum sections, cultural relics, and literature records in geologic time and human history. The researches on the desert environment evolution process and climate changes began during the 1920s. But some interdisciplinary studies such as cooperation among ecology, environment and climate started in recent years. For example, the paleo-environment in the Cretaceous Period is evident from trunk-fossil exposure sites and regional distribution. That of the later Quaternary was confirmed by analyzing desert lacustrine sediments and contrasting the evolutions of northern Xinjiang loess and the Tianshan Mountains. For the present desert, the general method used to reconstruct climate change sequences is statistical and simulation analyses of tree annual rings and observation records. From the above-mentioned research we found that the desert experienced normal and inverse evolution processes. Especially, this desert has an impressive response and feedback to the present environment and climate changes, which is totally different from other deserts. In this section, the latest research will be introduced including its past, present and future development, in order to evaluate and plan desert environment protection, resources exploitation and the grand engineering effect in western exploitation.

12.1.1 Summary

The Gurbantünggüt Desert is the third largest desert in China. It lies in the south central Junggar Basin (N 44°11′–46°20′, E 84°31′–90°00′). The area is 48.8×10^3 km^2, and it is made up of the Huojingnielixin, Dezuosuotengailisong, Suobugurbugelai, Kuobeibu and Akekum Deserts. There are 14 counties and dozens of farms nearby.

The topography character of the desert is an alternating distribution of alps and basins, and each topography unit has an obvious boundary and individual character. The desert is encircled by alps (Fig.12-1). The geologic structure and topography in the basin is characterized by concentric orbicular zones, and it can be classified into several basic topography zones from the basin periphery to its center: that is mountainous region-upland-proluvial, and alluvial gravel gobi in front of mountain-subsidence basin with sand desert. The hydrology is characterized by the centripetal water system originating from mountainous regions and converging into the basin center. The replenishment of underground water is mainly lateral percolation in the piedmont, and precipitation and snow infiltration in the plain. The climate is temperate continental climate which is controlled by the westerly. Consequently, the environment is arid with little precipitation, the environment is more fragile and the desert is distributed widely.

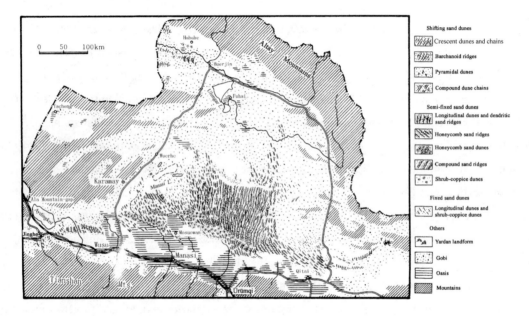

Fig. 12-1　The environment of the Gurbantünggüt Desert and sand dunes' types

The precipitation in the Gurbantünggüt Desert is snow in winter. The desert is usually covered with snow 30 cm in depth, which lasts for three months. The snow depth often differs among dune ridges because the depth is influenced not only by the transportation and redistribution from wind force, but also vegetations between dunes. Due to frequent inbreaking of northwestern cold airflow and the Cold Lake Effect, deep seasonal frozen soil is formed in the desert region, with a maximum depth of over 170 cm. Therefore, the melting of snow and frozen soil plays an important role in the survival vegetation and its regenesis in this desert region.

As early as the 1920s, the Soviet expert Vladimer Obrucher(В.А.Обручев) had investigated the Manasi Lake, and later in the 1950s, the Xinjiang Synthetically Science Investigation Team investigated the desert entirely. After that, the desert environment, climate changes and vegetation community distribution in the geologic time, human history and present period was successively investigated (Cheng Changdu 1983). Since the Cretaceous Period, the desert climate and environment had experienced several fluctuations from arid to humid and warm to cold, and the desert also went through periods of inverse development processes. Till 4,000 a BP the climate abruptly became arid and formed the current pattern. Once climate fluctuation occur in the desert, it will obviously reflect both the vegetation coverage and dynamical operation of aeolian weathering. Moreover, human influence is an important factor in the inverse development process of present aeolian desertification.

Sandy desert is the product of an arid climate; the spatial pattern is formed because of climate changes and environmental evolution over the long term. Therefore, in sandy desert research, only when the natural environment formation, evolution and important evolution period is known, and the normal and inverse evolution process of present sandy desert, influence degree and extent of nature and anthropogen is known, can we realize the global climate changes' impact on desertification and predict its future development trend with the theoretical and scientific warrant.

12.1.2　The past of the Gurbantünggüt Desert environment

The Gurbantünggüt Desert has experienced several climate and environment changes, and the present pattern was not formed until the end of the later Pleistocene. In the geologic evolution time, the Junggar Basin had experienced mountain erosion in the Mesozoic and early Tertiary, mountain uplift in the later Tertiary and at the beginning of the Quaternary. Especially in the Jurassic and Cretaceous Periods, the dating analysis of the exposed silicified tree-fossil in the middle and eastern basin indicated that the conditions of climate and environment were pleasant, and trees and vegetations were plentiful. The Study on the Tianshan Mountains Evolution, (Institute of Ecology and Geography, Chinese Academy of science, Xinjiang, 1986) revealed that in the Mesozoic Period, the stratum of the Bogda Mountains between Ürümqi and Mulei belongs to fluvial-lacustrine sediment, most of which are purple gravel, sandstone, clay and sandy clay interbeded with purple gray, gray green sandstone, and ostracoda and vertebrate fossil etc. All of these indicate that lakes covered the desert region, and vegetation or animals were abundant at that time. By the end of the Cretaceous Period, violent tectonic movement of crust made the Tianshan Mountains Paleozoic stratum uplift again. From then on, the mountain was lowered and the topography gradually became complanate because of long term denudation. Synchronously climate and environment changed greatly. The great changes of climate and environment happened in the Quaternary. Ancient aeolian sand was firstly found by Dong Guangrong (1995a) in the Ordos Plateau. Afterwards, Wei Wenshou and Dong Guangrong found the same ancient aeolian sand when they investigated the Gurbantünggüt Desert. Thus it can be seen that the desert was formed at the beginning of the Pleistocene, and experienced a series of normal and inverse evolution processes of drifting sand and fixed or semi-fixed sandy land. According to the dating by Wei Wenshou about the desert fringe sediments, the desert was bigger than now before 18 ka

BP. It basically was fixed during 18–8 ka BP, after 8 ka BP, the desert expanded. By the end of the later Holocene, the desert was aeolian sediment, and fluvial-lacustrine sediments obviously reduced in lower land. The blown sand increased obviously although there was fine sand, silt sand and sub-clay. About 4 ka BP gray fine sandy paleosol increased obviously in the lake sediment, which indicated that the desert shrunk at that time. At the end of the Holocene, the scope of shifting sand reduced and climate changed to warm and humid, although there was no broad swampy sediment, the granularity composition of fine sandy paleosol had a trend of becoming finer.

During the course of human history (2,000 a), the sandy desert environment was basically steady, and only at the southeastern and southwestern edge did the fixed and semi-fixed dunes change to shifting ones due to the impact of anthropogenic activity. According to research about historical record by Xia Xuncheng, the desert environment in the Tang Dynasty Censhen wrote poem like this "the sand is vast and expands into the sky in yellow" and that in Daoguang age in the Qing Dynasty Shanchang wrote poem like this "vast and yellow sand makes the sky dim". We can conclude that the sandy desert and dust from the Junggar Basin interior disserved to the northern Tianshan in history (Xia et al., 1991). For example, Yirbaka stoneware relic lies in shifting sand zone with a distance of 38 km from northern Mulei County (it was about 3,000 a BP). There were not only refined stoneware such as stone kernel, small stone foliage, stone arrowhead, stone scraping gallet, but also potsherd of the Tang Dynasty, and copper arrow head. Such cases indicated that the environment was desert steppe and fixed dunes, which was pleasant enough for people to live about 1,000 years ago. The present shifting dunes appeared no more earlier than the Tang Dynasty. Deducing from the north boundary of potsherd distributing, sand desert had spread southwardly about 1 km in the past 1,000 years.

Observed from an ancient path relic, there was "Camel Path" in the northern Mulei and the "Tang Dynasty Path" at the south edge of Qitai, Jisaer, Fukang, and Changjitian. There was the Haoshu Town relic of the Tang Dynasty in the desert edge of northern Qitai County, the circumambience is farmland. The Akemulala Beacon Tower relic is located on the "Tang Dynasty Road" which is located over 10 km westward from the Xiquan Farm of Fukang County. The terrain is broad with some brushy dunes scattered around the beacon tower. The dunes had been activated and moved southwardly around Donghu Village, Fukang County. Partial sects had exceeded the "Tang Dynasty Road" over the past 50 years. A poet who was in Qianlong age of the Qing Dynasty described the Tang Dynasty Road as "Seeing the pavilions at bottom land growing Haloxylones, green is upon all the trunks and branches" and "Tender tamarisks together with sand upon land bottom, why the colour like the red glow". But now the trunk of Haloxylones reduced largely at the desert edge, local people called the temporary assarts "Chuang Tian" far from their habitation which usually were arid fields relying on precipitation and natural fertilizer, and after one or two years of cultivation they would be discarded, resulting in aeolian desertification.

In the northern Qitai and Jimusar, the Huihu Road went across the Gurbantünggüt Desert from south to north in the Tang Dynasty. In 1,221 AD, the Yuan Dynasty, Changchun Zhenren called the desert as "Sand Top" in his *Western Travel Notes*. He described the sandy desert as "it is over hundred *li* from south to north, it is broad from west to east". Anyone who wanted to go through the sand desert must "hurry on with his journey night and day; if the weather is bad, the people and horses will be exhausted". He reined six horses and "Go through over one hundred sand ridges, like a boat sailing in the billow." Until going out of the sand desert and reaching the front of the Beitinggu City in Jimusar, did he meet axmen. The fact that he could walk through over one hundred sand ridges indicated that the vegetation was good and the extent of fixed sand desert was large at that time. Then after 600 years, during the time of Jiaqing (1796–1820 AD) in the Qing Dynasty, Li Luanxuan went to Jitaidao from Qitai northwardly. At that time, the desert was "There is no grass and trees on the mountain and blown sand prevails". He also experienced perplexed complexion "sand is deep enough for horse to immerse, stone is too flinty and can destroy wheel" near the Dishuiya Desert. Obviously, the desert had been activated at that time, and the blown sand movement and new sand deposits obstructed carriages passing. At the beginning of the 1920s, an investigation team once went to Dishuiquan from the Beidao Bridge of Qitai County by passing through the desert by bus. The condition was that the width of activation zone of semi-fixed dunes was 10 km, and the desert moved and seriously obstructed the bus from getting across. The dune activation situation was very evident and the harm of aeolian desertification was aggravated.

The southern edge of sand desert lies in the west of Wusu County, the southeastern Aibi Lake and northern Jinghe County. There were shifting dunes when Changchun Zhenren visited in 1221 AD.The condition was "Go by sand desert, fine sand will be blown off by wind. They assembles or disperses suddenly like terrifying waves. There is no grass or trees. Horses obstructed and carriages were immersed, after one day he went out". In 1821 AD, Xujian described in note *rivers in northwestern China* "the sandy field scope is from Jinghe to Tuoduoke, deposited sand has turned to sandy hills and it is hard to walk". According to his description, the height of sand dunes increased a bit. In May of 1917, Xiebing arrived at Shaquanyi (eastern Jinghe County), and described that "the shifting sand deposited as high as a wall"around the Longwang Temple with a distance of 40 km to Jinghe. From 1821 to 1917, the active dunes enhanced obviously.

12.1.3 Present desert

The present environment of the Gurbantünggüt Desert has been investigated since the 1920s, especially since the 1950s, by the general investigation of the Gurbantünggüt Desert by CAS Sand-control Team. They thought that the sand desert was fixed or semi-fixed. The precipitation was ample in 1958; the vegetation categories were abundant. They were both in the middle Asian shrub-coppice deserts and central Asian deserts. Therefore, the conclusion acquired in the investigation was that there was no shifting dunes and only small communities of ephemeral foliage. From then on, a lot of scholars have investigated the geographical environment, foliage community and land resources.

Huang Peiyou (1988), Wei Wenshou (2000) analyzed and reconstructed the sequences of climate and precipitation, and discovered that the climate of desert regions in Northern Xinjiang not only varied with the long term climatic changes, but also with the short-period climatic undulations. For example, after the arid stage in the 1960s, the temperature and precipitation were quite normal until the end of the 1980s when the temperature ascended obviously. Seen from the simple linear regression equation, the temperature ascended distinctly and precipitation increased slightly, but the humidity index declined because of the increase of evaporation quantity, which made the aeolian desertification spread.

In order to reasonably and practically estimate the response of the desert environment to climate changes, analysis with satellites images and climate changes were conducted. Satellites images from 1975, 1976 and 1991–1993 were selected, and the climate changes sequence of 1975–1993 was selected to represent the period of time in sand desert changes. Before 1975, northern Xinjiang was in a cold and arid period, especially in 1974, the precipitation had reached the lowest since there was observation data. The temperature fluctuated below the average line since 1969 which was the year with lowest temperatures. Both temperature and precipitation increased gradually after 1975, up to 1999 the short-period warm and arid condition continued.

According to analysis of satellites images, the Gurbantünggüt Desert area increased a bit during 1975–1991. The spread region of aeolian desertification mainly were at the eastern and western edges of Akekum, southwestern edge of Kuobubei and southern edge of Dezuosuotengailisong (Huang Chunchang, 2000). The aeolian desertification was developing prominently due to human impact in the southern edge of Dezuosuotengailisong, and formed shifting sand zones. But seen from the satellite images, the edge was quite clear. The major cause was that the speed of desert advance slowed down because the local climatic condition and environment limited the dynamical factors of desert movement after shifting dunes went into the resident places. On the other hand, people prevented and controlled the expansion of deserts by means of biological and engineering measures around resident area. In the Kuobubei Desert and the Akekumu Desert, the spread process of aeolian desertification is related to the the surface saud materials and local climate, especially it is affected by the local strong wind and denudation. On the southeastern edge of the Gurbantünggüt Desert, climate changes influenced the desert principally, because the dominating land type was salin-sodic, and the living conditions were poor and hard, the influence of human is trivial. For example, on the eastern edge of Akekumu and in the north of Sanquanzi, dunes and sandy lands had been activated because of the reduction in precipitation in arid and hot summer, and snow in winter, resulting in reduction of vegetation cover. On the other hand, owing to the influence of topography and local circumfluence, together with the former mentioned processes, aeolian erosion was strengthened and made some unstable dunes or lands reactivated.

The present environment changes in the Gurbantünggüt Desert are obviously a response to climate changes. The Kuobubei Desert in the north of Cainan Oil Field and the inter-place between the Akekumu Desert and the Dezuosuotengailisong Desert has formed the zonal crescent shifting dunes.

The Suobugurbugelai Desert has an obvious aeolian desertification trend since the 1940s. In its developing process, firstly the vegetation reduced, the sandy vegetation species simplified, secondly the *P.euphratica* Olivier seared, dunes became activated because of wind erosion processes on their windward slopes. In the southwest of the Kuobubei Desert and the Akekumu Desert, local desert boundary had clearly spread southwardly. Accordingly, as seen from the changes of desert conditions in the above regions, the factors directly affected by humans were less. Peculiarly in the southwest of Kuobubei and Akekumu and the inter-place between the Akekumu Desert and the Dezuosuotengailisong Desert, people hardly affected them, but the aeolian desertification continued to develop. Arid climate's impact on sand desert happens not only in the Gurbantünggüt Desert but also in southern Sahara edge. After the 1960s, the successive reduction of precipitation was the most serious since the 20th century. Both in China and in the world, aridization and aeolian desertification was increasingly serious and their area expanded in some regions, which happened just when the temperature turned relatively cold in the northern hemisphere.The cases were only obviously represented in the fixed and semi-fixed deserts and glacial areas. The normal and inverse process fluctuation of the Gurbantünggüt really reflected the natural environment changes, especially the climate changes in time and space. Therefore, natural climate changes determined the sandy desert environment changes and land aeolian desertification in the oasis fringe. The response process of sandy desert to climate changes reflected the sensitivity and hysteresis of arid climate accumulation. Of course, in arid climate conditions, the human economic activation, especially in oasis fringes, accelerated the aeolian desertification process.

The boundary of the Gurbantünggüt Desert spread continuously, which was manifested by the record in the beginning of the 20th century. According to the analysis of historical climate changes and desert evolution, together with the response of present period climate changes to the desert development process, climate played an important role in the activation of dunes or sand lands at the edge of desert and reduction of vegetation coverage. The response of desert to climate change can be proved in the Gurbantünggüt Desert. In changes in the northern edge of the desert, the influence of chopping, assarting and grazing was little, which made the environment remain aboriginal. The main reason caused the sand dune or sandy lands activate was the strengthening of wind erosion because of climate change, the a decline in the groundwater table, drying up of salina and perishing of sandy land vegetation. For example in the activation zone of northern Sangequan, the eastern zone was activated dune and the western zone was activated sandy land. On the eastern edge of the Akekumu, due to the arid climate,the groundwater replenishment quantity infiltrating from the Beita Mountains and the Altai Mountains to the basin was reduced, making the fount and swamp area decreased abruptly. The local northeast wind because of topographical channelling caused by the Beita Mt and the Altai Mt, and the obstruction of the Meilir Mountains result in strong wind erosion and the Yardan Physiognomy in the northern Meilir Mt, the southern Uulungur River and then eastern edge of the Akekumu Desert.

The contrast of the warm or cold stage and distribution of humidity index in the historical and present climate indicate that the same dynamical mechanism made the climate and environment change and let the shifting sand spread continuously, namely the climate aridization and aeolian desertification developed synchronously. The fact that climate process led to aeolian desertification can not be doubted in the coupling process of local arid or humid changes and global thermal condition varies in the long- or short-term. The sandy desert was the peculiar outcome in the global climate change process, by responding to the arid and humid or warm and cold climate changes, as well as sensitive area for arid climate changes. If seen from the global climate change macroscopically, climate change is influenced not only by environment changes from earth's exterior, but also by the aggregate operation among earth's five spheres adding the local condition change. If seen from the sandy desert region microcosmicly, when climate environment turn to humid stage, regional sandy desert would respond obviously and improve along with it. Consequently, while climate changes in global scale, sandy desert environment actively responds and improves itself. At the same time, sandy desert environments directly influences global changes.

In other words, a lot of sects on the southern edge of Gurbantünggüt were "lake with reed broad to fringe of sky, mud with deep water" in history, and flourished by *tamarisks, haloxylons, P.euphratica Olivier*, dominated by fixed and semi-fixed dunes. By the end of the 1950s, this type of desert accounted for 97% of the total Gurbantünggüt Desert. Up to the 1990s, the shifting sand area exceeded 8%. The cause was the frequent anthropogenic activity that destroyed the vegetation, which caused dune activation and severe land desertification. In arid regions, such cases occur not only around the oasis, but also in regions with fixed and semi-fixed dunes. For example ,in Manasi, Mosuowan and Xiayedi on the southwest edge of the Gurbantünggüt Desert, the width of dune activation belt increased from 1–2 km to 5–10 km. There is already 33 km^2 farmland that was threatened in Mosuowan. This activation zone ranges 350 km from Changji, Miquan, Fukang, Jimusar, Northern Qitai, and to northern Mulei easterly and westerly. Moreover, in the zone between the southeastern Anannuor Lake lying in the lower reach of the Manasi River and the big salt lake lying in the northwestern Gurbantünggüt Desert, the dune activation was also very obvious. Shifting sand area had expanded to 28% in the 1990s from 5% in the 1950s. In the middle of the desert,shifting sand scattered because of oil field exploitation and road construction.

12.1.4 The future changing trend of the desert environment

Climate has changed greatly throughout history, experiencing both cold glacial time and warm interglacial periods. But present evidence is insufficient to conclude whether the current weather will become cold or warm over the long term (Ding , 1997). Analyzing small fluctuations indicate that climate remains turning to warm, but we are not sure whether this change is controlled by natural variations, or led by the earth's surface atmosphere temperature increase due to anthropogenic influence and the increase of greenhouse gas since industrialization. The process is related to both interstellar influence and many factors such as aerosphere, hydrosphere, biosphere, lithosphere and cryosphere. Because there are many uncertainties in these factors, we also have many uncertainties to evaluate the global temperature increase. Consequently, there are two sorts of views on the present climate change factors and the future climate change trend. IPCC (1996) estimate that by 2030 the greenhouse gas concentration will be double that before industrialization. According to ocean-atmosphere model contrast by Washington and Meehl, if CO_2 increases by 1% per year, 30 years later, the temperature would increase 0.7 °C, if CO_2 doubles, the temperature will increase by 1.6°C annually. Using GIS model, Rind et al.(1999) concluded that the CO_2 would double in troposphere and stratosphere. And the surface temperature of sea would rise along with the increase of CO_2 concentration. Temperature rise caused by doubled CO_2 will happen in troposphere and in stratosphere temperature will decline which lead to the reduction of atmosphere atatic stability. Additionally, several people consider that interstellar and the five spheres cooperation affects global climate change. Anthropogenic influence is not necessarily the major factor affecting climate change but disturb the process of temperature increases and decreases. Along with global climate changes, precipitation and land drought or humidity condition change, too. Because of reduction in temperature gradient in longitude, atmosphere circumfluence and vapor transportation intensity from ocean to continent were weakened, leading to soil humidity reduction in the middle latitude continent and increase of precipitation and water runoff in high-latitude-continent. According to drought or humidity distribution in future climate conditions advanced by American meteorologist Kellogg, America, Canada, eastern Europe or Russia and central Asia will become noticeably, but Africa, India,the eastern coastland of southern China, Japan and Australia will become evidently wet. After that, Manabe and Wetherald (1975) studied the climate and CO_2 increase through a simple numerical circumfluence model, and concluded that earth surface reflection would reduce and evaporation capability would increase due to the melting of glacial and snow after temperature rises. Therefore, they acquired that the evaporation would increase in Russia and central Asia in 2025 according to synthesis of future temperature and radiance balance. Wei Wenshou considers that the climate in Xinjiang is controlled by westerly belt, representing the Mediterranean climate in Northern Xinjiang, its changing from aridity-humidity to cold - warm is not consistent with the climate changes in summer monsoon regions in China. Consequently, climate changes in Xinjiang had formed an individual unit in China. It also influence the fluctuation of summer monsoon is north boundary of eastern China and inverse development of the Gurbantünggüt Desert.

According to climate changes trend simulated by climate model in the IPCC's report, the atmosphere temperature would increase 1–3.5 °C from the 1990s to 2100 (Ren, 1997). All the predicted increasing rate of average temperature are bigger than that over the last 10,000 years. They predicted that global temperature would turn to warm according to the northern hemisphere temperature change, mean relative macula volume of solar activation period, revolution radius change on midwinter day when gigantic planet converges in the earth's core, and earth rotation speed etc. They also indicated that the northern hemisphere's climate would enter into a relatively cold period and then return back to be warm by 2020. At the beginning of the 22 century it may warm up rapidly. To China and Xinjiang even the Gurbantünggüt Desert, climate change trends follow that of the northern hemisphere. The climate fluctuation is the natural factor of aridization and aeolian desertification (Zhu, 1999). Over the past 30 years, because of human and nature influences, in desert regions in northern China, especially northwest regions, precipitation increased slightly, but the rapid increase of temperature increased evaporation, and reduced the humidity index. The aeolian desertification area expanded continuously. In the last 35 years (1960–1994), desert in China increased slowly (Dong et al., 1990). The desert and sandy land area in Xinjiang has reached 420,000 km^2 and the Gurbantünggüt Desert suffered from desertification in the same way. According to above-mentioned development trend, these deserts will face more rigorous aridization challenge.

The sandy desert changes in China are influenced by climate change, especially the East Asia monsoon affects not only the climate change of drought or waterlogging and cold or warm of the eastern China, but also the normal and inverse development of northern desert region environment (Gao et al., 1993). Along with climate fluctuations, desert changes in a normal and inverse alternating way. Climate changes in large scale determine the aeolian desertification processes and variations of sand desert modality and boundary. The small scale climate fluctuation will lead to changes of sandy desert environment and drought or humidity. Many studies have indicated that climate fluctuation would cause the sandy desert to spread or shrink in geologic time. But in the anthropic history, the spread or shrinking of sandy desert and alternative process of activation or natural fixed are caused not only by climate fluctuation, but also human activities and the social development. Along with economic development and the recognization of human effect, active measures have been taken to mitigate desertification.

Although the Gurbantünggüt Desert was formed early, but during every abrupt changes in the environment and climate, it experienced fixed-mobile-fixed evolution process, and belongs to the Mediterranean climate type. Especially in the period of modern desert evolution, this region is controlled by the westerly and the influences of the Pacific summer monsoon is weak. Besides, the sandy desert lacustrine sediment was not the result of monsoon operation before 18 ka, a fact proved by the lack of paleosol in the Taklimakan Desert.

Because of climate warming, humidity index reductions in arid regions and anthropic impact, the effect of aeolian desertification on the environment, economy and society is increasing. The environmental problems of the Taklimakan Desert has drawn global attention in earth science field. Peculiarly the deterioration of environment and lack of water resource are increasingly, affecting the human living condition. The Lop Nur and the Manasi River have dried up, the Tarim River has been discontinued, and the Taiterma Lake and the Ebinur Lake are drying up. This environmental deterioration and aeolian desertification present the West Construction Project important task of environmental protection. Consequently, society development need an evaluate on present and a forecast for future.

12.2 Taklimakan Desert

The Tarim Basin is the largest inland basin and encompasses the biggest sand desert in China. The Taklimakan Desert, lying in the center of the basin, is one of the most famous deserts in the world . Its area accounts for over half of desert area in China. Its expansion, roominess and mysteries have drawn many Chinese and foreign scholars, attention. But the environment is so severe that is difficult to be explored, which makes it a region least known on the earth. The word "Taklimakan" comes from Uigur, and its original meaning has been lost.Today it is usually explained as "If you go in,you will not come out". Swedish explorer Sven Hedin called it "Death Sea", after his experience of barely escaping with his life from the desert, and this has been used until now.

12.2.1 General description

12.2.1.1 Review of history

Literature on the Tarim Desert can be traced back to 2,000 years ago and was recorded in classical literature, such as *Yu Tribute* , *The Classic of Mountains and Seas·Xicierjing*, *The Classic of Mountains and Seas·Haineigongjing*, *Historical Records* in the Han Dynasty, *Hanshu Xiyu Biography Faxian biography* in the Jin Dynasty, *Da Tang Xiyu Recordation* in the Tang Dynasty and *Xiyu Shuidao Recordation* in the Qing Dynasty etc. Marco Polo described the desert in his travel notes. From the late 19 century to the first half of the 20th century, explorers and scholars in China and abroad investigated and explored the Taklimakan Desert and its surrounding regions. Stein and Sven Hedin had written many archaeological reports and literatures, and Huang Wenbi had written *Archaeology Recordation in the Tarim Desert*. They provided full and accurate historical and geographical data to study the Taklimakan Desert.

Comprehensive investigations on the Tarim Basin were carried out after the reunification of China. Since the 1950s, several investigations had been organized, such as the"Synthesis Investigation to the Taklimakan Desert" (1950–1960), "Lop Nur Science Investigation" (1980, 1981), "Agriculture Natural Resources Synthesis Inquisition in the Tarim River and Branches of the Hotan River and the Yerqiang River" (1982–1984), "Resource and Environment Remote Sensing Investigation on Both Sides of Tarim River"(1984–1988), "Synthesis Scientific Investigation of the Taklimakan Desert (the Second Time)"(1887–1990), "Chinese and Japanese Explanation for the Aeolian Desertification Form Mechanism" (1990–1994), "Remote Sensing Investigation of San Bei Shelter Belt" (Xinjiang part)(1987–1990). These investigations and researches analysed and studied the resource, environment and anthropogenic activity in the Tarim Basin in various aspects and different ways. A series of disquisition and monographs had been published, providing abundant information to recognize and study the Taklimakan Desert.

12.2.1.2　Summary of natural geography

The Tarim Desert lies between the Tianshan and the Kunlun Mountains in the center of the Eurasian continent and located far from the ocean. It is a closed inland basin, except for the wind gap in the eastern side; the other three sides are all surrounded by high mountains with a height of over 4,000 m. The south is the Qinghai–Tibet Plateau, the southwest is the Pamirs Plateau, the north and northwest is the Tianshan Mountains. The Tarim Basin inclines from southwest to northeast. Its south and southwest edges are 1,400–1,500 m high, and the northwest and northeast is 1,000–1,200 m high. The lowest place is the Lop Nur with a height of 780 m. The whole basin looks like an anomalous rhombus with a length of 1,425 km from west to east, a width of 810 km from south to north, and with an area of 542,200 km². The Taklimakan Desert which lies in the center of the basin has an area of 337,600 km², (E77°–90°, N37°–41°). It is the largest desert in China and the second largest sandy desert in the world (Fig. 12-2).

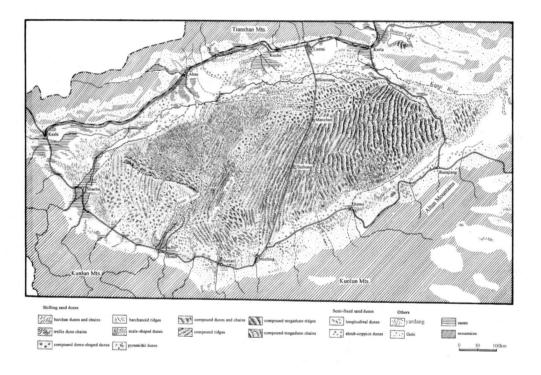

Fig. 12-2　Landforms in the Taklimakan Desert

The arid environment of the Tarim Basin can be traced back to the Cretaceous Period, but the arid sandy desert environment did not begin until the end of the Tertiary and formed at the beginning of the Quaternary. With the uplift of the Qinghai-Tibet Plateau, a lot of mountains around the Tarim Basin uplifted gradually, which intensifies the aridization. In the Early Pleistocene, blown sand started to appear in the east when strong wind occured. At the end of the Middle Pleistocene, a lot of sandy lands appeared (Zhou , 1982). In the Later Pleistocene, the Taklimakan Desert had a big size scale, but it formed and developed widely since the Middle Pleistocene (Zhu, 1981). As the Qinghai-Tibet Plateau and its surrounding mountainous uplifted continuously, the arid intensity of the Tarim Basin strengthened. In the whole Holocene it had an extremely arid environment, characterized by alternating cold and warm periods. The climate was very arid, with annual precipitation about 15–16 cm, and an aridity index over 20. In addition, the frequent strong wind made the ground surface even more arid. Water vapor in the Tarim Basin is imported from exterior (Xia et al., 1993). It includes: ① the westerly airflow; ② the cold airflow moving southwardly from north; ③ the southeast monsoon formed by subtropical high pressure that drive the air mass moving northwardly, and form precipitation after entering into basin; ④ the airflow crossing the Qinghai-Tibet Plateau and going down into the basin from the southeast or southwest, bringing precipitation in summer (Fig. 12-3). However, these water vapors only form a small quantity of precipitation at the edges of the basin, with little precipitation in the center of the basin. The desert gets most of its water from bigger rivers originating in the surrounding mountain region.

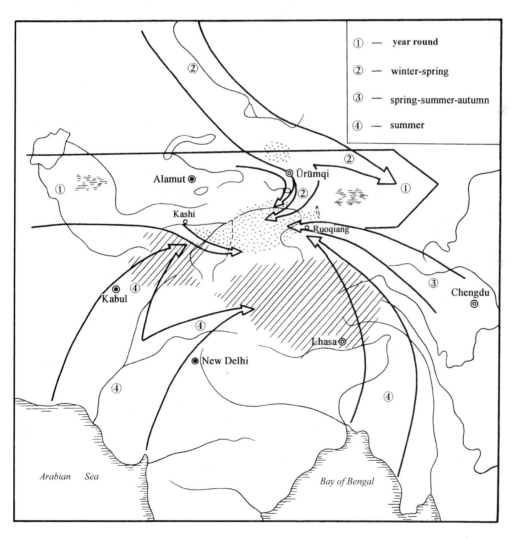

Fig. 12-3   Pathway of water vapor into the Tarim Basin

In the basin, the isotherm distributed annularly with the desert as the center because of surrounding alps. Mean annual temperature is about 10–12℃, the mean temperature of January and July is –5.6– –8.7℃ and 24.8–27.4℃, respectively: The western and southwestern regions of the basin are controlled by the westerly from the Pamir; the eastern region is controlled by northeast wind pouring into the basin from the northeast gap forming airflow convergent field in high-altitude at 82°–85°E.

All water systems coming from the Tianshan, the northern Kunlun Mountains and the Kala Kunlun Mountains converge into the basin (Fig. 12-4). The total runoff is 392.69×10^8 m³. The northern water system includes the Kashger River, the Aksu River,the Weigan River, the Dina River, the Kaidu River, the Tarim River and others with a total runoff as much as 222.79×10^8 m³. The mainstream of the southern water system mainly includes the Hotian River, the Keriya River, and the Qarqan River, which includes the Pishan River,the Qira River,the Niya River etc. The runoff quantity is 87×10^8 m³.

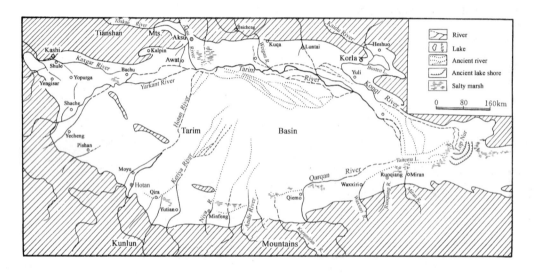

Fig. 12-4   Distribution of the hydrographical system in the Tarim Basin

The zonal soil type of the Tarim Basin is brown desert soil. The main non-zonal soil type is aeolian sand soil, saline soil, oasis albic soil etc, which can be classified into four regions: A. The brown desert soil and oasis albic soil region in northern plain and intermountain basin. In the west and north edges, the main soil type are brown desert soil, saline soil, oasis albic soil and humid soil; meadow soil, and blown sand soil occupies a bigger area. B. Gypsum saline brown desert soil and oasis albic soil regions in the southern plain: distributes on the south edge and the soil type is similar to that of the northern edge except that takyr soil are semi-developed, oasis albic soil and humidity soil area is small. C. Lop Nur plain Salina region: distributed in the eastern desert, the main soil is blown sand soil and salt soil. D. Taklimakan blown sand soil region: distributed widely in the desert and the soil develops weakly; only on the bank of desert river can meadow soil, salt soil be seen.

In the Taklimakan desert there are 22 families, 57 geniuses and 80 species of plants. The characteristics of vegetation is spare category, simple community structure, extremely low coverage, and vast bald sterile lands. The extremely arid climate determines that most vegetation can endure aridity, salina, leanness and aeolian sand. Riverside woods and meadow are mainly *P. enphratica Olivier, P. cathayana Dode*.

In the formation and evolution process of the Tarim Desert, all natural factors including physiognomy, climate, soil, hydrology and biology have individual roles, but they also influence each other and form a unitive and synthetically natural geologic process.

12.2.2 The formation and evolution of the desert

12.2.2.1 New tectonic movement and paleogeographical outline

The formation and evolution of the Taklimakan Desert is related to the tectonic movement and paleo-geographical modality. The India Block and Eurasia have intensively collided since the late Tertiary. From then on, the Qinghai-Tibet Plateau including the Kunlun Mountains, the Parims, the Altun Mountains and the Tianshan Mountains uplifted obviously, the Tarim Bay disappeared and the basin formed. after the basin was formed, alps around the basin blocked the periphery humid airflow reaching the basin. At the same time, the airflow sunk into the Tarim Basin from around mountainous regions has a foehn effect, which made air in the basin extremely dry. In addition the basin topography resulted in weathering materials from surrounding mountainous regions transported and deposited in the central section, providing abundant material for the sandy desert. Thus the Taklimakan Desert formed and developed.

1) Tectonic base of paleogeographical outline in the Quaternary.

The palaeo-geography figure in the Quaternary was formed via new tectonic movement developed on the basis of old tectonic. The Tarim movement in the Proterozoic Era finished the development of Tarim geosynclines, and formed the Tarim platform which was different from its northern and southern edges. Hercynian movement ended in Permian established the main geological construct pattern in Tarim area which includes, the central rising; the northeast and southwest subsidence which formed three construct units, and other sub-structure parts and ruptures (Fig. 12-5). With the returning of the south and north geosynclines, the Kurktage, Keping, Tieganlike and the Altun Mountains terrains, which lie on the edge of the terra, were uplifted. During the entire Mesozoic, the tensile stress was dominant which formed normal faults and the basin sunk in the fringe regions of the mountains. Over this course the Yanshan Movement was more assuasive, causing the basin to decend in the west part and uplift in the east part, which led to the Tethyan water inflooded into the southwest region from the Entrance of Alayi Strait in the Later Cretaceous. Other regions of the basin were terrigenous red sediment regions or denudation regions. In the later Oligocene, the Himalayan Movement caused the Alaiyi Strait uplift. At the same time, the surrounding geosynclines were activated and started to rise, and they were surrounded by two groups of deep and big ruptures in northeast and northwest directions. After the subsiding of the whole tectonic,the Tarim region began to evolve into a unitive inland basin, consisting of three tectonic regions: the periphery, the edge and the interior, while the other areas were some small tectonic regions. They corresponded to deep tectonic. The way of their distribution and movement not only controlled the sediment distribution, type and cover stratum distortion, but also influenced the development and evolution of tectonic physiognomy in the basin. New tectonic movements are happening on the base of this conformation.

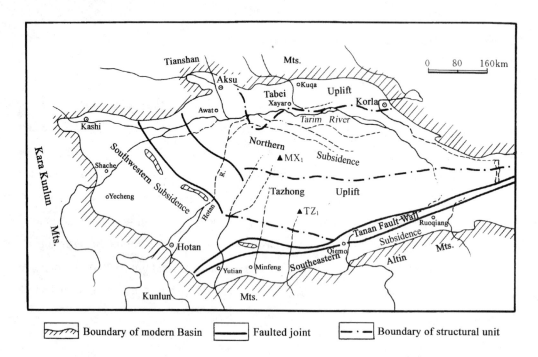

Fig. 12-5 Geological structure of the Tarim Basin (Mu Guijin, 1994)

2) New tectonic movement and evolution of the basin physiognomy.

Since the end of the Pliocene Period,the Qinghai-Tibet Plateau,the Tarim Basin and the whole of western China came into an intense phase of tectonic movement.The Qinghai-Tibet Plateau and the Tianshan Mountains began to uplift rapidly, and the Tarim Basin formed. New tectonic movement played a decisive role in the formation and evolution of all main physiognomy in the basin.

Tectonic movement was not fierce in the Mesozoic and the early Tertiary,and the topography difference between the Tarim Basin and peripheral region was minimal.The sedimentation center was in some unattached small basins such as southwest and Kuqa subsidence regions. Apophysis of the central Tarim part was low massif and denudation regions. The Yanshan Movement in the Late Cretaceous enlarged the basin range, and sea water once rushed into Kuqa subsidence region, and the denudation range correspondingly shrank. The abundance of gypsum layers and lack of organism in the sediment reflected that the climate was arid in the early Tertiary (Dong et al., 1995b). Thereafter, the whole Tarim Basin subsided, but because of the limitation of the Qinghai-Tibet Plateau and the Tianshan mountain uplift in the late Tertiary, the Tarim Basin appeared as a shallow and glacis basin initially and the regional climate was not influenced by the peripheral terrain but by the planet climatic belt. The physiognomy units had showed rudiment.

Since the early Pleistocene, as experienced since 3.0 Ma BP, the Qinghai-Tibet Plateau uplifted obviously, and the Xiyu formation of conglomerate widely accumulated in front of mountain regions and distributed zonally surrounding the whole basin. The apophysis of the Qinghai-Tibet Plateau was not high enough to block the humid airflow from coming in, so the network of river is denser than now. The water converged mainly to the subsidence region in front of the mountains, and the dune distribution range and the scale was far smaller than now.

In the early and middle Pleistocene, the extrusion stress intensified, the mountainous region around the basin uplifted rapidly,and the basin outline was much more evident. The general trend of the basin terrain established at that time was high in the west and low in the east. Strong extrusion resulted in return of subsidence region in front of mountain and the basin reduced. Deposits of piedmont were no longer distributed zonally. Influenced by the new tectonic movement, the former sunkage regions in front of the mountains disappeared, water system in the basin basically stablized after adjusting. The vertical shear from anaphase uplift movement, formed scalar form terra. The Tarim River was formed under the control of Avati subsidies fractured block and Luntai-Yuli fractured block. From then on, the basin water system converged and flew eastwardly. In the basin blown sand physiognomy gained adequate development, with oasis appearing only along the river.

In the Later Pleistocene and Holocene, the basin physiognomy did not change substantially. All kinds of case-hardened physiognomies such as rivers, lakes, blown sand physiognomy were continuously developing. Environmental effects of the Qinghai-Tibet Plateau on the Tarim Basin stabilized. The surface of piedmont and the Mazatage Mountains in the basin uplifted ulteriorly, while the Lop Nur River, the lower reach of the Qarqan River and the middle reach of the Tarim River slowly subsided. Other stable regions that fluviation can not reach developed into main part of the desert in the basin. Uplift of the surrounding-mountains deepened the basin day by day. Extra moisture was hard to come into, and the basin became arid continuously. The fluviation weakened, and blown sand and loess physiognomy expanded collectively.

About the formation age and development process of the Taklimakan Desert, some thought it was formed in the middle Pleistocene on a large scale (Xinjiang Ecology and Geography Institute, China Academy, 1986), and developed on the dry delta, alluvial plain and slope plain in front of mountain. Modern desert developed on the base of the middle Pleistocene. Also there were other views. According to macroscopical research on middle Asia, some earlier scholars thought that modern desert began to form in the later Quaternary, overlaying on the lacustrine sediment which widely developed in the earlier Tarim Basin. Zhou Tingru thought the desert had widely developed since the beginning of the Quaternary, and the compound crescent dunes in desert center were ancient aeolian physiognomy factors (Zhou Tingru, 1963, 1964). Since the 1980s, some scholars deduced that the Taklimakan Desert formed in the Miocene or new Tertiary by sludging ancient blown sand exposing in apophysis region and ambient mountainous regions (Liu et al., 1959; Dong et al., 1991). Based on more and more new discoveries about the desert formation age, augment of dating data and improvement of precision, and the increase of section density of underlying layers in the desert, comprehensive and further cognition would be achieved.

12.2.2.2　Arid climate and evolution of desert

1) Formation of arid climate

Shortage of rain was necessary for desert formation. At the global scale, climate aridity is related to latitude and circumfluence. The region between 15°–35° in southern or northern hemisphere where subtropical high lies is the aridity region on the earth. Under the control of subtropical high the atmosphere is stable, humidity is low, and clouds are scarce. The Taklimakan Desert lies in the temperate zone of 36°30′–41°36′, its arid climate moved northwardly under the influence of the distribution of sea and continent and topography, but it is also affected by circumfluence.

There are abundant evidence of lithology and biology to indicate that the arid environment appeared as early as the Cretaceous Period in the Tarim Basin (Zhou , 1963, 1964; Liu et al., 1959). In the early Tertiary, the Chinese climate was controlled by a planetary wind system. Because the polar position was different, at that time the Tarim Basin was controlled by a subtropical high pressure zone. The climate was arid and hot. In the middle Tertiary, strong lithosphere movement happened, the Paleo-Mediterranean Sea disappeared and Eurasia joined together. Due to the difference of thermal conditions between the sea and continent, monsoon circumfluence condition in eastern Asia was established. The height of the Qinghai-Tibet Plateau was only about 1000 m in the early Pliocene, and can not influence the planetary wind system circumfluence condition significantly. At the end of the Pliocene and beginning of Pleistocene, new tectonic movement was intense and the Qinghai-Tibet Plateau uplifted in a large scale, which disturbed the phases of dominating wind system of planet, and redistributed the climatic belt. The uplift of the Qinghai-Tibet Plateau, Tianshan Mountains and other periphery mountainous regions affected this region as follows: cold high-pressure were aroused by invading cold air masses from polar regions and moved southwardly to Mongolia-Siberia in winter or glacial periods, and was intensified and expanded, which led to a chill, desiccated and windy climate; In summer or inter-glacial periods, the Mongolian high-pressure retreated northwardly with the westerly mainstream lying above this region. Vapor was mostly dropped on windward slope of middle Asian mountain before the westerly arrived at this region, and flow is anticyclone. Terrain friction when passing the north edge of the plateau.Moreover, the region is affected by engender warm low-pressure over the plateau and the superficial warm low-pressure in the desert, which results in an extreme dry and hot climate (Dong , 1995b).

In other words, the causes of arid climate and sandy desert were different during different periods. In the pre-Quaternary including the Cretaceous and Tertiary,arid climate was mainly related to the location of sub-tropic dynamical high-pressure zones. In the Quaternary and Holocene, arid climate formation and development was related to the southward movement of biologic climatic belt caused by the glacial and adjustment of atmosphere circumfluence due to thermo-dynamical and dynamical operation led by uplift of the Qinghai-Tibet Plateau and periphery mountainous regions, and it was a non-zonal desert (Dong, 1995b).

2) Desert evolution and climate change

The desert is the result of arid climate and its evolution was controlled by climate changes, especially arid and humid changes. Dong Guangrong et al. analyzed and researched the sediment faces, lithology and granularity, chemical elements, sporo-pollen, carbonates, organic materials, heavy minerals, clay minerals, geomagnetism information, dune lamination trend etc. and symbols of desert in normal and inverse process. They cataloged by time of the climate and desert changes in the region, discussed the basic characters, and pointed out that the climate and desert changes can be divided into two stages: A. In the pre-Quaternary, including the Cretaceous and Tertiary, temperature decreased gradually, but in general it was dry and hot tropic to sub-tropic savanna and desert steppe. The sandy desert was the "Red Desert" that was mainly fixed and sub-fixed sand dunes. B. In the Quaternary, the whole region lies in a warm temperate zone and middle-cold temperate arid desert steppe to extreme arid desert. The desert changed to a "Yellow Desert", where the shifting sand increased and expanded gradually. In the early and middle Pleistocene, it was relatively warmer and more humid and belonged to an arid desert steppe. Desert scattered and the scope was small. From the later part of the early Pleistocene to middle Pleistocene, the arid climate and desert dominated by shifting sand were basically set. Since the late Quaternary, regional climate became arid once again, and desert expanded correspondingly, ultimately forming now extreme arid desert physiognomy.

Compared with the eastern region in China, the warm and cold fluctuations of this region were coincidence with that in the eastern region, indicating the influence of global changes on this region, but the precipitation was less and it belonged to arid to extreme arid climate, with the temperature and humidity combination characterized by alternation of warm arid and cold arid (Dong , 1997). Accordingly desert changes in this region were characterized by alternative drift, expansion or stablization, shrinkage of sand, which was different from the instance that fixed or sub-fixed dune account for a large proportion. In most regions the desert developed in normal direction and flowing dunes were dominant, excepting regions near river , lake and water areas with elevated groundwater table where the desert developed in inverse direction and fixed or sub-fixed dunes can be seen. Ren Zhengqiu thought there existed relative arid and humid fluctuation after the formation of the large desert. At millennial time scales the dry-humid fluctuation is consistent with the warm and humid-cold and arid fluctuation showed by global changes, which is characterized by the increase or reduction of solar radiation in middle or high latitude regions related to the changes of earth's movement parameters—global warming (or cooling)—summer monsoon strengthening (or weakening)—precipitation increase (or decrease), and led to a relatively humid (or much more arid) climate in this region. (Ren , 1994), but the desert expansion happened in the period when climate changed to cold and arid. According to research of paleoclimate and paleo-environment, Li Baosheng et al. pointed out that because it was far from sea and surrounded by huge mountains, it can hardly cast off aridity even in the Holocene high temperature times, only in pattern of arid blown sand physiognomy there was humid climate environment in some regions and usually it was short. But Mu Guijin (Mu,1994) thought there were two important development stages for the Taklimakan Desert, respectively in the Late Pleistocene and the middle Holocene, during which the basic outline of present desert physiognomy formed, and further developed to modern desert gradually. All of these illuminated that the desert developed on the basis of plains with broad fluvial sediment and a plain covered by blown sand deposits (Mu , 1994).

3) The source and characteristics of the sandy desert deposit

Arid climate is necessary for desert formation, of which an abundant sand source is the substance basis. Zhu Zhengda et al. thought the main sand source of the Taklimakan Desert was gigantic thick loose alluvial sand layers of the Quaternary in the Tarim Basin.

As early as the Tertiary, the Tarim Basin was glacis. There were denudated hill in the basin center, only in the western basin; the hypsography of depressions in front of mountains was lower and received deposits composed of fine grains. New tectonic movement led to the Tarim Basin hypsography incline northeastern, thereby influencing water system distribution and sediment character in the basin. At the beginning of the Quaternary, the global climate changed and the glacial age arrived . The mountains around the basin were not high enough to block moisture, and precipitation including snowfall increased, large-scale glaciers developed and expanded. During interglacial period thawing water from ice and snow made abundant water quantity converge to numerous rivers. Weathered materials in the surrounding mountainous regions were carried to deposit in the basin and formed the ample delta and alluvial plain.

In spacious regions of west, middle and south Taklimakan, delta from ancient streams was extremely upgrowth. Analysis of field investigation, aerophotos and satellite images indicate that vestiges of old streams stretched from the edges 200–250 km into the hinterland of the present desert. For example, the old Keriya River water once inflooded northwardly into the Tarim River; old riverbed vestige of the Qarqan River showed that it once flooded into the Taklimakan Desert center in the Quaternary. According to the fan like arrangement of dry river bed in desert center, Wu Zheng et al. thought in the relatively humid time of Quaternary, rivers originating from the Kunlun Mountains supplied abundant ice water, together with the Keriya River and the Hotan River that lies in the west, the Niya River that lies in the east , the Andir River etc, fashioned a huge delta plain (Wu, 1997). According to the drilling record of Pishan, Moyu, Yutian etc. the sediments was mainly composed of gray fine and silt sand, which indicates the plain deposits is fluvial and alluvial.

The northern Taklimakan Desert is alluvial and pluvial fan deposits caused by many rivers that originated from the south piedmont of Tian Shan Mountains and alluvial plain deposits of the Tarim River. The width of the Tarim River reaches 130 km, due to the gradual northward movement of the Tarim River. The old riverbed of the Paleo-Tarim River stretches from west to east, its southern boundary can expand into the desert with a distance of 80–100 km to the present riverbed (near the 40°20′N). Physical detecting data showed that the thickness of the Quaternary layer of alluvial plain in the Tarim upriver was 400–500 m, and most components were fine sand. Silt and sandy clay were found within 70 m deep (Xinjiang Synthetic Investigation Team, China Academy, 1965).

It can be deduced that the sand of the Taklimakan Desert was not from the same source, but was formed by the subsiding sand deposit layer in each place rised by wind in the same place, which can be illuminated by the comparable mineral constitution of dune sand and subsiding sediment sand in the same place, and in addition to difference of dune sand in various regions. Based on the sand material composition, mineral component and distribution in space, the Taklimakan Desert sand grain mainly were fine sand and extremely fine sand, with mean granularity of 0.093 mm.The finest one was in Yecheng and Pishan of the desert southwest edge (mean granularity was 0.06–0.10 mm). It was coarser in Minfeng of the southern edge (the mean granularity was 0.14–0.18 mm), but it lied between the two grains in the Lop Nur of the eastern part (the mean granularity was 0.11–0.18 mm) (Wu , 1997). In the same region, it became finer from upriver to downriver lengthwise and   the material near the riverbed became coarser breadthwisely.

Dune sand of paleo-alluvial plain in the whole Tarim River basin was much finer than that of alluvial plain in the north fringe of the Kunlun Mountains. The mean size of sand in the north segment of the Tarim Desert Road was 0.083 mm. The mineral component is different from south and north region. The source of sand in the southern region was the fluvial sediment of the Kunlun Mountains and the Altun Mountains. Hornblende is dominant in the heavy minerals of both blown sand and fluvial sand (30.5%–53.1%), with mica, epidotic and metal minerals also abundant, and the compound of heavy mineral was same. In blown sand and fluvial sand of the Tarim River, hornblende content reduced, and mica was the main component (43.8%). In the Lop Nur region of the eastern desert, hornblende was dominant (38.2%–51.0%), but the mica content was also high (19.6%–41.5%). In the Kashi delta region of west, mineral component was complex as riverhead was from various mountainous areas.

Scientific investigations, in the Taklimakan Desert between 1987–1990 revealed that the mean size of dune sand was 0.121 mm, of which the most was ultra fine sand and accounted for 45%. The mean size of subsiding sediment sand was 0.093 mm and that of alluvial sand was 0.101 mm, which illuminated that the dune sand comes from near sites. That was to say, the fine sand was taken away by wind and left coarse sand which from the dune sand. The content of silt in dune sand indicate that dune had high maturity degree in the eastern hinterland of the desert, while dune sand along the river bank and on the Gobi plain belonged to immature sand. Qian Yibing et al. took hundreds of samples from the Taklimakan Desert systemically, and analyzed their mineral ingredients, chemical elements, microelements, single mineral chemical ingredient, mica oxygen isotope component, and base rock mineral component etc. (Fig. 12-6, Table 12-1, Table 12-2). The result indicates that the heavy minerals in sand samples are characterized by high concentrations of stable—ultra stable minerals of magnetite, hematite and garnet, with the lowest concentrations in the Hotan drainage area and southern edge while it was intervenient in the northern edge and desert hinterland. Unstable mineral content of hornblende or biotite was higher in the desert hinterland than southwestern edge and lower than Hotan drainage area. The ratio of quartz and feldspar concentrations was the lowest in the southern edge, the highest along river area, and intervenient in desert hinterland. The content of Al_2O_3, K_2O and Na_2O in dune sand was higher than that in fluvial sand, but the content of Fe_2O_3, MgO, MnO, CaO were relatively higher in fluvial sand. The Ba and Sr content were highest in dune sand, lowest in fluvial sand, and intervenient in underlying sand. Hornblende chemical components in dune sand and fluvial sand are very similar. $\delta^{18}O$ in sandy material had the characteristics of metamorphic quartz. The sandy material in desert hinterland especially the chemical element was closest to the mean value of the Taklimakan Desert. Above mentioned characteristics showed that at the desert edge the sandy material from local source, while hinterland desert took external sources and homogenized. The similarity of dune sand and fluvial sand indicates they are closely related. The dune sand experienced the following evolution processes: class of base rock (most was metamorphic rock) —paleo-fluvial sand—dune sand. Mu Guijin et al. thought the source of blown sand had a close relation with surrounding big water systems by analyzing the sediment granularity in the Taklimakan Desert. Most aeolian sand was fine sand and was stable sediment in various structural characteristics.

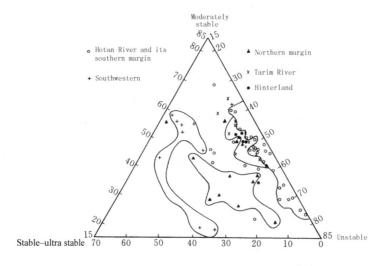

Fig. 12-6   Mineral composition of sand materials with different stabilities

Table 12-1 The quartz/feldspar ratio of the sandy material

Sampling area	Max	Min	Mean	N
Hotan River drainage area	1.94	0.65	1.26	28
Southwestern edge in desert	1.40	0.70	1.09	13
Northern edge of the desert	1.34	0.49	1.06	15
Tarim River drainage area	1.64	0.92	1.38	8
The desert hinterland	1.25	1.08	1.17	5

Table12-2 The main chemical component of sandy material (%)

Sampling area		Deposit type	Al_2O_3	Fe_2O_3	MnO	MgO	CaO	K_2O	Na_2O	TiO_2	P_2O_5	n
North margin of	Korla-Luntai-Aksu	Dune sand	11.03	2.01	0.06	1.03	5.77	3.33	2.48	0.72	0.19	4
desert		Fluvial sand	9.02	3.04	0.08	2.41	14.50	1.95	1.77	0.39	0.11	9
		River floodplain sand	11.83	2.71	0.06	1.92	7.37	2.85	2.52	0.32	0.12	4
Southwest margin of desert	Atushi-Kashi-Pishan	Dune sand	9.24	2.42	0.06	1.70	8.68	1.84	1.98	0.09	0.28	3
		Fluvial sand	8.49	3.13	0.08	1.72	9.02	1.58	1.55	0.38	0.11	12
		River floodplain sand	12.46	4.65	0.09	3.30	14.81	1.66	2.59	0.51	0.15	1
Hotan River and Keriya River		Dune sand	10.62	2.81	0.07	1.93	6.92	2.21	2.51	0.41	0.09	28
		Fluvial sand	11.15	3.49	0.08	2.07	7.09	2.30	2.33	0.45	0.13	13
		River floodplain sand and underlain sand	10.60	2.81	0.06	1.94	6.92	2.28	2.37	0.41	0.12	14
Hinterland of desert		Dune sand	9.82	2.18	0.05	1.65	7.83	2.23	2.34	0.33	0.08	7
		Fluvial sand	10.10	3.18	0.07	2.53	9.93	2.21	1.65	0.46	0.13	1
		Underlain sand	9.72	2.43	0.05	1.86	8.04	2.14	2.33	0.38	0.10	9
Average		Dune sand	10.18	2.36	0.06	1.58	7.30	2.40	2.33	0.39	0.16	
		Fluvial sand	9.69	3.21	0.08	2.18	10.13	2.01	1.83	0.42	0.12	
		River floodplain sand and underlain sand	11.15	3.15	0.07	2.26	9.27	2.23	2.45	0.41	0.12	

The mean size is related to material source characteristics, wind intensity, dune development history and dune position (Mu, 1990). Chen Weinan analyzed the sand granularity near the longitude of 84°E trans-Taklimakan, then concluded that dune sand was mainly ultra fine sand, with sand of 0.1–0.05 mm accounting for 60%–80%. The degree of sorting along the line of dune sand was low, which is related to both reparability degree of subsiding sandy material and the frequent sand movement with new component joined continuously. In the desert center, dune sand was well developed, but that was not good in edge region, which reflected that desert spread from the center to the periphery.

4) The changes of ancient water system in the Tarim Basin

The changes of the ancient water system in the Tarim Basin influenced the occurrence and evolution of the Taklimakan Desert. Physiognomy types under the desert, including diluvial and alluvial plain, dry delta and lacustrine plain etc., have a close inter-relation. On the other hand, because of lack of flow distance or changes of waterway, some natural oasis and paleo-artifical oasis disappeared and numerous lands were turned into sandy desert and some new oasis was formed at the same time.

In the Quaternary and human history, the Tarim Basin existed two colossal and interdependent water systems. One was the Tarim River water system in transmeridional, the other was the paleo-water system originating from the Kunlun Mountains and inflooding into desert hinterland northwardly in south-to-north direction (Fig. 12-7).

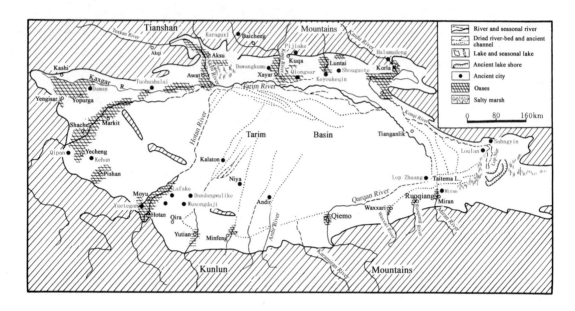

Fig. 12-7　Distribution map of ancient river-channels and oasis in the Tarim Basin

(1) The changes of water system in the Tarim Basin.

The Tarim River was a colossal hydrological network stream, the Kaxgar River, the Yerqiang River, the Hotan River; the Aksu River etc. all converged into the Tarim River. The Keriya River originated from the Kunlun Mountain, and the Kuqa River, the Weigan River and the Dina River originate from south piedmont of the Tianshan Mountains also once poured into the Tarim River. Flooded deposit of the Andi River once was carried to 39°52′N, 84°20′36″E, which was near to the paleo-Tarim River deposit region in the desert hinterland. The middle Tarim River moved frequently from south to north, and the extent reached 80–130 km. In the place 52 (south of Shaya) –111 km (south of Luntai) south of the present Tarim River bank, remains old stream of the paleo-Tarim River and *P.euphratica Olivier* still exists(Fig. 12-8). According to dating data of ^{14}C, the southeast of the paleo- Tarim River formed 1,000–5,000 years before.

Since the end of the Qing Dynasty, the Tarim River water system has degenerated rapidly. In recent 50 years, the degeneration is the worst. The Keriya River stopped flooding into the Tarim River 500–1,000 years ago, and the Kaxgar River, the Weigan River and the Dina River had disengaged from the Tarim River. By the end of 1970s to the beginning of the 1980s, the down stream of the Yerqiang River was in discontinuity condition. The quantity of river water inflooded into the Tarim River from Hotan reduced from 1,100–1,200 million m³/a in the past to 600–800 million m³/a in the 1980s. The

Peafowl River, the Tarim River had been in discontinuity condition, led to the disappearance of the Lop Nur and the Taitema Lake. The inevitable result was that aeolian desertification rapidly developed and spread in the Tarim River area. According to investigation, the Tarim River moved south to north in a width of 40 km in the southern Shaya, shifting sand area had increased from 15% to 82% (Zhu 1987). There was 1.5 km of riverbed in the end of the Tarim river which was entrenched by shifting dune. The Kulukekumu Desert and the Taklimakan Desert surrounded the "Green Corridor" in Tarim downriver.

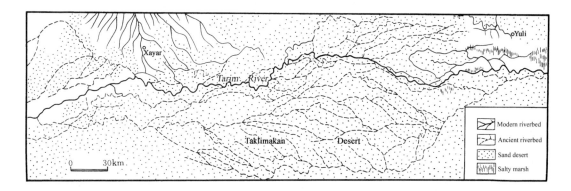

Fig. 12-8   Distribution of the paleo-Tarim River in the northern part of the Taklimakan Desert

The Lop Nur, where the Tarim River ended, was more than 20,000 km^2. Since middle Holocene it shrank southwestwardly. The satellite images clearly displayed the concentric veins and helix-like construction. The Ancient Konqi River (Kumu River) had ever breeded the paleo-oasis of Loulan. The river course changed entirely between 581–609 BC, and led to the abandonment of the Loulan paleo-oasis, which then changed into Yardangs.

(2) Variance of the Kunlun Mountains paleo-water-system.

After the streamed out its mountainous entrance, the Hotan River formed multilevel diluvial–alluvial fans. Clearly seen from aerophotos and satellite images, there were ancient watercourses distributed within 60–80 km west of the Kaxgar River and 50-60 km east of the Yulongkashi River. In the lower reaches of the Hotan River, at 38°45′N, 39°30′N and 39°55′N, there were 4 to 5 ancient watercourses paralleling with present main riverway and disappeared into desert northwardly. In the delta region of Hotan downriver, the ancient Hotan River once flew northeastwardly then continuously moved northwardly and westward because of the restriction of strong deposition and blown sand activities, leaving the old Hotan River, the Bositang River, the Ajike River and the past Hotan River (Fig. 12-9). Over the course of human history, the main river channel of Yulongkashi River moved westward and left Akesipir paleo-oasis in the desert. The Paleo-Keriya River once flew through desert lengthways and ended in the Tarim River. Dry delta stretching about 200 km into desert hinterland, once had Kaladun and Dandanwulike archaic castles in the Han and the Tang Dynasty. Later, the Keriya Riverway moved eastward and archaic castles turned into desert. Lots of lands lied in the downriver of the Keriya River and Damagou desertified as the result of the river way change and decreases in the flowing distance. The aeolian desertification of Jingjue Country in the Han Dynasty and Nirang City in the Tang Dynasty was the result of flowing distance shrinkage. The Qiemo River moved from the west to the east in history, and the Qarqan Kuoxienahar Ancient City on the high plain in the piedmont and the Qialemadan Ancient city on the old river bank stretching into desert suffering from aeolian desertification.

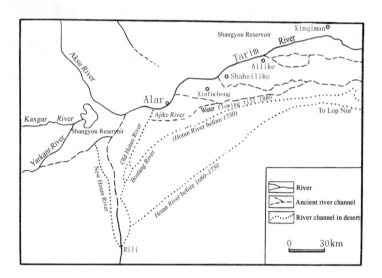

Fig. 12-9   Sketch map about the change of lower reaches of the Hotan River

Observed from these facts, at the southern edge of the Taklimakan Desert there are a lot of examples of paleo-oasis land degeneration and aeolian desertification because of river course shift. "Sand Advancing while Human Withdrawing" was essentially influenced by environment worsening due to "Water Withdrawing while Sand Advancing".

12.2.3   Modality types and evolution of blown-sand physiognomy

12.2.3.1   Wind field character and intensity of blown sand activation

1) Atmosphere circulation and wind field distribution

The Tarim Basin was surrounded by high mountains on three sides,the topography inclined from west to east, from 1,000–1,200 m to 780–820 m. In basin there were many smaller basins and different convexities and apophysises, which composed hypsography of various scales. Specific basin and surrounding topgraphy determined specifically circumfluence and more complicated local circumfluence characters,which is strengthened by the large desert and Gobi area.

In a winter half year, the Tarim Basin was controlled by high-pressure and anticyclone. The center of anticyclone lies near 40°N and 83°E with convergence line near the surface being close to the Niya River. At 3,000 m above the ground, airflow line is bent only on the northern slope of Kunlun Mt and south slope of Tianshan Mountains, which has little effect on desert (Ling, 1988). Above 3000 m, the direct influence of plateau on airflow was weakened obviously. In the prevailing wind field on the ground, the northeast system prevailed from Eastern Xinjiang to the eastern Tarim Basin, which is caused by the Mongolian high-pressure and the southward movement of northern branch of the westerly. The atmosphere circumfluence pattern of March and April was shown as Fig. 12-10. Airflow convoluted in the east and formed northeast wind when inflowing into the Tarim Basin. One branch flowed toward Korla and the other flowed Qiemo by passing Ruoqiang. The two branches of airflow were characterized by high-wind speed and dryness.At the time when ground temperature started to increase it was liable to produce strong sand dust. In the north of the Tarim Basin, dry north wind blown from the Tianshan Mountains. There is westerly wind system from the west of the basin pass over mountains near 40°N. In the southwestern there is high-temperature airflow from Pakistan crossing the Kunlun Mountains. All airflow blowing from these three directions were characterized by thermal wind which can not reach basin hinterland, and the updraft was weak.

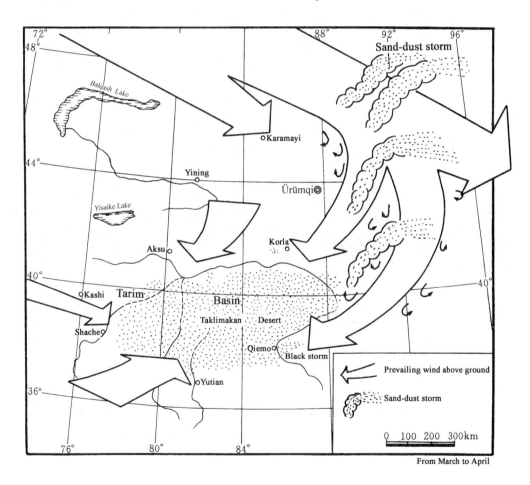

Fig. 12-10   Sketch map of prevailing wind and sand-dust storms at lower of convection layer in the
Tarim Basin (March-April) (Masatoshi, 1991)

In the summer or warm half year, average airflow over the desert was anticyclone in the east and cyclone in the west. The near surface convergence line was near the Niya River. The average height of the two airflows were 3,000 m and 4,000 m respectively.The whole basin was controlled by sub-tropic high-pressure, and westerly prevailed above 5,000 m. The basin was controlled by low-pressure near the surface . Because of forming and strengthening warm low-pressure, the pouring of east wind was strengthened and pushed the convergence line with the westerly 1° in longitude westward. Because of existence of Tianshan high-pressure, northly wind prevailed in northern basin. The three wind systems converged in the basin (Fig. 12-11). The Northwesterly was weak above basin, and the surface was influenced by local airflow. Convolution airflow of eastern basin and airflow from west convergence near the 83°–84°E and well represented in desert center. In addition, the convergence of Tian Shan airflow in the north, produced strong updraft leading to the development of cumulus which will bring precipitation. In 1988, in the desert area between 40°06′N and 83°06′E, 20 mm precipitation in half an hour had been observed (Li, 1995). Prevailing wind system was destroyed in piedmont and local wind system was formed and influenced the desert edge because of the effect of the surrounding mountains such as the northerly of southern Tianshan piedmont, the southerly and southwest of Kunlun northern piedmont. This kind of xerothermic wind generally accelerated aeolian desertification, which is well represented in basin's southern edge and eastern region.

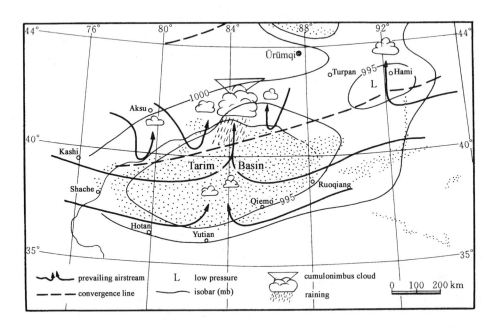

Fig. 12-11   Isobaric line of cumulus cloud and cumulonimbus cloud in the Tarim Basin (in July)
(Jiyezhengmin, 1991)

2) Blown sand activity intensity and its distribution.

The overall characteristics of dune configuration and distribution are closely related to the airflow field. The most possible sand carrying intensity reflected the airflow field of a region synthetically and effectively (Ling. 1988), namely airflow direction and wind speed fields influenced blown sand activity synthetically. The most possible sand carrying density is calculated according to effective wind of blowing-sand, and the vector synthetic direction was the synthetic sand carrying direction. The synthetic maximal intensity of carrying-sand was calculated based on effective blowing-sand wind from weather stations of the Taklimakan Desert edge. The maximum appear near Ruoqiang in southeastern desert, which was related to plateau topography and wind field. The accelerating of wind speed over large Gobi area and is also responsible for its strong sand carrying. The synthetic density of carrying-sand in Yuli region was not as strong as in Ruoqiang due to influence of eastward pouring airflow, and that of Hotan airport took the third place. Li Zhengshan et al., with additional data of 1992–1996 years at stations like Xiaotang, Mancan and Tazhong in interior desert, via research on blowing-sand wind condition during 1961–1970 years on the desert periphery (Fig. 12-12), and drew the following conclusions: northeast wind system was dominant in eastern edge of the desert, and northwest wind system prevailed in the western and southwestern edge of the desert. The two wind systems converged in Maigaiti, Jinxing and Minfeng. The northern edge of the desert, was mainly controlled by northly wind while in the desert, northeastly was dominant with the occurrence of northwestly and northsouthly. Wind speed in windward side was bigger than that in lee side and controlled the changes of wind speed in desert from west to east; the wind speed of desert interior was bigger than that of periphery and controlled wind speed changes from south to north (Li , 1999). The wind speed of Ruoqiang was the biggest which is related to the rushing east wind while in Yutian it was the smallest resulting from hardly arrival of northeastly and northwestly.

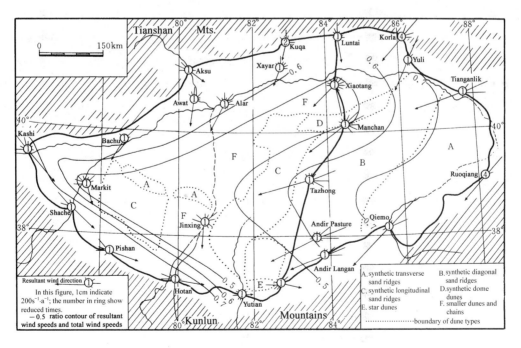

Fig. 12-12　Blowing-sand wind condition in the Taklimakan Desert (Li et al., 1999)

3) Relationship of wind field character , dune form and dune movement.

The present various physiognomys of the Taklimakan Desert are the result of long term wind action. The characteristics of dune, special distribution and movement direction are related to airflow field (including speed field and direction field) closely. Zhu Zhengda et al. thought the prevailing wind system could be divided using the line from southwestern Bachu to the middle Keriya River. The southwest of the borderline is controlled by northwestly and westerly winds, but it is mainly northeastely from Bachu to Keping.The wind and the northwestly converged in the Tuokelake Desert and turned to northly wind. The east of the borderline prevailed northeast wind. The area between them was controlled by alternate of the two wind systems. Along the Kunlun Mountains piedmont the prevailing wind was westerly or southwester in the west of the border because of mountain influence. The northeaster prevailed in the east of the borderline.

Dune modality and its distribution are related to the prevailing wind closely. In a region with single wind direction, the main modality was normally crescent dunes and dune chains. While the pyramidal dunes appeared in regions with various wind directions and equivalent wind speed, such as in south edge between Qiemo and Yutian. The transitional synthetic dunes appeared in regions where two group of wind directions were intersectant but the intersection angle was smaller. The relationship between wind condition and dune types has been studied in the Taklimakan Desert. According to wind compounding condition it can be classified into five type, also there were corresponding dune types with each of them (Table 12-3) (Li, 1999). The arrangement-direction of dunes is basically accordant with that of effective wind blowing-sand. In the western region of the desert, the main dune configuration was crescent dune chain and compounded crescent sand ridge, while in the north edge of the Mazhatage Mountains and the Qiaositage Mountains, there are mega star dunes and compound crescent dunes with a height of 100–150 m. Influenced by mountain, the dune extending direction is northeast-southwest in the northern edge of the mountains and northwest-southeast in its south edge. In the Buguli Desert in Yingjisha and Shache, the dominant dunes was crescent dunechains, while in the Tuokelake Desert the main dune type was crescent dunechain and lengthways sand ridge which was formed by means of wind blowing brushy sandpile, which moved southeastwardly. The middle part between the Hotan River and the Andir River is covered by shifting dune with a height of 100–150 m except for "Green Corridor" formed by several rivers. The majority was crescent dunechains and compounded crescents between the Keriya River and the Hotan River. The northern region between the Keriya River and the Niya River were compounded crescents with a height of 100–200 m; the southern region was lattice dunes led by alterative control of northeaster and northwester. The compounded dunes can reach over 100m in the east of the Niya River, with some star-shape dunes and lots of Tamarisk cones，the heights of them were 10–40 m.

Table 12-3   The main distribution characters of dunes in the Taklimakan Desert

Wind condition	Compound transverse sand ridge	Compound leaning sand ridge	Compound lengthways sand ridge	Compound arch sand ridge	Asteroidal dune
Wind condition type	Narrow wind condition	Broad wind condition	Obtuse angle double wind condition	Many wind with main direction	Three wind direction
Wind direction combination	NE, NW	NE, N, NW	NE, NW	NE, NW, Deflection S	NE, N, NW, SE
Distribution	Southeast desert Eastern edge Southwestern edge	The northwestern and middle desert	Along the Maigaiti, Jinxing, Minfeng in the southwestern desert	Yutian region	Xiaotang, Manshen

The overall movement direction of the Taklimakan Desert is shown in Fig. 12-13, and they are exactly consisent with the prevailing wind. In the boundary where northeaster and northwester were separated, dunes take an arcuate turn along the compounded wind direction, due to the alternative operation of these two wind systems. Dune movement directions also were diversified due to the influences of the surrounding high mountains and local apophysis in the interior of the desert.

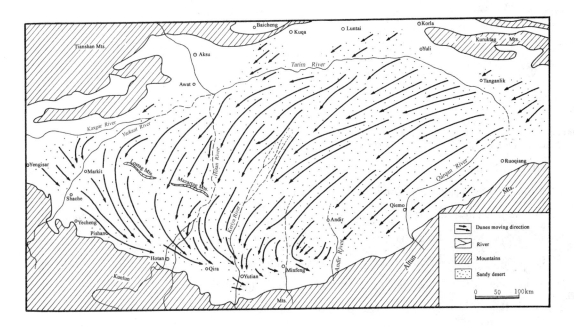

Fig. 12-13   The overall movement direction of sand dunes in the Taklimakan Desert

On the speed of dunes movement, according to the results of field observation for many years, Zhu Zhengda and Wu Zheng, revealed that dune movement mostly happened in windy season in Yingjisha, Shache and Pishan regions, especially during strong wind conditions. The movement during windy season accounted for 60%–80% of the movement in whole year (Zhu et al., 1981). The movement speed of dune in the region with single wind direction (such as Pishan) was much quicker than that of areas with compounded wind direction (such as Minfeng). The other factors that influence dune movement include the dune height, dune surface moisture condition, vegetation covering degree, the local physiognomy environment and ground conditions etc. According to speed of dune movement, this region can be classified into four types: slow movement type (forward movement is less than <1 m), middle movement type (1–5 m), quick movement type (5–10 m), and posthaste movement type (>10 m) (Table 12-4). The slow type distributes in spacious region in desert inerparts and pyramidal dune region of southern desert; the middle type distributes in Hotan downriver, low reaches of Kashi delta and the Tarim River bank region; the quick speed type distributes in western Shache, region between Qiemo and Ruoqiang; the posthaste speed distributes in desert fringe between Yecheng and Pishan, eastern Qiemo region etc.

Table 12-4　The distribution type of dune movement speed per year in the Taklimakan Desert region

Slow speed type (<1 m)	Middle-speed type (1–5 m)	Quick-speed type (6–10 m)	Posthastetype (>10 m)
The high dune region in Taklimakan desert hinterland; the pyramid dune region in Yutian and Minfeng of the southern desert; the high dune region in southwestern Qira	Along the Hotan and the Tarim River, in the oasis edge of the Hotan, Yutian and Qira, the west and south of Minfeng oasis, in the Tuokelake Desert	In the southeast Buguli Desert, northwest Pishan Oasis, west of the Mugui and Muji Oasis, southwest of Qira and the Minfeng Oasis, Washixia gorge	In the sandy land of the Kashi Delta, the southwest of the Pishan Oasis in southwest of the Taklimakan Desert, between Qiemo-Ruoqiang in the southeast of desert

(1) Other factors affecting the formation and development of blown sand physiognomy.

Wind is an important factor to form blown sand physiognomy which determines the main characters and array direction of blown sand physiognomy. There also were many factors related to blown sand physiognomy formation in the Taklimakan Desert such as ground materials composition, ground surface gurgitation, moisture condition, vegetation condition and so on.

The influence of ground material composition depends on the amount of sand supply which also determine dune development scope. The ground materials under dune in the Taklimakan Desert mainly can be classified into two groups: one is mainly coarse sand and gravel, with few middle and fine sand. In the middle part of proluvium fans in front of mountain, the gravel accounted for 65% and the sandy one 35%, which formed low dunes. The other was sand with various sizes in alluvial plain and front edge of proluvium fan; which formed higher dunes. Consequently, the dune in proluvium sector of desert edge is lower and the one distributed in alluvial plain of desert interior is higher.

The essence of the influence of ground surface gurgitation on blown sand physiognomy is the change of the ground denudation, sediment and wind regime which lead to different blown sand physiognomy. It usually was the base of some high dunes, and led to some peculiar modality. The Mazhatage Mountains lying in the desert center with a height of 200–300 m, a length of 140 km from west to east and a width of 2 km from south to north, influence the blown sand physiognomy at least in five aspects, namely: determining the dune types and distribution of south and north mountain. dune height and density; influencing the dune movement direction; the weathering matter from the mountain is the important source of dune sand; impeded surface and ground water, and affected precipitation (Zhao , 1991). The Minfeng apophysis which is 78 km long from east to west and 9–16 km wide from south to north and heigh of 153 m, influences the desert just like that of the Mazhatagte Mountains, but it is covered with gravel and deposited little blown sand, and had a quality of gobi. The longitudinal high compounded dunes extending from south to north is widely distributed in the east of the Keriya River, with the base of ridges and hillocks composed of pluvial—alluvial matters of the Quaternary (Zhou , 1995).

The influences of moisture on vegetation can be observed in different parts of the Taklimakan Desert. In front edge of proluvial fan, the underground water table is 1–3 m deep, and vegetation is good. In alluvial plain and dry delta on both sides of the rivers extended into desert interior, *P. euphratica* and *Tamarisks* formed green, corridor, due to temporary fluviation or the higher water table. Because in these regions the vegetation condition was good, the majority of dunes were fixed or sub-fixed dunes which distributed along both of the river banks and forward alluvial fan edge. But along some old riverbed, there was no water and the water condition turned bad, vegetation died, brushy dune was blown by wind and destroyed. The crescent dunes and dune chains began developing and formed landscape with the coexistence of shifting dune and brushy dune.

Besides the above-mentioned factors, the formation of dune in desert edge and oasis is also related the to anthropogenesis. Because the vegetation on the fixed or sub-fixed brushy dunes was destroyed, the shifting sand formed, such as dunes in oasis of the Lop Nur, Kashi and Shache. Or because sandy ground surface was eroded by wind after vegetation was destroyed and sand deposited in front of it, such as the downstream of the Yuepu Lake and so on. Or because of irrigation, river course was changed and shortened, on the dry riverbed, sand was blown on the spot and formed dunes such as shifting sand in the Shule and Yingjisha oases.

(2) The basic characters, form types and spacial distribution of sand blown aeolian physiognomy

Generally, according to the causes of underground layers, the Taklimakan Desert can be divided into four parts: the first is proluvium-alluvial plain on the southern piedmont of the Tianshan Mountains; the second is alluvial plain delta and lacustrine plain of the Tarim River; the third is hills or monadnock and ridge of hillock in the hinterland and the forth is proluvium-alluvial fan plain and delta in front of the Kunlun–Altun Mountains belt. In hinterland of desert, the alluvial and pluvial plain of the Tarim River converged with the proluvium-alluvial dry delta of northern piedmont of the Kunlun Mountains at N 40° and E 83°-85°, which is located at the south boundary of fornix-shape dunes. In the east of the Keriya River, Quaternary ridges and hillocks widely distributed from south to north. In the desert hinterland, there are the Mazhatage Mountains and Minfeng apophysis extending nearly from west to east. The eastern desert was alluvial plain of the Lop Nur and delta plain of downreaches of the Tarim River and the Konqi River.

①The characters of blown sand physiognomy.

Based on the above causes, it is seen that the wind acts with the sandy ground surface, and is influenced by ground configuration, moisture of vegetation condition and sand source replenishment, which form the unique blown sand physiognomy in the Taklimakan Desert (Fig. 12-2). Its four basic characters are:

A Aeolian erosion and sediment physiognomies coexist. The great coverage of dune bodies is from the erosion of same size.

B The shifting dune is the dominant one and accounts for 82% of dune area.

C Dunes are high and large, and physiognomy types are complicated. The dunes whose height is over 50 m account for 80% of the area of shifting dune. Dunes in the east are higher than the west. The types of dunes include the single dune, the combinatorial dune and compounded dune, and there were 13 sub-types totally. It is called "Museum of blown sand physiognomy in china".

D On a degree ,the blown physiognomy has a regular spatial pattern.

② Spacial distribution of dune type.

A Approximately the Keriya River is the boundary, to the east of the river dunes are high compounded dune chains, compounded sand ridges and intervals or billabong between them. To the west of the river dunes are crescent dunes, crescent dune chains, scalelike dunes, sand ridges and compounded sand ridges, inter-distributed.

B The south and southwest of the Taklimakan Desert are ancient alluvial plain. There are compounded dune chains with crescent dunes, crescent dune chains, sand ridges, tamarisk cones and silt billabongs appearing alternately.

C On the north slope of the Mazhatage Mountains in desert hinterland there are high compounded dune chains (star-shaped dunes on their tops partly), the south slope is aeolian structure plain with sand ridges and crescent dunes locally.

D In the middle and lower reaches of the rivers flowing into desert hinterland, from riverbed to their two sides, dunes are developing from fixed to sub-fixed dunes, from small to big, from single to compounded. Namely from fixed dunes of tamarisk and *P.euphratica Olivier* to sub-fixed or sub-shift dunes to crescent dunes, dune chains to high compounded dunes.

E In the lower reaches of the Tarim and the Keriya rivers and the exterior fringe of the ancient alluvial plain in the middle reach of the Tarim River there are fornix-shaped compounded dunes with crescent dunes and compounded crescented dune chains.

F High compound longitudinal sand ridges extending from south to north in hinterland and their intervals were mainly sandy plain with coarse sand ripples, scutellate dunes, crescent dunes (chains), sand ridges and scalelike dunes, etc.

G In the interior and edges of the desert, there were simple and younger crescent dunes and dune chains with fixed and sub-fixed brushy dunes and undulate sandy land.

H The edges of irrigated oasis formed by independent water systemes in the desert southern edge, is a special distribution that blocks of flowing dunes was adjacent with oasis farmlands, villages and small towns even counties because of destroy of desert vegetation belt.

Compartmentalization of the Taklimakan Desert aeolian physiognomy by Zhu Zhengda et al.was refined generalization to dune under physiognomy, dune configuration types and special distribution, it can be classified into nine parts and twenty-one sub-parts (Table 12-5).

Table 12-5   Compartmentalization of aeolian physiognomy in the Taklimakan Desert

1. The region of sabkha plain with yardangs and dunes
   ① The erosion plain region of Loulan
   ② The region with dune chains of the Kuluke Kum desert
2. The region of alluvial and pluvial plain covered with dunes on the piedmont of the Kunlun-Altun Mts
   ① the region of dune chains of the Kate Kum desert with crescent sand ridges
   ② region of star-shaped dunes in Yutian and Qiemo with sand ridges
   ③ brushy dune region in Qiemo-Minfeng
3. Region of alluvial plain in piedmont of the western Kunlun Mountains with dunes
   ① region of dune chains in Kala Kum
   ② region of dunes together with brushy dunes in Pishan-Qira
   ③ region of compounded dune chains in Peier Kum with compounded longitudinal ridges
4. Region of delta plain with dunes of Kashi
   ① region of ridges of the Tuoketuola Kum desert with dune chains
   ② region of dune chains in Buguli Kum
5. Region of plain in the north of the Mazar Tage Mountains with dunes
   ① region of compounded dune chains in Tage Kum with star dunes
   ② region of dune chains in Kumzhayinike with scalelike dunes
6. Region of delta plain with dunes in center of the Taklimakan desert
   ① Region of brushy dunes and dune chains in delta plain in the lower reach of the Keriya river with compounded crescent dunes
   ② region of longitudinal compounded ridges
   ③ region of compounded dune chains in the north of Minfeng
   ④ region of scalelike dunes with compounded longitudinal ridges between Hotan and Keriya rivers
7. Region of plain in the eastern of the Taklimakan Desert
   ① region of compounded dune chains in Kelakeshaali Kum
   ② region of dune chains in the north of Qiemo with compounded dune chains
8. Region alluvial plain of the Tarim river with dunes
   ① region of dune chains in the the northern of the Taklimakan desert
   ② region of brushy dunes along with the Tarim river with odd dune chains
9. Region of pluvial and alluvial plain in the south piedmont of the Tian Shan Mountains with odd shifting dunes

4) Atmospheric dust in the Tarim Basin

The surrounding mountains, extremely arid climate and frequent gales provided favorable physical and dynamical condition for forming atmospheric sand dust. The sand material of the Taklimakan Desert in basin center also provided abundant source for atmospheric sand dust, making this region one of severe sand dust regions in our country, especially the southern edge of the basin.

(1) Spatial and temporal distribution of dust fall.

The distribution of isolines of the mean annual days of floating dust occurence in the Tarim Basin takes on a closed bow-like shape. By synthetical analysis of the statistic data from 32 weather stations in basin periphery and hinterland (Fig. 12-14), the following dust fall distribution is found: the floating dust from the basin can affect the Pamirs to the west, northwardly from south of the Tianshan Mountains and southwardly to the east of the Kunlun Mountains of the northern Qinghai-Tibet plateau, and extended to 115°E eastwardly. In the basin, isolines of the mean annual days of floating dust is 40–220 days. The Taklimakan Desert is located in the 80-day isoline region. The number of days with floating dust in the south was more than that in the north, it is more in the west than in the east, and it is much in the hinterland than in the north and less than in the south. The maximal floating dust region is in the desert area which is 100 km wide in north of the belt of Moyu-Hotan-Qira-Minfeng. In the west area such as Kashi, there is region of local high. The number of floating dust days reduced with the increase of height above sea level. The dust can reach 3,000–4,000 m high, and the highest is 5,000–6,000 m. In the north of the basin, from the Tarim River (1,000 m a.s.l.) to the Tianshan Mountains area (2,500 m a.s.l.), the mean annual floating dust day reduced from 90 days to 0–2 days. In moutainous region with a height of 1,500 m to 3,000–5,000 m in the west and south of the basin, it reduced from 100–200 days to 0–10 days. The eastern region is relatively wide, floating dust extended eastwardly with the increase of height. The field measurement of atmospheric dustfall in the Tarim Basin revealed the same distribution pattern. Mean monthly dust fall in the edge of southern basin and Hotan regions can reach 542.10 t/km^2, that in Kashi region was 68.22 t/km^2, and that in eastern Bayinguoleng region was 26.25 t/km^2. The regions with least dust fall were Aksu region and Kezilesu autonomy county. The mean monthly dust fall respectively were 16.38 t/km^2 and 9.96 t/km^2, was high in the south and low in the north, high in the west and low in the east.

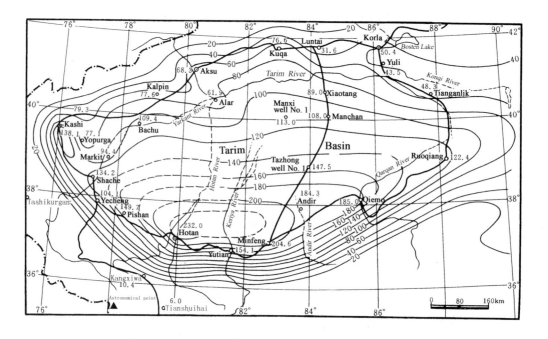

Fig. 12-14　Distribution map of mean annual floating dust days in the Tarim Basin (1961–1990)

Temporally, it can appear in any time in one day, mainly during afternoon to evening because of thermo-dynamical processes in the basin, and it lasts usually for 2–5 days. Seasonally, it mainly occurs in spring and summer (Fig. 12-15). The total of the two seasons accounted for 72.6% of that in the whole year. Spring was the season with maximum in Hotan region and account for 33.8% of the annual total. In summer, it reduce slightly; winter was the lowest in a year.

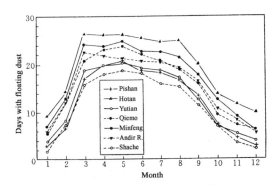

Fig. 12-15　Distribution map of monthly floating dust days in the Tarim Basin (1961–1990)

The change of dust fall at different heights in atmosphere is as following: it reduced with height below 6m, then rises above 6m and kept constant in 8–10m. It was not measured above 10m, It was different from the common cognition that the amount of dust fall reduced with the height, which is mainly related to turbulence process.It is obviously influenced by the amount of saltated sands below 6m high, which is mainly influenced by passing sand dust above 8m high from far away. At 2–10m above ground level, the dust fall was mainly composed of tiny sand with a content of 57.7%–80.3%, the second was coarser silt with a content of 15.6%–38.1%, which indicate that the main dust fall of atmosphere below 10m was sand.

　(2) The causes of dust fall distribution.

　The spatial and temporal distribution of dust fall in atmosphere in the Tarim Basin are related to the regional circulation closely. The routes of dust fall accompanied by blown sand movement is similar. The easterly airflow of eastern basin travelled westward and brought windy and sandy weather to Hotan. The wind power weakened and sandy dust resorted in high altitude then floating dust weather formed. The northwestern airflow of western basin advanced southeastwardly and brought sand dust which was blocked by the Kunlun Mountains on the south slopes, making floating dust increase in the region. Eastern and western airflow met the Keriya River and the Hotan and converged, making Hotan area a centre of floating dust and sand dust devil. The peak value of dust fall within a year is related to the occurrence and intensity of low level thermal low-pressure in the Tarim Basin. Essentially, the frequency of blown sand weather (including sand dust devil, raising sand and floating dust) determines the atmospheric sand dust content, but the blown sand weather frequency was determined by atmosphere circulation in basin.

　Sub-sandy soil and loess distributed on the north slope of the Kunlun Mountains and the Altun Mountains were regarded as aeolian deposit, and were related to atmosphere sand dust directly (Li　et al., 1988; Liu et al., 1985). Liu Yuzhang et al. analyzed the mineral component and granularity of dust fall samples in the Qira Observation Station, and discovered that the heavy mineral contents of the Taklimakan Desert dune sand (<.0.1mm), atmospheric dust fall of Gobi plain and sub-sandy soil of the north slope of the Kunlun Mountains were all low. The heavy mineral contents of the unstable, more stable, stable and extremely stable had the same order. The minerals mainly were hornblende type, epidotic and opacity mineral, which proved the loam-sandy soil deposit mainly was from the northern desert. Observed from granularity, the grain components of atmosphere sand dust fall and contents of each granularity group were between sub-sandy soil and loess, indicating that atmosphere dust fall include both the sub-sandy soil grain component and the loess. But the main component of the Taklimakan Desert was fine sand and extremely fine sand. Consequently, the desert sand—sub-sandy soil—loess zonal distribution from north to south in the north slope of the Kunlun Mountains was formed by the prevailing wind by long term transportation and separation. The fine sand with relatively coarser-grain mainly moved by saltation and deposited on the spot then formed desert sand. Some fine sand or grains and tiny sand were transported and suspended in atmosphere, then deposited in sequence from coarse to fine and formed sub-sandy soil and loess.

In summary, the Tarim Basin is one of the regions most seriously affected by sand dust in China. The dust fall was higher in south than in north, and the west was higher than the east, with the highest in Hotan to Qira area. The dust fall mainly appears in spring and summer, which was formed under the cooperation of ground prevailing wind system and basin thermal low-pressure.

12.2.4　The processes and causes of aeolian desertification

The Taklimakan Desert lies in inland basin and is formed in extremely arid and windy condition. Abundant sandy materials of alluvial, alluvial—lacustrine deposits supply the material source of active desert with large area and complex configuration. It was mainly formed from the middle Pleistocene to the Holocene.

The natural condition was the natural background of aeolian desertification. In human history and present time, the aeolian desertified land by human disturbance was about 28266 km^2 under the background of climate changes, and accounting for 9.2% of the total land area, of which 65.1% formed in human history, and 34.9% formed at present (Zhu, 1987).

In human history aeolian desertification process in this region mainly happened in downstream oasis in the south and east desert. River course changed and water table declined, paleo-plowland and dweller places were abandoned and caused aeolian desertification. In north region, on both sides of the Tarim River and some sectors of edges of proluvial and alluvial fans on south piedmont of the Tian Shan Mountains, because changes of river courses or long term unreasonable irrigation, led to the rise of groundwater and soil salinization. Sandy dry riverbed or abandoned cultivation region suffered wind erosion and turned to aeolian desertified land.

Because of human influence and improper utilization of natural resource in the latest 100 years, the fragile ecology system is destroyed, which accelerated aeolian desertification. Certainly, there were cases where dunes moved forward and resulted in aeolian desertification locally.

1) The processes and causes of aeolian desertification in human history

The history process of aeolian desertification refers to the processes of occurrence and development of aeolian desertification in human history, and regions influenced by it was called aeolian desertified land in history. Seen from its history, it is characterized by the aeolian desertification of downriver inland in the Taklimakan Desert or river banks of desert edge and oasis in plains and edges of fans in front of mountains (Xia et al., 1991)

(1) Aeolian desertification in history.

① Aeolian desertification of archaic oases in the eastern and southern desert.

From east to west, i.e. from Milan, Washixia, Qiemo, Andir, Minfeng, Yutian, Qira, Luopu, Hotan, and Pishan to Yecheng and so on, there are a lot of ruins of ancient cities in the outer periphery of oasis in desert (Fig. 12-16).

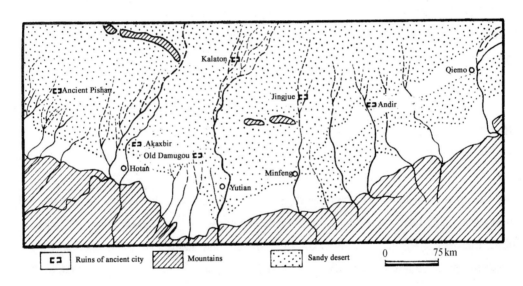

Fig. 12-16   Ancient oasis distribution in the south margin of the Taklimakan Desert

The Lop Nur region of Tarim downriver had "Loulan County" recorded in 176 BC with an area of 30,000 km^2 and population of 14,100. Its name was changed to Shanshan and the capital was moved to Nicheng in 77 BC. In the prosperous times it once governed southern part separately with Yudian country. About at the beginning of the 6th century, it turned into desolate and uninhabited ruins. According to the record of *Han Book·Xiyu Biography* by Bangu in the Eastern Han Dynasty: " Loulan country was the most flourishing in the Dongsheng, but in the Han Dynasty, there were white dragonlike piles and short of aquatic", Shanshan country " There were much sand and halid on the ground and few of plowland s... and many reeds, tamarisks, poons". It was obvious that at least 2,000 years ago, large area of pickled soils existed in this region and is called aeolian Yardangs today. In 399 BC when Faxian toured to the Lop Nur and Shanshan country, he saw "There are no birds and no beasts but bones on ground". After ancient country disappeared, the blown sand physiognomy process was accelerated, and fixed or sub-fixed sand piles turned to shifting dunes. After the delta of the Konqi River—Tarim downriver dried up entirely, the Kuluke Desert was dominated by shifting dunes taking on presence in front of people.

In desert hinterland, 100 km north to Qiemo County, there existed ancient Qiemo city beside north of the ancient Qiemo riverbed, with an area of 25,000 km^2, and subsisted more than 2,000 years. In the year of 645 BC, Tang Xuanzhuang passed this place and the city was consummate, but without man. Observing from the distribution, the ancient city was discarded when the Qiemo River changed eastwardly and flew into the Taitema Lake.

There were three ancient cities near the Andir River, namely Akekaoqikeranke, Tiyingmu and Dawuzileke. They can be tracked back to the Tang Dynasty, at least to the 15th century. Aeolian desertification should happen after the 15th century. Three ancient cities respectively lied in desert with distances of 15 km to the southwest and 27 km southeast to Andir pasture.

Jingjue Ancient City lied in Niya downriver and with a length of 22 km from south to north and width of 0.5 km from west to east. The house was made up of the mixtures of straw, sheep dejecta and mud and can fix sand. According to cultural relics, the aeolian desertification took place after the 4th–5th century. Now the ancient city is covered by crescented dunes. About 70 km south to Jingjue ancient city, the Tang Dynasty Nixiang City laid, its west is sandy soil; the east is "Drift sand flew allover and converged or scattered with wind" (644 BC). Nixiang City was abandoned in the 8th century.

Keriya downriver and Damagou downriver belonged to ancient Mi Country. In 138 it was firstly mentioned by Zhang Qian, *Han Book. Xiyu Biography* introduced that "Mi Country, the king governed the city...there are 3,340 households, 20,040 population, and 3,540 soldiers. It once was one of the biggest countries at southern edge of the Tarim Basin and turned to a small country, far smaller than Yudian, after the Eastern Han Dynasty. The Keladun Ancient City in the north of Mi County lied in the western delta of Keriya downriver with a distance of 200 km southwardly to Yutian County. Dating of ^{14}C indicate it is in Western Han era, and was discarded in the 4th–5th century. The aeolian desertification began in the 8th century. Dandanwulike, another northern ancient city of Mi country, with a distance of 90 km southward to Damagou, was active in the 4th–8th century. The *Poluomi Book* dug here made sure that the dating was 781–791 AD. It was degenerated into desertified land because of war. The place 60km south to Dandanwulike, and 15-50 km north to Damagou, was thought to be the hinterland of the ancient Mi Country oasis, but it degenerated into desert gradually in the 11th–15th century. The Old Damagou ruins, with a distance of 20–30 km south to Damagou, was discarded in the 1870s. It was obvious that the aeolian desertification of paleo-oasis in the Keriya River drainage area is earlier in the north than in the south.

Yudian country was established in the Hotan River drainage area about the 3th century BC. Its population was 19,300 in Western Han Dynasty (*Han Book·Xiyu Biography*) and 83,000 in the Eastern

Han Dynasty (*Laterly Han Book·Xiyu Biography*), and it once was the biggest paleo-oasis in southern fringe of the Tarim Basin. Zhaisadanna Country of Hotan region in the Tang Dynasty, which was "the around is two thousand kilometers and more than half of the sand field ", once was the Akesipir Ancient City, the east capital of Yudian Country. It lied in the south bank of the Dakumati River, which was the eastern branch of the Yulongkashi River. The city maintained from the Western Han Dynasty to the Kalahan Dynasty. According to the collected Qidan character in small copperplate it was after the 13th century. In the Qinmaqin Desert zone between the Karakax River and the Yurungkax River with a distance of over 30 km south to Hotan, many ancient relics of construction and channels were found. The Balemasi relic in its southern edge is testified that it had experienced the Han and the Tang dynasties, and was discarded in the 11th–12th century. The relic of ancient soldier's castle at Mazhatage in desert hinterland of Hotan downriver once was an important gate in the "Silk Road" along the Hotan River traversing the Taklimakan Desert in the Han and the Tang Dynasty, and it was discarded in the Southern and Northern Song Dynasties.

It is the evidence for aeolian desertification in history time that sand buried zone appeared in the southern path of "Silk Road". In the regions from Moyu to Yecheng and from Yutian to Minfeng, there remains ancient roads, balefire stages, pottery pieces and broken tiles among the lower dunes in the north of the present highway. In the zone with low dunes, the ancient road was about 5-10km to the southern fringe of present desert. Some scholars deduced the southern boundary of aeolian desertification in history by the rate of crescented dunes along the ancient road. But Zhou Xingjia thought the conjecture can not reflect the real condition. It was the river flowing into desert that make the ancient city existed in the environment with dunes. And it was discarded due to river course shift. The instance that ancient city was buried by southwardly invaded shifting sand have not been proved. The aeolian desertification condition of paleo-oasis in the eastern and southern edges of the Taklimakan Desert was shown in Table 12-6.

Table 12-6　The abandoned oasis and the aeolian desertification status in the east and south of the Taklimakan Desert

Rivers	Ancient country name	The nearby environment conditions during the existence of ancient oasis	The ancient town	Abandoned age	Causes of abandonment	Present aeolian desertification situation
Lower reaches of Konqi River and Tarim River, middle reaches of Milan River and Ruoqiang River	Loulan Country (Later called Shanshan Country) (Han and Jin Dynasties)	Many *Bailongdui* (Yardangs), sparse grass, little farmlands, many reeds, Chinese tamarisk, poons. Kumatag Desert at the east part.	Loulan	In the beginning of 6th century	River course shifting to south	eroded land
			Haitou	5th century	River course shifting to south	eroded land
			Yixun	5th century	War	Yixun became eroded shifting land, the oasis remained exist
			Hanni	5th century	War	Oasis
The ancient riverway flowing northwardly in	Qiemo Country (in Western	The east, north and west edges were desert	Qiemo Ancient Town	Not clear	River course shifting To east	The shifting dune and eroded land

Rivers	Ancient country name	The nearby environment conditions during the existence of ancient oasis	The ancient town	Abandoned age	Causes of abandonment	Present aeolian desertification situation
the lower reach of Qiemo River	Han Dynasty)					
The lower reaches of Andir River	Tihuoluo Country (Tang Dynasty)	The periphery of ancient town was desert.	Akekaoqikaran Ketiyingmu Dawuzileke	7th century 15th century 15th century	River course shifting to south River course shifting to west	The shifting dune and eroded land The shifting dune and eroded land The shifting dune and eroded land
The lower reaches of Niya River	Jingjue Country (Han Dynasty)	Land was the narrow and long oasis surrounding by sand ridge	Jingjue Country relic Nixiang City(the Tang Dynasty)	After 4th—5th century 8th century	River was discontinuous River was discontinuous	eroded and shifting land eroded and shifting land
Lower reaches of Keriya River and Damagou River	Yumi Country (Han Dynasty)	Shifting dunes, semi-fixed dunes and fixed dunes all existed.	Kaladun (the Western Han Dynasty)	7th—8th century	River course shifting Variance to west	eroded land and sub-fixed dune
			Dandanwulike	8th century	River course shifting or discontinuous	eroded and shifting land
			Wuzengtati and Wulizati	In the beginning of 11th century	River was discontinuous	Erosion and sub-fixed dune The half rampart was buried in sand
			Kalaqin Ancient Town	At the end of 15th century	The river was discontinuous	
			Tetergelamu	At the end of 11th century	The river was discontinuous	Erosion sub-fixed dune
			The old land of Hadelike	At the end of 9century	no clear	Erosion sub-fixed dune
			The old Damagou	In 70's of the 9th century	The river was discontinuous	Erosion sub-fixed dune
The middle and lower reaches of Hotan River	Yushen Country (Han Dynasty)	Most sand dunes, little soils. Often floating dusts.	Akesipir Ancient City Balemasi Relic Mazhatage Ancient Castle Yuetegan	After13th century 13th century 10th century 9th century	The river course shifting to west war war no clear	shifting dune shifting dune Erosion land Oasis
Each water system in Pishan County	Pishan Country	Big dunes on the road, some fixed dunes and semi-fixed dunes	Arsaihujia	9th century	River course shift	shifting dune and erosion land
			Aziwumujia	3th century	River course shift	shifting dune and erosion land
			Keziletamu	3th century	River course shift	shifting dune and erosion land
			Yujimilike	3th century	River course shift	shifting dune and erosion land
			Buteleke	10th century	River course shift	shifting dune and erosion land
			Yarqiwuyilike	13th century	River course shift	shifting dune and erosion land
			Erqimailike	15th century	River was discontinuous	shifting dune

② Aeolian desertification of the northern Tarim Basin in history.

As mentioned before, the Tarim River in the northern Taklimakan Desert once was a colossal hydrological network in history. Some rivers originated from the Kunlun Mountains and southern piedmont of the Tianshan Mountains and flooded into the Tarim River. The middle reach of the Tarim River frequently waved in south and north. There are present rivers, dry riverbeds, paleo-river ways, lakes and morasses, which are arranged in a crisscross pattern. Its lower river also accepts the Konqi River water and flow into the Lop Nur at last. When we investigated in the Taklimakan Desert hinterland in the end of the 1980s and beginning of the 1990s, we saw the southernmost Tarim River course blocked by blown sand. Under the surface of silty clay layers on the banks of old river ways, there were ancient aeolian sand layers having similar color and mineral component as dune sand. They hadn't the typical characteristics of the Tarim River alluvial sand that were gray (or white gray) and with much mica mineral. The paleo-blown sand had a yellow gray or gray yellow color with little mica, which indicate that they experienced long term wind carrying. Consequently, we can conclude that the ancient Tarim Rivers formed and developed in arid environment. There were *Haloxylons* and *Tamarisks* growing together with dunes on both banks of rivers. Moreover, the further the dunes are away from the riverway, the more active the dunes are. Certainly, when the integrated water system network existed, desertified soil distribution and intensity were restrained by the water condition. Generally, in the up or middle reaches of the paleo-Tarim River in Shaya County, the area of aeolian desertification was narrow, the dune height was below 5m. But in the middle and lower side of middle reaches of palaeo-Tarim River in southern Luntai, the area of aeolian desertification was wide, with dune height about 6–10 m, of which the biggest can reach 20–30m.

Huang Wenbi investigated the Kezi River's northern bank of the eastern part of Bachu County in 1929, and proved that there was Tangwang City relic sites on the ancient road of the northern Kezi River and paleo-road passing through from Kuqa to Shule, and there was ancient irrigation system with a width of 3m or more from east to west. Pieces of red potteries and beacon towers scattered all over. This region had become sandy soil or salted soil when Huang Wenbi investigated it. The archaic trench system mainly was buried by sand piles. It was obvious that aeolian desertification of northern old river way in lower reaches of the Kezi River happened after the Tang Dynasty.

The old Tarim River of the southern Shaya River (now dry riverbed) had water in the Tang Dynasty. We can still see relics of beacon towers, pottery pieces, kitchen ash and so on in the Tang Dynasty and paleo-road on both sides old river banks buried by shifting sand. Here the aeolian desertification only occurred after the Tang Dynasty.

Some archaic cultivation region were discarded because of secondary soil salinization on the north bank of the Tarim River and pluvial-alluvial plains in southern piedmont of the Tianshan Mountains. Many relics in fringes of oasis such as Kuqa, Xinhe, Shaya, Luntai, distributed in hemicycle shape. The cultivation region of the Han Dynasty distributed on the furthest periphery of the plain,and inner ward were relic sites in the Tang Dynasty (Fig. 12-17). Since then, by wind processes, sandy material deposited on the discarded plantations on the fringe of alluvial fan and dry riverbeds and formed aeolian desertified lands characterized by shrub sand mound and crescent dune chains. For instance, both the land with shifting dunes in the west of Kuqa, Xinhe and Shaya and the land of the Quner Kumu Desert between Kurle and Luntai were formed in human history.

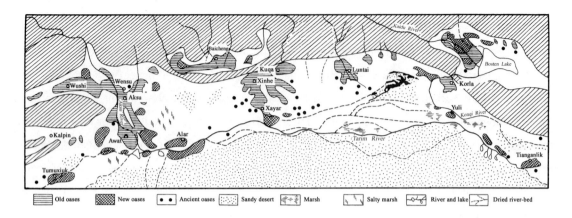

Fig. 12-17　Ancient oasis distribution in the Tarim River

About the formation age of the Qunrkumu Desert, some scholars thought it was in present period. But in the volume 192 of *General Book* in the Tang Dynasty, it is recorded "(Yanqi) to Hecheng (Xizhou) eastward by 900 li and westward to Guizi for 900 li, all was sand field." Censen, a poet in the Tang Dynasty, went to Anxi (now Kuqa): In 749, wrote in his poem that: "Hoping going to the sky (note: "Tianshan" means "sky mountains" in chinese, maybe also relate to that "the west sky" is same as "heaven", so mean the Kuqa was a very good place) by riding, having experienced two full moon after left my home. Where to live tonight? There is nobody in the boundless plain of sands!". As "Passing Sand Field" poem described: "Visitor got lost in yellow dust, the sky with clouds down to ground straightly when seeing around. It is said that when go to the end of ground it is also the end of the sky, but when I arrived at Anxi I can go westward further." The poet also left the verses such as "Man is worrying under the moon in sands" and "Horse hoofs are laborious in the western sand". It was obvious that the desert landscape had existed between Kurle and Kuqa in the southern piedmont of the Tianshan Mountains in the Tang Dynasty, although the aeolian desertification was not as serious as nowadays. Shifting crescent dune chains are dominating in the Quner kumu Desert today, but blowing and winnowing brushy sand mounds was dominant in the Tang Dynasty. Certainly, the shifting dunes should also exist; otherwise, the "yellow sand" would not appear in the above mentioned verses.

(2) The cause of aeolian desertification in history.

Arid climate, abundant sand source, exposed ground surface and blowing-sand wind were precondition of aeolian desertification in the Tarim Basin. But the aeolian desertification in history is related to natural factors including climate changes stages, water resources, new tectonic movements, etc., and anthropogenic factors including war, pestilence and irrigation, etc.

There were two aspects of cognition generally about aeolian desertification in history caused by climate changes, Zhou Xingjia et al., according to research on the development and evolution process of the Keriya River oasis, found that oasisification or aeolian desertification is determined by the abundance of water resource , movement direction and modality, while the water abundance is related to temperature fluctuations. Observed from climate changes, when temperature was high, ice or snow melt, consequently oasis develops, and vice visa. The research on desertification periods and alluvial periods in the Tarim Basin since 7,000 a BP, indicated the relationships between the alternation of the two and the global temperature fluctuation. In the warmest period in the Holocene in 8,500 –3,000 a BP, for instance, many climate fluctuations happened, which was conductive to oasis development. But in the global cold time in the latest hundreds of years, oasis were in shrank stage basically. Zhongwei et al., according to research on the Bositeng Lake and Damagou section and Tagele section of southern Xinjiang, concluded that climate in the southern Xinjiang was controlled by alternation of cool-humid time and warm-arid time. The period when "Silk Road" was flourishing and expedited, including the Western Han Dynasty, the Sui and the Tang Dynasties (581–907), and the Yuan Dynasty (1271–1368), corresponds with the relatively climatic cool and humid stages; and the periods that the "Silk Road" was relatively deserted and drowsy such as the Eastern Han Dynasty, the Weijing Dynasty, the Nonchao and the Beichao Dynasties (from beginning of AD to later of 6th century), the Wudai Dynasties and the southern and Northern Song Dynasties usually corresponds to warm and arid times. There is a common sense for the above two opinions of them taking the water resource changes led by climate fluctuation as the dominant cause of changes of oasis in flourish and withering.

The influence of new tectonic movement on development and evolution of oasis in the Tarim Basin should not be ignored. It was reflected that with the uplift of the Qinghai-Tibet Plateau, the Tarim Basin took on upward tectonic movement, and then spatially different lift make it higher in the south and lower in the north. This influenced the choices of rivers for their directions and locations. The research about the Keriya oasis indicated that since 16,500 years before, the oasis were shrinking. In warm times new oasis advanced northwardly as superposed tiles, and narrowed the range of river course shifting, in south of the Tarim River and north of end of the Keriya River oasis. The survey still indicated that the entire Tarim river way moved about 98km from south to north, which was related to the subsidence of the Tarim River northern edge and the biggest subsidence velocity was 2.4 mm/a. On a degree, new tectonic movement restricted water level condition in oasis, controlled the shift of direction and modality of runoff, and in turn influenced the oasis evolution.

Convulsions and water-using activity were important anthropogenic factors affecting oasis evolution. Records from the *Regions West of the Great Tang Empire*: in the place 150km east to present Hotan, one brutal war made the battle ground "no grass; the soil is red and black". In the second half of the 7th century AD, Tubo Tribe intruded into the southern edge of the Tarim Basin and destroyed oasis. The Dandanwulile was destroyed just at that time. During 971–1006 AD Yudian Country and Klahan Country experienced long term crusade, and the Lapu Ancient City in Yecheng County was destroyed in the battles. The Tarim Basin was in disruption condition in the Ming Dynasty. The long term warfare made Yudian Country change from "People are rich and joy" to the condition of "the adjacent countries are belligerent, the population are near10 thousand and all of them are living in mountains to avoid wars"(broad records in around areas). In the Qing Dynasty, many chaos happened in Southern Xinjiang. In 1865–1906 AD the Agubo Tribe intruded. They burned not only the houses, killed the people, pillaged the wealth, but also demolished water conservancy, which made the lower reaches not be irrigated and led to abandoned soil. Human activities changed the special and temporal distribution of water. Some rivers once broke off seasonally in the Tang Dynasty, just as in records from the *Regions West of the Great Tang Empire* "A great river is flowing northwardly in the southeast of Hotan town, with a distance of hundreds of kilometers, people use it for irrigation, latterly it broke off". The oasis which lied in lower reaches had no water for irrigation; people was forced to leave there.

In summary, the causes of aeolian desertification of the Tarim Basin in history include natural factors and anthropogenic factors. Recently more and more scholars referred it to "Anthropic-Telluric Relation". Research on coupling relation between natural and anthropogenic variance pointed out whether the natural factors or anthropogenic factors is the dominant factor of environment changes, can only be deduced from analysis in certain time scales combining with proper spatial scope, (Wang , 1995). In earlier human history, the natural factors were dominant for the entire environment evolution of the Tarim Basin. At that time, the water system network disintegration and aeolian desertification spread was resulted from arid environment since later Pleistocene. About 2,000 years ago human economic activities and wars etc. influenced the desert and oasis environment more and more. But in the latest hundreds of years, especially in the recent decades of years, human activity acted determinative operation. Aeolian desertification process also went into a new stage as present period.

2) Processes and causes of present aeolian desertification

The present process of aeolian desertification refers to that in the latest several hundred years and was caused by anthropogenic factors. The regions influenced by aeolian desertification was called aeolian desertified lands.

(1) Aeolian desertification led by lack of comprehensive programming on river water resource utilization.

The water was over used in the upper and middle reaches, and the quantity reduced in lower reaches, making vegetation degradation and malfunction of preventing wind and fixing sand. At the same time, the sandy dry riverbed acted as source for aeolian desertified lands. The following showed water quantity changes and aeolian desertification condition in some major rivers in the latest 50 years.

The Tarim River gathered water from a great deal of water systems originating from the Tianshan Mountains and the Kunlun Mountains. In the past, water was abundant and a water area of 3,000 km^2 was formed at its end, the Lop Nur. After the 1950s, because the large scale agriculture development took irrigated water in the upper and middle reaches, water in the lower reaches reduced continuously. The "Terminal Lake" was the Daxi Lake Reservoir. The water supplied to the lower reach following Tieganlike reduced from $(8-9)\times10^8$ m^3 in the 1950s to 3.6×10^8 m^3 in the 1960s, then to $(0.55-1.09)\times10^8$ m^3 in the 1970s, and in the 1980s basically there was no water supply. The lower reaches with a length of 302 km broke off since the middle of the 1970s. The groundwater level declined because of this, for instance: the water table of Alagan Well fallen from 3–5 m at the end of the 1950s to 11–13 m in 1986. Consequently, the 1.5km riverbed at the end of the Tarim River was buried by dune, and a number of vegetation withered and died. The aeolian desertification of the green corridor accelerated, and the Kuluke Desert in the east bank and the Taklimakan Desert in the west tend to merge because of forwardly dunes movement and shifting sandy-soil (Xia, 1991).

At the beginning of the 1950s, there was $(1.0–1.5)\times10^9$ m^3 water inflooded into the Tarim River, but after 1979 there was basically no water. About 100 km extension of wild *P.cathayana Rehd* and *P. euphratica Olivier* woods down the Xiahe forestry centre of Bachu County faded, and in the latest hundreds of years desertified soil spread with a rate of 20 m/a to oasis.

The mean quantity of water inflooded into the Tarim River from the Hotan River lower reaches was $(11–12)\times10^8$ m^3, but since the 1980s it was less than 8×10^8 m^3, and the least was only 0.4×10^8 m^3. The aeolian desertified area of *P.cathayana Rehd* and *P. euphratica Olivier* woodland in the Hotan River lower reaches had accounted 30%–40% of the entire woodland area. The crescent dune rudiment has formed in higher floodplain by present riverbed where no floods can reach. Sandy land with shifting dunes appeared in many river islands.

About 1,000 years ago, the Keriya River flowed northwardly into the ancient Tarim river. In the inner part of the desert 391 km to (in straight)northern Yutian county, there are intense desertified sites in old riverways, which had dried up since 400–500 a BP, and covered with shifting dunes presently. When Sven. Hedin went there to explore the area of the Keriya River in 1896, the floodwater could flow to 100 km north to Keladun. In the 1950s, the floodwater can reach Xiabulake, 305 km north to Yutian County. And in the 1980s, it reaches only to Daheyan (present village named Daliyaboyi) 225 km north to the city. The retreat of the seasonal runoff is nearly 80 km (Table 12-7).

Table 12-7　The estimated seasonal retreatment condition of the Keriya River

Age	Current type	The place that currently flow to	The distance to Yutian city(km)	The length of shrink age (km)
1950s	Floodwater	Xiabulake	305	
	Normal runoff	Tuobakealagan	265	
1960s	Floodwater	Xiaderang	255	50
	Normal runoff	Iraq	250	15
1970s	Floodwater	Aketuzi	245	60
	Normal runoff	Xiakeshimu	241	24
1980s	Floodwater	Daheyan	225	80
	Normal runoff	Misalai	160	

The Niya River shortened over 20km in one and a half century. At the end of the 19th century, its end was located 8 km north to Damazha. In 1981 it only can reach Damazha. The north to Damazha formed continuously pieces of desertified land.

From the above instances, "Sand Advanced and Human Withdrew" here really means "water withdrew and sand advanced", which was more typical in extremely arid southern Xinjiang. The aeolian desertified land resulting from unreasonable water resource utilization was 3,430 km^2 in the Taklimakan Desert, which accounted for 40% of the total aeolian desertified land area.

(2) Aeolian desertification caused by ignoring environmental protection in land exploiture process.

The mismanagement and misuse of water resource led to the reduction of large areas of vegetation along the river and lower reaches. The "excessive cultivation, cutting and grazing activities" around cultivation region made more and more farmlands degraded to desertified land.

The *P. euphratica Olivier* woodland area, acting as desert barrier, reduced from 520 thousand hm^2 in 1958 to 352.2 thousand hm^2 in 1978, reduced by 32%. The decadent woods area accounted for 10.5% of the total. The decadent woods area in the Tarim River also accounted for 18.7% of this region. During 1958–1978, *P. euphratica Olivier* woods area of lower reaches reduced from 54 thousand hm^2 to 16.4 thousand hm^2, namely it reduced by 69.6%, the rest decadent *P. euphratica Olivier* woodland mostly become into desertified *P. euphratica Olivier* woodland. The *P.cathayana Rehd* and *P. euphratica Olivier* woodland area in the Yerqiang River drainage area reduced from 171.3 thousand hm^2 in 1950s to 94.6 thousand hm^2 in 1985, reduced by 45%. The *P.cathayana Rehd* woods area in the lower reaches of the Kashiger River reduced from 0.7 thousand hm^2 in the beginning of the 1950s to 0.286 thousand hm^2 in 1984, and reduced by 59%. There was10.7 thousand hm^2 *P.cathayana Rehd* woods in the Hotan region between the Karakax River and the Yurungkax River at the beginning of the 1950s, and it was only 1173 hm^2 at the beginning of the 1980s, in addition to scatter woods it was only 3,100 hm^2, and reduced by 70%. Additionally, the vegetation of tamarisks also was destroyed badly. For example in the zone of Bachu County Sanchashankou to the Xiker Reservoir, there was 100 thousand hm^2 of tamarisk in 1958, while at the beginning of the 1980s it was only 6.7 thousand hm^{2}and shifting dune had harmed the Kashi Oasis. The 60% residents in Hotan, Moyu and Luopu counties took wood as their energy source, according to the least quantity of 2.5 t per household, 190 thousand households needed 47.5 thousand tons of wood each year. The annual biology production of three counties diversiform-leaved poplar woods only was 28.8 thousand tons,that of the tamarisk woods was 22.2 thousand tons, and that of the sparse woods was 1.2 t/a, the total of them was 6.5 thousand tons, adding up to 57.5 thousand tons which only was the 12% of the required quantity. Consequently, the desert vegetation of the periphery of Hotan oasis disappeared and shifting dunes connected with the oasis closely. Until now, local people still go into desert and dig and chop the woods.

Since the late 1970s, the environment was getting worse because of digging plants such as *G.uralensis Fisch, Clerodendrum cyrtophyllum* Turcz and *Apocynum lancifolum* L. The *G.uralensis Fisch* area was 3.8 million hm^2 in the past but now it is only 8,000 hm^2. 2 m^2 ground surface will be destroyed while 1 kg *G.uralensis Fisch* was dug. The pasture area, which was destroyed by digging *G.uralensis Fisch*, was 14 million hm^2 in Yuli County in the lower reach the Tarim River, leading to aeolian desertification of pasture and the increase of wind-sand days. The mean wind-sand days increased from 42 days per year in the 1960s to near 1/3 year (near 100 days) in the 1980s, and the aeolian desertified area enlarged by 14.7 million hm^2. According to incomplete statistics, among the 8,600 hm^2 farmland, which had been abandoned by five farming groups of the Tarim downriver areas, there was 2,000 hm^2 which had been buried by shifting sand. The Moyu County in Hotan region asserted more than 14,000 hm^2 abandoned lands in the upper of the Kalakashi River from 1958 to 1960, but more than 4,000 hm^2 were aeolian desertified.

In conclusion, there was 3,838 km^2 desertified land in the Taklimakan Desert because of neglection of environment protection, which accounted for 45% of the present aeolian desertified area.

(3) Aeolian desertification by shifting dunes encroachment.

The downward area of winds, such as forward plain in the piedmont of the Kunlun Mountains is within the range of dunes intrusion. When dune intrusion would occur can be calculated by to estimating dune configuration in typical area. For example, it is showed from the observed information in Pishan area that on sandy gravel plain without plants and in single-direction wind, it will need 3 years to finish the process from 10 cm high pie dune to scutellate dune to rudimental crescent dune to 2 m high dune. But the rate of forward shift was different and with a rate of 10–80 m /a, according to its relationship with the height of dune (Zhu, 1987). The mathematical relation is as follows:

$$D \text{ (value for dune advancement)} = 97.1 - 44.6H \text{ (height of dune)}$$

$$r \text{ (correlation coefficient)} = 0.96$$

In the region with multidirection wind, the effective wind speed making dune move forwardly was weak and low, because wind energy was consumed greatly by adapting new dynamic course. According to the observation in Minfeng region, the mathematical relation between advancement distance and height of dunes lower than 12m was:

$$D = 9.20 - 0.69H, \qquad r = 0.94$$

According to the above method, all kinds of low dunes in the desert fringe were regarded as the result of present wind, and its distribution range was the possible advancement scope of present dune. The intrusion region of the Taklimakan Desert edge can be calculated according to dune height in various areas, as shown in Table 12-8.

Table 12-8　The estimated area of land intruded by modern sand dunes under the force wind in the marginal area of the Taklimakan Desert

Region	Area intruded by modern sand dunes	Account for the overall intruded area (%)
The southwestern edge of the Taklimakan Desert (Yecheng to Hotan)	231	17.8
The middle and southern fringe (Cele to Qiemo)	279	21.5
The southwestern fringe of the Taklimakan Desert (Qiemo to Ruoqiang)	132	10.2
The eastern fringe of the Taklimakan Desert (the lower reaches of Tarim River)	302	23.3
The southern fringe of the Taklimakan Desert	170	13.1
The east of Buguli and the Tuokelake Desert	182	14.1
Total	1,296	100.0

Zhu Zhengda (1987) primarily calculated that the aeolian desertified area was 28,266 km^2 in the Taklimakan desert (Table 12-9).

Table 12-9　The statistics of aeolian desertified land area in the Taklimakan Desert region

The type of aeolian desertified land	The area of desertified land (km^2)	The ratio of the total desertified land (%)
The desertified land formed in history	19,702	69.7
Desertified land in modern time	8,564	30.3
thereinto: desertified land led by ignoring protect environment after assart	3,838	13.6
Desertified land led by unreasonable use of water resource	3,430	12.1
Desertified land led by inbreak of dune under the operation of wind force	1,296	4.6
Total	28,266	100

We can conclude from the statistics of Table 12-9:

① In total area of 3.26×10^5 km^2 of the Taklimakan Desert, the desertified land area accounted for 8.6%.

② In aeolian desertified land, anthropogenic part accounted for 84.9%, and the natural accounted for 15.1%, mainly by dune advancement. Human activities were the dominating factors of aeolian desertification. Therefore, when we exploit and utilize natural resources in the Taklimakan Desert region, effective prevention and control strategy on aeolian desertification should be taken.

3) The causes and evolution trends of aeolian desertification

(1) Aeolian desertification causes

In the human history, due to the influence of natural factors such as climate changes. and anthropogenic factors, the aeolian desertification of Tarim Basin experienced different stages. The intensity and evolution forms is diverse, especially in the latest decades, the strong economical activity deeply influenced the aeolian desertification development,which is characterized by the co-existence of aeolian desertification and oasification. In the upper river, a great deal irrigation works were built, the cultivated land continuously enlarged, indicating the artifical oasification . At the same time, because of the over-damming in upper and middle reaches, river was shortened even broke off, leading to obvious aeolian desertification in downstream regions.

According to aerial photograph and satellite images in 1959, 1983, 1992 and 1996, we mapped(all in scale as 1:100,000) and analyzed the land use changes of the Alaer area in upper river, the vegetation change of Yingbazha area in middle river and change of aeolian desertification of Alagan area in downriver. It is seen that the co-existence of aeolian desertification and oasification in Tarim downriver is manifested by: ① The rapid development of cultivated land in Upper River; ②obvious change of vegetation in middle river; ③continuously increased in aeolian desertified land area down river.

The cultivated land increased by 14,800 hm^2 from 22,900 hm^2 in 1959 to 37,700 hm^2 in 1996; the mean annual increase is 400 hm^2. During 1992–1996, it increased more rapidly; with mean annual increase of 975 hm^2, salinization of cultivated land were mitigated when cultivated land increased. The woods and grass land decreased, while the *P. euphraica Oliver* decreased by 3,666 hm^2, the brush wood decreased by 8,232.2 hm^2, the various grass land decreased by 7,150.5 hm^2, and the total is 19,048.5 hm^2. The river bank field and river way changed obviously and the bank were eroded seriously. The cropland destroyed by wind can reach 768.2 km^2 in southern bank.

In the middle reaches, poplar woods and shrub increased by 2,300 hm^2 and 174 hm^2 respectively, with an annual increase of 0.53% and 0.02%, because nature reserve of poplar was established and strengthened. The recovery of vegetation prevent the development of desert area. The increase rate of aeolian desertification was 0.27%–0.76% before 1983, and it decrease by − 0.14%−−1.12% after 1983. Researches on aeolian desertification in Yingbazha area in recent 30 years indicated that the area of aeolian desertified land accounted for 59.07% of the total area in the early 1960s, 67.67% in the late 1970s and the average annual increase was 0.76%. The desertified area accounted for 68.58% of the whole area in the early 1980s, and the average annual increase was 0.27%. The development of desertified land reduced, compared to that in the early 1960s and late 1970s, The desertified area accounts for 63.63% of the whole area in the early 1990s. The area is still large comparing with the late 1950s, but it was reduced compared with the late 1970s and the early 1980s. Aeolian desertification in this area decreased, and the annual average is 1.12% from the early 1980s to 1990s. The area of poplar is 2956 hm^2 in the 1996. The growth of poplar improved, because the area submerged by the super flood reached 2–6 km wide. Some dry river channels in the past was also filled with water, and the moisture condition of woodland was improved. But the area of brush and grass decreased by 5,176 hm^2, and some of them was led by vegetation damage. There were 387 hm^2 cultivated land in 1992, and it increased to 2,202 hm^2 in 1996. Many land was abandoned and became desert.

The aeolian desertified land in down river area increased by 123.1 km^2 in 1996 compared with 1959, which accounted for 94.34% of the inspected area. The average annual increase rate of aeolian desertification was 0.24%, 0.26% before 1983, and 0.12%–0.20% in 1983. This was related to the protection of vegetation remnant. The aeolian desertification degree increased, with severely aeolian desertified land increased from 6.08% of land area in 1959 to 11.7% in 1996 and extremely severe aeolian desertified land from 30.2% to 33.76%. According to the development trend and the worsening moisture condition, it is difficult to control.

(2) The evolution trend of aeolian desertification.

The aeolian desertification in Tarim developed and changed with the extension of human exploited and utilized natural resources. At the same time, the feedback of aeolian desertification on human economic society is more and more intense.

From the trend of population development, the population of Southern Xinjiang was 7.0582 million in 1990, and the natural growth ratio was 18%–22% (Wang, 1995). Based on this development ratio, the population will reach 150.907 million in 2020. Seen from the climate changes, the research of stratum sections in southern Taklimakan edge had proved that climate was arid and wind condition changed little in desert region since last glacial period. According to sporro-pollen analysis and ^{14}C dating in the Lop the Nur Basin Section, the arid desert climate has changed a little in the last 20 Ka. The palynological data analysis and ^{14}C dating of the Hotanyuetegan relic culture stratum also proved that the climate was arid and temperate since 2,500 a. The climate changes in history also indicated that the overall climate obviously changed into arid in the Tarim Basin and still continue. Consequently it can be estimated that the environment problem such as water resource shortage, aridity, and wind-sand disaster and land degradation will restrict human activation in the future decades.

On one hand, in oasis area surrounding the basin in front of mountains, there was adequate water for irrigation because that water source was stable. The underground fresh water belt had certain width, and irrigation works was constructed in long term, especially with the construction of preventing infiltration aqueduct and exploiture of water source. The establishment of forest protected farmland, and the land was fertilized and production capability increased. In addition, culture degree enhanced, and the oasis in this area has become base of meat, melon and vegetable. It can be predicted that the agriculture in this area would get better. The environmental quality of oasis improved, the volume of population and land carrying capacity increased along with the improvement of irrigation works and product ability. In some areas, wind blowing sand will be relieved and controlled through the realization of integrated repair and prevent sand project of aeolian desertification.

On the other hand, anthropic activity influenced to a certain extent. The surface water runoff is about 39.2 billion m^3 around Tarim. In history, the scale of oasis is not big, only part of the water inflows the oasis, mostly inflow to the desert margin and hinterland. Since the 20th century, with the increase of fore-mountain oasis, the river mostly flowed to oasis, and the quantity inflowed to margin and hinterland of desert become less. The development of economy needs more water resource. The industry and agriculture production and the city life water supply increased, especially land. Gas resource exploitation and petroleum industry development, make water resource become more and more intense. More water is required in developed area and it makes quantity of water inflowed to the margin and hinterland of desert become less and less. The imbalance of water resource will increase continually, making contradiction of the water and land imbalance in basin worse, and accelerate aeolian desertification.

Fortunately, the country had paid great attention to the problems of environment in the west. "The research on the evolution of ecological environment and its regulation and control in the arid area in west China" and "The research on the process of aeolian desertification in Northern China and its protect" projects have been listed in the developmental program of national key basic research. In the Tarim Basin, engineering work is ongoing, which will control the whole drainage area. The layout of the project is to stabilize the upper reaches, manage the middle reaches and protect the lower reaches. Through various adjustments and controlling measures, the anthropic activity and geography environment will be in the way of inter-adaptive, cooperative and development.

12.2.5 Natural resources and the evaluation in the Tarim Basin

12.2.5.1 General situations of socioeconomy

The Southern Xinjiang, including the Tarim Basin composed of Kashi, Hotan, Aksu and Kezilesukerkezi Automous Region, Bayinguole Mongolian Autonomous Region, adding up to five cities and 37 counties, has an area of about 1.066,2 million km^2, and total population of 7.214,4 million. The density is 7 people per km^2 which was 2 people less than the whole Xinjiang. It also borders on Kirghiziastan, Tajikestan, Afghanistan and India, and the boundary line is 2,200 km long. It has five ports which had been opened up or will be opened.

The eastern and northern parts of the Tarim basin including Bayinguole Mongolian Autonomous Region and Bayinguole-Aksu in Aksu region which lies in the eastern and northern Tarim Basin, have 2 cities and 16 counties totally. The an area was 60.769,8 million hm^2. The population density was 4 people per km^2 and there are 33 nationalities including Uigur, Hui, Han and Mongolian etc. The Minority population accounted for 70% of the total, and is the region with the biggest area and less population in Xinjiang Autonomous Region. The region connects Southern Xinjiang and Northern Xinjiang. The railway had been put to use by 2000. At the same time, it was the strategic passage from Xinjiang to Qinghai and hinterland and its strategic status is important. On the West it borders Kirghizistan Republic and had an opening port of Biedieli.

The Hotan region, Kashi region and Kashi-Kezilesukerkezi-Hotan region in Kezilesukerkezi autonomous Region lies in the western and northern Tarim Basin. There are 3 cities and 21 countries in total. The total land area was 45.852,4 million hm^2; the population density was 10 people per km^2 and was 359 people per km^2 in oasis region. The Minority population accounted for 94% of this region and they were inhabited in this region. It was also the important way and converge point of southern and middle "Silk Road", and was an important port that our country communicates with various countries in Middle and Southern Asian. The Hotan region borders on Kirghiziastan, Tajikestan, Afghanistan and India etc. The borderline is over 2,000 km^2. There are four ports such as Hongqisufu, Kalasu, Yishuerstan, and Tuerzate, but, the traffic is not convenient, the natural environment is not good, and the economy is not well developed. One fourth of the population was still in poverty.

12.2.5.2 Light and heat resource

The climate of this area is arid, belonging to typical warm temperate zone continental climate. The weather is much sunny with little precipitation. The atmosphere transparency is good, sunshine hour is long, light and heat resource is abundant, the ratio of sunlight is up to 60% –70%. The diurnal temperature difference is 14 –16 °C, and the frost tree period is 180 –240 days. All of these are propitious to accumulate sugar for vegetation. It is the major production region of melon and fruit, and most the region is developed for cotton production.

The sun radiation of Aksu area in Bayingolin Mongol Autonomous Region is 6,000–6,260 MJ/m^2. The annual sunlight hour is 2,800–3,000, and the accumulated temperature that is more than 10 °C is 3,800–4,300 °C. Period without frost is 210–230 days and the diurnal temperature difference is 12–14 °C. Heat increased from mountainous region to plain regions, it also increase a little from west to east. It is fit for planting caloric-tolerance crop such as continent cotton, long villas cotton, Kurle savory pear, Kuqa white apricot and Aksu golden coronal apple, all are popular. The red pigment content of tomato exceeds that of trump production in America and Italy. In the inter-valley of lower mountainous region and basin, the accumulated temperature that is more than 10 °C is 3,300–3,600 °C, the period without frost is 180 days. It is fit to plant wheat, oil plants and sugar beet, and it has one harvest time in a year or three harvest times in two years.

The zone of Kashi-Kezilesu-Hotan, except mountainous region, belongs to warm temperate arid climate, there are many mountains, the topography is complex and the difference is big in interior. In the plain zone, precipitation is little, and evaporation is intense. Sunlight is abundant, and light and heat resource is rich. The annual sun radiation quantity is about 6,000 MJ/m^2, and the annual sunlight time is 2,600–2,800 days, with period without frost of 210–240 days. The accumulated temperature that is more than 10 °C is 4,100–4,500 ℃, the Artux can reach 4,700 ℃, the diurnal temperature difference is 12–14 ℃. It is propitious for plant cotton, melon and fruit, grape, silkworm mulberry, and had two harvest times in a year. The region near desert has high temperature in summer and large diurnal temperature difference due to desert influence, here is propitious for planting long villus cotton. It has much excellent fruit that famous in our country such as Jiashi melon, megranate, almond, fig and peach. But the Kizilsu Kirgiz Autonomous Region has 90% mountainous land and little heat resource. The accumulated temperature more than 10 ℃ is 2,400–2,500 ℃ in Wuqia and Aheqi valley region. It is not propitious for planting crops. The accumulated temperature more than 10 ℃ is only 1,500 ℃ in Kashikuer region.

12.2.5.3　Water resource

The total available water resource in southern Xinjiang is 52.789 billion m^3, accounting for 48.11% of the whole Xinjiang. Meanwhile the surface river runoff is 39.269 billion m^3; the exploitation quantity of ground water is 13.5 billion m^3. The average water resource in the region is limited, and most fluvial runoff distributes unequally in various seasons. It is arid in spring but waterlogged in summer. Now the utilization ratio of water resource is nearly 50%.

In Bayinguole-Aksu, the climate is arid, the annual precipitation is 40–80mm in plain region, and it is less than 20mm in the southern area. The mountainous region has more precipitation, the south piedmont of the Tianshan Mountains is 200–400mm, the northern piedmont of the Altun Mountains is 100–300mm, and it decreases a little from west to east. The evaporation can reach 2,000–2,900 mm and is 25–100 times of the precipitation quantity. The total available water resource in this region is 25.871 billion m^3 and the average is 42,620 m^3/km^2, and it is 65% of the average in whole Xinjiang, but the individual available quantity in water resource is 1.4 times of that of whole Xinjiang. The surface water runoff is 19.049 billion m^3, and there are 60 rivers and the main are the Kaidu River, the Konqi River, the Tarim River, the Weigan River and the Aksu River. The groundwater exploitation is 6.822 billion m^3, which accounts for 22.50% and 27.28% of the whole Xinjiang separately. The water resource spatial distribution is very imbalanced, seen from surface water run off quantity distribution, the Aksu region has 12.6 billion m^3 and is abundant-water zone, the most regions in Bayingolin Mongol Autonomous Region have 6.0 billion m^3 and is middle-water zone, the Qiemo and Ruoqiang regions are most scarce, meanwhile the yearly run off quantity of the Cherchecheng River only is 0.54 billion m^3. The water area in this region accounts for 36% of the whole Xinjiang, the water that can be used for cultivation is 131 thousand hm^2 and accounts for 38.99% of the whole Xinjiang. The water area of the Bosten Lake—the biggest fresh water lake in Xinjiang is about 100 thousand hm^2 and belongs to middle nutrition water area, also it is the second biggest fishery base in Xinjiang. There are a lot of bulrush resources growing to weave and make paper. There are 7 families, 29 genera and 39 species of fishes in this region, meanwhile there are 2 families and 8 species of local fishes, there are 31 species of fishes with high economical value such as grass carp, chub, carp, bream fish and fresh-water bream.

In Kashi-Kizilsu Kirgiz-Hotan region, annual precipitation is less than 50mm in plain, it is 200–300mm in mountainous, and belongs to areas with little precipitation. But it still has some water resource because of the supplement of glaciers melt water and that the region is expansion. The total available water is 26.893 billion m^3 and the average is 58,665 m^3/km^2. The per capita is 5,773 m^3, they are 89% and 80% of the whole Xinjiang, respectively. And it belongs to deficit-water region. Meanwhile the surface run-off quantity is about 20.22 billion m^3 and accounts for 23.88% of the whole Xinjiang. The main rivers are the Yerqiang River,the Kaxgar River, the Hotan River, the Keriya River, the Andir River, the Kalamila River, the Gaizi River and the Kezi River etc. The groundwater exploitation is 6.673 billion m^3 and accounts for 26.68% of the whole Xinjiang. The theoretical reserve of water energy in the area is 1.200,75 million kW. there are 55 power stations whose capacity are over 12,000 kW, the total capacity is 2.626,9 million kW, which accounts for 35.79% of theoretical reserves of water energy and 30.78% of capacity of those of whole Xinjiang, respectively. They assemble in the above mentioned rivers such as the Kashiger River, the Yerqiang River, the Karakax River and the Yurungkax River.

12.2.5.4　Land resources

There are several kinds of arable land with a total area of 34.5802 million hm^2, accounting for 32.43% of the whole land, and the farming land is 2.397,6 million hm^2 accounting for 40.75% of Xinjiang. There are 2.943,1 million hm^2 bad lands can be exploited which account for 60.09% of the whole Xijiang land. There are 19.951,6 million hm^2 grasslands accounting for 41.56% of the Xijiang grass land, but the productivity and quality of the land is not good. The capability of domestic animals is 12.73 million sheep account for 39% of the whole Xijiang. The coverage of forest is 1.19%, which is

0.38% lower than the coverage of Xijiang. The forest area is 17,825 million hm², and the amount of growing trees is 419,716 million m³. This area is the main distributing region of plain desert forest and artificial forest. The desert forest area is 13,475 million hm², and the amount of growing trees is 139,219 million m³, accounting for 93.96% and 96.23% of plain desert forest in the whole Xinjiang respectively. The plain artificial forest is 0.315,6 million hm² and the amount of growing stock of standing trees is 163,342 million m³, accounting for 69.24% and 62.96% of plain artificial forest of the whole Xinjiang, respectively. The growth of vegetation in mountainous area is worse than that in the North Xijiang. The forest area and the amount of growing stock of standing tree only account for 7.65% and 5.34% of the whole Xinjiang respectively. The forest on the south slope of the Tianshan distributes as points and slices. There is no forest in the east of Yecheng on the north slope of the Kunlun Mountains.

There are several kinds of available lands with a total area of 18.7034 million hm² from Bayinguole to Aksu. The availability ratio of land is 30.78% which is 10.4% lower than that of the whole Xinjiang. There is farmland 1.103,3 million hm² accounting for 18.75% of the whole Xinjiang and the quality is well. The potential land resources are abundant, and there is 2.390,4 million hm² wildland can be exploited which account for 48.81% of the available land in whole Xinjiang, but the quality is low. The first and second grade of land only account for 33% which is mainly distributed in drainage areas like Kuqa, Shaya, Xinhe, Awati of Aksu, and the Konqi River drainage area in the Weigan river drainage area. The area suitable to forest is 1.235 million hm², and the quality is well. Thereinto, the first and second grade of the land which suitable to forest account for 55%, are mainly distributed in countries and cities like Hejing, Baicheng, Kuqa, Yuli, Shaya. The available area for grazing is 1.397,47 million hm² but, the quality of land is low, among which the areas of the first and second grade of the grazing available land accounts for 26%, mainly distributed in Hejing, Bayinbuluke, banks of the Kaidu River, and Baicheng, Heshuo, Kuqa, Yuli, Wensu, Aksu, Yanji bansin, Qiemo, Ruoqiang, etc. The forest area is 1.017,4 million hm², and the amount of growing stock of standing tree is 26.034,1 million m³. The among which area of diversiform-leaved poplar woods in plain desert is 0.822,6 million hm² and the the amount of growing tree is 9.087,4 million m² in plain desert, which accounts for 56.11% and 62.8% of those in whole Xinjiang respectively. The poplar wood is concentrated in this regions and the woodland area only accounts for 5.29%. The broad distribution of desert diversiform-leaved poplar woods with the tamarisks and reeds composed a green barrier on the fringe of desert, which plays an important role on maintaining oasis and desert environment. In plain the artificial woods area is 90,400 hm² and the amount of growing stock of standing tree is 6,003,700 m³, accounting for 19.84% and 23.14% of those in whole Xinjiang respectively. In mountainous region the woods area is 104,400 hm² and the amount of growing stock of standing tree is 10,943,000 m³, they are mainly distributed in Gongnaisi forest centre in the Tianshan Mountains. The available area of natural grassland is 28.1 hm² and the available stock capacity is 7,296,3 million sheep, which accounts for 24.11% and 22.63% of those in whole Xinjiang, respectively. Especially the Bayanbulak Grassland is the most famous and it is one of the most superior pastures in Xinjiang.

Kashi-Kizilsu Kirgiz-Hotan region has various kinds of available lands amounting to 15.876,8 million hm^2 and the available ratio is 34.63%. Now the farmland is 1.294,3 million hm^2 and accounts for about 22% of the Xinjiang. The potential land resources are abundant, and the area suitable for cultivation is 0.522,7 million hm^2 accounting for 11.29% of that in whole Xinjiang, with the most of them belonging to the third and fourth grades, accounts for 92%. The wildland suitable for cultivation is mainly distributed in the middle and lower reaches of the Yarkant River and the Kaxgar River, the Hotan River and the Keriya River drainage area. The available woodland area is about 0.607,6 million hm^2, and the first and second grade accounts for 58% and the quality is better. It is mainly distributed in drainage of the Yarkant River, the eastern mountainous region in Pamirs, middle and down of the Keriya River, the Yarkant River and the Hotan River drainage area. The available area for grazing is about 13.422,2 million hm^2, the first and second grade accounts for 58%. The land quality is worse and mainly distributes in drainages like Pamirs, the Yarkant River, the Hotan River, the Keriya River in mountainous region in east of Pamirs. The woods area is 0.765,1 million hm^2, the amount of growing tree is 15.937,5 million m^3, and most of them are plain desert woods and plain manual woods. The plain desert woods area is 0.524,9 million hm^2 and the amount of growing tree is 4.834,5 million m^3, accounting for 35.81% and 33.41% respectively to those of the whole desert woods in Xinjiang. Among them woods are 72,600 hm^2, accounting for 50.63% of plain desert woods in whole Xinjiang. It is one of the collective distribution region of desert woods with diversiform-leaved poplar in Xinjiang. They mainly distribute in the Yarkant River, the Hotan River, the Keriya River, the Andier River, the Kalamilan River, the Niya River banks and end of Kashiger River. The artificial woods area in the plain is 0.225 million hm^2 and the amount of growing stock of standing tree is 10.330,5 million m^3, accounting for 49.41% and 39.82% of the whole manual woods in Xinjiang. The main tree species are *Populus, E.angusifolia L, Morus alba L, Salix, valnut, almond, P. davidiana Franch, P. armeniaca* var. ansu *Maxim, U. pumila L and Periploca sepium Bge*. The available natural grassland area is about 8.376,2 million hm^2 and the available stock capacity is 5.233,3 million sheep units, accounting for 17.45% and 16.23% of the whole Xinjiang respectively. Good grasslands are little, and most of them are bad. The proportion of grassland area lack of water is big. The stock capacity is low. The forage grass in farm region is abundance. More *G.uralensis Fisch* resource distributes in desert plain of the Yarkant River and the Kaxgar River drainage area, there will be high economic value if they can be exploited and utilized.

12.2.5.5 Mineral resource

In southern Xinjiang, there are mineral resources such as oil, natural gas, jade, gypsum, iron, gold, vermiculite, asbestos, Irish diamond, copper, salt, gem, andalusite, limestone, Glauber's salt, argil, lead, coal, lazurite, phosphorite, magnesite, dolomite, natural sulphur, sulfur iron ore and so on, and most minerals are favorable, also the oil, natural gas, vermiculite, asbestos, sulphur, iron ore, Glauber's salt, jade are abundant, the coal is relatively scarce and lcocated in some areas and there exist great regions without coal.

The potential value of available reserves of mineral that had been proved by 1990 was 46.262 billion *yuan* in Bayinguole-Aksu region, the main preponderant minerals were oil, natural gas, asbestos, vermiculite, iron ore, coal, managesite, gypsum, limestone, dolomite, etc. The oil, natural gas, asbestos were important for the whole country. The prospecting of oil and gas resources in the northern Tarim acquired greatly breakthrough in recent years, not only the oil and gas are good, but also a passel oil and gas fields had been proved up and controlled in Lunnan, Yakela, Jilake, Sangtamu, Jiefangqu, etc. The available geological reserves of oil and gas fields had been proved up and controlled had increased drastically. It had been the strategic superseding region of oil and gas resources in our country. Our country has determined to build "the west gas is transported to the east" engineering from Lunnan to Shanghai which had accomplished primary design when exploiting the natural resource in Tarim. It is more delectable to exploit desert oil field in the center of the Tarim Basin; lots of reserve oil conformations had been discovered in desert hinterland, which had prefigured that there were many oil fields under the boundless sand sea. Qieganbulake vermiculite mine in Yuli County was the oversize mineral bed in the world. This region possesses our country maximum asbestos deposit belt, the asbestos reserve accounts for 98% of that in whole Xinjiang, all are distributed in Qiemo and Ruoqiang two counties. The coal resource is more abundant and the prognosticative reserve is more than 90 billion tons, the reserve proved is 2.515 billion tons and accounts for 2.7% of that in the whole Xinjiang. It distributes focusly in Yanqi basin, Kuqa and Baicheng and is the most important coal field in southern Xinjiang. The theoretic reserve of water energy is 5.871,2 million kW. There are 23 power stations with the designed capacity of more than 10,000 kW, and the total designed capacity reaches 1.731,4 million kW, accounting for 1/5 of the whole Xinjiang. The water energy of the Kaidu River drainage area distributes concentratedly and is convenient for various rundle exploiting.

The geological construction in Kashi-Kizilsu Kirgiz-Hotan region is complicated. There are six belts of ore with promising prospect passing this region, namely they are copper ore belt in Gaizitekelimansu, lead and zinc multiple metal ore belt in Gongger, nephrite ore belt in Hotan-Yutian, copper, sulphur, rare metals and gem mine zone in Qieliekeqi, gem ore belt in Aketaosubashi, rare metal, mica and gem ore belt in Sansu-Hongliutan. The mineral reserve of copper, gem and jade, gold, lead, zinc and rare metals is big, but the most mineral resource is not clear and the available reserve proved small. The latent value of proved reserve was 4.497 billion *yuan* in 1990. The available reserve of cement limestone was over 0.11 billion tons. The reserve of lead and zinc are proved to account for 69% and 96% of the whole Xinjiang's respectively. Distributing in the three counties of Atushi, Wuqia and Aketao, the natural sulphur and iron ore reserve accounts for 100% and 88.21% of the whole Xinjiang's respectively, the iron ore proved reserve was 65.58 million tons in Qiwliekeqi of Aketao County and was in the third place in Xinjiang. The future of oil and gas resources are promising, the depressed area in the southwestern Tarim Basin is 61,600 km^2, and is the most developed regions in Xinjiang, the prognosticative reserve of oil and gas resource is 5.6 billion tons, the Kekeya Oil Field and abundance oil and gas indication had been discovered. The condition for mineralization of coal is bad, the scale is small, the quality is poor, and coal beds are unstable and mostly distribute in mountainous region, belonging to lack coal region. The reserve proved is about 0.145 billion tons, which only accounts for 0.16% of the whole Xinjiang's. It is mainly distributed in Wuqia County in Kizilsu Kirgiz autonomous borough, Hotan City and Pishan County in Hotan region. A great deal of coal is imported from Aksu region annually because of little coal field there. In the countrysides the major fuel is biologic energy. The main reason that lots of desert vegetation had been destroyed is the lack of fuel.

12.2.5.6 Tourist resources

The tourist resources are abundant. There are peculiar arid natural scenery, high mountain sights, and colorful ethical customs. It also has many remains of ancient "Silk Road" and plenty regional and ethical products. All of these make it advantageous to develop traveling resources.

It is the only way of the middle and the south lines of the ancient "Silk road" from Bayingolin to Aksu, and the tourist resources are abundant. There are 123 cultural relics, and the focus and famous areas are in the vicinity of Kuqa. There are five famous Thou-Buddha Cavities in Xijiang, and four of them are in the vicinity of Kuqa. The Kezier Thou-Buddha Cavity in Baicheng County can compare with the Mogao Grotto in Dunhuang, the Yungang Grotto in Datong, and the Longmen Grotto in Luoyang. And the Kumulatu Thou-Buddha Cavity, the Shubashi Buddha Temple remains, the Guizi Old City Ruins, the Big Dragon Pool and the Little Dragon Pool,etc. Kuqa has unique charm. Moreover, there also are the Altun Mountains Natural Reserve, the Bayanbulak Swan Reserve, the Bayanbulak grassland, the Bositeng Lake, the Tiemenguan Pass, the Lop Nur Yardang landforms, the Loulan Old City, the Milan Old City, the Bogdaqin Old City, the Xikeqin Thou-Buddha Cavity, the Moleqia river rock portray, the Tomür Peak in western of the main Tianshan Mountains, and poplar woods on banks of the Tarim River. These tourist resources are more attractive and can be exploited.

The inland desert, plateau scenery and world-famous crest in Kashi-Kizilsu Kirgiz-Hotan area are natural tourist resources. There are many optimal fields suitable to travel and scientific investigation and explore, such as the second highest in the world- Qogir Summit, "Father of glaciers" Muztagata Summit and Kongurr Summit, the biggest and oldest oasis in Xijiang - Kashi, Shache, Hotan oasis, the vast Taklimakan Desert with Buguli and Tuohulake Deserts under oasis, has dune styles of complex and complete. Nations, folk-customs, religions, and histories are multi-combination, which make the human culture traveling resources miraculous and colorful. The ancient "Silk Road", Islamic religionary architectures, minority customs, folk-customs and culture arts all have special charm. There are many cultural relics such as the Xiangfei Tomb, the Aitigaer Mosque, the Aisikeshaer Ancient City Ruins, the Yushufumazha, the Suwen Ancient City, the Three-immortal Buddha Cavity, ancient-tomb-group of 10th century, and Gaizi Dak on the ancient "Silk Road". The most attractive subjects are the travelling of ancient "Silk Road", desert exploration and climbing mountains. The superiority of this area is there are many ports such as Konjirap and Tuerzate which are opened to outside. It also has fine conditions to develop domestic tourism.

Moreover, there are plenty of wildlife resources in south Xijiang such as kendyr, licorice, herba cistanches, reed, wapiti, wild yak, Tibetan antilope, bharal, argal, which have values for scientific research and economic utilization. It is the urgent affair to protect these resources. Since the foundation of the People's Republic of China, the water and land resources in Southern Xijiang are exploited constantly. The regional economy of agriculture and grazing as main bodies has been greatly developed. Presently it has become main producing region of melon, fruit and cotton in Xinjiang. And the stockbreeding in farm region also has important status. Recently, the largescale exploiting of petroleum, natural gas, vermiculite and asbestos minerals makes the development of natural resources enter into a new phase, which will be hoped to make the area become the important area of petrol industrial and base of nonmetal building materials.

12.3 Kumtag Desert

"Kumtag" means "sand hills" in Uigur. The Kumtag Desert is distributed to the north of the Altun Mountains, south of the Kezile Tagh Mountains, east of the Lop Nur, west of the Kala Tagh Mountains and Tuliangdao, from E 91°25' to 94°00', and N 38°20' to 40°50', with an extensive area of 20,000 km². Its width is 120 km, and the length is 280 km (Fig. 12-18). The area of aeolian yardangs is the largest in the vicinity of the Kumtag Desert and the Lop Nur. The Kumtag Desert takes on broomlike shape and is famous for its unique feather dunes in China.

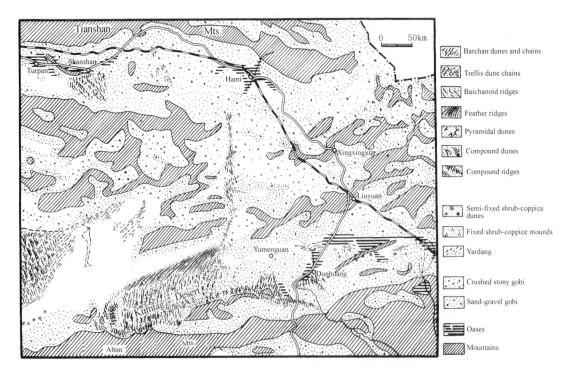

Fig. 12-18 Distribution map of the Kumtag Desert

12.3.1　Regional physical geographic features

Tectonically, the Kumtag Desert is comparable with the Taklimakan Desert. In the late Tertiary and early Quaternary, mountainous regions around the Tarim Basin were uplifted intensively due to tectonic movement, and formed the present basin configuration. Because of the intense uplift of the Kunlun Mountains in the southern basin margin, the Tarim Basin shifted from a terrain with high topography in the center to a terrain leaning from southwest to northeast. The topography characteristics controlled by tectonic movement influenced the water system distribution and deposition characteristics in the whole basin, and resulted in the rivers originating from the Tianshan Mountains, the Kunlun Mountains and the Altun Mountains to converge into one. This river then inflooded into the Lop Nur of the eastern basin, which made it become the lowest point and catchment center of the Tarim basin. The Tarim River and its branches transported a great deal of mountainous weathering materials to the Lop Nur region, then deposited and formed extensive deltas, alluvial plains and lacustrine plains. According to drilling recorder, the Quaternary deposite profile is as deep as 500 m in the district of Tieganlike. These fluvial and lacustrine deposits composed of fine sand, silty clay (Fig. 12-19), and the abundant sand beds were the main sources of the Kumtag Desert.

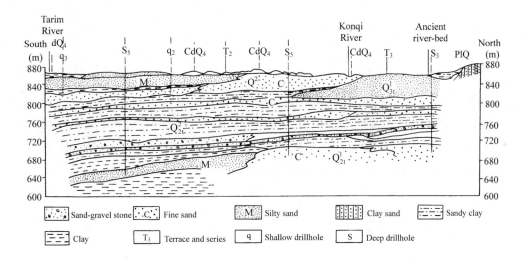

Fig. 12-19　Material sources of the Kumatag Desert

Influenced by new tectonic movements, the underlying physiognomy of the Kumtag Desert is an extremely arid denudated highlands with undulating monadnocks. The Annanba alluvial fan in the northern slopes of the Altun Mountains was cut into a ravine with a depth of 100–200 m by runoff, and most mountains developed dry valleys with directions from north to south. The desert was covered on the 1,250–2,000 m high lithoid mountain region, or covered on the alluvial plain.

The Kumtag Desert is distributed in the extremely arid region of China. The uplift of the Qilian

Mountains, the Tianshan Mountains, the Kunlun Mountains around the Tarim Basin are the main causes that make this region become arid. The uplifts of these high mountains severely destroyed the atmospheric circumfluence, water, and the heat equilibrium condition of the Northern Hemisphere. But the Qinghai-Tibet Plateau in the south fringe influences to a maximum extent. Its mean altitude is over 4,500 m and composes the "World Fastigium" with the highest topography on the earth. It also obstructs the southwest monsoon from flowing northward and makes it arid. Because the passage where the southwest monsoon entered into Xinjiang was maintained in the early Quaternary, the arid climate began in the early Quaternary and has lasted until the present. In the entire Quaternary period, although the climate of mountainous regions around the basin fluctuated, the arid climate characteristics changed very little. This was proven by the extensive gypsum beds and salt shuck mixing in exposed Quaternary deposits in the Lop Nur region. These deposits formed in an extremely arid condition or they were once in an extremely arid condition after formation. The long term arid climate was a necessary condition to form the desert in this region.

According to records between 1979–1981, the annual precipitation in this area is about 20 mm, and even only about 10 mm in desert regions. The annual evaporation capacity is 2,800–3,000 mm, and the annual mean temperature is about 10 °C. The January mean temperature is about –8°C. The July mean temperature is about 28 °C. The main wind is a strong northeaster, and the second is northwester. It sometimes appears as a 40–50 m/s gale near the northwest gale entrance in the Turpan Basin, where there are frequent sandstorms and floating dust weather. The number of days with over eight grade wind is over 10 days, and the dunes are shifting sand hills (dunes) with lower speed.

The height of the surface water runoff formation zone is over 2,500 m a.s.l. Because the glaciers are small and thawing water from snow is little in the Altun Mountains. But in places with heights of 2,500–3,000 m, the surface water had switched into underground, so the entire desert body has no surface water runoff, but there are a few springs exposed in valleys with a direction from north to south in the eastern desert. There is metamorphic cranny water in the southern desert edge and it is bicarbonate-chloride-sodium water. The mineralization degree is 1 g/L. Dune water is distributed in other regions, with a conjectured burying depth of about 30 m in depth in intervals, is chloride-vitriol-sodium water, and the mineralization degree is about 3–10 g/L. The desert belongs to a water area of thermo mineralization carried methane in an artesian basin. According to geology tectonics, there may be deep-seated artesian water in deserts and the water layer is thick.

The gypsum brown desert and oasis soil are distributed in the Shule River of the eastern Kumtag Desert. The salt-alkali soil with salt comes from the Lop Nur and downriver of Shule River in northern desert. Aeolian sandy soil, sub-sandy soil and extremely arid sandy entisol distribute in desert.

Except for the vegetation in the valley of the eastern desert, the other region had rare vegetation. The vegetation species are *Chenopodiaceae, Compositae, Tamarisk caceae, Leguminosae, Zygophyllaceae, Gramineae and Ephedra, Nitraria, Artemisia.*

12.3.2 The source and formation of desert sand

12.3.2.1 The source of desert sand

It can be learned from the composition character of desert sand matter that the desert sand mainly comes from underground sediment. Because of the differences among underground deposits, the sand material sources are various and affected by the underground sediment.

(1) From the ancient lacustrial sediments. The Lop Nur is the lowest region of the Tarim Basin, and is the center of water in the area,thus forming extensive lacustrine and fluvial sediment plains. The Yardang physiognomy in the northern edge of the Kumtag Desert exposed many Quaternary lacustrine sediments that are mainly composed of interlayers of silver sand and clay. The strong northeaster eroded the lacustrince sediments year by year just like a huge iron-comb would scrape and incise the ground;this eroded the loose sand layer, and left erosion-resistant skeletons of clay. All of these formations make up the Yardangs (Fig. 12-20). Because of the transit of the northeaster, the loose sand layer scraped away by the wind accumulates in the northern piedmont of the Altun Mountains, developing the Kumtag Desert.

Fig. 12-20　Typical Yandangs eroded by wind shaping lacustrince sediments at the margin of the Lop Nur

(2) From fluvial sediment. Historically,the Shule River deposited fluvial sediments in the eastern Kumtag Desert. These fluvial sediments are mainly composed of interlayers of fine sand, silt and clay (Fig. 12-21). By the action of wind, the sand in the loose sandy layers were eroded, transported, and deposited to form the eastern Kumtag Desert.

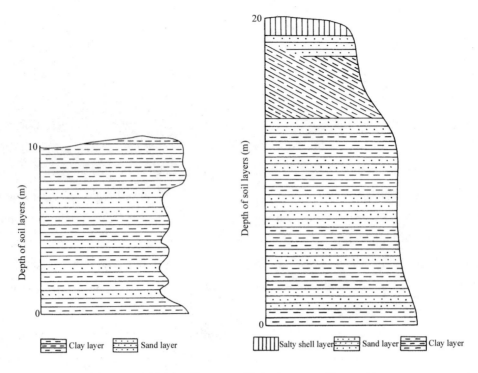

Fig. 12-21　Fluvial sediments profile in the eastern Kumtag Desert

(3) From proluvium. The area with diluvial sediments in the southern piedmont of the Kezile Tagh Mountains and north of Sanlongsha is large. The diluvial sediments are mainly composed of gravel mingling with coarse and fine sand (Fig. 12-22). The surface of the ground is mainly gravel, and the fine sand had been blown by the northeast wind, becoming one of the Kumtag Desert sand sources. Especially in the northeastern desert, many sand sources are from the Sanlongsha area. The sand from the sources areas is mainly relatively coarse diluvial sediment.

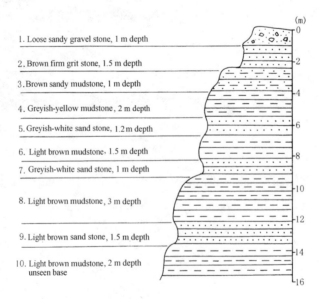

1. Loose sandy gravel stone, 1 m depth

2. Brown firm grit stone, 1.5 m depth

3. Brown sandy mudstone, 1 m depth

4. Greyish-yellow mudstone, 2 m depth

5. Greyish-white sand stone, 1.2 m depth

6. Light brown mudstone, 1.5 m depth

7. Greyish-white sand stone, 1 m depth

8. Light brown mudstone, 3 m depth

9. Light brown sand stone, 1.5 m depth

10. Light brown mudstone, 2 m depth
     unseen base

Fig. 12-22　Quaternary sediments profile in the southern piedmont of the Kezile Tagh Mountains

(4) From the eluvial and sloping deposits weathered from base rocks. There are hills composed of mudstone and sandstone of the Tertiary and pre-Tertiary on both sides of the Akeqi valley. Because of mechanical erosion, the layer is denuded into various size slices, and the fine sand is one of the sand sources of the Kumtag Desert.

12.3.2.2 The age of the desert formation

There is no available dating for the forming age of the Kumtag Desert, and it is difficult to judge. The age in this area can be roughly estimated according to the underlain sediments, by using the paleo-geological environment and the ^{14}C data.

(1) Underlain sediments of the desert. Some underlain sediments were exposed in the northern Kumtag Desert. These sediments are mainly made up of gravel mingling with light red and french grey muddy sand (Fig. 12-23). The cemented and loose sediments should belong to the Middle Pleistocene after comparison with the Quaternary stratum. The fact that the Kumtag Desert covers the Middle Pleistocene layer shows that its formation age is probably during the Middle Pleistocene.

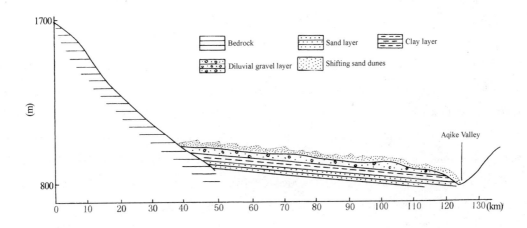

Fig. 12-23   The Quaternary sediments profile in the northern Kumtag Desert

(2) The Quaternary paleogeographical environment. After the early Pleistocene, the upheaval of the Qinghai-Tibet Plateau and the fringe mountains obstructed the monsoon from extending into the continent, causing the Tarim Basin climate to become arid. The characteristics of the arid climate include rare precipitation, acute changes of cold and heat, and frequent blown sand activity. These provided appropriate conditions for the formation of sandy deserts. Therefore, the Kumtag Desert was formed after the formation of the arid climate in the Tarim Basin.

(3) Dune morphology. Generally, the older dunes are bigger and more complex while the young dunes are smaller. The dunes in the Kumtag Desert are mainly higher in the south and lower in the north. The heights of the southern dunes are 70–80 m and the northern dunes are about 10 m, which have ladder-shapes which descend from south to north. These characteristics reflects that the

development process of the desert is constantly extending from south to north.

(4) The dating of ^{14}C age. The *T.chinentsis Lour* and *C. mongolicum Turcz* community that had withered away in ancient times was buried in dunes of the featherlike dune ridge distribution regions in the northern Kumtag Desert. The absolute age was 4,600±100 a by ^{14}C dating, indicating that vegetation grew in this area before 4,600 a BP, and dunes expanded after 4,600 a BP.

In summary, the Kumtag Desert appeared after the middle Pleistocene, and developed and expanded further in the later Pleistocene, then formed the present period scale. The beginning formation was in the south, then expanded northward, and is gradually spreading northward toward the Aqike valley.

12.3.3 The basic characters of blown sand physiognomy

12.3.3.1 The morphological characteristics of the regional blown sand physiognomy

1) Differentiation of desert physiognomy from northeast to southwest

The basic characteristics of desert physiognomy in distribution are showed not only by the regional changes of erosion and deposit shapes, but also by the regional difference of weathering and aeolian deposit processes. The blown sand physiognomy of this region was distributed orderly from the northeast to southwest. In the district of Tudaoliang in the eastern desert, the main physiognomy was wind eroded configuration-Yardangs with an area of 330 km^2. The ground was bumpy and fragmented, which was affected by wind erosion differentiation. The ridges and depressions are distributed alternately, the long ridge is usually 20–30 m high, and some can reach 50–80 m high. The extended direction is northeast with azimuth 20°–30° and is consistent with the main wind direction of the region. The lowland corridor between ridges became the natural wind passages. The ground surface was Gobi gravel with a 0.5 m high gravel wave. And its extended direction also was northeast with azimuth 20°–30°. In districts near the geodetic measurement point of I13, it transferred to concomitance of wind erosion physiognomy and aeolian deposit physiognomy. The sand is usually accumulated in the leeward sides of ridges and appears as sand ridges. The sand ridges normally were 5–10 m high and 30–50 m long, also extended towards northeast with azimuth 20°–30°, consistent with the regional dominating wind direction. The height of erosion ridges were 10–15 m high. It transferred to aeolian deposit dune region southwestwardly. The dune configuration was quite different, with the dune height gradually increasing from north to south, but the erosion configuration scattered and the height decreased to only 2–3 m. But in the region with one kind of dominating configuration, both the deflation and sedimentation processes of wind coexisted.

2) The desert is higher in the southwest and lower in the northeast

Controlled by tectonics in a direction from northeast-southwest, the sand materials cover the base rock ground in the southern edge of the desert.

The desert physiognomy is distributed scalariformly, high in the north and low in the south. Because the scalariform surface is influenced by tectonic movement, the southwest step was high (the height was 2,500 m a.s.l.) and the northeast was low (the height was 835 m a.s.l.). In the northern edge of desert, the steepy scalariform is toward the Aqike valley. The valley has standard characteristics of rift, developed deposits which is not deflated in the latest; the east end is as high as 827 m a.s.l., and the rift place near the Lop Nur is 803 m high. The alkali-resistant vegetation grew here such as bulrush, *Apocynum lancifolium* L. and tamarisks. The ground was composed of sand material. In the rift valley distributed 10 lake banks representing the Lop Nur Lake water winced from east to west and scattered some wind erosion monadnock. The place of southern rift valley bordered on the Kumtag Desert was a fault line in the northeast-southwest-direction. The fault incised through the middle Pleistocene stratum and formed a steep bank. The forward edge was 20 m high and had been deflated. Above the steepy ridge was a scalariform surface leaning from southwest to northeast. The scalariform surface can be classified into three levels: the first height was 840–900m a.s.l., the second was 925–1,100m a.s.l., the third was 1,150–1,500m a.s.l. There are featherlike dunes, broad and explanate sand lands, sand ridges, beehive dunes, pyramid dunes and sand hills. The third level mesa joined with arid denudation base rock in mountainous regions, the pyramid dune developed on mountainous windward side, the sand ridge appeared on the mountainous leeward side. The sheet crescent dune chain formed between mountainous valley, was 5–6m high and moved from north-northeast to south-southwest.

3) Dunes with complex type and unique form

The Kumtag Desert like a feather fan covers the inclined plain in front of the Altun Mountains. The dune types are composed of featherlike dunes, sand hills, pyramid dunes and honeycomb dunes, etc. In addition, there are other types such as crescent sand ridges and dunes, and the specific distribution are as follows.

(1) Dunes with complex type.

① Featherlike dune. The area of featherlike sand ridges is 4,000 km^2, which accounts for 1/5 of the whole desert area. It formed under the influence of northeastern wind, and extended along with the slope in northeast-southwest direction. It was composed of two kinds of dunes including the primary and secondary ridges. The lower secondary ridges distributed in intervals between the higher primary ridges. The two is near to be perpendicular in direction of each other, the primary ridge likes feather pipe, the secondary featherlike ridge on both sides of the pipe, and all of those formed the featherlike dune system. The primary ridge is about 10–20 m high with a gentle slope from 15°to 20°. The ridge body is as wide as 50 to 100 m. The interridge space was 500 to 1,000 m, with the length is 12 km to km. There are usually higher crescent sand mounds on the windward slope of the featherlike ridge. The secondary ridge generally is 2 m high with a windward gradient of 4°, and leeward 8°.

② Pyramidal dune. The pyramid dunes are mainly distributed on hills and mesas in the southern

Kumtag Desert and forward of the Altun Mountains. The dunes are caused by multi-direction winds, not only the northeaster but also the local airflow caused by the Altun Mountains. The dunes take on conic shape with triangular slope, acute angle top and narrow ridge line, usually three to four edges and faces, and each of the edges usually represents a wind direction. The dune body is very high and is usually 50 to 80 m and some even exceed 100–200 m. Sometimes they are distributed indiridually, and sometimes assembled as pyramid dune groups.

③ The semi-fixed shrub dune. In the Aqike valley, because the underground water table is higher, plants such as *Tamariks*, *C. Mongolicum* Turcz., *N. tangutorum* Bobr. are growing, making the duns semi-fixed. The volume of semi-fixed dunes is increasing constantly with the growth of its plants. This kind of dune presents roundness and eclipse on ichnography, and their heights are usually 1 to 5 m and up to 10 m influenced by plants. This kind of dune is only broadly distributed in the northern Kumtag Desert; although they also appear in eastern China, they are rare and small there.

④ Barchan chain. Barchan chains are distributed along the line from the southern Kumtag Desert edge to Sanlongsha. They are formed from the connection of single crescent dunes under conditions of an abundant sand supply. Usually they are composed of 3–4 dunes, sometimes there are dozens of them, generally with a height of 3–5 m, and some as high as 10 m. The configuration changed with the difference of regional wind direction. Influenced by the northeastern wind, the dunes remain the flexural camber trace of original crescent dune with two wings and had certain flexural. The plane character still reflected the crescent dune character. This kind of dune moves rapidly; along the line of Sanlongsha, the dune moved from the northeast to southwest with a rate of 5–10 m/a.

⑤ Complex longitudinal dune. They are mainly distributed in the southern Kumtag Desert, the extension direction is paralleled to the main wind direction or crossed in about 30° angle, and furled with several lines of sand ridges, with an area of 16,000 km², forming the main body of the Kumtag Desert. They stretched very long, usually 10–20 km ,even 40–50 km, 50–80 m high and 500–100 m wide, the width between two sand ridges is 400–600 m and there distributed the lower sand ridge and crescent dune chain. They usually are incised by valleys in south-north direction due to the influence of underlain topography and distributed on the ridge of mountainous slope.

(2) Cause of featherlike dune.

Many internal and oversea scholars have done special research on the causes of all kinds of dune configuration, but have done little on featherlike dunes. Xia Xuncheng et al. probed into the formation and development mechanism primarily according to field survey combined with analyzing data of aerophotos and satellite images in different period. They thought that there were some necessary conditions to form featherlike dune.

① Action of wind with single or near single direction. The prevailing wind direction is northeast in the Lop Nur region and accounts for 16%, the second is northern or northeast and accounted for 15% (Fig. 14-11). Seen from monthly data, the most frequent wind direction were northeaster.

② Broad and flat ground. Usually the longitudinal dune stretches very long, needs broad movement scope from several to tens of kilometers. The northern piedmont of the Altun Mountains is a large area with lacustrine deposits, the ground is flat and uplift a little with mountain region, and the topography is just fitting for.

③ Abundant sand material source. The Lop Nur region was all lacustrine deposit, and the main lithology is an interlayer of silver sand and clay. The abundant sand source is the base of longitudinal dune.

Featherlike dunes originally developed from crescent dunes according to field observations; the configuration of crescent dune was kept on the windward side of all featherlike ridges. After crescent dune formed they moved southwardly continuously with the influence of main wind direction. But to the northern piedmont of the Altun Mountains, wind direction changed obviously due to the restraining of mountain wind. There were both the north or northeast and northeast winds. In the condition that two wind directions took on an acute angle, the one wing of crescent dune stretched long forwardly, but the other wing moved back relatively, formed crescent dune of uncinate-shape. The complex crescent dune extended along the composition direction of wind force. It intersected in certain angle with two wind directions. Hanna thought that the main movement manner of atmosphere boundary air was one kind lengthways twist vortex that was near to parallel average airflow through observation in atmosphere laboratory and theoretic analysis of hydrodynamics stability. The huge lengthways twist atmosphere vortex led to the formation of longitudinal dune.

After the formation of crescent sand ridge, the evolution with twist movement manner was developed continuously. Sand transported and deposited along the stretching direction of sand ridge, form ridge body heighten continuously and stretch southwardly. Make the original crescent dune configuration inconspicuous even disappeared, and only left the sand ridge formed by one wing stretched. At the same time the sand ridge heightened continuously and stretched, the evolution with twist movement manner only can take away some sand for sand ridge heightening and stretching because of the abundant sand source in the Lop Nur region. The left sand deposited on both of the ridge sides or between the ridges, then formed small parallel sand banks plumbing with the sand ridge and formed special featherlike dune. In the region without abundant sand source, parallel sand banks would not appear after crescent dune formation. For example, the crescent sand ridge of the Altun piedmont in southeastern Qiemo, on both sides of the sand ridge there was not parallel sand banks distribution because the around area was gravel desert, and there was no sand source.

The featherlike ridge stretched continuously to the Altun Mountains slope because of topography and wind direction changes. The newly formed sand ridge joined in and made the distance between sand ridges shorten gradually, finally combined into compounded longitudinal dunes. For example, the 11 strip of sand ridges distributed in the east of Sanlongsha, the original width between each sand ridge was about 500 m. Over the course of sand ridge stretching southwardly, the distance between sand ridges narrows gradually, finally overlapping and combining into compounded longitudinal dunes.

12.3.4 Reconstruction and utilization

Only in the eastern Kumtag Desert there was village resident and small oasis area. The oasis environment would change a little because of small population density. In the east of the Lop Nur, south from the Altun Mountains, north to the east of the Tianshan Mountains even to boundary of China and Mongolia, the geology physiognomy and bio-climatic factors were extremely complex and had important scientific significance. So, climate and biology resource investigation and monitoring should be developed in the Kumtag Desert. According to the investigation of Zheng Ximing et al. a salt lake with an area of about 7,000 km^2 distributed in the Lop Nur region which is bigger than the Qarhan Salt Lake area (5,856 km^2) in the Qaidam Basin. The salt lake was composed of Luobei depression, Erlun region and new lake district of the Lop Nur from north to south. Meanwhile, there was 1,300 km^2 in Luobei and 5,600 km^2 in Erlun region, also the saltcast of halite distributed in the two regions. The kalium salt reserve is abundant in the Lop Nur; it has great significance for China kalium fertilizer production. The special physiognomy landscape and archaeological tourist resource have investigation and tour exploitation value such as Yardang physiognomy, white dragon pile, mesa and ancient beacon tower. But in the beginning attention should be paid to environment.

References

Cheng Changdu. 1983. The vegetation community system and basic characters of distribution in sandy land of the Gurbantünggüt Desert. Acta Phytoecologica Sinica, 7 (2): 89—98

Ding Yihui. 1997. IPCC. The main scientific outcome and problem of the scientific evaluation report in the second climate changes. Research of climate changes and the influence in China. China Meteorological Press, 21—25

Dong Guangrong, Chen Huizhong, Wang Guiyong et al. 1995a. The evolution of sandy land and desert and climate changes since 150 ka in northern China. Science in China (Series B), 25 (12): 271

Dong Guangrong, Chen Huizhong. 1991. The ancient aeolian sand of Cenozoic in the south edge of the Taklimakan Desert, the Quaternary glacier and environment of western China. Beijing: Science Press

Dong Guangrong, Jin Jiong, Gao Shangyu et al. 1990. Climate changes of desert regions in the north China since the Later Pleistocene. Quaternary Sciences, (3): 187—196

Dong Guangrong, Wang Guiyong. 1995b. The Quaternary geology of the Taklimakan Desert. In: the dissertation report material of synthesis scientific investigation in Taklimakan Desert

Dong Guangrong. 1997. New advancement of research on Quaternary geology in the Taklimakan Desert. Journal of Desert Research, 17(1)

Е·И·Селиванов. 1960. The operation of wind force and sand bed topography in the western of Middle-Asian. Geology Comment, 20 (4)

Gao Shangyu, Chen Weinan, Jin Heling et al. 1993. The primary research on the northwest edge of China monsoon region in the Holocene. Science in China, 23(3)

Huang Changchun. 2000. Environment Variance. Beijing: Science Press, 18—45

Huang Peiyou. 1988. The entironment research on Pipacai community in the middle Junggar Basin, Xinjiang. Acta Pedologica Sinica, 5 (3): 66—77

IPCC. 1996. Climate Change 1995: The Science of Climate Change, J T Houghton, L G Meira Filho, B A Callander, et al. Cambridge, UK: Cambridge University Press. 572

Li Jiangfeng. 1995. New cognition and discovery of the desert climate in the Taklimakan Desert. Arid Zone Research, Supplement

Li Zhengshan, Cheng Guangting. 1999. The blown-sand wind condition of the Taklimakan Desert. Journal of Desert Research, 19 (1)

Ling Yuquan. 1988. The relation of airflow characters and activity intensity of aeolian sand in the Taklimakan Desert. Journal of Desert Research, 8 (2)

Liu Dongsheng. 1985. Loess and Environment. Beijing: Science Press

Liu Juxiang, Zhang Shusen. 1959. The paleoclimate in geologic time of China. Scientia Geological Sinica, 33 (2)

Masatoshi Yoshino. 1991. The wind and rain in desert region of Xinjiang. Desert Research,1

Mu Guijin, Ji Qihui. 1990. The mechanism composing characters and meaning of Quaternary deposit in the Taklimakan Desert region. Arid Land Geography, 13 (2)

Manabe S and R T wetherald. 1975. The effects of doubling the CO_2 concentration on the climate of a general circulation model. Journal of Atmospheric Sciences, 32(1): 3—15

Mu Guijin. 1994. The formation epoch and development process of the Taklimakan Desert. Arid Land Geography, 17 (3)

Norim E. 1922. Quaternary Climate Changes within the Tarim Basin. Geographic Review, 22(4)

Ren Zhengqiu. 1994. The discussion of relation between wet or drought fluctuation and global temperature changes in the Taklimakan Desert region. Journal of Desert Research, 14(2)

Ren Zhengqiu. 1997. The deliberation to various problems of climate warm in modern times. Research of climate changes and influence in China. Beijing: China Meteorological Press, 43—47

Rind P,D Shindell, P Lonergan, and N K Balachandran. 1998. Climate change and the middle atmosphere. Part III:The doubled CO_2 climate revisited. J. Clim., 11, 876—894

Synthesis science investigation team of Xinjiang, Chinese Academy. 1965. The ground water of Xinjiang. Beijing: Science Press

Wang Jingfeng. 1995. The Evolution and Adjustment of the Relation between Human and Earth, Beijing: Science Press

Wei Wenshou. 2000a. The response and feedback of climate changes of modern desert—for example of the Gurbantünggüt Desert. Chinese Science Bulletin, 45(6): 636—641

Wei Wenshou. 2000b. The environment of modern desert and climate changes in the Gurbantünggüt Desert. Journal of Desert Research, 20 (2): 178—184

Wu Zheng. 1997. The research on China desert and coast dune. Beijing: Science Press

Xia Xuncheng, Li Chunshun, Zhou Xingjia et al., 1991, The control on Desertification and Aeolian Sand Disaster in Xinjiang. Beijing: Science Press. 10—31

Xinjiang Institute of Ecology and Geography, Chinese Academy of Science. 1986. The Evolution of Tianshan Mountains. Bejing: Science Press. 38—47

Zhao Yuanjie. 1991. The influence of Mazhatage Mountain to aeolian sand physiognomy along the both sides. Arid Zone Research, (1)

Zhou Tingru. 1963. The relation between the main type of terrestrial deposit in the Quaternary and physiognomy climate development in Xinjiang. Acta Geographica Sinica, 29 (3)

Zhou Tingru. 1964. About the paleogeography problems of the latest earth history times in Xinjiang. Journal of Beijing Normal University (Natural Sciences) (1)

Zhu Zhenda, Chen Yeping, Wu Zheng et al. 1981. Research on Aeolian Sand Geomorphology in the Taklimakan, Beijing: Science Press

Zhu Zhenda. 1987. Desertification process and development trend in the Taklimakan Desert region. Journal of Desert Research, 7 (3)

Zhu Zhenda. 1999. China Desert · Desertification · Treatment Countermeasure. Beijing: China Environmental Science Press, 25—133

Chapter 13
Deserts and Aeolian Desertification in the Qinghai-Tibet Plateau

On the Qinghai-Tibet Plateau, with a mean elevation over 4,000 m, there is thin air, intense solar radiation, cold climate, large diurnal temperature variations and a unique geographic environment. Firstly, the bare ground surface, sufficient sunshine and dramatic temperature change causes freeze-thaw weathering and thereby forms sand and gravel deserts. Secondly, dominated by the high level westerly air stream throughout the year, coupling with the influence of the relief, the plateau has frequent and strong winds with annual mean wind velocity larger than 4 m/s, and the annual number of strong wind days over much of the plateau exceeds 100 days.

The Qinghai-Tibet Plateau overall is a type of cold desert environment and the aeolian desertification process is also related to the evolution of the high-cold climate. The aeolian sand problems in three regions of the plateau have attracted people's attention: a. northeastern Qaidam Basin, the Qinghai Lake Basin and the Gonghe Basin; b. "Yarlung Zangbo River and Its Two Tributaries" region including the Yarlung Zangbo River, Lhasa River and Nyang Qu River; C. Ngari Highland.

13.1 Aeolian desertification in the Gonghe Basin of Qinghai Province

The Gonghe Basin, located between the Qinghai Nanshan range of the Qilian Mountains system and a dike of the Ela Range of the Kunlun-Qinling Mountains system, is a large Cenozoic downfaulted basin. It is 300 km long and 50–60 km wide, with an area of 13,800 km^2 (Fig. 13-1).

13.1.1 Location and distribution of aeolian desertified land

13.1.1.1 Land aeolian desertification types

According to surface features and changes in vegetation and soil, Dong Guangrong et al. (1993) divided the aeolian desertification development degree into four grades.

1) Potential aeolian desertified land

This refers to the lands that have potential natural conditions for aeolian desertification but there is no aeolian desertification at present. They include fixed sandy land, sandy loess hills, fenced grassland and irrigation fields, and mainly occur in the northwestern part of the basin and flood plain, with a total area of 7,743 km^2, accounting for 56% of the total area of the Gonghe Basin. They still maintain an

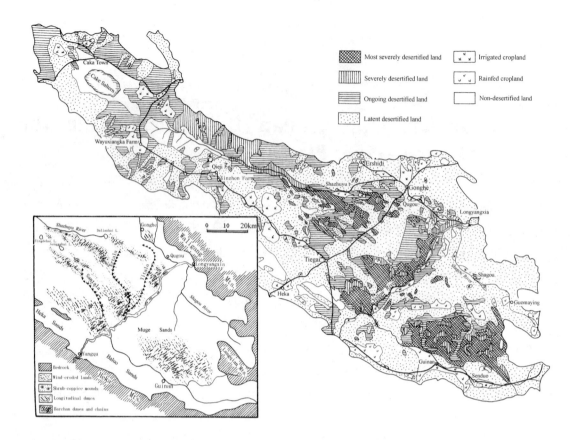

Fig. 13-1   Distribution of desertified lands in the Gonghe Basin

initial state of primary grassland surface, or only suffer from very slight aeolian erosion without obvious sand accumulation. Most of the region is covered by original vegetation. The edificators of the steppe zone include *Stipa krylovii* and *Artemisia frigida*; the edificator of arid desert steppe includes Stipa breviflora etc., with a vegetation cover of over 60%.

2) Developing aeolian desertified land

This refers to the land suffering from slight degrees of aeolian desertification, including semi-fixed sandy land (dunes), flat sandy land, wind-scoured depressions, abandoned cultivated land and arid land etc., with a total area of 3,246 km², accounting for 23% of the area of the Gonghe Basin. Such land basically has a fixed sand surface and sand movement takes place in local places when wind is strong enough. Ground surface is dominated by sheet deflation, with a depth of a few centimeters or so. There are different sizes of strips or patches of accumulated sand on the downwind sides of the wind- eroded land and most of shrubs and grasses are not buried by sand. Main edificators over much of the area have been replaced by psammophytes such as *Artemisia arenaria*, *Caragana spinifera*, *Oxytropis alpine* and *Nitraria tangutorum* etc., with a vegetation cover of 36%–40%. The organic layer in the original soil profile is being destroyed or has already been destroyed.

3) Intensely developing aeolian desertified land

This refers to the land at the rapid development stage of aeolian desertification, including semifluid sand dunes and flat sandy lands. They mainly occur in the piedmont belt of the Nanshan Mountain in the northwestern part of the basin, with a total area of 651 km^2, accounting for 4.7% of the area of the Gonghe basin. The original surface features of such land have been destroyed; there are numerous blowouts 0.1–1 m deep in holes, troughs, residual mounds and dense residual debris on the surface due to strong wind erosion. Sand accumulation is widespread on the downwind side of the wind-eroded land. Since the thickness of the accumulated sand exceeds the mean height of grasses, only a few shrubs can be seen on the interdune flats. Aeolian activity is frequent and the dune crests move forward during strong wind period. original vegetation is sparse or even absent and psammophytes are dominant, such as *Aneurolepidium dasystachys*, *Dsammochola villosa*, *Agriophyrum squarrosum*, *Corispermum tibeticum* and *Artemisia arenaria*, etc., with a vegetation cover of 15%–30%. The leached horizon of original soil has been partly or entirely destroyed or buried by sand.

4) Severe aeolian desertified land

This refers to the land suffering from a severe degree of aeolian desertification, including gobi desert and mobile dunes. Such land mainly occurs in the midstream valley of the Shazhuyu River and part of the Yellow River valley and covers an area of 1,028 km^2, accounting for 7.4% of the area of the Gonghe Basin. The original surface features have been entirely destroyed due to serious wind erosion and sand or dune encroachment. Furthermore, unvegetated pseudo gobi or wind-eroded badland occurs in patches and the downwind surface has been covered by sand dunes, dominated by barchan dunes, dune chains, transverse sand ridges, longitudinal dunes, and huge compound transverse and longitudinal dunes. There are no or only a few psammophytes such as *Agriophyllum arenarium, potaninia mongolica* and *Artemisia arenaria*, with a vegetation cover of less than 10% in the area. The original soil layer has entirely disappeared or there is only residual illuvial layer left or being buried by sand.

13.1.1.2　Distribution characteristics of aeolian desertified land

1) Aeolian desertified land proportion exceeds that of non-desertified land

The Gonghe Basin in Qinghai is one of the main aeolian desertification development regions in the steppe and desert steppe zones of China. Of its total area, the non-desertified land only occupies a small percentage, while the aeolian desertified land occupies a large percentage.

2) Various aeolian desertified lands distribution

Like other desertified steppe zones, severe aeolian desertified land, intensely developing aeolian desertified land, developing aeolian desertified land, potential aeolian desertified land, deflation districts, shifting sand districts, loess districts and fluviolacustrine flood land are alternatingly distributed in strips or patches in the region and their boundaries are difficult to delineate. This is quite different from the arid desert regions with well-defined boundaries of gobi and desert regions as the occurrence and development of aeolian desertification in the steppe and desert steppe zones have complex spatial distributions. In spite of this, the rough boundaries of modern wind erosion and deposition zones have be recognized; generally speaking, the Tanggem, Ahazhuyu and Yindeir townships in the northwestern part of the basin are dominated by wind erosion, and therefore gobi is widespread while sand mounds are rarely seen. Shifting sand is mainly distributed in three regions, namely, the Shazhuyu-Tanggen region, Longyangxia reservoir bank, and the Mugetan region, which consists of crescent dunes, crescent dune chains and barchan dune ridges, 2–20 m in height.

The large grassland around the shifting sand districts, especially the zones in front of and behind the Heka Mountains, Gahaitan, and the piedmont belt of the Guinan Mountains are the major deposition zones of modern loess.

13.1.2   Natural environment of aeolian desertification

The Gonghe Basin belongs to the steppe zone. Annual precipitation varies from less than 200 mm in the west to 300 mm or so in the east, and mainly falls between May and September, accounting for 80%–90% of the annual total; mean number of days with precipitation is 80–120 days. Aeolian sand activity mostly appears in spring due to arid climate and soil thawing. Statistical data of annual gale days and frequency is presented in Table 13-1.

Table 13-1   Gale days and frequency in different regions of the Gonghe Basin

Region		Spring (Mar. -May.)	Summer (Jun. -Aug.)	Autumn (Sep. -Nov.)	Winter (Dec. -Feb.)	Whole year
Caka	(d)	39.7	18.2	15.7	23.7	97.3
	Frequency	41	19	16	24	100
Gonghe	(d)	18.9	5.5	7.1	13.7	45.2
	Frequency	42	12	16	30	100

Note: Gales > Grade 8 refer to the wind speed >17.2 m/s.

According to observations, the longest duration of gales (≥Grade 8) was 22 days (Caka, March 12 to April 2 , 1962); this ranks first among all regions of Qinghai Province since the 1960s.

Grassland in the Gonghe Basin is mainly covered by xeric herbs, such as *Achnatherum splendens, stipa and Agropyron cristatum etc.* with about 10 species or at least 6–7 species. Since the habitat is arid, *Achnatherum splendens* grows poorly, with a height of 10–80 cm. Apparently, such grassland cannot effectively defer aeolian sand activities.

The prevailing wind direction in the Gonghe Basin is northwest by west due to the influence of the

Mongolian-Siberian high. According to statistical data of the Gonghe weather station (1961–1970), maximum wind velocity in January is 20 m/s with a wind direction of west and northwest; in April it is 20 m/s and the wind direction is west; in July it is 14 m/s with a NNW direction; in October it is 16 m/s with a W, WNW direction. The prevailing wind direction over the whole year is westward and north ward direction. The long axis of the Gonghe Basin is in WNW direction and parallels the prevailing wind direction. Furthermore, west of the Gonghe Basin is the Qaidam Basin, and they are separated by arid denuded low mountains that cannot prevent the penetration of strong northwest winds or even enhance wind force. As a result, large amounts of sand are transported by wind to the eastern part of the basin and thus form sand dunes in the region east of the Shazhuyu River. Controlled by the dominant wind direction, sand dunes are moving in a southeast direction of 60°–70°, for example, sand dunes at Talatai west the Yellow River are approaching the river bank.

13.1.3　Material source of aeolian desertification

The extensive development of sand dunes in the Gonghe Basin relies on an abundant sand supply, and the main sand source is the large and thick early Quaternary Fluviolacustrine deposits. This can be demonstrated by the strata of the Gonghe section and the analytical results of particle-size composition (Table 13-2). The four sand samples collected from the Gonghe Section contain all the sediment size grades from gravel to clay, dominated by dune sand fraction, while modern dune sands only include medium, fine and very fine sand. Of the four sand samples, mean fine sand content is 58.31%, and this is approximate to the content of medium and fine sands. Owing to selective entrainment by winds, the accumulated sands mainly consist of very fine to medium sand, dominated by fine sand, while the finer particles such as silt and clay can be transported by wind for a long distance. The mid-value of the particle size (M_d) is smaller than the dune sand of the Gonghe section.

Table 13-2　Grain-size composition of sand samples of the strata of the Gonghe Formation in the Gonghe Basin

Sand sample		Grain-size content (%)							(M_d)	S_o
		Gravel (>2mm)	Very coarse sand (2–1mm)	Coarse sand (1–0.5mm)	Medium sand (0.5–0.25mm)	Fine sand (0.25–0.125mm)	Very fine sand (0.125–0.063mm)	Silt,clay (<0.063mm)		
Gonghe Section	1	0.34	0.03	0.04	6.75	70.62	10.22	12.00	0.19	1.41
	2	2.32	0.42	0.15	4.22	41.44	12.80	40.96	0.13	3.03
	3	0.05	0.17	0.14	1.42	56.14	8.45	33.71	0.15	2.38
	4	0.10	0.70	0.51	3.43	65.04	10.72	19.47	0.16	1.63
	mean	0.70	0.33	0.21	3.96	58.31	10.55	26.54	0.16	2.11
Dune Sand	Ancient Dune			0.02	4.06	62.92	23.10	9.9	0.15	1.30
	New dune				32.87	66.60	0.53		0.23	1.13
	mean			0.02	18.47	64.76	11.82	9.9	0.19	1.22

According to analytical results of particle size in various environments, the M_d of dune sand generally varies between 0.15–0.35 mm and the mean M_d of dune sands of different periods in the region is 0.19 mm. This low value is related to the location of the Gonghe Basin lying at the margin of the desert zone in China. The sorting coefficient of the Gonghe Formation (S_o) is significantly higher than that of dune sand, whit a mean value of 2.11. This shows that well-developed meander results in the deposition of river flood plain and aeolian sand is the sorting result of the Gonghe section. The mean value of 1.22 is consistent with the partied-size parameter of aeolian environment.

The analytical results of heavy mineral composition of the Gonghe section and dune sand also demonstrate that the former is the primary sand source of the latter (Table 13-3).

Table 13-3　Heavy mineral content of the Gonghe section and dune sand in the Gonghe Basin (Grain size 0.25—0.01 mm, specific gravity > 2.9)

Sand sample		Gonghe section					Dune sand		
		1	2	3	4	mean	Old dune sand	New dune sand	mean
Relatively stable mineral	Tremolite	0.76	0.17	0.16	0.17	0.32	0.17		0.17
	Garnet	1.97	4.47	3.87	5.16	3.87	7.72		7.72
	Acanticone	18.97	20.10	20.28	20.10	19.84	16.98	41.18	29.08
	Zoisite	4.56	2.41	6.35	3.78	4.30	4.63	2.35	3.49
	Sphene	0.76	0.52	0.31	0.52	0.53	0.69	2.35	3.49
	Antonite	2.73	2.06	0.77	2.58	2.04	0.86	0.29	0.58
	Chorite	2.73	1.72	1.70	1.20	1.84	1.54		1.54
	Apatite	2.43	2.23	4.95	3.95	3.39	1.72	0.29	1.01
	Sillimanite	0.15		0.16	0.17	0.16	0.17		0.17
	Total	35.06	33.68	38.55	37.63	36.23	34.48	44.40	39.44
Very stable mineral	Ziroon	1.97	2.92	3.41	2.41	2.68	2.06		2.06
	Taltalite	2.28	1.20	2.17	1.38	1.76	1.89	0.59	1.24
	Rutile	0.30	0.34	0.46		0.37	0.17	0.54	0.38
	Corumdum	0.15				0.15			
	Mean	4.70	4.46	6.04	3.79	4.75	4.12	1.18	2.65
Unstable mineral	Hornblende	28.83	26.80	28.95	33.33	29.48	36.54	27.06	31.80
	Glaucophane						0.17		0.17
	Actinolite	2.28	3.44	3.72	2.92	3.09	2.40	0.29	1.35
	Augite	0.30	0.86	0.16	0.17	0.37	0.34	1.47	0.91
	Diopside	0.30		0.46		0.38	0.34	0.59	0.47
	Ficinite	0.15		0.16		0.16	0.34	0.88	0.53
	Black mica	0.15				0.15	0.17		0.17
	Total	32.01	31.10	33.45	36.42	33.25	40.13	30.29	35.21
Stable mineral	Ilmenite aimant	24.43	28.52	17.96	21.48	23.10	17.90	22.35	21.13
	Aetite	1.06	1.55	1.24	0.52	1.09	0.52	1.77	1.15
	Monacite	1.07				0.17			
	Mean	25.49	30.24	19.20	22.00	24.23	20.42	24.12	22.27
Debris		2.73	0.52	2.79	0.17	1.55	0.86		0.86
Total		99.99	100.00	100.03	100.01		100.01	99.99	

The four sand samples collected from the Gonghe section contain 23 kinds of heavy minerals, except very small amount of monacite (0.17%) and corundum (0.15%). The ancient dune sands contain all other 21 kinds of heavy minerals. This clearly indicates their inherited relation. New dune sands only contain 14 kinds of heavy minerals but the high-content minerals of the Gonghe section are mostly preserved. Especially the percentages of four types of minerals (unstable mineral, less stable mineral, stable mineral and very stable mineral) in the Gonghe section and dune sand are approximate similar. In addition, their weathering degree and sand roundness also show a certain difference. The primary ancient dunes sands have poor weathering degree and roundness, and half of them are subangular. But new dune sands have higher weathering degree and therefore they are mostly difficult to be identified by optical method; furthermore they have good roundness and mostly show a rounded shape. This shows that primary sands have been reworked by strong wind force.

13.1.4   Desert evolution and environmental changes

Sand dunes in the Gonghe Basin can be divided into two types based on their formation time: one is fixed ancient dunes and another is new dunes. [14]C dating of loessal subsand soil on the gravel layer of the Tamai terrace by Xu Shuying et al. in 1982 yielded an age of 17,300±250 a BP and the ^{14}C dating of organic carbon in ancient dune crests on the loessal subsand soil yielded an age of 6,180±80 a BP. This shows that ancient dunes were formed between 17,300–6,180 a BP.

A late episode in the late Pleistocene (25,000–1,000 a BP), namely the Younger Dryas Ice Age, was a very cold period, when there was aeolian sand formation in the Salawusu region of Inner Mongolia. It has been proven that the formation of ancient dunes in the desert worldwide is related to the last glaciation (Singh, 1971; Grove et al., 1968). The studies on the ice cover in Antarctica and Greenland and oceanic cores show that the period around 17,000 a BP was the peak of the Younger Dryas Ice Age. The loessal soil covered by ancient dunes in the region is periglacial loess formed 17,300 years ago. In the Younger Dryas Ice Age, the climate in the Gonghe Basin was very dry and cold, hence permafrost and ancient sand dunes were formed.

In the early Holocene the climate gradually turned warm and wet, sand dune development stopped, and paleosols with high organic matter content were formed in the surface layer. According to Nichols (1967), the period from 8,000–5,000 a BP was an optimal climatic stage in northwest Europe and Canada and the period around 6,500 a BP was the warmest and the most humid stage of the postglacial period. The warmest and the most humid stage in east Africa occurred between 8,625-4,960 a BP and the environmental changes in the early Holocene in the Gonghe Basin were consistent with those in other regions of the world.

The new sand dunes covered on the ancient sand dunes with well-deveolped paleosol on dune crests were formed later than 6,000 a BP. According to the observations at the inlet of the Qiabqia River flowing into the Yellow River, there is widespread shifting sand on the first terrace and peat in the interdune oxblow lake deposits, and ^{14}C dating yielded an age of $4,955+105$ a BP. This shows that there was a dry and active sand activity period about 5,000 a BP.

From numerous literature records and isotopic determination data Denton et al. (1973) suggested that the glaciers in neoglacial period in the Northern Hemisphere experienced three advance stages, namely 8,300–7,000, 5,800–4,900 and 3,300–2,400 a BP. If the sand dune formation and glacier development are synchronous, the new sand dunes would have been formed about 3,000 a BP.

According to existing ^{14}C dating data, the desert evolution and environment in the Gonghe basin since the late episode of the late Pleistocene has experienced the following changes.

(1) The first arid period corresponded to the last ice age of the late episode of the late Pleistocene, when there were aeolian loess and ancient sand dunes formed.

(2) The wet period corresponded to optimal climatic stage of the early Holocene, when the paleosols on dune crests and the peat layer on the first terrace of the Yellow River were formed, and there was a high water surface level of the three lakes in the Gonghe Basin.

(3) The second arid period corresponded to the glacier advance period of the neoglacial period at about 3,000 a BP, when large areas of mobile dunes formed, water surface of the three lakes in the basin fell; for example, the water surface of the Dalianhai Lake fell by 8 m or more.

13.2 Desert in the Qinghai Lake basin

The Qinghai Lake, located at the northeastern margin of the Qinghai-Tibet Plateau, is the largest inland lake of China. It is a Cenozoic downfaulted lake surrounded by high mountains exceeding 4,000 m in elevation. There are widespread rolling dunes on the eastern shore of the lake, and we call this the eastern shore desert of the Qinghai Lake, with an area of 475 km^2. The sand dunes on the western shore of the lake formed in the past several decades, and it has become the second largest blown sand area of the region and is tending to expand.

13.2.1 Distribution and types of sand dunes in the eastern shore desert of the Qinghai Lake

The eastern shore desert of the Qinghai Lake can be divided into three districts (Fig. 13-2). The first district is the lakeside plain between the Qinghai Lake and the Tongbao-Daban mountains, and it extends about 60 km from the mouth of the Ganzi River in the north to the northern piedmont of the Manlong Mountains, with a north-south width of 5–10 km, and an area of 320 km^2. The second district is the sand barrier and sand bank to the west of the Haiyan bay, with a sand-covered area of 90 km^2. It has been proven that large volumes of aeolian sand has deposited on the shallow lake floor and is called "underwater aeolian sand". The third district is the aeolian sandy land located at the basin and the Longma River of the Yellow River basin at the southeastern margin of the lake basin. This sandy land is 40 km to the north of the lake and can be viewed as a part of the eastern shore desert. Sand dunes in this area stretch about 7 km south to north, with an area of 65 km².

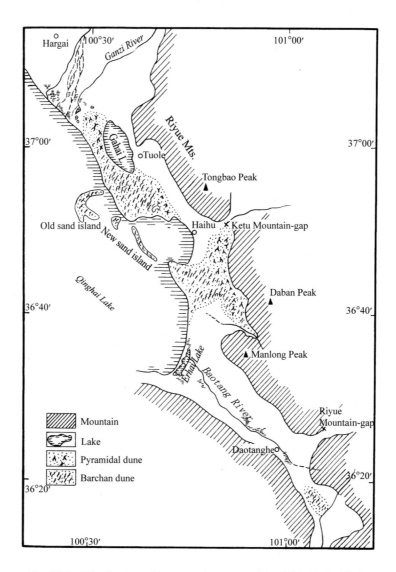

Fig. 13-2　Distribution of desert on the eastern side of the Qinghai Lake

In spite of a small area, the eastern shore desert of the Qinghai Lake is characterized by dense and huge sand dunes, of which the pyramid dunes are the most noticeable. Such dunes form three chains at the western edge of the Gahai, the northern side of the Yanhai Bay and the western piedmont of the Daban Mountains; the sand dune heights in these three areas are 40–60 m, 80–120 m and 100–140 m respectively. The highest pyramid dunes occur at the mouth of the Aobao Gully in front of the Daban Mountains, with a relative height of 160 m, the altitude of its crest is 3,592 m, and it is about 400 m above the lake surface. These dunes show a conical shape and have a sharp and narrow crest line. With some secondary barchan dunes and dune chains superimposed on the windward slopes, they exhibit a complex dune shape.

13.2.2 Distribution and types of sand dunes in the western shore desert of the Qinghai Lake

The deterioration of eco-environment in the Qinghai Lake region has become a quite prominent problem; especially the sand dunes on the western lakeshore have been spreading over the past 10 years and form the second largest blown sand zone in the lake region. Sand dunes in the region mainly occur to the northwest of the Haixi Mountains (Bird Island) and the northeastern margin of the delta of the Buha River. These sand dunes are 150–250 m away from the lake and arranged in a 10 km long and 0.5–1.5 km wide strip parallel to the lakeshore (Fig. 13-3). The main dune types include barchan dunes and barchan dune chains. The former is located on the lake shore and the latter at the land side. Single barchan dunes are generally 30–50 m wide, 1.5–2.0 m high, with asymmetric windward and leeward slopes. Sand dune chains are formed by mutually connected barchan dunes, with their main chains running in a south-north direction and their secondary chains in a northeast-southwest direction. They are formed by winds from opposite directions, of which the main chain is formed by the leading winds (lake winds). Strong lake winds result in the deposition of sand mountains and sand dunes on the eastern shore of the lake. Owing to the topographical obstruction of the Datong Mountains and the Heishan Mountains, the western wind and the northwestern wind on the western shore of the lake are weak but the eastern and the northeastern winds are relatively strong, and thus lakeshore dunes and dune chains form.

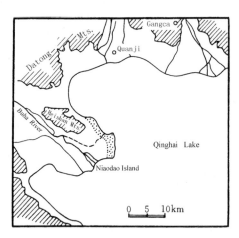

Fig. 13-3　Distribution of desert on the western side of the Qinghai Lake

13.2.3　Sand source and changes of the desert

Main sand sources of modern sand dunes are the lacustrine-alluvial deposits formed in the Buha

River, especially the fine sand deposits at the river mouth and the delta. The Qinghai Lake basin is a vast closed inland drainage system. A total of 50 rivers flows into the lake but these river systems are asymmetric, with large rivers emptying into the lake via the northern and western lakeshores while small rivers empty into the lake via the eastern and southern lakeshores. The most important rivers on western and northern shores are the Buha River and the Hargai River, respectively. The Buha River is the longest river, with a catchment area corresponding to one half of the total area of the Qinghai Lake basin. Its annual mean recharge is 33.7 m^3/s, and maximum recharge in the rainy season may reach 493 m^3/s. According to calculations, the mean annual sediment concentration of the Buha River is 0.38 kg/m^3. Sediment recharge 11.4 kg/s, and annual total sediment load 361,000 t. The deposition of huge amounts of sediments at the river mouth forms a 13 km long delta in the lake, and a shallow water zone with a depth smaller than 10 m extends about 7 km in the lake. Borehole data reveal that the frontal edge of the delta of the Buha River mainly consists of fine sand (0.25–0.125 mm), medium sand (0.5–0.25 mm) and reaches a thickness of 24 m, having the largest thickness of Holocene deposits in the lake area. The lakeside plain formed by the alluvial fan and delta of the Shaliu River and the Hargai River in the northern part of the lake region is also large, with a maximum width of 15 km, and it mainly consist of sand and silt.

Table 13-4 shows the analytical results of sand samples collected from the underwater delta and other places. The main sand source of modern sand dunes in the lake region is from the deltas at the river mouths of several big rivers on the western and northern lake shores. The wind transported materials from the delta of the Holocene Buha River formation deposit in the plain east of the lake.

Table 13-4　Analytical results of the grain size of sand samples from the Qinghai Lake floor

No.	Water Depth (m)	location	Grain-size content (%)						M_d (mm)	S_o
			Coarse sand >0.5mm			Coarse Silt 0.1–0.05mm	Fine Silt 0.05–0.01mm	Clay <0.01mm		
1	1.7	Haiyan bay		19.94	72.26	5.72	1.01	1.08	0.16	1.34
2	5.5	South of the ait	2.60	61.23	34.80	0.68	0.37	0.32	0.28	1.27
3	15	Mouth of the Buha River	1.55	12.11	79.16	6.26	0.44	0.48	0.17	1.30
4	21.5	Mouth of the Buha Alan River	0.37	10.12	78.26	6.46	0.75	4.04	0.16	1.31

The northeastern edge of the Qinghai-Tibet Plateau is one of the regions with the highest wind velocity and frequency in the plateau. According to statistical data, mean annual wind velocity in the lake region is 3.1–4.3m/s, with maximum wind velocities in different months reaching 13–22 m/s. The dominant wind direction in the lake region is northwest, although it may be affected by the southeast monsoon wind in summer. The sands on the western and northern lakeshores are transported by the strong wind to the southeastern part of the lake and are deposited there after encountering mountain barriers such as the Riyue Mountain etc. Such blown sand not only forms sand dunes on lakeside plain but also sand barriers and sand dikes. When deposited in the lake, some dammed lakes gradually separate from the lake proper and form a unique landscape on the eastern shore of the lake.

The delta deposits of the Buha River on the western shore of the Qinghai Lake are direct sand sources for sand dunes. The natural oscillations during the development of the river flow stopped the development of the northern edge of the delta. The deposits at the original plain and at the frontal edge were reworked into a sand bank and flood plain under the action of lake water and thereby constitute the material basis for the formation of sand dunes on the western shore of the lake. The persistent drought and serious rodent damages lead to vegetation degradation in the swamp and flood plain in the delta plain system of the Buha River, and this is one of the main factors leading to land aeolian desertification and desert expansion in this study region.

13.2.4　Desert evolution

Based on integrated data, Chen Kezao et al. mapped out the extent of the Qinghai Lake in the early Holocene, when the lake was about one–third larger than the present size and the lake level was about 100 m above the present lake level. It can be seen that the eastern shore of the lake, at that time, was close to the piedmont and the lake surface was close to the Ketu pass (103 m above the present lake surface). Sand dunes on the eastern shore of the lake appeared when the lake surface shrank and the lake floor was exposed after the early Holocene. Therefore, one might think that the eastern shore desert of the Qinghai Lake was formed not earlier than the late Pleistocene; instead it was actually the outcome of the lake retreat in the Holocene.

Many researchers pointed out that the shrinkage of the lake surface salinized the water and therefore aquatic species became simple. Furthermore, large-scale deposition of aeolian sand and the appearance of deserts in the lake region are closely related to the decrease in lake water volume.

Owing to the influence of neotectonic movement, the subsidence amplitude was larger in the western part of the lake than the eastern part and the sand carried by northwest winds continuously deposited in the eastern shallow water zone. As a result, the eastern shore desert enlarged and sand dunes formed. In addition, the rise of sand dikes in the lake divided the lake bay and thereby formed a series of sub lakes such as the Gahai Lake and the Erhai Lake, etc. It can be seen that owing to decreasing lake water levels since the Holocene, aeolian sand activity was exacerbated, sand dikes rose, and sub-lakes formed. However, the shrinkage of the lake and the spread of aeolian sand are not in the linear of form due to the influence of periodical Holocene climatic variations.

The shrinkage of the lake surface is mainly attributed to the decrease of inflow into the lake rather than precipitation changes. The changes of river discharge resulted from the periodical alternations between Holocene cold and warm periods. The headwaters of several large rivers on the western and northern shores of the Qinghai Lake are close to the modern snow line, therefore the river recharge is large in warm periods and small in cold periods. According to the study at the northeast edge of the Qinghai-Tibet Plateau, there were two cold periods in the region, namely the early Holocene cold period and the middle Holocene cold period, and the intermediate stage was a warm period. Correspondingly, there were two active periods of aeolian sand deposition and sand dune development.

As described above, the watershed area of the Daotang River is an aeolian sand deposition zone of the eastern shore of the Qinghai Lake. In the early Holocene, the water surface of the Qingahi Lake was close to the present Daotanghe Town and the aeolian sand deposition area was about 10 km south of the lake. Aeolian sands of the two different times have been identified in the region. Loose new dunes cover the calcareous cemented old dunes and between them exists a layer of paleosol with high humus content. ^{14}C dating shows that the paleosol formed at about 3,960±100 a BP. The paleosol marks a warm climatic period and the interrupted stage of aeolian sand deposition. From this it follows that the old sand dunes were formed in the Holocene cold period, while the new sand dunes were formed in the neoglacial period.

Huge pyramid dunes on the plain to the east of the lake are the products of long-term development. Since the conclusion of the neoglacial period, air temperature gradually rose and aeolian sand activities entered into a relatively stable period. Some plant species colonized sand dunes in the Daotang River watershed and the area north of the Erhai Lake. In areas where groundwater was high, fixed coppice dune formed. Viewed from the general trend, there were alternating active and stable periods for the lowering lake level and aeolian sand activity, and the climatic fluctuations on a 1,000-year timescale show that the modern time is in a relatively stable stage of aeolian sand activity.

13.3   Desert in the Qaidam Basin

The Qaidam Basin is a big inland basin in the northeastern part of the Qinghai-Tibet Plateau in northwestern Qinghai Province. With an elevation between 2,500–3,000 m, it is one of the highest desert regions of China. The eastern part of the basin falls in the desert steppe zone, mean annual air temperature is 2–4 °C, annual precipitation 50–170 mm, annual evaporation 2,000–2,500 mm, and aridity 2.1–9.0. The western part of the basin falls in the arid desert zone, mean annual air temperature is 1.5–2.5°C, annual precipitation 10–25 mm, annual evaporation 2,500–3,000 mm, and aridity 9.0–20.0. The basin exhibits an alternatingly distributed landscape of wind-eroded lands, sand dunes, gobi, salt lakes and salinized soil plains (Zhu Zhenda, 1980) (Fig. 13-4).

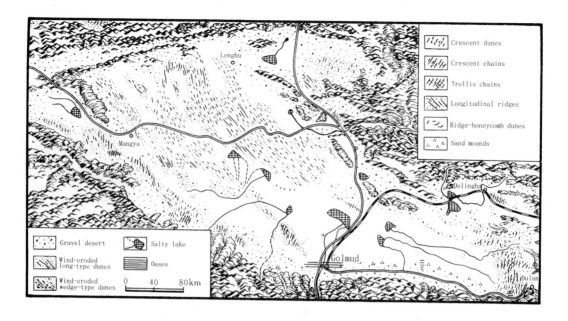

Fig. 13-4　Map of aeolian sand landforms in the Qaidam Basin

13.3.1　Aeolian sand landforms

The main characteristics of wind deposition and erosion landform landscapes in the Qaidam Basin are as follows.

(1) Sand dunes are scattered and mostly alternate with gobi in the piedmont diluvial plain. They are relatively concentrated in the northern piedmonts of the Qimatag and Ahasongwula Mountains in the southwestern part of the basin and roughly form a discontinuous northwest- southeast trending sand zone. Most sand dunes are shifting dunes, they account for 70% of the basin's total dunefield area and are dominated by crescent dunes, sand ridges and dune chains, generally 5–10 m in height. There are also small areas of high complex dunes (20–50 m high). Fixed and semi-fixed dunes mainly occur in the frontal edge of the northern piedmont plain with high groundwater table of the Kunlun Mountains, especially in the Hotiegui region sand dunes are gathered, dominated by coppice dunes, 3–5 m or 5–10 m high; main dune plant species are Tamarix chinensis and Haloxylon ammodendron etc.

(2) Aeolian eroded land is widespread and occupies about 67% of the basin's desert area and mainly occurs in the northwestern part of the basin. The northwest-southeast trending short-axial anticlinal structure consisting of Tertiary rock strata (mud shale, silt rock and sandstone) is well developed in the basin. Such rock strata are loose, contain soft-hard interbeds and cleavages. Under the actions of wind erosion and mechanical weathering they form wind-eroded mounds and badlands and are oriented in NW-SE and WNW-ESE direction, 10–15 m high or even 40–50 m high, 10–200 m long or even more than 1,000 m. There are sand patches, sand ridges or crescent dunes in the aeolian eroded lowland or windward slope of wind-eroded hills, but they only occupy about 5% of the total area of

aeolian eroded land.

Aeolian deposition landscapes are dominated by crescent dunes and dune chains, and they occur in the central part, river valleys at the northeastern edge and the intermontane basins at the southwestern edge of the basin. Their formation is related to sand entrainment and locally produced sand.

Gobi desert in the Qaidam Basin are mainly distributed in the piedmont plains at the margin of the basin, such as the northern piedmont of the Altun Mountains, and they are dominated by diluvial-alluvial sandy gravel gobi.

13.3.2   Material sources

The arid climate is a precondition for the formation of deserts in the Qaidam Basin, while various clastic deposits in the basin are the material basis for the formation of desert. Furthermore, different surface materials may form different types of deserts with different surface features.

(1) Northwestern part of the basin. Under persistent arid and windy conditions, the very thick layer of the late Tertiary and early Quaternary fine-grained lacustrine deposits were reworked by winds into aeolian eroded landform landscape, with an area of 24,000 km^2. The main aeolian eroded landscape types include deflation column, deflation bornhardt, deflation mushroom, Yardang, deflation wedge-shaped mound, deflation enlonged mound, wind-scoured depression and wind-scoured plain etc.

(2) Southeastern and eastern parts of the basin. Since the mountains including the Qiman Mountains at the southwestern edge of the basin were stable since the Neogene, the weathered and denuded deposits are fine. Several dried ancient river channels, 1–2 km in width, in Xiangide, Dulan and Xiariha in the eastern part of the basin extend in the interior of the desert. The thick layer of late Pleistocene deposits formed there are the main sand sources of the desert dunes. The northwest (west) winds carry large amounts of sand to the alluvial-diluvial plain to form the regularly distributed aeolian sand landforms. The dunefield area in the basin is about 11,000 km^2.

(3) The arid piedmont plain at the edge of the basin. Gravel surface occupy a very large proportion in the desert area of the basin, roughly accounting for 52% of the basin's desert area, which is closely related to the high mountains around the basin. According to preliminary statistics, about 70 mountain-originating rivers flow into the basin, and the alluvial and diluvial deposits carried by these rivers constitute a material basis for the formation of the gravel desert in the basin. Aeolian eroded mud desert ranks second in area and occupies 33% of the basin's desert area, and the sand dune area only occupies 15% of the basin's area. Lacustrine deposits in the basin are widespread and mainly consist of well consolidated mud and silt materials. Under the arid climatic conditions they form large areas of wind eroded mounds and wind scoured depression. This is different from the situation in the Tarim basin, where abundant alluvial-diluvial deposits dominated

by loose medium and fine sands form large area of desert dunes, also known as sand sea, which developed into the largest desert of China.

13.3.3 Modern aeolian sand deposition

Modern deposition processes develop on the basis of the sand dunes formed in the later episode of late-pleistocene. Developing dunes in the northwest of the basin are mainly distributed southeast of the Huahai Basin. The main dune types include crescent dunes, crescent dune chains, linear dune ridges and honey comb dunes. The heights of sand dunes are generally lower than 5 m and dominated by shifting dunes moving southeastward. There is also a sand dune zone in the southwestern part of the basin. It includes crescent dunes, crescent dune chains, linear dune ridges, honey comb dunes and star dunes, which are 10–30 m in height, with the maximum height exceeding 100 m.

Sand dunes in the eastern part of the basin are distributed in patches at the edge of the basin. The largest desert is the Dulan-Tiegui desert. Its western part is mobile, while the eastern part is fixed or semi-fixed, and sand dunes are mainly advancing in the ESE direction. Sand dune types are singular, mainly including reticulate dune chains, crescent dune chains and linear dune ridges. Sand dunes at the marginal areas are small and short but in the central part they are high, generally 20–40 m in height, with a maximum height of 60 m or more. Some of the highest reticulate dunes in China also occur in this region.

In the past several decades, as a result of irrational economic activities, some former fixed or semi-fixed dunes have been destroyed and shifting sand is spreading.

13.3.4 Desert evolution

Desert is the product of arid climate and the desert in the Qaidam Basin expands and shrinks with the wet-dry changes of the climate. In the Eogene, the mountains around the basin was low, generally lower than 1,000 m (Li, 1979), and the basin had a humid-hot climate. Water amount was large and the mountains were covered by sub-tropic coniferous forests. Until the early Tertiary, the basin still had a humid-hot climate with plentiful precipitation, and hence no salt deposits were found in the Miocene strata.

In the later episode of the Neogene, the climate of the basin gradually became dry, salt deposition took place and vegetation in surrounding mountains changed from a coniferous forest into desert grassland . The desert in the basin was most likely to occur in this period and mainly concentrated in the northwestern part of the basin, and the wind-eroded surface features were more likely to form. However, no ancient dunes in this period were found due to limited investigations.

In the early Pleistocene, the climate in the middle and eastern parts of the basin was warm and humid and the lake surface was vast. According to drilling data, no salt deposits were found in the early

Pleistocene strata. The occurrence of warm-humid climate were related to the establishment of new monsoon circulations and the disappearance of the old plateau (Li Jijun, 1979). However, the western part of the basin experienced dry period, which can be demonstrated by the presence of halite and gypsum deposits in the early Pleistocene strata.

In the mid-Pleistocene, the largest glacial period occurred in China. The climate was extremely dry and cold, lakes shrank, lacustrine deposits were exposed, desert development processes started,and wind-eroded surface features and sand dune landscapes occurred in the western and eastern parts of the basin. However, in the later episode of the mid-Pleistocene the climate turned warm and humid, and therefore the desert development processes stopped or slowed down.

In the early episode of the late Pleistocene, the last glacial period occurred in China, and the climate was very dry and cold and the lake surface shrank. Furthermore, owing to the influence of neotectonic movement, the northwestern part of the basin further uplifted, large areas of lacustrine deposits were exposed, wind erosion was prevalent, wind-eroded mounds and wind-scoured landscapes occurred at the southwestern edge and the eastern alluvial delta of the basin.

In the Holocene, the climate for much of the time, especially during the period of 7,000–3,000 a BP, was warm and wet. Therefore, the Dulan-Tiegui Desert was gradually fixed or partly fixed by vegetation, silt and clay; however the desert in the western part of the basin was still expanding. Owing to better water conditions at the southern edge of the basin, tamarisk spread very rapidly and formed numerous tamarisk sand mounds with a diameter was larger than that of today's tamarisk sand mounds, and in some places it was about one-third larger than current tamarisk sand mounds.

At present the basin is in an arid and warm-wet climatic environment which is relatively warmer and wetter; especially in the eastern part of the basin the shifting sand initially formed have been fixed by vegetation. This is evidence of the relatively wet and warm climate. But the climate in the western pert of the basin is always dry. It has been inferred that such climatic condition will continue for a long time.

13.4 Aeolian dune development and environmental changes in the adjoining region of Puruogangri ice sheet, North Tibetan Plateau

13.4.1 Introduction

Periglacial aeolian sand deposition is one of the special phenomena occurring under cold climatic conditions. In Europe, periglacial aeolian sand deposits are mostly located between 50°–54°N and 5°–25°E, and their southern boundaries roughly coincide with the Pleistocene Maximum ice sheet. In North America, larger sandy lands of these aeolian sand deposits are generally believed to have formed from the Wisconsin glacial epoch onwards. Hence, aeolian sands were formed under relatively humid and cold climatic conditions in Europe and North America. In contrast to Europe and North America, aeolian sand deposits in China are mainly distributed in the Qinghai-Tibet Plateau, which has a high altitude and dry-cold climate. Although there is a remarkable extent of aeolian deposits in the region, so far only few literature (Li et al., 1983; Yang et al., 1983; Xu et al., 1983; Zhao, 1991; Dong et al., 1993, 1996a; Zhang et al., 1999) have focused on it. Because aeolian sand deposits in different regions have different formational mechanisms, some problems remain to be solved. For example, the origin of the periglacial aeolian sands, the roles of the cryogenic processes in the evolution of aeolian dunes and the migration characteristics of sand dunes, and rare Holocene climatic information recorded in the periglacial sand dunes (Niessen et al., 1984) are very important to understand formational mechanism of the large aeolian dunes. Based on the survey of aeolian sands in the adjoining region of Puruogangri Ice Sheet that was carried out by an exploration team for drilling ice cores, a preliminary discussion is presented on the relationships between development of aeolian dunes and environmental changes.

13.4.2 Development of aeolian dune

Puruogangri ice sheet, lying between 33°41′–33°58′N and 88°42′–89°03′E, is the largest terrestrial ice sheet in China, with an area of 422 km^2. It is at the centre of the Qiangtang Plateau, the hinterland of the Qinghai-Tibet Plateau, and is influenced by the plateau's cold and arid monsoon. Because of formidable natural conditions, the region is uninhabited and has no meteorological records. Environmental degradation phenomena, such as rangeland desertification, salinization and permafrost degradation, are widespread. The glaciers, mountains, lake, gobi and aeolian dune together form a unique natural landscape. Well developed aeolian dunes and intensive sand stream is a distinct mark. Aeolian sands are mainly deposited on the relatively wider gobi area at the piedmont of the ice sheet, with a small area of 6 km×5 km. Large sand dune types are simple barchan dunes or chain dunes. The sand dunes are generally 200–600 m apart, suggesting that sand supply is seriously insufficient. However, the dunes are relatively high, generally ranging from 20–35 m, and its movement is very slow. Some crescent (chain) dunes have a crescent-shaped ponding at the leeward base. The profiles of some sand dunes have humus layers with weak chemical decomposition. In contrast to these, the majority of deserts and sandy lands in China are between 30°–50°N and 75°–125°E in the northern inland basins with larger and numerous well-developed aeolian dunes. Generally, in many deserts crescent dunes rarely contain paleosols layers because they move very fast. Their heights generally vary between 1m and 10 m and seldom exceed 15 m, and their moving speed rates generally range from 5–10 m/a (Wu, 1987). The large crescent dunes rarely exist in many deserts because of their fast movement. In the Tibetan Plateau, the aeolian landforms usually are crescent (chain) dunes and shrub sand mounds are below 10m high. The large crescent (chain) dunes rarely occur, particularly in the periglacial area because of their insufficient sand supply. Through study of the relationships between development characteristics of aeolian dunes, glacial activity and cryogenic environments in the periglacial area, it can provide a better understanding about the role of the cold environment in the formation of large crescent dunes.

13.4.3 Formation mechanism of large crescent dunes

The deposition of aeolian sand is closely related to the activity of glaciers in the cold environment (Wright, 2001). In the Tibetan Plateau, one of the most striking characteristics is the existence of aeolian dunes in wider river valleys, glacier-developed or glacier relic areas. For example, the largest area of aeolian dunes in the plateau occurs in Maquan River valley, the upper reaches of the Yarlu Zangbo River, where sands are fed by glacial melt-water from the Himalayan and Gangdise Mountains. In general, the formation of aeolian dunes requires several essential conditions: an abundant sand source, suitable depositional sites and certain wind power. Sand sources originated in the region as follows: ①Glacial abrasion produces large amounts of sands, and the sand is transported by glacial melt-water and deposited under river beds. With a decreasing water table in the cold seasons from October to May, a large amount of sands are exposed out of the water, then transported to suitable topographic sites to form sand dunes. ②Glacier retreat leaves a large area of sand-rich moraine sediments. Sand streams could form and aeolian sands accumulate in some places under the strong winds. Hence, moraine deposits are an important sand source. Nearby the aeolian dune area, some moraine ridges are mainly composed of sands mixed with a small amount of gravels. Their heights generally vary from 10–20 m. ③Widespread mechanical weathering, cryogenic weathering and freeze-thaw weathering can accelerate the disintegration of bedrock and gravels under sharp temperature changes, promoting the formation of sands.

The characteristics of glacial movement is therefore a main factor for determining the amount of sand deposits. To produce aeolian sands effectively, sufficiently large glaciers with grinding movement are required. The underlying lithologic characteristics of rock-beds also are very important. Rocks with uniform textures and moderate hardness, such as phyllites, psammites, schists and slates, can easily produce sands, silt and clay. Wright (2001) conducted simulations involving glacial grinding, fluvial comminution, aeolian abrasion, frost weathering and salt weathering. Mechanical procedures were found capable of producing sand-sized quartz to silt-sized particles under laboratory conditions. The findings also clearly demonstrated that glacial activity and cold weathering processes are not the sole processes responsible for providing a fine particle generation which should be produced under a variety of environments.

13.4.4 Characteristics of deposit grains

Analytical results show that mineral contents of sands are composed of quartz (40%), feldspar (45%) and debris (15%), with a low content of resistance mineral (Li et al., 2002). The sand deposits of moraine (gobi) and lacustrine are not only of coarse grain sizes but also contain a certain amount of silt (Table 13-5). The contents of coarse grain size and silt imply that they are produced in situ or transported over a short distance. They are mostly fluvial and alluvial sediments with poor sorting degrees, and experience cryogenic weathering and wind erosion. The grain size of modern sand dunes mainly consists of three grain fractions, i.e. medium sand, fine sand and very fine sand. On average, fine sand and very fine sand account for 40.32% and 51.26% respectively. Smaller grains have more preferential entrainment than coarse sand, so finer particles including silt and clay can be transported by wind over a long distance, leading to the deposition of fine sand and very fine sand. Furthermore, sands underlying moraine deposits mainly consist of fine sand and very fine sand, accounting for 31.39% and 51.36%, respectively; they also contain a certain amount of coarse particles and silt, which could distinguish them from aeolian sands. According to the analytical results of grain size in Chinese deserts, mean grain-sizes of dune sands mostly vary between 0.15–0.35 mm. The mean grain size of 0.15–0.20 mm in the region falls within the range, and the slightly low value of grain-size may be related to the environment in the high and cold region. Aeolian sands are the result of sorting by wind, and the sorting coefficient δ(0.37–0.73) suggests a fine to moderate sorting degree. The skewness SK (−0.13–0.25) mostly represents an extremely negative skewness, showing coarser sediments, and the kurtosis KG (0.84–0.17) shows a wider and bimodal distribution. All confirm that sands were derived from deposits of glacial moraines, then sorted by wind or water.

Table 13-5　Grain size and sorting of moraine sediments and sand dunes in the adjoining region of Puruogangri Ice Sheet

Surface type	Gravel	Very coarse sand	Coarse sand	Medium sand	Fine sand	Very fine sand	Silt	Clay	M_z	δ	SK	KG
	>2mm	−10mm	0-1mm	1-2mm	2-3mm	3-4mm	4-9mm	9-10mm				
Sand underlying moraine	Not counted	1.05	0.92	3.43	31.39	51.65	6.55	5.02	φ2.80	1.30	0.25	2.71
Glacier gobi desert	37.35	17.57	3.11	1.50	8.27	28.85	3.33	+	φ−0.46	2.78	0.33	0.55
Lakeshore deposits	36.59	11.57	7.39	11.01	11.26	11.94	7.85	2.37	φ−0.35	3.06	0.24	0.71
Sand 1 covered on glacier surface	5.59	11.95	22.95	38.50	13.72	4.85	2.64	+	φ0.43	1.52	−0.10	0.95
Sand 2 covered on glacier surface	3.42	2.45	13.62	30.06	13.27	23.41	11.74	2.02	φ1.65	1.90	0.01	0.94
Crescent dune	+	+	+	1.90	47.76	50.27	0.09	+	φ2.57	0.44	−0.21	1.17
Crescent dune	+	+	0.58	19.39	37.06	42.79	0.18	+	φ2.33	0.73	−0.25	0.84
Crescent dune	+	+	+	+	39.14	60.72	0.13	+	φ2.68	0.37	−0.13	1.09

13.4.5 Formational mechanism of large barchan dunes

The formation of sand dunes requires a certain wind power besides sand sources. The region, with an altitude of 5,400–5,600 m, is controlled by a westerly jet stream throughout the year,and it is one of the places with the strongest wind in China. In addition, the sediment materials on the surface are mainly composed of alluvial, lacustrine and aeolian sediments which have loose texture, poor cohesion, high fragility and sand content; hence, they are easily eroded by wind. Being a windy and sandy region, the annual mean blown sand days are 30 days, with a maximum number of 38 days (Gao et al., 1983). For example, in Bangoing County, which is nearest to the Puruogangri ice sheet region, the time that wind velocity is stronger than 17.2 m/s is 85.5 days per year, 75% of which occurs from November to the following May.

The region is the coldest region in the Qinghai-Tibet Plateau with widespread permafrost (Gao et al., 1983). For example, the northern part of the Qiangtang Plateau has a mean temperature of −18°C in the cold season from November to the following April, and is much lower in January. Under such low temperature conditions, the sand dune surface is usually in a frozen state. Coupled with the frequent occurrence of intensive convective airflow, precipitation or snowfall occurs more frequently, with an annual estimate of 150 mm (Gao et al., 1983). The sand dune surfaces are of higher moisture content; therefore, 2–50 cm thick frozen layers often form. The frozen layers play an important role in the development processes of sand dunes through exchange of material and energy. Winter and spring are cold periods with strong blown sand activity. During that period, vegetation is blasted and sparse, and glacial meltwater suffers from a shortage. Sands in river beds are often exposed out of the water, so there is a relatively abundant sand supply. Under the stress of strong winds, the dunes cannot move because of large areas of frozen surfaces. Sands extensively deposit along the windward and leeward slopes. Plant remains can be easily blown over the dune crests and deposited on leeward slopes of sand dunes, causing cross laminae of humus layers.

Summer and autumn are relatively quiet periods because blown sand activities are weak, glacial meltwater is in a flood stage and plants grow well. Large amounts of sediments carried by glacial meltwater mostly deposit under river beds. There are no sufficient sources of sands to supply sand dunes, so the sand stream is in an unsaturated state, leading to the erosion on the windward slopes and deposition on the leeward sides. As a result, the bases of barchan dunes gradually became wider, and the dune volumes can be enlarged further (Fig. 13-5).

The trends of cross laminae in sand dunes are a main geological indicator for reconstructing wind directions (Zhang et al., 2000). Based on the survey on three sand dunes, the trends of laminae are mainly in a range of 40°–120°, indicating that the prevailing wind direction is WNW-SW, which has not changed during the last ten thousand years.

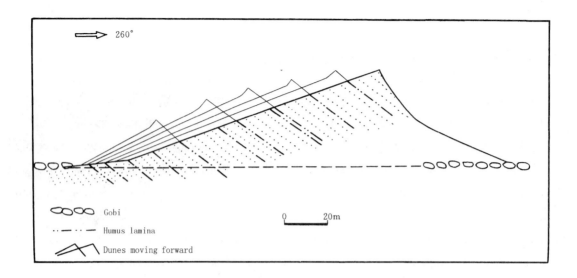

Fig. 13-5   Schematic formation of a large crescent dune

Generally, the development processes from small crescent dunes to large crescent dunes (ridges) are as follows: Deflation takes place on the windward slope of sand dunes, and then the sands are transported over the dune crest and deposited on the leeward slip face, forming high-angle (25°–32°) cross-beddings. The effect of "frozen dune surfaces" is vitally responsible for the very slow migrations of crescent dunes. As a result, the bases of the crescent dunes gradually became wider, and the dune volumes could further enlarge. This would facilitate the dunes to grow further vertically (Fig. 13-5). Environmental change also is an important factor to develop large sand dunes. On a large scale, the stabilization and mobilization of the dunes can essentially reflect climate changes just like the cycle of glacial-interglacial.

13.4.6   Environmental changes recorded from aeolian dune profiles

Shifting sands usually represent a dry-cold and windy environment or a period of sand dune re-activation. The humus layers of sand dunes (2 mm to 10 cm thick) represent a period from a few decades to a few hundred years when plants grew well, and the dunes were stabilized by vegetation. The studied sand dune is a 28 m high crescent dune chain at the east of Puruogangri ice sheet. Humus samples were collected from the stoss slope of the studied dune. ^{14}C dating was conducted in Cold and Arid Regions Environmental and Engineering Research Institute, Chinese Academy of Sciences. Table 13-6 shows the dating of humus layers in the studied sand dune, where the formation age should be much older than 10.8 ka BP as it attaches 3 m thick aeolian sand beneath the oldest humus layer; therefore, the aeolian dune was possibly formed during the Last Glacial Maximum. Much worldwide evidence demonstrates that there are some correlations between fossil dunes and the last glacial period during the late Pleistocene. Most widespread fossil dunes in the world can be dated back to an early age of 15 ka BP (Stokes et al., 1997; Lancaster et al., 2002).

According to Hovermann and Sussenberger (1986), a cold and dry interval occurred between 14 and 10 ka BP. Sedimentation of sandy facies of possible aeolian origin occurred at Qarhan (36°45′N, 95°20′E) around 16.4 ka BP (Bowler et al., 1986). According to the study in the Gonghe basin (36°21′N, 100°47′E) by Xu et al. (1983), the periglacial aeolian sandy loess or loessial soil in a fossil dune profile was formed at 17.3 ka BP. Extensive aeolian sands that are accumulated in the Gonghe Basin during 14.8–12.7 ka BP (Fang, 1991) reflect a large-scale reorganization of atmospheric circulation closely linked to the onset of glaciation in the northern hemisphere resulting from the uplift of the Tibetan Plateau. Viewed from the fluctuations of global dry-cold and humid-warm during a time scale of 10,000 years, the desert development in the monsoon region of China, which roughly synchronized with the spread of the global deserts, was also synchronous all over the world during the Last Glacial Maximum (Tchakerian, 1994). Gao et al., (1993) assured the intensity of the Asian monsoon circulation that controlled the occurrence, development and shrinkage of deserts, as well as the mobilization and stabilization of sand dunes.

The dating of humus layers of sand dunes (Table 13-6) in the Puruogangri correlates with the records of the Dunde ice cores (38°06′N, 96°24′E), the drills of Zhacancaca Lake (32°30′N, 82°20′E) and loessial paleosols profile in the Gonghe Basin. As depositional sequences of dunes are the records of environmental changes, precipitation is a key factor that reflects aeolian sand activity and the summer monsoon intensity. Located in high altitudes and a cold environment, the Puruoganri region is of relatively low evaporation and good moisture due to the formation of the crescent-shaped pondings at many leeward bases of dunes.

Besides relatively good water conditions, the temperature should be another important factor in determining the intensity of the summer monsoon because the region's heat energy mainly results from the solar radiation or the latent thermal from summer monsoon. As long as both water and thermal conditions are suitable, the plants will grow well, and sand dunes will be stabilized; otherwise, sand dunes are bare and re-activate. Yao et al. (1997, 1999) believes the monsoon intensity is an important driving factor mainly controlled by solar radiation (Clemens et al., 1991), and leads to the variations of temperature and moist air supply. Accordingly, in a longer time scale, an increase in temperature will accompany an increase in precipitation and vice versa.

Dai (1990) suggested that the Southwest monsoon has an obvious effect on the Qinghai-Tibet Plateau. Based on mean flow field at an altitude of 5,000 m between 1961–1970, a convergence line at the eastern part of the plateau was constituted at the troposphere and could reach 35°N from July to August. Its position and intensity are closely related to the displacement of the Western Pacific Subtropical High (Fig. 13-6). Fang et al. (1999) also proposed a swinging model for the westerlies. He pointed out that during high insolation periods (interglacials or mega interstadial) the Tibetan Low Pressure might remain strong because of little or no snow cover and more insolation absorption occurs than in other areas at the same latitude due to the high altitude. The westerlies may stay north of the

Table 13-6 Comparison of ¹⁴C dating of humus layers in Puruogangri with dating of the loessal paleosol profile, ice core and saline lake drills in other regions

¹⁴C dating of humus layers in the Puruogangri dune profiles (a BP)	¹⁴C dating of Ren Co and Hidden Lake's drills (a BP), southwest of Tibet (Tang et al., 1999)	Dating of loessial paleosols profile in Gonghe basin (a BP) (Dong et al., 1993)	δ¹⁸O of Duende ice core (a BP) (Yao and Shi, 1992)	¹⁴C dating of Zacang Caka Lake's drills (a BP), north of Tibet (Li et al., 1983)
980±70	1,600±120 (Ren Co)		840–980 (Cold period)	
1,820±70		1,450±70		1,400±690
(exist in other dune)	2,090±60 (Ren Co)		1,800–1,840 (Cold period)	
2,280±70			2,540–2,690 (Cold period)	
2,240±80		3,500±160	2,690–3,700 (Warm period)	3,000±810
(exist in other dune)	4,350±150 (Hidden Lake)	4,320±200	3,790–3,890 (Little warm period)	3,840±130
3,460±80		4,390±90	4,000–4,200 (Warm period)	
4,190±80			4,920–5,040 (Cold period)	4,780±180
(exist in other dune)	5,070±70 (Hidden Lake)	6,180±80	5,400 and 5,900 (Sub-low temperature)	5,600±150
4,420±80	6,540±70 (Ren Co)		5,760–5,890 (Warm period)	5,719±130, 6,500±160
	7,140±70 (Hidden Lake)	7,080±90	7,200–6,100 (Stable warm and humid)	7,000±110, 7,670±250
5,330±90	7,810±60 (Hidden Lake)	7,090±185 (Low temperature)	7,800;7,300 and 8,100 (Cold period)	7,800±210
5,970±95		8,350±100 (Low temperature)	8,350–8,520 (Strong high temperature)	8,000±130
7,450±100			8,650–8,990 (Strong low temperature)	
	9,570±90 (Ren Co)		9,000–9,200 (Warm period)	9,060±120
8,320±110	9,580±160 (Hidden Lake)			10,900±200
	11,360±120 (Hidden Lake)			13,400±160
9,540±130	17,320±620 (Ren Co)	17,300 (Xu et al., 1983)		15,400±160
10,780±130				
No data				

Fig. 13-6 Mean flow field in July at the 5,000 m level between 1961–1970 (Dai, 1990)

Tibet Plateau throughout the whole summer, causing a strong enhancement of the summer monsoon.

According to the dating sequence of the studied dune and previous studies (Li et al., 1983; Dong et al., 1996b) that were based on the Southwest monsoon intensity, the Holocene can be divided into three stages in the hinterland of the plateau:

(1) The early Holocene between 10,000–7,600 a BP was the stage when the intensity of the Southwest monsoon was gradually strengthened. The climate became warmer and more humid, blown sand activity was weakened, and sand dune development ceased. During this period, the temperature in the southern part of the Qinghai-Tibet Plateau was 4-5°C higher than today, and it was the region with the largest temperature-rises among the same latitudinal regions in China, even in the world. With the onset of the Holocene, the climate became warmer, and plants spread. In Puruogangri about 1–2 cm thick humus layers are mainly distributed at the lower base of the sand dunes. The ^{14}C dating of the humus layers is 10,780±130 and 9,549±130 a BP, respectively. Some 9 m thick aeolian sands were deposited between two humus layers. Estimated from the aeolian sand thickness between the humus layers and their related ^{14}C dating in the sand dune, the mean migration rate of the sand dune computed is about 0.7 cm·a^{-1}. According to the analytical results of Holocene strata in the Mandong Lake, the pollens of woody plants in diatomaceous earth had increased (Li et al., 1983). The drill records of the Zacang Caka Lake revealed that the pollen assemblage was dominated by herbs from the last glacial period to the early Holocene, and abundance and diversity of the species significantly increased (Li et al., 1983). ^{14}C dating of plant residues in a sand ridge on the lakeshore near eastern Wudaoliang, a place along the Qinghai-Tibet Highway, was 9,716±270 a BP (Zhao 1991). During 8.5–8.3 ka BP, the water table of the Bangong Lake (33°42′N, 79°00′E) was 30–35 m higher than the present time because of increasing precipitation.

(2) The mid-Holocene between 7,500–4,000 a BP was a developmental stage of the Southwest monsoon. There are five layers of humus, ranging from 3 to 5 cm in thickness, formed within the sand dune. The ^{14}C dating of the humus layers are 8,320±110, 7,450±100, 5,970±95, 5,330±90 and 4,420±80 a BP, respectively. Aeolian sands 68 m thick were deposited between 8,320±110 and 4,420±80 a BP of the humus layers. The mean migration rate of the sand dune is about 1.7 cm/a. The Dunde ice core records indicate that the period of 7.2–6.1 ka BP was a stable warm and humid stage. More than 30 sites of cultural relic remains from the Stone Age have been found in the northwestern part of the Qinghai-Tibet Plateau, which is currently unsuitable for human habitation today (Liu et al., 1991). The Zacang Caka Lake region was dominated by shrub steppe at that time. Compared to the previous stages, the broad-leaved species (e.g. *Alnus*) or hygrophytes (e.g. *Cyperus*) increased (Li et al., 1983) when the mean annual temperature was 2–5°C higher than today. In the Hidden Lake (29°48.77′N, 92°22.37′E) and Ren Co (30°43.97′N, 96°40.97′E), the paleo-vegetation was dominated by forest or forest-meadow during 8–5 ka BP. The precipitation was 200 mm more than the present. The intensity of the Southwest monsoon reached its acme by 7 ka BP, but gradually weakened from 5 ka BP. to the present. When the temperature and precipitation decreased, the paleo-vegetation was dominated by steppe (Tang et al., 1999).

(3) The late Holocene from 4,000 a BP to the present was the period when the Southwest monsoon was gradually weakened. With the Southwest monsoon weakening, the winter monsoon

became stronger again. The ^{14}C dating of humus layers in the studied dune are 3,460±80, 2,280±70, 980±70 a BP, respectively. A bed of 21 m thick aeolian sands were deposited between 3,460±80 and 980±70 a BP of humus layers. There are 30 m thick aeolian sands deposited on the latest humus layer, representing a gradual development of aeolian sand activity. The climate of the Qinghai-Tibet Plateau became drier and colder during the past 3,000 years, and the Zacang Caka Lake further shrank and salinized in 3,800 a BP (Li et al., 1983); therefore, aeolian sand was gradually re-activated. It should be noted out that the Qinghai-Tibet Plateau might still be in a cold state even though a warming trend makes snowline altitudes rise, glaciers retreat, permafrost degrade and the ground temperature of frozen soil rise.

13.4.7　Conclusions

(1) The study showed that glaciation is one of the major contributions to sand supply in a cold environment. Large amounts of sands are produced by glacial abrasion and freeze-thaw weathering, or from a large area of moraine. Aeolian sands could be deposited at the piedmont on a glacier-caused gobi through being transported by glacial melt-water and deposited under the control of strong winds.

(2) The evolution of aeolian dunes takes on some common environmental features and shows their own particularity. Large and simple sand dunes form under the control of unidirectional wind. The frozen surfaces of the dunes caused by cold climate are responsible for the development of large barchan dunes. Owing to frozen effects in the cold environment, the evolution of the sand dunes is dominated by expanding dune bases and vertical accretion, thereby forming large barchan dunes. In a longer scale the stabilization and mobilization of the dunes can essentially reflect the climatic changes just like a cycle of glacial-interglacial. The migration rate of large barchan dunes has an average rate of 1.7–0.7 cm/a.

(3) The temperature and water that control the environmental changes in the adjoining region of the Puruogangri ice sheet are the main factors in determining plant growth. Viewed from the region's heat, mainly resulting from the latent heat of the summer monsoon, the Southwest monsoon intensity might be a key factor. The monsoon intensity can lead to temperature change and moist air supply. An increase in temperature is proportional to precipitation and vice versa. As long as both water and thermal conditions are suitable, the plants will grow well, and the sand dunes will be stabilized. Otherwise, the sand dunes are bare and cause re-activation.

(4) Ice core records have much higher sensitivity than humus layers in sand dunes. However, the humus layers in the Puruogangri are perfectly preserved, which directly reflect environmental changes. In published literature, the sedimentary sequence in the sand dune is the most perfect representative model of Chinese deserts. This will be the exceptional and convictive evidence of environmental changes to verify the Puruogangri ice core records in the near future.

13.5 Aeolian desertification in the "Yarlung Zangbo River and its Two Tributaries" region in Tibet

The "Yarlung Zangbo River and its Two Tributaries" Region , namely the middle reaches of the Yarlung Zangbo River, Ihasa River and the Nyang Qu River, is located in the Zangnan valley in the mid-southern part of the Tibet Autonomous Region (Fig. 13-7). It borders Sangri to the east, Laz to the west, Zangnan Lake Basin to the south, and the southern piedmont of the Gandise-Nyainqentanglha Mountains to the north. Its geographic coordinate is $28°-31°$ N and $87°-93°$ E, the east-west length is 520 km, and the north-south width is 200 km, with a total area of 65,000 km^2.

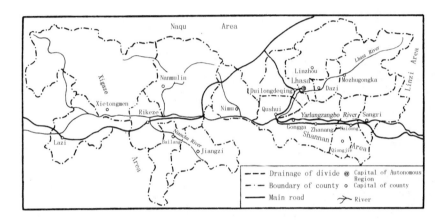

Fig. 13-7   Location of the midstream basin of "Yarlung Zangbo River and its Two Tributaries" in Tibet

The midstream basin of "Yarlung Zangbo River and its Two Tributaries" is one part of the high-cold region of the Qinghai-Tibet Plateau in China and also one of the regions with a fragile eco-environment. The region is now faced with various environmental problems such as debris flow, landslide and soil salinization etc., especially, the aeolian desertification problem is most prominent.

13.5.1   Status of aeolian desertification

The development degree of aeolian desertification is mainly manifested in aeolian sand landforms, and the environment elements including vegetation and soils change with the changes in aeolian sand landforms. Therefore, aeolian desertification types can be divided with aeolian sand landforms as the prominent factor, in combination with other indicators such as vegetation and soil changes (Table 13-7). According to surface material composition, the aeolian desertified land in the region can be divided into aeolian desertified land and gravelly aeolian desertified land. The gravelly aeolian desertification in the "Yarlung Zangbo River and its Two Tributaries" Region has three features: ① sand-gravel lands (e.g. ait, marginal shoal, alluvial-diluvial plain, dry river bed, and piedmont alluvial-diluvial fans) contain a certain amount of sand, and after freeze-thaw weathering produces new sand materials, it becomes an aeolian sand source area; ② under the action of sand-moving winds, wind erosion and deposition widely take place on the gravel land or even form scattered sand dunes; ③ sand-gravel lands are important grazing lands. Some canals and highways pass through such land, and cultivated lands were even developed on this land; hence it is a region suffering from aeolian desertification damages.

Table 13-7　Aeolian desertified land types and indicators in the midstream basin of "Yarlung Zangbo River and its Two Tributaries"

Indicator		Slightly aeolian desertified land		Moderately aeolian desertified land		Severely aeolian desertified land
Aeolian sand landform	Surface material composition	Sandy land (<10%)	Sand-gravel land (<10%)	Sandy land (<10%)	Sand-gravel land (>10%)	Sand-gravel land (<10%)
	Aeolian sand activity	Fixed surface without sand deflation	Semi-exposed surface with less obvious sand flow sand deposition	Semifixed surface with sand flow but no dune migration	Exposed surface with sand flow and local sand deposition	Wind erosion and sand flow exist,and dunes migrate
	Surface feature	Flat sandy land with fixed dune	Flat sand-gravel land with coppice dunes	Flat sandy land with semifixed dunes	Flat sandy land with scattered barchan dunes	Flat sandy land, sloping sandy land barchan dune, dune chains and huge complex dunes exist
	Dune density	<5%		30%—5%	5% or so	>30%
	Dune height	1—2m		1—3m		
Vegetation	Vegetation cover	>45%	>25%	10%—45%	<25%	<10%
	Main plant species	Sophora moorcroftiana, Caragana spinifera, Pinnisetum flaccidum, Stipa, Setarria viridis		Sophora moorcroftiana, Pennisetum flaccidum, Artenisia, Astragalus membranaceus		Pennisetum flaccidum, Oxytropis alpine, Salsola collina, Agriophyrum squarrosum
Soil	Soil	Fixed blown sand soil	Sand-gravel soil	Semifixed blown sand soil	Sand-gravel soil	Shifting blown sand soil

Aeolian desertification can be divided into three grades, namely slight, moderate and severe aeolian desertification; while gravel land only has two grades of slight and moderate aeolian desertification. The is because gravel land has limited sand sources and gravel layer has a certain protection ability, therefore the latter cannot reach a severe degree of aeolian desertification. Other aeolian desertification classification indicators are roughly the same for these two types of aeolian desertification .

13.5.1.1　Distribution of aeolian desertified land

There is a total of 1,860.9 km^2 of aeolian desertified land in this region, accounting for 2.8% of the region's total land area or corresponding to 97.5% of existing cultivated land area. The spatial distribution of the aeolian desertified land has five features.

(1) Aeolian desertified lands in the valleys of the "Yarlung Zangbo River and its Two Tributries" are distributed discontinuous strips, 58.7% of which occur on the river banks, especially in the wide

valleys of the Yarlung Zangbo River. Aeolian desertified land covers the largest area, for example, the area of Aeolian desertified land in Danada-Dazhuka, Qu shui-Zedang reaches 46.5% and 41.1%, and they all occur on the northern bank of the Yarlung Zangbo River. The distribution of aeolian desertified land in ait, marginal shoals, alluvial-diluvial plains and dry river beds is shown in Fig. 13-8, and they account for 25.7%, 17.8%, 10.6% and 4.5% of the total land area of the region. In addition, they also occur on the alluvial-diluvial fans and mountain slopes, and account for 34.1% and 7.2% of the region's total aeolian desertified land, respectively.

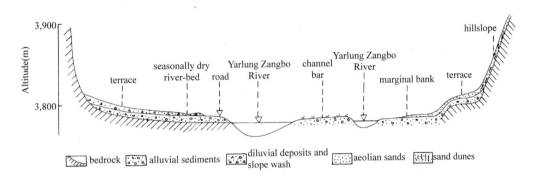

Fig. 13-8   The distribution of aeolian desertified land in different landform sites in the Yarlung Zangbo River valley

(2) Viewed from the administrative region boundary of aeolian desertified land, the Xigaze region has the largest aeolian desertified land, followed by the Shannan region, and Lhasa City has the least aeolian desertified land, which account for 52.5%, 29.1% and 18.4% of the total aeolian desertified land, respectively.

(3) Gravelly aeolian desertified land covers a total area of 944.5 km², accounting for 50.8% of the total desertified land. It is mainly distributed in ait, marginal shoals, terraces, dry river beds and alluvial-diluvial fans, accounting for 33.6%, 31.5%, 15.2%, 10.8% and 8.9% of the total area of sand-gravel land. The aeolian desertified land is the largest in the Rigze region, followed by Lhasa City, and least in the Shannan region. Aeolian desertified land in the region is 916.4 km², accounting for 49.2% of the region's total aeolian desertified land. It is mainly distributed in ait, marginal shoals, terraces, alluvial-diluvial fans and mountain slopes, accounting for 19.9%, 20.5%, 10.4%, 34.5% and 14.6% ,respectively.

(4) In the region, there are 578.6 km² of slightly aeolian desertified land, 752.8 km² of moderately aeolian desertified land and 530.5 km² of severely aeolian desertified land, accounting for 28.5%, 40.5% and 31.0% of the region's total aeolian desertified land, respectively It can be seen that the region is dominated by moderately and severely aeolian desertified land (the combined percentage is 71.5%). Therefore, this region belongs to the moderate-severe aeolian desertification region in the high-cold zone of the Qinghai-Tibet Plateau.

(5) According to the regional distribution of aeolian desertified land, the largest area of slight

aeolian desertified land is distributed in the Xigaze region followed by Lhasa City and the smallest area in the Shannan region. Similarly, the largest area of moderate aeolian desertified land is distributed in Xigaze, followed by Lhasa City, with the smallest area in Shannan.

13.5.1.2 Potential aeolian desertified land and aeolian non-desertified land

There are also potential aeolian desertified land and aeolian non-desertified land in the region. Aeolian non-desertified land refers to the lands where no aeolian desertification takes place, such as water bodies, rocky land, swamp meadows, towns and industrial lands (highway, airport, and industrial land). Potential aeolian desertified land refers to the land with aeolian desertification-prone conditions but no aeolian desertification at present, such as cropland, fallow land, and forest land, etc. Wind erosion is one of the main links of land aeolian desertified processes, and should be viewed as a symptom of slight or moderate aeolian desertification. If including potential areas, the aeolian desertified land area will double.

13.5.2 Causes of aeolian desertification

The "Yarlung Zangbo River and its Two Tributaries" region is located in the temperate semiarid steppe monsoon zone of the plateau. Its eco-environment is quite fragile, mainly manifested in abundant surface sand sources, dry, cold and windy climate,and sparse and dwarf vegetation etc.

13.5.2.1 Natural factors

(1) Abundant surface sand sources. Loose Quaternary deposits of different thicknesses are extensively distributed on the mountain slopes, valley terraces, river beds, cultivated lands, badland and sandy lands. Such deposits and soils contain a certain amount of sand and mostly have a higher fine and very fine sand content in addition to silt and clay (Table 13-8). Such deposits provide a material source for the development of aeolian desertification.

Surface sand material in the region mainly comes from the bedrock, especially the sandstone in the surrounding mountains. Located in the high-cold zone, there is strong solar radiation and large diurnal temperature variations, hence freeze-thaw weathering and mechanical physical weathering are widespread and vigorous. The weathering of mountain rocks produces large amounts of sand and silt sand they are transported, sorted and deposited by wind and finally transported to the Yarlung Zangbo River and its tributary system. The distribution of sand sources is unbalanced, and they mainly occur in the valleys of the "Yarlung Zangbo River and its Two Tributaries", especially at the junctions of various rivers. According to statistical data from four hydrological stations at Nugsha, Yangcun, Jiangzi and Lhasa, the annual sediment transport rates of the Lhasa River and Nyang Qu River are

Table 13-8　Surface material grain-size composition in the midstream basin of "Yarlung Zangbo River and its Two Tributaries"

No.	Location	Landform site and sample name	Grain-size composition (%)							
			Gravel	Very coarse sand	Coarse sand	Medium sand	Fine sand	Very fine sand	Silt	Clay
1	Duojiza	Slope sand		0.21	0.27	2.14	74.08	17.76	4.74	0.78
2		Slope wash	0.69	0.13	0.06	0.65	83.08	13.53	1.49	0.37
3	Duobtang	Slope loess			0.03	0.61	4.42	39.84	50.03	5.07
4	Xie tangmen	Slope loess				0.23	4.12	44.86	49.65	1.12
5		Slope buried sand			0.29	5.09	27.03	45.88	18.50	2.49
6	Duojiza	Sand and gravels on the top of diluvial fan	4.25	0.17	0.05	0.86	78.52	12.80	2.88	0.47
7	Sdang	Terrace sand		0.06	0.36	75.58	21.22	2.42	0.36	
8	Jiangdang	Farmland sandy loam	1.89	1.01	1.52	6.73	15.34	35.21	30.51	7.79
9	Aimagang	Farmland sandy soil	0.34	3.05	2.17	6.49	17.63	57.54	9.40	2.58
10		Bad land sandy soil	0.69	2.39	7.88	11.54	16.80	33.33	22.94	4.43
11	Duojiza	River bed sand				2.65	42.80	51.42	2.90	0.22
12	Qushui	River bed dand		0.07	0.68	6.95	17.82	57.72	13.03	2.93
13	Duojiza	Mobile dune sand				0.66	76.19	22.23	0.79	0.13
14	Jiangdang	Mobile dune sand			2.65	44.06	42.68	8.75	0.73	1.13
15	Duojiza	Interdune Aeolian sand			0.01	13.46	69.20	14.88	2.07	0.38

31.1 kg/s and 28.7 kg/s, respectively, and annual sediment discharges are 983,000 t and 904,000 t, respectively. In the two wide-valley basins of the Yarlung Zangbo River, the annual sediment transport rates are 458 kg/s and 466 kg/s, and their annual sediment discharges are (14.5–14.72) million t (Table 13-9). According to the calculation of sediment transport rate and sediment discharge, the annual sediment deposition amount in the Qushui-Zedang wide valley could reach 783,000 t or more.

Table 13-9　Annual sediment transport rate and sediment discharge in midstream basin of "Yarlung Zangbo River and its Two Tributaries"

River	Hydrological station	Mean annual sediment transport rate (kg/s)			Annual sediment discharge (10^4t)			Mean annual sediment concentration (kg/m^3)			Number of years with data (a)
		max	min	mean	max	min	mean	max	min	mean	
Yarlung Zangbo River	Nugsha	1,460	87.3	458	4,620	275	1450	1.53	0.261	0.737	14
	Yang village	660	194	466	4,620,611	1472	0.62	0.266	0.465	5	
Nyang Qu River	Jiangzi	58.0	9.67	28.7	183	30.5	90.4	1.99	0.601	1.25	5
Lhasa River	Lhasa	50.7	12.8	31.1	160	40.3	98.3	0.142	0.056	0.098	7

Sand sources in the region have seasonal and interannual variations. As a rule, its annual and interannual variations are consistent with the runoff changes. The period from October to April of the following year is the low-water stage, when the sediment transport rate and sediment deposition are the lowest; the other months are high-water periods, when the sediment transport rate and sediment deposition are the largest; the variations of annual sediment transport rate and sediment deposition are consistent with the runoff changes. The deposits in the wide-valley basin of the Yarlung Zangbo River and at the junctions of its tributaries are the main material sources of land aeolian desertification in the region.

(2) Dry, cold and windy climate. Dry, cold and frequent winds are the main climatic features of the "Yarlung Zangbo River and its Two Tributaries" region. Since the penetration of moist airstream from the Indian Ocean is impeded by the Himalayas, coupled with foehn effect, annual precipitation in the region is low (251.7–508 mm), annual evaporation is high (2,289–2,733 mm), aridity is 5–10, 80% of precipitation falls in May-September and thus forms obvious dry and wet seasons. Wind regime in the region is complex due to the influence of trade winds and wind direction is variable from region to region. Mean annual wind velocity is 1.7–3.1 m/s. The winds > 5 m/s can cause wind erosion and occurs almost every month. The largest wind velocity may reach 32 m/s, and the annual number of gale days varies between 27.5–90.7 days. Wind direction in the region is mainly controlled by the conversion of monsoon seasons and valley orientation, coupling with "funneling effect" wind velocity in summer half year (June–October) is larger.

(3) Sparse and dwarf vegetation. Habitat conditions such as dry, cold and windy climate and loose sand-gravel surface generally support very few plant species or even no vegetation. However, in the sand-gravel land and sandy land along the river banks some scattered patches of steppe and shrub grassland species can be found, such as *Stipa baicalensis*, *Aristida triseta*, *Pennisetum flaccidum*, *Stipa purpurea* and *Artemisia* etc., with a vegetation cover of 5%–75%. The height of most plant species is 5–50 cm and they grow poorly. The area of forest land, including natural forest and artificial forest in the region is only 155,000 hm^2, accounting for 2.34% of the region's total land area, the forest cover is 2.29% and in the river valley it is only 1.12%. Owing to low vegetation cover, sandy lands in the region are mostly in an exposed or semi-exposed state, therefore they are prone to wind erosion and cause the development of aeolian desertification.

13.5.2.2　Anthropogenic factors

The mid-stream basin of the "Yarlung Zangbo River and its Two Tributaries" is the political, economic and cultural center of Tibet. As a part of the Qinghai-Tibet plateau, the eco-environment of the region is fragile and prone to suffer from aeolian desertification. Rapid population growth and irrational land exploidation and use has upset the ecological balance and triggered aeolian desertification processes which has led to the expansion and exacerbation of aeolian desertification.

1) Over-reclamation

To meet the food requirements of a rapidly growing population, the grasslands in the region were uncontrolledly reclaimed without adopting any protective measures. As a result, cultivated land area greatly increased but primary vegetation and soil structure were seriously destroyed, and this largely aggravated soil wind erosion (Table 13-10). Wind erosion leads to fine particles blowing away, leaving behind coarse grains on the surface. This provides a sand source for aeolian desertification of the surrounding land, and it is therefore one of the important processes of aeolian desertification in the region.

Table 13-10   Comparative experiment results of soil deflation amounts in ploughed and unploughed farmland

Land type	Duration of wind Action (min)	Wind velocity (m/s)	Deflation Amount (g)	Modulus of wind erosion
Unploughed farmland	5	16.43	40.90	1.012
	5	21.20	893.62	22.102
	5	22.82	1,073.76	26.5772
Ploughed farmland	5	17.19	462.47	11.4408
	5	20.09	782.78	19.3604
	5	23.03	1,711.18	42.2652

2) Overgrazing

In the 32-year period from 1959–1990, the mean growth rate of livestock population in the region was 16.6%; in the same period the per capita share of natural grassland area decreased from 2.13 hm^2 to 1.27 hm^2, and the livestock number exceeded the grassland carrying capacity. Especially in winter and spring, overgrazing is very severe and the livestock trampling magnitude and frequency largely increase. As a result, grassland vegetation is destroyed; soil deflation and deposition are aggravated and thus cause grassland aeolian desertification (Table 13-11).

Table 13-11   Effects of livestock trampling and browsing on soil deflation

Soil condition	Deflation amount (kg)	Wind force (scale)	Duration of wind action (min)
Prior to trampling	0.00	10	15
Slight trampling and browsing	0.06	10	15
Moderate trampling and browsing	0.42	10	15
Severe trampling and browsing	1.18	10	15

3) Overcutting

In Tibet, coal and oil-gas resources are scarce, therefore the consumption of biological energy sources is very large. According to investigations, annual consumption of biological energy sources in Tibet is about 502,000 t, of which animal dung and fuelwood occupy 80,000 t and herdsmen consume about 175,000 t, accounting for 96%; city dwellers consume about 7,000 t, accounting for 4%. The fuelwoods mainly come from natural forest land, shrub forest land and shrub grassland. Overcutting activities seriously destroy the region's vegetation. It is estimated that each year about 4,000–7,000 hm^2 of natural shrub forest land were destroyed. Vegetation destruction results in the exposure of sandy ground surfaces, and the increase of the soil deflation rate (Table 13-12). Sand dunes are important causes responsible for aeolian desertification in this region.

Table 13-12　Comparison of deflation amounts in different cutting areas (wind force 10 blowing for 15 min)

Cutting area (%)	0	10	30	60	100
Soil deflation amount (kg)	0.34	0.40	1.46	4.68	9.12

References

Comprehensive Investigation Team of Qinghai-Tibet Plateau, Chinese Academy of Sciences. 1983a. Climate in Tibet. Beijing: Science Press. 168: 127—131

Comprehensive Investigation Team of Qinghai-Tibet Plateau, Chinese Academy of Sciences. 1983b. Quaternary Geology of Tibet. Beijing: Science Press

Comprehensive Investigation Team of Qinghai-Tibet Plateau, Chinese Academy of Sciences. 1983c. Topography of Tibet. Beijing: Science Press

Dai Jiaxi. 1990. Climate of Qinghai-Tibet Plateau. Beijing China: Meteorological Press, 133—135

Denton G H, Karlen W. 1973. Holocene climate variations: their pattern and possible cause. Quaternary Research, 3

Dong Guangrong, Gao Shangyu. 1993. Land Desertification and Control Ways in Gonghe basin of Qinghai, Beijing: Science Press

Fang Yong. 1963. Basic characteristics of landforms of Qinghai Lake basin, their causes and evolution, Memories of Journal of Geography, No.5. Beijing: Science Press

Grove A T, Warren A. 1968. Quaternary a landforms-and climate on the south side of the Sahara. Geographical Journal, 134

Lanzhou Institute of Desert Research, Chinese Academy of Sciences et al. 1979. Comprehensive investigation report of Qinghai Lake, Beijing: Science Press

Lanzhou Institute of Desert Research, Chinese Academy of Sciences. 1986. Land desertification and its control in Ih Ju Meng of Inner Mongolia. In Memorials of Institute of Desert, Chinese Academy of Sciences. No.3

Li Jijun. 1979. Uplift times, range and form of Qinghai-Tibet Plateau. Science in China, (6): 608—616

Nichols H. 1967. Central Canadian palynology and its relevance to north Western Europe in the late quaternary Period. Review Palaeobotany and Palanology, 2

Singh G. 1971. The Indus valley culture seen in the context of post glacial climate and ecological studies in north west India. Archaeology in Oceania, 6

Wang Tao. 1990. Several problems on the formation and evolution of Badain Jaran Desert. Journal of Desert Research, 10(1): 29—40

Yao Tandong, Lonnie G, Thompson et al. 1997. Climatic changes recorded in Guliya ice core since last interglacial period. Science in China (Series D), 27(5): 447—452

Yao Tandong. 1999. Sudden climatic changes of Qinghai-Tibet Plateau during last glacial period—comparative study of Guliya ice core and Greenland GRIP core. Science in China (Series D), 29(2): 175—184

Zhong Decai. 1986. Preliminary study of desert formation and evolution in Qaidam Basin. Memorials of Institute of Desert, Chinese Academy of Sciences, No.3

Zhu Zhenda, Chen Zhiping, Wu Zheng et al. 1981. Study of Aeolian Sand Landforms in Taklimakan Desert. Beijing: Science Press

Zhu Zhenda, Wu zheng, Liu Shu et al. Introduction to Desert of China. Beijing: Science Press

Chapter 14
Gobi Desert

"Gobi desert" means "a vast, boundless area of gravel plain" in both the Mongolian and Manchu languages. In the western Mongolian Plateau, it refers to the vast regions with flat surfaces, coarse materials, low or almost no vegetation cover and few human settlements. With the increase in geographical exploration in central Asia in the late 19th century, "gobi desert" became a proper term to describe such landforms or landscapes, and is generally referred to as the gravel or rocky deserts by geographers. It is usually formed in mountains or on high plains (plateaus) where large amounts of debris is produced by physical weathering on the surface under the conditions in a dry desert climate. The debris is then sorted by wind, resulting in the removal of fine grains while coarse grains remain on the land surface, forming the gobi desert landscape. This is the erosional type of gobi desert. Depositional gobi desert, another type of gobi desert, is formed on the diluvial-alluvial plains where large amounts of mixed deposits were transported by floods from the mountains to the piedmont. After exposure to strong winds, only debris or gravel remains on the surface and a gobi desert landform is developed.

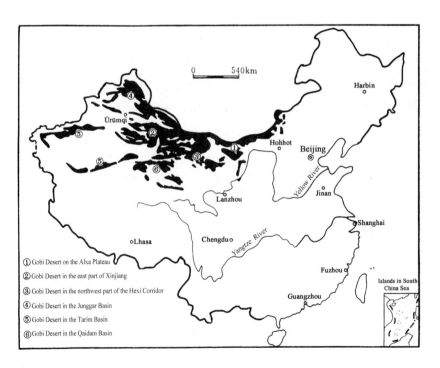

Fig. 14-1   The distribution of gobi deserts in China

Large areas of gobi deserts are distributed in the arid northwest China. In the late 1970s, the total area of gobi desert in China was about 569,500 km^2, equivalent to that of the sandy desert (Fig. 14-1) (Zhu et al., 1980). Among the gobi deserts, erosional ones account for about 32% of the total area and depositional ones account for 68%. In China, Gobi deserts mainly occur in extremely arid regions in the northwest. Continuous distribution of gobi desert occurs in eastern Xinjiang Uigur Autonomous Region, the Alxa Plateau in western Inner Mongolia Autonomous Region, and the northern Hexi Corridor. Besides these areas, some gobi deserts sporadically occur in the piedmont diluvial fans around the Junggar Basin in northern Xinjiang, the Tarim Basin in southern Xinjiang, and the Qaidam Basin in Qinghai.

14.1   Features and types of gobi deserts

The common features of gobi desert concluded by Zhao (1962) are:

(1) the dry climate gobi desert is usually formed in desert climates or desert-steppe climates, with prominent continental characteristics;

(2) surface materialsare composed of coarse grains of gravel or bedrock;

(3) plain surface compared to typical deserts;

(4) usually lacks water, has rare surface runoff and low groundwater levels;

(5) low fertility surface soils, such as the brown to grey-brown desert soils and the brown carbonate-rich soils;

(6) low vegetation cover, dominated by desert plants or desert-steppe plants; the vegetation cover is usually less than 30%, and in most areas it is only around 10%.

In the features mentioned above, the factor of surface material composition is particularly important. It not only affects other factors such as groundwater level and vegetation cover, but also determines the difficulty, to a large extent, of utilizing gobi deserts. Therefore it is an important criteria for classifying the gobi deserts. For example, on the erosional rocky gobi deserts in the peneplain, most of the surface materials are bedrocks cut by weathering processes and occasionally covered with a thin layer of debris or gravel. It is hard for plant growth and difficult to utilize. On the depositional gobi deserts covered with thick sediments, however, the surface materials are mainly gravel or sandy gravel, and the grains and structure vary in different locations. In the desert (except the desert steppe) area, the surface is characterized by an obvious gravel surface. As eroded by both wind and water, the fine materials are blown or washed away and coarse materials remains (Fig. 14-2). In these areas, the surface soils extremely lack water and nutrients. The temperature variation is extremely large (often reaching 60 °C to 70 °C or even 80 °C on gravel surfaces at noon in the summer). Under the gravel surface, there often exists a hard varnish layer preventing water penetration. All these characteristics are disadvantages for seeds to germinate and grow. On the other hand, this layer can also protect ground water and fine materials below.

Fig. 14-2 Wind eroded gobi desert

(scale in the figure is a coin of 1 *yuan*, RMB)

Controlled by geological tectonics and geomorphological processes, the surface material composition and other factors vary in different locations due to variations in weathering, erosion and deposition processes. Therefore, in gobi desert classifications, they are divided into two main types, namely erosional and depositional gobi deserts according to their geologic and geomorphological origin. Sub-types are further classified according to the surface material composition, such as the denudation-drift bedding-diluvial gravel and sandy gobi deserts, and the denudation-eluvial-drift bedding rocky and coarse debris gobi deserts etc.

Besides classifications according to formation processes, some scientists classify gobi deserts into 4 levels. Level 1 includes the desert and desert-steppe according to the zonal factors. In Level 2, erosional-depositional and depositional gobi deserts are included according to the interactions of the internal and external geomorphological agents. Level 3 includes diluvial, alluvial-diluvial, diluvial-alluvial and diluvial-drift bedding gobi deserts according to the formation processes and surface materials. Level 4 is the primary classification of gobi deserts, which is based on the combination of plant association and other natural factors. Beyond these two classifications, there are still other methods to classify gobi deserts. For example, according to the geomorphological locations, there are diluvial piedmont gobi deserts, and diluvial terrace gobi deserts. Here we find that in all these classifications, formation process and surface materials are the two most important factors. Therefore in this chapter, formation and surface materials gobi deserts are regarded as the main basis for the classification.

14.2 Distribution, types and features of gobi desert in different regions

14.2.1 Gobi desert on the Alxa Plateau

The Alxa Plateau generally refers to the area north of the Hexi Corridor, south of the China-Mongolia border, east of the Heihe River and west of the Helan Mountains. Administratively, it includes Alxa Zuoqi, Alxa Youqi, Ejin Qi and part of Bayanzhuo'er Meng in central Inner Mongolia. This is an area with many deserts in China and there is also large areas of gobi desert. The gobi deserts in this area are partly formed by diluvial-alluvial deposits, such as those located on both sides of the Heihe River (also called the Central Gobi), and partly composed of erosional gobi deserts, scattered in the mountains in the north of the Badan Jarin Desert and the Yamaleike Desert. On the piedmont plains of the Heli Mountains and northern Longshou Mountains, diluvial sandy gravels are the main surface materials of the gobi deserts. In the Mazong Mountains area to the west of the Heihe River, there are hilly erosional gobi deserts. In some intermontane plains, diluvial gobi deserts are the main type (Zhu, 1980).

Windy, large temperature variations and low precipitation are the typical characteristics of the climate in this area (Yu, 1962). Sharp temperature change causes severe weathering and denudation, resulting in large amount of loose deposits. The weathering remains are transported by temporary runoff formed during short concentrative rains to the lower reaches, providing the materials for gobi desert development. In addition, the wind blows the fine grains away, leaving coarse gravels or debris on surface, which compose the current gobi desert surface. The landscape and surface material composition vary distinctly as the formation process of gobi desert is different.

14.2.1.1 Gravel gobi desert of diluvial origin

This type of gobi desert is widely distributed and most gobi deserts in the Alxa Plateau belong to this type. In the eastern and northern parts of this area, the surface material is the Quaternary diluvial deposits overlaying the Tertiary red clay. In the west, East and West Ejin Gobi deserts are composed of diluvial layer deposits underlain by old lacustrine sediments. Therefore, this type of gobi desert is characterized by the Quaternary diluvial as the dominant surface material. Cut through by flowing water and wind erosion, the gobi desert surface often forms some wind erosional gullies with depths of 5 m. Especially, in the east gobi sandy desert boundary regions, where the wind erosion process is severe, wind erosional gullies are trough- or ellipse-shaped with diameters of 2 to 20 km.

In the eastern and northern gobi deserts, where the underlying material is the Tertiary red clay, the ground water level is 10 m below the surface. The water is the phreatic water in the red clay, with poor quality. It is Cl-Na type, with salinity of 13.5 g/L, the total hardness is 216.5° (German degree), tasting salty and bitter, and is called bitter water by the local residents. The East and West Ejin Gobi Deserts are relatively young, and the diluvial layer is thin and loose. The ground water level is high, and of good quality. It is also Cl-Na type, but the salinity is only 1.26 g/L and total hardness is 17° (German degree). It serves as drinking water for the local residents and domestic animals.

14.2.1.2　Rocky gobi deserts of denudation

This type of gobi desert is distributed in the vast area to the north of the Badain Jaran Desert, mainly composed of low denuded hills. The parent rocks are severely weathered and the debris is widely deposited. Cone-shaped and dome-shaped remnants exist on the gobi deserts and the surface is undulate with a relative height of 5 to 10 m. The groundwater lever is low.

14.2.1.3　Alluvial gobi deserts

This type of gobi desert is mainly distributed in the lower reaches of the Heihe River, including the banks of the east and west branch rivers and the region between the two branch rivers. It is a typical alluvial plain. The surface material is river alluvium. Alternating layers of gravel and sand can be found in sections, and the gravels in the sections have a definitive roundness. There is an abundant supply of ground water, and it has a shallow depth (usually 0 to 5 m). The water type is alkaline HCO^{3-}, the salinity is low with a total hardness of 17° to 34° (German degree).

As the annual precipitation decreases from east to west, the soils and vegetation also change regularly from east to west. Further west, they exhibit more desert-like features.

In the east diluvial gobi deserts, ordinary grey-brown desert soil develops. The soil is thick, mostly more than 1m. There is an abundant amount of gravel found in the upper layers of the soil. Above the gravel, there is often a thin layer of carbonates. Below the gravel, calcareous deposits decreas, and powder gypsum crystals appear.

In the west, the ordinary grey-brown desert soil is gradually substituted by gypsum desert soil. Large amounts of clastic or fibrous gypsum crystals begin to appear at 20 cm or even 10 cm below the surface. Gravel can be found in the whole soil profile. The soil is thin, and parent material is found 30 cm below the surface.

In addition, primitive grey-brown desert soil develops on the alluvial gobies and the diluvial gobi desert in western Ejin Qi. The groundwater level of this area is low. The soil has the general characteristics of ordinary grey-brown desert soil. Some of the soil have been salinized to different degrees.

By adaptation to the soils, dwarf shrubs and semi-shrubs have developed in the ordinary grey-brown desert soil area. The plant species are rich in diversity, and the total vegetation cover is 10% to 15%, sometimes reaching 20%. The main plant species are *Potaninia mongolica*, *Salsola passerine*, *Reaumuria soongarica*, and *Oxytropis aciphylla* etc. In the west, the diversity of plant species decreases. For example, *Potaninia mongolica* and *Oxytropis aciphylla* disappear, and *Salsola passerine* decreases. The dominant plant species are replaced by dwarf shrubs such as *Reaumuria soongarica* and *Nitraria sphaerocarpa* with a much lower vegetation cover of less than 5%. Sometimes there is no vegetation cover over large areas of land surface. The composition of the vegetation is very simple, and only *Halogeton arachnoideus* grows widely while *Reaumuria soongarica* and *Nitraria sphaerocarpa grow sparsely*. In the primitive grey-brown desert soil area, as the groundwater level is low and the soil is loose, *Haloxylon ammodendron* grows sparsely with concomitant species such as *Nitraria sphaerocarpa*, *Calligonum mongolicum* and *Zygophyllum xanthoxylon* etc. The total coverage is 3% to 5%. In the light colored meadow soil along the eastern and western branch rivers in the lower reaches of the Heihe River, there are sparse trees of *Populus euphratica* and *Elaeagnus moorcroftii* as well as halobiotic shrubs of *Tamarix chinentsis* and *Lycium ruthenicum*. This is the only region where there are natural arbor trees in the gobi deserts.

14.2.2　Gobi deserts in eastern Xinjiang

Eastern Xinjiang refers to the regions west of the Hexi Corridor, south of the Tianshan Mountains, east of the Turpan Basin and north of the Altun Mountains, and it is one of the most extreme arid regions in China. The annual precipitation is only 10 to 30 mm and aridity is 29 to 60. Gobi deserts are the main landscape in this area. They connect with those northwest of the Hexi Corridor. This is a region that gobi deserts are most densely distributed, not only in China but also in all of Eurasia. Diluvial gobi deserts are mainly distributed in the piedmonts of the Tianshan and Kuluktag Mountains; gobi deserts of denudation are mainly distributed to the south of Hami (Goshun Gobi), and the surface features are undulatory rocky denuded plain or rocky plain with hilly islands and terrace highlands (Zhu, 1980). The natural conditions in this area is extremely poor; the land surface is mostly covered by gravel or broken rocks with black, reluster varnish on the rock surface. Beneath the rocks or gravel is a layer of gypsum, with thick and hard salt pan located underneath in some regions. With lack of soil and water in this area, the plants are sparsely distributed, and the lands are even devoid of vegetation in large areas. According to the landforms where the gobies are located and the surface materials, gobi deserts in this area can be grouped into three types: gobi deserts with underlying soils, sand-gravel gobi deserts and rocky gobi deserts (The Desert Control Team, Chinese Academy of Sciences, 1961).

14.2.2.1　Gobi deserts with underlying soils

This type of gobi desert includes those in the margins of the diluvial fans in the piedmonts of the northern and the southern Tianshan Mountains, those around the Barkol Lake and the Tor Nur Lake in Yiwu County in the west, and those near the Yumenguan Farm in Dunhuang. Judging from its landform position, this type of gobi is also closely related to the alluvial processes of water flow besides just the diluvial processes. Therefore the natural conditions of this type of gobi desert are the best. There is generally a thick soil layer (30 to 50 cm) composed of fine gravel or coarse sand without gypsum. The groundwater level is about 4 to 6m below the surface. The percent of vegetation cover is higher than that in other regions (5% to 15%). The plants are mainly salt-enduring dwarf shrubs, such as *Nitraria sphaerocarpa*, *Reaumuria soongarica*, *Anabasis salsa*, *Nitraria tangutorum* and semi-shrubs like *Kalidium foliatum*, or perennial herbaceous plants such as *phragmites austrails* and *Alhagi sparsifolia* etc. This type of gobi desert is generally used as rangeland at present. Having good conditions for water drainage, the gobi desert in these regions usually have not been severely salinized and drought-resistant crops or pasture can be planted.

14.2.2.2 Sand-gravel gobi deserts

The gobi deserts on the northern and southern sides of the eastern Tianshan Mountains belong to this type, and it is the most widely distributed type of gobi deserts in this area. The surface is flat with gentle slopes, and the materials are exclusively gravel or coarse sands. Some sporadic denuded hills or remnants are distributed separately with a relative height between 10 to 50 m. Thick layers of gypsum, about 45 cm, exists below the ground surface and water and soil are lacking. The groundwater level is very low and no water can be used by plants. Except some sparse undershrubs and semi-shrubs growing in some dry channels (mainly *Ephedra Przewalskii* Stapf, *Eurotia*, *Nitraria sphaerocarpa*, *Iljinia regelii*, *Anabasis salsa*, and *Reaumuria soongarica* etc., with coverage of 5%–10%), there is no vegetation in this vast gobi desert.

14.2.2.3 Rocky gobi deserts

The Geshun Gobi Desert south of Hami, the large gobi desert in the west part of the northern Tianshan Mountains and the Nuoming gobi north of the Tianshan Mountains all are rocky gobi deserts. This area is a peneplain as the result of long-term denudation. The surface is slightly undulate, and is covered by debris formed by weathered bedrock. The bedrock is sometimes directly exposed to the land surface. The soil layer is very thin and impoverished. A gypsum layer lies beneath the pavement. Under the gypsum layer, there are usually thick salt pans of 15 cm /with the thickest reaching 30 to 40 cm. Below the salt pan, there is gypsum again. Because of the extremely dry climate, almost no surface runoff appears and the groundwater is deeply embedded. Much of the area is bare lands without vegetation, and only some drought-enduring and gypsum-loving plants such as *Iljinia regelii* and *Halocnemum glomeratus* survive in the dry channels, creating a desolate vision.

14.2.3　Gobi deserts in the northern Hexi Corridor

The Hexi Corridor, especially the area to the west of Jiuquan, is one of the largest areas of gobi desert distribution. The features of gobi deserts in the Hexi Corridor are noticeable. For example, on the north piedmont of the Qilian Mountains, the gravel layer of the gobi desert reaches 700 to 800 meters, which is rarely seen in other parts of China. The "black gobi" in the Mazong Mountains, however, lacks water and soil and no people live there, and it is called "the greatest gobi desert of gobi deserts" (Zhao, 1962). According to the geomorphological cause of formation and the material composition, there are two main types of gobi deserts, namely denuded (erosional)-depositional type and depositional type, along with 6 classified sub-types. Strongly controlled by modern geologic and geomorphologic processes, all types of gobi deserts are roughly parallel, extending in accordance with the Corridor's direction, and showing an east to west belt-like distribution. The typical characteristics are briefly introduced as follows.

14.2.3.1 Denudation (erosion)—depositional type

This type of gobi desert is distributed in the Mazong Mountains-North Mountains. The denudation (erosion) and deposition processes are equally important. Compared with other depositional gobi deserts, the surface material in this area is coarser and the land surface is more undulate. The deposited gravel layer is thinner, and the temperature is lower with slightly more precipitation. The vertical zonality is obvious. There are 3 sub-types (Xi'an Sand-Control and Research Center, 1960).

(1) Denuded-drift bedding diluvial gravel and sandy gobi deserts (Mazong Mountains–North Mountains).

This type of gobi desert occurs in the Mazong Mountains and North Mountains to the north of the Hongliuyuan-Xiadong-Red SpringSevenwell line (those between the Black Mountains-Jiashan Mountains and the Jieshan-Sanwei Mountains also belong to this type). Gobi deserts in this area are characterized by rocky hills and intermontane basins interlaced in distribution, sometimes continuous and sometimes sporadic.

Tectonically, this area is a part of the Precambrian Mazong Mountains-Alxa Platform, and this area had a stable uplift over a long time. The old rock was denuded and eroded to low remnant hills. The Himalaya Mountains-building Movement in the mid-Tertiary resulted in a series of East-West or NE-SW continental girders as this region is mainly affected by fault blocks. Between the girders are places for sinking fault blocks. Gobi deserts are distributed at the margins of these fault blocks, formed by the processes of strong denudation/erosion on the old rocks and drift bedding or deluvial. The land surface is roughly plain, composed of gravel and coarse sands. The compositions of the gravel is similar to those of the bedrocks in the mountains, consisting mainly of granites, gneisses, quartzites, quartz schists etc. The diameters of the gravel are 3 to 10 cm. In the granite area, there are more sand grains and the natural conditions are better. Generally there is an obvious black varnish surface, forming the "varnish Gobi Desert" or "Black Gobi Desert". The variation in temperature change on the gobi desert surface is large and there are often strong winds. Precipitation and surface runoff are rare. The groundwater level is often 10 to 20 m below the surface. The main soil is the infertile and thin brown gypsum desert soil, generally 50 to 60 cm in depth. In the soil profile, there is often a rock surface and a varnish layer. Under this is the red-brown gypsum layer, being the thickest in slope-deposition materials and disappearing in the alluvial materials. Vegetation in this area is also sparse with coverage lower than 5% to 10%. The plant species are dominated by *Reaumuria soongarica*, *Nitraria sphaerocarpa*, *Sympegma regelii*, and *Ephedra prezwalskii* etc. Compared with other gobi deserts in this area, the relatively high altitudes and better water condition, in addition to lower amounts of human disturbance, allow the survival of some shrubs such as *Haloxylon ammodendron* and *Caragana sinica*. Local vegetation cover can reach 20%–30%.

(2) Denudation-eluvium-drift bedding rocky and coarse gravel gobi deserts (peneplains on the piedmonts of the Mazong Mountains-North Mountains).

This type of gobi desert is occurs in a belt going from east to west and is located to the south of the above type of gobi desert on the piedmonts of the Mazong and North Mountains, The land surface is almost entirely covered by this gobi desert. The materials are mainly rocks and coarse gravel, while, fine gravel and sandy gobi desert is limited to some local low-lying lands.

Taking into account modern geologic and geomorphologic actions, this area is one in which the external agent of denudation is larger than the inner agent of uplift, and the phenomenon of peneplane is obvious. The mountains have been cut flat or exist as sporadic remnant hills. The bedrock is exposed or covered by a thin layer of gravel, forming the famous "black gobi desert". The gobi desert surface is slightly undulate and divided severely into channels or valleys. There are no perennial rivers and the groundwater level is lower than 10 to 20 m. In addition to the dry and windy climate, the soil is mostly infertile and thin gypsum brown desert soil. Ordinary brown desert soil and alluvial soil only appear in local lowlands. The sparse plants are dominated by sporadic *Reaumuria soongarica* and *Nitraria sphaerocarpa*, with coverage lower than 1%. The plants are short and in dormant or semi-dormant states. Only in the erosional trenches or small sandpiles can the coverage reach more than 5% and the plants are mainly clusters of *Sympegma regelii* that have better growth conditions.

(3) Erosional-drift bedding-diluvial gravel gobi desert (Qilian Mountains).

This type of gobi desert is distributed in the Qilian Mountains. Gravel gobi deserts, rocky mountains and the intermontane basins are interlaced in this area. Among these landscapes, the gobi desert area is relatively small and is mainly limited to northern valleys in the mountains.

The Qilian Mountains is, tectonically, a geosyncline that has been instable since its formation by the Haixi Mountains building movement in the late Paleozoic. After the Himalaya Mountains building movement in the mid-Tertiary, the fault block uplifted drastically, forming many NW-SE parallel high, middle and low mountains and intermontane basins. Upland erosion and denudation resulted in large amounts of rock debris, which was then drift bedded or flooded in situ, forming the gobi desert and grasslands. The gobi deserts formed by drift bedding-diluvial processes are characterized by coarse pieces of rocks and gravel in surface materials, though the sorting process is not obvious. The slope of the surface is relatively large. In addition to the relatively high altitude (especially in the south), vertical zonation is distinct. Snow and rain are more plentiful and the hydrological networks are densely distributed. The vegetation cover is better and the main species are *Kalidium foliatum*, *Reaumuria soongarica*, *Nitraria sphaerocarpa*, *Ephedra prezwalskii*, and *Sympergma regelii* etc.

14.2.3.2　Depositional Type

This type of gobi desert is mainly distributed between the Mazong-Beishan Mountains and Qilian Mountains. Depositional processes are dominant during the gobi desert formation. There are three sub-types.

(1) Diluvial gravel gobi desert located on the inclined plain on the southern piedmont of the Mazong-North Mountains. This type of gobi desert occurs in the transition area from the Mazong–North Mountains to the modern river valleys as a narrow belt extending in an east-west direction. The land surface is covered by gobi desert and materials are mainly Quaternary diluvial rock pieces and coarse gravel. The diameter of the gravel is between 2 to 10 cm with angularity. Varnish surface can be found on the gravel. The compositions of the gravel or rock pieces are silicic limestones, quartz schists, quartzites and granites, transported from the Mazong–North Mountains. The land surface is roughly a plane with a gentle slope of 1° to 3°, gradually decreasing in altitude from the northeast to the southwest. Dissected by the modern erosional valleys, the surface is slightly undulate. Surface runoff is rare (some floods occur in the rainy season) and the groundwater level is 5 to 10 m below the surface. The soil is dominated by the infertile brown gypsum desert soil, with lime nodules and a gypsum layer of 20 to 100 cm at the bottom of the profile. The vegetation composition is similar to that in the gobi desert of denuded- eluvial-drift bedding rocky and coarse gravel gobi desert, characterized by sparse, short and simple species. In the modern erosional valleys the plants are a little more luxuriant.

(2) Diluvial-alluvial gravel gobi desert (fans on the northern piedmont of the Qilian Mountains). This type of gobi desert is distributed on the northern piedmont of the Qilian Mountains from the east to the west as a belt. The land surface is mostly covered by gobi desert and is composed of Quaternary conglomerates (Jiuquan and Yumen conglomerates), which formed a little later than the gobi desert in the Qilian Mountains. The roundness of the gravel is good with diameters between 2 and 12 cm. They are grey and black in color and are cemented by mud or calcareous material. The gravel layer varies in thickness from tens to hundreds of meters intervened with sands and composed of limestones, marbles, and several metamorphic rocks. The land surface is nearly flat, though it inclines slightly from the north to the south with a gradient of 0.5° to 3°. The gradient increases when closer to the piedmont. Many rivers originate from here and cut deeply into the conglomerates, irrigating the oases in the valleys. Because of insufficient irrigation water, the water can't be used for rebuilding the gobi desert. The irrigation water in the gobi desert depends on water from springs and floods. In relatively higher locations (e.g. terraces), the soil is brown gypsum desert soil. In the low and flat locations, however, the soil is ordinary brown desert soil and alluvial soils (cultivated soil has developed on the oasis), thus being easier to reclaim. The plants grow better than those in the above type of gobi desert. More plant species are found, including *Reaumuria soongarica, Nitraria sphaerocarpa, Sympergma regelii, Ephedra prezwalskii, Asterothamnus centrali asiaticus, Gymnocarpos przewalskii, Convolvulus*

tragacanthoides, and *Peganum harmala* etc.

(3) Alluvial-diluvial sand-gravel gobi desert (intermontane valleys between the Qilian-Mazong-North Mountains). This type of gobi desert lies in the ancient and modern river valleys, spreading in the oasis and salt-alkaline lowlands, and the total area is small. Its natural conditions are the best among all gobi desert types. The surface is flat and materials are mainly river alluvial-diluvial sand-gravels. The roundness of the gravel is good and the diameter varies from 1 to 3 cm. The main compositions are quartzites, quartz sandstones, schists and phyllites etc. The water condition is good and groundwater levels are less than 5m below the land surface, which makes it easy for digging wells and irrigation. On the alluvial soils that have high fertility, plants grow well, and are dominated by *Alhagi sparsifolia*, *Ephedra prezwalskii*, and *Nitraria sphaerocarpa* etc. This area is the main distribution area for oases in the northern Hexi Corridor, where there are dense human settlements as well as an urgent need to reclaim and make use of gobi desert land.

14.2.4 Gobi desert in the Junggar Basin

The Junggar Basin lies in northern Xinjiang. In this basin is the Gurbantünggüt desert, China's third largest desert, and it encompasses large areas of gobi desert. Diluvial-alluvial gobi deserts mainly occur in the piedmont plains and some intermontane basins, such as the Tacheng Basin. Denuded gobi deserts are mostly terrace-like or denuded plateaus with island hills, spreading widely on both banks of the paleo-Wulun River in northern Gurbantünggüt Desert and in Xiazijie (Zhu, 1980).

The diluvial-alluvial gobi desert is made up of Quaternary gravel alluvial-diluvial fans of different sizes. The land surface dips toward the Basin center with a gradient of 5° to 10°, composed of screes, gravels and sands which are zonal obviously. They transition in an order of screes, gravels and sand from the top of the alluvial-diluvial fans to fine-grained slity-sand and sandy silt that appear at the margins of the fans. The porosity and permeability of the deposits decline along the land surface, indicating that the groundwater movement weakens along the land surface. This area contains rich phreatic water. In the margins of the alluvial-diluvial fans, clay layers increase and shallow layers of confined water can be found. The alluvial-diluvial gravel layer in the western JunggarBasin is usually 15 to 25 m, and locally is thicker than 30 m. In the gravel layers near the piedmont, the water amount is affluent and the quality is good. The salinity is less than 1 g/L and the water is $HCO_3^- - SO_4^{2-}$ type. In the southern part of the basin, gobi deserts are distributed along the piedmont in narrow strips, whose gravel layer reaching 300m. The groundwater level changes regularly from the piedmont to the center of the basin, namely becoming shallower with the lithology. The chemical composition of the water in these regions transit form bicarbonate to bicarbonate-sulphate types (Zhao, 1964). Some drought-enduring plants such as *Haloxylon persicum* and *Haloxylon ammodendron* spread in the southwest gravel gobi desert where there is more gravel, but they are short, only 50 cm. The concomitant species is *Anabasis aphylla*, with small amounts of *Salsola arbuscula*, *Artemisia. frigida*, and *Calligonum mongolicum* etc. In the northern basin, the alluvial-diluvial gobies are distributed on the high girders, where the major plants are *Anabasis* Formation. In the northern piedmont of the Tianshan Mountains and the southern piedmont of the Altai Mountains, plants of Artemisia genus spread on the loam soils (Li, 1962).

Denuded gobi desert area consists of Tertiary horizontal strata, which formed terrace-like table hills and cuestas through the subsequent intermittent tectonic uplifts and differential denudation. The precipitous ridges of the table hills and the cuestas are exposed to physical weathering and temporary water flows and wind erosion, resulting in peculiar badland gullies and the narrow depositional zone for the alluvial on the piedmont. Through the weathering of grits on the top of the table hills and the cuestas, a layer of sand and gravel spread on the surface, forming gobi desert and thin sandlots. The size and composition of the gravels on the gobi desert are variable; most of them are round with good roundness and are partly covered by varnish. In the drainage of the paleo-Wulun River and Xiazijie, there is an affluent amount of confined water. The salinity is 2 to 5 g/L, belonging to HCO_3^--Cl^--Na^+, SO_4^{2-}-Cl^--Na^+ and Cl^--SO_4^{2-}-Na^+ types (Hu, 1962). The vegetation is semi-shrubs dominated by *Anabasis salsa* (Li, 1962).

14.2.5   Gobi deserts in the Tarim Basin

The Tarim Basin is the largest inland basin in China. Surrounded by the Kunlun and Tianshan mountains,which tower higher than 5,000 m in the north, west and South, the climate in the basin is extremely dry. Large amount of debris carried by numerous rivers flowing into the basin is deposited in the piedmonts, forming a belt of diluvial-alluvial fans around the basin, namely the piedmont gravel belt. The gravel belt is wide in the piedmont of the Kunlun Mountains, with the width generally reaching 10 to 15 km. In the Tianshan Mountains, as divided by intermontane basins, the mountain is narrow and the material is relatively fewer, and the gravel belt is narrow, only 10 to 15 km (Zhu et. al., 1962, 1980). The gravels on the north piedmont mainly come form the bedrocks in the mountains nearby, and are thick in the south and east, thin in the north and west, with a maximum of 600 to 900 m, and a minimum of 100 to 150 m. Horizontally, the diameters decrease from the gravels and screes in the piedmont up the sandy gravels further up the mountain. In the section, the diameters become smaller from the top to the bottom vertically. There is abundant groundwater with levels changing from 100 m in the piedmont to 50–100 m in the middle and finally less than 50 m in the tail of the piedmont. The salinity of the phreatic water also varies from 0.5 g/L in the nearby mountain to 0.5–1.0 g/L in the middle and marginal parts, with some higher than 1.0 g/L locally. The chemical composition of the water is mostly HCO_3^--Ca^{2+}-Na^+ type, with minor SO_4^{2-}-Na^+-Mg^{2+} type (Li, 1964). The vegetation is dominated by *Ephedra prezwalskii* and *Nitraria sphaerocarpa*, with few concomitant species such as *Zygophyllum gobicum*, *Artemisia arenaria*, and *Calligonum mongolicum* etc. (Li, 1962). The diluvial plain on the southern piedmont of the Tianshan Mountains is small in size and silts are contained in the gravels, which decrease the water permeability. The phreatic water level and the salinity also have zonality, but the dimension is small.

The diluvial plain in the piedmont of the Altun Mountains in the east of the basin is also a major area for gobi desert distribution. This area connects the Altun Mountains in the south and terminates at the alluvial plain on the piedmont, occupying the whole gravel diluvial-alluvial fan and inclining from the south to the north. It is cut by many gullies, with a thick layer of sandy gravels, coarser in the east and finer in the west. The groundwater level is extremely low.

14.2.6 Gobi deserts in the Qaidam Basin

The Qaidam Basin is a large inland basin in the northeast of the Tibet Plateau, lying in the northwest of Qinghai Province. The altitude of the basin is 2,500 to 3,000 m. The area of gobi desert is large at 31,400 km^2. The gobi deserts are interlaced with sand dunes, mainly distributed on the piedmont diluvial plain in the margins, such as the northern piedmont of the Kunlun Mountains and the southern piedmont of the Altun Mountains, dominated by diluvial-alluvial sandy gravel gobi desert (Zhu et al., 1980). The gobi deserts in this region are mainly diluvial gobi, located on the middle and upper parts of the diluvial plains. The width and thickness of gobi desert are different between the northern and southern basin; generally wide and thick in the south, and narrow and thin in the north. Mechanical composition of the surface materials becomes finer form the mountains to the center of the basin. They can be identified as gravels, sand-gravels and gravel-sands according to the proportion. The natural condition in the latter two compositions is better. There is another type of gobi desert overlain on the Tertiary stratum, which is thin and has high salt content. Lacking water, this type of gobi desert is hard for utilization (Yang Renzhang et al., 1962). In the gravel gobi deserts where the water condition is good, there is also good vegetation. The plants are composed of *Achnatherum spendens*, *Melilotus albus* Medic ex Desr., *Caragana korshinskii*, *Alhagii sparsifolia* and Ephedras. The groundwater level is low in most sandy gravel gobi desert areas and no water can be used by plants. In locations where there is surface running water, Ephedras, *Caragana korshinskii*, Eurotia, and *Haloxylon ammodendron* can grow. In locations where there is gypsum and salt crust, there are small amount of halophytes (Golmud Experiment station of Desert Control, 1959).

14.3   Reclamation and use of gobi deserts

Gobi desert is the main landform type in northwest China. It not only covers a large area but also has rich resources such as solar energy, wind energy and all kinds of mineral resources. On the other hand, the natural conditions of there deserts are harsh. For example, the extremely dry climate, the infertile grey-brown desert soils and the deeply embedded groundwater have greatly influenced the development of the local economy and the improvement of people's living standard. Therefore, how to promote the beneficial aspects and abolish the harmful aspects of gobi deserts, as well as reclaiming and utilizing different types of gobi deserts, rationally, are important issues.

Before reclaiming and utilizing different types of gobi deserts, in different areas, we need to analyze the local natural and social economical situation thoroughly and carefully. The purpose is to make full use of the advantageous conditions and avoid or overcome the disadvantageous ones. Among the natural factors, water is a crucial issue. Without water, reclaiming or making use of the gobi deserts is just a dream. Therefore, making use of water rationally is the guiding principle. The irrigation water source and amount should be considered first, including the surface water source, amount, and possibility for utilization, the reserves of groundwater, the groundwater levels and the quality etc. Secondly, the material composition and features (including the grain size and thickness) of gobi desert and the land surface conformation (making use of the lowland where there are good natural conditions) should be considered. Finally, it is important to look into the soil, vegetation and climate. The main task is to cultivate the gravel surface and change the structure of soils. However, the gravel surface can't be cultivated completely, otherwise shifting sand disasters will occur. The arbor, shrub and grass species suitable for planting in gobi deserts should be selected carefully. We should also make efficient use of the local solar and wind energies and control drifting sands. Among the social-economical factors, labor forces should be considered first, then the economical cost and the benefit. Finally we also need to consider the historical development, the economical structure and the standard for production and living (Zhao, 1962). After the analyses of the local natural and social factors, we should start from the reality of the natural conditions and the requirements of production, promote the beneficial aspects and abolish the harmful aspects, develop the industry, agriculture, forestry, stock raising and subsidiary production. For example, at the margins of diluvial fans and oasis regions where there is an abundant amount of irrigation water and sunlight, cotton, vegetables and food crops can be planted. In the diluvial gobi deserts where the natural conditions are good, with affluent mineral resources which are needed urgently by the national economy, we can develop the industrial cities; the suburban areas can grow vegetables, giving attention to the development of forestry, animal husbandry and avocations to satisfy the requirements of industrial construction. In the coarse gravel gobi deserts where the natural conditions are abominable, according to the objective requirements, livestock raising should be developed in order to save labor forces and adapt to the natural conditions. The animals should be sheep or goats that can eat the coarse fodder, but rotational grazing should be practiced to prevent overgrazing. At the same time, we also need to protect the existing grassland, trees and shrubs. For afforesting oases and protecting railways, the arbor, shrub species should be selected and planted in suitable locations. Agriculture production should be vegetables, melons and fruits based on experiments in favorable locations before popularization.

For different types of gobi deserts, we should take different measures to reclaim or utilize them. Taking water as an example, we should make full use of spring water (improving the management of irrigation water) and the flood water (build channels and dams). Following the guiding principle in water utilization, we can reclaim the gobi deserts and improve the soils. It's also necessary to summarize the experiences of local people in channeling water and afforestation. The following experiences, for instance, are prospective useful and worth being considered in utilization the gobi deserts. ① Planting farm land shelter belts. ② Making use of the lowlands such as the modern erosional gullies where water conditions are favorable. ③ Improving soils step by step with biological measures. In the gobi deserts where the natural conditions are poor, local shrub and grass species should be selected first since they can endure droughts and infertile soils. After the water and soil conditions are improved, they can be replaced with big trees or shrubs and grasses that have high economical values. ④ In the gobi deserts where the natural conditions are extremely poor, enclosure may be the best choice to save the labor force and funds.

Taking the Turpan Basin as an example, the local people have adopted efficient measures in making use of the gobi deserts. Here we introduce the experiences briefly.

Gobi deserts spread widely in the Turpan Basin, accounting for 30% of the total land area of the county. Therefore, the measures of reclaiming and utilizing gobi deserts are capable of not only making full use of the heat (sunlight), water and soil resources, but also eliminating the shifting sand hazards and preventing the sand encroachment on the gravel gobi deserts. Considering the natural conditions in the gobi deserts in the basin and the biological features of grapes, local people grow grapes in making use of the gobi desert. The preconditions for growing grapes in gobi deserts include channeling water for irrigation and planting trees to check winds. Leveling the land and improving the management during the growing season are two important issues that need attention. Local people diverted water to wash salts in soils first, and then fill the pits for planting grapes with fertile improved soil imported from other places. After the grapes survived and grew, people still paid attention to fertilization and training the stems of grapes, made the plants short and the fruit bearing shoots compact. Such plants have the potential to prevent the winds. After adopting these measures, grapes can grow well on the gravel gobi deserts and the maximum output can reach 60 tons per hectare. Therefore, the main experience in growing grapes in the gravel gobi deserts is to make full use of the thermal energy artificial replenishment of water and nutrients (Summary of the people's experiences in sand control in Turpan Basin, 1979).

The experiences in the Turpan Basin show that the exploitation and utilization of the land resources in the extremely dry regions needs to take full consideration of the features of the ecosystem, and the efficient protection and exploitation measures in accordance with the natural laws. Only in this way can we prevent the occurrence and spreading of desertification, consolidate the oasis, and increase productivity.

References

Central Station of Anxi Desert Control Research. 1960. Geomorphy and gobi desert types of Beigangou region of Anxi. 1—3

Desert Control Team, Chinese Academy of Sciences. 1961. Investigation Report of gobi desert of eastern Xinjiang and western Hexi Corridor. 7—10

Golmud Experiment Station of Desert Control. 1959. Classification of site types in desert area and forestry partition and forestry planning

Hu Shizhi, Lu Yunting, Wu Zheng et al. 1962. Desert investigation of Junggar Basin. In: Desert Control Team of Chinese Academy of Sciences. Desert Control Study (No. 4). Beijing: Science Press. 43—61

Investigation Group of Desert Control in Turpan Region. 1979. Wind prevention, desert controlling, and transformation of gobi desert—a case study of Turpan in Xinjiang region. In: Study of Desert in China and Its Controlling. Lanzhou: Lanzhou Institute of Desert Research, Chinese Academy of Sciences

Li Baoxing, Zhao Yunchang. 1964. Groundwater in the Tarim Basin and its formation condition. In: Desert Control Team of Chinese Academy of Sciences. Desert Control Study (No. 6). Beijing: Science Press. 131—211

Li Bo. 1962. Preliminary study of vegetation of desert area in Northwest China and its transformation and utilization. In: Desert Control Team of Chinese Academy of Sciences. Desert Control Study (No. 4). Beijing: Science Press. 134—142

Yang Renzhang, Su Shirong, Xu Tingguan et al. 1962. Investigation on Qaidam Desert. In: Desert Control Team of Chinese Academy of Sciences. Desert Control Study (No. 3). Beijing: Science Press. 65—77

Yu Shouzhong, Li Bo, Cai Weiqi et al. 1962. Investigation on Gobi desert and Badain Jaran Desert of western Inter Mongolia. In: Desert Control Team of Chinese Academy of Sciences. Desert Control Study (No. 3). Beijing: Science Press. 96—108

Zhao Songqiao. 1962. Preliminary study of gobi desert's types and its form and utilization of northwestern Hexi Corridor. In: Desert Control Team of Chinese Academy of Sciences. Desert Control Study (No. 3). Beijing: Science Press. 78—89

Zhao Yunchang. 1964. Groundwater in Junngar Basin. In: Desert Control Team of Chinese Academy of Sciences. Desert Control Study (No. 6). Beijing: Science Press. 75—76

Zhu Zhenda, Liu Huaxun, Chen Enjiu et al. 1962. Natural characteristics of southwestern Taklimakan Desert and its formation and utilization of northwestern Hexi Corridor. In: Desert Control Team of Chinese Academy of Sciences. Desert Control Study (No. 3). Beijing: Science Press

Zhu Zhenda, Wu Zheng, Liu Su et al. 1980. An introduction to desert in China (Revised edition). Beijing: Science Press

Chapter 15
Special Types of Sandy Lands and Aeolian Desertification

15.1 Sandy Lands on the Huang-Huai-Hai Plain

Eastern China is influenced by the East Asian Monsoon, and precipitation is unevenly distributed and the dry and rainy seasons are distinct. There is more rain in summer in the northern semi-humid region. In northern China and the central plains, the precipitation is concentrated from July to August. The winter half-year is both a dry and windy season, and the sand-driving wind mainly occurs in the dry season in northern China. As the dry and windy seasons are synchronous, wherever land surfaces are composed of sand material and the vegetation during this season can't protect the underlying surface, wind force will act on the land surface and result in sandstorms. The ground surface exhibits a rolling sand dune landscape, which is similar to the aeolian desertification area, also known as blown sand lands (Zhu, 1980).

The Huang-Huai-Hai Plain is the largest alluvial plain in China, extending over a large area. From administrative regionalization, it covers five provinces–Hebei, Henan, Shandong, Anhui, Jiangsu, and two cities—Beijing and Tianjing. According to strict geographical concepts, the plain of the lower reaches of the Yellow River (Huanghe River), Huaihe River basin and Haihe River basin, all belong to the Huang-Huai-Hai Plain. If considering the consistency of the agricultural resource conditions and the cropping system, the similarity of the major measures in controlling natural hazards, and people's historical habits, the plain in the lower reach of the Luanhe River is also included in the Huang-Huai-Hai Plain. Its southern boundary is the Huaihe River and the eastern boundary is close to the Huanghai Sea, Bohai Sea and the southern mountain region in Shandong Province. The northern and western borders are the Yanshan Mountains, Taihang Mountains and Fuliushan Mountains. It is generally called the North China Plain, covering an area or a large part of Beijing, Tianjin, Hebei, Shandong, Henan, Anhui and Jiangsu provinces (Yang, 1989). The ground slope is gentle, and the altitude ranges from 100 m in the west to 2–5 m above sea level in the east coast. Viewed from the mountain relief, plains in Hebei, Shandong and Henan are located in the corridor of the Taihang Mountains and Tai Mountains. In winter it is the passage for the northern cold air current to go southward. In spring and autumn, however, it is the corridor for the joining of cold and warm air masses.

The total area of the Huang-Huai-Hai Plain is about 350,000 km^2, and the area of aeolian desertified land is 20,330 km^2, accounting for 5.8% of the total land area. The Yellow River alluvial plain in Shandong Province borders the Bohai Sea in the northeast and the Tai Mountains in the east and southeast. The Yellow River crosses the alluvial plain obliquely. The sandy land in this alluvial plain is about 9,300 km^2 which takes up 45.7% of the total sandy land area of the Huang-Huai- Hai Plain. The sandy land in Henan Province is about 8,150 km^2, accounting for 40.1% of the total (Wu, 1999), distributed in Xinxiang-Neihuang's sand band, and mostly centralized in Yanjin and Neihuang counties (Gao, 2000). There is about 4,500 km^2 aeolian desertified land in Yanjin County. The sandy land in the Beijing Plain is mainly distributed in the three river basins of the Yongding River, Chaobai River, and Wenyu River. Especially concentrated in the Yongding River basin, the aeolian desertified land area is 5,900 km^2, accounting for 3.6% of the Beijing Plain's total area. The sand materials originate mainly from various river's alluvial deposits, which are most abundant in the Yongding River basin, followed by the Chaobai River.

15.1.1 Natural conditions for the formation of the sandy land in the Huang-Huai-Hai Plain

15.1.1.1 Climate

The sandy lands in the Huang-Huai-Hai Plain belong to the semi-arid and semi-humid monsoon climate region in the warm-temperate zone, which has sufficient sunlight and appropriate temperatures. The rainy season is concentrated in the summer and the four seasons are distinct. The total amount of solar radiation is 460.5–565.2 kJ/cm^2 and the annual accumulative temperature >10 °C is 3,800–4,900 °C, consistent with that in the inland desert areas (3,000–5,000 °C) in China. The frost-free period is 180–220 days and the annual precipitation is 500–1,100 mm (Yang, 1989). Therefore the climatic conditions are comparatively superior. For example, there is more heat than the northeast sandy lands and the moisture conditions are better than the northwest sandy lands. The Shandong Plain lies in the monsoon climate district of the temperate zone. Controlled respectively by the Subtropical High and the Mongolia High, the climate there shows obvious continentality, characterized by "dry and windy springs, hot and rainy summers, mild and appreciably dry autumns, cold and snow-less winters". The prevailing wind directions (wind force ⩾4) in Dezhou, Liaocheng and Heze districts are NNE to N, SSE and S. The cities of Binzhou and Dongying are influenced by the sea-land wind. The prevailing wind in Binzhou City is dominated by the south-east wind, with a northerly wind in winter and the southerly wind between spring and summer. Dongying City is dominated by a SSE wind, and the SSW wind is secondary. Strong winds (wind force ⩾8) are distributed unevenly, occurring more frequently along the coasts than in inland regions. On average, there are 18.9 days with strong winds in Dezhou and 27.9 days in Leling.

Days of blown sand (wind speed ⩾ 4m/s) in the north are more than those in the south, with 161 days in Dezhou and 141 days in Liaocheng and 71 days in Heze annually. Sand driving wind appears in spring more frequently, with 70% in Dezhou, 46% in Liaocheng, and 47% in Heze respectively (Chen, et al., 1989). The aridity of the Huang-Huai-Hai Plain Sandy Land conforms with the general climate trend. The aridity of Shan County, which lies in Heze of southern Shandong, is 0.3–0.6, because of the less precipitation in the rain shadow area in the north of Tai Mountains, the aridity of Liaocheng is (even more) 1.7–1.9. Annual variability is huge in precipitation, the rainy season is obvious and storm rainfalls occur frequently. For example, the annual precipitation in Xiajin of Dezhou reached 1,320.9 mm in 1961, the precipitation was 1,126.0 mm in the rainy season (June, July, August, September), 4 storm rainfall events occurred in that year, and the total amount of storm rainfall reached 672.8 mm, and it reached 466.2 mm in just 24 hours. But annual total precipitation was only 277.3 mm in this area in 1968, and only 143.1 mm in the whole rainfall season (Chen, 1989).

Annual total radiation is 522.4 kJ/cm^2 for seasonal aeolian desertified land in the Yu Cheng region in Shandong Province, and is 441.3 kJ/cm^2 during the farming period. The heat is sufficient and the sunshine is long, with 2,639 hours in the whole year, and close to 2,500–3,000 hours in the northern desert area in China. The sunshine duration is 780 hours in April-July and 669 hours in July-September. Average annual temperature in this region is 13.1 °C, with the extreme highest temperature of 42.2 °C and the extreme lowest temperature of –25 °C. This region's accumulative temperature ($\geqslant$10 °C) is 4,440.9 °C. The frost period is from October 20 to about April 2 of the following year, and the frost-free period is 200 days. The days with high temperatures varies from year to year. The yearly temperature difference is 29 °C and the daily temperature difference is 10.8 °C. The annual and interannual precipitation variability of this region is great, and this region is prone to occurrences of droughts and floods. Concentrated in the rainy season, the storm rainfall erodes the soil seriously, and the average annual precipitation is 616 mm, with maximum annual precipitation of 1,144.4 mm and minimum value of 239.0 mm in this region.

The amplitude of annual precipitation is very large with a maximum of 697.0 mm. It is dry in spring and wet in summer, and annual precipitation is concentrated in June-August, which accounts for 68.1% (of the total precipitation of the whole year). Annual potential evaporation capacity is 2,229 mm, which is 3.6 times the annual total precipitation. Precipitation is extremely variable from year to year. The probability of a normal year, dry year and wet year is 0.53, 0.16, 0.31, respectively (Su Peixi, 1996). The drought/flood calamities take place every other year. Located in the central part of the Huang-Huai-Hai Plain and at the border of Hebei, Shandong and Henan Provinces, the average annual temperature of Xiajin County is 12.7 °C, the length of the frost-free season is 192 days, and its average annual precipitation is 565.5 mm (Yang Xilin, et al., 1996).

The average annual temperature in sandy lands of Henan Province is 13.4–14.5 °C, the annual sunshine duration is 2,240–2,530 hours, annual total precipitation is 574–741 mm, which is mainly concentrated in July, August and September, annual evaporation is 1,509–2,067 mm, and the frost-free period is 205–244 days. The average annual temperature in the Yanjin experimental area is 14.0 °C, and the frost-free period is 216 days with the first frost occurring in the last ten days of October and the late frost in the last ten days of March or the first ten days of April. Annual accumulative temperature ($\geqslant 10$°C) is 479.3 °C, average annual sunshine duration is 2,504.8 hours, and total solar radiation for the whole year is 499.9 kJ/cm^2 (Wu, et al., 1999; Gao, et al., 2000).

Annual total radiation in the Beijing region is 560.5 kJ/cm^2, annual sunshine duration is 2,600–2,800 hours, and the Average annual temperature is 11.5 °C, with a highest temperature of 43.5 °C and a lowest temperature of –27.4 °C. Annual accumulative temperature ($\geqslant 10$ °C) is 3,400–4,200 °C, and frost-free period is 180–200 days. Average annual precipitation is 500–700 mm. Geographical environments in the Beijing region differs greatly, and the frequency of aeolian sand activities differs locally. Average annual blown sand days (includes floating dust, dust storm and blown dust days) is up to 26 days. The pattern of aeolian sand activities is also different. For example, blown dust prevails in some places, floating dust prevails in other places, and dust storms occur more frequently in the Yanqing Basin.

Wind is the driving force for aeolian sand activities and aeolian desertification processes. Wind force and strong wind frequency determine the intensity of the sand activities, and wind-direction frequency determines the direction of net sand transport. In the Yucheng region of Shandong Province, the average wind speed is 3 m/s, with the strongest wind speed of 27 m/s. The strong wind (wind force >7) is concentrated in March, April and May, which accounts for 55% of the whole year, and the main wind direction is SSW. The aeolian sand season is prolonged in extremely dry years. Because of relatively fine soil particles and low water content in soil in spring, the threshold wind velocity to initiate sand movement is relatively lower. Generally, sand movement will appear when the wind speed is equal to or above 4 m/s. Wind speed varies greatly within a year, and wind speed is the biggest in April with a monthly average of 4.2 m/s and sand-moving wind speed of 4.0 m/s. Aeolian sand activities at this period are extremely frequent, and result in the greatest damage. After this month, wind speed drops, with a minimum wind speed of 2.2 m/s occurring in August. In autumn, vegetation begins to wither, surface coverage reduces, and wind speed strengthens gradually. Aeolian sand activities on sandy land of the Huang-Huai-Hai Plain is frequent in spring.

In general, climate conditions of the Huang-Huai-Hai Plain Sandy Land is better than that in the northern desert area, with synchronous increases in temperature and rainfall, plentiful precipitation, long frost-free period, and sufficient sun light, which is suitable for growing many kinds of crops, forest and grass. Located in the semi-humid climate area of warm-temperate zone, the sandy land can carry on the cultivation systems of growing 3 crops every 2 years or growing 2 crops each year.

15.1.1.2 Hydrology

Moisture content of the Huang-Huai-Hai Plain Sandy Land is relatively more adequate than that in the northern desert area. In large parts of the Henan Sandy Land, groundwater depth is 2–10 m and mineralization degree is 1–3 g/L with good water quality. It is an excellent water resource for industry, agriculture and drinking. In Yucheng, the groundwater level is relatively high, and groundwater depth varies topographically, with depths of 1–2 m, 3–5 m, and 5–7 m in grass beach, flat sandy land, and sand dune slope respectively. By reclaiming sandy lands into farmland, and diverting water by building canals, this will not only utilize groundwater resources, but also utilize the Yellow River water. On the sandy lands, peach, apricot, cherry and plum trees grow well in normal years. But in flood years, because of high water levels, roots are submerged for a long time, their breathing is blocked, and this can even result in the death of fruit trees.

Water quality in this area is good (Table 15-1). The groundwater mineralization degree in the sandy land of Yucheng is about 0.5—1 g/L, and pH value is 7.8. The mineralization degree of canal water is similar to well water.

Table 15-1　Quality of different types of water sources in the Yucheng Sandy Land

Type of water	Content of cation (mg/L)					Content of anion (mg/L)				
	K^+	Na^+	Ca^+	Mg^+	Total	Cl^-	SO_4^{2-}	HCO_3^-	CO_3^{2-}	Total
Canal water	12.08	50.05	27.73	17.32	107.18	55.53	98.83	108.24	0	262.60
Well water	4.32	19.93	48.94	34.64	107.83	10.80	17.95	341.04	0	369.79

Table 15-2　Plant species and soil wind erosion intensity of different sand lands

Land types		Plant species	Covering season of vegetation	Intensity of soil wind erosion	Remarks
Farmland	Winter wheat land	Winter wheat, peanut, corn, etc.	Whole year	Light	To plant winter wheat in the first twenty days of October of the previous year; interplant summer peanut in early June or plant summer maize in the first twenty days of June after harvesting the wheat
	Spring land	Peanut, cotton, soybean, etc.	From last 20 days of May to October	Serious	Bare ground surface in spring
	Orchard	Apple, pear, hawthorn, peach, apricot, grape,etc.	The whole year	Relatively light	Liable to erosion before leaf expansion in windy season, reducing wind force after expansion
Badland	About 1m water level	Reed, scirpus triqueter etc.	The whole year	Light	Consolidation of the weeds, difficult to blow sand particles
	Below 2m water level	Cogongrass, horsetail,etc.	April to the first ten days of September	Serious	Weeds withered in September to the following March, and ground surface is exposed
Sand dunes	Fixed	Cogongrass, cynodon dactylon etc.	Above 40% coverage from April to the first ten days of November	Medium	
	Semi-fixed	Cogongrass, ziziphus jujube etc.	20%—40% coverage from April to the first ten days of November	Serious	
	Shifting	Cogongrass	Naked year-round	Extremely serious	Scarce weeds

15.1.1.3 Vegetation

There are abundant biotic resources in the sandy areas of the Huang-Huai-Hai Plain. They are mainly crops, industrial crops and commercial forest, such as wheat, peanut, maize, watermelon, muskmelon, soybeans, cotton, apple, pear, peach, jujube, grape, poplar, paulownia imperial, cera sinensis, grain, oil, melons, fruits, vegetables, forest and weeds. There are domestic animals and fishery, such as ox, horse, sheep, pig, chicken, and duck, as well as soil microorganisms and small animals. There are a great variety of plants in this area. But the withering season of vegetation is synchronous with the beginning of aeolian sand activities. Soil wind-erosion intensity varies with different kinds of land, which is determined by vegetation species, coverage and covering season (Table 15-2). Wind speed at 1 m above the surface of shifting dunefield is 7.7 m/s; wind erosion depths reach 3.7, 2.8, and 2.1 cm per hour when coverage is 0, 16%, and 20% respectively. With plants sprouting and growing, vegetation coverage increases and desert landscape disappears gradually. This is followed by farmland weed hazards. Orchard weeds begin to grow vigorously in the last ten days of April. If no control measures are adopted immediately, this will greatly influence the fruit tree's growth.

15.1.1.4 Soil

The soil parent material in the Huang-Huai-Hai Plain originates from Quaternary alluvial sediments, which contain a small amount of organic matter of 0.5%. The fertility is relatively poor, and soils are mainly sandy and loamy.

The mechanical composition of blown sand soil is mainly fine sand. Fine sand in the 0–25 cm layer accounts for 70.5% of total grain content, and 80.1% at the 25–50 cm soil layer (Table 15-3). The degree of porosity is about 40% (Table 15-4). Soil structure is loose, and deep seepage of water and nutrients is serious. Because of small clay content, cementation is low and prone to deflation. The threshold velocity for sand movement is 4 m/s on bare sandy land, and it is 4.8 m/s when the vegetation coverage is 25%.

In Yucheng of Shandong Province, soil texture is loose sand, with poor structure and low organic matter contents (Table 15-5). The content of N, P and K is poor and the pH value is 8.2. The nutrient content in different types of sandy land is obviously different (Table 15-6) (Yang Xilin, et al., 1996). At the beginning of cultivation, compared with the northern desert area, the sandy land is more fertile and contains trace elements such as Fe, Zn, Mn, and B.

Table 15-3　Mechanical composition of sandy land of Yucheng in Shandong Province

Depth(cm)	Content of various grain size(%)						HCl leaching loss	Physical sand grain (>0.01mm)	Physical clay (<0.01mm)
	Coarse-medium sand(1–0.25mm)	Fine sand (0.25–0.05mm)	Coarse silt (0.05–0.01mm)	Medium silt(0.01–0.005mm)	Fine silt (0.005–0.001mm)	Clay (<0.001mm)			
0–25	0.27	70.51	16.55	1.22	1.40	3.20	6.85	87.33	5.82
25–50	0.08	80.12	9.83	0.63	0.69	1.93	6.72	90.03	3.25

Table 15-4 Physical constant of soil moisture
in newly cultivated sand ground vineyards of Yucheng in Shandong Province

Soil bulk density (g/cm^3)	Soil specific gravity (g/cm^3)	Porosity (%)	Capillary rise (cm)	Coefficient of moisture absorption (%)	Field moisture capacity (%)	Saturated water content (%)	Wilting percentage (%)	Wilting coefficient (%)
1.46	2.39	38.92	92.1	1.14	20.97	27.86	1.69	1.65

Table 15-5 Nutrient content of sandy land of Yucheng in Shandong Province

Sampling depth(cm)	Organic matter content (g/kg)	Total nutrient (g/kg)			Available nutrient (mg/kg)		
		N	P$_2$O$_5$	K$_2$O	N	P$_2$O$_5$	K$_2$O
0–25	3.2	0.23	1.06	20.55	19.7	2.7	50.0
25–50	1.9	0.17	0.97	20.55	20.8	1.6	38.0

Table 15-6 The nutrient content of different sandy lands of Xiajin in Shandong Province

Sandy land type	Depth (cm)	Organic matter (g/kg)	C/N	Total nutrient (g/kg)			Available nutrient (mg/kg)		
				N	P$_2$O$_5$	K$_2$O	N	P$_2$O$_5$	K$_2$O
Shifting dune	0–60	1.0	8.16	0.07	0.72	18.4	13.4	3.3	47.0
Wind erosion hillock	0–69	2.2	8.54	0.15	0.92	15.8	14.4	2.1	52.0
Wind erosion farmland	0–55	4.6	8.81	0.20	1.02	16.4	43.5	3.1	70.0

15.1.2 Formation causes and characteristics of sandy land

An obvious characteristic of humid and semi-humid sandy areas is that aeolian sand activities occur only in the dry season, and hence it can be defined as seasonal wind-blown sandy land.

15.1.2.1 Formation of sandy land

There are some limitations and laws in the distribution of the Huang-Huai-Hai Plain Sandy Land. There are three main reasons for the formation.

(1) Abundant sand material is the foundation for the formation of blown sand land. Three rivers, the Huaihe river, the Yellow River, and the Haihe River, flow through the Huang-Huai-Hai Plain, and the sand sources originate from sediment deposition. Secondly, sediment deposition is caused by diverting water from the Yellow River. For example, there are 6-8 billion m^3 of Yellow River water which was diverted to Shandong Province every year, carrying about 40.8–50.4 million m^3 of sand (Chen, et al., 1989).

(2) The synchronization of the windy season and dry season, together with the consistency of vegetation growing-withering cycles and windy-arid seasons, are the climatic factors of aeolian sand formation in this area. An obvious characteristic is that the appearance of sand landscape is consistent with the seasonal variation of vegetation. When vegetation withers, a desert landscape

appears.

(3) Uncontrolled reclamation, excessive cultivation and irrational utilization of sandy land, together with rapid population growth, are human factors for land desertification in this region.

According to historical records, since 602 BC (The fifth year of the Emperor Zhouding), the Yellow River had shifted 6 times over the past 2,600 years, breached 26 times, and flooded more than 1,590 times (Fig. 15-1).

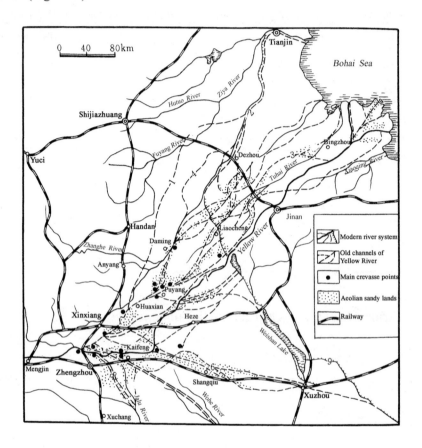

Fig.15-1　Map showing watercourse changes in lower reaches of the Yellow River

1. Yuhe riverway; 2. 602 BC–11 AD; 3. 11–1048 AD; 4. 1048–1194 AD; 5. 1194–1494 AD; 6. 1494–1855 AD; 7. 1855–1937 AD (Present watercourse); 8. 1938–1946 AD; 9. Canal

Because of great migration and diversion, huge amounts of fine sand were deposited in the main stream area and the middle-upper part of breached fans, while loam and clay were deposited far away from the main stream line.

15.1.2.2　Sandy land landforms

After each migration and diversion of the Yellow River, alluvial landforms formed in the plain include: batture, sandy river-trough depression, breached fan terrace, river-related depression outside the dyke, depression between fan terraces (Chen et al., 1989).

15.1.2.3 Characteristics of aeolian sandy land

Besides the characteristics similar to the aeolian landforms of desertified land, blown sandy land also has its own unique characteristics:

(1) Seasonal variations in its landscape. In the dry and windy season, sand sheet landscapes are commonly present. In the rainy-hot-windless season, they are not very obvious or might have even disappeared. In the spring windy-sandy season on sandy plains along the Yellow River, strong wind erosion troughs, deflation hillocks, sand drifts and sand sheet often appear on the aeolian sandy land, and different kinds of farmland landscapes appear in summer and autumn (Zhu, 1986).

(2) Barren soil is related to water loss and soil erosion. In densely populated and economically developed regions, the peasants are the poorest population. The aeolian sand activities seriously affect the local living environment and the development of agriculture. Taking the northwest blown sand area in Shandong Province as an example, of the 739 thousand hm^2 of wind-eroded cultivated land, about 21.3369 million t of soil were removed by wind per year. The aeolian sand activities are mainly manifested in farmland soil erosion. Soil wind erosion is the main form of blown sand hazards, and soil nutrient loss results in barren soil. According to Zhu Zhenda et al. (1994), annual nutrient loss by wind erosion in cultivated land is equal to 15%–20% of the amount of fertilizer applied in the area.

(3) It is easy to control. Generally, the aeolian sandy land of the Huang-Huai-Hai Plain can only develop small sand dunes, Which are easily leveled. In addition, natural conditions are better with more precipitation, abundant surface water and groundwater resources, high air temperature, long growing season, and fine blown sand soil. On one hand, the ecological environment there is fragile and prone to aeolian desertification, but on the other hand, aeolian desertification is easy to reverse.

(4) It is usually accompanied by other types of aeolian desertification. Because the sandy land is of river deposits, there are not only positive landforms such as sandy hillock mounds, there are also many negative landforms such as river-trough depressions, depressions between fans, and depressions between sand dunes. There is a high groundwater level in these depressions, usually suffering from water logging and secondary salinization and also accompanied by flooding and alkalization.

15.1.2.4 Classification of aeolian sandy land

Aeolian sandy land can be classified based on comprehensive principles of its developing stages, landform features and utilization methods (Table 15-7). There is little shifting sand in this area, and it occurs mainly on sandy hillock tops of old watercourses and current alluvial flats, the main diverting canal from the Yellow River, and both sides of deposited sand land. Lower limit of vegetation coverage between semi-stabilized sandy land and stabilized sandy land is 35%, while semi-stabilized sandy land has no lower limit of vegetation coverage.

Table 15-7   Classification of blown sand land in the alluvial plain of the Yellow River
in Shandong province (Chen et al., 1989)

Development stages	Landform	Utilization
shifting sandy land	crescent dune chain	
	undulating shifting sand land	
semi-stabilized sandy land	sandy hillock	forest land
	undulating sandy land	
	flat or undulating sandy land	
stabilized sandy land	sandy hillock	orchard
	undulating sand land	weeds land
	flat or undulating sandy land	
wind eroded farmland	strongly wind-eroded farmland	agro-forestry land
	general wind eroded farmland	
	improved sandy land	

Sandy land is a valuable land resource. Its ecological environment is fragile and susceptible to aeolian desertification, but it is easy to reverse and control. With the rapid development of the national economy and population growth, the need for food and agricultural products increase sharply. How can this issue be resolved? One way is to enlarge the area of cultivated land, and the other way is to enhance yield per unit area. The purpose of comprehensive management for sandy land is to enlarge land-utilizing area and utilize potential land productivity. Therefore, reasonable development and comprehensive utilization play an ever increasing important role in national economic construction. Compared to Chinese arid and semiarid regions, this kind of sandy land has relatively abundant light, heat and water resources, as well as a long agricultural production history. As long as we give full play to the potential of water and soil resources, along with following the principles of "taking measures suitable to local conditions", taking care of "water conservancy and forest network construction, fruit-crop intercropping, using and protecting land", remarkable economic benefits can be obtained, and achieve a healthy cycle for the ecological environment. This will finally achieve all-round development of society and economy in this region.

15.2   Coastal Sandy Lands

The coastal zone is a region where interactions between the continent, the ocean and the atmosphere occur and the sand along the coast is the product of such interactions. The total continental coastline of China is longer than 18,000 km, of which the sandy coast is about 3,000 km. Of the 3,000 km sandy coastline, sand dunes occur in about 585 km in different sections. The area of blown sand land is about 1,755 km². Wind blown sand problems are a problem for all the coastal provinces/regions (including the west coast of Taiwan) except for Jiangsu Province. For example, 65 km of the coastline of Liaoning Province, 75 km of Hebei, 95 km of Shandong, 50 km of Taiwan,

100 km of Guangdong and 50 km of Hainan are subject to blown sand hazards. In Zhejiang Province, the sandy coasts are mainly located in the east or southeast of the Zhoushan Islands, with a length of 60 km (Zhu, 1994).

The characteristics of blown sand along the coasts are:

(1) It is widely distributed from the semi-humid coasts in the temperate zone in the north to the humid tropical and sub-tropical coasts in the south. The most typical coastal sandy lands are the tropical savanna in southwest Hainan Island, mostly located near the river mouth. These sands are transported by the rivers to the river mouth and then are pushed back by waves and ocean currents, forming material sources for coastal deserts.

(2) The formation of coastal deserts is related to local wind regime, sand source and landforms that develop into dunes. Specifically, the abundant sandy sediments, strong and stable sea wind, relatively small slope (average $1:1,000$), and the medium tidal range are favorable for the formation of wide beaches (Gao et al., 2000).

(3) In addition to natural factors such as sand sources and strong wind, human destruction of local vegetation is also closely related to the formation and development of coastal deserts. For example, Pingtan in Fujian Province was once grassland for grazing horses during the Tang and Song Dynasties according to historical records. But it was covered by shifting sand by 1723–1735 during the Qing Dynasty. The coast in eastern Fujian was also farming lands decades before the Guangxu Emperor (1871–1908) and became sandy lands later. These indicate that frequent human activities destroyed the vegetation resulting in the spreading of shifting sand. Therefore, the coastal sandy lands also are a complicated system of the interactions between natural and human factors.

(4) The grain size features of the coastal dune sands indicate that they are mainly medium to fine sands, with diameters between $\varphi 0.4$–2.2, with an average of $\varphi 1.5$ (0.35 mm) (Cai et al., 1983), which is consistent with the southern humid climate. The grain size of the coastal dune sands is an order of magnitude larger than that of inland desert sand and that of the deposited sands transported by the Yellow River, with good to excellent sorting and nearly symmetric with a negative skew.

(5) The material composition of the coastal sandy lands is mainly terrestrial debris with a certain amount of marine shells. The surface features of the quartz sand grains indicate that they both inherited and reshaped the beach sands. In addition, the imprint of the windy environment has been imposed on the surface of the sand grains (Wu, 1997), making it different from the inland desert sands. The stratification is mainly large-scale salty or sphenoid cross-bedding with high angles, and semi-contemporaneous deformations can be identified, which is another important feature different form the inland desert sands.

(6) Geomorphologically, the coastal sandy lands are not as typical and regular as the inland desert dunes. The forms and types of dunes are relatively simple, mainly including the foreshore dunes, transverse dunes, crescent dunes (chains), parabolic dunes, longitudinal dunes, sand sheets or climbing dunes, and grass-shrub dunes. The foredunes and sand sheets are the most characteristic

dune types in coastal sandy lands. The former develops above the high-tide line, being the closest dunes parallel to the sea shore. They have unique binary sedimentary structures: the upper part has an aeolian structure and the lower part has a typical beach structure. The latter is wide and flat, lying on the inner side of the back edge of the beach dune bands. Its formation and development are related to several factors such as dynamical coastal conditions and sand sources. Specifically, as the sands are transported by the onshore winds, and the frictional resistance increases along the way, the wind becomes weaker the further away from the shore, the sand grains carried by the wind are deposited along the wind path and the sand source gradually decreases. If there exists low-lying landforms or depressions in the downwind direction transverse the beach with high levels of ground water, the wet surface will restrict sand movement and dune development and thus sand sheets will form. Climbing dunes are formed by the wind blown towards land on beach dunes, when blocked by hills, the sand will deposit along the slopes, this repeated process will result in dunes climbing toward the hills. Climbing dunes are located on bed rock hills, terraces and the windward slopes near the shore.

(7) The typical development pattern of the coastal dunes can be summarized as follows: the sands are transported to shore by the onshore wind and then continue to move to the beach, forming transverse dunes, crescent dunes, parabolic dunes and longitudinal dunes, as well as forming dune bands along the beaches. At the back edge of the sand dune bands are sand sheets (Wu, 1995; Chen et al., 1996; Fu et al., 1997).

In this section, the distribution features of blown sand hazards in typical regions along the coast line are introduced.

15.2.1   The blown sand on the west shore of the Liaodong Bay

The coast from the Liugu River to the mouth of the Luanhe River is the most typical coast of dune development in Hebei and Liaoning Provinces. Sparse sands appear south of the Luanhe River mouth, near Lianhuachi and Binhai Village in Leting County, Hebei Province. To the north of the Luanhe River mouth, however, most rivers are carrying large amounts of sands to the lower reaches. Especially, the Luanhe River, originating on the Mongolian Plateau and flowing through the Onqin Daga Sandy Land and the crystalline rock of the Yanshan Mountains, formed the sandy lands in Qian'an, Luan Xian County and South Luan Xian County on the alluvial plain, the remaining sandy material is transported to the nearby shore of the Bohai Sea. Under the actions of waves and tides, most of the sands are moved toward the north of the Liaodong Bay, forming the sandy lands. A small portion of the sand is moved southward to the sand spit of Dagang in the northern Bohai Bay.

From the Yanghe river mouth to the Luanhe River mouth east of Changli County in Hebei Province, there is a dune group 45 km long and 1–2 km wide, and it is the largest scale of coastal dunes in China (Fig 15-2). The dune group extends NNE in direction; the height of dunes in the north is 5 to 7 m, and more than 30 m in the south (Wang et al., 1987). The main dune types are transverse dunes, crescent dune chains, star dunes and flat sandy lands. The transverse dunes are close to the shore forming the main dune belt and are best developed in the Qixing Lagoon. To the north of Xinkaikou and south of Xinlizhuang, the volume of the transverse dunes becomes smaller and lower, accompanied by star dunes. The crescent dune chains mainly appear on the landward side of the main dunes (transverse dunes), with an oblique angle to the main dunes. They are best developed east of Qili Sea. Star dunes mainly occur south of Xinlizhuang and north of Xinkaikou, at the junction of the two reversed S-shaped main dunes. The flat sandy lands are in the landward margin of the dunes. The altitude of the sandy lands is 1–3 m. Crescent dunes occur occasionally in the sandy lands west of the dune belt and north of the Dapu River.

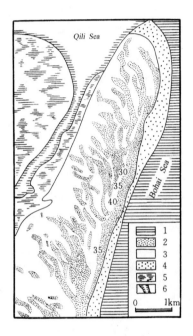

Fig. 15-2   The coastal dunes north of the Luanhe River mouth and south of Xinkaikou on the western
shore of the Bohai Bay (Li, 1987)

1. Sea; 2. Dunes; 3. Interdune depressions; 4. Coastal sandy lands; 5. Swampland; 6. Lagoons [the figures in the graph indicate the dune heights (m)]

The interdunes of the coastal dunes are square or pinch-and-swell in form, and parallel to the shore. Those between the crescent dune chains are oblique to the coastline. The altitudes of the interdune depressions decrease gradually from the sea shore to inland, from 4–5 m to 1–2 m. The dunes are active in late autumn and early winter when the wind is strong. The dominant wind direction is NE and the secondary wind direction is NW. In the late 1970s, many trees (*Robiniai pseudoacacia* and *populus*) were planted in these interdune depressions. But because the dunes were bald, these trees didn't play a role in preventing the drifting sand, and Populus were eventually buried by the drifting sand in the leeward side of the dunes.

The coastal dune area along Changli was opened up as a holiday tour area at the end of the 20th century and is now attracting tourists by the beaches, dunes and sea.

15.2.2 Blown sand in the sandy coast of the Shandong Peninsula

Coastal dunes and sandy flats are widely distributed in the sandbars of the islands from the Shahe River mouth to Rongcheng County south of the eastern shore of the Laizhou Bay. However, on the sandy coast in Lanshantou, Rizhao City, located southwest of Shidao, there are few dunes as the aeolian activity is weak.

As the coast on the eastern shore of the Laizhou Bay is oriented in a NE to SW direction with a slight angle in the dominant wind direction of NNW, and the dune size is small and most are sandy flats. The lagoons between the feather-shaped sand piles near Diaolongzui haven't been filled with sands as the sandbanks are in the same direction of the dominant wind and located a far distance from sand sources, such as the lagoon in Qinglinpu sandbar. On the other hand, the sandbars are relatively young in age and the blown sand doesn't have enough time to fill the lagoon, such as the new sandbar north of Diaolongzui.

The coastal sand in the east of Longkou on the northern shore of the Shandong Peninsula has the following characteristics: ① dunes are sparse with different scales; ② The blown sands often cover hill slopes;③ sand-covered lagoon flats are widely seen (Fig. 15-3).

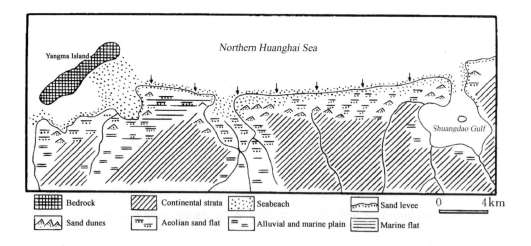

Fig. 15-3   Blown sand in the northern shore of the Shandong Peninsula
(Cai et al., 1983)

The best developed coastal dunes in this area are those near the bay of lagoons, namely those on the inner side of sandbars extending into the bays. The size of dunes is not large but in a developing stage. For example, dunes in three places north of Mouping City all developed near the bay of a lagoon, and the highest height reaches 25 m. The dunes are not high along relatively straight coastlines and their growth slowly increases as they climb up hill slopes.

Coastal sand landforms are well developed along the shore of the Taozi Bay near Yantai City in the north of Shandong Peninsula, which was under alluvial processes of the Dagujia River and marine accumulation processes during the Holocene. Three arrays of dunes developed on both side of the river mouth of the Dagujia River, roughly parallel to the coastline with heights of 5 to 7 m. The front margin of the coastal dunes is flat sandy beach 100 to 200 m wide (Zhang, 1995).

15.2.3 Coastal sandy lands around the Zhoushan Islands in Zhejiang Province

The coastal sandy lands in Zhejiang Province mainly occur on the Zhoushan Islands, such as Zhujiajian Island, Putuo Island, Sijiao Island and Taohua Island, and are distributed on the seaward shores extending NNE or nearly N to S.

On the southeast shore of Zhujiajian Island, sand landforms develop in some small bays. For example, 1 to 2 arrays of dunes develop on the shores of the Li'a, Qianbushe and Dongsha Bays, and 3 arrays of dunes exist on the shore of the Nansha Bay. They form a dune belt of 300 to 500 m wide, 5 to 10 m higher than the high tide line. Sands are sometimes blown to the windward slope of bedrock beak heads forming a sand slope 1,000 to 3,000 m long with a maximum height of 30 m. The dunes extend in a direction nearly parallel to the shores of the bays, NE-SW or nearly N-S. The inner side (landward side) is eluvium broken rocks or farmland and the outer side is the modern tidal beach 500 to 1,000 m wide.

Sand landforms also develop on the shores in the northeast of Putuo Island. One array of dunes occurs in the north of the Putuo Temple in the form of a sandbank connecting to the island, and is about 2 m higher than the high tide line. The sandbank is about 200 m wide and 200 long, connected to the tidal beach which is also about 200 m wide. No obvious dunes occur in Duisha, Qianbushe and Baibushe islands. The sands are piled on the shores, 200 to 400 m wide. The back edge of the sand piles climb 30 to 40 m high on the bed rock shore and the front edge is connected to the tidal beach which is 200 to 500 m wide. The dunes along the coast of Sijiao Island mainly occur in the bays in the form of sandbars, about 350 to 400 m wide and 1,800 m long. The top of the sandbar is 3 to 7 m higher than the high tide line. The front edge of the dunes is the modern tidal beach 200 to 300 m wide. Dug by human, the sand structure was destroyed and wind blown sand disasters are also serious. The sands of various sand-covered areas around the Zhoushan Islands and the beaches are all fine sands with good sorting, and active when there is strong wind. The local residents try to stabilize the sands with flagstones but the effect is not apparent. Trees were planted at the back margin of the sand piles in the 1990s (Zhu, 1994).

15.2.4　Coastal dunes in Fujian Province

The coastal dunes in Fujian Province are mainly distributed along the coast south of the mouth of the Minjiang River. Dunes develop best on the sandy coasts in Changle County, Pingtan County, Pujiang County, Putian County and Dongshan Island. The aeolian sand activities occur at close to the sea side of the river mouths.

15.2.4.1　Dunes on the eastern coast of Changle County

Being the largest river in Fujian, the Minjiang River transports 10.192 million tons of sands annually. Owing to the fact that the coast line is almost perpendicular to the NE monsoon, the vegetation around the river mouth is destroyed by the local people in Changle, and the aeolian sand activities are more serious than in other places. The dunes spread from Meihua on the south bank of the Minjiang River to Zhishou, roughly parallel to the coast. The dunes are 8 to 10 m high, with maximum height of 25 m consisting of pure sands. Besides the dunes in the coast plains, there are also dunes that cover the hills (Fig. 15-4).

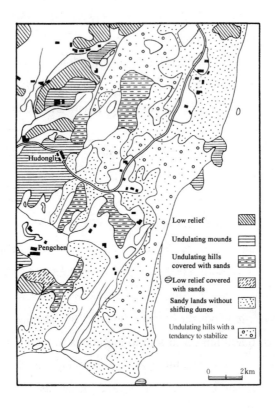

Fig. 15-4　Aeolian sandy lands on the eastern coast of Changle County, Fujian Province

On the northern coast from Meihua to Zhanggang near the Minjiang River mouth, all kinds of dunes developed. Foredunes are parallel to the coast with a height of 2 m. Transverse dunes of large scale exist in the inner side of the foredunes. They average 6 to 8 m high in Daliuhu and Shibi and the highest ones can reach more than 10 m. Plants such as horsetail beefwood have been grown on the dunes to stabilize sands. Therefore most of the dunes have become stabilized or semi-stabilized. In the back of the transverse dunes lies a large tract of sandy flat, which is 13 km in length and 35 km in width. The sandy land slightly undulates with small sand ridges, parabolic dunes and dome dunes on it. Most of the sandy land has been planted with horsetail beefwood or has been cultivated. The central coast from Zhanggang to Zhangkan is where sand dunes are most dense and highest. For example, the Wenwu sand spit is 7 km long, extending to Shabian Village. Besides one row of transverse dunes 2–3 km long and 6–10 m high parallel to the coast in a nearly north-south direction on the eastern shore of the sand spit, all the other places are occupied by crescent dune chains 1–2 km long and more than 10 m high. At the southern end of the sand spit, some parabolic dunes and dome dune develop. On the coast plain from Dongshan to Zhangquan, high crescent dunes are formed. The south coast from Zhangban to Keminglou, as acted by strong onshore winds and waves, the foredunes have been destroyed, and high transverse dunes are close to the coast. They are 700 to 1,800 m long and 15 to 20 m high. On the coast from Xiasha to Zhishou, foredunes 1 to 2 m high are advancing. Semi-stabilized dune chains, sand ridges and dome dunes 5 to 10 m high are distributed on the inner side of the foredunes. Further on the inner side there is slightly waving sandy ground. Horsetail beefwood has been planted on the dunes and the sandy ground, and the coverage has reached more than 50 percent.

15.2.4.2　Dunes on Haitan Island

Haitan Island is the largest island in Fujian Province with an area of 251 km^2. Hilly terraces are distributed in the north and south and the middle is the flat Luyangpu Plain. Wind blown sand sediments spread throughout the island in flats and depressions, the area of which is about 86.65 square kilometers, accounting for 34.6% of the whole island (Zhang, 1997) (Fig. 15-5). Sand hazards have been serious since historical times. The north and northeast coasts of the island are now retreating from serious erosion. As the Luyangpu Plain is 13 km long and 5 to 6 km wide with low and flat topography, the sands in the beaches of Botang to Paitangpao in the northeast could be transported by the NNE onshore winds directly southwest of the island, such as the Zhuyu area. As a result, a large sand sheet of 6,800 hm^2, 3 to 5 m in altitude is formed (Cai, 1992) on the Luyangpu Plain and sparse sandy lands are distributed on the plain southeast of Tianmei. The sand sediments are 3 to 10 m thick on the sand sheet, on which there exist sparse linear dunes and crescent dunes of less than 2 m. On the reddish old sandstone terraces where there is flowing water, many coppice dunes developed. They look like domes or steamed bread. In Jingsha, located behind Junshan, the climbing dunes have covered the hill slopes as high as 97.6 m in altitude.

Since protective forest of horsetail beefwood was planted and reasonable land use since the

1960s, the environment of the island is becoming more beautiful. It was designated by the Central Government as a China National Park in March 1994.

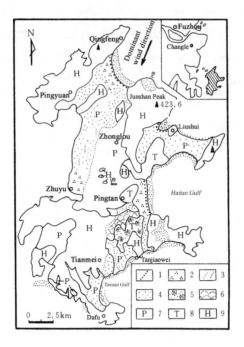

Fig. 15-5　Map of sand landforms on Haitan Island

1. Fore-dunes; 2. Dome dunes; 3. Linear dunes; 4. Sandy flat; 5. Sand-covered terraces; 6. Sand-covered hills; 7. Plains; 8. Terraces; 9. Hills

15.2.4.3　Dunes on Dongshan Island

The sands on Dongshan Island are distributed on the eastern coast as sandbanks connecting to the island in the Dongshen Bay and Gongqian in the south. The Dongshen Bay is a lagoon bay covered by sands. The sands are expanding toward the hill slopes, reaching 70 m above sea level. The thickness of the sands is different, generally increasing from the shore to inland. The area of sands around the Dongshen Bay is 1,000 hm^2. The sand source in Gongqian sandbank is plentiful, resulting in a wide distribution of blown sand of 3,000 hm^2. Small fore dunes 1–2 m high occur above the high tide line around the Huidong Bay east of the sandbank. In the middle part of the sandbank, however, there exist large crescent dunes and dune chains. South of the sandbank, there is a large tract of sandy flat located from Chishi to Xigang. According to core data, the sand sediments below the flat exceed 6 m and are a maximum of 20 m (Cai et al., 1992). The sands moved along the northern and eastern slopes of Damao Hill, reaching 60 to 70 m on the slopes.

15.2.4.4　Dunes on the Gulei Peninsula

The Gulei Peninsula in Zhangpu south of the west bank of the Taiwan Strait is actually a large scale sandbank. The north section of the sandbank is consistent with the dominant wind direction (NE). The sandbank near Gangkou Village changes direction to N-S, oblique to the dominant wind direction (Cai, 1989). The northern sandbank is sandy flat 1.5 to 2.0 m above sea level, with gramineous grass and horsetail beefwoods growing on it. Small embryonic dome and crescent dunes occur beginning from the Cai Village to the southwest. To the south of Xincuo and Huli, crescent dunes and dune chains occur and the size increases gradually from 10 m to 20 m. Many sand ridges and parabolic dunes develop in the downwind side of the crescent dunes and dune chains in the west of the sandbank. The total area of dunes and sandy lands is 4,600 hm^2.

The development of blown sand hazards along the coasts in Fujian Province is, to a large extent, related to human activities over the past 300 years due to population growth and vegetation destruction.

15.2.5　Coastal aeolian sandy lands in Taiwan Province

The blown sand in Taiwan Island is mainly located on the western coasts (Cai et al., 1983). The coast from Tainan to the Dajia Stream is extruding and is subject to attacks from the strong northeast monsoon. In addition, the streams of Zengwen, Zhushui, Dadu, Dajia, and Da'an all have high contents of suspended grains, providing abundant sand material. Therefore, the west coast is the major area for aeolian sand activities (Zhu et al., 1983). Dunes are fairly well developed in the southwest. But the few small scale dune that occur in the northwest have been reclaimed into agricultural lands. The coastal dunes in the southwest can be divided into two regions: the first is near the sea plain where the dunes are sparse with a sand source from the old sandbanks and the current riverbed fine sands near the river mouths; the other is the chain-shaped sandbars. The former still has sand movement with a maximum migration rate of 1.75 m/yr, and the latter is continuously expanding.

The dunes on the near sea plain are mainly distributed on the alluvial plains of the rivers (Fig. 15-6). The forms of dunes vary frequently from crescent dunes to sand ridges either parallel or perpendicular to the coastlines. The coastal sections with many dunes along the Zhushui Stream are: ① the southern bank of the Dongluo Stream. From Chuanhe to Fengtianli, the dunes are lower than 15 m. Dunes extend east-west ward near the section from Xidiliao to Wanheli, with a height of 10–25 m and an area of 100 m×3,000 m; ② the southern bank of the Xiluo Stram. The dunes are also extending east-west ward, with a height of 22 to 28 m west of the Yangxian Village and 15 to 20 m near Zhouzi. The average height of dunes in this area is between 15 and 20 m; ③ the area between the Huwei Stream and the New Huwei Stream. Many small scale dunes occur in this region. The dunes near Daji and in southern Zhonghu are mostly lower than 20 m, with a maximum height 30m (Wang, 1980).

On the chain-shaped sandbars and sand banks, the dunes are lower than 15 m. Dense dunes are distributed on the outer Sandingzhou sandbar. In the interdune depressions there is fresh water. There

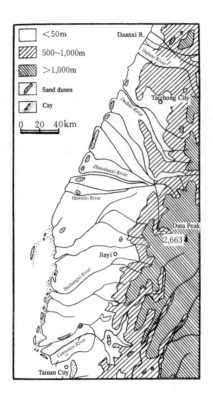

Fig. 15-6 Dunes or sand ridges in the west coast of Taiwan Province (Zhu et al., 1994)

are also many dunes on the sandbar in Haixianzhou between the two river mouths of the Baxian Stream and the Jishui Stream. The big dunes in the center are covered by dense horsetail beefwoods which have stabilized the sands effectively, but there are no trees at the margin and dunes are increasing in height. Except for the protective forests in the north of the sandbar in Ezhou in the north of the Zengwen Stream, there are no trees on other sandbars and dunes are exposed. Dunes are also frequently seen around the lagoons between the sandbars in Jiayi. An old beach 12 km×4 km large lies here, and its age is unclear. The sands in dunes and sandbars on the west coast of Taiwan are mostly fine sands, 95 percent of which have diameters between $\varphi 2.2$–2.7(Wang, 1980).

15.2.6 Coastal sandy lands in Guangdong Province

The coastal dunes in Guangdong Province include those in East Guangdong and West Guangdong. Large dunes appear in the coast extending eastward, northeastward or NNE and are rarely seen in the coasts facing south or southwest.

15.2.6.1 Coastal dunes in East Guangdong

In East Guangdong, coastal dunes mainly occur in Chenghai, Shantou, Chaoyang and Lufeng (Wu, 1995). The Xi and Dong Rivers southwest of the Hanjian Delta between Chenghai and Shantou have large runoff volumes and carry a large amount of sands, providing abundant sand materials for the development of sandbars. The sea at the river mouths of the Xi and Dong Rivers is open and wide with strong wave actions, also providing good dynamical conditions for the development of sandbars. Therefore the sandbars develop well in the southwest and the sand deposition process is prominent. On the contrary, the number of sandbars in the northeast is fewer with a weak sand deposition process (Fig. 15-7). Besides, the coast between the Haimen Bay and the Jieshi Bay is a typical lagoon coast in Guangdong Province and sandbars (or sandbanks and sand spits) are composed of well-sorted medium to fine sands. They are easily blown by winds and the dunes develop well. In this area, typical crescent dunes, parabolic dunes and sand ridges are not only widely spread on the whole sand spit, but also extend to alluvial-marine accumulation plains with heights of 5 to 15 m, such as those in Tianxin, Jinghai and Nanhai in Huilai, Jiazi, Donghu and Wukan in Lufeng. The coast in Nanhai, Huilai is a region with typical dunes covering a relatively large area in East Guangdong.

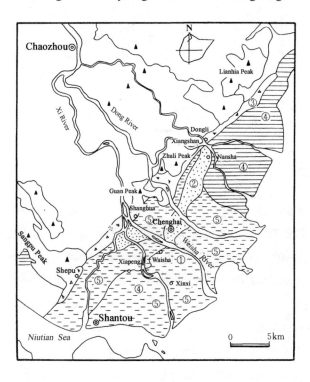

Fig. 15-7　Map of coastal sand distribution in the southern Hanjiang Delta
① Sandbars and dunes; ② Flat sandy lands; ③ Shell sandbars; ④ Coastal lowlands; ⑤ Dried lagoons

15.2.6.2　Coastal dunes in West Guangdong

Coastal dunes in West Guangdong mainly occur in Pinggang, Xitou, Hailing Island, Dianbai, Bohe and Shuidong (Wu, 1995). Large areas of blown sand lands exist on the east coast of the Leizhou Peninsula, including the islands between Wuchuan County in the north and Xujian County in the southeast, such as Donghai Island, Nansan Island and Dongli Island. The total area exceeds

30,000 hm^2. Three types of sand landforms can be recognized according to their formation ages, namely the old, medium and young (Han, 1985) (Fig. 15-8).

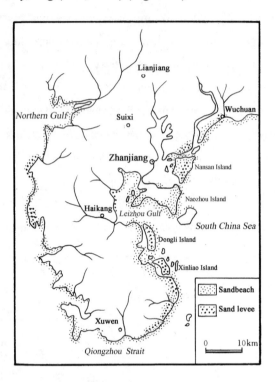

Fig. 15-8   Blown sand lands in the Leizhou Peninsula (Han, 1985)

(1) Old sandbars. They are composed of dark red fine sands, with weak cementation. These sandbars are distributed in Tiantou on Nansan Island, Dutou on Dongli Island, and Liuwei, Xiaze and Yunzi in Xuwen County, most of which have been covered by the medium sandbars. There are still debates as to the formation of these old red sands. Some researchers argue that they are a type of marine deposits of recent origin while other scholars believe they are aeolian sands. For example, Wu et al., (2000) thinks that they are aeolian deposits formed in the late Pleistocene. The periods between 56–42 ka and 30–10 ka are the two major deposition periods for the old red sands.

(2) Medium sandbars. They extend extensively in strips or sand ridges roughly parallel to the coast. The width of a single sand ridge is generally 200 to 1,600 m, with a maximum of 3,000 m in Leixi on Nansan Island. The average width of the sandbar is 1 to 4 km and the maximum width also occurs in Nansan Island, reaching 5 km. Sandbars and dunes spread continuously. Five to seven parallel ridge-shaped sandbars extend NE-SW along the coast from Bomao to Wuyang in Wuchuan County in the northeast, with an area of 4,000 hm^2. The sand deposits increase in thickness from the northeast to the southwest. Transverse dunes, crescent dunes and parabolic dunes are all well developed.

(3) The young sandbars. They were formed in the past 20 to 30 years and are composed of grey fine sands. These sandbars mainly occur between Dengta to Leixi on Nansan Island, Wuyang in

Wuchuan County, Xinliao Island and Wailuo to Longtang in Xuwen County, generally lower than 5 m and more than 10 m in width. Dunes are mainly small crescent dunes, crescent dune chains and coppice dunes. As most of them are moving, blown sand hazards are frequent.

15.2.7 Coastal sands in Hainan Province

Coastal sands in Hainan Province are widely distributed in Wenchang, Qionghai and Wanning in the east, and Zhan Xian County, Changjiang, Dongfang and Ledong County stretching from the northwest to the southwest in Hainan Island.

15.2.7.1 The coast in Wenchang, northeast Hainan Island

This section of coast is composed of marine terraces and plains. The coast extends NW or nearly N-S, causing active sand movement under the action of NW waves in winter and the SE waves in summer. Besides the transverse movements, the sands also move longitudinally to the south in winter and to the north in summer, forming wide sand beaches and lagoon plains. A dune belt of 100 km long, extending from the Puqian Bay, Mulantou to Tongguling, was formed by strong onshore winds and typhoons which blew sands from the beaches to the sandbars and lagoon plains. The dune belt is 3 to 5 km wide, exceeding 10 km in local places (Wu, 1995). The dune types from the shore to inland are foredunes, dune belts (mainly large transverse, crescent, parabolic and longitudinal dunes), and sandy flats (Fig. 15-9).

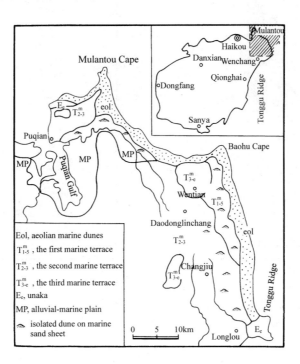

Fig. 15-9   Sketch map showing the distribution of coastal blown sand in Wenchang, northeast Hainan Island

15.2.7.2　West Hainan Island

The coast in Dongfang, from Sigeng in the north to Banqiao in the south, is a narrow belt with

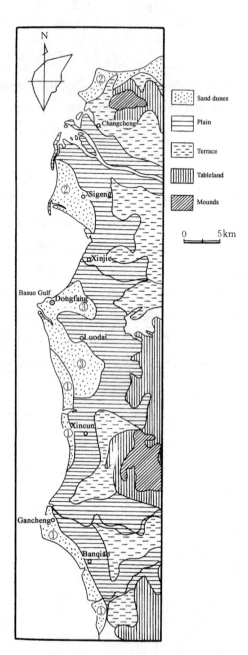

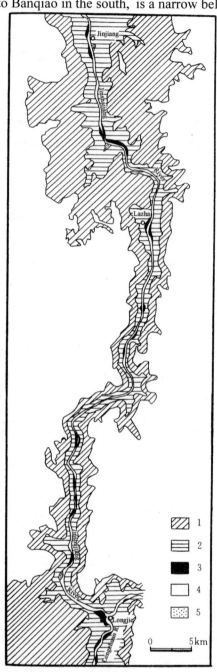

Fig. 15-10　Distribution of coastal sands in
Dongfang, west Hainan Island
① Crescent dunes and sand ridges; ② Coppice dunes;
③ Sandy flats

Fig. 15-11　Sketch map of relief and sandy
lands distribution in the Jinsha
River valley
1. Altitude 1,200—1,500 m; 2. Altitude<1,200 m;
3. Sand landforms; 4. Altitude >1,500 m; 5. Alluvial
fans

discontinuous dunes and sandy lands covering 7,911 hm^2. Coppice dunes, crescent dunes and sand ridges develop on this coast. The dunes range in height from several meters to more than 10 meters (Wu, 1995) (Fig. 15-10). Located west of the Wuzhi Mountains, the western coast of Hainan Island lies in the rain shadow of the northeast and southwest monsoons. Also affected by the southwest dry-hot winds, it is hot all the year round with strong evaporation. These factors make it the hottest and driest area on the Island. Taking Ledong as an example, the mean annual temperature is 24.5 °C. The precipitation is 998.9 mm annually, but the potential evaporation reaches 2,390 mm, 2.4 times the precipitation. The annual aridity is 1.3 to 1.5. The number of dry months (precipitation <40 mm) reaches 5.1 to 5.5. Furthermore, the land surface materials of the coastal plains and terraces consist of red-brown, yellow brown sands, with good water permeability and poor fertility. In addition, the open topography favours strong wind generation (wind force 5-6). Aeolian sand activity in Ledong is severe and the widely spread dunes make it look like a desert, with the potential desertified land of a savanna. The blown sand lands there is different form other coasts. The plants on the dunes, mainly drought-enduring plants, are sparse and short, such as cacti (*Opuntia*) and other psammophytes. Some dunes are bare and devoid of any plants, forming the shifting dunes.

Because of the extremely inconsistent heat and moisture conditions of the ecological environment and severe human activities in western Hainan Island, drought is exacerbated and the land degradation process is similar to that in Africa, with a shift from tropical forest to Savanna and finally to deserts (Zhu, 1986).

15.3 Sandy lands in the dry-hot valleys in southwest China

Rivers of different magnitudes flow through western Sichuan and the Hengduan Mountains of Yunnan in southwest China. Most rivers, except the lower reaches of the Jinsha River and the middle reaches of the Nanpan River, flow in a north-south direction, with a dissected depth exceeding 1,000 m and forming many deep valleys. For example, the mountains on both sides of the Jinsha River valley below Shigu are 3,000 m above the river surface. As the deep valleys are in the leeside of the southwest or southeast monsoons, are blocked by high mountains in the east and west, local dry environments have developed. In addition to large amounts of latent heat emitted by the strong updrafts, the foehn effect reduces most moisture at the leeside and increases the temperature, making these valleys dry and hot. The dry and wet seasons are clearly divided in these valleys. During the wet season, the precipitation accounts for 80 to 90 percent of the annual total. During the dry season, however, rainfall is rare and precipitation is only 10 to 20 percent of the annual total (Wu, 1989). For instance, the annual precipitation in the Jinsha River valley is only 610–770 mm, but the mean annual temperature is 20–22 °C. The annual potential evaporation even reaches 2,500–3,900 mm. In some valleys where there are sandy flats, wind blows the sandy sediments, making the surface look like a desert landscape. Embryonic crescent dunes, crescent dunes and dune chains occur in the river valleys, especially in large valleys with a N-S directions. Bare crescent dunes or dune chains are often seen on convex sandy flats spreading downwind. Windblown sand hazards mainly occur in the dry-hot river valleys of the Minjiang River, Dadu River, Yalong River and Jinsha River in Sichuan Province (Fig. 15-11).

Owing to a limited sand source, the size of dunes is usually not large. The dune heights are generally 0.5–1 m. In the rainy season, except for the sands on the terraces, most sands are submerged by floods. Blown sands, therefore, appear seasonally.

Below is a brief discussion on the rehabilitation of the blown sand lands in these dry-hot river valleys, using those in the dry-hot river valley in Yuanmou, Yunnan Province as examples.

The transport and deposition processes of the Longchuan River resulted in the sand landforms in the dry-hot river valley in Yuanmou, Yunnan Province. Embryonic crescent dunes, sand ridges and patches of shifting sands 1.5 m high developed during the dry season. Currently the area with typical sand landforms has reached 20 hm^2. On the other hand, as the bedrock is exposed and subject to strong weathering, large amount of debris deposited on the slopes, and a rocky desert landscape formed. Compared with the sand landforms in the north arid and semi-arid regions, the sand landforms in the dry-hot river valleys are sparsely distributed and sand activities show seasonality.

Specific rehabilitation measures include:

(1) Reinforcing fundamental education and enhancing public awareness about environmental protection. Educating the farmers to reform the cultivation system. Controlling rapid population growth and popularizing the energy-saving cooking utensils.

(2) Planting trees for water and soil conservation, including economic forests and firewood forests. The natural forest should be enclosed. Considering the special environments in the dry-hot river valleys, drought-enduring herbs and shrubs could be introduced artificially with regards to ecological principles. After 10 years of rehabilitation, the environment could be improved.

(3) Protection and reasonable use of the existing grasslands. For the grassland in the river valley in Yuanmou, overgrazing should be forbidden. For the grassland where degradation has appeared, enclosure measures should be taken. Artificial cultivation, such as planting grasses of high quality and evergreen small arbors, is also necessary. Experiments carried out in a 0.4 hm^2 land 1,300 m above sea level indicate that if siratros and soy beans are planted at the time of enclosure, the grassland could be restored 1 year later, and the grass coverage could reach more than 90% 2 years later. Therefore, enclosure and artificial cultivation are the main approaches for the restoration of the degraded grasslands in this area.

(4) Basic construction for irrigation and water conservancy. Modern agricultural techniques such as sprinkler irrigation and drop irrigation should be popularized to enhance the utilization efficiency of water resources and stabilize food production.

References

Cai Aizhi, Cai Yue'er. 1983. Cause and characteristics of aeolian deposits along the coast of China. Journal of Desert Research, 3(3): 1—10

Cai Aizhi, Cai Yue'er. 1989. Transgression and diffusion of aeolian sand on Gulei Peninsula in the south of Fujian Province. Marine Geology and Quaternary Geology, 9(4): 41—47

Cai Aizhi, Cai Yue'er. 1990. Formation of Gongqian Tombolo in Dongshan Island. Marine Geology and Quaternary Geology, 10(1): 81—91

Cai Aizhi, Cai Yue'er. 1992. Transgression and eolian sand sequence in Luyangpu Plain, Haitan Island, Fujian. Journal of Oceanography in Taiwan Strait, 11(2): 112—117

Chen Fang, Zhu Dakui. 1996. Dune formation and evolution along the south coast of Minjiang Estuary. Journal of Desert Research, 16(3): 233—239

Chen Guangting, Yang Taiyun, and Zhang Weimin. 1989. Study of sandy land on alluvial plain of the Yellow River section in Shandong Province. Journal of Desert Research, 9(1): 19—33

Chen Guangting, Zhang Jixian et al. 1995. Aeolian sand and its control. See: Proceedings of Lanzhou Institute of Desert Research, Chinese Academy of Sciences. (Number 4). Beijing: Science Press. 1—120

Cui Shuhong. 1995. Land degradation and its management policy of dry-hot river valley of Yuanmou in Yunan province. Geographical Research, 14(1): 66—71

Fu Mingzuo, Xu Xiaoshi, Xu Xiaowei. 1997. The aeolian geomorphical types in the coastal areas of the Yellow Sea and Bohai Sea, and their distribution patterns and development models. Oceanologia et Limnologia Sinica, 28(1): 56—65

Gao Qianzhao, Liu Famin. 2000. Agricultural ecological system construction and sustainable development of Yanjing Sandy Land. Journal of Desert Research, 20(suppl): 107—113

Han Chaoqun. 1985. Preliminary study of aeolian characteristics and cause of Zhanjiang in the southwest of Guangdong Province. Journal of Desert Research, 5(1): 27—29

Li Congxian. 1987. Preliminary study of aeolian sediments to the north coast of the Mian River. Journal of Desert Research, 7(2): 12—21

Li Shanwei, Liu minhou, Wang Yongji et al. 1985. Eolian sand dunes along the coast of Shandong Peninsula. Oceanology & Huang Sea and Bohai, 3(3): 47—55

Su Peixi. 1996. Characteristics of seasonal aeolian land and study of fruit trees development. Journal of Ecological Agriculture, 4(2): 54—58

Wang Xin. 1980. Geographical Landscape in Taiwan. Taibei: Taiwan Vocation Press, 64—73

Wang Yin, Zhu Dakui. 1987. Discussion of formation of coastal sand dunes. Journal of Desert Research, 7(3): 29—40

Wu Jicheng, Wang Shenghou, Ren Sukun, et al. 1999. Trend analysis on sustainable development for agriculture in sandy land of Henan province. In: Tang Dengyin et al., Proceedings of Agricultural Sustainable Development on Huang-Huai-Hai Plain. Beijing: China Meteorological Press, 98—103

Wu Wei. 1989. Preliminary study of desertification in mountain areas of southern China. Journal of Desert Research, 9(3): 36—43

Wu Zheng, Wang Wei, Tan Huizhong et al. 2000. The age of the "old red sand" on the coast of south Fujian and west Guangdong, China. Chinese Science Bulletin, 45(5): 533—537

Wu Zheng, Wu Kegang. 1987. Sedimentary structure and development pattern of coastal sand dunes in the northeastern part of Hainan Island. Acta Geographica Sinica, 42(2): 129—141

Wu Zheng. 1995. Aeolian Geomorphy in Southern China. Beijing: Science Press

Wu Zheng. 1997. Desert and Coastal Sand Dunes in China. Beijing: Science Press

Yang Xilin, Wei Xinghu, Zhao Xingliang. 1996. Comprehensive development and management of sandy land. Journal of Desert Research, 16(1): 43—49

Yang Zhengming. 1989. Management of Low-yield Land and Its Effect on Huang-Huai-Hai Plain. Beijing: Agricultural Press, 1—10

Zhang Jianping. 1997. Human-made effect of land desertification in dry-hot river valley of Yuanmou. Mountain Research, 15(1): 53—56

Zhang Wenkai. 1997. Basic characteristic of eolian sand and its development and utilization. Journal of Desert Research, 17(2): 138—143

Zhang Zhenke. 1995. Preliminary study of coastal eolian geomorphy near Yantai. Journal of Desert Research, 15(3): 210—215

Zhu Zhenda, Chen Guangting. 1994. Sandy Desertification of Land of China. Beijing: Science Press, 68—70

Zhu Zhenda. 1986. Land desertification in humid and semi-humid zones. Journal of Desert Research, 6(4): 1—12

Part IV
Control of Deserts and Aeolian Desertification

Chapter 16
Strategy of Aeolian Desertification Control

Aeolian desertification is not only an important ecological problem, but also a very critical economic and social problem, which hampers the sustainable development of China's economy and society. At the beginning of the founding of the PRC, the government started the process of combating aeolian desertification. Although significant achievements have been made in aeolian desertification control, yet only a small proportion of the aeolian desertified land has been improved, and in most regions the situation has become worse. We think there is an urgent need to review why long-term efforts have so far only achieved minimal results, and where the crux of the problem lies. Today, the most urgent task for aeolian desertification control is the innovation of aeolian desertification control models and institutions.

16.1 Principles and approaches to control aeolian desertification

In the process of researching the control of deserts and aeolian desertification, the concepts of deserts and aeolian desertification are always confused. It is very important to distinguish the causes of aeolian desertification and the vulnerability of natural environments around the aeolian desertified land. Owing to the lack of water resources, the environment in the arid region is very vulnerable. Climate change and unreasonable human economic activities can result in environment degradation. Lack of precipitation, abundant sand materials on the ground surface, and lack of vegetation in the arid region are the foundations which cause aeolian desertification, while climate change and human activities are conditions that cause aeolian desertification. It is clear that aeolian desertification is different from deserts in the arid region. The definition of desertification in the "United Nations Convention to Combat Desertification" puts stress on climate change and unreasonable human economic activities as the cause for land desertification. Most notably, unreasonable human economic activities are the main cause of desertification. It has been argued that aeolian desertification occurring in arid desert steppe and semi-humid sylvosteppe was mainly caused by over-reclamation, over-cutting, and over-grazing. And some aeolian desertified land around the margin of oases in the arid region is mainly caused by lack of water resources and irrational use of water resource. Aeolian desertification in China mainly developed in the past 2,000 years, and especially since the 1850s. Along with population growth and economic development, aeolian desertification also extended rapidly.

To control deserts and aeolian desertification, we cannot change the natural environment that causes deserts and aeolian desertification. A desert is mainly a natural environment with relief features. It is hard to control the desert. Therefore, we mainly discuss the strategy of aeolian desertification control in this chapter.

16.1.1 Fundamental principles of aeolian desertification control

16.1.1.1 Basic principles

The objective of aeolian desertification control is to rehabilitate the degraded ecosystem and build an artificial eco-economic system, which can ensure the sustainable development of the ecological environment, natural resources and socioeconomic growth.

Ecological environments in aeolian desertified areas is a critical factor. Once human economic activity pressure exceeds the environmental limit, land will suffer aeolian desertification; as soon as such pressure is relieved, it can recover automatically (Zhu et al., 1994). This self-resilience is dependent upon the quality of natural environments around the aeolian desertified area, with moisture being the most important condition. The annual precipitation is above 200 mm in some semiarid regions of northeast China. In the southeast of the Songnen Sandy Land, the Horqin Sandy Land, and the Mu Us Sandy Land, the annual precipitation can even reach 400 mm. Studies shows that, if the human activity is removed in such regions, the aeolian desertified land will recover automatically after 5–7 years. The annual precipitation of the Hulun Buir Sandy Land and the Onqin Daga Sandy Land is 250–355 mm. Studies also show that if the human activity is removed in these areas, the aeolian desertified lands can also recover automatically after 7–8 years. With the same precipitation, slightly aeolian desertified land easily recovers, and severely aeolian desertified land is difficult to recover, while the very severely aeolian desertified land with active sand dunes cannot self-restore without some artificial measures. Therefore, we think that aeolian desertification control should pay close attention to the slightly aeolian desertified land, especially to the potential aeolian desertified land with heavy human activity pressure. This is because it becomes harder to control slightly and potentially aeolian desertified land after their situations become severe.

(1) The principle of prevention first. Prevention first is a general principle for any natural disaster. In aeolian desertification control, we should first salvage the potentially and slightly aeolian desertified land, so as to control the aeolian desertified land expansion. And then, we make an effort to combat the severely aeolian desertified land step by step.

(2) The principle of consistency in benefiting the society the economy and the ecology. When combating aeolian desertification, we should not only consider its ecological environment, but also consider the population and socioeconomic development problems in the aeolian desertified area. If there is a contradiction between economical benefit and ecological benefit, we should first consider the ecological benefit.

(3) The principle of consistency in land utilization and aeolian desertification control. In the aeolian desertified transitional areas of farming and grazing, it is important to balance the land use of agriculture, forestry, grazing, and grassland rationally. Efforts should be made to change current farming structures, to popularize grain-grass intercropping, to introduce fodder grasses into the cropland farming system, to develop a three-crop rotation for grain, forage, and other cash crops to enhance soil fertility, to develop animal husbandry, and to form a stable eco-agricultural system.

(4) The balancing of long-term ecological benefits and short-term economical interest. Improving the environment is a long-term process. We can obtain short-term economical interest from natural resource exploitation, such as agriculture and pastures. However, we have to protect the long-term ecological benefit in the aeolian desertified area because of its vulnerable ecological environment.

(5) The management by the government. Environment is a public matter. Aeolian desertification control is a nation wide job. Favorable policies, financial assistance, and technology should be given to the aeolian desertified region to help local people combating aeolian desertification.

(6) Research and experiments. Aeolian desertification researches should contain: ① dynamic monitoring of aeolian desertification and environment changes, and establishing a network of monitoring and surveillance all over the country; ② establishing experimental and demonstration bases; ③ providing information and advisory services; ④ comprehensive research of the relationship of society, economy, and aeolian desertification, to work out an overall aeolian desertification control plan.

16.1.1.2 Ecological principles

The integrative aeolian desertification control measures based on ecological theory are also called ecological engineering of aeolian desertification control. This ecological engineering not only deals with the energy and material circulation theory, but also contains the economic development system and sandy damage control engineering system.

(1) Control and exploitation: double objective principle. Aeolian desertification is one kind of land degradation. Eco-environment protection is the first step of aeolian desertification control. Economic interest should not be the only objective of the artificial ecological economic system. It should follow the double objective principle, namely, ecological benefit and economical interest. That is to say, ecological benefit is foremost and economical interest is secondary.

(2) Moderate resource development principle. In the aeolian desertification control process, it is important to balance energy input and energy output of the whole ecosystem. So, resource development should not go beyond the environmental limit. Different economic behavior has different development indexes, such as grassland livestock number index, farmland multiple crop index, and forestland cutting cycle index etc. The common principle for all these indexes is sustainable development of our ecological environment and recyclable resources.

(3) Multinomial complementary principle. In the potential and on-going aeolian desertification area, the social and economical system should be a compound system due to its vulnerable ecological condition. When one section of the whole system breaks down, the other sections can complement that section. This is the meaning of the multinomial complementary principle. In fact, multinomial complement is an ensemble that contains diversified economic departments and management vocations in the production system. In the potential and on-going aeolian desertification area, multinomial complement contains three important aspects (Fig. 16-1).

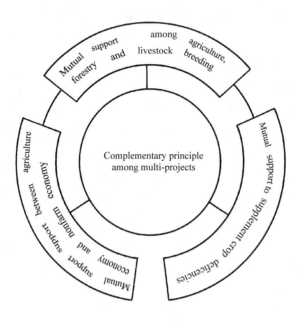

Fig. 16-1   Complementary net

(a) Agriculture, animal husbandry, and forestry complement each other.

(b) Different crops complement each other.

(c) Farm and non-farm production complement each other.

1) Farm and non-farm production complementing each other

The land-dependent economic activities such as agriculture, animal husbandry, and forestry should combine with non-farm production to complement each other. Traditional agriculture, animal husbandry, and forest industry are strongly dependent on natural conditions, especially in the fragile ecological environment in aeolian desertified areas. Land-dependent activity has low economic effect and instability. It is clear that the traditional production pattern can only lead to resource depletion and eco-environment degradation in the aeolian desertified area. If non-farm production and population is increased (such as 40% of the total population), the regional economic condition and household income can be greatly improved, and the land pressure will greatly decreased, and thereby favor the regional sustainable development. The effect of this kind of complement is very obvious.

2) Agriculture, animal husbandry, and forestry complementing each other

Readjusting the structure of agriculture, animal husbandry, and forestry can improve their function of complementing each other. The investigation in the southern Horqin Sandy Land and the Mu Us Sandy Land shows the optimal structure: farmland occupies 20%–30% of the total land area, forestry 30%, grassland 40%–50%. The agriculture income occupies 40%–50% of the gross income, forestry about 20%, and animal husbandry about 30%.

3) Different crops complementing each other

Reasonable planting design of crops will benefit the soil organic matter and nutrient elements. Different crops have different features and effects on soil: barley and Indian corn are nutrient-consuming crops, medic can increase soil nutrient, while bean cultures such as soya can fix nitrogen by their nodule bacteria.

The effect of this multinomial complementary net is higher than the effect of the individual constituent. Such a complementary ecosystem is suitable to potential and on-going aeolian desertification areas. The relationship of the principles are illustrated by Fig. 16-2.

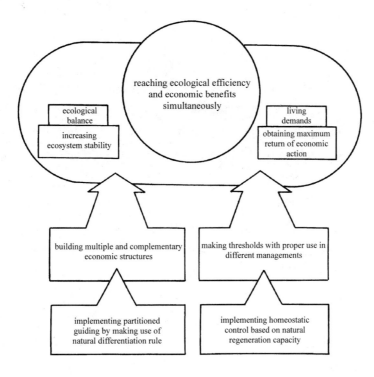

Fig. 16-2   Complementation among Multi-constituents

4) Synthetic system principle

From the above analysis, it is clear that aeolian desertification results from the interaction between human development and their eco-environment. To control aeolian desertification effectively, it is necessary to adopt synthetic measures. The synthetic measures deal with interdisciplinary fields such as sociology, economics, and natural sciences. In addition, we should strengthen education and establish relevant laws. People can be educated by television programs, film, broadcasting, magazines, newspapers etc. In this way, people's environmental awareness can be improved and therefore, they are willing to participate in the aeolian desertification control.

The aeolian desertification control principles discussed above are interrelated and mutually complement each other. According to the regional characteristics, establishing complementary economic structures can enhance the stability of the ecosystem. According to the regional carrying capacity and establishing a moderate resource development threshold, ecological balance can be recovered, and people can obtain the maximum economic benefit.

16.1.2　Approaches to control aeolian desertification

16.1.2.1　Fundamental approaches of aeolian desertification control

Strong wind action, loose sandy surface, and sparse vegetation are the three key factors of aeolian desertification. In order to control aeolian desertification, we have to remove these factors. However, the wind action and loose sandy surfaces are impossible to remove with present science and technology. A great deal of practices on aeolian desertification control in China and other countries indicate that using biological measures to increase ground cover is feasible. Therefore, biological measures are the fundamental approach of aeolian desertification control. And some engineering measures should be used as temporary measures. The biological measure can be divided into two major approaches: spontaneous recovery and establishing artificial vegetation.

Spontaneous recovery is simple but it is impractical in China because the vegetation recovery period is very long. Vegetation recovery may take several years or even decades. Moreover, aeolian desertification can hinder the spontaneous recovery of vegetation. In addition, owing to rapid population growth, it is impossible to stop production and society. So, it is impossible to widely use the spontaneous approach in all the aeolian desertified area in China. Artificial vegetation can enhance the land productivity in aeolian desertified area, thereby enhancing the population carrying capacity, making economic development sustainable, as well as getting better ecological, economical, and social benefits. Therefore, the establishment of artificial vegetation should be a primary approach to combat aeolian desertification in China.

Considering aeolian desertification causes, development trends, and status, the fundamental countermeasures of aeolian desertification control in China include five aspects:

(1) Controlling population growth and reducing population pressure. To ensure sustainable ecological environments and economic development, it is necessary for population growth, economic increases and resource regeneration to develop harmoniously. otherwise natural resources will be overused. Once the vegetation is destroyed, aeolian desertification will be exacerbated in the critical arid regions of northern China. Therefore, controlling population growth, defining a suitable population capacity, and relieving population pressures in desertified area are all very important to aeolian desertification control in China.

(2) Increasing ground cover and establishing vegetation protection systems. Vegetation can weaken the wind force and reduce deflation in the arid region. So, it is an important measure for aeolian desertification control.

(3) Enhancing productivity levels and combating aeolian desertification. The unreasonable land use system and land use pattern should be modified in the desertified area, so as to enhance agricultural productivity, and to resolve the contradictions between population growth and land carrying capacity.

(4) Modifying energy structure, resolving fuel problems. In the rural areas of northern China, most farmers cut and collect vegetation for their fuel. This is an important cause of aeolian desertification aggravation. To control aeolian desertification in the rural area, efforts should be made to alter existing energy structures by introducing oil and coal from other regions or using solar energy or electric power.

(5) Adopting different measures to cope with different degrees of aeolian desertification. The severity or degree of aeolian desertification is different from place to place. So, different aeolian desertification control measures should be adopted in different regions according to its severity and extent.

16.2 Strategies and measures to combat aeolian desertification

16.2.1 Strategies to combat aeolian desertification

16.2.1.1 Strategic objective to combat aeolian desertification in China

Strategic objectives to combat aeolian desertification in China include coordinating the relationship between the natural environment and economical development in arid, semi-arid and parts of semi-humid regions as well as establishing a socioeconomic system which not only can control aeolian desertification but also can promote the development of social economy. Its objective is to adopt suitable and feasible land use patterns and systems to recover land productivity damaged by aeolian desertification; to develop and utilize aeolian desertified land; to improve living standards of local people, including family planning, sanitation, health etc.

In short, the ultimate objective is to reduce and eliminate the factors which can result in aeolian desertification, to recover and reestablish a new ecological balance and environment of high quality that is suitable for human survival and development. So far as aeolian desertified land is concerned, two goals need to be achieved:

(1) To control further land aeolian desertification. This includes the expansion of aeolian desertification and the aggravation of aeolian desertification severity. Except for severely aeolian desertified land, other aeolian desertified lands still have a certain productive potential, hence, they can be used for agricultural production and grazing. The basic principle of aeolian desertification control is to protect the productivity of this kind of land from further loss and ensure people can live a normal life in desertified areas.

(2) To rehabilitate all kinds of aeolian desertified lands. Aeolian desertified lands can expand on its own. If it is not controlled, people's livelihood will be affected. However, if it is reversed, the productivity will be recovered or improved.

16.2.1.2 Strategic steps to combat aeolian desertification

China has a vast territory, with different socioeconomic and natural conditions in different regions. There are also great differences between aeolian desertification status in different regions. Because of limited financial and material resources, it's impossible to rehabilitate all of the aeolian desertified lands in the country. Combating aeolian desertification must be carried out with knowledge of local conditions and step by step.

Strategic steps to combat aeolian desertification in northern China are as follows: firstly, special attention should be paid to the slightly aeolian desertified land in arid, semi-arid and parts of semi-humid regions. These lands should be used appropriately and reasonably according to local ecological characteristics and natural conditions to avoid the occurrence of new aeolian desertified land; secondly, measures should be taken to control moderately aeolian desertified land and recover its productivity; at last, great efforts should be made to avoid the expansion of severely and very severely aeolian desertified land.

In order to control aeolian desertification as early as possible and promote harmonious development of the ecological environment and economy in China, the above-mentioned strategic steps will be implemented according to the following schedule:

By 2005, an advanced land use system should be adopted, and land should be utilized reasonably to avoid the spread of aeolian desertified land. It includes: stabilize rainfed farmland areas, adopt advanced management systems for soils and crops, and improve aeolian desertified farmlands, as well as to adopt advanced techniques to manage grassland, and rehabilitate slightly and moderately aeolian desertified grasslands.

By 2010, based on reasonable land use, through developing and introducing suitable and advanced farming and stockbreeding techniques to establish product processing and market installations, we can realize the integration of aeolian desertification control and economic development. In the mean time, we should plant and grasses on a large scale to recover vegetation and fix shifting sand.

By 2020, some severely aeolian desertified land will be improved and put into agricultural production and very severely aeolian desertified land should be protected to promote its natural restoration.

16.2.2　Measures to combat aeolian desertification

Based on strategies of aeolian desertification control and considering the differences of natural and economic conditions and aeolian desertification status in different areas, different measures will be adopted to combat aeolian desertification in different areas. Furthermore aeolian desertification control should be carried out in light of local conditions.

The measures used to control aeolian desertification in arid and semiarid zones include: ① protecting natural vegetation; ② surveying land use structure and enlarging the ratio of forest land and grassland area; ③ constructing a shelterbelt system; ④ returning cropland to forest and grassland and constructing capital farmland; ⑤ using grassland appropriately and constructing an artificial fodder base; ⑥ controlling population growth and livestock number so as not to exceed the carrying capacity of grassland. In arid areas, measures to combat aeolian desertification are as follows: ① taking an inland river basin as an ecological unit and rationally allocating water resources to upstream, midstream and downstream basins; ② constructing a protective forest system around oases; ③ developing water-saving farming; ④ engineering and ecological measures are combined to stabilize shifting sand around oases and to promote the reversal of aeolian desertification.

Aeolian desertification control is a complicated system project. It can only be accomplished through working out scientific planning with all people's involvement.

16.2.2.1　Vegetation re-establishment should be implemented with knowledge of local conditions

(1) Land use structure should be adjusted and dry farmland should account for the largest percentage in the agro-pastoral ecotone where most land is aeolian desertified. Lands with good water conditions suitability for cultivation should be fully utilized. The Cropland Conversion Program should be implemented to enlarge the area of forest and grassland. In addition, over cultivation, over grazing and over cutting should be strictly prohibited.

(2) Work should be done to strengthen the construction of pasture, to decide livestock number

according to the carrying capacity of the grassland, and to maintain the equilibrium between livestock and grassland. At the same time, it is important to accelerate investments and enhance the commercial rate to maintain economic benefits, reduce grassland pressure and promote the restoration of degraded grassland.

For severe and very severe aeolian desertified lands, different measures such as enclosure etc. should be taken to avoid aeolian desertified lands' expansion.

Some examples of aeolian desertification control show that both economic and ecological benefits will be obtained after aeolian desertification is controlled successfully. Appraisals of input and output for aeolian desertification control is shown in Table 16-1.

Table 16-1　Assessment of input and output for aeolian desertification control

Types	Main measures	Input (*yuan/mu*)	Output (*yuan/mu*)
Developing aeolian desertified land	Plant trees and grass, cultivate farmland with good water and soil conditions;	37	96.1
Intensively developing aeolian desertified land	Implement cropland conversion program, enclosure;	44	60
Severely aeolian desertified land	Construct sand barrier, plant shrubs and grasses;	69	86

Analyses of the ratio of output to input show that the ratio of single agriculture benefit is not high, ranging from 0.2 to 0.5, while forestry and stockbreeding benefits are 1–1.4 and 0.4–0.6 respectively. It implies that the development of single agriculture is not wise to combat aeolian desertification, while the combination of agriculture, forestry, and stockbreeding can attain better ecological and economic benefits.

16.2.2.2　Control population growth strictly and reduce pressure exerted by the population on the land

The conflict between population and resources results in environmental degradation and it is also the main cause of aeolian desertification. It is generally agreed that the rate of population growth exceeds that of resources all over the world. Man is not only the producer but also the consumer. The quantity and quality of consumable materials are determined by the land productivity under certain technical conditions. As far as a special area is concerned, the rate of population growth must be consistent with the actual productivity of land resources. If the land productivity can't afford to maintain rapid population growth, it will lead to over utilization of land resources. The essence of aeolian desertification is man's resource extraction exceeding the land capacity. So population control is the best way to mitigate land pressure, restore vegetation, reconstruct the ecological environment and to adjust the relationship between man and the environment.

Resolving population problem can start with two aspects. First, special attention should be paid to family planning policies, including establishing regional populations to control population growth; Second, rural populations should be transferred to other industries, such as secondary and tertiary industry to mitigate population pressure on aeolian desertified land and improve their economic status.

Today, the population density of 20–80 persons per sq km is relatively large in aeolian desertified areas, especially in the agro-pastoral ecotone in China. Many farmlands, pastures, and settlements are facing the problem of sand dunes encroachment. Specific measures to control population growth in aeolian desertified area are as follows:

(1) Working out regional population programming. Population in aeolian desertified areas must be controlled and shouldn't exceed the prescribed limit. The implementation of the family planning policy reduces the rate of population growth. For example, the rate of population growth in some areas of southeastern Ningxia decreased from 33.6‰ to 26.7‰ in 1972; annual population growth rate in some areas of central Gansu Province decreased from 35.8‰ in 1975 to 12.9‰ in 1981.

(2) Reducing population in severely aeolian desertified areas to promote the restoration of environments. For example, some places with better water resources in aeolian desertified areas were chosen to construct new settlements and water projects to change current unstable productive conditions. Resettlement of the surplus population from severely aeolian desertified areas can improve their living standard, lighten population pressures on the land, and benefit aeolian desertification control and environmental sustainable development.

(3) Increasing non-agricultural population and decrease agricultural population in aeolian desertified areas. In aeolian desertified areas, a single economic structure with a high proportion of agricultural populations (Table 16-2) almost entirely depend on land. Increasing the proportion of non-agricultural industries and transferring the agricultural population to industrial and commercial industries (successful examples proved that an industrial population accounting for 40% is suitable considering current productivity levels) are positive countermeasures to improve the economic status and lighten population pressures on land in aeolian desertified areas.

Table 16-2　Percentage of agricultural population in aeolian desertified areas
(located within northern Shaanxi Province)

County	Percentage of agricultural population (%)	Percentage of non-agricultural population (%)
Yulin	82.6	17.4
Shenmu	93.2	6.8
Hengshan	96.6	3.4
Jingbian	96.1	3.9
Dingbian	92.1	7.9

16.2.2.3　Strengthening capital construction of agricultural and pastural industries and improving management

Over-reclamation, over-cutting and over-grazing are not only related to a large population, irrational agricultural structure, distribution and management, but also related to traditional large-scale production methods. Agricultural production and stock raising mainly depend on natural conditions, and especially dry, cold and windy climatic changes resulted in instability of agricultural and animal husbandry in aeolian desertified areas. To improve their living standards, farmers have to reclaim more farmlands or enlarge their grazing area. Their behaviors destroyed vegetation and soil structure, finally leading to the occurrence of aeolian desertification of farmland and grasslands. In most areas, with the increase in population and livestock number, per capita arable land and per animal share of grassland area decreased constantly, intensity of pasture utilization increased, and degraded grassland and aeolian desertified land also increased. Due to the long-term excessive utilization of land, original grassland severely degraded. What should be pointed out is that this kind of extensive management of land violates the principle of sustainable development. It meets people's immediate needs, but result in crises for their future survival and development. So, work need to be done to reinforce capital construction of agricultural and pastoral industries, improve management and change extensive land use into intensive land use.

For the animal husbandry industry, the following measures should be taken in the near future: ① Determine grazing animal number by pasture productivity, gradually improve livestock variety, adjust stock population structure and accelerate stock population turnover; ② Measures such as enclosure, irrigation, and rotational grazing should be adopted to protect natural pastures and appropriate use; ③ Work should be done to construct and expand high-yield grassland and fodder bases, as well as develop forage or fodder processing industries actively; ④ Increase shelters or semi-enclosed feeding systems; ⑤ Rationally arrange grazing and drinking points and roads to mitigate pasture pressure, improve pasture productivity, prevent further degradation and aeolian desertification of pastures, promote further development of the pastoral industry and maintain the equilibrium between livestock population and pasture.

As for agriculture, measures should be taken to prohibit reclaiming grassland, to decrease the area of dry farmland, to prohibit cultivating steep land with a slope of more than 20°–25°, and to transform irrigable land into stable and high yield farmland. In doing so, much more labor, land and funds can be used to plant trees and grasses, combat aeolian desertification and develop animal husbandry.

At the same time, work should be done to protect vegetation and soil. Firstly, measures such as construction of fuel forests, encouraging using coal as fuel, popularizing firedamp, solar stoves, and coal-saving stoves are taken to solve energy source shortage problems of local farmers, herdsmen and citizens; secondly, contracts should be signed between commercial departments and local people to develop reasonable hunting and trading systems and corresponding award and punishment systems to control excessive digging and hunting. In addition, roads and other construction projects should be included in the agenda to try to protect natural vegetation and soil.

16.2.2.4 Construction of modern ecological agricultural system

As mentioned above, transformation from extensive management to intensive management can temporarily mitigate or partly resolve the conflict between aeolian desertification and economic development, but it can't resolve the conflict completely. Though this measure mitigates unreasonable human behaviors such as over-cultivation, over-cutting and over-grazing, it is still impossible to entirely halt aeolian desertification. The best way to halt aeolian desertification is to improve land productivity. Namely, minimum input should be used to get the maximum ecological, economic and social benefits.

Ecological agriculture is the latest development stage of agriculture following primitive agriculture, traditional agriculture and petroleum agriculture. In brief, ecological agriculture is a multitiered, polyschematic, multifunctional agricultural productive system based on past successful examples and ecological and economic theories (Liu Shu, 1982).The basic characteristics of ecological agriculture show that it has the following advantages: maximum green vegetation cover, maximum biological production, most reasonable utilization of photosynthetic products, best economic benefits and best dynamical balance between land and the ecological environment. Ecological agriculture is a complicated system. As far as the material cycle and the process of biological production are concerned, ecological agriculture has two prominent characteristics: first, it is a regeneration system for the material cycle and multitiered utilization of energy based on soil-crop-animal. In this system, biological resources are not only food and fodder but also fuel and fertilizer; each substance can be utilized completely and repeatedly. According to the energy transferring principle, the shorter the food chain, the simpler the structure, and this will result in higher net output. Ecological agriculture makes full use of this principle. For example, in ecological agriculture, straws from crops are not only production energy sources, but also fuel and fertilizer. For instance, after straws have been sugared or aminated, they can be used as livestock fodder and increase the output of livestock. At the same time, livestock dejection can be used to grow edible mushrooms and the remnants of edible mushrooms also can feed earthworms, at last, the remnants utilized by earthworms can be returned to farmland as fertilizer. During this process, all biological products and excrements can be efficiently utilized and transferred. Second, living creatures in ecological agriculture are not isolated but are closely related to and integrated into environment. Ecological agriculture is a process with interaction between humans and their environment. In certain areas, it acts as a dissipative ecological structure with a variable function. Namely it is influenced by both nature and human economic activities, and the important point is that humans regulate and control agricultural productive systems, determine its components, and even interfere in and change natural ecological systems according to their desires. During the process where natural vegetation is replaced by artificial vegetation, all kinds of artificial measures will be taken to strengthen the material and energy cyclic process of ecological systems in order to obtain quality and high biomass and create quality productive conditions and living environments. Ecological agriculture increases the output of primary products greatly, which solves the inconsistency between humans, stock needs and natural resources. Therefore, a large area of degraded pastures can be enclosed and the reversal of aeolian desertification may be accomplished.

16.2.2.5　Different measures to combat different kinds of aeolian desertified lands

According to different degrees of aeolian desertification, there are four kinds of aeolian desertified lands. Different degrees of aeolian desertification can cause different hazards, so different methods or measures are taken to control different kinds of aeolian desertified lands.

(1) Aeolian desertification-prone land (natural pasture or fixed sand dunes). There are almost no or very little significant traces of wind erosion and shifting sand on this kind of land, so most of this kind of land can be utilized continuously. Among these, land with silty soil can be used as agricultural land. Land with sandy soil or aeolian sand can tolerate normal grazing. When used for cultivation or grazing, the most important consideration is that the soil layer shouldn't be destroyed so that underlying paleo-aeolian sand is outcropped, which can result in the occurrence of new sand resources. In isolated locations where there is wind-eroded ground or flakes of shifting sand, measures should be taken to prevent this area from expanding.

(2) Developing aeolian desertified land. This type of land includes silty-soil land and blown sand soil; there is no significant shifting sand, but it generally suffers from soil drifting. Land with thick silty soil can be used as pasture or the base of ecological agriculture. Semi-fixed sandy land can tolerate moderate grazing. The key consideration is to not destroy the surficial layer of silty soil or semi-fixed blown sand soil, otherwise this can lead to the mobilization and advancement of semi-fixed sand dunes. For parts of areas where there is severe soil drifting or shifting sand encroaching, similar measures should be taken to prevent it from further development.

(3) Intensively developing aeolian desertified land. This type of land is completely sandy soil and semi-fixed, with vegetation in interdune areas or at the foot of dunes. Special attention should be paid to this kind of land, because it's a cross between mobile and semi-fixed sandy land. Whether it is treated appropriately or not can result in completely different results. For this kind of land, measures such as natural or artificial enclosures etc. are taken to fix this land step by step. If necessary, grass at interdune area can be cut, but grazing and cultivation are forbidden on this kind of land.

(4) Severe aeolian desertified land. The soil of this land is mobile blown sand soil, with sparse vegetation at interdunes. This land is the source of shifting sand. To prevent enlarging sand hazards while increasing the area of useful land, measures to combat aeolian desertification should be carried out. There is great difficulty in controlling this kind of aeolian desertification. There are two measures. First, if there are good water conditions, water can be channeled to irrigate farmlands and interdune lowlands to construct arboreal and shrubby forests, which can then be partitioned and enclose sand dunes in order to prevent shifting sandy land from advancing or expanding. Because wind force and front sand sources decrease with the forest belt's growth and expansion, each isolated shifting dune is denuded and plant species settle in interdune area. Generally, shifting sand can be fixed about 3–4 years later. After an area of shifting sand has been fixed in this way, water will be channeled to another area of shifting sand to irrigate. This method can be done repeatedly. Secondly, if there are no irrigating conditions or there are great sand dunes that water can hardly reach, mechanical or engineering measures combined with biological measures can be taken to combat

aeolian desertification comprehensively. Before the rainy season comes, clay and plant materials are used to build parallel mechanical sand protection barriers which are 20 cm high, 20–40 cm wide at the foot, with a space of 200 cm to 400 cm between two barriers, and these barriers will be located in the lower 1/3 level of windward slopes. C. *intermedia* Kuang and *Artemisa arenaria* DC. will be planted between barriers, and they can germinate and grow during the rainy season. Because interdune areas and parts of the 1/3–2/3 level of windward slope can almost be fixed this way, the bare top of sand dunes will be denuded by wind, and then the denuded top and leeward slope of sand dunes will be treated in the same way. In this way, a large area of shifting sand will be fixed or semi-fixed. During the course of combating aeolian desertification, the target area should be enclosed to prevent disturbances from humans or livestock. What should be specially pointed out is that low mobile sand dunes around reservoirs or along rivers can be first treated in this measure.

16.2.2.6 Powerful measures to combat aeolian desertification

Combating aeolian desertification is a great ecological construction project, which can change the nature, socioeconomic activity and traditional production ways as well as people's lifestyle customs. This is a shared responsibility for all government officials and peoples and will require a persistent struggle for many generations. So, to ensure the implementation of the above-mentioned measures, the following tasks are essential.

(1) Improving people's awareness through dissemination. Aeolian desertification control is an enormous issue concerning national welfare and people's livelihood, and its success depends on the entire society's hard work. All kinds of ways should be taken to strengthen dissemination of information: aeolian desertification control is to protect national land, to ameliorate the ecological environment and to promote economic development, helping officials and people understand the importance and task of aeolian desertification control, as well as their responsibilities. The occurrence of environmental degradation and aeolian desertification are partly attributed to people and officials' ignorance of ecological and aeolian desertification problems.

(2) Ensuring the right to land use and signing contract responsibility for production and the environment. In China, the state has the right of land ownership, but state-owned enterprises, collectives or people have the right to use land. If the right to use land is not determined, the conflict between land use and land protection will emerge, and over-cultivation, over-cutting and over-grazing will take place. So, it's necessary to confirm the right of land use among state-owned enterprises, collectives and individuals. Although the system of contracted responsibility has been implemented in some areas, contractors only make contracts for production, so they only care about production without considering environmental protection. Therefore, it's imperative to sign contracts for both production and environmental protection. This will encourage contractors to manage their contracted land, pasture, forest and water resources carefully and prevent over-utilization. Furthermore, the intensity of resource utilization should not exceed the elastic limit for

environmental self-recovery. the Chinese Government has promulgated the Land Law, Steppe Law, Forest Law, Environmental Protection Law and Combating Aeolian Desertification Law to protect these resources and environments from destruction. Any person or enterprise that devastates resources or environment will be punished, and will be rewarded for environmental preservation.

(3) Implementation of aeolian desertification control policies. The Chinese central government promulgated several policies to control aeolian desertification, to utilize resources reasonably in desertified areas, to ameliorate ecological environments and promote agricultural or pastoral production. First, aeolian desertification control should be carried out with a planning. Measures should be taken to protect vegetation and prohibit over-cultivation, over-cutting and over-grazing. Secondly, the governments at all levels are in charge of local aeolian desertification control work. The governments in desertified areas should work out detailed plans for aeolian desertification control in consideration of local conditions. Third, the governments should delineate the boundary of desert or desertified land that needs to be fenced to prevent livestock use. All kinds of nature reserves should be gradually built where rare animals and plants live. Enterprises engaging in mining, soil exploitation, road construction and other projects must pay special attention to aeolian desertification control. Funds used to combat aeolian desertification should be raised as much as possible. Fourth, materials used for aeolian desertification control projects such as fertilizer, pesticide, petrol, woods etc. should be included in the national plan for material supplies. Fifth, research projects on desert control and resource exploitation and utilization can be included in national scientific research plans. Measures should be taken to encourage scientists to do research or implement advanced techniques in desertified areas.

(4) Application of science and techniques to control aeolian desertification. We must give top priority to scientific research in the control of aeolian desertification. Furthermore, the aeolian desertification control plan should be worked out based on sufficient surveys and evaluations to further strengthen vegetation protection and ecological agriculture in desertified areas, as well as by generalizing and spreading effective aeolian desertification control experiences and progress. At present, great progress has been made in aeolian desertification control technologies, and there are many successful experiences. These should be widely used to transform scientific achievement into productivity and to accelerate the step of combating aeolian desertification.

16.3 Rehabilitation patterns of aeolian desertified lands in different climatic zones

According to the status of aeolian desertification in China, problems in aeolian desertification control and the integration of ecological, economical and social benefits, more than 50 years of experience in aeolian desertification control can be generalized into several patterns that are suitable to different climatic zones and different natural conditions.

16.3.1 Rehabilitation pattern of aeolian desertification in semi-arid regions

Firstly, the occurrence of aeolian desertification is influenced by a fragile environment, but in the semi-arid region, the aeolian desertification process can cease and will spontaneously restore once intensive human disturbances are removed. In other words, semi-arid zones have ecological resilience. The grazing exclusion method is generally adopted in semi-arid regions (Table 16-3). Even in slightly desertified areas, it's also an effective way. For example, slightly aeolian desertified land around Chaohaimiao of Horqin Zuoyi Houqi in the eastern Horqin Sandy Land gradually recovered by itself with increased vegetation cover and biomass (Table 16-4) after 3 years of enclosure without other artificial measures.

Table 16-3   Effect of enclosures on aeolian desertified land control

Location	Status before enclosure	Period	Vegetation coverage after enclosure (%)
Al Horqin	Shifting sands	1975–1981	70–80
Around Duolun	Abandoned cropland	1968–1981	60
Xi Ujimqin	Semi-fixed sandy lands with spots of shifting sands	1976–1981	65
Ulan Odu of Onugiud Qi	Degraded sandy grassland	1972–1981	80–90

Table 16-4   Changes of vegetation cover and biomass after enclosures around Chaohaimiao of Horqin Zuoyi

Plant Species	Without enclosure		1-year enclosure		2-year enclosure		3-year enclosure	
	Coverage (%)	Output (g/m^2)	Coverage (%)	Output (g/m^2)	Coverage (%)	Output (g/m^2)	Coverage (%)	Output (g/m^2)
A. frigida Willd	30	130	45	228	50	255	65	271
A. halodendron Turcz. ex Bess	30	483	40	642	45	755	45	733
Stechm forbs	45	219	55	310	60	321	70	386
Bothriochloa ischaemum Keng	35	183	40	304	60	392	65	364

Secondly, it is a good measure to readjust the existing land use pattern that does not conform with ecological principles. That is to say, it is essential to change the farming management which is characterized by extensive cultivation and poor harvest, to employ grains as the basis for dry farming, and to enlarge the proportion of forestry and grazing to make them beneficial to both the ecology and the economy. The main points for readjusting the farming structure include cutting down areas of farmland which are influenced by aeolian desertification and to concentrate intensive farming on the beach flats of lake basins and on river valley plains where water conditions are better. The efficacy of readjusting the desertified lands in some typical regions illustrate this issue clearly. For example, Huanghua Tala Commune of Naiman Qi, Inner Mongolia, was sandy grassland with an annual precipitation of about

360 mm. The areas of the desertified lands developed to 81% of the total land area in the commune due to over-reclamation and over-cutting. Since the 1970s, the land used for dry farming has been readjusted. Consequently the proportion of forest and forage has been enlarged; measures such as combining tree, shrubs and grass, and planting tree belts and woodlots have been adopted. At present, the proportion of agriculture, forestry and grazing lands has been readjusted to 21 : 52 : 27. The desertified lands have been preliminarily controlled, the total grain output has been increased by 3.36 times, and the aeolian desertification process has been basically brought under control.

The readjustment of land use structure centered on dry farming in Sijinzi Village of Tongyu County in western Jilin Province represents a successful example of controlling aeolian desertification. Sijinzi Village of Tongyu County is located northwest of the county city where aeolian desertification was developing and aeolian desertification land accounts for 34.9% of total area with an annual precipitation of 407.2 mm. Owing to over-reclamation of grassland, natural vegetation had been destroyed and the forestry and grazing lands were replaced by agricultural lands. As a result, the proportion of agriculture, forestry and grazing lands was changed from 2 : 1.5 : 6.5 in the late 1950s to 4 : 1 : 5 in the 1970s. In the late 1970s, land use patterns centered on dry farming was changed, and the proportion of agriculture, forestry and grazing lands was adjusted to 1 : 1 : 3. In 1984, it was readjusted to 1.5 : 2.5 : 6, and vegetation cover increased from 6.8% to 16.3%. Therefore, the ecological environment was ameliorated and shifting sands were controlled. After the construction of field protective forest, the intensity of wind erosion decreased. As a result, per livestock share of forage was increased from 1,850 kg to 3,000 kg; the cultivated area decreased by 58.33%, but gross yield increased by 1.4% because of the increased per unit output. Peasants in this village only engaged in agriculture, but now they engaged in mixed farming, so per capita income increased from 177 *yuan* to 500 *yuan*, and the economy of this village was greatly improved. At the same time, aeolian desertified land has been reversed, and both ecological and economic benefits were gained. The same examples can be seen in Mangkeng Village of Yulin County in the Mu Us Sandy Land.

According to research work of land use structure in typical areas, the optimal proportion of land use is different in different aeolian desertified aeolian areas (Table 16-5). It's partly due to different aeolian desertification degrees and landscape. The more severe the aeolian desertification, and the more complicated the landscape structure, the proportion of forest and grass should be higher.

Table 16-5   The optimal proportion of land use in different aeolian desertified areas

Characteristics of aeolian desertified land	Proportion of land use (%)		
	Farming	Forestry	Grazing
The developing aeolian desertified land with slight wind erosion and sand deposition	61	20	19
The developing aeolian desertified land with coarsening surface	47	27	26
The developing aeolian desertified land with coppice dunes	29	30	41
Intensively developed aeolian desertified land with shifting sands and fixed, semi-fixed dunes	15	30	55
Severely developed aeolian desertified land with beach flat in lake basins and mobile sandy dunes	10	40	50

The adjustment of land use structure should be combined with the construction of capital farmland, and enlarging the proportion of forestry and grazing land can gain ecological and economic benefits. For example, Baiyin Tala of Eleshun in Hure Qi of the southern Horqin Sandy Land was a desertified area with mobile sand dunes and interdune area in the past. After adopting measures to combat aeolian desertification, each farmer had 0.33 hm^2 farmland, 0.5 hm^2 woodlands and 6 heads of livestocks, with an annual income of about 300 *yuan*, what's more, 82% of aeolian desertified land has been controlled.

Thirdly, the proportion of forestry and livestock raising should be increased. Besides enlarging the proportion of forestry and grazing land, the system of shelter feeding or half shelter feeding should be popularized. This will require establishment of proper artificial grassland and forage farms to supplement the insufficient forage supply on the natural grazing fields. Owing to the combination of livestock breeding and farmland, both straw and green manure can be use as supplemental forage. This method possesses very important significance to livestock development, and also provides an example of economic efficacy. For example, in the counties in the sandy areas of Yulin, the value created by each person engaged in livestock breeding is 1.38 times more than that created by each person engaged in agriculture.

Fourthly, another measure includes recovering the natural vegetation on the desertified lands without decreasing productive potential. The exclusion of grazing animals should be emphasized. Afforestation should be practiced on sand dunes. Shrub or grass should be planted in depressions. The fixation of shifting sands on both sides of the railway near Naiman in the Horqin Sandy Land and Dayijianfang, Zhanggutai and Hongshixia, Yulin in the Mu Us Sandy Land are successful examples. There was severely desertified land with numerous mobile sand dunes along the Naiman section of the Jing–Tong Railway. Vegetation was planted to fix mobile sandy dunes, and engineering measures were also taken. The protection system consists of arbor (mainly *P.silvestris* L. var. mongolica Litv), shrub (mainly *A. halodendron* Turcz. Ex Bess, *S. gordejevii* Chang et Skv. and *C. microphylla* Lam), tame grassland and enclosed natural vegetation, which prevented the development of shifting sands and ensured the smooth operation of the railway. As a result, the vegetation cover increased from less than 10% before treatment to the current 30%–50%, and the velocity of sand flow decreased by 60%–70%; the content of surficial organic matters also increased and was 6–8 times that of shifting sands; the content of fine particles less than 0.01 mm increased by 2–4 times. The severely aeolian desertified land began to reverse. Table 16-6 is an example of environmental changes after aeolian desertified land has been controlled.

Table 16-6   Environmental changes after aeolian desertified land has been controlled (Sanjiazi Zhangwu)

Contrast	Percentage of different landscape (%)			
	Patch of shifting sand	Land slightly eroded by wind	Speckled shifting sand	Slightly desertified land
Past	44	25	9	22
Present	8	4	6	82

The farmland protection networks should be established in the beachflats. Also the tree networks should be planted on the alluvial plains of rivers to prevent the basic farmland from being damaged by wind and sand. The Yuxi River Basin in Yulin County in the southern Mu Us Sandy Land is a typical example.

In other words, the land use structure of grazing, forestry and agriculture integrated organically should be established in semi-arid regions with consideration of local conditions, namely by integrating the structure of commercial stockbreeding, protective forestry and self-sufficient agriculture. This structure should center on beachflats and river valley plains. Aeolian desertified land in the agro-pastoral ecotone will be controlled step by step only if the above mentioned artificial ecological system is established.

The above measures can be generalized as a rehabilitation pattern shown in Fig. 16-3.

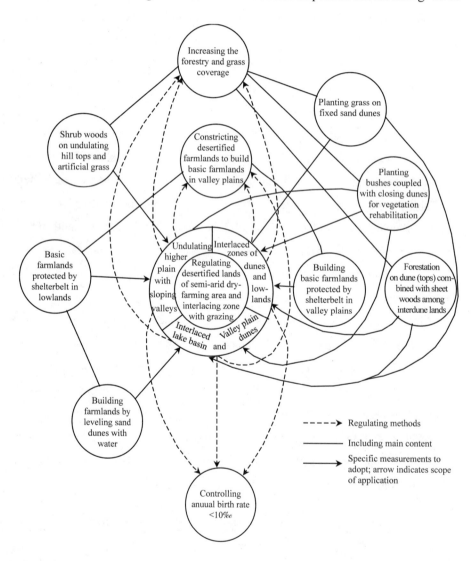

Fig. 16-3 Rehabilitation pattern of aeolian desertified land in the agro-pastoral ecotone of semi-arid regions

Besides determining reasonable carrying capacity, popularizing reasonable rotational grazing and establishing a grassland and forage base, aeolian desertification land control in grazing areas of semi-arid regions still requires appropriate allocation of well density and road construction.

16.3.2 Rehabilitation pattern of aeolian desertified land in arid regions

The development of aeolian desertification in arid region is attributable to the irrational utilization of water resources in the downstream basin, but also results from vegetation destruction at the margin of oases which leads to the activation and advancement of sand dunes. So, measures should be taken shows as follows:

(1) Using the inland river basin as an ecological unit to develop an overall plan. In accordance with the principles of overall consideration of all factors in the upper, middle and lower reaches of rivers it's important to unify the management and utilization of surface and underground water resources, to reasonably allocate the water supply along the river, to implement the regulation of regional general layout and the structure of irrigated oases which rely on water supply, and to establish stable and highly efficient artificial ecosystems in the river valley. Therefore, it's necessary to adjust the degree of land use and exploitation to correspond with the maximum irrigating capacity, namely to determine the area of farmland according to the volume of available water resources.

(2) Using irrigated oases as a center to plant sand blocking belts of grasses (using the surplus water in the winter season) at the outskirts of oases, to plant sand break forests consisting of trees and shrubs at the margin of oases, and to establish farmland protection networks and windbreaks in the interior of oases, such as in Turpan and the Hotan Oasis.

(3) Regarding the shifting dunes around the edges of oases, sand barriers should be planted on shifting dunes and sand binders should be planted inside, and sand barriers and shrubs should be established in the interdune areas to create a comprehensive protective system, like Pingchuan in the northern Linze Oasis in Gansu province. At the same time, measures should be taken to protect natural forest and shrub clumps in the marginal area of oases and in deserts.

During the rehabilitation process of aeolian desertified land in arid regions, efforts should be made to rehabilitate land in the marginal areas of desert and on inland river banks with good water and soil conditions by using these methods in combination with the construction of irrigation works, establishment of farmland protection networks and soil a melioration. The Shihezi–Kuitun area at the southwestern edge of the Gurbantünggüt Desert and some oases in middle reaches of the Tarim River at the northern edge of the Taklimakan Desert are typical examples.

The fixation of shifting sands to exploit available land resources around oases in arid regions, as well as the construction of new oases, are essentially the combination of reconstructing and utilizating aeolian desertified land, which are also the two basic points of aeolian desertification control. The commutative combination and supplement of these two aspects can only ensure the gain of ecological and economic benefits. The data in Table 16-7 show the changes of landscapes around oases before and after combating aeolian desertification. On one hand, it shows the decrease of severe aeolian desertified land and intensely developing aeolian desertified land; on the other hand, it shows that part of the aeolian desertified land has been changed into woodland and orchards, the productivity of degraded land has recovered, and aeolian desertification is beginning to reverse.

For the areas encroached by mobile sand dunes in arid regions, measures to fix shifting sands should be taken, especially where roads pass through.

Table 16-7   Changes in landscape area around oases before and after combating aeolian desertification
(Pingchuan sand control station in Linze)

Landscape	Area　(%)	
	Before	After
Intensively developing aeolian desertification land	17.8	0.4
Shifting sand dunes	54.6	9.4
Reversed aeolian desertification land	9.0	52.4
Insusceptible farmland	8.9	37.8
Badland	9.7	

According to many people's experience in the rehabilitation of aeolian desertified land and related experiments in the marginal areas of deserts in arid regions, the measures to combat aeolian desertification can be generalized into the patterns shown in Fig. 16-4.

Fig. 16-4   Main techniques to control aeolian desertification

16.4　Measures to control aeolian desertification

16.4.1　Vegetative method

National and international practices have proven that vegetative or biological methods to combat desertification are basic measures to fix shifting sand and control aeolian desertification. Mechanical sand barriers (artificial sand barrier) and spraying chemicals are temporary measures. They can be used to stabilize sand surfaces and create a stable ecological environment for the establishment of artificial vegetation or for the rehabilitation of natural vegetation on sand dunes and wind-eroded lands (Zhu et al. 1998).

The vegetative method primarily includes the establishment of artificial vegetation or rehabilitation of natural vegetation; establishment of sand break forest belts to prevent shifting sand from encroaching on oases, traffic lines, towns and other facilities; establishment of protective forest nets to prevent farmland from being eroded by wind and pasture from degradation; protection of natural vegetation to prevent fixed and semi-fixed sand dunes and sandy grassland from suffering aeolian desertification.

It should be pointed out that the type of protection system in sandy regions of China has been transformed from the traditional ecotype to an eco-economic type. Namely, during the processes of shifting sand stabilization and aeolian desertification control over a large area, there should be appropriate construction of timber, economic, and fuel forests, reconstruction of vegetation in pastures, rational utilization of artificial vegetation, enlargement of present oases and capital farmland and development of agriculture, forestry, stockbreeding, fishery and other industries to improve the living standard of people in sandy regions.

Using the vegetative method for combating desertification has the following six main points:

(1) The artificial, artificial-natural and natural vegetation on mobile and semi-fixed sand dunes can prevent sand dunes and sandy land from wind erosion and make them fixed permanently by covering the sand surface and reducing wind velocity;

(2) The constructed vegetation can improve the properties of barren shifting sand and promote the formation of sandy soil;

(3) The constructed vegetation can ameliorate the ecological conditions above and under the covered area, which is beneficial for living organisms' reproduction;

(4) The constructed vegetation can propagate and regenerate by itself, even short life-span pioneer plants constructed on mobile sand dunes can evolve into stable ecological systems with abundant plant species through automatic adjustment;

(5) The combined arbor-shrub-subshrub-forage vegetation is not only appropriate for grazing but also supply firewoods and timber;

(6) A sand dune is a complicated system, and it includes sand dunes, interdune areas, flat interdune bottomland (meadow) and sandy flat. After the advancement of shifting sand and wind erosion is controlled by vegetation, farmlands, orchards, melon land and forage bases, and even new villages can be established on fertile lands protected by vegetation.

Obviously, vegetal sand stabilization is by no means an easy job. The choice of sand-binding species depends on biogeographic zone, and therefore different sand-binding plants are chosen in consideration of local conditions all over the world. At the same time, the choice of sand-binding plants and afforestation tree species is also limited by local ecological conditions. Moreover, the success or failure of the vegetative method depends on the amount of sand surface wind erosion that can be controlled.

16.4.2　Checkerboard sand barriers

During the practice of sand control, mechanical measures are generally taken to fix a large area of shifting sand, and different standard grids or rows of sand barriers made of different kinds of materials (such as straw, reed, clay, and gravel) are extensively adopted. In general, several rows of sand barriers are adopted where the prevailing wind direction is singular, and the checkerboard sand barrier is used where the prevailing wind is multi-directional. A sand barrier is a basic protection measure to control blown sand hazards. It alters the properties of the underlying surface and increases the roughness of the ground surface.

When sand flows over straw checkerboard sand barriers, eddy and sand deposition take place. After long term wind erosion and deposition, a stable and smooth concave curved surface develops, with an average ratio of maximum depth to sand barrier border length of approximately $1:10$. Regular wavy underlying surfaces composed of this kind of stable curved surface can produce an uplifting force, which ensures that surficial sand can't be blown away and sand blown from other places can pass. Because this kind of underlying surface has an "uplifting effect", it can lift up sand that comes from other places.

A checkerboard sand barrier is characterized by increasing surficial roughness, decreasing the velocity of near surface airflow, thereby decreasing airflow's capacity for transporting sand and changing the transportation rate distribution at different heights. Checkerboard sand barriers are effective where the prevailing wind is multi-directional. When a checkerboard sand barrier is built, an upright sand barrier is also constructed at the windward side to prevent sand from depositing in front of the sand-fixation belt and resulting in a more efficient sand-fixation belt. A $1:10$ height to width ratio for the checkerboard sand barrier is best. The general standard for checkerboard sand barriers is 1 m×1 m, and this is cheap and effective. Plastic net made into larger 2 m×2 m or 3 m×3 m checkerboard sand barriers in Algeria were also effective. Flexible materials are better than rigid ones. It has been proven that sand barriers made of rigid concrete bars are not effective for blocking wind and could easily cause wind erosion. Stripe sand barriers are effective where the prevailing wind is unidirectional and sand barriers can be installed vertical to the prevailing wind direction. Debris leftover from a highcrop in farmlands is an effective measure to prevent sand hazards in farmland near deserts. Vegetative method combined with chemical measures to fix sand are the most effective methods in industrial and mining areas or along road lines where sand hazards are very severe.

16.4.3　Upright sand fences

Sand-fixing measures have a very obvious protective effect, but sand deposited in front of sand fences often causes a large area of sand-fixing belts to lose their function. This can result in the formation of new passages of sand flow and the occurrence of new sand hazards. Therefore, sand-fixing measures should be combined with sand-blocking measures.

Upright sand fences are built at the upwind frontal edges to block sand sources and promote the formation of high sand-blocking dikes which can prevent sand from depositing at the upwind frontal edges and change the transporting capacity of airflow. But it only can be built at the upwind edges, above 2/3 the height of the windward slope and beneath the crest line, and it should be set vertical to the prevailing wind direction (Zhu et al. 1998).

16.4.3.1　Influencing factors

(1) Height. The height of sand fences is determined by the local transportation rate. If it is too low, it will be quickly buried by sand. If sand fences are rebuilt frequently, it's expensive and in convenient. But if the sand fence is too high, it's very difficult to be fixed. In general, 1 m is a suitable height.

(2) Porosity. Indoor and field experiments have proven the porosity of sand fences is the most important factor influencing its protective effect. The protective effect includes: ① Sand-trapping capacity; ② Effective protection distance. For dense fences with a porosity of zero, it also can block sand, but its protective range in front of and behind the fence is shorter than its height. With an increase in porosity, the protective range and effect also increase. When the porosity is 30%–40%, the protective effect is optimal.

(3) Relationship between sand source, wind regime, possible transportation rate and fence location. Sand source, wind velocity and duration determine the sand transport rate. Sand transport rate determines the choice of fence. The fence should be located at a high position and at an area where it can't be eroded by wind. To prevent the erosion of the fence base, 2–4 rows of checkerboard sand fences are built at the windward base.

In order to assess the protective effect of sand fences, we define the ratio (K%) of the fence's sand-trapping quantity (Q_0) per unit width (m) to the corresponding possible maximum sand transport rate (Q_p) per unit width, namely K= Q_0/ Q_p×100%, as the sand-trapping efficiency of sand fences, which is closely related to fence height, porosity, strike and fence location. It should be pointed out that the sand-trapping efficiency of sand fences is variable and it decreases with the increase of deposited sand volume. Because sand flow is blocked, sand flow direction becomes parallel to the sand mound strike. In fact, multi-directional wind also influences sand-trapping efficiency directly. For example, the average K value is 70%–80% in the Shapotou area, with a maximum value of 96.5%, and the protective range is 7.5–11.3 times the height of the fence.

16.4.3.2　Applicable conditions and range sand fences

(1) Sand fences are effective in shifting sand areas where the prevailing wind direction is singular. If combined with sand-fixing measures, the protection system of "laying emphasis on fixation in combination with block" can prevent sand hazards effectively. For coarse flat sandy land or gravel land, single sand fences can be used, but they should be built on the windward side at a long distance from the protected target. If necessary, a sand-blocking system of multilevel sand fences can be adopted.

(2) Upright sand fences have been widely used to block sand and snow abroad. For example, to control snow on roads, the former USSR and America set a slot at the bottom of barriers which causes the airflow to accelerate and blow away snow on the road to deposit at the leeward side of the road. So, sand can deposit constantly and much sand accumulation can result in a new hazard; the cost is expensive. In the sand-preventing experiments along the Nanjiang Railway and snow-preventing experiments along the Tianshan Road in China, the "Feathered Transporting Sand (Snow) Measure" was adopted. It divides fences into many little segments, and the single fence is arranged parallel according to certain trend spacing. It's characterized by utilizing the energy conversion function to change the direction of sand flow, accelerate wind velocity and blow sand away, with a transportation rate of 65%–90%.

Of course, there are also other sand-transporting measures which can divert sand flow. For example, the section of road in desert can be designed in a streamlined form or with a 1 ：8 gentle slope, which thereby enhance sand transport capacity, and therefore no sand deposition takes place near the road shoulder. Gravel platforms along both sides of the railway in desert ares has a double protection function: first, the gravel layer can fix shifting sand; second it has a strong rebound function for sand particles and has a non-accumulative transport function for the passing sand flow.

The above-mentioned four kinds of sand control measures are also known as "fixation, block, transport and diversion" measures. Theoretic analysis and practices have proven that sand-fixing measures are the most practical and effective measures to prevent sand damages. Because this measure can dissipate wind energy, sand-blocking is a necessary measure that ensures the sand-fixing measure can be completely effective. Under special conditions, the sand-fixing measure also can be used alone with obvious results.

Practices also showed that different measures should be taken in consideration of local conditions. Moreover, different measures should be appropriately combined because no single measure is perfect.

16.4.4 Combination of different measures

Construction and arrangement of protective systems are determined by the characteristics of flow field and method or intensity of sand movement. Common arrangement schemes are as follows:

16.4.4.1 Protective system dominated by "fixation" and combined with "block" and "transport" and "diversion"

This is a sand control measure suitable for controlling large areas of shifting sand. It's not only effective and practical but also accords with the principles of theoretical aeolian sand physics. Concretely speaking, sand-blocking belts at the front edge can effectively control sand sources; sand-fixing belts can stabilize the sand surface, change the property of the underlying surface and control the condition of sand movement efficiently or creates conditions for vegetative sand stabilization. If local natural conditions are better, plants can be used as fences, which are called "living sand barriers". The length of this protective system should be determined in accordance with the protected targets (such as railway or roads).

The width of the protective system (protection width) is entirely determined by the migration speed of local mobile sand dunes, or by the local possible maximum resultant transportation rate and direction. According to experiences in Shapotou, the effective protection width is 130 m on the northern side of the railway. Even in extremely arid regions, we believe the protective width of 150–200 m is wide enough when the migration speed of mobile sand dunes is less than 1m/a.

16.4.4.2 Protective system dominated by "block" and combined with "transport"

This method is applicable to coarse flat sandy land and gravel land. There may be two possible situations: the sand source is distant and not abundant, or the sand source is close, but it has an uneven distribution, such as low barchan dunes area at the edge of the desert and interdune flats in the desert interior.

The common characteristics of these areas are flat and open topography, strong wind, and a course and limited sand source. With sand movement processes, once it encounters obstacles such as a roadbed, vegetation, etc., shifting sand will deposit and can result in sand damage. Therefore, sand-blocking belts need to be built on the windward side located far from the protected target. Because no protective measures are taken between sand-blocking belts and the protected target, small amounts of sand material may be transported and deposited near the protective system and lead to slight sand damage. Sand- transporting and sand-passing measures can be taken to resolve this kind of sand damage. In practice, a single protection measure can also be adopted; for instance, clay or gravel is used to completely cover the surface of sand dunes.

16.4.5　Chemical dune stabilization

In the 1930s, oil-prospecting workers in deserts sprayed crude oil on sand dune surfaces to prevent blown sand hazards and protect oil equipment. From then on, the concept of chemical dune stabilization came into existence, which gave birth to a new and active research field. Inspired by dune stabilization using crude oil, people have done more work to develop new sand-fixing materials. As a result, a series of sand-fixing materials and organic or inorganic stabilizers have been developed.

Up to now, chemical dune stabilization has a history of 70 years, but it developed rapidly and has become one of the important sand-fixing measures in arid regions threatened by blown sand damages, especially in desert zones with abundant oil resources. Chemical dune stabilization can be divided into the following forms:

(1) Covering sand surface. Asphalt petroleum products or latex are sprayed on sand surfaces. Due to strong absorption and electrical function of sand particles, they can only form a thin and weak protective layer.

(2) Binding function. Almost all chemical sand-fixing materials have this property. After a chemical sand-fixing liquid occupies the interspaces between sand particles, the action between particles can be increased, and hence they form a bonding layer.

(3) Hydration. For instance, action between concrete and sand particles can form a strong and hard bonding layer.

(4) Sedimentation function. When water glass and intensifiers are used as sand-fixing materials, they infiltrate and occupy the interspaces between sand particles, and the intensifier deposits and forms a strong and hard protective structure.

(5) Polymerization. As polymer and latex are used to control sand, they can form an elastic or rigid bonding structure.

The principles of chemical dune stabilization are complicated; it's not only related to the properties (such as chemical composition and mechanical composition) of sand particles, but also related to the chemical and physical properties (such as molecular structure, absorbability, and viscosity) of chemical sand-fixing materials.

References

Dong Guangrong, Gao Shangyu. 1993. Land Aeolian Desertification and Prevention Measures in Gonghe Basin of Qinghai Province. Beijing: Science Press

Liu Shu. 1982. The application of ecological principles in aeolian desertification land control. Journal of Biology, (1): 2–9

Liu Xinmin. 1982. Discussion of aeolian desertification control in northern Linze Oases of Gansu Province. Journal of Desert Research, 2 (3): 9–15

Shapotou Station of Desert Experimental Research, Cold and Arid Region Environmental and Engineering Institue, CAS. 1980. Study of Shifting Sand Control in Shapotou in Tengger Desert. Yinchuan: Ningxia People's Publishing House

Zhu Zhenda, Chen Guangting. 1994. Aeolian Desertification in China. Beijing: Science Press

Zhu Zhenda, Liu Shu, Di Xingmin. 1989. Aeolian Desertification and Control in China. Beijing: Science Press

Zhu Zhenda, Zhao Xingliang, Ling Yuquan et al. 1998. Sandy Land Rehabilitation Engineering. Beijing: Science Press

Zhu Zhenda. 1992. The trend of aeolian desertification land in China and basic sand control pattern. China Science Fund, (1)

Chapter 17
Blown Sand Hazards and Their Control Measures

17.1 Causes of blown sand hazards and their basic features

Wind is one of the active agents for shaping landforms in northern China, and its related blown sand hazards can cause some of the most serious natural calamities in desert regions of northwest China. The area of arid and semi-arid regions suffering from blown sand hazards in northern China accounts for 30% of the total land area in China. If including the wind-blown sandy land in the Qinghai-Tibet Plateau, its area will reach up to 50%. Chinese dry agriculture and animal husbandry are primarily distributed in these regions, where there are extensive soil resources, abundant biologic resources and mine materials, and also many human inhabitants. Blown sand hazards resulting from sand drifting activity heavily affects people's health and economic development. Along with the more harmonious development between the social economy and the environment, utilization of new resources, and increasing environmental protection awareness, blown sand hazards need to be understood more completely to develop a theoretical basis and methods for preventing blown sand hazards.

17.1.1 Causes of the formation of blown sand hazards

Blown sand movement includes materials deflation, transportation and re-deposition under wind power conditions. Blown sand hazards are mainly wind and sand-drift flow that destroy crops, farm implements and constructions over a long term. Blown sand movement is the outcome of aeolian desertification. Therefore, blown-sand hazards assist aeolian desertification. Formation of blown sand activity requires two conditions: one is sufficient strong wind as a dynamic condition and the other is easily entrained loose surface deposits as a material base.

17.1.1.1 Dynamic conditions for blown-sand activity

Not all wind acting on sandy surfaces can cause blown-sand activity, and only a critical wind velocity greater than the threshold wind velocity for sand entrainment can cause blown sand activity. Different underlying surfaces have different values of threshold wind velocity, which is closely related to grain size composition, vegetation canopy above a surface, etc.

(1) The climate background of wind conditions. Because of atmospheric pressure distribution patterns and monsoon cyclical systems caused by the ocean-land distribution of Eurasia and the Pacific Ocean as well as the uplift of the Qinghai-Tibet Plateau, the northern region of China, located a far distance from oceans in the continental interior, suffers from the Siberian-Mongolian cold high pressure system in winter, so the climate is cold and arid; but in summer, within the shelter of high mountains and plateaus, the moist monsoon hardly these regions, and the climate is mainly characterized by high temperatures and low rainfall. Therefore, the weather is dry and has an obvious territorial climate in most regions of northern China. The four characteristics are aridity and less rain, intense sunlight, violent temperature change and strong wind power. Vegetative canopies are very small, due to weathering and accumulation of salinity action under arid climates and strong wind conditions. Moreover, large areas of desert and Gobi in northwest China make wind power more strong and wind action is the main agent shaping topographical features.

(2) Seasonal change of wind power. There is an obvious seasonal change of wind power action in northern China. Wind power and its occurrence frequency are very high in winter and spring, especially strong winds larger than force 8. These Types of days are mainly concentrated in the spring, accounting for 40%–70% of the number of days with strong wind in a year. This is because the Siberian-Mongolian cold high pressure system controls the Mongolian Plateau and the Siberian region in winter, and a unique cold high pressure airflow caused by the Qinghai-Tibet Plateau and intensifies the effects of the ridge. When high-pressure airflow moves southward, it has a direct and strong impact on northern China. Because the Siberian-Mongolian high pressure system is relatively weaker and its activity is more frequent in spring, there are always strong winds and cold airflow. Therefore, blown-sand activity in the sand regions of northern China is very frequent in winter and spring, though most notably in spring.

17.1.1.2　Material base for blown sand activity (earth surface and its coverage)

The formation of blown sand activity is closely related to the material composition above the surface, including grain size, loose or clay aggregated: moisture, and the vegetation cover.

(1) Granularity composition. The granularity here not only refers to the size of seperated sand particles, but also refers to soil aggregates and clods. According to previous research, the size of sand grains entrained under a given wind velocity has more difference. Under normal conditions, the size of grains entrained by wind is less than 1mm, but under strong enough wind conditions, grains with 2–3 mm diameter can be blown away. The grain size in deserts and aeolian desertified land in China is mostly centralized in the range of 0.1–0.25 mm. For normally dry and bare sandy surfaces, with many experiment and observations in field, sand particles begin to initiate and form sand-drifting flow when wind velocity at the high of 2 m above the surface reaches to 4 m/s ($\geqslant$5 m/s wind vane wind velocity at the meteorological station).

(2) Moisture conditions. When sand is in a wet condition, its surface can form a layer of moisture film which can bind neighboring particles together. Static gravitation among water molecule can make grain-grained viscidity increase, and increase the binding energy between particles. Therefore, threshold of entrainment for sand grains will be enhanced (Table 17-1).

Table17-1　Influence of sand grain size and percentage of containing water on threshold of entrainment

Sand grain size (mm)	Initiated wind velocity(m/s)				
	Dry conditions	Percentage of containing water (%)			
		1	2	3	4
2.0–1.0	9.0	10.8	12.0		
1.0–0.5	6.0	7.0	9.5	12.0	
0.5–0.25	4.8	5.8	7.5	12.0	
0.25–0.175	3.8	4.6	6.0	10.5	12.0

17.1.1.3　Vegetation conditions

Vegetation conditions include earth surface property and canopy status of plants and other shelters. Earth surface property determines roughness length. Initiated velocity of sand grain under coarseness surface will be increased due to more friction drag.

Soil moisture and vegetation conditions in a region depend on the precipitation. Inter-annual amplitude and seasonal distribution of precipitation have obvious differences in most regions of northern China. For example, between 1949 to 1989 the highest amount of precipitation in the Beijing region was 1,406.0 mm (1959), but the lowest amount of precipitation was 261.5 mm (1965). Owing to large amplitude of precipitation, inter-annual change of vegetation canopy above the surface, especially for herbage vegetation, takes place often. Even after a severe drought year, vegetation canopy begins to decrease rapidly, and needs several or ten years to restore its original canopy. The decrease in vegetation coverage makes the earth surface bare, provides advantageous conditions for wind action on sandy surfaces, and results in more frequent blown sand hazards. In addition, there is a severe disparity in the seasonal distribution of precipitation. Under normal conditions, the precipitation is very low in winter and spring, and is relatively abundant in summer and autumn. In the Horqin Sandy Land and the Ulanqab grassland region, precipitation in spring only accounts for 8%–13% of the total precipitation in a year. Especially in spring, the lower precipitation not only makes surfaces dry and limits water content of the soil, but also restricts surface plants from striking root, coming into bud and reviving. Therefore, the vegetation canopy restores slowly in spring and it is also the lowest in the year. But in this period, wind power is also the strongest in a year. Therefore, the concurrence of arid season and strong wind provides advantageous conditions for blown sand hazards at this time (Table 17-2).

Table 17-2　Percentage of strong wind and precipitation in spring during a year in northern sandy region of China

Site	Percentage of strong wind (%)	Percentage of precipitation (%)
Tonyliao	61.71	11.90
Ganqika	64.86	12.81
Erlian	49.70	10.90
Zhurihe	40.70	12.30
Damao Qi	42.90	8.20
Shangdu	41.20	13.10

From Zhu, Z.D., et al. (1989)

17.1.1.4　Function of climate change in the formation of wind-blown sand hazards

Eastern of China is located in the East Asian monsoon region, but the Qinghai-Tibet Plateau affects the total climate situation. The location of Mongolia high pressure, intensity of southeast subtropical high pressure directly impacts climate changes every year, such as the regions with rain, precipitation intensity, the actions of strong wind and cold wave, and the numbers of typhoon landing and its intensity. These factors of climate have a cyclical variation. From the data of the Beijing region, it can be found, since the 1950s that both the number of strong wind events and their intensity increased in the 1970s.

Geophysicists always seek for the reason of climate change in earth from El Nino and La Nina events, except for sunspots and sun storms. These two phenomena have already been explained in the previous chapter, so we don't give unnecessary details. Either the normally short-term fluctuation of precipitation or long-term dry-wet changes resulted by global warming will affect the formation of blown sand hazards and their intensity. Annual precipitation variation impacts vegetation distribution and its canopy. Sustained drought over several years will make rivers dry or cause diversion, and decreasing levels of underground water Thus indirectly limits vegetation distribution and its canopy. All of the above factors accelerate the formation and intensity of blown sand hazards, and sometimes can even exceed the action of wind power. Contrarily, if the precipitation increases, vegetation cover and distribution will be increased thus effectively preventing or restricting blown-sand hazards.

17.1.1.5　Function of human activities in the formation of blown sand hazards

Effects of human activities on the formation of blown sand hazards are due to in-harmonious development between excessive economic activities and environmental resources, which destroys vegetation in vulnerable ecological environments directly or indirectly, and causes the sandy surface originally covered with vegetation to become bare. Under conditions of wind erosion, the sand-driving wind occurs and does harm to people's life and production.

(1) Excessive human activities directly destroy the vegetation canopy. Excessive cultivation,

grazing and wood-chopping in grassland regions characterized by strong winds are the main human activities that damage vegetation cover.

(2) Irrational human activities change ecological conditions in vegetation distribution region, and this indirectly damages vegetation conditions. For example, changing water systems and water resources distribution will lead to irreversible deficiency of water conditions in some regions. Altering anti-erosion capacity and vegetation canopy condition, the surface will be exposed to wind forces, and the sand-driving wind begins to occur (Zhu, 1998).

17.1.2　Basic characteristics of blown sand hazards

17.1.2.1　Temporal and spatial characteristics of blown sand hazards

(1) Temporal characteristics of blown sand hazards. The temporal characteristics of blown sand hazards still rely on natural and human factors and their interaction. Inter-annual variations of blown sand hazards is determined by dry-wet fluctuations in climate, wind regime, and the impacted degree of human actions on ground vegetation. When the climate remains dry for several years and the destruction of human actions on vegetation is very serious, blown sand hazards are also intensified. Seasonal change of blown sand hazards is closely related to apparent continental climate attribution and seasonal feature of agricultural production. Blown sand hazards are mainly concentrated in winter and spring in most northern regions of China, though most notably in spring. Because it has more wind and a drier climate in spring, vegetation is in a dormant state and its canopy is the lowest of the year. In addition, once sandy surface has been plowed and loosened in winter, it will supply enough erodible materials for the formation of blown sand hazards.

(2) Spatial characteristics of blown sand hazards. Blown sand hazards are mainly distributed over arid, semiarid and even some semi-humid areas in northern China, as well as the entire Qinghai-Tibet Plateau. They include the western region of northeast China and the northern and northwest regions of northern China, and they effect Inner Mongolian Autonomous Region, Xinjiang Uygur Autonomous Region, Tibet, Gansu, Qinghai, Ningxia, Shanxi, Shaanxi, Hebei, Liaoning, and Jilin Province. There is not a lot of research concerning spatial differentiation of blown sand hazards degree. Some scholars have assessed and partitioned aeolian desertification hazards danger in northern China, and divide 16 danger regions of aeolian hazards, in which the most severity has five, named: ① severe regions of Horqin with 7 counties (Qi); ② severe regions of the Bashang and Houshan including Bashang of Hebei Province, south five Qis of Xilin Gol Meng and some regions of Houshan in Ulanqab Meng; ③ severe regions of Ordos including 5 counties in northern Shanxi Province and 6 counties of Yikzhao Meng in Inner Mongolia, in most of which is in farming-pastoral zone; ④ severe regions of Ningxia Hui Autonomous Region including Shizuishan City and Zhongwei County; ⑤ severe regions of the Qinghai-Tibet Plateau including the entire

northern Tibet Plateau, "Yarlung Zangbo River and its two tributaries" of south Tibet, and " three basins", "three-river fountain" regions of Qinghai Province. These five regions can basically be regarded as regions with severe blown sand hazards.

17.1.2.2　Modes of blown sand hazards

(1) Damage of blown sand to agriculture and pasture. Once a surface suffers from wind erosion, soil fertility of farmland and pasture will degrade and their yields will decrease, with organic content and nutrient blow away by wind. For example, there is 0.877 million hm^2 of farmland in the Houshan area of Ulanqab Meng, 0.327 million hm^2 of them has 1cm-thick erosion surface soil every year, and 0.067 million hm^2 of them has 3 cm-thick one. Because of sand cutting or sand burying of sand-driving wind on crop and forage grasses, normally growth of plant will be limited. If seeds of plants have been entrained or sand burying, people have to replant them. Besides, due to deposition of wind blown sand, farmland and pasture will suffer from burying of sand accumulation. Even more, it can form some sand dunes and directly cause soil resources loss.

(2) Damage of blown sand to residential area, mine base, cultural relic and buildings, and so on. Damage of blown sand to residential areas is that encroachment of drifting sand breaks down building and houses, and people have to move and then become ecological refugees. Damage to cultural relics and buildings is mainly referred to abrasion of wind drifting sand on large-scale equipment in the field and burying building. Taking Dunhuang as a typical case, sand-driving wind from the east of the Mingsha Mountains causes grottos region sand accumulating greatly, blocks plank roads and collapse brim of grottos. Wind erosion not only causes fading of open-air frescos, but also thins peak of grottos, and even exposes some super peak of grottos to sun.

(3) Damage of blown sand to traffic, water conservancy, and communication establishment. Damages of blown sand to traffic mainly bury and erode railway, roadbed of highway, road surface, and stop transportation. Damages to water conservancy are mostly manifested in silting hydraulic engineering and river. A typical example is that of the Longyangxia Reservoir of Qinghai Province, the blown sands entering the reservoir is about 1.41×10^6 m^3 every year. Damages to communication establishment present not only on collapsing electrical wire poles, breaking wire by wind, but also on existing blown sand electric phenomenon around wire. According to observations in the field, voltage of blown sand electric phenomenon around wire reaches up to 2,700 V, which strongly disturbs communication and electricity transmitting and even endangers human security.

(4) Damage of blown sand to environment. A sudden sandstorm always causes a series of hazards, such as strong soil deflation by wind, sand dune advancing, and dust blowing and driftings. Sand-dust weather not only makes atmosphere muddy, impedes people working normally, but also disrupts civil aviation and causes economic loss. Moreover, these dust materials consisting of quartz, microelement and salinity directly damage people health.

17.2 Quantitative evaluations of blown sand hazards

Most regions in northern China are subject to wind-blown sand damage in different degrees. Only evaluating the degree of blown sand hazards quantitatively, can the proper sand-combated policies and sand-controlled countermeasures be carried out. About quantitative evaluation on wind-blown sand hazards, there is not a suit authorized measure to judge it so far, only estimating the grade of blown sand hazards from different points of view.

17.2.1 Evaluation of danger degree of aeolian desertification hazards

Evaluation of danger degree of aeolian desertification hazards is an important embranchment of blown sand hazards evaluation. Danger degree of aeolian desertification hazards is the grades of directly harming or latent threat to social economic development in a region. Some researchers have established the danger degrees of aeolian desertification in the northern region of China (Dong, 1997), and considered the aeolian desertification as an areal complex, which is interaction between natural progress and social economic progress, in a certain geographical region. Both aeolian desertification progress and social economic conditions determine the formation and development of aeolian desertification hazards, in which the level of social economic development mostly manifest in the two aspects of population and economic increases, while the intensity of aeolian desertification progress mainly depends on the formation condition of aeolian desertification (including latent natural conditions, population pressure and livestock pressure) and its present status and developmental rate. Therefore the seven aspects of population level, economic level, latent aeolian desertification condition, population pressure, livestock pressure, and the present status of aeolian desertification and its developmental rate all impact on the occurrence of aeolian desertification and its development. Making an evaluation of aeolian desertification hazards must follow these seven aspects, then frame specific evaluation indexes, establish mathematical models, calculate the index of aeolian desertification hazards degree, and finally rank and divide different danger regions of aeolian desertification hazards. According to all the above mentioned, there are 15 danger regions of aeolian desertification hazards, in which six fall into light degree regions, five middle degree regions, and four severe regions. The six light degree regions are Hulunbeir region, the middle and western regions of northeast plain, the northern region of the west of Shaanxi Province, the Shaanxi-Gansu-Ningxia region, the Qaidam region, and the Mongolian-Xinjiang region respectively. The five middle degree regions are the new Inner Mongolia-Gansu-NingXia region, the southern region of the north in Shanxi Province, the Mongolia-Shanxi region, the Gonghe Basin region, and the Junggar Basin region respectively. The four severe degree regions are the Horqin region, the Bashang and Houshan region, the Ordos region, and Ningxia Hui Autonomous Region respectively.

17.2.2   Quantitative evaluation of wind erosion

The measure for wind erosion quantity in field is usually accomplished by measuring the depth of wind erosion in a given period. In a wind tunnel, experiments measures the weight of surface soil on an erosion bed over a certain period of time, and the erosion quantity can be obtained. By analyzing the content of nutrition composition in soil, its loss quantity in a region during a certain time can be estimated. We can evaluate the blown sand hazards in farmlands or pastures preliminarily by this method. Investigation shows that on average, about 2.805×10^4 ton fertile soil has been blown away in Houshan region of Ulanqab Meng every year because of wind erosion, of which 3,825 kg is organic matter, 3,090 kg N, and 6,000 kg P.

17.2.3   Evaluation of deflation and accumulation quantity of blown sand in a region

We can calculate the deflated and accumulated mass of blown sand in the entire region, after measuring sand flux in different typical sectors, and ascertaining sand-transporting area and cross section of different types with the methods of remote sensing interpretation and local investigation. Using this method, blown sand quantity entering into reservoirs, rivers, and traffic roads can be estimated preliminarily. Somebody estimated the deflation quantity of blown sand in border regions between Shaanxi, Shanxi Province and Inner-Mongolia Autonomous Region, and found that the total deflation quantity in this region is about 1.09 billion $t \cdot a^{-1}$, and average erosion intensity is 1,600 t/(a · km).

17.2.4   Evaluation of blown sand hazards to traffic roads

The danger degree of blown sand hazards along the Tarim desert highway running through the Taklimakan Desert varies greatly. Dong (1997) established a mathematical model for the degree of blown sand hazards as follows.

$$S = \frac{v^2}{H^8} \tag{17-1}$$

where, S is sand transport, v is average wind speed，H is relative humidity of air. The degree of wind-blown sand hazards along the desert highway can be evaluated by this formula.

17.2.5 Evaluation of direct economic loss caused by blown sand hazards

It is necessary in routine duties to evaluate reduction of crops and pastures yield caused by blown sand hazards, economic loss of ruined croplands and replanting crops during a strong wind or a dust storm, and economic loss of people and livestock casualty, collapsed buildings and houses, interruption of traffic and communication resulted from blown sand. For example, 20.7×10^3 hm^2 need to replant in 80×10^3 hm^2 farmland threatening aeolian desertification in Zhangbei County of Hebei Province every year, and seeds for replanting in 1984 are high to 485×10^4 kg. Rare 12–degree southeast wind caused 226.1 km railway in Hami region to suffer from blown sand, and 59 sections had sand accumulation with the total mass of 74918 m^3 during May in 1984.

17.3 Basic approaches to control blown sand hazards

Blown sand hazards in northern China have different formation causes and various natural conditions. To control and combat sand hazards, we must follow the principle of adjusting measures to local conditions and harm types.

17.3.1 Basic principles of controlling blown sand hazards

Wind-blown sand hazards are that wind-blown sand movement causes disruptions to people's production, living and other economic actions. Commonly, highly possibly reducing the intensity of wind-blown sand movement can achieve the aim of controlling wind-blown sand hazards. The essence of wind-blown sand movement is the process of producing aeolian saltation cloud when wind velocity larger than threshold velocity of sand grain entrainment acts on sandy surface. Aeolian saltation cloud is the magnificent exhibition of three recycle segments of sand grain deflation, transportation, and re-deposition by wind. The center of wind-blown sand combating is to weaken wind power causing aeolian saltation cloud and shifting dune, reduce sand content in airflow, reinforce sandy surface, and enhance its anti-erosion capacity. Based on fundamental principle mentioned above, there are three measures for controlling wind-blown sand hazards, termed as sand-fixation with vegetation, sand-prevention by mechanic ways, and sand-fixation with chemicals. Sand-fixation with vegetation includes the recovery of natural vegetation and establishment of manual vegetation. Although the effects of vegetation measures are slow, protection time is relatively long once these vegetation are grown up and exert protected action. They not only have the characteristic of integration of reformation with utilization, but also can ameliorate local microclimate and are the extensively adopted sand-controlling measures. However, sand-fixation with vegetation is always limited by natural environment conditions, especially by water condition.

Commonly, sand-fixation with vegetation mostly has been adopted in the region with annual mean precipitation more than 200 mm and no irrigation condition. If the annual mean precipitation in an area is less than 200 mm, the measure of sand combating should firstly consider mechanical one. Annual mean precipitation in the Shapotou area of Ningxia Hui Autonomic Region around the southeast margin of the Tengger Desert is about 188 mm, and this is usually considered the annual precipitation limit for sand-fixation with vegetation. Certainly, redistribution of precipitation in some sections and local planting for sand combating under irrigation condition is not included due to topographic factor. Sand-prevention with mechanics mainly includes all kinds of barriers and wind-derived plank. Mechanical measure for sand combating has the advantage of no limitation of water condition, and can get good effect soon, but its protection time is short and need to renew and maintain regularly. Therefore, they are often adopted in the regions with severe blown sand hazards, such as along traffic roads, around farmland and residential sites, and are combined with vegetation measures. Sand-fixation with chemicals is mainly to spray artificial concrete substances to cut airflow directly interacting with sand-bed. Chemical measure can have a quick get effect, but with high cost, and so can be applied in the region suffering from very severe blown sand hazards and with difficulty to adopt to vegetation, such as, along very important traffic roads, mine, and residential sites. No matter what kind of measures it may be, it is hardly adopted alone. When applying them under concrete condition, people always combine these three measures to form a entire protected system for getting good effects after analyzing the types of blown sand hazards and natural conditions. Recently, we generalize some complex measures, according to the characters of protection region, combating sand hazards in the oasis regions in desert belts, harnessing aeolian desertification soil in desert steppes and grasslands, and preventing sand hazards along railway and highway. Now, they are discussed respectively as follows.

17.3.2 Basic approaches for controlling blown sand hazards

17.3.2.1 Combating sand hazards in oasis region of desert belt

1) Rational utilization of water resources in desert belts

Water resource is the vital factor for an oasis within a desert belt. Storage capacity of water resource directly determines vegetation status, and then affects the intensity of blown sand hazards in oasis region of desert belt. If utilizing water resources rationally in desert belt, we must consider the entire situation of water resource in this region, think over the harmony of water-using mass in upper, middle and lower reaches of a river, avoid water shortages in lower reaches due to excessive interception of water resources in upper and middle reaches, and exploit underground water within reason to prevent vegetation in an oasis and its fringe from dying because of deteriorating water conditions and declining ground water levels.

2) Establishing complex protection forestry systems

Irrigation oasis in desert belt is surrounded by gobi desert and aeolian desert, and suffers from sand-driving wind and hazards of dune encroaching farmland. At present, in order to combat blown sand hazards, we usually adopt the protection forestry system composed of establishing grass-reared to fix sand in the adjacent regions between an oasis and aeolian or gobi desert, establishing sand-blocking forestry belts in the fringe of oasis, and establishing crop-protected forestry nets within oases (Fig 17-1).

Fig. 17-1　Protection forestry belt in the fringe of an oasis

(1) The belt of rearing grass to fix sand in the adjacent regions between oasis and aeolian desert or Gobi desert. Oasis in the desert belt of China are mostly distributed around Gobi desert with sand-driving wind or in the fringe of low dunes with wide inter-dune depressions, and some are even located at the edge of fixed or semi-fixed dunes, except for a few around huge shifting dunes, sparse vegetation is distributed there with different degrees. According to this characteristic, we adopted the protected measures of rearing grasses or trees to fix sand dunes in different regions and stopping tree-chopping and herd-grazing, in order to renew some high fecundity xerophytes in the usage of natural seeding and increase vegetation coverage. For example, in the Turpan district of Xinjiang Uygur Autonomous Region, by means of artificial irrigation and planting, vegetation easily grows and rejuvenates, and forms a natural barrier in front of an oasis. After irrigating in the belt of growing grass to fix the sand, xerophilous shrubs can germinate new seedlings and increase its coverage within a vegetation period. Projective canopy of vegetation will exceed 30% after three years in the Turpan district. Because the measure of growing grasses to fix sand has advantages of easily establishing and exerting protection benefits quickly, and can take a role of protecting sand-controlling forestry belts and young forests in the initial stages, it is a pioneer measure in protection system. After establishing the belt of growing grass to fix sand, because of sand-driving wind from the periphery of irrigation oases entering into the grass belt, airflow close to the surface is affected by shrub vegetation, and the aim of preventing blown sand can be attained as the wind velocity near the surface decreases.

(2) Sand-defending forestry belt at the fringe of oases. The function of sand-defending forestry belts at the fringe of oases is to continuously weaken the velocity of sand-driving wind over grasses belt, and form front sand-defending protection belt combined with the belt of rearing grasses to fix sand. In order to exert a sand-defending role, we should pay attention to the structure and width of the sand-defending forestry belt. Due to different natural conditions and varied ways of blown sand hazards at the fringe of a certain oasis, their protection forestry belts also have different characteristics. Such as, sand-defending forestry belt is commonly consisted of banding and strip in Linze and Gaotai regions of the Hexi Corridor. Specifically, people first built sparse-structured forestry belt with 50–60 m width along dry canals at the fringe of oasis, and then establish striped forestry along inter-dune depressions distributed by this forestry belt using irrigation of free-farming water and underground water to make dune surrounded by forestry belts and striped forestry, and to reduce the numbers of exotic sand sources due to the forward moving of sand dunes. We constructed relative wide sparse-structured forestry belt in the side close to oasis of northeastern region of the Ulan Buh Desert, and adopted the measure of planting shrub together with measure of rearing grasses to fix sand. Observation data show that average wind speed will reduce 50%–60% within the distance of 30 times height of trees, and 70% sand content in the airflow near to ground (0–20 cm above ground) has been blocked in the front of forestry belt. But for the Turpan district in the front regions of sand and gravel desert or blow-land, multiple-row forestry belt similar to compact-structured sand-defending forestry belt usually constructed at the fringe of oasis with the main hazards of strong wind and wind-blown sand. According to those stated above, the structure and width of sand-defending forestry belts varied greatly in different oasis, based on the primary experiential summarization of productive practice. But it is still absent for systematically theoretic research.

(3) Crop-protected forestry belts within oasis. While establishing the belts of rearing grasses to closed sand and sand-controlling forestry belts, we must build crop-protecting forestry grids within oasis. Only uniting these three measures to form a protected system, the effective function of defending blown sand can be got. Commonly, the configure pattern is high arbors dominant in tree specie adopted, such as all kinds of *Populus,* and narrow forestry belts or little grids. Narrow forestry belt mentioned in this book is referred to 6–12 m width belt consisted of 4-6 rows tree, but the little grid reduces space distance of main forestry belt less than 20H. Observation at the Chepaizi District in the west margin of the Gurbantünggüt Desert showed that wind velocity within little grid reduced greatly than that of big grid.

3) Sand-fixation with mechanical barrier.

Sand-driving wind will directly endanger the oasis whose periphery is distributed great shifting sand dunes. In this situation, the surface of shifting sand dune needs to fix with the measure of building mechanical barrier. The materials of barrier commonly come from local, such as clay soil, wheat, reed, and other plant's tress, and its aim is to increase the roughness length of sand surface and its drag, weaken wind speed, and reduce sand content in wind-blown sand.

17.3.2.2 Combating sand hazards in grassland region

According to natural environmental condition, especially in the differences of water condition, grasslands are divided into desert grassland, dry grassland, and forest grassland. There exists an close relation between blown sand hazards of grassland and its natural environmental background. For half a century, extensive reclamation of sandy grassland and other human unreasonable economical activities contribute to expanding range of blown sand harm and its deterioration. For example, Bashang and its adjacent districts in Hebei Province, including those from Bashang to the south of Onqin Daga Sandy Land and the Houshan area of Ulanqab Meng, are the regions with rapidly spread rate of aeolian desertification soil in recent years. Therefore, blown sand combating in grassland must combine the adjusting of soil structure with sand-defending and sand-combating work.

(1) Adjusting unreasonable soil-utilized structure. For those grasslands mostly located in the farming-pastoral zone of northern China, dry farming agriculture gradually substitutes for original grassland stock farming. In addition, the increasing number of livestock exceeds the capacity of grassland, and accelerates soil blown away. In order to combating wind-blown sand hazards in this region, we must start with adjusting soil-utilized structure, reducing the proportion of dry farming land, and restoring land for grass and stock farming, managing intensively the land with good condition of water and fertilize, and building crop-protected forestry grid. Establishment of artificial forage base in the farmland-withdrawal and abandoned land can relief the contradiction between livestock and forage. Therefore, we must have consciousness of ecologic environment protection, and properly deal with the relationship between ecological benefit and economic benefit at the cost of losing local benefit at present.

(2) Building integrated protection system. Being better water content, vegetation canopy conditions compared with those of desert, wind-blown sand hazards of grassland are relative smaller, so the responsive preventing and controlling system is mainly to increase vegetation canopy. As for the low-and middle-degree aeolian desertified grassland, the measure is to develop grassland and to add sowing to accelerate natural vegetation recovery and renewal exuberance. For heavy aeolian desertified grassland with shifting sand dunes, the measure is to fix sand with arbors and shrubs. Specifically, we construct slice-liked forestry with arbors in the inter-dune depression, and build shrub forestry in the windward slope of sand dune. Arbor forestry in the inter-dune depression not only takes a role of defending wind to fix sand, but also their tender tress can be used as forage and fuel. Shrub forestry also is regarded as firewood to settle the question of fuel shortage for people, except for its protected action.

(3) Controlling population number and livestock in grassland. Since nearly half a century, the

main reason for wind-blown sand hazards intensifying in grassland is excessively reclamation and grazing, due to rapidly increase of population. Therefore, controlling population number and livestock of grassland can defend wind-blown sand hazards radically. It needs to take a precise estimation for population capacity and stock capacity in grassland under present productivity level and living standard, and engage all kinds of action limited in the range of soil bearing capacity, and make human action to harmonize resource environment.

17.3.3 Degradation of grassland in western China and prevention of blown sand harm

17.3.3.1 Deteriorated status of natural pasture in the west of China

Grassland degradation is the first step for the development of aeolian desertification. Five big pastures are distributed in the west of China (Inner Mongolia Autonomous Region, Xinjiang Uygur Autonomous Region, Qinghai Province, and Tibet). The area of natural grassland in the 12 provinces of west China is about 331 million hm^2, accounting for 48.2% of the total area in the western region, and accounting for 84.37% of national total area of natural grassland. It is obvious that stock farming on pasture takes a leading role in the economy of west region. The 90% grassland of 3.9 billion hm^2 in China was degenerated with different degree, with the middle-degree degradation area of grassland 3.9 billion hm^2. The area of deteriorated grassland in Ningxia Hui Autonomous Region and Shanxi Province accounts for 90%–97%.

The extent of deteriorated grassland in Gansu, Xinjiang Uygur Autonomous Region, and Inner Mongolia Autonomous Region varies from 42% to 87%. In contrast to that in the middle of the 1980s, the area of degenerated grassland is still extending. Take Inner Mongolia Autonomous Region as a typical case, the area of deteriorated grassland is about 213,369.28 km^2 in the end of the 1970s, accounting for 35.57% of the area of available pasture. But, it increases to 386,988.35 km^2 in 1995, accounting for 60.08%. The area of deteriorated grassland increases 173,619 km^2 within 15 years, with expanding rate of 11,575 km^2 every year.

17.3.3.2 Causes of grassland degradation

The direct and specific causes of grassland degradation are identified to show Varing in different regions, and can be summed in three aspects: nature, human, and policy factors. Natural factors mainly includes climate change, and drought caused by the increase of evaporation due to reduction of precipitation and rising of temperature. Meteorological data show that the climate has not taken great change in grassland region in north China during recent 100 years, but shown an obvious fluctuation. Climate change in grassland of Inner Mongolia Autonomous Region is stable in recent 50 years, such as, average precipitation is about 371 mm in the east region of temperate grassland from 1959 to 1968, and it is 369 mm from 1979 to 1988. Two continued droughts occurred in Inner Mongolia Autonomous Region from the end of the 1920s to the begin of the 1930s, and caused inland lake dry up, shifting sand expand, but did not cause large-area grassland degradation in large scale. For all mentioned above, we could draw a conclusion that climate change is not a main reason for grassland degradation in larger scale.

Many researches show that human irrational economic activities cause large scale grassland degradation in recent 30 years, mainly including grazing exceeded stock capacity of grassland, reclamation in blindness, excessive picking, and some negative influence in the development of mine.

Excessive pasturing is a general issue in stock farming of grassland in western China, and also is the main reason for grassland degradation. In present, average overload pasture in natural grassland accounts for 20%–30%, and 50%–120% in the seasonal grassland of desert and high elevation cold region, even reach up to 300% in some local regions. There are 11.664 million sheep in the 12 provinces of west China in 1986, but in 1997 it reaches 14.732 million, and increase 3.068 million in 11 years. Take Inner Mongolia as a typical case, a sheep possesses 4.1 hm^2 grasslands in 1947 and its utilized intensity is very slow. After 18 years, due to the increasing of livestock, possessing a sheep needs only 0.97 hm^2 grasslands in 1965 and already exceed stock capacity of natural grassland. After another 20 years, the number of livestock fluctuated about 7 million. Long-period pasture over stock capacity of grassland restrained pasturage and other vegetation grows, and with livestock's trample, caused grassland degradation.

People always regard soil with land leveling, fertility, deep soil layers and good vegetation as grassland for farming and reclamation object. Since 1994, large area of grassland in China has suffered from several reclamations in order to solve grain problem. From the 1950s to the 1970s, there are three reclamations in large scale in northwest China, and already reclaimed grassland has 0.667 million hm^2 at the end of the 1960s. According to investigation from Chinese Academy of Sciences, reclamation in 33 mengs of east Inner Mongolia is 970, 851 hm^2 in ten years before and after 1998. Soil degradation is very severe and rapid after grassland suffered from reclaimation, due to extensive cultivation and little harvest.

On one hand, grassland with good natural condition has always been reclaimed, and on the another hand, biological yield of grassland begins to reduce, and even become barren land. Excessive pasture on remained grassland is more severe, and its degradation become worse land.

Unreasonable wood-chopping and mowing also leads to grassland degradation. Grassland degradation caused by long-term mowing unreasonably without input has already been validated by many experiments. For example, mowing for successive years leads to more output than input, nutrition element imbalance, grassland yield decreasing, vegetation height and single plant weight falling, and then grassland begin to deteriorate in a long time. Wood-chopping and excessive picking is also another important reason for grassland degradation. A great deal of digging medical plants, such as *liquorices, ephedra, anemarrhena, astragalus* root in Inner Mongolia and other economic plants, such as mushroom and Fachai, severely destroyed grassland vegetation, soil structure and initiated grassland degradation. Pits are all over the Ordos grassland due to excessive digging of *liquorices* and *ephedra* over a long period. Investigation shows that digging 1kg *liquorices* will destroy 0.5–0.67 hm^2 grassland, and according to this estimation, the area of grassland resulting from digging liquorices about 2.67×10^4 hm^2 in this region every year. The loss of stock farming production in Gansu Province caused by excessively digging *liquorices* exceed 10 million *yuan* RMB in 1994. There are 77.82 km^2 grasslands at Liudun village in Shawo countryside of Ningxia Hui Autonomic Region, being digging *liquorices*, 5.21 km^2 of them turned into shifting sand region, and blown sand emerged in 66.5% of grassland during 15 years. 13 million hm^2 grasslands were destroyed by pulling down *Fachai* in Inner Mongolia Autonomic Region, accounting for 19.5% of the entire grassland.

Degenerated grassland, sparse and low community structure and living-conditions are widened, and catch of their natural enemy all provided a suitable condition for mouse to exist and multiply. Mouse burrowed on grassland, chewed plant root, and destroyed grassland vegetation, and then accelerated its degradation. The area with pest and mouse hazards is 39.31 hm^2 in 11 provinces of northern China in 1996, of which rat hazards accounts for 78.7%. Mouse hazards are the outcome of grassland degradation and also the reason for accelerating grassland degenerated further.

Mineral resources in grassland regions of China are very abundant, such as coal, petroleum, natural gas, salt, saltpeter, and alkali. In recent years, owing to exploitation of these mineral resources, the economic level in pasture developed quickly. But in the processes of exploitation, it also caused some negative effects, such as trampling grassland vegetation, burying grassland by ore tailing and accelerating grassland degradation around mine region or aeolian desertification. The main factor of grassland degradation is unreasonable human activities for a long period, including policy-guiding question. As is well known, China is a big nation with a large population. Most of them are living on planting and have formed a conception of regarding agriculture but not pasture, despised the ecological function of grassland, invested less on grassland for a long time, and gets more output than input on ecological system of grassland. Statistics show that the expense invested by a nation on building grassland and pasture was only 4.6 billion *yuan* RMB from 1949 to 1989, and on average, 1 hm^2 area of grassland got less than 0.45 *yuan* RMB. It was much less for Qinghai Province, as the investment was 0.128 billion *yuan* RMB and 1 hm^2 area of grassland only got 9.6 *fen* (one hundred *fen* equal to one *yuan*) RMB a year.

17.3.3.3 Effects of grassland degradation on economy and society in west regions

A negative consequence of grassland degradation is that primary productivity begins to decline. According to different degree of grassland degradation, the falling extent of productivity also varied greatly, namely, light degradation with 20%–35%; middle degradation with 35%–60%; severe degradation with 60%–85%; and very severe degradation with more than 85%, respectively. Using a typical grassland as an example, primary productivity over-ground vegetation is only 1,200–1,000 kg/hm^2, 1,000–600 kg/hm^2, 600–200 kg/hm^2, and <200 kg/hm^2, respectively. The drop of productivity over-ground vegetation will lead to the decreasing of stock capacity. Investigation shows that stock capacity on natural grassland of Inner Mongolia Autonomic Region in the 1980s is about 75% of that in the 1950s, and 80% in the 1960s. In addition, due to increasing livestock number, more burden of grassland will be added to lead to decrease weight of livestocks living on natural grassland. According to the investigation from Qinghai Province, average weight of cattle and sheep is 82.5 kg and 20.7 kg respectively in the 1960s, but in 1979 it fell into 62 kg and 15.9 kg, with dropping 25% and 23% respectively. Sheep weight in Uxin Qi of Inner Mongolia Autonomic Region decreased from 25 kg in the 1950s to 20 kg in the 1960s and to 15 kg in the 1980s.

The second evil consequence of grassland degradation is the change of structure, height, coverage of phytocommunity and its appearance. Although the number of plant species on degenerated grassland does not change, the function and proportion of different plant population varied greatly. The proportion of quality forage on degenerated grassland reduced, but the toxic and harmful grasses increased. Furthermore, the height and coverage of phytocommunity on degenerated grassland decreased, and single plant's height reduced. Commonly, average height of phytocommunity on degenerated grassland is only about one fifth of that on natural grassland. Otherwise, parts of them underground grow very badly, and their number decreases and presents decked characteristics.

The ecological conditions on degenerated grassland deteriorated greatly, such as compacted soil surface layer, big mass in unit volume, porosity reducing, bad water penetrating and other bad physical condition, even with characteristics of aeolian desertification. Not only all mentioned above, due to the reduction of organic content of soil and nutrition elements for plant, fertility of soil decline conspicuously, and it takes disadvantage for plant to grow and accelerates grassland degradation.

Deteriorated ecological condition on degenerated grassland aggravated the process of soil erosion by wind and other agents, and possibly provided sand sources for sandstorm. In addition, lower biological yield and productivity of degenerated grassland will accelerate the occurrence of other calamities.

With the development of degenerated grassland, reduction of biological productivity and stock capacity, for herders relying on livestock, it greatly accelerates the degree of poverty and even affects social stability and solidification. There are 101 national poor counties in some pasturing area with severely degenerated grassland in China, accounting for 17.1% of entire poor counties, and poverty population in these regions is about 15 million, accounting for a fourth of that in China. In some region, due to grassland degradation, land aeolian desertification, houses and stalls buried by shifting dunes, some herders became ecological refugees and had to remove. 500 houses were destroyed in Sonid Zuoqi of Xilin Gol Meng, and its government was also forced to remove.

Pasturing areas in grassland are mostly in minority residential region. There are 31 minorities in pasturing areas in grassland, with about 22 million populations, accounting for one-third of the entire minority population in China. Land degradation, long-term poverty and economic disparity will affect national unity and social stability. Statistics show that accumulative loss reach 0.96 billion *yuan* RMB, due to destruction of infrastructure on grassland resulting from pulling Facai. A great deal of achievement has been obtained in the aspect of controlling degenerated grassland in China since the 1990s. In recent ten years, we adopted the measures of planting grass artificially, seeding with plane, and closed rearing with enclosure to restore grassland and get some obvious effect in some regions. Averagely, the area of grass-planting exceeds 2.7 million hm^2, and accumulative reserving area of artificial grassland is about 1.5 million hm^2, and 1 million of them was fenced. Up to the end of 2,000, the area of farmland substituted by grasses or trees is about 1.363×10^5 hm^2 in 193 counties of 12 provinces in west China.

17.3.3.4 Countermeasures of preventing and combating grassland degradation and blown sand hazards

Preventing and combating grassland degradation is a systematic engineering, and it is needed to adopt integrated measures and get attention from all inspects.

(1) Converting ideas, altering bias towards grass and grassland, and highly recognizing the function of grassland on the aspects of maintaining ecological security, establishing ecological barrier, exerting ecological effect, and regarding grassland establishment and vegetarian feeding greatly as a basic national policy and bringing it into agriculture system. We also should increase investment on stock farming and make it form complement with grain production and pig-breeding and farm birds consuming grain.

(2) Strictly protecting and reasonably utilizing natural pasture. Because natural pasture is an important renewed resource. We show it scientifically and reasonably, and establish code of protecting natural grassland. In addition, the number of livestock on it should be determined by primary productivity of grassland and its stock capacity, and by the balance principle between grasses and livestock. We should avoid pasturing on grassland exceeding its stock capacity and limit this case, establish grazing system in given period, divide the no-grazing region, stop pasturing in no-grazing region, strictly manage all activities which may destroy natural pasture, strictly prohibit reclaiming grassland as farmland and the conception of turning grassland into wasteland and wild region for farming.

(3) Establishing artificial grassland with different proportion according to the specific conditions. We should increase the forage provision in winter and spring, make seasonal stock farming free from time, and take extensive stock farming into intensive one. According to experiences from home and abroad, China needs to build 33-million hm^2 artificial grassland. After building, production value will increase manifold, provided that per hm^2 artificial grassland yields 3000–3750 kg of hay.

(4) Insisting on the plan of planting grass on farmland and consolidating its achievement. Since China has decided to exploit the west Region, many achievements have been obtained, especially in the aspect of degenerated grassland harnessing, and it is necessary to stick to this doing for a long time.

(5) Integrated harnessing for degenerated pasture. Ecological system has self-recovered capacity. If the environmental condition does not change, degenerated ecological system can restore original condition for enough long time on the condition of eliminating the factor for its degradation. Without disturbance from pasture and other factors, grassland can restore on itself. For example, in typical grassland region of Inner Mongolia Autonomous Region, degenerated grassland with *cold wormwood, spear grass, guinea grass*, and *wheat grass* as its main species has been restored after seven years, and biological yield over ground also increased from 1.1 t/hm^2 to 1.9 t/hm^2, added about 73%. The coverage of grass community also added from 48% to 55% and its height correspondingly enhanced from 10 cm to 30 cm. The proportion of gramineous plant mainly including *guinea grass* and *wheat grass* increased from 38% to 71%, of which *guinea grass* increased from 9% to 35.7%. But the proportion of *Compositae* plant decreased greatly from 31% to 9%, of which cold wormwood decreased from 27% to 4.7%. The proportion of leguminous plant increased conspicuously and the quality of grassland improved.

For some degenerated grassland ecological system, its self-restoration is very slow. Ecological recovery is to recognize and eliminate limiting factors for its recovery, and attain the aim of rapid recovery with low investment. In the course of restoring and meliorating ecological system in grassland, many measures have been adopted, including the measures of meliorating soil physical characters, such as earth loosening, shallow plowing, the measures of improving soil nutritional condition, such as fertilization, especially nitrogenous fertilizer, the measure of replanting quality pasture to increase the rate of vegetation recovery and the measure of proper grazing to accelerate grassland recovery.

Plowing shallow and loosening earth has obvious effect on the ecological system recovery of degenerated grassland. For example, for the degenerated grassland in typical grassland region of Inner Mongolia Autonomous Region, after loosening earth the aerated characteristics of soil improved and its porosity also increased 6.4%, which accelerated animals and animalcule activities in soil. In addition, observation shows that shallow plowing and earth loosen can cut underground stem of some quality pasture to accelerate its germination, to increase the density of tress, and to improve it's renewed rate. After loosening earth on natural grassland, its yield will increase 27%–87%. However, only meliorating physical character of soil, its benefit does not last long without radically ameliorating necessary nutritional elements for plant growing, based on the point of material recycle of ecological system.

Fertilizing grassland is to ensure the material balance between input and output of ecological system and also is an important measure to achieve system-sustaining production.

Replanting fodder grasses is an effective measure of accelerating some quality of grass multiplication and its expanding speed. In Yangcao grassland region in Inner Mongolia Autonomic Region, replanting guinea grass can make grassland renewed in 2–3 years. Replanting or mix-planting *leguminosae* grass is also another measure to renew or improve the quality of degenerated grassland. Because nitrogen of soil on degenerated grassland is very deficient, replanting *leguminosae* grass can add the fertilization of soil, increase the productivity of grassland plant, and speed its recovery.

Reasonably controlling livestock herds can ameliorate material recycle of ecological system on grassland, and accelerate plant growing and better the pasture conditions.

(6) Increasing the proportion of yard fattening and improving its level. Grassland stock farming in west region of China is dominated by grazing for a long time. It has not only low productivity, but also shows unfavorable to protect the resources on natural grassland. According to the balanceable principle between livestock and grass, we should reduce the time for grazing in winter and spring possibly and increase the time for yard fattening in this period on the condition of utilizing natural grassland resources adequately and grazing in summer.

(7) Exerting multifunction of grassland, developing some new industries such as tourism, and green food, to increase the income of herders in order to reduce the pressure of grassland.

(8) Developing mine industry, traffic industry, and carrying out the system of "one must harness it if he destroyed it".

(9) Establishing sustainable management for grassland ecological system. The present status of the grassland control in China is harness and degradation existing at the same time, and degradation is more severe, so establishing a suitable grassland sustainable management system is the essential measure for preventing the grassland degrading and the restoring of degraded grassland. For example, sustained usage is more rational when the grassland resource is in shortage; the using way of high strength in short time is more advantage to the plant growing than the way of low strength in a long time. But the suitable grassland management system varied on the basis of the type of the grassland. So the clarification of such things are essential for the suitable management system making, such as the first productivity and the stock capacity of the grassland, the effect of different graze type and time, the action mode of the grassland productivity and the graze intensity, the mechanism of grassland biodiversity maintenance. At the same time it is the higher-level strategy of optimizing the land using management system for the grassland ecology system management.

17.4 Combating and preventing blown sand hazards along railway and highway in sand region of China

China is one of the countries in the world with large area desert, extensive distribution and severe aeolian desertification. The Baotou-Lanzhou Railway began to be put into use in 1957, which initiated a precedence of building highway in desert. Some railways, which run through desert or Gobi, such as the Jining-Erenhot Railway, the Gantang-Wuwei Railway, the Lamzhou-Xingjiang Railway Qing hai–Tibet (sector from Xining to Golmud), Jitong, and Baoshen et al., have finished construction. The Baotou–Yan'an Railway is also on the edge of being finished and will be used, and the railway track in the desert is more than 1,400 km, for the sector of this railway damaged by sand is up to more than 200 points, and the length is near 1,000 km, the sector secured effectively accounts for the half of it, and the rest are being regulated. There are lots of roads run through deserts in China, for example, the Xilinhot–Zhangjiakou road runs through Onqin Daga Sandy Land, the Baotou-Yulin road run through the Hobq Desert and Mu Us Sandy Land, and the Tarim Desert Highway. As we know, the first road protected along the whole way is Ying (shuiqiao)–Yan (hu) railway located in Zhongwei county of Ningxia Hui Automatic Region runs through the Tengger Desert. The Tarim Desert Highway was completed in 1995, with 447 km through shifting dune, which was recorded in Jinis as the first and longest desert highway built with pitch and concrete in 1999. The first-term sand-combating system along highway using mechanical sand-fixed measure is the greatest sand-combating system of desert highway in the world.

It is the best way to build biological protection belt with arbor, shrub and grass. But, because of limitation of natural conditions, it is very difficult to build biological sand-preventing system in arid region. Even in some regions with good natural conditions, restoring and building artificial vegetation need a certain period, and we have to adopt mechanical measures to sustain long time in extreme arid regions before building biological sand-preventing system. Sand-fixed system in Yingshuiqiao-Gantang section of the Baotou–Lanzhou Railway has been build for 40 years, but it is necessary to maintain sand-blocking barriers in the front of railway and renew sand-fixed belt with straw checkerboard sand barriers.

Traditionally, sand-combating measures can be divided into three classes, biological, mechanical and chemical measures. Author thinks that sand-fixation with natural or artificial synthetic sand-fixation liquor does not produce chemical action between sand grain and liquor, so does not merge into physical (mechanical) measure and term it as sand-fixation with chemicals. Sand-cementation with chemical liquor is one of the mechanical measures. With great difference between east and west of China, although many regions along railway and highway adopted integrated sand-fixation measures combined mechanical with biological ways, their priorities varied greatly. In the eastern region of China, biological measure is the priority, and then engineering measures, but in extreme arid region of the west, engineering is the major. In the middle region of China with precipitation more than 200 mm, the integrated system with biological and engineering measure is first to be considered for getting a long-term benefit.

17.4.1 Preventing and combating blown sand hazards along railway in shifting dunes region (taking protection system in Shapotou Section of the Baotou–Lanzhou Railway as a typical case)

The project of "protection system in Shapotou section of the Baotou–Lanzhou Railway" attained a Special Award of National Science and Technology Progress in 1986. The section from Yingshuiqiao to Gantang of the Baotou–Lanzhou Railway traversing the southeast region of the Tengger Desert is the earliest railway built in desert and its protection system is of pioneering character. It is a typical integrated protection system with biological and engineering measure, taking sand-fixation as its main aim, combined with sand-blocked, and with the action of transporting and diverging.

Aeolian geomorphology is characterized by reticulate shifting dunes with 15–20 m relative height in Shapotou region. Annual precipitation is about 185 mm. Underground water level exceeds dozens meters and plant cannot reach for growth. Stable water content in wet-sand layer under dry-sand layer (3–20 cm) is about 2%–3%. In this region, natural *psammophyte* are *Agriophyllum squarrosum, Pugionium cornutum, Stilpnolepis centiflora, Artemisia sphaerocephala, Hedysarum scoparium,* and so on, and their coverage is only 1%–2%.

The earliest protection system along the Yingshuiqiao-Gantang Railway has two sand-fixation and sand-blocked belts, and can be divided into four belts according to their functions. The first is sand-blocked belt in front of the railway, which is composed of 1m-high standing barriers with different materials. Before establishing barriers, we built 1–2 row barriers with straw in the sides of railway to prevent the basement of railway from wind erosion. The second, as the principal portion of protection system, is sand-fixation belt with 1m×1m vegetation under no irrigation condition. The third is arbor or shrub forestry belt under irrigation condition. The fourth is the sand-transporting belt on gravel platform acting as buffer(Fig.17-2). In fact, there is only about 2 km long section of railway with complete four belts, including 9 km long section with 2–4 belts, and the rest is composed of sand-fixation belt and sand-transporting platform. In the investigated region from K701 to K715, the width of protection belt is commonly 235–580 m, and its average width is 335.5 m, in which, the width of sand-fixation belt is about 150–480 m, and its average width is 241 m, the width of forestry belt is about 17–90 m, and its average width is 67.7 m. In view of the sand-combating effect, the width of protection belt is on the big side. After calculation, the width of reasonable sand-preventing belt in agreement with the principle of wind-blown sand physics is about 130 m. But practice shows that sand-blocked belt with good effect is necessary, and building as more as possible. Sand-blocked belt can block most sand grain and protect sand-fixation belt effectively. Otherwise, sand-fixation belt will be buried by shifting sand quickly.

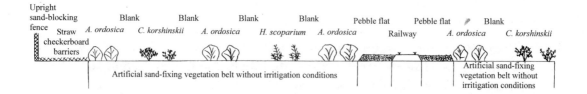

Fig. 17-2　Cross-section diagram of sand-fixation system along railway in Shapotou region

After many seed introducing tests, we selected some plant suited for building vegetation sand-fixation belt with shrub and grass, such as *Artemisia ordosica, Caragana Korshinskii, C. intermedia, C. microphylla, and Hedysarum aev*. But as plant grows, its water consumption increases, and water quality in sand layer become worsen. Therefore, artificial vegetation appears recession and succession gradually, and its coverage begins to decrease. In addition, a great deal of crust and lowly plant, such as moss and algae, appears on sand surface. Degradation of artificial vegetation manifests two points as follows. One is gradually falling of vegetation canopy. Sand-fixation belt with vegetation was built in 1956, and extended in the 1960s. Investigation showed that vegetation canopy was usually about 30%, some reached 43.7% in 1973, but in 1976, it decreased to 30%, such as the canopy of *Caragana Korshinskii*, decreased from 47.6% to 22.5%. The other is changing population structure. After seed introduction, because of the changing of living conditions (such as losing the condition of sand-burying once shifting sand has been fixed), even some quality indigenes do not bloom, or only bloom without fruit, and cannot renew themselves, then will be kicked out. While *Artemisia ordosica* can renew naturally, vegetation type were substituted by single *Artemisia ordosica* gradually.

As mentioned above, the reduction of vegetation canopy does not affect sand-fixation, because crust layer concreted the surface of dune. For three or four years after building artificial vegetation, sand dune surface will appear 0.1–0.2 cm thick crust, and it will develop 0.5 cm after 8 years, and 1.2 cm after 25 years. The firstly formed crust is loose and brittle, and there is sand soil under it with the same character as shifting sand. But as time continues, the texture of crust will be more compact gradually. Investigation showed that the color of crust formed in 24-year old artificial vegetation will become gray-brown, with compacted texture and strong resisting wind erosion, and there is 3–4 cm gray-brown block-structured soil layer under it. The formation of crust is under the action of vegetation, and stable sand surface and dust deposited on it will provide environmental condition and granule materials. Bacteria, epiphyte, blue algae, diatom and cryptogams such as moss, all joined in the formation process of crust. Analyses show that there is more nitrifying bacteria, amonifying bacteria, and fibrin decomposing bacteria in crust than shifting sand and also there exist self-generating azotobacteria, silicate bacteria, and so on. Blue algae includes *Microcoleus vainatus, Oscillatoria pseudogeminata, Phormidium amblguum, Schizothrix rupicola*, etc., in total of 20 kinds. Diatom has *Navicula minima var atomoides, Hantzschia amphioxys,* and so on. Moss has *Barbula ditrichoides* and *Bryum argenteum* propagated in the 1 cm thick surface soil layer.

With the development of crust and evolvement of soil-forming process, *Bassia dasyphylla*, *Corispermum* and *Eragrostis poaeoides* multiplied rapidly, *Salsola ruthenica*, *Setaria viridis*, *Echinops gmelini*, *Allium mongolicum*, *Scorzonera divaricata*, and other herbage plant begin to intrude. The more thickness surface soil layer become, the more species of herbage plant appear. Sand dune will be further fixed after forming more compacted grass layer in the years with normal water or rich water.

There are several dozen kinds of arbor, shrub and semi-shrub planted in Shapotou region through test since 1956, and most of them do not adapt to formidable natural conditions. Even the arbor doesn't grow well due to limited water condition and short nutrition in sand dune, such as, *Elaeagnus angustifolia,* as a indigene with high adaptive capacity, grown into shrub-shaped. After building forestry belt of arbor (*Robina pseudoacacia, Populus simonii, Populus gansuensis, and Pinus sylvestris*) and shrub (*Salix gordejevii, Amorpha fruticosa*) with water-irrigation using Yellow River in 1966, they grew well and can exert the double action of wind-defending and greening. But it must need water source as irrigation condition to build forestry belt, special arbor, in arid region.

17.4.2 Preventing and combating blown sand hazards along railway in Gobi region (taking protection system in Yumen Section of the Lanzhou–Xinjiang Railway as an example)

Many railways in China traverse Gobi desert region, with strong wind, but short of sand source, and un-saturation aeolian saltation cloud. The behaviors of wind-blown sand over gobi desert surface commonly manifest wind erosion. About 60% milestone of the Lanzhou–Xinjiang Railway traverse gobi desert region. The project of "sand-combating system in Yumen section of the Lanzhou–Xinjiang Railway" attained the first award of National Science and Technology Progress in 1994 and can be taken as a typical engineering of combating wind-blown sand to protect railway over gobi desert region.

There are deflation pier, sand drifting with grass and shrub, and small sand dunes with 1–3 m height distributed on both sides of the railway, except for somewhat fluctuating gravel with 2–20 cm grain size. Annual precipitation is about 61.3–85.3 mm, and varies greatly in different period. For example, it is 25–41.5 mm in dry year, 165 mm in wet year. Precipitation in July accounts for a quarter of that in a year. Sometimes, there is about 140 successive days without precipitation in spring and winter. Average wind speed is 3.3–4.7 m/s in spring and winter, and the days with strong wind in a year is about 42. All of theses are disadvantage factor for plant growth. Water sources on the earth surface include the Changma River, the Chijin River, the Baiyang River, and the Shiyou River, which are located at the foot of the Qilian Mountains. Surface water and shallow underground water is fresh water, which can provide irrigation condition for building forestry belt.

According to the character of strong wind, shortage of sand sources and strong wind erosion of blown sand, the main aim along railway in Yumen section is to reduce wind speed and cut off sand supplies from sources. Local people adopted the configuration mode of "blocking together with protection, front compact and back sparse", and build forestry belt with different width and strips in the region parallel with railway, and match other biological or engineering measures to form an integrated sand-blocking and wind-preventing system with forestry belt as its body. The material of high vertical sand-blocking barrier located in the front of protection system was taken from the local place. People use tress stumped from *willow* and other shrub to weave 1.5 m high barriers with two-line arrangement or feather-liked structure. Forestry belt was started to be built in the region of 10–15 m from barrier, and selected different mode according to the condition of wind regime and sand source. Commonly, there are three classes. ① Common protection mode. One or two forestry belt was built along the perpendicular side of the dominant wind direction, and the first width in the front of protection system is about 20–30 m. In the upwind regions, people established two-line shrub, and plant 3–5 line arbor in the downwind region. The second wind-preventing forestry belt is 50 m away from the first, and its width is usually about 20 m and mix-planted with arbor and shrub. In order to avoid disturbing engine driver's line of sight, forestry belt is 40 m away from railway. In the side of hypo-main wind, the width of forestry belt is 20 m; mix-planted with arbor and shrub, and it is about 35 m away from railway. The total width of sand-blocking and wind-preventing system is 195 m. ② Hypo-emphatic protection mode. There are two-line wind-preventing barriers in the side of dominant wind and the width of front sand blocking and wind-preventing forestry belt increased up to 40–50 m on the basis of common protection mode. Its space interval between lines is still 5 m. There are 3–4 belts of shrub in the front of protection system and 6–7 belts of arbor behind it. We can increase the width of forestry belt in the hypo-main wind direction up to 20–25 m. The total width of protection system is 210–220 m. ③ Emphatic protection mode. On the basis of hypo-emphatic protection mode, we have increased one sand-blocking and wind-preventing forestry belt, with 40–50 m wide, in the side of dominate wind, with shrub in the front region and arbor in the back region, and with 100 m away from the second belt. The width of protection forestry belt in the side of hypo-main wind properly increases up to 25–30 m. The total width of protection system in the emphatic section is 370 m (Fig. 17-3). It must protect natural vegetation beside protection system, and accelerate them to grow with flood-irrigation. In addition, the measure of covering sand with dregs from oil refining factory and wasted liquor from paper mill has been adopted in both sides of railway of Yumen section.

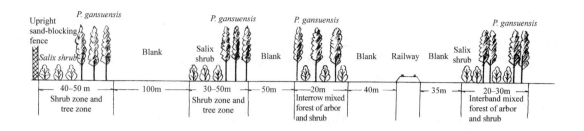

Fig. 17-3　Cross-section diagram of sand-prevention system in Yumen section of the Lanzhou–Xinjiang Railway

The choices of tree species rely on the different aims of blocking sand or preventing wind. The tree species of sand-blocking forestry commonly are xerophytic shrub or semi-shrub with rapid growth rate, strong renewing capacity, more canopy and strong main root and branch root, and resist sand burying and cutting, grow adventitious root rapidly after buried by sand, bourgeon adventitious bud after wind erosion, and can bear common drought and physiological drought. Protection forestry are long-span and xerophytic arbor with high trunk, luxuriant branches and leaves, rapid growth rate, strong root system, and to resist falling, breaking by wind, and able to bear drought, leanness.

After the introduction and selection, the species of arbor, not only adapt to local environment but also agree with the above-mentioned conditions, which include *Populus gansuensis*, *P. alba*, *P. alba* var. *pyramidalis*, *P. hopeiensis*, *P. opera*, *P. nigra*, and *Elaeagnus angustifolia*. The species of shrub includes *Hippophae rhamnoides*, *Haloxylon ammodendron*, and other *Caragana*.

Being more gravel and little soil within soil layer in gobi desert region, the survival ratio of tree is low, or tree is live but grow badly and cannot form forestry due to water and fertilizer leaking. In the course of building protection forestry along railway, according the rule that blown sand flow will deposit and accumulate when moved on fluctuation landform or obstacles, people plant trees in the ditch and get actual effect. Wind-accumulated soil in ditch is loosen and has some certain fertility, good capacity of water-sustaining and water conservation, due to deadwood or leaves falling into the ditch, and can provide a good condition for trees, especially in its infancy period, to grow, and increase its survival rate.

Sand-preventing and sand-combating engineering along railway in Yumen section of the Lanzhou–Xinjiang Railway began to make investigation and design in May of 1966. Up to 1994, 96 km sand-defending forestry belt (about 560 hm^2) has been built in the sides of Junkenyierdao ditch, from the Sanshili well to the Gongchang River region. In addition, people also built about 120 km long irrigation ditch. With many green barriers in both sides of railway, it effectively controlled the attacking of wind-blown sand to railway, ensured the safety of traveling train, and get accumulative benefit up to several hundreds million *yuan* RMB.

17.4.3 Preventing and combating blown sand hazards along highway in extremely arid sand region (taking sand-defending engineering along the Tarim Desert Highway as an example)

Taklimakan Desert is the biggest desert in China, and the second in the world in area. The area of shifting dune accounts for 85% of that total area, and the active intensity of sand dune is the most in the world. About 92% of length of the desert highway transverses through the active dunes. The desert consists of active sand dune with different configurations and heights. The relative height of sand dune in the back desert is about 70 m. Field observation shows that the annual moving rate of about 1 m high crescent dunes is 5–20 m, with 1,000–2,300 m^3 sand transport in every kilometer section. It is very difficulty to build highway in that formidable natural condition, and more difficulty to combat wind-blown sand hazards to ensure that highway be expedite.

Annual precipitation is about 32–48 mm along desert highway, but evaporation capacity is high to 3,200–3,400 mm. Annual relative humidity of air is 45%, and only 10% in the end of spring or early summer. The highest temperature of sand surface is up to 74 °C in summer, and the lowest is about −23 °C in winter. The thickness of dry-sand layer on dune surface is about 20–40 cm. Underground water level in some inter-dune depression exceeds 8 m, and it is mostly salted water with 4.5 g/L of mineralized degree, even up to 25 g/L in some regions, except for fresh water in a few old river-way regions. All this environmental conditions makes sand combating with biology very difficult. Therefore, a sand-combating road has been guided that people adopted sand-fixation with biology to build and restore ecological balance, with chemicals as assistant measure on the basis of adopting sand-fixation with mechanical to ensure that highway to be expedite. Specifically, the first way was to build sand-blocking barriers and mechanical sand-defending system dominated by straw checkerboard. The second was to build "green corridor" using irrigation with salty water to create advantage condition.

In the sand-fixation with mechanical measure, sand blocking, fixing, transporting, diverging and controlling measures should be adopted comprehensively according to specific condition. Since the project of desert highway in Tarim was carried out, sand-combating work have begun. On understanding of the movement of wind-blown sand in the desert, designers kept the highway away form the region with severe blown sand hazards, and make route located in the middle or lower regions of longitudinal complex sand ridge with unsaturated sand flow. In the wind gap with strong wind or flat sand region, it must design sand-through section in the course of designing roadbed and road surface, and clear obstacles in the sides of road to transport sand freely without accumulation. Under the condition of dominant wind direction and the included angle between dominant wind direction and highway less than 45°, sand-blocking barriers always have been distorted to form feather-like arrangement in different sections.

Existing sand-defending system along the Tarim Desert Highway is dominated by sand-blocking barriers and sand-fixing straw checkerboard. Macromolecule materials, emulsifying pitch and salt liquor have been sprayed to fix sand surface in some experimental regions. The materials of sand-blocking barriers come from a local place, such as reed, and afterward in order to get execution rapidly, they were substituted by nylon net in large scale. The width of protection belt agreed with the degree of blown sand hazards in different morphogenetic regions, commonly 50–80 m in the side of dominant wind direction, and 30 m in the side of hypo-main wind direction (Fig. 17-4). There are 893 km sand-blocking barriers and 5.352 million m^2 straw checkerboard.

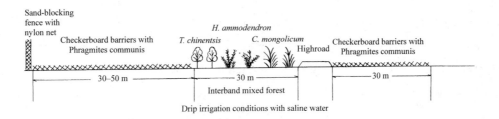

Fig. 17-4　Sand-combating engineering system along the Tarim Desert Highway

Sand-prevention with biology along the Tarim Desert Highway went through some test stage, such as tree species selection, irrigation with salty water and selected several kinds of shrub and herbage. Sand-defending system ensures that highway be expedite and accelerate petroleum exploration in the back of desert. The project of the Tarim Desert Highway was gain one of the ten National Science and Technology Achievement Award in 1995 and the First Award of National Science and Technology Progress in 1990.

The above exemplifications illuminated that combating sand along railway or highway must agree with environmental conditions and wind-blown sand regularity in a region and follow the wind-blown sand physical principle, and adopt integrated sand-combating measures with biology and mechanic, namely sand-blocking, sand-fixating, sand-transporting and sand-diverging.

17.5　Combating and preventing wind-blown sand hazards in farmland

In the large regions of northern China, from Da Hinggan Ling Mountains in the east to Pamirs Plateau in the west, are covered by expansive gob, desert, aeolian desert sand and sandy grassland, where strong wind-blown sand movement harmed agricultural production and pasture yield.

17.5.1 Types of wind-blown sand hazards and its present status

17.5.1.1 Types of wind-blown sand hazards

Hazards of wind-blown sand on farmland are caused by sand-driving wind. Sand dunes advances forward through driving by wind-blown sand flow, and deflation in sandy soil, and sand sources pervading down the wind in semi-fixed sand and blown land. Commonly, their hazards in farmland can be divided into three classes (Lanzhou Desert Institute of the Chinese Academy of Sciences, 1977).

(1) Soil deflation. Soil deflation is a main manner of wind-blown sand hazards in farmland. It is just windy season when seeds are sowed in spring. In this time, sandy farmland is commonly vulnerable to wind erosion for powerful wind, exposed state and soft surface soil. Furthermore the just sowed seeds and seedlings are easily blown away and destroyed on topsoil. Sometimes the seeds can survive after three–four times sowed. In addition, cultivation layer becomes thin and fertile in soil decreases due to the erosion of silt soil or organic content and the increase of sand-content. Therefore, with low yield of farmland, people have to abandon it afterwards. This kind of blown sand hazards is prone to occur in the reclamation regions of grassland.

(2) Sand-cutting seedlings of cereal crops. Sand grains will beat seedlings of crops in the moving process of sand flow due to wind erosion, commonly in farmland, semi-fixed sand and blown land around farmland. Leaves of seedlings were usually damaged and with bad growth, even more withered and it leads to later ripe or no harvest.

(3) Sand-burying croplands. Large-area shifting dunes and part sand dunes may bury croplands in the process of continuous forward moving. At the same time, a spreading belt of blown sand will form in the front of dunes and make soil became sandy. In the action of wind condition, sand-occurring in farmland and sand-driving wind from other regions all together harm croplands.

These three kinds of wind-blown sand hazards were caused by a series of sand activities in the process of wind erosion on farmland, such as sand grain deflation, transportation and deposition and mobile sand dune forward moving. The type of blown sand hazards in different regions is not the same due to different sand sources. In a word, the type of blown sand hazards in croplands of semi-arid regions of east China is dominated by mobile sand dune forward moving and cultivated soil deflation, but for croplands in irrigated oasis regions of west China, the main types is mobile sand dune forward moving and sand-driving wind, and for croplands in semi-humid desert regions, wind erosion and sand beating seedling is the most hazard.

17.5.1.2 Present status of wind-blown sand hazards

Aeolian desertification farmland is distributed extensively in China, with an area of 2.562×10^6 hm^2, accounting for 1.93% of the area of farmland (Table 17-3), of which light and middle degree aeolian desertification farmland is 2.1886×10^6 hm^2, accounting for 85.42%, and strong degree, 3.734×10^5 hm^2, accounting for 14.58%. The area of aeolian desertification farmland in west China is up to 110,776 hm^2, accounting for 2.24% of total farmland in this regions, and 43.24% of the total farmland in China, of which, the area of aeolian desertification in arid regions of the northwest and loess plateau regions accounts for 21.06% and 10.70% respectively. In the farming-pastoral zone of Inner Mongolia Autonomic Region, aeolian desertification is very severe, such as in rain-feeding farmland region of Houshan. Informations (Zhu, 1989) shows that the area of aeolian desertification already accounts for 32.4 of that of local farmland in Shangqiu County in the end of the 1980s. In addition, Chen (1994) researched Houshan area of Ulanqab Meng and other five Qis in the south regions of Xilin Gol Meng for ten years and put forward that the area of aeolian desertification will reach 127.53×10^4 hm^2 in 2000, and increased 35.07% compared with that in the middle of the 1980s. The investigation at the beginning of the 1990s showed that part cultivated layer and grass-growing layer were blown away, calcareous crust and sand-gravel layer under them were exposed and the land production capacity almost lost.

Table 17-3   Area of aeolian desertification of dry farmland in west region of China (hm^2)

Province	Total area of dryland in wind-erosion regions	Area of aeolian desertification	Percentage (%)
Ningxia	205,554	108,281	52.68
Shanxi	242,616	5,745	2.37
Qinghai	168,779	425	0.39
Inner mongolia	2,877,380	2,694,789	93.65
Tibet	26,159	22,245	85.04
Xinjiang	1,399,763	354,248	25.31
Gansu	1,022,671	364,328	35.63
Sichuan	7,883	7,869	99.82
Total	5,890,806	3,557,929	60.40

Data from: General Office of National Environmental Protection: "Investigation report of the present statue of ecological environment in the Western Region of China".

In addition, it is estimated that losing organics content, nitrogen and phosphor in soil is about 0.559 hundred million tons, amounting to 2.68 hundred million ton chemical fertilizer, equal to 17 billion *yuan* RMB. It must take long time to make severe aeolian desertification farmland restore the original nutrition condition of soil and physical-chemical character, even adopting artificial measures. The deterioration of soil quality will lead to the decreasing of grain single production gradually. For example, in the rain-feeding dry farmland regions, single production of grain is 1,335 kg/hm^2 in the 1960s, 1,275 kg/hm^2 in the 1970s, 900 kg/hm^2 in the 1980s, and only 450 kg/hm^2 in the 1990s, and more less in drought year about 150 kg/hm^2.

Seven Qis of the Houshan area in Ulanqab Meng of the Inner Mongolia Autonomous Region suffered from severe aeolian desertification, and there are 32×10^4 hm^2 dry farmland where the 1cm thick surface soil layer has been blown away by wind every year, including 840.48 tons organic content, 54,096 tons nitrogen and 8.30×10^6 tons physical clay particles. With continuous wind erosion, original chestnut soil mould cover with deep soil layer has been blown away and calcareous crust was exposed. In the northern region of Shangqiu County of the Inner Mongolia Autonomous Region, organic content in soil was about 4.129% at the beginning stage of reclamation, and decreased to 1.189% in the period of middle aeolian desertification, and to mere 0.757% in the period of severe aeolian desertification and abandoning cultivation. Using the Houshan area of Ulanqab Meng as a criterion, losing chemical fertilizer of aeolian desertified land in China is about $17,047.44 \times 10^4$ tons every year, with total value of 10.575 billion *yuan* RMB (Zhu, 1994). Another estimation of loss of organic content, nitrogen and phosphorus in soil due to wind erosion is up to 0.595 hundred million tons, amounting to 2.68 hundred million ton chemical fertilizer, equal to 17 billion *yuan* RMB.

Shifting sand dune belts in the Pingchuan regions north of the Heihe River is about 40 km long, and with an area of 12 km^2. Blown sand severely damaged oasis in the periphery of dune, especially deflation of wind-blown sand on soil. Average deflation depth of soil in cropland is about 3–5 cm, and organic content lose 400–700 kg/(hm^2 a), due to conspicuous losing of fine grain and organic content. Because of these, aeolian desertified land in the Pingchuan Oasis in the north of the Heihe River was 8% in the 1940s, and increased to 20% in the beginning of the 1960s even increased up to 30% in some severe sections, with coverage less than 3%. Some croplands had to be abandoned due to encroachment of shifting sand dunes, and farmland have moved southward 200–500 m. Crescent dunes, barchan chains, coppice mounds and deflation land developed extensively on abandoned farmland.

Mobile sand dunes moved forward 8–10 m in the Qingtuhu district of Minqin County, sand dunefields in the eastern Wuwei, Yumen and Jinta, etc., with 12.7×10^4 hm^2 cropland in the oasis before shifting dune severely abandoned due to sand-burying and other wind-blown sand hazards. There were 679 villages suffering from sand burying along wind-blown-sand road.

A strong sandstorm occurred on 28th April 1983, which caused 14 people dead, 37 wounded, and 44,837 livestock dead, 101 civilian houses damaged, 378 stalls damaged, 195 wells buried, and 9 km of communication routes damaged in Ih Ju Meng. Some resident sites in desert commonly had to move for 3–4 years due to encroachment from shifting sand dune.

The depth of surface soil layer in grassland is about 30–50 cm in the eastern region of Xilin Gol grassland, with 50%–60% fine sand grain content in soil layer less than 0.5 mm. Surface soil layer was blown away within 2 years after reclamation, and its deflation depth was about 20–25 cm, amounting to 2,000–2,500 m^2 surface soil loss in one hectare land. But on the bit ridged windward sections, even subsoil and parent sand material exposed on surface, and fine sand grain content of 0.05 mm diameter increased to 60%–90% (Zhu, 1989).

The precipitation of 13 villages in the middle of Naiman Qi of Horqin region is about 30 mm from March to July in 1980. With long-term drought, blown sand is very strong and the days with strong wind in spring and summer are about 15, which causes a seed-planting period delay for 7–15 days. The area of damaged planting is about 0.91 hm^2, and 0.41×10^4 hm^2 buckwheat and grain without harvest in the entire Qi. 33.3 hm^2 fertile lands were buried by shifting sand dunes in Yaoledianzi Village in mere 20 years, with average reduction of 1.67 hm^2 every year. Due to the decreasing of farmland, people have to reclaim barren and lead to aeolian desertification, agricultural ecological environment further deteriorated (Lin, 1993). Seedling and leaves of corn and other crops were withered and dead by wind-blown sand in Yaoledianzi Village in a strong wind lasting 5–6 days in June of 1985, with 30% damaged area, and made corn ripeness later for about 10 days, broomcorn ripeness later for half month (Lin, 1993).

With abusively reclaiming fixed dune, farmlands within 100 m in the side of leeward were buried by sand in the experimental field of Jiangqiao Village in Tailai County of Heilongjiang Province in merely one year in 1973, with 4.2 cm thick sand-cover layer averagely. 9 hm^2 farmland in Hamutai Village was blown into 9,000 m^3 sand soil within three years, with 10 cm thick sand-cover layer averagely.

The area of land suffering from blown sand hazards was about 280 hm^2 in Tongyu County of Jilin Province in the 1950s and up to 1.44 hm^2 in the 1970s. The accumulative area of seeds blown out, of seedling beat by wind-blown sand, and of damaged planting was about 21.58×10^4 hm^2 in 32 years from 1949 to 1980. Average damaged planting area was about 280 hm^2 in a year, and up to 1.87×10^4 hm^2 in 1972. There was 700 hm^2 farmlands without harvest due to wind erosion and sand buried in 1982, and the reduction was about 45×10^4 tons. The area of aeolian farmland in Maxiagen Village of Xinhua countryside in this county was 20 hm^2 in the 1950s, which increased to 60 hm^2 in the 1960s, 136.7 hm^2 in the 1970s, and up to 250 hm^2 in the 1980s. There is a sand ridge trended from southeast to northwest in Houmaxiagen Village. With extensive reclamation and pasturing, the boundary of shifting sand dune extended 500 m toward east, and already attacked the west regions of village. 40 residents have to remove because wind blown sand encroached their houses, stalls and wells (Ma, 1985).

For the regions with extra sand sources besides farmlands, because croplands suffered from sand burying and attacked by blown sand from other places, people mainly build sand-fixation forestry belts and grass rearing to fix or control and block sand movement in their sources. For the case that sand source came from the inner of farmland, sand occurred in farmland due to wind erosion. The combating measure is to build crop-protected forestry grids and adopt agricultural cultivation measure in order to weaken wind speed near earth surface, ameliorate physical character of soil and increase soil capacity of resisting deflation. According to the condition of sand sources, character of wind-blown sand hazards on croplands and natural status in a region, it can be divided into three sand-combating types, namely, irrigated croplands in oasis, semi-arid croplands in sand region, cropland in aeolian desertification section in semi-humid region.

17.5.2 Combating measures of wind-blown sand hazards

17.5.2.1 Preventing wind-blown sand hazards in irrigated croplands of oasis

This region is mainly located in the west of the Helan Mountains and the Wushaolin Mountains. Croplands in these regions commonly distributed in oasis, and croplands suffered from wind-blown sand harmed is mostly from shifting sand dune outside oasis, dry riverbed, gobi, shifting sand dune within oasis, semi-fixed sand dune and wind-erosion regions. In the fringe of oasis, people built sand-blocking forestry belt and grass-rearing belt from farmland to sand source region to fix, control and block sand, and to prevent farmland from sand burying and attacking. Within oasis people built sand-fixed vegetation and constructed cropland-protected forestry grids to weaken wind speed near earth surface and reduce the sand occurring occasion in the local place. The main measures are listed as follows.

(1) To build sand-sealing and grass-rearing belts.

① With wind-blown sand movement in long term, it is to build fixed and semi-fixed sand dune belts with different widths in the fringe of oasis and the region bordered on desert. The plants on coppice mound mostly are *Tamarix* and *Nitraria* because of its little fluctuant. On lower sand between inter-dunes, the vegetation is commonly *Alhagi Gagneb*, *Glycyrrhiza uralensis*, *Artemisia ordosica*, *Artemisia arenaria*, *Sophora alopecuroides* and other psammophytes. With very strong reproductive performance of these plants, although suffering from damage, and once closed in and especially in irrigated condition, their coverage can restore to more than 40%–50% after 3–5 years and can provide the sand-fixing action.

② Width of grass-rearing and sand-closed region was determined by sand source distribution on windward slope and the width of semi-fixed dune formed natural condition. In initial stage, planning width is about 500–1,500 m in the region between desert and oasis, due to sparse vegetation and strong wind-blown sand movements. Planning region is the important protection object, and strictly prohibits grazing, cutting firewood, digging vegetation root, mowing grass, digging medicinal materials and other human activities in planning region. The belt bordered on planning region is taken as buffer region, and strictly control the scale of grazing and firewood cut with dig-root manner to make psammophytes grow and spread.

③ In closed and rearing region, people plant trees and replant psammophytes to increase their restoration with utilization of spare water irrigation for farmland. Commonly after 3–4 years, the coverage of *Alhagi Gagneb*, *Artemisia ordosica*, *Psammochloa villosa*, *Phragmites communis*, *Sophora alopecuroides,* and other natural vegetation increased from 20%–30% to 50%–60%, and shifting sand dune tends toward stable.

④ It is to plant *Elaeagnus angustifolia*, *Popupus*, shrubs of *Salix*, and other arbors on lowland between inter-dunes of closed and rearing region, and built tightly structured sand-prevented forestry belts composed of *Elaeagnus anustifolia*, *Popupus*, *Salix* and so on. Therefore, an integrated protection system of rearing grass and sand-closed integrated with artificial forestry is formed to prevent croplands from wind-blown sand hazards.

⑤ If grass-rearing and sand-closed region is an original base for grazing and firewood cutting in oasis, the canopy of psammophyte can increase to more than 60%–70% for several years closed and prohibition. For sprouted shrubs such as *Tamarix* and *Nitraria,* it can cut stubble near earth surface properly as to materials for weaving basketry, firewood, and can urge shrubs to sprout and rejuvenate (Lanzhou Desert Institute of Chinese Academy of Sciences, 1977; Fan, 1996).

(2) Building sand-preventing and blocking forestry belts.

① According to the principal of adjusting measures to local conditions and setting countermeasures for different hazards, sand-preventing and blocking forestry belts should be distributed with lamina, block and belt structure. Trees are mostly planted on the lowlands between inter-dunes, deflation lands and lower flat sand regions, and less possess farmland or land for farming beside oasis as possible, and should not stay far away from oasis, otherwise it is difficult for them to survive due to bad water and soil conditions, and hardly irrigation, even for temporary irrigation to live, but finally will be withered.

② Building sand-preventing and blocking forestry belts, we should follow a principal of building from near to far and from easy to difficult. It means that at first trees planted in the periphery of oasis and then extended out. For the section with sand dunes, it firstly plant trees with the configure of former blocking and back pulling sand on the lowlands between inter-dunes to surround sand dunes with inter-dune forestry. As sand dune peak was shaped lower by wind, it replanted trees in the bank of sand dune to extend the area of forestry. Therefore, a dense sand-blocking forestry belt was formed without any mechanical measures such as barriers to fix sand.

③ Sand-blocking forestry belts were composed of arbors and shrubs and adopted mix-planted in different rows. The proportion of shrubs should increase by the side of sand sources for forming tight structure to block sand dune moving forward and wind-blown sand from far way out of the fringe of forestry belts and make farmland in the side of downwind within forestry belts from wind erosion.

④ Width of sand-blocking forestry belt depends on the status of sand sources. In the former region of oasis suffered from large-area shifting sand dunes encroachment, with strong wind-blown sand and difficult utilization for agriculture, these regions should be used for planting trees and the width of forestry belt is 200–300 m at small scale, and 800–900 m even more than 1,000 m at large scale. When active sand dunes move close to oasis, orderly arranged dunes before it, it can build 50–100 m width forestry belt near the fringe of sand dune and the width of forestry belt can be reduced 30–50 m in the border region between oasis and sand dune with fixed or semi-fixed dunes.

If the border region between oasis and desert was covered with fixed or semi-fixed sand dunes, slow flat sand, and deflation land, due to no more sand accumulation, it should build sand-blocking forestry belt in the fringe of oasis with the width of 10–20 m and not exceeding 30–40 m. For example, people planted 3–5 rowed *Tamarix* in windward side of oasis in the Turpan Basin to block wind-blown sand flow from gobi desert or wind-eroded land, and form fixed sand ridge with *Tamarix* gradually with protection of arbor forestry belt located in the downside of sand ridge.

⑤ Building large sand-blocking forestry belt must integrate with grass-rearing and sand-closed measure. It utilized spared water irrigation for croplands or provides water irrigation to increase natural vegetation growth on sand dunes or gobi desert, and finally formed multi-layers sand-fixed and blocked barriers with arbors, shrubs and herbages. In the planning regions of sand-blocking forestry belt with large or part dunes, it should fix sand with vegetation gradually.

Practices showed that the arbors for building sand-blocking forestry belt in the periphery of oasis of northwest China mostly are *Elaeagnus angustifolia*, *Populus simonii*, *P. gansuensis*, *P. alba*, *P.nigra*, *P.canadensis*, *P. cathayana*, *Salix matsudana*, *S. alb*, *Ulmus pumila*, etc., and the shrubs mostly are *Haloxylon ammodendron*, *Tamarix chinensis*, *Hippophae rhamnoides*, *Caragana korshinskii*, *Hedysarum scoparium*, *Calligonum mongolicum*, etc. (Lanzhou Desert Institute of Chinese Academy of Sciences, 1977).

(3) Building cropland-protected forestry grids.

① In order to increase wind-preventing action of protected forestry grids, it is best to build narrow forestry belts with ventilation structure or sparse structure. Average wind speed will reduce 40%–50%, in contrast to open field, in the regions from leeward side of forestry belt to 15 times height of forestry belt for no matter what structures, and reduce 20% at 20 times height of forestry belt.

② The building of cropland-protected forestry grids: over all planning should be made, combined with strip-liked and square cropland, and water, soil and forestry should be comprehensively controlled. After the formation of forestry belts, it usually does not need to irrigate perennial due to side infiltration and lower underground water.

③ Configuration of forestry belt: Being frequent strong wind, violent blown sand movement and sometime company with sandstorms and black storms in the northwestern region of China, it is best to build narrow forestry belt, small cropland-protected forestry grids. Commonly, the space of main forestry belt is about 200–300 m, and that of subsidiary forestry belt is 500–600 m. It is meaning that the area of strip-liked cropland in a grid is about 10–18 hm^2. On sandy land, the space of main forestry belt can be reduced to 150–200 m and the space of subsidiary forestry belt can be reduced to 400–500 m. The narrow forestry belt should consist of 2–3 rowed arbors and no exceed 5 rows at most.

④ With good water and soil condition in oasis regions, fast growing arbor species should be chosen for cropland-protected grid. The tree species for forestry grid are *Salix matsudana*, *Populus simonii*, *P.nigra*, *P. albla*, *P.nigra*, and so on in north reclamation region of the Ulan Buh Desert and the Hetao irrigation region, P. gansuensis, *P. albla*, and so on, in the Hexi Corridor, *P. cathayana* in the Qaidam Basin, and *P. albla*, *P.nigra*, *Salix alba*, etc., in some oasis and new reclamation regions in Xinjiang (Li, 1987).

　　(4) Mechanical measures.

　　① Clay barrier(Fig.17-5).

Fig. 17-5　Clay barrier

　　There are two kinds of clay barriers, one is to dig clay on the spot silt soil to pave several small low banks of earth, which is paralleled with each other, in the windward slope of dunes, perpendicular with dominant wind direction, and increase several longitudinal small low banks of earth in necessary. The other is, based on the pavement of row structure, repave several small low banks of earth paralleled with main wind direction, also named clay-checkered barriers. When paving row structured clay barriers, the space of barriers does not exceed 4 m at most, and usually is 2–3 m, with 15–20 cm height and 30–40 cm width of its bottom. The standard of clay-checkered barriers commonly is 1m×1.5 m or 2 m×3 m, with 150 cm height and 30 cm width of its bottom (Lanzhou Desert Institute of Chinese Academy of Sciences, 1977).

　　Sand fixation of clay barriers mostly manifested three aspects. (a) Sand bed in the middle of barriers began to descend due to wind erosion and appeared sand-accumulation beside barriers after a wind season. The space of barriers is, the more deep sand bed in the middle of barrier deflated by wind, but commonly its most depth of wind erosion does not exceed 1/10 space of barriers, and usually is about 1/12. When the depth of wind erosion between barriers is up to a certain value, a stable concave curve formed and it does not suffer from wind erosion and sand accumulation any longer. Therefore, if people wanted to plant *Haloxylon ammodendron* or direct seed psammophyte on shifting sand dune, it must pave clay barriers in advance to avoid wind erosion period of sand bed between barriers for providing a stable environmental condition for seedling survival. (b) Wind speed within 20 cm above earth surface in the middle of barriers reduced about 20%–30% as compared with that on shifting sand dune, and the wind speed on 2 m above sand bed reduced more than 40%. The early-formed stable concave between barriers has an effective role of collecting rain to ameliorate water condition of sand layer. After rain, the depth of sand layer with the same humidity within clay barriers is more 10–15 cm than that on adjacent shifting sand dune. Water content of sand layer between 0–50 cm within clay barriers usually increases 20% compared with that on shifting sand dunes. (c) The materials for clay barrier come from local with more economic and last protection compared with straw barrier, and can ameliorate physical structure of shifting sand dune, increase its capacity of resisting wind erosion. Clay barrier usually can last more than 4–5 years and the psammophyte planted on it can form forestry after 3–4 years.

②Straw barrier.

The materials for straw barrier can be used with broomcorn stalk, corn stalk, reed, *Achnatherum splendens*, branches and so on. Commonly, in the fringe of farmland, it built single rowed or double rowed standing barriers with 0.5–1.0 m height and the space of double rowed barriers is about 1–2 m. On shifting sand dunes in the fringe of farmland, it can build semi-covered ranked barrier or checkered barrier, and their height usually does not exceed 20 cm. The space of ranked barriers is about 1–2 m, and standard of checkered barriers is 1 m×1 m and 1.5 m×2 m. Observation shows that the character of underlying surface has been altered greatly after building straw barriers on shifting sand dunes. When 1m×1m semi-covered straw barriers were built on shifting sand dunes, its roughness is up to 1.571 cm and increased 205–600 times in contrast to that on bare shifting sand surface. On shifting sand dune, the threshold velocity for sand grain shifting is about 4.5 m/s at 2 m high, but in the middle parts of 1m×1m semi-covered straw barriers, the value will increase to 9–10 m. This weakened vortex intensity for sand grain ascended in the middle of barriers. Wind speed at 2 m above surface between barriers decreased 30%–40% compared with that on bare shifting sand surface. Therefore, straw barriers can play a role of fixing sand surface (Lanzhou Desert Institute of Chinese Academy of Sciences, 1977).

After straw barriers are fixed on dune, a special concave surface can be formed due to complex interaction between airflow and straw barrier. But the deflation depth of sand surface between barriers is not like that on clay barrier and the depth commonly does not exceed 1/10 of the space of adjacent barriers. Once a stable concave curve was formed, sand surface tended to be stabilized. When standing barriers was set along the edge of shifting sand dunes and wind-eroded land, effective distance of wind weakened in leeward side is up to 10–20 *H* (*H* is the height of barrier), which has a conspicuous action of preventing cropland from attacking by wind-blown sand flow.

(5) Agricultural technology measures.

① Properly choosing and collocating crops.

Practice showed that crops tolerated sand cutting are hemp, wheat, barley, highland barely, millet, potato, broomcorn, and so on. Monocot crops can grow new leaves and has low mortality under irrigated condition, when total or part leaves are withered after sand cutting, because its terminal bud is wrapped in leaves.

For example, cotton was usually planted in small plot with lower sand content in Turpan region of Xinjiang, while wheat, broomcorn and other crops bearing wind-blown sand were planted in farmland with higher sand content. In this region, it also planted hemp in the fringe of sand dune and broomcorn in the small bank of cotton field. Hemp and broomcorn, as high-stem crops, growing fast have capacity of resisting wind-blown sand, and can exert the role of artificial sand barriers.

Experimental observation in reclamation region of northern Ulan Buh Desert shows that seedling of hemp and corn planted in newly reclaimed barren land easily suffers from wind erosion and sand cutting. If planted wheat-bearing sand cutting with high density, the blown sand hazards will reduce, and herm and corn planted in leeward will be protected.

② Sandy soil cultivation.

The proportion of summer-harvested crops is very big in oasis. How to prevent bare farmland from wind erosion and keep soil moisture content of fertilized land is an important problem of sandy soil cultivation. In order to increase roughness of earth surface, sandy soil plough up across with dominant wind direction to weaken wind speed near earth surface and prevent soil from wind erosion, because of uneven furrow.

③ Planting technology.

Because the seedling period of crops is not able to endure wind-blown sand, it must adjust the period of planting and make seedling period avoid of wind season. According to local seasonal changes of wind-blown sand and the characters of crops in Hexi region, for the farmland suffering from severe wind erosion, people plant millet suited for later seeding and other short-term growth crops to avoid of strong wind season, even summer-planted crops, such as corn, cotton, were planted later properly to reduce the time experienced in wind season and also weaken wind power via weed in the cropland. As for wheat, sunflower, hemp and other crops commonly carry out early seeding, because soil is relatively humid after unfreezing and does not suffer from wind erosion. In addition, once this kind of crops grows up, they have a strong character of resisting wind-blown sand hazards.

After increasing planting quantity, seedlings-kept rate is on the lower side because sandy soil suffered from wind erosion. In order to keep adequate density of crops in unit area, it usually increases seed quantity. Take wheat as an example, seed quantity on a hm^2 sandy soil commonly increases 22.5–37.5 kg compared with that on farmland, which can improve seedling's capacity of resisting wind erosion.

All mentioned engineering technology measures and agricultural technology measure are very necessary for preventing or reducing wind-blown sand hazards on cropland and also for getting effective protection before cropland-protected forestry girds, sand-blocking forestry belt and grass-rearing and sand-closed belt exert protected function, although they don't prevent wind erosion and attack wind-blown sand from extra places.

17.5.2.2 Preventing blown sand hazards in croplands of semi-arid sand region

These regions mainly include the east area of the Helan Mountains, the western area of Baicheng and Kangping, and the northern sandy cropland of Zhangwu, Duolun, Shangdu, Yuci, Yanchi and Jingtai (Zhu et al., 1994). Croplands, shifting sand dune, fixed dunes and semi-fixed dunes in these regions take belt-liked interlinked distribution or mosaic distribution. Wind-blown sand hazards for croplands in Tandi and Dianzi region are mainly the farmlands which were buried by shifting sand and seedlings of cropland attacked by wind-blown sand. The main combating measure is to build sand-blocking forestry belts in the border region between sand dunes and farmlands, and plant grass-rearing belts to fix shifting sand dune beside the forestry belts. The hazards for croplands on flat region mostly come from wind erosion itself, and so its combating measure is mainly to build cropland-protected forestry belts and main prevented measures are listed as follows.

(1) Fathering active sand dunes.

① Blocking in front of it and pulling behind it, pushing it forward with the wind.

In sandy regions of Ordos, people planted several rowed wild seedlings or tress of *Artemisia ordosica* with 2–3 years old along contour line of sand dunes and perpendicular with dominant wind direction in the middle and lower regions of windward slope of dunes in later autumn and early spring, with 10–20 roots in a pit, planted depth of 30–40 cm and exposed height of 10–20 cm, spacing in the row of 0.5–1.0 m and row spacing of 1.5–2.0 m. In the fixed and semi-fixed sand dunes region far away from *Artemisia ordosica,* it commonly used *Salix matsudana* to fix sand and planted one or two rowed tress of *Salix matsudana* with 2–3 years old in lower region of windward slope of sand dunes, with 4–5 roots in a pit, spacing in the row of 0.5–1.0 m and row spacing of 2.0–3.0 m even increasing to 4.0–5.0 m. When planting sand-fixed plants with density in the middle and lower regions of windward slope of sand dunes, wind erosion on sand dunes surface tends to be gentle and may plant sand-fixed trees and species of arbor.

While in sandy regions of Horqin, people firstly planted several belted wild seedlings of *Artemisia* with density or inserted tress of *Salix sinica* in the middle and lower regions of windward slope of shifting sand dunes, with 0.5–1.0 m width of each belt and planted 2–4 rows, spacing in the row of 0.5 m and distance of belts of 1–2 m. When sand dune crest was smoothed flat by wind, it may be planted with some shrubs in large scale areas. Commonly shifting sand dunes can be fixed after 3-4 years using seedlings of *Pinus*. In order to ameliorate soil fertility and increase sand-fixed action, it may seed *Caragana microphylla* or plant seedling of *Lespedeza bicolor* with 2 years old in the regions between belts of *Salix sinica* or *Artemisia* before plant *Pinus*. Because seedlings of *Pinus* are not able to endure light wind erosion, sand cutting and sand burying, when planting them in the regions between belts of sand-fixed plants, it commonly properly paves some weeds to make them live and grow (Liu et al., 1993, 1996; Fan 1996; Li, 1987).

② Planting arbors and shrubs in inter-dune depression.

In sandy regions of Ordos, it planted 1–2 rowed *Salix matsudana, Populus simonii,* and *Populus canadensis* with 3–4 years old, 3–4 m long and 4–5 m thick in the regions of leeward slope or the foot of shifting sand dunes in spring, and its planted depth was determined by the level of underground water and commonly was 1–2 m with spacing of the rows of 2 m×3 m. It planted seedlings or tress of *Salix matsudana, Artemisia arenaria, Amorpha fruticosa,* and *Populus* in the low regions of inter-dunes before arbor forestry without planting sand-fixed plants in windward slope at first. When sand dunes moving forward and entered into lower regions of inter-dunes, seedlings of high-stem belt forestry are grown more quickly as more frequently suffering from sand burying. After 2–3 years, sand dune crest has been shaped by wind and became flat sand dunes and then planted sand-fixed plants on its windward slope.

But in sandy regions of Horqin, it commonly planted *Populus simonii, Populus pseudo-simonii, Amorpha fruticosa* and Salix sinica in the lower regions of inter-dunes. If the level of underground water is usually about 2–3 m and without temporary water-accumulated phenomenon on earth surface during rain season, it may mix-plant *Pinus,* and also builds mixed broadleaf-conifer forest.

③ Combining arbors with shrubs to fix sand dunes.

It planted arbors and shrubs in leeward slope of sand dunes and lower region between dunes to pull sand dunes flat gradually and then properly planted *Amorpha fruticosa* and other sand-fixed plants or seeded daghestan sweet clover or in virtue of natural grasses to fix sand dune completely.

④ Comprehensively planting arbors, shrubs and grasses.

It planted species of arbor and shrub bearing sand buried in the regions between sand dunes, and planted sand-fixed plants in the lee regions of windward slope of sand dunes. As sand dunes moves forward, seedlings in low regions of inter-dunes suffered from sand burying and were grown strongly. Because sand-fixed plants controlled the lee region of windward slope, sand dunes' crest has been smoothed flat by wind gradually and then may plant sand-fixed plants entirely in this region. In addition, it may seed forage such as *Melilotus suaveolens* under forestry in inter-dunes depression. Due to good water condition here, *Melilotus suaveolens* grow very well and not only ameliorate soil structure but also provide forage.

Investigation showed that in sandy regions of Ordos, sand dunes can be controlled through "Blocking before it and pulling behind it, pushing it forward with the wind". This method can cause coverage of arbors and shrubs increasing more than 50% after 5–6 years, and coverage of artificial seeding grass or natural grass increasing to 40%. Sand dunes can be basically fixed with the integrated planting measure of arbors, shrubs and grass. In Horqin regions, following this method, shifting sand dunes can be controlled and turned into 2 m high lush *Pinus* forestry within 10 years.

As time continues, *Pinus* forestry grows more quickly, with its height of 5–6 m and chest diameter of 6–7 m after 17 years (Fan, 1996; Zhu, 1998).

(2) Fencing and rearing protection belt.

It built closed protection belt for rearing in the periphery of forestry belts with width of 1–2 km. Closed rearing belt not only improve the canopy of vegetation, but also consolidate the result of farthing shifting sand dunes, and then reduce sand sources for forming wind-blown sand and take protection for croplands.

In Maowuliegan district of Ejin Horo Qi of the Mu Us Sandy Land, though the measure of rearing grass and closed sand since 1952, it made psammophyte dominated by *Amorpha fruticosa* restore very well, and made pasture increase to 1220 hm^2, accounting for 78.3% of the entire area.

In fixed sand dune and flat sand with *Amorpha fruticosa* as its dominated vegetation within the Mu Us Sandy Land, after 3 years, the height of natural seeding *Amorpha fruticosa* shrubs on abandoned deflation region is about 35 cm, with crest breadth of 30–35 cm. Commonly it is closed for 4–5 years, the height of vegetation will reach 60–70 cm.

The precipitation is about 300 mm in Otog Qi. If closed for 1–2 years, the coverage of natural herbages such as *Eragrostis pilosa, Setaria viridis, Zygophyllaceae,* and other weed is about 70%. It continued to be closed for 3–5 years, *Pennisetum centrasiaticum* and other rooted plants began to breed, and closed for 6–10 years, it was near to original vegetation status, and with domination by *Artemisia frigida, Melilotus suaveolens, Astragalus adsurgens, Lespedeza davurica, Stipa glareosa, Stipa gobica* (Fan, 1996; Hu, 1990; Zhu, 1991).

(3) Protected forestry belt in cropland.

① In relative humid valley-bottom or bottomland with irrigated condition, arbors can grow 15–20 m. When build cropland-protected grids along ditch, cropland, and road, the spacing of main forestry belt across with dominant wind direction is about 300–400 m, and that of assistant forestry belt is about 600–800 m. On farmland with strong wind erosion, grids of forestry belts may be small and the spacing of main forestry belt is about 100–150 m or 200–300 m, and that of assistant forestry belt is about 200–300 m. Commonly, the spacing of main forestry belt is determined by 15–29 times height of tree.

② Main forestry belt is usually 2–3 rows and 5–6 m wide in order to protect little land.

③ In order to prevent cultivated soil from wind erosion, shrub belts will be planted in the regions between main forestry belt and assistant forestry belt when building cropland-protected forestry grids.

④ Either for farmland with irrigation or dry farmland, if there is shifting or semi-fixed sand dunes in periphery of it, especially in the side of main wind direction, people should build sand-blocking forestry belt beside farmland and plant psammophyte in the section with sand dunes to avoid shifting sand enter into cultivated regions.

⑤ Planting tree species of cropland-protected grids. Arbors are *Populus simonii, P. albla, Salix matsudana*, *Elmus pumila*, etc., and shrubs are *Salix psammophila*, *Artemisia halodendron*, *Hippophae rhamnoides*, *Hedysarum*, *H. fruticosum*, *Lespedeza bicolor*, *Caragana korshinskii*, *C. microphylla*, *Salix gerdejevii*, *Prumus armeniaca*, *Elmus pumila*, and so on. These indigenous tree species have strong adaptability, and most are pioneer tree species with strong sand-fixed action. The species of arbor are *Populus simonii*, *P. cathayana*, *P. Canadensis*, *Pinus sylvestris*, *Salix matsudana*, and so on (Liu, 1996; Zhu, et al., 1993).

17.5.2.3 Preventing wind-blown sand hazards in croplands of humid and semi-humid aeolian desertification region

Humid and semi-humid aeolian desertification regions mainly include lower reaches of the Nenjiang River, west region of Jilin Province, the Huang-Huai-Hai Plain and south sandy land along river (Zhu, 1981). Annual precipitation in these regions is commonly 400–700 mm, and 1,500 mm at most. And there is herbage, shrubs vegetation and several-year growth herbage even in sand dunes activated section. Because of good natural conditions, sand-prevented measures for croplands in these sections mainly manifested harness of activated sand dunes and improve canopy of vegetation to reduce cutting of wind-blown sand on crops. Constructing of cropland-protected forestry aims to prevent soil from wind erosion and ameliorate local environment.

① Sufficiently utilizing water resources to develop irrigated agriculture and emphasizing on using underground water to develop irrigation with well, burying plastic pipes to develop spray irrigation, drip irrigation and other water-saving technology. Utilization of sandy land changed from original one ripe for a year to three ripe for two years or two ripe for a year to improve its utilization efficiency.

② Establishing wind-prevented system with narrow forestry belts, small grids, integrated measures between arbors and shrubs or shrubs and herbage. At the same time according to different cases, local people planted crops by the measures of belt-liked coverage in cropland, grid-liked coverage on sand dunes and kept stubbles of high stem crops such as cotton and corn to prevent soil from wind erosion.

③ Commonly, exploitation and utilization of sandy land get effects for 2–3 years. Such as planting fruit trees on these regions, in order to get economic effect quickly, it need to plant melons and annual oil plants, which can get benefit in the same year. Practices showed that in order to develop fruit tree on sandy desert soil, it needed to plant crops to foster fruit with first three years, took fruit for 4–5 years, and began to take fruit to foster crops after 6 years.

④ Part activated sand dunes and sand ridges may be closed naturally for rearing, and they can restore for 3–5 years. Artificial measures also can accelerate the speed of sand dune fixation. For example, in lower reaches of Nenjiang River and the west regions of Jilin Province, it is mainly to plant *Caragana sinica, Lespedeza bicolor, Amorpha fruticosa, Artemisia halodendron* to fix shifting sand dunes. While in Nanchang Province people planted monocotyledons, which can not only fix sand surface but also take as medicine plants (Zhu, 1998).

17.5.3 Successful cases

17.5.3.1 Hotan Prefecture of Xinjiang—representing combating wind-blown sand hazards in oasis in extreme arid regions

Around the center of an oasis, the sand-combating system was constructed. Specifically, local people adopt closed measure for rearing in the semi-fixed sand dune region of oasis's periphery to protect natural vegetation, adopt irrigation with inducing flood to restore and build protection belts together with shrubs and herbage to avoid attacking of wind-blown sand as well as to provide a good condition for developing stock farming. They also built 358 km long sand-blocking forestry belts with 100–300 m wide at the fringe of oasis. Within oasis, people built cropland-protected forestry grid with dominants of narrow forestry grids, configured *Juglans regia, Morus alba, Amygdalus, Vitis vinifera,* and other fruited trees, and took intercrop of forestry and grain or forestry and cotton to make the canopy of forestry in oasis increase to 40.2%.

Except for adopting closed measure for rearing in the periphery of oasis, people flatted dune for isolated shifting sand dune region, induced flood for irrigation and built belted forestry in the regions between dunes, and fix sand through setting barriers of reeds or straw on dunes' surface for vast stretches of shifting sand dunes. In some regions with good conditions, they also flushed sand dunes out making use of inducing flood and leveled land to increase the area of farmland by utilizing flood period of from July to September.

After adopting these measures, local environment was improved, wind speed in cropland protected by forestry net reduced 25% compared with that of open field, and sand content in wind-blown sand decreased 40%–60%. Economic benefit was also conspicuous. Compared to the beginning of the 1990s with 1970s, total production of grain, cotton and oil in entire county increased 1.17 times, 1.1 times and 2.31 times respectively, and the single production of grain increased 3.3 times with improved 7.5 times of income per capita (Fan, 1996).

17.5.3.2 Linze County of Hexi Corridor in Gansu Province —representing combating wind-blown sand hazards in oasis in desert grassland regions

Because the regions between north Pingchuan oasis of Linze County and shifting sand dunes has narrow inter-dunes lowlands and can irrigate them with spare water for cropland. Firstly, sand-prevented forestry belts compose of *Pupolus gansuensis, Elaeagnus angustifolia* was built along dry ditch in the fringe of oasis, with the width of 10–50 m. *Pupolus gansuensis* is of conspicuous wind-prevented effect and mostly planted on the sections with underlying soil. While Russian olive is of good wind-blocked effect because of luxuriated branches and leaves, and is mostly adapted on relative low-nutrient soil. During constructing sand-prevented forestry, cropland-protected forestry nets composed of *Pupolus gansuensis, P. nigra* var. *thevestina, Salix matsudana* and *Ulmus pumila* was built within oasis and its scale was 300 m×500 m. Local people planted many kinds of sand-fixed forestry at inter-dunes in the fringe of oasis or on dunes, set clay or reed barriers (including other plants tress) firstly, and then planted *Haloxylon persicum, Hedysarum scopaium, Caragana korshinskii, Tamarix chinentsis* within barriers due to their protection. Therefore, a protection system with strip-liked distribution and surrounded clump by clump was formed in the fringe of oasis. In order to prevent sand sources from extra regions, grass-rearing and sand-closed belts were built beside protection system mentioned above in some regions with shifting sand dunes, and grazing is prohibited to accelerate natural vegetation recovery. The plants of grass-rearing and sand-closed belt have *Artemisia arenaria, Agriophyllum squarrosum, Bassia dasyphylla, Calligonum mongolicum, Corispermum declinatnm, Alhagi sparsifolia, Salsola colina*, etc., with width of 800–1000m. In winter, utilization of irrigated spare water of cropland can accelerate vegetation recovery. Therefore, take oasis as a center, an integrated sand-defending system combined with blocking, fixing and closed measures were formed from fringe to periphery of oasis. Specifically, grass-rearing and sand-closed belts were built at the fringe of oasis, sand-fixed belt composed of setting barriers and planting sand-fixed plants were built at the section with dunes in the periphery of oasis, and sand-blocked belts were built at the fringe of oasis. Certainly, during constructing this sand-defending system, it needs to link with restoring productivity of aeolian desertification land, namely, to dig ditches for leading water, to build cropland-protected forestry net, and ameliorate soil in original abandoned regions. For example, new developed area of oasis is 2,935 hm^2 in Gongchengtan regions, with the yield of grain of 5,527.5 kg/hm^2, and income per capita of 768.3 *yuan* RMB every year, which not only prevents shifting sand dunes but also restores the productivity of soil and ecological environment.

17.5.3.3 Yanchi County of Ningxia—representing combating wind-blown sand hazards in transition belts between dry grassland and desert grassland

Different combating modes were adopted in Yanchi County aimed at different cases. In semi-agricultural and semi-grazing region with bottomland, shifting sand dunes, fixed and semi-fixed sand dunes, the combating mode is, take bottomland as a center, to exploit underground water, dig ditches for leading water, level soil land, bury sand with clay, ameliorate soil with increasing fertilizer, build cropland-protected forestry nets combined with popularized quality variety, thin film covered technology, and build basic cropland, at that time, is to reduce the area of dry cropland suffering from aeolian desertification hazards on sand dunes or sandy land. As for sand dunes beside bottomland, local people adopt the measure of composed of shrubs and herbage to fix sand dunes and replant pasture to determine the number of livestock by the mass of forage, except for protecting natural vegetation on sand dunes. Therefore, it forms a small combating mode of artificial ecological system consisting of "defending, controlling, utilization" in oasis. During the process of carrying out, it adopt the way of " ecological door", which not only suits for disperse characteristics of residents in sand region, but also agrees with distributed pattern for dune bottomland and land for agriculture and pasture, and easily achieves ecological, economic and social benefits together (Zhu, 1989; 1998).

17.5.3.4 Naiman Qi of Jirem Meng in Inner Mongolia—representing combating wind-blown sand hazards in forest grassland in semi-humid regions.

In wave-liked sandy region with development of aeolian desertification, the typical case is Huanghua Tala located south region of Naiman Qi. Because the development of aeolian desertification land is caused by excessive reclamation of wave-liked sandy grassland and its area account for 81% of total area, the basic measures is to adjust existing land-utilized structure without agreement with ecological principle, alter existing extensively-planted but little-income dry-agricultural economy dominated by planting grain, and extend the proportion of forestry and grass. Adjusted measure is to reduce the area of dry farmland suffering from aeolian desertification, plant forestry or grass on farmland, and intensively manage flat bottomland with good water condition. In addition, cropland-protecting forestry net system was build to form a small ecological system in each grid. Owing to different regions with different conditions, local people make different countermeasures, such as developing agriculture in region with good water and soil condition. Therefore, a multi-structure and multi-function ecological nets consisting of forestry belts, forestry nets and strip-liked forestry was formed, and the utilized structure of agriculture, forestry and livestock farming was adjusted to 21：52：27. Because of reversion of aeolian desertified land, the canopy of vegetation increased to 35%, single yield of grain improved 5 times and its total production increased 3.~6 times, and income per capita also improved 1–3 times.

In those aeolian ,ertified regions mainly used for grazing which consisting of interlacing of dunes and smaller interdunes lowlands, lowlands and residential area as well as surrounding farmlands were usually taken as base centers to exploit underground water and to develop irrigated farming for constructing basic farmlands and to build sand-break consisted of arbor, shrub and grass. Enveloping periphery sandy lands and planting sheet woods in interdunes and combining with planting foliage used for fixing dunes on the surface of dunes, and seeding some pasturage, can fix shifting dunes in one aspect and prepare for future rangelands. This kind of mode not only avoids shifting dunes to invade and to activate dunes, and to change ecological environment, but also can integrate with developing farming economy. Just adopting this kind of manner controlled aeolian desertified lands of Baiyintala in Naiman Qi.

In those aeolian desertified regions mainly used for agriculture consisting of interlacing of dunes and wider interdunes lowlands, they will begin from fixing shifting dunes and enveloping grasslands, and combining with readjusting land use structure, and lowlands will be taken as basic farmlands construction center to protect ecological environment and to resume land productivity. Yaoledianzi is a key case. There are 1,300 hm^2 lands in Yaoledianzi, thereinto, and aeolian desertified lands cover 77%, with vegetation canopy being less than 15%. In order to fix shifting dunes, some foliage (like *A. halodendron* and *S. gordejevii*) will be planted on the surface of dunes firstly. Adopting alive sandbreak to fix shifting dunes, and compressing farmlands endangered by aeolian desertification through returning farmlands to pasture, wide lowlands were taken as a base to dig wells and irrigate and level off lands for constructing basic farmlands. In addition, such cash crops as melon and some fruits will be increased in single cereal crops. In addition, assisting some devotion, fertilizer and new techniques will be incorporated. This will not only change the environment, but also develop the economy. As a result, the shifting dunes area had increased to 25% of the total land area, and the vegetation canopy had increased to 30%, and the total yield of crops had increased by 70%, and the annual income had increased by 1.26 times (Liu et al., 1996; Zhu et al., 1998).

17.5.3.5 Zhanggutai region of Liaoning Province—representing combating wind-blown sand hazards in loess hilly area in transition belt between semi-arid and semi-humid region

The spacing of forestry belt and the magnitude of forestry grids mainly depend on the degree of wind-blown sand hazards, local environmental condition and the growth height of main tree species in Zhuanggutai of Liaoning Province. Commonly, the spacing of main forestry belt is 250–500 m with width of 3–5 rows, and that of minor forestry belt is 1,000–2,000 m with width of 2–3 rows. Species of arbor are *Pupolus simonii*, *P. pseudosimonii*, *P. cathayana*, *P. Canadensis*, *Salix matsudana*, *Ulmus pumila*, and so on, and that of shrub are *Amorpha fruticosa*, *Lespedeza bicolor*, *Prunus armeniaca* and so on.

When canopy of vegetation exceeds 70%–80%, wind erosion commonly does not occur. But when canopy is about 50%–70%, intensity of wind erosion is about 0.5–2.9 cm/a. while the canopy is 30%–50%, intensity of wind erosion increases to 2.5–20 cm/a.

There is 25 hm^2 farmland distributed on the northeast fringe of shifting sand dunes, and shifting sand dunes an front of forestry belts move forward 1.4 m every year and cover 0.56hm^2 farmlands. Cropland-protected forestry belt was built in 1970 and began to exert function in 1973. It reduced 10.08 hm^2 cropland covered by shifting sand dunes up to 1986, amounting to 64.2 tone production of corn, and made the production corn increase 29.9%. Net value was about 7.2×10^4 *yuan* RMB without regard of production invest. Because forestry belts possess land and affect production of crops, net increased production efficiency is 8.0% and total economic value is 4.89×10^4 *yuan* RMB (Jiao, 1989).

17.6 Controlling wind-blown sand hazards on grasslands

There are $1.341,21 \times 10^8$ hm^2 of natural grassland in desert regions of China, accounting for 34.14% of total area of natural grassland in China (Zhang et al., 1998). In recent years, owing to harsh natural conditions and human activities, the grassland degradation and aeolian desertification is showing an accelerating trend. This has brought about serious damages to eco-system and animal husbandry in these regions. And it also causes many negative effects on local people's livelihood and economic development. Therefore, to strengthen the control of grassland blown sand hazards, control is of great significance to protect ecosystem, promote economic, especially the animal husbandry development in desert regions.

17.6.1 Lightening the grazing intensity and adopting rational grazing system to restore grassland vegetation

Overgrazing is one of the fundamental causes leading to grassland degradation and aeolian desertification. So lightening grazing intensity and adopting rational grazing system are the most economic and effective method for controlling wind-blown sand hazards on grasslands (Huang, 2000). By doing that, the damaged grassland can restore refreshment and propagation.

17.6.1.1 Lightening grazing intensity

The grasslands formed under different environmental conditions have different community composition, productivity, grazing tolerance and thereby the stock capacity. In the desert regions of northern China, due to arid climate, cold winter and strong sand-drift activity, the grassland usually has low productivity. The grass has low edibility and poor trampling resistance. Therefore, the grassland in northern China has low stock capacity. For example, the grass yield of grassland in northeast China, with highest yield in China, is only about 5,016 kg/hm^2, and the figure in northwest China is only about 1,000–2,000 kg/hm^2. In the desert regions of northwest China, the average pasture edible grass ratio is about 50.02% and the theoretical stock capacity is only about 0.52 sheep unit per hectare. However, because the local people only demands the largest stock number, the actual stock capacity may reach 0.92 sheep unit per hectare, overloading about 77.6% (Zhang et al., 1998).

Lightening the grazing intensity means to reduce the livestock number in the over-grazing grassland and make the actual stock capacity approximate the theoretical value, and finally make the grassland recover. The utilization ratio of fodder grass can be expressed in the following equations:

$$\text{Utilization ratio} = \frac{\text{Feed intake}}{\text{Total forage weight}} \times 100\% \qquad (17\text{-}2)$$

$$\text{Stock capacity} = \frac{\text{Forage storage}\left(\text{kg}/\text{hm}^2\right) \times \text{Utilization ratio}}{\text{Daily intake}\left(\text{kg}/\text{d}\right) \times \text{Grazing days}} \qquad (17\text{-}3)$$

Table 17-4 gives the vegetation changes of a rangeland, which was heavily grazed at first and then enclosed by barbed wire and lightly grazed. By comparing these data we can see that after reducing the grazing pressure, the plant coverage, grass height and total biomass increase obviously. The increase of grass height and coverage can raise the surface roughness effectively. It not only can reduce the wind power but also can make the moving sand deposited. The increases of underground biomass can hold soil, lighten soil erodibility, and finally halt the aeolian desertification of grassland.

Table 17-4　Vegetation changes of a grassland under heavily and slightly grazing conditions

Items	Grassland utilization degree	1992	1993	1994	1995	1996
Plant coverage (%)	Heavily grazing	47.7	55.7	64.3	62.3	57.7
	Slight grazing	48.7	67.3	75.0	76.7	81.0
Grass height (cm)	Heavily grazing	9.5	8.0	12.2	5.7	8.7
	Slight grazing	11.5	13.7	32.1	22.9	21.2
Above-ground yield (g/m^2 dry weight)	Heavily grazing	80.1	74.1	106.0	98.6	73.7
	Slight grazing	70.3	117.0	158.5	172.4	216.9
Root weight (g/m^2 dry weight)	Heavily grazing	178.1	220.8	225.4	195.4	102.1
	Slight grazing	200.1	528.9	380.2	241.5	201.4

Note: the root weight refers to the root weight within 0-30 cm soil layer.

17.6.1.2　Adopting rational grazing system

Each type of grassland has its own growth regular pattern. In addition, different grasses have different response to grazing at different periods. So adopting rational grazing system can reduce the effects of browsing and trampling on grassland. In such case, the grassland plants can be restored after being browsing by livestock. This is of importance to control grassland aeolian desertification.

Grazing system can be divided into seasonal grazing, rotational grazing and continuous grazing and so on (Zhang et al., 1998; Huang, 1981). The seasonal grazing can be also divided into grassland into Summer–Autumn grazing and Winter–Spring grazing according to pasture's type, character and hydrothermal conditions. In general, the Summer–Spring grazing should select the grasslands with good water sources, flat terrain and forage grasses, such as flood land, lowland meadow, dry meadow and high-cold mountainous area. This type of grassland is cold and windy and its grass yield has great changes in winter and spring, so only suitable to grazing between summer and autumn, while the Winter–Spring grazing should select the dunes-distributed grassland. This type of grassland has undulate terrain and the plants are mainly shrubs and semi-shrubs. This is favorable for livestock to escape wind and cold. In addition, the snow cover in winter can also supply drinking water for them partly.

Seasonal utilization is a method for utilizing grassland rationally and preventing to destroy the grassland. The rotational grazing means that we can divide the one grassland into several plots according to grass growth and livestock's fodder demand, and then rotationally let them graze at different times. This pattern makes the grass have short restoration time, and ensures the grass' better development and regeneration (Table 17-5). It can raise the grassland utilization efficiency and reduce the disease hazard of livestock.

Table 17-5　Rowen changes of grassland in growing season under different grazing intensities

Items	June		July		August		September		Average	
	Increased height(cm)	Rowen yield(g/m^2)	Increased height(cm)	Rowen yield(g/m^2)	Increased height(cm)	Rowen yield(g/m^2)	Increased height(cm)	Rowen yield(g/m^2)	Increased height(cm)	Rowen yield(g/m^2)
Heavily grazing	10.2	34.0	9.4	90.6	4.7	46.5	2.6	11.4	6.7	45.6
Moderately grazing	6.1	35.6	8.5	70.5	5.4	68.8	1.4	3.2	5.4	44.5
Slightly grazing	1.6	35.8	8.5	104.4	4.4	49.0	2.3	19.1	4.2	52.1

17.6.2　Enclosing grassland, planting trees and restoring vegetation

When grasslands become desertified very severely, it is very hard to recover its vegetation by reducing the grazing intensity and taking rational grazing system. Once the grassland has begun to be eroded by wind, it desertification will be exacerbated during arid and windy years. If no effective measures are taken, the aeolian desertification will expand more quickly than ever. Therefore, it is necessary to adopt more effective measures, such as grassland enclosure, supplementary seeding and planting trees to control, the aeolian desertification spreading and occurrence of blown sand hazard.

17.6.2.1　Grassland fencing

Grassland fencing is one of the most economic methods for controlling wind-blown sand hazards occurred in grassland. This method means that fence some severely desertified grassland, no human activities such as grazing and cutting are allowed during this period, and therefore the grassland vegetation can be restored gradually. In general, the vegetation of lightly desertified grassland in semi-arid regions can be restored after 1–2 year's enclosure. As to the severely desertified grasslands, the time for vegetation recovery has great differences due to the difference in the height and distribution scope of sand dunes, but the vegetation will be recovered or improved obviously after 5–10 years of fencing. In arid regions, the recovery speed of vegetation is affected by arid climate, however, the vegetation will be recovered slowly if given enough time and low input.

Grassland fencing can be divided into three types, i.e. long-term, short-term and temporary fencing. We should choose them on the basis of the size, form and degradation degree of grassland. In general, for large, continuous and severely desertified grassland or active sand dunes, long-term fencing is the first selection. Even in some extremely arid regions, permanent fencing is also necessary. But for slightly desertified grassland, short-term fencing should be selected. Experiments show that in semi-arid region, even for the severely degraded grassland the vegetation will be recovered quickly after 2–3 years of fencing. The vegetation coverage, grass height and their biomass will increase obviously (Table 17-6). When the ground surface is entirely covered by vegetation, rational grazing is feasible.

Table 17-6　Effects of short-term enclosure on vegetation of degraded grassland

Items		First year	Second year	Third year	Fourth year	Fifth year
Coverage (%)	Heavily grazing	46.6	34.7	42.3	29.1	15.1
	Enclosure	70.0	80.3	89.0	80.0	57.7
Height (cm)	Heavily grazing	4.9	4.1	5.8	3.0	2.0
	Enclosure	32.6	24.9	33.7	20.6	33.1
Above-ground yield (g/m^2 dry weight)	Heavily grazing	41.9	26.7	23.9	23.7	15.1
	Enclosure	267.0	347.0	432.9	220.4	240.2
Root weight (g/m^2 dry weight)	Heavily grazing	117.4	174.8	137.4	52.7	31.3
	Enclosure	359.9	508.9	447.6	251.5	360.2
Ratio of bare land (%)	Heavily grazing	—	6.3	21.8	39.5	42.4
	Enclosure	—	1.5	0	0	0

The time of short-and temporary-fencing can be determined according to specific situation. For example, fencing could be carried out in whole year, summer, winter, spring, or spring and summer, and even only 1–2 month. In general, for fencing in summer and grazing in winter, the shrub pasture should be selected. Because this type of grassland has dense vegetation, thus favorable to avoid wind damages in winter and grazing can be done after snowing. In summer, the fencing should be carried out in July or so. Because in this month, fodder grasses have the maximum recovery ability, the grasses of different degree desertified rangeland can achieve a higher yield (Table 17-7), especially the severely desertified rangeland.

Table 17-7　Effects of enclosure of different degrees of degraded grassland in different months

Items	June		July		August		September	
	Increased height (cm)	Rowen yield (g/m^2)	Increased height (cm)	Rowen yield (g/m^2)	Increased height (cm)	Rowen yield (g/m^2)	Increased height (cm)	Rowen yield (g/m^2)
Heavily degradation	10.2	34.0	9.4	90.6	4.7	46.5	2.6	11.4
Slightly degradation	6.1	35.6	8.5	70.5	5.4	68.8	1.4	3.2
Undegraded	1.6	35.8	8.5	104.4	4.4	49.0	2.3	19.1

17.6.2.2　Reseeding

In order to accelerate the recovery speed of desertified grassland, range reseeding is necessary sometimes. Range reseeding means that sowing fodder grass on desertified rangeland directly without destroying the original vegetation. Under a certain protective condition, grass seeds can germinate and grow normally and can cover the ground surface gradually. The rangeland established by this method is called semi-artificial rangeland. Practices show that reseeding on desertified rangeland is an effective way to control grassland aeolian desertification. It can recover the vegetation quickly and improve the yield and quality of grasses obviously (Zhang et al., 1998; Liu et al., 1993).

The reseeding methods include aerial seeding and manual seeding. The former is applicable in those regions with flat and open topography and large area. It has the advantages such as large-scale and quick speed, but its cost is high and has many restrictive conditions. The latter is applicable for village or household to reseed in small rangeland. It is the most widely used method in sand regions due to low cost, simple operation and few restrictive conditions.

(1) Selection of grass seed. With dry climate and strong sand blown activities in desert grasslands, the selection of grass seed must be careful (Table 17-8). The plants are suitable to plant in semi-wet grassland mainly include *Astragalus adsurgen*, *Melilotus suaveolen*, *Leymus chinense*, *Artemisia halodendron*, etc. Seeds suitable to plant in semi-arid grassland are *Caragana microphylla*, *Hippophaë rhamnoides*, *Hedysarum scoparium*, *H. leave*, *Artemisia sphaerocephal*, *A. ordosica*, *Agriophyllum squarrosum*, *Lespedeza davurica*, etc. While some seeds such as *Artemisia sphaerocephala*, *Calligonum mongolicum*, *Hedysarum scoparium* and *Holoxylon ammodendnon* are suitable to plant in arid and extremely arid regions (Table 17-9) (Liu et al., 1996; Qiu et al., 2000).

Table 17-8　Evaluation criterion of aerial seeding site types and distribution of suitability index

Evaluation factors		Evaluation criterion and distribution of suitability index			
		Class one	Class two	Class three	Class four
Degree of gentleness	Degree of slope (°)	<6	6–12	12–16	>16
	Index	10	7	5	2
Sand dune height	Height (m)	<2	2–5	5–10	>10
	Index	10	7	4	1
Sand dune density	Density (%)	<20	20–30	30–45	>45
	Index	10	7	4	1
Degree of fixation	Ratio of fixation (%)	<5	5–15	15–40	>40
	Index	10	7	3	1
Thickness of dry sand layer	Thickness (cm)	<10	10–20	20–30	>30
	Index	10	7	5	3
Soil moisture content	Moisture content (%)	>5	5–3	3–1	<1
	Index	10	7	5	2
Depth of flood water	Depth (mm)	>200	200–100	100–50	<50
	Index	10	7	5	2
Groundwater level	Water level (m)	<0.8	0.8–1.5	1.5–3.0	>3.0
	Index	10	7	5	2
Index of adaptability		80	56	36	14
Importance index		100	70	45	17.5
Range of importance index		100–80	79–55	54–35	34–17.5

Table 17-9　Quality requirement of several seeds for re-seeding

Seeds	Thousand-grain weight (g)	Purity (%)	Germination percentage (%)	Moisture content (%)
Hedysarum scoparium	28–32	95	85	10
Hedysarum mogolicum	14–16	90	50	10
Artemisia sphaero cephyalla	0.7–0.9	95	80	10
Astragalus adsurgens	1.8–2.5	95	90	10
Hippophae hammoides	7–9	90	80	10
Caragana microphylla	28–34	95	75	10

(2) Seed rate. Seed rate is closely related to survival ratio of seedlings in unit area. It not only depends on seed size, but also must consider other natural factors such as damages of rats, insects, rabbits and sunshine scorching. In general, the seed rate of big-grained seeds is about 15–25 kg/hm^2, and small-grained seed is about 7.5–15 kg/hm^2. Table 17-10 is seed rate for different grass seeds. No matter it is artificial seeding or aerial seeding, the seed quality must be considered carefully.

Table 17-10　Seed rate of re-seeding for different grass seeds

Items	Weight sum of one thousand seeds (g)	Aerial seeding	Artificial seeding	Line seeding	Remarks (Row spacing for line seeding)
Artemisia halodendron	0.65–0.67	3–5	3–5	1–2	1.0–1.5 m
Caragana microphylla	23–32	6–10	6–10	4–7	1.0–1.5 m
Hedysarum fruticosum	10	45	45	10–20	1.5–2.0 m
Astragalus adsurgens	1.3–2.4	20–40	20–40	15–30	1.5–2.0 m
Melilotus officinalis	1.9–3	30–40	30–40	20–30	0.5–1.0 m

17.6.2.3　Vegetation re-establishment and afforestation of grassland

When grassland has changed into drifting sand dunes, it can't be controlled in a short time by fencing. If re-seeding is made in these regions, seeds can't grow properly due to wind erosion. Therefore, the most effective method is to re-establish vegetation and plant trees. Sand stabilization and afforestation can restore grassland vegetation and prevent sand dunes encroachment on surrounding rangelands, farmlands, villages and roads. However, due to harsh natural conditions in the regions, only by adopting suitable techniques can the moving sand successfully be controlled.

1) Afforestation on shifting sand dunes

For planting trees on shifting sand dunes, the windward slope should be fixed with some bush or semibush species such as *Artemisia halodendron, Salix flarida, Caragana microphylla, and*

Hippophylla rhammoides. When shifting sand has been fixed, some drought-tolerant and wind-proof shrub species such as *Elaeagnus angustifolia, Salix matsudana, Ulmus glaucescens and Pinus silvestris*, should be planted among bush barriers. In interdune depressions or wetlands, tree species can be planted directly. For shifting sandy dunes, sand stabilization and reforestation should be carried out firstly in their interdune depressions and lower part of windward slope. When the dune crest and lee slope has been eroded flat by wind, afforestation can be conducted in this part. This method has two advantages. Firstly, low and flat dune topography is close to groundwater. Secondly, flatted dune crests reduce wind erosion and is favorable for plant growth.

2) Establishment of protective forest

In arid and semi-arid regions of northern China, large-scale establishment of protective forest in rangeland is not practical. In fact, in some semi-arid regions with precipitation of 300–450 mm, when suitable tree species and correct techniques are selected, protective forest can be established. In some sandy lands with adequate groundwater source such as the Horqin Sandy Land and the Mu Us Sandy Land, the establishment of protective forest is feasible.

The selection of tree species is critical for constructing protective forest. In desert regions, tree species selection should consider the hydrothermal factors (Table 17-11, Table 17-12). Those trees with low water consumption, strong drought resistance, sand blast tolerance and fast-growing speed should be chosen firstly. In semi-arid and mixed farming-grazing regions of northern China, the suitable tree species for constructing protective forest mainly include *Pinus silvestris, P.tabulaeformis, Salix gordejevii, S.matsudana, Ulmus pumila, Amorpha fruticosa, Caragana korshinskii, C.microphylla, Lycium chinens, Prunus armeniaca*, etc. In some regions with adequate groundwater, some poplars can also be selected.

Table 17-11　Increment investigation of several shrub species on sandy land

Tree species	Age	Increment (cm)		Remarks
		Height (average)	Diameter (average)	
Hippophae rhammoides	1	67.88	0.86	Plant seedlings
	2	115.0	1.19	Plant seedlings
	3	256.0	3.84	Plant seedlings
Caragana microphylla	2	77.47	0.77	Plant seedlings
	5	122.0	1.05	Plant seedlings
Lespedeza bicolor	1	49.1	0.60	Plant seedlings
	2	45.0	0.55	Direct seeding
Salix flarida	1	67.0	0.67	Cuttage (after stumping)
	2	128.0	1.21	Cuttage (after stumping)
	3	22.6		Cuttage (after stumping)
Armenica siberica	1	15.7	18	Plant seedlings on fixed sandy land
Artemisia halodenron	1	35.0		Plant seedlings
Hedysayu scoparium	3	31.85	0.26	Plant seedlings

Table 17-12 Survey results of annual growth of *Pinus syvestris*

Dune position	1985 Height/Diameter	1986 Height/Diameter	1987 Height/Diameter	1988 Height/Diameter	1989 Height/Diameter	1990 Height/Diameter
Dune foot	10.8/1.17	15.4/1.22	24.2/1.39	33.6/1.60	46.2/1.79	70.0/2.41
Dune midslope	8.4/0.39	9.8/1.11	19.9/1.15	23.7/1.29	32.8/1.50	55.4/2.22

17.6.3 Protection of grassland vegetation and control of new sand sources

Human destruction is the main cause of grassland aeolian desertification. To control sand damages of grassland, it is very important to prevent the formation of new sand sources.

17.6.3.1 Prevention of over-digging medical plants

Some plants such as *Ephedra simica, Radix liguritiae, Cistanche sala* and *Cordyceps sinensis* are rare medicinal herbs, and due to demand that exceeds supply, people dig them excessively. This not only depletes resources, but also destroys natural vegetation seriously and leads to grassland aeolian desertification. Especially, over-digging *Radix liguritiae* has severely damaged grassland. In some districts, over-digging of *Radix liguritiae* has led to exposure of soil to wind erosion. Therefore, to control grassland aeolian desertification, the over-digging of medical plants must be stopped.

17.6.3.2 Prohibition of woodcutting in grasslands

Natural grassland species in desert region and arid desert regions are mainly bushes and semi-bushes. They can increase surface roughness, reduce wind speed and relieve aeolian desertification of grassland. But, due to high heat value and long duration of combustion, these plants are cut as fuel. According to investigations, 21% of fuels in the Horqin Sandy Land come from psammophytes. On average, each household consumes about 654 kg of psammophytes per year, equal to 0.6–1.0 hm^2 of grassland plants (Liu et al., 1993). In addition, in order to obtain fuel, residents in some small towns cut firewood in grassland around these towns. As a result, vegetation around these towns has been entirely damaged, thus causing aeolian desertification. According to Zhu (1994), of the total area of land aeolian desertification in China, about 33.2% was caused by vegetation damages such as fuelfood cutting. Therefore, preventing grassland vegetation damaging from cutting is one of the basic measures to control grassland aeolian desertification (Zhu et al., 1994).

17.6.3.3 Controlling of rodent damages

Rodent damage is one of the main causes for the degradation of sandy grassland. Rats can eat the aerial part of pasture plants. According to statistical data, one rat can eat 30–500 g of pasture plants per day, and a 10-rat food consumption amount is equal to that of one sheep per day. Obviously, if the rat number is large, their food consumption will be very great. When rats dig their holes underground, a large quantity of soil will be dug out to form mounds on ground surface. On one hand, it makes the effective grassland area decrease. On the other hand, the grassland will be desertified due to wind erosion. For example, in Bortungu of Shawan County of Xinjiang, in some severely damaged plots there are an average of 4,000 rat holes per hectare, and the maximum is about 6802.

Rats in grassland can be killed by a poison bait method. The most widely used poison baits and their dosages are presented in Table 17-13 and Table 17-14.

Table 17-13　Lethal dosages of some rodenticides and their operating dosages (mg/kg)

Animal name	Zinic phosphide	Sodium diphacinone	Amine fluoroacetate	Sodium fluoroacetate	GlyFtor	Gophacide	Rat Killer
Microtus daurica	43			0.30	4.50	23.43	0.25
Rattus losea	29.7	0.87	22.6			16.93	
Microtus brandti						12.10	
Meriones unguiculatus	12.0	0.09–1.00	1.70	0.65	10.00	11.00	0.66
Mus musculus	150–200			8.00			
Ochotona alpina		3.17–8.68	0.71		3.40		
Ochotona daurica						7.00	
Sheep			1.50	0.30	4.00	3.10–5.60	
Dog			0.50	0.06	6.00	26.0–30.0	
Dosage	5–8	0.2–0.3	0.2–2.0	0.05–0.2	0.5–3.0	0.5–1.0	0.05–0.2

Table 17-14　Application rate of zinc phosphide by different bait-feeding methods

Feeding method of baits	Row spacing (cm)	Sowing width (m)	Amount of bait used		Note
			(kg/km^2)	(kg/hm^2)	
Artificial feeding	25	Place in hole	69–206	0.69–2.06	15 pills per hole in 1-2 grade zone
Animal power feeding	20	0.5–1	750	7.5	3–4 grade zone
Drilling method	20	3.6	750	7.5	2 grade zone
Car-spraying	30	3.0	990	9.9	2 grade zone
Air-spraying	50	35–40	150	1.5	Less than 30m height

17.6.3.4　Pest control

The pests in grasslands in desert regions mainly include locusts, caterpillars, aphids, chafers and pulse beetles and so on, in which the locust hazard is most serious. For example, in Qinghai province, the area damaged by insects reached 97×10^4 hm^2 in the past several years. The density of insect about 200 ind/m^2 in some severely damaged regions. In such cases, the grass yield decreased by 30%–50%, or even 60%–90%. During 1977–1988, the insects hazard occurred almost every year in the Chifeng region in Inner Mongolia. The affected area was about 6×10^4 hm^2 and the insect density ranged from 30 to 50 ind/m^2, with a maximum value of 120–200 ind/m^2.

At present, the main method to control insect damages is to use chemical insecticides. For example, we can use a mixture of 20% Marathont, 10% DDVP and 70% Solvent spray plants; the spray dose is about 1,500 g/hm^2. We can also spray DM or 2.5% Marathont by airplane, and its spray dose is 22.5–37.5 kg/hm^2. These chemicals can pollute the environment and harm livestock and homans, so some effective and low-toxicity chemicals such as chrysanthmum chloride can be widely used (Table 17-15).

Table 17-15　Experimental results of pest control using chemical insecticides

Chemicals	Dose	Insect density before spraying (ind/m^2)	after 24 hours		after 48 hours	
			Death number (ind/m^2)	Efficiency (%)	Death number (ind/ cm)	Efficiency (%)
40% Methyl systox	1,125 (ml/hm^2)	67.2	59.2	88.09	63.2	94.05
5% Chrysanthmum chloride	450 (ml/hm^2)	35.2	29.4	83.52	31.2	88.64
50% Malathion	1,125 (ml/hm^2)	26.4	21.6	81.82	24.0	90.91
	750 (ml/hm^2)	18.6	10.4	55.91	14.4	77.42
75% 3911	450 (ml/hm^2)	32.8	11.2	34.14	17.6	53.66
5% Caricide	15 (kg/hm^2)	31.4	1.3	4.14	2.7	8.6
	22.5 (kg/hm^2)	32.1	4.1	12.77	6.7	20.87

17.7　Monitoring and forecast of blown sand hazards

The basic principle for controlling blown-sand hazards is to emphasize on prevention and rehabilitation. This is a universal principle for controlling all natural disasters. To control sand blown damages, their monitoring and prediction are essential(Fig.17-6).

Fig. 17-6 Dust trapper installed near desert

The aim of monitoring and prediction of blown-sand hazards is to monitor aeolian desertification processes and its developing trend. The monitoring contents of land aeolian desertification include: (a) aeolian desertification factors (natural and artificial); (b) sand activities such as wind erosion rate, sand flux near ground surface, dust content in air and dust deposition amount; (c) changes of aeolian sand geomorphology; (d) vegetation changes (coverage and composition); (e) soil (grain size, moisture content and nutrient) and other geographical conditions. Up to now, this work still has not been carried out fully in desert regions of China except for some local sites.

In the early stages, aeolian desertification monitoring in China was carried out by Lanzhou Institute of Desert, CAS (see Chapter 10). The Institute issued two sets of aeolian desertification data successively. These data showed that there were $33.4 \times 10^4 \, \text{km}^2$ aeolian desertified land in the 1970s, and the expanding rate was about $1,560 \times 10^4 \, \text{km}^2$ per year from the 1950s to 1970s. It also showed there were $37.1 \times 10^4 \, \text{km}^2$ aeolian desertified land in the 1980s and the expanding speed rate was about $2,100 \times 10^4 \, \text{km}^2$ per year in the 1980s. According to the remote-sensing monitoring results conducted by CAREERI, there were $38.57 \times 10^4 \, \text{km}^2$ of desertified land in northern China in 2000. Limited by various factors, the monitoring was not conducted systematically. Because of great differences in aeolian desertification definitions and classification indicators, the statistical data obtained by related departments have great differences and can't provide a scientific basis for making decisions.

Table 17-16 Classification of aeolian desertification in northern China

Aeolian desertification type / Degree of aeolian desertification	A Dune re activation or mobile sand encroachment	B Shrub aeolian desertification	C Gravelly aeolian desertification	D Wind-eroded badland	E Cultivation-caused aeolian desertification in dry farming field
Distributed regions	East sandy land, desert of west China, or river banks in desert	Desert in west China, edge of east sandy land, middle part of Inner Mongolia	Gobi edge, middle and west part of Inner Mongolia	Lop Nur in Xinjiang, edge of Yardan zone at east side of Alun Mts; South Inner Mongolian Plateau (Bashang in Hebei)	Reclamation district in east grassland, north part of loess plateau
1 Original state (Potential aeolian desertification)	1a Fixed dunes or oasis grassland, farmland	1b Steppe or desert steppe, steppified desert	1c Desert steppe or steppified desert	1d Steppe or desert steppe, steppified desert	1e Dry-farming cropland
2 Slight aeolian desertification	2a Blowouts occurs on windward slopes of dunes, area of shifting sand spots occupy 5%—25%, primary vegetation cover>90%	2b Shrubs grow well, shrub sand mound and sand spits of various shape occur	2c Gravels are enriched on ground surface	2d shallow wind-eroded pits occur but no obvious steep bench formed	2e Sand accumulated in furrows in spring, ridges exhibit obvious wind erosion evidences
3 Moderate aeolian desertification	3a Sand dunes exhibit obvious wind-eroded slope and slip face differentiation, area of shifting sand occupies 25%—50%, vegetation cover is 50%—90% of primary state	3b Leaved shrubs cannot entirely cover sand mounds. Shifting sand occurs on the windward side of sand mounds, loose sand or gravels occur in inter-ridge flats	3c Coarse sand and gravels cover ground surface, there are sparse plants, grass cover >25%, ground exhibits a gravel pastureland landscape	3d Blowouts are mostly exposed, small steep benches occur on ground	3e Small patches of shifting sand occur in loessial farmlands, wind-eroded cropland has very low fertility, 50% of humus layer is blown away
4 Heavy aeolian desertification	4a Sandy land is in a semi-fixed state, area of shifting sand exceeds 50%, vegetation cover is smaller than 50% of primary state	4b Large area of shrubs begins to die, vegetation cover <25%, area of shifting sand exceeds 50%	4c Ground surface is almost entirely covered by gravels, sands exist between gravels, vegetation cover is 10%—25%	4d Residual wind-eroded benches occur on ground surface, grasses are scattered between low-class deflation residual hills, gravelly farmlands are abandoned	4e Humus layer in wind-eroded farmland is almost entirely blown away, calcium horizon and soil parent material are exposed shifting sand area of desertified croplands >25% and hence mostly abandoned
5 Severe aeolian desertification	5a Mobile dune field, vegetation cover <10%	5b Undulated shifting sand land, vegetation cover <10%	5c Ground surface is entirely covered by gravels, vegetation cover <10%	5d Wind-eroded badlands become the main body of ground surface	5e Flat sand land or gravel land vegetation cover<10%

The monitoring of blown sand hazards should have an organization, a work team and a monitoring network. The earth resources' information transmitted by earth resource terrestrial satellite (ERTS) and meteorological satellite (MS) provides a firm basis for monitoring land aeolian desertification. However, the conversion of remote sensing information still remains at the stage of visual interpretation. The so-called man-machine conversation is also finished by interpreter's experience and knowledge, and the computer only computes localization and drawing function. At present, remote-sensing experts are trying to seek the auto-interpretation method of computer by amplifying certain spectrum, extension and other physical methods. We hope this issue will soon be successfully solved.

Aeolian desertification monitoring or unified surveying must have a uniform classification system, otherwise the monitoring results can't check each other and is insignificant. Regrettably, up to now, there is no unified classification system and uniform criteria for evaluation. Table 17-16 is the classification system used in the aeolian desertification interpretation by the project of aeolian desertification process and its control in 2001.

Because there have no monitoring network in whole country, the fundamental monitoring for blown-sand hazards has not been carried out so far in China. Therefore, the predictions of blown sand hazards mainly rely on long-term weather forecasting issued by meteorological departments integrated with the analysis of various factors of aeolian desertification development. The prediction of land aeolian desertification mainly uses an epitaxial method of development trend curve or are calculated through the latest-obtained speed rate. We hope that the related departments can pay more attentions to blown-sand hazards and strengthen the monitoring and prediction of land aeolian desertification.

References

Cong Zili. 1997. Comprehensive control of tailing land aeolian desertification in Jinchang City. Journal of Desert Research, 17(3): 317–321

Dong Yuxiang. 1997. Regional risk factor evaluation of aeolian desertification in north China. Acta Geographica Sinica, 52(2)

Fan Zili. 1996. Land Development and Its Influence on Eco-environment and Countermeasures. Beijing: China Meteorological Press, 1996

He Daliang, Chen Guangting. 1991. Present status of sand-drifting activities in Beijing. Geographical Research, 10(4)

He Xingdong. 1993a. Preliminary study on community characteristics of simple-leaf-Vitex trifolia and its adability for sandy land in Houtian area. Chinese Journal of Ecolony, (4): 37–42

He Xingdong. 1993b. Preliminary study on forestation of wetland pine in sands of subtropical zone. Journal of Desert Research, 13(1): 57–63

He Xingdong. 2000. Irrigation units and its calculation formula of sand-fixation plants in sand dunes. Journal of Desert Research, 20(1): 63–66

Hu Binqing. 1990. Aeolian desertification in Zhelimu Meng. Journal of Desert Research, 10(1)

Huang Zhaohua. 1981. Pasture utilization, aeolian desertification and control in Yikezhao Meng, Inner Mongolian. Journal of Desert Research, 1(1)

Huang Zhaohua. 2000. Problems of Rational Utilization of Grassland in Semi-arid and Arid Regions in China. Lanzhou: Gansu Cultural Press.

Jiao Shuren. 1989. Structure and Function of Ecological System of Sand Stabilization Forest in Zhanggutai. Shenyang: Liaoning Science and Technology Press

Lanzhou Institute of Desert, CAS. 1977. Blown Sand Damage Control in Farm Field. Beijing: Science Press

Li Zhi. 1987. Controlling strategy of aeolian desertification in reclaimed area of northern Wulanbuhe Desert. Journal of Desert Research, 7(4): 46

Liu Xinming, Zhao Halin, Zhao Aifen. 1996. Wind-blown Sand Environment and Vegetation in Horqin Sands. Beijing: Science Press

Liu Xinming, Zhao Halin. 1993. Study on Integrated Controlling of Eco-environment in Horqin Sands. Lanzhou: Gansu Science and Technology Press

Ma Wenlin. 1985. Present status and trend of aeolian desertification in Songnen Plain. Journal of Desert Research, 15(3): 46

Qiu Mingxing. 2000. Vegetation in Desert of China. Lanzhou: Gansu Cultural Press

Zhang Linyuan, Wang Nai'ang. 1994. Desert and Oasis in China. Lanzhou: Gansu Educational Press

Zhang Peifang, Yuan Jiazu. 1996. Eco-environmental Evaluation, Zoning and Suggestion of Forestry in China. Beijing: Chinese Economic Press

Zhang Qiang, Zhao Xue, Zhao Halin. 1998. Grassland in Desert Regions of China. Beijing: China Meteorological Press

Zhu Linyi, Baoyin. 1993. Site Quality Evaluation of Tree and Bush in Mu Us Sands. Beijing: China Forestry Publishing House

Zhu Zhenda, Chen Guangting. 1994. Aeolian Desertification in China. Beijing: Science Press

Zhu Zhenda, Liu Su, Di Xinming. 1989. Aeolian desertification and its Control in China. Beijing: Science Press

Zhu Zhenda, Zhao Xingliang, Ling Yuquan et al. 1998. Desert Control Engineering. Beijing: Chinese Environmental Press.

Zhu Zhenda. 1991. Fragile ecological belt and land aeolian desertification in China. Journal of Desert Research, 11(4): 3

Zhu Zhenda. 1998. Land aeolian desertification in China: conception, origin and control. Quaternary Research, (2)

Chapter 18
Regionalization of Aeolian Desertification Control in China

18.1 Regionalization of aeolian desertification control in China

In order to formulate policies and measures to prevent and control aeolian desertification, the regional planning of deserts and aeolian desertification control must be done according to the characteristics of deserts and desertified land distribution, and their development processes. Regionalization is restricted to the aeolian desertified lands and potential areas of aeolian desertification. As far as the eight big deserts in China, they are all mobile sandy lands and there is no need to be control them as they do not pose a direct danger to people's lives or the production of industry and agriculture. The so-called desert expansion actually is caused by the destruction of natural vegetation in the marginal insulating belts of the desert. The insulating belts at desert margins, generally fixed and semi-fixed dunes, are a screen for the oasis. Observations show that the sand flux penetrating the destroyed belts reached $14m^3/m$. Insulating belts can block and trap sand; psammophytes can also trap sand even if the vegetation is scarce. Meanwhile, the wind velocity near the soil surface can be slowed down, so the sand inflow to the oasis and croplands will decrease. At present, the control of desert encroachment mainly lies in the rehabilitation of desertified land.

18.1.1 Regionalization principles

(1) The principle of natural zones. The causes, processes and characteristics of aeolian desertification as well as their control measures are different under different natural conditions. We can divide the desertified areas in China into five regions according to natural conditions.

(2) The principle of aeolian desertification development degree. In areas with the same natural conditions, the control measures are different based on different development degrees. Therefore, the four development degrees of slight aeolian desertification, moderate aeolian desertification, severe aeolian desertification and very severe aeolian desertification will be regarded as secondary indicators.

(3) The principle of the consistency of natural conditions, agricultural natural resources and exploitation direction. In a natural zone, aeolian desertification causes, the patterns of land use, the direction of resource exploitation and the basic conditions of environmental protection are significantly different; especially in the utilization of agricultural resources, the difference is more

evident. Therefore, they are regarded as third-tier indicators.

18.1.2　Regionalization for aeolian desertified land rehabilitation

According to the principles of aeolian desertified land distribution and its development degree as well as Zhu Zhenda's work "The Aeolian Desertification Processes and Regionalization for its Control in northern China", the rehabilitation of aeolian desertified land is divided into five major zones and thirty-one sub-zones. They include:

18.1.2.1　Aeolian desertified land rehabilitation in the humid zone

The humid zone is located south of the Qinling Mountains and the Huaihe River, with more than 800 mm of annual precipitation and no more than 0.99 aridity. Although the precipitation is adequate, it is erratic and shows strong seasonal variation. Meanwhile, these areas are located in a subtropical zone with high temperature, high evaporation and the differentiation of a rainy season and a dry season. The dry season is from October to the following April in southern China, from September to the following May in central China, and in the Yangtze River basin, there is a short dry season between Meiyu Season in early July and a rainy period in mid August. The soil water erosion occurs in the rainy season and wind erosion takes place in the dry season. The area of desertified lands is limited and scattered in some regions of Jiangxi Province, Hunan Province, Guangxi Zhuang Autonomous Region, Guizhou Province, Yunnan Province, Sichuan Province, Fujian Province, Zhejiang Province, Hubei Province, Anhui Province and Henan Province.

(1) Moderately blown sand land control in the middle reaches of the Yangtze River. The area includes the riverside area of the Yangtze River, the area north of the Dongting Lake and the Poyang Lake and the riverside areas in some regions of Hubei Province and Jiangxi Province.

(2) Moderately blown sand land in the dry and hot river valley in the Hengduan Mountains region. The Hengduan Mountains is located far from the ocean and deeply cut by the Jinsha River, the Lancang River and the Nujiang River, so the valleys are dry and hot due to the "Foehn Effect". Wind blown sand disasters mainly occur in the dry and hot valleys of the Minjiang River, the Dadu River, the Yalong River and the Jinsha River in Sichuan Province and there are barchan dunes or barchan dune chains in some valleys.

18.1.2.2　Aeolian desertified land in the sub-humid zone

Aeolian desertified lands caused by deflation in this zone are mostly distributed in the Songnen Plain, Huang-Huai-Hai Plain and some coastal plains. They are all located in the downstream plains and related to high-terrace deposits and vegetation destruction.

(1) Moderately aeolian desertified land in the lower reaches of the Nenjiang River and west of Jilin Province. This area includes the downstream banks of the Nenjiang River in Heilongjiang

Province, the Changlin, Kaitong and the northeast of Shuangliao to the south of Baicheng City in western Jilin Province as well as Fuyu County. The desertified lands are formed after vegetation was destroyed by overgrazing and irrational grassland reclamation and show a patchy shifting sand landscape.

(2) Moderately aeolian desertified land in the center of the Huang-Huai-Hai Plain. This area includes the alluvial plain of the Yellow River, comprising the aeolian desertified lands in Beijing, Tianjin, Hebei, Henan, Shandong, Jiangsu and Anhui.

18.1.2.3　Aeolian desertified land in the semi-arid steppe, dry farming region and desert steppe zone

This area includes the land to the east of the Helan Mountains, west of Kangping and Baichengzi, north of Zhangwu, Duolun, Shangdu and Jingtai, and south of the China-Mongolia border. Moisture and vegetation conditions in these areas are better than those in the arid desert zone but the ecosystem is quite fragile and land is prone to aeolian desertification. These areas are concentrated regions of desertified land distribution in China. All this land resulted from local natural conditions such as the simultaneous occurrence of drought, frequent wind, and sandy surface.

(1) Severely aeolian desertified land in the Bashang area of Hebei. This area, including land north of Zhangbei, Guyuan, Kangbao, Shangyi and Fengning as well as northwest of enclosed pastures in Hebei Province, is a rapid development region for land desertification. Adverse human economic activities such as over-reclamation and over-deforestation are the reasons for the aeolian desertification.

(2) Slightly aeolian desertified land in northeastern Inner Mongolia. This area extends from the region west of Hulun Lake in Hulun Buir to the north of Xilin Gol Meng. Natural vegetation in the area in is dominated by undershrub and weeds and it is a natural grazing area. However, over-grazing in the grassland has destroyed the natural vegetation and led to slight aeolian desertification.

(3) Moderately aeolian desertified land in Hulun Buir. This area, extending from the west of the Da Hinggan Ling Mountains to the east of the Hulun Lake, and to the north of the China-Mongolia border, is an undulating high plain and also a natural pasture land. Aeolian desertified lands in the region include two types: one is sandy hill covered mostly with *Pinus sylvestris* and distributed in high plains or river terrace with scattered blowouts; the other is sandy high plain formed by the encroachment of shifting sand due to grassland reclamation.

(4) Moderately aeolian desertified land in Xilin Gol Meng. This area includes the lands east of Sonid Youqi to the west of the Xi Ujimqin Qi, and north of the Onqin Daga Sandy Land. Aeolian desertification in this area is caused by over-reclamation and irrational use of the grassland.

(5) Severely aeolian desertified land in Onqin Dage Sandy Land. This area, located in the south of Qagan Nur and north of Zhengxiangbai Qi and Zhenglan Qi, is a sandy land with fixed and semi-fixed dunes. Its aeolian desertification occurred in the historical period and modern intensive human activities (woodcutting and overgrazing) aggravate the aeolian desertification processes.

(6) Slightly aeolian desertified land in the northern part of Ulanqab Meng. This area, which includes land to the north of the Bayanlairi and the Bailin Temple and south of the China-Mongolia border, is a desert grassland. Overgrazing resulted in patchy shifting sand on sand-gravel surfaces as well as aeolian desertification around water wells and residential areas.

(7) Moderately aeolian desertified land in the Houshan region of Ulanqab Meng and central Qahar. The areas extending from the south of Damao Qi and Duolun to the southeast of Urad Zhongqi, and eastern Taipusi Qi are natural pastureland with comparatively favorable natural conditions and 400–250 mm of annual precipitation. Aeolian desertification of this area is caused by over-reclamation of the grassland and overgrazing.

(8) Severely aeolian desertified land in the west of Horqin. This area, extending from the south of the Xar Moron River in the western Horqin Grassland to the north of Ongniud Qi, is grassland between the Balin Bridge and the Laoha River. The aeolian desertification of this area was caused by the excessive agro-pastoral land use over the past 200 years and the degree of aeolian desertification is very severe.

(9) Severely aeolian desertified land in the east of Horqin. This area, extending from the east of the Laoha River to the west of the mainstream of the Xiliao River, is characterized by an alternating distribution of meadow and dune. The patchy mobile dunes resulted from grassland reclamation and woodcutting in the past century.

(10) Moderately aeolian desertified land north of Horqin. This region, extending from the north of the Xiliao River to the west of the Zhenjia Village and Tuquan, and to the southeast of Lindong and Linxi and Tuquan, includes some areas of the alluvial-diluvial plains of the Xiliao River and the alluvial-diluvial plains of the rivers in the southeast piedmont of the Da Hinggan Ling Mountains. Aeolian desertification in this area is expanding due to vegetation degradation caused by adverse human activities.

(11) Severely aeolian desertified land east of Ordos. This area, one part of the Ordos high-plain, includes the area south of Ejin Horo Qi and Otog Qi and north of the Great Wall in northern Shaanxi and Yanchi in Ningxia, is grassland. However, due to frequent human disturbances, aeolian desertification in this region is very severe.

(12) Moderately aeolian desertified land in the western and central Ordos. This area, including west of Otog Qi, east of Wuhai City, north of Ejin Horo Qi and Uxin Qi, southeast of Hanggin Qi and west of Dongsheng, is located in the steppe zone with 200–250 mm of annual precipitation. Aeolian desertification is rapidly developing, especially in the southeast of Hanggin Qi and the west of Otog Qi.

(13) Severely aeolian desertified land north of Ordos. This area, including a large part of Hanggin Qi, part of Dalad Qi and Jungar Qi and Dongsheng City, belongs to steppe zone. Due to overgrazing and over-cultivation, desertification in this area is developing rapidly and results in serious disasters.

(14) Moderately aeolian desertified land along the Great Wall. This area, including the northwestern part of Shanxi, south of Ulanqab Meng in Inner Mongolia, and the northeastern part of

Shaanxi, is largely sandy loess ridges, undulating hills and the ancient Yellow River (Huanghe River) terraces. The area is very prone to aeolian desertification as a result of disturbances from human activities.

(15) Severely aeolian desertified land west of Hetao. This area includes north of the Ulan Buh Desert and Delunbuluge, the sporadic desertified lands occurring in the Hetao Plain and shifting sand occurring on the west bank of the Yellow River from Dengkou to Wuda.

(16) Severely aeolian desertified land in the southeast of Ningxia. This area includes most of southeast Ningxia, such as Yanchi, Lingwu, Taole, Tongxin, Zhongning and Zhongwei. In terms of the aeolian desertification causes, most desertified lands are caused by overgrazing, over-cutting and reclamation of the grassland, and a part of desertified lands are caused by encroachment of sand dunes in the southeast Tengger Desert.

18.1.2.4 Sand dune activation and shifting sand encroachment in arid desert zones

This zone is located west of the Helan Mountains and the Wushaoling Mountains. Aeolian desertified land is caused by: ① Human activities around the edge of oases, mainly caused by over-cutting; ② Destruction of insulating vegetation around the desert, for example north of Gulang County at the edge of the Tengger Desert; ③ Irrational use of the water resources, for example in the lower reaches of the Heihe River and the Tarim River; ④ Overgrazing in gravel deserts.

(1) Moderately aeolian desertified land east of Alxa. This area includes the vast region to the west of Helan Mountains, east of the Bayanwula Mountains and the Tengger Desert and north of Zhaobi Mountains, and lies at the eastern margin of arid desert zone with less than 200 mm of annual precipitation. Aeolian desertification is mainly caused by: ① destruction of shrubs at the desert edge and on fixed and semi-fixed dunes; ② overgrazing on piedmont plains; ③ shifting sand encroachment on the edge of deserts.

(2) Slightly aeolian desertified land in Bayinnuoergong. This area includes some land between the Badain Jaran Desert, the Tengger Desert, the Yamaleike Desert and the Bokedi Desert. Overgrazing and irrational wood-cutting caused the aeolian desertification.

(3) Slightly aeolian desertified land southwest of Alxa. This area, located between the Heli Mountains, the Longshou Mountains, the Badain Jaran Desert and the desert in western Minqin, is a pastoral zone. Due to overgrazing, aeolian desertification is developing around the grazing sites, water-wells and residential areas, as well as along the railway and highways.

(4) Severely aeolian desertified land in the Hexi Corridor region. Desertified land in the area is located between the Qilian Mountains, the Heli Mountains and the Longshou Mountains, distributed in patches and caused by shifting sand spread and sand dune encroachment on oases.

(5) Moderately aeolian desertified land in the lower reaches of the Heihe River. This area includes the region west of the Badain Jaran Desert and east of the denudation-accumulation gravel desert in the Mazun Mountains. Vegetation degradation caused by a decrease in water supplies due to over-use of

river water in upper and middle reaches and over-cutting caused the aeolian desertification.

(6) Moderately aeolian desertified land south of the Junggar Basin. This area extends from Qitai in the east to Kuitun in the west and to the plain at the northern piedmont of the Tianshan Mountains in Jinghe and the marginal zone of the Gurbantünggüt Desert. Due to over-cutting, fixed and semi-fixed dunes have become reactivated.

(7) Severely aeolian desertified land in the middle and lower reaches of the Tarim River. This area, including the middle and lower reaches of the Tarim River in the northern and eastern margin of the Taklimakan Desert, is an ancient desertfied land. Destruction and degradation of natural vegetation, such as *Populus euphratica* and *Tamarix Chinensis*, caused by the drying up of the river resulted in desertification in the lower reaches. Excessive wood-cutting resulted in aeolian desertification in the middle reaches.

(8) Severely aeolian desertified land in the southern Tarim Basin. This area includes the southern fringe of the Taklimakan Desert and the piedmont plain of the Kunlun Mountains. The development of aeolian desertification resulted from the activation of fixed and semi-fixed dunes, encroachment of dunes of the Taklimakan Desert as well as the degradation of vegetation.

18.1.2.5　Aeolian desertified land in high and cold regions of western China

A series of basins (altitudes ranging from 2,500 m to 3,500 m) in the northeast have aeolian sand landforms, the main part (altitude above 4,000 m) of the Qinghai-Tibet Plateau, located in the westerly circulation zone, also has aeolian desertified land due to cold, dry and windy climate, destruction of vegetation and serious soil erosion.

(1) Severely aeolian desertified land in the Qaidam Basin. This area includes the piedmont plains at the northeast and southern margins of the Qaidam Basin. Aeolian desertification is developing rapidly in cultivated regions and overgrazing areas.

(2) Aeolian desertified land around the Qinghai Lake and in the Gonghe Basin. This area includes the desertified land around the Qinghai Lake, resulting from the decrease of the inflow and dropping water levels of the lake due to over-use of water resources; the desertified land from Shazhuyu in the Gonghe Basin to the first, second, and third Tala, as well as Mugetan on the banks of the Yellow River, is caused by overgrazing.

(3) Aeolian desertified land in the "one river and two tributaries" zone of Tibet. This area includes the valley of the Yarlung Zangbo River and its tributary valleys, Lhasa City and Xikaze City. Aeolian desertification is mainly caused by over-cultivation, firewood collection and overgrazing.

The following are a few examples of desertified land control, mainly including the rehabilitation and use of desertfied lands in the Huang-Huai-Hai Plain, semi-arid agricultural-pastoral zone in eastern Inner Mongolia, bordering areas of Shanxi, Shaanxi and Inner Mongolia, arid desert oases and the Qinghai-Tibet Plateau.

18.2 Blown sandy land development and rehabilitation in the sub-humid Huang-Huai-Hai Plain

With relatively adequate precipitation and favorable natural conditions, surplus manpower but insufficient land resources, the general guiding principle for land management in this region is "promoting rehabilitation through development and rehabilitation during the development processes".

The Huang-Huai-Hai Plain has a long development history but the occurrence of sandy land has a short history. Historic documents show that the sandy lands in Hebei, Shandong and Henan Provinces in the 1940s were still covered by forest and there were forests and fruit trees on the hillocks such as *Pear, White Mulberry, China Hawthorn, Apricot* and *China Jujube* before the 1950s–1960s. With the rapid population growth in the last 50 years, two large-scale human activities, such as removal of forests and grasses and land reclamation, greatly changed the sandy lands. First, the sand ridges that posed a serious threat to agricultural production rapidly decreased. Second, the seasonal wind erosion was exacerbated by land reclamation. Third, diverting water from the Yellow River to irrigate has brought large amounts of sand to croplands.

Many experiences and lessons have been learned from sandy land reclamation and utilization over the past 50 years. However, there is still a need to work out rehabilitation planning with consideration of local conditions.

18.2.1 Principles of combating aeolian desertification

Aeolian desertified lands in the Huang–Huai–Hai Plain have great product potential due to adequate sunlight, heat and water resources and relatively favorable natural conditions. However, due to its fragile ecosystem, desertified land area may expand if land resources are misused. In order to scientifically and rationally use the desertified lands in the sub-humid Huang-Huai-Hai Plain, we should adhere to the principle of combining economic benefits with ecological benefits and taking into consideration the sustainable development of population, resources, environment, society and economy.

(1) In consideration of local conditions to work out an overall planning to ameliorate blown sand lands, area by area.

(2) Working out suitable measures to control disasters and improve the environment.

(3) Giving full play to local advantages to enhance rehabilitation effects and achieve high-benefits and sustainable use.

18.2.2　Design of aeolian desertification control schemes

18.2.2.1　General principles

The general principle for the rehabilitation of blown sandy land in the sub-humid Huang-Huai-Hai Plain is: irrigation facilities must be first constructed and protective forest must be matched; economic forest and agro-pasture should be developed according to local conditions. The desertified lands in the Huang-Huai-Hai Plain have large agricultural production potential and are dominated by flat sandy lands. Local farmers cultivated crop in humid years but the harvest was smaller due to the fluctuating water resources. Some of this land was reclaimed by local farmers but later abandoned due to lack of water resources. Sandy lands located far from rivers can be reclaimed if irrigation facilities are constructed and the following patterns can be adopted.

Pattern one: low-lying and flat sandy lands with scattered small dunes can be irrigated by the Yellow (Huanghe) River water. The fundamental construction projects, including irrigation and drainage systems, roads, forests and farmland, should be designed and arranged together.

Pattern two: high sandy lands with fewer high dunes and relatively less surface water resources can be transformed into farmland through irrigation by using the Yellow River water and groundwater.

Pattern three: sandy lands located a far distance from rivers and with high dunes can be used to develop mixed agriculture, forestry and stockbreeding through constructing well irrigation and drainage systems.

18.2.2.2　Design of protective forests, canals, roads and croplands

Different land use types and aeolian desertification control measures, including biological and mechanical measures and cropping systems should be adopted according to the characteristics of sand damage and topographic conditions. In the design of irrigation and drainage systems, special consideration should be given to flood carrying capacity during rainstorm periods.

1) The selection of afforestation tree species

Indigenous tree species including arbor and shrub, which have the characteristics of fast growths, endurance of impoverished soils and use as timber, should be chosen for the shelter forest. The main tree species include: *Populus ussuriensis*, *Populus tomentosa*, *Salix matsudana*, *Robinia pseudoacacia*, *Paulownia* and *Amorpha fruticosa* and the accessory tree species include: *Toonaa sinensis*, *Tamarix chinensis*, *Fraxinus*, *Armeniaca sibirica*, *Salix babylonica*, *Populus nigra var. italica*, *Robinia pseudoacacia*, *Ulmus pumila* and *Cupressus*, etc. The shelter forest belt should include trees, shrubs and grasses. The grass species include *Medicago sativa*, *Astragalus adsurgens*, *Melilotus officinalis* and *Henerocallis citrine*.

2) Design of canals, roads, forests and croplands

The construction of a perfect irrigation system is an important measure to rehabilitate sandy lands in the Huang-Huai-Hai Plain. Canals, forests and road systems should be built simultaneously. The irrigation system, including sprinkling and drip irrigation, can be adopted in some areas. The irrigation and drainage canals vary in length from 8 m to 15 m and in depth from 1.5 m to 2 m. The width of main roads varies from 6 m to 8 m and the width of farm path is 4 m. The area of sandy cropland enclosed by shelter forest varies from 3 hm^2 to 5 hm^2. The distance between the main shelter forest belt including trees, shrubs and grasses is 200–250 m and the distance between the accessory shelter forest belts, which is vertical with the main shelter forest belt, is 150–200 m.

(1) The flat sandy lands with irrigation canals. The sandy lands in Yucheng in Shandong Province is a good example of this kind, which has a canal system linked with the surrounding irrigation network. With the Yellow River water as a water source, the irrigation system in Yucheng consists of a branch canals and some lateral canals. The distance between two branch canals is 500 m and between two lateral canals is 600 m. And the square irrigation check that is divided into grid lands is 250 m×200 m in size. Considering the effect of groundwater and the drainage function of irrigation canals, the designed bed of branch and lateral canals should be close to the lowest level of ground water during the year and about lower 2.0–3.5 m than the cropland surface. The cross-section of branch and lateral canals should be wide and shallow with a side slope ratio of 2.5 and canal gradient of approximately 1/1,000 (Fig. 18-1).

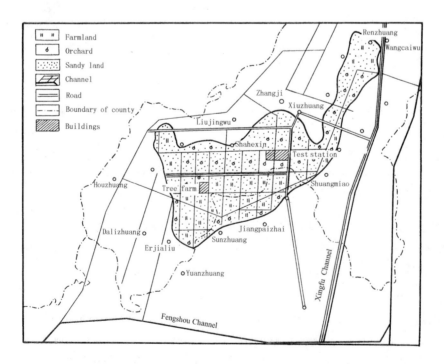

Fig. 18-1　Agro-development area in Yucheng City, Shandong Province

(2) The high sandy lands with irrigation canal. The sandy land in Xiajin of Shandong Province is a good example of this kind, with a cropland grid of 150 m×250 m. The forest shelter belt, canal and road account for 23%–25% of the grid area and the area of cropland is 2.8–2.9 hm² with a utilization percentage of 74%–77%. After 10–15 years, the four rows of trees around the cropland can be cut and the forest land can be reclaimed into cropland (Fig. 18-2).

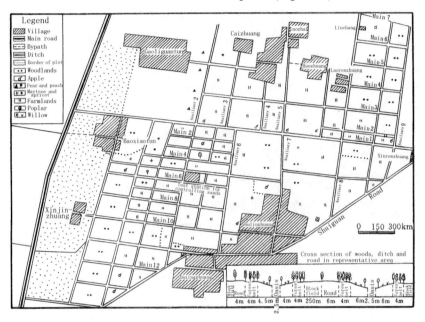

Fig. 18-2   Agro-development area in Xiajin, Shandong Province

(3) The sandy lands located a far distance from rivers and without irrigation canal. The sandy land in Yanjin of Henan Province is representative of the type where ground water level is 7–8 m deep. In the course of agro-development, the well irrigation and ditch system and shelter forest system should be constructed and the area ratio of fruit trees, farmland and forest land is 3:4:3 (Fig.18-3).

3) Scheme of sand-fixing forest

Sand dunes with a height of 4–5 m or more are the main origin of sand resources that result in sand damages in the region. If they are fenced in to protect them from grazing, they can be naturally fixed. They can also be fixed by planting sand binders. Tree species used to fix sand include *Amorpha fruticosa, Robinia pseudoacacia, Salix matsudana, Armeniaca sibirica, Aillanthus altissima, Ulmus pumila, Platycladus orientalis* and *Pinus sylvestris* var. *mongolica* and fodder grasses such as *Medicago sativa, Melilotus officinalis, Onobrychis viciaefolia* and *Trifolium pretense.*

4) Economic forest scheme

The establishment of economic forest utilization is the main way to increase economic and ecological benefits in sandy lands. When fruit-trees are planted, some technology measures should be

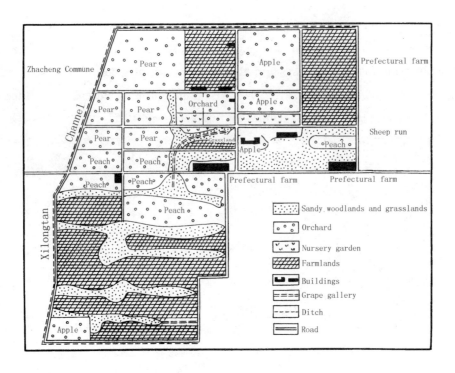

Fig. 18-3　Agro-development area in Yanjin of Henan Province

adopted to increase the survival rate. For the surviving trees, some matched management technology should be adopted to ensure the trees grow well. Once the environment is improved, some new species should be planted to form a characteristic orchard in sandy land (Su, 1996). The suitable tree species are *Vitis vinifera*, *Malus pumila*, *Pyrus*, *Amygdalus persaca*, *Armeniaca vulgaris*, *Rataegus pinnatifida*, *Ziphus jujube*, *Diospyros kaki*, *Cerasus pseudocerasus* and *Juglans* (Fig. 18-4).

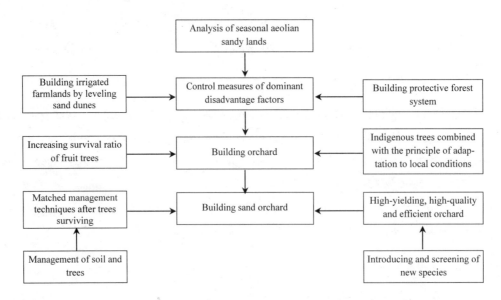

Fig. 18-4　The model of fruit-tree development in sandy lands in the Huang-Huai-Hai Plain

5) Crop planting scheme

In order to increase land cover to prevent soil wind erosion during the windy season, planting winter wheat is an effective method. Several varieties such as *Xiaoyan No.6* and *Xinjinan No.13* are suitable to be planted in newly-reclaimed impoverished sandy lands, with a yield of 3,750 kg/hm^2. Soybean species include *No.502* and *E15,* which are suitable to sow in spring, *Ludou No.4* and *E40,* which are suitable to sow in summer, and *Kefeng No.6* which is suitable to sow in spring or summer (Yang et al., 1996).

18.3   Agro-pastoral zone of eastern Inner Mongolia

The agro-pastoral zone is a natural zone extending from eastern to western China and is suitable for both agricultural and pastoral activities. In terms of the climatic conditions, the agro-pastoral zone is located between the northern limit of the agricultural zone and the southern limit of the pastoral zone in China. However, in the past century, along with the population growth, large areas of grassland have been reclaimed and therefore the agro-pastoral zone has extended beyond the original zonal scope. Especially from the 1950s to 1970s, land desertification in the agro-pastoral zone became more and more severe (Fig.18-5); this not only impacted the economic development but also threatened the eco-environment.

Fig. 18-5   Stele for indicating the project area of the northern Onqin Daga Sandy Land rehabilitation

18.3.1   Demarcation of the agro-pastoral zone

Because the agro-pastoral zone extends 4,000 km from eastern to west China and crosses the semi-humid zone, semi-arid zone, arid zone and other transitional zones, it has complicated geographic conditions, a diverse climate, and different intensities of human activities; therefore, along its boundary demarcation is consistent in the eastern zone but the boundary demarcation in the western area is more contested.

Scientists of the Gansu Weather Bureau suggest that the semi-arid area in central Gansu, with a precipitation of 450 ± 30 mm and accumulative temperatures (⩾0°C) of 3,000 °C, should be regarded as an agro-pastoral zone. According to the scientists of the Weather Bureau of Inner Mongolia, the dividing line between agricultural, pastoral, and forest areas in arid and semi-arid regions is: when the wind day (wind force ⩾8) exceeds 20 days in chestnut soil areas and 10 days in brown soil areas, this area should be used as pastoral area. Li Shikui et al. (1982) proposed that the area where the precipitation is 400 ± 30 mm should be an agro-pastoral zone.

According to Li Shikui, all agro-pastoral zones in China, except for that extending from south to north in Hulun Buir Meng, is distributed like a strip extending from east to west (Fig. 18-6). The agro-pastoral zone starts from the east of the Hulun Buir Plateau and forms a strip from south to north along the west foot of the Da Hinggan Ling Mountains; then it extends from the piedmont hill of the Da Hinggan Ling Mountains along the Ulan Hot, north of Tailai County, Tongyu, Tongliao, Chifeng, Weichang, Bashang area in Zhangjiakou, Datong, Hohhot, Yulin, the north of Huan County, northern Guyuan, and Huining County to Lanzhou. The above mentioned line forms the southeast boundary of

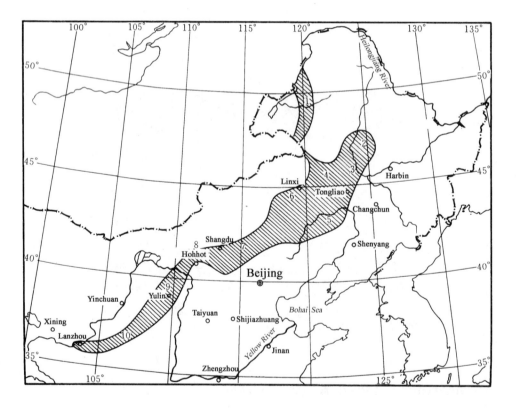

Fig. 18-6 Distribution of agro-pastoral zone in China

1. Eastern Hulun Buir; 2. Nenjiang region; 3. Baicheng region; 4. Northern Horqin; 5. Southern Horqin; 6. Southeast Xilin Gol-Meng; 7. Qahar Steppe; 8. Southern Ulanqab grassland; 9. Ordos; 10. Southern Ningxia

the agro-pastoral zone. The line extending from west Hailar, to eastern Xilin Gol, Xi Ujimqin Qi, Huade, the Houshan area in Ulanqab Meng, eastern Baotou, eastern Ih Ju Meng, eastern Yanchi, central Ningxia to Lanzhou, form the northwest boundary of the agro-pastoral zone.

18.3.2 The economic characteristics, land use and protection of agro-pastoral zones

18.3.2.1 Economic activities in agro-pastoral zones

The history of human activities is actually not very long in the agro-pastoral zone. For example, in the Liao Dynasty, Han people started to arrive in the Horqin Sandy Land and reclaim farmland (Li, 1991). Until the late nineteenth century, a large-scale reclamation was started in northern Liaoning and Horqin Zuoyi Houqi (Jing, 1992). The development of agriculture in this zone mainly occurred between the 1950s–1970s, and this is consistent with the occurrence and development of aeolian desertification in terms of the time line(Zhu, 1994).

The eastern part of the agro-pastoral zone in Inner Mongolia has better conditions to develop agriculture; the main crops are maize and legumes and the main livestock are cattle and sheep. In the western part, the main crops are maize and wheat and the main livestock are also cattle and sheep.

Irrational land use has led to serious eco-environmental degradation. Although great efforts have been made to effectively utilize the existing land resources and improve the degraded environment over the past several decades, we have only achieved limited results.

18.3.2.2 The status of the eco-environment

The agro-pastoral zone in Inner Mongolia, where aeolian desertification is developing rapidly, is an important part of the fragile eco-zone in northern China. Aeolian desertification has not only resulted in the degradation of grassland and forest, reduction of cropland productivity and the loss of arable land, but also resulted in the frequent occurrence of wind-blown sand damages.

Aeolian desertification in the agro-pastoral zone in eastern Inner Mongolia has posed a serious threat to 2 million hm^2 of cultivated field in about 20 counties or Qis and the livelihood of 3 million farmers and herdsmen. Wind erosion has resulted in the loss of organic matter and soil fertility. In the Horqin Sandy Land, the proportion of desertified land increased from 20% (in the 1950s) to about 70% (in the 1980s) (Liu et al., 1993). In seven counties in the Houshan area of Ulanqab Meng near the agro-pastoral zone in eastern Inner Mongolia, some 32,000 hm^2 of land is suffering from wind erosion, with an annual deflation depth of 1 cm, amounting to an annual loss of 840.48 t of organic matter and 8.30 million t of clay. Although some achievements have been obtained after several decades of control, the aeolian desertification is still developing and the desertified area (2,031.4 km^2) accounted for 4.4% of the total area in the mid-1970s and 8.7% of the total area in the mid-1980s with an annual increase rate of 8.3% (Nature Protection Department of the Environment Protection Agency of China, 1999).

The agro-pastoral zone has become a dust source area affecting the eco-environment of all of northern China and Beijing. The Xilin Gol Grassland and northern piedmont of the Yinshan Mountains of Inner Mongolia is the source area for dust which blows over all of northern China and Beijing.

18.3.2.3　The protection and use of the agro-pastoral zone

Aeolian desertification in the agro-pastoral zone is a severe ecological, social and economic problem. However, through 50 years of hard work, great progress has been made in aeolian desertification control (the study team of aeolian desertification of China, 1998). For example, in the Yulin region, according to the different types of land degradation, some areas with relative high groundwater level had patchy forests planted between dunes, barriers were set up to fix the mobile dunes and narrow shelter forest belts were established around farmlands to form an eco-engineering system; as a result, obvious ecological, social and economic benefits have been achieved. The forest coverage increased from the previous 18% to 36.7% in 1994; about 3,400 km^2 of mobile dunes have been fixed; some 1,000 km^2 of farmland have been protected by a shelter forest net; and more than 1,500 km^2 of grassland have been improved.

In the Naiman area, the annual precipitation is about 360 mm; annual number of gale days is 25–30; and dust storms occur 25–30 days per year. Since the beginning of the twentieth century, the vegetation had been gradually destroyed due to over-reclamation and over-grazing. Especially in the 1950s–1970s, the population growth and irrational land-use led to rapid desertification. The desertified land area increased from 20% in the 1950s to more than 50% in the middle of the 1970s and to about 70% at the end of the 1980s. Over the past several decades, an effective aeolian desertification control and land use model, with an "eco-household" as a "little biosphere", a hamlet as a "complex ecosystem" and a village as an "ecosystem net", have been adopted. As a result, the aeolian desertification development trend has basically been restrained. For example, in Yaole Dianzi Village, the demonstration plot at Naiman Station of Lanzhou Desert Institute, Chinese Academy of Sciences, the desertified land area decreased from 75%–80% in the 1970s to 15%–20% in 1995 and per capita income increased from 170 *yuan* to 1,500 *yuan*.

18.4　Semi-arid agro-pastoral zones in Shanxi, Shaanxi and Inner Mongolia

The Shanxi-Shaanxi-Inner Mongolia borderland areas lie in the Loess and Ordos Plateaus in the middle reaches of the Yellow River, including Hequ, Baode, Pianguan and Xing County of Shanxi Province; Yulin, Shenmu, Fugu, Dingbian, Hengshan County of Shaanxi Province; and Ejin Horo Qi, Dalad Qi, Jungar, Dongsheng, Qingshuihe, and Togtoh County of Inner Mongolia; in total, there are 16 Counties (or cities), with a total area of 6.9×10^4 km^2.

18.4.1 Background

18.4.1.1 Natural conditions

Influenced by hydro-thermal conditions, the geographic landscape in the region varies from a grassland in the northeast to a desert in the southwest, with the Mu Us Sandy Land and the Hobq desert occurring in this region.

This region is a transition zone between the monsoon climate in eastern China and an arid climate in the northwest. Roughly with the Great Wall as the boundary, the area to the south is warm temperate zone and north is temperate zone. The climate of the region changes from semiarid in the northwest to semi-humid in the southeast. Annual precipitation in Ejin Horo Qi is 355 mm and in Shenmu County 446 mm. Soil erosion in the region is severe. The annual wind velocity in the region is 2.7 m/s and the number of sand storm days is 12.8 per year.

The land types in this region are diversified, including river valleys, fan-like lands, loess hills and gullies, bottomland of loess hills, arenaceous rock hills, limestone hills, wind blown sand land and blown sand bottomland (Guo et al., 1995).

The amount of surface and underground water resources in the region is $48.48 \times 10^8 \, m^3$, and average inflow of the Yellow River per year in the region is $247 \times 10^8 \, m^3$.

Water and soil loss, land aeolian desertification and soil salinization are the main environmental problems in this region. Total aeolian desertification land in the region is 37,359 km^2; soil erosion area is 36,195 km^2, most of which is distributed along the Yellow River and in loess hills of the southern part; and salinized land area is $9.87 \times 10^4 \, hm^2$, which is mainly distributed in Dalad Qi, Togtoh Qi, Dingbian County, Ejin Horo Qi, Junggar Qi and Qingshuihe County.

18.4.1.2 Socio-economic status

This region historically was an agricultural, pastoral and agro-pastoral zone, and there was almost no industry. There were 1,055 independent industrial enterprises in the region by the end of 1990; the total value of industrial output was $15.7 \times 10^8 \, yuan$. The regional industrial output exceeded the agricultural output in 1991 (Guo et al., 1995).

This region has abundant energy resources and the coal resources in the region occupy 26.2% of that in China. Proved reserves of natural gas in Shaanxi, Gansu and Ningxia Basin is more than $1,000 \times 10^8 \, m^3$, and proved reserves of natural gas field in Jingbian and Dingbian are about $632 \times 10^8 \, m^3$.

There are several development areas in this region, including the Shenfu-Dongsheng coalfield development area, Jungar coalfield development area, hydroelectric power and thermal power development areas along the Yellow River, Yulin development area, Jingbian natural gas development area and coal, electric power and aluminium development areas in Hequ, Baode, Pianguan and Xing County (Guo et al., 1995).

18.4.2　Problems of land aeolian desertification

The aeolian desertified land in this region is 37,359.42 km², which is about 54.16% of the total land area of the region. Its distribution in various counties is shown in Table 18-1.

Table 18-1　Areas of aeolian desertified land in the Shanxi-Shaanxi-Inner Mongolia borderland

County, (Qi, City)	Total area (km²)	Potential aeolian desertified area (km²)	Light aeolian desertified area (km²)	Moderately aeolian desertified area (km²)	Severely aeolian desertified area (km²)
Xing County	3,168.40				
Pianguan	1,685.40	1,068.45			73.29
Hequ	1,322.56	1,082.00			52.48
Baode	977.53	990.40			7.13
Ejin Horo	5,958.12	582.71	2,341.91	2,309.35	724.15
Jungar	7,535.01	335.51	2,320.40	820.27	1,041.83
Dalad	819.5	1,983.15	1,812.51	2,070.15	2,332.69
Togtoh	141.77	260.35	613.10	233.41	31.57
Qingshuihe	2,818.52	642.16	362.34	417.04	21.92
Dongsheng	2,136.42	8,028.0	816.08	325.09	193.07
Fugu	3,200.53	2,165.12	1,035.41		
Shenmu	7,537.73	2,305.94	2,487.90	953.31	1,782.08
Yulin	6,834.87	1,453.73	1,163.02	1,137.78	3,080.14
Hengshan	4,179.00	2,269.18	596.64	610.21	702.97
Jingbian	4,974.40	2,227.28	1,131.02	553.52	1,062.58
Dingbian	6,863.73	4,720.17	1,175.35	603.75	364.46
Total	6?,827.49	25,905.95	15,855.18	10,033.88	11,470.36

(Guo Shaoli et al., 1995)

There are 51.07 ×10⁴ hm² of mobile sand dunes with vegetation coverage only about 10%, of which Yulin and Dalad Qi accounts for 13.33×10⁴ hm², 6.67×10⁴ hm² in Shenmu, 4.67×10⁴ hm² in Hengshan, 2.4 ×10⁴ hm² in Dingbian and about 0.20–0.67 ×10⁴ hm² in the other counties. The area of semi-fixed sand dunes with vegetation coverage of 10%–40% is about 56.2×10⁴ hm², Yulin County and Dalad Qi nearly occupies 10×10⁴ hm², and other counties occupy nearly 1,000 hm² each. The area of fixed sand dunes with vegetation coverage of 40%–50% is about 85.64×10⁴ hm² in the region.

Aeolian desertified land has expanded 35 km south of the Great Wall in the past 150 years. In Ih Ju Meng, about 17,106.88 km² of land in 4 cities and Qis has been desertified. The situation of grassland and farmland degradation in some counties (or cities) in the Shanxi-Shaanxi-Inner Mongolia borderland is presented in Table 18-2.

Wind is the main external agent of aeolian desertified land, so it also has an effect on wind erosion and aeolian desertified land. According to statistics, the average wind velocity in the region tends to decline from northwest to southeast. It is 3 m/s in the northwest and 2.2 m/s in the loess hills in the southeast.

Table 18-2　Situation of grassland and farmland degradation in some counties (or Qis, cities) in the Shanxi-Shaanxi-Inner Mongolia borderland

County (Qi, City)	Grassland area (km²)	Desertified grassland area (km²)	Percent of desertified grassland (%)	Farmland area (km²)	Desertified farmland (km²)	Percent of desertified farmland (%)
Dalad	4,874.40	2,404.64	49.3	608.00	69.00	11.4
Dongsheng	1,487.36	173.44	11.7	226.00	13.25	5.9
Junggar	2,618.28	1,033.19	38.5	627.60	63.5	10.1
Ejin Horo	3,374.12	1,973.75	58.5	237.60	5.4	2.3
Qingshuihe	849.32	27.12	2.19	511.47	9.47	1.9
Shenmu	3,739.62	940.55	25.2	1,021.87	85.83	8.4
Fugu	1,282.64	26.27	2.1	655.53	4.36	0.7
Dingbian	3,427.92	426.94	12.5	2,166.73	220.32	10.2
Jingbian	1,603.89	352.25	22.0	1,486.80	88.75	6.0
Hengshan	929.32	73.22	7.9	960.47	106.18	11.1
Yulin	2,854.21	2,032.44	71.2	818.40	94.93	11.6

(Guo et al., 1995)

The annual precipitation in the region decreases from southeast to northwest, and the aridity index increases from southeast to northwest. Aridity not only influences the physical characteristics of the surface substance but also influences vegetation and thereby has an effect on wind erosion and aeolian desertified land in the region.

Surface soil substances in the region mainly include fluviolacustrine deposits, original rock covered by sand and sandy loess. The grain-size composition of different types of sediment varies greatly. Observations show that the higher the sand-clay ratio, the stronger the wind erosion.

Many kinds of human activities can lead to aeolian desertified land. As far as this region is concerned, this includes over-reclamation, fuel collection, overgrazing and large-scale industrial construction which destroys the structure of surface soil.

Industrial construction and mining constructions in the region have led to severe aeolian desertification. There are two ultra coalfields in the region with a total area of about 17,203 km². The Shenfu-Dongsheng Coalfield occupies 16,205.9 km² of land area and 3,083.2 km² of it is severely aeolian desertified, accounting for 19.03% of the total land area; moderately desertified land is 2,440.35 km², occupying 15.06%; slightly aeolian desertified land is 7,735.3 km², occupying 47.73%. The total aeolian desertified land is 13,258.85 km², occupying 81.81% of the total land area. The area of the Jungar coalfield is 997.5 km² and 109.65 km² of it is severely aeolian desertified land, occupying 10.99% of the total land area; moderately aeolian desertified land is 26.25 km², occupying 2.63%; slightly aeolian desertified land 73.75 km², occupying 7.39%. The total aeolian desertified land in the region is 209.645 km², occupying 21.02% of the total coalfield land area.

The main road in the region is 1,077.0 km long. An early investigation showed that 750.5 km of this road was damaged by sand, which is 69.68% of the total length and 176.75 km was severely damaged by sand, occupying 16.41% of the total length of the road.

18.4.3　Researches on aeolian desertification control

Research on aeolian desertification control in the region has a long history. In 1958, people began to plant sand-binding plants using a plane in Yulin (Fig.18-7). In 1959, a comprehensive aeolian desertification control station was set up in Yulin by the Chinese Academy of Sciences and local departments, and they began to conduct experiments on the introduction of sand-binding plants and mechanical sand-fixing measures (Li et al., 1963; Yang et al., 1998).

Fig. 18-7　Aeolian desertified land and shelterbelts along the Great Wall in Yulin, northern Shaanxi

Zhu Zhenda et al. (1982) first studied aeolian desertification problems along the Great Wall in northern Shaanxi. Extensive research was conducted with the implementation of the comprehensive scientific investigation of the Loess Plateau (Yang et al., 1993; Wen et al., 1993; Zhang, 1993) and the agricultural development and environmental restoration project in the Shanxi-Shaanxi-Inner Mongolia borderland area (Guo et al., 1995).

18.4.4　Control districts

According to the principles of consistency between natural conditions and natural resources, human activities and the direction of economic development, regional systematic control and environmental improvement, and maintaining the integrity of administrative border, Guo Shaoli et al. (1995) divided the region of the Shanxi-Shaanxi-Inner Mongolia borderland into 5 districts. These include: ① aeolian desertification and salinization control and agricultural, forestry and pastoral comprehensive development region along the Yellow River; ② soil and water conservation and a comprehensive development region for agriculture, forestry and pastoral in the loess hills; ③ wind check and sand fixation, soil and water conservation, and a comprehensive development region for pastoral, forestry and agriculture in dune zones; ④ wind check and sand fixation, and a comprehensive development region for agriculture, forestry and pasture in sand dunes and sandy land; ⑤ soil and water conservation, land aeolian desertification control, and a comprehensive development region for pastoral, forestry and agricultural in undertake plains. The team of Chinese Land Aeolian Desertification Control Research (1998) gave priority to the comprehensive management of the Shenfu-Dongsheng-Jungar sandy land environment, the utilization of sandy land along the Great Wall at the southern edge of the Mu Us Sandy Land and the coalfield environments and natural gas field.

18.4.5 Aeolian desertification control

Technical measures to control desertified land in the region proposed   by Zhu Zhengda et al. (1982) include: establishing forest nets for protecting cropland in the valley and bottomland; planting tree-shrub sand-break forest at the edge; and protecting vegetation in the surrounding area.

Yang Gensheng et al. (1998) described aeolian desertification control methods of shifting sand fixation, establishing enclosed pasture, aerial seeding, developing high-benefit agriculture and forestry on sandy lands, wind erosion control ands soil erosion control.

Techniques to fix shifting sand include afforestation in lowlands between dunes and on the slopes. Plant species used to fix shifting sand include *Salix psammophila*, *Hedysarum fruticosum*, *Hedysarum scoparium*, *Caragana korshinskii*, *Caragana intermedia*, *Pinus sylvestris* L. var. *mongolica*, *Salix matsudana*, *Populus alba* L. var. *pyramidalis*, *Populus canadensis*, *Populus hopeiensis*, *Robinia pseudoacacia*, *Ulmus pumila* etc. Plant species suitable to aerial seeding in the region are *Hedysarum fruticosum*, *Artemisia salsoloides*, *Astragalus adsurgens*, *Melilotus officinalis*.

Building enclosed pastures is an efficient way to enclose and protect degraded grassland. Cultivation techniques to protect cropland from wind erosion include: stubble mulch farming, strip cultivation, band planting, and zero tillage.

Yang Gensheng et al. (1998) introduced the shelterbelt system in the Dongsheng Coalfield. The shifting sand control system in the Dongsheng Coalfield is an integrated mode set up around the water source, residential areas, traffic lines, mining fields, borrow areas, industrial squares, etc. Specific methods include: building sand-fixing belts with trees and shrubs to prevent sand from damaging the mine field and residential areas and checker board sand barriers using *Artemisia ordosica* and *Pinus tabulaeformis*, *Pinus sylvestris* L. var. *mongolica*, *Populus* etc.; building sand barriers using *Artemisia ordosica* and *Salix psammophila* along highways; fixing natural sand sources by building biotic sand barriers and planting trees and shrubs to reclaim mine districts.

18.5 Aeolian desertification control of oases in arid desert zones

According to statistics (Zhu et al., 1994), the total area of inland arid zones in northwest China is 306×10^4 km^2, accounting for about 1/3 of China's total land area. Most of the region is covered by gobi, desert and wind-eroded land, with the exception of some high mountains, and human activities are limited in oases. Therefore, the focus of sustainable socio-economic development and eco-environmental conservation in arid regions of northwest China is to prevent and control oasis aeolian desertification.

18.5.1 Characteristics of the desert oasis eco-system

The desert eco-system is a zonal ecosystem in arid regions of northwest China which is characterized by arid climatic conditions, rare precipitation, high evaporation, high diurnal temperature range, abundant sand, frequent wind-sand activities, denuded surfaces, large sand and gravel content and poorly-developed soil. The main features of the desert oasis ecosystem formed in such a harsh environment are: ① vegetation is sparse and simple in species composition, generally consisting of only one or two species; ② the main plant species are xerophytic and most of them are shrubs and half-shrubs, and almost all of the main plant and animal species have the structure and function to adapt to the extreme environment, and are therefore important sources for gene banks; ③ the primary and secondary production of the ecosystem and its utilization rate are low, and its ability to support human development is low; ④ structure of flow and circulation and the transfer of energy, material, and information in the system are not perfect; therefore, it is difficult to recover once damaged and the remaining land may become a sand source that threatens surrounding areas.

Oases can be divided into natural oases, semi-artificial oases and artificial oases according to the influential extent of human activities. With the increase of population pressure and rapid economical development, almost all oases were disturbed by human activities, and oasis ecosystems in arid regions of China currently are severely effected by human beings.

The oasis is an ecosystem in arid regions with an excellent structure and function, active life activities, and the highest production potential compared to its surroundings. It is quite different from the desert ecosystem surrounding it, but it is inevitably affected by the desert environment. The main features of oases include:

(1) Complexity in structure. An oasis ecosystem has more complex structure and life activities than the desert surrounding it. An artificial oasis is a combined system of natural, economic, social and other subsystems. Various subsystems have diversified components and form a composite structure. In the natural subsystem, the perfect combination of environmental factors such as water, temperature,

soil, landform and others, especially the dense biotic population and reticular food chains formed by them, are the bases for various active processes in the oasis ecosystem. The economic subsystem includes different level of structures such as industry (the first, second and third-tier industries), land use, planting, fishery and poultry raising and shelterbelt systems. The social subsystem includes administrative and economic management systems, as well as organizations for education, culture, public health and environment. There is a complex interdependence and mutual containment among different subsystems; they affect each other through energy flow, substance and information. Such features are similar in agricultural ecosystems in non-arid regions, but compared with natural ecosystems in non-arid regions, natural oases have simple species structure. Communities within these oases are always formed by single species such as *Populus euphratica* forest, *Tamarix chinensis* shrub, Phragmites communis meadow bog, etc., and auxiliary species are monotonic, therefore, the resilience threshold value in harsh natural environments is lower.

(2) High production efficiency. Plains, alluvial and diluvial fans in desert regions have high biological production potential due to excellent temperature and sunshine conditions, but the limiting factor is water. For example, in the plains region in the middle reaches of the Heihe River, fresh grass yield available for livestock of desert vegetation is 567 kg/hm^2 and every 1.13 hm^2 of grassland can support a sheep unit, but in the low and wet meadow grassland it is 1.341 kg/hm^2 and every 1.1 hm^2 of grassland can support a sheep unit. Desert vegetation is monotonic and sparse, and livestock raised in these areas must be strictly controlled, but oases are suitable for the growth of numerous species. Since the 1950s, the Hexi Corridor oases have bred and introduced more than 500 crop varieties, 100 fruit trees and forest species, 20 fodder grass species and many livestock species, and have realized artificial systems of diversification.

(3) Dependence on water. Where there is water, there will be an oasis; otherwise, the area is desert. Water sources in oases are mainly water passing through and underground water, and underground water is essentially the conversion of surface water upstream. The scale, distribution and production potential of oases are determined by the total volume of water resources. According to data (Han Deling, 1995), the quantity of water required to maintain 1 hm^2 of an oasis is 54.2×10^4 m^3 (including underground water), the average water consumption of an oasis is 5,420 m^3 per hm^2. Irrational use of water resources will lead to waste of water resources, soil salinization and shrinkage of oases at the lower reaches of rivers or even lead to collapse of the oasis system.

(4) Close relationship to mountain and desert systems. The dependence of oases on water makes it impossible to exist alone. First, almost all the water used by oases are from high mountains in arid regions, and the forest, shrub and grassland ecosystems in mountains are water-storage reservoirs that have a function to conserve and adjust water. Second, there is a distinct boundary between oasis ecosystems and deserts. Transition belts between them are narrow or even non-existent. But arid inland oasis river basins, the upper, middle and lower reaches of rivers, and the relationship of mountain-oasis-desert are compound ecosystems that depend on one another, as well as flourish and

decline together.

(5) Fragility. The environmental base of oases is fragile. Water, its lifeline, comes from outside the oases, and theoases are surrounded by desert, controlled by arid and windy climate, and their landforms are low-lying and closed; therefore, their resistance to disturbance is limited. Such disturbances are mainly man-made, including irrational water use, excessive cultivation, overgrazing, excessive fuel collection, excessive medicinal herb collection, excessive building, excessive road construction, irrational irrigation and discharge of industrial waste. Such activities not only affect an oasis, but also affect mountain and desert ecosystems. Such disturbances often cause eco-environmental problems such as water system changes, oasis shrinkage, shelterbelt destruction, sand encroachment and soil salinization, and once this happens, it is very difficult to restore.

18.5.2　Oasification and aeolian desertification

According to Wang Jiuwen (1997), oasification and aeolian desertification are the two leading geographic processes in arid region. The two processes are entirely opposite and weaken each other.

18.5.2.1　Characteristics of oasification

Oasification is a process creating an oasis landscape through the enrichment and use of water in areas with a background of arid climate and a desert environment. It has the following five characteristics:

(1) Enrichment of water. Includes the expansion of the land area moistened by surface water and underground water under natural conditions, and the expansion of artificial irrigation land.

(2) Increase of vegetation coverage. Includes the increase of plant species under natural conditions; plant life-forms and ecological types evolving from ultra-xerophytic shrubs to mesophytic trees, shrubs and grasses; plant community developing from a sparse one to an abundant one; an artificial oasis is made from man-made vegetation systems such as shelterbelt systems, artificial timber forests, orchards, artificial grassland, cropland and greenbelt.

(3) Increase of crop yield. Per unit area yield increases greatly, and can even increase tens or hundreds of times. This means a significant enhancement of output and quality of products.

(4) Changes in soil. Includes changes of desert soil under natural conditions into meadow soil swamp soil, and the evolution of desert soil and salinized meadow soil into irrigation-warping soil through cultivation, irrigation and fertilization, soil fertility will thus greatly increase.

(5) Improvement of local microclimate. The reduction of wind speed, aeolian sand activities, temperature differences and the increase in humidity will lead to a "wet island effect", and this is more distinct in large oases.

Oasification processes include two aspects. One is the extension of the oasis area, including the extension of the original oasis and the construction of a new oasis through diverting water. Owing to limited water resources, the extensions of oases in most inland basins in northwest China have reached their limit. The other oasification process is the improvement of the structure and function of oasis ecosystems.

18.5.2.2　Characteristics of aeolian desertification

There are great differences in aeolian desertification between arid region and semi-arid and semi-humid zones. The zonal ecosystems in semi-arid and semi-humid zones are not desert, instead they are forest land and grassland with higher productivity than desert. They easily recover into their original state and increase land productivity once the destruction is stopped. The zonal ecosystem in arid regions is desert, and human activities are concentrated in an intrazonal ecosystem (oasis), therefore, the aeolian desertification process in arid regions is the inverse process of oasification, namely reduction in size or even disappearance of an oasis due to scarcity of water supply and irrational human activities, and evolvement of land production and landscape to zonal desert. The characteristics of oasis aeolian desertification in arid regions are as follows:

1) Water shortage and irrational human activities are the main factors resulting in aeolian desertification

Water shortage may be caused by persistent drought in water source zones and the irrational use of water resources by human beings, such as, excessive water use in the middle reaches results in an insufficient water supply at the lower reaches.

2) Vegetation degradation, soil salinization and shifting encroachment are the main characteristics

Salinized land scattered in low-lying areas with poor drainage conditions in a midstream oasis is mainly caused by irrational irrigation methods. Water in the lower reaches has high salinity due to multiple conversion of surface water into underground water and strong evaporation. Vegetation degradation is mainly caused by water shortages and over-cutting. Therefore aeolian desertification in oases develops rapidly. Taking the Hexi Corridor of Gansu Province as an example, according to a survey (1994–1996), there was 536.5×10^4 hm^2 of different degrees of desertified land in the Hexi region (Table 18-3), accounting for more than 95% of total aeolian desertified land area in the province. The oasis eco-environment is also severely threatened by blown sand (Table 18-4).

The net increased area of aeolian desertified land in the Hexi region during the 44 years from 1949 to 1995 is 79.03×10^4 hm^2, an increase of 17.49%, and an average annual increase rate of 0.40%. However, the aeolian desertification development tended to become slow since the 1990s. The areas of fixed sand dunes and semi-fixed sand dunes increased by 80.2×10^4 hm^2 during those 44 years, with an increase of 44.8%, and an average annual increase rate of 1.02%. The ratio between expanded and controlled rate is 1 ∶ 2.55; this indicates that the measures to combat aeolian desertification are efficient.

Table 18-3 Different degrees of aeolian desertified land in the Hexi region (10^4hm^2)

Districts	Jiuquan	Wuwei	Zhangye	Jiayuguan	Jinchang	Hexi (in Gansu)
Area of aeolian desertified land(10^4hm^2)	340.08	154.14	33.46	0.45	8.37	536.5
Fixed sand land(10^4hm^2)	107.06	40.56	4.57	0.01	0.34	152.54
(non-biotic engineering control) (10^4hm^2)	(0.17)		(0.21)			(0.38)
Slightly aeolian desertified land area(10^4hm^2)	107.24	41.03	4.78	0.01	0.34	153.4
Slightly aeolian desertified land area /total desertified land (%)	31.53	26.62	14.29	2.22	4.06	28.59
Semi-fixed sand area(10^4hm^2)	67.04	15.95	13.86	0.16	7.96	104.97
Moderately aeolian desertified land(10^4hm^2)	67.04	15.95	13.86	0.16	7.96	104.97
Moderately aeolian desertified land / total desertified land (%)	19.71	10.35	41.42	35.56	95.1	19.57
Shifting sand dune(10^4hm^2)	158.58		14.82	0.28	0.07	270.91
Aeolian residual hill (10^4hm^2)	7.22	97.16				7.22
Severely aeolian desertified land (10^4hm^2)	165.8		14.82	0.28	0.07	278.13
Severely aeolian desertified land /total desertified land (%)	48.75	63.03	44.29	62.22	0.84	51.84

Source: 1996. Report on Survey of Desertified Land in Gansu Province. 1(1). 20

Table 18-4 Land area damaged from aeolian desertification in the Hexi Corridor of Gansu

	Jiuquan	Jiayuguan	Zhangye	Jinchang	Wuwei	Shule River basin	Heihe River basin	Shiyang River basin	Hexi Corridor
Farmland ($10^4 hm^2$)	4.69	0.29	6.37	0.91	4.55	2.27	9.07	5.47	16.81
Grassland ($10^4 hm^2$)	352.16	0.53	16.61	1.73	21.84	339.41	29.89	23.57	392.87
Villages	1442	17	515	23171	2170	1160	814	25341	27315
(destroyed area)	(537)	(14)	(254)	(1,286)	(2,078)	(374)	(431)	(3,364)	(4,169)
Railway (km)	711.8	133.4	162.8	165	93.5	444.8	563.2	258.5	1,266.5
(destroyed length) (km)	(384)	(35)	(133.9)	(50)	(760)	(249)	(303.9)	(126)	(678.9)
Highway (km)	3,869.2	118.9	672.6	348	2,106	2,542.2	2,118.5	2,454	7,114.7
(destroyed length) (km)	(1,258.7)	(36)	(398.2)	(114)	(727)	(1,030.5)	(662.4)	(841)	(2,533.9)
Canal (km)	8,938.6	87.6	2,340.1	9,055	2,537	5,441.5	5,924.8	11,592	22,958.3
(destroyed length) (km)	(4,980.1)	(29.8)	(1,025.9)	(1,553)	(946)	(2,567.9)	(3,467.9)	(2,499)	(8,534.8)
Loss per year ($10^4 yuan$)	20,412.1		1,670.9	650.6	3,231	1,846.5	20,236.5	3,881.6	25,964.6

3) Larger difficulty in combating aeolian desertification in arid regions than in non-arid regions

Once aeolian desertification has in oases, especially after dunes or bare salinized land have appeared, a lot of manpower, financial and material resources and time are required to restore it, and sometimes restoration is impossible. Hence, the prevention of aeolian desertification is more important than controlling aeolian desertification.

4) Mutual conversion of desertification and oasification

In arid desert regions, if there is water, the land might become an oasis. And if there is no water, it might become a desert. When water is in short supply, the desert is enlarged and the oasis shrinks. When water is adequate, the oasis will enlarge or recover gradually. But while some desertified lands become oases, some oases will possibly become desertified. Historically, the variations of an oasis was always caused by changes in the water system; the appearance of man-made oases and the disappearance of natural oases have proven this. However, when the exploitation of water resources of an inland river basin reaches or exceeds its limit, the enlargement of an oasis is impossible. Oasification can only be achieved by mitigating aeolian desertification expansion in parts of the oasis.

18.5.3   Protection and construction of a desert-oasis eco-environment

The priority in developing of western China is the infrastructure construction and eco-environmental construction (Fig.18-8). In this respect, some basic strategies and measures to protect eco-environments and to combat aeolian desertification should be proposed according to sustainable development principles.

Fig. 18-8   Protective forest net for an oasis in the Hexi Region

18.5.3.1   Guiding ideas on the construction of an oasis ecosystem and economic development

(1) Using the inland river basin as a unit, establishing comprehensive management of water, ecosystems and the economy. An inland river basin is a unit of ecological function, in which mountainous areas and plains, oases and deserts, surface water and ground water are closely related. Irrational distribution of water resources and water waste has become a common problem in arid areas of China, or even in central Asia. For example, some oases in the lower reaches of the Shiyang River in the Hexi region and the Tarim River in Xinjiang have become deserts after several decades

of development. Only by adopting integrated management of water, ecosystems and the economy by using the river basin as a unit can we scientifically develop and utilize water resources, protect the eco-environment and realize the sustainable development of the economy.

(2) Stopping further land reclamation and tapping existing potential using advanced science and technology. At present, the exploitation of water resources in oasis in arid northwest China has been reaching its limit. So the development of the oasis economy should rely on enhancing water use efficiency, adjusting land use structure, adopting advanced technologies and management rather than expanding oasis area.

(3) Giving priority to prevention in aeolian desertification control. The development and reconstruction of oases need lots of money, manpower and time. Sometimes, it is even impossible to reconstruct once the oasis has been destroyed. So we should pay special attention to the prevention of aeolian desertification. Various human activities including production and management should avoid destroying plants and water resources. On the basis of prevention, corresponding measures are adopted to restore the eco-environment. Those lands that are impossible to be restored can be abandoned.

18.5.3.2 Basic measures to protect oasis environment

(1) Control population growth and improve the quality of labor. Population growth accelerates land aeolian desertification. To realize sustainable development, we must control population increases. For this purpose, the family plan policy should first be carried out strictly; second, the non-agriculture industry should be encouraged to mitigate the tremendous pressure on primary resources such as water and land; and third, some people should be moved to areas with better water and land conditions.

(2) Rational use and distribution of water resources. According to Li Fuxing et al. (1998), if the net irrigation norm for farmland in the Hexi region is decreased from 6,940.5 m^3/hm^2 to 3,300 m^3/hm^2 and the industrial water consumption is decreased from 675.7 m^3 to 170 m^3 per ten thousand *yuan*, the conflict between water supply and demand can be solved. Agriculture uses the largest amount of water; water-saving technology is a key to save water. The main water-saving measures include perfecting management, canal seepage control, leveling land, conveying water by pipeline, and using sprinkle irrigation and drop irrigation techniques etc.

(3) Readjust industrial and planting structure and develop artificial grassland. Ren Jizhou's research results show that the coupling of mountain and oasis systems can enhance the production profit by 6–60 times. He points out that the oasis-desert transition belt can be developed into a new pastoral base belt. The coupling of mountain, oasis and desert agricultural ecosystems can greatly increase the output value of water units. The main measures include: strictly control livestock numbers in the upstream mountain and desert plain grasslands, and convert the binary grain-cash crops structure into the ternary grain crop-cash crop-livestock raising structure. Stopping grazing in the downstream riparian forest land and establishing artificial grassland are effective measures to restore the *Populus euphratica* and *Tamarix chinensis* forest and they also contribute to increase vegetation coverage and halt wind erosion.

Table 18-5　Main eco-environmental problems in arid regions

Types	Problems and their effect	Improvement principles	Damages	Methods of management
I	Protected objects are irreplaceable and have great potential value; once they are destroyed, they can not be recovered.	Such loss should be avoided.	Endemic species and their habitats decline.	Establishing a protected area; avoiding harmful construction works in the main habitat.
II	Protected objects are vital for regional economic development and maintain a favorable ecoenvironment.	Protection is more important than exploitation	Destruction of water conservation forest in the mountain.	Strengthen management, aviod destructive development, and reduce population pressure.
III	Effect of the problem is vast, the damaging process is slow, loss is hysteretic and accumulated, mainly manifesting in the reduction of land productivity.	Take regional sustainable development as a core; adjust the structure and rebuild the eco-environment.	1. Land aedian desertification 2. Grassland degeneration	Improve shelterbelts at the edge of oases and carefully utilize sandy land; establish artificial grassland and reduce the pressure on natural grassland; and develop pastoral farming.
IV	Local disaster: multiple loss might be caused by a single factor, and it is difficult to recover or even cannot be recovered when the situation is severe.	Protection is the main methods, land that is easily destroyed must be utilized carefully ; adjust water and land use structure in area of utilization, and abandon destroyed region if necessary.	1. Soil secondary salinization and nutrient leaching loss. 2. Vegetation disappears due to dwindling rivers and lakes and ground water drawdown. 3. Pollution of water body. 4. Decrease of species that are not endemic but have high economic and environmental value.	Adopt water-saving techniques, adjust land use and planting structure, abandon severely destroyed region. Improve water resource allocation, rebuild drought-enduring vegetation, immigrate when necessary. Reform pollution source to reach discharge standard. Establishing protective area or artificial breeding base, and strengthen legal system.
V	Sudden ecological disaster, ecoenvironmental problem caused by irrational use of water resources and land coupling with abrupt climate change.	Put protection first and adopt remedial measures once it happens.	1. Sand storm 2. Insect pest occurs suddenly over a vast area. 3. Flood	Improve shelterbelt system of cropland, residential region; use different kinds of economic and defense facilities.Mixed crop field with forest and grassland.Control soil erosion in the mountain; improve channel discharge capacity.

(4) Establishing a water-saving shelterbelt system. A shelterbelt system is essential for the development of an oasis economy. Oasis shelterbelt systems can reduce wind speed, alleviate wind erosion, and prevent shifting sand encroachment. The oasis shelterbelt system is comprised of four parts, namely a cropland protective forest network inside the oasis, a sand break forest belt consisting of trees and shrubs at the edge of an oasis, barriers outside the sand break forest and sand binders inside the barriers, and conservancy belt outside. In order to save water, the area proportion of forest land should be reduced through adjustment of the forest structure.

(5) Comprehensive rehabilitation of eco-environments using different measures. According to the characteristics of eco-environments and economic development in arid zones, the

eco-environment problems and countermeasures are put forward in Table 18-5.

18.6 Pastoral area of the Tibetan Plateau

The Tibet Autonomous Region lies between 26°50′–36°53′N and 78°25′–99°06′E, the longest distance from west to east is 2,000 km and from south to north is 1,000 km, with an area of 120.48×10^4 km^2 (Land Management Bureau of the Tibet Autonomous Region, 1994).

18.6.1 Background

18.6.1.1 Survey of Tibet's natural environment

The Tibetan Plateau lies above 4,000 m and was formed by violent crustal uplift movement over the past several million years. It has experienced changes from ocean to land, and from a tropical and subtropical climate of low-altitude to a plateau climate (Luo, 1996).

The macroscopic topographical features of the Tibetan Plateau are: surrounded on all sides by high mountains and deep canyons, and the interior is vast highland and a variety of lakes. Running water is one of the active factors that reshapes the surface configuration through erosion, transport and deposition. Freeze-thawing action is an important external agent of the plateau and mountain. Glaciation shaped the special erosion and deposition landform of the Qinghai-Tibet Plateau. Debris flow and wind action also contributed a lot to the development of modern landforms (Luo, 1996).

As the main part of the Tibet an Plateau, most parts of the Tibet Autonomous Region are above 4,000 min altitude (Table 18-6), and 76% of it is mountain and hills.

Table 18-6   The ground surface of different altitudes in the Tibet Autonomous Region

Altitude(m)	>5,000	4,000–5,000	3,000–4,000	2,000–3,000	1,500–2,000	<1,500	Water field
Proportion (%)	34	51.1	8	2	0.9	2	2

Source: Land Management Bureau of the Tibet Autonomous Region, 1994

The proportion of different landform types in the Tibet Autonomous Region is shown as Table 18-7.

Table 18-7   The proportion of different landform types in the Tibet Autonomous Region

Land form	Flat ground	Hills	Mountain
Proportion(%)	23.5	25.3	51.2

Source: Land Management Bureau of the Tibet Autonomous Region, 1994

Temperature in most parts of Tibet is lower than that in the regions of the same altitude in eastern China, and annual mean temperature of Tibet is 4.2 °C; the highest annual mean temperature is 16.0 °C

(Medog) and the lowest is −3 °C (Amdo). Mean temperatures in the coldest month vary from −15 °C (Amdo) to −8.4 °C (Medog), and those in the warmest month change from 7.6 °C (Cona) to 22.2 °C (Medog) (The Land Management Bureau of The Tibet Autonomous Region, 1994).

Annual precipitation decreases from southeast to northwest, from 2,357.6mm in Muotuo to 50 mm in northern Ali, and the temporal distribution is uneven, and most rain falls between June and September.

Solar radiation in Tibet is about 586.6–796.1 k J/(cm^2 · a), and it decreases from northwest to southeast. Hours of sunshine in Tibet are above 3,000 every year and the sunshine ratio is 65%–78%.

The frost-free season in most areas of Tibet is short. In Medog, Zayu and other areas, it is more than 270 days, and in valleys of the Yarlung Zangbo River and rivers in eastern Tibet it is between 150–200 days. In most regions it is shorter than 100 days, even only 9 days (Bange), so frost climate prevails in the region.

There are many rivers in Tibet. Incomplete statistics shows that there are more than 20 rivers with a drainage area above 10,000 km^2, and more than 100 rivers above 2,000 km^2. In addition, there are more than 1,500 lakes of different areas, most of which are above 4,000 m in altitude.

Due to complex and multiple types of soil-forming processes, remarkable physical weathering, violent freezing effects, accumulation of soil organic matter, and other factors, soil formation in Tibet is very different from the surrounding low-altitude region. Soil types in Tibet vary greatly from the mountains in the southeast to the plateau in the northwest, and soil types are: forest soil→ subalpine meadow soil and alpine meadow soil→alpine steppe soil→alpine desert soil. The soil types on the plateau surface from south to north are: subalpine steppe soil→alpine steppe soil→ alpine desert rangeland soil and other sub-zonal soil (from southern to northern Tibet) and sub-alpine desert soil→alpine desert soil and other sub-zonation soil (from southern to northern Ali) (The Land Management Bureau of the Tibet Autonomous Region, 1994).

The vegetation in Tibet is characterized by its complex flora composition, multiple plant types and various mountain vegetation. Due to differences in water and temperature conditions, the vegetation types from southeast to northwest are: tropical and subtropical upland forest→upland shrub rangeland→high and cold meadow→high and cold rangeland→high and cold desert and other vegetation belts. Tropic or subtropic evergreen broad-leaved forest, mixed broadleaf-conifer forest, dim-coniferous forest, subalpine shrub meadow and alpine meadow are distributed from bottom to top in alpine regions (Integrated Scientific Investigation Team of the Qinghai-Tibet Plateau, Chinese Academy of Sciences, 1998).

18.6.1.2 Status of the social economy in Tibet

The population in Tibet was 228.88 × 10^4 in 1993, 197.46 × 10^4 of which was an agricultural population and the other 31.42 × 10^4 was a non-agricultural population; 216.79 × 10^4 were Tibetan, occupying 94.7% of the total population. Agriculture and animal husbandry are main industries of Tibet (Table 18-8).

Total output value of agriculture and industry (10^4 *yuan*)	Total output value of agriculture (10^4 *yuan*)	Proportion of total agricultural output value (%)
276,600	230,600	83.37

(From Luosang Lingzhiduojie, 1996)

Total farmland area in Tibet was 36.05×10^4 hm^2, 25.57×10^4 hm^2 of which was irrigable land, and there are $6,479.68 \times 10^4$ hm^2 of different types of grassland (The Survey Bureau of the Tibet Autonomous Region, 1995).

Distributions of rangeland in Tibet are: 40.6% is meadow, 45.6% is grassland, 4.6% is desert steppe, and 9.2% is shrub and steppe. About 2.13 hm^2 of grassland is required for per unit sheep. Forest cover in Tibet is 5.84%.

Per capita income of Tibet in 1992 was: 3,448 *yuan* in the town and 930 *yuan* in agricultural and pastoral areas. Average per capita consumption was 903 *yuan*, herdsman and farmer consumption was 594 *yuan*, others totaled 2,032 *yuan*.

18.6.2 Aeolian desertification in Tibet

Aeolian desertified land in Tibet mainly occurs in straths in the Yarlung Zangbo River and the Shiquan River basins (The Land Management Bureau of the Tibet Autonomous Region, 1994). Aeolian desertified land distribution in Tibet exhibits a difference between the plateau and lake basins, wide valley and incised valley, different precipitation and temperature belts, and different economic zones (Li, 1998).

The middle part of the "Yarlung Zangbo River and its Two Tributaries" basin (the Yarlung Zangbo River, the Lhasa River and the Nyang Qu River in Tibet) lies between 28°–31° N and 87°–93° E, including 18 counties which covers an area of 6.57×10^4 km^2, and has 1,860.9 km^2 of aeolian desertified land, including 578.6 km^2 of severely desertified land, 752.8 km^2 of moderately desertified land and 529.5 km^2 of slightly desertified land; this is a typical desertified region. Severely desertified land is mainly distributed in river breaches, river terraces, diluvial fan edges, dry riverbeds or valley slopes (Dong et al., 1996; Li, 1998). The main aeolian landforms include: crescent dunes, barchan chains, longitudinal dunes, pyramidal dunes, echo dunes, climbing dunes, falling dunes, patchy dunes and coppice dunes (Table 18-9).

One-third of the farmland in the middle reaches of the "Yarlung Zang bo River and Its Two Tributaries" area has degraded due to aeolian desertification, and the sand deposition thickness on farmland in winter can reach 5 to 10 cm (Dong Guangrong et al., 1996). Aeolian desertification also severely damages grasslands, roads, water channels and villages (Liu, et al., 2001).

Table 18-9   Distribution and characteristics of different sand dunes in Xigaze and the adjacent region

Types	Distribution	Characteristics
Crescent dunes	Terrace, flood plain	Crescent shape with two asymmetric wings, south wing is round and north slender, and the strike 70° and the height is about 2.6–13.4 m
Barchan chains	Terrace, marginal bank	Formed by 2–4 barchans with a height of 3.0–12.0 m
Longitudinal dunes	North slope of the Yarlung Zangbo River valley	The strike is about 270°, length 60m, height 2–3 m, the section is symmetric and dip angle of the two sides are 26°–28°
Pyramid dunes	High flood plain in the southern bank of the Yarlung Zangbo River	Dune has flat top with a height of about 3.5 m, three sand ridges extend from it and formed three slip faces, gradient of 20°–26°, it's direction is WSW, NNW and E
Hill slope covered by sand	Valley slope	There are three types of dunes, namely echo dune, climbing dune and falling dune
Patchy, sheet and coppice dunes	Terrace, channel bare, marginal bank, flood plain with better water condition	Flat sandy land, less than 2.0 m thick and no slip face slope. The height is 1–5 m, with *Sophora moorcroftiana* Pennisetum centrasiaticum, etc. growing on it

18.6.3   Regionalization of aeolian desertification control in Tibet

Aeolian desertification control was divided into different districts according to the experiences of other regions and, the formation and distribution features of land aeolian desertification.

The climates in Tibet were divided into 5 zones, namely tropical mountain climate, subtropical mountain climate, plateau temperate climate, plateau subfrigid climate and plateau frigid climate by the Land Management Bureau of the Tibet Autonomous Region (1994). Landforms in Tibet were divided into the Himalayas, intermontane lake basin in southern Tibet, plateau lake basin in northern Tibet and plateau canyon in eastern Tibet by the Survey Bureau of the Tibet Autonomous Region (1995). And 8 agricultural districts were divided by the Integrated Scientific Investigation Team of the Qinghai-Tibet Plateau, Chinese Academy of Sciences (1984), including the pastoral area in northeast Tibet; pastoral area in northwest Tibet; pastoral and agricultural area in western Tibet; pastoral and agricultural area in southern Tibet; agricultural area in central Tibet; forestry and agricultural area in eastern Tibet; forestry, pastoral and agricultural area in eastern Tibet, and forestry and agricultural area at the southern margin of Tibet. These regionalizations reflect natural and social economic characteristics of Tibet and therefore can be used as a reference for aeolian desertification control regionalization.

Aeolian desertification control in Tibet is divided into 4 districts according to its climatic factors (including temperature, precipitation), topographic factors (position, altitude) and agricultural economic activities, namely the eastern Tibet zone including the region east of Baqing, Suoxian, Jiali, Jiacha, Nongzi and Cuola; the southern Tibet zone including the region south of Muozhugongka, Linzhou, Yangbajin, Nimu, Nanmulin, Xietongmen, Angren and Jinong; western Tibet zone including the 4 counties of Pulan, Zhada, Ga'er and Ritu.

Eastern Tibet has better natural conditions and it is a forest area of Tibet (Table 18-10, Table 18-11). Sand dunes mainly occur in valleys and have become a hazard to a limited extent.

	Annul temperature (°C)	Annul precipitation (mm)	Proportion of precipitation in June to Sep.(%)	Frost-free season	Annul gale days	≥10accumulative temperature (°C)	Geomorphic conditions
Eastern Tibet	1.5–18.1	245–2,358	25.8–80.5	31–274	0.2–87.4	472–5,010	Mountain, coulee, low hills, valley below 4,000 m
Southern Tibet	−8.8	236.1–614.7	50.7–96.8	38–188	2–112.5	207.7–2,176.9	Medium dissected mountain, valley plain and plateau lake basin at altitude of 3,400–4,500 m
Western Tibet	0.1	68.9	74.6	95	36	1159	Medium and deep dissected mountain, river valley at altitude of 2,900–4,500 m
Northern Tibet	−6.2	246–680.6	76.1–92.6	9–94	15.2–139.4	24.2–726.7	Broad valley, low hills and lake basin. The altitude of valley and basin is about 4,200–5,000 m

(Source Integrate Research Team for the Tibet Plateau of CAS, 1984)

Table 18-11　Agricultural economic situations of various districts

	Percent of land area in Tibet/(%)	Percent of grassland area in Tibet/(%)	Percent of woodland area in Tibet/(%)	Percent of farmland area in Tibet/(%)	Rural population density (person/km²)	Farmland area occupied by each laborer (hm²)	Livestock numbers occupied by each laborer (sheep)
East Tibet	22.2	14.6–55.5	10.06–40.47	0.04–0.44	0.35–3.77	3.3–4.3	12.1–40.4
South Tibet	11.1	67.3–85.7	—	0.5–2.38	2.25–13.18	5.1–6.2	18.5–44.3
West Tibet	4.6	73.2	—	0.04	0.22	3.9	65.6
North Tibet	62.1	77.3–90	—	0.006–0.04	0.18–2.04	0.6–1.0	114.0–176.5

(Source: Integrate Research Team for the Tibetan Plateau of CAS, 1984)

Natural conditions in southern Tibet are relatively good and farmland occupies a high proportion and the population density in the region is also high. This region lies in the middle reaches of the Yarlung Zangbo River and suffers from severe land aeolian desertification.

Western Tibet is the aridest region in Tibet and it is also an agricultural and pastoral production region. In the valley below Shiquanhe town, human activities, especially felling of Elegant Falsetamarisk (*Myricaria elegans*), have led to land aeolian desertification, which results in the increase of sand flow, and fixed and semi-fixed dunes.

Natural conditions in northern Tibet are not suitable for planting crops, so this region is a traditional pastoral area with low population density and high per capita livestock share. The Zhongba County at the headwaters of the Yarlung Zangbo River is suffering from severe aeolian desertification and there is a vast expanse of sand dunes.

18.6.4　Aeolian desertification control in Tibet

(1) Eastern Tibet. East Tibet has better natural conditions, and aeolian desertified land mainly occurs in river valleys. The main tasks for land aeolian desertification control are to prevent shifting sand from spreading. Main methods of control are: fixing shifting sand in the valleys. Branch

barriers can be used to block sand, and some tree species with good germination power such as *Salix* and *Hippophae rhamnoides* can be used to establish sandbreak forest belts. Sand dunes can be fixed by several rows of fences consisting of branches or shrubs of indigenous trees. *Pinus densata* can be planted in sandy land to prevent aeolian desertification.

(2) Southern Tibet. Southern Tibet is suffering from severe land aeolian desertification. Aeolian desertification control in the region involves many aspects, such as cropland, grassland, communication, water conservancy works, villages and towns. The shelterbelt system used in oasis regions can be used to protect cropland and grassland, including physical sand barriers at the front edge, sand-fixing belts consisting of shrubs and grasses around sand dunes, sandbreak forest belts and forest nets inside oases. Protective forests along the Yarlung Zangbo River is an important part of the protective system. Tree species used for forest shelterbelt establishment include *Salix longistamina, Salix paraplesia* var. *subintegra, Hippophae rhamnoides, Populus beijingensis* and *Populus alba*, etc.

Sand protection along traffic lines consists of sand-blocking belts at the front edge and sand-fixing belts at the roadside. Sand-blocking belts at the front edge can be physical or biological. Sand-fixing belts are a combination of physical and biological techniques, and the former includes building straw check-boarder barriers and paving a layer of gravel on sand surfaces. Sand-fixing plant species include *Artemisia salsoloides, Sophora moorcroftiana, Caragana spinifera*. Tree species used for blocking sand include *Salix longistamina* and *Hippophae rhamnoides*.

Measures to protect canals are generally the same for the road, and the canals in desertified regions can be protected using gravel materials.

In most cases, the measures to protect villages and towns are to plant large-scale forest belts around them, and their function is to dissipate wind energy, block and fix shifting sand.

(3) Western Tibet. The main tasks in the region are protecting villages and towns, and the plant species used include *Caragana versicolor* and *Myricaria elegans*.

(4) Northern Tibet. Aeolian desertification control in the region is mainly to protect natural grassland. It can be enclosed or use a rotational grazing pattern.

References

Chen Huaishun, Liu Zhimin. 1997a. The characteristics of the vegetation composition of Jiangdang and its adjacent area at Rizaze of Xizang. Journal of Desert Research, 17(1): 63–69 (In Chinese)

Chen Huaishun, Liu Zhimin. 1997b. Vegetation dynamics in Xigaze valley of Tibet. Researches on Resources and Ecoenvironmental Web, 8(1). (In Chinese)

Chen Huaishun, Liu Zhimin. 1997c. Characteristics of *Sophora moocroftiana* population and its function on vegetation in river valley. Researches on Resources and Ecoenvironmental Web, 8(3). (In Chinese) Collections of Essays on Chinese Historical Geography, (3). (In Chinese)

Chen Longheng, Li Fuxing, Di Xinmin. 1998. Aeolian Sandy Soil in China. Beijing: Science Press. (In Chinese)

Chen Guangting, Yang Taiyun, Zhang Weimin. 1989. Studies on blown sand land in the Yellow River alluvial plain, Shandong Province. Journal of Desert Research, 9 (1): 19–33. (In Chinese)

Cheng Weixin. 1993. Amelioration of Wetland and Environmental Ecology. Beijing: Science Press, 154–174. (In Chinese)

Dong Guangrong, Dong Yuxiang, Li Sen et al. 1996. Study on the Planning of Land Aeolian Desertification Control in the Middle of Yarlung Zangbo River and Its Two Tributaries Basin, Tibet in China. Beijing: China Environmental and Science Press. (In Chinese)

Dong Guangrong, Jin Jong, Shao Liye. 1991. Situation of land desertification in the Yarlung Zangbo River and its two tributaries basin, Xizang. Journal of Desert Research, 11(1): 59–61.

Gao Qianzhao, Liu Famin. 2000. Construction of ecosystem and sustainable development for sandy land agriculture of Yanjin. Journal of Desert Research, 20(suppl. 1): 107–113. (In Chinese)

Grove A T. 1986. Desertification in southern Europe. Climatic Change, (9): 49–57.

Guo Shaoli. 1995. Study on agricultural development and environmental realignment in Shanxi-Shaanxi-Inner Mongolia. area. Beijing: China Science and Technology Publishing House. (In Chinese)

Han Deling. 1995. Some understandings on oasis problems. Journal of Arid Land Resources and Environment, 9(3): 13–31. (In Chinese)

Jing Ai. 1992. Cultivation on Horqin in the Qing Dynasty. Collections of Essays on Chinese Historical Geography, (3). (In Chinese)

Kassas M. 1995. Desertification: a general review. Journal of Arid Environments, (30): 115–128.

Le Houerou H N. 2000. Utilization of fodder trees and shrubs in the arid and semiarid zones of West Asia and North Africa. Arid Soil Research and Rehabilitation, (14): 101–135.

Li Bingyuan. 1998. Some questions on aeolian desertification in the Qinghai-Tibet Plateau. Journal of Desert Research. 18 (supp. 1): 13–18. (In Chinese)

Li Chunlu. 1994. Examination and research on techniques to plant shelterbelt forest in southern mountain region of the Yarlung Zangbo River. In: Zeng Weili, ed., Collection of Researches on Tibetan Forestry. Lhasa: Xizang People's Publishing House. 16–27. (In Chinese)

Li Fuxing, Yao Jianhua. 1998. Comprehensive Study on Economic Development and Environmental Recondition in Hexi Corridor. Beijing: China Environmental Science Press. (In Chinese)

Li Lingfu. 1991. Recovery and extension of farming area in northeast China during the early period of the Qing Dynasty. Collections of Essays on Chinese Historical Geography, (2). (In Chinese)

Li Minggang, Gao Shangwu, Zhang Hanhao et al. 1963. Summary on sand-fixing and forestation test. In: Researches on Sand Control (5). Beijing: Science Press, 19–36. (In Chinese)

Li Shikui, Wang Shili. 1982. A preliminary discussion on agricultural districts in China. Collection of Meteorologic Science and Technology. (In Chinese)

Li Shikui. 1988. Discussion of demarcation line between agriculture and animal husbandry area in half arid climate of north China. In: China Society of Natural Resources. Natural Resources Study of Arid and Semi-Arid District in North China. Beijing: Science Press. (In Chinese)

Li Xiaoyun. 2000. Studies on technique exploitation of fruit trees for high-yield and superior quality on sandy land in northern Henan Province. Journal of Desert Research, 20 (supp. 1): 114–119. (In Chinese)

Liu Lianyou, Liu Zhimin, Zhang Jiashen et al. 1997. Sand source material and modern aeolian desertification process in Jiangdang valley of the Yalung Zangbo River basin. Journal of Desert Research, 17(4): 377–382. (In Chinese)

Liu Xianwan, Li Sen & Shen Jianyou. 1999. Wind tunnel simulation experiment of mountain dunes. Journal of

Arid Environments, (42): 49–59.

Liu Xinmin, Zhao Halin. 1993. Study on Comprehensive Control of Eco-environment in Horqin Sandy Land. Lanzhou: Gansu Science and Technique Press. (In Chinese)

Liu Yanhua. 1992. Land System in Mid-Reach Area of Yalung Zangbo River, Tibet. Beijing: Science Press. (In Chinese)

Liu Z, Zhao W. 2001. Shifting sand control in central Tibet. AMBIO

Liu Zhimin. 1997. Comparative studies on the introducing of sand-fixing plant in Xigaze, Tibet. Journal of Desert Research, 17(1). (In Chinese)

Luosang Lingzhiduojie. 1996. Generality on Environment and Development of the Qinghai-Tibet Plateau. Beijing: China Tibetan Study Publishing House. (In Chinese)

Ma Shiwei, Ma Yuming, Yao Honglin et al. 1998. Desert Science. Hohhot: Inner Mongolia People's Publishing House. (In Chinese)

Mitchell D J, Fullen M A, Truman I C, Fearnehough W. 1998. Sustainability of reclaimed desertified land in Ningxia, China. Journal of Arid Environments, (39): 239–251.

Natural Protection Department of China Environmental Protection Bureau. 1999. Ecological Problems in China. Beijing: China Environmental Science Press. (In Chinese)

Perry R A. 1986. Desertification processes and impacts in irrigated regions. Climatic Change, (9): 43–47.

Rapp A. 1986. Introduction to soil degradation processes in drylands. Climatic Change, (9): 19–31.

Sanders D W. 1986. Desertification processes and impacts in rainfed agricultural regions. Climatic Change, (9): 33–42.

Shen Weishou. 1986. Status of Aordosica in sandy-vegetation succession in Shapotou.

Shen Weishou. 1996. Floristic characters of the middle reach of the Yalung Zangbo River area. Acta Phytotaxonomica Sinica, 34(3): 276–281. (In Chinese)

Skidmore E L. 1986. Wind erosion climatic erosivity. Climatic Change, (9): 195–208.

Su Peixi. 1996. Study on characters of seasonal wind-blown sand land and development of fruit trees on it. Journal of Ecological Agriculture Research, 4(2): 54–58. (In Chinese)

Team of "Chinese land aeolian desertification (land degradation) control research". 1998. Study on Aeolian Desertification (Land Degeneration) Control in China. Beijing: China Environmental Science Press. (In Chinese)

The Bureau of Land Management of Tibet Aut. Reg. 1994. The Land Resources of Tibet Aut. Reg. Beijing: Science Press. (In Chinese)

The Comprehensive Scientific Expedition to Qinghai-Tibet Plateau, Chinese Academy of Sciences. 1984. Agricultural Geography of Tibet. Beijing: Science Press. (In Chinese)

The Comprehensive Scientific Expedition to Qinghai-Tibet Plateau, Chinese Academy of Sciences. 1988. The Series of the scientific Expedition to the Qinghai-Tibet Plateau: Vegetation of Tibet. Beijing: Science Press. (In Chinese)

The Mapping Bureau of the Tibet Aut. Reg. 1995. Map of the Tibet Aut. Reg. Beijing: SinoMaps Press. (In Chinese)

Wang Jiuwen. 1997. Discussion on oasis, oasisization process and oasis construction. In: Committee of Arid Region Research of China Natural Resource Institute. The Theory and Practice on Oasis Construction. (In Chinese)

Wei Xinghu, Liu Zhimin, Xie Zhongkui et al. 1996. Test on watermelon planting on sandland in Xigaze valley of Tibet. Journal of Desert Research, 16(4). (In Chinese)

Wen Zixiang, Zhang Qiang, Chen Maocai. 1993. Resources exploitation and land aeolian desertification renovation in north Shaanxi. In: The Comprehensive Scientific Expedition to the Loess Plateau, Chinese Academy of Sciences. The Proceedings of Comprehensive Management and Exploitation in the Loess Plateau Area. Beijing: China Environmental Sciences Press, 65–73. (In Chinese)

Yang Gensheng, Liu Lianyou, Chen Weinan et al. 1993. Evaluation on land aeolian desertification in wind-blown sand region in the north of the Loess Plateau area and in commodity grain base along the Yellow River basin in Inner Mongolia. In: The Comprehensive Scientific Expedition to the Loess Plateau, Chinese Academy of Sciences. The Proceedings of Comprehensive Management and Exploitation in the Loess Plateau Area. Beijing: China Environmental Science Press, 52–63. (In Chinese)

Yang Gensheng, Lu Rong. 1998. Aeolian-desertification and Techniques to Control in Ikezhao League of Inner Mongolia. Beijing: China Environmental Science Press. (In Chinese)

Yang Gensheng. 1993. Land aeolian desertification in Shenfu-Dongsheng mining area and its influence on sediment flow to the Yellow River. In: The Comprehensive Scientific Expedition to the Loess Plateau, Chinese Academy of Sciences. The Proceedings of Comprehensive Management and Exploitation in the Loess Plateau Area. Beijing: China Environmental Science Press, 74–82. (In Chinese)

Yang Xilin, Wei Xinghu, Zhao Xingliang. 1996. Study on comprehensive management and exploitation of wind-blown sand land. Journal of Desert Research, 16(1): 43–49. (In Chinese)

Yang Yichou. 1984. A preliminary observation on aeolian sand landform in Yalung Zangbo River valley. Journal of Desert Research, 4(3): 12–15. (In Chinese)

Zha Y, Gao J. 1997. Characteristics of aeolian desertification and its rehabilitation in China. Journal of Arid Environments, (37): 419–432.

Zhang Hongye. 2000. Amelioration and effective use of the sandy land in the northwestern Shandong Province. Acta Geograghica Sinica, 55(2): 219–227. (In Chinese)

Zhang Qiang. 1993. Development of agriculture, forestry and pastoral farming in wind-blown sand area of Shanxi-Shaanxi-Inner Mongolia. In: The Comprehensive Scientific Expedition to the Loess Plateau, Chinese Academy of Sciences. The Proceedings of Comprehensive Management and Exploitation in the Loess Plateau Area. Beijing: China Environmental Science Press, 119–133. (In Chinese)

Zhang Tianzeng. 1993. General Discussion of the Loess Plateau. Beijing: China Environmental Science Press. (In Chinese)

Zhao Wenzhi. 1998. A preliminary study on the arenaceous adaptability of Soghora Moorcroftiana. Acta Phytoecologica Sinica, 22 (4): 379–384. (In Chinese)

Zhao Xingliang. 1991. Discussion on problems of sand-fixing of plants in Shapotou area. In: Studies on Shifting Sand Control in Shapuotou Area of Tengger Desert (2). Yinchuan: Ningxia People's Publishing House, 27–57. (In Chinese)

Zhu Zhenda, Chen Guangting. 1994. Land Aeolian Desertification in China. Beijing: Science Press. (In Chinese)

Zhu Zhenda, Liu Shu, Di Xingmin et al. 1989. Aeolian Desertification and Rehabilitation in China. Beijing: Science Press. (In Chinese)

Zhu Zhenda, Liu Shu, Shen Jingqi et al. 1982. The historical process and approach to exploit and use of researches along the Great Wall in north Shaanxi and Ningxia and in the Hexi Corridor. In: Collection of Lanzhou Institute of Desert, CAS. (2). Beijing: Science Press, 1–13. (In Chinese)

Zhu Zhenda, Liu Shu. 1986. Study on Aeolian Desertification and Its Control Districts in North China. Beijing: China Forestry Publishing House. (In Chinese)

Afterward

"Deserts and Aeolian Desertification in China" is a summary of the research carried out over fifty years from 1950 until 2000 at the former Institute of Desert Research, Chinese Academy of Sciences. The original Chinese version of "Deserts and Aeolian Desertification in China" was published in 2003 by Hebei Science and Technology Press. Resulting from the large number of contributors, their diverse specialties and backgrounds, as well as the various perspectives and discourses relating to the research, excluding certain content was unavoidable. However, the inherent value of the academic and theoretical standards included in this book was reaffirmed by various experts who were in attendance at the 2004 Publishing Conference, which convened in April in Beijing. Mr. Lu Dadao, then president of the Geographical Society of China, and Academician of the Chinese Academy of Sciences, indicated: "The publication of this book has resulted in a systematic summary of desert science over the past several decades, and it not only has high academic value, it is also a new beginning into the research and control of deserts and desertification in China." Mr. Liu Dongsheng, recipient of the State Science and Technology Prize (the highest honor in science and technology in China), and an Academician of the Chinese Academy of Sciences, emphasized: "A compilation of the research and practices over the past several decades resulting in a work like 'Deserts and Aeolian Desertification in China' represents our growth in the field of deserts and desertification and has become an important component of international scientific research." Mr. Chen Shupeng, Academician of the Chinese Academy of Sciences, expressed that the publication of this book is a symbolic representation of the growth of scientific research and researchers. He also pointed out the international significance of the research on deserts and desertification in China: "Though our research concerns temperate deserts, our theories and experiences from several projects that combat desertification have already made great contributions to the research and rehabilitation of tropical deserts in Third World countries. Furthermore, it is extremely important that we have trained such a large number of experts talented in both research and technology, and this is yet another mark of our appearance on the global scene." Mr. Zheng Du, one of the original veteran researchers who established the 1959 Sand Control Team (the predecessor of the Institute of Desert Research), as well as an Academician of the Chinese Academy of Sciences, has shown complete approval of this book: "Under extremely harsh conditions in blown sand environments, we have developed desert and aeolian desertification research, and achieved results that have been acknowledged at both the national and international level. We should especially celebrate the fact that there are a bountiful number of successors who can continue to carry out this research."

Our decision to translate and publish an English version of this book was made after receiving the encouragement and support of the scientific community, along with our desire to share the results of our research and control of deserts and aeolian desertification with other scientists and scholars in the international community. First, we developed an abridgement of the original Chinese version, and then we organized a group of young researchers (including graduate students) to carry out the translation. This work was a process of translation and then translating once again, and the extensive amount of time devoted to this project was partly because of limited knowledge concerning certain scientific issues, as well as obstacles with the English language. By 2006, Science Press had produced an English manuscript, which we then sent to experts in related fields to provide feedback. We not only made many corrections and additions, including new research results, but we also proofread the English once again. We would especially like to thank Kara Hill of the Department of East Languages and Literature at The Ohio State University. Ms. Hill not only agreed to work in Lanzhou for nearly three months to assist with the editing and translation, but she also worked long hours every day to complete the final version of this work.

From 2002, China began implementing the "Law of the People's Republic of China on the Prevention and Control of Desertification." This not only established laws for the prevention and control of desertification, but has also become a standard for the various levels of government and people in China. China has successively launched policies and measures, as well as implemented significant projects for preventing and controlling desertification, such as the "Three-North" project, which is the continuing development of the third and fourth phase of a shelterbelt system; the project around Beijing-Tianjin for Controlling the Sources of Blown Sand; and returning reclaimed farmland into forests and grasslands, also known as "Grain for Green." All of these projects have helped to relieve the pressure from unreasonable land use in areas of desertification in northern China, and have allowed the ecological balance to reestablish a beneficial cycle. After entering the 21st Century, the trend of desertification has undergone fundamental changes, namely from a situation of "regional control, but overall deterioration" in the last half of the 20th Century, to "regional control and overall stabilization." In many areas, the process of desertification has begun to reverse. For example, "The Processes of Oasification-Desertification and their Responding to Human Activities & Climatic Change and their Regulation in the Arid Region of China," is part of China's National Key Basic Research Development Program (973). According to the latest remote sensing results from this project, there has been a decreasing trend in the total area of desertified land, but we still need to pay attention to the following points: (I) Several areas of desertification are in an overall state of deterioration, such as arid grasslands that suffer from pressures that continue without mitigation, such as an arid climate and the overgrazing of animals. Additionally, oases in the upper and lower reaches of rivers in northwestern China continue to expand, affecting the depletion of water resources at the lower reaches. As a result, the environment deteriorates, and desertification continues unabated. And (II) Since the 1990s, the high increase over long periods of extremely severe and severe desertified land has yet to be alleviated; this has also increased the difficulty in controlling desertification.

Our experience in controlling desertification has conveyed that the policies that have been instituted in China; the theoretical research and practice models in our system; their adaptability to create feasible and practical plans; and necessary investments are all essential for preventing and controlling desertification.

The collaboration between the studies of the natural sciences, the humanities, and socio-economics has transformed into one discipline of deserts and desertification. Though the land in deserts and desertified areas can have national boundaries, but it is obvious that the experiences and accomplishments achieved in researching and controlling deserts and desertification do not have boundaries. We hope to continue and share these experiences and accomplishments with our colleagues and friends in other countries.